Born in 1802, the son of a high officer in Napoleon's army, Victor Hugo spent his childhood against a background of military life in Elba, Corsica, Naples, and Madrid. After the Napoleonic defeat, the Hugo family settled in straitened circumstances in Paris, where, at the age of fifteen, Victor Hugo commenced his literary career with a poem submitted to a contest sponsored by the Académie Française. Twenty-four years later, Hugo was elected to the Académie, having helped revolutionize French literature with his poems, plays, and novels. Entering politics, he won a seat in the National Assembly in 1848; but in 1851, he was forced to flee the country because of his opposition to Louis Napoleon. In exile on the Isle of Guernsey, he became a symbol of French resistance to tyranny; upon his return to Paris after the Revolution of 1870, he was greeted as a national hero. He continued to serve in public life and to write with unabated vigor until his death in 1885. He was buried in the Pantheon with every honor the French nation could bestow.

LES MISÉRABLES

BY

Victor Hugo

A new unabridged translation
by Lee Fahnestock and
Norman MacAfee,
based on the classic
C. E. Wilbour translation

A SIGNET CLASSIC

SIGNET CLASSIC
Published by the Penguin Group
Penguin Putnam Inc., 375 Hudson Street,
New York, New York 10014, U.S.A.
Penguin Books Ltd, 27 Wrights Lane,
London W8 5TZ, England
Penguin Books Australia Ltd, Ringwood,
Victoria, Australia
Penguin Books Canada Ltd, 10 Alcorn Avenue,
Toronto, Ontario, Canada M4V 3B2
Penguin Books (N.Z.) Ltd, 182–190 Wairau Road,
Auckland 10, New Zealand

Penguin Books Ltd, Registered Offices:
Harmondsworth, Middlesex, England

Published by Signet Classic, an imprint of Dutton Signet,
a member of Penguin Putnam Inc.

First Printing, March, 1987
24 23 22 21 20 19 18 17

Library of Congress Catalog Card Number: 86-62313

Printed in the United States of America

Introduction

Les Misérables is a vast novel built to the measure of Victor Hugo's humanity and vision. The culminating work of his long career, it was published in 1862, when the author was sixty. An instant success with the public, the book has stood since then as a masterpiece of fiction, both for the emotional intensity of its dramatic story and for a richness that defies any simple description. Undoubtedly readers come to the book for the deeply engrossing characters and stay on, as the author himself predicted, for the wider social and historic panorama.

The political timing of the publication was auspicious. Isolated by exile from the empire of Napoleon III, whose authoritarianism was relaxing as his effectiveness and popularity were waning, Hugo found a ready audience for his progressive fervor. Despite his long list of works in poetry, fiction, and drama, Hugo had been most widely known before this novel as a public figure, defender of the national conscience. And now, homesick for France but unwilling to accept the amnesty offered by the emperor he despised, he was eager for the chance to remind France at large of his presence.

A friend reported to him that all of Paris was raving about the book. As for the critics, Hugo clearly took it as a compliment that his liberal views had enraged the reactionary, the conservative Catholic, and the Bonapartist journals. The gratifying enthusiasm of the younger critics, however, was not unanimously sustained, for the book had appeared outside of its time. When he began writing it in 1845, the Romantic traditions of intense sentiment and crusading idealism were prevalent. François-René de Chateaubriand, Alphonse de Lamartine, George Sand, and Honoré de Balzac were the literary leaders.

By the time *Les Misérables* appeared almost twenty years later, however, the despair of Gustave Flaubert's *Madame Bovary* and the rich decadence of Baudelaire's *Les fleurs du mal* were already part of the literary climate. A new group, the Realists, objected to what they saw as Hugo's excesses of sentiment and rhetoric, and disparaged the poetic and humanitarian idealism that interfered with the credibility of his scenes.

And yet, rising above the fluctuations of literary criticism, the book has always retained a powerful hold on the public, and writers have continued to turn to Hugo for inspiration. Diverse authors such as Arthur Rimbaud, Stéphane Mallarmé, and Paul Claudel were influenced by this giant of Romanticism. André Gide called him the greatest master of images and sonorities, of symbols and language forms, in all of French literature.

Hugo was born in 1802, during Napoleon's rule as First Consul, and was to experience all the social upheaval and radical swings of French political life through the coming of the Third Republic in 1870 and beyond. His early childhood was spent in Italy, Spain, and many different parts of France, as the family of five went from one post to the next following the father, Léopold Hugo, a career officer made a count and then a general under Napoleon. Seriously buffeted by the discord between mismatched parents, the young Victor and his older brothers, Abel and Eugène, joined their mother in Paris when the couple separated. There Victor's fondest memories were of an apartment on the Impasse des Feuillantines whose huge walled garden was a place of idyllic happiness, where he and Eugène both fell in love with the young Adèle Foucher, later Victor's bride.

With his mother he attended Royalist salons, and attitudes learned there were part of his thinking until a reconciliation with his father led him on to a Napoleonic fervor. Gifted in languages, Hugo began to write poetry as a boarding student in Paris, where he grew to admire the great Romantic writer and statesman Chateaubriand. He continued to write, and edited a conservative literary journal with Eugène, while ostensibly studying law to please his father. Hugo gained considerable notice for his early fiction and particularly for his poetry, but it was as a playwright that he made his first assault on the literary barricades. His own Romantic manifesto, contained in a celebrated preface to his play *Cromwell*, declared war on prevailing Classical restrictions in favor of freer, more realistic forms and characterizations. Two years later, in 1830, with a carefully orchestrated riot in the audience on its opening night, his play *Hernani* won a place for Romantic drama. It also brought him financial success and the acknowledged leadership of the young Romantics, including Balzac, Alexandre Dumas, Gérard de Nerval, and Hugo's closest friend, Charles-Augustin Sainte-Beuve.

Hugo married Adèle Foucher in 1823, "when together their ages did not add up to forty" (to paraphrase the poem recited at the barricade by the students on page 1105). By 1831 he was the father of four children and a figure in public demand. In that year he suffered a deep personal blow when Adèle formed a liaison with Sainte-Beuve. Crushed, Hugo himself soon took up with a young actress, Juliette Drouet, in an intense companionship that was to last fifty years. For the rest of his life an abiding ambivalence propelled Hugo to seek out romantic conquests while at the same time maintaining a longing for innocence, the side of him that appears in his fiction. This ambivalence, combined with his willing stance of genius, made him a difficult man to live with. Though he could be intensely generous, his divided attention left none of his various households completely satisfied.

As a young man Hugo received honors from three kings, was awarded the Légion d'Honneur and elected to the august Académie Française, but his temperament was not suited to a safe career under royal patronage. The protagonists of his verse dramas, outcasts combating corrupt or unjust power, caused the royal banning of two productions. The failure of a final play, *Les Burgraves*, brought a virtual end to his dramatic career in 1843.

In 1845 he began to write a book called *Les Misères*. In the same year Louis-Philippe, the so-called bourgeois king, made him *pair de France*, with a title for life and a seat in the upper legislative body. From then on his life, writing, and politics were inseparable, linked by his firm belief in the civilizing obligation of the poet. His first speeches were against the death penalty and against the horrifying prison conditions he had observed. He urged the adoption of laws to improve the lot of women, recommending universal free education and general suffrage as the means to relieve poverty. Though his political position was confused by a lingering attachment to Bonapartism and monarchy—they too had their Romantic appeal—he matched with an evolving credo of his own the nation's painful struggle toward the equality and well-being promised by the revolution of 1789.

The writing went smoothly for Hugo until the massive uprising of 1848 that unseated Louis-Philippe and brought on the short-lived Second Republic. Then, at the chapter called "The Blotter Talks" (page 1148), he abruptly left off writing for a full-time role in politics. During the rebellion Hugo was a conspicuous figure, plunging fearlessly into angry crowds, speaking for conciliation. As a conservative deputy for Paris he advocated the presidency of Louis-Napoleon. But in the continuing governmental chaos he made an abrupt switch to the left, finally aligning his politics with the humanitarian principles he had always advocated.

For his opposition to the coup d'état by which Napoleon III became emperor, Hugo was forced to flee through Belgium to the British Channel Islands, an exile that would last twenty years. His continued political agitation, including satires aimed at "the little Napoleon," required a further move from Jersey to Guernsey, with a trunk of manuscripts, among them *Les Misérables*, almost lost overboard on the way.

In 1843—already rocked by the deaths of both his parents, of an infant son, and of his brother Eugène, who had gone mad on Victor's wedding day—the writer suffered a permanently devastating loss. At nineteen his adored eldest daughter, Léopoldine, drowned with her husband in a boating accident. It was a shock that effectively divided his life into "before" and "after." He gradually confronted his grief in what was probably his greatest series of lyric poems, *Les Contemplations*, which was released for publication five years into his island existence.

The years of exile encouraged other contemplations as well. Gazing back at the troubled shores of France, Hugo filled sketchbooks with paintings of mystic landscapes; he explored the occult; and he published the first part of a monumental work, projected as an epic history of mankind.

In 1860 he finally returned to *Les Misérables,* the book he had never expected to complete, and wrote through to the end. Then, in a move quite uncharacteristic of this writer who preferred to move forward rather than revise, he went back to insert many sections that brought the book into line with his liberalized views and perspectives gained offshore. In one of his rare trips back to the mainland, he went to Belgium. There, writing the Waterloo section last, he finished *Les Misérables* beside the actual battlefield, in Mont-Saint-Jean. He was certain that he had created a masterpiece.

With the downfall of Napoleon III in 1870, Hugo returned to Paris. He received a hero's welcome as the champion of democracy, delivering four separate speeches to the huge crowd gathered at the railway station. It was the so-called "terrible year," dominated by the rout of the French army and a German siege of Paris. When peace was restored, he served as a senator under the more stable Third Republic, continuing his appeals for progress and mercy.

Hugo lived on like one of the old men he drew so perceptively, curiosities because they have lasted beyond their time. Having outlived his wife and Juliette Drouet, having outlived his two sons, he was left with only his institutionalized daughter, Adèle, and two well-loved grandchildren about whom he wrote a fine book of poems, *The Art of Being a Grandfather*. His death in 1885 was nationally mourned; two million Frenchmen turned out for the procession that followed the casket from the Arc de Triomphe to the Panthéon.

When Hugo first began writing *Les Misérables,* it was as if he had been gathering the material all his life. Many of the characters show traces of his own personal experience, and the book's philosophical stance mirrors the concerns of his political existence. His first published story, of a black slave in Santo-Domingo betrayed by an influential white friend, shows the same concern for outcasts that pervades the novel and that later led Hugo to plead for the life of the American abolitionist John Brown. Early research into prison conditions had produced two short fictional works, and around 1835 Hugo had investigated accounts of a bishop in the Midi who succored a released convict.

The principal action opens in 1815, the year Napoleon's Hundred Days interrupted the reign of Louis XVIII, beginning with Napoleon's triumphant return from Elba and ending in his defeat at Waterloo. By the story's close eighteen years later, the last Bourbon king, Charles X, has given way to the constitutional monarchy of Louis-Philippe. It is in frustration against Louis-Philippe's slow-moving regime that the students and workers are driven to the barricades at the book's climax.

Very early, Hugo conceived of the book as the story of a saint, a man, a woman, and a little girl. The story begins with a rather leisurely section revealing Bishop Myriel's gentle humor and sanctity. Then, in what may for many readers be the first strong indication of the book's dramatic power, a confrontation takes place between the churchman and a dying pariah, a former deputy to the Revolutionary Convention that had sentenced Louis XVI to death (page 35). This highly emotional scene, followed by less intense, discursive chapters on the ecclesiastic attitudes of the times, demonstrates Hugo's deliberate method of alternating dramatic action and passages of historic background, a process that produces an account of astonishing depth and clarity.

At the center of the narrative is Jean Valjean, a good man made a petty thief by poverty, whose life and dignity are restored by a bishop's trust and by his own unselfish love for a little girl. Valjean's progress is halting, marked by inward debate, by error, and by the unending flight from adversaries. Chief among these is Javert, the implacable police officer made dangerous by an obsessive sense of duty. At the same time Thénardier, the completely false inkeeper, not even a good criminal, stalks Valjean for his own evil gain. Much of the book's suspense comes from their persistent tracking down of the outcast hero.

A second outcast, Fantine, who first appears (page 120) as a trusting young seamstress, becomes the victim of bourgeois callousness. Only the longing innocence remains as desperation drives her to prostitution. In a sense of obligation to her, Valjean undertakes the care of her daughter, Cosette. Fantine's child becomes the luminous center of Valjean's life. Anyone aware of Hugo's own parental loss will see a poignant source of Valjean's all-consuming love for Cosette, his jealousy of Marius, and the terrible sacrifices he must make in her behalf.

A host of secondary figures repeatedly reveals Hugo's delight in writing a character or scene for its own sake. It would be hard to forge the feisty royalist, Monsieur Gillenormand, frozen in the attitudes and fashions of a bygone era, or the street urchin, Gavroche, who lacks everything but seems to possess the city through his wit and insolence. Without an overt display of tight organization, the huge cast in fact moves very precisely toward the denouement.

The expository passages, a remarkable feature of the novel, deserve brief mention here through a couple of examples. The long sequence on the battle of Waterloo—that name which has passed into our language—beginning on page 301 is justly famous for the brilliance of its sweeping panorama highlighted by ironic detail, and for the analysis of the battle's role, as European history wheeled and turned. The protest occasionally heard, that the sequence has little to do with the plot, overlooks the wider scope of the book, which Baudelaire called "the legend of the nineteenth century."

A very different sort of chapter added to "Fantine" from exile, "The Year 1817" (page 114), catalogs a random series of seeming trivia that caught the Parisian fancy, or failed to, during a brief span of euphoria in that year. Here we see such things as the Napoleonic N being erased from the Louvre and Chateaubriand dictating to his secretary every morning as he stood in front of his window cleaning his teeth. It scarcely matters that many of the names and events recalled by Hugo so much later are now unknown, some even incorrect. Like references throughout the book, they are there for the tone they help to set; the sharp contrasts and dismissive attitudes in the chapter convey a strong sense of misplaced public values.

One of the book's particular joys is Hugo's contagious love of Paris, the center and symbol of France, first described in terms of its people, who are seen as wrongheaded at times, but always resourceful and witty. Obvious affection is also lavished on the physical city, the landmarks and streets where much of the action unfolds. Hugo follows the characters through their winding itineraries, mentioning each street by name. For instance, there is Marius' progress toward the barricade from the rue Plumet—across the Pont des Invalides and down the Champs-Elysées, through what was then the Place Louis XV and is now the Place de la Concorde, past the fashionable strollers on the Rue de Rivoli and on into the pitch-black battle zone near the markets.

Today, though the custom of renaming Paris thoroughfares for new heroes continues, there has been for some time an Avenue Victor-Hugo in the sedate sixteenth arrondissement. And much else remains as history performs new scenes on old sets: Couples stroll through the same Jardin du Luxembourg; a metro stop almost under the site of the barricade at Corinth bears the name of Les Halles (though that great central market has now given way to a subterranean shopping mall); and a brief tour of the Paris sewers begins across the Seine, one bridge away from the shore where Valjean emerged with his unconscious burden. Paris ways persist, for the student uprising of May 1968 saw modest versions of the same barricades constructed of overturned vehicles and paving blocks, though muskets and artillery were replaced by tear gas and fire hoses.

Reading *Les Misérables* today, nobody would deny that Victor Hugo's prodigious flow of words occasionally produces moments of excess, when we might wish he had shown more restraint. But to Albert Lacroix, the young Belgian who first published the book, the author refused cuts as he had to all other editors. He finally permitted the excision of one chapter on prostitution and woman's lot which, as the author would smile to see, now appears in some French editions as an appendix. While several abridged editions exist in English, that expedient seems a mistake. It is almost impossible to predict the individual detail, the flashing image or human quirk precisely observed, that will burn its way into a reader's mind for good. The sound solution is to honor the author's wishes. If the heightened rhetoric of elation and despair occasionally strains our patience or credulity, the quiet perception on the next page generally restores it.

The classic translation done by Charles E. Wilbour was completed in time for publication by the A. L. Burt Company of New York in 1862, the same year the novel appeared in French, an incredible feat actually duplicated by several translators in various languages. An interesting figure, Wilbour trained as a lawyer, seems to have had some political connections, and translated two other books by his friend Hugo before turning to the study of Egyptology.

For this revised edition, our aim has been to move the phrasing and vocabulary forward, closer to contemporary usage and occasionally closer to what we take as the author's intent, but never to lose the basic fabric, which is still Wilbour's Hugo, the version that has endured.

—L.F.

LES MISÉRABLES

So long as there shall exist, by reason of law and custom, a social condemnation which, in the midst of civilization, artificially creates a hell on earth, and complicates with human fatality a destiny that is divine; so long as the three problems of the century—the degradation of man by the exploitation of his labor, the ruin of woman by starvation, and the atrophy of childhood by physical and spiritual night—are not solved; so long as, in certain regions, social asphyxia shall be possible; in other words, and from a still broader point of view, so long as ignorance and misery remain on earth, there should be a need for books such as this.

Hauteville House, 1862

So long as there shall exist, by reason of law and custom, a social condemnation which, in the midst of civilization, artificially creates a hell on earth, and complicates with human fatality a destiny that is divine; so long as the three problems of the century—the degradation of man by the exploitation of his labor, the ruin of woman by starvation, and the atrophy of childhood by physical and spiritual night—are not solved; so long as, in certain regions, social asphyxia shall be possible; in other words, and from a still broader point of view, so long as ignorance and misery remain on earth, there should be a need for books such as this.

Hauteville House, 1862

Contents

FANTINE

COSETTE

MARIUS

SAINT-DENIS

JEAN VALJEAN

FANTINE

Book One

AN UPRIGHT MAN

I

MONSIEUR MYRIEL

In 1815 Monsieur Charles-François-Bienvenu Myriel was Bishop of Digne. He was then about seventy-five and had presided over the diocese of Digne since 1806.

Although it in no way concerns our story, it might be worthwhile, if only for the sake of accuracy, to mention the rumors and gossip about him that were making the rounds when he first came to the diocese. Whether true or false, what is said about men often has as much influence on their lives, and particularly on their destinies, as what they do.

M. Myriel was the son of a judge of the Superior Court of Aix, with the rank acquired by many in the legal profession. It was said that his father, expecting him to inherit his position, had arranged a marriage for the son at the early age of eighteen or twenty, following the custom among these privileged families. Despite his marriage, Charles Myriel had attracted a great deal of attention. Handsome, though not very tall, he was elegant, graceful, and witty. His early years had been devoted to worldly pleasures. With the Revolution, events moved quickly. Hunted down, decimated, or forced into exile, these families were soon dispersed. At the first outbreak of the Revolution, M. Charles Myriel emigrated to Italy. After a protracted illness his wife ultimately died there of a lung disease. They had no children. What happened next to M. Myriel? The collapse of the old French society, the downfall of his own family, the tragic scenes of 1793, still more terrifying perhaps to the exiles who witnessed them from afar, magnified by horror—did these inspire him with thoughts of renunciation and solitude? In the midst of the flirtations and diversions that consumed his life at that time was he suddenly overcome by one of those mysterious, inner blows that sometimes strike the heart of the man who could not be shaken by public disasters of his life and fortune? Who could say? We do know that when he returned from Italy he was a priest.

In 1804, M. Myriel was curé of Brignolles. He was already an old man and living in deep seclusion.

About the time of Napoleon's coronation, some trifling business of his parish—no one remembers precisely what it was—took him to Paris. Among other influential people, he went to see Cardinal Fesch on behalf of his parishioners. One day—when the emperor had come to call on his uncle the cardinal—our worthy priest happened to be waiting as his Majesty went by. Noticing that the old man looked at him with a certain curiosity, Napoleon turned around and said brusquely, "Who is this good man looking at me?"

"Sire," replied M. Myriel, "you are looking at a good man, and I at a great one. May we both be the better for it."

That evening the emperor asked the cardinal the priest's name. Still later, M. Myriel was totally surprised to learn he had been appointed Bishop of Digne.

Beyond this, who could tell how much truth there was in the stories concerning M. Myriel's early years? Few families had known the Myriels before the Revolution.

M. Myriel had to submit to the fate of every newcomer in a small town, where many tongues talk but few heads think. Although he was bishop (in fact, because he was), he had to submit. But after all, the gossip linked with his name was only gossip: rumor, talk, words, less than words—*palabres*, as they say in the lively language of the South.

Be that as it may, after nine years of residence as

bishop of Digne, all these tales, which are initially engrossing to small towns and petty people, were entirely forgotten. Nobody would have dared to speak of them or even remember them.

When M. Myriel came to Digne he was accompanied by an old unmarried lady, Mademoiselle Baptistine, his sister, ten years younger than himself.

Their only servant was a woman about the same age as Mademoiselle Baptistine, Madame Magloire, who, already the servant of the priest, now took the double title of Mademoiselle's maid and the Bishop's housekeeper.

Tall and thin, Mademoiselle Baptistine was a pale and gentle person. She was the incarnation of the word "respectable," whereas to be "venerable," a woman should also be a mother. She had never been pretty; her whole life, which had been a succession of pious works, had finally cloaked her in a kind of transparent whiteness, and in growing old she had acquired the beauty of goodness. What had been thinness in her youth was in her maturity a transparency, and this ethereal quality permitted glimmers of the angel within. She was more of a spirit than a virgin mortal. Her form seemed made of shadows, scarcely enough body to convey the thought of sex—a little substance containing a spark—large eyes, always downcast, a pretext for a soul to remain on earth.

Madame Magloire was a little old woman, white-haired, plump, bustling, always out of breath, because of her constant activity and also her asthma.

On his arrival, M. Myriel was installed in his bishop's palace with the honors prescribed by the imperial decrees, which rank the bishop right below the field marshal. The mayor and the presiding judge called on him first, and he, for his part, paid like honor to the general and the prefect.

The installation complete, the town waited to see its new bishop at work.

II

MONSIEUR MYRIEL BECOMES MONSEIGNEUR BIENVENU

The bishop's palace at Digne was next to the hospital. A beautiful, spacious stone structure, it was built around the beginning of the last century by Monseigneur Henri Pujet, a doctor of theology of the Faculty of Paris, Abbé of Simore, who was Bishop of Digne in 1712. The palace was truly sumptuous. There was an air of grandeur about it all, the bishop's apartments, the reception rooms and bedrooms, the vast courtyard surrounded by arcades in the old Florentine style, and a garden planted with magnificent trees.

The dining hall was a splendid long gallery at ground level, opening onto the garden. There Monseigneur Henri Pujet had given a great banquet on July 29, 1714, to Archbishop Charles Brûlart de Genlis, Prince of Embrun; Antoine de Mesgrigny, a Capuchin and Bishop of Grasse; Philippe de Vendôme, Grand Prior of France, the Abbé of Saint Honoré de Lérins; François de Berton de Grillon, Lord Bishop of Vence; Cesar de Sabran de Forcalquier, Lord Bishop of Glandève; and Jean Soanen, priest of the oratory, preacher in ordinary to the king, Lord Bishop of Senez; the portraits of these seven reverend persons decorated the hall, and this memorable date, July 29, 1714, appeared in letters of gold on a white marble tablet.

The hospital was a narrow two-story building with a small garden.

Three days after the bishop's arrival, he visited the hospital; when the visit was over, he invited the director to come with him back to the palace.

"Monsieur," he said, "how many patients do you have right now?"

"Twenty-six, Monseigneur."

"That is what I counted," the bishop said.

"The beds," the director continued, "are closely packed together."

"So I noticed."

"The wards are only small rooms, and are difficult to ventilate."

"So it seemed to me."

"And then, when the sun does shine, the garden is too small for all the convalescents."

"That was what I was thinking."

"Among the epidemics, we've had typhus this year; two years ago we had military fever, with a hundred patients at times, and we didn't know what to do."

"It's a problem."

"What can we do, Monseigneur?" the director asked. "We just have to resign ourselves to it."

This conversation took place in the dining hall on the first floor.

The bishop was silent a few moments, then he turned suddenly toward the director.

"Monsieur," he said, "how many beds do you think this hall alone would contain?"

"Your Lordship's dining hall!" exclaimed the director, stupefied.

The bishop ran his eyes over the hall, measuring and calculating.

"It will hold twenty beds," he said to himself; then, raising his voice, he said, "Listen, Monsieur Director, here's what I think. Obviously this is wrong. There are twenty-six of you in five or six small rooms; there are three of us in space enough for sixty. That is wrong, I assure you. You have my house and I am in yours. Give me back mine and this will be your home."

Next day the twenty-six indigent patients were installed in the bishop's palace, and the bishop was in the hospital.

M. Myriel had no property; his family had been impoverished by the Revolution. His sister had an annual income life estate of five hundred francs, which in the church residence sufficed for her personal needs. As bishop, M. Myriel received fifteen thousand francs from the government. The very day he took up his residence in the hospital building, he resolved to allocate this sum once and for all to the following uses. This is the estimate he wrote.

"Budget for My Household Expenses

"For the little seminary, fifteen hundred livres.
Mission congregation, one hundred livres.
For the Lazaristes of Montdidier, one hundred livres.
Seminary of foreign missions in Paris, two hundred livres.
Congregation of the Saint-Esprit, one hundred and fifty livres.
Religious establishments in the Holy Land, one hundred livres.
Maternal charitable societies, three hundred livres.
For that of Arles, fifty livres.
For the improvement of prisons, four hundred livres.
For the relief and release of prisoners, five hundred livres.
For the liberation of fathers of families imprisoned for debt, one thousand livres.
Additions to the salaries of poor schoolmasters of the diocese, two thousand livres.
Public storehouse of the Hautes-Alpes, one hundred livres.
Association of the ladies of Digne, of Manosque and Sisteron for free instruction of indigent girls, fifteen hundred livres.
For the poor, six thousand livres.
My personal expenses, one thousand livres.
Total, fifteen thousand livres."

M. Myriel made no alteration in this plan during the time he held the see of Digne; he always called it the budget for his household expenses.

Mademoiselle Baptistine accepted this arrangement with utter submission. To this saintly woman, M. Myriel was at once her brother and her bishop, her companion by ties of blood and her superior by ecclesiastical authority. She loved and venerated him unabashedly. When he spoke, she listened; when he acted, she gave him her cooperation. Only their servant, Madame Magloire, grumbled a little. The bishop, as we can see, had allocated only a thousand francs for himself; this, added to the income of Mademoiselle Baptistine, gave them fifteen hundred francs a year, on which the three old people subsisted.

Thanks, however, to Madame Magloire's rigid economy and Mademoiselle Baptistine's excellent management, whenever a curate came to Digne, the bishop found the means to offer him hospitality.

One day, about three months after the installation, the bishop said, "With all this I feel quite embarrassed."

"I should think so," said Madame Magloire. "Monseigneur has not even asked for the sum due him from the province for his carriage expenses in town and on trips around the diocese. It used to be the practice with all bishops."

"Why yes!" the bishop said. "You're right, Madame Magloire."

He made his application.

Some time afterward the county council took up his request and voted him an annual stipend of three thousand francs under this heading: "Allowance to the bishop for carriage expenses, and travel expenses for pastoral visits."

The bourgeoisie of the town were quite worked up about it, and a senator of the empire, formerly a member of the Council of Five Hundred who had backed the Eighteenth Brumaire, now provided with a rich senatorial seat near Digne, wrote to M. Bigot de Préameneu, Minister of Public Worship, a carping, confidential letter, from which we extract the following:

"Carriage expenses! What can he want with that in a town of less than 4,000 inhabitants? Expenses of pastoral visits! In the first place, what good do they do? And then, how is it possible to travel by carriage in this mountainous region? There are no roads; he can only go on horseback. Even the bridge over the Durance at Château-Arnoux is barely passable for oxcarts. These priests are always the same: greedy and miserly. This one played the good apostle at the outset; now he's behaving like all the rest; he must have a carriage and post-chaise. He must have luxury like the former bishops. Bah! Priests! Monsieur le Comte, things will never get better till the emperor delivers us from the whole pack of them. Down with the pope! As for me, I render everything unto Caesar," and so on and so forth. (Relations with Rome were touchy at that time.)

On the other hand, the application pleased Madame Magloire. "Good," she said to Mademoiselle Baptistine.

"Monseigneur began with others, but he has found out at last that he must take care of himself. He has settled all his charities, and so now here are three thousand francs for us."

That same evening the bishop wrote the following note and handed it to his sister:

"Carriage and Traveling Expenses

"Beef broth for the hospital, fifteen hundred livres.
The Aix Maternal Charity Association, two hundred and fifty livres.
The Draguignan Maternal Charity Association, two hundred and fifty livres.
Foundlings, five hundred livres.
Orphans, five hundred livres.
Total, three thousand livres."

Such was the budget of M. Myriel.

As for the official perquisites, marriage licenses, dispensations, private baptisms and preaching, consecrations of churches or chapels, marriages, and so on, the bishop collected them from the wealthy with as much rigor as he dispensed them to the poor.

In a short time donations of money began to come in. Those who had and those who had not, knocked at the bishop's door; some came to receive alms that others had just bestowed, and in less than a year he had become the treasurer of all the benevolent and the dispenser to all the needy. Large sums passed through his hands. Nevertheless, nothing changed his way of life or added the slightest luxury to his simple life.

Quite the contrary. As there is always more misery at the lower end than humanity at the top, everything was given away before it was received, like water on parched soil. No matter how much money came to him, he never had enough. And then he robbed himself. Since it was the custom for all bishops to put their baptismal names at the head of their orders and pastoral letters, the poor of the district had chosen by a sort of affectionate instinct, from among the bishop's names, the one that meant most to them, and so they always called him Monseigneur Bienvenu. We shall follow their example. Besides, it pleased him. "I like the name," he said. "The 'welcome' of Bienvenu counterbalances the Monseigneur."

We do not claim that the portrait we present here is a true one, only that it comes close.

III

GOOD BISHOP—DIFFICULT DIOCESE

The bishop, though he had converted his carriage into alms, still made his regular round of visits, and in the diocese of Digne this was exhausting. There was little flat terrain, many mountains, and hardly any roads. Thirty-two parishes, forty-one curacies, and two hundred and eighty-five subcuracies. To visit all of them took some effort, but the bishop managed. He traveled on foot in his own neighborhood, in a cart when he was on the plains, and in a *cacolet*, a basket strapped on the back of a mule, in the mountains. The two women usually accompanied him, but when the journey was too difficult for them he went alone.

One day, riding on a donkey, he arrived at Senez, formerly the seat of a diocese. His purse being empty at the time, he could not afford any better conveyance. The mayor of the city, coming to receive him at the gate of the bishop's residence, was mortified to see him dismount from his donkey. Several citizens stood nearby, laughing. "Monsieur Mayor," the bishop said, "and good citizens, I can see why you are shocked; you think it shows pride for a poor priest to use the same conveyance used by Jesus Christ. I have done it from necessity, I assure you, and not from vanity."

On his visits he was indulgent and gentle, and he preached less than he talked. He made virtue accessible. He never used far-fetched examples or reasoning. To the inhabitants of one region he would cite the example of a neighboring region. In the cantons where the needy were treated with severity, he would say, "Look at the people of Briançon. They have given the poor and widows and orphans the right to mow their meadows three days before anyone else. When their houses are in ruins they rebuild them free of charge. And so it is a countryside blessed by God. For a whole century they have not had a single murderer."

In villages where the people were greedy for profits and rich crops, he would say, "Look at Embrun. If at harvest time a man's sons are in the army and his daughters are working in the city, and if he is slowed down by illness, the priest mentions him in his sermons, and after mass on Sunday the whole population of the village, men, women, and children, go into the poor man's field and harvest his crop, and store the straw and grain in his granary." To families divided by questions of property and inheritance, he would say, "Look at the mountain people of Devolny, a country so wild that the nightingale is heard less than once in fifty years. Well now, when the father dies, the boys go off to seek their fortunes and leave the property to the girls, so they can find husbands." In cantons inclined to legal disputes and where the farmers were ruining themselves over notarized papers, he would say, "Look at those good peasants of the valley of Queyras. There are three thousand souls there. Why, it is like a little republic! You never see a judge or a constable. The mayor does everything. He apportions the duty, taxes each one in good faith, decides their quarrels without charge, distributes their patrimony without fees, renders judgments at no expense. And he is obeyed, because he is a just man among simple-hearted men." In villages where he found no schoolmaster he would again cite the valley of Queyras. "Do you know what they do?" he would ask. "Since a little district of twelve or fifteen houses cannot always support a teacher, their schoolmasters are paid by the whole valley and go from village to village, spending a week teaching in one place and ten days in another. These masters appear at the fairs, where I have seen them. They are known by the quills they wear in their hatbands. Those who teach only reading have one quill; those who teach reading and arithmetic have two; and those who teach reading, arithmetic, and Latin have three. They are considered great scholars. But what a shame to be ignorant! Do like the people of Queyras."

He would talk like that, gravely and paternally, inventing parables when he lacked examples, going straight to the point with a few phrases and a lot of images, with the very eloquence of Christ, convincing and persuasive.

IV

WORKS TO MATCH WORDS

His conversation was cheerful and pleasant. He adapted himself to the level of the two old women who lived with him, but when he laughed, it was a schoolboy's laughter.

Madame Magloire sometimes called him "Your Highness." One day, rising from his armchair, he went to his library for a book. It was on one of the upper shelves, and as the bishop was rather short, he could not reach it. "Madame Magloire," said he, "bring me a chair. My highness cannot reach that shelf."

One of his distant relatives, the Countess of Lô, rarely missed an occasion to enumerate in his presence what she called "the expectations" of her three sons. She had several relatives, very old and near death, of whom her sons were the legal heirs. The youngest of the three was to receive from a great-aunt a hundred thousand livres in income; the second was to take his uncle's title of duke; the eldest would succeed to the peerage of his grandfather. The bishop customarily listened in silence to these innocent and pardonable maternal displays. Once, however, he appeared more absentminded than usual while Madame de Lô went through all the successions and expectations. Stopping suddenly, with some impatience, she exclaimed, "My goodness, Cousin, what are you thinking about?" "I am thinking," he replied, "of something odd from, I believe, Saint Augustine: 'Place your expectations in Him to whom there is no succession!' "

On another occasion, as he read a letter announcing the death of a gentleman from nearby and listing at great length, not only the high positions of the departed but also the feudal and titular honors of all his relatives, he exclaimed, "What a broad back death has! What a marvelous load of titles will he cheerfully carry, and what stamina must men have who use the tomb to feed their vanity!"

At times he used gentle raillery, almost always charged with serious meaning. Once, during Lent, a young vicar came to Digne, and preached in the cathedral. The subject of his sermon was charity, and he treated it very eloquently. He called upon the rich to give alms to the poor, if they were to escape the tortures of hell, which he pictured in the most fearful colors, and enter paradise, which he portrayed as desirable and inviting. There was a wealthy retired merchant at the service, somewhat inclined to usury, a M. Géborand, who had accumulated an estate of two million from manufacturing coarse cloth and woolens. Never in all his life had M. Géborand given alms to the unfortunate; but from the day of this sermon it was noticed that regularly every Sunday he gave a penny to the old beggar women at the door of the cathedral. There were six of them to share it. One day the bishop, seeing him perform this act of charity, said to his sister with a smile, "There's Monsieur Géborand, buying a pennyworth of paradise."

When soliciting aid for any charity, he was never silenced by a refusal; he was never at a loss for words that would set the hearers thinking. One day, he was seeking alms for the poor in a salon gathering, where the Marquis de Champtercier, old, rich, and miserly, was present. The marquis managed to be, at the same time, an ultra-royalist and an ultra-Voltairean, a species of which he was not the only representative. Coming to him in his turn, the bishop touched his arm and said, "Monsieur le Marquis, you must give me something." The marquis turned and answered drily, "Monseigneur, I have my own poor." "Give them to me," the bishop said.

One day he preached this sermon in the cathedral: "Dearest brethren, my good friends, in France there are one million three hundred and twenty thousand peasants' cottages that have only three openings; one million eight hundred and seventeen thousand that have two, the door and one window; and finally, three hundred and forty-six thousand cabins with only one—the door. And this is because of the tax on doors and windows. Imagine poor families, aged women and small children living in these huts, and think of the fever and disease. Alas! God gives light to men, and the law sells it. I do not blame the law, but I bless God. In l'Isère, in the Var, and in the Upper and Lower Alps, the peasants do not even have wheelbarrows; they carry the manure on their backs; they have no candles, but burn pine knots, and bits of rope soaked in pitch. And the same is true all through the Upper Dauphiné. They make bread once in six months and bake it by the heat of dried cowdung. In winter they have to break it with an ax and soak it in water for twenty-four hours before they can eat it. My brethren, be compassionate; see how much suffering there is around you."

Born a Provençal, he had familiarized himself with all the dialects of the South. He would say, *"Eh, bé! moussu, sès sagé?"* as in Lower Languedoc; *"Onté anaras passa?"* as in the Lower Alps; *"Puerte un bouen montou embe un bouen froumage grase,"* as in the Upper Dauphiné. This pleased the people and contributed not a little to giving him ready access to their hearts. He was equally at home in a cottage and on the mountains. He could say the loftiest things in the simplest language; and as he could speak all dialects, his words penetrated every soul.

He behaved the same with the rich as with the poor.

He condemned nothing hastily or without taking account of circumstances. He would say, "Let's see how the fault crept in."

Being, as he smilingly described himself, an ex-sinner, he had none of the inaccessibility of a rigid moralist, and would boldly profess without the raised eyebrows of the ferociously virtuous, a doctrine that might be loosely summarized as follows:

"Man has a body that is both his burden and his temptation. He drags it along and gives in to it.

"He ought to watch over it, keep it in bounds, repress it, and obey it only as a last resort. It may be wrong to obey even then, but if so, the fault is venial. It is a fall, but a fall onto the knees, which may end in prayer.

"To be a saint is the exception; to be upright is the rule. Err, falter, sin, but be upright.

"To commit the least possible sin is the law for man. To live entirely without sin is the dream of an angel. Everything on this earth is subject to sin. Sin is like gravity."

When he heard people raising a hue and cry, easily finding fault, "Oh ho!" he would say, with a smile. "It would seem that this is a great crime that everyone commits. See how an offended hypocrisy is quick to protest and run for cover."

He was indulgent toward women and the poor, upon whom the weight of society falls most heavily. He would say, "The faults of women, children, and servants, and of the weak, the indigent, and the ignorant, are the faults of their husbands, fathers, and masters, of the strong, the rich, and the wise." Or he would say, "Teach the ignorant as much as you can; society is guilty in not providing universal free education, and it must answer for the night it produces. If the soul is left in darkness, sins will be committed. The guilty one is not he who commits the sin, but the one who causes the darkness."

Clearly, he had his own strange way of judging things. I suspect he acquired it from the Gospels.

In a salon one day he heard an account of a criminal case about to be tried. A miserable man—because of love for a woman and the child she had borne him—had been making counterfeit coins, his real money gone. At that time counterfeiting was still punished by death. The woman was arrested for passing the first piece he had made. She was held prisoner, but there was no proof against her lover. She alone could testify against him, and lose him through her confession. She denied his guilt. They insisted, but she was obstinate in her denial. At that point, the king's state prosecutor devised a shrewd plan. He maintained that her lover was unfaithful and by means of fragments of letters skillfully put together succeeded in persuading the unfortunate woman that she had a rival and that the man had deceived her. Inflamed with jealousy, she denounced her lover, confessed everything, and proved his guilt. He was to be tried in a few days, at Aix, with his accomplice, and his conviction was certain. The story was told and retold, and everybody was delighted by the magistrate's cleverness. Bringing jealousy into play, he had brought truth to light by means of anger, and justice had sprung from revenge. The bishop listened to all this in silence. When it was finished he asked, "Where are this man and woman to be tried?"

"At the Superior Court."

"And where is the king's prosecutor to be tried?"

A tragic event occurred at Digne. A man had been condemned to death for murder. The unfortunate prisoner was a poorly educated but not entirely ignorant man who had been a juggler at fairs and a public letter writer. The townspeople were fascinated with the trial. The evening before the day appointed for the execution of the condemned, the prison chaplain fell ill. A priest was needed to be with the prisoner in his last moments. The curé was sent for, but he refused to go, saying, "This is no concern of mine. I want nothing to do with that mountebank; anyway, I'm sick, myself; and, in addition, it is not my responsiblity." When this reply was reported to the bishop, he said, "The curé is right. It is not his responsibility; it is mine."

Immediately going to the prison, he went down into the dungeon to the "mountebank," called him by his name, took him by the hand, and talked with him. He spent the whole day with him, forgetting food and sleep, praying to God for the soul of the condemned, and urging the man to join with him. He told him the greatest truths, which are the simplest. He was father, brother, friend to him—and a bishop only for blessings. He taught him everything by encouraging and consoling him. This man would have died in despair. Death, for him, was like an abyss. On his feet and trembling before the dreadful abyss, he had recoiled with horror. He was not ignorant enough to be indifferent. The terrible shock of his sentence had in some way broken that wall which separates us from the mystery of things beyond and which we call life. Through these mortal breaches, he was constantly looking beyond this world and seeing nothing but darkness; the bishop showed him the light.

The next day, when they came for the poor man, the bishop was with him. He followed him and appeared before the crowd in his violet robes, with his bishop's cross at his neck, side by side with the miserable creature bound with ropes.

He climbed onto the cart with him, ascended the scaffold with him. The sufferer, so desolate and overwhelmed the day before, was now radiant with hope. He felt that his soul was reconciled, and he trusted in God. The bishop embraced him, and as the ax was about to fall, he said to him, "He whom man kills God restores to life; he whom his brothers drive away finds the Father. Pray, believe, enter into life! The Father is here." When he climbed down from the scaffold, something in his look made the people fall back. It would be hard to say which was the more inspiring, his pallor or his serenity. As he entered the humble house which he smilingly called his *palace,* he said to his sister, "I have been officiating pontifically."

Because the loftiest things are often the least understood, there were those in the city who said, in commenting on the bishop's conduct, that it was affectation. But such ideas were confined to the upper classes. The people, who do not look for malice in holy works, marveled and were touched.

As for the bishop, the sight of the guillotine was a shock to him, from which he recovered only slowly.

Indeed, the scaffold, when it is there, set up and ready, has a profoundly hallucinatory effect. We may be indifferent to the death penalty and not declare ourselves, either way so long as we have not seen a guillotine with our own eyes. But when we do, the shock is violent, and we are compelled to choose sides, for or against. Some, like Le Maistre, admire it; others, like Beccaria, execrate it. The guillotine is the law made concrete; it is called the Avenger. It is not neutral and does not permit you to remain neutral. Whoever sees it quakes, mysteriously shaken to the core. All social problems set up their question mark around that blade. The scaffold is vision. The scaffold is not a mere frame, the scaffold is not an inert mechanism made of wood, iron, and ropes. It seems like a creature with some dark origin we cannot fathom, it is as though the framework sees and hears, the mechanism understands, as though the wood and iron and ropes have their own will. In the hideous nightmare it projects across the soul, the awful apparition of the scaffold fuses with its terrible work. The scaffold becomes the accomplice of the executioner; it devours, eats flesh, and drinks blood. The scaffold is a sort of monster created by judge and carpenter, a specter that seems to live with an unspeakable vitality, drawn from all the death it has wrought.

Thus the impression was horrible and profound; on the day after the execution, and for many subsequent days, the bishop seemed overwhelmed. The violent calm of the fatal moment had disappeared; the phantom of social justice took possession of him. He, who ordinarily looked back on all his actions with such radiant satisfaction, now seemed to be filled with self-reproach. At times he would talk to himself, muttering dismal monologues. One evening his sister overheard and jotted down the following: "I didn't believe it could be so monstrous. It's wrong to be so absorbed in divine law as not to perceive human law. Death belongs to God alone. By what right do men touch that unknown thing?"

With time these impressions faded away and probably disappeared. Nevertheless, it was remarked that the bishop always avoided passing the execution square.

M. Myriel could be called at all hours to the bedside of the sick and the dying. He well knew that there was his highest duty, his most important work. Widowed or orphan families did not need to send for him; he came on his own. He would sit silently for long hours beside a man who had lost the wife he loved or a mother who had lost her child. Just as he knew the time for silence, he also knew the time for speech. Oh, admirable consoler! He did not seek to drown grief in oblivion, but to exalt and dignify it through hope. He would say, "Be careful how you think of the dead. Don't think of what might have been. Look steadfastly and you will see the living glory of your beloved dead in the heights of heaven." He believed that faith gives health. He sought to counsel and calm the despairing by pointing out the Man of Resignation, and to transform the grief that contemplates the grave by showing it the grief that looks up to the stars.

V

HOW MONSEIGNEUR BIENVENU MADE HIS CASSOCK LAST SO LONG

The private life of M. Myriel was filled with the same thoughts as his public life. To one who could have seen it with his own eyes, the voluntary poverty in which the Bishop of Digne lived would have been a somber but charming sight.

Like all old men and most thinkers, he slept very little, but that little was sound. In the morning he devoted an hour to meditation and then said mass, either at the cathedral or in his own house. After mass he had his breakfast of rye bread and milk and then went to work.

A bishop is a very busy man; he has to receive the report of the clerk of the diocese, usually a canon, every day, and nearly every day his general. He has congregations to superintend, licenses to grant, ecclesiastical bookselling to examine, parish and diocesan catechisms, prayer books, and so on, instructions to write, sermons to authorize, curates and mayors to make peace between, a clerical correspondence, an administrative correspondence, on the one hand the government, on the other the Holy See, a thousand matters of business.

Whatever time these various affairs and his devotions and his breviary left him, he gave first to the needy, the sick, and the afflicted; what time the afflicted, the sick, and the needy left him, he gave to work. Sometimes he would dig in his garden, and sometimes he would read and write. He had only one name for these two kinds of work: gardening. "The spirit is a garden," he said.

At noon he would have his lunch, much the same as his breakfast.

Toward two o'clock, when the weather was good, he would go out for a walk in the fields or in the city, often visiting the cottages and cabins. He would be seen plodding along, wrapped in thought, his eyes lowered, leaning on his long cane, wearing his violet quilted cloak, violet stockings, and heavy shoes, and his flat tricornered hat, with three golden fringed tassels protruding from its points.

His coming was cause for celebration. It was as though he gave off warmth and light as he passed along. Old people and children would come to their doors for the bishop as they would for the sun. He blessed and was blessed in return. Anyone in need of anything was shown the way to his house.

Now and then he would stop and talk to the little boys and girls—and give a smile to their mothers. When he had money, his visits were to the poor; when he had none, he visited the rich.

To hide the fact that he made his cassock last a long time, he never went out without his violet cloak. In summer this was rather a nuisance.

On his return he had dinner, a meal just like his breakfast.

At half-past eight in the evening he had supper with his sister, Madame Magloire standing behind them and waiting on the table. Nothing could be more frugal than this meal. If, however, the bishop had one of his curés to supper, Madame Magloire used that occasion to serve her master some excellent fish from the lakes or some fine game from the mountain. Every curé was a pretext for a special meal; the bishop did not interfere. With these exceptions, there was rarely more than boiled vegetables, or bread warmed in oil. And this gave rise to a saying in the town: "When the bishop does not entertain a curé, he entertains a Trappist."

After supper he would chat for half an hour with Mademoiselle Baptistine and Madame Magloire then go back to his own room and write, sometimes on loose sheets, sometimes on the margin of one of his folios. He was a well-read, even learned man. He has left five or six rather curious manuscripts, among them a dissertation on this passage in Genesis: "In the beginning the spirit of God moved upon the face of the waters." He contrasts this with three other versions: the Arabic, which has "the winds of God blew"; Flavius Josephus, who says, "a wind from on high fell upon all the earth"; and finally the Chaldean paraphrase of Onkelos, which reads "a wind coming from God blew upon the face of the waters." In another dissertation, he examines the theological works of Hugo, Bishop of Ptolemais, a great-great-uncle of the writer of this book, and proves that various little tracts published in the last century under the pseudonym of Barleycourt should be attributed to that prelate.

Sometimes in the midst of his reading, no matter what book he might have in his hands, he would suddenly fall into deep meditation, and when it was over, write a few lines on the open page. These lines often have no connection with the book in which they are written. We have before us a note he penned on the margin of a quarto volume entitled *The Correspondence of Lord Germain with Generals Clinton, Cornwallis, and Admirals of the American Station* (Versaille: Poinçot Bookseller; Paris: Pissot, Quai des Augustins).

And this is the note: "Oh Thou who art! Ecclesiastes names thee the Almighty; Maccabees names thee Creator; the Epistle to the Ephesians names thee Liberty; Baruch names thee Immensity; the Psalms name thee Wisdom and Truth; John names thee Light; the Book of Kings names thee Lord; Exodus calls thee Providence; Leviticus, Holiness; Esdras, Justice; Creation calls thee God; man names thee Father; but Solomon names thee Compassion, and that is the most beautiful of all thy names."

Toward nine in the evening the two women would go up to their rooms on the second floor, leaving him alone until morning on the ground floor.

Here we should give an exact idea of the Bishop of Digne's house.

VI

HOW HE PROTECTED HIS HOUSE

As we have said, the house he lived in consisted of a ground floor and a second story; three rooms on the ground floor, three on the second, and an attic above. Behind the house was a garden of about a quarter of an acre. The two women occupied the upper floor; the bishop lived below. The room that opened upon the street was his dining room, the second was his bedroom, and the third his oratory. You could not leave the oratory without passing through the bedroom, or the bedroom except through the dining room. At one end of the oratory there was an enclosed alcove, with a bed for an occasional guest. The bishop kept this bed for the country curés when business or the needs of their parish brought them to Digne.

The former hospital pharmacy, a little building adjoining the house and extending into the garden, had been transformed into a kitchen and storeroom.

In the garden, there was also a stable, the former hospital kitchen, where the bishop now kept a few cows. Invariably, every morning, he sent half the milk they gave to the sick at the hospital. "I pay my tithes," he said.

His room was quite large and difficult to heat in bad weather. As wood is expensive in Digne, he conceived the idea of having a room with a tight plank ceiling partitioned off from the cow barn. In the coldest weather he spent his evenings there, and called it his winter parlor.

In this winter parlor, as in the dining room, the only furniture was a square white wooden table and four rush-seated chairs. The dining room, however, was furnished with an old sideboard stained red. A similar sideboard,

suitably draped with white linen and imitation
served for the altar that decorated the oratory.

His rich penitents and the pious women of Digne had often contributed money for a beautiful new altar for his oratory; he had always taken the money and given it to the poor. "The most beautiful of altars," he said, "is the soul of an unhappy man who is comforted and thanks God."

In his oratory he had two prie-dieu rush chairs, and an armchair, also rush-seated, in the bedroom. When he happened to have seven or eight visitors at once—the prefect, the general, the major of the regiment in the garrison, or some pupils from the secondary school, he had to go to the stable for the chairs in the winter parlor, to the oratory for the prie-dieu, and to the bedroom for the armchair; this way he could gather up to eleven seats for his visitors. With each new visitor a room was stripped.

It happened sometimes that there were twelve; then the bishop concealed the embarrassment of the situation by standing before the fire if it were winter or by walking with his guests in the garden if it were summer.

There was another chair in the guest's alcove, but it had lost half its rushes, and had only three legs, so that it could only be used propped against the wall. In her room, Mademoiselle Baptistine also had a large easy chair, which had once been gilded and covered with flowered silk, but as it had to be hoisted into her room through the window, the stairway being too narrow, it could not be counted among the movable furniture.

It had once been Mademoiselle Baptistine's ambition to be able to buy a parlor sofa, with cushions of Utrecht velvet, roses on a yellow background, while the mahogany should be in the form of swans' necks. But this would have cost at least five hundred francs, and as she had been able to save only forty-two francs and ten sous for the purpose in five years, she had finally given up. But whoever attains the ideal?

Nothing could be plainer in arrangement than the bishop's bedroom. A French window opening onto the garden; facing this, an iron hospital bed with green serge curtains; in the shadow of the bed, behind a screen, the grooming articles that betrayed the elegant habits of the man of the world; two doors, one near the fireplace, leading into the oratory, the other near the bookcase, opening into the dining room. The bookcase, a large closet with

lled with books; the fireplace, cased with
ntel painted to imitate marble, usually without
the hearth, a pair of andirons decorated with
es of flowers, once plated with silver, which was
of episcopal luxury; above the mantle, where one
ally puts a mirror, a copper crucifix, with traces of silver, attached to a piece of threadbare black velvet in a wooden frame from which the gilt was almost gone. Near the French window, a large table with an inkstand, strewn with papers and heavy volumes. In front of the table was the rush-seated armchair. In front of the bed, a prie-dieu from the oratory.

On either side of the bed hung two portraits in oval frames. Small gilt inscriptions on the background of the canvas indicated that one portrait represented the Abbé de Chaliot, Bishop of Saint Claude, the other the Abbé Tourteau, vicar general of Agde, Abbé of Grandchamps, Cistercian order, diocese of Chartres. The bishop found these portraits when he succeeded the hospital patients in this room, and left them untouched. They were priests and probably donors to the hospital—two reasons why he should respect them. All that he knew of them was that the king had given the one his diocese, the other his clerical benefits, on the same day, April 27, 1785. When Madame Magloire had taken down the pictures for dusting, the bishop found this odd detail written in faded ink on a little square of paper, yellowed with age, stuck with four seals to the back of the portrait of the Abbé of Grandchamps.

At his window he had an antique curtain of coarse woolen material, which finally became so old that, to save the expense of a new one, Madame Magloire put a large patch in the very middle of it. The bishop often called attention to the patch, which was in the form of a cross. "How apt," he would say.

Every room in the house was whitewashed, as is the custom in barracks and in hospitals.

Later, however, as we shall eventually see, Madame Magloire found under the wallpaper some paintings decorating Mademoiselle Baptistine's room. Before it was a hospital, the house had been a sort of gathering place for the town's leading citizens, hence these decorations. The floors of the rooms were paved with red tiles, which were scoured every week, and straw matting was spread beside the beds. The two women kept the house exquisitely neat from top to bottom. This was the only luxury the bishop would permit. He would say, "That takes nothing from the poor."

Yet we must confess that of his former possessions, he still kept a set of silver cutlery for six and a ladle, which Madame Magloire contemplated every day with new joy as they shone on the coarse white linen tablecloth. And as we are drawing the portrait of the Bishop of Digne just as he was, we must add that more than once he had said, "It would be difficult for me to give up eating with silver."

To the silverware should be added two massive silver candlesticks inherited from a great-aunt. These held wax candles, and stood on the bishop's mantel. When anyone came to dinner, Madame Magloire lit the two candles and placed the candlesticks on the table.

In the bishop's room, at the head of his bed, there was a small cupboard in which Madame Magloire put away the silver cutlery and the large ladle every evening. But the key was never taken out of it.

The garden, somewhat marred by the ugly structures already mentioned, was laid out with four walks crossing at a dry well in the center. Another walk around the garden skirted the white wall that enclosed it. These walks left four square plots bordered with boxwood. In three of them Madame Magloire grew vegetables; in the fourth the bishop had planted flowers and here and there a few fruit trees. Madame Magloire once said to him in a kind of gentle reproach, "Monseigneur, you are always eager to make everything useful, yet here is a useless plot. It would be much better to have salads there than bouquets."

"Madame Magloire," the bishop replied, "you are mistaken. The beautiful is as useful as the useful." He added after a moment's pause, "Perhaps more so."

This plot, consisting of three or four beds, occupied the bishop nearly as much as his books. He would spend an hour or two there, trimming, weeding, making holes in the ground and planting seeds. He was not as hostile to insects as a gardener might have wished. He had no botanical pretensions and knew nothing of species and classification; he did not care to decide between Tournefort and the natural method; he took no sides, either for the utricles against the cotyledons or for Jussieu against

Linnaeus. He did not study plants; he loved flowers. He had great respect for the learned, but still more for the ignorant, and, while fulfilling his duty in both directions, he watered his beds every summer evening with a tin watering can painted green.

No door in the house had a lock. The door of the dining room, which, we have mentioned, opened onto the cathedral grounds, was formerly fortified with bars and bolts like the door of a prison. The bishop had had all this ironwork taken off, and the door, night and day, was shut with only a latch. Any passerby, whatever the hour, could open it with a simple push. At first the two women had been worried because the door was never locked. But the Bishop of Digne said to them, "Have bolts put on your own doors, if you like." Eventually they shared his confidence, or at least acted as if they did. Madame Magloire alone had occasional attacks of fear. As for the bishop, his reasoning is explained, or at least indicated, in these three lines he wrote on the margin of a Bible: "This is the difference: The door of a physician should never be closed; the door of a priest should always be open."

In another book, *The Philosophy of Medical Science*, he wrote this: "Am I not a physician as well? I too have my patients. First I have the physician's, whom he calls the sick; and then I have my own, whom I call the unfortunate."

Again he wrote: "Do not ask the name of him who asks you for a bed. It is precisely he whose name is a burden to him who most needs sanctuary."

It occurred to a worthy curé—I am not sure whether it was the one from Couloubroux or Pomprierry—to ask him one day, probably at the instigation of Madame Magloire, if the bishop were quite sure there was not a degree of imprudence in leaving his door, day and night, open to whoever might wish to enter, and if he did not fear that some evil would befall a house so poorly defended. The bishop touched him gently on the shoulder and said, *"Nisi Dominus custodierit domum, in vanum vigilant qui custodiunt eam."*[1]

NOTE: Author's footnotes are indicated by the initials V.H. All other footnotes are the translators'.

[1] Unless God protects a house, they who guard it watch in vain.—(V.H.)

And then he changed the subject.

He would often say, "There is a bravery for the priest as well as for the colonel of dragoons. . . . Only, ours should be peaceable."

VII

CRAVATTE

This is the proper place for an incident that we must not omit, for it clearly shows the sort of man the Bishop of Digne was.

After the destruction of the band of Gaspard Bès, which had infested the gorges of Ollivolles, one of his lieutenants, Cravatte, took refuge in the mountains. He hid for some time with his bandits, the remnant of Gaspard Bès's band, in the countryside near Nice, then made his way to the Piedmont, and suddenly reappeared in France near Barcelonnette. He was first seen at Jauziers, then at Tuiles. He hid in the caverns of the Joug de l'Aigle and from there descended on the hamlets and villages by the ravines of Ubaye and Ubayette.

He even pushed as far as Embrun, and one night broke into the cathedral and stripped the sacristy. His robberies devastated the countryside. The gendarmes were put on his trail, but he always got away, sometimes using armed resistance. He was a bold devil. In the midst of all this terror, the bishop made his visit to Chastelar. The mayor came to see him and urged him to turn back. Cravatte held the mountains as far as l'Arche and beyond; it would be dangerous even with an escort. It would expose three or four poor gendarmes to useless danger.

"So then," the bishop said, "I'll go without an escort."

"Don't even think of such a thing," exclaimed the mayor.

"I think so much of it that I absolutely refuse the escort, and I am going to leave in an hour."

"To leave?"

"To leave."

"Alone?"

"Alone."

"Monseigneur, you must not."

"Up on the mountain," replied the bishop, "there's a little village I haven't seen for three years; they are good friends of mine, kind and honest shepherds. They own one goat out of thirty that they pasture. They make pretty woolen yarn of various colors, and they play their mountain tunes on small six-holed flutes. Occasionally they need someone to talk to them about God. What would they say of a bishop who was afraid? What would they say if I shouldn't go there?"

"But, Monseigneur, the bandits?"

"True enough," said the bishop, "you're right. I may meet them. They too must need someone to tell them of God's goodness."

"Monseigneur, but it's a gang! A pack of wolves!"

"Monsieur Mayor, perhaps Jesus has made me the shepherd of that very flock. Who knows the way of Providence?"

"Monseigneur, they'll rob you."

"I have nothing."

"They'll kill you."

"A simple old priest who passes along muttering prayers? No, no; what good would it do them?"

"But suppose you meet them!"

"I would ask them for alms for my poor."

"Monseigneur, don't go, in heaven's name! You're risking your life."

"Monsieur Mayor," said the bishop, "I am in this world to care not for my life, but for souls."

He would not be dissuaded. He set out, accompanied only by a child who offered to go as his guide. His stubbornness was the talk of the countryside, and everyone feared the outcome.

He would not take his sister or Madame Magloire with him. He crossed the mountain on a mule, met no one, and arrived safe and sound among his "good friends," the shepherds. He spent two weeks there, preaching, administering the holy rites, teaching and exhorting. About to leave, he decided to chant a Te Deum with ceremony. He talked with the curé about it. But what could be done? There was no episcopal furniture. They could only give him a paltry village sacristy with a few old robes of worn-out damask, trimmed with fake braid.

"No matter," said the bishop. "Monsieur le curé, at the sermon announce our Te Deum. It will take care of itself."

All the nearby churches were searched, but the collective finery of these humble parishes could not have suitably clothed a single cathedral choir member.

While they were trying to figure a way out of this fix, a large chest was delivered to the priest's house and left for the bishop by two unknown horsemen, who immediately rode away. The chest was opened; it contained a cope of gold cloth, a miter decorated with diamonds, an archbishop's cross, a magnificent crosier, all the pontifical raiment stolen a month before from the treasury of Notre Dame d'Embrun. In the chest was a paper with these words: "Cravatte to Monseigneur Bienvenu."

"I said that it would take care of itself," said the bishop. Then he added with a smile, "To him who is contented with a curé's surplice, God sends an archbishop's cope."

"Your Lordship," murmured the curé, with a shake of the head and a smile, "God—or the devil."

The bishop trained his eyes on the curé, and replied with authority: "God!"

On his way back to Chastelar, all along the road, the people came to see him out of curiosity. At the priest's residence in Chastelar he found Mademoiselle Baptistine and Madame Magloire waiting for him, and he said to his sister, "Well, wasn't I right? The poor priest went to those poor mountaineers with empty hands; he returns with hands filled. I went forth placing my trust in God alone; I bring back the treasures of a cathedral."

In the evening before going to bed he added, "Have no fear of robbers or murderers. They are external dangers, petty dangers. We should fear ourselves. Prejudices are the real robbers; vices the real murderers. The great dangers are within us. Why worry about what threatens our heads or our purses? Let us think instead of what threatens our souls."

Then turning to his sister: "My sister, a priest must never take any precaution against a neighbor. What his neighbor does God permits. Let us confine ourselves to prayer when we feel danger looming, pray not for ourselves, but that our brother not fall into crime because of us."

Such events were rare in his life. We repeat those we know of; but his life was usually spent doing the same things at the same hours. A month of his year was like an hour of his day.

As to what became of the "treasures" of the Cathedral of Embrun, questions on that point would embarrass us. They were fine things certainly, very tempting, and very good to steal for the benefit of the unfortunate. Stolen they already were, by others. Half the work was done; it only remained to change the course of the theft, to turn it to the benefit of the poor. We say nothing more on the subject. Except that, among the bishop's papers was found a rather obscure note, possibly connected with this affair, which reads as follows: "The question is, whether this ought to be returned to the cathedral or to the hospital."

VIII

AFTER-DINNER PHILOSOPHY

The senator referred to above was an intelligent man who had made his way in life with a directness of purpose that disregarded such obstructions as conscience, sworn testimony, faith, justice, and duty; he had marched straight to his objective without swerving. Formerly a public prosecutor, mollified by success, he was not a bad man at all, doing all the little kindnesses that he could for his sons, sons-in-law, his other relatives, and even his friends, having wisely taken the pleasant side of life, accepting all benefits that came his way. Anything else seemed stupid. He was witty and just enough of a scholar to think himself a disciple of Epicurus, though he was probably simply a product of Pigault-Lebrun. He laughed freely and pleasantly at infinite and eternal things and at the "crotchets of the good bishop." He laughed at them sometimes, with a patronizing air, in front of M. Myriel himself, who merely listened.

At some semiofficial ceremony, the Comte de ——— (this senator) and M. Myriel stayed to dine with the prefect. At dessert, the senator, in rather high spirits, though still dignified, exclaimed, "Good Lord, Monsieur Bishop, let's talk. It's difficult for a senator and a bishop to look each other in the eye without blinking. We are two prophets. I must confess to you, I have a philosophy of my own."

"And you're right," the bishop answered. "As a man makes his philosophy, so he rests—you are on the purple bed, Monsieur Senator."

Encouraged by this, the senator proceeded: "Let's be good fellows."

"Good devils, even," said the bishop.

"I assure you," the seantor resumed, "that the Marquis d'Argens, Pyrrho, Hobbes, and M. Naigeon are not villains. I have all my philosophers in my library, gilt-edged."

"Like yourself, Monsieur le Comte," interrupted the bishop.

The senator went on: "I hate Diderot; he's an ideologue, a demagogue, and a revolutionary, basically believing in God, and more bigoted than Voltaire. Voltaire mocked Needham, and he was wrong; for Needham's eels prove that God is unnecessary. A drop of vinegar in a spoonful of dough supplied the *fiat lux*. Imagine the drop greater and the spoonful larger, and you have the world. Man is the eel. Then what is the use of an eternal Father? Monsieur Bishop, the Jehovah hypothesis bores me. It's good for nothing except to produce people with skinny bodies and empty heads. Down with this great All; how he irritates me! Hail, Zero! He leaves me alone. Between you and me, both to get it off my chest and confess to my pastor, as one should, I admit I have good common sense. I'm not wild about your Jesus, who preaches renunciation and self-sacrifice in every field. A miser's advice to beggars. Renunciation, for what? Self-sacrifice, to what? I do not see one wolf immolating himself for the benefit of another wolf. So let us stay with nature. We're at the summit, so let's have a superior philosophy. What's the use of being better off if we can't see further than the next man's nose? Let's live for pleasure. Life is all we have. Man has another life elsewhere, above, below, anywhere? I don't believe a word of it. Ah! Self-sacrifice and renunciation are recommended to me. I am warned I should take care what I do; I must struggle over questions of good and evil, justice and injustice; over the *fas* and the *nefas*. Why? Because I shall have to render an account for my acts. When? After death. What a splendid dream! After I'm dead it will take minute fingers to pinch me. I'd like to see a ghost grab a handful of ashes. Let us, the initiated, who have raised the skirt of Isis, speak the truth: There is neither good nor evil, there is only vegetation. Let us look for the real, down deep, right to the bottom. We should sniff out the truth, dig underground, and grab it. Then it gives you exquisite joy. Then you grow strong, and you laugh. I'm firmly convinced, Monsieur Bishop, that the immortality of man is a will-o'-the-wisp. Oh! lovely promise. Trust it if you like! Adam's letter of recommendation! We have souls; we'll be angels, with blue wings at our shoulders. Tell me, now, isn't it Tertullian who says the blessed will go from one star to another? Fine. We'll be the grasshoppers of the universe. And then we'll see God. Ridiculous, all this heaven. God is a monstrous myth. I wouldn't say that in the *Moniteur,* of course, but I whisper it among my friends. *Inter pocula*. Sacrificing earth to paradise is like leaving your fortune to a corpse. I'm not that stupid. Duped by the Infinite! I am nothing; I call myself Count Nothing, the senator. Did I exist before my birth? No. Will I after my death? No. What am I? A little dust surrounding an organism. What do I have to do on this earth! I have the choice of pain or pleasure. Where will pain lead me? To nothing. But I will have suffered. Where will pleasure lead me? To nothing. But I will have enjoyed. My choice is made. I must eat or be eaten, and I choose to eat. It is better to be the tooth than the grass. That's my philosophy. After which, there is the gravedigger—the pantheon for *us*—but all fall into the great gulf—the end; *finis;* total liquidation. This is the vanishing point. Death is dead, believe me. Laughable, the idea that there is anyone there with anything to say to me. Fairy tales all: Goblins for children; God for men. No, our tomorrow is night. Beyond the grave, all are only equal nothings. You have been Sardanapalus or Vincent de Paul—it amounts to the same nothing. Live, then, above all else; use your self while you have it. In fact, I tell you, Monsieur Bishop, I have my own philosophy, and I have my philosophers. I don't allow myself to be beguiled by nonsense. But there should be something for those beneath us, the barefooted, knife grinders and other miserable souls. They're given myths and chimeras for nourishment, about the soul, immortality, paradise, and stars. They munch on it, spread it on their dry bread. He who has nothing else has the good Lord—the least good he can have. I have no objection to that, but I keep Monsieur Naigeon for myself. The good Lord is good enough for the people."

The bishop clapped his hands.

"That's the idea," he exclaimed. "Materialism is excellent, truly marvelous; reject it at your risk. Ah! Once you have it, you're no one's fool; you don't stupidly allow yourself to be exiled like Cato or stoned like Stephen or burned alive like Joan of Arc. Those who have acquired this admirable materialism have all the joy of feeling irresponsible, of thinking they can calmly devour everything—high positions, sinecures, honors, power rightly or wrongly acquired, lucrative retractions, useful betrayals, delectable lapses of conscience—and that they will enter their graves with it all totally digested. How nice! I'm not referring to you, my dear Senator. Nevertheless, I must congratulate you. You great lords have, as you say, your very own philosophy—exquisite, refined, accessible to the rich alone, good for all occasions, admirably seasoning the pleasures of life. This philosophy comes from great depths, unearthed by specialists. But you are good princes, and you are quite willing to let belief in the good Lord be the philosophy of the people, much as a goose with onions is the turkey with truffles of the poor."

IX

THE BROTHER PORTRAYED BY THE SISTER

To give some idea of the household of the Bishop of Digne, and the way these two good women subordinated their actions, thoughts, even their easily disturbed womanly instincts to the bishop's habits and plans so that he did not even have to express them aloud, we can do no better than to copy this letter from Mademoiselle Baptistine to Madame la Viscontesse de Boischevron, a childhood friend:

Digne, Dec. 16, 18–.

"My dear Madame: Not a day goes by without talk of you. That is usual enough, but now we have another reason. Would you believe that in washing and dusting the ceilings and walls, Madame Magloire made some discoveries? Our two bedrooms, once covered with old wallpaper, later whitewashed, would at present do credit to a château like yours. Madame Magloire has torn off all the paper; it had something underneath. My unfurnished parlor, which we use for drying clothes, is fifteen feet high, eighteen feet square, and has a ceiling, once painted and gilded, with beams like those in your house. This was covered with canvas when it was used as a hospital. And then there is wainscoting from our grandmothers' time. But it is my own room you ought to see. Madame Magloire has discovered under at least ten layers of paper some paintings, which, though not good, are quite tolerable. Telemachus on horseback meeting Minerva in one; and in another, he is in the garden—I forget the name—where the Roman ladies would go for one night. There is much more: I have Romans, men and women [*here a word is illegible*], and their full retinue. Madame Magloire has cleaned it all up, and this summer she is going to repair some damages, varnish it, and my room will be a veritable museum. In a corner of the attic she also found two antique pier tables. They wanted almost six livres to regild them, but it is far better to give that to the poor; besides, they are very ugly, and anyway, I would prefer a round mahogany table.

"I am still happy; my brother is so good. He gives all he has to the poor and sick. We are sometimes left with little. The weather here is very harsh in winter, and one must do something for those in need. At least we have some warmth and light, which are great comforts, as you know.

"My brother has his own ways. He says that a bishop ought to be like this. Just imagine, the door is never locked. Whoever enters is immediately my brother's guest. He is afraid of nothing, not even at night; he says it is his form of bravery.

"He wants neither me nor Madame Magloire to fear

for his safety. He exposes himself to every danger and wants us to appear unaware of it. It takes a lot to understand him.

"He goes out in the rain, walks through puddles, travels in winter. He has no fear of darkness or of dangerous roads, or of strangers.

"Last year he went alone to an area overrun with bandits. He would not take us. He was gone two weeks, and when he came back, though we had thought him dead, nothing had happened to him and he was well. He said, 'See, how they have robbed me!' And he opened a trunk containing the jewels of the Embrun Cathedral that the bandits had returned to him.

"That time on his return, since I had gone out with some of his friends to meet him, I could not keep from scolding him a little, making sure to speak only while the carriage made noise, so no one overheard us.

"At first I used to say to myself, no danger worries him, he's incorrigible. Now I've become used to it. I motion to Madame Magloire not to oppose him, and he runs whatever risks he chooses. I call Madame Magloire away and go to my room, pray for him, and fall asleep. I am calm, for I know very well that if any harm came to him, it would be my death. I would go to the good Lord with my brother and my bishop. Madame Magloire has had more difficulty getting used to what she calls his imprudence. Now we have adapted; we pray together; we are afraid together, and then we go to sleep. Even if Satan came into the house, no one would interfere. After all, what is there to fear in this house? There is always One with us who is the strongest. Satan may visit our house, but the good Lord lives here.

"That is enough. Now my brother does not need to say a word. I understand him without his speaking, and we commend ourselves to Providence.

"So it is with a man whose soul is so noble.

"I asked my brother for the information you requested concerning the Faux family. You know how much he knows and remembers, because he is still a good royalist. It really is a family from Caen. There were, five centuries ago, a Raoul de Faux, Jean de Faux, and Thomas de Faux, all gentry, one of them a lord of Rochefort. The last was Guy Etienne Alexandre, a colonel who held some rank in the light horse of Brittany. His daughter

Marie Louise married Adrien Charles de Gramont, son of Duke Louis de Gramont, a peer of France, colonel of the Gardes Françaises, and lieutenant general of the army. It is written Faux, Fauq, and Faouq.

"Will you please, my dear madame, ask your holy relative, Monsieur le Cardinal, to pray for us? As for your precious Sylvanie, she is wise not to waste her brief time with you in writing to me. She is well, you say, works as you wish, and loves me still. That is all I could desire. Her greetings reached me through you and made me happy. My health is tolerable, though I grow thinner every day.

"Farewell. My page is filled and I must stop. With a thousand warm good wishes.

"BAPTISTINE.

"P.S. Your sister-in-law is still here with her little family. Your great-nephew is charming. Can you believe he is almost five? Yesterday he saw a horse going by on which they had put knee pads, and he cried out, 'What is wrong with his knees?' The child is so sweet. His little brother drags an old broom around the room for a carriage, and says, 'Giddy-up!' "

As this letters shows, these two women knew how to conform to the bishop's way of life, with that womanly talent of understanding a man better than he himself can. Beneath the invariably gentle, open manner of the Bishop of Digne, he sometimes performed great, daring—even grand—deeds, seemingly unaware of them himself. The women shuddered but did not interfere. Sometimes Madame Magloire would venture a rebuke beforehand, never at the time, or afterward. No one ever disturbed him by so much as a word, once an action was begun. At certain times, when he had no need to say it, when, perhaps, he was hardly conscious of it, so complete was his artlessness, they vaguely felt that he was acting as bishop, and at such moments they became merely two shadows in the house. They waited on him passively, and if to obey was to disappear, they would do so. With charming and instinctive delicacy they knew that obtrusive attentions would annoy him. So even when they thought him in danger, they understood—I will not say his thought—but rather his nature, to the point of ceasing to watch over him. They entrusted him to God's care.

Besides, as we have just seen, Baptistine said that his death would be hers, too. Madame Magloire did not say so, but she felt the same.

X

THE BISHOP IN THE PRESENCE OF AN UNFAMILIAR LIGHT

A short while after the date of the letter quoted above, the bishop did something that the whole town found far more dangerous than his excursion across the bandit-infested mountains.

In the countryside near Digne, there was a man who lived alone. This man, to state the startling fact right off, had been a member of the National Convention. His name was G———.

The narrow world of Digne spoke of the former deputy with a sort of horror. A revolutionary conventionist, think of it! That was in the time when people thee-and-thoued one another and called everyone "Citizen." This man was practically a monster. He had not exactly voted for the execution of the king, but almost; he was half a regicide. Why then, with the restoration of the legitimate monarchy, had they not arraigned him before the provost court? He would not have been beheaded, probably, but even if clemency prevailed, he might have been banished for life. Besides, he was an atheist, like the others. Bab-blings of geese against a vulture!

But was this G——— a vulture? Yes, if one should judge him by the savageness of his isolation. Because he had not voted for the king's execution, he was not in-cluded in the sentence of exile and could remain in France.

He lived about an hour's walk from town, far from any hamlet or road, in a desolate ravine of a wild valley. He was said to have a sort of shelter there, some clearing. He had no neighbors and nobody even passed by. Since he had come, the path leading to the place had become overgrown, and people spoke of it as they would of a hangman's house.

From time to time, however, the bishop thoughtfully gazed at the spot on the horizon where a clump of trees indicated the former conventionist's ravine, and he would say, "There lives a lonely soul." And deep down, he would add, "I owe him a visit."

But we must confess that this idea, natural enough at first glance, seemed strange, impracticable, almost repulsive, after a few moments' reflection. For at heart he shared the general impression, and the conventionist inspired him somehow with that feeling, akin to hatred, so well expressed by the word "aversion."

The shepherd should not recoil from the diseased sheep. Oh, but such a black sheep!

The good bishop was confused; sometimes he would start out in that direction but then turn back.

At last, one day the news was circulated in town that the young shepherd who served the conventionist in his retreat had come for a doctor; that the poor man was dying, that he was paralyzed, and could not live through the night. "Thank God!" some said.

The bishop took his cane, put on his cloak because he wanted to hide the badly worn cassock and also because the night wind would be rising, and set out.

The setting sun had nearly touched the horizon when the bishop reached the accursed spot. A certain quickening of the pulse told him he was near the lair. He jumped over a ditch, cleared a hedge, made his way through a brush fence, found himself in a dilapidated garden, and after boldly walking across the open ground, suddenly, behind some high shrubbery, he caught sight of the retreat.

It was a low, impoverished hut, small and clean, with a little vine clinging to the front.

In front of the door, in an old peasant chair on rollers, sat a man with white hair, smiling toward the setting sun.

The young shepherd stood beside him, handing him a bowl of milk.

As the bishop watched, the old man spoke.

"Thank you," he said. "I won't need anything else." And his smile moved from the sun to rest on the boy.

The bishop stepped forward. At the sound of his footsteps the old man turned his head, and his face expressed as much surprise as one can feel at the end of a long life.

"This is the first time since I have lived here," he said, "that I have had a visitor. Who are you, monsieur?"

"My name is Bienvenu Myriel," the bishop replied.

"Bienvenu Myriel? I have heard that name before. Are you the one the people call Monseigneur Bienvenu?"

"I am."

The old man went on, half smiling: "Then you are my bishop?"

"In a way."

"Welcome, monsieur."

The conventionist extended his hand to the bishop, who did not take it. He only said, "I am glad to find that I have been misinformed. You do not appear to be very ill."

"Monsieur," replied the old man, "I will soon be better." He paused then added, "In three hours I will be dead."

Then he went on: "I am something of a physician; I know the steps by which death approaches; yesterday only my feet were cold; today the cold has crept to my knees, now it has reached the waist; when it reaches the heart, all will be over. The sunset is lovely, don't you think? I had myself wheeled out for one last look at nature. You can speak to me; that won't tire me. You were right to come to see a dying man. It is right that these moments should have witnesses. Everyone has his dream; I would like to live till dawn, but I know I have less than three hours left. It will be night, but no matter. Dying is simple. It does not take daylight. So be it: I will die by starlight."

The old man turned toward the shepherd. "Little one, go to bed. You stayed up all last night. You're tired."

The child went into the hut.

The old man followed him with his eyes and added, as though to himself, "While's he's sleeping, I'll die. The two slumbers are good brothers."

The bishop was not as moved as he might have been. This did not seem a godly death. We must tell everything, for the little inconsistencies of great souls should be mentioned. He who had laughed so heartily at "His Highness" was still slightly shocked at not being called

Monseigneur and was almost tempted to answer "Citizen." He felt a desire for the brusque familiarity common enough with doctors and priests, but not proper for him.

This conventionist, after all, this representative of the people, had wielded power on this earth; and perhaps for the first time in his life the bishop felt in a mood to be severe. The conventionist, however, treated him with modest consideration and cordiality, in which one might perceive a humility proper to one so nearly dust unto dust.

The bishop, for his part, though generally free from curiosity—which he found almost offensive—could not keep from examining the conventionist with an attention that, as it did not spring from sympathy, would have seemed unconscionable regarding any other man. But he regarded a conventionist as an outlaw, even beyond the law of charity.

G———, with his calm, almost erect figure, and resonant voice, was one of those noble octogenarians who are the marvel of doctors. The Revolution produced many such men equal to the era. One felt that here was a man tested by life. Though so near death, he appeared healthy. His bright glances, his firm speech, and the muscular movements of his shoulders seemed almost enough to disconcert death. Azrael, the Islamic angel of the sepulcher, would have turned back, thinking he had the wrong door. G——— appeared to be dying because he wished to die. There was liberty in his dying; only his legs were paralyzed. His feet were cold and dead, but his head lived in the full power of life and clarity. At this solemn moment G——— seemed like the king in the oriental tale, flesh above and marble below. The bishop seated himself on a nearby stone. Their conversation began abruptly.

"I congratulate you," he said, in a tone of reprimand. "At least you did not vote for the king's execution."

The conventionist did not seem to notice the bitter emphasis placed on the words "at least." The smile vanished from his face. "Do not congratulate me too much, Monsieur; I did vote for the destruction of the tyrant."

And the tone of austerity confronted the tone of severity.

"What do you mean?" asked the bishop.

"I meant that man has one tyrant, Ignorance. I voted

for the abolition of that tyrant. That tyrant fathered royalty, which is authority springing from the False, whereas science is authority springing from the True. Man should be governed by science."

"And conscience," added the bishop.

"They are the same: Conscience is science."

Monsieur Bienvenu listened with some amazement to this language, as it was new to him.

The revolutionary went on: "As to Louis XVI, I said no. I do not believe I have the right to kill a man, but I feel it a duty to exterminate evil. I voted for the downfall of the tyrant, that is, for the abolition of prostitution for woman, of slavery for man, of darkness for the child. In voting for the republic I voted for that: I voted for fraternity, for harmony, for dawn. I helped to overthrow prejudice and error: Their downfall brings light! We brought down the old world—a jug of misery overturned, becomes a vessel of joy to humanity."

"Joy alloyed," said the bishop.

"You might say troubled joy, and at present, after this fatal return of the past that we call 1814, vanished joy. Alas! the work was imperfect, I admit; we demolished the ancient order of things physically, but not entirely in the idea. To destroy abuses is not enough; habits must also be changed. The windmill has gone, but the wind is still there."

"You have demolished. To demolish may be useful, but I distrust destruction made in anger!"

"Justice has its anger, Monsieur Bishop, and the wrath of justice is an element of progress. No matter what they say, the French Revolution is the greatest advance taken by mankind since the coming of Christ. Incomplete it may be, but it is sublime. It loosened all the secret chains of society, it softened all hearts, it calmed, appeased, enlightened; it caused waves of civilization to flow over the earth; it was good. The French revolution is the consecration of humanity."

The bishop could not help murmuring, "Yes? And '93!"

The former deputy sat up in his chair with an almost mournful solemnity, and as well as a dying person could, he exclaimed, "Ah! Of course! '93! I was expecting that. A cloud had been forming for fifteen hundred years; at the end of fifteen centuries it burst. You are condemning the thunderbolt."

Without perhaps acknowledging it, the bishop was moved. However, he regained his composure and replied, "The judge speaks in the name of justice, the priest in the name of pity, which is only a more exalted justice. Such a thunderbolt should not make mistakes." And he added, glaring at the revolutionary: "Louis XVII?"

The conventionist stretched out his hand and seized the bishop's arm. "Louis XVII. Let's see! For whom do you weep?—for the innocent child? Good! I weep with you. For the royal child? I ask time to reflect. In my view the brother of Cartouche, an innocent child, hung by a rope under his arms in the Place de Grève till he died, for the sole crime of being the brother of Cartouche, is a no less painful sight than the grandson of Louis XV, an innocent child murdered in the tower of the Temple for the sole crime of being the grandson of Louis XV."

"Monsieur," the bishop said, "I disapprove of this coupling of names."

"Cartouche or Louis XV; for which one are you concerned?"

There was a moment of silence; the bishop almost regretted that he had come, and yet he felt strangely and inexplicably moved.

The former deputy went on: "Oh, Monsieur Priest! You do not like the harshness of truth, but Christ loved it. He took a scourge and purged the temple; his flashing whip was a rude truth teller; when he said '*Sinite parvulos,*' he made no distinctions among the little ones. He was not pained at coupling the dauphin of Barabbas with the dauphin of Herod. Monsieur, innocence is its own crown! Innocence can only be noble! She is as august in rags as in the fleur de lys."

"That's true," the bishop said, quietly.

"I repeat," the old man continued, "you've mentioned Louis XVII. I agree, let's weep together for all the innocent, all the martyrs, all the children, humble as well as mighty. I'm for that. But then, as I said, we must go further back than '93, and our tears must start before Louis XVII. I will weep for the children of kings with you, if you will weep with me for the children of the people."

"I weep for them all," the bishop said.

"Equally," G——— exclaimed, "and if the balance tips, let it be on the side of the people: They have suffered longer."

There was silence again, broken at last by the old man. He raised himself up on one elbow, pinched one of his cheeks, as one does unconsciously in examining and forming an opinion, then addressed the bishop with a look full of all the energies of dying. It was like an explosion.

"Yes, Monsieur, the people have been suffering for a long time. And then, sir, that's not all; why do you come to question me and to speak to me of Louis XVII? I don't know you. Since I have been in this region I have lived within these walls all alone, never going beyond them, seeing no one but this child who helps me. Your name has, it is true, reached me confusedly, and I must say not without respect, but no matter. Clever men have so many ways of impressing the good and simple people. For instance, I did not hear the sound of your carriage. You undoubtedly left it behind the thicket, down there at the fork in the road. You have told me you are the bishop, but that tells me nothing about your moral integrity. Now, then, I repeat my question, Who are you? You are a bishop, a prince of the church, one of those men covered with gold, insignia, and wealth, a fat sinecure—the see of Digne, fifteen thousand francs per year, ten thousand francs contingent, total twenty-five thousand francs—you have kitchens and retinues, give fine dinners, eat good poultry on Friday, show off in your gaudy coaches like peacocks, lackeys in front and lackeys behind, you have palaces, and travel about in the name of Jesus Christ, who walked barefoot. You are a prelate; rents, palaces, horses, valets, a good table, all the sensuous pleasures of life, you have these like all the rest, and like all the rest you enjoy them. Very well, but that says too much and not enough; it does not enlighten me as to your intrinsic worth, what is unique to yourself, you who probably come with the claim of bringing me wisdom. To whom am I speaking? Who are you?"

The bishop bowed his head and replied, "*Vermis sum.*"

"An earthworm in a carriage!" grumbled the old man.

It was the turn of the conventionist to be haughty and the bishop to be humble.

The bishop replied gently, "Monsieur, so be it. But explain to me how my carriage, which is there a few steps beyond the trees, how my good table and Friday poultry, how my twenty-five thousand livres of income, how my palace and my lackeys, prove that pity is not a virtue, that kindness is not a duty, and that '93 was not an outrage?"

The old man passed his hand across his forehead as if to dispel a cloud.

"Before answering you," he said, "I beg your pardon. I have wronged you, monsieur. You are my guest. I should be more polite. You are discussing my ideas; I should confine myself to combatting your reasoning. Your wealth and your possessions are advantages I have over you in the debate, but it is not in good taste to dwell on them. I promise I won't use them again."

"Thank you," the bishop said.

G——— went on: "Let us return to the explanation you asked me to give. Where were we? What were you saying to me? That '93 was an outrage?"

"An outrage, yes," said the bishop. "What do you think of Marat applauding at the guillotine?"

"What do you think of Bossuet chanting the Te Deum during the persecution of the Huguenots?"

The response was severe, but it reached its target like a dagger. The bishop was staggered, speechless; it shocked him to hear Bossuet spoken of in that manner. The best men have their blind spots, and sometimes they feel almost crushed at how little respect logic can show them.

The conventionist began to gasp; the agonizing asthma that mingles with the last breath broke his voice; yet his lucid soul still shone in his eyes. He went on: "Let's say a few more words—I would like that. Beyond the revolution, which, taken as a whole, is an immense human affirmation, '93, alas! is a reply. You think it an outrage, but the whole monarchy, monsieur? Carrier is a bandit; but what can you say about Montrevel? Fouquier-Tainville is a wretch; but what is your opinion of Lamoignon Bâville? Maillard is frightful, but what of Saulx-Tavannes? The elder Duchêne is ferocious, but what epithet will you furnish me for the elder Letellier? Jourdan-

Coupe-Tête is a monster, but less than the Marquis de Louvois. Monsieur, monsieur, I mourn Marie Antoinette, archduchess and queen, but I also mourn that poor Huguenot woman who, in 1685, under Louis le Grand, monsieur, while nursing her child, was stripped to the waist and tied to a post, while her child was held before her; her breast swelled with milk and her heart with anguish; the baby, weak and famished, seeing the breast, cried in agony; and the executioner said to the nursing mother, 'Recant!' giving her the choice between the death of her child and the death of her conscience. What do you say to this Tantalus torture inflicted on a mother? Monsieur, remember this: The French revolution had its reasons. Its anger will be pardoned by the future; its result is a better world. Its most terrible blows are a caress for the human race. I must be brief. I must stop. I have too good a cause; and I am dying."

And, no longer looking at the bishop, the old man concluded his thought with these few tranquil words: "Yes, the brutalities of progress are called revolutions. When they are over, men recognize that the human race has been harshly treated but that it has moved forward."

The revolutionary did not know that he had successively demolished all the bishop's interior defenses, one after the other. There was one left, however, and from it, the last resource of Monseigneur Bienvenu's resistance, came forth these words, in which nearly all the harshness of the opening reappeared.

"Progress ought to believe in God. The good cannot have an impious servant. An atheist is an evil leader of the human race."

The old representative of the people did not answer. He was trembling. He looked up into the sky, and a tear gathered slowly in his eye. When the lid was full, the tear rolled down his ashen cheek, and he said, almost stammering, low, talking to himself, his eyes gazing inward:

"Oh thou! O ideal! Thou alone dost exist!"

The bishop felt an inexpressible emotion.

After a brief silence, the old man raised his finger toward heaven, and said, "The infinite exists. It is there. If the infinite had no *me*, the *me* would be its limit; it would not be the infinite; in other words, it would not be. But it is. Then it has a *me*. This *me* of the infinite is God."

The dying man pronounced these last words in a loud

voice and with a shudder of ecstasy, as if he saw someone. When he had spoken, his eyes closed. The effort had exhausted him. It was evident that in one minute he had lived through the few hours remaining to him. What he had said had brought him near to the One who is in death. The last moment was at hand.

The bishop realized that time was pressing. He had come as a priest; from extreme coldness he had gone gradually to extreme emotion; he glanced at those closed eyes, he took that old, wrinkled, icy hand and drew close to the dying man.

"This is the hour of God. Do you not think it would be sad if we had met in vain?"

The conventionist reopened his eyes. Calm was imprinted on his face, already touched with shadow.

"Monsieur Bishop," he said with a deliberation that came perhaps still more from the dignity of his soul than from the waning of his strength, "I have spent my life in meditation, study, and contemplation. I was sixty years old when my country called me and ordered me to take part in her affairs. I obeyed. There were abuses, I fought them; there were tyrannies, I destroyed them; there were rights and principles, I proclaimed and professed them. The soil was invaded, I defended it; France was threatened, I offered her my breast. I was not rich; I am poor. I was one of the masters of the state, the vaults of the bank were piled with coins, so we had to strengthen the walls or they would have fallen under the weight of gold and silver; I dined in the Rue de l'Arbre-Sec at twenty-two sous for the meal. I succored the oppressed, I solaced the suffering. True, I tore the drapery from the altar; but it was to dress the wounds of the country. I have always supported the forward march of humanity toward the light, and I have sometimes resisted a progress that lacked pity. On occasion, I have protected my own adversaries, your friends. At Peteghem in Flanders, at the very spot where the Merovingian kings had their summer palace, there is a monastery of Urbanists, the Abbey of Sainte Claire in Beaulieu, which I saved in 1793; I did my duty according to my strength, and what good I could. After that I was hunted, hounded, pursued, persecuted, slandered, railed at, spit upon, cursed, banished. For many years now, with my white hairs, I have noticed that some people believed they had a right to despise me; to the poor, ignorant crowd I have the face of the damned, and hating no man myself I accept the isolation of hatred. Now I am eighty-six years old; I am about to die. What have you come to ask of me?"

"Your blessing," said the bishop. And he fell to his knees.

When the bishop raised his eyes, the face of the old man looked noble. He had died.

The bishop went home profoundly absorbed in thought. He spent the whole night in prayer. The next day, some individuals, their curiosity piqued, tried to talk to him about the conventionist G———, but he simply pointed to heaven.

From that moment he redoubled his tenderness and brotherly love for the weak and the suffering.

Every allusion to "that old scoundrel G———" sent him into a strange reverie. No one could say that the passing of that soul in his presence, and the reflection of that great conscience upon his own, had not had its effect on his approach to perfection.

This "pastoral visit" was of course an occasion for gossip in the local circles.

"Was the bedside of such a man the place for a bishop? Of course he could expect no conversion there. All these revolutionaries are backsliders. Then why go? What had he gone there to see? He must have wanted to see a soul carried away by the devil."

One day a dowager, of the impertinent sort that believe themselves witty, remarked, "Monseigneur, people ask when Your Lordship will wear the red bonnet." "Ah ha! That is a mighty color," replied the bishop. "Luckily, those who hate it in a bonnet worship it in a chapeau."

XI

A QUALIFICATION

It would be quite wrong to suppose from this that Monseigneur Bienvenu was "a philosopher bishop" or "a patriot curé." His meeting, which we might almost call his communion, with the conventionist G——— left him somewhat stunned and made him still more charitable; that was all.

Although Monseigneur Bienvenu was anything but a politician, we ought perhaps to indicate here briefly his position regarding the events of the day, if indeed Monseigneur Bienvenu ever consciously adopted a position.

For this we must go back a few years.

Some time after M. Myriel became a bishop, the emperor made him a baron of the empire, along with several other bishops. The arrest of the pope took place, as we know, on the night of July 5, 1809; on that occasion, M. Myriel was called by Napoleon to the synod of the bishops of France and Italy convened in Paris. This synod was held at Notre Dame, beginning its sessions on June 15, 1811, under the presidency of Cardinal Fesch. M. Myriel was one of the ninety-five bishops present. But he attended only one session and three or four private conferences. Bishop of a mountain diocese, living so close to nature, in rustic conditions and privation, he seemed to bring these eminent personages ideas that changed the tone of the synod. He returned early to Digne. When asked about this sudden return, he answered, "I annoyed them. The mountain air came in with me. I had the effect of an open door."

Another time, he said, "What do you expect? Those prelates are princes. I'm only a poor peasant bishop."

The fact is that he had offended them. Among other strange things, he had dropped the remark one evening when he happened to be at the house of one of his highest-ranking colleagues: "What fine clocks! fine carpets! fine liveries! It must all be very bothersome. How loath I would be to have all these superfluities forever crying in my ears: 'There are people who are starving! There are people who are cold! What about the poor? What about the poor?' "

We should say, by the way, that the hatred of luxury is not an intelligent hatred. That would imply a hatred of the arts. Nevertheless, among churchmen, if taken beyond their rituals and ceremonies, luxury is a fault. It appears to indicate habits that are not truly charitable. A wealthy priest is a contradiction. He ought to stay close to the poor. But who can be in continual contact night and day with every distress, every misfortune and privation, without picking up a little of that holy poverty, like the dust of labor? Can you imagine a man near a fire who does not feel warm? Can you imagine a laborer working constantly at a furnace who has not one hair singed, nor a nail blackened, nor a drop of sweat, nor a speck of ashes on his face? The first proof of charity in a priest, and especially a bishop, is poverty.

That is undoubtedly what the Bishop of Digne believed.

It must not be thought, however, that, in some delicate matters, he shared what could be called "the ideas of the age." He had little to do with the theological quarrels of the moment and kept his peace on questions where church and state were compromised; but if hard-pressed, he would have proved more Ultramontane than Gallican. Because we are drawing a portrait, and want to conceal nothing, we are compelled to add that he was very cool toward Napoleon in the decline of his power. After 1813, he acquiesced in and even applauded all the hostile demonstrations. He refused to see him as he passed on his return from Elba, and declined to require, in his diocese, public prayers for the emperor during the Hundred Days.

Besides his sister, Mademoiselle Baptistine, he had two brothers; one a general, the other a prefect. He wrote quite often to both. He felt a coolness toward the first, because, being in command in Provence at the time of the landing at Cannes, the general placed himself at the head of twelve hundred men and pursued the emperor as if he wished to let him escape. His correspondence was more affectionate with the other brother, the ex-prefect, a brave and worthy man who lived in retirement in Paris on the Rue Cassette.

So even Monseigneur Bienvenu had his hour of partisan spirit, his hour of bitterness, his clouds. The shadow of the moment's passions passed over this great and gentle soul occupied with eternal things. Certainly, such a man deserved to escape political opinions. Let no one misunderstand; we do not confuse so-called political opinions with that great yearning for progress, with that sublime patriotic, democratic, and human faith which, in our days, should be the basis of all generous thought. Without going further into questions that have only an indirect bearing on the subject of this book, we would simply say, it would have been better if Monseigneur Bienvenu had not been a royalist and if his eyes had never been averted for a single instant from that serene contemplation, steadily shining above the conflicts of human affairs, in which are seen those three pure luminaries, Truth, Justice, and Charity.

Although we contend that it was not for a political function that God created Monseigneur Bienvenu, we could have understood and admired a protest in the name of law and liberty, a fierce opposition, a perilous and just resistance to Napoleon when he was all-powerful. But what pleases us in those who are rising is less pleasing in those who are falling. We do not admire the combat when there is no danger; and in any case, the combatants of the first hour alone have the right to be the exterminators in the last. He who has not been a determined accuser during prosperity should hold his peace in adversity. He alone who denounces the success has a right to proclaim the justice of the downfall. As for ourselves, when Providence intervenes and strikes the blow, we take no part; 1812 began to disarm us. In 1813, the cowardly breach of silence on the part of that taciturn legislative body, emboldened by catastrophe, deserved more than indignation, and it was base to applaud it; in 1814, seeing those traitorous marshals, seeing that senate passing from one gutter to the next, insulting what they had deified, seeing that idolatry recoiling and spitting upon its idol, it was a duty to turn away in disgust; in 1815, when the air was filled with final disasters, when France felt the thrill of their sinister approach, when Waterloo could already be dimly perceived opening in front of Napoleon, the sad acclamations of the army and people to the man condemned by destiny were not proper subjects for laughter; and having every possible reservation about the despot, a heart like that of the Bishop of Digne ought not perhaps to have refused to see what was noble and touching, on the brink of the abyss, in the final embrace of a great nation and a great man.

To conclude: He was always and in all things just, true, fair, intelligent, humble, worthy, beneficent, and benevolent, which is another beneficence. He was a priest, a sage, and a man. We must even say that in those political opinions that we have been criticizing and that we are disposed to judge almost severely, he was tolerant and yielding, perhaps more than we who now speak.

To take an example—The doorkeeper of the City Hall

had been placed there by the emperor. He was an old subaltern officer of the Old Guard, a legionaire of Austerlitz, and as staunch a Bonapartist as the eagle. This poor fellow sometimes thoughtlessly allowed words to escape him that the law at that time defined as seditious. Since the profile of the emperor had disappeared from the Legion of Honor, he never dressed in regulation uniform, so that he might not be forced, as he would say, to bear his cross. He had devotedly removed the imperial effigy from the cross that Napoleon had given him; it left a hole, and he would put nothing in its place. "Better die," said he, "than wear the three toads over my heart." He was always railing loudly at Louis XVIII. "Old gouty-foot with his English spats!" he would say, "let him go to Prussia with his wig-tail," happily uniting in the same insult the two things he most hated, Prussia and England. He said so much that he lost his job. There he was, without bread and in the street with his wife and children. The bishop sent for him, scolded him a little, and made him doorkeeper at the cathedral.

In the diocese, M. Myriel was the true pastor, the friend of all. In nine years, by dint of holy works and gentle manners, Monseigneur Bienvenu had filled the city of Digne with a kind of tender and filial veneration. Even his conduct toward Napoleon had been accepted and pardoned in silence by the people, a good, meek flock who adored their emperor but loved their bishop.

XII

THE SOLITUDE OF MONSEIGNEUR BIENVENU

There is almost always a squad of young abbés around a bishop, just as there is a flock of young officers around a general. They are what the charming St. Francis de Sales somewhere calls "white-billed priests." Every profession has its aspirants who make up the cortège of those who are at the summit. No power is without its worshipers, no fortune without its court. The seekers of the future revolve around the splendid present. Every capital, like every general, has its staff. Every influential bishop has his patrol of undergraduates, cherubs who make the rounds and keep order in the bishop's palace, and who stand guard over the monseigneur's smile. To please a bishop puts a foot in the stirrup for a subdeacon. Each must make his own way; the apostolate never disdains the canonicate.

And as elsewhere there are top brass, in the church there are rich miters. There are bishops who stand well at court, wealthy, well endowed, adroit, accepted in the world, knowing how to pray no doubt, but also knowing how to ask favors; with few scruples about making themselves the viaduct of advancement for a whole diocese; hyphens between the sacristy and diplomacy; more abbés than priests, prelates rather than bishops. Lucky are they who get near them. Men of influence as they are, they rain about them, upon their families and favorites, and upon all of these young men who please them, fat parishes, sinecures, archdeaconates, chaplaincies, and cathedral functions—steps toward a bishop's dignities. In advancing themselves they advance their satellites; it is a whole solar system in motion. The rays of their glory color their retinue purple. Their prosperity scatters its crumbs to those behind the scenes, in the guise of nice little promotions. The larger the diocese of the patron, the larger the curacy for the favorite. And then there is Rome. A bishop who can become an archbishop, an archbishop who can become a cardinal, leads you to the conclave; you enter into the rota, you have the pallium, there you are an auditor, you are a chamberlain, you are a monseigneur, and from Grandeur to Eminence there is only a step, and between Eminence and Holiness there is nothing but the smoke of a ballot. Every cowl may dream of the tiara. In our day the priest is the only man who can regularly become a king, and what a king! The supreme king. So, what a nursery of aspirations is a seminary. How many blushing choir boys, how many young abbés, have the ambitious dairymaid's pail of milk on their heads! Who knows how easily ambition disguises itself under the name of a calling, possibly in good faith and deceiving itself, in sanctimonious confusion.

Monseigneur Bienvenu, a humble, poor, private person, was not counted among the rich miters. This was plain from the complete absence of young priests around him. We have seen that in Paris he did not fit in. No glorious future dreamed of alighting upon this solitary old man. No budding ambition was foolish enough to ripen in his shadow. His canons and his grand vicars were good old men, rather common like himself, and like him immured in that diocese from which there was no road to promotion, and they resembled their bishop, with this difference, that they were finished, and he was perfected. The impossibility of getting ahead under Monseigneur Bienvenu was so plain that fresh from the seminary, the young men ordained by him procured recommendations to the Archbishop of Aix or of Auch, and left immediately. For after all, we repeat, men like advancement. A saint addicted to abnegation is a dangerous neighbor; he is very likely to infect you with an incurable poverty, a stiffening of the articulations necessary to advancement, and, in fact, more renunciation than you would like; and men flee from this contagious virtue. Hence the isolation of Monseigneur Bienvenu. We live in a sad society. Succeed—that is the advice which falls drop by drop from the overhanging corruption.

In passing, we might say that success is a hideous thing. Its false similarity to merit deceives men. To the masses, success has almost the same appearance as supremacy. Success, that pretender to talent, has a dupe—history. Juvenal and Tacitus only reject it. In our day, an almost official philosophy has entered into its service, wears its livery, and waits in its antechamber. Success: That is the theory. Prosperity supposes capacity. Win in the lottery, and you are an able man. The victor is venerated. To be born with a caul is everything. Have luck alone and you will have the rest; be happy, and you will be thought great. Beyond the five or six great exceptions, the wonders of their age, contemporary admiration is nothing but shortsightedness. Gilt is gold. To be a chance comer is no drawback, provided you have improved your chances. The common herd is an old Narcissus, who adores himself and applauds the common. That mighty genius, by which one becomes a Moses, an Aeschylus, a Dante, a Michelangelo, or a Napoleon, the multitude attributes at once and by acclamation to whoever succeeds in his object, whatever it may be. Let a notary rise to be a deputy; let a sham Corneille write *Tiridate;* let a eunuch come into the possession of a harem; let a military

Prudhomme accidentally win the decisive battle of an era; let a pharmacist invent cardboard soles for army shoes and put aside, by selling this cardboard as leather for the army of the Sambre-et-Meuse, four hundred thousand livres in income; let a peddler marry usury and have her bear seven or eight million, of which he is the father and she the mother; let a preacher become a bishop by talking platitudes; let the steward of a good house become so rich that on leaving service he is made Minister of Finance—men call that Genius, just as they call the face of Mousqueton, Beauty, and the bearing of Claude, Majesty. They confuse heaven's radiant stars with a duck's footprint left in the mud.

XIII

WHAT HE BELIEVED

We need not examine the Bishop of Digne on his orthodoxy. Before such a soul, we feel only inclined toward respect. The conscience of an upright man should be taken for granted. Moreover, given certain natures, we admit the possible development of all the beauties of human virtue in a faith different from our own.

What he thought of this dogma or that mystery are secrets of the innermost faith known only in the tomb, where souls enter stripped bare. But we are sure that his religious difficulties never resulted in hypocrisy. No corruption is possible with the diamond. He believed as much as he could. *Credo in Patrem,* he often exclaimed, deriving, besides, from his good deeds that measure of satisfaction that meets the demands of conscience and says in a low voice, "Thou art with God."

We feel obliged to note that, outside of and, so to speak, beyond his faith, the bishop had an excess of love. It is on that account, *quia multum amavit*, that he was considered vulnerable by "serious men," "sober persons," and "reasonable people"—favorite phrases in our sad world, where egotism gains its keynote from pedantry. What was this excess of love? It was a serene benevolence, going beyond humans, as we have already indicated, and, on occasion, extending to inanimate things. He lived without disdain. He was indulgent toward God's creation. Every man, even the best, has some unconsidered severity that he holds in reserve for animals. The Bishop of Digne had none of this severity peculiar to most priests. He did not go as far as the Brahmin, but he appeared to have pondered these words of Ecclesiastes: "Who knows whither goeth the spirit of the beast?" Ugliness of appearance, monstrosities of instinct, did not trouble or irritate him. He was moved and touched by them. He seemed to be thoughtfully seeking, beyond apparent life, for its cause, its explanation, or its excuse. He seemed at times to ask God for commutation. He examined without passion, and with the eye of a linguist deciphering a palimpsest, the portion of chaos which there is yet in nature. These reveries sometimes drew strange words from him. One morning, he was in his garden and thought himself alone, but his sister was walking behind him; all at once he stopped and looked at something on the ground: a large, black, hairy, horrible spider. His sister heard him say, "Poor thing! It's not his fault."

Why not recount this almost divine childish goodness? Puerilities, perhaps, but these sublime puerilities were those of St. Francis of Assisi and of Marcus Aurelius. One day he sprained an ankle rather than crush an ant.

So lived this upright man. Sometimes he went to sleep in his garden, and then he seemed most worthy of veneration.

According to accounts of his youth and early manhood, Monseigneur Bienvenu had formerly been a passionate, even violent man. His universal tenderness was less an instinct of nature than the result of a strong conviction filtered through life into his heart, slowly dropping into him, thought by thought; for a character, as well as a rock, may have holes worn into it by drops of water. Such marks are ineffaceable; such formations are indestructible.

In 1815, we probably have said already, he reached his seventy-sixth year, but he did not appear to be more than sixty. He was not tall; he was somewhat portly, and frequently took long walks to avoid becoming more so; he had a firm step and was but slightly bent: a circumstance from which we do not claim to draw any conclusion—

Gregory XVI, at eighty years, was erect and smiling, which did not prevent him from being a bad bishop. Monseigneur Bienvenu had what people call "a handsome air," but so benevolent that you forgot it.

When he talked with that childlike gaiety that was one of his charms, and of which we have already spoken, everyone felt at ease in his presence, and joy seemed to radiate from his whole being. His ruddy, fresh complexion and white teeth, all of which were well preserved, and which showed when he laughed, gave him that open easy air that makes us say of a man: He is a good fellow; and of an old man: He is a good man. This was, we remember, the effect he produced on Napoleon. On first sight, and to anyone meeting him for the first time, he was indeed nothing more than a good man. But if one spent a few hours with him and saw him even briefly in a thoughtful mood, little by little the good man became transfigured, and took on something imposing; his wide and serious forehead, made noble by his white hair, became noble also through meditation; majesty radiated from this goodness, yet the radiance of goodness remained; and the emotion was something like the experience of seeing a smiling angel slowly spread his wings without ceasing to smile. Respect, ineffable respect, penetrated by degrees and made its way to your heart; and you felt that you had before you one of those strong, tested, and indulgent souls, where the thought is so great that it cannot be other than gentle.

As we have seen, prayer, celebration of the religious offices, alms, consoling the afflicted, the cultivation of a little piece of ground, fraternity, frugality, hospitality, self-sacrifice, confidence, study, and work filled up each day of his life. Filled up is exactly the phrase; and in fact, the bishop's day was full to the brim with good thoughts, good words, and good actions. Yet it was not complete if cold or rainy weather prevented him from passing an hour or two in the evening, when the two women had retired, in his garden before going to sleep. It seemed as though it were a sort of rite with him, to prepare himself for sleep by meditating in the presence of the great spectacle of the starry firmament. Sometimes late at night, if the two women were awake, they would hear him slowly walking the paths. He was out there alone with himself, composed, tranquil, adoring, comparing the serenity of his heart with the serenity of the skies, moved in the darkness by the visible splendors of the constellations and the invisible splendor of God, opening his soul to the thoughts that fall from the Unknown. In such moments, offering up his heart at the hour when the flowers of night emit their perfume, lit like a lamp in the center of the starry night, expanding in ecstasy in the midst of creation's universal radiance, perhaps he could not have told what was happening in his own mind; he felt something floating away from him, and something descending upon him; mysterious exchanges of the soul with the universe.

He contemplated the grandeur, and the presence of God; the eternity of the future, that strange mystery; the eternity of the past, a stranger mystery; all the infinities hidden deep in every direction; and, without trying to comprehend the incomprehensible, he saw it. He did not study God; he was dazzled by Him. He reflected on the magnificent union of atoms, which give visible forms to Nature, revealing forces by recognizing them, creating individualities in unity, proportions in extension, the innumerable in the infinite, and through light producing beauty. These unions are forming and dissolving continually, from which come life and death.

He would sit on a wooden bench leaning against a decrepit trellis and look at the stars through the irregular outlines of his fruit trees. This quarter of an acre of ground, so sparingly planted, so cluttered with shed and ruins, was dear to him and satisfied him.

What more was needed by this old man, who divided the leisure hours of his life, where he had so little leisure, between gardening in the daytime and contemplation at night? Was this narrow enclosure with the sky for a background not space enough for him to adore God in his most beautiful, most sublime works? Indeed, is that not everything? What more do you need? A little garden to walk in, and immensity to reflect on. At his feet something to cultivate and gather; above his head something to study and meditate on; a few flowers on earth and all the stars in heaven.

XIV

WHAT HE THOUGHT

A final word.

As these details may—particularly in these times, and to use an expression now in fashion—give the Bishop of Digne certain "pantheistic" features and lead to the belief, whether to his blame or to his praise, that he had one of those personal philosophies peculiar to our age, which sometimes spring up in solitary minds gathering and growing until they replace religion, we insist that no one who knew Monseigneur Bienvenu would have felt justified in holding any such idea. What enlightened this man was the heart. His wisdom was formed from the light emanating from there.

He had no systems but many deeds. Abstruse speculations are full of pitfalls; nothing indicates that he risked his mind in mysticisms. The apostle may be bold, but the bishop should be timid. He would probably have hesitated to delve too deeply into certain problems reserved in some sense for great and terrible minds. A sacred horror hovers near the approaches to mysticism; somber openings lie gaping there, but something tells you, as you near the brink—Do not enter. Woe to him who does! There are geniuses who, in the fathomless depths of abstraction and pure speculation—situated, so to speak, above all dogmas—present their ideas to God. Their prayer audaciously offers an argument. Their worship questions. This is direct religion, filled with anxiety and responsibility for those who would scale its walls.

Human thought has no limit. At its risk and peril, it analyzes and dissects its own fascination. We could almost say that, by a sort of splendid reaction, it fascinates nature; the mysterious world surrounding us returns what it receives; it is likely that the contemplators are contemplated. However that may be, there are men on earth—if they are nothing more—who distinctly perceive the heights of the absolute in the horizon of their contemplation and who have the terrible vision of the infinite mountain. Monseigneur Bienvenu was not one of those men; Monseigneur Bienvenu was not a genius. He would have dreaded those sublime heights from which even some very great men like Swedenborg and Pascal have slipped into insanity. Certainly, these tremendous reveries have their moral use; and by these arduous routes there is an approach to ideal perfection. But for his part, he took the short cut—the Gospels.

He did not attempt to give his robe the folds of Elijah's mantle; he cast no ray of the future on the dark scroll of events; he did not seek to condense the glimmer of things into flame; he was nothing of the prophet and nothing of the magician. His humble soul loved, and that was enough.

That he raised his prayer to a superhuman aspiration is probable; but one can no more pray too much than love too much; and, if it was a heresy to pray beyond the written form, St. Theresa and St. Jerome were heretics.

He inclined toward the distressed and the repentant. The universe appeared to him a vast disease; he perceived fever everywhere, he auscultated suffering everywhere, and, without trying to solve the enigma, he endeavored to stanch the wound. The formidable spectacle of created things prompted a tenderness in him; he was always busy finding for himself and inspiring in others the best way of sympathizing and comforting; the whole world was to this good and rare priest a permanent subject of sadness seeking to be consoled.

There are men who work for the extraction of gold; he worked for the extraction of pity. The misery of the universe was his mine. Grief everywhere was only an occasion for good always. *Love one another:* He declared that to be complete; he desired nothing more, and it was his whole doctrine. One day, that man who considered himself "a philosopher," the senator mentioned before, said to the bishop, "See now, what the world shows us: each fighting against all others; the strongest man is the best man. Your *love one another* is *stupidity*." "Well," replied Monseigneur Bienvenu, without arguing, "if it is stupidity, the soul ought to shut itself up in it, like the pearl in the oyster." And he did shut himself up in it, he lived in it, he was absolutely satisfied with it, leaving the mysterious questions that attract and discourage, the unfathomable depths of abstraction, the precipices of metaphysics—all those profundities,—to the apostle converging upon God, to the atheist upon annihilation:

destiny, good and evil, the war of being against being, the conscience of man, the thoughtlike dreams of the animal, the transformation of death, the recapitulation of existences contained in the tomb, the incomprehensible grafting of successive affections upon the enduring *me*, the essence, the substance, the Nothing and the Being, the soul, nature, liberty, necessity; difficult problems, sinister depths, toward which are drawn the gigantic archangels of the human race; fearful abyss that Lucretius, Manou, St. Paul, and Dante contemplate with that flaming eye that seems, looking steadfastly into the infinite, to kindle the very stars.

Monsieur Bienvenu was simply a man who accepted these mysteries without examining them, without stirring them up, and without troubling his own mind about them; and who had in his soul a deep respect for the mystery that surrounded them.

Book Two

THE FALL

I

THE NIGHT AFTER A DAY'S WALK

An hour before sunset, on the evening of a day in the beginning of October, 1815, a man traveling on foot entered the little town of Digne. The few people who were then at their windows or doors, viewed this traveler with a sort of distrust. It would have been hard to find a figure who looked less prepossessing. He was thick-set of medium height, stout and hardy, in his full maturity; he might have been forty-six or -seven. A slouched leather cap half hid his face, burnt by the sun and wind, and dripping with sweat. His shaggy chest was exposed through the coarse yellow shirt fastened at the neck by a small metal anchor; he wore a tie twisted like a rope, coarse blue trousers, worn and shabby, white on one knee, and with holes in the other, a ragged old gray blouse, patched on one side with a piece of green cloth sewn with twine. On his back was a well-filled knapsack, firmly buckled and new. In his hand he carried an enormous gnarled stick. His stockingless feet were in hobnailed shoes, his hair was cropped and his beard long.

The sweat, the heat, his long walk, and the dust, added an indescribably sordid quality to his tattered appearance.

His hair was shorn, but bristly, for it had begun to grow a little, and seemingly had not been shaved for some time. Nobody knew him; he was evidently a traveler. Where had he come from? From the south—perhaps from the sea; for he was entering Digne by the same road that, seven months before, the Emperor Napoleon had taken from Cannes to Paris. The man must have been walking all day long, for he appeared very weary. Some women of the old city at the lower part of the town had seen him stop under the trees of the Boulevard Gassendi and drink at the fountain at the end of the promenade. He must have been very thirsty, because some children who followed him saw him stop two hundred steps farther on and drink again at the fountain in the marketplace.

When he reached the corner of the Rue Poichevert he turned left and went toward the mayor's office. He went in and a quarter of an hour later emerged.

The man humbly raised his cap to a gendarme seated near the door on the stone bench where General Drouot had stood on March 4, to read to the terrified inhabitants of Digne the proclamation of the *Golfe Juan*.

Without returning his salutation, the gendarme looked him over attentively, watched him for some distance, and then went into the town hall.

There was at the time in Digne a good inn called La Croix de Colbas; its keeper was one Jacquin Labarre, a man held in some esteem in the town because he was related to another Labarre, who kept an inn at Grenoble called Trois Dauphins and who had served in the Guides. At the time of the Emperor's landing there had been much talk in the countryside about this inn of the Trois Dauphins. It was said that General Bertrand, disguised as a wagon driver, had made frequent trips there in January and had distributed crosses of honor to the soldiers and handfuls of Napoleons to the peasants. The truth is that the emperor, when he entered Grenoble, refused to stay at the prefecture, saying to the prefect, after thanking him, "I am going to the house of a brave man, an old acquaintance," and he went to the Trois Dauphins. This glory of the Labarre of the Trois Dauphins was reflected twenty-five miles to the Labarre of the Croix de Colbas. They would say of him: "He is the cousin of the man from Grenoble!"

The traveler turned toward this inn, which was the best for miles around, and immediately went into the kitchen, which opened onto the street. All the stoves were fuming, and a great fire was burning briskly in the fireplace. The innkeeper, who was also head cook, was going from the fireplace to the saucepans, very busy superintending an excellent dinner for some wagon drivers, who were laughing and talking noisily in the next room. Whoever has traveled knows that nobody fares better than wagon drivers. A fat marmot, flanked by white partridges and goose, was turning on a long spit above the fire; on the stoves were cooking two large carp from Lake Lauzet and a trout from Lake Alloz.

The host, hearing the door open, and a newcomer enter, said, without raising his eyes from his ranges, "What will Monsieur have?"

"Something to eat and a room."

"Nothing easier," said the host, but on turning his head and taking in the traveler, he added, "for pay."

The man drew from his pocket a large leather purse and answered, "I have money."

"Then," said the host, "I am at your service."

The man put his purse back into his pocket, took off his knapsack and put it down by the door, and keeping his stick in hand, sat down on a low stool by the fire. Digne being in the mountains, October evenings are cold.

However, as the innkeeper went back and forth, he kept a careful eye on the traveler.

"Is dinner almost ready?" said the man.

"Almost," the innkeeper answered.

While the newcomer was warming himself with his back turned, the worthy innkeeper, Jacquin Labarre, took a pencil from his pocket and tore off the corner of an old newspaper lying on a little table near the window. On the margin he wrote a line or two, folded it, and handed the scrap of paper to a child who served him as lackey and kitchen help. The innkeeper whispered a word to the boy, who ran off in the direction of the town hall.

The traveler saw nothing of this.

He asked a second time, "Is dinner almost ready?"

"Soon," said the host.

The boy came back with the paper. The host unfolded it hurriedly, as one who is expecting an answer. He seemed to read carefully, then, tilting his head, thought for a moment. Finally he stepped toward the traveler, who seemed drowned in troubled thought.

"Monsieur," he said, "I cannot receive you."

The traveler half rose from his seat.

"Why? Are you afraid I won't pay you, or do you want me to pay in advance? I have money, I tell you."

"It's not that."

"What then?"

"You have money—"

"Yes," said the man.

"And I," said the host, "I have no room."

"Well, put me in the stable," the man replied quietly.

"I can't."

"Why?"

"Because the horses take up all the room."

"Well," the man responded, "a corner in the attic; a bale of hay; we'll see to that after dinner."

"I cannot give you any dinner."

This declaration, made in a measured but firm tone, appeared serious to the traveler. He got up.

"But I'm dying with hunger. I have been walking since sunrise; I have come thirty-five miles. I will pay, and I want something to eat."

"I have nothing," said the host.

The man burst out laughing, and turned toward the fireplace and stoves.

"Nothing! And all that?"

"All that is spoken for."

"By whom?"

"By them, the wagon drivers."

"How many of them are there?"

"Twelve."

"There is enough there for twenty."

"They have ordered and paid for it all in advance."

The man sat down again and said, without raising his voice, "I am at an inn. I am hungry, and I will stay."

The innkeeper leaned over him, and said in a voice that made him tremble, "Go away!"

At these words the traveler, who was bent over, poking some embers in the fire with the iron-shod tip of his stick, turned around suddenly and opened his mouth, as if to reply, when the host, looking steadily at him, added in the same low tone: "Stop, enough of this. Shall I tell you your name? Your name is Jean Valjean. Now shall I tell you *who* you are? When I saw you come in, I suspected something. I sent to the mayor's office, and here is the reply. Can you read?"

So saying, he held out the paper that had just come from the mayor. The man glanced at it. After a short silence, the innkeeper said, "It is my custom to be polite to everyone: Now go!"

The man bowed his head, picked up his knapsack, and went out.

He took the main street, walked at random, slinking near the houses like a sad, humiliated man. Not once did he turn around. If he had, he would have seen the innkeeper of the Croix de Colbas, standing in his doorway with all his guests, and the passersby gathered about him, speaking excitedly, and pointing at him; and from the looks of fear and distrust that were exchanged, he would have guessed that before long his arrival would be the talk of the whole town.

He saw nothing of all this: People weighed down with troubles do not look back; they know only too well that misfortune stalks them.

He walked along in this way for some time, going haphazardly down unknown streets and forgetting fatigue, as happens with sorrow. Suddenly he felt a pang of hunger; night was coming, and he looked around to see if he could not find some lodging.

The good inn was closed to him; he sought some humble tavern, some poor cellar.

Just then a light shone at the end of the street; he saw a pine branch, hanging from an iron bracket against the white sky of the twilight. He went toward it.

It was a tavern on the Rue Chaffaut.

The traveler stopped a moment and looked through the little window into the tavern's low hall, lit by a small lamp on a table, and a great fire in the hearth. Some men were drinking and the host was warming himself; an iron pot hanging over the fire was simmering in the blaze.

Two doors lead into this tavern, which is also a sort of restaurant—one from the street, the other from a small court full of manure.

The traveler did not dare to enter by the street door; he slipped into the court, stopped again, then timidly raised the latch, and pushed open the door.

"Who is it?" the host asked.

"Someone who wants supper and a bed."

"All right. Here you can eat and sleep."

He went in. All the men who were drinking turned

toward him. The lamp shining on one side of his face, the firelight on the other, they examined him for some time as he was taking off his knapsack.

The host said to him, "There is the fire; the supper is cooking in the pot; come and warm yourself, friend."

He seated himself near the fireplace and stretched out his feet toward the fire, half dead with fatigue. An inviting odor came from the pot. All that could be seen of his face under his slouched cap took on a vague appearance of comfort, which tempered that other aspect given him by long suffering.

His profile was strong, energetic, and sad, a physiognomy strangely constructed: At first it seemed humble but soon turned severe. His eyes shone from under his eyebrows like a fire beneath a thicket.

However, one of the men at the table was a fisherman who had left his horse at the stable of Labarre's inn before entering the tavern on the Rue de Chaffaut. It so happened that he had met, that same morning, this suspicious-looking stranger traveling between Bras d'Asse and—I forget the place, I think it is Escoublon. Now, on meeting him, the man, who seemed already very tired, had asked him to take him up behind, to which the fisherman responded only by doubling his pace. The fisherman, half an hour before, had been one of the throng around Jacquin Labarre and had just related his unpleasant meeting with him to the people of the Croix de Colbas. He motioned to the tavern keeper, who came over to him. They exchanged a few words in a low voice; the traveler had again lapsed into thought.

The tavern keeper returned to the fire, and laying his hand roughly on the man's shoulder, said harshly, "You have to clear out."

The stranger turned around and said mildly, "Ah! So you know, too!"

"Yes."

"They sent me away from the other inn."

"And we're turning you away from this one, too."

"But where can I go?"

"Anywhere else."

The man picked up his stick and knapsack and left. As he went out, some children who had followed from the Croix de Colbas, and seemed to be waiting, threw stones at him. He turned angrily, threatening them with his stick, and they scattered like a flock of birds.

He passed the prison. An iron chain hanging from the door was attached to a bell. He rang.

The grating opened.

"Jailer," he said, respectfully removing his cap, "would you open up and let me spend the night?"

A voice answered, "A prison is not a tavern. Get arrested and we'll gladly welcome you."

The grating closed.

He went into a small street where there are many gardens; some of them are enclosed only by hedges, which brighten up the street. Among them he saw a pretty little one-story house with a light in the window. He peered in as he had done at the tavern. It was a large whitewashed room, with a bed covered in Indian-print calico and a cradle in the corner, some wooden chairs, and a double-barreled gun hung against the wall. In the center of the room a table was set. A brass lamp lit the coarse white tablecloth, a tin mug full of wine shone like silver, and the brown soup bowl was steaming. At this table sat a man about forty years old; he had a joyful, open expression and was bouncing a little child on his knee. Nearby a young woman was nursing another child; the father and child were laughing, and the mother was smiling.

For a moment the traveler stayed there, contemplating this gentle, touching scene. What was he thinking? Only he could have said. Probably that this happy home would be hospitable and that where he saw so much happiness, he might perhaps find a little pity.

He tapped faintly on the window.

No one heard him.

He tapped a second time.

He heard the woman say, "Did you hear a knocking?"

"No," the husband replied.

He tapped a third time. The husband got up, took the lamp, and opened the door.

He was a tall man, half peasant, half artisan. He wore a large leather apron reaching to his left shoulder, and forming a pocket containing a hammer, a red handkerchief, a powderhorn, and all sorts of other things held up by the belt. He raised his head; his shirt, open and folded back, showed his bull-like neck, white and bare. He had thick brows, enormous black sideburns, prominent eyes, a large jaw, and a quite indescribable air of being at home.

"Monsieur," said the traveler, "I beg your pardon; I have money. Could you give me a plate of soup and a corner of the shed in your garden to sleep in? Could you? I can pay."

"Who are you?" asked the master of the house.

The man replied, "I have come from Puy-Moisson. I have walked all day. I have come thirty-five miles. Can you, if I pay?"

"I wouldn't refuse to lodge any proper person who would pay," said the peasant, "but why don't you go to the inn?"

"There's no room."

"That's not possible! It's neither a fair nor a market day. Have you been to Labarre's house?"

"Yes."

"Well?"

The traveler replied hesitatingly, "I don't know; he didn't take me."

"Have you been to that place in the Rue Chaffaut?"

The embarrassment of the stranger increased. He stammered: "They didn't take me, either."

The peasant's face assumed an expression of distrust; he looked over the newcomer from head to foot, and suddenly exclaimed with a sort of shudder, "Are you the man?"

He looked again at the stranger, stepped back, put the lamp on the table, and took down his gun.

On hearing the words "Are you the man," his wife jumped up and, clasping her two children, precipitately took refuge behind her husband; she looked at the stranger with horror, her neck bare, her eyes dilated, muttering in a low tone: "*Tso maraude!*"[1]

All this happened in less time that it takes to read; after examining the man for a moment, as one would a viper, the master of the house came back to the door and said, "Get out!"

"For pity's sake, a glass of water," said the man.

"A gunshot," said the peasant, and then he closed the

[1] Patois of the French Alps for "chat de maraude" (marauding cat). —(V.H.)

door violently, and the man heard two heavy bolts being drawn. A moment later the shutters were closed, and noisily barred.

Night was steadily falling; the cold Alpine winds were blowing. By the light of the dying day the stranger glimpsed in one of the gardens facing the street a kind of shed that seemed to be made of turf. He boldly scaled a wooden fence and found himself in the garden. He neared the hut; its door was a narrow, low entrance; in construction, it was like the shanties that road workers put up for temporary shelter. He undoubtedly thought that it was, in fact, such a lodging. He was suffering both from cold and hunger. He had resigned himself to the latter; but here at least was a shelter from the cold. These huts are not usually occupied at night. He got down and crawled in. It was warm there and he found a good bed of straw. He rested a moment on his bed, motionless from fatigue; then, as his knapsack on his back troubled him, and it would make a good pillow, he began to unbuckle the straps. Just then he heard a ferocious growl and looking up saw the head of an enormous bulldog at the opening of the hut.

It was a kennel!

As he was vigorous and agile, he seized his stick, made a shield of his knapsack, and got out of the hut as best he could, but not without enlarging the tears in his already tattered garments.

He also made his way out of the garden, but backward; being obliged, out of respect to the dog, to rely on a maneuver with his stick that adepts at this sort of fencing call *la rose couverte*.

When he had, not without difficulty, gotten over the fence, he again found himself alone in the street with no lodging, roof, or shelter, driven even from the straw bed of that miserable kennel. He collapsed rather than seated himself on a stone, and it seems that someone passing by heard him exclaim, "I'm not even a dog!"

Soon he got up and began to walk again, making his way out of town, hoping to find some tree or haystack where he could take shelter. He walked on for some time, his head bowed. When he thought he was far away from all human habitation he raised his eyes and looked around. He was in a field; in front of him was one of those low hillocks covered with stubble that after the harvest looks like a shaved head. The sky was very dark; it was not simply the darkness of night, but there were very low clouds, which seemed to lean on the hills and, ascending, covered the whole sky. A little of the twilight, however, lingered in the zenith; and as the moon was about to rise, the clouds formed in mid-heaven a vault of whitish light, from which a glow fell to earth.

So the earth was lighter than the sky, which produces a peculiarly sinister effect, and the hill, poor and stunted in outline, loomed dim and pale against the gloomy horizon. The whole prospect was hideous, hateful, grim, and desolate. There was nothing in the field or on the hill, only one ugly tree, a few steps from the traveler, which seemed to be twisting tremulously.

The man was clearly far from possessing those delicate perceptions of intelligence and feeling that produce a sensitivity to the mysterious side of nature; still, in the sky, in the hill, plain, and tree, there was something so profoundly desolate that after a moment of motionless contemplation, he abruptly turned back. There are moments when nature seems your enemy.

He retraced his steps; the gates of Digne were closed. Digne, which sustained sieges during the religious wars, was still surrounded in 1815 by old walls flanked by square towers, later demolished. He passed through a gap and entered the town.

It was about eight in the evening. Not knowing the streets, he again wandered.

Soon, he came to the prefecture, then to the seminary; on passing by the cathedral square, he shook his fist at the church.

At the corner of the square stands a printing office. It is there that first were printed the proclamations of the emperor and of the Imperial Guard to the army, brought from the island of Elba and dictated by Napoleon himself.

Exhausted and lacking all hope, he lay down on a stone bench in front of the printing office.

Just then an old woman came out of the church. She saw him and asked, "What are you doing there, friend?"

He replied harshly, angrily, "You can see, my good woman, I'm trying to sleep."

This good woman, who really deserved that description, was Madame la Marquise de R———.

"On the bench?" she asked.

"For nineteen years I've had a wooden mattress," said the man; "tonight I have a stone one."

"You were a soldier?"

"Yes, my good woman, a soldier."

"Why don't you go to the inn?"

"Because I have no money."

"Alas!" said Madame de R———, "I have only four sous in my purse."

"Give them over then."

He took the four sous, and Madame de R——— continued, "You cannot find lodging for so little at an inn. But have you tried? You cannot spend the night this way. You must be cold and hungry. They should have given you lodging out of charity."

"I have knocked at every door."

"Well, what then?"

"Everybody has driven me away."

The good woman touched the man's arm and pointed out to him, on the other side of the square, a little house beside the bishop's palace.

"You have knocked at every door?" she asked.

"Yes."

"Have you knocked at that one there?"

"No."

"Knock there."

II

CAUTIONARY ADVICE TO THE WISE

That evening, after his walk around town, the Bishop of Digne stayed in his room quite late. He was busy with his great work on Duty, which unfortunately he never completed. He was carefully dissecting all that the Fathers and Philosophers have said on this serious topic. His book was divided into two parts: first, the duties of all; secondly, the duties of each, according to one's position in life. The duties of all are the principal duties; there are four, as set forth by St. Matthew: duty toward God (Matt. 6); toward ourselves (Matt. 5:29, 30); toward our neighbor (Matt. 7:12); and toward animals (Matt. 6:20, 25). As to other duties, the bishop found them defined and prescribed elsewhere; those of sovereigns and subjects in the Epistle to the Romans; those of magistrates, wives, mothers, and young men by St. Peter; those of husbands, fathers, children, and servants in the Epistle to the Ephesians; those of the faithful in the Epistle to the Hebrews; and those of virgins in the Epistle to the Corinthians. He was carefully combining these injunctions into a harmonious whole, which he hoped to offer the faithful.

At eight he was still at work, writing with some inconvenience on little slips of paper, holding a large book open on his knees, when Madame Magloire, as usual, came in to take the silver from the cupboard near the bed. A moment later, the bishop, knowing that the table was laid and that his sister was perhaps waiting, closed his book and went into the dining room.

This dining room was oblong, with a fireplace and a door onto the street, as we have said, and a window on the garden.

Madame Magloire had just finished putting down the silver.

While setting the table, she was talking with Mademoiselle Baptistine.

There was a lamp on the table, near the fireplace, where a good fire was burning.

One can easily imagine these two women, both past their sixtieth year: Madame Magloire, small, fat, and quick; Mademoiselle Baptistine, sweet, thin, fragile, a little taller than her brother, wearing a puce-colored silk dress, a shade quite fashionable in 1806, the year she had bought it in Paris. To use a popular comparison, which says in a few words what a page could barely express, Madame Magloire looked like a peasant and Mademoiselle Baptistine like a lady. Madame Magloire wore a white funnel-shaped cap, a gold cross at her neck, the only bit of feminine jewelry in the house, a snowy fichu just peering out above a heavy black wool dress, with wide short sleeves, a green-and-red-checked calico apron tied at the waist with a green ribbon, its bib pinned up in front; she wore coarse shoes and yellow stockings like the women of Marseilles. Mademoiselle Baptistine's dress, in the style of 1806, had a short waist, narrow skirt, sleeves with epaulettes, and flaps and buttons. Her gray hair was hidden under a frizzy wig called *à l'enfant*. Madame Magloire had an intelligent, clever, lively air; the two corners of her mouth raised unevenly, and the upper lip protruded beyond the lower, making her seem somewhat rough and imperious. So long as the bishop was silent, she talked to him without inhibition though with respect; but once he spoke, as we have seen, she would implicitly obey, like Mademoiselle. Mademoiselle Baptistine, however, did not speak. She confined herself to obeying and endeavoring to please. Even when young, she had not been pretty; she had very prominent blue eyes and a long pinched nose, but her whole face and person, as we said at the outset, breathed an indescribable goodness. She had been preordained to meekness, but faith, charity, hope—the three virtues that gently warm the heart—had gradually elevated this meekness to sanctity. Nature had made her a lamb; religion had made her an angel. Poor, sainted woman! Tender, long-vanished memory.

Mademoiselle Baptistine so often told what happened at the bishop's house that evening, that many still alive can recall the tiniest details.

Just as the bishop entered, Madame Magloire was speaking vivaciously. She was talking to Mademoiselle on a familiar subject, one to which the bishop was quite accustomed. It was a discussion about the way to secure the front door.

It seems that while Madame Magloire was shopping for supper, she had heard the news in various places about an evil-looking runaway, a suspicious vagabond, who had arrived and was lurking somewhere in town; some unpleasant adventures might happen to any who came home late that night; also, there was talk the police were not doing their jobs, because the prefect and the mayor did not like one another and each was hoping to injure the other by provoking incidents; it was up to intelligent people to protect themselves; so everyone ought to be careful to shut up, bolt, and bar his house properly, and secure his door thoroughly.

Madame Magloire emphasized these last words, but the bishop, having come from a cold room, sat down in front of the fire and began to warm himself, and so he was thinking of something else. He did not hear a word of what Madame Magloire had just said, and she repeated it. Then Mademoiselle Baptistine, trying to satisfy Madame Magloire without displeasing her brother, ventured to say timidly, "Brother, did you hear what Madame Magloire said?"

"I vaguely heard some of it," the bishop said. Then turning his chair half around, putting his hands on his knees, and raising to the old servant his good-humored face, which the firelight illuminated, he said, "Well, then! What's the matter? Are we in any great danger?"

Madame Magloire began her story again, unconsciously exaggerating it a little more. It appeared that a barefoot gypsy, some sort of dangerous beggar, was in town. He had gone for lodging to Jacquin Labarre, who had refused him; he had been seen entering the town by the Boulevard Gassendi and roaming through the streets at dusk. A man with a knapsack and a rope and a terrible-looking face.

"Really?" said the bishop.

This willingness to question her encouraged Madame Magloire; it seemed to indicate that the bishop was actually almost worried. She continued triumphantly, "Yes, Monseigneur, it's true. Something will happen tonight in town; everybody says so. The police are so badly organized. To live in this mountainous country and not even have streetlamps! If you go out, it's black as your pocket! And I say, Monseigneur, and Mademoiselle agrees—"

"Me?" interrupted the sister. "I say nothing. Whatever my brother does is fine."

Madame Magloire went on as if she had not heard this protest, "We say this house is not safe at all; and if Monseigneur will allow me, I will go and tell Paulin Musebois, the locksmith, to come and put the old bolts back in the door; we have them right here, and it will only take a minute. I say we must have bolts, if only for tonight; nothing could be worse than a door that can be opened from the outside by the first comer; and anyway the Monseigneur has the habit of saying, 'Come in,' even at midnight. But, my heavens! There's no need even to ask permission—"

At this moment there was a violent knock on the door.

"Come in!" said the bishop.

III

THE HEROISM OF PASSIVE OBEDIENCE

The door opened.

It opened quickly, quite wide, as if someone were pushing it boldly and energetically.

A man entered.

We already know him. It was the traveler we saw wandering in search of food and shelter.

He came in, took a step, and paused, leaving the door open behind him. He had his knapsack on his back, his stick in his hand, and a rough, hard, tired, and fierce look in his eyes. Seen by firelight, he seemed a hideous, sinister apparition.

Madame Magloire had not even the strength to scream. She stood trembling, her mouth agape.

Mademoiselle Baptistine turned, saw the man enter, and started up half alarmed; then, slowly turning back again toward the fire, she looked at her brother, and her face resumed its usual profound serenity.

The bishop gazed tranquilly at the man.

As he was opening his mouth to speak, undoubtedly to ask the stranger what he wanted, the man, leaning with both hands on his club, glanced from one to another in turn, and without waiting for the bishop to speak, said loudly, "Listen here! My name is Jean Valjean. I was a convict. I have spent nineteen years in prison. Four days ago I was freed and started out for Pontarlier. For four days I have been walking from Toulon. Today I walked thirty-five miles. When I reached this place this evening I went to an inn, and they sent me away because of my yellow passport, which I had shown at the mayor's office, as the law requires. I went to another inn. They said, 'Get out!' First one, then the other. Nobody would have me. I went to the prison, and the jailer would not let me in. I crept into a kennel. The dog bit me and chased me away as if he were the man, and I the dog. I went into the fields to sleep under the stars; there were no stars. It looked like rain—and where was the good Lord to stop the drops?—so I came back to town to find shelter in some doorway. In the square I was resting on a stone when a good woman pointed to your house and said, 'Knock there!' I have knocked. What is this place? Are you an inn? I have money; my savings, one hundred and nine francs and fifteen sous that I earned in the chain gang over nineteen years. I'll pay. What do I care? I have money. I'm so tired—thirty-five miles on foot, and I'm so hungry. Won't you let me stay?"

"Madame Magloire," said the bishop, "another place, please."

The man took three steps toward the lamp on the table. "Look," he exclaimed, as if he had not understood, "did you understand? I'm a convict—I'm just out of prison." He drew from his pocket a large sheet of yellow paper which he unfolded. "There's my passport, yellow, as you can see. That's enough to have me kicked out wherever I go. Would you read it? Me, I know how to read. I learned in prison. There's a school there for anyone who wants to. See, here is what they put in the passport: 'Jean Valjean, a liberated convict, a native of ———,' that part doesn't concern you, 'has been in prison nineteen years; five years for burglary; fourteen years for four attempted escapes. This man is highly dangerous.' There you are! Everybody else has thrown me out; will you take me in? Is this an inn? Can you give me something to eat, a place to sleep? D'you have a stable?"

"Madame Magloire," said the bishop, "put some sheets on the bed in the alcove."

We have already described the brand of obedience practiced by these two women.

Madame Magloire went off to fulfill her orders.

The bishop turned to the man: "Monsieur, sit down and warm yourself. We are going to have supper in a moment, and your bed will be made while you eat."

At last the man did understand; his expression, which up till then had been gloomy and hard, now showed stupefaction, doubt, and joy—an extraordinary transformation. He began to stammer like a madman.

"What! You'll let me stay? You won't send me away? A convict! You call me *Monsieur* and don't say 'Get out, dog!' like everybody else. I thought you'd send me away, too, so I told you who I am right away. Oh! the fine woman who sent me here! I'll have something to eat! A bed like other people with a mattress and sheets—a bed! It's nineteen years since I've slept in a bed. You're really willing for me to stay? You're good people! Besides, I have money: I'll pay well. I beg your pardon, Monsieur Innkeeper, what's your name? I'll pay all you say. You are a fine man. You are an innkeeper, aren't you?"

"I am the priest who lives here," said the bishop.

"A priest," said the man. "Oh, noble priest! Then you don't want any money? You're the priest of this big church? Yes, that's it. How stupid I am; I didn't notice your cap."

While speaking, he had put down his knapsack and walking stick in the corner, returned his passport to his pocket, and sat down. Mademoiselle Baptistine was gazing at him sympathetically. He went on, "You are humane, Monsieur Curé; you don't despise me. A good priest is a good thing. Then you don't even want me to pay you?"

"No," said the bishop, "keep your money. How much do you have? You said a hundred and nine francs, I think."

"And fifteen sous," added the man.

"One hundred and nine francs and fifteen sous. And how long did it take you to earn that?"

"Nineteen years."

"Nineteen years!"

The bishop heaved a deep sigh.

The man continued, "I still have all my money. In four days I've spent only twenty-five sous, which I earned by unloading wagons at Grasse. Because you're an abbé, I want you to know, we have a chaplain in the galleys. And then one day I saw a bishop; Monseigneur, they called him. It was the Bishop of la Majore, from Marseilles. He's the curé that's over the other curés. You know—sorry—I say it so badly, but for me, it's so far off! You know what we are. He said mass in the middle of the place on an altar; he had a pointed gold thing on his head. It shone in the sun. It was noon. We were lined up, on three sides. With guns and lighted matches in front of us. We couldn't see him too well. He spoke to us, but he wasn't near enough, we didn't understand him. That's what a bishop is."

While the man was talking, the bishop went to the door, which was still open wide, and shut it.

Madame Magloire brought the silver and set it on the table.

"Madame Magloire," said the bishop, "set the places as near the fire as you can." Then turning toward his guest, he added, "The night wind is raw in the Alps; you must be cold, monsieur."

Everytime he said this word "monsieur," with his gently solemn and heartily hospitable voice, the man's face lit up. *Monsieur* to a convict is a glass of water to a man dying of thirst at sea. Ignominy thirsts for respect.

"This lamp," said the bishop, "gives very poor light."

Madame Magloire understood him, and going to his bedroom, took the two silver candlesticks off the mantel, lit the candles, and placed them on the table.

"Monsieur Curé," said the man, "you are truly good. You don't despise me. You take me into your house. You light your candles for me, and I haven't hidden from you where I come from, and how miserable I am."

The bishop, who was sitting beside him, touched his hand gently and said, "You didn't have to tell me who you are. This is not my house; it is Christ's. It does not ask any guest his name but whether he has an affliction. You are suffering; you are hungry and thirsty; you are welcome. And don't thank me; don't tell me that I am taking you into my house. This is the home of no man, except the one who needs a refuge. I tell you, a traveler, you are more at home here than I; whatever is here is yours. Why would I have to know your name? Besides, before you told me, I knew it."

The man opened his eyes in surprise. "Really? You knew my name?"

"Yes," answered the bishop, "your name is my brother."

"Listen, Monsieur Curé," exclaimed the man. "I was famished when I came in, but you are so kind that now I don't know what I am; it's all gone."

The bishop looked at him again and said, "You have suffered a great deal?"

"Oh, the red tunic, the ball and chain, the plank to sleep on, the heat, the cold, the work gang, back to the prison ship every night, the lash, the double chain for nothing, solitary confinement for one word—even when sick in bed, the chain. The dogs, a dog is happier! Nineteen years! And I am forty-six, and now a yellow passport, just that!"

"Yes," answered the bishop, "you have left a place of

suffering. But listen, there will be more joy in heaven over the tears of a repentant sinner than over the white robes of a hundred just men. If you are leaving that sad place with hatred and anger against men, you deserve compassion; if you leave it with goodwill, gentleness, and peace, you are better than any of us."

Meantime Madame Magloire had served up supper; it consisted of soup made of water, oil, bread, and salt; a little pork, a scrap of mutton, a few figs, a green cheese, and a large loaf of rye bread. On her own she had added to the bishop's usual dinner a bottle of fine old Mauves wine.

The bishop's countenance suddenly lit up with the expression of pleasure peculiar to hospitable natures. "Do be seated!" he said briskly. As was his habit when he had a guest, he seated the man on his right. Mademoiselle Baptistine, perfectly accommodating and natural, sat down on his left.

The bishop said the blessing and then served the soup himself, as usual. The man began eating greedily.

Suddenly the bishop said, "It seems to me something is missing on the table."

The fact is that Madame Magloire had set out only the three places that were necessary. Now it was the custom of the house, when the bishop had anyone to supper, to set all six of the silver services on the table, an innocent display. This graceful appearance of luxury was a sort of charming childishness in this gentle but austere household, elevating poverty to dignity.

Madame Magloire understood the remark; without a word she went out, and a moment later the three sets for which the bishop had asked were shining on the cloth, symmetrically arranged before each of the three diners.

IV

SOME FACTS ABOUT THE DAIRIES OF PONTARLIER

Now, in order to give an idea of what went on at this table, we could not improve upon a passage in a letter from Mademoiselle Baptistine to Madame de Boischevron, in which the conversation between the convict and the bishop is related in naïve detail.

"The man paid no attention to anyone. He ate with the voracity of a starving man. After supper, however, he said, 'Monsieur Curé, all this is too good for me, but I must say that the wagon drivers, who wouldn't let me eat with them, live better than you do.'

"Between you and me, the remark shocked me just a bit. My brother answered, 'But they get more tired out than I do.'

" 'No,' replied this man; 'they just have more money. You're poor, I can see. Perhaps you're not even a curé. Are you only a curé? Ah! If God is just, you deserve to be a curé.'

" 'God is more than just,' said my brother.

"A moment later he added, 'Monsieur Jean Valjean, are you going to Pontarlier?'

" 'A compulsory journey.'

"I am pretty sure that's what the man said. Then he went on, 'I have to be on the road tomorrow morning at daybreak. It's a hard journey. If the nights are cold, at least the days are warm.'

" 'You are going,' said my brother, 'to a fine part of the country. During the revolution, my family was ruined. I first took refuge in Franche-Comté, and supported myself there for some time by manual labor. I was willing, and I found plenty of work there. I had only to choose. There are paper mills, tanneries, distilleries, oil factories, large clock-making establishments, steel mills, copper foundries, at least twenty iron foundries—four of them, at Lods, Châtillion, Audincourt, and Beure, are very large.'

"I don't think I'm mistaken that these are the names my brother mentioned. Then he broke off and said to me, 'Dear sister, don't we have relatives in that part of the country?'

"I answered, 'We did; among others Monsieur Lucenet, captain of the gates at Pontarlier under the old régime.'

" 'Yes,' replied my brother, 'but in '93 no one had relatives; it was every man for himself. I worked. In the region of Pontarlier where you are going, Monsieur Valjean, they have an industry that is quite patriarchal and very charming—their cheese dairies, which they call *fruitières*.'

"Then my brother, while giving this man something to eat, explained to him in detail what these *fruitières* were—that there were two kinds: the *great barns*, belonging to the rich, and where there are forty or fifty cows producing from seven to eight thousand cheeses during the summer; and the associated *fruitières*, which belong to the poor; these consist of peasants living in the mountains who put their cows into a common herd and divide the proceeds. They hire a cheesemaker, whom they call a *grurin;* the *grurin* takes in the milk of the associates three times a day and notes the quantities in duplicate. It's toward the end of April that the dairy work starts up, and about the middle of June the cheesemakers drive their cows into the mountains.

"The man revived as he ate. My brother gave him some good Mauves wine, which he does not drink himself, because he says it is too expensive. My brother gave him all these details with that easy gaiety you well know, mingling his words with compliments to me. He kept coming back to the good position of a *grurin*, as if he wanted this man to understand, without advising him directly and pointedly, that it would be refuge for him. One thing struck me. This man was all that I have told you. Well, during supper and the rest of the evening, with the exception of a few words about Jesus, when he entered, my brother did not say a word that could recall to this man who he himself actually was or indicate to him who my brother was. It was certainly a golden opportunity to get in a little sermon and to set the bishop above the convict in order to make an impression on his mind. Perhaps it would have appeared to some as a duty, having this unfortunate man in hand, to feed the mind at the same time as the body, and to give some reproach, seasoned with morality and advice, or at least a little pity accompanied by an urging to behave better in the future. My brother did not ask him about either his birthplace or his life story; for his crime lay in his past, and my brother avoided everything that could recall it to him. At one time, my brother was speaking of the mountaineers of Pontarlier, who have *pleasant work close to heaven, and who,* he added, *are happy, because they are innocent,* but he stopped short, fearing that in this word that had escaped him there might be something that could hurt the man's feelings. On reflection, I think I understand what was going on in my brother's mind. He undoubtedly thought that this man, who was called Jean Valjean, had his misery all too constantly in his mind, that it was better to make him think of other things, and have him believe, if only for a moment, that he was a person like anyone else, by treating him in this normal way. Isn't this a true understanding of charity? Isn't there, dear lady, something truly evangelical in this tact, which refrains from sermonizing, moralizing, and making allusions? Isn't it most sympathetic, when a man has a bruise, not to touch it at all? It seems to me that this was my brother's guiding principle here. At any rate, all I can say is, if he had all these ideas, he did not show them even to me: From beginning to end, he was the same as other evenings, and he ate with this Jean Valjean as if dining with Monsieur Gédéon, the provost, or with the curé of the parish.

"Toward the end, at dessert, someone pushed the door open. It was mother Gerbaud with her child in her arms. My brother kissed the child and borrowed fifteen *sous* that I had with me to give to mother Gerbaud. The man, meanwhile, paid little attention to what was going on. He did not speak and seemed very tired. The poor woman left, my brother said grace, and then turned to this man, saying, 'You must be very tired.' Madame Magloire quickly removed the cloth. I understood that we ought to retire so this traveler could sleep, and we both went to our rooms. However, a few moments later, I sent Madame Magloire to put on the man's bed a Black Forest roebuck skin, from my room. The nights are cold, and this hide retains the warmth. It is a pity that it is quite old, and the hair is dropping off. My brother bought it when he was in Germany, at Totlingen, near the source of the Danube, along with the little ivory-handled knife I use at meals.

"Madame Magloire came back immediately, we said our prayers in the parlor, which we use as a drying room, and then we went to our rooms without a word."

V
TRANQUILITY

After saying goodnight to his sister, Monseigneur Bienvenu took one of the silver candlesticks from the table, handed the other to his guest, and said, "Monsieur, let me show you to your room."

The man followed him.

As must be clear from what has been said, the house was so arranged that one could reach the alcove in the oratory only by going through the bishop's bedroom. Just as they were going through this room Madame Magloire was putting the silver away in the cupboard at the head of the bed, the last thing she did every night before going to sleep.

The bishop left his guest in the alcove, in front of a clean white bed. The man placed the candlestick on a small table.

"Now," said the bishop, "a good night's sleep to you. Tomorrow morning, before you go, you'll drink a cup of warm milk from our cows."

"Thank you, Monsieur l'Abbé," said the man.

Scarcely had he pronounced these words of peace, when suddenly he made a strange gesture that would have horrified the two women of the house, if they had witnessed it. Even now it is hard for us to understand what impulse he obeyed at that moment. Did he intend to give a warning or threat? Or was he simply obeying a sort of instinctive impulse, obscure even to himself? He turned abruptly toward the old man, crossed his arms, and glaring at his host, exclaimed harshly, "So, now! You let me stay in your house, as near to you as that!"

He checked himself, and added, with a laugh that had a trace of something horrible, "Have you thought I might be a murderer?"

The bishop replied, "God will take care of that."

Then gravely, moving his lips like one praying or talking to himself, he raised two fingers of his right hand and blessed the man, who, however, did not bow; and without turning his head or looking behind him, went toward his room.

When the alcove was in use, a heavy serge curtain was drawn in the oratory, concealing the altar. Before this curtain the bishop knelt as he passed and offered a short prayer.

A moment later he was walking in the garden, surrendering mind and soul to a dreamy contemplation of these grand and mysterious works that God shows at night to eyes still open.

As to the man, he was so completely exhausted that he did not even avail himself of the clean white sheets; he blew out the candle with his nostril, as convicts do, collapsed onto the bed, fully dressed, and into a sound sleep.

Midnight struck as the bishop came back to his room.

A few moments later, the little house was all asleep.

VI

JEAN VALJEAN

Toward the middle of the night, Jean Valjean awoke.

Jean Valjean was born into a poor peasant family in the Brie region. In his childhood he had not been taught to read. When he had come of age, he chose the occupation of a pruner at Faverolles. His mother's name was Jeanne Mathieu, his father's Jean Valjean or Vlajean, probably a nickname, a contraction of *Voilà Jean*.

Jean Valjean was thoughtful though not sad, a characteristic of affectionate natures. On the whole, however, there was something immature and passive, to all appearances at least, in Jean Valjean. He had lost his parents when he was very young. His mother died of a poorly treated milkfever, his father, a pruner before him, was killed when he fell from a tree. Jean Valjean now had only one relative left, his older sister, a widow with seven children, girls and boys. This sister had brought up Jean Valjean, and as long as her husband lived, she had taken care of her younger brother. Her husband died, leaving the eldest of these children at eight, the youngest one year old. Jean Valjean was just twenty-five. Taking the father's place, he supported the sister who had reared him. He did it naturally, as a duty, but with a trace of surliness. His youth was spent in rough and poorly paid labor; he was never known to have a sweetheart; he had no time to be in love.

At night he came in weary and ate his soup without a word. While he was eating, his sister, Mother Jeanne, frequently took out of his bowl the best of his meal—a bit of meat, a slice of bacon, the heart of the cabbage—to give to one of her children. Eating steadily, his head down nearly in the soup, his long hair falling over his dish, hiding his eyes, he did not seem to notice and let it happen. At Faverolles, not far from the Valjeans' house on the other side of the road there was a farmer's wife named Marie Claude; the Valjean children, always famished, sometimes went in their mother's name to borrow a pint of milk, which they would drink behind a hedge, or in some nook of the lane, snatching away the pitcher so greedily one from another that the little girls would spill it on their aprons and throats; if their mother had known, she would have punished the delinquents severely. Jean Valjean, rough and grumbler as he was, paid Marie Claude; their mother never knew, and so the children escaped punishment.

In the pruning season he earned eighteen sous a day; after that he hired out as a reaper, a workman, teamster, or laborer. He did whatever he could find to do. His sister worked also, but what could she do with seven little children? It was a sad group, gradually held tighter and tighter in the grip of misery. One very severe winter, Jean had no work, the family had no bread. Literally, no bread, and seven children.

One Sunday night, Maubert Isabeau, the baker on the Place de l'Eglise, in Faverolles, was just going to bed when he heard a crash against the barred window of his shop. He got down in time to see an arm thrust through the opening made by the blow of a fist against the glass.

The arm seized one loaf of bread and took it. Isabeau rushed out; the thief was making off at top speed; Isabeau pursued and caught him. The thief had thrown away the bread, but his arm was still bleeding. It was Jean Valjean.

This happened in 1795. Jean Valjean was brought before the tribunals of the time for "burglary at night, in an inhabited house." He had a gun, which he used as well as any marksman in the world, and was something of a poacher, which worked against him, there being a natural prejudice against poachers. The poacher, like the smuggler, is nearly a brigand. But we must note in passing, that there is still a deep gulf between that sort of man and the horrible assassin of the city. The poacher lives in the forest, and the smuggler in the mountains or on the sea; cities produce ferocious men, because they produce corrupt men. Mountains, the forest, and the sea make men savage; they develop fierceness but usually without destroying the human.

Jean Valjean was found guilty: The terms of the penal code were explicit. In our civilization there are fearful times when the criminal law wrecks a man. How mournful the moment when society draws back and permits the irreparable loss of a sentient being. Jean Valjean was sentenced to five years in prison.

In Paris on April 22, 1796, came the announcement of the victory of Montenotte, achieved by the commanding general of the army of Italy, whom the message of the Directory to the Five Hundred, of the second Floréal, year IV, called Buonaparte. That same day a great chain was riveted at Bicêtre. Jean Valjean was a part of that chain. An old prison guard, now nearly ninety, clearly remembers the miserable man, who was shackled at the end of the fourth chain in the north corner of the court. Sitting on the ground like the rest, he seemed to take in nothing of his position, except its horror. Probably with the vague ideas of a poor ignorant man, there was also a notion of something excessive in the penalty. While they were riveting the bolt of his iron collar behind his head with heavy hammer strokes, he wept. The tears choked his words, and he only managed to say from time to time, "I was a pruner at Faverolles." Then still sobbing, he raised his right hand and lowered it seven times, as if touching seven heads of unequal height, and from this gesture one could guess that whatever he had done had been to feed and clothe seven little children.

He was taken to Toulon, where he arrived after a journey of twenty-seven days, on a cart, the chain still around his neck. At Toulon he was dressed in the red tunic. All his past life was erased, even his name. He was no longer Jean Valjean; he was Number 24,601. What became of the sister? What became of the seven children? Who worried about that? What becomes of the handful of leaves of the young tree when it is felled?

It is an old story. The poor little lives, these creatures of God, thereafter without support, guidance, or shelter, wandered aimlessly, who knows where? Each took a different path, perhaps, sinking little by little into the chilling haze that swallows up solitary destinies, that sullen gloom where so many ill-fated souls are lost in the somber advance of the human race. They left the region; the church of what had been their village forgot them; the stile of what had been their field forgot them; after a few years in prison, even Jean Valjean forgot them. Where that heart had been wounded, there was a scar. That was all. While he was at Toulon, he heard only once of his sister. I think that was at the end of the fourth year of prison. I have forgotten how the news reached him. Someone who had known him at home had seen his sister. She was in Paris, living in a poor street near Saint-Sulpice, the Rue du Gindre. Only one child, the youngest, a little boy, was still with her. Where were the other six? Perhaps even she did not know. Every morning she went to a bindery, No. 3 Rue du Sabot, where she worked as a folder and book stitcher. She had to be there by six in the morning, long before the winter dawn. In the same building with the bindery was a school, where she sent her little boy of seven. But as the school did not open until seven and she had to be at work by six, the child had to wait in the yard an hour, until the school opened—a cold dark hour in the winter. They would not let the child wait in the bindery, because he was troublesome, they said. The workmen, as they passed in the morning, saw the poor little fellow sometimes sitting on the pavement nodding with weariness, often sleeping in the dark, crouched and bent over his basket. When it rained, an old woman, the door keeper, took pity on him;

she let him come into her lodge, furnished with only a pallet bed, a spinning wheel, and two wooden chairs; and the little one slept there in a corner, hugging the cat to keep himself warm. At seven o'clock the school opened and he went in. That is what they told Jean Valjean. It was as if a window had suddenly been opened onto the fate of those he had loved, and then everything closed again, and he heard nothing more, ever. Nothing more reached him; never would he see them again! And for the rest of this sad story, they will not be seen again.

Near the end of this fourth year, came Jean Valjean's chance for freedom. His comrades helped him as always in that dreary place, and he escaped. For two days he wandered at liberty through the fields; if it is freedom to be hunted, to cock your head constantly, to tremble at the slightest noise, to be afraid of everything, of the smoking chimney, a man going by, the baying of a dog, a galloping horse, the striking of a clock, of the day because you see and of the night because you do not, of the road, the path, the underbrush, sleep. The evening of the second day he was captured. He had neither eaten nor slept for thirty-six hours. The maritime tribunal extended his sentence three years for this attempt, making eight. In the sixth year his turn to escape came again; he tried it but failed again. He did not answer at roll call, and the alarm cannon was fired. At night a patrol discovered him hidden beneath the keel of a vessel on its cradle; he resisted the galley guard that seized him. Escape and resistance, as provided by the special code, were punished by an additional five years, two with the double chain. Thirteen years. The tenth year his turn came around again, and he made another attempt with no better success. Three more years for this new attempt. Sixteen years. And finally, I think it was in the thirteenth year, he made yet another, and was retaken after an absence of only four hours. Three years for these four hours. Nineteen years. In October, 1815, he was freed; he had entered in 1796 for having broken a pane of glass and taken a loaf of bread.

This is a place for a short parenthesis. This is the second time, in his studies on the penal question and regal sentences, that the author of this book has met with the theft of a loaf of bread as the starting point for a ruined life. Claude Gueux stole a loaf of bread; Jean Valjean stole a loaf of bread; English statistics show that in London starvation is the immediate cause of four out of five thefts.

Jean Valjean entered the galleys sobbing and trembling; he left hardened. He entered in despair; he left sullen.

What had happened within this soul?

VII

PROFOUNDEST DESPAIR

Let us try to give an answer.

Society absolutely must look into these things since they are its own work.

He was, as we have said, ignorant, but he was not stupid. The natural light was burning within him. Misfortune, which also has its illumination, added to the faint glow that existed in his mind. Under the whip, under the chain, in the cell, in fatigue, under the searing sun of the galleys, on the convict's plank bed, he turned inward to his own conscience, and he thought things over.

He set himself up as a tribunal.

He began by arraigning himself.

He recognized he was not an innocent man unjustly punished. He acknowledged he had committed an extraordinary and reprehensible act; that the loaf might not have been refused him, if he had asked for it; that in any event it would have been better to wait, either for pity or for work; that it is not altogether an unanswerable reply to say, "Could I wait when I was hungry?"; that, in the first place, it is very rare that anyone dies of actual hunger; and that, fortunately or unfortunately, man is so made that he can suffer long and hard, morally and physically, without dying; that he should, therefore, have had patience; that that would have been better even for the poor little ones; that it was an act of folly in him—a poor, worthless man—to grab all of society forcibly by the collar and imagine he could escape from misery by theft; that, in any event, it was a bad door for getting out of misery, by entering into infamy; in short, that he had done wrong.

Then he asked himself if he were the only one who had done wrong in the course of his disastrous story. If, in the first place, it was not a serious thing that he, a workman, could not have found work and he, an industrious man, should have been without bread. If, moreover, the fault committed and confessed, the punishment had not been cruel and excessive. If there were not a greater abuse on the part of the law, in the penalty, than there had been, on the part of the guilty, in the crime. If there were not too much weight on one side of the scales—on the side of the expiation. If the excess of the penalty were not the eradication of the crime; and if the result were not a reversal of the situation, replacing the wrong of the delinquent with the wrong of the repression, to make a victim of the guilty, and a creditor of the debtor, and actually to put the right on the side of the one who had violated it. If that penalty, in conjunction with its successive extensions for his attempted escapes, were not finally a sort of outrage of the stronger on the weaker, a crime of society upon the individual, a crime committed afresh every day, a crime that was committed for nineteen years.

He asked himself whether human society could rightfully make its members submit equally, in the one case by its unreasonable carelessness and in the other by its pitiless care; and to hold a poor man forever between a lack and an excess, a lack of work, an excess of punishment.

If it was not outrageous that society should treat with such rigid precision those of its members who were most poorly endowed in the chance distribution of wealth and were therefore most deserving of tolerance.

With these questions asked and answered, he condemned society and sentenced it.

He sentenced it to his hatred.

He made it responsible for his fate, and promised himself that he perhaps would not hesitate someday to call it to account. He declared to himself that there was no equity between the injury he had committed and the injury committed on him; he concluded, in short, that his punishment was not merely an injustice but, beyond all doubt, a gross injustice.

Anger may be foolish and absurd, and one may be wrongly irritated, but a man never feels outraged unless in some respect he is fundamentally right. Jean Valjean felt outraged.

And then, human society had done him nothing but injury; never had he seen anything of her but the wrathful face she calls justice, when showing it to those she strikes down. No man had ever touched him except to bruise him. All his contact with men had been by blows. Never, since infancy, since his mother, since his sister, never had he been greeted with a friendly word or a kind look. Through suffering upon suffering he gradually came to the conclusion that life is a war and that in that war he was the vanquished. He had no weapon but his hatred. He resolved to sharpen it in the chain gang and take it with him when he left.

At Toulon there was a school for the prisoners conducted by some rather ignorant friars, where the essentials were taught to any of these poor men who were willing. He was one. At forty he went to school and learned to read, write, and do arithmetic. He felt that to increase his knowledge was to strengthen his hatred. In certain cases, instruction and enlightenment can actually work to underscore the wrong.

Sad to say, after having tried society, which had caused his misfortunes, he tried Providence, which created society, and he condemned it as well.

Thus, during those nineteen years of torment and slavery, this soul rose and fell at the same time. Light entered on the one side and darkness on the other.

Jean Valjean was not, we have seen, born evil. He was still good when he arrived at the prison. There, he condemned society and felt himself becoming wicked; he condemned Providence and felt himself becoming impious.

At this point, it is difficult not to reflect a moment.

Can human nature be so entirely transformed inside and out? Can man, created good by God, be made wicked by man? Can the soul be completely changed by its destiny, and turn evil when its fate is evil? Can the heart become distorted, contract deformities and incurable infirmities, under the pressure of disproportionate grief, like the spinal column under a low ceiling? Is there not in every human soul—was there not particularly in Jean

Valjean's soul—a primitive spark, a divine element, incorruptible in this world and immortal in the next, which can be developed by goodness, kindled, lit up, and made to radiate, and which evil can never entirely extinguish.

Grave and obscure questions; to the last one, any doctor would probably have unhesitatingly answered no, if he had seen at Toulon, during rest hours, which to Jean Valjean were for thought, this gloomy prisoner, seated, with folded arms, on the bar of some windlass, the end of his chain stuck into his pocket so as not to drag, serious, silent, and pensive, a pariah of the law, which views man with wrath, and condemned by civilization, which views heaven with severity.

Certainly, a doctor would have seen in Jean Valjean an incurable misery; he would perhaps have pitied this man sickened by the law, but he would not even have attempted a cure; he would have turned from the sight of the caverns glimpsed in that soul; and, like Dante at the gate of Hell, he would have erased from that existence the word that the finger of God has nonetheless written on the brow of everyone—*Hope!*

Was that state of mind that we have attempted to analyze as perfectly clear to Jean Valjean as we have tried to make it for our readers? After their formation, did Jean Valjean clearly see and had he seen, while they were forming, all the elements of his moral misery? Had this rough, illiterate man taken accurate account of the succession of ideas by which he had risen and fallen, step by step, till he had reached that sad state which for so long had been the internal horizon of his mind? Was he aware of all that had happened inside him, and all that was stirring there? We dare not say so; in fact, we do not believe it. Jean Valjean was too ignorant, even after so much ill fortune, for neat discrimination in these matters. At times he did not even know exactly what he felt. Jean Valjean was in the dark, suffering in the dark, hating in the dark. He lived constantly in darkness, groping blindly, like a dreamer. Except, at times, there broke over him suddenly, from inside or out, a shockwave of anger, an overflow of suffering, a sudden white flash that lit up his whole soul and showed all around him in front and behind in the glare of a hideous light the fearful precipices and dark perspectives of his fate.

The flash passed away, night fell again, and where was he? He no longer knew.

The peculiarity of punishment of this kind, in which the pitiless or brutalizing part predominates, is to transform gradually by a slow numbing process a man into an animal, sometimes into a wild beast. Jean Valjean's repeated, obstinate attempts to escape are enough to prove the strange effect of the law on a human soul. Jean Valjean had repeated these attempts, so completely useless and foolish, when the opportunity arose, without a moment's thought of the outcome or of trials already undergone. He escaped impetuously, like a wolf on seeing his cage door open. Instinct said, "Go!" Reason said, "Stay!" But before so mighty a temptation, reason disappeared, and only instinct remained. The beast alone was reacting. When he was recaptured, the new punishment inflicted on him only made him fiercer.

We must not omit one important fact: In physical strength Jean Valjean far surpassed all the other inmates of the prison. At hard work, at twisting a cable, or turning a winch, he was equal to four men. He would sometimes lift and hold up enormous weights on his back, occasionally taking on the role of "jack," or what was called in old French an *orgeuil*—whence came the name, incidentally, of the Rue Montorgeuil near les Halles in Paris. His comrades nicknamed him Jean the Jack. At one time, while the balcony of Toulon's City Hall was being repaired, one of Puget's marvelous caryatids that support the balcony slipped and was about to fall; Jean Valjean, who happened to be there, held it up with his shoulder till the workmen came.

His agility was even greater than his strength. Certain convicts, constantly planning escape, have developed a veritable science of strength and skill combined—the science of the muscles. A mysterious system of statics is practiced daily by prisoners, eternally envying birds and flying insects. To scale a wall, to find a foothold where you could hardly see a projection, was a game for Jean Valjean. Given an angle in a wall, with the pressure of his back and his knees, with elbows and hands braced against the rough face of the stone, he would ascend, as if by magic, to the third floor. Sometimes he climbed up in this way to the prison roof.

He talked little and never laughed. Only some extreme emotion would draw from him, once or twice a year, that mournful laugh of the convict, like the echo of a devil's cackle. He seemed continually absorbed in looking at something terrible.

In fact he was absorbed.

Through the sick perceptions of an incomplete nature and a vanquished intelligence, he vaguely felt a monstrous weight was on him. In that wan half light where he crouched, whenever he turned his head and tried to raise his eyes, he would see, with mingled rage and terror, forming, massing, rising out of view above him with horrible ramparts, a frightening accumulation of laws, prejudices, men, and acts, whose outlines escaped him, whose weight appalled him—it was that prodigious pyramid we call civilization. Here and there in that shapeless, seething mass, sometimes near, sometimes far, or at inaccessible heights, he could make out some group, some vivid detail, here the jailer with his cudgel, here the gendarme with his sword, there the mitered archbishop, and high up, in a blaze of glory, the emperor crowned and resplendent. It seemed to him that these distant splendors, far from dissipating his night, made it blacker, deathlier. All this—laws, intolerance, actions, men, things—came and went above him, according to the complicated, mysterious movement God imposes on civilization, walking over him and crushing him with an indescribably serene cruelty, an inexorable indifference. Souls sunk to deepest misfortune, unfortunate men lost in the depths of limbo where they are no longer visible, the rejects of the law, feeling on their heads the whole weight of human society, so formidable to those outside it, so terrible to those beneath it.

From his position, Jean Valjean meditated. What sort of reflections could they be?

If a millet seed under a millstone had thoughts, undoubtedly it would think as Jean Valjean did.

All this, realities full of specters, phantasmagoria full of realities, had finally produced in him an almost inexpressible mental state.

Sometimes in the midst of his prison work he would stop and begin to think. His reason, more mature and yet more disturbed than before, would rebel. All that had happened to him would appear absurd, everything surrounding him impossible. He would say to himself, "This is a dream." He would look at the jailer standing a few steps away like some phantom; suddenly this phantom would strike him with a club.

The external world scarcely had an existence. It would be almost true to say that for Jean Valjean there were no sun, no beautiful summer days, no radiant sky, no fresh April dawn. Some dim light from a small, high window was all that shone in his soul.

In conclusion, in the course of nineteen years, Jean Valjean, the inoffensive pruner of Faverolles, the miserable convict of Toulon, had become capable—thanks to prison training—of two types of crime: first, a sudden unpremeditated act, rash, instinctive, a sort of reprisal for the wrong he had suffered; second, a serious, premeditated act, debated in his conscience and mulled over with the false ideas such a fate will produce. His premeditations went through the three successive phases to which certain natures are limited—reason, will, and obstinacy. As motives, he had habitual indignation, bitterness, a deep sense of injury, a reaction even against the good, the innocent, and the upright, in the unlikely event he encountered them. The beginning and end of all his thoughts was hatred of human law; that hatred which, if not checked in its growth by some providential event, becomes in time a hatred of society, then hatred of the human race, then hatred of creation, revealing itself by a vague, incessant desire to injure some living being, no matter who. So, the passport was right in describing Jean Valjean as "a very dangerous man."

From year to year this soul had progressively withered, slowly but inevitably. A dry eye goes with a dead soul. When he left prison, he had not shed a tear for nineteen years.

VIII

DEEP WATERS, DARK SHADOWS

Man overboard!

Who cares? The ship sails on. The wind is up, the dark ship must keep to its destined course. It passes on.

The man disappears, then reappears, he sinks and rises again to the surface, he hollers, stretches out his hands. They do not hear him. The ship, staggering under the gale, is straining every rope, the sailors and passengers no longer see the drowning man, his miserable head is only a point in the vastness of the billows.

He hurls cries of despair into the depths. What a specter is that disappearing sail! He watches it, follows it frantically. It moves away, grows dim, diminishes. He was just there, one of the crew, he walked up and down the deck with the rest, he had his share of air and sunlight, he was a living man. Now, what has become of him? He slipped, he fell, it's all over.

He is in the monstrous deep. There is nothing beneath his feet but the yielding, fleeing element. The waves, torn and scattered by the wind, close around him hideously; the rolling abyss bears him away; tatters of water are flying around his head; a populace of waves spit on him; vague openings half swallow him; each time he sinks he glimpses yawning precipices full of dark; frightful unknown tendrils seize him, bind his feet, and draw him down; he feels he is becoming the great deep; he is part of the foam; the billows toss him back and forth; he drinks in bitterness; the voracious ocean is eager to devour him; the monster plays with his agony. It is all liquid hatred to him.

He tries to defend, to sustain himself; he struggles; he swims. With his poor exhausted strength, he combats the inexhaustible.

Still he struggles on.

Where is the ship? Far away. Barely visible on the pallid horizon.

The wind blows in gusts; the billows overwhelm him. He raises his eyes but sees only the ashen clouds. In his dying agony, he is part of the sea's immense insanity, tortured by its immeasurable madness. He hears sounds unknown to man, seemingly come from some terrible kingdom beyond.

There are birds in the clouds, even as there are angels above human distresses, but what can they do for him? They fly, sing, and soar, while he gasps.

He feels buried by the two infinities together, the ocean and the sky, the one a tomb, the other a shroud.

Night falls; he has been swimming for hours, his strength almost gone; the ship, a distant far-off thing, where there were men, is gone; he is alone in the terrible gloom of the abyss; he sinks, he strains, he struggles, feels beneath himself invisible shadowy monsters; he screams.

Men are gone. Where is God?

He screams. Help! Someone! Help! He screams over and over.

Nothing on the horizon. Nothing in the sky.

He implores the lofty sky, the endless waves, the reefs; all are deaf. He begs the storms; but impassive, they obey only the infinite.

Around him, darkness, storm, solitude, wild, unconscious tumult, the ceaseless churning of fierce waters. Within him, horror and exhaustion. Beneath him the devouring abyss. No resting place. He thinks of the shadowy adventures of his limp body in the limitless gloom. The biting cold paralyzes him. His hands cramp shut and grasp at . . . nothing. Winds, clouds, whirlwinds, blasts, stars, all useless! What can he do? He yields to despair; worn out, he seeks death, no longer resists, gives up, lets go, tumbles into the mournful depths of the abyss forever.

O implacable march of human society! Destroying men and souls in its way! Ocean, repository of all that the law lets fall! Ominous disappearance of help! O moral death!

The sea is the inexorable night into which the penal code casts its victims. The sea is measureless misery.

The soul drifting in that sea may become a corpse. Who shall restore it to life?

IX

NEW GRIEVANCES

When the time came for leaving prison, and the strange words "You are free" sounded in Jean Valjean's ears, the moment seemed improbable and unreal; a ray of vivid light, a ray of true light of living men suddenly penetrated his soul. But it quickly faded. Jean Valjean had been dazzled with the idea of liberty, had believed in a new life. He soon saw what sort of liberty comes with a yellow passport.

And there were other bitter blows besides. He had calculated that his savings, during his prison stay, should amount to a hundred and seventy-one francs. True, he had forgotten to take into account the compulsory rest on Sundays and holidays, which, in nineteen years, meant a deduction of about twenty-four francs. However that might be, his savings had been reduced by various local charges to the sum of a hundred and nine francs and fifteen sous, counted out to him at his departure.

He understood nothing of this and thought himself wronged or, more to the point, robbed.

The day after his liberation, he saw, before the door of an orange flower distillery at Grasse, some men unloading bales. He offered his services. They needed help and accepted him. He set to work. He was intelligent, strong, and skilled; he did his best; the foreman seemed satisfied. While he was at work, a gendarme passed, noticed him, and asked for his papers. He had to show the yellow passport. Jean Valjean resumed his work. A while before, he had asked one of the workmen how much they were paid per day for this work, and the reply was thirty sous. That evening, because he planned to leave town the next morning, he went to the foreman and asked for his pay. The foreman did not say a word but handed him fifteen sous. He protested. The man replied, "That's good enough for you." He persisted. The foreman glared at him: "Watch out for the chain gang."

Here again he felt he had been robbed.

Society, the state, in reducing his savings, had robbed

him, wholesale. Now, at the retail level, the individual was robbing him, too.

Liberation is not deliverance. A convict may leave prison behind but not his sentence.

That was what happened to him at Grasse. And we have seen the welcome he received at Digne.

X

THE MAN WAKES UP

As the cathedral clock struck two, Jean Valjean awoke.

It was incongruous, what awakened him: too much comfort. For nearly twenty years he had not slept in a bed, and, though tonight he had not even undressed, the sensation was too novel not to disturb his sleep.

He had slept over four hours. His fatigue was gone. He was not accustomed to many hours of sleep.

He opened his eyes and looked for a moment into the darkness around him, then closed them to go to sleep again.

When many different sensations have disturbed the day, when the mind is preoccupied, we can fall asleep once but not a second time. Sleep comes at first more readily than it returns. Such was the case for Jean Valjean. He could not get to sleep again, and so he began to think.

He was in one of those times when our minds are agitated with ideas. There was a kind of vague ebb and flow in his brain. His oldest and his most recent memories floated pell-mell and mingled confusedly, losing shape, swelling beyond measure, then abruptly disappearing as if in a muddy, troubled stream. Many thoughts came to him, but one kept reappearing, driving out all others. That thought was this: He had noticed the silver place settings and the large spoon that Madame Magloire had put on the table.

Those six silver sets obsessed him. There they were, a few steps away. At the very moment he was going through the middle room to reach the one he was now in, the old servant was placing them in a little cupboard at the head of the bed. He had carefully noticed that cupboard: on the right, coming from the dining room. They were solid, old silver. With the big serving spoon, they would bring at least two hundred francs, double what he had made in nineteen years' labor. True—he would have got more if the "government" had not "robbed" him.

His mind wavered a whole long hour, in agitation and struggle. The clock struck three. He opened his eyes, rose up hastily in bed, reached out his arm and felt for his knapsack which he had put into the corner of the alcove, then he swung his legs and put his feet on the ground, finding himself, somehow, seated on his bed.

He stayed for some time lost in thought in that position, which would have looked rather ominous had anyone seen him there in the dark—he the only one awake in the sleeping house. All at once he stooped down, took off his shoes, and put them softly on the mat in front of the bed, then resumed his thinking posture and was still again.

In that hideous meditation, the ideas we have been describing persistently stirred up his mind, entered, left, returned, became a sort of weight on him; and then he thought, too, without knowing why, in a mechanical obstinate reverie, of a convict named Brevet, whom he had known in prison, and whose trousers were only held up by a single cotton knit suspender. The checked pattern of that suspender kept coming to his mind.

He stayed in this position, and would perhaps have remained so until daybreak if the clock had not struck the quarter or the half hour. It seemed to be saying, "Come on!"

He rose, hesitated a moment, and listened; the house was still; he walked straight and cautiously toward the window, which he could just see. The night was not very dark; there was a full moon, across which flashed large clouds driven by the wind. Outside this produced alternative light and shade, eclipses and illuminations, and indoors a kind of twilight. This glimmer, enough for him to find his way, changing with the passing clouds, was like that sort of pale light that falls through a cellar window crossed back and forth by pedestrians. On reaching the window, Jean Valjean examined it. It had no bars, opened into the garden, and was fastened in country fashion, merely with a little wedge. He opened it; but because the cold, crisp air rushed into the room, he closed it again immediately. He looked into the garden with an intensity that studies rather than sees. The garden was enclosed by a white wall, quite low and easy to scale. Beyond, against the sky, he distinguished the tops of trees at regular intervals indicating that this wall separated the garden from an avenue or a lane planted with trees.

Following this observation, he turned like a man whose mind is made up, went to his alcove, picked up his knapsack, opened it, fumbled in it, took out something, which he laid on the bed, put his shoes into one of his pockets, tied up his bundle, swung it over his shoulders, put on his cap, with the visor pulled down over his eyes, groped for his stick, and went to put it in the corner of the window, then returned to the bed, and resolutely took up the object he had laid there. It looked like a short iron bar, pointed at one end like a spear.

In the darkness it would have been hard to make out the intended use of this piece of iron. Could it be a lever? Or a club?

By daylight, it would have been recognized as nothing but a miner's drill. At that time, the convicts were sometimes employed in quarrying stone on the high hills surrounding Toulon, and they often used miners' tools. Miners' drills are of solid iron, terminating at the lower end in a point, by which they are sunk into the rock.

Taking the drill in his right hand and holding his breath, he moved stealthily toward the door of the next room, the bishop's, as we know. On reaching the door, he found it ajar. The bishop had not closed it.

XI

WHAT HE DOES NEXT

Jean Valjean listened. Not a sound.

He pushed the door.

He pushed it lightly with the tip of his finger, with a

cat's stealthy, timorous care. The door yielded to the pressure with a silent, imperceptible movement widening the opening slightly.

He waited a moment, then pushed the door again more firmly.

It yielded gradually and silently. The opening was now wide enough for him to pass through, but there was a small table beside the door creating a troublesome angle that blocked the entrance.

Jean Valjean saw the obstacle. At any risk, the opening had to be widened.

He made up his mind and gave the door a third push, harder than before. This time a poorly oiled hinge suddenly let out a harsh and prolonged creak into the darkness.

Jean Valjean trembled. The noise sounded in his ears as clear and terrible as the last trumpet on Judgment Day.

In the fantastic exaggeration of this instant, he almost imagined that the hinge had become animate and suddenly endowed with a terrible life, that it was barking like a dog to waken all sleepers.

He stopped, shuddering, bewildered, and dropped from his tiptoes to his feet. He felt the pulses of his temples throb like trip hammers, and it seemed as though his breath was coming from his chest like the roar of wind from a cavern. It seemed impossible that the horrible sound of this irritated hinge had not shaken the whole house with the shock of an earthquake: The door he pushed had given the alarm; the old man would rise; the two old women would scream; help would come; in a quarter of an hour the town would be alive with it and the gendarmes in pursuit. For a moment he thought he was lost.

He stood stock still, petrified like the pillar of salt, not daring to stir. Some minutes passed. The door had swung wide open; he ventured a look into the room. Nothing had moved. He listened. Nothing was stirring in the house. The noise of the rusty hinge had wakened nobody.

This first danger was over, but still he felt a frightful inner turmoil. Nevertheless he did not flinch. Not even when he thought he was lost had he flinched. His only thought was to make a quick end of it. With one step he was in the room.

A deep calm filled the bedroom. Here and there, indistinct, confused forms could be distinguished, which by day were papers scattered over a table, open folios, books piled on a stool, an armchair with clothes on it, a prie-dieu, but now were only dark crannies and whitish spots. Jean Valjean advanced, carefully avoiding the furniture. At the far end of the room he could hear the even, quiet breathing of the sleeping bishop.

Suddenly he stopped: He was near the bed, he had reached it sooner than he thought.

Sometimes nature mingles her effects and spectacles and our acts with a serious, intelligent appropriateness, as if she wanted us to reflect. For almost half an hour a great cloud had darkened the sky. At the moment when Jean Valjean paused before the bed the cloud broke up as if deliberately, and a ray of moonlight crossing the high window suddenly lit up the bishop's pale face. He slept peacefully. He was almost completely dressed in bed, because of the cold Basse-Alpes nights, with a dark woolen garment that covered his arms to the wrists. His head was tilted back on the pillow in the unstudied attitude of sleep; over the side of the bed hung his hand, ornamented with the pastoral ring, and which had done so many good deeds, so many pious acts. His face was lit up with a vague expression of contentment, hope, and happiness. It was more than a smile and almost a radiance. On his forehead rested the indescribable reflection of an unseen light. The souls of the upright in sleep contemplate a mysterious heaven.

A reflection from this heaven shone upon the bishop.

But it was also a luminous transparency, for this heaven was within him; it was his conscience.

At the instant when the moonbeam overlay, so to speak, this inward radiance, the sleeping bishop appeared as if in a halo. But it was mild and veiled in an inexpressible twilight. The moon in the sky, drowsing nature, the garden without a quiver, the quiet house, the hour, the moment, the silence, added something strangely solemn and unutterable to the venerable repose of this wise man, and enveloped his white locks and closed his eyes with a serene, majestic glory, this face all hope and confidence —this old man's head and infant's slumber.

There was something close to divine in this man, something unconsciously noble.

Jean Valjean stood in the shadow with the iron drill in his hand, erect, motionless, terrified by this radiant figure. He had never seen anything like it. This confidence terrified him. The moral world has no spectacle more powerful than this: a troubled, restless conscience on the verge of committing a crime, contemplating the sleep of a just man.

This sleep in this isolation, with a neighbor such as he, contained a touch of the sublime, which he felt, vaguely but powerfully.

No one could have told what was happening inside him, not even himself. To attempt to realize it, the utmost violence must be imagined in the presence of the most extreme mildness. Not even in his face could anything be read with certainty. It was a sort of haggard astonishment. He was looking at it; that was all. But what were his thoughts; it would have been impossible to guess. It was clear that he was moved and overwhelmed. But what was this emotion?

He did not take his eyes off the old man. The only thing clearly visible in his attitude and expression was a strange indecision. It was as though he were hesitating between two realms, that of the doomed and that of the saved: He seemed ready either to crack this skull or to kiss this hand.

In a few moments he raised his left hand slowly to his forehead and took off his hat; then, letting his hand fall again slowly, Jean Valjean resumed his meditations, his cap in his left hand, his club in his right, and his hair bristling on his fierce-looking head.

Under this frightful gaze the bishop still slept in profoundest peace.

The crucifix above the mantelpiece was dimly visible in the moonlight, apparently extending its arms toward both, with a benediction for one and a pardon for the other.

Suddenly Jean Valjean put on his cap, then moved quickly along the bed, without looking at the bishop, straight to the cupboard, which he could make out near its head; he raised the drill to force the lock; the key was in it; he opened it; the first thing he saw was the basket of silverware; he took it, crossed the room hastily, heedless of noise, reached the door, entered the oratory, took his stick, stepped outside, put the silver in his knapsack, threw away the basket, ran across the garden, leaped over the wall like a tiger, and escaped.

XII

THE BISHOP AT WORK

The next day at sunrise, Monseigneur Bienvenu was walking in the garden. Madame Magloire ran toward him quite beside herself.

"Monseigneur, Monseigneur," she cried, "does Your Lordship know where the silver basket is?"

"Yes," said the bishop.

"God be praised!" she said. "I did not know what had become of it."

The bishop had just found the basket on a flower bed. He gave it to Madame Magloire and said, "Here it is."

"Yes," she said, "but there's nothing in it. Where's the silver?"

"Ah!" said the bishop. "It's the silver then that troubles you. I don't know where that is."

"Good heavens! It's stolen. That man who came last night stole it!"

And in the twinkling of an eye, with all the agility of her age, Madame Magloire ran to the oratory, went into the alcove, and came back to the bishop. The bishop was bending with some sadness over a cochlearia des Guillons, which the basket had broken in falling. At Madame Magloire's cry he looked up.

"Monseigneur, the man has gone! The silver is stolen!"

While she was uttering this exclamation, her eyes fell on a corner of the garden where she saw traces of the escape. A capstone of the wall had been dislodged.

"See, that is where he got out; he jumped into Cochefilet Lane. The wretch! He stole our silver!"

The bishop was silent for a moment, then raising his serious eyes, he said mildly to Madame Magloire, "Now first, did this silver belong to us?"

Madame Magloire was speechless. After a moment the bishop continued, "Madame Magloire, for a long time I have wrongfully been withholding this silver. It belonged to the poor. Who was this man? A poor man, quite clearly."

"Alas! alas!" returned Madame Magloire. "It's not on my account or Mademoiselle's; it is all the same to us. But it's for you, Monseigneur. What is Monsieur going to eat with now?"

The bishop looked at her with amazement. "But don't we have any pewter cutlery?"

Madame Magloire shrugged her shoulders. "Pewter smells."

"Well, then, iron."

Madame Magloire grimaced.

"Iron has a taste."

"Well, then," said the bishop, "wooden implements."

In a few minutes he was breakfasting at the table where Jean Valjean sat the night before. While breakfasting, Monseigneur Bienvenu pleasantly remarked to his sister, who said nothing, and Madame Magloire, who was grumbling to herself, that there was really no need even of a wooden spoon or fork to dip a piece of bread into a cup of milk.

"Was there ever such an idea?" said Madame Magloire to herself, as she went back and forth: "To take in a man like that, and to give him a bed at his side; and yet what a blessing he did nothing but steal! Oh, good Lord! It gives me the chills just to think of it!"

As the brother and sister were rising from the table, there was a knock at the door.

"Come in," said the bishop.

The door opened. A strange, fierce group appeared on the threshold. Three men were holding a fourth by the collar. The three men were gendarmes; the fourth Jean Valjean.

A brigadier of gendarmes, who appeared to head the group, was near the door. He advanced toward the bishop, giving a military salute.

"Monseigneur," he said—

At this word Jean Valjean, who was sullen and seemed entirely dejected, raised his head with a stupefied air. "Monseigneur!" he murmured. "Then it is not the curé!"

"Silence!" said a gendarme. "It is his lordship, the bishop."

In the meantime Monseigneur Bienvenu had approached as quickly as his great age permitted: "Ah, there you are!" he said, looking at Jean Valjean. "I'm glad to see you. But I gave you the candlesticks, too, which are silver like the rest and would bring two hundred francs. Why didn't you take them along with your cutlery?"

Jean Valjean opened his eyes and looked at the bishop with an expression no human tongue could describe.

"Monseigneur," said the brigadier, "then what this man said was true? We met him. He was acting like a fugitive, and we arrested him in order to find out. He had this silver."

"And he told you," interrupted the bishop, with a smile, "that it had been given to him by a good old priest at whose house he had slept. I see it all. And you brought him back here? It's all a mistake."

"If that's so," said the brigadier, "we can let him go."

"Please do," replied the bishop.

The gendarmes released Jean Valjean, who shrank back.

"Is it true they're letting me go?" he muttered, as if talking in his sleep.

"Yes! You can go. Don't you understand?" said a gendarme.

"My friend," said the bishop, "before you go away, here are your candlesticks; take them."

He went to the mantelpiece, took the two candlesticks, and handed them to Jean Valjean. The two women observed without a word, gesture, or look that could disturb the bishop.

Jean Valjean was trembling all over. He took the two candlesticks distractedly, with a bewildered expression.

"Now," said the bishop, "go in peace. By the way, my friend, when you come again, you needn't come through the garden. You can always come and go by the front door. It is only closed with a latch, day or night."

Then turning to the gendarmes, he said, "Messieurs, you may go." The gendarmes left.

Jean Valjean felt like a man about to faint.

The bishop approached him and said, in a low voice,

"Do not forget, ever, that you have promised me to use this silver to become an honest man."

Jean Valjean, who had no recollection of any such promise, stood dumbfounded. The bishop had stressed these words as he spoke them. He continued, solemnly, "Jean Valjean, my brother, you no longer belong to evil, but to good. It is your soul I am buying for you. I withdraw it from dark thoughts and from the spirit of perdition, and I give it to God!"

XIII

PETIT-GERVAIS

Jean Valjean left the city as if he were escaping. He hurried into the open country, taking the first lanes and byways at hand, without noticing that he was retracing his steps. He wandered this way all morning. He had eaten nothing, but did not feel hungry. He was prey to a mass of new emotions. He felt somewhat angry, without knowing at whom. He could not have said whether he was touched or humiliated. At times, there came over him a strange relenting, which he tried to resist with the hardening of his past twenty years. This condition wore him out. He was disturbed to see within him that that frightful calm which the injustice of his fate had given him was now somewhat shaken. He asked himself what might replace it. At times he would really have preferred to be in prison with the gendarmes, and free from this new development; it would have troubled him less. Although the season was well along, there were still here and there a few late flowers under the hedges, whose odor he caught as he walked, reminding him of his childhood. The memories were almost unbearable, it was so long since they had occurred to him.

Inexpressible thoughts gathered in his mind this way all day long.

As the sun was sinking toward the horizon, lengthening the shadow of the smallest pebble, Jean Valjean was seated behind a thicket in an absolutely deserted large russet plain. There was no horizon but the Alps. Not even the steeple of a distant village church. Jean Valjean might have been ten miles from Digne. A path cutting across the plain went by a few steps from the thicket.

In the midst of this meditation, which would certainly have contributed to the frightening effect of his rags on anyone who might have met him, he heard a joyful sound.

He turned his head and saw coming along the path a little Savoyard, a chimneysweep, about ten years old, singing, with a small hurdy-gurdy at his side, and a pack on his back. One of those cheerful boys who go from place to place, with their knees poking through their trousers.

Still singing, the boy stopped from time to time, playfully tossing up a few coins he had in his hand, probably his entire fortune. Among them was a forty-sous piece.

Without noticing Jean Valjean, the boy stopped beside the thicket and tossed up his handful of coins; until that moment he had skillfully caught them on the back of his hand.

This time the forty-sous piece got away from him and rolled toward the thicket, near Jean Valjean.

Jean Valjean put his foot on it.

The boy, however, had followed the piece with his eye and had seen where it went.

He was not frightened and walked right up to the man.

It was a totally secluded place. There was no one to be seen on the plain or on the path. The only sound was the faint cry of a flock of birds of passage, flying across the sky at an immense height. The child turned his back to the sun, which made his hair like threads of gold and flushed the savage face of Jean Valjean with a lurid glow.

"Monsieur," said the little chimneysweep, with a childish confidence composed of ignorance and innocence, "my money?"

"What's your name?" said Jean Valjean.

"Petit Gervais, Monsieur."

"Go away," said Jean Valjean.

"Monsieur," repeated the boy, "give me my coin."

Jean Valjean looked down and did not answer.

The child began again. "My money, Monsieur!"

Jean Valjean's eyes remained fixed on the ground.

"My money!" exclaimed the boy. "My silver coin! My money!"

Jean Valjean did not seem to understand. The boy took

him by the shirt collar and shook him. And at the same time he made an attempt to move the big, iron-tipped shoe standing on his treasure.

"I want my money, my forty sous!"

The child began to cry. Jean Valjean raised his head. He remained seated. He was troubled. He looked at the boy with an air of bewilderment, then reached out toward his stick, and said gruffly, "Who is it?"

"Me, sir," answered the boy. "Petit Gervais! Me! Me! Give me my forty sous, please! Take away your foot, sir, please!" Then becoming angry, small as he was, and almost threatening: "Come on, will you move your foot? Why don't you move your foot?"

"Ah! You still here!" said Jean Valjean, and rising hastily to his feet, without releasing the piece of money, he added, "You'd better get moving!"

The boy looked at him in terror, then began to shake from head to foot, and after a few dumfounded seconds, took off and ran with all his strength, not daring to turn his head or cry out.

Soon, however, he stopped, out of breath, and Jean Valjean, still distracted, heard him sobbing.

In a few minutes the boy was gone.

The sun had set.

The shadows were deepening around Jean Valjean. He had not eaten all day; he probably had a fever.

He was still standing, had not budged since the child fled. His chest heaved with deep breaths at irregular intervals. His eyes were trained on a spot ten or twelve steps ahead of him, and seemed deeply absorbed in the shape of an old piece of blue crockery lying in the grass. All at once he shivered; he had just begun to feel the cold night air.

He pulled his cap down over his forehead, absently tried to close and button his shirt around him, stepped forward, and stooped to pick up his stick.

At that instant he noticed the forty-sous piece that his foot had half buried in the ground, now glistening among the pebbles. It was like an electric shock. "What is that?" he said, between his teeth. He drew back a step or two, then stopped, unable to dislodge his gaze from the spot his foot had covered the instant before, as if the thing that glistened there in the shadows were an open eye staring at him.

After a few minutes, he sprang convulsively toward the piece of money, seized it, and, straightening up, looked away across the plain, peering in all directions, standing still and trembling like a frightened animal seeking a place of refuge.

He saw nothing. Night was falling, the plain was cold and bare, thick purple mists were rising in the clear twilight.

He said, "Oh!" and began to walk rapidly in the direction in which the boy had gone. After some thirty steps, he stopped, looked around, and saw nothing.

Then he called with all his might, "Petit Gervais! Petit Gervais!"

He listened and waited.

There was no answer.

The countryside was desolate and gloomy. There were vast open stretches on all sides, nothing around him but a shadow in which his gaze was lost and a silence in which his voice was lost.

A biting north wind was blowing, which gave a kind of dismal life to everything around him. The bushes shook their thin arms with incredible fury, as though threatening and pursuing somebody.

He began to walk again, then quickened his pace to a run, and from time to time stopped and called out in that solitude, in a desolate and terrible voice: "Petit Gervais! Petit Gervais!"

Surely, if the child had heard him, he would have been frightened, and would have stayed hidden. But undoubtedly the boy was already far away.

He met a priest on horseback. He went up to him and said, "Monsieur curé, did you see a child go by?"

"No," said the preist.

"Petit Gervais was his name?"

"I haven't seen anybody."

He took two five-franc pieces from his bag and gave them to the priest. "Monsieur curé, this is for your poor. Monsieur curé, he is a little fellow, about ten years old, with a pack, I think, and a hurdy-gurdy. He went this way. One of those Savoyards, you know?"

"I haven't seen him at all."

"Petit Gervais? Is his village near here? Can you tell me?"

"If it is as you say, my friend, the little fellow is a

foreigner. They roam around the countryside. Nobody knows them."

Jean Valjean hastily took out two more five-franc pieces, and gave them to the priest.

"For your poor," said he.

Then he added wildly, "Monsieur abbé, have me arrested. I am a robber."

The priest spurred his horse and fled, terrified.

Jean Valjean began to run again in the direction he had first taken.

He went on this way for quite a while, looking around, calling and shouting, but met nobody else. Two or three times he left the path to look at what seemed to be somebody lying down or crouching; it was only low bushes or rocks. Finally, at a place where three paths met, he stopped. The moon had risen. He strained his eyes in the distance and called out once more, "Petit Gervais! Petit Gervais! Petit Gervais!" His cries died away into the mist, without even awaking an echo. Again he murmured, "Petit Gervais!" but with a feeble, almost inaudible voice. That was his last effort; his knees suddenly bent under him, as if an invisible power suddenly overwhelmed him with the weight of his bad conscience; he fell exhausted onto a large rock, his hands clenched in his hair, and his face on his knees, and cried out, "I'm such a miserable man!"

Then his heart swelled, and he burst into tears. It was the first time he had wept in nineteen years.

When Jean Valjean left the bishop's house, as we saw, his thoughts were unlike any he had ever known before. He could understand nothing of what was going on inside him. He stubbornly resisted the angelic deeds and the gentle words of the old man, "You have promised me to become an honest man. I am purchasing your soul. I withdraw it from the spirit of perdition, and I give it to God!" This kept coming back to him. In opposition to this celestial tenderness, he summoned up pride, the fortress of evil in man. He dimly felt that this priest's pardon was the hardest assault, the most formidable attack he had ever sustained; that his hardness of heart would be complete, if it resisted this kindness; that if he yielded, he would have to renounce the hatred with which the acts of other men had for so many years filled his soul, and in which he found satisfaction; that, this time, he must conquer or be conquered, and that the struggle, a gigantic and decisive struggle, had begun between his own wrongs and the goodness of this man.

Faced with all these things, he reeled like a drunk. While he kept on walking this way with a haggard look, did he have any distinct perception of what might be the result of his adventure at Digne? Did he hear those mysterious murmurs that alert or entice the spirit at certain moments of life? Did a voice whisper in his ear that he had just passed through the decisive hour of his destiny, that there was no longer a middle course for him, that if, thereafter, he were not the best of men, he would be the worst, that he must now, so to speak, climb higher than the bishop or fall lower than the convict; that, if he wanted to become good, he must become an angel; that, if he wanted to remain evil, he must become a monster?

Here we must again ask those questions we have already posed elsewhere: Was some confused shadow of all this gathering in his mind? Certainly misfortune, as we have said, educates the intelligence, but it is doubtful that Jean Valjean was able to realize all that we are suggesting here. If these ideas did occur to him, he glimpsed rather than saw them, and they only managed to throw him into an intolerable, almost painful confusion. He was just out of that monstrous, somber place called prison and the bishop had hurt his soul, as too vivid a light would have hurt his eyes on coming out of the dark. The future life, the possible life offered to him, all pure and radiant, filled him with trembling and anxiety. He no longer really knew where he was. Like an owl seeing the sun suddenly rise, the convict had been dazzled and blinded by virtue.

One thing was certain, though he did not suspect it, that he was no longer the same man, that all was changed in him, that it was no longer in his power to prevent the bishop from having talked to him and having touched him.

In this frame of mind, he had met Petit Gervais and stolen his coin. Why? He certainly could not have explained it. Was it the final effect, the final effort of the evil thought he had brought from prison, a remaining impulse, a result of what is called in physics "acquired force"? It was that, and perhaps it was also even less than that. To put it plainly, it was not he who had stolen, it was not the man, it was the beast that, from habit and instinct, had stupidly set its foot on that money, while the intellect was struggling in the midst of so many new and unknown influences. When the intellect awoke and saw this act of the brute, Jean Valjean recoiled in anguish and cried out in horror.

It was a strange phenomenon, possible only in his current condition, but the fact is that in stealing this money from the child, he had done a thing of which he was no longer capable.

However that may be, this last offense had a decisive effect upon him; it rushed across the chaos of his intellect and dissipated it, set the light on one side and the dark clouds on the other, and acted on his soul, in the state it was in, as certain chemical reagents act on a murky mixture, by precipitating one element and producing a clear solution of the other.

At first, even before self-examination and reflection, distractedly, like someone trying to escape, he sought the boy to give him his money back; then, when he found this was futile, he stopped in despair. At the very moment when he exclaimed, "I'm such a miserable man!" he saw himself as he was, and was already so far separated from himself that he felt he was no more than a phantom and that he had there before him, in flesh and bone, stick in hand, a shirt on his back, a knapsack filled with stolen articles on his shoulders, with his set and gloomy face and his thoughts full of abominable projects, the hideous convict Jean Valjean.

Excessive misfortune, as we have noted, had made him somehow a visionary. This then was like a vision. He truly saw this Jean Valjean, this ominous face, in front of him. He was on the point of asking himself who the man was, and he was horrified at the idea of asking himself such a question.

His brain was in one of those violent, yet frighteningly calm, states where reverie is so profound it swallows up reality. We no longer see the objects before us, but we see, as if outside of ourselves, the forms we have in our minds.

He saw himself then, so to speak, face to face, and at the same time through that hallucination he saw, at a mysterious distance, a sort of light, which he took at first to be a torch. Looking more closely at this light dawning on his conscience, he recognized it had a human form, that it was the bishop.

His conscience considered in turn these two men placed before it, the bishop and Jean Valjean. Anything less than the first would have failed to soften the second. By one of those singular effects peculiar to this kind of ecstasy, as his reverie continued, the bishop grew larger and more resplendent to his eyes; Jean Valjean shrank and faded away. For one instant he was no more than a shadow. Suddenly he disappeared. The bishop alone remained.

He filled the whole soul of this miserable man with a magnificent radiance.

Jean Valjean wept for a long time. He shed hot tears, he wept bitterly, more powerless than a woman, more terrified than a child.

While he wept, the light grew brighter and brighter in his mind—an extraordinary light, a light at once entrancing and terrible. His past life, his first offense, his long expiation, his exterior degradation, his interior hardening, his release made sweet by so many schemes of vengeance, what had happened to him at the bishop's, his recent act, this theft of forty sous from a child, a crime all the meaner and more monstrous in that it came after the bishop's pardon—all this returned and appeared to him, clearly, but in a light he had never seen before. He could see his life, and it seemed horrible; his soul, and it seemed frightful. There was, however, a gentler light shining on that life and soul. It seemed to him that he was looking at Satan by the light of Paradise.

How long did he weep? What did he do after weeping? Where did he go? Nobody ever knew. It was simply established that, that very night, the stage driver who at that hour rode the Grenoble route and arrived at Digne about three in the morning, on his way through the bishop's street saw a man kneeling in prayer, on the pavement in the dark, before the door of Monseigneur Bienvenu.

Book Three

IN THE YEAR 1817

I

THE YEAR 1817

The year 1817 was the one Louis XVIII, with a certain royal presumption not devoid of stateliness, called the twenty-second year of his reign. It was the year of M. Bruguière de Sorsum's fame. All the hairdressers' shops, hoping for the return of powder and birds of paradise, were bedecked with azure and fleur-de-lis. It was the candid time when Comte Lynch sat every Sunday as churchwarden on the official bench at Saint-Germain-des-Prés, dressed as a peer of France, with his red ribbon and long nose and that majesty of profile peculiar to a man who has done a brilliant deed. The brilliant deed committed by M. Lynch was that, being mayor of Bordeaux on March 12, 1814, he had surrendered the city a little too soon to the Duke of Angoulême. Hence his peerage. In 1817 it was the fashion to engulf little boys from four to six years old in large morocco caps with earflaps similar to Eskimo stovepipes. The French army was dressed in white in Austrian style; regiments were called legions and wore, instead of numbers, the names of the Départements. Napoleon was at St. Helena and, as England would not give him green material, had had his old coats turned. In 1817, Pellegrini sang, Mademoiselle Bigottini danced, Potier reigned, Odry did not yet exist. Madame Saqui succeeded Forioso. There still were Prussians in France. M. Delalot was a celebrity. Legitimacy had just asserted itself by cutting off the fist and then the head of Pleignier, Carbonneau, and Tolleron. Prince Talleyrand, the grand chamberlain, and Abbé Louis, the designated minister of finance, looked each other in the face, laughing like two clairvoyants; both had celebrated the mass of the Federation in the Champ-de-Mars on July 14, 1790; Talleyrand had said it as bishop, Louis had served him as deacon. In 1817, along the pathways of this same Champ-de-Mars, one could see huge wooden cylinders, painted blue, with traces of eagles and bees, that had lost their gilt, lying in the rain, rotting away in the grass. There were the columns that, two years before, had supported the emperor's rostrum in the Champ-de-Mai. They were blackened here and there from the campfires of the Austrians bivouacked near the Gros-Caillou. Two or three of these columns had disappeared in these bivouac fires and had warmed the huge hands of the kaiserlicks. The Champ-de-Mai was remarkable because it was held in June on the Champ-de-Mars. In the year 1817, two things were popular—Voltaire-Touquet and Chartist snuffboxes. The latest Parisian sensation was the crime of Dautun, who had thrown his brother's head into the fountain of the Marché-aux-Fleurs. At the Ministry of the Navy an investigation was opened concerning that ill-fated frigate *The Medusa,* which would cover Chaumareix with shame and Géricault with glory. Colonel Selves went to Egypt, there to become Suleiman-Pasha. The palace of the Thermes, Rue de La Harpe, was turned into a cooper's shop. One could still see, on the platform of the octagonal tower of the Hotel de Cluny, the little wooden shed that had served as observatory to Messier, the astronomer of the navy under Louis XVI. The Duchess of Duras read the manuscript of *Ourika* to three or four friends in her boudoir, furnished with cross-legged stools in sky-blue satin. The N's were erased from the Louvre. The Pont d'Austerlitz abdicated its name and became the bridge of the Jardin-du-Roi, a double enigma disguising both the Pont d'Austerlitz and the Jardin-des-Plantes. Louis XVIII—absently scanning Horace with the tip of his fingernail while thinking about heroes that had become emperors, and shoemakers that had become dauphins—had two concerns, Napoleon and Mathurin Bruneau. The French Academy gave as a prize theme, *The Happiness Procured by Study.* M. Bellart was eloquent, officially. In his shadow could be seen taking root the future Attorney General, de Broë, destined for sarcasms of Paul Louis Courier. There was a counterfeit Chateaubriand called Marchangy, as later there was to be a counterfeit Marchangy called d'Arlincourt. *Claire d'Albe* and *Malek Adel* were masterpieces; Madame Cottin was declared the first writer of the age. The Institute struck from its list the academician Napoleon Bonaparte. A royal ordinance established a naval school at Angoulême since, with the Duke of Angoulême being Grand Admiral, it was obvious that the town of Angoulême had by right all the qualities of a seaport, without which the monarchical principle would have been compromised. The question was tossing about in the cabinet as to whether the pictures representing acrobats which were spicing up Franconi's posters and attracting street urchins should be tolerated. M. Paër, the author of *L'Agnese,* an honest man with square jaws and a wart on his cheek, directed the small, select concerts of the Marchioness de Sassenaye, Rue de la Ville-l'Evêque. All the young girls sang *l'Ermite de Saint-Avelle,* words by Edmond Géraud. The *Nain jaune* was transformed into the *Miroir*. The Café Lemblin stood behind the emperor against the Café Valois, which favored the Bourbons. A marriage had just been made to a Sicilian princess by M. le duc de Berry, who was already regarded with suspicion by Louvel. Madame de Staël had been dead a year. Mlle. Mars was hissed by the bodyguards. The large newspapers were very small. The format was restrained, but the freedom broad. *Le Constitutionnel* was constitutional; *La Minerve* called Chateaubriand "Chateaubriant." This provoked much laughter among the citizens at the expense of the great writer.

In corrupt journals, prostituted journalists insulted the exiles of 1815; David no longer had talent, Arnault no longer had wit, Carnot no longer had any decency, Soult had never won a battle; it is true that Napoleon no longer had genius. Everybody knows that letters mailed to an émigré rarely reach their destination, the police considering it their religious duty to intercept them. This fact is by no means new; Descartes complained of it in his exile. Now, David displayed some pique in a Belgian newspaper at not receiving the letters addressed to him, and this seemed ludicrous to the royalist papers, which took this opportunity to ridicule the exile. To say "regicides" instead of "voters," "enemies" instead of "allies," "Napoleon" instead of "Bonaparte," separated two men by more than an abyss. All people of common sense agreed that the era of revolutions had been closed forever by King Louis XVIII, dubbed "the immortal author of the Charter." At the terrace of the Pont Neuf, the word "Redivivus" was sculpted on the pedestal awaiting the statue of Henri IV. At Rue Thérèse, No. 4, M. Piet was sketching the plan of his secret assembly to consolidate the monarchy. The leaders of the Right said, in a grave dilemma, "We must write to Bacol." Messrs. Canuel O'Mahony and Chappedelaine made a start, not altogether without the approval of Monsieur, the king's eldest brother, of what was afterward to become the "conspiracy of the Bord de l'Eau." L'Epingle Noire plotted on its side. Delaverderie held interviews with Trogoff. M. Decazes, to a certain extent a liberal spirit, prevailed. Chateaubriand, standing every morning at his window at No. 27 Rue Saint-Dominique, in pajama pants and slippers, his gray hair covered with a madras kerchief, a mirror before his eyes, and a complete case of dental instruments open before him, cleaned his teeth, which were excellent, while dictating versions of *La Monarchie selon la Charte* to M. Pilorge, his secretary. The critics in authority preferred Lafon to Talma. M. de Féletz signed himself A.; M. Hoffman signed himself Z. Charles Nodier was writing *Thérèse Aubert*. Divorce was abolished. The *lycées* called themselves *collèges*. The students, their collars decorated with a golden fleur-de-lis, pommeled each other over the King of Rome. The secret police of the palace denounced to her royal highness, Madame, the portrait of the Duc d' Orleans, shown everywhere, who looked better in the uniform of general of hussars than the Duc de Berry in the uniform of general of dragoons—a serious matter. The city of Paris regilded the dome of the Invalides at its own expense. Sober citizens wondered what M. de Trinquelague would do in such and such a case; M. Clausel de Montals differed on sundry points from M. Clausel de Coussergues; M. de Salaberry was not amused. Comedy writer Picard, of that Academy to which comedy writer Molière could not belong, played *Les deux Philiberts* at the Odeon, on whose pediment the removal of the letters still permitted a clear reading of the inscription: THÉÂTRE DE L'IMPÉR-

ATRICE. People took sides for or against Cugnet de Montarlot. Fabvier was factious; Bavoux was revolutionary. The bookseller Pelicier published an edition of Voltaire under the title *Works of Voltaire, of the French Academy*. "That will attract buyers," said the naive publisher. The general opinion was that M. Charles Loyson would be the genius of the age; envy was beginning to nibble at him, a sign of glory, and this joke about him made the rounds:

"Même quand Loyson vole, on sent qu'il a des pattes."[1]

Cardinal Fesch refusing to resign, M. de Pins, Archbishop of Amasie, administered the diocese of Lyons. The quarrel of the Vallée des Dappes began between France and Switzerland with a report from Captain, later General, Dufour. Saint-Simon, unknown, was constructing his sublime dream. There was a celebrated Fourier in the Academy of Sciences whom posterity has forgotten, and an obscure Fourier in some unknown garret whom the future will remember. Lord Byron was beginning to flower; a footnote to a poem by Millevoye introduced him to France as "a certain Lord Baron." David d'Angers was attempting to knead marble. The Abbé Caron spoke with praise, to a small group of Seminarists in the cul-de-sac of the Feuillantines, about an unknown priest, Félicité Robert by name, who later became Lamennais. A thing that smoked and clacked along on the Seine, making the noise of a swimming dog, came and went beneath the windows of the Tuileries, from the Pont Royal to the Pont Louis XV; it was a machine of little value, a kind of toy, the daydream of a visionary, a utopia—a steamboat. The Parisians regarded the useless thing with indifference. M. Vaublanc, wholesale reformer of the Institute by coup d'état and royal ordinance and distinguished maker of several academicians, after having made them, could not make himself one. The Faubourg Saint-Germain and the Pavillon Marsan desired M. Delaveau for prefect of police, because of his piety. Dupuytren and Récamier quarreled in the amphitheater of the Ecole de Médicine, and shook their fists in each other's faces, over the divinity of Christ. Cuvier, with one eye on the book of Genesis and the other on nature, was endeavoring to

[1] Even as Loyson soars, we sense his earthbound feet.

calm reactionary bigotry by reconciling fossils with texts and making the mastodons support Moses. M. François de Neufchâteau, the praiseworthy cultivator of the memory of Parmentier, was making every effort to have *pomme de terre* pronounced *parmentière*, though without success. Abbé Grégoire, ex-bishop, ex-member of the National Convention, and ex-senator, had changed to the status of the "infamous Grégoire" in royalist polemics. The expression we have just used, "changed to the status of," was denounced as a neologism by M. Royer-Collard. The new stone could still be distinguished by its whiteness under the third arch of the Pont d'Jéna, which, two years before, had been used to block the entrance of the mine bored by Blücher to blow up the bridge. Justice summoned to her bar a man who had said aloud, on seeing Count d'Artois entering Notre-Dame, "O damn! I long for the time I saw Bonaparte and Talma entering the Bal-Savage, arm in arm." Seditious language. Six months' imprisonment.

Traitors showed themselves openly, stripped even of hypocrisy; men who had gone over to the enemy on the eve of a battle made no secret of their bribes and shamelessly walked abroad in daylight in the cynicism of wealth and honor; deserters of Ligny and Quatre-Bras, brazen in their purchased shame, nakedly exposed their devotion to monarchy, forgetting the notices posted on the interior walls of public toilets in England: *Please adjust your dress before leaving*.

Such was the confused mass of the now-forgotten events that floated like flotsam on the surface of the year 1817. History ignores almost all these minutiae: it cannot do otherwise; it is under the dominion of infinity. Nonetheless, these details, which are incorrectly termed little —there being neither little facts in humanity nor little leaves in vegetation—are useful. It is the features of the years that makes up the face of the century.

In this year, 1817, four young Parisians had a good laugh on four others.

II

DOUBLE QUARTET

One of these Parisians was from Toulouse, another from Limoges, the third from Cahors, and the fourth from Montauban; but they were students, and to say student is to say Parisian; to study in Paris is to be born in Paris.

These young men were insignificant; everybody has seen the type; the four first comers will serve as examples; neither good nor bad, neither learned nor ignorant, neither talented nor stupid; handsome in that charming April of life we call twenty. They were four Oscars; for at this time, Arthurs did not yet exist. "Burn the perfumes of Araby in his honor," exclaims the romance. "Oscar approaches! Oscar, I am about to see him!" Ossian was everywhere, elegance was Scandinavian and Caledonian; the pure English type was not prevalent till later, and the first of the Arthurs—Wellington—had only just won the victory of Waterloo.

The first of these Oscars was called Félix Tholomyès, of Toulouse; the second, Listolier, from Cahors; the third, Fameuil, from Limoges; and the last, Blacheville, from Montauban. Of course each had his mistress. Blacheville loved Favourite, so-called because she had been in England; Listolier adored Dahlia, who had taken the name of a flower as her *nom de guerre;* Fameuil idolized Zéphine, the diminutive of Josephine, and Tholomyès had Fantine, called "the Blonde," because of her beautiful hair, the color of the sun.

Favourite, Dahlia, Zéphine, and Fantine were four enchanting girls, perfumed and sparkling, still somewhat working girls, since they had not wholly given up the seamstress's needle, agitated by love affairs yet preserving on their countenances a remnant of labor's serenity, and in their souls that flower of purity which in woman survives the first fall. One of the four was called the child, because she was the youngest; and another was called the old one—the Old One was twenty-three. To conceal nothing, the three first were more experienced, more careless, and better versed in the ways of the world than

Fantine the Blonde, who still maintained her first illusions.

Dahlia, Zéphine, and particularly Favourite could not say as much. There had been already more than one episode in their scarcely begun romance, and the lover named Adolphe in the first chapter reappeared as Alphonse in the second and Gustave in the third. Poverty and coquetry are fatal counselors; the one scolds, the other flatters, and the beautiful daughters of the people have both of them whispering in their ears, one on each side. Their ill-guarded souls listen. Thence their fall, and the stones that are cast at them. They are overwhelmed with the splendor of all that is immaculate and inaccessible. Alas! Was the Jungfrau ever hungry?

Favourite, having been to England, was the idol of Zéphine and Dahlia. At a very early age she had had a home of her own. Her father was a brutal, boasting old professor of mathematics, never married, and a rake despite his years. When young, he one day saw the dress of a chambermaid catch on the fireplace fender, and fell in love through the accident. Favourite was the result. Occasionally she saw her father, who tipped his hat to her. One morning, an old woman with a wild air entered her rooms, and asked, "You do not know me, Mademoiselle?"

"No."

"I am your mother." The old woman immediately opened the buffet, ate and drank her fill, sent for a mattress that she had, and made herself at home. This mother was a gossip and grouch; she never spoke to Favourite, stayed for hours without uttering a word, breakfasted, dined and supped for four, and went down to the concierge's lodge to see visitors and talk ill of her daughter.

What had involved Dahlia with Listolier, with others perhaps, with indolence, was her beautiful, rosy fingernails. How could such nails do work! She who will remain virtuous must have no compassion for her hands. As for Zéphine, she had conquered Fameuil by her rebellious yet caressing little way of saying "Yes sir."

The young men were comrades, the young girls were friends. Such loves are always reinforced by such friendships.

Wisdom and philosophy are two different things; a proof of this is that, with all necessary reservations for these little, irregular households, Favourite, Zéphine, and Dahlia were philosophical and Fantine was wise.

"Wise!" you will say, and Tholomyès? Solomon would answer that love is a part of wisdom. We limit ourselves to saying that Fantine's love was a first, an only, a faithful love.

She was the only one of the four who had been touched by one alone.

Fantine was one of those beings who are brought forth from the heart of the people, so to speak. Sprung from the most unfathomable depths of social darkness, she bore on her brow the mark of the anonymous. She was born at Montreuil-sur-mer. Who were her parents? Who can say? She had never known either father or mother. She was called Fantine—Why? Because she had never been known by any other name. At her birth, the Revolutionary Directory was still in power. She could have no family name, because she had no family; she could have no baptismal name, because at the time there was no church. She was named at the whim of the first passerby who found her, an infant wandering barefoot in the streets. Her name came to her like water from the clouds on her forehead when it rained. She was called little Fantine. Nobody knew anything more about her. At age ten, Fantine left the city and went into service among the farmers in the suburbs. At fifteen, she came to Paris, to "seek her fortune." Fantine was beautiful and remained pure as long as she could. She was a pretty blonde with fine teeth. For dowry, she had gold and pearls; but the gold was on her head and the pearls were in her mouth.

She worked to live; then, also to live, for the heart too has its hunger, she loved.

She loved Tholomyès.

To him, it was an affair; to her a passion. The streets of the Latin Quarter, swarming with students and grisettes, or working girls, saw the beginning of this dream. In those labyrinths of the hill below the Pantheon, where so many ties are knotted and loosened, Fantine fled from Tholomyès over several months, but always in such a way as to meet him again. There is a way of avoiding a person that resembles a search. In short, the idyll took place.

Blacheville, Listolier, and Fameuil made up a sort of

group of which Tholomyès was the head. He was the wit of the company.

Tholomyès was an older student of the old style; he was rich, having an income of four thousand francs—a splendid sum on the Montagne Sainte-Geneviève. He was a high liver, thirty years old, and in poor shape. He was wrinkled, his teeth falling out, and he was beginning to show signs of baldness, of which he said, gaily, "The head at thirty, the knees at forty." His digestion was poor, and he had a weeping eye. But as his youth died out, his gaiety increased; he replaced his teeth with jests, his hair with joy, his health with irony, and his weeping eye was always laughing. He was dilapidated, but bedecked with flowers. His youth, exiting long before its time, was retreating in good form, bursting with laughter but showing no loss of fire. He had had a play refused at the Vaudeville; he wrote poetry now and then on any subject; beyond that, he doubted everything with an air of superiority—a great power in the eyes of the weak. So, being bald and ironic, he was the leader. Could the word *iron* be the root from which irony is derived?

One day, Tholomyès took the three others aside and said to them with an oracular gesture: "For nearly a year, Fantine, Dahlia, Zéphine, and Favourite have been asking us to give them a surprise; we have solemnly promised them one. They are constantly reminding us of it, me especially. Just as the old women of Naples cry to Saint January, '*Faccia gialluta, fa o miracolo,* yellow face, do your miracle,' our pretty ones are always saying, 'Tholomyès, when are you going to deliver on your promise?' At the same time our parents are writing for us. Two birds with one stone. It seems to me the time has come. Let's talk it over."

Thereupon, Tholomyès lowered his voice, and mysteriously articulated something so ludicrous that a prolonged and enthusiastic giggling arose from the four throats at once, and Blacheville exclaimed, "What an idea!"

A smoke-filled alehouse appeared before them; they entered, and the rest of their conference was lost in murk.

The result of this mystery was a brilliant pleasure party, which took place on the following Sunday, the four young men inviting the four young girls.

III

FOUR FOR FOUR

Today it is difficult to imagine a country party of students and grisettes as it was forty-five years ago. Paris no longer has the same outskirts; the look of suburban Parisian life has completely changed in half a century; in place of the crude, one-horse chaise, we now have the railroad car; in place of the pinnace, we have now the steamboat; we say Fécamp today, as we then said Saint-Cloud. The Paris of 1862 is a city that has France for its suburbs.

The four couples painstakingly accomplished all the country follies then available. It was the beginning of vacation time, a warm, clear summer's day. The night before, Favourite, the only one of the women who knew how to write, had written to Tholomyès for her four: "Early rise gets the prize." So they rose at five in the morning. Then they went to Saint-Cloud by the coach, looked at the dry cascade, and exclaimed, "How beautiful it must be when there's water!" breakfasted at the Tête-Noire, which Castaing had not yet visited, amused themselves with a game of tossing quoits by the great five-sided basin, climbed to Diogenes' lantern, played roulette with macaroons on the Sèvres bridge, gathered bouquets at Puteaux, bought creampuffs at Neuilly, ate apple turnovers everywhere, and were perfectly happy.

The girls chirped and chatted like uncaged warblers. They were delirious with joy. Now and then they would playfully cuff the young men's ears. Intoxications of life's morning! Enchanted years! The wing of the dragonfly trembles! Oh reader, whoever you may be, do you have such memories? Have you walked in the underbrush, pushing aside branches for the charming head behind you? Have you slid, laughing, down some slope wet with rain, with the woman you loved, who held you by the hand, crying out: "Oh, my new shoes! Just look at them now!"

Let us add that that joyous annoyance, the sudden shower, was withheld from this good-natured company, although Favourite had said on setting out, with a magisterial and maternal air: "The snails are crawling in the paths. A sign of rain, children."

All four were ravishingly beautiful. A good old classic poet, then renowned, a good man who had an Eléanore, the Chevalier de Labouïsse, who was walking that day under the chestnut trees of Saint-Cloud, saw them pass by about ten in the morning and exclaimed, with the Graces in mind, "One too many!" Favourite, Blacheville's friend, the Old One of twenty-three, ran forward under the broad green branches, leaped across ditches, madly sprang over bushes, and took the lead in the gaiety with the verve of a young deer. Zéphine and Dahlia, whom chance had endowed with a kind of beauty that was heightened and perfected by contrast, kept together through the instinct of coquetry still more than through friendship, and, leaning on each other, affected English attitudes; the first "keepsakes" had just appeared, melancholy was in vogue for women, as Byronism later was for men, and the hair of the tender sex was just beginning to be left in disheveled locks. Zéphine and Dahlia wore theirs in rolls. Listolier and Fameuil, discussing their professors, explained to Fantine the difference between M. Delvincourt and M. Blondeau.

Blacheville seemed to have been created expressly to carry Favourite's old shawl over his arm all Sunday.

Tholomyès followed, presiding over the group. He was in high spirits, but one felt his governing powers; there was dictatorship in his joviality; his principal adornment was a pair of nankeen trousers, cut in the elephant-leg fashion, with stirrups of copper-colored braid; he had a huge rattan can worth two hundred francs in hand and, as he denied himself nothing, a strange thing called a cigar in his mouth. Nothing being sacred to him, he was smoking.

"This Tholomyès is astonishing," said the others, with veneration. "What trousers! Such energy!"

As to Fantine, she was joy itself. Her splendid teeth had evidently been endowed by God with one function—laughter. She carried in hand, rather than on her head, her little hat of stitched straw, with long, white ties. Her thick blond tresses, inclined to blow about, easily coming undone, obliging her continually to do them up again, seemed designed for the flight of Galatea under the willows. Her rosy lips babbled with enchantment. The corners of her mouth, turned up voluptuously like the antique masks of Erigone, seemed to encourage impudence, but her long, shadowy eyelashes were discreetly cast down on the lower part of her face as if to check its festive tendencies. Her whole outfit was indescribably harmonious and enchanting. She wore a dress of mauve challis, little reddish-brown boots, the laces of which were crossed over her fine, white, open-worked stockings, and that type of jacket, invented in Marseilles, the name of which, *canezou,* a corruption of the words *quinze août* in the Canebière dialect, signifies beautiful weather, warmth, and noon. The three others, less timid as we have said, wore low-necked dresses, which in summer, beneath bonnets covered with flowers, are full of grace and allure; but beside this daring attire, the canezou of the blond Fantine, with its transparencies, indiscretions, and reticence, at once concealing and disclosing, seemed a provoking godsend of decency; and the famous court of love, presided over by the Viscountess de Cette, with the sea-green eyes, would probably have given the prize for coquetry to this canezou, which had entered the lists for that of modesty. Sometimes the simplest is the wisest. That's how it is.

A brilliant face, delicate profile, eyes of a deep blue, heavy eyelashes, small, arching feet, wrists and ankles neatly turned, the white skin here and there showing the azure aborescence of veins; a cheek small and fresh, a neck robust as that of Aegean Juno; the nape firm and supple, shoulders modeled as if by Coustou, with a voluptuous dimple in the center, just visible through the muslin; a gaiety tempered with dreaminess; sculptured and exquisite—this was Fantine, and you could imagine underneath this dress and these ribbons a statue, and inside this statue a soul.

Fantine was beautiful, without really being conscious of it. Those rare dreamers, the mysterious priests of the beautiful, who silently compare all things with perfection, would have dimly perceived in this working girl, through the transparency of Parisian grace, an ancient sacred euphony. This daughter of obscurity had breeding. She possessed both types of beauty—style and rhythm. Style is the force of the ideal, rhythm its movement.

We have said that Fantine was joy; she was also modesty.

An observer who had studied her attentively would have found through all this intoxication of her age, of the season, and of love, an unconquerable expression of reserve and modesty. She remained a bit wide-eyed. This chaste wonder is the nuance that separates Psyche from Venus. Fantine had those long white slender fingers of the vestals who stir the ashes of the sacred fire with a golden rod. Although she would have refused nothing to Tholomyès, as could all too clearly be seen, her face in repose was supremely virginal; a kind of serious, almost austere dignity suddenly possessed it at times, and nothing could be stranger or more disquieting than to see gaiety vanish and reflection instantly succeed delight. This sudden seriousness, sometimes quite pronounced, resembled the disdain of a goddess. Her forehead, nose, and chin presented that equilibrium of line, quite distinct from the equilibrium of proportion, which produces harmony of features; in the characteristic interval separating the base of the nose from the upper lip, she had that almost imperceptible but charming fold, the mysterious sign of chastity, which caused Barbarossa to fall in love with a Diana found in the excavations of Iconium.

Love is a fault; be it so. Fantine was innocence floating upon the surface of this fault.

IV

THOLOMYÈS IS SO HAPPY, HE SINGS A SPANISH SONG

That day was sunshine from start to finish. All nature seemed to be on a vacation. The flower beds and lawns of Saint-Cloud were balmy with perfume; the breeze from the Seine vaguely stirred the leaves; the boughs were gesticulating in the wind; the bees were pillaging the jasmine; a whole bohemian crew of butterflies had settled in the yarrow, clover, and wild oats. The stately park of the King of France was invaded by a swarm of vagabonds, the birds.

The four joyful couples glowed in concert with the sunshine, the flowers, the fields, and the trees.

And in this paradisaical community—talking, singing, running, dancing, chasing butterflies, gathering bindweed, soaking their openwork stockings in the high grass, fresh, wild but not wicked, each stole kisses from another indiscriminately now and then, all except Fantine, who was closed up in her vague, dreamy, fierce resistance, and who was in love. "You always look out of sorts," Favourite said to her.

These are the true pleasures. These moments in the lives of happy couples are a profound appeal to life and nature and call forth endearment and light from everything. Once upon a time there was a fairy who created meadows and trees expressly for lovers. Whence that eternally bosky school for lovers, which is always opening up again and which will last so long as there are thickets and students. Whence the popularity of spring among thinkers. Patrician and knife grinder, duke and peasant, men of the court and men of the town, as they used to say, all are subjects of this sprite. They laugh, they seek each other out, the air seems filled with the clarity of exhaltation; what a transfiguration it is to love! Notary clerks become gods. And the little shrieks, the pursuits in the grass, the waists encircled by stealth, the jargon that is melody, the adoration that breaks through in the way a syllable is said, those cherries snatched from one pair of lips by another—it all catches fire and turns into celestial glories. Beautiful girls lavish their charms with sweet prodigality. We imagine it will never end. Philosophers, poets, painters behold these ecstasies and don't know what to make of them, they are so dazzling. The departure for Cythera! exclaims Watteau; Lancret, the painter of the commons, contemplates his bourgeoisie soaring in the sky; Diderot stretches out his arms to all these loves, and d'Urfé mixes them with the Druids.

After lunch, the four couples went to see, in what was then called the king's square, a plant newly arrived from the Indies, the name of which escapes us at present, and which at this time was attracting all Paris to Saint-Cloud: It was a strange and beautiful shrub with a long stalk, the innumerable branches of which, fine as threads, tangled and leafless, were covered with millions of little, white blossoms, which gave it the appearance of flowing hair, powdered with flowers. There was always a crowd admiring it.

When they had viewed the shrub, Tholomyès exclaimed, "I propose donkeys," and making a bargain with a donkey driver, they returned through Vanvres and Issy. At Issy, there was an incident. The park, Bien-National, owned at the time by the supply officer Bourguin, was by sheer good luck open. They had passed through the gateway, visited the mannikin anchorite in his grotto, and tried the mysterious little effects of the famous cabinet of mirrors—a lascivious trap worthy of a satyr become millionaire or Turcaret metamorphosed into Priapus. They had swung energetically in the great swinging net attached to the two chestnut trees, touted by the Abbé de Bernis. While swinging the girls, one after the other, which produced folds of flying skirts that Greuze would have found worth his study, the Toulousian Tholomyès, who was something of a Spaniard—Toulouse is cousin to Tolosa—sang in a melancholy key, the old *gallega* song, probably inspired by some beautiful damsel swinging in the air between two trees.

Soy de Badaioz.
Amor me llama.
Toda mi alma
Es en mi ojos
Porque enseñas
A tus piernas.

Fantine alone refused to swing.

"I don't like it when people put on airs like that," Favourite whispered rather sharply.

They left the donkeys for a new pleasure, crossed the Seine in a boat, and walked from Passy to the Barrière de l'Etoile. They had been on their feet, it will be remembered, since five in the morning, but "There's no weariness on Sunday," said Favourite. "On Sunday, fatigue has the day off." Toward three o'clock, the four couples, delirious with happiness, were running down the Russian mountains, a singular structure then occupying the heights of Beaujon, the serpentine line of which could be seen above the trees of the Champs Elysées.

From time to time Favourite would say, "But the surprise? I want the surprise."

"Patience," answered Tholomyès.

V

BOMBARDA'S

Having exhausted the Russian mountains, the happy eight now thought of dinner and, a little weary at last, ended up at Bombarda's, a branch set up in the Champs Elysées by the famous restaurateur Bombarda, whose sign at that time hung on the Rue de Rivoli near the Delorme arcade.

A large though ugly room, with an alcove containing a bed at the far end (the place was so full this Sunday that they had had to make do with this perch); two windows from which they could see, through the elms, the quay and the river; a magnificent August light glancing across the windows; there were two tables; one was laden with a triumphant mountain of bouquets, mingled with hats and bonnets, while at the other, the four couples were gathered around a joyful pile of plates, napkins, glasses, and bottles; jugs of beer and flasks of wine; little order on the table, some disorder under it.

Says Molière:

> Ils faisaient sous la table,
> Un bruit, un trique-trac epouvantable.[1]

Here was where the pastorale, begun at five in the morning, was to be found at half-past four in the afternoon. The sun was declining, and with it their appetite.

The Champs Elysées, full of sunshine and people, was nothing but glare and dust, the two elements of glory. Marly's horses, those neighing marbles, were rearing in a golden cloud. Carriages were coming and going. A magnificent squadron of bodyguards, trumpets at the head, was coming down the avenue of Neuilly; the white flag, faintly tinged with red by the setting sun, was floating over the dome of the Tuileries. The Place de la Concorde, at the time called Place Louis XV again, was overflowing with happy promenaders. Many wore the silver fleur-de-lis suspended from white moiré ribbon that in 1817 had

[1] And under the table they beat
A fearful tattoo with their feet.

not wholly disappeared from the buttonholes. Here and there, ringed in by applauding spectators, circles of little girls let fly a Bourbon ditty deriding the Hundred Days, the chorus of which ran:

Rendez-nous notre père de Gand,
Rendez-nous notre père.[1]

Crowds of people from the surrounding faubourgs in their Sunday clothes, sometimes even decked with fleurs-de-lis like the city dwellers, were scattered over the great square and the carré Marigny, riding the wooden horses of the carousel and trying to catch the silver ring; others were drinking; a few, printer's apprentices, wore paper caps; their laughter resounded through the air. Everything was radiant. It was a time of uncontested peace and profound royal security; it was the time when a private and special report of Prefect of Police Anglès to the king on the faubourgs of Paris, ended with these lines: "All things considered, sire, there is nothing to fear from these people. They are as carefree and lazy as cats. The lower classes in the provinces are restless, those in Paris are not. They are all small men, sire, and it would take two of them, one on top of the other, to take on one of your grenadiers. There is nothing at all to fear from the populace of the capital. It is remarkable that this segment of the population has also decreased in height during the last fifty years; and the people of the faubourgs of Paris are smaller than before the Revolution. They are not dangerous. In sum: *dependable riffraff.*"

That a cat may change into a lion, prefects of police do not believe possible; this can happen, nonetheless, and this is the miracle of the Parisian people. Besides, the cat, so despised by the Comte Anglès, had the esteem of the republics of antiquity; to their eyes it was the incarnation of liberty and, as if to serve as a pendant to the wingless Minerva of Piraeus, there was in the public square at Corinth, the bronze colossus of a cat. The naive police of the Restoration looked too optimistically on the Parisians. They were by no means such dependable riffraff as believed. The Parisian is to Frenchmen what the Athenian was to Greeks: Nobody sleeps better than he,

[1] Give us back our *Père de Gand.*
Give us back our sire.

nobody is more frivolous and idle than he, nobody seems to forget things more easily than he; but best not trust him, nonetheless; he has adapted to all sorts of indolence, but when there is glory to be gained, he is wondrous at every kind of fury. Give him a pike, and he will play the tenth of August; give him a musket, and you will have an Austerlitz. He is the support of Napoleon, and the resource of Danton. Is France in danger? He enlists; is liberty in danger? He tears up the pavement. Beware! His hair-raising rage is epic; his shirt can suddenly become a Greek's chlamys. Take care! Out of the first Rue Grenétat to come along, he will create the humiliations of a Caudine Forks. When the tocsin sounds, this denizen of the faubourgs will grow; this little man will rise, his look will be terrible, his breath will be a tempest, and a blast will go forth from his poor, frail breast that could shake the wrinkles out of the Alps. It is thanks to the men of the Paris faubougs that the Revolution, infused into the armies, conquered Europe. He sings; it is his joy. Proportion his song to his nature, and then you'll understand. So long as the Carmagnole was his sole refrain, he overthrew only Louis XVI; let him sing the Marseillaise, and he will liberate the world.

Having made this note in the margins of the Anglès report, we will return to our four couples. The dinner, as we have said, was over.

VI

A CHAPTER OF SELF-ADMIRATION

Table talk and lovers' talk are equally elusive; lovers' talk is clouds, table talk is smoke.

Fameuil and Dahlia hummed tunes; Tholomyès drank, Zéphine laughed, Fantine smiled. Listolier blew a wooden trumpet bought at Saint-Cloud. Favourite looked tenderly at Blacheville, and said, "Blacheville, I adore you."

This elicited a question from Blacheville: "What would you do, Favourite, if I stopped loving you?"

"Me!" cried Favourite. "Oh! don't say that, not even

as a joke! If you stopped loving me, I'd run after you, I'd scratch you, I'd pull your hair, I'd throw water at you, I'd have you arrested."

Blacheville smiled with the sensual complacency of a man whose self-esteem is tickled. Favourite continued: "I'd call out the guards! I'd be very upset—don't you forget it! Beast!"

Blacheville, in ecstasy, leaned back in his chair and closed his eyes with a satisfied air.

Dahlia, still eating, whispered to Favourite through the hubbub, "Are you really so fond of your Blacheville, then?"

"I detest him," answered Favourite, in the same tone, lifting her fork. "He's stingy; I'm in love with the boy across the street from me. He's so nice; do you know him? Anybody can see he was born to be an actor! I love actors. The moment he comes in, his mother hollers, 'Oh, dear! My peace of mind is ruined. My boy, you're such a trial!' Just because he goes into the attic among the rats, into the dark corners, as high as he can, and sings and carries on—How do I know? They can hear him downstairs! He gets twenty sous a day already by writing some stupidities for an attorney. He's the son of an old choir member of Saint-Jacques-du-Haut-Pas! Oh, he's so nice! He adores me so that one day, watching me make dough for pancake batter he said: 'Mamselle, make your gloves into fritters and I'll eat them.' Nobody but artists can say things like that. I'm going crazy about this boy. No matter, I tell Blacheville that I adore him. How I lie! Oh, how I lie!"

Favourite paused, then went on, "Dahlia, you see I'm sad. It has done nothing but rain all summer; the wind makes me edgy and just doesn't let up. Blacheville is so stingy; there are hardly any green peas in the market yet, people care for nothing but eating; I have 'the spleen,' as the English say; butter is so expensive! And then, just look—it's horrible! We're dining in a room with a bed in it. I'm disgusted with life!"

VII

THE WISDOM OF THOLOMYÈS

In the meantime, while some were singing, the rest were all noisily talking. There was absolute pandemonium. Tholomyès interfered.

"Don't let's talk so much and so fast!" he exclaimed. "We should take time to reflect, if we want to be brilliant. Too much improvisation leaves the mind stupidly empty. Flowing beer gathers no foam. Gentlemen, less haste. Let's mix dignity with festivity, eat with deliberation, feast slowly. Take your time. Look at the spring; if it hurries, it's ruined—frozen. Excessive zeal kills peach and apricot trees. Excessive zeal kills the grace and joy of good dining. No zeal, gentlemen! Grimod de la Reynière agrees with Talleyrand."

"Tholomyès, leave us alone," Blacheville said.

"Down with the tyrant!" Fameuil cried.

"Bombarda, Bombast, Bamboozle!" Listolier exclaimed.

"Sunday still exists," Listolier resumed.

"We're sober," Fameuil added.

"Tholomyès," Blacheville said, "observe my calm [*mon calme*]."

"You are its marquis," replied Tholomyès.

This uninspired play on words had the effect of a stone thrown into a country pond. The Marquis de Montcalm was a celebrated royalist of the time. All the frogs fell silent.

"My friends!" Tholomyès exclaimed, in the tone of a man resuming command. "Compose yourselves. This pun, though it falls from heaven, should not be welcomed with too much wonder. Everything that falls this way is not necessarily worthy of enthusiasm and respect. The pun is the droppings of the soaring spirit. The jest falls where it will. And the spirit, after freeing itself from stupidity, seeks the skies. A white spot flat on a rock does not prevent the condor from soaring above. Far be it from me to insult the pun! I honor it in proportion to its merits—not beyond. Everyone, the most august, most sublime, and most charming in humanity and perhaps outside of humanity, has played on words. Jesus Christ made a pun on St. Peter, Moses on Isaac, Aeschylus on Polynices, Cleopatra on Octavius. And note, that this pun of Cleopatra's preceded the battle of Actium and that without it no one would have remembered the city of Toryne, a Greek name meaning ladle. This conceded, I return to my exhortation. My brethren, I repeat, no zeal, no commotion, no excess, even in witticisms, mirth, gaiety, and puns. Listen here, have the prudence of Amphiaraüs, and the baldness of Caesar. There has to be a limit, even for rebuses. *Est modus in rebus*. There must be a limit even for dinners. You may like your apple turnovers, my ladies, but don't abuse them. Even in dumplings, there must be good taste and art. Gluttony punishes the glutton. Gula punishes gulax. Indigestion is charged by God with enforcing morality on the stomach. And remember this: Each of our passions, even love, has a stomach that must not be overloaded. We must in all things write the word *finis* in time; we must restrain ourselves, when it becomes urgent, draw the bolt on the appetite, play a fantasia on the violin, then break the strings with our own hand.

"The wise man is he who knows when and how to stop. Have some confidence in me. Because I have studied law a little, as my examinations will prove, because I know the difference between the moot question and the pending question, because I have written a Latin thesis on the method of torture in Rome at the time when Munatius Demens was questor of the Parricide; because I am about to become a doctor, so it seems, it does not necessarily follow that I'm a fool. I recommend to you moderation in all your desires. As sure as my name is Félix Tholomyès, I speak wisely. Happy is he who, when the hour comes, takes a heroic resolve and abdicates like Sylla or Origenes."

Favourite listened with profound attention. "Félix!" she said, "what a pretty word. I like this name. It is Latin. It means happy."

Tholomyès continued, "*Quirites,* gentlemen, *caballeros, miei amici,* would you feel no passion, dispense with the nuptial couch, and defy love? Nothing's easier. Here's a recipe: lemonade, overexercise, hard labor; tire yourselves out, haul logs, do not sleep, stay up late, gorge yourselves with carbonated drinks and water-lily teas; drink emulsions of poppies and agnuscastus; enliven this with a rigid diet, starve yourselves, and add cold baths, girdles of herbs, the application of a leaden plate, lotions of Goulard's extract and fomentations with vinegar and water."

"I prefer a woman," Listolier said.

"Woman!" resumed Tholomyès. "Be careful. Unhappy is he who surrenders himself to the changing heart of woman! Woman is perfidious and tortuous. She detests the serpent through competition. The serpent is the shop across the street."

"Tholomyès," cried Blacheville, "you're a drunk."

"I am not!" Tholomyès said.

"Then be cheerful," Blacheville replied.

"Agreed," Tholomyès answered.

Then, filling his glass, he stood up. "Honor to wine! *Nunc te, Bacche, canam.* Pardon, ladies, that's Spanish. And here is the proof, *señoras;* like cask, like people. The arroba of Castile contains sixteen liters, the cantaro of Alicante twelve, the almuda of the Canaries twenty-five, the cuartin of the Baleares twenty-six, and the boot of Czar Peter thirty. Long live the czar, who was great, and long live his boot, which was still greater! Ladies, some friendly advice! Deceive your neighbors, if it seems good to you. The characteristic of love is to rove. Love was not made to cower and crouch like an English housemaid whose knees are callused with scrubbing. Gentle love was made to rove gaily! It has been said to err is human; I say, to err is loving. Ladies, I idolize you all. Oh Zéphine, our Josephine, face more than annoyed, you would be charming if less cross. Yours is like a beautiful face, upon which someone has sat down by mistake. As for Favourite, oh nymphs and muses, one day as Blacheville was crossing the Rue Guerin-Boisseau, he saw a beautiful girl with white, well-gartered stockings, who was showing off her legs. The prologue pleased him, and Blacheville loved. She whom he loved was Favourite. Oh, Favourite! Thou hast Ionian lips. There was a Greek painter, Euphorion, who was nicknamed painter of lips. This Greek alone would have been worthy to paint thy mouth. Listen! before thee, there was no creature worthy of the name. Thou wert made to receive the apple like Venus or to eat it like Eve. Beauty begins with thee. I have spoken of Eve; she was of thy creation. Thou deservest the patent for the invention of beautiful women. Oh, Favourite, I cease to thou you, for I pass from poetry to prose. You spoke just now of my name. It moved me, but whatever we do, let us not trust names; they may be deceitful. I'm called Félix, but I'm not happy. Words deceive. Do not blindly accept what they seem to mean. It would be a mistake to write to Liège for corks or to Pau for gloves. Miss Dahlia, in your place, I should call myself Rose. The flower should have fragrance, and woman should have wit. I say nothing about Fantine, she is visionary, dreamy, pensive, sensitive; she is a phantom with the form of a nymph and the modesty of a nun, who has strayed into the life of a grisette but takes refuge in illusions and sings, and prays and gazes at the blue sky without knowing clearly what she is seeing or what she is doing, and who, with eyes fixed on heaven, wanders in a garden among more birds than exist there. Oh, Fantine, know this: I, Tholomyès, am an illusion—but she does not even hear me—the fair daughter of chimeras! Nevertheless, everything about her is freshness, gentleness, youth, soft, the clarity of morning. Oh, Fantine, worthy to be called Marguerite or Pearl, you are a jewel of the purest water.

"Ladies, a second piece of advice—do not marry; marriage is a graft; it may take hold or not. Shun the risk. But what am I saying? I'm wasting my words. Women are incurable on the subject of weddings, and all that we wise men can say will not hinder vestmakers and spats-stitchers from dreaming about husbands loaded with diamonds. Well, that's how it is; but, my beauties, remember this: You eat too much sugar. Women have only one fault, nibbling sugar. Oh, consuming sex, the pretty, little white teeth adore sugar. Now, listen carefully! Sugar is a salt. Every salt is desiccating. Sugar is the most desiccating of all salts. It sucks up the liquids from the blood through the veins; from this comes the coagulation, then the solidification of the blood, followed by tubercles in the lungs, followed by death. And that is why diabetes borders on consumption. Munch no sugar, therefore, and you will live! Now I turn my attention to the men: Gentlemen, make conquests. Rob each other without remorse of your beloved. Crisscross and double cross. In love, there are no friends. Wherever there's a pretty woman, there's open warfare. No holds barred; fight to the death.

A pretty woman is a *casus belli;* a pretty woman is a *flagrans delictum*. All the invasions of history have been determined by petticoats. Woman is the right of man. Romulus carried off the Sabine women; William carried off the Saxon women; Caesar carried off the Roman women. The man who is not loved hovers like a vulture over the sweethearts of others; and for my part, to all unfortunate widowers, I issue the sublime proclamation of Bonaparte to the army of Italy, 'Soldiers, you lack everything. The enemy has everything.' "

Tholomyès stopped.

"Catch your breath, Tholomyès," said Blacheville.

At the same time, Blacheville, aided by Listolier and Fameuil, to a tune of lament launched into one of those workshop songs, made up of the first words that came, rhyming richly and not at all, devoid of sense as the movement of the trees and the sound of the winds that are born from the smoke of the pipes, dissipate and take flight with it. This is the verse with which the group replied to Tholomyès' harangue:

Les pères dindons donnèrent
De l'argent à un agent
Pour que mons Clermont-Tonnerre
Fût fait pape à la Saint-Jean;
Mais Clermont ne put pas être
Fait pape, n'étant pas prêtre;
Alors leur agent rageant
Leur rapporta leur argent.

This was not likely to calm Tholomyès' improvisations; he emptied his glass, filled it, and began again. "Down with wisdom! Forget all I've said. Let's be neither prudes, nor prudent, nor Prud'hommes! I drink to joy; let's be joyful. Let's finish our course of study with folly and food. Indigestion and the Digest. Let Justinian be the male, and revelry the female. Joy in the abysses. Live, oh creation! The world is one big diamond! I'm happy. The birds are astonishing. Such festivities everywhere! The nightingale is an Elleviou gratis. Summer, I salute thee. Oh, Luxembourg! Oh, Georgics of the Rue Madame, and the Allée de l'Observatoire! Oh, daydreaming infantry! Oh those charming nursemaids who, while watching children. amuse themselves by starting some of their own. The pampas of America would delight me, if I did not have the arcades of the Odeon. My soul flies off toward virgin forests and savannas. Everything is beautiful. Flies hum in the sunbeams. The hummingbirds whizz in the sunshine. Kiss me, Fantine!"

And, by mistake, he kissed Favourite.

VIII

DEATH OF A HORSE

"The food is better at Edon's than Bombarda's," exclaimed Zéphine.

"I like Bombarda better than Edon," said Blacheville. "There's more luxury. It's more Asiatic. Look at the lower hall. There are looking glasses on the walls."

"I prefer meringues glacées on my plate," said Favourite.

Blacheville persisted.

"Look at the knives. The handles are silver at Bombarda's, and bone at Edon's. Silver is more precious than bone."

"Except when it's on the chin," observed Tholomyès.

At this moment he was looking out at the dome of the Invalides, visible from Bombarda's windows.

There was a pause.

"Tholomyès," Fameuil cried, "Listolier and I have just been having a discussion."

"A discussion is good," replied Tholomyès, "a quarrel is better."

"We were discussing philosophy."

"I have no objection."

"Which do you prefer, Descartes or Spinoza?"

"Désaugiers," said Tholomyès.

This decision rendered, he sipped at his drink and resumed: "I consent to live. All is not over on earth, since we can still be irrational. For that I thank the immortal gods. We lie, but we laugh. We affirm, but we doubt. The unexpected erupts from a syllogism. Splendid. There are still men on earth who know how to open and shut the surprise boxes of paradox with joy. Know, ladies, that this wine you are drinking so calmly is Madeira from the vineyard of Coural das Freiras, which is three hundred and seventeen fathoms above sea level. Watch out while you drink! Three hundred and seventeen fathoms! And M. Bombarda, this magnificent restaurateur, gives you these three hundred and seventeen fathoms for four francs, fifty centimes."

Fameuil interrupted again.

"Tholomyès, your opinions are law. Who's your favorite writer?"

"Ber—"

"Quin?"

"No. Choux."

And Tholomyès went on. "Honor to Bombarda! He would equal Munophis of Elephanta if he could procure me an almée and Thygelion of Chaeronea if he could bring me a hetaera! Because, oh, ladies, there were Bombardas in Greece and Egypt; this is what Apuleius teaches us. Alas! Always the same thing and nothing new. Nothing original left in all the Creator's creation! *Nil sub sole novum*, says Solomon; *Amor omnibus idem*, says Virgil; and Carabine climbs into the barge with Carabin at Saint-Cloud, as Aspasia embarked with Pericles onto the fleet of Samos. One final word. Do you know who this Aspasia was, ladies? Though she lived in a time when women did not yet have a soul, she was a soul; a soul of a rose and purple shade, more glowing than fire, fresher than dawn. Aspasia was a being in whom the two extremes of woman met—she was the prostitute goddess. She was Socrates plus Manon Lescaut. Aspasia was created in case Prometheus needed a floozy."

Tholomyès, once started, would have found it hard to stop, had a horse not fallen down at that moment on the quay. The shock arrested both cart and orator. It was a skinny old mare, ready for the bone-heap, harnessed to a heavy cart. On reaching Bombarda's, the beast, worn and exhausted, had refused to budge. The incident attracted a crowd. Scarcely had the driver, swearing and indignant, had time to utter with suitable vehemence the decisive word "Nag!" backed by a terrible snap of the whip, than the animal fell for the last time. At the hubbub of the passers-by, Tholomyès' merry auditors turned their heads, and Tholomyès profited by it to close his address with this melancholy parody:

Elle était de ce monde où coucous et carrosses
Ont le même destin;
Et, rosse, elle a vécu ce que vivent les rosses,
L'espace d'un matin!

"Poor horse!"sighed Fantine.

Dahlia exclaimed, "Now we have Fantine sympathizing with horses! Have you ever seen anything so absurd?"

At this moment, Favourite, crossing her arms and throwing her head back, stared at Tholomyès and said, "Come on! The surprise?"

"Precisely. The moment has come," replied Tholomyès. "Gentlemen, the hour has come for surprising these ladies. Ladies, wait for us a moment."

"It begins with a kiss," Blacheville said.

"On the forehead," Tholomyès added.

Each one gravely placed a kiss on the forehead of his mistress; after which they went toward the door, one after the other, laying a finger on their lips.

Favourite clapped her hands as they went out.

"It's fun already," she said.

"Don't be too long," murmured Fantine. "We're waiting for you."

IX

JOYFUL END OF JOY

Abandoned, the girls leaned on the window sills in couples, and chatted, tilting their heads and speaking from one window to the other.

They saw their young men leave Bombarda's, arm in arm, turn around, wave to them with a laugh, then disappear in the dusty Sunday crowd that takes possession of the Champs-Elysées once a week.

"Don't be long!" Fantine cried.

"What are they going to bring us?" Zéphine said.

"Let's hope something pretty," Dahlia said.

"Me, I hope it'll be gold," Favourite replied.

They were soon distracted by a commotion on the

water's edge, which they could make out through the branches of the tall trees and which they found quite entertaining. It was the moment for the departure of the mails and stagecoaches. At that time, almost all the stages to the south and west drove by the Champs-Elysées. Most of them followed the quay and went out through the Barrière Passy. Every minute some huge vehicle, painted yellow and black—heavily laden and noisily harnessed, distorted with trunks, tarpaulins, and valises, full of heads popping in and out the windows, disappearing, grinding the roadway, turning the paving stones into flints—would hurtle through the crowd, throwing out sparks like a forge, with dust for smoke, and an air of fury. This hubbub delighted the young girls. Favourite exclaimed, "What a racket! You'd think piles of chains were flying off into the heavens."

It so happened that one of these vehicles, which could be distinguished with difficulty through the dense foliage of the elms, stopped for a moment, then set off again at a gallop. This surprised Fantine.

"That's strange," she said. "I thought the stagecoaches never stopped."

Favourite shrugged. "This Fantine is surprising, very curious. She's amazed at the simplest things. Suppose I'm a traveler and say to the stagecoach drivers, 'I'm going ahead: pick me up on the way by the quay.' The stagecoach passes, sees me, stops and picks me up. This happens every day. You know nothing of life, my dear."

Some time passed this way. Suddenly Favourite started as if from sleep.

"Well!" she said. "And the surprise?"

"Yes," returned Dahlia, "the famous surprise."

"They are taking a long time!" Fantine sighed.

As Fantine finished her sigh, the boy who had waited on them at dinner came in. He had something in his hand that looked like a letter.

"What is that?" asked Favourite.

"A paper the gentlemen left for these ladies," he replied.

"Why didn't you bring it at once?"

"Because the gentlemen ordered me not to give it to the ladies till an hour had gone by," the boy answered.

Favourite snatched the paper from his hands. It was really a letter.

"Well!" she said. "There's no address; but look what is written on it:

THIS IS THE SURPRISE.

She hastily unsealed the letter, opened it, and read (she knew how to read):

"Dear lovers—

"Understand, we have parents. Parents—you barely know the meaning of the word, they are what are called fathers and mothers in the civil code, simple but honest. Now these parents bemoan us, the old people clamor for us, these good men and women call us prodigal sons, they desire our return and offer to kill the fatted calf for us. Being virtuous we obey them. At the moment you read this, five mettlesome horses will be bearing us back to our papas and mamas. We are striking our tents, as Bossuet says. We are going, we are gone. We are fleeing to the arms of Laffitte and on the wings of Caillard. The Toulouse coach snatches us from the abyss, and you are this abyss, our beautiful darlings! We are returning to society, to duty and order, at a full trot and the rate of nine miles an hour. It is necessary to our country that we become, like everybody else, prefects, fathers of families, country policemen, and councilors of state. Venerate us. We are sacrificing ourselves. Mourn us quickly, replace us rapidly. If this letter tears your heart, tear it apart. Adieu.

"For nearly two years we have made you happy. Bear us no ill will for it.

"*Signed:* BLACHEVILLE,
FAMEUIL,
LISTOLIER,
FÉLIX THOLOMYÈS

"P.S. The dinner is paid for."

The four girls gazed at each other.

Favourite was the first to break the silence.

"Well!" she said, "it's still a good joke."

"It's quite amusing," said Zéphine.

"It must have been Blacheville's idea," Favourite went on. "This makes me finally fall in love with him. No sooner loved than left. That's our story."

"No," Dahlia said, "it was Tholomyès' idea. That's clear."

"In that case," Favourite returned, "down with Blacheville, and long live Tholomyès!"

"Long live Tholomyès!" Dahlia and Zéphine cried.

And they burst out laughing.

Fantine laughed like the others, but an hour later, when she was back in her room, she wept. It was her first love, as we have said; she had given herself to Tholomyès as to a husband, and the poor girl had his child.

Book Four

TO TRUST IS SOMETIMES TO SURRENDER

I

ONE MOTHER MEETS ANOTHER

During the first quarter of the present century, at Montfermeil, near Paris, there was a cheap tavern, which is no longer there. It was kept by a man and wife named Thénardier in the Ruelle Boulanger. Above the door, nailed flat against the wall, was a board on which something was painted that looked like a man carrying on his back another man wearing the heavy epaulettes of a general, gilt and with large silver stars; red blotches signified blood; the rest of the picture was smoke and probably represented a battle. At the base was this inscription: THE SERGEANT OF WATERLOO.

Nothing is more ordinary than a cart or wagon in front of the door to an inn; nevertheless the vehicle or, more properly speaking, the fragment of a vehicle obstructing the street in front of the Sergeant of Waterloo one evening in the spring of 1818 certainly, by its bulk, would have attracted the attention of any passing painter.

It was the front part of one of those trolleys for carrying heavy articles, used in wooded regions for hauling joists and tree trunks. It consisted of a massive iron axletree with a pivot to which a heavy pole was attached and which was supported by two enormous wheels. The whole thing was squat, crushing, and misshapen. It might have been mistaken for a gigantic gun-carriage.

The roads had covered the wheels, rims, hubs, axle, and the shaft with a coating of hideous yellowish mud, similar in color to that with which cathedrals are sometimes decorated. The wood had disappeared beneath mud and the iron beneath rust.

Under the axletree hung a garland of huge chain fit for an imprisoned Goliath.

This chain made one think, not of the beams it was used to carry, but of mastodons and mammoths it might have harnessed; it had a prison look about it, but a Cyclopean, superhuman prison, and seemed as if unriveted from some monster. With it Homer could have bound Polyphemus, or Shakespeare Caliban.

Why was this vehicle in this place on the street? First to obstruct the lane, and then to complete its work of rusting. In the old social order we find a host of institutions like this across our path in the full light of day, with no reasons for being there.

The middle of the chain was hanging close to the ground under the axle, and on the arc, as on a swinging rope, two little girls were sitting that evening, an exquisite pair, the smaller, eighteen months old, in the lap of the larger, two and a half years old.

A cleverly tied bandana kept them from falling off. A mother, seeing this frightful chain, had said, "Now there's a toy for my children!"

The radiant children, attractively dressed, were like two roses twined on the rusty iron, with their perfect, sparkling eyes and their fresh, laughing faces. One was a rosy blonde, the other a brunette, their artless faces two delightful surprises; the perfume shed by a flowering shrub nearby seemed their own breath; the smaller one had her pretty little stomach bared with the chaste indecency of infancy. Above and around the delicate heads, steeped in joy and bathed in light, the gigantic hulk, black with rust and almost frightful with its tangled curves and sharp angles, arched like the mouth of a cave.

The mother, a woman whose appearance was somewhat forbidding, but touching at this moment, was sitting on the doorstep of the inn, swinging the two children by a long rope, tenderly following them with her eyes for fear of accident, with that animal yet celestial expression peculiar to motherhood. At each swing the hideous links let out a strident noise like an angry cry; the little ones were in ecstasy, the setting sun mixed with the joy, and nothing could be more charming than this whim that made of a Titan's chain a swing for angels.

While rocking the children the mother sang, out of tune, a then popular song: "Il le faut, disait un guerrier."

Singing and watching her children prevented her from hearing and seeing what was going on in the street.

Someone, however, had approached her as she was beginning the first couplet of the song, and suddenly she heard a voice say quite near her ear: "You have two lovely children, madame."

"A la belle et tendre Imogine," answered the mother, singing on; then she turned her head.

A woman was standing in front of her a few steps away; she also had a child, in her arms.

In addition she was carrying a large carpetbag, which seemed heavy.

This woman's child was the loveliest creature imaginable: a little girl of two or three. She could have competed with the other little ones for the most appealing attire; there were ribbons at her shoulders and Valenciennes lace above the fine linen wings on her cap. The folds of her skirt were raised enough to show her plump white thighs. She was charmingly rosy and healthful. One wanted to nibble at the pretty little creature's cheeks. We can say nothing of her eyes except that they must have been large and had lashes. She was asleep.

She was sleeping in the absolutely confident slumber of her age. Mothers' arms are made of tenderness, and sweet sleep blesses the child who lies within.

As for the mother, she seemed poor and sad; she looked like a working woman intending to return to peasant life. She was young—and pretty? Possibly, but in her clothes beauty could not show through. Her hair, one blond mesh of which had slipped loose, seemed very thick, but it was severely fastened up beneath an ugly, tight nun's headdress, tied under the chin. Laughing shows fine teeth when one has them, but she did not laugh. Her eyes seemed not to have been tearless for a long time. She was pale; she looked very weary, and somewhat sick. She gazed at her child, asleep in her arms, with that look peculiar to a mother who nurses her own child. Her figure was clumsily masked by a large blue kerchief like those used by invalids folded across her bosom. Her hands were tanned and spotted with freckles, the forefinger hardened and pricked with the needle; she wore a coarse brown wool mantle, a calico dress, and heavy shoes. It was Fantine.

Yes, Fantine. Hard to recognize, yet with a closer look, you could see she still retained her beauty. A sad line, like a touch of irony, had marked her right cheek. As for her clothing—that airy web of muslin and ribbons that seemed made of gaiety, folly, and music, full of baubles and perfumed with lilacs—that had vanished like the beautiful sparkles of hoarfrost, which we take for diamonds in the sun; they melt, and leave the branch a dreary black smudge.

Ten months had slipped by since the "good joke."

What had happened during those ten months? We can well imagine.

After recklessness comes trouble. Fantine had lost sight of Favourite, Zéphine, and Dahlia; the tie, broken by the men, loosened for the women; they would have been astonished if anyone had said two weeks later they were friends; they no longer had any reason to be so. Fantine was left alone. The father of her child gone—alas! such partings are irrevocable—she found herself absolutely isolated, with the habit of labor lost, and the taste for pleasure acquired. Led by her liaison with Tholomyès to disdain the simple work she knew how to do, she had neglected her opportunities; now they were all gone. No resources. Fantine could scarcely read and did not know how to write. She had only been taught in childhood how to sign her name. She had a letter written by a public letter-writer to Tholomyès, then a second, then a third. Tholomyès had replied to none of them. One day, Fantine heard some old women saying as they saw her child, "Do people ever take such children seriously? They only shrug their shoulders at them!" Then she thought of Tholomyès, who shrugged his shoulders at his child, and who did not take this innocent creature seriously, and her heart turned dark at the place that had been his. But what should she do? She had no one to ask. She had made a mistake, but, deep down, we know she was modest and virtuous. She had a vague feeling of being on the brink of danger, of slipping into the streets.

She had to have courage; she had it, and continued bravely. She had the idea of returning to her native village Montreuil-sur-mer; there perhaps someone would remember her and give her work. Yes, but she would have to hide her mistake. And she had a confused notion of a possibly necessary separation still more painful than the first. Her heart ached, but she made up her mind. We will see that Fantine possessed fierce courage. She had already valiantly given up her finery, was dressed in calico, and had put all her silks, her trinkets, her ribbons, and laces on her daughter—the only vanity that remained, and that a sacred one. She sold all she had, which gave her two hundred francs; when her little debts were paid, she had only about eighty left. At twenty-two years of age, on a fine spring morning, she left Paris, carrying her child on her back. Anyone seeing the two of them go by would have pitied them. The woman had nothing in the world but this child, and this child had nothing in the world but this woman. Fantine had nursed her child; that had weakened her chest somewhat, and she coughed slightly.

We shall have no further need to speak of M. Félix Tholomyès. We will only say that twenty years later under King Louis Philippe, he was a fat provincial attorney, rich and influential, a wise voter and rigid juror, but as always, a man of pleasure.

Toward noon, after having, for the sake of her health, traveled from time to time at a cost of a penny a mile, in what they then called the petites voitures of the outskirts of Paris, Fantine reached Montfermeil, and stood in the Ruelle Boulanger.

As she was passing by the Thénardier inn, the two little children happily perched on their monstrous swing had a dazzling effect upon her, and she paused before this vision of joy.

Magic charms do exist. These two little girls were one for this mother.

Brimming with emotion, she watched them. The presence of angels is a herald of paradise. She thought she saw above this inn the mysterious "here" of Providence. These children were so clearly happy: She gazed at them, admired them, so much affected that as the mother was taking a breath between verses of her song, she could not help saying what we have just read.

"You have two lovely children there, madame."

The most ferocious animals are disarmed by caresses to their young.

The mother raised her head and thanked her, and made the stranger sit down on the stone step, she herself being in the doorway: The two women began to talk.

"My name is Madame Thénardier," said the mother of the two girls. "We run this inn."

Then going on with her song, she sang between her teeth:

"Il le faut, je suis chevalier
Et je pars pour la Palestine."

This Madame Thénardier was a red-headed, large but angular woman, the soldier's wife type in all its horror, with, strangely enough, a languid air gained from novel reading. She was unrefined but simpering. Old romances impressed on the imaginations of mistresses of restaurants have such effects. She was still young, scarcely thirty. If this woman, now seated bent over, had been upright, perhaps her towering form and broad shoulders, those of a movable colossus, fit for a market woman, would have dismayed the traveler, disturbed her confidence, and prevented what we have to tell. A person seated instead of standing: Fate hangs on just such a thread.

The traveler told her story, somewhat modified.

She said she was a working woman, and her husband was dead. Unable to find a job in Paris she was going to search for it elsewhere, in her own province; she had left Paris that morning on foot; carrying her child she had become tired, and meeting the Villemomble stage had gotten in; from Villemomble she had come on foot to Montfermeil; the child had walked a little, but not much, she was so young; she had had to carry her, and the jewel had fallen asleep.

And at these words she gave her daughter a passionate kiss, which wakened her. The child opened her large eyes, blue like her mother's, and saw—what? Nothing, everything, with that serious, sometimes severe look of little children, which is one of the mysteries of their shining innocence before our shadowy virtues. It is as though they felt themselves angels and knew us to be human.

Then the child began to laugh, and, although the mother held her back, she slipped to the ground with the indomitable energy of a little one that wants to run around. All at once she caught sight of the two others in their swing, stopped short, and put out her tongue in token of admiration.

Mother Thénardier untied the children and took them off the swing saying, "Play together, the three of you."

At that age, acquaintance is easy, and in a moment the little Thénardiers were playing with the newcomer, digging holes in the ground to their intense delight.

This newcomer was very cheerful; the goodness of the mother is written in the gaiety of the child; she had taken a small piece of wood, which she used as a spade, and was energetically digging a hole fit for a fly. The gravedigger's work is fun when done by a child.

The two women went on chatting.

"What's her name?"

"Cosette."

For Cosette, read Euphrasie. The name of the little one was Euphrasie. But the mother had made Cosette out of it, by that sweet and charming instinct of mothers and of the people, who change Jósefa into Pepita, and Françoise into Sillette. It is a kind of derivation that confuses and disconcerts the entire science of etymology. We knew a grandmother who succeeded in changing Théodore to Gnon.

"How old is she?"

"Going on three years."

"The same age as my first."

The three girls were grouped in an attitude of profound anxiety and bliss; a great event had occurred; a large worm had come out of the ground; they were both afraid of it and in ecstasies over it.

Their bright foreheads touched: three heads in one halo of glory.

"Children!" exclaimed the Thénardier mother. "How quickly they get to know one another. Look at them! One would swear they were three sisters."

These words were the spark the other mother was probably awaiting. She seized the hand of Madame Thénardier, looked right at her and said, "Will you keep my child for me?"

Madame Thénardier made a gesture of surprise, neither consent nor refusal.

Cosette's mother went on, "You see, I can't take my child into the country. The work will prevent it. With a child I couldn't find a job there; they're so backward in that district. It is the good Lord who led me to your inn. The sight of your little ones, so pretty and clean and happy, immediately overwhelmed me. I said, There's a good mother; they will be like three sisters, and then it will not be long before I come back. Will you keep my child for me?"

"I must think it over," Madame Thénardier said.

"I will give six francs a month."

Here a man's voice was heard from within: "Not less than seven francs, and six months paid in advance."

"Six times seven is forty-two," the wife said.

"I'll pay it," said the mother.

"And fifteen francs extra for the first expenses," added the man.

"That's fifty-seven francs," Madame Thénardier said, and in the midst of her reckoning she sang indistinctly: "Il le faut, disait un guerrier."

"I'll pay it," said the mother. "I have eighty francs. That will leave me enough to reach my part of the country if I walk. I'll earn some money there, and as soon as I have some, I will come for my little love."

The man's voice responded, "Does the child have clothes?"

"That is my husband," said Madame Thénardier.

"Of course she has, the poor darling. I could tell it was your husband. And a fine wardrobe, too, an extravagant wardrobe, everything in dozens, and silk dresses like a lady's. They're in my carrying bag."

"You have to leave that here," put in the man's voice.

"Of course, I'll give it to you," said the mother. "It would be odd if I left my child naked."

The face of the master appeared. "All right," he said.

The bargain was concluded. The mother spent the night at the inn, gave her money and left her child, repacked her bag, much lighter now, minus her child's clothes, and set off the next morning, expecting to return soon. These partings appear tranquil but are full of despair.

A neighbor of the Thénardiers met this mother on the street after she had left her child, and she came in, saying, "I have just met a woman in the street, who was crying as if her heart would break."

When Cosette's mother had gone, the man said to his wife, "That's enough for my debt of 110 francs, which falls due tomorrow; I was fifty francs short. Do you realize a sheriff would have come and they'd have brought charges against me? You've built a good mousetrap with your little ones."

"Without even knowing it," the woman said.

II

FIRST SKETCH OF TWO EQUIVOCAL FACES

The captured mouse was very puny, but the cat exults even over a lean mouse.

What were the Thénardiers like?

We will say just a word right here; later the sketch will be completed.

They belonged to that bastard class composed of rough people who have risen and intelligent people who have fallen, which lies between the so-called middle and lower classes and unites some of the faults of the latter with nearly all the vices of the former, without possessing the generous impulses of the worker or the respectability of the bourgeois.

They were among those dwarfish natures, which, if they happen to be heated by some sullen fire, easily become monstrous. The woman was at heart a brute, the man a blackguard, both in the highest degree capable of that hideous sort of progression that can be made toward evil. There are souls that, crablike, crawl continually toward darkness, going backward in life rather than advancing, using their experience to increase their deformity, growing continually worse, and becoming steeped more and more thoroughly in an intensifying viciousness. That was the case with this man and this woman.

The man especially would have been a puzzle to a physiognomist. We have only to look at some men to distrust them, for we feel the darkness of their souls in two directions. They are restless as to what is behind them, and threatening as to what is in front of them. They are full of mystery. We can answer no more for what they have done than for what they will do. The shadows in their eyes give them away. Hearing them utter a single word, or seeing them make one gesture, we catch glimpses of guilty secrets in their past and dark mysteries in their future.

This Thénardier, if we can believe him, had been a soldier, a sergeant he said; he probably had been in the campaign of 1815, and had even been brave, it seems. Later, we shall see what his bravery consisted of. The sign of his inn was an allusion to one of his feats of arms. He had painted it himself, for he knew how to do a little of everything—all badly.

It was the time when the old classic romance—which, after being *Clélie,* sank to *Lodoïska,* still noble but becoming more and more vulgar, falling from Mademoiselle de Scuderi to Madame Barthélemy-Hadot, and from Madame de Lafayette to Madame Bournon-Malarme—was enflaming the romantic souls of the concierges of Paris, and causing some devastation even in the suburbs. Madame Thénardier was just intelligent enough to read such books. She fed on them. She drowned what little brain she had in them; and they had given her, while she was still young, and even later, a kind of pensive attitude toward her husband, a genuine villain, a ruffian, educated almost to the point of grammar, at once coarse and fine, but so far as sentimentality was concerned, reading Pigault Lebrun, and for "all related to the weaker sex," as he put it, a totally correct dolt. His wife was about twelve or fifteen years younger than he. At a later period, when limp romantic locks began to gray, when Mégère parted company with Pamela, Madame Thénardier was only a gross mean woman who had relished stupid novels. People do not read stupidities with impunity. The result was that her eldest child was named Eponine, and the youngest, who had just escaped being called Gulnare, owed to some chance pleasure wrought by a novel by Ducray Duminil, the less problematic name of Azelma.

However, let us say in passing that all things are not

ridiculous and superficial in this singular era to which we are alluding, and which might be termed the anarchy of baptismal names. Besides this romantic element we have just noted, there is the social symptom. Today it is not infrequently that we see shepherds named Arthur, Alfred, and Alphonse, and viscounts—if viscounts still exist—named Thomas, Peter, or James. This change, which places the "elegant" name on the plebeian and the country appellation on the aristocrat, is only an eddy in the tide of equality. The irresistible penetration of new inspiration is there as in everything else: Beneath this apparent discord there is a great and profound reality—the French Revolution.

III

THE LARK

To be vicious does not ensure prosperity—the inn, in fact, was not doing well.

Thanks to Fantine's fifty-seven francs, Thénardier had been able to avoid a lawsuit and honor his signature. The next month they were still in need of money, and the woman carried Cosette's wardrobe to Paris and pawned it for sixty francs. When this sum was spent, the Thénardiers began to look on the little girl as a child they sheltered for charity and treated her accordingly. Her clothes being gone, they dressed her in the castoff skirts and blouses of the little Thénardiers—that is, in rags. They fed her on everyone's leftovers, a little better than the dog but a little worse than the cat. The dog and cat were her messmates. Cosette ate with them under the table off a wooden dish like theirs.

Her mother, who, as we shall later see, had found a job at Montreuil-sur-mer, wrote, or rather had someone write for her, every month, asking for news of her child. The Thénardiers invariably replied, "Cosette is doing wonderfully well."

The six months passed; the mother sent seven francs for the seventh month and continued to send this sum regularly month after month. The year was not over before Thénardier said, "It's not enough! What does she expect us to do for her seven francs?" And he wrote demanding twelve francs. The mother, persuaded that her child was happy and doing well, agreed and forwarded the twelve francs.

There are certain natures that cannot have love on one side without hatred on the other. Madame Thénardier passionately loved her own little ones and therefore detested the young stranger. It is sad to realize that a mother's love can have such a dark side. Little as was the place Cosette occupied in the house, it seemed to her that this little was taken from her children, and that Cosette decreased the air her girls breathed. This woman, like many of her kind, had a certain amount of caresses and a certain amount of blows and hard words to dispense each day. If she had not had Cosette, surely her daughters, idolized as they were, would have received it all, but the little stranger did them the service of attracting the blows to herself; her children had only the caresses. Cosette could not stir without drawing down on herself a hailstorm of undeserved and severe chastisements. A frail, gentle little one who must not have understood anything of this world, or of God; continually ill-treated, scolded, punished, beaten, she saw beside her two other young things like herself, who lived in a halo of glory!

The woman was unkind to Cosette, and Eponine and Azelma were unkind, too. Children at that age are simply copies of the mother; only the size is reduced.

A year passed and then another.

People in the village said, "What good folk those Thénardiers are! They're not rich, and yet they bring up a poor abandoned child."

They thought Cosette was forgotten by her mother.

Meanwhile Thénardier, having learned in some obscure way that the child was probably illegitimate and that her mother could not acknowledge her, demanded fifteen francs a month, saying that the "creature" was growing and eating, and threatening to send her away. "She won't get around me!" he exclaimed. "I'll drop the brat right down in her hideout. I have to have more money." The mother paid the fifteen francs.

From year to year the child grew, and her misery, too.

So long as Cosette was very small, she was the scapegoat of the two other children; as soon as she began to grow a little, that is to say, before she was five years old, she became the servant of the house.

Five years old! It will be said that's hard to believe, but it's true; social suffering can begin at any age. Didn't we see recently the trial of Dumollard, an orphan turned bandit, who, from the age of five, say the official documents, being alone in the world, "worked for his living and stole"!

Cosette was made to run errands, sweep the rooms, the yard, the street, wash the dishes, and even carry heavy loads. The Thénardiers felt doubly authorized to treat her this way, as the mother, who still remained at Montreuil-sur-mer, began to be remiss in her payments. Some months remained due.

Had this mother returned to Montfermeil, at the end of these three years, she would not have known her child. Cosette, so fresh and pretty when she came to that house, was now thin and pale. She had a peculiarly restless air. A sneak! said the Thénardiers.

Injustice had made her sullen, and misery had made her ugly. Only her eyes remained beautiful, and they were painful to look at, because, large as they were, they seemed to increase the sadness.

It was harrowing to see the poor child, in winter, not yet six years old, shivering under the tatters of what was once a calico dress, sweeping the street before daylight with an enormous broom in her little red hands and tears in her large eyes.

In the neighborhood she was called the Lark. People like figurative names and were happy to give a nickname to this child, no larger than a bird, trembling, frightened, and shivering, first to wake every morning in the house and the village, always in the street or in the fields before dawn.

Except that the poor lark never sang.

Book Five

THE DESCENT

I

HISTORY OF AN IMPROVEMENT IN MAKING JET BEADS

Meanwhile, what had become of the mother, who, according to the people of Montfermeil, seemed to have abandoned her child? Where was she? What was she doing?

After leaving her little Cosette with the Thénardiers, she went on to Montreuil-sur-mer.

This, it will be remembered, was in 1818.

Fantine had left the province some twelve years before, and Montreuil-sur-mer had changed in appearance. While Fantine had been slowly sinking deeper and deeper into misery, her native village was prospering.

Within about two years, there had been one of those industrial changes that constitute the great events of small communities.

These circumstances were important, and so we will give some of the details.

From time immemorial the particular occupation of the inhabitants of Montreuil-sur-mer had been the imitation of English jet beads and German black glass trinkets. The industry had always been slow because of the high price of the raw material. At the time of Fantine's return to Montreuil-sur-mer a complete transformation had been carried out in the production of these "black goods." Toward the end of 1815, an unknown man had come to settle in the city and had conceived the idea of substituting shellac for resin in the manufacturing process; and for bracelets, in particular, he made the clasps by simply bending the ends of the metal together instead of soldering them.

This minor change had caused a revolution. It had in fact reduced the price of the raw material enormously, and this had made it possible, first, to raise the wages of the workers—a benefit to the district; secondly, to improve the quality of the goods—an advantage for the consumer; and third, to sell them at a lower price even while making three times the profit—a gain for the manufacturer.

Thus we have three results from one idea.

In less than three years the inventor of this process had become rich, which was good, and had made all those around him rich, which was better. He was a stranger in the region. Nothing was known about where he came from and little about his early history.

The story went that he came to the city with very little money, a few hundred francs at most.

From this slender capital, under the inspiration of an ingenious idea, made productive by order and attention, he had extracted a fortune for himself and a fortune for the whole region.

On his arrival at Montreuil-sur-mer he had the clothes, the manners, and the language of a laborer.

It seems that the very day on which he obscurely entered the little city, just at dusk on a December evening, with his bundle on his back, and a thorn stick in his hand, a great fire had broken out in the town hall. This man rushed into the fire and, risking his life, saved two children, who proved to be those of the captain of the gendarmerie, and in the hurry and gratitude of the moment no one thought to ask him for his passport. He was known from that time by the name Father Madeleine.

II

MADELEINE

A man of about fifty, he was good-natured but always seemed preoccupied; this was all that could be said about him.

Thanks to the rapid progress of this industry, which he had so successfully recast, Montreuil-sur-mer had become a good-sized business center. Huge purchases were made there every year for the Spanish markets, where there is a large demand for jet work, and Montreuil-sur-mer, in this branch of trade, almost competed with London and Berlin. The profits of Father Madeleine were so great that by the end of the second year he was able to build a large factory, in which there were two immense workshops, one for men and the other for women: Anyone in need could go there and be sure of finding work and wages. Father Madeleine required the men to be willing, the women to have good morals, and all to be honest. He divided the workshops, and separated the sexes so that the girls and the women might not lose their modesty. On this point he was inflexible, although it was the only one in which he was in any degree rigid. This severity was justified by the opportunities for corruption that abounded in Montreuil-sur-mer, as a garrisoned city. All in all his coming had been a blessing, and his presence was a providence. Before the arrival of Father Madeleine, the whole region was stagnant; now it was all alive with the healthy strength of labor. An active circulation stimulated everything and penetrated everywhere. Unemployment and misery were unknown. There was no pocket so dark that it did not contain a little money and no dwelling so poor that it did not contain some joy.

Father Madeleine employed everybody; there was only one prerequisite: "Be honest!"

As we mentioned, in the midst of this activity, of which he was the cause and pivot, Father Madeleine had made his fortune, but what was strangest about this simple businessman was that this fact did not appear to be his principal concern. It seemed that he thought a lot about others, and little about himself. In 1820, it was known that he had six hundred and thirty thousand francs standing to his credit in the bank of Laffitte; but before setting aside this six hundred and thirty thousand francs for himself, he had spent more than a million for the city and for the poor.

The hospital was poorly endowed, and he made provision for ten additional beds. Montreuil-sur-mer is divided into the upper city and the lower city. The lower city, where he lived, had only one school, a miserable hovel that was fast going to ruin; he built two, one for girls and the other for boys. He paid the two teachers, out of his own pocket, double the amount of their meager salary from the government; and one day, he said to a neighbor who expressed surprise at this: "The two highest functionaries of the state are the wet-nurse and the school teacher." He built, at his own expense, a house of refuge, an institution then almost unknown in France, and provided a fund for old and infirm laborers. Around his factory, a new section of the city had rapidly grown up, containing many indigent families, and he established a pharmacy that was free to all.

At first, when he began to attract public attention, the good people would say, "This is a man who wants to get rich." When they saw him enrich the country before himself, the same good people said, "He is ambitious." This seemed the more probable, since he was religious and observed the forms of the church, even the practice to a certain extent, a thing much approved in those days. He went regularly to hear mass every Sunday. The local deputy, who scented rivalry everywhere, was not slow to worry about Madeleine's religion. This deputy, who had been a member of the legislative body of the Empire, shared the religious ideas of a Father of the Oratory, known by the name of Fouché, Duke of Otranto, whose protégé and friend he had been. In private he jested a little about God. But when he saw the rich manufacturer Madeleine go to low mass at seven o'clock, he foresaw a possible rival candidate, and he resolved to outdo him. He took a Jesuit confessor and went to both high mass and vespers. At that time ambition was in a real sense a steeplechase. The poor, as well as God, gained by the terror of the honorable deputy, for he endowed two beds at the hospital, making twelve.

At length, in 1819, it was reported in the city one morning that on the recommendation of the prefect, and in consideration of the services he had rendered to the area, the king had appointed Father Madeleine mayor of Montreuil-sur-mer. Those who had pronounced the newcomer ambitious eagerly seized this opportunity, which all men desire, to exclaim; "There! What did I say?"

Montreuil-sur-mer was all rumor. And the report proved to be well founded, for, a few days afterward, the nomination appeared in the *Moniteur*. The next day Father Madeleine declined.

In the same year, 1819, the results of the new process invented by Madeleine had a place in the Industrial Exhibition, and on the report of the jury, the king named the inventor a Chevalier of the Legion of Honor. Here was a new rumor for the little city. "So! it was the Cross of the Legion of Honor that he wanted." Father Madeleine declined the Cross.

This man was definitely an enigma, and the good people made the best of it, saying, "He must be some sort of adventurer."

As we have noted, the area owed a great deal to this man, the poor owed him everything; he was so effective that everyone finally had to respect him, and so kind that no one could help loving him; his workmen in particular adored him, and he received their adoration with a melancholy gravity. Once he was recognized as rich, those who constituted "society" bowed to him when they met, and, in the city, he began to be called Monsieur Madeleine; but his workers and the children continued to call him "Father Madeleine," and at that name his face always lit up with a smile. As his wealth increased, invitations rained down on him. "Society" claimed him. The exclusive little salons of Montreuil-sur-mer, which were carefully guarded, and in earlier days had naturally been closed to the artisan, opened their doors wide to the millionaire. A thousand advances were made to him, but he refused them all.

And again the gossips were not at a loss. "He's an ignorant man and poorly educated. No one knows where he came from. He doesn't know how to behave in society. It is by no means certain he even knows how to read."

When they saw him making money, they said, "He is a merchant." When they saw the way in which he scattered his money, they said, "He is ambitious." When they saw him refuse honors, they said, "He is an adventurer." When they saw him repel the advances of the fashionable, they said, "He is a brute."

In 1820, five years after his arrival at Montreuil-sur-mer, the services he had rendered the region were so spectacular, and the wishes of the whole population so unanimous, that the king again appointed him mayor of the city. He refused again, but the prefect resisted his determination, the principal citizens came and urged him to accept, and the people in the streets begged him to do so; the insistence was so strong that at last he yielded. It was remarked that what particularly seemed to convince him was the almost angry exclamation of an old woman belonging to the poorer class, who cried out to him from her doorstep, with some anger, "A good mayor is a good thing. Are you afraid of the good you might do?"

This was the third step in his ascent. Father Madeleine had become Monsieur Madeleine, and Monsieur Madeleine now became Monsieur the Mayor.

III

MONEY DEPOSITED WITH LAFFITTE

Nevertheless he remained as simple as at first. He had gray hair, a serious eye, the tanned complexion of a laborer, and the thoughtful expression of a philosopher. He usually wore a hat with a wide brim, and a long coat of coarse cloth, buttoned to the chin. He fulfilled his duties as mayor, but beyond that his life was solitary. He talked with very few. He shrank from compliments and with a touch of the hat would walk on rapidly; he smiled to avoid talking and gave to avoid smiling. The women said of him, "What a good bear!" His pleasure was walking in the fields.

He always ate his meals alone reading out of a book open in front of him. His library was small but well chosen. He loved books; books are cold but sure friends. As his growing fortune gave him more leisure, it seemed that he took advantage of it to cultivate his mind. Since he had been at Montreuil-sur-mer, it was noted that from year to year his language became more polished, more carefully chosen, and gentler.

In his walks he liked to carry a gun, though he seldom used it. When he did so, however, his aim was frighteningly accurate. He never killed an inoffensive animal and never fired at any of the small birds.

Though he was no longer young, it was reported that he had prodigious strength. He would offer a helping hand to anyone needing it, help a fallen horse, push a mired wagon, or grab a rampaging bull by the horns. He always had his pockets full of money when he went out, and empty when he returned. When he walked through a village the ragged little youngsters would run after him with joy and surround him like a swarm of flies.

It was supposed that he must have formerly lived out in the country, for he had all sorts of useful secrets that he taught the peasants. He showed them how to get rid of grain moths by sprinkling the granary and washing the cracks of the floor with a solution of common salt, and how to drive away weevils by hanging up all around the ceiling and walls, in the pastures, and in the houses, orviot flowers. He had recipes for clearing a field of rust, of vetches, of moles, of doggrass, and all the weeds that compete with the grain. He protected a rabbit warren against rats with nothing but the odor of a little Barbary pig that he placed there.

One day he saw some peasants busily pulling out nettles; he looked at the heap of plants, uprooted, and already wilted, and said, "They're dead; but it would be good if we knew how to put them to some use. When the nettle is young, the leaves make excellent greens; when it grows old it has filaments and fibers like hemp and flax. Cloth made from the nettle is as good as cloth made from hemp. Chopped up, the nettle is good for poultry; pounded, it is good for cattle. Neetle seeds mixed with animals' fodder gives a luster to their hides; the roots, mixed with salt, produce a beautiful yellow dye. And it makes excellent hay, because it can be cut twice in a season. And what does nettle need? Very little soil, no care, no culture; except that the seeds fall as fast as they ripen, and it is difficult to gather them, that's all. If we took a little time, the nettle would be useful; we neglect it, and it becomes harmful. Then we kill it. Men are so like the nettle!" After a short silence, he added, "My friends, remember this: There are no bad herbs, and no bad men; there are only bad cultivators."

The children loved him still more because he knew how to make charming toys out of straw and coconuts.

When he saw the door of a church shrouded with black, he would go in: He sought out funerals as others seek out christenings. The bereavement and the misfortune of others attracted him, because of his great kindness; he mingled with friends in mourning, with families dressing in black, with the priests bereaved around a corpse. He seemed glad to take as text for his thoughts the funeral psalms, full of the vision of another world. With his eyes raised to heaven, he listened with a sort of longing toward all the mysteries of the infinite, to the sad voices that sing on the brink of death's dark abyss.

He did a multitude of good deeds as secretly as bad ones are usually done. He would steal into houses in the evening and furtively mount the stairs. Some poor devil, on returning to his garret, would find that his door had been opened, sometimes even forced, during his absence. The poor man would cry out, "Some thief has been here!" Once inside, the first thing he would see would be a piece of gold lying on the table. "The thief" was Father Madeleine.

He was good-natured and sad. The people used to say, "There is a rich man who does not show pride. There is a fortunate man who doesn't seem self-satisfied."

Some pretended that he was a mysterious individual and declared that no one ever went into his room, which was a true anchorite's cell furnished with hourglasses, and decorated with death's heads and cross-bones. So much of this nature was said that some of the more mischievous among the elegant young ladies of Montreuil-sur-mer called on him one day and said, "Monsieur Mayor, will you show us your room? We have heard it is a grotto." He smiled, and immediately admitted them to this "grotto." They were well punished for their curiosity. It was a room with mahogany pieces, ugly as all furniture of that kind is, and the walls covered with cheap paper. They could see nothing unusual beyond two old-fashioned candlesticks that stood on the mantel and appeared to be silver, "for they had identification marks," an observation typical of the spirit of these small towns.

But none the less did the word persist that nobody ever went into that room, that it was a hermit's cave, a place of dreams, a hole, a tomb.

It was also whispered that he had "immense" sums deposited with Laffitte, with the special condition that they were always at his immediate command, in such a way that, it was added, Monsieur Madeleine might arrive in the morning at Laffitte's, sign a receipt and carry away his two or three millions in ten minutes. In reality these "two or three millions" dwindled down, as we have said, to six hundred and thirty or forty thousand francs.

IV

MADELEINE IN MOURNING

In early 1821, the newspapers announced the passing of M. Myriel, Bishop of Digne, known as Monseigneur Bienvenu, who died in the odor of sanctity at the age of eighty-two.

The Bishop of Digne, to add a detail that the journals omitted, had been blind for several years before he died but was content because his sister was with him.

Let us say in passing, to be blind and to be loved, is in fact—on this earth where nothing is complete—one of the most strangely exquisite forms of happiness. To have continually at your side a woman, a girl, a sister, a charming being, who is there because you need her, and because she cannot do without you, to know you are indispensable to someone necessary to you, to be able at all times to measure her affection by the degree of her presence that she gives you, and to say to yourself: She dedicates all her time to me, because I possess her whole love; to see the thought if not the face; to be sure of the fidelity of one being in a total eclipse of the world; to imagine the rustling of her dress as the rustling of wings; to hear her moving to and fro, going out, coming in, talking, singing, and to think that you are the cause of those steps, those words, that song; to show your personal attraction at every moment; to feel even more powerful as your infirmity increases; to become in darkness, and by reason of darkness, the star around which this angel gravitates; few joys can equal that. The supreme happiness of life is the conviction that we are loved; loved for ourselves—say rather, loved in spite of ourselves; this conviction the blind have. In their calamity, to be served is to be caressed. Are they deprived of anything? No. Light is not lost where love enters. And what a love! A love wholly founded in purity. There is no blindness where there is certainty. The soul gropes in search of a soul, and finds it. And that soul, found and proven, is a woman. A hand sustains you, it is hers; lips lightly touch your forehead, they are her lips; you hear breathing near you, it is she. To have her wholly, from her devotion to her pity, never to be left alone, to have that sweet shyness as your aid, to lean on that unbending reed, to touch Providence with your hands and be able to grasp it in your arms; God made palpable, what transport! The heart, that dark celestial flower, bursts into a mysterious bloom. You would not give up that shade for all the light in the world! The angel soul is there, forever there; if she goes away, it is only to return; she fades away in dream and reappears in reality. You feel an approaching warmth, she is there. You overflow with serenity, gaiety, and ecstasy; you are radiant in your darkness. And the thousand little cares! The trifles that are enormous in this void. The most ineffable accents of the womanly voice used to comfort you, and replacing for you the vanished universe! You are caressed through the soul. You see nothing, but you feel yourself adored. It is a paradise of darkness.

It was from this paradise that Monseigneur Bienvenu passed to the other.

The announcement of his death was carried in the local paper of Montreuil-sur-mer. M. Madeleine appeared next morning dressed in black with a black band on his hat.

This mourning was noticed all over the town, and there was talk. It appeared to throw some light on M. Madeleine's origins. The conclusion was that he was in some way related to the venerable bishop. "He's wearing black for the Bishop of Digne," was the talk of the drawing rooms; it elevated M. Madeleine very much and gave him suddenly marked consideration in the noblest circles of Montreuil-sur-mer. The microscopic Faubourg Saint-Germain of the little place considered lifting the quarantine on M. Madeleine, the probable relative of a bishop. M. Madeleine perceived the advance he had obtained, in increasing nods from old ladies and more frequent smiles of young ladies. One evening, one of the dowagers of that little social world, curious by right of age, ventured to ask him, "The mayor is undoubtedly a relative of the late Bishop of Digne?"

He said, "No, madame."

"But," the dowager persisted, "you wear mourning for him?"

He answered, "In my youth I was a servant in his family."

Another remark going the rounds was that whenever there was seen passing through the city a young Savoyard who was tramping around the country in search of chimneys to sweep, the mayor would send for him, ask his name, and give him money. The little Savoyards told each other, so many of them came that way.

V

VAGUE FLASHES ON THE HORIZON

Little by little with the passing of time all opposition was dropped. At first there had been—as always for those who rise by their own efforts—slander and calumnies against M. Madeleine, soon this was reduced to mean remarks, then it was only wit, then it vanished entirely; respect became complete, unanimous, cordial, and there came a moment, around 1821, when the words "Monsieur the Mayor" were pronounced at Montreuil-sur-mer with almost the same accent as the words "Monseigneur the Bishop" at Digne in 1815. People came from thirty miles around to consult Monsieur Madeleine. He settled differences, he prevented lawsuits, he reconciled enemies. Everybody voluntarily chose him as judge. He seemed to have learned the book of natural law by heart. A contagion of veneration had, in the course of six or seven years, progressively spread over the whole country.

One man alone, in the city and its environs, kept himself entirely free from this contagion, and whatever Father Madeleine did, he remained indifferent, as if a sort of unchangeable, imperturbable instinct kept him awake and on the watch. It would seem that in some men there is indeed the true instinct of a beast, pure and unassailable like all instinct, which creates antipathies and sympathies, which separates one nature from another forever, which never hesitates, never is perturbed, never keeps silent, and never admits to being in the wrong; clear in its obscurity, infallible, imperious, refractory under all counsels of intelligence and all solvents of reason, and which, whatever may be their destinies, secretly warns the dog-man of the presence of the cat-man, and the fox-man of the presence of the lion-man.

Often, when M. Madeleine passed along the street, calm, affectionate, followed by the benedictions of all, it happened that a tall man, wearing a flat hat and an iron-gray coat and armed with a stout cane, would turn around abruptly behind him and follow him with his eyes until he disappeared, crossing his arms, slowly shaking his head, and raising his upper and lower lips to his nose, a sort of significant grimace that might be rendered as "Who is that man? I'm sure I've seen him somewhere before. In any event, I at least am not fooled by him."

This individual, with an almost threatening gravity was one of those who, even in a hurried interview, command the attention of the observer.

His name was Javert, and he was one of the police.

At Montreuil-sur-mer he carried out the unpleasant but useful function of inspector. He was not there at the time of Madeleine's arrival. Javert owed his position to the protection of Monsieur Chabouillet, the secretary to the minister of state, Comte Anglès, then prefect of police in Paris. When Javert arrived in Montreuil-sur-mer, the fortune of the great manufacturer had already been made, and Father Madeleine had become M. Madeleine.

Some police officers have a peculiar expression, combining an air of meanness with an air of authority. Javert had this, without the meanness.

It is our conviction that if souls were visible to the eye we would clearly see the strange fact that each individual of the human species corresponds to some species of the animal kingdom; and we would easily recognize the truth, scarcely perceived by thinkers, that from the oyster to the eagle, from the pig to the tiger, all animals are in man, and that each of them is in each man; sometimes even several of them at a time.

Animals are merely the forms of our virtues and vices, wandering before our eyes, the visible phantoms of our souls. God shows them to us to make us reflect. Though, as animals are merely shadows, God has not made them capable of education in the complete sense of the word. Why should He? On the contrary, our souls being realities with their own particular purpose, God has given them intelligence, that is to say, the possibility of education. A sound social education can always draw out of a soul, whatever it may be, any usefulness it contains.

This is said, of course, from the restricted point of view of apparent earthly life, and without prejudice to the deep question of the anterior or ulterior personality of beings that are not man. The visible *me* in no way authorizes the thinker to deny the hidden *me*. With this qualification, let us proceed.

Now, if we admit for a moment that in every man there is one of the animal species, it will be easy for us to describe the guardian of the peace Javert.

The peasants of the Asturias believe that in every litter of wolves there is one pup that is killed by the mother for fear that on growing up it would devour the other little ones.

Give a human face to this wolf's son and you will have Javert.

Javert was born in prison. His mother was a fortune-teller whose husband was in the galleys. He grew up thinking himself outside of society, and despaired of ever entering it. He noticed that society irrevocably closes its doors on two classes of men, those who attack it and those who guard it; he could choose between these two classes only; at the same time he felt that he had a powerful foundation of rectitude, order, and honesty based on an irrepressible hatred for that gypsy race to which he belonged. He entered the police. He succeeded. At forty he was an inspector.

In his youth he had been stationed with the work gangs in the South.

Before going further, let us describe Javert's human face.

It consisted of a snub nose, with two deep nostrils, bordered by large, bushy sideburns covering both his cheeks. One felt ill at ease on first seeing those two forests and those two caverns. When Javert laughed, which was rarely and terribly, his thin lips parted, showing not only his teeth, but his gums; a cleft as broad and wild as on the muzzle of a fallow deer formed around his nose. When serious, Javert was a bulldog; when he laughed, he was a tiger. Beyond that, a small head, large jaws, hair hiding the forehead and falling over the eyebrows, between the eyes a permanent central crease like an angry star, a gloomy look, a pinched and ferocious mouth, and an air of fierce command.

This man was a compound of two sentiments, simple and good in themselves, but he made them almost evil by his exaggeration of them: respect for authority and hatred of rebellion; and in his eyes theft, murder, all crimes were merely forms of rebellion. In his strong and implicit faith he included everyone with a function in the state, from the prime minister to the constable. He had nothing but disdain, aversion, and disgust for all who had once overstepped the bounds of the law. He was absolute, admitting no exceptions. On the one hand he would say, "A public official cannot be deceived; a magistrate is never wrong!" And on the other, "They are irremediably lost; no good can come of them." He fully shared the opinion of those extremists who attribute to human laws an indescribable power of making, or, if you will, of determining, demons, and who place a Styx at the bottom of society. He was stoical, serious, austere: a dreamer of stern dreams; humble and haughty, like all fanatics. His stare was cold and piercing as a gimlet. His whole life was contained in two words: waking, watching. He marked out a straight path through all that is most tortuous in the world; his conscience was bound up in his usefulness, his religion in his duties; and he was a spy as others are priests. Woe to any who fell into his hands! He would have arrested his own father if he escaped from prison and turned in his own mother for breaking parole. And he would have done it with that sort of interior satisfaction that springs from virtue. His life was one of privations, isolation, self-denial, and chastity—never any amusement. It was implacable duty, the police as central to him as Sparta to the Spartans; a pitiless detective, fiercely honest, a marble-hearted informer, Brutus united with Vidocq.

Javert's whole being expressed the spy and the sneak. The mystic school of Joseph de Maistre, which at that time enlivened what were known to be ultraconservative journals with pretentious cosmogonies, would have said that Javert was a symbol. You could not see his forehead, which disappeared under his hat; you could not see his eyes, which were lost under his brows; you could not see his chin buried in his cravat; you could not see his hands drawn up into his sleeves, you could not see his cane carried under his coat. But when the time came, all at once would spring from this shadow, as from an ambush, a steep and narrow forehead, an ominous look, a threatening chin, enormous hands, and a monstrous club.

In his leisure moments, which were rare, although he hated books, he would read; so he was not entirely illiterate. This was also perceptible in a certain pomposity in his speech.

He was free from vice, as we have said. When he was satisfied with himself, he allowed himself a pinch of snuff. That proved he was human.

It will be readily understood that Javert was the terror of the whole class which the annual statistics of the Minister of Justice include under the heading "Persons without a fixed abode." To speak the name of Javert would put them to flight; the sight of Javert's face petrified them.

Such was this intimidating man.

Javert was like an eye always fixed on M. Madeleine, an unblinking eye full of suspicion and conjecture. M. Madeleine finally noticed all this, but seemed to consider it of no consequence. He never questioned Javert, he neither sought him out nor shunned him, he endured this unpleasant, annoying stare without appearing to pay any attention to it. He treated Javert as he did everybody else, with ease and kindness.

From some words Javert had let drop, it was guessed that he had secretly hunted up, with that curiosity belonging to his race, and which is as much a matter of instinct as of will, all traces of his previous life that Father Madeleine had left elsewhere. He appeared to know, and he sometimes said in a covert way, that somebody had gathered certain information in a certain region about a certain missing family. Once he happened to say, speaking to himself, "I think I've got him!" Then for three days he was moody, not saying a word. It seems that the clue he thought he had proved inconclusive.

But—and this is the necessary corrective to an excess of absolute meaning that certain words may have presented—there can be nothing really infallible in a human creature, and the very peculiarity of instinct is that it can be disturbed, and thrown off course. Were this not so, it would be superior to intelligence, and the beast would possess a purer light than man.

Javert was evidently somewhat disconcerted by the completely natural air and tranquility of M. Madeleine.

One day, however, his strange behavior appeared to make an impression on M. Madeleine. The occasion was as follows.

VI

FATHER FAUCHELEVENT

One morning M. Madeleine was walking along an unpaved alley in Montreuil-sur-mer. He heard a shout and, seeing a crowd a short way off, he went over. An old man called Father Fauchelevent had fallen under his cart, and his horse was lying on the ground.

This Fauchelevent was one of the few who were still enemies of M. Madeleine at the time. When Madeleine first arrived in the region, the business of Fauchelevent, who was a notary of long standing and very well read for a peasant, was already beginning to decline. Fauchelevent had seen this mere artisan grow rich, while he himself, a professional man, had been going to ruin. This had made him jealous, and he had taken every opportunity to injure Madeleine. Then came bankruptcy, and the old man, having nothing left but a horse and cart, as he had no family or children, was compelled to earn his living as a carter.

The horse had broken both thighs, and could not get up. The old man was caught between the wheels. Unfortunately he had fallen so that the whole weight rested on his chest. The cart was heavily loaded. Father Fauchelevent was groaning in pain. They had tried to pull him out, but in vain. An uncoordinated effort, inexpert help, a false push, might crush him. It was impossible to extricate him other than by raising the wagon from underneath. Javert, who came up at the moment of the accident, had sent for a jack.

Then M. Madeleine appeared. The crowd fell back with respect.

"Help," cried old Fauchelevent. "Who will save an old man?"

Monsieur Madeleine turned toward the bystanders. "Does anybody have a jack?"

"They've gone for one," a peasant answered.

"How soon will it be here?"

"We sent to the nearest place, to the blacksmith in Flachot; but it will take at least a quarter of an hour."

"A quarter of an hour!" exclaimed Madeleine.

It had rained the night before, the road was soft, the cart was sinking deeper by the minute, and pressing more and more on the old carter's chest. It was obvious that in less than five minutes his ribs would be crushed.

"We can't wait a quarter of an hour," Madeleine said to the peasants.

"We have to!"

"But it will be too late! Don't you see the wagon is sinking?"

"It can't be helped."

"Listen," resumed Madeleine, "there is still room enough under the wagon for someone to crawl in, and lift it with his back. In half a minute we'll have the poor man out. Isn't there anybody here with enough strength and courage? Five louis d'ors for him!"

Nobody stirred in the crowd.

"Ten louis," said Madeleine.

The bystanders dropped their eyes. One of them muttered, "He'd have to be all brawn. And then he'd risk getting crushed."

"Come on," said Madeleine, "twenty louis."

The same silence.

"It's not the goodwill that they lack—" said a voice.

Monsieur Madeleine turned and saw Javert. He had not noticed him when he arrived.

Javert continued, "—but strength. It would take an incredible man to lift a wagon like that on his back."

Then, staring at M. Madeleine, he went on, emphasizing every word: "Monsieur Madeleine, I have known only one man able to do what you are asking."

Madeleine shuddered.

Javert added, with a casual air, but without taking his eyes off of Madeleine: "He was a convict."

"Ah!" said Madeleine.

"From the prison at Toulon."

Madeleine turned pale.

Meanwhile the cart was slowly settling. Father Fauchelevent roared and yelled, "I'm dying! My ribs are breaking! A jack! Anything! Oh!"

Madeleine looked around: "Isn't there anybody who wants twenty louis to save this poor old man's life?"

None of the bystanders moved. Javert went on: "I have known only one man who could take the place of a jack; it was that convict."

"Oh! It's crushing me!" the old man cried.

Madeleine raised his head, met the falcon eye of Javert still fixed on him, looked at the immovable peasants, and smiled sadly. Then, without a word, he fell to his knees, and even before the crowd had time to cry out, he was under the cart.

There was an awful moment of suspense and silence.

Madeleine, lying almost flat under the fearful weight, was twice seen trying in vain to bring his elbows and knees closer together. They cried out to him, "Father Madeleine! Come out of there!" Old Fauchelevent himself said, "Monsieur Madeleine! Go away! I must die, you can see that; leave me! You'll be crushed, too." Madeleine did not answer.

The bystanders held their breath. The wheels were still sinking and it would now be almost impossible for Madeleine to extricate himself.

All at once the enormous mass shook, the cart rose slowly, the wheels came half out of the ruts. A smothered voice was heard, crying, "Quick! help!" It was Madeleine, who had just made a final effort.

They all rushed in. The devotion of one man had given strength and courage to all. The cart was lifted by twenty arms. Old Fauchelevent was safe.

Madeleine arose. He was very pale, though dripping

with sweat. His clothes were torn and covered with mud. Everyone was weeping. The old man kissed his knees and called him the good Lord. Madeleine himself wore on his face an indescribable expression of joyous and celestial suffering, and he looked with a tranquil eye at Javert, who was still watching him.

VII

FAUCHELEVENT BECOMES A GARDENER IN PARIS

Fauchelevent had broken his kneecap in his fall. Father Madeleine had him carried to the infirmary he had set up for his workers in the same building as his factory, which was served by two sisters of charity. The next morning the old man found a thousand-franc bill on the stand by the side of the bed, with this note in the handwriting of Father Madeleine: "I have purchased your horse and cart." The cart was broken and the horse was dead. Fauchelevent got well, but he had a stiff knee. Monsieur Madeleine, through the recommendations of the sisters and the curé, got the old man a job as gardener at a convent in the Quartier Saint Antoine in Paris.

Some time later M. Madeleine was appointed mayor. The first time that Javert saw M. Madeleine wearing the municipal sash that gave him full authority over the city, he felt the same sort of shudder a bulldog would feel on scenting a wolf in his master's clothes. From that time on he avoided him as much as he could. When his official duties absolutely demanded it, and he could not avoid contact with the mayor, he spoke to him with profound respect.

The prosperity that Father Madeleine had created at Montreuil-sur-mer, in addition to the visible signs that we have pointed out, had another symptom that, although not visible, was nonetheless significant. It never fails. When the population is suffering, when there is lack of work, when trade falls off, the taxpayer, constrained by poverty, resists taxation, exhausts and overruns the delays allowed by law, and the government spends a great deal of money in the costs of levy and collection. When work is abundant, when the country is rich and happy, the tax is easily paid and costs the state little to collect. It may be said that poverty and public wealth have an infallible thermometer, the cost of tax collection. In seven years, that cost had been reduced three quarters in the district of Montreuil-sur-mer, so that that district was frequently held up as an example, particularly by M. de Villèle, then minister of finance.

Such was the situation of the region when Fantine returned. No one remembered her. Luckily the door of M. Madeleine's factory was like the face of a friend. She went there, and was admitted into the workshop for women. The business was entirely new to Fantine; she could not be very proficient and consequently did not receive much for her day's work; but that little was enough; the problem was solved; she was earning her living.

VIII

MADAME VICTURNIEN SPENDS THIRTY-FIVE FRANCS ON MORALITY

When Fantine realized that she was making a living, she had a moment of joy. To live honestly by her own labor —what a heavenly gift! The will to work returned to her. She bought a mirror, was pleased with the sight of her youth, her lovely hair and fine teeth, forgot many things, thought of nothing except Cosette and future possibilities, and was almost happy. She rented a small room and furnished it on credit, a remnant of her former disorderly ways.

Not being able to say that she was married, she was careful, as we have already related, not to speak of her little girl.

At first, as we have seen, she paid the Thénardiers punctually. Because she only knew how to sign her name she had to use a public letter-writer.

She wrote often; that was noticed. They began to whisper in the women's workshop that Fantine "wrote letters" and that "she put on airs." For prying into other people's affairs, none are equal to those of whom it is no concern. "Why does this gentleman never come till dusk?" "Why doesn't Mr. So-and-so ever hang his key on the nail on Thursday? Why does he always take the sidestreets?" "Why does Madame always leave her carriage before getting to the house?" "Why does she send for a package of writing paper when her portfolio is full of it?" etc., etc. There are those who, to solve one of these enigmas, which are completely irrelevant to them, spend more money, waste more time, and give themselves more trouble than ten good deeds would take—and they do it for the pleasure of it, without being paid for their curiosity in any other way than with more curiosity. They will follow this man or that woman all day long, stand guard for hours at street corners, under the entrance of a passageway, at night, in the cold and in the rain, bribe messengers, get carriage drivers and lackeys drunk, pay a chambermaid, or bribe a porter. For what? For nothing. Pure craving to see, to know, to find out. Pure itching for scandal. And often when these secrets are made known, these mysteries published, these enigmas brought into the light of day, they lead to catastrophes, duels, failures, the ruin of families, and make lives miserable, to the great joy of those who have "discovered all" without any ulterior motive, from pure instinct. A sad thing.

Some people are malicious from the mere necessity of talking. Their conversation, chatter in the drawing room, gossip in the antechamber, is like those fireplaces that rapidly burn up wood; they need a great deal of fuel; the fuel is their neighbor.

So Fantine was watched.

In addition to this, more than one was jealous of her fair hair and white teeth.

It was reported that in the workshop, with all the others around her, she often turned aside to wipe away a tear. Those were moments when she thought of her child, perhaps also of the man she had loved.

It is painful to break the sad links to the past.

It was known that she wrote, at least twice a month, and always to the same address, and that she prepaid the postage. They succeeded in learning the address: *Monsieur Thénardier, innkeeper in Montfermeil.* The public letter writer, a simple old fellow who could not fill his stomach with red wine without emptying his brain of his secrets, revealed this at a tavern. In short, it became known that Fantine had a child. "She must be that sort of a woman." And there was one old gossip who went to Montfermeil, talked with the Thénardiers, and said on her return, "For my thirty-five francs, I've found out all about it. I've even seen the child!"

The busybody who did this was a harridan named Madame Victurnien, keeper and guardian of everybody's virtue. Madame Victurnien was fifty-six years old and wore a mask of old age over her mask of ugliness. Her voice trembled, and she was capricious. It may seem strange, but this woman had once been young. In her youth, in '93, she married a monk who had escaped from the cloister in a red cap and had passed from the Bernardines to the Jacobins. She was dry, rough, sour, sharp, crabbed, almost venomous, never forgetting her monk, whose widow she was and who had ruled and controlled her harshly. She was a nettle bruised by a frock. At the restoration she became a bigot, and so energetically, that the priests had pardoned her monk episode. She had a little property, which she had bequeathed with much ado to a religious community. She was in very good standing at the bishop's palace in Arras. So this Madame Victurnien went to Montfermeil and returned saying, "I've even seen the child!"

All this took time; Fantine had been at the factory more than a year when one morning the overseer of the workshop handed her, on behalf of the mayor, fifty francs, saying that she was no longer wanted in the shop, and enjoining her, on behalf of the mayor, to leave the city.

This was the very same month in which the Thénardiers, after asking twelve francs instead of six, had demanded fifteen francs instead of twelve.

Fantine was devastated. She could not leave the city; she was in debt for her room and her furniture, and fifty francs was not enough. She stammered out some words of supplication. The overseer made it clear that she had to leave the workshop instantly. After all, Fantine was only a mediocre worker. Overwhelmed with shame even more than despair, she left the workshop, and returned to her room. Her mistake, then, was now known by everyone!

She felt no longer strong enough to say even a word. She was advised to see the mayor; she did not dare. The mayor had given her fifty francs because he was kind, and he had sent her away because he was just. She had bowed to that decree.

IX

MADAME VICTURNIEN'S VICTORY

The monk's widow then proved capable of some good.

M. Madeleine had known nothing about all of this. Life is filled with such combinations of events. M. Madeleine scarcely ever entered the women's workshop.

As head of this shop he had appointed an old spinster whom the curé had recommended to him, and he had every confidence in this overseer, a very respectable person—firm, just, upright, full of the charity that consists of giving, though to some extent lacking the charity that consists of understanding and pardoning. M. Madeleine left everything up to her. The best men are often compelled to delegate their authority. It was in exercising this full power with the conviction that she was doing right that the overseer had framed the indictment, tried, condemned, and executed Fantine.

As to the fifty francs, she had given them from a fund that M. Madeleine had entrusted to her for alms giving and aid to working women, and of which she rendered no account.

Fantine offered herself as a servant in the neighborhood; she went from house to house. Nobody wanted her. She could not leave the city. The secondhand dealer to whom she was in debt for her furniture—and what furniture!—had said to her, "If you go away, I'll have you arrested as a thief." The landlord, to whom she owed rent, had said to her, "You're young and pretty, you can find some way to pay." She divided the fifty francs between landlord and dealer, returned to the dealer three quarters of his goods, kept only what was necessary, and found herself without work, without position, owning nothing but her bed and still owing about a hundred francs.

She began to make coarse shirts for the soldiers of the garrison and earned twelve sous a day. Her daughter cost her ten. It was then that she began to fall behind with the Thénardiers.

However, an old woman, who lit her candle for her when she came home at night, taught her the art of living in misery. Below living on a little lies the art of living on nothing. They are two rooms; the first is dim, the second totally dark.

Fantine learned how to do entirely without fire in winter, how to give up a bird that eats a few millet seeds every other day, how to make a coverlet of her petticoat, and a petticoat of her coverlet, how to save her candle by eating her meals by the light of a window across the way. Few know how much some feeble souls, who have grown old in privation and honesty, can extract from a sou. This eventually becomes a talent. Fantine acquired this sublime talent and gained a little courage.

During these times, she said to a neighbor, "I say to myself: by sleeping only five hours and working all the rest at my sewing, I'll always more or less manage to earn some bread. And then, when one is sad, one eats less. Sufferings, troubles, a little bread on the one hand, a little anxiety on the other—all that will keep me alive."

In this distress, to have had her little daughter with her would have been a strange happiness. She thought of having her come. But why make her share this poverty? And then, she was in debt to the Thénardiers. How could she pay them? And the journey—how to pay for that?

The old woman, Marguerite, who had given her lessons in poverty, was a pious woman, a person of genuine devotion, poor and charitable to the poor, and even to the rich, knowing how to write just enough to sign *Margeritte*, and believing in God, which is knowledge.

There are many of these virtues in lowly places; someday they will be on high. This life has a day after.

At first, Fantine was so ashamed she did not dare go out.

In the street, she imagined that people turned around behind her and pointed her out; everybody looked at her and no one greeted her; the sharp and cold disdain of passersby penetrated her, body and soul, like a north wind.

In small towns, an unfortunate woman seems to be laid bare to the sarcasm and the curiosity of all. In Paris, at least, nobody knows you, and that obscurity is a shelter. Oh! How she longed to go to Paris! Impossible.

She simply had to become accustomed to disrespect, as she had to poverty. Little by little she resigned herself to the inevitable. After two or three months she shook off her shame and went out as if nothing had happened. "It makes no difference to me," she said.

She came and went, her head high and with a bitter smile, and felt that she was becoming shameless.

From her window Madame Victurnien sometimes saw her going by, noticed the distress of "that creature," "thanks to me put back to her place," and congratulated herself. The malicious have a dark happiness.

Excessive work fatigued Fantine, and her slight dry cough got worse. She sometimes said to her neighbor, Marguerite, "Just feel how hot my hands are."

In the morning, however, when with an old broken comb she combed her lovely hair, which flowed in silky waves, she enjoyed a moment of coquettish happiness.

X

OUTCOME OF THE SUCCESS

She had been fired toward the end of winter; summer passed, winter returned. Short days, less work. In winter there is no heat, no light, no noon, evening touches morning, there is fog, and mist, the window is frosted, and you can't see clearly. The sky is a dungeon window. The whole day is a cellar. The sun has the look of a beggar. Horrible season! Winter changes into stone the water of heaven and the heart of man. Her creditors harassed her.

Fantine earned too little. Her debts had increased. The Thénardiers, being poorly paid, were constantly writing letters to her, the contents of which saddened her, while the postage was ruining her. One day they wrote to her that her little Cosette had no clothing at all for the cold weather, that she needed a wool skirt and that her mother must send at least ten francs for that. She received the letter and held it crumpled in her hand all day. That evening she went into a barber's shop at the corner of the street and pulled out her comb. Her beautiful fair hair fell below her waist.

"What beautiful hair!" exclaimed the barber.

"How much will you give me for it?" she said.

"Ten francs."

"Cut it off."

She bought a knit skirt and sent it to the Thénardiers.

This skirt made the Thénardiers furious. It was the money that they wanted. They gave the skirt to Eponine. The poor lark still shivered.

Fantine thought, "My child is no longer cold, I have clothed her in my hair." She put on a little round cap, which concealed her shorn head, so she was still pretty.

But a gloomy process was going on in Fantine's heart.

When she saw she could no longer comb her hair, she began to look with hatred on everything around her. She had long shared in the universal veneration of Father Madeleine; nevertheless by dint of repeating to herself that it was he who had turned her away, that he was the cause of her misfortunes, she came to hate him particularly. If she passed the factory when the workers were at the door, she would force herself to laugh and sing.

An old working woman who saw her singing and laughing this way, said, "That girl will come to a bad end."

She took a lover, the first comer, a man she did not love, out of bravado, and with rage in her heart. He was a lazy wretch, a street musician, who beat her and left her, as she had taken him, with disgust.

She worshiped Cosette.

The lower she sank, the darker everything became around her, the more the sweet little angel shone out in her innermost heart. She would say, "When I'm rich, I'll have my Cosette beside me"; and she would laugh. The cough did not leave her, and she had night sweats.

One day she received a letter from the Thénardiers saying: "Cosette has come down with a disease that's sweeping the area; 'Military fever,' they call it. The necessary medicines are expensive. It is ruining us, and we can no longer pay for them. Unless you send us forty francs within a week the little one will die."

She burst out laughing, and said to her old neighbor, "Oh! They're nice! Forty francs, just think! That's two Napoleons! Where do they think I can get all that? What fools they are, these peasants!"

However, she went to the staircase near a dormer window and reread the letter.

Then she went downstairs and outside, running and jumping, still laughing.

Somebody who met her said, "What's the matter with you—so cheerful all of a sudden?"

She answered, "A stupid joke that some country people have just written me. They're asking for forty francs, the peasants!"

As she passed through the square, she saw a crowd gathered around an odd-looking carriage on the top of which stood a man in red clothes, declaiming. He was a juggler and a traveling dentist and was offering to the public complete sets of teeth, opiates, powders, and elixirs.

Fantine joined the crowd and began to laugh with the rest at this harangue, with its mixture of slang for the crowd and jargon for the better educated. The puller of teeth saw this beautiful girl laughing and suddenly called out, "You have pretty teeth—you, the laughing girl there. If you'll sell me your two incisors, I'll give you a gold Napoleon for each of them."

"What's that? What are my incisors?" asked Fantine.

"The incisors," resumed the professor of dentistry, "are the front teeth, the two upper ones."

"How horrible!" cried Fantine.

"Two Napoleons!" grumbled a toothless old hag who stood by. "She's the lucky one!"

Fantine fled away and stopped her ears not to hear the shrill voice of the man calling after her: "Think it over, my beauty! Two Napoleons! You could think of ways to use them! If you have the courage, come this evening to the inn of the Tillac d'Argent; you'll find me there."

Fantine went home, furious, and told the story to her neighbor Marguerite: "Can you believe that? Isn't he abominable? Why do they let people like that go all around the countryside? Pull out my two front teeth! Why I'd look horrible! The hair can grow back, but teeth! What a monster! I'd rather thow myself from the sixth floor, headfirst! He told me he'd be at the Tillac d'Argent this evening."

"And what did he offer you?" Marguerite asked.

"Two Napoleons."

"That's forty francs."

"Yes," Fantine said, "that makes forty francs."

She turned thoughtful and went about her work. In a quarter of an hour she left her sewing and went to the stairs to read the Thérnardiers' letter again.

On her return she said to Marguerite, who was working near her, "What does this mean, a military fever? Do you know?"

"Yes," answered the old woman, "it's a disease."

"Then it needs a lot of medicines."

"Yes, awful medicines."

"How does it start up?"

"It's a disease you just get."

"Does it attack children?"

"Children particularly."

"Do people die from it?"

"Very often," said Marguerite.

Fantine left and reread the letter on the stairs.

In the evening she went out, and she was seen going toward the Rue de Paris where the inns are.

The next morning, when Marguerite went into Fantine's bedroom before daybreak, for they always worked together, making one candle do for the two, she found Fantine seated on her bed, pale and icy. She had not been to bed. Her cap had fallen onto her knees. The candle had burned all night, and was almost gone.

Marguerite stopped in the doorway, petrified by this wild disarray, and exclaimed, "Good Lord! The candle is all burned out. Something has happened."

Then she looked at Fantine, who sadly turned her shorn head toward her.

During the night Fantine had grown ten years older.

"Bless us!" said Marguerite. "What's the matter with you, Fantine?"

"Nothing," said Fantine. "Quite the contrary. My child will not die from that terrible disease because I couldn't send help. I'm satisfied."

So saying, she showed the old woman two Napoleons that lay glistening on the table.

"Oh! good God!" said Marguerite. "But that's a fortune! Where did you get them?"

"I got them," answered Fantine.

At the same time she smiled. The candle lit up her face. It was a sickening smile, the corners of her mouth were stained with blood, and there was a black hole where her two front teeth had been.

They had been pulled out.

She sent the forty francs to Montfermeil.

Actually, the Thénardiers had lied to her to get the money. Cosette was not sick at all.

Fantine threw her mirror out the window. Long before that she had left her tiny room on the second floor for an attic room closed only with a latch; one of those garret rooms where the ceiling slants down to the floor and you constantly hit your head. The poor cannot go to the far end of their rooms or to the far end of their lives, except by continually bending more and more. She no longer had a bed; she kept a rag she called her coverlet, a mattress on the floor, and a worn-out rush chair. Her little rose bush had dried up in the corner, forgotten. In the other corner was a butter-pot for water, which froze in the winter, and the different levels at which the water had stood stayed marked a long time by circles of ice. She had lost her modesty, she was losing her coquetry. The last sign. She would go out with a dirty cap. Either from want of time or from indifference she no longer washed her linen. As fast as the heels of her stockings wore out she drew them down into her shoes. This could be deduced from some perpendicular wrinkles. She mended her old, worn-out corsets with bits of calico that tore with the slightest motion. Her creditors quarreled with her and gave her no peace. She would see them in the street, she would see them again on her stairs. She spent whole nights weeping and thinking. There was a strange brilliance in her eyes, and a constant pain in her shoulder near the top of her left shoulder blade. She coughed a great deal. She hated Father Madeleine profoundly, and she never complained. She sewed seventeen hours a day; but a contractor who was using prison labor suddenly cut the price, and this reduced the day's wages of free laborers to nine sous. Seventeen hours of work, and nine sous a day! Her creditors were more pitiless than ever. The secondhand dealer, who had taken back nearly all his furniture, kept saying to her, "When will you pay me, woman?"

Good God! What did they want her to do? She felt hunted down, and something of the wild beast began to develop within her. About the same time, Thénardier wrote to tell her that really he had waited with too much generosity and that he must have a hundred francs immediately, or else little Cosette, just convalescing after her severe sickness, would be turned out of doors into the cold and onto the highway, and that she would fend for herself as best she could, and would perish if she must. "A hundred francs," thought Fantine. "But where is there a way to earn a hundred sous a day?"

"All right!" she said, "I'll sell what's left."

The unfortunate creature became a woman of the streets.

XI

CHRISTUS NOS LIBERAVIT

What is this story of Fantine about? It is about society buying a slave.

From whom? From misery.

From hunger, from cold, from loneliness, from desertion, from privation. Melancholy barter. A soul for a piece of bread. Misery makes the offer; society accepts.

The holy law of Jesus Christ governs our civilization, but it does not yet permeate it. They say that slavery has disappeared from European civilization. That is incorrect. It still exists, but now it weighs only on women, and it is called prostitution.

It weighs on women, that is to say, on grace, fraility, beauty, motherhood. This is not the least among man's shames.

At this stage in the mournful drama, Fantine has nothing left of what she had formerly been. She has turned to marble in becoming corrupted. Whoever touches her feels a chill. She goes her way, she endures you, she ignores you; she is the incarnation of dishonor and severity. Life and the social order have spoken their last word to her. All that can happen to her has happened. She has endured all, borne all, experienced all, suffered all, lost all, wept for all. She is resigned, with that resignation resembling indifference as death resembles sleep. She shuns nothing now. She fears nothing now. Every cloud falls on her, and the whole ocean sweeps over her! What does it matter to her? The sponge is already saturated.

So she believed at least, but it is wrong to imagine that one can exhaust one's destiny or fully plumb the depths of anything.

Alas! What are all these destinies driven helter-skelter? Where do they go? Why are they what they are?

He who knows that sees all darkness.

He is alone. His name is God.

XII

THE IDLENESS OF M. BAMATABOIS

There is in all small towns, and there was at Montreuil-sur-mer in particular, a set of young men who nibble their fifteen hundred livres' annual income in the country with the same airs as their fellows devour two hundred thousand francs in Paris. They are beings of the great neuter species: geldings, parasites, nobodies who have a little land, a little folly, and a little wit, who would be clowns in a drawing room, and think themselves gentlemen in a barroom, who talk about "my fields, my woods, my peasants," whistle at actresses in the theater to prove they are persons of taste, quarrel with the officers of the garrison to show that they are gallant, hunt, smoke, gawk, drink, take snuff, play billiards, stare at passengers getting out of the coach, live at the café, dine at the inn, have a dog that eats the bones under the table and a mistress who sets the dishes on it, hold tight to a sou, overdo the fashions, admire tragedy, scorn women, wear out their old boots, copy London as seen through Paris, and Paris as seen through Pont-à-Mousson, grow stupid as they grow old, do no work, do no good but not much harm.

M. Félix Tholomyès, if he had remained in his province and never seen Paris, would have been such a man.

If they were richer, we would say they are dandies; if they were poorer, we should say they are tramps. They are simply idlers. Among them are some that are bores and some that are bored, some dreamers and some jokers.

In those days, a dandy was made up of a large collar, a large necktie, a watch loaded with chains, three waistcoats of different colors worn one over the other, the red and blue inside, a short-waisted olive-colored coat with a fishtail, a double row of silver buttons close together and going right up to the shoulder, and trousers of a lighter olive, decorated on the two seams with an odd number of ribs varying from one to eleven, a limit never exceeded. Add to this, Blucher boots with little iron caps on the heel, a high-crowned, narrow-brimmed hat, hair brushed out, an enormous cane, and conversation spiced with Potier's puns. Above all, spurs and a mustache. In those days, mustaches meant civilians, and spurs meant pedestrians.

The provincial dandy wore longer spurs and fiercer mustaches.

It was the time of the war between the South American Republics and the King of Spain, of Bolívar against Morillo. Hats with narrow brims were Royalist and were called Morillos; the liberals wore hats with wide brims called Bolívars.

So, eight or ten months after what has been related in the preceding pages, or in early January 1823, one evening when it had been snowing, one of these dandies, a "right-thinking" man because he wore a Morillo, very warmly wrapped in one of those large cloaks that completed the fashionable costume in cold weather, was amusing himself with tormenting a creature who was walking back and forth before the window of the officers' café, in a low-cut ball dress, and flowers on her head. The dandy was smoking, for that was decidedly in fashion.

Each time the woman walked past him, he threw out at her, with a puff of smoke from his cigar, some remark he thought witty and pleasant as, "My, but you're ugly!" "Why don't you try hiding your face?" "You've lost your two front teeth!" etc., etc. This gentleman's name was M. Bamatabois. The woman, a sad, overdressed specter walking back and forth in the snow, did not answer, did not even look at him, but continued pacing in silence with a dismal regularity that put her back under his sarcasm every five minutes, like the condemned soldier who at stated periods submits again to the rod. This lack of attention undoubtedly irked the idler, who, taking advantage of the moment when she turned, came up behind her stealthily and, stifling his laughter, stooped over, seized a handful of snow from the sidewalk, and threw it hastily down her back between the naked shoulders. The girl roared in rage, turned, bounded like a panther, and rushed at the man, burying her nails in his face, and using the most shocking words, usually heard only in the barracks. These insults were thrown out in a voice roughened by brandy, from a hideous mouth minus two front teeth. It was Fantine.

At the noise, the officers came out of the café, a crowd gathered, and a large circle was formed, laughing, jeering and applauding, around this tornado composed of two beings who could hardly be recognized as a man and a woman, the man defending himself, his hat knocked off, the woman kicking and thumping, her head bare, shrieking, toothless, hairless, her face gray with a terrible wrath.

Suddenly a tall man advanced quickly from the crowd, seized the woman by her muddy satin dress, and said, "Follow me!"

The woman raised her head; her furious voice died out at once. Her eyes were glassy, from ashen she turned pale, and she shuddered with terror. She recognized Javert.

The dandy took advantage of the incident to steal away.

XIII

SOLUTION OF SOME QUESTIONS OF THE MUNICIPAL POLICE

Javert brushed aside the bystanders, broke up the circle, and walked off rapidly toward the police station, at the far end of the square, dragging the poor creature after him. She did not resist, but followed listlessly. Neither spoke a word. The flock of spectators, in a paroxysm of joy, followed with their quips. Deepest misery is an occasion for obscenities.

When they reached the police station, a low hall warmed by a stove, watched by a guard, with a grated glass door looking out on the street, Javert opened the door, entered with Fantine, and closed the door behind him, to the great disappointment of the curious crowd, which stood up on tiptoe and stretched their necks in front of the dirty window of the guardhouse, trying to see. Curiosity is gluttony. To see is to devour.

On entering, Fantine collapsed in a corner, motionless and silent, crouching like a frightened dog.

The sergeant of the guards placed a lighted candle on the table. Javert sat down, drew from his pocket a sheet of stamped paper, and began to write.

By our laws these women are placed entirely under the discretion of the police, who can do what they want with them, punish them as they see fit, and confiscate at will those two sad things they call their industry and their liberty. Javert was impassible; his grave face betrayed no emotion. He was, however, seriously and earnestly preoccupied. It was one of those moments in which he exercised without restraint, but with all the scruples of a strict conscience, his formidable discretionary power. At this moment he felt that his policeman's stool was a bench of justice. He was conducting a trial. He was trying and condemning. He called up all the ideas of which his mind was capable for the great thing he was doing. The more he examined the conduct of this girl, the more it revolted him. Clearly he had seen a crime committed. He had seen, there in the street, society, represented by a property-holding voter, insulted and attacked by a creature who was an outlaw and an outcast. A prostitute had assaulted a citizen. He, Javert, had seen that himself. He wrote in silence.

When he had finished, he signed his name, folded the paper, and handed it to the sergeant of the guard, saying, "Choose three men, and take this girl to jail." Then turning to Fantine, "You are in for six months."

The unfortunate woman shuddered.

"Six months! Six months in prison!" she cried. "Six months earning seven sous a day! But what will become of Cosette! My daughter! My daughter! I still owe more than a hundred francs to the Thénardiers, Monsieur Inspector, do you know that?"

Without getting to her feet, she dragged herself along the floor, dirtied by the muddy boots of all these men, clasping her hands, on her knees.

"Monsieur Javert," she said, "I ask for your pity. I assure you that I was not in the wrong. If you had seen the beginning, you would understand. I swear to you by the good Lord that I was not in the wrong. That gentleman, whom I don't know, threw snow down my back. Do they have the right to throw snow down our backs when we are going along quietly like that without harming anybody? That made me wild. I'm not very well, don't you see? And then he had already been saying things to me for some time. 'My, you're ugly!' 'Where are your teeth!' I know only too well that I've lost my teeth. I didn't do anything; I thought, 'He's a gentleman who's having a little fun.' I wasn't immodest with him, I didn't speak to him. That was when he put the snow on me. Monsieur Javert, good Monsieur Inspector! Wasn't there anyone there who saw it, who could tell you that's true! Perhaps I was wrong to get mad. You know, at that moment, we can't control it. We get excited. And then to have something that cold thrown down your back when you're least expecting it! I was wrong to spoil the gentleman's hat. Why did he go away? I'd ask his pardon. Oh! I wouldn't mind asking his forgiveness. Have pity on me just this once, Monsieur Javert. Look, you don't know how it is, in the prisons they only earn seven sous; that's not the fault of the government, but they earn seven sous, and just think that I have a hundred francs to pay, or else they'll send away my little one. O God! I can't have her with me, what I do is so awful! O my Cosette, O my little angel of the good, blessed Virgin, what will become of her, poor starved child! I tell you the Thénardiers are innkeepers, peasants, they have no consideration. They only think of getting their money. Don't put me in prison! Don't you see, she's a little dear, they'll put her out on the highway, to fend for herself, in the middle of winter; you must pity such a thing, good Monsieur Javert. If she were older, she could earn her living, but at her age she can't. I'm not a bad woman at heart. It's not laziness and greed that have brought me to this; I've drunk brandy, but it was from misery. I don't like it, but it dazes you. When I was happier, you'd just have had to look in my closet to see that I was not a disorderly woman. I had clothes, so many! Have pity on me, Monsieur Javert."

She talked this way, bent double, shaken with sobs, blinded by tears, her chest bare, wringing her hands, coughing a dry, short cough, stammering quietly with agony in her voice. Great grief is a divine and terrible radiance that transfigures the wretched. At that instant Fantine had again become beautiful. At certain moments she stopped and tenderly kissed the policeman's coattail. She would have softened a heart of granite; but you cannot soften a heart of wood.

"Come on," said Javert, "I've heard you out. Are you through now? Six months! The Eternal Father in person couldn't help you now."

At those solemn words, "The Eternal Father in person couldn't help you now," she understood that her sentence had been pronounced. She collapsed, whispering, "Mercy!"

Javert turned his back.

The soldiers grabbed her by the arms.

A few minutes earlier a man had entered unnoticed. He had closed the door and stood with his back against it, and heard Fantine's desperate plea.

When the soldiers put their hands on the wretched girl, who did not want to get up, he stepped forward out of the shadow and said, "One moment if you please!"

Javert raised his eyes and recognized M. Madeleine. He took off his hat, and bowing with a sort of angry awkwardness said, "Excuse me, Monsieur Mayor—"

These words, "Monsieur Mayor," had a strange effect on Fantine. She sprang to her feet at once like a ghost rising from the ground, pushed back the soldiers with her arms, walked straight to M. Madeleine before they could stop her, and gazing at him fixedly, with a wild look, she exclaimed, "Ah, so you're the mayor!"

Then she burst out laughing and spit in his face.

M. Madeleine wiped his face and said, "Inspector Javert, set this woman free."

Javert felt as though he were about to lose his mind. At that moment he experienced, blow after blow and, almost simultaneously, the most violent emotions he had known in his life. To see a prostitute spit in the face of a mayor was so monstrous that, in his wildest conjecture, even to imagine it would have seemed sacrilege. On the other hand, in his innermost thoughts, he made a dim and hideous association between what this woman was and what this mayor might be, and then glimpsed with horror something indescribably simple in this prodigious assault. But when he saw this mayor, this magistrate, wipe his face quietly and say, "Set this woman free," he was stupefied; thought and speech alike failed him; the sum of possible astonishment had been surpassed. He remained speechless.

The mayor's words were no less strange to Fantine. She raised her bare arm and clung to the damper handle of the stove as though quaking. Meanwhile she looked all around and began to talk in a low voice, as if to herself: "Free! They let me go! I'm not going to jail for six months! Who said that? Nobody could have! I misunderstood. It can't be this monster mayor! Was it you, my good Monsieur Javert, who told them to set me free? Oh! Don't you see? I'll tell you and you'll let me go. This monster mayor, this old devil of a mayor, he's the cause of it all. Think of it, Monsieur Javert, he turned me out because of a pack of beggars who gossiped in the workshop. Wasn't that horrible! Turning away a poor girl who does her work honestly. Since then I couldn't earn enough, and all the trouble began. To start with, there's a change you gentlemen of the police ought to make—that is, stop prison contractors from doing wrong to poor people. I'll tell you how it is; just listen. You earn twelve sous at shirtmaking, which falls to nine sous, not enough to live on. Then we have to make do. I had my little Cosette, and I just had to turn to the streets. Now you see it's this beggar of a mayor who did it all. And then, I did step on the hat of the gentleman in front of the officers' café. But he, he had spoiled my dress with the snow. We have only one silk dress, for the evenings. You see, I never meant to do wrong, truly, Monsieur Javert, and everywhere I see women much worse than me who are much more fortunate. Oh, Monsieur Javert, it is you who said that they must let me go, isn't it? Go and ask, speak to my landlord; I pay my rent, and he'll tell you I'm honest. Oh Lord, I'm so sorry, I've touched—I didn't realize—the damper on the stove, and it's smoking."

M. Madeleine listened with profound attentiveness. While she was talking, he had fumbled in his waistcoat, had taken out his purse and opened it. It was empty. He had put it back in his pocket. He said to Fantine, "How much did you say you owed?"

Fantine, who was looking only at Javert, turned to him: "Who said anything to you?"

Then turning to the soldiers, "Say, see how I spat in his face? Ah! You old devil of a mayor. You came here to scare me, but I'm not afraid of you. I'm afraid of Monsieur Javert. I'm afraid of my good Monsieur Javert!"

As she said this she turned back toward the inspector: "Now, you see, Monsieur Inspector, you have to be just. I know you're just, Monsieur Inspector; in fact, it's all very simple, a man who has some fun putting snow down a woman's back, that makes them laugh, the officers, they have to amuse themselves somehow, and we're there just for their amusement. And then, you, you come along, you're obligated to keep order, you arrest the woman who's done wrong, but now I see, since you're good, you tell them to set me free, it's for my little one, because six months in prison, that would keep me from supporting my child. Just don't come back again, wretch! Oh! I'll never come back again, Monsieur Javert! They can do anything they like to me now, I won't budge. Only, today, don't you see, I hollered because it hurt me. I just didn't expect that snow from that gentleman, and then, I've told you, I'm not very well, I cough, I have something in my chest like a burning ball, and the doctor tells me, 'Take care of yourself.' There, feel, give me your hand, don't be afraid, here it is."

She had stopped crying; her voice was caressing; she placed Javert's huge rough hand on her delicate white chest and smiled as she looked at him.

All of a sudden, she smoothed down the folds of her dress, which, as she crawled, had risen almost up to her knees, and she walked toward the door, saying in an undertone to the soldiers, with a friendly nod, "Boys, Monsieur Inspector said you must free me. I'm going."

She put her hand on the latch. One more step and she would be in the street.

Until that moment Javert had stood, rooted, his eyes fixed on the ground, looking out of place in the middle of the scene, like a statue waiting to be put back in position.

The sound of the latch roused him. He raised his head with an expression of sovereign authority, an expression always that much more frightening when power is vested in lower beings—ferocious in the wild beast, vicious in the undeveloped man.

"Sergeant," he exclaimed, "don't you see that this tramp is escaping? Who told you to let her go?"

"I did," said Madeleine.

Hearing Javert's words, Fantine trembled and dropped the latch, as a thief who is caught drops what he has stolen. When Madeleine spoke, she turned, and from that moment, without saying a word, without even daring to breathe freely, she looked in turn from Madeleine to Javert and from Javert to Madeleine, as one or the other was speaking.

It was clear that Javert must have been thrown off balance, or he would not have allowed himself to address the sergeant as he did, after the mayor's instructions to free Fantine. Had he forgotten about the mayor's presence? Had he finally decided within himself that it was impossible for someone in authority to give such an order, and that quite simply the mayor must have said one thing when he meant another? Or, in view of the enormities he had witnessed over the last two hours, was he saying to himself that he had to resort to extreme measures, that the lesser had to make itself greater, for the detective to turn into a magistrate, the policeman become a judge, and that in this shocking turnabout, order, law, morality, government, society itself, were personified in him, Javert?

However that may be, when M. Madeleine said, "I

did," Javert turned toward the mayor and—pale, cold, with blue lips, a frantic stare, his whole body rocked by an invisible tremor, and, an unheard-of thing—said to him, with a downcast look, but a firm voice, "Monsieur Mayor, that cannot be done."

"Why?" said M. Madeleine.

"This wretched woman has insulted a citizen."

"Inspector Javert," replied M. Madeleine, in a calm, conciliatory tone, "listen. You're an honest man, and I have no objection to setting this straight with you. The truth is this: I was on my way through the square when you arrested this woman; there was still a crowd there; I heard everything; I know all about it; it is the citizen who was in the wrong; it is he who, with proper police work, would have been arrested."

Javert responded, "This wretch has just insulted Monsieur the Mayor."

"That is my concern alone," said M. Madeleine. "The insult is to me. I can do what I please about it."

"I beg Monsieur the Mayor's pardon. The insult does not belong to him, but to justice."

"Inspector Javert," replied M. Madeleine, "the highest justice is conscience. I have heard this woman's story. I know what I'm doing."

"And as for me, Monsieur Mayor, I don't understand what I am seeing."

"Then be satisfied with obeying."

"I obey my duty. My duty requires that this woman spend six months in prison."

M. Madeleine answered mildly, "Listen to me carefully. She will not spend a single day there."

At these decisive words, Javert had the effrontery to look the mayor in the eye, and said, though still in a tone of profound respect, "I am very sorry to resist Monsieur the Mayor; it is the first time in my life, but he will permit me to observe that I am within the limits of my own authority. I will speak, since the mayor desires it, on the matter of the citizen. I was there. This girl fell upon Monsieur Bamatabois, who can vote and owns that fine house with a balcony at the corner of the esplanade, three stories high, and all of cut stone. Indeed, some things in this world must be considered. However that may be, Monsieur Mayor, this matter belongs to the police; this concerns me, and I detain the woman Fantine."

At this M. Madeleine folded his arms and said in a severe tone that nobody in the city had ever heard, "The matter of which you speak resides with the municipal police. By the terms of articles nine, eleven, fifteen, and sixty-six of the code of criminal law, that is within my jurisdiction. I order that this woman be set free."

Javert endeavored to make a last attempt.

"But, Monsieur Mayor—"

"I refer you to article eighty-one of the law of December 13, 1799, concerning illegal imprisonment."

"Monsieur Mayor, permit—"

"Not another word."

"However—"

"You may go," said Monsieur Madeleine.

Javert received the blow, standing full front and straight to the breast like a Russian soldier. He bowed deeply before the mayor and went out.

Fantine stood by the door and in a daze looked at him as he went past her.

Meanwhile she also was in the grips of a strange turmoil. She had just seen herself somehow disputed by two opposing powers. Before her eyes she had seen a struggle between two men who held in their hands her liberty, her life, her soul, her child; one of these men was drawing her to the side of darkness, the other was leading her toward the light. In this contest, seen through the magnifying distortion of fear, these two men had appeared to her like two giants; one spoke as her demon, the other as her guardian angel. The angel had vanquished the demon and the thought made her shudder from head to toe: This angel, this deliverer, was the very man whom she abhorred, this mayor whom she had so long considered the author of all her woes—this Madeleine!—and at the very moment when she had insulted him hideously, he had saved her! Had she then been deceived? Would she have to change all her beliefs? She did not know; she trembled. She listened with dismay, looked around with alarm, and at each word that M. Madeleine uttered, she felt the fearful darkness of her hatred melt within her and flow away, while an indescribable and ineffable warmth of joy, of confidence, and of love welled up in her heart.

When Javert was gone, M. Madeleine turned toward her, and said slowly and with difficulty, like a man struggling not to weep, "I have heard you. I had known nothing of what you have said. I believe it is true and I feel it is true. I did not even know that you had left my workshop. Why did you not apply to me? But now, I will pay your debts, I will have your child come to you, or you will go to her. You shall live here, in Paris, or wherever you wish. I take charge of your child and you. You will not have to work anymore, if you do not want to. I will give you all the money you need. You will become honest in again becoming happy. More than that, listen. I declare to you from this moment, if everything is as you say, and I do not doubt it, that you have never ceased to be virtuous and holy before God. Poor woman!"

This was more than poor Fantine could bear. To have Cosette! To leave this infamous life! To live, free, rich, happy, respected, with Cosette! To see suddenly springing up in the midst of her misery all these realities of paradise! She looked astonished at the man speaking to her, and began weeping quietly. Her limbs gave way, she fell to her knees in front of M. Madeleine, and, before he could prevent it, he felt that she had seized his hand and carried it to her lips.

Then she fainted.

Book Six

JAVERT

I

NOW, REST

M. Madeleine had Fantine taken to the infirmary, which was in his own house. He entrusted her to the sisters, who put her to bed. A violent fever had come on, and she spent part of the night delirious. Finally, she fell asleep.

Toward noon the following day, Fantine woke up. She heard someone breathing near her bed, drew aside the curtain, and saw M. Madeleine standing, gazing at something above his head. His look was full of compassionate, prayerful agony. She followed its direction and saw it was fixed on a crucifix nailed against the wall.

From that moment M. Madeleine was transfigured in the eyes of Fantine; to her he seemed bathed in light. He was absorbed in a kind of prayer. She gazed at him for a long while without daring to interrupt; at last she said timidly, "What are you doing here?"

M. Madeleine had been there for an hour waiting for Fantine to wake up. He took her hand, felt her pulse, and asked, "How do you feel?"

"Very well. I slept," she said. "I think I'm getting better—this will be nothing."

Then he said, answering the question she had first asked him, as though she had just asked it, "I was praying to the martyr on high."

And inwardly he added, "—for the martyr here below."

M. Madeleine had spent the night and morning learning

about Fantine. He knew everything now, including her past history in all its poignant details.

He went on, "You've suffered so, poor mother, but don't be sad, you are now among the elect. It is in this way that mortals become angels. It is not their fault; they do not know how to go about it otherwise. This hell you have just left is the first step toward Heaven. You had to begin there."

He sighed deeply, but she smiled, with that sublime smile that was minus two teeth.

That same night, Javert wrote a letter. In the morning he carried it to the post office of Montreuil-sur-mer. It was directed to Paris and bore this address: "To Monsieur Chabouillet, Secretary to Monsieur the Prefect of Police." As news of the affair at the police station had been gotten around, the postmistress and some others who saw the envelope before it was sent and who recognized Javert's handwriting in the address thought he was sending in his resignation. M. Madeleine wrote immediately to the Thénardiers. Fantine owed them a hundred and twenty francs. He sent them three hundred francs, telling them to pay themselves out of it and bring the child at once to Montreuil-sur-mer, where her mother, who was sick, wanted her.

This astonished Thénardier.

"What the devil!" he said to his wife, "we won't let go of the child. It just might be our little lark will become a milk cow. I guess some silly fellow's fallen for the mother."

He replied with a bill for five hundred and some odd francs carefully drawn up. In this bill figured two incontestable items for above three hundred francs, one from a physician and the other from an apothecary who had attended and supplied Eponine and Azelma during two long illnesses. Cosette, as we have said, had not been ill. There was only a substitution of names. Thénardier wrote at the bottom of the bill: "Received on account three hundred francs."

M. Madeleine immediately sent three hundred francs more and wrote: "Bring Cosette quickly."

"Christ!" said Thénardier, "we'll never let the girl go!"

Meanwhile Fantine had not recovered. She was still in the infirmary.

It was not without some repugnance, at first, that the sisters received and cared for this girl. Anyone who has seen the low reliefs at the Cathedral of Rheims will recall the distension of the lower lip among the wise virgins beholding the foolish virgins. This ancient contempt of vestals for less fortunate women is one of the deepest instincts of womanly dignity; the sisters had experienced it with the intensification of Religion. But within a few days Fantine had disarmed them. The motherly tenderness within her, with her soft and touching words, moved them. One day the sisters heard her say in her delirium, "I have been a sinner, but when I have my child with me, that will mean God has forgiven me. While I was bad I would not have had my Cosette with me; I couldn't have stood the sadness and surprise in her eyes. It was for her, though, that I sinned, and that's why God has forgiven me. I shall feel His benediction when Cosette comes. I will gaze at her; the sight of her innocence will do me good. She knows nothing of it all. She's an angel, sisters. At her age, the wings haven't fallen off yet."

M. Madeleine came to see her twice a day, and at each visit she asked him, "Will I see Cosette soon?"

He answered, "Perhaps tomorrow. I expect her any moment."

And the mother's pale face would brighten.

"Ah!" she would say, "how happy I will be."

We have just said she did not recover: On the contrary, her condition seemed to worsen week by week. That handful of snow applied to the naked skin between her shoulder blades had caused a sudden stoppage of perspiration, and so the disease, which had been incubating for some years at last attacked her violently. At that time they were just beginning to diagnose and treat lung diseases, following the advanced theory of Laennec. The doctor sounded her lungs and shook his head.

M. Madeleine said to him, "Well?"

"Doesn't she have a child she is anxious to see?" said the doctor.

"Yes."

"Well then, bring her here quickly."

M. Madeleine gave a shudder.

Fantine asked him, "What did the doctor say?"

M. Madeleine tried to smile.

"He told us to bring your child at once. That will restore your health."

"Oh!" she cried. "He's so right. But why are the Thénardiers keeping my Cosette from me? Oh! She is coming! Here at last I see happiness near me."

The Thénardiers, however, did not let go of the child; they gave a hundred bad reasons. Cosette was too delicate to travel in the wintertime, and then there were a number of little debts, they were collecting the bills, etc., etc.

"I will send somebody for Cosette," said M. Madeleine. "If necessary, I will go myself."

He wrote at Fantine's dictation this letter, which she signed.

"Monsieur Thénardier:

You will deliver Cosette to the bearer.

He will settle all small debts.

I have the honor of greeting you with kind regards,

FANTINE"

In the meantime a serious matter interfered. Though we chisel away as best we can at the mysterious block from which our life is made, the black vein of destiny continually reappears.

II

HOW JEAN CAN BECOME CHAMP

One morning M. Madeleine was in his office arranging some pressing business of the mayoralty, in case he should decide to go to Montfermeil himself, when he was informed that Javert, the inspector of police, wished to speak to him. On hearing this name spoken, M. Madeleine could not repress a feeling of displeasure. Since the affair at the police station, Javert had more than ever avoided him, and M. Madeleine had not seen him at all.

"Have him come in," he said.

Javert entered.

Monsieur Madeleine remained seated near the fire, pen in hand, looking over a bundle of papers on which he was making notes and which contained the reports of the police patrol. He did not interrupt his work for Javert: He could not help thinking of poor Fantine, and it was right that he receive him very coldly.

Javert respectfully greeted the mayor, who had his back to him. The mayor did not look up but continued to make notes on the papers.

Javert advanced a few steps and paused without breaking the silence.

A physiognomist, if he had been familiar with Javert's nature, if he had made a study for years of this savage in the service of civilization, this odd mixture of Roman, Spartan, monk, and corporal, this spy incapable of a lie, this virgin detective—a physiognomist, if he had known his secret and inveterate aversion for M. Madeleine, his contest with the mayor on the subject of Fantine, and he had seen Javert at that moment, would have said, "What's happened to him?"

It would have been obvious to anyone knowing this conscientious, clearheaded, straightforward, sincere, upright, austere, fierce man, that Javert had suffered some great interior turbulence. There was nothing in his mind that was not shown on his face. He was, like all violent people, subject to sudden changes. Never had his face been stranger or more startling. On entering, he had bowed to M. Madeleine with a look in which was neither rancor, anger, nor defiance; he had paused some steps behind the mayor's chair and was now standing in a soldierly attitude with the natural, cold rigor of a man who was never kind, but has always been patient; without saying a word or making any gesture, he waited in genuine humility and tranquil resignation, until it should please Monsieur the Mayor to turn toward him, calm, serious, hat in hand, and eyes cast down with an expression between that of a soldier in front of his officer and a prisoner before his judge. All the feeling as well as all the memories we should have expected of him had disappeared. Nothing was left on this face, simple and impenetrable as granite, except a gloomy sadness. His whole being expressed abasement and steadfastness, an indescribably courageous dejection.

At length, the mayor laid down his pen and turned part way around.

"Well, what is it? What's the matter, Javert?"

Javert remained silent a moment as if collecting himself, then raised his voice with a sad solemnity, which did not, however, exclude simplicity: "A criminal act has been committed, Monsieur Mayor."

"What act?"

"A subordinate in the government has been lacking in respect to a magistrate, in the gravest manner. I come, as is my duty, to bring the fact to your attention."

"Who is this subordinate?" asked M. Madeleine.

"I am," said Javert.

"You?"

"Me."

"And who is the magistrate who has cause to complain of this agent?"

"You, Monsieur Mayor."

M. Madeleine straightened up in his chair. Javert continued, with serious looks and eyes still downcast.

"Monsieur Mayor, I come to ask you to be so kind as to make charges and procure my dismissal."

Amazed, M. Madeleine opened his mouth. Javert interrupted him: "You will say that I might tender my resignation, but that is not enough. To resign is honorable; I have done wrong. I ought to be punished. I must be dismissed."

And after a pause he added, "Monsieur Mayor, you were severe to me the other day, unjustly. Be justly so today."

"Oh, indeed! Why? What's all this nonsense? What does it all mean? What is the criminal act committed by you against me? What have you done to me? How have you wronged me? You accuse yourself: Do you wish to be relieved?"

"Dismissed," said Javert.

"Dismissed it is then. It's very odd. I don't understand."

"You will, Monsieur Mayor," Javert sighed deeply, and continued sadly and coldly. "Monsieur Mayor, six weeks ago, after that scene about that girl, I was enraged and I denounced you."

"Denounced me?"

"To the Prefecture of Police at Paris."

M. Madeleine, who did not laugh much more often than Javert, began to laugh: "As a mayor having encroached upon the police?"

"As a former convict."

The mayor's face turned ashen.

Javert, who had not raised his eyes, continued, "I had suspected it. For a long time I had had the idea. A similarity, information you obtained at Faverolles, your immense strength; the affair of old Fauchelevent; your skill as a marksman; your leg that drags a little—and actually I don't know what other stupidities; but at last I took you for a man named Jean Valjean."

"Named what? What is that name?"

"Jean Valjean. He was a convict I saw twenty years ago, when I was a guard of the chain gang at Toulon. After leaving prison, this Valjean, it appears, robbed a bishop's palace, then he committed another robbery with weapon in hand, on a highway, against a little Savoyard chimneysweep. For eight years his whereabouts have been unknown, and a search has been made for him. I imagined—in short, I have done this thing. Anger convinced me, and I denounced you to the prefect."

M. Madeleine, who had taken up the file of papers again, a few moments before, said with a tone of perfect indifference, "And what answer did you get?"

"That I was crazy."

"Well!"

"Well, they were right."

"It is fortunate that you think so!"

"It must be so, for the real Jean Valjean has been found."

The paper that M. Madeleine held fell from his hand; he raised his head, looked steadily at Javert, and said in an inexpressible tone, "Ah!"

Javert continued, "Let me tell you the story, Monsieur Mayor. There was, apparently, in the countryside, near Ailly-le-Haut-Clocher, a simple sort of man called Father Champmathieu. He was very poor. Nobody paid any attention to him. Such people get by, one hardly knows how. Finally, this last fall, Father Champmathieu was arrested for stealing cider apples from—but that's not important. There was a theft, a wall scaled, branches of trees broken. Our Champmathieu was arrested; he still had the branch of an apple tree in his hand. The rogue was locked up. So far, it was nothing more than a correctional matter. But now enters the hand of Providence. Since the jail was in poor condition, the penitentiary justice thought it best to take him to Arras, to the prison of the province. In this prison at Arras there was a former convict named Brevet who is there for some trifle and who, for his good conduct, has been made turnkey. No sooner was Champmathieu brought in than Brevert cried out, 'Ha, ha! I know that man. He's a former convict.'

" 'Look at me, you. You're Jean Valjean.' 'Jean Valjean, who is Jean Valjean?' Champmathieu acts surprised. 'Don't play dumb,' said Brevet. 'You are Jean Valjean; you were in the work gang in Toulon. It is twenty years ago. We were there together.' Champmathieu denied it all. Heavens! You understand; they went into it in depth. The case was investigated and this was what they found. Thirty years ago this Champmathieu was a pruner in various places, particularly in Faverolles. There we lose trace of him. A long time after we find him in Auvergne; then in Paris, where he is said to have been a wheelwright and to have had a daughter—a laundress, but that's not proven, and finally in this part of the country. Now, before going to prison for burglary, what was Jean Valjean? A pruner. Where? At Faverolles. Another fact. This Valjean's baptismal name was Jean; his mother's family name, Mathieu. Nothing could be more natural, on leaving prison, than to take his mother's name for disguise; then he would be called Jean Mathieu. He goes to Auvergne, the pronunciation of that region could make *Chan* of *Jean*—they would call him Chan Mathieu. Our man adopts it, and now you have him transformed into Champmathieu. You follow me, don't you? A search has been made at Faverolles; Jean Valjean's family is no longer there. Nobody knows where they are. You know among those classes such disappearances of families often occur. You search but find nothing. Such people, when they are not mud, are dust. And then as the beginning of this story dates back thirty years, there is nobody now at Faverolles who knew Jean Valjean. But a search has been made in Toulon. Besides Brevet, there are only two convicts who have seen Jean Valjean. They are convicts for life; their names are Cochepaille and Chenildieu. These men were brought from the galleys and confronted with the alleged Champmathieu. They did not hesitate. To them as well as to Brevet it was Jean Valjean. Same age; fifty-four years old; same height; same appearance, in fact the same man; it's him. It was at this time that I sent my denunciation to the Prefecture at Paris. They replied that I was out of my mind, that Jean Valjean was at Arras in the hands of justice. You can imagine how astonished I was, I who believed that I had here the same Jean Valjean. I wrote to the justice; he sent for me and brought Champmathieu before me."

"Well," interrupted M. Madeleine.

Javert replied, with an incorruptible and sad face, "Monsieur Mayor, the truth is the truth. I'm sorry about it, but that man is Jean Valjean. I recognized him, too."

M. Madeleine said in a very low voice, "Are you sure?"

Javert began to laugh with the suppressed laugh indicating profound conviction.

"Oh yes, positive!"

He remained a moment in thought, unconsciously taking up pinches of the powdered wood used to dry ink, from the box on the table, and then added, "And now that I see the real Jean Valjean, I do not understand how I ever could have believed anything else. I beg your pardon, Monsieur Mayor."

In uttering these serious and supplicating words to him, who six weeks before had humiliated him before the entire guard, and had said "You may go!" Javert, this haughty man, was unconsciously filled with simplicity and dignity. M. Madeleine answered his request, by this abrupt question: "And what did the man say?"

"Oh, Lord! Monsieur Mayor, it's an ugly business. If it is Jean Valjean, it is his second offense. To climb a wall, break a branch, and take apples—for a child that's only a trespass; for a man it is a misdemeanor; for a convict it is a crime. Scaling a wall and theft includes everything. It is a case not for a police court but for the superior court. It is not a few days' imprisonment, but life imprisonment. And then there is the affair of the little Savoyard, who will, I hope, be found. Devil take it! That is enough to struggle against, isn't it? It would be for anybody but Jean Valjean. But Jean Valjean is a sly fellow. And that's just where I recognize him. Anybody else would realize he was in hot water, and rant and rave, as the teakettle sings on the fire; he would say that he was not Jean Valjean, et cetera. But this man pretends not to understand; he says, 'I am Champmathieu; I have no more to say.' He puts on a look of surprise; he plays dumb. Oh, that one is cunning! But no matter, the evidence is there. Four people have recognized him, and the old villain will be condemned. It has been taken to the superior court at Arras. I'm going to testify. I've been summoned."

Monsieur Madeleine had turned back to his desk and was quietly looking over his papers, reading and writing alternately, like a man pressed with business. He turned again toward Javert.

"That will do, Javert. Actually, all these details interest me very little. We are wasting time, and we have urgent business. Javert, go at once to the house of the good woman Buseaupied, who sells herbs at the corner of Rue Saint-Saulve; tell her to make her complaint against the carter Pierre Chesnelong. He is a brutal fellow, he almost crushed this woman and her child. He must be punished. Then you will go to Monsieur Charcellay, Rue Montre-de-Champigny. He has complained that when it rains the gutter of the next house pours water onto his house and is undermining the foundation. Then you will inquire into the offenses that have been reported to me, at the widow Doris's, Rue Guibourg, and Madame Renée le Bossé's, Rue du Garraud-Blanc, and make out reports. But I am giving you too much to do. Didn't you tell me that you were going to Arras in eight or ten days on this matter?"

"Sooner than that Monsieur Mayor."

"What day then?"

"I think I told Monsieur that the case would be tried tomorrow, and that I should leave by tonight's stagecoach."

M. Madeleine made an imperceptible gesture.

"And how long will the matter last?"

"One day at most. Sentence will be pronounced at the latest tomorrow evening. But I shall not wait for the sentence, which is certain; as soon as my testimony is given, I'll return."

"Very well," said M. Madeleine.

And he dismissed him with a wave of his hand.

Javert did not go.

"Your pardon, monsieur," said he.

"What more is there?" asked M. Madeleine.

"Monsieur Mayor, there is one thing more to which I desire to call your attention."

"What is it?"

"It is that I ought to be dismissed."

M. Madeleine rose.

"Javert, you are a man of honor and I esteem you. You exaggerate your fault. Besides, this is an offense that concerns only me. You deserve promotion, not disgrace. I want you to keep your job."

Javert looked at M. Madeleine with his calm eyes, in whose depths it seemed that one beheld his conscience, unenlightened, but stern and pure, and said in a tranquil voice: "Monsieur Mayor, I cannot agree to that."

"I repeat," M. Madeleine said, "that this matter concerns only me."

But Javert, with his one idea, continued, "As to exaggerating, I don't exaggerate. This is my reasoning: I unjustly suspected you. That is nothing. It is our job to suspect, although it may be an abuse of our right to suspect our superiors. But without proof and in a fit of anger, with revenge as my aim, I denounced you as a convict—you, a respectable man, a mayor, and a magistrate. This is a serious matter, very serious. I have committed an offense against authority in your person, I, who am the agent of authority. If one of my subordinates had done what I have, I would have pronounced him unworthy of the service, and sent him packing. Well, listen a moment longer, Monsieur Mayor. In my life I have often been severe toward others. It was just. I was right. Now if I were not severe toward myself, all I have justly done would become injustice. Should I spare myself more than others? No. You see! If I had been eager only to punish others and not myself, that would have been despicable! Those who say 'That scoundrel Javert' would be right. Monsieur Mayor, I do not wish you to treat me with kindness. Your kindness, when it was for others, enraged me quite enough; I do not wish it for myself. The kindness that consists of defending a woman of the streets against a citizen, a police agent against the mayor, the inferior against the superior, that is what I call ill-begotten kindness. Such kindness disorganizes society. Good God, it is easy to be kind, the difficulty is to be just. If you had been what I thought, I would not have been kind to you; not I. You would have seen, Monsieur Mayor. I ought to treat myself as I would treat anybody else. When I arrested malefactors, when I dealt severely with offenders, I often said to myself, 'If you ever trip up, if ever I catch you doing wrong, watch out!' I have tripped, I have caught myself doing wrong. So much the worse! I must be sent away, broken, dismissed—that is just. I have hands, I can till the ground. It doesn't matter to me. Monsieur Mayor, the good of the service demands an example. I simply ask the dismissal of Inspector Javert."

All this was said in a tone of proud humility, a desperate and resolute tone, which gave an indescribably bizarre grandeur to this oddly honest man.

"We shall see," said M. Madeleine.

And he held out his hand to him.

Javert started back and said fiercely, "Excuse me, Monsieur Mayor. A mayor does not give his hand to an informer."

He added between his teeth, "Yes, a spy, from the moment I abused the power of my position, I've been no better than a spy!"

Then he bowed deeply and went toward the door.

There he turned around, his eyes still downcast.

"Monsieur Mayor, I will continue in the service until I am replaced."

He went out. Monsieur Madeleine sat musing, listening to the firm resolute step as it died away along the corridor.

Book Seven

THE CHAMPMATHIEU AFFAIR

I

SISTER SIMPLICE

The events that follow were never entirely known at Montreuil-sur-mer. But the few that did leak out have left such memories in that town that it would be a serious omission of this book not to relate them down to the most minute details.

Among these details, the reader will find two or three improbable circumstances, which we preserve out of respect for the truth.

In the afternoon following Javert's visit, M. Madeleine went as usual to see Fantine.

Before going to Fantine's room, he sent for Sister Simplice.

The two nuns attending the infirmary, Lazarists as all these Sisters of Charity are, were called Sister Perpétue and Sister Simplice.

Sister Perpétue was an ordinary village girl who had become in general terms a Sister of Charity; she entered the service of God as she would have entered service anywhere. She was a nun as others are cooks. This type is not very rare. The monastic orders glady accept this heavy peasant clay, easily shaped into a Capuchine or an Ursuline. Such country people are useful for the coarser duties of devotion. There is no shock in the transition from shepherd to Carmelite; the one becomes the other without any huge effort; the common basis of ignorance of a village and a cloister is a ready-made preparation and immediately puts the peasant on an even footing with the monk. Enlarge the smock a little and you have the frock. Sister Perpétue was a stout nun from Marines, near Pontoise, fond of her dialect, psalm singing, and muttering, sugaring a nostrum according to the bigotry or hypocrisy of the patient, treating invalids harshly, rough with the dying, almost dashing God in their faces, belaboring the death agony with angry prayers, bold, honest, and florid.

Sister Simplice was white with a waxen clarity. In contrast to Sister Perpétue she was a sacramental taper by the side of a tallow candle. Saint Vincent de Paul has spiritually portrayed the figure of a Sister of Charity in these admirable words in which he unites so much freedom with so much servitude. "Her only convent shall be the house of sickness; her only cell, a rented room; her chapel the parish church; her cloister the streets of the city, or the wards of the hospital; her only wall obedience; her cloister bars the fear of God; her veil modesty." This ideal was embodied in Sister Simplice. No one could have guessed her age; she had never been young and seemed as if she would never have to be old. As a person—we dare not say a woman—she was gentle, austere, companionable, cold, and she had never told a lie. She was so gentle as to appear fragile; though in fact she was stronger than granite. She touched the unfortunate with charming fingers, delicate and pure. There was, so to speak, silence in her speech; she said just what was necessary, and she had a tone of voice that would have both edified a confessional and enchanted a drawing room. This delicacy adapted itself to the serge dress, finding in its harsh touch a continual reminder of Heaven and God. Let us emphasize one circumstance. Never to have lied, never to have spoken for any purpose whatever, even carelessly, a single word that was not the truth, the sacred truth, was the distinctive trait of Sister Simplice; it was the mark of her virtue. She was almost celebrated in the Community for this imperturbable veracity. The Abbé Sicard speaks of Sister Simplice in a letter to the deaf-mute Massieu. Sincere and pure as we may be, we all have the mark of some little lie on our truthfulness. She had none. A little lie, an innocent lie, can such a thing exist? To lie is the absolute of evil. To lie a little is not possible; whoever lies, lies a whole lie; lying is the very face of the Devil. Satan has two names: He is called Satan, and he is called the Liar. That is what she thought. And as she thought, she practiced. The result was that whiteness we have mentioned, a whiteness whose radiance covered even her lips and eyes. Her smile was white, her look was white. There was not a spider's web, not a speck of dust on the glass of that conscience. When she took the vows of Saint Vincent de Paul she had taken the name of Simplice by special choice. Simplice of Sicily, it is well known, is that saint who preferred to have both her breasts torn off rather than answer, having been born at Syracuse, that she was born at Segesta, a lie that would have saved her. That patron saint was fitting for this soul.

On entering the order, Sister Simplice had two faults that she corrected gradually; she had had a taste for good food and loved to receive letters. Now she read nothing but a prayerbook in large type and in Latin. She did not understand Latin, but she understood the book.

The pious woman had become fond of Fantine, probably sensing in her some latent virtue, and had devoted herself almost exclusively to her care.

M. Madeleine took Sister Simplice aside and commended Fantine to her with an unusual insistence, which the sister remembered later.

On leaving the sister, he went up to Fantine.

Fantine waited each day for M. Madeleine's appearance as one waits for a ray of warmth and joy. She would say to the sisters, "I live only when the mayor is here."

That day she had a high fever. As soon as she saw M. Madeleine, she asked him, "Cosette?"

He answered with a smile, "Very soon."

M. Madeleine seemed just the same as usual with Fantine. Only he stayed an hour instead of half an hour, to Fantine's great satisfaction. He gave a thousand instructions to everybody so the sick woman would lack nothing. It was noticed that at one moment his expression turned very somber. But this was explained when it was known that the doctor had, bending close to his ear, said to him, "She is sinking fast."

Then he returned to the mayor's office, and the office boy saw him attentively examine a road map of France that hung in his room. He jotted a few figures in pencil on a piece of paper.

II

ASTUTENESS OF MASTER SCAUFFLAIRE

From the mayor's office he went to the outskirts of the city, to a Flemish man, Master Scaufflaer, Frenchified into Scaufflaire, who kept horses for hire and "carriages if desired."

To get to Scaufflaire's, the shortest way was by a rarely traveled street, on which was the rectory of the parish in which M. Madeleine lived. The curé was, it was said, a worthy, respectable man and a good counselor. At the moment when M. Madeleine arrived in front of the rectory, there was only one person going by in the street, and he noticed this: The mayor, after passing by the curé's house, stopped, paused a moment, then turned back and retraced his steps as far as the rectory's door, a large door with an iron knocker. He seized the knocker quickly and raised it; then he stopped again, stood a short time as if in thought, and after a few seconds, instead of letting the knocker fall loudly, replaced it gently and resumed his walk with a sort of haste he had not shown before.

M. Madeleine found Master Scaufflaire busy repairing a harness.

"Master Scaufflaire," he asked, "do you have a good horse?"

"Monsieur Mayor," said the Fleming, "all my horses are good. What do you mean by a good horse?"

"I mean a horse that can do sixty miles in a day."

"The devil!" said the Fleming. "Sixty miles!"

"Yes."

"Harnessed to a chaise?"

"Yes."

"And how long will he rest after the journey?"

"He must be able to start again the next day if need be."

"To do the same thing again?"

"Yes."

"The devil! And you say sixty miles?"

M. Madeleine drew from his pocket the paper on which he had penciled the figures. He showed them to the Fleming. They were the figures 15, 18, 26.

"You see," he said."Total, fifty-nine—rounded off, sixty miles."

"Monsieur Mayor," resumed the Fleming, "I have just what you want. My little white horse, you've probably seen him sometimes going by; he is a little animal from the Lower Boulonnais. He's full of fire. They tried at first to make a saddle horse out of him. But no! He kicked; he threw everybody off. They thought he was vicious; they didn't know what to do with him. I bought him. I put him in front of a chaise; Monsieur, that was what he wanted; he's as gentle as a girl, he goes like the wind. But, for example, it won't do to get on his back. He doesn't want to be a saddle horse. Everybody has his own ambition. To pull, yes, to carry, no: He must have said that to himself."

"And he can make the trip?"

"Your sixty miles all the way at full trot, and in less than eight hours. But there are some conditions."

"Name them."

"First, you must let him catch his breath for an hour when you've gone halfway; he'll eat, and somebody must be there while he eats to prevent the tavern boy from stealing his oats; I've noticed that at taverns, oats are more often drained off by stable boys than eaten by horses."

"Somebody will be there."

"Secondly—is the chaise for Monsieur the Mayor?"

"Yes."

"Monsieur the Mayor knows how to drive?"

"Yes."

"Well, Monsieur the Mayor will travel alone and without baggage, so as not to overload the horse."

"Agreed."

"But Monsieur the Mayor, having no one with him, will be obliged to take the trouble of seeing to the oats himself."

"Agreed."

"I must have thirty francs a day, the days he rests

included. Not a penny less, and the animal's fodder at the expense of Monsieur the Mayor."

Monsieur Madeleine took three Napoleons from his purse and laid them on the table.

"There is two days, in advance."

"Fourthly, for such a trip, a chaise would be too heavy; that would tire the horse. Monsieur the Mayor must consent to travel in a little tilbury that I have."

"I consent to that."

"It is light, but it is open."

"It doesn't matter."

"Has Monsieur the Mayor reflected that it is winter?"

M. Madeleine did not answer; the Fleming went on, "That it is very cold?"

M. Madeleine kept silent.

Master Scaufflaire continued, "That it may rain?"

M. Madeleine raised his head and said, "The horse and the tilbury will be in front of my door tomorrow at half-past four in the morning."

"Agreed, Monsieur Mayor," answered Scaufflaire, then scratching a stain on the top of the table with his thumbnail, he went on with the careless air that Flemings know so well how to mix with their astuteness: "Why, I just remembered! Monsieur the Mayor has not told me where he's going. Where is Monsieur the Mayor going?"

He had thought of nothing else since the beginning of the conversation, but without knowing why, he had not dared ask.

"Does your horse have good forelegs?" said M. Madeleine.

"Yes, Monsieur Mayor. You will hold him up a little going downhill. Is there much downhill between here and where you are going?"

"Don't forget to be at my door precisely at half-past four in the morning," answered M. Madeleine, and he went out.

The Fleming was left "dumfounded," as he said himself sometime later.

The mayor had been gone two or three minutes, when the door opened again; it was the mayor.

He had the same impassive and absentminded air as before.

"Monsieur Scaufflaire," he said, "what price would

you estimate for the horse and the tilbury that you are hiring out to me, taking the one with the other?"

"The one pulling the other, Monsieur Mayor," said the Fleming with a loud laugh.

"Whatever. How much?"

"Does Monsieur the Mayor want to buy them?"

"No, but in any event I want to guarantee them to you. On my return you can give me back the amount. What price do you place on the horse and chaise?"

"Five hundred francs, Monsieur Mayor!"

"Here it is."

M. Madeleine placed a banknote on the table, then left and this time did not return.

Master Scaufflaire regretted terribly that he had not said a thousand francs. In fact, the horse and tilbury were worth a hundred crowns.

The Fleming called to his wife and told her about the affair. Where the deuce could the mayor be going? They talked it over. "He's going to Paris," the wife said. "I don't think so," the husband said. Monsieur Madeleine had forgotten the paper on which he had marked the figures, leaving it on the mantel. The Fleming picked it up and studied it. Fifteen, eighteen, twenty-six? This must mean the relay stations of the post. He turned to his wife: "I've figured it out." "How?" "It's fifteen miles from here to Hesdin, eighteen from Hesdin to Saint Pol, twenty-six from Saint Pol to Arras. He is going to Arras."

Meanwhile M. Madeleine had reached home. To return from Master Scaufflaire's he had taken a longer road, as if the door of the rectory were a temptation to him and he wished to avoid it. He went up to his room and shut himself in, which was nothing remarkable, since he usually went to bed early. However, the concierge of the factory, who was also M. Madeleine's only servant, noticed that his light was out at half-past eight, and she mentioned it to the cashier, who came in, adding, "Is Monsieur the Mayor sick? I thought he was behaving somewhat strangely."

The cashier occupied a room right underneath M. Madeleine's. He paid no attention to the concièrge's words, went to bed and right to sleep. Toward midnight he suddenly woke up; in his sleep, he had heard a noise overhead. He listened. It was footsteps going back and forth, as if someone were pacing in the room above. He listened more attentively and recognized M. Madeleine's footstep. That seemed strange to him; ordinarily no noise at all emanated from M. Madeleine's room before he got up. A moment later, the cashier heard something that sounded like the opening and shutting of a cupboard, then a piece of furniture was moved, another silence, and the footsteps began again. The cashier sat up in bed, woke all the way up, looked out, and through his windowpanes saw on an opposite wall the reddish reflection of a lighted window. From the direction of the rays, it could only be the window of M. Madeleine's room. The reflection trembled as though coming from a bright fire rather than from a candle. The cashier could not see the shadow of the sash, indicating that the window was wide open. Because it was so cold out, this open window was surprising. The cashier fell asleep again. An hour or two later he woke up again. The same footsteps, slow and regular, were going back and forth constantly over his head.

The reflection was still visible on the wall, but it was now pale and steady like the light of a lamp or candle. The window was still open.

Let us see what was happening in M. Madeleine's room.

III

A TEMPEST WITHIN A BRAIN

The reader has undoubtedly guessed that M. Madeleine is none other than Jean Valjean.

We have already looked into the depths of that conscience; the time has come to look there again. We do so not without emotion and trepidation. There is nothing more terrifying than this kind of contemplation. Nowhere can the mind's eye find anything more dazzling or more obscure than in man; it can focus on nothing more awe-inspiring, more complex, more mysterious, or more infinite. There is one spectacle greater than the sea: That is the sky; there is one spectacle greater than the sky: That is the interior of the soul.

To write the poem of the human conscience, if only of one man, even the most insignificant man, would be to swallow up all epics in a superior and definitive epic. The conscience is the chaos of chimeras, lusts, and temptations, the furnace of dreams, the cave of the ideas that shame us; it is the pandemonium of sophisms, the battlefield of the passions. At certain moments, penetrate the ashen face of a human being who is thinking and look at what lies behind; look into that soul, look into that obscurity. There, beneath the external silence, giants are doing battle as in Homer, melées of dragons and hydras, and clouds of phantoms as in Milton, ghostly spirals as in Dante. Such gloom enfolds that infinity which each man bears within himself and by which he measures in despair the desires of his will and the actions of his life!

One day Alighieri found himself hesitating in front of an ominous door. Here is one now facing us, on whose threshold we hesitate. Let us enter nonetheless.

We have little to add to what the reader already knows concerning what had happened to Jean Valjean since his adventure with Petit Gervais. From that moment on, as we have seen, he was a different man. What the bishop had wished for him, he had carried out. It was more than a transformation—it was a transfiguration.

He succeeded in disappearing from sight, sold the bishop's silver, keeping only the candlesticks as souvenirs, quietly slipped from city to city across France, came to Montreuil-sur-mer, had the idea we have described, accomplished what we have related, succeeded in making himself unassailable and inaccessible, and, finally established at Montreul-sur-mer, happy to feel his conscience saddened by his past and the last half of his existence giving the lie to the first, he lived peaceably, reassured and hopeful, with two remaining thoughts: to conceal his name, and to sanctify his life; to escape from men and to return to God.

These two thoughts were so closely associated in his mind that they fused into one; both were equally absorbing and imperious and ruled his smallest actions. Ordinarily they harmonized in regulating the conduct of his life; they turned him toward the dark side of life; they made him benevolent and simplehearted; they counseled him to the same things. Sometimes, however, there was a conflict between them. In such cases, it will be remembered, the man, whom the countryside around Montreuil-sur-mer called M. Madeleine, did not waver in sacrificing the first to the second, his security to his virtue. Thus, despite all reserve and all prudence, he had kept the bishop's candlesticks, worn mourning for him, called and questioned all of the little Savoyard chimneysweeps who passed through, gathered information about families in Faverolles, and saved the life of old Fauchelevent, in spite of Javert's disquieting insinuations. It would seem, as we have already noted, that he thought, following the example of all who have been wise, holy, and just, that his highest duty was not toward himself.

In any event, it must be said, nothing like the present occasion had ever occurred. Never had the two ideas that governed the unfortunate man whose sufferings we are relating come into so serious a conflict. He understood this confusedly, but thoroughly, from the first words that Javert had pronounced on entering his office. At the moment when that name he had so deeply buried was so strangely uttered, he was dazed, and as if stunned by the sinister grotesqueness of his destiny, and through that stupor he felt the shudder that precedes great shocks; he bent like an oak before a storm, like a soldier before an attack. He felt clouds of thunder and lightning gathering above his head. Even while listening to Javert, his first thought was to go, to run, to give himself up, to drag this Champmathieu out of prison, and go back in his place; it was as painful and poignant as an incision into living flesh, but faded away, and he said to himself, "Let's see! Let's see!" He repressed the first generous impulse and recoiled before such heroism.

Undoubtedly it would have been splendid if, after the holy words of the bishop, after so many years of repentance and self-denial, in the midst of a penitence so admirably begun, even in the presence of so terrible a conflict, he had not faltered an instant, had continued to march on steadily toward that yawning precipice at whose far end was heaven; this way would have been fine, but it was not the case. We must describe what was taking place in that soul, and we can relate only what was there. What first took over was the instinct of self-preservation; he hastily rallied his thoughts, stifled his emotions, took into consideration Javert's presence, the great danger, postponed any decision with the steadiness of terror, put out of his mind all consideration of the course he should pursue, and resumed his calm as a gladiator picks up his shield.

For the rest of the day he was in this state, tempest within, perfect calm without; he took only what might be called precautionary measures. Everything was still confused and colliding in his brain; the agitation there was such that he did not distinctly see any idea; and he could not have said a thing about himself, unless it were that he had just received a terrible blow. As usual he went to Fantine's bedside and prolonged his visit, by instinctive kindness, saying to himself that he ought to do so, and to commend her earnestly to the sisters, in case he should have to be absent. He vaguely felt that it would perhaps be necessary for him to go to Arras; and without having in the least decided on this journey, he said to himself that, entirely free from suspicion as he was, there would be no disadvantage to being a witness to what might occur, and he hired Scaufflaire's tilbury in order to be prepared for any emergency.

He ate dinner with a reasonable appetite.

Returning to his room he collected his thoughts.

He examined the situation and found it unprecedented; so unprecedented that in the midst of his reverie, by some strange impulse of almost inexplicable anxiety, he rose from his chair and bolted his door. He feared something more might enter. He was barricading himself against all possibilities.

A moment later he blew out his candle. It bothered him.

It seemed to him that somebody could see him.

Who?

Alas! What he wanted to keep outside had come in, what he wanted to blind was looking at him. His conscience.

His conscience, or God.

At first, however, he deluded himself; he had a feeling of safety and solitude; with the bolt drawn, he believed himself impregnable; with the light out, he felt invisible. Then he took possession of himself; he placed his elbows on the table, rested his head on his hand, and began his meditations in the darkness.

"Where am I? Am I dreaming? What have I heard? Is it really true that I saw this Javert, and that he talked to me this way? Who can this Champmathieu be? So he looks like me, does he? Is that possible? When I think that yesterday I was so calm, and so far from suspecting anything! What was I doing yesterday at this time? What does this incident mean? How will it turn out? What can I do?"

This was his torment. His brain had lost the power to retain its ideas; they went by like waves, and he grasped his forehead with both hands to stop them.

Out of this tumult, which overwhelmed his will and his reason, and from which he tried to draw a certainty and a resolution, nothing emerged but anguish.

His brain was burning. He went to the window and threw it wide open. There was not one star in the sky. He went back and sat down by the table.

The first hour rolled by this way.

Little by little, however, vague outlines began to take shape and hold fast in his meditations; he could perceive, with the precision of reality, not the whole of the situation, but a few details.

He began by recognizing that, however extraordinary and critical the situation was, he was completely the master of it.

His daze only deepened.

Independently of the severe and religious aim of his actions, everything he had done up to now was merely a hole he was digging in which to bury his name. What he had always most dreaded, in his hours of self-communion, in his sleepless nights, was the thought of ever hearing that name pronounced; he felt that would be the end of everything for him; that the day on which that name reappeared, his new life would vanish from around him, and, who knows, even perhaps his new soul from within him. He shuddered at the mere thought. Surely, if anyone had told him then that an hour would come when the hideous name would resound in his ear, when Jean Valjean would suddenly emerge from the night and stand before him, when the shocking glare destined to dissipate his enveloping mystery would suddenly gleam above his head, and that this name would not menace him, and the glare would only deepen his obscurity, that this rending of the veil would increase the mystery, that this earthquake would consolidate his structure, that this prodigious event would have no other result, if it seemed good to him, to himself alone, than to make his existence both more brilliant and more impenetrable, and that, from his encounter with the phantom of Jean Valjean, the good and worthy citizen M. Madeleine would come forth more honored, more peaceful, and more respected than ever—if anyone had said this to him, he would have shaken his head and taken the words as nonsense. Well, precisely that had happened; the whole accumulation of the impossible was now a fact, and God had permitted these absurdities to become real things!

His musings continued to grow clearer. He was getting a better and better understanding of his position.

It seemed as though he had just awakened from some strange sleep and found himself sliding down a slope in the middle of the night, on his feet, shivering, recoiling in vain, on the very brink of an abyss. In the gloom he distinctly saw an unknown man, a stranger, whom fate had mistaken for him and was shoving into the gulf in his place. For the gulf to be closed, someone had to fall in, he or the other.

All he had to do was leave things alone.

The clarity became total, and he recognized this: That his place in prison was empty, that do what he could it was always awaiting him, that robbing Petit Gervais sent him back there, that this empty place would await him and attract him until he returned there, that this was his inevitable fate. And then he said to himself: At this very moment he had a substitute, that a man named Champmathieu had that bad luck, and that as for himself, present hereafter in the person of this Champmathieu, present in society under the name of M. Madeleine, he had nothing to fear, provided he did not prevent men from sealing over the head of this Champmathieu the stone of infamy that, like the stone of the sepulcher, falls once never to rise again.

All this was so violent and strange that he suddenly felt the sort of indescribable inner movement no man experiences more than two or three times in his life, a sort of convulsion of the conscience that stirs up everything dubious in the heart, which is composed of irony, joy, and despair, and which might be called a burst of inner laughter.

He hastily relit his candle.

"Well, then!" he said, "what am I afraid of? Why am

I pondering these things? Now I'm safe. It's all over. There was only a single half-open door through which my past could invade my life; that door is now walled up! Forever! This Javert who has troubled me so long, that fearful instinct which seemed to have guessed the truth, that had guessed it, in fact, and that followed me everywhere, that terrible bloodhound always trailing me, he is thrown off the track, busy elsewhere, absolutely baffled. He is satisfied, he will leave me in peace, he caught his Jean Valjean! Who knows, he will probably even want to leave the city! And all this accomplished without me. And I had nothing to do with it! Ah, yes, but what misfortune is there in all this? People seeing me truly would think that some catastrophe had happened to me! After all, if any harm has been done to anybody, it is in no way my fault. Providence has done it all. This is what He apparently wants. Have I the right to change what He arranges? What am I asking for now? Why would I interfere? It doesn't concern me. I'm not satisfied! But what do I need? The goal I have been aiming at for so many years, my nightly dream, the object of my prayers to heaven—security—I have gained. It is God's will. I must do nothing contrary to the will of God. And why is it God's will? So I may carry on what I have begun, so I may do good, may one day be a great and encouraging example, so it may be said that there was finally some happy result from this suffering I have undergone and this virtue to which I have returned! Really I don't understand why I was so afraid of going to the honest curé and confessing the whole story and asking his advice; this is clearly what he would have said to me. It is decided. Leave the matter alone! Let's not interfere with God."

This is the way he debated in the depths of his conscience, hanging over what might be called his own abyss. He rose from his chair and began to pace the room. "Come on," he said, "let's forget it. The decision is made!' " But he felt no joy.

Quite the contrary.

One can no more keep the mind from returning to an idea than the sea from returning to a shore. For the sailor, this is called the tide; in the case of the guilty, it is called remorse. God stirs up the soul as well as the ocean.

After a few moments, despite all efforts, he returned to this somber dialogue, in which it was he who spoke and he who listened, saying what he wanted to stifle, listening to what he did not wish to hear, yielding to the mysterious power that said to him, "Think!" as it said two thousand years ago to another condemned man, "Walk!"

Before going on, and to be quite clear, we should emphasize one point.

Certainly we talk to ourselves; there is no thinking being who has not experienced that. One could even say that the word is never a more magnificent mystery than when, within a man, it travels from his thought to his conscience and returns from his conscience to his thought. This is the only sense of the words, so often used in this chapter, "he said," "he exclaimed"; we say to ourselves, we speak to ourselves, we exclaim within ourselves, without breaking the external silence. There is great tumult within; everything within us speaks, except the tongue. The realities of the soul, though not visible and palpable, are nonetheless realities.

So he asked himself what point he had reached, he questioned this decision. He confessed to himself that everything he had been arranging in his mind was monstrous, that to let the matter alone, not to interfere with God, was simply horrible, to let this mistake of fate and men be accomplished, not to prevent it, to lend himself to it by his silence, to do nothing, was ultimately to do everything! It was the last degree of hypocritical wrong! It was a base, cowardly, lying, abject, hideous crime!

For the first time in eight years, the unhappy man had just tasted the bitter flavor of a wicked thought and a wicked action.

He spit it out with disgust.

He continued questioning himself, sternly asking what he had meant by this: "My goal is achieved." He told himself that his life did truly have a goal. But what goal? To conceal his name? To deceive the police? Was it for so petty a thing that he had done all he had done? Had he no other goal, the great one, the true one? To save, not his body, but his soul. To become honest and good again. To be an upright man! Was not that above all, that alone, what he had always wanted, and what the bishop had urged? To close the door on his past? But he was not closing it, great God! He was reopening it by committing a vile act! He would be a robber again, and the most despicable of robbers! He was robbing another man of his existence, his life, his peace, his place in the world, he would be a murderer in a moral sense; he was killing a miserable man, inflicting on him that terrible living death, that live burial called prison! On the contrary, to give himself up, to save this man stricken by so ghastly a mistake, to reassume his name, becoming again out of duty the convict Jean Valjean; that was really the way to his resurrection, to closing forever the hell from which he had emerged! To fall back into it in appearance was in reality to emerge! He must do that! All he had done was nothing, if he did not do that! His whole life was useless, his suffering lost. He could only ask, "What is the use?" He felt the bishop's presence all the more since he had died, that the bishop was staring at him, that henceforth Mayor Madeleine with all his virtues would be abominable to him, and the convict Jean Valjean would be splendid and pure in his sight. That men could see his mask, but the bishop saw his face. That men saw his life, but the bishop saw his conscience. So he had to go to Arras, save the false Jean Valjean, turn in the true one. Alas! That was the greatest sacrifice, the most poignant victory, the final step to be taken, but he had to do it. Painful fate! He could only enter into holiness in God's eyes, by returning to infamy in men's!

"Well," he said, "let's take this course—do our duty! Let's save this man!"

He said these words without noticing that he was speaking aloud.

He took his books, checked them, and put them in order. He threw in the fire a package of notes he held against needy small traders. He wrote a letter, which he sealed, and on the envelope of which might have been read, if there had been anyone in the room at the time: Monsieur Laffitte, banker, Rue d'Artois, Paris.

From a desk he took a billfold containing some banknotes and the passport he had used that same year in going to the elections.

Anyone seeing him going through these various motions so pensively and seriously would not have suspected what was going on inside him. Still, at times his lips quivered; at others he raised his head and stared at some point on the wall, as if he saw just there something he wanted to clear up or question.

The letter to M. Laffitte finished, he put it in his pocket as well as the billfold, and began to pace again.

His thought had not varied. He still saw his duty clearly written in luminous letters flaring out before his eyes and moving with his gaze: "*Go! Give thy name! Denounce thyself!*"

He also saw, as if they were laid bare before him in palpable forms, the two ideas that up to then had been the double rule of his life, to conceal his name and to sanctify his soul. For the first time, they appeared absolutely distinct, and he saw the difference separating them. He recognized that one of these ideas was necessarily good, while the other might become evil; that the former was devotion, and the latter selfishness; that the one said, "neighbor," and the other said, "me"; that the one came from light, and the other from night.

They were fighting with each other. He saw them fighting. While he watched, they had expanded before his mind's eye; they were now colossal; and he seemed to see struggling within him, in that infinity of which we spoke just now, in the midst of darkness and gloom, a goddess and a giantess.

He was horrified, but it seemed that the good thought was gaining the upper hand.

He felt he had reached the second decisive movement of his conscience and his destiny; that the bishop had marked the first phase of his new life, and that this Champmathieu marked the second. After the great crisis, the great trial.

Meanwhile the fever, calmed for an instant, gradually returned. A thousand thoughts flashed through him, but they strengthened his determination.

One moment he had said that perhaps he took the matter too seriously, that after all this Champmathieu was not interesting, that in fact he had committed a theft.

He answered, If this man has in fact stolen a few apples, that is a month in prison. There is a wide distance between that and years in chains. And who even knows? Has he committed a theft? Is it proven? The name of Jean Valjean overpowers him and seems to dispense with proofs. Don't prosecuting officers habitually act this way? They think he is a robber because they know he is a convict.

At another moment the idea occurred to him that, if he should turn himself in, perhaps the heroism of his action, and his honest life for the past seven years, and what he had done for the region, would be considered, and he would be pardoned.

But this notion quickly vanished, and he smiled bitterly at the thought that the robbery of the forty sous from Petit Gervais made him a second offender, that that matter would certainly reappear, and by the precise terms of the law he would be condemned to hard labor for life.

He turned away from all illusion, became more and more detached from the earth, and sought consolation and strength elsewhere. He said to himself that he must do his duty; that perhaps he should not be more unhappy after having done his duty than after having evaded it; that if he let matters alone, if he stayed at Montreuil-sur-mer, his reputation, his good name, his good works, the deference, the veneration he commanded, his charity, his riches, his popularity, his virtue, would be tainted with a crime, and what pleasure would there be in all these holy things tied to that hideous thing? Whereas, if he carried out the sacrifice, in prison, with his chain, his iron collar, his green cap, his perpetual labor, his pitiless shame, they would be consecrated.

Finally, he said to himself that it was necessity, that his destiny was so fixed, that it was not for him to derange the arrangements of God, that in any event he must choose; either public virtue and private abomination or private sanctity and public infamy.

In examining so many gloomy ideas, his courage did not fail, but his brain was fatigued. He began unconsciously to think of other things, of unimportant things.

His temples throbbed. He paced back and forth incessantly. Midnight struck first from the parish church, then from the city hall. He counted the twelve strokes of the two clocks and compared the sound of the two bells. It reminded him that, a few days before, he had seen in a junkshop an old bell for sale, inscribed with this name: Antoine Albin de Romainville.

He was cold. He lit a small fire. He did not think to close the window.

Meanwhile he had fallen into his daze again. It took no little effort to recall what he was thinking of before the clock struck. At last he succeeded.

"Ah! Yes," he said, "I had resolved to turn myself in."

And then all at once he thought of Fantine.

"But wait!" he said. "That poor woman!"

Here was a new crisis.

Abruptly appearing in his reverie, Fantine was like a ray of unexpected light. It seemed to him that everything around him changed; he exclaimed, "Ah! Yes, indeed! So far I have only been thinking of myself! I have only considered my own convenience! Whether I should keep silent or denounce myself—conceal my body or save my soul—be a despicable and respected magistrate, or an infamous and venerable convict: It is myself, always myself, myself alone. But, good God! All this egotism. Different forms of egotism, but still egotism! Suppose I should think a little of others? The highest duty is to think of others. Let's see, let's examine! I'm gone, taken away, forgotten; what will become of all this? I turn myself in? I'm arrested, this Champmathieu is released, I'm sent back to the chain gang; very well, and what then? What happens here? Ah! Here, there is a district, a city, factories, a business, laborers, men, women, old grandfathers, children, poor people! I have created all this, I keep it all alive; wherever a chimney is smoking, I have put the fuel in the fire and the meat in the pot; I have produced comfort, circulation, credit; before me there was nothing; I have aroused, enlivened, animated, quickened, stimulated, enriched, the whole region; without me, the soul is gone. I take myself away; it all dies—and this woman who has suffered so much, who is so virtuous in her catastrophe, whose misfortunes I have unconsciously caused! And that child I wanted to bring here, whom I have promised to the mother! Don't I owe something to this woman too, in reparation for the wrong I have done her? If I should disappear, what happens? The mother dies. The child becomes whatever she may. This is what happens if I turn myself in; and if I do not reveal myself? Let's see, if I don't reveal myself?"

After asking this question, he stopped; for a moment he hesitated and shuddered; but the moment was brief, and he answered calmly, "Well, this man goes to the galleys, it's true, but, so what? He stole! It's useless for me to say he didn't, he did! As for me, I stay here, I go on. In ten years I'll have made ten millions; I scatter it over the countryside, I keep nothing for myself; what is it to me? What I am doing is not for myself. Everyone's prosperity goes on increasing, industry is quickened and grows, factories and workshops multiply, families—a hundred families, a thousand families—are happy; the population grows; villages spring up where there were only farms, farms spring up where there was nothing; poverty disappears, and with poverty disappear debauchery, prostituion, theft, murder, all vices, all crimes! And the poor mother raises her child! And the whole country is rich and honest! Yes! How foolish, how absurd I was! How could I think of turning myself in? This certainly demands reflection, and nothing can be hurried. Because it would have pleased me to do the grand and generous thing! After all that's very melodramatic! Because I was only thinking of myself, of myself alone, wasn't I? To save a thief from punishment perhaps a little too severe, but in reality fair, nobody knows who, an odd one at any rate. Must an entire countryside be destroyed? Must a poor unlucky woman die in the hospital! Must a poor little girl die on the street! Like dogs! Ah! That would be abominable! And the mother not even see her child again! And the child hardly knowing her mother! And all for this miserable old thief, who, beyond all doubt, deserves the chain gang for something else, if not for this. Fine scruples that save an old tramp who has, after all, only a few years to live, and who will hardly be more unhappy in prison than in his hovel, but sacrifice a whole population, mothers, wives, children! This poor little Cosette who has no one in the world but me, and who is undoubtedly at this very moment blue with cold in the Thénardiers' hovel! They too are miserable people! And I would fail in my duty toward all those poor humans! And I should go away and reveal myself? And I should commit this stupid blunder! Take it at the very worst. Suppose there were a fault for me in this, and that my conscience should someday reproach me; for the good of others, the acceptance of these reproaches that weigh only on me, of this fault that affects only my own soul—why, that is devotion, that is virtue."

He rose and resumed his pacing. This time it seemed to him he was satisfied.

Diamonds are found only in the dark bowels of the earth; truths are found only in the depths of thought. It seemed to him that after descending into those depths, after long groping in the blackest of this darkness, he had at last found one of these diamonds, one of these truths, and that he held it in his hand; and it blinded him to look at it.

"Yes," he thought, "that's it! I am on the road to truth. I have the solution. I must ultimately hold on to something. My choice is made. Let the matter rest! No more vacillation, no more shrinking. This is in the interests of all, not in my own. I am Madeleine, I remain Madeleine. Woe to him who is Jean Valjean! He and I are no longer the same. I do not recognize that man, I no longer know what he is; if it happens that someone is Jean Valjean now, let him fend for himself. It does not concern me. That is a deadly name floating in the dark; if it stops and settles on any man, so much the worse for him."

He looked at himself in the little mirror hanging over his mantelpiece and said, "Yes! Reaching a decision has comforted me! I am quite another man now!"

He took a few steps more, then he stopped short.

"That's it!" he said. "I must not hesitate before any of the consequences of the decision I have reached. There are still some threads that bind me to this Jean Valjean. They must be broken! In this very room, there are objects that still accuse me, silent things that would be witnesses; they must all disappear."

He felt in his pocket, drew out his purse, opened it, and took out a little key.

He put this key into a lock whose hole was scarcely visible, lost as it was in the darkest shading of the figures on the paper covering the wall. A secret door opened; a kind of false cupboard built between the corner of the wall and the chimney casing. There was nothing in this closet but a few trifles; a yellow smock, an old pair of trousers, an old knapsack, and a large thorn stick, iron-tipped at both ends. Those who had seen Jean Valjean when he passed through Digne in October 1815 would easily have recognized all the remnants of his miserable outfit.

He had kept them, as he had kept the silver candlesticks, to remind him at all times of what he had been. But he concealed what came from prison, and left out in plain sight the candlesticks that came from the bishop.

He cast a furtive look toward the door, as if fearing it would open in spite of the bolt that held it; then with a quick and hasty gesture, and at a single armful, without even glancing at these things he had kept so religiously and at great peril over so many years, he took it all—rags, stick, knapsack—and threw it onto the fire.

He shut up the secret compartment and, increasing his precautions, useless from then on, since it was empty, concealed the door behind a heavy piece of furniture he pushed against it.

In a few seconds, the room and the wall opposite were lit up with a great red flickering glare. Everything was burning; the thorn stick cracked and threw out sparks into the middle of the room.

The knapsack, as it was consumed with the hideous rags it contained, left something uncovered which glistened in the ashes. By bending down to it, one could easily have recognized a piece of silver. It was undoubtedly the forty-sous piece stolen from the little Savoyard.

But he did not look at the fire; he continued walking to and fro, always at the same pace.

Suddenly his eyes fell on the two silver candlesticks on the mantel, which were glistening dimly in the reflection.

"Wait!" he thought, "all of Jean Valjean is contained in them, too. They too must be destroyed."

He took the two candlesticks.

There was enough fire to melt them quickly into an unrecognizable ingot. He bent over the fire and warmed himself for a moment. It felt really comfortable to him. "Such good warmth!" he said.

He stirred the embers with one of the candlesticks.

A minute more, and they would have been in the fire.

At that moment, it seemed to him that he heard a voice crying within him, "Jean Valjean! Jean Valjean!"

His hair stood on end; he was like a man hearing something terrible.

"Yes! That's it, finish the work!" said the voice. "Complete what you are doing! Destroy these candlesticks! Annihilate this memorial! Forget the bishop! Forget everything! Ruin this Champmathieu! Go on, that's it! Pat yourself on the back! So it's arranged, it's decided, it's done. There is a man, an old graybeard who doesn't know what he's accused of, who has done nothing, maybe, an innocent man, whose misfortune is caused by your name, upon whom your name weighs like a crime, who will be taken instead of you, and be condemned, will end his days in misery and horror! Very well. Be an honored man yourself. Remain, Monsieur Mayor, remain honorable and honored, enrich the city, feed the poor, bring up the orphans, live happily, virtuous and admired, and all this time while you are here in joy and in light, there will be a man wearing your red tunic, bearing your name in ignominy, and dragging your chain in the work gang! Yes! This is a perfect arrangement! Oh, misery!"

The sweat rolled off his forehead. He looked at the candlesticks with haggard eyes. Meanwhile the voice that spoke within him was not finished. It continued, "Jean Valjean! Around you there will be many voices that will make a great noise, that will speak very loud and bless you; and one alone that nobody will hear that will curse you in the darkness. Well, listen, wretch! All these blessings will fall before they reach Heaven; only the curse will climb up into the presence of God!"

This voice, at first quite feeble, which rose from the most obscure depths of his conscience, had gradually become horrendous, and he heard it now shouting into his ear. It seemed to him it had emerged from himself and was now speaking from the outside. The last words he heard seemed so distinct that he looked around the room with a kind of terror.

"Is anybody here?" he asked, aloud, startled.

Then he went on with a laugh like the laugh of an idiot, "That's stupid! No one could be here."

There was One; but He who was there no human eye can see.

He put the candlesticks on the mantel.

Then he resumed the monotonous, dismal pacing that disturbed the man asleep below in his dreams and wakened him out of his sleep.

This walk soothed and excited him at the same time. It sometimes seems that on most momentous occasions we put ourselves in motion in order to ask advice from whatever we might meet on the way. After a few moments he no longer knew where he was.

He now recoiled with equal horror from each of the resolutions he had formed. Each of the two ideas confronting him appeared to him as doomed as the other. What a destiny! What a bizarre coincidence that this

Champmathieu was mistaken for him! To be hurled down headlong by the very means Providence first seemed to have used for his affirmation.

For a moment he contemplated the future. Denounce himself, great God! Give himself up! With infinite despair he saw all he would have to leave, all he must take up again. He would bid farewell to this existence, so good, so pure, so radiant; to this universal respect, to honor, to liberty! No more would he go out to walk in the fields, never again would he hear the birds singing in the month of May, never give alms to the little children! No longer would he feel the sweet looks of gratitude and love! He would leave this house that he had built, this little room! Everything looked charming to him now. Never again would he read these books, write on this little white wooden table! His old concierge, the only servant he had, would no longer bring him his coffee in the morning. Great God! Instead of that, the work gang, the iron collar, the red shirt, the chain on his ankle, exhaustion, the dungeon, the plankbed, all these familiar horrors! At his age, after having been what he was! If only he were still young! But so old, to be insulted by the first comer, to be manhandled by the prison guard, struck by the jailer's stick! To have his bare feet in iron-bound shoes! Morning and evening to submit his leg to the hammer of the watchman who tests the chains! To endure the curiosity of strangers, who would be told, "This one is the famous Jean Valjean, who was once mayor of Montreuil-sur-mer!" At night, dripping with sweat, overwhelmed with weariness, the green cap over his eyes, climbing two by two, under the sergeant's whip, the ship's ladder of the floating prison. Oh, what misery! Can fate then be malign like an intelligent being and turn monstrous like the human heart?

And whatever he did, he always fell back onto this paradox at the core of his thought. To remain in paradise and become a demon! To re-enter hell and become an angel!

What should he do, great God! What should he do?

The torment from which he had emerged with so much difficulty, broke loose anew inside him. His ideas again began to turn confused. They took that indescribable, dazed and mechanical form peculiar to despair. The name of Romainville returned constantly to his mind, with two lines of a song he had once heard. He reflected that Romainville is a little woods near Paris where young lovers go to gather lilacs in April.

He tottered, physically as well as within. He walked like a little child just left to walk on its own.

Now and then, struggling against his fatigue, he made an effort to rouse his intellect. He tried to state, finally and conclusively, the problem over which he had in some sense fallen exhausted. Must he reveal himself? Must he be silent? He could see nothing distinctly. The vague forms of all the reasonings thrown out by his mind trembled and dissolved one after another in smoke. But this much he felt, that whichever decision he might make, necessarily and with no possibility of escape, something of himself would surely die; that he was entering a sepulcher to the right and left; that he was suffering a death agony, the death agony of his happiness or the death agony of his virtue.

Alas! All his irresolutions were on him again. He was no further forward than when he began.

In this way, his unhappy soul struggled with its anguish. Eighteen hundred years before this unfortunate man, the mysterious Being, in whom all the sanctities and all the sufferings of humanity come together, He too, while the olive trees trembled in the fierce breath of the Infinite, had brushed away the fearful cup that appeared before him, streaming with shadow and running over with darkness, in the star-filled depths.

IV

FORMS ASSUMED BY SUFFERING DURING SLEEP

The clock struck three. For five hours he had been pacing this way, almost without interruption, when he dropped into his chair.

He fell asleep and dreamed.

This dream, like most dreams, bore no relation to the situation beyond its mournful poignant character, but it made an impression on him. This nightmare struck him so forcibly that he afterward wrote it down. It is one of the papers in his own handwriting that he left behind. We think we should copy it here word for word.

Whatever this dream may mean, the story of that night would be incomplete if we were to omit it. It is the gloomy adventure of a sick soul.

It is as follows: On the envelope we find this line: "*The dream I had that night.*"

"I was in a field. A vast, grassless, sad field. It did not seem to be day or night.

"I was walking with my brother, the brother of my childhood; this brother of whom I must admit I never think and whom I scarcely remember.

"We were talking, and we met others who were walking. We were speaking of a former neighbor, who, because she lived by the street, always worked with her window open. Even while we talked, we felt cold because of that open window.

"There were no trees in the field.

"We saw a man passing nearby. He was entirely naked, ashen-colored, riding a horse the color of earth. The man was hairless; we saw his skull and the veins in his skull. He was holding a stick that was limber, like a twig of grape vine, and heavy as iron. This horseman passed by and said nothing.

"My brother said to me, 'Let's take the deserted road.'

"There was a narrow, deep-cut road where we saw not a bush or even a sprig of moss. All was earth colored, even the sky. A few steps farther, and no one answered me when I spoke. I noticed that my brother was no longer with me.

"I entered a village that I saw. I thought that it must be Romainville (why Romainville?).[1]

"The first street I entered was deserted. I turned into a second street. At the corner of the two streets a man was standing against the wall. I said to him, 'What is this place? Where am I?' He did not answer. I saw the open door of a house; I went in.

"The first room was deserted. I went into the second.

[1] This parenthesis is in the hand of Jean Valjean [V.H.].

Behind the door of this room a man was standing against the wall. I asked him, 'Whose house is this? Where am I?' The man did not answer. The house had a garden.

"I went out of the house and into the garden. The garden was deserted. I found a man standing behind the first tree. I said to this man, 'What is this garden? Where am I?' The man did not answer.

"I wandered through the village, and I realized it was a city. All the streets were deserted, all the doors were open. No living being was going by in the streets or moving in the rooms or walking in the gardens. But behind every turn of a wall, behind every door, behind everything, there was a man standing in silence. Only one could ever be seen at a time. These men looked at me as I passed by.

"I left the city and began to walk in the fields.

"After a while, I turned and I saw a great crowd following me. I recognized all the men I had seen in the city. Their heads were strange. They did not seem to be hurrying, and yet they walked faster than I. They made no sound as they walked. Suddenly, this crowd came up and surrounded me. Their faces were earth-colored.

"Then the first one I had seen and questioned as I entered the city said to me, 'Where are you going? Don't you know you've been dead for a long time?'

"I opened my mouth to answer, and I realized no one was there."

He woke up. He was freezing. A wind as cold as the morning wind swung the open sashes of the window on their hinges. The fire had gone out. The candle was low in the socket. The night was still dark.

He got up and went to the window. There were still no stars in the sky. From his window he could look into the courtyard and street. A harsh, rattling noise suddenly resounding from the ground made him look down.

Below him he saw two red stars, whose rays danced back and forth grotesquely in the shadows.

His mind was still half submerged in the midst of his dream. "Of course," he thought, "there are none in the sky. Now they're on earth."

This confusion, however, faded away; a second noise like the first awakened him completely; he looked and realized that these two stars were the lamps of a carriage.

By their light he could make out the shape of a carriage. It was a tilbury drawn by a small white horse. The noise he had heard was the sound of the horse's hoofs on the paving stones.

"What is that carriage?" he said to himself. "Who could be coming so early?"

At that moment there was a soft tap at the door of his room.

He shuddered from head to foot and called out harshly, "Who's there?"

Someone asnwered, "Me, Monsieur Mayor."

He recognized the voice of the old woman, his concièrge.

"Well," he said, "what is it?"

"Monsieur Mayor, it is exactly five o'clock."

"And so?"

"Monsieur Mayor, it is the coach."

"What coach?"

"The tilbury."

"What tilbury?"

"Didn't Monsieur Mayor order a tilbury?"

"No," he said.

"The driver says that he has come for Monsieur Mayor."

"What driver?"

"Monsieur Scaufflaire's driver."

"Monsieur Scaufflaire?"

That name startled him as if lightning had flashed in front of his face.

"Oh, yes!" he said. "Monsieur Scaufflaire!"

If the old woman had seen him at that moment she would have been frightened.

There was a long silence. He gazed confusedly at the candle flame, took some of the melted wax from around the wick, and rolled it between his fingers. The old woman was waiting. She spoke up again: "Monsieur Mayor, what shall I say?"

"Say I'm coming down."

V

STICKS IN THE SPOKES

The postal service from Arras to Montreuil-sur-mer was still carried out at that time by little mail wagons dating from the Empire. These wagons were two-wheeled cabriolets, lined with buckskin, hung on jointed springs, with only two seats, one for the driver, the other for the passenger. The wheels were armed with those long threatening hubs that keep other vehicles at a distance, still seen on German roads. The letters were carried in a huge oblong box placed behind the cabriolet and forming a part of it. This box was painted black and the cabriolet yellow.

These vehicles, unlike any in use today, were indescribably misshapen and clumsy, and, when seen from a distance crawling along some road against the horizon, they were like those insects, termites, I think, whose slender forequarters drag along a heavy rear section. They went, however, very fast. The mails that left Arras every night at one, after the arrival of the mail courier from Paris, arrived at Montreuil-sur-mer a little before five in the morning.

That night coming down to Montreuil-sur-mer by the road from Hesdin, the mail wagon, taking a corner as it was entering the city, ran into a little tilbury drawn by a white horse, which was going in the opposite direction and in which there was only one person, a man wrapped in a cloak. The wheel of the tilbury was hit severely. The courier cried out to the man to stop, but the traveler did not listen and kept on his way at a rapid trot.

"There is a man in a devil of a hurry!" said the courier.

The man in such a hurry was the one we have seen struggling in such pitiable internal debate.

Where was he going? He couldn't have said. Why was he in a hurry? He didn't know. He was going forward as chance dictated. Where? To Arras, no doubt; but perhaps he was going somewhere else, too. At moments he suspected so and shuddered at the thought. He was plunging into the dark as into a yawning gulf. Something was pushing him, something drew him on. What ever was going on inside him, no one could describe, but everyone will understand. Who has not entered, at least once in his lifetime, this dark cavern of the unknown?

But he had resolved nothing, decided nothing, determined nothing, done nothing. None of the acts of his conscience had been final. More than ever he was just as he had been at the start.

Why was he going to Arras?

He repeated what he had already said to himself when he hired Scaufflaire's cabriolet, that, whatever the outcome, there could be no objection to seeing with his own eyes and judging the case for himself; that it was in fact a sound idea, that he ought to know what happened; that he could decide nothing without having observed and analyzed; that from a distance we make every little thing seem like a mountain; that after all, when he had seen this Champmathieu, some poor wretch, his conscience would be fully reconciled to letting him go to prison in his place; that it was true Javert would be there, and Brevet, Chenildieu, Cochepaille, old convicts who had known him, but would surely not recognize him; what an idea! that Javert was a hundred miles off track; that all conjecture and supposition were trained on Champmathieu, and that nothing is so stubborn as supposition and conjecture; that there was, therefore, no danger.

That it was undoubtedly a dark hour, but that he would get through it; that after all he held his fate, evil as it might chance to be, in his own hands; that he was master of it. He clung to that thought.

In fact, to tell the truth, he would have preferred not to go to Arras.

Still, he was on the way.

Although absorbed in thought, he whipped his horse, which raced along at that regular, sure, full trot that covers eight miles an hour.

As the tilbury went forward, he felt something within him holding back.

At daybreak he was in the open country; the town of Montreuil-sur-mer was a long way behind. He saw the horizon growing lighter; without seeing them, he watched all the frozen forms of a winter dawn pass before his eyes. As much as evening, morning has its ghosts, too. He did not see them, but unconsciously, and by an almost physical kind of penetration, those black outlines of trees and hills added to the turmoil of his soul an indescribable gloom and apprehension.

Every time he passed one of the isolated houses by the side of the road, he said to himself, "And yet, there are people asleep inside!"

The trotting of the horse, the rattling of the harness, the wheels on the paving stones, made a gentle, monotonous sound. These things are charming when a person is joyful, but mournful when one is sad.

It was daylight when he arrived at Hesdin. He stopped in front of an inn to let his horse catch his breath and to give him some oats.

The horse was, as Scaufflaire had said, of that small breed from Le Boulonnais, which has too much head, too much belly, and not enough neck, but with a broad chest, a large rump, fine and slender legs, and a firm foot; a homely breed; but strong and sound. The admirable animal had gone fifteen miles in two hours and was as fresh as at the start.

He did not get out of the tilbury. The stable boy stooped down suddenly and examined the left wheel.

"Are you going to go far like this?" asked the boy.

He answered, almost without breaking up his train of thought, "Why?"

"Have you come far?" the groom went on.

"Fifteen miles from here."

"Ah!"

"Why do you say ah?"

The boy stooped down again, was silent for a moment, with his eyes fixed on the wheel, then he rose up saying, "Well, to think that this wheel has just come fifteen miles, that's possible, but it's sure it won't go another half a mile."

He sprang down from the tilbury. "What do you mean, my friend?"

"I mean that it's a miracle you've come fifteen miles without taking a spill, into some ditch along the way, you and your horse. Look for yourself."

The wheel in fact was badly damaged. The collision with the mail wagon had broken two spokes and loosened the hub so the nut was no longer holding.

"My friend," he said to the stable boy, "is there a wheelwright around here?"

"Certainly, monsieur."

"Would you do me the favor of going to get him."

"There he is, right here. Oh, Master Bourgaillard!"

Master Bourgaillard the wheelwright was on his own doorstep. He came over and examined the wheel, with the grimace of a surgeon studying a broken leg.

"Can you mend that wheel on the spot?"

"Yes, monsieur."

"When can I start again?"

"Tomorrow!"

"Tomorrow!"

"It is a good day's work. Is monsieur in a hurry?"

"A great hurry. I must leave in an hour at the latest."

"Impossible, monsieur."

"I will pay whatever you like."

"Impossible.'"

"Well! in two hours."

"Impossible today. There are two spokes and a hub to be repaired. Monsieur cannot start again before tomorrow."

"My business cannot wait till tomorrow. Instead of mending this wheel, can't it be replaced?"

"How do you mean?"

"You are a wheelwright?"

"Certainly, monsieur."

"Don't you have a wheel you can sell to me? I could start away at once.

"A wheel to exchange?"

"Yes."

"I have no wheel made for your cabriolet. Two wheels make a pair. Two wheels don't go together by chance."

"In that case, sell me a pair of wheels."

"Monsieur, not every wheel fits on every axle."

"Just try."

"It's no use, monsieur. I have only cartwheels. It's a small place here."

"Can you rent me a cabriolet?"

The wheelwright, at the first glance, had seen that the tilbury was a hired vehicle. He shrugged his shoulders.

"Fine care you take of the cabriolets you rent! I'd have one a good long while before I'd let you take it."

"Well, sell it to me."

"I don't have one."

"What! Not even a carriole? I'm not hard to please, as you can see."

"This is a small town. True, under the old shed there," added the wheelwright, "I have an old chaise belonging to a neighbor in town, who has me keep it, and who uses it every 29th of February. I'd rent it to you, of course, it's nothing to me. But the owner mustn't see it go by; and then, it's clumsy; it would take two horses."

"I'll take two post-horses."

"Where is monsieur going?"

"To Arras."

"And monsieur would like to get there today?"

"I would."

"By taking post-horses?"

"Why not?"

"Would monsieur agree to getting there around four tomorrow morning?"

"No, indeed."

"I mean, you see, there's something I'd have to say about taking post-horses. Monsieur has his passport?"

"Yes."

"Well, by taking post-horses, monsieur will not reach Arras before tomorrow. We're on a side road. The relays are poorly supplied, the horses are in the fields. The ploughing season has just begun; heavy teams are needed, and the horses are taken from everywhere, including the post. Monsieur will have to wait at least three or four hours at each relay, and then they go at a walk. There are a good many hills to climb."

"Well, I'll go on horseback. Unhitch the cabriolet. Somebody nearby can surely sell me a saddle."

"Certainly, but can you saddle this horse?"

"True, I'd forgotten, you can't."

"Then—"

"But in the village I can surely find a horse for hire?"

"A horse to go to Arras without stopping?"

"Yes."

"It would take a better horse than what there is around here. You would have to buy him too, since nobody knows you. But neither to sell nor to hire, neither for five hundred francs nor a thousand, will you find such an animal."

"What should I do?"

"The best thing to do, in this case I tell you honestly,

is for me to repair the wheel and for you to continue your journey tomorrow."

"Tomorrow will be too late."

"Damn!"

"Isn't there a mail wagon going to Arras? When does it go by?"

"Tonight. Both mails make the trip at night, the up mail as well as the down."

"And—you need a whole day to repair a wheel?"

"A whole day, and a long one!"

"If you put two workmen on it?"

"If I put ten."

"If you lashed the spokes with cords?"

"The spokes I could, but not the hub. And the rim is in bad condition, too."

"Isn't there a livery stable in town?"

"No."

"Is there another wheelwright?"

The stable boy and the wheelwright answered at the same time, with a shake of the head—"No."

He felt an immense joy.

It was clear that Providence was involved. It was Providence that had broken the wheel of the tilbury and stopped him on his way. He had not given in to the first obstacle; he had just exerted all possible efforts to continue his journey; he had faithfully and scrupulously exhausted every means; he had shrunk from neither the weather nor fatigue nor expense; there was no reason to reproach himself. If he went no step farther, it no longer concerned him. Now it was not his fault; it was not the act of his conscience but the act of Providence.

He took a breath. He breathed freely and deeply for the first time since Javert's visit. It seemed to him that the iron hand that had gripped his heart for twenty hours had just relaxed.

It seemed that now God was for him, God was clearly on his side.

He said to himself he had done all he could and now he had only to retrace his steps, calmly.

If his conversation with the wheelwright had taken place in a room of the inn, it would have had no witnesses, nobody would have heard it, the matter would have rested there, and it is probable that we should not have had to relate any of the events to follow, but the conversation took place in the street. Any discussion in the street inevitably gathers a crowd. There are always people who ask nothing better than to be spectators. While he was questioning the wheelwright, some of the passersby had stopped around them. After listening for a few minutes, a young boy whom no one had noticed separated from the group and ran off.

As the traveler, after the internal deliberation we have just indicated, was making up his mind to go back, this boy returned. He was accompanied by an old woman.

"Monsieur," said the woman, "my boy tells me you're anxious to rent a cabriolet."

This simple speech, uttered by an old woman brought there by a boy, made the sweat stream down his back. He imagined he saw the hand from which he was just freed reappear in the shadow behind him, ready to seize him again.

He answered, "Yes, madame, I'm looking for a cabriolet."

And he was quck to add, "But there is none available."

"Yes, there is," the woman said.

"Where?" the wheelwright interrupted.

"At my house," she replied.

He shuddered. The fatal hand had closed on him again.

The old woman did have, in fact, under a shed, a sort of willow carriole. The blacksmith and the boy at the inn, irritated that the traveler might escape them, intervened.

"It was a frightful go-cart, it had no springs, it was true the seat was held up by leather straps, it would not keep out the rain, the wheels were rusty and rotten, it couldn't go much further than the tilbury, a real rattletrap! This gentleman would be unwise to use it," etc., etc.

This was all true, but this go-cart, this rattletrap, this thing, whatever it might be, could stand on its own two wheels and could go to Arras.

He paid what was asked, left the tilbury to be mended at the blacksmith's against his return, had the white horse harnessed to the carriole, got in, and continued the route he had been following since morning.

The moment the carriole started, he acknowledged that an instant earlier he had felt a certain joy at not being able to go where he was heading. He examined that joy with a kind of anger, and thought it absurd. Why should he feel joy at going back? After all, he was making a journey of his own accord. Nobody was forcing him into it. And certainly, nothing could happen that he did not choose to have happen.

As he was leaving Hesdin, he heard a voice crying out, "Stop! Stop!" He stopped the carriole with a hasty movement, in which there was still something strangely feverish and convulsive that resembled hope.

It was the woman's little boy.

"Monsieur," said he, "it was I who got the carriole for you."

"Well!"

"You haven't given me anything."

He, who gave to all, and so freely, felt this claim was exorbitant and almost odious.

"Oh! It's you, beggar!" he said. "Nothing for you!"

He whipped up the horse and started away at a quick trot.

He had lost a good deal of time at Hesdin and wished to make it up. The little horse was plucky, and pulled enough for two; but it was February, it had rained, the roads were bad. And then, it was no longer the tilbury. The carriole ran hard and was very heavy. And besides there were many steep hills.

He took almost four hours to go from Hesdin to Saint Pol. Four hours for eighteen miles.

At Saint Pol he drove to the nearest inn and had the horse taken to the stable. As he had promised Scaufflaire, he stood by while the horse was eating. He was thinking sad and confused thoughts.

The innkeeper's wife came into the stable.

"Wouldn't monsieur like some lunch?"

"Why, that's true," he said. "I'm actually very hungry."

He followed the woman, who had a fresh and pleasant face. She led him into a low hall, where there were some tables covered with oilcloth.

"Please hurry," he said, "I have to start off again. I am in a hurry."

A big Flemish servant girl waited on him rapidly. He looked at the girl with a feeling of well-being.

"This is what was the matter," he thought. "I hadn't eaten breakfast."

His breakfast was served. He seized the bread, bit a

piece, then slowly put it back on the table, and did not touch anything more.

A teamster was eating at another table. He said to this man, "Why is their bread so bitter?"

The teamster was German and did not understand him. He returned to the stable and his horse.

An hour later he had left Saint Pol and was driving toward Tinques, which is only fifteen miles from Arras.

What was he doing during the trip? What was he thinking about? As he had during the morning, he watched the trees go by, the thatched roofs, the cultivated fields, and the dissolving views of the countryside that change at every turn of the road. Scenes like that are sometimes enough for the soul, and almost eliminate the need for thought. To see a thousand objects for the first and last time, what could be more profoundly melancholy? Traveling is a constant birth and death. It may be that in the murkiest part of his mind, he was drawing a comparison between these changing horizons and human existence. All aspects of life are in perpetual flight before us. Darkness and light alternate: after a flash, an eclipse; we look, we hurry, we stretch out our hands to seize what is passing; every event is a turn in the road; and suddenly we are old. We feel a slight shock, everything is black, we can make out a dark door, the gloomy horse of life that was carrying us stops, and we see a veiled and unknown form that turns him out into the darkness.

Twilight was falling just as the children coming out of school saw the traveler entering Tinques. The days were still short. He did not stop at Tinques. As he was driving out of the village, a man who was repairing the road raised his head and said, "Your horse is very tired."

In fact, the poor animal was not moving faster than a walk.

"Are you going to Arras?" added the road mender.

"Yes."

"At this rate, you won't get there soon."

He stopped his horse and asked the worker, "How far is it from here to Arras?"

"A good twenty miles."

"How can that be? The map book only shows sixteen."

"Ah!" replied the workman, "then you don't know the

road is being repaired. You'll find it cut off a quarter of an hour from here. No way to go on."

"Really!"

"You'll take the left, the road to Carency, and cross the river; when you reach Camblin, you'll turn to the right; that's the road from Mont Saint-Eloy to Arras."

"But it's dark, I'll lose my way."

"You don't come from around here?"

"No."

"Besides, they are all country roads. Look, monsieur," the road mender went on, "d'you want some advice? Your horse is tired; go back to Tinques. There is a good inn there. Sleep there. You can go on to Arras tomorrow."

"I have to be there tonight—this evening!"

"That changes it. Then go back all the same to that inn, and take an extra horse. The boy that'll go with the horse can guide you through the crossroads."

He followed the man's advice, retraced his steps, and a half hour later he passed the same place, but at a full trot, with a good extra horse. A stable boy, who called himself a postilion, was sitting on the shaft of the carriole.

He felt, however, that he was losing time. It was now quite dark.

They turned onto the shortcut. The road conditions became awful. The carriole tumbled from one rut to the next. He said to the postilion, "Keep up a trot and you'll get double the tip."

In one of the jolts the whiffletree broke.

"Monsieur," said the postilion, "the whiffletree is broken; I don't know how to harness my horse now, this road is very bad at night, if you'll turn back and stay at Tinques, we can be at Arras early tomorrow morning."

He answered, "Do you have a piece of string and a knife?"

"Yes, monsieur."

He cut off a branch and made a whiffletree out of it.

This caused another twenty-minute loss, but they started off at a gallop.

The plain was dark. A low fog, thick and black, was creeping over the hilltops and drifting away like smoke. There were glimmering flashes in the clouds. A strong wind, coming from the sea, sounded all around the horizon like someone moving furniture. Everything seemed brushed with terror. How things shudder under the vast breath of night!

The cold penetrated him. He had not eaten since the evening before. He vaguely recalled his other night adventure in the great plain near Digne, eight years before; and it seemed like yesterday to him.

Some distant bell struck the hour. He asked the boy, "What time is that?"

"Seven o'clock, monsieur; we'll be in Arras at eight. We've got only nine miles to go."

At this moment he thought for the first time, and it seemed strange it had not occurred to him sooner, that perhaps all the trouble he was taking might be useless; that he did not even know the time of the trial; that he should at least have found that out; that it was foolish to be going on at this rate, without knowing whether it would be of any use. Then he made some mental calculations; that ordinarily the sessions of the superior court began at nine in the morning; that this case would not take long; the theft of some apples would go very quickly; that there would be nothing but a question of identity; four or five witnesses and a little to be said by the lawyers —that he would get there after it was all over!

The postilion whipped up the horses. They had crossed the river and left Mont Saint-Eloy behind.

The night grew darker and darker.

VI

SISTER SIMPLICE PUT TO THE TEST

Meanwhile, at that very moment, Fantine was in ecstasies.

She had spent a very bad night. Terrible cough, elevated fever; she had had nightmares. In the morning, when the doctor came, she was delirious. He appeared alarmed and asked to be informed as soon as M. Madeleine arrived.

All morning she was in low spirits, spoke little and

folded tucks in the sheets, whispering some calculations that seemed to be distances. Her eyes were sunken and staring. Their light seemed almost gone, but then, at moments, they would light up and gleam like stars. It seems as though at the approach of a certain dark hour, the light of heaven fills those who are leaving the light of earth.

Whenever Sister Simplice asked her how she was, she answered invariably, "Well, thank you, but I would like to see Monsieur Madeleine."

A few months earlier, when Fantine had lost the last of her modesty, her last shame, and her last happiness, she was a shadow of herself; now she was a ghost of herself. Physical suffering had completed the work of moral suffering. This creature of twenty-five had a wrinkled forehead, flabby cheeks, pinched nostrils, shriveled gums, a leaden complexion, a bony neck, protruding collarbones, emaciated limbs, dun-colored skin, and her fair hair was mixed with gray. How illness mimics old age.

At noon the doctor came again, left a few prescriptions, inquired if the mayor had been to the infirmary, and shook his head.

M. Madeleine usually came at three o'clock to see the sick woman. Since promptness is kindness, he was always prompt.

At about half-past two, Fantine grew restless. In the space of twenty minutes, she asked the nun more than ten times, "Sister, what time is it?"

The clock struck three. At the third stroke, Fantine rose up in bed—ordinarily she could hardly turn over—she joined her two shrunken yellow hands in a sort of convulsive clasp, and the nun heard rising from her one of those deep sighs that seem to lift a great weight. Then Fantine turned and looked toward the door.

Nobody came in; the door did not open.

She sat this way for a quarter of an hour, her eyes fixed on the door, motionless, and as if holding her breath. The sister did not dare to speak. The church clock struck the quarter. Fantine fell back on her pillow.

She said nothing, and again began folding tucks in the sheet.

A half hour passed, then an hour, but no one came; every time the clock struck, Fantine sat up and looked toward the door, then she fell back.

Her thoughts could be clearly seen, but she spoke no

name, she did not complain, she found no fault. She only coughed mournfully. One would have said that something dark was settling down upon her. She was ashen, and her lips were blue. At times she smiled.

The clock struck five. Then the sister heard her speak very softly and gently: "But since I am going away tomorrow, he is wrong not to come today!"

Sister Simplice herself was surprised at M. Madeleine's delay.

Meanwhile, Fantine was looking up at the canopy of her bed. She seemed to be trying to recall something. All at once she began to sing in a voice faint as a whisper. The nun listened.

Nous achèterons de bien belles choses
En nous promenant le long des faubourgs.

Les bleuets sont bleus, les roses sont roses,
Les bleuets sont bleus, j'aime mes amours.

La vierge Marie auprès de mon poêle
Est venue heir en manteau brodé;
Et m'a dit:—Voici, caché sous mon voile,
Le petit qu'un jour tu m'as demandé.
Courez à la ville, ayez de la toile,
Achetez du fil, achetez un dé.
  Nous achèterons de bien belles choses
  En nous promenant le long des faubourgs.

Bonne sainte Vierge, auprès de mon poêle
J'ai mis un berceau de rubans orné;
Dieu me donnerait sa plus belle étoile,
J'aime mieux l'enfant que tu m'as donné.
Madame, que faire avec cette toile?
Faites en trousseau pour mon nouveau-né.
  Les bleuets sont bleus, les roses sont roses,
  Les bleuets sont bleus, j'aime mes amours.

Lavez cette toile.—Où?—Dans la rivière.
Faites-en, sans rien gâter ni salir,
Une belle jupe avec sa brassière
Que je veux broder et de fleurs emplir.
  L'enfant n'est plus là, madame, qu'en faire?
  Faites-en un drap pour m'ensevelir.

Nous achèterous de bien belles choses
En nous promenant le long des faubourgs.

Les bleuets sont bleus, les roses sont roses,
Les bleuets sont bleus, j'aime mes amours.[1]

It was an old lullaby with which she had sung her little Cosette to sleep, and which she had forgotten during the five years since she had lost her child. She sang it in a voice so sad, and to a melody so sweet, that it made even the nun weep. The sister, accustomed to discipline as she was, felt a tear on her cheek.

The clock struck six. Fantine did not seem to hear. She appeared not to be paying attention to anything around her.

Sister Simplice sent a girl to ask of the concierge if the

[1] We'll buy some lovely little things,
Strolling on the avenue.

Violets are blue, and roses are red,
Violets are blue, and my love is true.

The Virgin Mary came to my room
Yesterday in an embroidered cloak
And told me: "Here beneath my veil
Is the baby you once asked me for."
"Run to town, get fine linen,
Buy some thread and a thimble too."
We'll buy some lovely little things,
Strolling on the avenue.

Good holy Virgin, by my bed
I've put a cradle draped with ribbons;
If God gave me his fairest star,
I'd love the child you gave me all the more.
"Madame, what shall we do with this linen?"
"Make a trousseau for my baby."
Violets are blue, and roses are red,
Violets are blue, and my love is true.

Launder this linen. "Where?" Down by the river.
Make it a skirt, without spoiling or soiling,
A pretty, long skirt, with its own linen vest,
Which I'll embroider and fill up with flowers.
"The child is gone, madame, what more can we do?"
"Make it a shroud for burying me."

We'll buy some lovely little things
Strolling on the avenue.
Violets are blue, and roses are red,
Violets are blue, and my love is true.

mayor had come in, and if he could come to the infirmary very soon. The girl returned in a few minutes.

Fantine was still motionless and seemed absorbed in thought.

In a whisper the servant told Sister Simplice that the mayor had gone away that morning before six in a little tilbury drawn by a white horse, cold as the weather was; that he had gone alone, without even a driver, that no one knew what route he had taken, that some said he had been seen turning off on the road to Arras, that others were sure they had met him on the road to Paris. That when he went away he seemed, as usual, very kind, and that he simply told the concièrge that he need not be expected that night.

While the two women were whispering with their backs turned to Fantine's bed, the sister questioning, the servant conjecturing, Fantine, with that feverish vivacity common to some organic diseases, which mingles the free movement of health with the frightful exhaustion of death, had risen to her knees on the bed, her shriveled hands resting on the bolster, and with her head peeking through the opening of the curtains, she listened. All at once she exclaimed, "You're talking about Monsieur Madeleine! Why are you talking so softly? What has he done? Why doesn't he come?"

Her voice was so hoarse and rough that the two women felt they were hearing a man's voice; frightened, they turned toward her.

"Why don't you answer?" cried Fantine.

The servant stammered, "The concièrge told me he could not come today."

"My child," said the sister, "be calm, lie down again."

Without changing her position, Fantine went on in a loud voice, and in a tone at once piercing and imperious, "He can't come. Why not? You know the reason. You were whispering it there between you. I want to know."

The servant whispered quickly in the nun's ear, "Answer that he is busy with the City Council."

Sister Simplice blushed slightly; it was a lie that the servant had proposed to her. On the other hand, it did seem to her that to tell the truth to the sick woman would surely be a terrible blow, and that it was dangerous in Fantine's state. The blush did not last long. The sister turned her calm, sad eyes on Fantine, and said, "The mayor has gone away."

Fantine sprang up and sat on her feet. Her eyes sparkled. A marvelous joy spread over that mournful face.

"Gone away!" she exclaimed. "He has gone for Cosette!"

Then she stretched her hands toward heaven, and the expression on her face became indescribable. Her lips moved; she was praying in a whisper.

When her prayer was ended, "My sister," she said, "I'm quite willing to lie down again, I'll do whatever you say; I was wrong just now, pardon me for having talked so loud; it's bad to talk so loud; I know it, my good sister, but you see I'm so happy. God is kind, Monsieur Madeleine is good; just think of it, that he has gone to Montfermeil for my little Cosette."

She lay down again, helped the nun to arrange the pillow, and kissed a little silver cross she wore at her neck and which Sister Simplice had given her.

"My child," said the sister, "try to rest now, and don't talk anymore."

Fantine took the sister's hand between hers; the sister was sorry to feel that they were moist.

"He started this morning for Paris. In fact he needn't even go through Paris. Montfermeil is a little to the left as you come. You remember what he said yesterday, when I spoke to him about Cosette: 'Very soon, very soon!' He wanted to surprise me. You know, he had me sign a letter to take her away from the Thénardiers. They'll have nothing to say, will they? They'll give up Cosette. Because they've been paid. The authorities wouldn't let them keep a child when they're paid. My sister, don't ask me not to talk. I'm so happy, I'm doing very well. I have no pain at all, I'm going to see Cosette again, I'm even hungry. It's been almost five years since I last saw her. You do not, you cannot imagine what a hold children have on you! And then she'll be so sweet, you'll see! If you only knew what pretty little rosy fingers she has! She'll have very beautiful hands. At a year old she had ridiculous hands—like this! She must be tall now. She's seven, a little lady. I call her Cosette, but her name is Euphrasie. Now, this morning I was looking at the dust on the mantel, and it gave me the idea that I'd see Cosette again very soon! Oh, dear! How wrong to go for years without seeing one's children! We ought to remember that life is not eternal! Oh! How good the mayor is to go. Is it true, that it's very cold? Did he have his cloak, at least? He'll be here tomorrow, won't he? That will make tomorrow a holiday. Tomorrow morning, my sister, remind me to put on my lace cap. Montfermeil is a country place. I made the trip on foot once. It was a long way for me. But the stagecoaches go very fast. He'll be here tomorrow with Cosette! How far is it from here to Montfermeil?"

The sister, who had no notion of distances, answered, "Oh! I feel sure he'll be here tomorrow."

"Tomorrow! Tomorrow!" Fantine said. "I'll see Cosette tomorrow! See, good Sister of God, I'm well now. I feel wild; I'd dance, if anyone asked me."

Anyone who had seen her a quarter of an hour before would not have believed this. Now she was all rosy; she was talking in a lively, natural tone; her whole face was a smile. At times she laughed, whispering to herself. A mother's joy is almost like a child's.

"Well," the nun continued, "now you're happy, obey me—don't talk anymore."

Fantine laid her head upon the pillow, and said softly, "Yes, lie down again; be good now that you're going to have your child back. Sister Simplice is right. Everyone here is right."

And then, without moving, or turning her head, she began gazing all around with eyes wide open and a cheerful look, and she said no more.

The sister closed the curtains, hoping she would sleep.

Between seven and eight o'clock the doctor came. Hearing no sound, he supposed that Fantine was asleep, went in softly, and up to the bed on tiptoe. He drew open the curtains, and by the glow of the night light he saw Fantine's large eyes gazing up at him calmly.

She said to him, "Monsieur, you will let her lie by my side in a little bed, won't you?"

The doctor thought she was delirious. She added, "Look, there is just room."

The doctor took Sister Simplice aside, who explained the matter to him, that with M. Madeleine away somewhere for a day or two, they had thought it best not to enlighten the sick woman, who believed the mayor had gone to Montfermeil; that it was possible, after all, that she had guessed correctly. The doctor approved of this.

He returned to Fantine's bed, and she went on. "Then you see, in the morning, when she wakes up, I can say good morning to the poor kitten; and at night, when I'm awake, I can hear her sleep. Her gentle breathing is so sweet it will do me good."

"Give me your hand," said the doctor.

She reached out her hand, with a laugh.

"Oh, of course! It's true you don't know that I am cured. Cosette is coming tomorrow."

The doctor was surprised. She was better. Her breathlessness was gone. Her pulse was stronger. A sort of new life was suddenly reviving this poor exhausted being.

"Doctor," she asked, "has the sister told you that Monsieur the Mayor has gone for my little kitten?"

The doctor recommended quiet, and that she avoid all painful emotion. He prescribed an infusion of pure quinine, and, in case the fever should return in the night, a soothing potion. In leaving he said to the sister, "She is better. If by some good fortune the mayor really should come back tomorrow with the child, who knows? Some crises are so strange. We've seen diseases instantly cured by great joy; I know very well that this is an organic disease, and far advanced, but it is all a mystery! Perhaps we will save her!"

VII

THE TRAVELER ARRIVES AND PROVIDES FOR HIS RETURN

It was nearly eight in the evening when the carriole that we left on its way drove into the yard of the Hotel de la Poste at Arras. The man whom we have followed thus far got out, answered the greetings of the inn's people absentmindedly, sent back the extra horse, and took the little white one to the stable himself; then he opened the door of a billiard room on the first floor, took a seat, and leaned his elbows on the table. He had spent fourteen hours on this trip, which he had expected to make in six. He did himself the justice of feeling that it was not his fault, but basically he was not sorry about the delay.

The landlady entered. "Will monsieur have a bed? Will monsieur have supper?"

He shook his head.

"The stable boy says that monsieur's horse is very tired!"

Here he broke his silence. "Won't the horse be able to start again tomorrow morning?"

"Oh, monsieur! He needs at least two days' rest."

He asked, "Is the post office near?"

"Yes, sir."

The landlady took him to the post office; he showed his passport and asked if there were some way to return that same night to Montreuil sur-mer by mail coach; only one seat was vacant, beside the driver; he reserved and paid for it. "Monsieur," said the booking clerk, "don't fail to be here ready to start at precisely one o'clock in the morning."

This done, he left the hotel and began to walk around the city.

He did not know Arras, the streets were dark, and he walked aimlessly. Nevertheless, he seemed to refrain stubbornly from asking his way. He crossed the little Crinchon River and found himself in a labyrinth of narrow streets, where he was soon lost. A resident came by with a lantern. After some hesitation, he decided to speak to this man, but not until he had looked around furtively, as if afraid somebody might overhear the question he was about to ask.

"Monsieur," he said, "where is the courthouse, if you please?"

"You're a stranger here, monsieur?" said the citizen, a rather old man. "Well, follow me, I'm going right by the courthouse, the city hall that is. They're repairing the courthouse, so the courts are sitting at the city hall, temporarily."

"Does the superior court sit there?" he asked.

"Certainly, monsieur; you see, what is the city hall today was the bishop's palace before the revolution. Monsieur de Conzié, who was bishop in 'eighty-two, had a large hall built. The court is held in that hall."

As they walked along, the citizen said to him, "If Monsieur wants to see a trial, he is rather late. Usually the sessions end at six o'clock."

However, when they reached the great square, the citizen showed him four long lighted windows on the front of a vast dark building.

"Just look, monsieur, you're still in time: you are lucky. D'you see those four windows? That's the superior court. The lights are still burning. So they haven't finished. The case must have dragged on and they're having an evening session. Are you interested in this case? Is it a criminal trial? Are you a witness?"

He answered: "I have not come on business; I simply wish to speak to a lawyer."

"That's different," said the citizen. "Look, monsieur, here's the door. The doorkeeper is up there. You only have to go up the main stairway."

He followed the citizen's instructions, and in a few minutes found himself in a crowded hall with scattered groups of lawyers in their robes whispering.

It is always chilling to see these clumps of men in black, talking among themselves in low voices on the threshold of the courtrooms. There is seldom any charity or pity in their words. What are more often heard are sentences pronounced in advance. To a passing observer all the groups seem like so many gloomy hives where buzzing spirits are building in common all sorts of dark structures.

The hall, which, though spacious, was lit by a single lamp, was a former hall of the bishop's palace, and served as a waiting room. A double paneled door, now closed, separated it from the large room in which the superior court was in session.

The darkness was such that he had no fear in addressing the first lawyer he met.

"Monsieur," he said, "how are they coming along?"

"It's finished," said the lawyer.

"Finished!"

The word was said in such a tone that the lawyer turned around.

"Pardon me, monsieur, are you a relative, by any chance?"

"No. I don't know anyone here. And was there a sentence?"

"Of course. It could hardly have been otherwise."

"To hard labor?"

"For life."

He continued in a voice so faint that it could scarcely be heard, "So the identity was established?"

"What identity?" the lawyer responded. "There was no identity to be established. It was a simple matter. The woman had killed her child, the infanticide was proved, the jury discounted the possibility of any premeditation; she was sentenced for life."

"It's a woman, then?" he said.

"Certainly. The girl from Limoges. What else did you mean?"

"Nothing, but if it's finsihed, why is the hall still lit up?"

"The other case, which began about two hours ago."

"What other case?"

"Oh! That's a clear-cut one, too. A sort of thief, a second offender, a convict, a case of robbery. I forget his name. He really looks like a bandit. For his face alone, I'd send him to prison."

"Monsieur," he asked. "is there any way to get into the hall?"

"I don't really think so. There's a large crowd. However, they are taking a recess. Some people have come out, and when the session resumes, you could try."

"How do you get in?"

"Through that large door."

The lawyer left him. Within a few seconds, he had felt almost simultaneously, almost mingled, all possible emotions. The words of this disinterested man had alternately pierced his heart like icicles and fiery blades. When he learned that it was not over, he drew a deeper breath, but he could not have said whether it was from satisfaction or pain.

He approached several groups and listened to their conversation. The calendar of the term being very heavy, the judge had set down two short, simple cases for that day. They had begun with the infanticide, and were now on the convict, the second offender, an old man who had stolen some apples, but that did not appear to be very well proved; what was proved was that he had already been in prison at Toulon. This was what ruined his case. His interrogation was over, and the testimony of the witnesses had been given, but there were still to come the argument of the counsel and the summing up of the prosecuting attorney; it would hardly be finished before midnight. The man would probably be condemned; the prosecuting attorney was very good, and never failed with his defendants; he was a talented fellow who wrote poetry.

A bailiff stood near the door opening into the courtroom. He asked this officer, "Monsieur, will the door be opened soon?"

"It will not be opened," said the officer.

"What do you mean! It won't be opened when the session resumes? Isn't there a recess?"

"The session has just resumed," answered the bailiff, "but the door will not be opened again."

"Why not?"

"Because the hall is full."

"What! There are no more seats?"

"Not a one. The door is closed. No one can enter."

After a pause the officer added, "There are in fact two or three places still behind Monsieur the Judge, but Monsieur the Judge admits no one but public functionaries to them."

So saying, the officer turned his back.

The stranger went off with his eyes to the ground, crossed the antechamber, and walked slowly down the staircase, seeming to hesitate at every step. He was probably holding counsel with himself. The violent combat that had been going on inside him since the previous evening was not over; and with every passing moment, he fell upon some new twist. When he reached the stairway landing, he leaned against the railing and folded his arms. Suddenly he opened his coat, drew out his billfold, took out a pencil, tore off a sheet, and by the light of the single lamp rapidly wrote this line: "Monsieur Madeleine, Mayor of Montreuil-sur-mer"; then he went upstairs again rapidly, passed through the crowd, walked straight to the bailiff, handed him the paper, and said to him with authority, "Hand this to Monsieur the Judge."

The officer took the paper, glanced at it, and obeyed.

VIII

ADMISSION BY PRIVILEGE

Without being aware of it, the mayor of Montreuil-sur-mer had a certain celebrity. For seven years his virtuous reputation had been extending throughout Lower Boulonnais; it had finally crossed the boundaries of the little county and spread into the two or three neighboring regions. Besides the considerable service he had rendered to the principal town by reviving the jet-work industry, there was not one of the hundred and forty-one communes in the district of Montreuil-sur-mer that was not indebted to him for some favor. When necessary, he had even supported and stimulated the industries of the other districts. In this way he had, as the occasion demanded, sustained with his credit and his own funds the tulle factory at Boulogne, the flax-spinning factory at Frévent, and the linen mill at Boubers-sur-Canche. Everywhere the name of Monsieur Madeleine was spoken with veneration. Arras and Douai envied the lucky little town of Montreuil-sur-mer its mayor.

Like everyone else, the judge of the Royal Court of Douai, who was presiding at this term of the superior court in Arras, was familiar with this profoundly and universally honored name. When the officer, quietly opening the door that led from the counsel chamber to the court room, bent behind the judge's chair and handed him the paper on which was written the line we have just read, adding, "This gentleman wishes to witness the trial," the judge made a hasty gesture of deference, took a pen, wrote a few words at the bottom of the paper, and handed it back to the officer, saying to him, "Let him enter."

The unhappy man whose story we are telling had remained near the door of the hall, in the same place and the same attitude as when the officer left him. Through his thoughts he heard someone saying to him, "Will monsieur do me the honor to follow me?" It was the same officer who had turned his back on him the minute before; he was now bowing deeply before him. At the same time the bailiff handed him the paper. He unfolded it, and, as he happened to be near the lamp, he was able to read,

"The judge of the superior court presents his respects to Monsieur Madeleine."

He crumpled the paper in his hands, as though those few words had left some strange and bitter aftertaste.

He followed the officer.

In a few minutes he found himself alone in a small room, severely paneled, lit by two wax candles placed on a table covered with green cloth. The last words of the bailiff who had just left him still rang in his ears, "Monsieur, you are now in the counsel chamber; just turn the brass knob of that door and you'll be in the courtroom, behind the judge's bench." These words were associated in his thoughts with a vague memory of the narrow corridors and dark stairways through which he had just passed.

The officer had left him alone. The decisive moment had arrived. He vainly tried to collect his thoughts. Particularly at those moments when we have sorest need of grasping the sharp realities of life do the threads of thought snap off in the brain. He was in the very place where the judges deliberate and decide. With a glazed tranquility he gazed at the silent and formidable room where so many lives had been shattered, where his own name would soon be heard, and which his fate was crossing at this moment. He looked at the walls, then he looked at himself, astonished that it could be this chamber, and that this could be he.

He had eaten nothing for more than twenty-four hours; he was bruised by the jolting of the carriole, but he did not feel it; he seemed to feel nothing.

He went up to a black frame hanging on the wall, which contained under glass an old autographed letter written by Jean Nicolas Pache, mayor of Paris and minister, dated, undoubtedly by mistake, *June* 9th, year II, in which Pache sent to the commune the list of ministers and deputies they held under arrest. A spectator, if he had seen and watched him then, would no doubt have imagined that this letter seemed quite remarkable to him, for he did not take his eyes off it, but he read it two or three times. He was reading without paying any attention and without knowing what he was doing. He was thinking of Fantine and Cosette.

While still musing, he unconsciously turned, and his eyes took in the brass knob of the door that separated him from the hall of the superior court. He had almost forgotten that door. His expression, at first calm, now fell. His eyes, fixed on that brass knob, became set and wild and little by little filled with dismay. Drops of sweat started above the hairline and rolled down his temples.

At one moment, with a kind of authority united to rebellion, he made that indescribable gesture that says and says so well, *And who says I have to?* Then he quickly turned, saw in front of him the door by which he had entered, went to it, opened it, and went out. He was no longer in that room; he was outside, in a corridor, a long, narrow corridor, broken by steps and side doors, making all sorts of angles, lit here and there by lamps hung on the wall similar to nightlights for the sick; it was the corridor by which he had come. He took a deep breath and listened; not a sound behind him, not a sound in front of him; he ran as if pursued.

When he had rounded several of the turns of this passage, he listened again. There was still the same silence and the same shadow around him. He was out of breath, he tottered, he leaned against the wall. The stone was cold; the sweat was icy on his forehead; he roused himself with a shudder.

Then and there, alone, standing in that darkness, trembling with cold and, perhaps, with something else, he reflected.

He had reflected all night, he had reflected all day; now he heard only one voice within him, saying, "Alas!"

A quarter of an hour went by this way. Finally, be bowed his head, sighed with anguish, let his arms droop, and retraced his steps. He walked slowly and as if overwhelmed. It was as though he had been caught in flight and brought back.

He entered the counsel chamber again. The first thing he saw was the door handle. That handle, round and made of polished brass, shone out for him like an ominous star. He looked at it as a lamb might look at the eye of a tiger.

His eyes could not leave it.

From time to time, he took another step toward the door.

Had he listened, he would have heard, as a kind of confused murmur, the noise of the neighboring hall; but he did not listen and he did not hear.

Suddenly, without himself knowing how, he found himself near the door, he seized the knob convulsively; the door opened.

He was in the courtroom.

IX

A PLACE FOR CONVICTIONS

He took a step, automatically closed the door behind him, and remained on his feet, taking in what he saw.

It was a rather large space, dimly lit, filled in turn with noise and silence, where all the machinery of a criminal trial was unfolding with its petty yet solemn gravity, in the midst of the crowd.

At one end of the hall, where he happened to be, judges in threadbare robes were distractedly biting their fingernails or closing their eyelids; at the other end was a rabble in rags; there were lawyers in all sorts of positions; soldiers with honest, hard faces; old, stained wainscoting, a dirty ceiling, tables covered with serge, more nearly yellow than green; doors blackened by fingermarks; tavern lamps giving off more smoke than light, hanging on nails in the paneling; candles in brass candlesticks on the tables; everywhere shadows, ugliness, sadness; and from this emanated an austere and august impression; for men felt there the presence of that great humane thing called law, and that great divine thing called justice.

Nobody in this throng paid any attention to him. All eyes converged on a single point, a wooden bench placed against a little door, along the wall to the left of the judge. On this bench, lit by several candles, sat a man between two gendarmes.

This was the man.

He did not look for him, he saw him. His eyes went toward him naturally, as if they had known in advance where he was.

He thought he was seeing himself, older, undoubtedly, not exactly the same in features, but alike in attitude and appearance, with that bristling hair, those wild restless eyes, with that shirt—just as he had been on the day he entered Digne, full of hatred, and concealing in his soul that hideous hoard of frightful thoughts he had spent nineteen years harvesting on the prison floor.

He said to himself, with a shudder, "Great God! Will I return to that?"

This individual seemed at least sixty years old. There was something indescribably crude, dull-witted, and terrified in his appearance.

At the sound of the door opening, people had stood aside to make room. The judge had turned his head, and supposing the person who entered to be the mayor of Montreuil-sur-mer, greeted him with a bow. The prosecuting attorney, who had seen Madeleine at Montreuil-sur-mer, where he had been called more than once by the duties of his office, recognized him and bowed also. He scarcely noticed them. He gazed around him, as though hallucinating.

Judges, clerk, gendarmes, a throng of heads, cruelly curious—he had seen them all once before, twenty-seven years earlier. Once again he had fallen on these disastrous things; they were there before him, they moved, they existed. It was no longer an effort of his memory, a mirage of his fancy, but real gendarmes and real judges, a real throng, and real men of flesh and bone. It was done; he could see reappearing and existing again around him, in all their cruel reality, the monstrous visions of his past.

All this was looming before him.

Horror-stricken, he closed his eyes and cried out from the depths of his soul, "Never!"

And by a tragic trick of fate that was stirring up all his ideas and driving him almost insane, it was another self that faced him. This man on trial was being called Jean Valjean!

Right before his eyes he had an unthinkable vision, a sort of re-creation of the most horrible moment of his life, being played by his shadow.

It was all there—the same paraphernalia, the same time of night—almost the same faces, judge and assistant judges, soldiers and spectators. But above the head of the judge was a crucifix, something not in courtrooms at the time of his sentence. When he was tried, God had been absent.

There was a chair behind him; he sank into it, terrified of being observed. When seated, he took advantage of a pile of folders on the judges' desk to hide his face from the whole room. He could now see without being seen. He fully regained a sense of reality; by degrees he recovered his composure, and reached that degree of calm in which it is possible to listen.

Monsieur Bamatabois was one of the jurors.

He looked for Javert but did not see him. The witnesses' seat was hidden from him by the clerk's table. And then, as we have just said, the hall was very dimly lit.

As he had entered, the counsel for the prisoner was finishing his plea. Everyone's attention was fully engaged; the trial had been in progress three hours. During these three hours, the spectators had seen a man, an unknown, wretched being, thoroughly stupid or thoroughly artful, gradually bending beneath the weight of a terrible similarity. This man, as we already know, was a vagrant who had been found in a field, carrying a branch heavy with ripe apples, which had been broken off a tree in a nearby orchard called the Pierron enclosure. Who was this man? An examination had been held, witnesses had been heard, they had been unanimous, light had been shed on every aspect of the case. The prosecution said, "We have here not merely a fruit thief, a robber; we have here, in our hands, a bandit, an outlaw who has broken his parole, a former convict, a most dangerous outlaw, a former offender. Jean Valjean, whom justice has long been seeking, and who, eight years ago, on leaving the prison at Toulon, committed an armed highway robbery on the person of a young Savoyard, Petit Gervais, a crime specified in Article 383 of the Penal Code and for which we reserve the right of further prosecution once his identity is judicially established. He has now committed a new theft. He is a repeated offender. Convict him for the new crime and he will be tried later for the previous one." Faced with this accusation, before the unanimity of the witnesses, the principal emotion displayed by the accused was astonishment. He made gestures signifying denial, or else he gazed at the ceiling. He spoke with difficulty, answered with embarrassment, but from head to foot his whole person denied the charge. He seemed like an idiot in the presence of all these intellects ranged in battle around him, and like a stranger in the midst of this society by whom he had been seized. Nevertheless, a most threatening future awaited him; the probability increased every moment; and every spectator was looking more anxiously than he himself for the calamitous sentence that seemed to be hanging over his head with ever increasing certainty. One contingency even suggested the possibility, beyond prison, of capital punishment if his identity were established and if the Petit Gervais affair later resulted in a conviction. Who was this man? What was the nature of his apathy? Was it imbecility or artifice? Did he know too much or nothing at all? These were questions on which the spectators took sides, and which seemed to divide the jury. There was something fearful and something mysterious in the trial; the drama was not merely somber but puzzling.

The counsel for the defense had made a very good plea in the provincial language that long constituted the eloquence of the bar and was formerly used by all lawyers, in Paris as well as in Romorantin or Montbrison, but whch, now considered classic, is used by few except the official orators of the bar, to whom it is suited by its solemn sonority and majestic cadence; a language in which husband and wife are called "spouses," Paris, "the center of arts and civilization," the king, "the monarch," a bishop, "a holy pontiff," the prosecuting attorney, "the eloquent interpreter of the vengeance of the law," arguments, "the accents just heard," the time of Louis XIV, "the illustrious age" a theater, "the temple of Melpomene," the reigning family, "the august blood of our kings," a concert, "a musical solemnity," the general in command, "the illustrious warrior who," etc., students of theology, "those tender Levites," mistakes imputed to newspapers, "the imposture that distills its venom into the columns of these organs," etc., etc. The counsel for the defense had begun by explaining the theft of the apples—a thing poorly suited to a lofty style; but Bénigne Bossuet himself was once compelled to mention a hen in the midst of a funeral oration and acquitted himself with dignity. The counsel established that the theft of the apples was not in fact proved. His client, whom in his role as counsel he persisted in calling Champmathieu, had not been seen scaling the wall or breaking off the branch. He had been arrested in possession of this branch (which the counsel preferred to call "bough"), but he said that he had found it on the ground. Where was the proof to the contrary? Undoubtedly this branch had been broken and carried off after a scaling of the wall, then thrown away by the alarmed robber; undoubtedly, there had been a thief. But what evidence was there that this thief was Champmathieu? One thing alone. That he was a former convict. The counsel would not deny that this fact unfortunately appeared to be fully proved; the defendant had resided at Faverolles; the defendant had been a pruner, the name of Champmathieu might well have had its origin in that of Jean Mathieu; all this was true, and finally, four witnesses had positively and without hesitation identified Champmathieu as the convict Jean Valjean; to these circumstances and this testimony the counsel could oppose nothing but the denial of his client, a self-serving denial; but even supposing him to be the convict Jean Valjean, did this prove he had stolen the apples? That was a presumption at most, not a proof. The accused, it was true, and the counsel "in good faith" must admit it, had adopted "a mistaken system of defense." He had persisted in denying everything, both the theft and the fact that he had been a convict. An admission on the latter point would certainly have been better and would have secured him the indulgence of the judges; the counsel had advised him to take this course, but the defendant had obstinately refused, expecting probably to escape punishment entirely by admitting nothing. It was a mistake, but should the poverty of his intellect not be taken into consideration? The man was clearly dull-witted. Long suffering in prison, long suffering outside of prison had deadened him, etc., etc.; if he made a bad defense, was this a reason for convicting him? As for the Petit Gervais affair, the counsel had nothing to say, it did not concern this case. He concluded by entreating the jury and court, if the identity of Jean Valjean appeared obvious to them, to apply to him the legal penalties prescribed for the breaking of parole, and not the fearful punishment decreed for the convict found guilty of a second offense.

The prosecuting attorney replied to the counsel for the defense. He was violent and flowery, like most prosecuting attorneys.

He complimented the counsel for his "candor," of which he shewdly took advantage. He attacked the accused through all the concessions his counsel had made.

The counsel seemed to admit that the accused was Jean Valjean. He accepted the admission. This man then was Jean Valjean. This fact was conceded to the prosecution and could be no longer contested. Here, by an adroit autonomasia, going back to the sources and causes of crime, the prosecuting attorney thundered against the immorality of the romantic school—then in its dawn, under the name of the "Satanic school," conferred upon it by the critics of the *Quotidienne* and the *Oriflamme;* and not implausibly, he attributed to the influence of this perverse literature the crime of Champmathieu, or rather of Jean Valjean. These considerations exhausted, he passed to Jean Valjean himself. Who was Jean Valjean? Description of Jean Valjean: a monster vomited from, etc. The model of all such descriptions may be found in the story of Théramène, which as tragedy is useless, but which does great daily service to judicial eloquence. The audience and the jury "shuddered." This description finished, the prosecuting attorney summed up with a burst of oratory designed to arouse the enthusiasm of the *Journal de la Préfecture* to the highest pitch the next morning. "And it is such a man as this," etc. etc. A vagabond, a beggar, without means of support, etc., etc. Accustomed through his existence to criminal acts and profiting little from his life in prison, as is proved by the crime committed on Petit Gervais, etc., etc. It is such a man as this who, found on the highway in the very act of theft, a few paces from a wall that had been scaled, still holding in his hand the stolen object, denies the act in which he is caught, denies the theft, denies the scaling, denies everything, denies even his name, denies even his identity! Besides a hundred other proofs, to which we will not return, he is identified by four witnesses—Javert—the incorruptible inspector of police. Javert—and three of his former companions in disgrace, the convicts Brevet, Chenildieu, and Cochepaille. What has he to oppose this overwhelming unanimity? His denial. What depravity! You will do justice, gentlemen of the jury, etc., etc.

While the prosecuting attorney was speaking, the accused listened opened-mouthed, with a sort of astonishment, not unmingled with admiration. He was evidently surprised that a man could speak so well. From time to time, at the most "forceful" parts of the argument, at those moments when eloquence, unable to contain itself, overflows in a stream of withering epithets, and swirls around the prisoner like a tempest, he slowly turned his head from right to left, and from left to right—a sort of sad, mute protest, to which he had limited himself from the beginning of the argument. Two or three times the spectators nearest him heard him say in a low tone, "This all comes from not asking for Monsieur Baloup!" The prosecuting attorney pointed out to the jury this air of stupidity, clearly put on, and denoting, not imbecility but address, artifice, and the habit of deceiving justice; and which showed in its full light the "deep-rooted perversity" of the man. He concluded by entering his reservations on the Petit Gervais affair, and demanding a sentence to the full extent of the law.

This was, for this offense, as will be remembered, hard labor for life.

The counsel for the prisoner rose, began by complimenting "Monsieur, the prosecuting attorney, on his admirable argument," then replied, as best he could, but in a weaker tone; the ground was evidently giving way under him.

X

THE SYSTEM FOR DENIALS

The time had come for closing the case. The judge commanded the accused to rise, and put the usual question: "Have you anything to add to your defense?"

The man, standing, and twirling a hideous cap in his hands, seemed not to hear.

The judge repeated the question.

This time the man heard and appeared to understand. He started like someone waking from sleep, glanced around him, looked at the spectators, the gendarmes, his counsel, the jurors, and the court, placed his huge fists on the bar in front of him, looked around again, and, suddenly staring at the prosecuting attorney, began to speak. It was like an eruption. From the way in which the words escaped his lips, incoherent, impetuous, jostling each other helter-skelter, it seemed as though they were all eager to escape at the same time. He said, "I have this to say: I have been a wheelwright in Paris; it was at M. Baloup's. It's a hard life to be a wheelwright; you always work out of doors, in yards, under sheds when you have good bosses, never in shops, because you have to have room, you see. In winter it's so cold you shake your arms to warm up; but the bosses won't allow that; they say it's a waste of time. It's hard work to handle iron when there's ice on the pavements. It wears a man out fast. You get old very young in this trade. A man is used up by forty. I was fifty-three; it wasn't easy. And then the workmen are a bad group! When a poor man isn't young, they call you old bird, old beast! I earned only thirty sous a day, they paid me as little as they could—the bosses took advantage of my age. Then there was my daughter, a washerwoman by the river. She earned a little for herself; between us two, we got by. It was hard work for her too. All day long up to the waist in a tub, in rain, in snow, with wind that cuts your face when it freezes, but the washing has to get done; there are folks who don't have much linen and are waiting for it; if you don't wash you lose your customers. The planks are badly joined and the water drips all over you. Your clothes get wet through and through. It sinks right in. She did washing too in the laundry of the Enfants-Rouges, where the water comes in through pipes. There you're not in the tub. You wash in front of you under the pipe, and rinse behind you in the trough. It's under cover, and you're not so cold. But there is a hot lye bath that's terrible and ruins your eyes. She'd come home at seven o'clock at night, and go to bed right away, she was so tired. Her husband used to beat her. She's dead. We weren't very happy. She was a good girl; she never went to dances and was very quiet. I remember one Mardi Gras she went to bed at eight o'clock. Look here, I'm telling the truth. Just ask if it isn't true. But how stupid of me! Paris is a chasm. Who there even knows Father Champmathieu? But I tell you there's M. Baloup. Go and see M. Baloup. I don't know what more you want of me."

The man stopped speaking, but stayed on his feet. He had spoken these things in a loud, rapid, hoarse, harsh, and guttural tone, with a sort of angry and savage simplicity. Once, he stopped to nod to somebody in the crowd. The sort of affirmations that he seemed to fling out at random came from him like hiccups, and he punctuated each one with the gesture of a man chopping wood. When he had finished, the spectators burst out laughing. He looked at them, and seeing them laughing and not knowing why, began to laugh himself.

That was a bad sign.

The judge, a considerate, kindly man, raised his voice.

He reminded the "gentlemen of the jury" that M. Baloup, the former master wheelwright by whom the prisoner said he had been employed, had been summoned, but had not appeared. He had gone bankrupt and could not be found. Then, turning to the accused, he ordered him to listen to what he was about to say, and added, "You are in a position that demands reflection. The gravest accusations are weighing against you, and may lead to fatal results. On your own behalf, I question you one last time, explain yourself clearly on these two points. First, did you or did you not climb the wall of the Pierron enclosure, break off the branch, and steal the apples, that is to say, commit the crime of theft, and breaking into an enclosure? Secondly, are you or are you not the discharged convict Jean Valjean?"

The prisoner shook his head with a knowing look, like a man who understands perfectly, and knows what he is going to say. He opened his mouth, turned toward the presiding judge, and said, "In the first place—"

Then he looked at his cap, looked up at the ceiling, and fell silent.

"Prisoner," the prosecuting attorney continued in a severe tone of voice, "pay attention. You have answered nothing that has been asked you. Your confusion condemns you. It is clear that your name is not Champmathieu, that you are the convict Jean Valjean, disguised under the name at first of Jean Mathieu, which was that of his mother; that you have lived in Auvergne; that you were born at Faverolles, where you were a pruner. It is obvious that you have stolen ripe apples from the Pierron orchard and broken into the enclosure. The gentlemen of the jury will consider this."

The accused had at last resumed his seat; he rose abruptly when the prosecuting attorney had ended, and exclaimed, "You're a very bad man, I mean you. This is what I wanted to say. I couldn't think of it at first. I never stole anything. I'm a man who don't get something to eat every day. I was coming from Ailly, walking alone after a shower, which had made the ground all yellow with mud, so that even the ponds were running over, and you only saw little bits of grass sticking out of the sand along the road, and I found a broken branch on the ground with apples on it; and I picked it up not knowing what trouble it would give me. It's three months that I've been in prison, being pushed around. More I can't say. You talk against me and yell at me 'Answer!' The gendarme, who's all right, nudges my elbow, and whispers, 'Just answer.' I can't explain myself; I never went to school; I'm a poor man. You're all wrong not to see I didn't steal. I picked up off the ground things that were there. You talk about Jean Valjean, Jean Mathieu—I don't know any such people. They must be villagers. I've worked for Monsieur Baloup, Boulevard de l'Hôpital. My name is Champmathieu. You must be very smart to tell me where I was born. Me, I never knew. Everybody can't have houses to be born in; that would be too handy. I think my father and mother kept on the move, but I don't know. When I was a child they called me Little One; now, they call me Old Man. Those are my names. Take 'em as you like. I've been in Auvergne, I've been in Faverolles. Good Lord! Can't a man have been in Auvergne and Faverolles without having been in prison, too? I tell you I never stole anything, and that I'm Father Champmathieu. I've been there at Monsieur Baloup's; I lived in his house. I'm getting tired of all this nonsense. What is everybody after me for?"

The prosecuting attorney was still standing; he addressed the judge. "Sir, in the presence of the confused but adroit denials of the accused, who attempts to pass for an idiot but will not succeed—we warn him—we request that it may please you and the court to call back to the bar the convicts Brevet, Cochepaille, and Chenildieu, and Police Inspector Javert, and to submit them to a final interrogation, concerning the identity of the accused with the convict Jean Valjean."

"I must remind the prosecuting attorney," said the presiding judge, "that Police Inspector Javert, recalled by his duties to the chief town of a neighboring district, left the hall and the city as soon as his testimony was taken. We granted him this permission, with the consent of the prosecuting attorney and the counsel of the accused."

"True," the prosecuting attorney replied. "In the absence then of Monsieur Javert, I think it my duty to recall to the gentlemen of the jury what he said here a few hours ago. Javert is a well-respected man, who does honor to inferior but important functions through his rigorous and strict honesty. These are the terms of his testimony: 'I do not even need moral assumptions and material proofs to contradict the denials of the accused. I recognize him perfectly. This man's name is not Champmathieu; he is a former convict, Jean Valjean, hardened and feared. He was freed at the expiration of his term, but with extreme regret. He served out nineteen years at hard labor for burglary; five or six times he attempted to escape. Besides the Petit Gervais and Pierron robberies, I suspect him also of a robbery committed on his lordship, the late Bishop of Digne. I often saw him when I was adjutant of the chain-gang guard at Toulon. I repeat; I recognize him perfectly.' "

This declaration, in precise terms, seemed to produce a strong impression on the public and jury. The prosecuting attorney concluded by insisting that, in the absence of Javert, the three witnesses, Brevet, Chenildieu, and Cochepaille, should be heard again and solemnly interrogated.

The judge gave an order to an officer, and a moment later the door of the witness room opened, and the officer, accompanied by a gendarme ready to lend assistance, led in the convict Brevet. The audience was in breathless suspense, and all hearts beat as though at a single command.

The former convict Brevet was clad in the black and gray jacket of the central prisons. Brevet was about sixty years old; he had the face of a businessman and the air of a rogue. They sometimes go together. He had become something like a turnkey in the prison—to which he had been brought for new crimes. He was one of those men of whom their superiors say, "He tries to make himself useful." The chaplain testified to his religious habits. It must not be forgotten that this happened under the Restoration.

"Brevet," said the judge, "you are serving out a sentence that includes loss of civil rights and cannot give sworn testimony."

Brevet lowered his eyes.

"Nevertheless," continued the judge, "even in the man whom the law has degraded there may remain, if divine justice permits, a feeling of honor and equity. To that feeling I appeal in this decisive hour. If it still exists in you, and I hope it does, reflect before you answer me; consider on the one hand this man, whom a word from you may destroy; on the other hand, justice, which a word from you may enlighten. It is a solemn moment, and there is still time to retract if you think yourself mistaken. The accused will rise. Brevet, look closely at the prisoner; call on your memory, and say, on your soul and conscience, whether you still recognize this man as your former comrade in the galleys, Jean Valjean."

Brevet looked at the prisoner, then turned back to the court.

"Yes, your honor, I was the first to recognize him, and still do. This man is Jean Valjean, who came to Toulon in 1796 and left in 1815. I left the year after. He looks like a brute now, but he must have grown dull with age; in prison he was sullen. I recognize him, absolutely."

"Go sit down," said the judge. "Prisoner, remain standing."

Chenildieu was brought in, a convict for life, as was shown by his red shirt and green cap. He was serving out his punishment in the prison at Toulon, and had been let out for this occasion. He was a little man, about fifty, active, wrinkled, lean, yellow, brazen, restless, with a sort of sickly weakness in his limbs and whole person, and immense power in his eye. His companions in the prison had nicknamed him Je-nie-Dieu, or I-deny-God.

The judge spoke nearly the same words to him as to Brevet. When he reminded him that his sentence had deprived him of the right to take the oath, Chenildieu raised his head and looked the spectators in the face. The judge requested him to collect this thoughts and asked him, as he had Brevet, whether he still recognized the prisoner.

Chenildieu burst out laughing.

"God! Do I recognize him! We did five years on the same chain. Frown at me, will you, old man?"

"Be seated," said the judge.

The officer brought in Cochepaille; this other life convict, brought from prison and dressed in red like Chenildieu, was a peasant from Lourdes and part bear from the Pyrenees. He had tended flocks in the mountains, and from being a shepherd had slipped into banditry. Cochepaille was no less uncouth than the accused and appeared still more stupid. He was one of those unfortunate men whom nature turns out as wild beasts and society finishes as convicts.

The judge attempted to move him by a few serious and pathetic words, and asked him, as he had the others, whether he still recognized without hesitation or difficulty the man standing before him.

"It is Jean Valjean," said Cochepaille. "The one they called Jean-the-Jack, he was so strong."

Each of the assertions of these three men, obviously sincere and in good faith, had raised from the audience a murmur of evil portent for the accused—a murmur that increased in force and duration each time a new declaration was added to the preceding one. The prisoner himself listened to them with that astonished expression that, according to the prosecution, was his principal means of defense. At first, the gendarmes by his side heard him mutter between his teeth: "Oh, well! So much for him!" After the second, he said in a louder tone, with an expression close to satisfaction, "Good!" At the third, he exclaimed, "Splendid!"

The judge addressed him, "Prisoner, you have heard. What do you have to say?"

He replied, "I say—splendid!"

A buzz ran through the crowd and almost reached the jury. It was obvious that the man was lost.

"Bailiffs," said the judge, "enforce order. I am about to sum up the case."

At this moment there was a movement near the judge. A voice was heard crying out, "Brevet, Chenildieu, Cochepaille, look this way!"

So mournful, and so terrible was this voice that those who heard it felt their blood run cold. All eyes turned toward the point from which it came. A man, who had been sitting among the privileged spectators behind the court, had risen, pushed open the low gate that separated the tribunal from the bar, and was standing in the center of the hall. The judge, the prosecuting attorney, Monsieur Bamatabois, twenty persons recognized him, and cried out simultaneously, "Monsieur Madeleine!"

XI

CHAMPMATHIEU MORE AND MORE ASTONISHED

It was indeed he. The clerk's lamp lit up his face. He had his hat in hand; there was no disarray in his clothing; his overcoat was carefully buttoned. He was very pale, and trembled slightly. His hair, already gray when he came to Arras, was now perfectly white. It had turned white during the hour he had been there.

Every head was raised. The sensation was indescribable. There was a moment of hesitation among the spectators. The voice had been so agonized, the man standing there appeared so calm, that at first nobody could understand. They wondered who had cried out. They could not believe that this serene man had uttered that appalling cry.

This indecision lasted only a few seconds. Even before the judge and prosecuting attorney could say a word, before the gendarmes and court officers could make one move, the man, whom everyone up to this moment had called M. Madeleine, moved toward the witnesses, Cochepaille, Brevet, and Chenildieu.

"Don't you recognize me?" he asked.

All three stood dazed, and indicated by a shake of the head that they did know him. Cochepaille, intimidated, gave the military salute. Turning toward the jurors and court, M. Madeleine said in a mild voice, "Gentlemen of the jury, release the accused. Your honor, order my arrest. He is not the man you seek; I am. I am Jean Valjean."

Not a breath stirred. The first commotion of astonishment had given way to a sepulchral silence. The hall was touched with the sort of religious awe that grips a throng when something immense has taken place.

Yet the judge's face reflected sympathy and sadness;

he exchanged glances with the prosecuting attorney, and a few whispered words with the assistant judges. He turned to the spectators and asked in a tone that was understood by all, "Is there a physician in the hall?"

The prosecuting attorney spoke up, "Gentlemen of the jury, this strange and unexpected incident disturbing the hearing inspires us, like you, with only one feeling we have no need to express. You all know, at least by reputation, the honorable Monsieur Madeleine, mayor of Montreuil-sur-mer. If there is a doctor in the audience, we join with his honor the judge in asking him to kindly help Monsieur Madeleine and take him to his residence."

M. Madeleine did not allow the prosecuting attorney to finish, but interrupted him in tones of indulgence and authority. These are the words he spoke; here they are verbatim, just as they were written down immediately after the trial by one of the witnesses—as they still ring in the ears of those who heard them, nearly forty years ago.

"I thank you, Monsieur Prosecuting Attorney, but I am not mad. You'll see. You were on the point of committing a grave error; release that man. I am carrying out a duty; I am the unfortunate convict. I am the only one who can see this clearly, and I am telling you the truth. What I am doing at this moment, God on high is witnessing, and that is enough. You can take me, since here I am. Yet I have done my best. I have hidden under another name, I have become rich, I became a mayor; I wanted to live again among honest people. It seems this cannot be. There are many things I cannot say, I won't tell you the story of my life; someday you will know it. I did rob Monseigneur the Bishop—that is true; I did rob Petit-Gervais—that is true. They were right in telling you that Jean Valjean was wicked. But all the blame may not belong to him. Please listen, your honors; a man as unworthy as I has no protest to make to Providence, nor advice to give society; but, you see, the infamy from which I have sought to rise is pernicious. The prison makes the convict. Make of this what you like. Before prison, I was a poor peasant, unintelligent, a sort of idiot; prison changed me. I was stupid, I became wicked; I was a log, I became a firebrand. Later, I was saved by indulgence and kindness, as I had been lost by severity. But, pardon me, you cannot understand what I am saying. In my house you will find, among the ashes of the fireplace, the forty-sous piece I stole seven years ago, from Petit Gervais. I have nothing more to add. Take me. Good God! the prosecuting attorney shakes his head. You are saying 'Monsieur Madeleine has gone mad'; you do not believe me. That is hard to bear. At least do not condemn that man! How is it these men do not recognize me! I wish Javert were here. He would recognize me!"

Nothing could express the kind yet terrible melancholy of the tone that accompanied these words.

He turned to the three convicts. "Well! I recognize you, Brevet, do you remember—"

He paused, hesitated a moment, and said, "Do you remember those checkered, knit suspenders you had in prison?"

Brevet started as if in surprise, and glared at him from head to foot. He went on, "Chenildieu, you nicknamed yourself to repudiate God! Your entire left shoulder has been deeply burned from laying it on a stove full of embers one day, to erase the three letters T.F.P., which are still there nonetheless. Answer me, is this true?"

"It's true!" said Chenildieu.

He turned to Cochepaille. "Cochepaille, on your left arm, near where you have been bled, you have a date marked in blue letters with burned powder. It is the date of the emperor's landing at Cannes, March 1st, 1815. Pull up your sleeve."

Cochepaille pulled up his sleeve; all eyes around him were turned to his naked arm. A gendarme brought a lamp; the date was there.

The unhappy man turned toward the spectators and the court with a smile, the thought of which still wrenches the hearts of those who saw it. It was the smile of triumph; it was also the smile of despair.

"So you see," he said, "I am Jean Valjean."

Within that space there were no longer either judges or prosecutors or gendarmes; there were only staring eyes and hearts that were moved. Nobody could remember the part he had to play; the prosecuting attorney forgot he was there to prosecute, the judge that he was there to preside, the counsel for the defense that he was there to defend. Strange to say no question was asked, no authority intervened. It is peculiar to transcendent spectacles that they take possession of every soul and make every witness a spectator. Nobody, perhaps, was positively conscious of what he experienced; and, undoubtedly, nobody told himself that he saw a great gleaming light, yet all felt inwardly dazzled.

It was clear that Jean Valjean was standing there before them. That fact was beyond dispute. The arrival of this man had been enough to clear up the case, so obscure a moment before. Without need for any further explanation, the whole crowd, as if by a sort of electric revelation, instantly understood, and at one glance, this simple and marvelous story of a man giving himself up so that another man would not be condemned in his place. The details, the possible hesitation, the slight reluctance were lost in this immense, luminous fact.

It was an impression that quickly passed, but for the moment it was irresistible.

"I will not disturb the proceedings further," continued Jean Valjean. "I am leaving, since you are not arresting me. I have many things to do. Monsieur Prosecuting Attorney knows who I am, he knows where I am going, and will have me arrested when he chooses."

He walked toward the outer door. Not a voice was raised, not an arm stretched out to prevent him. All stood aside. There was at this moment an indescribable divinity about him that makes the multitudes fall back and give way before such a man. He walked slowly through the throng. It was never known who opened the door, but it is certain that the door was open when he got to it. On reaching it he turned and said, "Monsieur Prosecuting Attorney, I remain at your disposal."

Then he addressed the spectators.

"All of you, everyone here, you think me pitiful, don't you? Great God! When I think of what I have been on the point of doing, I consider myself worthy of envy. Still I wish that all of this had not happened!"

He went out, and the door closed as it had opened, for those who do supremely great deeds are always sure to be served by somebody in the crowd.

Less than an hour later, the verdict of the jury discharged from all accusation the said Champmathieu; and Champmathieu, immediately set free, went on his way, stupefied, thinking all men mad and understanding nothing of this whole fantastic vision.

Book Eight

COUNTER-STROKE

I

THE MIRROR IN WHICH M. MADELEINE LOOKS AT HIS HAIR

Day began to dawn. Fantine had spent a night that was feverish and sleepless but filled with happy visions; at daybreak she fell asleep. Sister Simplice, who had sat up with her, took advantage of this sleep to go and prepare a new dose of quinine. For a few moments the good sister had been in the infirmary laboratory, bending over her vials and drugs, looking at them very closely because of the mist that dawn casts over everything, when suddenly she turned her head and gave a faint cry. M. Madeleine was standing in front of her. He had just come in silently.

"You, Monsieur Mayor!" she exclaimed.

"How is the poor woman?" he answered in a low voice.

"Better just now. But we have been very anxious."

She explained what had happened, that Fantine had been gravely ill the night before, but was better now, because she believed that the mayor had gone to Montfermeil for her child. The sister did not dare question the mayor, but she clearly saw from his manner that that was not at all where he had been.

"Very good," he said. "You did well not to disappoint her."

"Yes," responded the sister, "but now, Monsieur Mayor, when she sees you without her child, what shall we tell her?"

He reflected for a moment, then said. "God will inspire us."

"But, we cannot lie to her," the sister said under her breath.

Daylight streamed into the room and lit up M. Madeleine's face. The sister happened to raise her eyes.

"O God, monsieur," she exclaimed. "What has happened to you? Your hair is all white!"

"White!" he said.

Sister Simplice had no mirror; she rummaged in a case of instruments, and found a little one the infirmary physician used to see whether the breath had left the patient's body. M. Madeleine took the mirror, looked at his hair, and said again, "White!"

He said the word with a lack of interest, as if thinking of something else.

The sister felt chilled by some unknown thing she glimpsed in all this.

He asked, "Can I see her?"

"Won't Monsieur Mayor bring back her child?" asked the sister, scarcely daring to venture a question.

"Certainly, but it will take two or three days at least."

"If she doesn't see Monsieur Mayor between now and then," the sister went on timidly, "she won't know that he has returned; it would be easy to encourage patience, and when the child comes, she will naturally think that Monsieur Mayor has just arrived with her. Then we won't have to tell her a fib."

M. Madeleine seemed to reflect for a few moments, then said with his calm gravity, "No, my sister, I must see her. I may not have much time."

The nun did not seem to notice this "may," which gave an obscure and singular meaning to the mayor's words. She answered, respectfully, lowering her eyes and voice, "In that case, she is asleep, but monsieur can go in."

He made a few remarks about a door that shut poorly, whose noise might awaken the sick woman; then he entered Fantine's room, went up to her bed, and opened the curtains. She was sleeping. She exhaled with that tragic sound peculiar to these diseases, which rends the hearts of poor mothers watching over the sleep of their doomed children. But this labored breathing scarcely disturbed an ineffable serenity resting on her face and transfiguring her in her sleep. Her pallor had become whiteness, and her cheeks were flushed. Her long, fair eyelashes, the only beauty left from her maidenhood and youth, quivered as they lay against her cheek. Her whole person trembled as if to the feel of an unseen fluttering of wings ready to unfold and bear her away. To see her like this, no one would have believed that hope for this life was almost gone. She looked more likely ready to soar away than to die.

When a hand is stretched out to pick the flower, the stem quivers, and seems in effect to shrink back and offer itself at the same time. The human body shares something of this trepidation at the moment when the mysterious fingers of death are about to gather in the soul.

M. Madeleine stood still for some time beside the bed, looking in turn at the patient and the crucifix, as he had done two months before, on the day when he first came to see her in this shelter. They were still there, both in the same attitude, she sleeping, he praying; only now, two months later, her hair was gray and his was white.

The sister had not come in with him. He stood by the bed, his finger to his lips, as if there were someone in the room to silence. She opened her eyes, saw him, and calmly said with a smile, "Cosette?"

II

FANTINE HAPPY

She did not give a start of surprise or joy; she was joy itself. The simple question "Cosette?" was asked with such deep faith, with so much certainty, with such a complete absence of worry or doubt, that she was at a loss for words. She went on, "I knew you were there; I was asleep, but I saw you. I've been seeing you for a long time; I've followed you with my eyes all night. You were in a halo of glory, and all sorts of celestial forms were hovering around you!"

He raised his eyes toward the crucifix.

"But tell me, where's Cosette?" she resumed. "Why didn't you put her on my bed so I might see her the moment I woke up?"

He answered something absent-mindedly, which he later could not recall.

Fortunately, the doctor, alerted to all this, had arrived. He came to M. Madeleine's aid.

"My child," he said, "be calm, your daughter is here."

Fantine's eyes beamed with joy, lighting up her whole face. She clasped her hands with an expression filled with the most violent and most gentle entreaty. "Oh!" she exclaimed, "bring her to me!"

A mother's touching illusion: To her Cosette seemed a little child who could be carried.

"Not yet," continued the doctor, "not right now. You still have some fever. The sight of your child will excite you and make you worse. First we must cure you."

She interrupted him impetuously.

"But I am cured! I tell you I am! Is this doctor a fool? Really! I do want to see my child!"

"You see how worked up you get!" said the physician. "As long as you're in this state, I can't let you see her. It's not enough to see her, you have to live for her. When you're more reasonable, I will bring her to you myself."

The poor mother bowed her head.

"Sir, I am sorry. I sincerely ask your pardon. Once I would never have spoken the way I did just now, but so many painful things have happened to me that sometimes I don't know what I'm saying. I understand, you're afraid of too much emotion. I'll wait as long as you like, but I swear to you it would not have harmed me to see my daughter. Already I can see her, I haven't taken my eyes off her since last night. Do you see? If they bring her to me now, I'll just talk to her very gently. That's all. Isn't it natural that I'd want to see my child, when they've been to Montfermeil on purpose just to bring her to me? I'm not angry. I know I'm going to be very happy. All night long, I saw figures in white, smiling at me. As soon as the doctor likes, he can bring Cosette. My fever's gone; I'm cured; I feel there's almost nothing the matter with me; but I'll act as if I'm sick, and not move, just to please the ladies here. When they see how calm I am, they'll say, 'You must give her the child.' "

M. Madeleine was sitting in a chair by the side of the bed. She turned toward him, visibly trying to appear calm and "very good," as she put it, in that debility that resembles childhood, so that seeing her so peaceful, there could be no objection to bringing her Cosette. Yet, although restraining herself, she couldn't help asking M. Madeleine a thousand questions.

"Did you have a good trip, Monsieur Mayor? Oh! how kind you were to go for her! Just tell me how she is. Did she travel well? Oh! She won't recognize me. In all this time, she's forgotten me, poor kitten! Children can't remember. They're like birds. Today they see one thing and tomorrow another, and they don't remember a thing. Just tell me, did she have clean clothes? Did the Thénardiers keep her neat? How did they feed her? Oh, if you only knew how I've suffered, asking myself all these things in my misery! Now, it's over. I'm happy. Oh! How I want to see her! Monsieur Mayor, did you think she is pretty? Isn't my daughter beautiful? You must have been very cold in the coach? Couldn't they bring her here for one little moment? They could take her away immediately. Tell them, please, you're the master here!"

He took her hand. "Cosette is beautiful," he said. "Cosette is well; you will see her soon, but be quiet. You're talking too much; you're taking your arms out of the covers, which makes you cough."

In fact, coughing fits did interrupt Fantine at almost every word.

She did not complain, afraid she had weakened the confidence she wanted to inspire by overeager pleas, and she began to talk about unimportant things.

"Montfermeil is a pretty place, isn't it? In summer people go there on outings. Do the Thénardiers do a good business? Not a great many people pass through that part of the country. Their inn is a—a cheap place."

M. Madeleine still held her hand and looked at her anxiously. It was obvious that he had come to tell her things he now hesitated to mention. The doctor had made his visit and left. Sister Simplice alone remained with them.

But in the midst of the silence, Fantine cried out, "I hear her! Oh, Lord! I hear her!"

She lifted her right hand for them to be still around her, held her breath, and listened in ecstasy.

There was a child playing in the court—the child of the concierge or of some working girl. It was one of those chance things that always happen and seem to make up a part of the mysterious staging of tragic events. The child, a little girl, was running up and down to keep warm, singing and laughing out loud. Alas! Is there anyplace where children's games are absent? It was that little girl Fantine had heard singing.

"Oh!" she said, "it's my Cosette! I know her voice!"

The child left as she had come, and the voice died away. Fantine listened for some time. A shadow crossed her face, and M. Madeleine heard her whisper, "How wicked it is of that doctor not to let me see my child! That man has a bad face!"

Yet her happy train of thought returned. With her head on the pillow she continued to talk to herself. "How happy we'll be! First we'll have a little garden; Monsieur Madeleine has promised me. My daughter will play in the garden. She must know her letters by now. I'll teach her to spell. She'll run on the grass chasing butterflies, and I'll watch her. Then there'll be her first communion. Ah! When will her first communion be?"

She began to count on her fingers.

"One, two, three, four. She's seven. In five years. She'll have a white veil and open-work stockings, and she'll look like a little lady. Oh, my good sister, see how foolish I am; here I am thinking already about my child's first communion!"

And she began to laugh.

He had let go of Fantine's hand. He was listening to the words as one listens to the wind blowing, his eyes on the ground, his mind absorbed in unfathomable reflection. Suddenly she stopped talking, and he automatically raised his eyes. Fantine looked appalling.

She did not speak; she did not breathe; she half-raised herself on the bed, the high-gown fell off her emaciated shoulders; her face, radiant just a moment before, turned deathly pale, and her eyes, wide with terror, seemed to fasten on something terrible facing her at the other end of the room.

"Good God!" he exclaimed. "Fantine, what's the matter?"

She did not answer; she did not take her eyes from the object she seemed to see, but touched his arm with one hand, and with the other gestured for him to look behind him.

He turned and saw Javert.

III

JAVERT SATISFIED

This is what had happened.

The half hour after midnight was striking when M. Madeleine left the hall of the Arras Superior Court. He had returned to his inn just in time to catch the mail coach, in which it will be remembered he had reserved a seat. A little before six in the morning he had reached Montreuil-sur-mer, where his first concerns had been to mail his letter to M. Laffitte, then go to the infirmary and visit Fantine.

Meanwhile he had scarcely left the hall of the superior court when the prosecuting attorney, recovering from his first shock, addressed the court, deploring the insanity of the honorable Mayor of Montreuil-sur-mer, declaring that his convictions were in no way altered by this remarkable incident, on which more light would surely later be shed, and demanding meanwhile the conviction of Champmathieu, obviously the real Jean Valjean. The prosecuting attorney's persistence visibly contradicted the general view of the public, the court, and the jury. The defense attorney had little difficulty in rebutting this harangue and establishing that, in consequence of the revelations of M. Madeleine—that is, of the real Jean Valjean—the case was overturned and the jury now had before them an innocent man. The counsel drew from this a few passionate appeals, unfortunately not very new, in regard to judicial errors, etc., etc.; the judge, in his summing up, sided with the defense; and the jury, after a few moments' deliberation, acquitted Champmathieu.

Yet the prosecuting attorney required a Jean Valjean, and having lost Champmathieu he took Madeleine.

Right after the discharge of Champmathieu, the prosecutor closeted himself with the judge. The topic of their conference was, "Of the necessity of the arrest of the person of Monseiur the Mayor of Montreuil-sur-mer." This sentence, containing a great many "of's," is the prosecuting attorney's, written by his own hand, on the minutes of his report to the attorney general.

With the first emotions over, the judge made few objections. Justice must take its course. Then to confess the truth, although the judge was a kind man and quite intelligent, he was at the same time a strong, almost zealous royalist, and had been shocked when the mayor of Montreuil-sur-mer, in speaking of the landing at Cannes, had said "the Emperor" instead of "Buonaparte."

The order of arrest was therefore granted. The prosecuting attorney sent it to Montreuil-sur-mer by courier, at top speed, to Police Inspector Javert.

It will be recalled that Javert had returned to Montreuil-sur-mer immediately after testifying.

Javert was just waking up when the courier brought him the warrant and order of arrest.

The courier was himself a policeman and an intelligent man who, in a few words, apprised Javert of what had happened at Arras. The order of arrest, signed by the prosecuting attorney, was couched in these terms: "Inspector Javert will arrest Monsieur Madeleine, Mayor of Montreuil-sur-mer, who has this day been identified in court as the discharged convict Jean Valjean."

Seeing Javert in the infirmary's entrance hall, anyone not knowing him could not have guessed what was going on, and would have thought he looked quite natural. He was cool, calm, grave, with his gray hair perfectly smooth across his temples, and he had climbed the stairs with his customary deliberation. But anyone who knew him well and had looked him over carefully would have shuddered. The buckle of his leather collar, instead of being at the back of his neck, was under his left ear. This denoted extraordinary agitation.

Javert was always in character, without a wrinkle in his duty or his uniform, methodical with villains, rigid with his coat buttons.

For his collar buckle to be awry, he must have just had one of those shocks that could be called inner earthquakes.

He came unostentatiously, had taken a corporal and four soldiers from a nearby station house, had left the soldiers in the courtyard, had been shown to Fantine's room by the unsuspecting concierge, accustomed as she was to seeing armed men asking for the mayor.

On reaching Fantine's room, Javert turned the knob, pushed the door open as gently as a nurse or a police spy, and entered.

Properly speaking, he did not enter. He remained standing in the half open doorway, his hat on his head, and his left hand in his overcoat, which was buttoned to the chin. In the bend of his elbow could be seen the leaden head of his enormous cane, which disappeared behind him.

He remained there for nearly a minute unnoticed. Suddenly, Fantine raised her eyes, saw him, and made M. Madeleine turn around.

As Madeleine's glance met that of Javert, Javert, without stirring, without moving, without coming closer, became terrifying. There is no human feeling that can ever be so appalling as joy.

It was the face of the devil who has just regained his victim.

The certainty of finally having Jean Valjean revealed on his face all that was in his soul. The troubled depths rose to the surface. The humiliation of having lost the scent somewhat, of having been in error for a while about Champmathieu, was erased by the pride of having guessed so well at first, and having so long held to a correct instinct. Javert's satisfaction radiated from his commanding attitude. The deformity of triumph spread across his narrow forehead. It was the full quotient of horror that only a gratified face can display.

At that moment Javert was in heaven. Without a clear notion of his own feelings, yet with a confused intuition of his need and his success, he, Javert, personified justice, light, and truth, in their celestial function as destroyers of evil. He was surrounded and supported by infinite depths of authority, reason, precedent, legal conscience, the vengeance of the law, all the stars in the firmament; he protected order, he hurled forth the thunder of the law, he avenged society, he lent aid to the absolute; he stood erect in a halo of glory; there was in his victory a trace of defiance and combat; standing haughty and resplendent, he displayed in full glory the superhuman beastiality of a ferocious archangel; the fearful shadow of the deed he was accomplishing, making visible in his clenched fist the uncertain flashes of the social sword; happy and indignant, he had gnashed his heel on crime, vice, rebellion, perdition, and hell, he was radiant, exterminating, smiling; there was an incontestable grandeur in this monstrous St. Michael.

Javert, though hideous, was not base.

Probity, sincerity, candor, conviction, the idea of duty, are things that, when in error, can turn hideous, but—even though hideous—remain great; their majesty, peculiar to the human conscience, persists in horror. They are virtues with a single vice—error. The pitiless, sincere joy of a fanatic in an act of atrocity preserves some mournful radiance that inspires veneration. Without suspecting it, Javert, in his dreadful happiness, was pitiful, like every ignorant man in triumph. Nothing could be more poignant and terrible than this face, which revealed what might be called all the evil of good.

IV

AUTHORITY GAINS ITS POWER

Fantine had not seen Javert since the day the mayor had saved her from him. Her sick brain could not grasp anything except that she was sure he had come for her. She could not bear this hideous face, she felt as though she were dying, she hid her face with both hands, and shrieked in anguish, "Monsieur Madeleine, save me!"

Jean Valjean—from here on we will call him by no other name—had stood up. He said to Fantine in his gentlest and calmest tone, "Don't be afraid. He hasn't come for you."

He then turned to Javert and said, "I know what you want."

Javert answered, "Hurry up."

In the inflection of those words there was an inexpressible something, part wild beast part madman. Javert did not say, "Hurry up!" he said, "Hur-up!" No spelling could express the tone in which this was said; it was no longer human speech; it was a howl.

He did not go through the usual ceremony; he made no speeches; he showed no warrant. To him Jean Valjean was a sort of mysterious and intangible antagonist, a shadowy wrestler with whom he had been struggling for five years, without being able to throw him. This arrest was not a beginning, but an end. He merely said, "Hurry up!"

While saying this, he did not budge, but threw Jean Valjean a look like the crampon that he used to drag miserable people to him.

It was the same look Fantine had felt penetrating the very marrow of her bones, two months earlier.

At Javert's command, Fantine had opened her eyes again. But the mayor was there, what could she fear?

Javert advanced to the middle of the room, exclaiming, "All right now, are you coming?"

The unhappy woman looked around her. There was no one but the nun and the mayor. To whom could this contemptuous familiarity be addresssed? To herself alone. She shuddered.

Then she saw an outrageous thing, so outrageous that nothing like it had ever appeared in the darkest delirium of her fever.

She saw the spy Javert seize the mayor by the collar; she saw the mayor bow his head. The world seemed to vanish before her eyes.

Javert, in fact, had taken Jean Valjean by the collar.

"Monsieur Mayor!" Fantine cried out

Javert burst into a horrible laugh, displaying all his teeth.

"There's no Monsieur Mayor here anymore!" he said.

Jean Valjean did not attempt to remove the hand that grasped the collar of his coat. He said, "Javert—"

Javert interrupted him, "Call me Monsieur Inspector!"

"Monsieur," Jean Valjean went on, "I would like to speak a word with you in private."

"Aloud, speak out loud," said Javert, "people speak out loud to me."

Jean Valjean went on, lowering his voice.

"It is a request that I have to make of you—"

"I tell you to speak up."

"But this should not be heard by anyone but yourself."

"What do I care? I won't listen."

Jean Valjean turned to him and said rapidly and very softly, "Give me three days! Three days to go for the child of this unhappy woman! I'll pay whatever it takes. You may accompany me if you like."

"Are you laughing at me!" cried Javert. "Look! I didn't think you were that stupid! You're asking for three days to get away, and you tell me you're going for this girl's child! Ha, ha, that's a good one!"

Fantine shuddered.

"My child!" she exclaimed, "going for my child! Then she is not here! Sister, tell me, where is Cosette? I want my child! Monsieur Madeleine, Monsieur Mayor!"

Javert stamped his foot.

"Now there's the other one! Hold your tongue, whore! Miserable town, where convicts are magistrates and prostitutes are nursed like countesses! Ha, but all that will be changed; high time!"

He stared at Fantine, and added, grabbing Jean Valjean's tie, shirt, and coat collar again, "I tell you there is no Monsieur Madeleine, and that there is no Monsieur the Mayor. There's a thief, a bandit, a convict named Jean Valjean, and I've got him! That's what there is!"

Fantine sat upright, supporting herself on her rigid arms and hands; she looked at Jean Valjean, then at Javert, and then at the nun; she opened her mouth as if to speak; a guttural sound came from her throat, her teeth clamped shut, she stretched out her arms in anguish, convulsively spreading her fingers, and groping like someone drowning; then suddenly fell back against the pillow.

Her head struck the head of the bed and fell forward on her breast, the mouth gaping, the eyes open and glazed.

She was dead.

Jean Valjean put his hand on that of Javert, which was holding him, and opened it as he would have opened the hand of a child; then he said, "You have killed this woman."

"Stop this!" cried Javert, furious. "I'm not here to listen to sermons; save all that; the guard is downstairs. Come right now or it's the handcuffs!"

In a corner of the room stood an old iron bedstead in dilapidated condition, which the sisters used as a campbed when they watched over a patient at night. Jean Valjean went to the bed, wrenched out the loose head bar—an easy thing for muscles like his—in the twinkling of an eye, and with the bar in his clenched fist, looked at Javert. Javert retreated toward the door.

His iron bar in hand, Jean Valjean walked slowly toward Fantine's bed. On reaching it, he turned and said to Javert in a voice that could scarcely be heard, "I advise you not to disturb me now."

Nothing is more certain than the fact that Javert shuddered.

He thought of calling the guard, but Jean Valjean might take advantage of his absence to escape. So he remained, grasped the small end of his cane, and leaned against the framework of the door without taking his eyes from Jean Valjean.

Jean Valjean rested his elbow on the bedpost, his head on his hand, and gazed at Fantine stretched out motionless in front of him. He stayed this way, silent and absorbed, evidently oblivious of everything in this life. His face and body expressed nothing but inexpressible pity. After a few moments' reverie, he bent down to Fantine, and spoke to her in a whisper.

What did he say? What could this condemned man say to this dead woman? What were the words? They were heard by no one on earth. Did the dead woman hear them? Certain touching illusions may be transcendent realities. One thing is beyond doubt; Sister Simplice, the only witness to what went on, has often said that as Jean Valjean whispered in Fantine's ear, she distinctly saw an ineffable smile spread across those pale lips and those dim eyes, full of the wonder of the tomb.

Jean Valjean took Fantine's head in his hands and arranged it on the pillow, as a mother would have done for her child, then fastened the string of her nightgown, and tucked her hair under her cap. This done, he closed her eyes.

At this instant Fantine's face seemed strangely luminous.

Death is the entrance into great light.

Fantine's hand hung over the side of the bed. Jean Valjean knelt before this hand, gently lifted it, and kissed it.

Then he rose and, turning to Javert, said, "Now, I am at your disposal."

V

A FITTING GRAVE

Javert put Jean Valjean in the city prison.

M. Madeleine's arrest produced a sensation, or rather an extraordinary commotion, at Montreuil-sur-mer. We are sorry not to be able to disguise the fact that, merely because of the sentence "He was a convict," almost everybody abandoned him. In less than two hours, all the good he had done was forgotten, and he was "nothing but a convict." It is fair to say that the details of the scene at Arras were not yet known. All day long, conversations like this were heard all over town: "Don't you know, he was a freed convict!" "He! Who?" "The mayor." "Bah! Monsieur Madeleine?" "Yes." "Really?" "His name was not Madeleine; he has a dreadful name, Béjean, Bojean, Bonjean!" "Oh! Good Lord!" "He's been arrested." "Arrested!" "In prison, in the city prison until his transfer." "His transfer! Where will he be taken?" "To the superior court for a highway robbery he once committed." "Well! I always did suspect him. The man was too good, too perfect, too sweet. He refused fees and gave money to every little devil he met. I always thought there must be something bad behind all of this."

"The drawing rooms," above all, were entirely of this opinion.

An old lady, a subscriber to the *Drapeau Blanc,* made this remark, the depth of which it is almost impossible to fathom: "I am not sorry about it. That will teach the Bonapartists!"

This is how the phantom that had been called M. Madeleine was dispelled at Montreuil-sur-mer. Three or four persons alone in the whole city remained faithful to his memory. The old concierge who had been his servant was among them.

On the evening of this same day, the honorable old woman was sitting in her lodge, still quite bewildered and sunk in sad reflections. The factory had been closed all day, the carriage doors were bolted, the street was deserted. There was no one in the house but the two nuns,

Sister Perpétue and Sister Simplice, who were at their vigil beside Fantine's body.

At about the time when M. Madeleine had usually come home, the honest doorkeeper unconsciously rose, took the key of his room from a drawer along with the taper stand he used at night to light himself up the stairs, then hung the key on a nail where he had usually picked it up, and put the taper stand beside it, as if she were expecting him. She then sat down again in her chair and went back to her reflections. The poor old woman had done all this without being aware of it.

More than two hours had elapsed when she awoke from her reverie and exclaimed, "Why, bless me! I've hung his key on the nail!"

Just then, the window of her lodge opened, a hand passed through the opening, took the key and stand, and lit the taper with the candle.

The concierge raised her eyes; she was dumfounded, a stifled cry in her throat.

She knew the hand, the arm, the coatsleeve.

It was M. Madeleine.

She was speechless for some seconds, thunderstruck, as she herself said later, in giving her account of the affair.

"My God! Monsieur Mayor!" she finally exclaimed, "I thought you were—"

She stopped; the end of her sentence would have lacked in respect to its beginning. To her, Jean Valjean was still Monsieur Mayor.

He completed her thought.

"In prison," he said. "I was there; I broke a window bar, dropped off from the top of a roof, and here I am. I'm going to my room; go for Sister Simplice. She is undoubtedly beside the poor woman."

The old servant hastily obeyed.

He gave her no warnings, very sure she would guard him better than he would guard himself.

Nobody ever knew how he had managed to get into the courtyard without opening the carriage door. He had, and always carried with him, a pass key that opened a little side door, but he must have been searched, and had this taken from him. This point has not been cleared up.

He climbed the stairs to his room. On reaching the top, he left his taper stand on the last stair, opened his door, making almost no noise, felt his way to the window and closed the shutter, went back for his taper, then into the room.

The precaution was not useless; we recall that his window could be seen from the street.

He glanced around him, at his table, his chair, his bed, which had not been slept in for three days. There was no trace of the disorder from the night before the last. The doorkeeper had cleaned the room. Except that she had picked up from the ashes and neatly laid on the table the metal tips of the stick and the forty-sous piece, blackened by the fire.

He took a sheet of paper and wrote: "These are the ends of my iron-tipped stick and the forty-sous piece stolen from Petit Gervais, which I mentioned at the superior court"; then he placed the two pieces of iron and the silver coin on the sheet in such a way that it would be the first thing seen on entering the room. From a wardrobe he took out an old shirt, which he tore into several pieces and in which he wrapped up the two silver candlesticks. In all this there actually seemed to be no haste or commotion. And while he packed the bishop's candlesticks, he was eating a piece of black bread. It was probably prison bread that he had brought in his escape.

This was determined through bread crumbs found on the floor of the room, when the court afterward ordered a search.

Two gentle taps were heard at the door.

"Come in," he said.

It was Sister Simplice.

She was pale, her eyes were red, and the candle she was holding trembled in her hand. The shocks of fate have this peculiarity, that however subdued or disciplined our feelings may be, they draw out the human nature from the depths of our souls and compel us to show it outwardly. In this day's turmoil the nun had again become a woman. She had wept, and she was trembling.

Jean Valjean had written a few lines on a piece of paper, which he handed to the nun, saying "Sister, you will give this to the curé."

The paper was not folded. She glanced at it.

"You may read it," he said.

She read: "I beg Monsieur the Curé to take charge of all that I leave here. From it he will please defray the expenses of my trial, and of the burial of the woman who died this morning. The remainder is for the poor."

The sister wanted to speak, but could scarcely stammer out a few inarticulate sounds. However, she managed to say, "Doesn't Monsieur Mayor wish to see the poor woman one last time?"

"No," he said, "I am being pursued; I would simply be arrested in her room; it would disturb her."

He had scarcely finished when there was a loud noise on the staircase. They heard the clump of climbing feet, and the old concierge exclaiming in her loudest and most piercing tones, "Kind sir, I swear to you in the name of God, that nobody has come in here the whole day or the whole evening; I have not even once left my door!"

A man replied, "Yet, there is a light in the room."

They recognized Javert's voice.

The room was so arranged that in opening, the door hid the corner of the wall to the right. Jean Valjean blew out the taper and placed himself in this corner.

Sister Simplice fell on her knees near the table.

The door opened.

Javert entered.

The whispering of several men and the protests of the concierge could be heard in the hall.

The nun did not raise her eyes. She was praying.

The candle was on the mantel, and gave only a dim light.

Javert saw the sister, and stopped, shamed.

It will be remembered that Javert's very foundation, his natural element, the medium in which he breathed, was veneration for all authority. He was all of a piece, admitting no objection or restriction. To him, of course, ecclesiastic authority was the highest of all; he was devout, superficial, and correct on this point as on all others. In his eyes, a priest was an infallible spirit, a nun was a being who never sinned. They were souls walled away from this world, with a single door that never opened except for the release of truth.

On seeing the sister, his first impulse was to leave.

But there was also another duty that held him and urged him imperatively in the opposite direction. His second impulse was to remain and to venture at least one question.

This was the Sister Simplice who had never lied in her

life. Javert knew this, and venerated her particularly because of it.

"Sister," he said, "are you alone in this room?"

There was a terrible moment during which the poor concierge felt her limbs falter beneath her. The sister raised her eyes and replied, "Yes."

Then Javert continued, "Excuse me if I persist, it is my duty—have you seen this evening a person, a man—he has escaped, and we are searching for him—Jean Valjean—you have not seen him?"

The sister answered, "No."

She lied. Two lies in succession, one upon another, without hesitation, quickly, as if she were adept at it.

"Your pardon!" said Javert, and he withdrew, bowing reverently.

Oh, holy maiden! For many years now, you are gone from this world; you have joined in glory your sisters, the virgins, and your brothers, the angels; may this lie be counted for you in Paradise.

The sister's statement was something so decisive for Javert that he did not even notice the singularity of the taper, just blown out, and smoking on the table.

An hour later, a man, walking rapidly through the fog beneath the trees, was leaving Montreuil-sur-mer going toward Paris. The man was Jean Valjean. It has been determined from the testimony of two or three wagon drivers who passed him, that he was carrying a bundle and was dressed in a workman's smock. Where did he get this smock? No one ever knew. However, an old laborer had died in the factory infirmary a few days earlier, leaving nothing but his smock. That must have been the one.

A last word in regard to Fantine.

We have all one mother—the earth. Fantine was restored to this mother.

The curé thought best, and perhaps he was right, to reserve the largest amount possible out of what Jean Valjean had left for the poor. After all, who was involved?—a convict and a woman of the streets. This was why he simplified Fantine's burial, reducing it to that bare necessity called the potter's field.

And so Fantine was buried in the common grave of the cemetery, which belongs to everybody and to nobody, and in which the poor are lost. Fortunately, God knows where to find the soul. Fantine was laid away in the darkness among the homeless bodies; she suffered the promiscuity of dust. She was thrown into the public pit. Her grave was like her bed.

COSETTE

Book One

WATERLOO

I

WHAT YOU SEE ON THE WAY FROM NIVELLES

On a beautiful morning in May of last year (1861), a traveler, the author of this story, was going from Nivelles toward La Hulpe. He was traveling on foot between two rows of trees, he was following a wide paved road, snaking across hills that one after the other, lift it up and let it drop again, like enormous waves. He had passed Lillois and Bois-Seigneur-Isaac. To the west he saw the slate-roofed steeple of Braine-l'Alleud, which takes the form of an inverted vase. He had just passed a wooded hill and at the corner of a crossroad, beside a sort of worm-eaten signpost bearing the inscription FORMER TOLL-GATE, NO. 4, a tavern with this sign: THE FOUR WINDS. ECHABEAU, PRIVATE CAFÉ.

Half a mile beyond this tavern, he reached a little valley, where a stream flowed under an arch dug into the embankment of the road. The cluster of trees, widely spaced but very green, that fills the vale on one side of the road, spreads out on the other side into meadows and sweeps away in graceful disarray toward Braine-l'Alleud.

On the right, and beside the road, there was an inn,

II

HOUGOMONT

Hougomont—this was a fateful spot, the beginning of the resistance, the first obstacle encountered at Waterloo by the great forester of Europe called Napoleon, the first knot under the axe.

It was a château; now it is nothing more than a farm. Hougomont, to the antiquary, is *Hugomons*. This manor was built by Hugo, lord of Somerel, the same who endowed the sixth chaplaincy of the Abbey of Villiers.

The traveler pushed open the door, brushed against an old carriage under the porch, and entered the court.

The first thing that struck him in this yard was a sixteenth-century door, which seemed like an archway, everything having fallen down around it. A monumental aspect is often produced by ruin. Near the arch another doorway with keystones from the time of Henry IV opens in the wall, revealing the trees of an orchard. Beside this door were a dung-hill, mattocks and shovels, some carts, an old well with its flagstone and iron pulley, a frisky colt, a strutting turkey, a chapel topped by a little steeple, an espaliered pear tree in bloom, against the wall of the chapel; such was the court whose conquest was Napoleon's dream. This bit of earth, if he could have taken it, would perhaps have given him the world. The hens are scattering the dirt with their beaks. There is a growling: It is a large dog, who bares his teeth, taking the place of the English.

The English fought there admirably. The four companies of guards under Cooke held their ground for seven hours, against the fury of an assaulting army.

Seen on the map, Hougomont laid out geometrically, buildings and enclosure taken together, presents a sort of irregular rectangle, one corner of which is cut off. At that corner is the southern entrance, protected by the wall, which is within pointblank musket range. Hougomont has two entrances: the southern, that of the château, and the northern, that of the farm. Napoleon sent his brother Jerome against Hougomont. The divisions of Guilleminot, Foy, and Bachelu were hurled against it; almost the whole corps of Reille was used there and defeated there, and the bullets of Kellermann were exhausted against this heroic section of wall. It was too much for Bauduin's brigade to force Hougomont on the north, and Soye's brigade could only batter it on the south—it could not be taken.

The farm buildings rim the southern side of the court. A small portion of the northern door, broken by the French, hangs dangling from the wall. It is composed of four planks, nailed to two cross-pieces, and on it can be seen the scars of the attack.

The northern door, forced by the French, to which a piece has been added to replace the panel hung on the wall, stands half open at the foot of the courtyard; it is cut squarely into a wall made of stone below and brick above, which closes the court on the north. It is a simple cart-door, such as one finds on all small farms, a large double door, made of rough planks; beyond this are the meadows. This entrance was furiously contested. For a long time all sorts of bloody handprints could be seen on the door. It was there that Bauduin was killed.

You still feel the storm of combat in this court: Its horror is visible; the upheaval of conflict is petrified there; it lives, it dies; it was only yesterday. The walls are still in death throes; the stones fall, the breaches cry out; the holes are wounds; the trees bend and shudder, as if making an effort to escape.

In 1815, the court was more built up than it is today. Structures that have since been pulled down formed projecting redans, angles, and squares.

The English barricaded themselves in there; the French managed to penetrate but could not maintain their position. Beside the chapel, one wing of the château, the only existing remnant of the Hougomont manor, stands crumbling, one might almost say disemboweled. The château served as dungeon; the chapel served as blockhouse. Mutual extermination was done there. The French, targeted from all sides, from behind the walls, from the barn roofs, from the bottom of the cellars, through every window, through every air hole, through every chink in the stones, brought bundles of sticks and set fire to the walls and the men: The storm of balls was answered by a tempest of flame.

In the ruined wing, through the iron-barred windows,

with a four-wheeled cart in front of the door, a large bundle of stakes for hop plants, a plough, a pile of dry brush near a live hedge, some lime smoking in a square hole in the ground, and a ladder lying next to an old shed with mangers for straw. A young girl was digging up weeds in a field, where a large yellow poster, probably for a traveling show at some annual fair, was fluttering in the wind. At the corner of the inn, beside a pond in which a flotilla of ducks was navigating, a rough footpath disappeared into the brush. The traveler took this path.

After a hundred paces, passing a fifteenth-century wall topped by a steep gable of crossed bricks, he found himself opposite a huge stone doorway, its arch springing from rectilinear imposts, in the solemn style of Louis XIV, with plain medallions on the sides. Over the entrance was a severe façade, and a wall perpendicular to the façade almost touched the doorway, flanking it at an abrupt right angle. On the meadow in front of the door lay three harrows, through which were blooming, as best they could, all the flowers of May. The entrance was closed. It was shut by a decrepit double door, decorated with an old rusty knocker.

The sunshine was enchanting; the branches of the trees had that gentle tremor of May that seems to come from the birds' nests more than from the wind. A hardy little bird, probably in love, was desperately singing away in a tall tree.

The traveler paused and examined in the stone at the left of the door, near the ground, a large circular excavation like the hollow of a sphere. Just then the door opened, and a peasant woman came out.

She saw the traveler, and noticed what he was examining.

"A French cannon ball did that," she said.

And she added, "What you see there, higher up in the door, near a nail, is the hole made by a Biscay musket. The bullet did not go through the wood."

"What's the name of this place?" asked the traveler.

"Hougomont," the woman answered.

The traveler straightened up. He took a few steps and looked over the hedges. On the horizon he could see through the trees a sort of hillock and on this hillock something in the distance that looked like a lion.

He was on the battlefield of Waterloo.

one can glimpse the dismantled rooms of a main building; the English guards lay in ambush there; the spiral staircase, broken from foundation to roof, looks like the interior of a broken seashell. The stairway has two landings; the English, besieged in this place, and crowded onto the upper steps, had cut away the lower ones. They are large slabs of blue stone, now heaped together among the nettles. A dozen steps still cling to the wall: On the first is cut the image of a trident. These inaccessible steps are firm in their sockets; all the rest looks like a toothless jawbone. Two old trees are there; one is dead, the other is wounded at the foot and does not leaf out until April. Since 1815 it had begun to grow across the staircase.

There was a massacre in the chapel. The interior, again restored to quiet, is strange. No mass has been said there since the carnage. The altar remains, however—crude, wooden, backed by a wall of rough stone. Four whitewashed walls, a door opposite the altar, two little arched windows, over the door a large wooden crucifix, above the crucifix a square opening blocked up with a bundle of straw; in a corner on the ground, an old glazed sash all broken—such is the chapel. Near the altar hangs a wooden fifteenth-century statue of St. Anne; the head of the infant Jesus was knocked off by a musket shot. The French, momentary masters of the chapel, then dislodged, set it on fire. The flames filled this ruin; it was a furnace; the door was burned, the floor was burned, the wooden Christ did not burn. The fire ate its way to his feet, whose blackened stumps alone are visible, then it stopped. A miracle, say the country people. The infant Jesus, decapitated, was not so fortunate as the Christ.

The walls are covered with inscriptions. Near the feet of the Christ we read this name: *Henquinez*. Then these others: *Conde de Rio Maïor. Marques y Marquesa de Almagro (Habana)*. There are French names with exclamation points, tokens of anger. The wall was newly whitewashed in 1849. The nations were insulting each other on it.

At the door of this chapel a body was found with an ax in its hand. This body was that of Second Lieutenant Legros.

On coming out of the chapel, a well can be seen on the left. There are two in this yard. You ask, Why is there no bucket and no pulley to this one? Because no water is drawn from it now. Why is no more water drawn from it? Because it is full of skeletons.

The last man to draw water from that well was named Guillaume Van Kylsom. He was a peasant who lived in Hougomont and was gardener there. On June 18, 1815, his family fled and hid in the woods.

For several days and nights the forest around the Abbey of Villiers concealed the scattered and frightened local population. Even now some vestiges remain, such as old trunks of scorched trees, marking the sites of the poor trembling bivouacs in the depths of the thickets.

Guillaume Van Kylsom remained at Hougomont "to take care of the château" and hid in the cellar. The English discovered him there. He was torn from his hiding place and, with blows of the flat of their swords, the soldiers forced this terrified man to serve them. They were thirsty; this Guillaume brought them drink. It was from this well that he drew the water. Many had their last drink from it. This well, where so many of the dead drank, was also to die.

After the action, there was a haste to bury the corpses. Death has its own way of embittering victory, and its glory is followed by pestilence. Typhus comes with triumph. This well was deep, and they made it a sepulcher. Three hundred dead were thrown into it. Perhaps too hastily. Were they all dead? Tradition says no. It appears that on the night after the burial, feeble voices were heard calling out from the well.

This well is isolated in the middle of the courtyard. Three walls, half brick, half stone, folded back like the leaves of a screen and imitating a square turret, surround it on three sides. The fourth side is open. That is the side where the water was drawn. The back wall has a sort of shapeless bull's eye, perhaps a shell hole. This turret had a roof, of which only the beams remain. The iron bracket sustaining the wall on the right is in the shape of a cross. You bend over the well, the eye is lost in a deep brick cylinder, filled with an accumulation of shadows. All around it, the bottom of the walls is hidden by nettles.

This well does not have in front of it the large blue flagstones that usually surround Belgian wells. The blue stone is replaced by a crossbar on which rest five or six misshapen wooden stumps, knotty and hardened like huge bones. There is no longer either bucket, or chain, or pulley; but the stone basin is still there for the overflow. The rainwater gathers there, and from time to time a bird from the nearby forest comes to drink and flies away.

One house among these ruins, the farmhouse, is still inhabited. The door of the house opens on the courtyard. Beside a pretty Gothic lock plate on the door there is an iron handle in trefoil, on a slant. As the Hanoverian Lieutenant Wilda was grabbing it to take refuge in the farmhouse, a French sapper struck off his hand with the blow of an ax.

The grandfather of the family occupying the house was the former gardener Van Kylsom, long since dead. A gray-haired woman said to us, "I was there. I was three years old. My older sister was scared and cried. They carried us off into the woods; I was in my mother's arms. They laid their ears to the ground to listen. As for me, I mimicked the cannon: *boom, boom.*"

As we mentioned, one of the yard gateways, on the left, opens into the orchard.

The orchard is awful.

It is in three parts, one might almost say in three acts. The first part is a garden, the second is the orchard, the third is a wood. These three parts have a common enclosure, on the entrance side the château buildings and the farm, to the left a hedge, to the right a wall, at the far end a wall. The right wall is brick, the back wall is stone. You enter the garden first. It is sloping, planted with currant bushes, choked with weeds, and closed in by a terrace of cut stone, with double-swelled balusters. It is a manor house garden, in the early French style that preceded the work of Lenôtre; today it is in ruins, and covered wth briers. The pilasters are surmounted by globes like stone cannonballs. There are forty-three balusters still in place; the others are lying in the grass; nearly all show some abrasion from gunshot. One broken baluster stands upright like a broken leg.

It was in this garden, which is lower than the orchard, that six of the First Light Infantry, having penetrated there, and unable to escape, caught and trapped like bears in a pit, battled it out against two Hanoverian companies, one of which was armed with carbines. The Hanoverians were ranged along the balusters, and fired from above. The intrepid infantrymen, answering from below, six against two hundred, with only the currant bushes for shelter, took a quarter of an hour to die.

You go up a few steps, and from the garden pass into the orchard proper. There, in these few square yards, fifteen hundred men fell in less than a hour. The wall seems ready to take up the combat again. The thirty-eight loopholes, pierced by the English at irregular heights, are still there. In front of the sixteenth lie two English granite tombs. There are no loopholes except in the south wall, the principal attack came from that side. This wall is concealed on the outside by a large hedge; the French came up, thinking there was nothing in their way but the hedge, crossed it, and found the wall, an obstacle and an ambush, the English Guards behind it, the thirty-eight loopholes pouring out their fire at once, a storm of grapeshot and cannonballs; and Soye's brigade was broken there. Thus began Waterloo.

The orchard, however, was taken. They had no scaling ladders, but the French climbed the wall with their fingernails. They fought hand to hand under the trees. All this grass was soaked with blood. A battalion from Nassau, seven hundred men, was annihilated there. On the outside, the wall against which Kellermann's two batteries were trained, is gnawed by grapeshot.

This orchard is as responsive as any other to the month of May. It has its golden blossoms and its daisies, the grass is tall, farm horses are grazing, lines with drying clothes cross the gaps between the trees, making visitors bend their heads; you walk over that green sward, and your foot sinks into mole tracks. In the midst of the grass, an uprooted trunk, lying on the ground, is still growing green. Major Blackman leaned back against it to die. Under a large tree nearby fell the German general Duplat, of a French family that fled on the revocation of the Edict of Nantes. Close beside it leans a diseased old apple tree swathed in a bandage of straw and clay. Nearly all the apple trees are falling from old age. There is not one that does not show its cannon ball or its musket shot. Skeletons of dead trees abound in this orchard. Crows fly into the branches; beyond it is a wood full of violets.

Bauduin killed, Foy wounded, fire, slaughter, carnage, a creek of English blood, German and French blood, mingled in fury; a well filled with corpses, the Nassau regiment and the Brunswick regiment destroyed, Duplat killed, Blackman killed, the English Guards crippled, twenty French battalions out of the forty of Reille's Corps decimated, three thousand men, in this one ruin of Hougomont, sabered, slashed, slaughtered, shot, burned; and all so that today a peasant can say to a traveler, "Monsieur, give me three francs and I'll describe the Battle of Waterloo!"

III

JUNE 18, 1815

Let us go back, for such is the storyteller's right, and place ourselves in the year 1815, a little before the beginning of the action narrated in the first part of this book.

If it had not rained on the night of June 17, 1815, the future of Europe would have been different. A few drops more or less tipped the balance against Napoleon. For Waterloo to be the end of Austerlitz, Providence needed only a little rain, and an unseasonable cloud crossing the sky was enough for the collapse of a world.

The battle of Waterloo—and this gave Blücher time to come up—could not begin before half-past eleven. Why? Because the ground was soaked. It was necessary to wait for it to firm up somewhat so the artillery could maneuver.

Napoleon was an artillery officer, and he never forgot it. The foundation of this prodigious captain was the man who, in his report to the Directory about Aboukir, said, "Each one of our cannonballs killed six men." All his battle plans were drawn up for projectiles. To have the artillery converge on a given point was his key to victory. He treated the strategy of the hostile general as a citadel and battered it for an opening. He overwhelmed the weak point with grapeshot; he entered and resolved battles with cannon. There was marksmanship in his genius. To destroy battle squares, pulverize regiments, break lines, crush and disperse masses, this was everything to him, to strike, strike, strike incessantly, and he entrusted this duty to the cannonball. A formidable method, which, linked to genius, made this somber prizefighter of war invincible for fifteen years.

On June 18, 1815, he counted on his artillery all the more because he had the advantage in numbers. Wellington had only a hundred and fifty-nine guns; Napoleon had two hundred and forty.

If the ground had been dry and the artillery able to move, the action would have been started at six in the morning. The battle would have been won by two o'clock, three hours before the Prussians tipped the scale of fortune.

What share of the blame for this defeat is Napoleon's? Should the shipwreck be imputed to the pilot?

Was Napoleon's evident physical decline accompanied at the time by a corresponding mental deterioration? Had his twenty years of war worn down the sword as well as the sheath, the soul as well as the body? Was the veteran detrimental to the captain? In a word, was that genius, as many good historians have thought, in eclipse? Had he put on a frenzy to disguise his declining powers from himself? Was he beginning to waver under the confusion of a random blast? Was he becoming—a grave fault in a general—careless of danger? In that class of great physical men who may be called the giants of action, is there an age when their genius becomes shortsighted? Old age has no hold on the geniuses of the ideal; for the Dantes and the Michelangelos, to grow older is to grow greater; for the Hannibals and the Bonapartes, is it to diminish? Had Napoleon lost his direct sense of victory? Could he no longer recognize the shoal, no longer detect the snare, no longer discern the crumbling edge of the abyss? Had he lost the instinct of disaster? Was he—who formerly knew all the paths to victory and who, from the height of his chariot of lightning, pointed them out with sovereign finger—now under such dark hallucination as to drive his tumultuous train of legions over the precipices? Was he gripped, at forty-six, by a supreme madness? Was this titanic driver of Destiny now only a monstrous suicide?

We think not.

His battle plan was, everyone agrees, a masterpiece. To march straight to the center of the allied line, pierce the enemy, cut them in two, push the British half toward Hal and the Prussian half toward Tongres, to make Wellington and Blücher into two fragments, carry Mont-Saint-Jean, seize Brussels, throw the Germans into the Rhine and the English into the sea. All this, for Napoleon, was in the battle plan. After that, he would see.

We do not, of course, claim to be giving the history of Waterloo; one of the key scenes of the drama we are telling hangs on that battle; but the history of the battle is not our subject; that history moreover has been told, and told in a masterly way, from one point of view by Napoleon, from the other point of view by a whole pleiad of historians (Walter Scott, Lamartine, Vaulabelle, Charras, Quinet, Thiers). As for us, we leave the historians to their struggle; we are merely a distant witness, a passerby on the plain, a researcher bending over this ground steeped in human flesh, perhaps taking appearances for realities; we have no right in the name of science to cope with a mass of facts undoubtedly tainted with mirage; we have neither the military experience nor the strategic ability to justify a system; in our opinion, a chain of accidents overruled both captains at Waterloo; and when destiny, that mysterious defendant, is called in, we judge like the people, that naive judge.

IV

A

If you want a clear idea of the battle of Waterloo, you have only to draw on the ground mentally a capital *A*. The left stroke of the *A* is the road from Nivelles, the right stroke is the road from Genappe, the cross of the *A* is the sunken road from Ohain to Braine l'Alleud. The top of the *A* is Mont-Saint-Jean, Wellington is there; the left-hand lower point is Hougomont, Reille is there with Jerome Bonaparte; the right-hand lower point is La Belle-Alliance, Napoleon is there. A little below the point where the crossbar of the *A* meets and cuts the right stroke, is La Haie-Sainte. At the middle of this crossing is the precise point where the final word of the battle was spoken. There the lion is placed, the involuntary symbol of the Imperial Guard's supreme heroism.

The triangle contained by the top of the *A*, between the two strokes and the crossing, is the plateau of Mont-Saint-Jean. The struggle for this plateau was the whole of the battle.

The wings of the two armies extended to the right and left of the two roads from Genappe and from Nivelles, d'Erlon being opposite Picton, Reille opposite Hill.

Behind the peak of the *A*, behind the plateau of Mont-Saint-Jean, is the forest of Soignes.

As to the plain itself, we must imagine a vast undulating area, each wave commanding the next, and these undulations rising toward Mont-Saint-Jean, bounded by forest.

Two opposing armies on a field of battle are two wrestlers. Their arms are locked. Each seeks to throw the other. They grasp at everything; a thicket is a strong point; a corner of a wall is a support for the shoulder; for lack of a few sheds to back them up, a regiment loses its footing; a depression in the plain, a movement of the soil, a convenient crosspath, woods, a ravine, may catch the heel of this colossus called an army and prevent him from falling back. He who leaves the field is beaten. Hence, for the responsible leader, the need to examine the smallest tuft of trees and appreciate the slightest details of contour.

Both generals had carefully studied the plain of Mont-Saint-Jean, now called the plain of Waterloo. Already in the preceding year, Wellington, with the sagacity of prescience, had examined it as a possible site for a great battle. On this ground and for this contest Wellington had the favorable side, Napoleon the unfavorable. The English army was above, the French army below.

To sketch here the appearance of Napoleon, on horseback, spyglass in hand, on the heights of Rossomme, at dawn on June 18, 1815, would be almost superfluous. Before we point him out, everybody has seen him. That calm profile under the little cocked hat of the school of Brienne, the green uniform, the white facings concealing the stars on his breast, the gray overcoat concealing the epaulets, the bit of red sash under the waistcoat, the leather breeches, the white horse with his saddle blanket of purple velvet with crowned *N*'s and eagles on the corners, the Hessian boots over silk stockings, the silver spurs, the Marengo sword, this whole image of the last

Caesar is alive in the imagination, applauded by half the world, rebuked by the rest.

That image has long been fully illuminated; it did have that obscurity through which most heroes pass, and which always veils the truth for a while, but now the history is luminous and complete.

This light of history is pitiless; it has a strange and divine quality that, luminous as it is, and precisely because it is luminous, often casts a shadow just where we saw a radiance; out of the same man it makes two different phantoms, and the one attacks and punishes the other, the darkness of the despot struggles with the splendor of the captain. Hence a truer measure in the final judgment of the nations. Babylon violated diminishes Alexander; Rome enslaved diminishes Caesar; massacred Jerusalem diminishes Titus. Tyranny follows the tyrant. Woe to the man who leaves behind a shadow that bears his form.

V

THE QUID OBSCURUM OF BATTLES

Everybody knows the first phase of this battle; the confused opening, uncertain, hesitant, threatening for both armies, but for the English still more than for the French.

It had rained all night; the ground was spongy from the shower; water lay here and there in hollows on the plain as in basins; at some points the wheels sank in up to the axles; the horses' girths dripped with liquid mud; if the wheat and rye flattened by that multitude of advancing carts had not filled the ruts and made a bed under the wheels, all movement, particularly in the valleys toward Papelotte, would have been impossible.

The affair began late; Napoleon, as we have explained, had a habit of holding all his artillery in hand like a pistol, aiming now at one point, now at another point of the battle, and he had wanted to wait until the field batteries could wheel and gallop freely; for this the sun had to come out and dry the ground. But the sun did not come out. This was not the field of Austerlitz. When the first gun fired, the English General Colville looked at his watch and noted that it was thirty-five minutes past eleven.

The battle was begun furiously, more so than the emperor may have wished, by the left wing of the French forces at Hougomont. At the same time Napoleon attacked the center by hurling Quiot's brigade at La Haie-Sainte, and Ney pushed the right wing of the French against the left wing of the English based on Papelotte.

The attack on Hougomont was partly a feint; to draw Wellington that way, to make him incline to the left, this was the plan. This plan would have succeeded, if the four companies of the English Guards, and the brave Belgians of Perponcher's division, had not resolutely held the position, enabling Wellington, instead of massing his forces at that point, to limit himself to reinforcing them with only four additional companies of guards and a Brunswick battalion.

The attack of the French right wing on Papelotte was intended to overwhelm the English left, cut the Brussels road, bar the passage of the Prussians, should they come, to carry Mont-Saint-Jean, drive Wellington back to Hougomont, from there to Braine-l'Alleud, from there to Hal; nothing could be clearer. With the exception of a few difficulties, this attack succeeded. Papelotte was taken; La Haie-Sainte was carried.

One detail should be noted. In the English infantry, particularly in Kempt's brigade, there were many new recruits. These young soldiers, confronting our formidable infantry, were heroic; though inexperienced, they fought boldly. They did particularly well as skirmishers; the soldier as a sharpshooter, to some extent left to himself, becomes, so to speak, his own general; these recruits exhibited something of French invention and French fury. This raw infantry showed enthusiasm. That displeased Wellington.

After the capture of La Haie-Sainte, the battle wavered.

From noon to four o'clock on that day, there was a hazy interval; the middle of the battle is rather indistinct and characterized by the density of the conflict. Twilight was gathering. Vast fluctuations could be seen in this mist, a giddy mirage, paraphernalia of war now almost unknown, the flaming Napoleonic calpacs, the fluttering sheaths, the crossed shoulder belts, the grenade cases, the hussars' dolmans, the red boots with a thousand creases, the heavy shakos festooned with fringe, the almost black uniforms from Brunswick mingled with England's scarlet infantry, the English soldiers with great white circular pads on their sleeves for epaulets, the Hanoverian light horse with their oblong leather helmets banded in copper with flowing red horse-hair plumes, the Scotch with bare knees and kilts, the large white gaiters of our grenadiers; these are tableaux, not strategic lines, the needs of Salvatore Rosa, not of Gribeauval.

A battle always involves a certain amount of tempest. *Quid obscurum, quid divinum.* Each historian traces the particular lineament that pleases him in this hurly-burly. Whatever the combinations of the generals, the shock of armed masses has incalculable impact; in action, the two plans of the two leaders become telescoped and each deforms the other. This point of the battlefield swallows up more combatants than any other, as the more or less spongy soil drinks up water thrown on it faster or slower. You are obliged to pour out more soldiers there than you would like. An unforeseen expenditure. The line of battle floats and twists like a thread; streams of blood flow regardless of logic; the army fronts undulate; regiments entering or retiring create promontories or gulfs; all these reefs continually sway back and forth in front of one another; where infantry was, artillery appears; where artillery was, cavalry rushes up; battalions are wisps of smoke. Something was there; look for it; it is gone; vistas are displaced; the somber folds advance and retreat; a sort of sepulchral wind pushes forward, falls back, swells and disperses these tragic multitudes. What is a hand-to-hand fight? An oscillation. The immobility of a geometric plan tells the story of a minute and not a day. To paint a battle requires those mighty artists with chaos in their brush. Rembrandt is better than Vandermeulen. Vandermeulen, exact at noon, lies at three o'clock. Geometry deceives; the hurricane alone is true. This is what gives Folard the right to contradict Polybius. We should add that there is always a certain moment when the battle degenerates into a combat, particularizes itself, scatters into innumerable details, which, to borrow the expression of Napoleon himself, "belong rather to the biography of the regiments than to the history of the army." In that case the historian clearly has the right to abridge. He can only seize upon the principal outlines of the struggle, and it is given to no narrator, however conscientious he may be, to fix absolutely the form of the horrible cloud that is called a battle.

This, which is true of all great armed encounters, is particularly applicable to Waterloo.

However, at a certain point that afternoon, the battle assumed a recognizable shape.

VI

FOUR O'CLOCK IN THE AFTERNOON

Toward four o'clock the English army's situation was grave. The Prince of Orange was in command of the center, Hill the right wing, Picton the left wing. The Prince of Orange, desperate and intrepid, cried out to the Hollando-Belgians: *Nassau! Brunswick! never retreat!* Hill, exhausted, had fallen back on Wellington. Picton was dead. At the very moment when the English had taken the French colors of the 105th of the line, the French had killed General Picton with a shot through the head. For Wellington the battle had two key points, Hougomont and La Haie-Sainte; Hougomont still held out, but was burning; La Haie-Sainte had been taken. Of the German battalion defending it, only forty-two men survived; all the officers except five were dead or taken prisoner. Three thousand combatants were massacred in that barn. A sergeant of the English Guards, the best boxer in England, considered by his comrades invulnerable, had been killed by a little French drummer. Baring had been driven out, Alten put to the sword. Several regimental colors had been lost, including one belonging to Alten's division, and one to the Luneburg battalion, borne by a prince of the Deux-Ponts family. The Scotch Grays existed no more; Ponsonby's heavy dragoons had been cut to pieces. That valiant cavalry had given way before the lancers of Bro and the cuirassiers, the armored cavalry of Travers; of their twelve hundred horses there remained six hundred; of three lieutenant colonels, two lay on the ground, Hamilton wounded, Mather killed. Ponsonby had fallen, pierced with seven thrusts of a lance. Gordon was dead, Marsh was dead. Two divisions, the fifth and the sixth, were destroyed.

With Hougomont yielding, La Haie-Sainte taken, there was only one point left, the center. That still held. Wellington reinforced it. He ordered in Hill, who was at Merbe-Braine, and Chassé, who was at Braine-l'Alleud.

The center of the English army, slightly concave, very dense and very compact, held a strong position. It occupied the plateau of Mont-Saint-Jean, with the village behind it and in front the slope, quite steep at that time. The rear backed up on the strong stone house, then an outlying property of Nivelles, that marks the intersection of the roads, a sixteenth-century mass so solid that the balls richocheted off without injuring it. All around the plateau, the English had cut away the hedges here and there, made embrasures in the hawthorns, stuck the mouth of a cannon between two branches, chopped loopholes in the thickets. Their artillery was lying in ambush under the shrubbery. This punic labor, undoubtedly fair in war, which allows snares, was so well done that Haxo, sent by the emperor at nine in the morning to reconnoiter the enemy batteries, saw none of it, and returned to tell Napoleon that there was no obstacle, except the two barricades across the Nivelles and Genappe roads. It was the season when grain is tall; on the brink of the plateau, a battalion of Kempt's brigade, the 95th, armed with carbines, was lying in the tall wheat.

Thus supported and protected, the center of the Anglo-Dutch army was well situated.

The danger of this position was the forest of Soignes, then contiguous to the battlefield and cut through by the ponds of Groenendael and Boitsfort. An army could not retreat there without breaking up; regiments would immediately have been dispersed and the artillery would have been lost in the swamps. A retreat, in the opinion of many military men—contested by others, it is true—would have been an utter rout.

Wellington reinforced this center with one of Chassé's

brigades, taken from the right flank, and one of Wincke's from the left in addition to Clinton's division. To his English, to Halkett's regiments, to Mitchell's brigade, to Maitland's guards, he gave as supports the Brunswick infantry, the Nassau contingent, Kielmansegge's Hanoverians, and Ompteda's Germans. "The right flank," as Charras says, "was bent back behind the center." An enormous battery was reinforced with sandbags at the spot where the Waterloo Museum now stands. Wellington had besides this, in a slight dip in the ground, Somerset's Horse Guards, fourteen hundred strong. This was the other half of that English cavalry, so justly celebrated. Ponsonby destroyed, Somerset was left.

The battery, which, if finished, would have been almost a redoubt, was placed behind a very low garden wall, hastily sheathed with sandbags and a broad bank of earth. The work was not finished; there had not been time to stockade it.

Wellington, anxious, but impassive, was on horseback, and stayed there the whole day in the same position, slightly in front of the old mill of Mont-Saint-Jean, which is still standing, under an elm that an Englishman, an enthusiastic vandal, has since bought for two hundred francs, cut down, and carried away. Wellington was coolly heroic there. The bullets rained down. His aide-de-camp, Gordon, had just fallen at his side. Lord Hill, showing him a bursting shell, said, "My Lord, what are your instructions, and what orders do you leave us, if you allow yourself to be killed?" "To follow my example," answered Wellington. To Clinton, he said laconically, "Hold this spot to the last man." The day was clearly going badly. Wellington cried out to his old companions of Talavera, Vittoria, and Salamanca, "Boys! We must not be beaten. What would they say of us in England!"

About four o'clock, the English line staggered backwards. Suddenly only the artillery and the sharpshooters could be seen on the crest of the plateau; the rest had disappeared; the regiments, driven by French shells and bullets, fell back into the valley still crossed by the cowpath of the farm of Mont-Saint-Jean; a retrogressive movement took place, the English battlefront was slipping away. Wellington gave ground. Beginning of retreat! cried Napoleon.

VII

NAPOLEON IN A GOOD MOOD

The emperor, although sick, and in pain on horseback because of a local affliction, had never been in such good humor as on that day. Since morning, his impenetrable countenance had worn a smile. On June 18, 1815, that profound soul masked in marble was radiant. The somber man of Austerlitz was cheerful at Waterloo. The greatest must display these contradictions. Our joys have shadows. The perfect smile belongs to God alone.

Ridet Caesar, Pompeius flebit, said the legionnaires of the Fuliminatrix Legion. This time Pompey was not to weep, but it is certain that Caesar laughed.

Since the previous night at one o'clock, exploring the hills near Rossomme on horseback in the storm and the rain with Bertrand, and gratified to see the long line of English fires lighting up the horizon from Frischemont to Braine-l'Alleud, he felt that destiny, with which he had an appointment for a certain day on this field of Waterloo, was punctual; he reined in his horse, and stayed motionless for some time, watching the lightning and listening to the thunder; and this fatalist was heard to utter in the darkness these mysterious words: "We are in accord." Napoleon was mistaken. They were no longer in accord.

He had not taken a moment for sleep; every instant of that night had brought him new joy. He had passed along the whole line of the advanced guards, stopping here and there to speak to the pickets. At half-past two, near the woods of Hougomont, he heard the tread of a marching column; for a moment he thought that Wellington was falling back. He said, "It's the English rear guard starting to get away. I'll capture the six thousand Englishmen who've just arrived at Ostend." He chatted freely; he had recovered the animation of the landing of March 1, when he showed the Grand Marshal the enthusiastic peasant of Golfe Juan crying, "Well, Bertrand, there is a reinforcement already!" On the night of June 17, he made fun of Wellington: "The little Englishman needs to be taught a lesson." The rain increased; it thundered while the emperor was speaking.

At half-past three in the morning one illusion was gone; officers sent out on a reconnaissance announced to him that the enemy was not moving. Nothing was stirring, not a bivouac fire was extinguished. The English army was asleep. Deep silence covered the earth; there was no noise except in the sky. At four o'clock, a peasant was brought to him by the scouts; this peasant had acted as guide to a brigade of English cavalry, probably Vivian's brigade on its way to take up position at the village of Ohain, at the far left. At five o'clock, two Belgian deserters reported to him that they had just left their regiment and that the English army was expecting a battle. "So much the better!" exclaimed Napoleon. "I'd prefer to knock them down than repulse them."

In the morning, he had stepped down in the mud, on the high bank at the turn of the road from Plancenoit, had a kitchen table and a peasant's chair brought from the farm of Rossomme, sat down, with some straw for a carpet, and spread out on the table the plan of the battlefield, saying to Soult, "Lovely checkerboard!"

Because of the night's rain, the convoys of provisions, mired in the softened roads, had not arrived at dawn; the soldiers had not slept, were wet, and had not eaten; but for all this Napoleon cried out joyfully to Ney, "We have ninety chances out of a hundred." At eight o'clock the emperor's breakfast was brought. He had invited several generals. While breakfasting, it was related that two nights earlier, Wellington had been at a ball in Brussels given by the Duchess of Richmond; and Soult, rough rider that he was, with his archbishop's face, had said, "The ball will be today." The emperor joked with Ney, who said, "Wellington will not be so simple as to wait for your majesty." This was his usual way. "He was fond of joking," says Fleury de Chaboulon. "The basis of his character was his playful humor," says Gourgaud. "He was full of little jokes, bizarre rather than witty," says Benjamin Constant. This playfulness of a giant is worth considerable attention. He called his grenadiers "the growlers"; he would pinch their ears and pull their mustaches. "The emperor did nothing but play tricks on us," one of them said. During the mysterious crossing from the island of Elba to France, on February 27, on the open sea, when the French brig-of-war *Zephyr* met the brig *Inconstant,* on which Napoleon was concealed, and asked the *Inconstant* for news of Napoleon, the emperor, who still had on his hat the purple and white cockade, decorated with bees, which he adopted on the island of Elba, took the speaking trumpet with a laugh, and answered himself, "The Emperor is fine." He who laughs in this way is on familiar terms with events. Napoleon had several of these bursts of laughter during his Waterloo breakfast. After breakfast, for a quarter of an hour, he collected his thoughts; then two generals sat down on the bundle of straw, pen in hand, paper on knee, and the emperor dictated the order of battle.

At nine, the moment when the French army, drawn up and set in motion in five columns, was deployed, the divisions in two lines, the artillery between the brigades, music in the lead, playing marches, with rolling drums, and blaring trumpets—mighty, vast, joyous—a sea of helmets, sabers, and bayonets against the horizon, the emperor, excited, cried out, "Magnificent! Magnificent!"

Between nine and half-past ten, the whole army, incredibly, was in position drawn up in six lines, taking, to repeat the emperor's expression, "The form of six *V*'s." A few moments after the formation of the battle line—in the profound silence, as at a gathering storm, preceding the fight, watching the procession of the three batteries of twelve pounders, detached by his orders from the three corps of D'Erlon, Reille, and Lobau, and destined to begin the action by attacking Mont-Saint-Jean at the intersection of the roads from Nivelles and Genappe—the emperor had tapped Haxo on the shoulder, saying, "There are twenty-four pretty girls, General."

Sure of the outcome, he had encouraged with a smile, as they passed in front of him, the company of sappers from the first corps, which he had detailed to barricade themselves in Mont-Saint-Jean, as soon as the village was taken. But all this serenity was disturbed by a word of haughty pity. On seeing to his left—a spot where today there is a large tomb—the gathering of those splendid Scotch Grays with their magnificent horses, he said, "Such a pity."

Then he mounted his horse, rode forward from Rossomme, and chose for his vantage point a narrow grassy ridge, to the right of the road from Genappe to Brussels, which was his second station during the battle. The third station, at seven o'clock, between La Belle-Alliance and

La Haie-Sainte was awesome; it is rather a high hill, which can still be seen and behind which the Guard was massed in a depression of the plain. Around this hill the balls ricocheted on the paved road close to Napoleon. Just as at Brienne, cannon balls and bullets whistled over his head. Almost at the spot where his horse had stood, battered bullets have been found, as well as old saber blades, and misshapen projectiles eaten away by rust. *Scabra rubigine*. A few years ago, a sixty-pound shell was unearthed there, still unexploded, the fuse broken off at the casing. It was at this last station that the emperor said to his guide Lacoste, a hostile peasant, frightened, tied to a hussar's saddle, turning away at every volley of grapeshot, and trying to hide behind Napoleon: "Idiot, this is shameful. You'll get yourself shot in the back." The writer of these lines himself has found in the loose soil of that slope, by digging in the gravel, the remains of a bomb, disintegrated by forty-six years of rust, and some bits of old iron, which broke like alder twigs in his fingers.

The curves of the variously tilted plains, where the encounter between Napoleon and Wellington took place, are, as everyone knows, no longer what they were on June 18, 1815. In taking from that deadly field the wherewithal to make its monument, its real form was destroyed: History, disconcerted, can no longer recognize itself there. To glorify it, it was disfigured. On seeing Waterloo again two years later, Wellington exclaimed "They have changed my battlefield." Where today the great pyramid of earth stands surmounted by the lion, there used to be a ridge that fell away toward the Nivelles road as a passable ramp, but which, toward the Genappe road, was almost an escarpment. The elevation of this escarpment can still be measured today by the height of the two great burial mounds banking the road from Genappe to Brussels; the English tomb at the left, the German tomb at the right. There is no French tomb. For France the whole plain is a sepulcher. Thanks to thousands and thousands of cartloads of earth used in the mound a hundred and fifty feet high and a half mile in circumference, the plateau of Mont-Sainte-Jean is now accessible as a gentle slope; on the day of the battle, especially on the side of La Haie-Sainte, its approach was steep and abrupt. The incline there was so steep that the

English artillery could not see the farm below them at the bottom of the valley, the center of the combat. On June 18, 1815, the rain had gullied out this steep descent still more; the mud made the ascent still more difficult; it was not merely laborious: The men actually got stuck in the mire. Along the crest of the plateau ran a sort of ditch, which could not possibly have been detected by a distant observer.

What was this ditch? Let us explain. Braine-l'Alleud is a village in Belgium; Ohain is another. These villages, both hidden by the swells of the land, are connected by a road about four miles long across a broken plain, often digging into the hills like a furrow, so that at certain points it is a ravine. In 1815, as now, this road cut through the crest of the plateau of Mont-Saint-Jean between the two roads from Genappe and Nivelles; except that today it is level with the plain, whereas then it was sunk between high banks. Its two slopes were taken away for the monumental mound. That road was and still is a trench for the greater part of its length; a trench in some parts a dozen feet deep, the slopes of which are so steep that they crumble away here and there, particularly in winter after rainstorms. Accidents happen there. The road was so narrow at the Braine-l'Alleud entrance that a pedestrian was once crushed by a wagon, as attested by a stone cross standing near the cemetery, which gives the name of the dead, *Monsieur Bernard Debrye, merchant of Brussels,* and the date of the accident, February 1637.[1] It was so deep at the plateau of Mont-Saint-Jean that a peasant, Mathieu Nicaise, had been crushed there in 1783 by the collapse of the bank, as another stone cross attested, the top of which disappeared during the alterations, though its overturned pedestal is still visible on the sloping bank to the left of the road between La Haie-Sainte and the farm of Mont-Saint-Jean.

[1] The inscription is as follows:

DOM
CY A ETE ECRASE
PAR MALHEUR
SOUS UN CHARIOT
MONSIEUR BERNARD
DE BRYE MARCHAND
A BRUXELLE LE (illegible)
FEVRIER 1637

On the day of the battle, this sunken road, of which nothing gave any warning, running along the crest of Mont-Saint-Jean—a ditch at the summit of the escarpment, a trench concealed by the ground—was invisible, and therefore terrible.

VIII

THE EMPEROR ASKS THE GUIDE LACOSTE A QUESTION

So, on the morning of Waterloo, Napoleon was pleased.

He was right; the battle plan he had conceived, as we have shown, was indeed excellent.

Once the battle was begun, its very diverse fluctuations, Hougomont's resistance, the tenacity of La Haie-Sainte, Bauduin killed, Foy put *hors de combat*, the unexpected wall that broke Soye's brigade, Guilleminot's fatal blunder in having neither grenades nor gun powder, the miring down of the batteries, the fifteen pieces without escort cut off by Uxbridge in a deeply cut road, the slight effect of the bombs that fell within the English lines, burying themselves in the rain-softened soil, only managing to raise volcanoes of mud, so the explosion was reduced to a splash, the futility of Piré's show of force against Braine-l'Alleud, all that cavalry—fifteen squadrons—practically destroyed, the English right wing scarcely disturbed, the left wing scarcely moved, Ney's strange mistake in massing, instead of spreading out, the four divisions of the first corps, a depth of twenty-seven ranks and a front of two hundred men thereby offered up to grapeshot, the frightful gaps in these ranks, made by the cannonballs, the lack of coordination between attacking columns, the oblique battery suddenly unmasked on their flank, Bourgeois, Donzelot, and Durutte jeopardized, Quiot repulsed, Lieutenant Vieux—that Hercules sprung from the Polytechnic School—wounded as he was chopping down with an ax the door of La Haie-Sainte under the direct fire of the English barricade barring the turn of the road from Genappe to Brussels, Marcognet's division caught between infantry and cavalry, shot point-blank, in the wheatfield toward Best and Pack, cut down by Ponsonby's sabers, his battery of seven pieces spiked, the Prince of Saxe-Weimar holding and keeping Frischemont and Smohain in spite of Comte d'Erlon, the colors of the 105th taken, the colors of the 43rd taken, a Prussian Black Hussar brought in by the scouts of the flying column of three hundred chasseurs scouring the countryside between Wavre and Planchenoit, the disquieting things this prisoner had said, Grouchy's delay, the fifteen hundred men killed in less than an hour in the orchard of Hougomont, the eighteen hundred men fallen in still less than that around La Haie-Sainte—all these stormy events, passing like battle clouds before Napoelon, had hardly disturbed his countenance and had not darkened its imperial expression of certainty. Napoleon was accustomed to looking intently at war; he never added up figure by figure the tedious sum of details; the figures mattered little to him, provided they gave this total: Victory. Though beginnings might go wrong he was not alarmed, he who believed himself master and possessor of the end; he knew how to wait, believing in himself beyond question, and he treated destiny as an equal. He seemed to say to Fate: You wouldn't dare.

Half light and half shadow, Napoleon felt himself protected when right and tolerated when wrong. He had, or believed he had, a connivance, one might almost say complicity, with events, equivalent to the ancient invulnerability.

However, when one has Beresina, Leipzig, and Fontainebleau in the background, it seems as though one might distrust Waterloo. The trace of a mysterious frown is emerging in the far reaches of the sky.

At the moment when Wellington began to draw back, Napoleon gave a start. He saw the plateau of Mont-Saint-Jean suddenly laid bare and the front of the English army disappear. It was rallying, but under cover. The emperor half rose in his stirrups. The flash of victory glinted in his eyes.

Wellington falling back on the forest of Soignes and destroyed would be the final overthrow of England by France; it was Cressy, Poitiers, Malplaquet, and Ramillies avenged. The man of Marengo was wiping out Agincourt.

The emperor then, contemplating this terrible turn of

events, swept his glass for the last time over every point of the battlefield. His Guard standing behind with grounded arms looked up to him with a sort of religious awe. He was reflecting; he was examining the slopes, noting the ascents, scrutinizing the clump of trees, the square rye field, the footpath; he seemed to count every bush. He looked for some time at the English barricades on the two roads, two large clearings of trees, the one on the Genappe road above La Haie-Sainte, armed with two cannon, which alone, of all the English artillery, were within clear view of the bottom of the battlefield, and that of the Nivelles road where the Dutch bayonets of Chassé's brigade glistened. Near that barricade he noticed the old chapel of Saint-Nicholas, painted white, which is at the corner of the crossroad toward Braine-l'Alleud. He bent over and spoke in an undertone to the guide Lacoste. The guide gave a negative shake of the head, probably deceitfully.

The emperor straightened up and reflected. Wellington had fallen back. It only remained to complete this repulse with a crushing charge.

Napoleon, turning abruptly, sent off a courier at full speed to Paris to announce that the battle was won.

Napoleon was one of those geniuses who give off thunder.

He had found his thunderbolt.

He ordered Milhaud's cuirassiers to take the plateau of Mont-Saint-Jean.

IX

THE UNEXPECTED

There were three thousand five hundred of them. They formed a line half a mile long. They were gigantic men on colossal horses. There were twenty-six squadrons, and behind them they had as support Lefebvre-Desnouettes' division, the hundred and six crack gendarmes, the Chasseurs of the Guard, eleven hundred and ninety-seven men, and the Lancers of the Guard, eight hundred and eighty lances. They wore helmets without plumes, and cuirasses of wrought iron, with pistols in their saddle holsters, and long saber swords. That morning, they had been the pride of the whole army, when at nine o'clock, with trumpets blaring, and all the bands playing *Veillons au salut de l'empire,* they had come up in a dense column, one of their batteries on their flank, the other at their center, and deployed in two ranks between the Genappe road and Frischemont, took up their battle position in this powerful second line, so wisely set up by Napoleon, which, with Kellermann's cuirassiers at its far left, Milhaud's cuirassiers at its far right, had, so to speak, two wings of iron.

The aide-de-camp Bernard delivered the emperor's order. Ney drew his sword and placed himself at their head. The enormous squadrons began to move.

It was an awesome spectacle.

All that cavalry, with sabers drawn, banners waving, and trumpets sounding, formed in column by division, charged evenly and as one man—with the precision of a bronze battering-ram opening a breach—down the hill of La Belle-Alliance, sank into that awesome trough where so many men had already fallen, disappeared in the smoke, then, rising from this valley of shadows reappeared on the other side, still compact and close, riding at a full trot, through a hail of grapeshot bursting against them, up the frightful mud slope of the Mont-Saint-Jean plateau. They rose, grave, menacing, imperturbable; in the intervals between the musketry and artillery the colossal sound of the hoofbeats could be heard. Being in two divisions, they formed two columns; Wathier's division had the right, Delord's the left. From a distance they could be taken for two immense steel serpents stretching toward the crest of the plateau. They coursed through the battle like a miracle.

Nothing like it had been seen since the taking of the great redoubt at La Muscova by the heavy cavalry; Murat was not there, but Ney was. It seemed as if this mass had become a monster with a single mind. Each squadron undulated and swelled like the coils of a polyp. They could be seen through occasional breaks in the thick smoke. It was a jumble of helmets, cries, sabers; a furious bounding of horses' rumps among the cannon fire and flourishing trumpets, a terrible and disciplined tumult; over everything, the armored breastplates, like the scales of a hydra.

These accounts seem to belong to another age. Something like this vision undoubtedly appeared in the old Orphic epics telling of centaurs, those titans with human faces and the bodies of horses, who scaled Olympus at a gallop, horrible, invulnerable, sublime, at once gods and beasts.

In odd numerical coincidence, twenty-six battalions were waiting for these twenty-six squadrons. Behind the crest of the plateau, under cover of the masked battery, the English infantry, formed in thirteen squares, two battalions to the square, and in two lines—seven on the first, and six on the second—with muskets raised and trained, waiting calm, silent, and immovable. They could not see the cuirassiers, and the cuirassiers could not see them. They listened to the rising of this tide of men. They heard the growing sound of three thousand horses, the alternating measured strike of their hoofs at a full trot, the rattling of armor, the clicking of sabers, and a sort of ferocious roar of the advancing horde. There was a moment of fearful silence, then, suddenly, a long line of raised arms brandishing sabers appeared above the crest, and the helmets, and the trumpets, and the banners, and three thousand faces with gray mustaches crying "Vive l'empereur!" All this cavalry emerged onto the plateau, and it was like the start of an earthquake.

All at once, and tragically, at the English left, and on our right, the head of the cuirassiers' column reared with a frightening din. Reaching the culminating point of the crest, going at full tilt, full of fury and bent on the extermination of the squares and cannons, the cuirassiers saw between themselves and the English a ditch, a grave. It was the sunken road to Ohain.

It was a moment of terror. There was the ravine, unexpected, gaping right at the horses' feet, twelve feet deep between its banks. The second rank pushed in the first, the third pushed in the second; the horses reared, lurched backward, fell onto their rumps, and struggled writhing with their feet in the air, piling up and throwing their riders; no means to retreat; the whole column was nothing but a projectile. The momentum to crush the English crushed the French. The inexorable ravine could not yield until it was filled; riders and horses rolled in together helter-skelter, grinding against each other, making common flesh in this dreadful gulf, and when this grave was full of living men, the rest marched over them and went on. Almost a third of Dubois's brigade sank into the abyss.

Here began the loss of the battle.

A local tradition, clearly exaggerated, says that two thousand horses and fifteen hundred men were buried in the sunken road of Ohain. This undoubtedly includes all the other bodies thrown into the ravine on the day after the battle.

We would note in passing that it was this Dubois brigade, so mortally tried, which an hour earlier and attacking alone, had carried off the colors of the Lunebourg batallion.

Before ordering this charge of Milhaud's cuirassiers, Napoleon had examined the ground, but could not see this sunken road which did not show even a dip on the surface of the plateau. Warned, however, and put on his guard by the little white chapel that marks its junction with the Nivelles road, and probably on the likelihood of some obstacle, he had put a question to the guide Lacoste. The guide had answered no. It may almost be said that from this shake of a peasant's head came Napoleon's downfall.

Other strokes of fate were still to come.

Might it have been possible for Napoleon to win this battle? We answer no. Why? Because of Wellington? Because of Blücher? No. Because of God.

For Bonaparte to be conqueror at Waterloo was no longer within the law of the nineteenth century. Another series of acts was under way in which Napoleon had no place. The ill-will of events had long been coming.

It was time for this titan to fall.

The excessive weight of this man in human destiny disturbed the equilibrium. This individual alone counted for more than the whole of mankind. This plethora of all human vitality concentrated within a single head, the world rising to the brain of one man, would be fatal to civilization if it endured. The moment had come for incorruptible supreme equity to look into it. Probably the principles and elements on which regular gravitation in the moral and material orders depend had begun to mutter. Reeking blood, overcrowded cemeteries, weeping mothers—these are formidable plaintiffs. When the earth is suffering from a surcharge, there are mysterious moanings from the deeps that the heavens hear.

Napoleon had been impeached before the Infinite, and his fall was decreed.

He annoyed God.

Waterloo is not a battle; it is the changing face of the universe.

X

THE PLATEAU OF MONT-SAINT-JEAN

At the same time as the incident of the ravine, the artillery came out of hiding.

Sixty cannon and the thirteen squares thundered and flashed at the cuirassiers point-blank. The brave General Delord gave the military salute to the English battery.

At a gallop all the English light artillery took up position within their formations. The cuirassiers did not even have time to catch a breath. The disaster of the sunken road had decimated but not discouraged them. These were men who, diminished in number, grew stronger in spirit.

Wathier's column alone had suffered disaster; Delord's, which Ney had sent off obliquely to the left, as if he had some foreboding of the trap, arrived unscathed.

The cuirassiers hurled themselves at the English formations.

At a full gallop, with free rein, sabers between the teeth and pistols in hand, the attack began.

There are moments in battle when the soul hardens a man to the point of changing the soldier into a statue, all flesh turning to granite. The English battalions, desperately assailed, did not yield an inch.

So it was appalling.

The English formations were attacked on all sides at once. A frenzied whirlwind enveloped them. The coolheaded infantry remained impassable. The first rank, with knee to the ground, received the cuirassiers on their bayonets, the second shot them down; behind the second rank, the cannoneers loaded their guns, the front of the square opened, made way for a blast of grapeshot, and closed again. The cuirassiers answered by crushing them. Their huge horses reared, trampled on the ranks, leaped over the bayonets, and fell, gigantic, in the midst of the four living walls. The bullets made gaps in the ranks of the cuirassiers, the cuirassiers made breaches in the squares. Files of men disappeared, ground beneath the horses' feet. Bayonets were buried in the bellies of these centaurs. Hence a gruesome display of wounds never perhaps seen elsewhere. The formations, eroded by this raging cavalry, closed up without wavering. Inexhaustible in grapeshot, they kept on firing in the midst of their attackers. It was a monstrous sight. These formations were no longer battalions, they were craters; the cuirassiers were no longer cavalry, they were a tempest. Each formation was a volcano attacked by a thundercloud; lava fought with lightning.

The formation to the extreme right, the most exposed of all, being in the open field, was almost annihilated in the first wave. It was made up of the 75th regiment of Highlanders. The piper in the center, while the work of extermination was going on, profoundly oblivious to all around him, lowering his melancholy eye filled with the reflections of forest and lakes, seated on a drum, his bagpipe under his arm, was playing his highland airs. These Scots died thinking of Ben Lothian, as the Greeks died remembering Argos. The saber of a cuirassier, striking down the pibroch and the arm that played it, stopped the song by killing the player.

The cuirassiers, relatively few in number, diminished by the catastrophe of the ravine, had to contend with almost the entire English army, but they multiplied in effectiveness, each man becoming the equal of ten. Nonetheless some Hanoverian battalions fell back. Wellington saw it and remembered his cavalry. Had Napoleon, at that very moment, remembered his infantry, he would have won the battle. This oversight was his great fatal blunder.

Suddenly the assailing cuirassiers felt assailed. The English cavalry was at their backs. Before them the formations, behind them Somerset; Somerset, with the fourteen hundred dragoon guards. Somerset had on his right Dornberg with his German light-horse, and on his left Trip, with the Belgian carabineers. The cuirassiers, attacked front, flank, and rear by infantry and cavalry, were compelled to face in all directions. What was that to them? They were a whirlwind. Their valor surpassed words.

Besides, behind them they had the ever-thundering artillery. All of that was necessary in order to wound such men in the back. One of their cuirasses, with a hole in the left shoulder-plate from a musket ball, is in the collection of the Waterloo Museum.

For such Frenchmen it took no less than the likes of these Englishmen.

It was no longer a conflict, it was a darkness, a fury, a giddy vortex of souls and courage, a hurricane of flashing swords. In an instant the fourteen hundred horse guards were only eight hundred; Fuller, their lieutenant colonel, fell dead. Ney rushed up with the lancers and Lefebvre-Desnouettes's chasseurs. The plateau of Mont-Saint-Jean was taken, retaken, taken again. The cuirassiers left the cavalry to return to the infantry, or more precisely, all this terrible multitude wrestled with each other without letting go. The squares still held. There were twelve assaults. Four horses were killed under Ney. Half of the cuirassiers lay on the plateau. This struggle lasted two hours.

The English army was terribly shaken. There is no doubt that if they had not been crippled in their first blow by the disaster of the sunken road, the cuirassiers would have overwhelmed the center, and secured the victory. This extraordinary cavalry astounded Clinton, who had seen Talavera and Badajos. Wellington, though three fourths conquered, was struck with heroic admiration. He said, half aloud, "Splendid!"

The cuirassiers annihilated seven squares out of thirteen, took or spiked sixty pieces of artillery, and took from the English six regimental colors, which three cuirassiers and three chasseurs of the guard carried to the emperor at the farm of La Belle-Alliance.

Wellington's situation was growing worse. This strange battle was like a duel between two wounded zealots who, while still fighting and resisting, lose all their blood. Which of the two would be first to fall?

The struggle of the plateau continued.

How far did the cuirassiers penetrate? No one can say.

One thing is certain: The day after the battle, a cuirassier and his horse were found dead under the frame of the hay scales at Mont-Saint-Jean, at the point where the four roads from Nivelles, Genappe, La Hulpe and Brussels meet. This horseman had pierced the English lines. One of the men who took away the body still lives at Mont-Saint-Jean. His name is Dehaze; he was then eighteen years old.

Wellington felt that he was giving way. The crisis was quickly approaching.

The cuirassiers had not succeeded, in the sense that the center was not broken. With everyone holding the plateau, nobody held it, and in fact it remained for the most part with the English. Wellington held the village and the crowning plain; Ney held only the crest and the slope. Both sides seemed rooted to this funereal soil.

But the weakening of the English appeared irremediable. The hemorrhage of their army was horrible. Kempt, on the left flank, called for reinforcements. "There are none," answered Wellington. "Let him die!" Almost at the same moment—a singular coincidence that indicates the exhaustion of both armies—Ney sent to Napoleon for infantry, and Napoleon exclaimed, "Infantry! Where does he think I could get them! Does he expect me to make them?"

However, the English army was farthest gone. The furious onslaughts of these great squadrons with iron cuirasses and steel breastplates had ground up the infantry. A few men around a flag marked a regiment; battalions were now commanded by captains or lieutenants. Alten's division, already so badly cut up at La Haie-Sainte, was almost destroyed; the intrepid Belgians of Van Kluze's brigade were strewn on the ryefield along the Nivelles road; there was hardly anything left of those Dutch grenadiers who, in 1811, among our ranks in Spain, fought against Wellington, and who, in 1815, rallied to the English side, fought against Napoleon. The loss in officers was heavy. Lord Uxbridge, whose leg was buried the next day, had a fractured knee. If, on the French side, in this struggle of the cuirassiers, Delord, Lhéritier, Colbert, Dnop, Travers, and Blancard were disabled, on the English side Alten was wounded, Barne was wounded, Delancey was killed, Van Merlen was killed, Ompteda was killed, Wellington's entire staff was decimated, and

England had the worst share in this balance of blood. The second regiment of foot guards had lost five lieutenant colonels, four captains, and three lieutenants; the first battalion of the thirtieth infantry had lost twenty-four officers and one hundred and twelve soldiers; the seventy-ninth Highlanders had twenty-four officers wounded, eighteen officers killed, and four hundred and fifty soldiers slain. Cumberland's Hanoverian hussars, an entire regiment, under Colonel Hacke, who was afterward court-martialed and broken, had turned in the face of fight, and were fleeing through the Forest of Soignes, spreading panic as far as Brussels. Carts, ammunition wagons, baggage wagons, wagons full of wounded, seeing the French gain ground and approach the forest, fled; the Dutch, cut down by the French cavalry, cried for help. From Vert-Coucou to Groenendael, over a distance of nearly six miles going toward Brussels, the roads, according to the testimony of witnesses still living, were choked with fugitives. This panic was such that it reached the Prince of Condé at Malines and Louis XVIII at Ghent. With the exception of the small reserve drawn up in echelon behind the field hospital set up at the farm of Mont-Saint-Jean, and the brigades of Vivian and Vandeleur flanking the left wing, Wellington's cavalry was exhausted. Numerous artillery units lay dismounted. These facts are acknowledged by Siborne; and Pringle, exaggerating the disaster, even says that the Anglo-Dutch army was reduced to thirty-four thousand men. The Iron Duke remained calm, but his lips were pale. The Austrian Commissioner, Vincent, the Spanish Commissioner, Alava, present at the battle on the English staff, considered the duke lost. At five o'clock Wellington drew out his watch and was heard to murmur these somber words: "Blücher, or darkness!"

It was about this time that a distant line of bayonets glistened on the heights beyond Frischemont.

Here is the turning point in this colossal drama.

XI

BAD GUIDE FOR NAPOLEON, GOOD FOR BÜLOW

We know Napoleon's bitter mistake; Grouchy anticipated, Blücher's arrival; death instead of life.

Destiny has such turnings. He was expecting the throne of the world, but Saint Helena rose into view instead.

If the little shepherd who acted as guide to Bülow, Blücher's lieutenant, had advised him to leave the forest above Frischemont rather than below Planchenoit, the shape of the nineteenth century would perhaps have been different. Napoleon would have won the battle of Waterloo. By any other approach than below Planchenoit, the Prussian army would have wound up at a ravine impassable to artillery, and Bülow would not have arrived.

Now, an hour of delay, as the Prussian general Muffling declares, and Blücher would not have found Wellington in position; "the battle was lost."

It was high time, as we see, for Bülow to arrive. He was actually very late. He had bivouacked at Dion-le-Mont, and started out at dawn. But the roads were impassable, and his divisions were mired down. The cannon sank to the hubs in the ruts. Furthermore, he had to cross the Dyle on the narrow Wavre bridge; the road leading to the bridge had been set on fire by the French; the caissons and artillery wagons, being unable to pass between two rows of burning houses, had to wait till the fire was extinguished. It was noon before Bülow was able to reach Chapelle-Saint-Lambert.

Had the action begun two hours earlier, it would have been finished at four o'clock, and Blücher would have come upon a field already won by Napoleon. Such are the immense chances, in proportion to an infinity that escapes us.

As early as noon, the emperor, first of all, with his field glass, saw on the far horizon something that caught his attention. He had said: "Over there I see a cloud that looks to me like troops." Then he asked the Duke of Dalmatia, "Soult, what do you see toward Chapelle-Saint

Lambert?" The marshal, turning his field glasses that way, answered, "Four or five thousand men, sire. Grouchy, of course." However, it remained motionless in the haze. The field glasses of the whole staff studied "the cloud" pointed out by the emperor. Some said, "They are columns halting." Most said, "It is trees." The fact is that the cloud was not moving. The emperor detached Domon's division of light cavalry to reconnoiter this obscure point.

Bülow, in fact, had not moved. His vanguard was very weak and could do nothing. He had to wait for the bulk of his corps, and he was ordered to concentrate his force before entering the line; but at five o'clock, seeing Wellington was in danger, Blücher ordered Bülow to attack with these remarkable words: "We must give the English army a breathing spell."

Soon afterward, the divisions of Losthin, Hiller, Hacke, and Ryssel deployed in front of Lobau's corps, the cavalry of Prince William of Prussia came out of the Paris woods, Plancenoit was in flames, and the Prussian bullets began to rain down even onto the ranks of the Guard in reserve behind Napoleon.

XII

THE GUARD

The rest is known; the attack of a third army, the battle disrupted, eighty-six pieces of artillery suddenly belching fire, Pirch the First coming up with Bülow, Ziethen's cavalry led by Blücher in person, the French driven back, Marcognet swept off the plateau of Ohain, Durutte dislodged from Papelotte, Donzelot and Quiot retreating, Lobau taken at an angle, a new battle at nightfall hurled at our dismantled regiments, the whole English line assuming the offensive and pushed forward, the gigantic gap made in the French army, the English and the Prussian grapeshot lending mutual aid, extermination, disaster in front, disaster on the flank, the Guard entering the line amid this terrible collapse.

Feeling they were going to their death, they cried out, "Vive l'Empereur!" There is nothing more poignant in history than the death agony bursting out in acclamations.

The sky had been overcast all day. All at once, at that very moment—it was eight o'clock in the evening—the clouds on the horizon parted, and through the elms on the Nivelles road streamed the sinister red light of the setting sun. The rising sun had been seen at Austerlitz.

For this final effort, each battalion of the Guard was commanded by a general. Friant, Michel, Roguet, Harlet, Mallet, Poret de Morvan, were there. When the tall helmets of the grenadiers of the guard with their large eagle plaques appeared, symmetrical, drawn up in line, calm, in the haze of that conflict, the enemy felt respect for France; they seemed to see twenty victories coming onto the battlefield, with wings extended, and those who were conquerors, thinking themselves conquered, recoiled; but Wellington cried, "Up, guards, and aim straight!" The red regiment of English guards, lying behind the hedges, rose up, a hail of grapeshot riddled the tricolored flag fluttering around our eagles, everything was hurled forward, and the final carnage began. In the lengthening shadows, the Imperial Guard felt the army giving way around them and the vast shudder of the rout; they heard "Every man for himself!" which had replaced the "Vive l'Empereur!" and, with flight behind them, they held to their course, battered harder and harder and dying more at every step. There were no weak souls or cowards there. The privates of that band were as heroic as their generals. Not a man flinched from the suicide.

Ney, desperate, great in all the grandeur of accepting death, bared himself to every blow in this tempest. His fifth horse was killed under him. Streaming with sweat, fire in his eyes, froth on his lips, his uniform unbuttoned, one of his epaulets half cut away by the saber stroke of a horse guard, his great eagle badge dented by a ball, bloody, covered with mud, magnificent, a broken sword in his hand, he said, "Come and see how a marshal of France dies on the battlefield!" But in vain, he did not die. He was haggard and indignant. He flung this question at Drouet D'Erlon. "What! Aren't you going to die?" He cried out in the midst of all this artillery crushing a handful of men, "What? Nothing for me? How I wish all these English bullets were buried in my body!" Unfortunate man! You were reserved for French bullets!

XIII

THE CATASTROPHE

The route behind the Guard was grim.

The army fell back rapidly on all sides at once, from Hougomont, from La Haie-Sainte, from Papelotte, from Planchenoit. The cry of "Treachery!" was followed by the cry "Every man for himself!" An army breaking ranks is like a thaw. Everything bends, cracks, floats, snaps, rolls, falls, crashes, dashes, plunges. Mysterious disintegration. Ney borrows a horse, leaps up on it, and without hat, scarf, or sword, blocks the Brussels road, stopping both the English and the French. He tries to hold the army, he calls them back, he insults them, he grapples with the rout. He is outflanked. The soldiers flee from him, crying, "Long live Marshal Ney!" Durutte's two regiments come and go, frightened, and as though tossed between the sabers of the Uhlans and fire from the brigades of Kempt, Best, Pack, and Rylandt; rout is the worst of all conflicts; friends kill each other in their flight; squadrons and battalions are crushed and dispersed against each other, enormous foam of battle. Lobau at one extremity, like Reille at the other, is rolled away in the flood. In vain Napoleon makes walls with the remains of the guard; in vain he expends his headquarters squadron in one last effort. Quiot retreats before Vivian, Kellermann before Vandeleur, Lobau before Bülow, Moraud before Pirch, Domon and Lubervic before Prince William of Prussia. Guyot, who had led the emperor's squadrons in the charge, falls under the feet of the English horse. Napoleon gallops along the lines of the fugitives, harangues them, urges, threatens, entreats. The mouths, which were crying *vive l'Empereur* in the morning, are now agape; he is hardly recognized. The Prussian cavalry, just come up and fresh, hurtle forward, fling themselves upon the enemy, slash, cut, hack, kill, exterminate. Teams balk, the guns are left on their own; the soldiers of the artillery trains unhitch the caissons and take the horses for their escape; upset wagons, their four wheels in the air, block the road, and are accessories to massacre. Men crush and crowd; they trample the living and the dead. Arms are useless. A swarming multitude fills roads, paths, bridges, plains, hills, valleys, woods, choked by this flight of forty thousand men. Cries, despair, knapsacks, and muskets cast into the rye, passage forced at swordpoint; no more comrades, no more officers, no more generals; inexpressible terror. Ziethen slashing away at France. Lions become calves. Such was this flight.

At Genappe there was an effort to turn back, to form a line, to make a stand. Lobau rallied three hundred men. The entrance to the village was barricaded, but at the first volley of Prussian grapeshot, all took flight again and Lobau was captured. The marks of that volley are still to be seen on the old gable of a brick ruin to the right of the road, a short distance from Genappe. The Prussians rushed into Genappe, furious, no doubt, at having conquered so little. The pursuit was monstrous. Blücher gave orders to kill all. Roguet had set this sad example by threatening death to every French grenadier who brought him a Prussian prisoner. Blücher surpassed Roguet. The general of the Young Guard, Duhesme, caught beside the door of a tavern in Genappe, gave up his sword to a Hussar of Death, who took the sword and killed the prisoner. The victory was completed by the assassination of the vanquished. Let us punish, since we are history: Old Blücher disgraced himself. This ferocity topped off the disaster. The desperate rout passed through Genappe, passed through Quatre-Bras, passed through Grosselies, passed through Frasnes, passed through Thuin, passed through Charleroi, and only stopped at the frontier. Alas! Who was now fleeing this way? The Grand Army.

This madness, this terror, this fall of the loftiest bravery ever to have astonished history, can it be without cause? No. The shadow of an enormous right hand rests on Waterloo. It was the day of Destiny. A power beyond man controlled that day. Hence the breakdown of minds in horror; hence all these great souls yielding their swords. Those who had conquered Europe collapsed to the ground, with no more to say or do, feeling a terrible dark presence approach. *Hoc erat in fatis*. That day the perspective of the human race changed. Waterloo is the hinge of the nineteenth century. This disappearance of the great man was necessary for the coming of the great century. One, to whom there can be no reply, took it in hand. The panic of heros can be explained. In the battle of Waterloo, there was more than a cloud, there was a meteor. God passed over it.

In the approaching night, on a field near Genappe, Bernard and Bertrand stopped with a tug at his coattail a haggard, pensive, gloomy man, who, dragged this far by the current of the rout, had just dismounted, slipped the reins of his horse under his arm, and, wild-eyed, was turning back alone toward Waterloo. It was Napoleon, still trying to advance, mighty sleepwalker of a vanished dream.

XIV

THE LAST SQUARE

A few formations of the Guard, immovable in the flow of the rout like rocks in running water, held out till nightfall. With night approaching, and death as well, they waited for this double shadow, and yielded unfaltering to its embrace. Each regiment, isolated from the others, and having no further communication with the shattered army, was dying alone. They had taken up a position, for this last struggle, some on the heights of Rossomme, others in the plain of Mont-Saint-Jean. There—abandoned, vanquished, terrible—these somber formations suffered agonizing martyrdom. Ulm, Wagram, Jena, Friedland, were dying with them.

At dusk, toward nine in the evening, at the foot of the plateau of Mont-Saint-Jean, there remained only one. In the deadly valley below that slope, scaled by the cuirassiers, now overrun by the mass of English, under the converging fire of the enemy's victorious artillery, under a terrifying howl of projectiles, this formation fought on. It was commanded by an obscure officer named Cambronne. With every volley, the square diminished, but returned the fire. It answered grapeshot with bullets, continually shrinking its four walls. Far off the fugitives, momentarily pausing for breath, listened to this dismal thunder decreasing in the darkness.

When this legion was reduced to a handful, when their banner was no more than shreds, when their muskets, out of ammunition, were nothing but clubs, when the pile of corpses was larger than the band of the living, a sort of sacred terror spread among the conquerors, for these sublime martyrs, and the English artillery, stopping to catch their breath, fell silent. It was a respite of sorts. Around them the combatants had, as it were, a throng of specters, the outlines of men on horseback, the black profile of the cannons, the white sky seen through the wheels and the gun carriages; the colossal death's head that heroes always see in the smoke of battle was advancing on them, glaring at them. In the twilight they could hear the loading of the artillery, the lighted matches like tigers' eyes in the night made a circle around their heads; all the linstocks of the English batteries approached the guns, when, touched by their heroism, suspending the moment of death above these men, an English general—Colville according to some, Maitland according to others—cried out to them, "Brave Frenchman, surrender!" Cambronne answered, "*Merde!*"

XV

CAMBRONNE

Out of respect to the French reader, the finest word, perhaps, that a Frenchman ever uttered cannot be repeated to him. We are prohibited from applying the sublime to history.

At our own risk and peril, we violate that prohibition.

Among all these giants, then, there was one Titan—Cambronne.

To speak that word, and then to die, what could be greater! For to accept death is to die, and it is not this man's fault, if, in the storm of grapeshot, he survived.

The man who won the battle of Waterloo is not Napoleon put to rout; nor Wellington giving way at four o'clock, desperate at five; not Blücher, who did not fight; the man who won the battle of Waterloo was Cambronne.

To burst out with such a word at the thunderbolt that kills you is victory.

To give this answer to disaster, to say this to destiny, to supply this base for the future lion, to fling down this reply to the rain of the previous night, to the treacherous wall at Hougomont, to the sunken road of Ohain, to Grouchy's delay, to Blücher's arrival, to be ironic in the sepulchre, to act so as to remain upright after falling, to drown the European coalition in two syllables, privies that the Caesars were already privy to, to make the last of words the first, by associating it with the glory of France, to close Waterloo insolently with a Mardi Gras, to complete Leonidas with Rabelais, to sum up this victory in one supreme word that cannot be spoken, to lose the field and to recover history, after this carnage to have the laugh on his side, is immense.

It is an insult to the thunderbolt. It attains the grandeur of Aeschylus.

This word of Cambronne's has the effect of a fracture. It is the breaking of a heart by scorn; it is a surplus of agony in explosion. Who conquered? Wellington? No. Without Blücher he would have been lost. Blücher? No. If Wellington had not begun, Blücher could not have finished. This Cambronne, coming at the final hour, this unknown soldier, this infinitesimal particle of war, senses a lie within a catastrophe, doubly bitter, and at the moment when he is bursting with rage, he is offered this mockery—life? How could he restrain himself?

They are there, all the kings of Europe, the fortunate generals, the thundering Jupiters, they have a hundred thousand victorious soldiers, and behind the hundred thousand, a million, their guns, with matches lit, stand open-mouthed; they have the Imperial Guard and the Grand Army under their feet, they have just crushed Napoleon, and Cambronne alone remains; none but this earthworm is left to protest. He will protest. So he looks for a word as one looks for a sword. Froth comes to his mouth, and this froth is the word. Faced with this prodigious and mediocre victory, this victory without victors, the desperate man draws himself up, he suffers its enormity, but he recognizes its nothingness; and he does more than spit on it; overwhelmed in numbers and material strength he finds in his soul a means of expression—excrement. We repeat. To say that, to do that, to find that, is to be the conqueror.

The spirit of great days entered this unknown man at that fatal moment. Cambronne finds the word for Waterloo, as Rouget de l'Isle finds the Marseillaise, through an inspiration from above. A breath from the divine maelstrom passes across these men, and they tremble, and the one sings the supreme song, the other utters the terrible cry. This word of titanic scorn Cambronne throws out not merely at Europe, in the name of the Empire, that would be but little; he throws it out at the past, in the name of the Revolution. It is heard, and men recognize in Cambronne the old soul of the giants. It is as though Danton were speaking or Kleber roaring.

To this word from Cambronne, the English voice replied, "Fire!" the batteries flared, the hill trembled, from all those brazen throats went forth a final terrible vomiting of grapeshot; vast clouds of smoke, dusky white in the light of the rising moon, rolled away, and when the smoke settled, there was nothing left. That formidable remnant was annihilated; the Guard was dead. The four walls of the living redoubt had fallen, hardly could a quivering be detected here and there among the corpses; and thus the French legions, grander than the Roman legions, expired at Mont-Saint-Jean on ground soaked in rain and blood, in the somber wheatfields, at the spot where today at four in the morning, whistling, and gaily whipping up his horse, Joseph drives by with the mail from Nivelles.

XVI

QUOT LIBRAS IN DUCE?

The battle of Waterloo is an enigma. It is as obscure to those who won it as to the one who lost it. To Napoleon it is a panic;[1] Blücher sees in it only fire; Wellington

1. "A battle ended, a day finished, false measures repaired, greater successes assured for tomorrow, all was lost by a moment of panic."—(Napoleon, *Dictations at St. Helena.*)

understands none of it. Look at the reports. The bulletins are confused, the commentaries are foggy. The former stammer, the latter falter. Jomini separates the battle of Waterloo into four periods; Muffling divides it into three tides of fortune; Charras alone, though on some points we differ, has perceived the characteristic contours of that catastrophe of human genius struggling with divine destiny. All the other historians are blinded by the glare and are left to grope in that blindness. A day of lightning, indeed, the collapse of the military monarchy—which, to the great amazement of kings, drew along with it all kingdoms—the downfall of force, the ruin of war.

In this event, bearing the imprint of superhuman necessity, man's share is nothing.

Would taking away Waterloo from Wellington and from Blücher detract anything from England and Germany? No. Neither illustrious England nor august Germany is in question in the problem of Waterloo. Thank heaven, nations are great aside from the dismal ventures of the sword. Neither Germany nor England nor France is held in a scabbard. Nowadays when Waterloo is merely a click of sabers, above Blücher Germany has Goethe, and above Wellington England has Byron. A vast rising of ideas is peculiar to our century, and in this dawning England and Germany have their magnificent share. They are majestic because they think. The higher plane they bring to civilization is intrinsic to them; it comes from themselves, and not by accident. The advances they have made in the nineteenth century do not spring from Waterloo. It is only barbarous nations that experience sudden growth after a victory. It is the fleeting vanity of the streamlet swelled by the storm. Civilized nations, especially in our times, are neither exalted nor degraded by a captain's good or bad luck. Their specific importance in the human race results from something more than a combat. Their honor, thank God, their dignity, their light, their genius, are not numbers that heroes and conquerors, those gamblers, can cast in the lottery of battles. Often a battle lost is progress attained. Less glory, more liberty. The drum is stilled, reason speaks. It is the game in which he who loses gains. So let us speak calmly of Waterloo on both sides. Let us render unto Fortune the things that are Fortune's, and unto God the things that are God's. What is Waterloo? A victory? No. A winning lottery ticket.

Won by Europe, paid by France.

It was not really worthwhile to put a lion there.

Waterloo is actually the strangest encounter in history. Napoleon and Wellington. They are not enemies, they are opposites. Never has God, who takes pleasure in antitheses, made a more striking contrast and a more extraordinary meeting. On one side, precision, foresight, geometry, prudence, retreat assured, reserves economized, obstinate composure, imperturbable method, strategy to profit from the terrain, tactics to balance battalions, carnage straight as a plumb line, war directed watch in hand, nothing left voluntarily to chance, ancient classic courage, absolute correctness; on the other, intuition, inspiration, a military marvel, a superhuman instinct; a flashing glance, a mysterious something that gazes like the eagle and strikes like the thunderbolt, prodigious art in disdainful impetuosity, all the mysteries of a deep soul, intimacy with Destiny; river, plain, forest, hill, commanded, and in some sense forced to obey, the despot going so far as to tyrannize the battlefield; faith in a star united with strategic science, increasing it, but disturbing it. Wellington was the Barrême of war, Napoleon was its Michelangelo, and this time genius was vanquished by calculus.

On both sides they were expecting somebody. It was the exact calculator who succeeded. Napoleon expected Grouchy; he did not come. Wellington expected Blücher; he came.

Wellington is classic war taking its revenge. Bonaparte, in his dawn, had met it in Italy, and defeated it superbly. The old owl had fled before the young vulture. Ancient tactics had been not only crushed but also scandalized. What was this Corsican of twenty-six? What was the significance of this brilliant novice who, with everything against him, nothing for him, with no provisions, no munitions, no cannon, no shoes, almost without an army, with a handful of men against multitudes, rushed at an allied Europe and absurdly gained victories out of the impossible? Where did this thundering madman come from who, almost without pausing for breath, and with the same set of the combatants in hand, pulverized one after the other the five armies of the Emperor of Germany, toppling Beaulieu onto Alvinzi, Wurmser onto Beaulieu, Melas onto Wurmser, Mack onto Melas? Who was this newcomer in war with the effrontery of destiny? The academic military school excommunicated him as it gave ground. Thence an implacable hatred of the old system of war against the new, of the correct saber against the flashing sword, and of the checkerboard against genius. On June 18, 1815, this hatred had the last word, and under Lodi, Montebello, Montenotte, Mantuna, Marengo, Arcola, it wrote: Waterloo. Triumph of the commonplace, generous to majorities. Destiny consented to this irony. In his decline, Napoleon again found Wurmser before him, but young. In fact to produce Wurmser, it would have been enough to whiten Wellington's hair.

Waterloo is a battle of the first rank won by a captain of the second.

What is truly admirable in the battle of Waterloo is England, English firmness, English resolution, English blood; the superb thing England had there—may it not displease her—is herself. It is not her captain, it is her army.

Wellington, strangely ungrateful, declared in a letter to Lord Bathhurst that his army, the army that fought on June 18, 1815, was a "detestable army." What does this dark assembly of bones, buried beneath the furrows of Waterloo, think of that?

England has been too modest in regard to Wellington. To make Wellington so great is to belittle England. Wellington is only one hero, among many. Those Scotch Grays, those Horse Guards, those regiments of Maitland and Mitchell, that infantry of Pack and Kempt, that cavalry of Ponsonby and Somerset, those Highlanders playing the bagpipe under the storm of grapeshot, those battalions of Rylandt, those raw recruits who hardly knew how to handle a musket, holding out against the veteran bands of Essling and Rivoli—all that is great. Wellington was tenacious, that was his merit, and we do not undervalue it, but the least of his foot soldiers or his horsemen was quite as firm as he. The iron soldier is as good as the Iron Duke. As for us, all glory goes to the English soldier, the English army, the English people. If there is to be a trophy, it goes to England. The Waterloo column would be more just if, instead of the statue of a man, it lifted to the clouds a sculpture of the nation.

But this great England will be offended at what we say here. Even after her 1688 and our 1789, she still has the feudal illusion. She believes in hereditary right, and in the hierarchy. This people, surpassed by none in might and glory, values itself as a nation, not as a people. So much so that as a people they subordinate themselves willingly, and take a Lord for a head. Workmen, they submit to being scorned; soldiers, they submit to whippings. We remember that at the battle of Inkerman a sergeant who, so it seems, had saved the army, could not be mentioned by Lord Raglan, since the English military hierarchy did not permit any hero below the rank of officer to be mentioned in a report.

What we admire above all, in an encounter like that of Waterloo, is the prodigious skill of fortune. The night's rain, the wall at Hougomont, the sunken road of Ohain, Grouchy deaf to cannon, Napoleon's guide who deceives him, Bülow's guide who leads him right; all this cataclysm is wonderfully carried out.

Taken as a whole, let us be frank, Waterloo was more of a massacre than a battle.

Of all great battles, Waterloo is the one that has the shortest line in proportion to the numbers engaged. Napoleon, two miles, Wellington, a mile and a half; seventy-two thousand men on each side. From this density came the carnage.

Calculations have been made and these proportions established: Loss of men: at Austerlitz, French, fourteen percent; Russians, thirty percent; Austrians, forty-four percent. At Wagram, French, thirteen percent; Austrians, fourteen. At La Moscowa, French, thirty-seven percent; Russians, forty-four. At Bautzen, French, thirteen percent; Russians and Prussians, fourteen. At Waterloo, French, fifty-six percent; Allies, thirty-one. Average for Waterloo, forty-one percent. A hundred and forty-four thousand men; sixty thousand dead.

The field of Waterloo today has that calm belonging to the earth, impassive support for man, and it looks like any other plain.

At night, however, a sort of visionary mist arises from it, and if some traveler is walking there, if he looks, if he listens, if he dreams like Virgil on the deadly plains of Philippi, he will be possessed by hallucinations of the disaster. The terrifying 18th of June lives again; the artificial hill of the monument fades away; this lion, whatever it be, is dispelled; the battlefield resumes its reality; the lines of infantry undulate in the plain, furious gallops cross the horizon; the bewildered dreamer sees the flash of sabers, the glistening of bayonets, the bursting of shells, the awful intermingling of the thunders; he hears, like a death rattle from the depths of a tomb, the vague clamor of the phantom battle; these shadows are grenadiers; these flickers are cuirassiers; this skeleton is Napoleon; that skeleton is Wellington; all this is gone, and yet it still clashes and struggles; and the ravines run red, and the trees shudder, and there is fury up to the sky, and, in the darkness, all those savage heights, Mont-Saint-Jean, Hougomont, Frischemont, Papelotte, Plancenoit, appear confusedly crowned with whirlwinds of specters exterminating one another.

XVII

SHOULD WE APPROVE OF WATERLOO?

There is a much-respected liberal school that admires Waterloo. We are not among them. To us Waterloo is simply the unconscious date of liberty. For such an eagle to come from such an egg was certainly unexpected.

Waterloo, if we see it as an end, is, in intention, a counterrevolutionary victory. It is Europe against France; it is Petersburg, Berlin, and Vienna against Paris; it is the status quo against the initiative; it is June 14, 1789, attacked by March 20, 1815; it is the monarchies clearing the decks for action against the indomitable French Revolution. Finally to extinguish the volcano of this vast people, twenty-six years in eruption, was the dream. It was the solidarity of the Brunswicks, the Nassaus, the Romanoffs, the Hohenzollerns, and the Hapsburgs, with the Bourbons. Waterloo has the divine right riding on the back of its saddle. It is true that since the empire was despotic, royalty, by natural reaction, was forced to become liberal, and that a constitutional order has reluctantly sprung from Waterloo, to the great regret of the conquerors. The fact is that revolution cannot really be conquered, and that being providential and absolutely decreed, it keeps reappearing, before Waterloo in Bonaparte throwing down the old thrones, after Waterloo in Louis XVIII granting and submitting to the charter. Bonaparte places a postilion on the throne of Naples and a sergeant on the throne of Sweden, employing inequality to demonstrate equality; Louis XVIII at Saint-Ouen countersigns the Declaration of the Rights of Man. If you wish to understand what Revolution is, call it Progress; and if you wish to understand what Progress is, call it Tomorrow. Tomorrow performs its work irresistibly, and it does it from today. It always accomplishes its aim through unexpected means. It uses Wellington to make Foy, who was only a soldier, an orator. Foy falls at Hougomont and rises again at the rostrum. Thus progress proceeds. There can be no wrong tools for this workman. Never distracted, it adapts to its divine work the man who strode over the Alps and the good old tottering patient at the Père Elysée. It employs the cripple king as well as the conqueror, the conqueror without, the cripple within. Waterloo, by cutting short the demolition of European thrones by the sword, has had no other effect than to continue the revolutionary work in another way. The swordsmen are gone, the time of the thinkers has come. The age that Waterloo would have liked to check has marched across it and proceeded on its way. This inauspicious victory has been conquered by liberty.

All in all and incontestably, what triumphed at Waterloo; what smiled behind Wellington; what brought him all the marshals' batons of Europe, among them, it is said, the baton of marshal of France; what cheerfully wheeled barrows of earth filled with bones to erect the lion's mound; what triumphantly wrote on that pedestal the date: June 18, 1815; what encouraged Blücher slashing at the fugitives; what, from the height of the plateau of Mont-Saint-Jean, was hanging over France as over a prey, was Counterrevolution. It was Counterrevolution that murmured the infamous word—dismemberment. Reaching Paris, it had a close view of the crater; it felt that the ashes were burning its feet, and had second thoughts. It came back lisping of a charter.

Let us see no more in Waterloo than what there is in Waterloo. Of intentional liberty, nothing. The Counterrevolution was involuntarily liberal, as, by a corresponding phenomenon, Napoleon was involuntarily revolutionary. On June 18, 1815, Robespierre on horseback was thrown from his saddle.

XVIII

REVIVAL OF DIVINE RIGHT

End of the dictatorship. The whole European system fell.

The Empire sank into a darkness resembling that of the expiring Roman world. It rose again from the depths, as in the time of the barbarians. Except that the barbarism of 1815, which should be called by its special name, the counterrevolution, was short-winded, soon out of breath, and quickly over. The empire, we must acknowledge, was mourned by heroes' tears. If there is glory in the scepter-sword, the Empire had been glory incarnate. It had spread across the earth all the light that tyranny can give—a somber light. Let us say further—an obscure light. Compared to real day, it is night. This disappearance of night had the effect of an eclipse.

Louis XVIII returned to Paris. The circle dancing of July 8 erased the enthusiasms of March 20. The Corsican became the antithesis of the Béarnais. The flag on the dome of the Tuileries was white. The exile mounted the throne. Hartwell's pine table took its place facing Louis XIV's chair decorated with fleur-de-lis. Men talked of Bouvines and Fontenoy as of yesterday, Austerlitz being out of date. The altar and the throne fraternized majestically. One of the most unquestionably safe forms of society in the nineteenth century was established in France and on the Continent. Europe adopted the white cockade. Trestaillon became famous. The motto *non pluribus impar* reappeared in the stone sun rays on the façade of the barracks on the Quai d'Orsay. Where there had been an imperial guard, there was a red house. The Arc du Carrousel—covered with awkwardly gained victories—disowned by these new times, and perhaps a little ashamed of Marengo and Arcola, made do with the statue of the Duke of Angoulême. The cemetery de la Madeleine, the terrible potter's field of '93, was covered with marble and jasper, the bones of Louis XVI and Marie-Antoinette being in its dust. In the moat of Vincennes, a sepulchral column rose from the ground, recalling the fact that the Duc d'Enghien died in the very same month in which Napoleon was crowned. Pope Pius VII, who had performed this consecration very close to the time of his death, tranquilly blessed the fall as he had blessed the elevation. At Schöenbrunn there was a little shadow four years old whom it was seditious to call the King of Rome. And those things were done, and those kings resumed their thrones, and the master of Europe was put in a cage, and the *ancien régime* became the new, and all the light and all the shadow of the earth changed places, because, in the afternoon of a summer's day, a shepherd said to a Prussian in the woods, "Go this way, not that way!"

This 1815 was a sort of gloomy April. The old unhealthy and poisonous realities took on new shapes. Falsehood espoused 1789, divine right masked itself under a charter, fictions became constitutional, prejudices, superstitions, and mental reservations, with Article 14 at heart, put on the varnish of liberalism. Serpents changing their skins.

Man had been both enlarged and diminished by Napoleon. The ideal, under this splendid material reign, had received the strange name of ideology. Serious recklessness of a great man, to turn the future into derision. The people, however, that cannon fodder so fond of the cannoneer, looked for him. Where is he? What is he doing? "Napoleon is dead," said a visitor to a disabled veteran of Marengo and Waterloo. "He dead!" cried the soldier. "Not that one!" Imagination deified this prostrate man. The heart of Europe, after Waterloo, was dark. An enormous void remained long after Napoleon's disappearance.

Kings threw themselves into this void. Old Europe took advantage of it to assume a new form. There was a Holy Alliance. Belle-Alliance, the deadly field of Waterloo, had already said it in advance.

In its presence and confronting this ancient Europe reformed, the outlines of a new France began to appear. The future, ridiculed by the emperor, made its entrance.

It had on its brow that star, Liberty. The passionate eyes of rising generations turned toward it. Strange to tell, men were smitten at the same time with this future, Liberty, and this past, Napoleon. Defeat had magnified the vanquished. Bonaparte fallen seemed higher than Bonaparte in power. Those who had triumphed were frightened. England guarded him through Hudson Lowe, and France watched him through Montchenu. His folded arms became the anxiety of thrones. Alexander called him "My Insomnia." This terror arose from the quantity of revolution he had within him. This is what explains and excuses Bonapartist liberalism. This phantom made the old world quake. Kings reigned ill at ease with the rock of Saint Helena in the horizon.

While Napoleon was dying at Longwood, the sixty thousand men fallen on the field of Waterloo tranquilly moldered away, and something of their peace spread over the world. The Congress of Vienna made the treaties of 1815 from it, and Europe called that the Restoration.

Such is Waterloo.

But what difference does it make to the Infinite? This entire tempest, this vast cloud, this war, then this peace, all of this darkness, do not disturb for one moment the light of that infinite Eye, before which the smallest insect leaping from one blade of grass to another equals the eagle flying from spire to spire among the towers of Notre-Dame.

XIX

THE BATTLEFIELD AT NIGHT

We return, for the requirements of this book, to the deadly battlefield.

On June 18, 1815, the moon was full. Its light favored the ferocious pursuit of Blücher, revealed the tracks of the fugitives, delivered this helpless mass to the bloodthirsty Prussian cavalry, and aided in the massacre. Night sometimes lends such tragic assistance to catastrophe.

When the last gun had been fired, the plain of Mont-Saint-Jean remained deserted.

The English occupied the French camp; it is the usual verification of victory to sleep in the bed of the vanquished. They set up their bivouac beyond Rossomme. The Prussians, let loose on the fugitives, pushed forward. Wellington went to the village of Waterloo to make his report to Lord Bathurst.

If ever the *sic vos non vobis* were applicable, it is surely to this village of Waterloo. Waterloo did nothing, and was two miles away from the action. Mont-Saint-Jean was cannonaded, Hougomont was burned, Papelotte was burned, Plancenoit was burned, La Haie-Sainte was taken by assault, La Belle-Alliance saw the conflagration of the two conquerors; these names are scarcely known, and Waterloo, which had nothing to do with the battle, has all the honor.

We are not among those who glorify war; when the opportunity presents itself we tell its realities. War has a frightful beauty, which we have not concealed; it has also, we must admit, some ugliness, such as the eager stripping of the dead after a victory. The day after a battle dawns on naked corpses.

Who does this? Who sullies the triumph like this? Whose is this hideous furtive hand that slips into the pocket of victory? Who are these pickpockets plying their trade in the wake of glory? Some philosophers, Voltaire among others, say they are the very ones who achieved the glory. It is the same ones they say, there is no switch; those on their feet pillage those on the ground. The hero of the day is the vampire of the night. A man surely has a right, after all, to strip a corpse whose maker he is.

As for us we do not believe this. To gather laurels and to steal the shoes from a dead man seem to us impossible for the same hand.

One thing is certain: After the conquerors come the thieves. But let us place the soldier, especially the contemporary soldier, beyond this charge.

Every army has a wake, and there the accusation should lie. Bat-beings, half brigand and half valet, all species of night bird engendered by this twilight called war, bearers of uniforms who never fight, sham invalids, formidable cripples, interloping sutlers, traveling, sometimes with their wives, on little carts and stealing what they sell, beggars offering themselves as guides to officers, army servants, marauders: ancient armies on the march—we are not speaking of the present time—were followed by all these, to such an extent that, in technical language, they are called camp followers. No army and no nation were responsible for these beings; they spoke Italian and followed the Germans; they spoke French and followed the English. It was by one of these wretches, a Spanish camp follower who spoke French, that the Marquis of Fervacques, deceived by his Picardy gibberish, and taking him for one of us, was treacherously killed and robbed on the same battlefield during the night after the victory of Cerisoles. From marauding came the marauder. The detestable maxim, "Live off your enemy," produced this leper, which only rigid discipline can cure. There are illusory reputations; it is not always known why certain generals, great though they were, have been so popular. Turenne was adored by his soldiers because he tolerated pillage; the permission to do wrong is part of kindness: Turenne was so kind that he allowed the Palatinate to be burned and put to the sword. There were fewer or more marauders in the wake of armies according to a commander's degree of severity. Hoche and Marceau had no camp followers; Wellington—to his credit—had few.

However, during the night of June 18, the dead were stripped. Wellington was firm; he ordered that anyone taken in the act be put to death; but pillage perseveres. The marauders were robbing in one corner of the battlefield and being shot in another.

The moon shone ominously on the plain.

Toward midnight a man was prowling or rather crawling near the sunken road of Ohain. To all appearances, he was one of those we have just described, neither English nor French, peasant nor soldier, less man than ghoul, attracted by the scent of corpses, counting theft as victory, coming to rifle Waterloo. He had on a tunic that was partly a cape; he was wary yet daring, looking behind as he moved ahead. Who was this man? Night probably knew more of his doings than day! He had no knapsack, but obviously large pockets under his cape. From time to time he would stop, examine the plain around him as though to see if he were observed, suddenly stoop down, move something that was on the ground silent and motionless, then rise up and skulk away. His gliding movement, his attitudes, his rapid and furtive gestures, made him seem like those twilight specters that haunt ruins and are called the Alleurs in old Norman legends.

Certain nocturnal waterbirds make such movements in marshes.

An eye carefully penetrating all this haze might have noticed at some distance, standing as if it were concealed behind the ruin on the Nivelle road near the route from Mont-Saint-Jean to Braine-l'Alleud, a sort of little vendor's wagon, covered with tarred osiers, harnessed to a starving nag chawing nettles through her bit, and in the wagon some sort of woman sitting on trunks and bundles. Perhaps there was some connection between this wagon and the prowler.

The darkness was serene. Not a cloud was in the zenith. No matter that the earth was red; the moon stayed white in the indifferent heavens. In the meadows, branches of trees broken by grapeshot, but not fallen, still holding by the bark, swung gently in the night wind. A breeze moved the brushwood. There was quivering in the grass that seemed like departing souls.

The tread of the patrols and watchmen of the English camp could be heard dimly in the distance.

Hougomont and La Haie-Sainte continued to burn, making, one in the east and the other in the west, two great flames, to which was attached, like a necklace of rubies with two smooth garnets at its extremities, the cordon of English campfires, extending in an immense semicircle over the hills of the horizon.

We have told of the catastrophe of the Ohain road. The heart shrinks with terror at the thought of such a death for so many brave men.

If anything is horrible, if there is a reality that surpasses our worst dreams, it is this: to live, to see the sun, to be in full possession of manly vigor, to have health and joy, to laugh heartily, to rush toward a glory that lures you on, to feel lungs that breathe, a heart that beats, a mind that thinks, to speak, to hope, to love; to have mother, wife, children, to have sunlight, and suddenly, in less time than it takes to cry out, to plunge into an abyss, to fall, to roll, to crush, to be crushed, to see the heads of grain, the flowers, the leaves, the branches, unable to catch hold of anything, to feel your sword useless, men under you, horses over you, to struggle in vain, your bones broken by some kick in the darkness, to feel a heel gouging your eyes out of their sockets, raging at the horseshoe between your teeth, to stifle, to howl, to twist, to be under all this, and to say, "Just then I was a living man!"

There, where the terrible disaster had been, all was now silent. The cut of the sunken road was filled with horses and riders inextricably heaped together. Horrible entanglement. There were no slopes left to the road; dead bodies filled it level with the plain, right to the brim like a well-measured bushel of barley. A mass of dead above, a river of blood below—such was this road on the evening of June 18, 1815. The blood ran all the way to the Nivelles road and oozed through in a large pool in front of the clump of felled trees that barred the road, at a spot that can still be seen. It was, it will be remembered, at the opposite end, toward the road from Genappe, that the cuirassiers' headlong interment took place. The thickness of the mass of bodies was in proportion to the depth of the sunken road. Toward the middle, at a spot that was shallower, where Delord's division had crossed, this layer of death became thinner.

The night prowler we just introduced to the reader was going in that direction. He ferreted through the immense grave. He looked around. He passed an indescribably hideous review of the dead. He walked with his feet in blood.

Suddenly he stopped.

A few steps in front of him, in the sunken road, at a point where the mound of corpses ended, from under the mass of men and horses appeared an open hand, lit by the moon.

The hand had something gleaming on one finger, a gold ring.

The man stooped down, stayed crouched for a moment, and when he rose again there was no ring on that hand.

He did not exactly straighten up, but stayed in a sinister and startled attitude, turning his back to the pile of dead, scrutinizing the horizon, on his knees, his upper body resting on his two forefingers, peering over the rim of the hollow road. The four paws of the jackal are well adapted to certain actions.

Then, deciding upon his course, he stood up.

At that moment he was startled. He felt something holding him from behind.

He turned; it was the open hand, which had closed, seizing the hem of his cape.

An honest man would have been frightened. This one began to laugh.

"Oh," he said, "it's only the dead man. I prefer a ghost to a gendarme."

However, the hand relaxed and let go. Strength is soon exhausted in the tomb.

"What's this!" the prowler added, "is this dead man alive? Let's see."

He bent over again, rummaged among the heap, pushed aside whatever impeded him, grabbed the hand, seized the arm, freed the head, drew out the body, and a few moments later he was dragging a lifeless man, at least one who was unconscious, in the shadow of the sunken road. It was a cuirassier, an officer; and an officer of some rank; a heavy gold epaulet protruded from under his breastplate, but he had no helmet. A furious saber cut had disfigured his face, where nothing but blood could be seen. It did not seem, however, that he had any broken bones; and by some happy chance, if the word is possible here, the bodies had hurled right over him, saving him from being crushed. His eyes were closed.

On his breastplate he wore the silver cross of the Legion of Honour.

The prowler tore off this cross, which disappeared in one of the gulfs under his cape.

After that he felt the officer's fob, found a watch there, and took it. Then he rummaged in his vest and found a purse, which he pocketed.

When he had reached this phase of the succor he was tendering the dying man, the officer opened his eyes.

"Thank you," he said feebly.

The rough movements of the man handling him, the cool of the night, and the fresh air breathed freely, had roused him from his lethargy.

The prowler did not answer. He raised his head. The sound of a footstep could be heard on the plain; probably it was some approaching patrol.

The officer murmured, for there was agony still in his voice, "Who won the battle?"

"The English," answered the prowler.

The officer went on, "Search my pockets. You'll find a purse there and a watch. Take them."

This had already been done.

The prowler made a pretense of executing the command and said, "There's nothing there."

"I've been robbed," replied the officer. "I'm sorry. They would have been yours."

The tread of the patrol was growing more and more distinct.

"Somebody is coming," said the prowler, making a movement as if to go.

The officer, raising himself painfully on one arm, held him back. "You've saved my life. Who are you?"

The prowler gave a quick whisper: "Like yourself, I belong to the French army. I have to go. If I'm taken I'll be shot. I've saved your life. Now help yourself."

"What's your rank?"

"Sergeant."

"What's your name?"

"Thénardier."

"I won't forget that name," said the officer. "And you, remember mine. My name is Pontmercy."

Book Two

THE SHIP ORION

I

NUMBER 24601 BECOMES NUMBER 9430

Jean Valjean had been retaken.

Excuse us for passing rapidly over the painful details. We shall merely reproduce a couple of items published in the newspapers of the day, some few months after the remarkable events that occurred at Montreuil-sur-mer.

The articles are somewhat laconic. It will be remembered that the *Gazette des Tribunaux* did not yet exist.

The first is from the *Drapeau Blanc*, dated July 25, 1823:

"A district in the Pas-de-Calais has just been the scene of an unlikely occurrence. A newcomer to the region known as Monsieur Madeleine, had within a few years, thanks to certain new processes, restored the manufacture of jet and black glass ware—formerly a local industry. He had made his own fortune by it, and in fact that of the entire district. In acknowledgment of his services he had been appointed mayor. The police have discovered that Monsieur Madeleine was none other than an escaped convict, condemened in 1796 for robbery, one Jean Valjean. This Jean Valjean has been sent back to prison. It appears that before his arrest, he managed to withdraw from Laffitte's a sum amounting to more than half a million, which he had deposited there and which incidentally, he had quite legitimately earned from his business. Since his return to the prison at Toulon, it has been impossible to discover where Jean Valjean concealed the money."

The second article, which goes into a little more detail, is taken from the *Journal de Paris* of the same date:

A former convict named Jean Valjean has recently been brought before the superior court of the Var, under circumstances bound to attract attention. This villain had succeeded in eluding detection by the police; he had changed his name and managed to procure the position of mayor in one of our small towns in the North. He had established a very considerable business in this town, but was ultimately unmasked and arrested, thanks to the indefatigable zeal of the public authorities. He kept as his mistress a prostitute, who died of the shock at the moment of his arrest. This wretch, who is endowed with herculean strength, managed to escape, but, three or four days later, the police picked him up again in Paris, just as he was getting into one of the small vehicles that ply between the capital and the village of Montfermeil (Seine-et-Oise). They say that he had availed himself of these three or four days of freedom to withdraw a considerable sum deposited by him with one of our principal bankers. The amount is estimated at six or seven hundred thousand francs. According to the bill of indictment, he has concealed it in some place known only to himself, and authorities have been unable to seize it; however that may be, the said Jean Valjean has been brought before the Superior Court of the Department of the Var under indictment for an armed assault and robbery on the high road committed some eight years ago on the person of one of those honest lads who, as the patriarch of Ferney has written in immortal verse,

> . . . De Savoie arrivent tous les ans,
> Et dont la main légèrement essuie
> Ces longs canaux engorgés par la suie.[1]

[1] . . . Who come from Savoy every year,
And whose hand deftly sweeps out
Those long channels choked with soot.

This bandit attempted no defense. It was proved by the able and eloquent representative of the crown that others were involved in the robbery, and that Jean Valjean was part of a band of robbers in the South. Consequently, Jean Valjean, being found guilty, was condemned to death. The criminal refused to appeal to the higher courts, and the king, in his inexhaustible clemency, deigned to commute his sentence to that of hard labor for life. Jean Valjean was immediately forwarded to the prison at Toulon."

It will not be forgotten that Jean Valjean had at Montreuil-sur-mer certain religious habits. Some of the newspapers, among them the *Constitutionnel,* held up this commutation as a triumph of the clerical party.

Jean Valjean's new prison number was 9430.

While we are at it, let us note, before leaving the subject, that with M. Madeleine, the prosperity of Montreuil-sur-mer disappeared; everything he had foreseen, in that feverish night of irresolution, happened; he gone, the *soul* was gone. In Montreuil-sur-mer after his disgrace, there was that egotistic partitioning that follows the fall of great men—that fatal carving up of prosperous enterprises, a hidden daily occurrence in human society and one that history has noted only once, and then because it took place after the death of Alexander. Generals crown themselves kings; foremen assumed the position of manufacturers. Jealous rivalries arose. The spacious workshops of M. Madeleine were closed; the building fell into ruin, the workers dispersed. Some left the region, others abandoned the business. From that time on, everything was done on a small scale, instead of a large one, and for gain rather than for good. There was no longer any center; competition and venom on all sides. M. Madeleine had ruled and directed everything. With him fallen, it was every man for himself; the spirit of strife succeeded to the spirit of organization, bitterness to cordiality, hatred of each against each instead of the good will of the founder toward all; the threads woven together by M. Madeleine became entangled and were broken; the workmanship was debased, the products were degraded, confidence was killed; customers diminished, there were fewer orders, wages decreased, the shops became idle, bankruptcy followed. And nothing was left for the poor. Everything disappeared.

Even the state noticed that someone had been crushed somewhere. Less than four years after the decree of the superior court establishing the identity of M. Madeleine and Jean Valjean, to the benefit of the prison, the expense of tax collection had doubled in the district of Montreuil-sur-mer; and M. de Villèle remarked as much on the floor of the Assembly, in the month of February 1827.

II

IN WHICH SEVERAL LINES WILL BE READ THAT MAY HAVE COME FROM THE DEVIL HIMSELF

Before proceeding further, we should relate in some detail a remarkable incident that took place around the same time at Montfermeil and that might coincide with certain conjectures of the public authorities.

In the neighborhood of Montfermeil there is a venerable superstition, all the more precious and rare in that a popular superstition in the vicinity of Paris is like an aloe tree in Siberia. We are among those who respect the rare. Here, then, is the superstition of Montfermeil: They believe there that the Devil has from time immemorial chosen the forest as the hiding place for his treasure. The good wives of the vicinity assert that it is not unusual to meet, at sundown, in the secluded portions of the woods, a grim man, possibly a cattle driver or a woodcutter, wearing wooden clogs and breeches and smock of coarse linen, and recognizable because, instead of a cap or hat, he has two immense horns on his head. That certainly ought to make him recognizable. This man is usually busy digging holes. There are three ways of handling any encounter with him.

The first is to approach the man and speak to him. Then you realize that he is just a peasant, that he looks black because it is twilight, that he is not digging a hole at all but merely cutting grass for his cows, and that what had been taken for horns is his pitchfork, which he carries on his back and whose prongs, thanks to night vision, seemed to grow out of his head. You go home, and you die within a week. The second method is to watch him, wait until he has dug the hole, filled it in, and gone away, then, running quickly to the spot, open it and get the "treasure" that the grim man has, of course, buried there. You die within a month. The third alternative is not to speak to the dark man or even look at him, and to run away as fast as you can. You die within the year.

As all three of these methods have their drawbacks, the second, which at least offers some advantages, among others that of possessing a treasure, though it be only for a month, is the one generally adopted. Therefore, the daring who never pass up a good opportunity, have often it seems, reopened the holes dug by the grim man and tried to rob the Devil. The operation does not appear, however, very profitable—at least, if we are to believe tradition, and particularly two enigmatic lines in barbarous Latin left us on this subject by a doubtful Norman monk named Tryphon, who dabbled in the black arts. This Tryphon was buried in the abbey of Saint-Georges de Bochervile near Rouen, and his grave is a major producer of toads.

So the treasure seeker makes a tremendous effort, as the holes are generally dug very deep; he sweats, he digs, he works away all night, because that is the time to do it; his shirt is soaked, his candle burns down, he chips his pickax, and when at length he has reached the bottom of the hole, when he puts his hand on the "treasure," what does he find? What is the Devil's treasure? A penny—sometimes a crown; a stone, a skeleton, a bleeding corpse, sometimes a ghost folded twice like a letter in an envelope, sometimes nothing. Tryphon's lines seem to suggest as much to the indiscreet and prying:

Fodit, et in fossa thesauros condit opaca,
As, nummos, lapides, cadaver, simulacra, nihilque.

It seems that nowadays they also occasionally find a powder horn with bullets or a dirty pack of greasy old cards evidently used by the Devil. Tryphon never mentions these articles, since Tryphon lived in the twelfth century, and it does not appear that the Devil was clever enough to invent gunpowder before Roger Bacon or playing cards before Charles VI.

Besides, whoever plays with the cards is sure to lose all he has, and as for the powder in the flask, it has the peculiarity of making your gun explode in your face.

Now, very shortly after the time when authorities took it into their heads that the liberated convict Jean Valjean had, during his few days at large, been prowling around Montfermeil, it was remarked, in that village, that a certain old road worker named Boulatruelle had "a fancy" for the woods. People in the neighborhood claimed to know that Boulatruelle had been in prison; he was under police surveillance, and, since he could not find work anywhere, the government employed him at half wages as a repairman on the crossroad from Gagny to Lagny.

Boulatruelle was distrusted by the people of the neighborhood; he was too respectful, too humble, quick to doff his cap to everybody, he always trembled and smiled at the gendarmes, was probably in league with bands of robbers, and was suspected of lying in wait in the hedges, at nightfall. He had nothing in his favor except that he was a drunkard.

What had been observed was this:

For some time past Boulatruelle had been leaving his work of stone breaking and road maintenance very early, and going into the woods with his pick. He would be seen toward evening in the remotest glades and the wildest thickets, looking like somone looking for something, or sometimes digging a hole. The housewives who passed that way took him at first for Beelzebub, then they recognized Boulatruelle, which was no more reassuring. These chance meetings seemed to disconcert Boulatruelle considerably. He was clearly trying to hide himself and what he was doing.

The village gossips said, "It's obvious that the Devil has been around here recently, and Boulatruelle saw him and is looking for his treasure. He's just the fellow to rob the Devil."—The Voltairians added, "Will Boulatruelle catch the Devil or the Devil catch Boulatruelle?" The old women took to crossing themselves a lot.

But Boulatruelle's visits to the woods stopped and he went back to his regular labor on the road. People began to talk about other things.

A few souls, however, remained curious, thinking that

the affair might involve, not the fabulous treasures of the legend, but some windfall more substantial than the Devil's banknotes, and that Boulatruelle was partly onto the secret. The most puzzled of all were the schoolmaster and the tavernkeeper Thénardier, who was everybody's friend and who had not disdained to strike up an intimacy with even Boulatruelle.

"He has been in prison," said Thénardier. "Good Lord! You never know who's there now or might wind up there!"

One evening, the schoolmaster remarked that, in another era, the authorities would have inquired into what Boulatruelle was up to in the woods, and that he would have been forced to speak—answer, even tortured, if need be—and that Boulatruelle would not have held out, if he had been put to the question by water, for instance.

"Let's put him to the question by wine," said Thénardier.

So they made up a party and plied the old road mender with drink. Boulatruelle drank copiously, but said little. He combined with admirable art and in masterly proportions the thirst of a drunk with the discretion of a judge. However, by dint of returning to the charge and by putting together and twisting the obscure expressions he did let slip, Thénardier and the schoolmaster made out, so they thought, the following:

One morning about daybreak as he was going to work, Boulatruelle had been surprised to see concealed under a bush in the woods, a pickax and spade. However, he supposed that they were the pick and spade of old Six-Fours, the water carrier, and thought no more about it. But, that same evening, he had seen without being seen himself, as he was hidden behind a large tree, "a person who did not come from that region, and whom he, Boulatruelle, knew very well"—or, as Thénardier translated it, "an old comrade from prison"—turn off from the high road toward the thickest part of the wood. Boulatruelle obstinately refused to tell the stranger's name. This person carried a package, something square, like a large box or a small trunk. Boulatruelle was surprised. Seven or eight minutes, however, elapsed before it occurred to him to follow the "person." But he was too late. The person was already in the dense woods, night had come on, and Boulatruelle did not manage to overtake him. Thereupon he made up his mind to watch the edge of the woods. "There was a moon." Two or three hours later, Boulatruelle saw this person come out of the woods, this time carrying not the little trunk but a pick and spade. Boulatruelle let the person go by because, as he thought to himself, the other was three times as strong as he, was armed with a pickax, and would probably murder him, on recognizing him and seeing that he, in turn, was recognized. Touching display of feeling in two old companions unexpectedly meeting. But the pick and spade were a gleam of light to Boulatruelle; he hurried to the underbrush in the morning, and found neither one. From this he concluded that this person, on entering the wood, had dug a hole with his pick, had buried the chest, and filled up the hole with his spade. Now, as the chest was too small to contain a corpse, it must contain money; hence his continued searches. Boulatruelle had explored, delved, and combed through the whole forest, and had dug in every spot where the earth seemed to have been freshly disturbed. But all in vain.

He had turned up nothing. Nobody thought any more about it at Montfermeil, except for a few gossips, who said, "I'm sure the road worker from Gagny didn't make all that fuss for nothing: The Devil was certainly there."

III

IN WHICH WE SEE THAT THE SHACKLE MUST HAVE UNDERGONE SOME PREPARATION TO BE BROKEN BY ONE HAMMER BLOW

Toward the end of October, in that same year, 1823, the inhabitants of Toulon saw returning to port, after stormy weather and in order to repair some damages, the ship *Orion,* which was later used at Brest as a school ship, and which now formed a part of the Mediterranean fleet. This ship, crippled by the sea's pounding, made a strong impression as it entered the roadstead. It flew a pennant that entitled it to a regulation salute of eleven guns, which it returned shot for shot—in all, twenty-two. It has been estimated that in salutes, royal and military compliments, exchanges of courteous hubbub, signals of etiquette, roadstead and citadel formalities, rising and setting of the sun saluted daily by all fortresses and all vessels of war, the opening and closing of gates, etc., etc., the civilized world, in every part of the globe, fires off daily one hundred and fifty thousand useless cannon shots. At six francs per shot, that amounts to nine hundred thousand francs a day, or three hundred million a year, gone up in smoke. This is only one item. Meanwhile, the poor are dying of hunger.

The year 1823 was what the Restoration has called the "time of the Spanish War."

That war comprised many events in one and numerous peculiarities. It was a great family affair of the Bourbons; the French branch aiding and protecting the branch at Madrid, that is to say, performing the duties of seniority; an apparent return to our national traditions, mixed up with subservience and obligation to the cabinets of the North; the Duc d'Angoulême, dubbed by the liberal journals "the hero of Andujar," repressing with a triumphant attitude—rather contradicted by his peaceful mien—the old and very real terrorism of the Holy Office, in battling the chimerical terrorism of the Liberals; the sans-culottes revived, to the great alarm of all the old dowagers, under the name of *descamisados;* monarchists trying to impede progress, which they called anarchy; the theories of '89 rudely interrupted in their undermining advances; a cry of halt from all of Europe delivered to the French idea of revolution making its tour of the globe; side by side with the generalissimo son of France, the Prince de Carignan —later Charles-Albert—enlisting in this crusade of the kings against the people as a volunteer with a grenadier's epaulets of red wool; the soldiers of the Empire returning to the field, but after eight years of rest, grown old, sad, wearing the white cockade; the tricolor displayed abroad by a heroic handful of Frenchmen, as the white flag had been at Coblentz, thirty years before; monks mingling with our troopers; the spirit of liberty and innovation set straight by bayonets; principles struck dumb by cannon shot; France undoing by her weapons what she had done with her mind; to cap the climax, the leaders on the other side sold, their troops hesitant; cities besieged by millions in currency; no military dangers, and yet some possible explosions, as is the case in every mine entered and taken by surprise; but little bloodshed, little honor gained; shame for a few, glory for none. Such was this war, brought about by princes descended from Louis XIV, and carried out by generals sprung from Napoleon. It had this sad fate, that it invoked the image of neither a great war nor great politics.

A few feats of arms were serious matters; the taking of Le Trocadero, among others, was a handsome military exploit; but, all in all, we repeat, the trumpets of this war give off a cracked and feeble sound, its general effect was suspect, and history approves the unwillingness of France to accept so false a triumph. It seemed clear that some Spanish officers entrusted with the resistance yielded too easily, the notion of bribery seemed inherent in the victory; it appeared as though the generals rather than the battles had been won, and the victorious soldier returned humiliated. It was war grown petty indeed, where *Bank of France* could be read on the folds of the flag.

Soldiers from the war of 1808, under whose feet Saragossa had so heroically crumbled, knit their brows at this ready surrender of citadels, and found themselves regretting Palafox. It is a trait of France to prefer a Rostopchine to a Ballesteros.

On a still graver point, which should be emphasized too, this war, which ruffled the military spirit of France, enraged the democratic spirit. It was a scheme of subjugation. In this campaign, the object held out to the French soldier, son of democracy, was the conquest of a yoke for someone else's neck. Hideous contradiction. France exists to arouse the soul of the nations, not to stifle it. Since 1792, all the revolutions of Europe have been the French Revolution: France radiates liberty. That is a fact as clear as day. Those who do not see it are blind. Bonaparte is the one who said it.

The war of 1823, an outrage against the generous Spanish nation, was at the same time an outrage against the French Revolution. This monstrous act of violence was committed by France but out of compulsion; for, aside from wars of liberation, all that armies do they do by compulsion. The words "passive obedience" tell the tale. An army is a strange composite masterpiece, in which strength results from an enormous sum total of utter weaknesses. Thus only can we explain a war waged by humanity against humanity in spite of humanity.

As for the Bourbons, the war of 1823 was fatal to them. They took it for a success. They did not see what danger there is in attempting to kill an idea by a military watchword. In their naïveté, they blundered to the point of introducing into their establishment, as an element of strength, the immense debility of a crime. The spirit of ambuscade and lying in wait entered their policy. The seed of 1830 lay in 1823. In their councils the Spanish campaign became an argument on behalf of violent measures and intrigues favoring divine right. Having restored *el rey neto* in Spain, France could certainly restore the absolute monarchy at home. They fell into the tremendous error of mistaking the obedience of the soldier for the acquiesence of the nation. That fond delusion destroys thrones. No one can afford to fall asleep either in the shade of a poisonous tree or in the shadow of an army.

But let us return to the ship *Orion*.

During the operations of the army of the Prince-generalissimo, a squadron was cruising the Mediterranean. We have said that the *Orion* belonged to that squadron and that it had been driven back to the port of Toulon by bad weather.

The presence of a warship in port has something about it that attracts and occupies the mob. It is because it is imposing, and the throng likes imposing things.

A ship of the line is one of the most magnificent encounters of human genius with the forces of nature.

A vessel of the line is composed at once of the heaviest and lightest materials, because it has to contend simultaneously with the three forms of matter, the solid, the liquid, and the fluid. She has eleven iron claws to grasp the rock at the bottom of the sea, and more wings and feelers than a butterfly to catch the breezes in the sky. Her breath is expelled through her hundred and twenty guns as through enormous trumpets, and proudly answers the thunderbolt. The ocean strives to lead it astray in the frightful similarity of its billows, but the ship has a compass, its soul, always counseling it and always pointing toward the north. On dark nights, its lanterns take the place of the stars. So, to oppose the wind, it has its ropes and canvas; against the water its timber; against the rock its iron, copper, and lead; against the darkness, light; against immensity, a needle.

To get some idea of the gigantic proportions whose sum is a ship of the line, you only have to pass under one of the covered building sheds, six stories high, at Brest or Toulon. The vessels under construction can be seen there as though under glass. That colossal beam will be a spar. That huge column of timber lying on the ground and reaching out of sight will be the mainmast: From its root in the hold to its summit in the clouds, it is three hundred and sixty feet long and three feet in diameter at its base. The English mainmast rises two hundred and seventeen feet above the waterline. Anchor lines in the time of our fathers were of rope; ours use chain. Now the mere coil of chains for a hundred-gun ship is four feet high, twenty feet broad, and eight feet thick. And for the construction of this vessel, how much timber is required? It is a floating forest.

And yet, note that we are speaking here only of the warship of some forty years ago, the mere sailing craft; steam, then in its infancy, has since added new wonders to this prodigy called a man-of-war. At present the sailing vessel with auxiliary power is a surprising mechanism moved by a spread of canvas measuring four thousand square yards of surface and by a steam engine of twenty-five hundred horsepower.

Without referring to these newer marvels, the old-fashioned ship of Christopher Columbus and De Ruyter is one of the noblest works of man. It is as inexhaustible in force as the breadth of infinity; it gathers up the wind in its canvas, it is firmly fixed in the immense chaos of the waves, it floats and it reigns.

But a moment comes when the white squall breaks that sixty-foot spar like a straw, when the wind bends that three-hundred-and-sixty-foot mast like a reed, when that anchor, weighing its tons upon tons, is twisted in the maw of the wave like the angler's hook in the jaws of a pike, when those monster guns utter plaintive and futile roars that the tempest whirls off into space and darkness, when all this might and majesty are engulfed in a superior might and majesty.

Whenever immense strength is put forth only to end in immense weakness, it makes men meditate. That is why in seaports, the curious, without knowing exactly why, flock to these wonderful instruments of war and navigation.

Every day, then, from dawn to dusk, the quays, wharves, and piers of Toulon harbor were crowded with saunterers and idlers whose occupation consisted of gazing at the *Orion*.

The *Orion* was a ship that had long been in bad condition. During earlier voyages, thick layers of shellfish had accumulated on its bottom to the point of seriously impeding its progress; it had been put up in the dry dock the year before to be scraped, then gone to sea again. But this scraping had damaged the bolts in the hull.

In the latitude of the Balearic Islands, its planking had loosened and opened up, and since in those days there was no copper sheathing, the ship had leaked. A violent equinoctial storm blew up, which stove in the port bows and a porthole and damaged the foremast chain plates. Because of these injuries, the *Orion* returned to port in Toulon.

It was moored near the arsenal. It was in commission, and they were repairing it. The hull had not been injured on the starboard side, but a few planks had been taken off here and there, according to custom, to allow air into the framework.

One morning, the throng witnessed an accident.

The crew was busy furling sail. The seaman whose duty was to take in the starboard head of the main topsail lost his balance. He was seen tottering; the dense throng gathered on the arsenal wharf cried out, the man tipped over head first and he spun across the yard, his arms outstretched toward the deep; as he went by, he grabbed the foot-rope, with one hand, and then the other, and hung suspended there. The sea lay far below him at a dizzying depth. With the shock of his fall, the rope had parted near the mast, and the poor fellow dangled back and forth at the end of this line, like a stone in a sling.

Anyone going to his aid would run a terrible risk. None of the crew, who were all coastal fishermen new to the service, dared try. In the meantime, the poor seaman was tiring; his agony could not be seen in his face, but his body showed his increasing weakness. His arms strained in horrible contortions. Every attempt he made to pull himself up only increased the swinging of the rope. He did not cry out, for fear of wasting his strength. The spectators could only await the moment when he would let go of the line, and at times they looked away so as not to see him fall. There are moments when a rope's end, a pole, the branch of a tree, is life itself, and it is frightful to see a living being lose his hold on it and fall like ripe fruit.

Suddenly, a man was seen clambering up the rigging with the agility of a wildcat. He was dressed in red—a convict; he wore a green cap—a convict for life. As he reached the round top, a gust of wind blew off his cap revealing an entirely white head: He was not a young man.

As a matter of fact one of the convicts working on board in some prison chore had at the first alarm run to the officer of the watch, and in the midst of the crew's confusion and hesitation, while all the sailors trembled and shrank back, had asked permission to save the seaman's life at risk of his own. At a nod from the officer he broke the chain riveted to the iron ring at his ankle with one hammer blow, then grabbed a rope and sprang to the shrouds. At the time nobody noticed with what ease the chain was broken. It was only later that anybody remembered it.

In a twinkling he was up on the yard. He paused a few seconds and seemed to measure it with his glance. Those seconds, during which the wind swung the sailor to and fro at the end of the rope, seemed an eternity to the onlookers. Finally, the convict raised his eyes to heaven and took a step forward. The crowd drew a long breath. They saw him run along the yard. On reaching its very tip, he fastened one end of the rope he had with him and let the other hang full length. At this point, he began to let himself down this rope hand over hand, and then there was a pervasive, inexpressible feeling of terror; instead of one man, two were now dangling at that dizzying height.

You could have said it was a spider coming to seize a fly, except that in this case the spider was bringing life, not death. Ten thousand eyes were trained on the pair. Not a cry, not a word was uttered; the same emotion creased every brow. Nobody dared breathe, as though afraid to add the least whisper to the wind swaying the two unfortunate men.

However, the convict had managed to make his way

down to the seaman. It was just in time; one minute more, and the man, exhausted and despairing, would have fallen into the deep. The convict firmly tied him to the rope to which he clung with one hand while he worked with the other. Finally, he could be seen moving back up to the yardarm, hauling the sailor after him; he supported him there, for a moment, to let him recover his strength, and then, lifting him in his arms, carried him, as he walked along the yard, to the crosstrees, and from there to the roundtop, where he left him in the hands of his messmates.

Then the throng applauded; seasoned prison guards wept, women hugged each other on the wharves, and on all sides voices exclaimed, with emotion-choked enthusiasm, "This man must be pardoned!"

He, however, had made it a point of duty to climb down again immediately, and go back toward his work. To get there sooner, he slid down the rigging and started to run along a lower yard. Every eye followed him. Suddenly, terror ran through the crowd. Whether from fatigue or dizziness, he hesitated and staggered. All at once, the crowd shouted; the convict had fallen into the sea.

The fall was dangerous. The frigate *Algesiras* was moored close to the *Orion,* and the poor convict had plunged between the two ships. It was feared he would be drawn under one or the other. Four men sprang immediately into a boat. The people cheered them on, once more gripped by apprehension. The man had not come back up to the surface. He had disappeared in the sea, without even a ripple, as though he had fallen into a cask of oil. They sounded and dredged the place. All in vain. The search was continued until nightfall, but not even the body was found.

The next morning, the *Toulon Journal* published the following item: "November 17, 1823. Yesterday a convict at work on board the *Orion,* on his return from rescuing a sailor, fell into the sea and was drowned. His body has not been recovered. It is presumed that it was caught under the piling at the pier head of the arsenal. This man was registered under the number 9430, and his name was Jean Valjean."

Book Three

FULFILLMENT OF THE PROMISE MADE TO THE DEPARTED

I

THE WATER QUESTION AT MONTFERMEIL

Montfermeil is between Livry and Chelles, on the southern slope of the high plateau separating the Ourcq from the Marne. At present, it is quite a large town, graced throughout the year with stuccoed villas, and on Sundays with citizens in full regalia. In 1823 Montfermeil had neither so many white houses nor so many contented citizens; it was nothing but a village in the woods. Of course here and there you would find a few country houses from the last century, recognizable by their grand appearance, their ironwork balconies, and those long windows whose little panes cast all shades of green on the white of the closed shutters. But Montfermeil was nonetheless a village. Retired dry-goods merchants and adoptive villagers had not yet discovered it. It was a peaceful, charming spot, not on the road to anywhere, the inhabitants inexpensively enjoyed a luxuriant and easygoing country life. But water was scarce there because of the height of the plateau.

They had to go a considerable distance for it. The end of the village toward Gagny drew its water from the magnificent ponds in the forest on that side; the other end, around the church and toward Chelles, could only find drinking water at a little spring on the side of the hill, near the road to Chelles about fifteen minutes' walk from Montfermeil.

So its water supply was a serious matter for each household. The great houses, the aristocracy, even the Thénardier tavern, paid a penny a bucketful to an old man who made it his business and whose income from the Montfermeil waterworks was about eight sous a day; but this man only worked up to seven o'clock in summer and five in the winter, and once night had fallen and the first-floor shutters were closed, whoever had no drinking water went to get it or went without.

This was the terror of the poor creature the reader may not have forgotten—little Cosette. It will be remembered that Cosette was useful to the Thénardiers in two ways, they got pay from the mother and work from the child. When the mother ceased entirely to pay—we have seen why in the preceding chapters—the Thénardiers kept Cosette. She became their servant. In that capacity she was the one who ran for water when it was needed. So the child, always terrified by the idea of going to the spring at night, made sure that the house always had water.

Christmas 1823 in Montfermeil was particularly beautiful. The early part of the winter had been mild; there had been neither frost nor snow. Some players from Paris had obtained permission from the mayor to set up their stalls in the main street of the village, and a wandering band of peddlers had, by the same license, put up their booths in the church square and even in the Ruelle du Boulanger, on which, as the reader perhaps remembers, the Thénardiers' shabby inn was situated. This filled up the taverns and pubs and gave this quiet little place a noisy, joyful atmosphere. We should also say, to be the faithful historian, that, among the curiosities displayed in the square, there was a menagerie in which hideous clowns, dressed in rags and come from who knows where, were in 1823 exhibiting to the peasants of Montfermeil one of those horrible Brazilian vultures, a specimen of which our Royal Museum only obtained in 1845 and whose eye is a tricolored cockade. Naturalists call this bird, I believe, Caracara Polyborus; it belongs to the order of the Apicidae and the family of the vultures. Some good old retired Bonapartist soldiers in the village went to see the bird as a matter of faith. The players pronounced the tricolored cockade a unique phenomenon, made expressly by God for their menagerie.

On that Christmas Eve, several wagon drivers and peddlers were seated at a table with four or five candles and drinking in the low hall of the Thénardier tavern. This room was like all barrooms; tables, pewter mugs, bottles, drinkers, smokers; little light, a lot of noise. However, the date, 1823, was indicated by the two things then in vogue among the bourgeoisie, which were on the table, a kaleidoscope and a mottled tin lamp. Mme Thénardier was seeing to supper, which was cooking before a bright blazing fire; the husband, Thénardier, was drinking with his guests and talking politics.

Aside from the political discussions, the principal subjects of which were the Spanish war and the Duc d'Angoulême, local items were heard amid the hubbub, like these:

"Down around Nanterre and Suresnes the vintage is turning out well. Where they expected ten casks they're getting twelve. That's a good yield from the press."

"But the grapes can't have been ripe?"

"Oh, in those parts you never harvest ripe, or else the wine turns ropy by spring."

"It's all light wine, then?"

"They're a good deal lighter than they make around here. You have to harvest green."

And so forth.

Or else a miller might be grousing: "Are we responsible for what's in the bags? We find a heap of little seeds there, but we don't have time to pick them all out, and of course we've got to let 'em go through the stones; there's darnel, there's fennel, there's cockles, there's vetch, there's hemp, there's foxtail, and a lot of other weeds, not counting the pebbles you get in some wheat, particularly Breton wheat. I don't like to grind Breton wheat, no more than carpenters like to saw beams with nails in 'em. Just think of the dirt all that makes in the till. And then they complain about the flour. It's their own fault. They can't blame us for the flour."

Between two windows, a reaper sitting at a table with a farmer, who was bargaining for a piece of work to be done in spring, was saying, "There's no harm if the grass is damp. It cuts better. The dew's a good thing. It doesn't matter, that grass of yours is young, and hard to cut. It's so green, it bends under the scythe."

And so forth.

Cosette was at her usual place, sitting on the cross-brace of the kitchen table, near the fireplace; she was in rags; her feet were in wooden shoes, and by the light of the fire she was knitting woolen stockings for the little Thénardiers. A young kitten was playing under the chairs. In a neighboring room two clear childish voices were heard laughing and chatting: it was Eponine and Azelma.

In the chimney corner, a cowhide lash hung from a nail.

At times, the cry of a very young child, somewhere around the house, was heard above the noise of the bar-room. It was a little boy the woman had had some winters before. "I don't know why," she said; "it was the cold weather,"—and now a little more than three years old. The mother had nursed him, but did not love him. When the brat's insistent racket became too much to bear, "Your boy is squalling," Thénardier said. "Why don't you go and see what he wants?"

"Aah!" the mother answered. "I'm sick of him." And the poor little fellow went on crying in the darkness.

II

TWO PORTRAITS FILLED IN

Up to now the Thénardiers have only been seen here in profile; the time has come to look at them from all sides.

Thénardier has just passed his fiftieth year; Mme Thénardier had reached her fortieth, which is the fiftieth for woman; so that there was an equilibrium of age between the husband and wife.

Since her first appearance, the reader perhaps remembers something of this huge Thénardiess—for such we shall call the female of this species—tall, blond, red, fat, brawny, square, enormous, and agile; she belonged, as we have said, to the race of those colossal wild women who pose at fairs with paving-stones hung in their hair. She did everything around the house, the beds, the rooms, the washing, the cooking; and generally did just as she pleased. Cosette was her only servant—a mouse in the service of an elephant. Everything trembled at the sound of her voice, windows and furniture as well as people. Her broad face was covered with freckles, like the holes in a skimming ladle. She had a beard. She had the look of a market porter dressed in petticoats. She swore splendidly; she prided herself on being able to crack a nut with her fist. Apart from the novels she had read, which at times produced odd glimpses of the affected lady under the ogress, it would never have occurred to anyone to say: That's a woman. This Thénardiess was a cross between a whore and a fishwife. To hear her speak, you would say this was a policeman; to see her drink, you would say this was a cartman; if you saw her handle Cosette, you would say this was the hangman. When at rest, a tooth protruded from her lips.

The other Thénardier was a little man, skinny, pale, angular, bony, and puny, who looked sick but was healthy; that is where his skulduggery began. He smiled habitually as a matter of good business and tried to be polite to everybody, even to the beggar to whom he was refusing a penny. He had the look of a weasel and the air of a man of letters. He bore a close resemblance to portraits of the Abbé Delille. He made it a point to drink with wagon drivers. Nobody ever saw him drunk. He smoked a large pipe. He wore a smock, and under it an old black coat. He had pretensions to literature and materialism. Certain names he often pronounced in support of whatever he might be saying. Voltaire, Raynal, Parny, and, oddly enough, Saint Augustine. He professed to have "a system." In general, a great swindler. A fellow-sopher: There is such a thing. It will be remembered that he pretended to have been in the service; he would tell with some pomp how at Waterloo, as a sergeant in a Sixth or Ninth Light something, he alone, against a squadron of Hussars of Death, had covered with his body, and saved amid a shower of grapeshot, "a dangerously wounded general." Hence the flamboyant picture on his sign, and the name of his inn, which was spoken of in the region as the "tavern of the sergeant of Waterloo." He was liberal, both classic, and Bonapartist. He had subscribed to the Champ d'Asile. It was said in the village that he had studied for the priesthood.

We believe he had studied in Holland only to be an innkeeper. This composite upstart was, according to the situation, a Fleming from Lille in Flanders, a Frenchman in Paris, a Belgian in Brussels, conveniently on the fence between the two frontiers. We know about his prowess at Waterloo. As we have seen, he exaggerated it somewhat. Ebb and flow; wandering, adventure, was his element; a torn conscience leads to an unraveled life; and no doubt, at the stormy period around June 18, 1815, Thénardier belonged to that species of marauding sutlers we have described, roaming the countryside, robbing here and selling there, traveling as a family, man, woman, and children, in some rickety wagon, in the wake of marching troops, with the instinct for always attaching himself to the victorious army. With this campaign over, and having, as he put it, "some funds," he had opened his tavern in Montfermeil.

This quibus, composed of purses, watches, gold rings, and silver crosses, gathered at the harvest in the furrows sown with corpses, did not form a great total and had not lasted this sutler turned tavern keeper very long.

Thénardier had that indescribable rigidity of gesture that, with a curse, reminds you of the barracks and, with a sign of the cross, the seminary. He was a fine talker. He liked being thought learned. Nevertheless, the schoolmaster remarked that he made mistakes in pronunciation. He made out travelers' bills in a high style, but practiced eyes sometimes found spelling mistakes in them. Thénardier was sly, greedy, lazy, and clever. He never turned his nose up at servant girls, and so his wife did not hire them. This giantess was jealous. It seemed to her that this skinny little yellow man must be the object of universal desire.

Thénardier, above all a man of astuteness and poise, was a rascal of the temperate variety. This is the worst sort, because hypocrisy is involved.

Not that on occasion Thénardier was incapable of anger, at least as much as his wife; but that was very rare, and at such times, as though he were at war with the whole human race, as though he had in him a deep furnace of hatred, as though he were among those who are perpetually avenging themselves, who accuse everybody around them of every evil that befalls them, and are always ready to throw at the first comer, as legitimate grievance, the sum total of deceptions, failure, and calamities of their life; when all this frustration worked in him and boiled up into his mouth and eyes, he was frightful. Woe to anyone who came within reach of his fury at such a moment!

Besides all his other qualities, Thénardier was attentive and penetrating, silent or talkative as occasion required, and always with great intelligence. He had something of the look of sailors accustomed to squinting through spyglasses. Thénardier was a statesman.

Every newcomer who entered the tavern would say, on seeing the Thénardiess, "That's the master of the house." A mistake. She was not even the mistress. The husband was both master and mistress. She performed, he created. He directed everything by a sort of invisible and continuous magnetic action. A word sufficed, sometimes a sign; the mastodon obeyed. Thénardier was to her, without her really being aware of it, a sort of being apart and sovereign. She had the virtues of her personality; never would she have differed in any detail with "Monsieur Thénardier"—nor—impossible to suppose—would she have publicly disagreed with her husband, on any matter whatsoever. Never had she committed "before company" that fault of which women are so often guilty, and which is called in parliamentary language "exposing the crown." Though their accord had no other result than evil, there was food for contemplation in the submission of the Thénardiess to her husband. This bustling mountain of flesh moved under the little finger of the frail despot. It was, viewed from its dwarfed and grotesque side, the great universal fact: the homage of matter to spirit; for some deformities have their origin in the very depths of eternal beauty. There was something of the unknown in Thénardier; hence the absolute empire of this man over this woman. At times, she saw him as a lighted candle; at others, she felt him like a claw.

This woman was a formidable creation, who loved nothing but her children, and feared nothing but her husband. She was a mother because she was a mammal. Actually, her maternal feelings ended with her girls and, as we shall see, did not extend to boys. The man had only one thought—to get rich.

He did not succeed. His great talents lacked a worthy opportunity. In Montfermeil Thénardier was ruining himself, if ruin is possible at zero. In Switzerland, or in the Pyrenees, this penniless rogue would have become a millionaire. But the innkeeper must graze where fate has placed him.

It is understood that the word "innkeeper" is employed here in a restricted sense and does not extend to an entire class.

In this same year, 1823, Thénardier owed about fifteen hundred francs in pressing debts, which worried him.

However obstinately unjust destiny was to him, Thénardier was one of those men who best understood, to the greatest depth and in the most modern style, that which is a virtue among the barbarians, and a commodity among the civilized—hospitality. He was, besides, an admirable poacher and an excellent shot. He had a certain cool, quiet laugh that was particularly dangerous.

His theories of innkeeping sometimes gushed out of him in flashes. He had certain professional aphorisms that he inculcated in his wife's mind. "The duty of the innkeeper," he said to her one day, emphatically, and in a low voice, "is to sell the first comer, food, rest, light, fire, dirty linen, servants, fleas, and smiles; to stop travelers, empty small purses, and honestly lighten large ones; to receive families who are traveling, with respect: fleece the man, pluck the woman, and pick over the child; to charge for the open window, closed window, chimney corner, sofa, chair, stool, bench, featherbed, mattress, and straw bed; to know how much the reflection wears the mirror down and to tax that; and, by five hundred thousand devils, to make the traveler pay for everything, including the flies his dog eats!"

This man and this woman were cunning and rage married—a hideous and terrible pair.

While the husband calculated and schemed, the Thénardiess gave no thought to absent creditors, did not worry either for yesterday or tomorrow, living passionately in the present moment.

Such were these two beings. Cosette was between them, undergoing their double pressure, like a creature at the same time bruised by a millstone and lacerated with pincers. The man and the woman each had a different way. Cosette was beaten unmercifully; that came from the woman. She went barefoot in winter; that came from the man.

Cosette ran upstairs and downstairs; washed, brushed, scrubbed, swept, slaved away, breathless, lifted heavy things, and, puny as she was, did the hardest work. No pity; a ferocious mistress, a spiteful master. The Thénardier tavern was like a web in which Cosette had been caught and was trembling. The ideal of oppression was realized in this dismal servitude. It was something like a fly serving spiders.

The poor child was passive and silent.

Finding themselves in such a world at the dawn of their existence, so young, so defenseless, what must go on in these souls fresh from God?

III

MEN MUST HAVE WINE AND HORSES WATER

Four new guests had just come in.

Cosette was musing sadly; for, though only eight years old, she had already suffered so much that she brooded with the mournful air of an old woman.

She had a bruised eyelid from a blow of the Thénardiess's fist, which made the Thénardiess say from time to time, "How ugly she is with her black eye."

Cosette was thinking it was dark outside, late in the evening, that the bowls and pitchers in the rooms of the last travelers to arrive had needed to be filled, and that there was no more water in the cistern.

One thing comforted her a little: They did not drink much water chez Thénardier. There were plenty of people there who were thirsty; but it was the kind of thirst that reaches toward the jug rather than the pitcher. Had anybody asked for a glass of water among these glasses of wine, he would have seemed a savage to all those men. However, there was an instant when the child trembled; the Thénardiess raised the cover of a kettle that was boiling on the stove, then took a glass and quickly went over to the cistern. She turned the faucet; the child had raised her head and followed all her movements. A thin stream of water ran from the faucet and filled the glass half full.

"Well," she said, "there's no more water!" Then she was silent for a moment. The child held her breath.

"Damn!" continued the Thénardiess, examining the half-filled glass, "this will be just enough."

Cosette went back to her work, but for more than a quarter of an hour she felt her heart leaping in her chest like a great ball.

She counted the minutes as they rolled by, and eagerly wished it were morning.

From time to time one of the drinkers would look out into the street and exclaim, "It is as black as an oven!" or "It would take a cat to go out on the street without a lantern tonight!" And Cosette shuddered.

All at once, one of the peddlers who lodged in the tavern came in and said in a harsh voice, "You haven't watered my horse."

"Oh yes we have," said the Thénardiess.

"I tell you no, ma'am," replied the peddler.

Cosette came out from under the table.

"Oh, yes, monsieur!" she said, "the horse did drink; he drank out of the bucket, the whole bucketful, and I carried it to him, and I talked to him."

It was not true. Cosette lied.

"Here is a girl as big as my fist, who can tell a lie as big as a house," exclaimed the peddler. "I tell you that he has not had any water, little wench! He has a way of blowing I know quite well when he hasn't had any water."

Cosette persisted, and added in a barely audible voice stifled with anguish, "But he did drink a good deal."

"Come on," continued the peddler, enraged, "that's enough; give my horse his water and shut up."

Cosette went back under the table.

"Well, of course that's right," said the Thénardiess. "If the animal hasn't had any water, it must have some."

Then looking around her: "Well, what's become of that girl?"

She stooped down and discovered Cosette crouched at the other end of the table, almost under the feet of the drinkers.

"Are you going?" cried the Thénardiess.

Cosette came out from where she had hidden. The Thénardiess continued, "Little Miss Nameless, go get some water for the horse."

"But, madam," said Cosette faintly, "there isn't any water."

The Thénardiess threw the street door wide open.

"Well, go fetch some!"

Cosette hung her head and went for an empty bucket by the chimney corner.

The bucket was larger than she, and the child could have sat down in it comfortably.

The Thénardiess went back to her range and tasted what was in the kettle with a wooden spoon, grumbling all the while. "There's some at the spring. She's the worst girl there ever was. I think I should have left out the onions."

Then she fumbled in a drawer where there were some pennies, some pepper, and garlic.

"Here, Little Miss Toad," she added, "on the way back get a big loaf at the baker's. Here's fifteen sous."

Cosette had a little pocket at the side of her apron; she took the coin without saying a word and put it in that pocket.

Then she remained motionless, bucket in hand, the open door in front of her. She seemed to be waiting for somebody to come to her aid.

"Get out!" cried the Thénardiess.

Cosette went out. The door closed.

IV

A DOLL ENTERS THE SCENE

The row of booths stretched along the street from the church, the reader will remember, as far as the Thénardier tavern. These booths, because of the impending approach of the citizens on their way to the midnight mass, were all illuminated with candles, burning in paper lanterns, which, as the schoolmaster of Montfermeil, at that moment seated at one of Thénardier's tables, had said, produced a magical effect. On the other hand there was not a star in the sky.

The last of these stalls, set up right opposite Thénardier's door, was a toy shop, all glittering with trinkets, glass beads, and magnificent things made of tin. In the first row in front, the merchant had placed, on a bed of white napkins, a huge doll nearly two feet tall in a dress of pink crepe with gold garlands on its head, with real hair and enamel eyes. All day, this marvel had been displayed to the wonder of the passersby under ten years of age, but there had not been found in Montfermeil a mother rich enough or prodigal enough to give it to her child. Eponine and Azelma had spent hours gazing at it, and Cosette herself, furtively it is true, had dared to look at it.

The moment Cosette went out, bucket in hand, all gloomy and overwhelmed as she was, she could not help raising her eyes toward this wonderful doll, toward "the lady," as she called it. The poor child stopped petrified. She had not seen this doll up close before.

The whole booth seemed a palace to her; this doll was not a doll, it was a vision. It was joy, splendor, riches, happiness, and it appeared in a sort of chimerical radiance to this unfortunate little being, buried so deeply in a cold and dismal misery. Cosette was measuring with the sad and simple wisdom of childhood the abyss that separated her from that doll. She was saying to herself that one must be a queen, or at least a princess, to have a "thing" like that. She gazed at the beautiful pink dress, the beautiful smooth hair, and she was thinking, "How happy that doll must be!" Her eyes could not leave this fantastic booth. The longer she looked, the more she was dazzled. She thought she saw paradise. There were other dolls behind the large one that appeared to her to be fairies and genies. The merchant walking back and forth behind his stall seemed like the Eternal Father.

In this adoration, she forgot everything, even the errand on which she had been sent. Suddenly, the Thénardiess' harsh voice brought her back to reality: "What is this, halfwit, haven't you gone yet? Just you wait; I'm coming after you! I'd like to know what she's doing there. You little monster!"

The Thénardiess had glanced into the street and seen Cosette in ecstasy.

Cosette fled with her bucket, running as fast as she could.

V

THE LITTLE GIRL ALL ALONE

Since the Thénardier tavern was in the part of town near the church, Cosette had to go to the spring in the woods toward Chelles to draw water.

She did not look again at the displays in the booths. As long as she was on the Ruelle Boulanger and near the church, the illuminated booths lighted the way, but soon the last gleam from the last stall disappeared. The poor child found herself in the darkness. She plunged on into it. Only, as she fell prey to certain feelings, she rattled the handle of the bucket as much as she could while she walked. That made a noise, which kept her company.

The farther she went, the denser became the dark. There was nobody left in the streets. However, she met a woman, who turned around on seeing her go by and stood still, muttering between her teeth, "Where in the world can that child be going? Is it a fairy child?" Then the woman recognized Cosette. "Oh," she said, "it's the lark!"

So Cosette passed through the labyrinth of crooked deserted streets, at the end of the village of Montfermeil going toward Chelles. As long as she had houses, or even walls, on the sides of the road, she went on boldly enough. From time to time, she saw the gleam of a candle through the cracks of a shutter; it was light and life to her; there were people there; that kept up her courage. However, as she progressed, her speed slackened as if automatically. When she was past the corner of the last house, Cosette stopped. To go beyond the last booth had been difficult; to go further than the last house became impossible. She put the bucket on the ground, buried her hands in her hair, and began to scratch her head slowly, a motion peculiar to terrified and hesitating children. This was Montfermeil no longer, it was open country; dark and deserted space was before her. She looked with despair into this darkness where there was nobody, where there were beasts, where perhaps there were ghosts. She looked intently, and she heard the animals walking in the grass, and she distinctly saw the ghosts moving in the trees. Then she grabbed her bucket again; fear gave her boldness: "Never mind," she said, "I'll tell her there isn't any more water!" And she went back into Montfermeil.

She had scarcely gone a hundred steps when she stopped again and began to scratch her head. Now, it was the Thénardiess that appeared to her; the hideous Thénardiess, with her hyena mouth and anger flashing from her eyes. The child cast a pitiful glance in front of her and behind her. What could she do? What would become of her? Where should she go? In front of her, the specter of the Thénardiess; behind her, all the phantoms of night and the forest. It was from the Thénardiess that she recoiled. She took the road to the spring again and began to run. She ran out of the village; she ran into the woods, seeing nothing, hearing nothing. She only stopped running when she was out of breath, and even then she kept going. She kept right on, desperate.

Even while running, she felt like crying.

The nocturnal tremor of the forest wrapped around her completely.

She thought nothing more; she saw nothing more. The immensity of the night confronted this little child. On one side—the infinite shadow, on the other—an atom.

It was only seven or eight minutes' walk from the edge of the woods to the spring. Cosette knew the road from traveling it several times a day, and so she did not lose her way. A remnant of instinct guided her blindly. But she turned her eyes neither right nor left, for fear of seeing things in the trees and bushes. This way she reached the spring.

It was a small natural basin, made by the water in the clay soil, about two feet deep, surrounded with moss, and with that long pocked grass called Henry the Fourth's ruff, and paved with a few large stones. A brook trickled out of it with a gentle murmur.

Cosette did not take time to breathe. It was very dark, but she was used to coming to this spring. She felt with her left hand in the darkness for a young oak that bent across the pool and usually served her as a support, found a branch, hung onto it, leaned down, and plunged the bucket in the water. For a moment she was so intent that her strength was tripled. While she was bent over this way, she did not notice that the pocket of her apron emptied into the spring. The fifteen-sous piece fell into the water. Cosette neither saw it nor heard it fall. She drew out the bucket almost full and set it on the grass.

This done, she felt that all her strength was used up. She was anxious to start at once, but the effort of filling the bucket had been so great that it was impossible for her to take a step. She simply had to sit down. She dropped onto the grass and stayed there crouching.

She closed her eyes, then opened them, without knowing why, but unable to do otherwise. At her side, the water whirling in the bucket made circles like serpents of white fire.

Above her head, the sky was covered with vast black clouds like sheets of smoke. The tragic mask of night almost seemed to bend over this child.

Jupiter was setting.

Startled, the child looked at that great star, which she did not know and which made her afraid. The planet, in fact, was at that moment very near the horizon and was crossing a dense layer of mist that gave it a horrible red glow. The mist, mournfully lurid, magnified the star. It seemed a luminous wound.

A cold wind was blowing off the plain. The woods were dark, without the least rustling of leaves, without any of that vague, fresh glow of summer. Great boughs rose hideously. Mean and shapeless bushes hissed in the glades. The tall grass wriggled under the north wind like eels. The brambles writhed like long arms seeking to seize their prey in their claws. Some dry weeds driven by the wind blew rapidly past, and appeared to flee with dismay as though pursued. On all sides, the prospect was dismal.

Darkness is dizzying. We need light; whenever we plunge into the opposite of day we feel our hearts chilled. When the eye sees darkness, the mind sees trouble. In an eclipse, at night, in the sooty darkness, even the strongest feel anxiety. Nobody walks alone at night in the forest without trembling. Darkness and trees, two formidable depths—a chimeric reality appears in the indistinct distance. An outline of the Inconceivable emerges a few steps away with a spectral clarity. You see floating in space or in your brain something strangely vague and unseizable like the dreams of sleeping flowers. There are fierce shapes on the horizon. You breathe in the odors of the great black void. You are afraid and are tempted to look behind you. The socket of night, the haggard look of everything, taciturn profiles that fade away as you advance, obscure dishevelments, angry clumps, livid pools, the gloomy reflected in the funereal, the sepulchral immensity of silence, the possible unknown beings, swaying of mysterious branches, frightful torsos of the trees, long wisps of shivering grass—you are defenseless against all of it. There is no bravery that does not shudder and feel the proximity of anguish. You feel something hideous, as if soul were melting into shadow. This penetration of the darkness is inexpressibly sinister for a child.

Forests are apocalypses; and a tiny soul's beating wings make an agonizing sound beneath their monstrous vault.

Without being conscious of what she was experiencing, Cosette felt seized by this black enormity of nature. It was not merely terror that held her but something even more terrible. She shuddered. Words fail to express the peculiar strangeness of that shudder, which chilled her through and through. Her eyes had become wild. She felt that perhaps she would be compelled to return there at the same hour the next night.

Then, by some sort of instinct, to get out of this singular state, which she did not understand but which terrified her, she began to count aloud, one, two, three, four, up to ten, and when she had finished, she began again. This restored her to a real perception of things about her. Her hands, which were wet from drawing water, felt cold. She stood up. Her fear had returned, a natural and insurmountable fear. She had only one thought, to flee; to flee at top speed, across woods, across fields, to the houses and windows and lighted candles. Her eyes fell on the bucket there in front of her. Such was the dread the Thénardiess inspired in her she did not dare leave without the bucket of water. She grasped the handle with both hands. She could hardly lift it.

She went a dozen steps this way, but the bucket was full, it was heavy, she had to rest it on the ground. She caught her breath an instant, then grasped the handle again, and walked on, this time a little longer. But she had to stop again. After resting a few seconds, she started on. She walked bending forward, her head down, like an old woman; the weight of the bucket strained and stiffened her thin arms. The iron handle was numbing and freezing her little wet hands; from time to time she had to stop, and every time she stopped, the cold water that sloshed out of the bucket splashed onto her bare knees. This took place in the depth of the woods, at night, in the winter, far from all human sight; she was a child of eight. At that moment only the Eternal Father saw this sad thing.

And undoubtedly her mother, alas!

For there are things that open the eyes of the dead in their grave.

Her breath came as a kind of painful gasp; sobs choked her, but she did not dare weep, so great was her fear of the Thénardiess, even at a distance. She always imagined the Thénardiess nearby.

However, she could not make much headway this way and was moving along very slowly. As hard as she tried to shorten her resting spells, and to walk as far as possible between them, she anxiously realized that it would take her more than an hour to return to Montfermeil at this rate, and that the Thénardiess would beat her. This anguish added to her dismay at being alone in the woods at night. She was worn out and was not yet out of the forest. Reaching an old chestnut tree she knew, she made one last halt, longer than the others, to rest up well, then she gathered all her strength, took up the bucket again, and began to walk on courageously. Meanwhile the poor little despairing thing could not help crying: "Oh my God! Oh God!"

At that moment she suddenly felt that the weight of the bucket was gone. A hand, which seemed enormous to her, had just caught the handle, and was carrying it easily. She looked up. A large dark form, straight and erect, was walking beside her in the darkness. A man who had come up behind her and whom she had not heard. This man, without saying a word, had grasped the handle of the bucket she was carrying.

There are instincts for all the crises of life.

The child was not afraid.

VI

WHICH MAY PROVE THE INTELLIGENCE OF BOULATRUELLE

During the afternoon of that same Christmas Day, 1823, a man walked for a long time on the most deserted portion of the Boulevard de l'Hôpital in Paris. This man had the look of someone searching for lodgings and seemed to stop by preference in front of the most modest houses of this dilapidated part of the Faubourg Saint-Marceau.

We shall see further on that this man did in fact rent a room in this isolated neighborhood.

This man, in his clothing as in his whole person, exemplifed what might be called the beggar of good society —extreme misery combined with extreme neatness. This is a rare combination, which inspires in intelligent hearts the double respect we feel for someone who is very poor and for someone who is very worthy. He wore a round hat, very old and carefully brushed, a long coat, completely threadbare, of coarse yellow cloth, a color that was not particularly unusual at that time, a large waistcoat with old-fashioned pockets, black trousers worn gray at the knees, black wool socks, and heavy shoes with copper buckles. One would have thought him a former tutor from a good family, returned from exile. From his hair, which was entirely white, from his wrinkled brow, from his gray lips, from his face in which everything breathed exhaustion and weariness of life, one would have supposed him much older than sixty. From his firm though slow step and the remarkable vigor evident in all his movements, one would hardly have thought him fifty. The wrinkles on his forehead were well placed, and would have favorably impressed anyone who studied him attentively. His lip contracted with a strange expression, which seemed severe yet humble. In the depths of his eye there was an indescribably tragic serenity. He carried in his left hand a small package tied in a handkerchief; with his right he leaned on a sort of staff cut from a hedge. This staff had been finished with some care and did not look very fierce; the knots were smoothed down, and a coral head had been formed of red wax; it was a cudgel, and it seemed a cane.

There are few pedestrians on that boulevard, particularly in winter. The man appeared to avoid them rather than approach them but not in an obvious way.

At that epoch, the king, Louis XVIII, went to Choisy-Le-Roy nearly every day. It was one of his favorite rides. Around two o'clock, almost invariably, the carriage and the royal cavalcade were seen going by at full speed along the Boulevard de l'Hôpital.

This took the place of watch and clock for the poor women of the quarter, who would say, "It's two o'clock, there he is going back to the Tuileries."

And some hurried over, and others lined up, for whenever a king goes by, there is always a tumult. Actually, the appearance and disappearance of Louis XVIII produced a certain effect in the streets of Paris. It was rapid, but majestic. This gout-ridden king loved fast driving; not being able to walk, he wanted to run; this cripple would have glady been chaffeured by the lightning. He went past tranquil and stern, surrounded by naked sabers. His massive golden coach, with large lily branches painted on the panels, rumbled along. One hardly had time to catch a glimpse of it. In the back corner on the right, one could see, on cushions covered with white satin, a broad face, firm and ruddy, a forehead freshly powdered à la bird of paradise, a proud, keen eye, and the smile of the well-read, two large epaulets of bullion floating above civilian clothes, the Golden Fleece, the cross of Saint Louis, the cross of the Legion of Honor, the silver badge of the Holy Spirit, a fat belly, and a large blue ribbon; that was the king. Outside of Paris, he held his hat with white feathers on his knees, which were enclosed in tall English gaiters; when he re-entered the city, he replaced his hat on his head, bowing seldom. He looked coldly at the people, who returned the look. When he appeared for the first time in the Quartier Saint-Marceau, all he succeeded in eliciting were these words by a resident to his comrade: "It's that big guy who's the government."

So this invariable passing of the king at the same hour was the daily event of the Boulevard de l'Hôpital.

The strolling man in the yellow coat obviously did not belong to the neighborhood, and probably not to Paris, because he was ignorant of this occurrence. At two o'clock when the royal carriage, surrounded by a squad of silver-trimmed bodyguards, turned into the boulevard, after passing La Salpêtrière, he seemed surprised, almost frightened. There was no one else on the crosswalk, and he quickly retreated behind a projecting corner of wall, but this did not prevent the Duc d'Havré from seeing him. The Duc d'Havré, as captain of the guards-in-waiting that day, was seated in the carriage opposite the king. He said to His Majesty, "There is a man with a rather unsavory look." Some policemen, who were clearing the way for the king, also noticed him; one of them was ordered to follow him. But the man plunged into the little empty streets of the Faubourg, and as night was coming on the officer lost track of him, as is stated in a report addressed on the same evening to the Comte Anglès, Minister of State, Prefect of Police.

When the man in the yellow coat had thrown the officer off his trail, he turned around, not without looking back many times to be sure he was not being followed. At a quarter after four, that is to say, after dark, he passed in front of the theater of the Porte Saint-Martin, where the play that day was *The Two Convicts*. The poster, lit up by the theater lights, seemed to impress him; although he was hurrying, he stopped to read it. A moment later, he was in the Impasse de la Planchette, and entered the Pewter Platter, which was then the office of the stagecoach to Lagny. This stage left at four-thirty. The horses were harnessed, and the travelers, who had been called by the driver, were hastily climbing the vehicle's tall iron steps.

The man asked, "Do you have a seat?"

"Only one, beside me on the box," said the driver.

"I'll take it."

"Get up then."

Before starting, however, the driver glanced at the traveler's shabby clothing and his small bundle, and took his pay.

"Are you going through to Lagny?" asked the driver.

"Yes," said the man.

The traveler paid through to Lagny.

They started. When they had passed the city gates, the driver tried to start up a conversation, but the traveler answered only in monosyllables, so the former began whistling and swearing at his horses.

The driver wrapped himself up in his cloak. It was

cold, but the man did not seem to notice. Like that, they passed through Gournay and Neuilly-sur-Marne. About six in the evening, they drew into Chelles. The driver stopped to let his horses breathe, in front of the stage coach inn in the former buildings of the royal abbey.

"I'll get off here," said the man.

He took his bundle and stick and jumped down from the stage.

A moment later he had disappeared.

He did not go into the tavern.

When, a few minutes after, the stage started off for Lagny, it did not overtake him in the main street of Chelles.

The driver turned to the inside passengers. "There," he said, "is a man who is not from these parts, because I don't know him. He looks like he doesn't have a sou, but he doesn't care about money: He pays to Lagny, and he only goes to Chelles. It's night, all the houses are shut, he doesn't go to the tavern, and we don't overtake him. Ergo, he must have sunk into the ground!"

The man had not sunk into the ground at all but had hurried in the darkness along the main street of Chelles, and turned left, before reaching the church, into the crossroad leading to Montfermeil, as though he knew the area and had been that way before.

He rapidly followed this road. At the spot where it intersects the old road bordered with trees that goes from Gagny to Lagny, he heard footsteps approaching. He concealed himself hastily in a ditch, and waited there until the people had gone a good distance. The precaution was almost superfluous, because, as we have said, it was a dark December night, with scarcely two or three stars in the sky.

It is at this point that the hill begins to rise. The man did not return to the Montfermeil road; he turned to the right, across the fields, and reached the woods with rapid strides.

When he got there, he slackened his pace, and began to look carefully at all the trees, pausing at every step, as if he were seeking and following a mysterious route known only to himself. There was a moment when he seemed to lose the way and stopped, undecided. By continual groping, he finally reached a glade where there was a heap of large whitish stones. He made his way quickly toward these stones and examined them attentively in the dark as if he were passing them in review. A large tree, covered with the excrescences that are the warts of vegetation, was a few steps from the heap of stones. He went up to the tree and passed his hand over the bark of the trunk, as if trying to recognize and count all the warts.

Opposite this tree, an ash, there was a chestnut tree wounded in the bark, which had been staunched with a tacked-on bandage of zinc. He rose on tiptoe and touched that band of zinc.

Then he stamped for some time on the ground in the space between the tree and the stones, like someone who wanted to be sure that the earth had not been freshly dug.

This done, he reoriented himself and resumed his walk through the woods.

This was the man who had fallen in with Cosette.

As he made his way through the copse toward Montfermeil, he had seen that little shadow struggling along with a sob, setting her burden on the ground, then taking it up and going on again. He had approached her and seen that it was a very young child carrying an enormous bucket of water. Then he had gone to the child and silently taken hold of the bucket's handle.

VII

COSETTE SIDE BY SIDE WITH THE UNKNOWN MAN IN THE DARK

Cosette, we have said, was not afraid.

The man spoke to her. His voice was serious, and almost a whisper.

"My child, that's very heavy for you, what you're carrying there."

Cosette raised her head and answered, "Yes it is, monsieur."

"Give it to me," the man continued, "I'll carry it for you."

Cosette let go of the bucket. The man walked along with her.

"It certainly is very heavy," he said to himself. Then he added, "Little girl, how old are you?"

"Eight, monsieur."

"And have you come a long way like this?"

"From the spring in the woods."

"And are you going far?"

"A good quarter of an hour from here."

For a moment the man did not speak, then he said abruptly, "Don't you have a mother?"

"I don't know," answered the child.

Before the man had time to say a word, she added, "I don't think I do. Everyone else does. But I don't have one."

And after a pause, she added, "I don't think I ever had one."

The man stopped, put the bucket on the ground, stooped down, and put his hands on the child's shoulders, trying to look at her and see her face in the darkness.

The thin and puny face of Cosette was vaguely outlined in the dim light of the sky.

"What is your name?" said the man.

"Cosette."

It was as though the man had an electric shock. He looked at her again, then letting go of her shoulders, took up the bucket, and walked on.

A moment after, he asked, "Little one, where do you live?"

"At Montfermeil, if you know where that is."

"Is that where we are headed?"

"Yes, monsieur."

Another pause, then he began again, "Who sent you out into the woods for water at this time of night?"

"Madame Thénardier."

The man resumed in a tone of voice intended as casual though it still trembled oddly: "What does she do, Madame Thénardier?"

"She is my mistress," said the child. "She keeps the tavern."

"The tavern," said the man. "Well, I'm going there to stay tonight. Show me the way."

"We're heading there," said the child.

The man walked very fast. Cosette followed him without difficulty. She was no longer tired. From time to time, she looked up at this man with a sort of calm and inexpressible confidence. She had never been taught to turn to Providence and pray. However, she felt in her heart something resembling hope and joy, which rose toward heaven.

A few minutes passed. The man spoke, "Isn't there a servant at Madame Thénardier's?"

"No, monsieur."

"Are you alone?"

"Yes, monsieur."

There was another pause. Cosette raised her voice, "I mean, there are two little girls."

"What little girls?"

"Ponine and Zelma."

That is the way the child simplified the romantic names dear to the mother.

"What are Ponine and Zelma?"

"Madame Thénardier's daughters."

"And what do they do?"

"Oh!" said the child, "they have beautiful dolls, things with gold in them; all sorts of things. They play, they have fun."

"All day long?"

"Yes, monsieur."

"And you?"

"Me! I work."

"All day long?"

The child raised her large eyes, whose tears could not be seen in the darkness, and answered softly, "Yes, monsieur."

After a pause she went on, "Sometimes, when I've finished my work and they're willing, I play too."

"What do you play with?"

"Anything I can. They leave me alone. But I don't have many toys. Ponine and Zelma won't let me play with their dolls. I only have a little lead sword no longer than that."

The child showed her little finger.

"And it doesn't cut?"

"Yes, monsieur," said the child, "it cuts lettuce and flies' heads."

They reached the village; Cosette guided the stranger through the streets. They passed by the bakery, but Cosette did not think of the bread she was supposed to have brought back. The man had stopped asking her questions, and now stayed mournfully silent. When they had passed the church, the man, seeing all the booths in the street, asked Cosette, "So is it fairtime here?"

"No, monsieur, it's Christmas."

As they drew near the tavern, Cosette timidly touched his arm: "Monsieur?"

"What, my child?"

"Here we are near the house."

"Well?"

"Will you let me take the bucket now?"

"Why?"

"Because, if madame sees that someone carried it for me, she will beat me."

The man gave her the bucket. A moment later they were at the tavern door.

VIII

INCONVENIENCES OF ENTERTAINING A POOR MAN WHO MAY BE RICH

Cosette could not help casting one look toward the large doll still displayed in the toy booth, then she knocked. The door opened. The Thénardiess appeared with a candle in her hand.

"Oh! It's you, you little beggar! My Lord, but you've taken your time! She's been playing, the wretch!"

"Madame," said Cosette, trembling, "there is a gentleman who is coming for lodging."

The Thénardiess very quickly replaced her surly look with her amiable sneer, an instant change typical of innkeepers, and looked for the newcomer with eager eyes.

"Is it you, monsieur?" she said.

"Yes, madame," answered the man, touching his hat.

Rich travelers are not so polite. The gesture and the sight of the stranger's clothes and baggage, which the Thénardiess took in at a glance, made the amiable sneer disappear and the surly look return. She added drily, "Come in, fellow."

The "fellow" entered. The Thénardiess cast a second

glance at him, particularly his long coat, which was absolutely threadbare, and his hat, which was somewhat dented, and with a nod, wink, and wrinkle of the nose, consulted her husband, who was still drinking with the wagon drivers. The husband answered by that imperceptible shake of the forefinger which, supported by a protrusion of the lips, signifies in such a case "complete destitution." Thereupon the Thénardiess exclaimed, "Ah! my good man, I'm very sorry, but I don't have a room."

"Put me wherever," said the man, "in the attic, in the stable. I will pay as though I had a room."

"Forty sous."

"Forty sous. Very well."

"In advance."

"Forty sous," whispered a wagon driver to the Thénardiess, "but it's only twenty sous."

"It's forty sous for him," replied the Thénardiess in the same tone. "I don't lodge poor people for less."

"That's true," added her husband quietly, "it ruins a house's reputation to have that sort."

Meanwhile the man, after leaving his stick and bundle on a bench, sat down at a table on which Cosette had been quick to place a bottle of wine and a glass. The peddler who had asked for the bucket of water had gone to carry it himself to his horse. Cosette had resumed her place under the kitchen table and her knitting.

The man, who hardly touched his lips to the wine he had poured, was contemplating the child with a strange intensity.

Cosette was ugly. If happy, she might have been pretty. We have already sketched this pitiful little face. Cosette was thin and pale; she was about eight years old, but one would hardly have thought her six. Her large eyes, sunk in a sort of shadow, were dimmed by continual weeping. The corners of her mouth had that curve of habitual anguish seen in the condemned and the terminally ill. Her hands were, as her mother had guessed, covered with chilblains. The light of the fire shining upon her made her bones stand out and her emaciation hideously visible. Because she was always shivering, she had acquired the habit of drawing her knees together. Her clothing was only rags that would have provoked pity in the summer and that elicited horror in the winter. She had on nothing but cotton, and that full of holes, not a speck of wool. Her skin showed here and there, and on it, bruises, where the Thénardiess had grabbed her. Her naked legs were red and rough. The hollows below her collarbones were enough to make you weep. Everything about this child, her walk, her attitude, the sound of her voice, the pauses between one word and another, her look, her silences, her slightest gesture, expressed and portrayed a single idea: fear.

Fear was spread all over her; she was, so to speak, covered with it; fear squeezed her elbows against her sides, drew her heels up under her skirt, made her shrink into the least possible space, prevented her from breathing more than absolutely necessary, and had become what might be called her bodily habit, without possible variation, except to increase. In the depths of her eyes, there was an expression of astonishment mingled with terror.

This fear was such that on coming in, wet as she was, Cosette had not dared dry herself by the fire but had gone back silently to her work.

The expression on the face of this child of eight was habitually so sad and occasionally so tragic that it seemed, at certain moments, as if she were on the way to becoming an idiot or a demon.

Never, as we have said, had she known what it is to pray, never had she set foot inside a church. "How can I spare the time?" the Thénardiess said.

The man in the yellow coat did not take his eyes off Cosette.

Suddenly, the Thénardiess exclaimed, "Oh! I forgot! That bread!"

Cosette, as was her habit whenever the Thénardiess raised her voice, came out quickly from under the table.

She had entirely forgotten the bread. She took recourse to the expedient of constantly terrified children. She lied.

"Madame, the baker was shut."

"You ought to have knocked."

"I did knock, madame."

"Well?"

"He didn't open."

"I'll find out tomorrow if that's true," said the Thénardiess, "and if you're lying, you'll do a little dance. Meanwhile, give me back the fifteen sous."

Cosette poked her hand into her apron pocket and turned pale. It was not there.

"Come on," said the Thénardiess, "didn't you hear me?"

Cosette turned her pocket inside out; there was nothing there. What did she do with the money? The desperate little girl could not utter a word. She was petrified.

"Have you lost my fifteen-sous piece?" screamed the Thénardiess, "or are you trying to steal it from me?" At the same time she reached toward the cowhide strap hanging in the chimney corner.

This menacing gesture gave Cosette the strength to cry out, "Forgive me! Madame! Madame! I won't do it anymore!"

The Thénardiess took down the whip.

Meanwhile, unnoticed, the man in the yellow coat had been fumbling in his waistcoat pocket. The other travelers were drinking or playing cards and paid no attention to anything else.

Cosette was anxiously huddling in the chimney corner, trying to squeeze together and hide her poor half-naked limbs. The Thénardiess raised her arm.

"I beg your pardon, madame," said the man, "but I just saw something fall out of the pocket of that little girl's apron and roll away. That may be it." At the same time he stooped down and appeared to look around the floor for a moment.

"Just as I thought, here it is," he said, rising.

And he handed a silver piece to the Thénardiess.

"Yes, that's it," she said.

That was not it; it was a twenty-sous piece; but the Thénardiess did not mind the profit. She put the coin in her pocket and contented herself with glaring at the child and saying, "Don't let that happen again, ever."

Cosette went back to what the Thénardiess called "her hole," and her large eyes, fixed on the unknown traveler, began to take on an expression they had never known before. It was still only an artless astonishment, but a sort of blind confidence had crept into it.

"Oh! You want supper?" the Thénardiess asked the traveler.

He did not answer. He seemed deep in thought.

"Who is this man?" she said between her teeth. "He's just some awful pauper. He hasn't a penny for his supper.

Is he even going to pay me for his lodging? Still, it's very lucky he didn't think to steal the money on the floor."

Meanwhile a door opened, and Eponine and Azelma entered.

They were really two pretty little girls, more city girls than peasants, very charming, one with her shiny auburn tresses, the other with her long black braids falling down her back, and both so lively, neat, plump, fresh, and healthy that it was a pleasure to look at them. They were warmly dressed, but with such maternal art that the thickness of the material detracted nothing from the daintiness of fit. Winter was taken care of without smothering spring. These two little girls shed light around them. Besides, in the tavern, they were royalty. In their clothing, their gaiety, the sounds they made, there was authority. When they came in, the Thénardiess said to them in a scolding tone full of adoration, "Ah! There you are, you two!"

Then, taking them onto her knees one after the other, smoothing their hair, retying their bows, and finally letting them go with that gentle sort of shake peculiar to mothers, she exclaimed, "Aren't they a mess!"

They went and sat down by the fire. They had a doll they turned back and forth on their knees with all sorts of cheerful babbling. From time to time, Cosette raised her eyes from her knitting and watched them sadly as they played.

Eponine and Azelma did not notice Cosette. To them she was like the dog. The three little girls did not have twenty-four years among them, and they already represented the whole of human society: on one side envy, on the other scorn.

The Thénardier sisters' doll was very faded, and very old and broken, but it seemed no less wonderful to Cosette, who had never in her life even had a doll, *a real doll,* to use an expression all children understand.

All at once, the Thénardiess, who was constantly going back and forth around the room, noticed that Cosette's attention was wandering and that instead of working she was watching the little girls playing.

"Ah! I've caught you!" she cried. "That's the way you work! I'll make you work with a whip, I will."

Without leaving his chair, the stranger turned toward the Thénardiess.

"Madame," said he, smiling almost diffidently. "Why not let her play!"

Spoken by any traveler who had eaten a slice of mutton and drunk two bottles of wine with his supper, and who did not have the look of "an awful pauper," such a wish would have been a command. But for a man who wore such a hat to allow himself a desire, and for a man who wore such a coat to permit himself a wish, was more than the Thénardiess thought she should tolerate. She replied sharply, "She has to work, since she eats. I don't feed her to have her do nothing."

"What is she making?" said the stranger, in that gentle voice, which contrasted so strangely with his beggar's clothes and his porter's shoulders.

The Thénardiess condescended to answer. "Stockings. Stockings for my little girls, who have none worth speaking of and would soon have to go barefoot."

The man looked at Cosette's poor red feet, and went on, "When will she finish that pair of stockings?"

"It will take her at least three or four good days, the lazy thing."

"And how much would this pair of stockings cost, when it is finished?"

The Thénardiess glanced at him scornfully.

"At least thirty sous."

"Would you take five francs for them?" said the man.

"Good God!" hooted a wagon driver who was listening, "five francs? You can bet on it! Five bullets!"

Thénardier now thought it was time to speak.

"Yes, monsieur, if that's your wish, you can have that pair of stockings for five francs. We can't refuse anything to travelers."

"You'll have to pay for them now," said the Thénardiess, in her curt and peremptory way.

"I'll buy that pair of stockings," answered the man, "and," he added, taking a five-franc piece out of his pocket and laying it on the table, "I'll pay for them."

Then he turned toward Cosette.

"Now your work belongs to me. Play, my child."

The wagon driver was so surprised by that five-franc piece that he left his glass and went to look at it.

"It's really true!" he exclaimed, drinking it in. "The real thing! No counterfeit!"

Thénardier approached and silently put the piece in his pocket.

The Thénardiess had nothing to say. She bit her lips, and her face took on an expression of hatred.

Meanwhile Cosette was trembling. She ventured to ask, "Madame, is it true? Can I play?"

"Play!" said the Thénardiess in a fearsome voice.

"Thank you, madame," said Cosette. And, while her mouth thanked the Thénardiess, all her little soul was thanking the traveler.

Thénardier returned to his drink. His wife whispered in his ear, "Who can that yellow man be?"

"I have seen," answered Thénardier, in an authoritative tone, "millionaires with coats like that."

Cosette had left her knitting, but she had not moved from her spot. Cosette always stirred as little as possible. From a little box behind her she had taken out a few old rags and her little lead sword.

Eponine and Azelma paid no attention to what was going on. They had just performed a very important operation; they had caught the kitten. They had thrown the doll on the floor, and Eponine, the elder, was dressing the kitten, in spite of her meows and contortions, in clothes and red and blue rags. While she was doing this serious and difficult work, she was talking to her sister in that sweet and charming language of children, whose grace, like the splendor of butterfly wings, escapes when we try to catch it.

"Look! Look, this doll is more fun than the other one. She moves, she cries, she's warm. Come on, let's play with her. She'll be my little girl; I'll be a lady. I'll come visit you, and you look at her. Bit by bit you will see she has whiskers, and then you have to act surprised. And then you'll see her ears, and then you'll see her tail, and that will surprise you. And you must say to me, 'Oh! Good heavens!' and I'll say to you, 'Yes, madame, my little girl is like this. Little girls are like this nowadays.' "

Azelma listened to Eponine admiringly.

Meanwhile, the drinkers were singing a bawdy song, at which they laughed enough to make the ceiling shake. Thénardier encouraged and accompanied them.

As birds make nests out of anything, children do the same with dolls. While Eponine and Azelma were dressing up the cat, Cosette had dressed up the sword. That done, she had cradled it on her arm and was singing it softly to sleep.

The doll is one of the most imperative needs, and at the same time one of the most charming instincts, of feminine childhood. To care for, clothe, adorne, dress, undress, dress over again, teach, scold a little, rock, cuddle, put to sleep, pretend that something is somebody—the whole future of the woman is there. Even while dreaming and chattering, while making little wardrobes and baby clothes, while sewing little dresses, little shirts and jackets, the child becomes a little girl, the little girl becomes a big girl, the big girl becomes a woman. The first baby takes the place of the last doll.

A little girl without a doll is almost as unfortunate and just as impossible as a woman without children.

So Cosette had made a doll out of her sword.

As for the Thénardiess, she went up to the yellow man. "My husband is right," she thought; "it may be Monsieur Laffitte. Some rich men are odd."

She came and rested her elbow on the table where he was sitting.

"Monsieur," she said.

At this word "monsieur," the man turned. The Thénardiess had called him before only "yellow" or "good man."

"You see, monsieur," she continued, putting on her most sugary expression, which was even more unbearable than her ferocious manner, "I am very willing for the child to play, I'm not opposed to it; it is good for once, because you are generous. But, you see, she's poor. She has to work."

"The child is not yours, then?" asked the man.

"Oh dear! No, monsieur! It's a little waif we've taken in out of charity. A sort of imbecile child. She must have water on her brain. Her head is big, as you see. We do all we can for her, but we're not rich. We've written in vain to her part of the country; for six months we haven't had an answer. We think her mother must be dead."

"Ah!" said the man, and he fell back into his reverie.

"This mother was not much," added the Thénardiess. "She abandoned her child."

During this whole conversation, Cosette, as if some

instinct had warned her they were talking about her, had not taken her eyes from the Thénardiess. She listened. She heard a few words here and there.

Meanwhile, the drinkers, all of them three-quarters drunk, were repeating their foul chorus with increased gaiety. It was highly spiced with jokes, in which the names of the Virgin and baby Jesus were often heard. The Thénardiess had gone to take part in the hilarity. Cosette, under the table, was looking into the fire, which reflected in her staring eyes; she had gone back to rocking the sort of rag baby she had made, and as she rocked it, she sang in a low voice, "My mother is dead! My mother is dead! My mother is dead!"

At the repeated insistence of the hostess, the yellow man, "the millionaire," finally consented to eat supper.

"What will monsieur have?"

"Some bread and cheese," said the man.

"He is definitely a beggar," thought the Thénardiess.

The revelers kept on singing their songs, and the child, under the table, also sang hers.

Suddenly Cosette stopped. She had just turned and seen the little Thénardiers' doll, which they had dropped for the cat and left on the floor, a few steps from the kitchen table.

Then she let go of the swaddled sword, which only half-satisfied her, and ran her eyes slowly around the room. The Thénardiess was whispering to her husband and counting some change, Eponine and Azelma were playing with the cat, the travelers were eating or drinking or singing, nobody was looking at her. She didn't have a moment to lose. She crept out from under the table on her hands and knees, made sure once more that nobody was watching her, then darted to the doll, and grabbed it. An instant later she was in her spot, sitting still, but turned in such a way as to cast a shadow on the doll she held in her arms. The joy of playing with a doll was so rare to her that it had all the force of rapture.

Nobody had seen her, except the traveler, who was slowly eating his simple supper.

This joy lasted for nearly a quarter of an hour.

But in spite of Cosette's precautions, she did not notice that one of the doll's feet stuck out and that the fire showed it very vividly. This bright, rosy foot protruding from the shadow suddenly caught Azelma's eye, and she said to Eponine, "Look!"

The two little girls stopped, amazed; Cosette had dared to take their doll.

Eponine got up, and without letting go of the cat, went to her mother and began to tug at her skirt.

"Leave me alone," said the mother. "What do you want?"

"Mother," said the child, "look at that!"

And she pointed at Cosette.

Cosette, wholly absorbed in the ecstasy of her possession, did not see or hear anything else.

The face of the Thénardiess assumed the peculiar expression composed of the terrible mingled with the commonplace that has given this variety of women the name of fury.

This time wounded pride augmented her anger. Cosette had transgressed all barriers. Cosette had laid her hands on the doll of "those young ladies." A czarina who had seen a muzhik trying on the grand sash of her imperial son would have had the same expression.

She cried with a voice harsh with indignation, "Cosette!"

Cosette shuddered as if the earth had quaked beneath her. She turned around.

"Cosette!" repeated the Thénardiess.

Cosette took the doll and placed it gently on the floor with a sort of veneration mingled with despair. Then, without moving her eyes, she clasped her hands, and—frightful to say of a child of that age—she wrung them; then, what none of the emotions of the day had managed to draw from her—neither the trip through the woods nor the weight of the water bucket nor the loss of the money nor the sight of the whip nor even the stern words she had heard from the Thénardiess—she burst into tears. She sobbed.

Meanwhile the traveler rose to his feet.

"What's the matter?" he said to the Thénardiess.

"Don't you see?" said the Thénardiess, pointing to the *corpus delicti* lying at Cosette's feet.

"Well, what of that?" said the man.

"That beggar," answered the Thénardiess, "has dared to touch the children's doll."

"All this noise about that?" said the man. "Well, what if she did play with the doll?"

"She has touched it with her dirty hands!" continued the Thénardiess, "with her awful hands!"

Here Cosette sobbed all the harder.

"Shut up!" cried the Thénardiess.

The man walked straight to the street door, opened it, and went out.

As soon as he had gone, the Thénardiess took advantage of his absence to give a severe kick under the table to Cosette, who shrieked in response.

The door opened again, and the man reappeared, holding the fabulous doll we have mentioned, which had been the admiration of all the youngsters in the village since morning; he stood it up before Cosette, saying, "Here you are, this is for you."

It is likely that during the time he had been there—more than an hour—in the midst of his reverie, he had caught confused glimpses of the toy booth lit up with lamps and candles so splendidly that it shone through the barroom window like an inspiration.

Cosette raised her eyes; she saw the man approach her with that doll as she would have seen the sun approach; she heard those astounding words: "This is for you." She looked at him, she looked at the doll, then she backed up slowly and went to hide all the way under the table in the far corner of the room.

She was no longer weeping, she looked as though she no longer dared to breathe.

The Thénardiess, Eponine, and Azelma were so many statues. Even the drinkers stopped. A solemn silence descended over the whole barroom.

The Thénardiess, petrified and mute, started up her inward conjectures again: "What could this old fellow be? Is he a pauper? Is he a millionaire? Perhaps he's both: a robber."

The face of her husband presented that expressive wrinkle that marks the human countenance whenever the dominant instinct appears with all its bestial power. The innkeeper contemplated the doll and the traveler in turn; he seemed to be sniffing out this man as he would have sniffed a bag of money. This only lasted a moment. He approached his wife and whispered to her, "That thing cost at least thirty francs. No mistake about it. Down on your knees before the man!"

Coarse natures have this in common with artless natures, that they have no transitions.

"Well, Cosette," said the Thénardiess in a voice that meant to be sweet and was entirely composed of the sour honey of vicious women, "aren't you going to take your dolly?"

Cosette ventured out of her hole.

"My little Cosette," the Thénardiess went on cajolingly, "Monsieur's giving you a doll. Take it. It's yours."

Cosette was looking at the wonderful doll with a sort of terror. Her face was still flooded with tears, but her eyes began to fill, like the sky at daybreak, with the strange glow of joy. What she experienced at that moment was almost what she would have felt if someone had said to her suddenly, "Little girl, you are now Queen of France!"

It seemed to her that if she touched that doll, thunder would erupt from it.

Which was true to some extent, for she thought that the Thénardiess would scold her and beat her.

However, the attraction overcame her. She finally approached and timidly murmured, turning toward the Thénardiess, "Can I, madame?"

No expression could describe her look, at once filled with despair, dismay, and ecstasy.

"Good Lord!" said the Thénardiess. "It's yours. Monsieur is giving it to you."

"Is it true, is it true, monsieur?" said Cosette. "Is the lady for me?"

The stranger's eyes seemed to be brimming with tears. He seemed to be at that stage of emotion in which one does not speak for fear of weeping. He nodded to Cosette and put the hand of "the lady" in her little hand.

Cosette hastily removed her hand, as if "the lady" had burned her, and looked down at the floor. We are forced to add that at that moment she stuck out her tongue. All at once she turned and seized the doll eagerly.

"I'll call her Catherine," she said.

It was an odd moment when Cosette's rags met and pressed against the ribbons and fresh pink muslin of the doll.

"Madame," she said, "may I put her in a chair?"

"Yes, my child," answered the Thénardiess.

Now it was Eponine and Azelma who looked at Cosette with envy.

Cosette placed Catherine on a chair, then sat down on the floor in front of her, motionless, without saying a word, in an attitude of contemplation.

"Why don't you play, Cosette?" said the stranger.

"Oh! I am playing," answered the child.

This stranger, this unknown man, who seemed like a visitor from Providence to Cosette, was at that moment the being whom the Thénardiess hated above all else in the world. However, she had to control herself. Her emotions were more than she could endure, accustomed though she was to pretense through attempts to copy her husband in all her actions. She sent her daughters to bed immediately, then asked the yellow man's *permission* to send Cosette to bed—"who is very tired today," she added, with a motherly air. Cosette went off to bed, holding Catherine in her arms.

From time to time the Thénardiess went to the other end of the room where her husband was, "to soothe her soul," she said. She exchanged a few words with him, which were all the more furious because she did not dare speak them aloud:

"The old fool! What's he got in his head, coming here and bothering us! Wanting that little monster to play! Giving her dolls! Giving forty-franc dolls to a brat I wouldn't give forty sous for. Any more, and he'll be calling her 'Your Majesty' like she's the Duchesse de Berry! He's got to be crazy, that old duck!"

"Why? It's very simple," replied Thénardier. "If that's what pleases him! It pleases you for the girl to work; it pleases him to let her play. That's his right. A traveler can do what he likes if he pays for it. If this old bird is a philanthropist, what's that to you? If he's crazy, it's none of your business. Why interfere, as long as he has money?"

A master's language and an innkeeper's reasoning, which in neither case permits reply.

The man had leaned his elbows on the table and resumed his attitude of reverie. All the other travelers, peddlers, and wagon drivers had moved off somewhat, and were no longer singing. They looked at him from a distance with a sort of respectful fear. This solitary man, so poorly dressed, who took five-franc pieces from his pocket so easily and lavished gigantic dolls on little brats in wooden clogs, was certainly a magnificent and formidable individual.

Several hours passed. The midnight mass was said, Christmas Eve was over, the drinkers had gone, the house was closed, the room with its low ceilings was deserted, the fire had gone out, the stranger remained in the same place and the same position. From time to time he changed the elbow on which he was leaning. That was all. But he had not spoken a word since Cosette was gone.

The Thénardiers alone out of propriety and curiosity had remained in the room.

"Is he going to spend the whole night like this?" grumbled the Thénardiess. When the clock struck two in the morning, she acknowledged defeat and said to her husband, "I'm going to bed. You can do what you like." The husband sat down at a table in a corner, lit a candle, and began to read the *Courrier Français*.

A good hour went by this way. The worthy innkeeper had read the *Courrier Français* at least three times, from the date of the issue to the name of the printer. The stranger did not stir.

Thénardier moved, coughed, spat, blew his nose, and creaked his chair. The man did not move. "Is he asleep?" thought Thénardier. The man was not asleep, but nothing could arouse him.

Finally, Thénardier took off his cap, approached softly, and ventured to say, "Is monsieur not going to rest?"

"Not going to bed" would have seemed to him much too familiar. "To rest" implied luxury, and there was respect in it. Such words have the mysterious and wonderful property of swelling the bill in the morning. A room in which you "go to bed" costs twenty sous; a room in which you "rest" costs twenty francs.

"Yes," said the stranger, "you're right. Where is your stable?"

"Monsieur," said Thénardier, with a smile. "I will show monsieur."

He took the candle, the man took his bundle and his staff, and Thénardier led him into a room on the second floor, which was very showy, furnished entirely in mahogany, with a high-post bedstead and red calico curtains.

"What's this?" said the traveler.

"It's actually our bridal chamber," said the innkeeper. "My spouse and I occupy another just like it. This one is not open more than three or four times a year."

"I would have liked the stable just as well," the man said bluntly.

Thénardier did not appear to hear this not very civil answer.

He lit two entirely new wax candles, which were displayed on the mantel; a good fire was blazing in the fireplace. On the mantel, under a glass case, there was a woman's headdress of silver thread and orange flowers.

"What's this?" said the stranger.

"Monsieur," said Thénardier, "it is my wife's bridal cap."

The traveler looked at the object with a look that seemed to say, "There was a moment, then, when the monster was a virgin."

Thènardier had lied, however. When he had leased the decrepit building to turn it into a cheap inn, he found the room fully furnished and bought this furniture and found these secondhand orange flowers, thinking that this would cast a gracious light over "his spouse" and that the house would derive from them what the English call respectability.

When the traveler turned back, the host had disappeared. Thénardier had discreetly absented himself without daring to say goodnight, not wishing to treat with disrespectful cordiality a man whom he proposed to skin royally in the morning.

The innkeeper retired to his room; his wife was in bed, but not asleep. When she heard her husband's step, she turned to him and said, "You know what, I'm going to kick Cosette out tomorrow."

Thénardier coolly answered, "Really?"

They exchanged no further words, and in a few moments their candle was blown out.

As for the traveler, he had put his staff and bundle in a corner. The host gone, he sat down in an armchair, and stayed there for some time in thought. Then he took off his shoes, picked up one of the two candles, blew out the other, opened the door, and went out of the room, looking around as though searching for something. He went down a hall, and came to the stairway. There he heard a very soft sound, like the breathing of a child. Guided by this sound he came to a sort of triangular nook built under the stairs, or, rather, formed by the staircase itself. This hole was nothing but the space beneath the stairs. There, among all sorts of old baskets and old rubbish, in the dust and among the cobwebs, was a bed—if a mattress so full of holes that the straw was showing, and a covering so full of holes that the mattress poked through, can be called a bed. There were no sheets. It was placed on the floor right on the tiles. In this bed Cosette was sleeping.

The man went over and looked at her.

Cosette was sleeping soundly. She was dressed. In winter she did not undress because of the cold. She held the doll clasped in her arms; its large open eyes gleamed in the darkness. From time to time she sighed deeply, as if about to awake, and she hugged the doll almost convulsively. There was only one of her wooden shoes beside her bed. An open door near Cosette's nook revealed a large dark room. The stranger went in. At the far end, through a glass door, he could see two little beds with very white spreads. They were those of Azelma and Eponine. Half hidden behind these beds was a curtainless willow cradle, in which the little boy, who had cried all evening, was sleeping.

The stranger assumed that this room adjoined the Thénardiers'. He was about to leave when his eye fell on the fireplace, one of those huge tavern hearths where there is always such a small fire, when there is fire at all, and which are so cold to the eye. In this one there was no fire, there were not even any ashes. What there was, however, attracted the traveler's attention. It was two little children's shoes, dainty in shape and of different sizes. The traveler remembered the graceful and immemorial custom of children putting their shoes on the hearth on Christmas Eve, to wait there in the darkness in expectation of some shining gift from the good fairy. Eponine and Azelma had not forgotten this, and each had put one of her shoes on the hearth.

The traveler bent over them.

The fairy—that is to say, the mother—had already paid her visit, and shining in each shoe was a beautiful new ten-sous piece.

The man straightened up and was on the point of going away when he perceived farther along, by itself, in the darkest corner of the fireplace, another object. He looked and recognized a shoe, an ugly wooden clog of the clumsiest kind, half broken and covered with ashes and dried mud. It was Cosette's. Cosette, with that touching confidence of childhood, which can always be betrayed without ever being discouraged, had also placed her shoe on the hearth.

What a sublime, sweet thing is hope in a child who has never known anything but its opposite!

There was nothing in this clog.

The stranger fumbled in his waistcoat, bent over, and dropped into Cosette's shoe a gold Louis.

Then he went back to his room with stealthy tread.

IX

THÉNARDIER MANUEVERING

On the following morning, at least two hours before daybreak, Thénardier, seated at a table in the barroom, candle by his side and pen in hand, was making out the bill for the traveler in the yellow coat.

His wife was standing, half bent over him, following him with her eyes. Not a word passed between them. It was, on one side, a profound meditation, on the other that religious admiration with which we observe a marvel of the human mind springing up and expanding. A noise was heard in the house; it was the lark, sweeping the stairs.

After a good quarter hour and some erasures, Thénardier produced his masterpiece:

Bill of Monsieur in No. I.

Supper .... 3 frs.
Room .... 10 frs.

Candle	5 frs.
Fire	4 frs.
Service	1 frs.
Total	23 frs.

Service was written *servisse*.

"Twenty-three francs!" exclaimed the woman, with an enthusiasm that mingled with some hesitation.

Like all great artists, Thénardier was not satisfied.

"We-ell," he said.

It was the accent of Castlereagh drawing up for the Congress of Vienna the bill that France was to pay.

"Monsieur Thénardier, you're right, he certainly owes it," murmured the woman, thinking of the doll given to Cosette in the presence of her daughters. "It's right, but it's too much. He won't pay it."

With his cold laugh Thénardier said, "He'll pay."

This laugh was the supreme sign of certainty and authority. What was said that way must be. The woman did not insist. She began to arrange the tables; the husband walked back and forth in the room. A moment later he added, "I owe, at least, fifteen hundred francs!"

He seated himself thoughtfully in the chimney corner, his feet in the warm ashes.

"Ah ha!" replied the woman, "you're not forgetting that I'm kicking Cosette out of the house today? The monster! It tears my guts to see her with her doll! I'd rather marry Louis XVIII than keep her in the house another day!"

Thénardier lighted his pipe and answered between two puffs: "You'll present the bill to the man."

Then he left.

He was scarcely out of the room when the traveler came in.

Thénardier reappeared immediately behind him and stood motionless in the half-open door, visible only to his wife.

The yellow man carried his staff and bundle in his hand.

"Up so soon?" said the Thénardiess. "Is monsieur going to leave us already?"

While speaking, she turned the bill in her hands with an embarrassed look, making creases in it with her nails.

Her hard face displayed an unaccustomed touch of timidity and doubt.

To present such a bill to a man who had the appearance of a pauper seemed too awkward to her.

The traveler appeared preoccupied and absent-minded.

He answered, "Yes, madame, I am going away."

"Monsieur, then, had no business at Montfermeil?" she asked.

"No, I'm only passing through. Madame," he added, "what do I owe?"

The Thénardiess, without answering, handed him the folded bill.

The man unfolded the paper and looked at it, but his thoughts were evidently elsewhere.

"Madame," he replied, "do you do a good business in Montfermeil?"

"So-so, monsieur," answered the Thénardiess, stupefied at not seeing an explosion.

She continued in a tragic, plaintive strain, "Oh! Monsieur, the times are very hard, and then we have so few rich people around here! It is a very little place, as you see. If we only had rich and generous travelers now and then, like monsieur! We have so many expenses! Why, that little girl eats us out of house and home."

"What little girl?"

"Why, you know, the little one! Cosette! The lark, as they call her around here!"

"Ah!" said the man.

She went on, "How stupid these peasants are with their nicknames! She looks more like a bat than a lark. You see, monsieur, we don't ask charity, but we aren't able to give it. We earn nothing and have a great deal to pay. The license, the excise, the doors and windows, a tax on everything! Monsieur knows that the government demands a deal of money. And then I have my own girls. I don't need to pay for other people's children."

The man replied in a tone that he attempted to make indifferent, and in which there was a slight tremor.

"Suppose you were relieved of her?"

"Who? Cosette?"

"Yes."

The woman's face lit up with a hideous expression.

"Ah, monsieur! My good monsieur! Take her, keep her, take her away, carry her off, sugar her, stuff, drink, feed her, and be blessed by the holy Virgin and all the saints in heaven!"

"Agreed."

"Really! You will take her away?"

"I will."

"Immediately?"

"Immediately. Call the child."

"Cosette!" cried the Thénardiess.

"In the meantime," continued the man, "I will pay my bill. How much is it?"

He glanced at the bill and could not repress a gesture of surprise. "Twenty-three francs?"

He looked at the hostess and repeated, "Twenty-three francs?"

There was, in the pronunciation of this repeated sentence, the nuance that lies between the exclamation point and the question mark.

The Thénardiess had had time to prepare herself for the shock. She replied with assurance, "Yes, of course, monsieur! It is twenty-three francs."

The stranger placed five five-franc pieces on the table.

"Go for the little girl," he said.

At this moment Thénardier moved to the middle of the room and said, "Monsieur owes twenty-six sous."

"Twenty-six sous!" exclaimed the woman.

"Twenty sous for the room," continued Thénardier coldly, "and six for supper. As for the little girl, I must talk with monsieur about that. Leave us alone, my dear."

The Thénardiess was dazzled by one of those unexpected flashes given off by talent. She felt that the great actor had entered the scene, answered not a word, and went out.

As soon as they were alone, Thénardier offered the traveler a chair. The traveler sat down, but Thénardier remained standing, and his face assumed a strange expression of good nature and simplicity.

"Monsieur," said he, "listen, I must say I adore this child."

The stranger looked at him steadily. "What child?"

Thénardier continued: "It's strange how we become attached! What is all this silver? Take back your money. I adore this child."

"Who do you mean?" asked the stranger.

"Oh, our little Cosette! And you want to take her away

from us? Indeed, I must speak frankly, truly, as you are an honorable man, I cannot consent to it. I would miss her. I've had her since she was very small. It's true, she costs us money; it's true she has her faults, it's true we aren't rich, it's true I paid four hundred francs for medicine one time when she was sick. But we must do something for God. She has neither father nor mother; I raised her. I have bread enough for her and for myself. In fact, I'm fond of this child. You understand, we all have affections; I'm a simple sort, myself; I don't think; I love this little girl; my wife is hot-headed, but she loves her, too. You see, she's like our own child. I feel the need of her chatter around the house."

The stranger was staring at him all the time. He continued, "Pardon me, excuse me, monsieur, but one does not give up this child just like that to a stranger. Aren't I right? After that, I'm not saying—you are rich, you look like a very fine man—if it is for her advantage? But I have to know about that. You see? On the supposition that I should let her go and sacrifice my own feelings, I would want to know where she is going. I would not want to lose sight of her, I would want to know who she was with, so I could come and see her now and then, so she would know that her good foster father was still watching over her. Well, there are some things that simply aren't possible. I don't even know your name. If you should take her away, I would say, where has the little lark gone? I must, at least, see some poor slip of paper, a bit of passport, something."

The stranger, without lifting his gaze, which went to the depths of the conscience, answered severely and firmly.

"Monsieur Thénardier, people do not take a passport to come fifteen miles from Paris. If I take Cosette, I take her. That is the end of it. You will not know my name, you will not know my address, you will not know where she is going, and my intention is that she shall never see you again in her life. Do you agree to that? Yes or no?"

As demons and genii recognize by certain signs the presence of a superior god, Thénardier understood that he had to deal with a very powerful individual. It came like an intuition; he understood it with keen, quick clarity. Though he had been drinking with the wagon drivers, smoking, and singing bawdy songs throughout the previous evening, he was observing the stranger, watching him like a cat, studying him like a mathematician. He had been peering at him on his own account, for pleasure and instinctively, and at the same time lying in wait as though being paid for it. Not a gesture, not a movement of the man in the yellow coat had escaped him. Even before the stranger had so clearly shown his interest in Cosette, Thénardier had guessed it. He had caught the searching glances of the old man constantly returning to the child. Why this interest? What was this man? Why, with so much money in his purse, this miserable clothing? These were questions he asked himself without being able to answer them, and they irritated him. He had been thinking it over all night. This could not be Cosette's father. Was it a grandfather? Then why did he not make himself known at once? When a man has a right, he shows it. This man evidently had no right to Cosette. Then who was he? Thénardier was lost in conjectures. He glimpsed everything but saw nothing. However it might be, when he began talking to this man, sure that there was a secret in all this, sure that the man had an interest in remaining unknown, he felt strong; at the stranger's clear, firm answer, when he saw that this mysterious person was mysterious and nothing more, he felt weak. He had been expecting nothing of the kind. His conjectures were routed. He rallied his ideas. In a second he weighed it all. Thénardier was one of those men who judge a situation at a glance. He decided that this was the moment to advance straight ahead and swiftly. He did what great captains do at that decisive moment they alone can recognize. He abruptly showed his hand.

"Monsieur," he said, "I must have fifteen hundred francs."

The stranger took an old black leather pocketbook out of his side pocket, opened it, and removed three banknotes, which he placed on the table. He then put his large thumb down on the bills and said to the tavern keeper, "Bring Cosette."

While this was going on, what was Cosette doing?

As soon as she awoke, Cosette had run to her wooden shoe. She had found the gold piece in it. It was not a Napoleon with its laurel wreath, but one of the new twenty-franc pieces of the Restoration. Cosette was dazzled. Her good fortune began to make her giddy. She did not know it was a piece of gold; she had never seen one before; she hastily concealed it in her pocket as if she had stolen it. Although she felt it was really hers, she guessed where the gift had come from, and she felt a joy filled with awe. She was happy; above all she was dazed. Such magnificent and beautiful things seemed unreal to her. The doll scared her, the gold piece scared her. She vaguely trembled before this munificence. The stranger himself did not make her afraid. On the contrary, he reassured her. Since the night before, through all her surprise, and in her sleep, she was thinking in her little child's mind of this man who looked so old and poor and sad, and who was so rich and kind. Since she had met him in the woods, everything seemed changed. Cosette, less happy than the smallest swallow in the sky, had never known what it is to take refuge under a mother's wing. For five years, as far back as she could remember, the poor child had shivered and shuddered. She had always been naked under the biting north wind of misfortune, and now it seemed to her she was clothed. Before, her soul had been cold; now it was warm. Cosette was no longer afraid of the Thénardiers. She was no longer alone. Somebody was there.

She hurriedly went about her morning tasks. The Louis, which she had placed in the same pocket of her apron from which the fifteen-sous piece had fallen the night before, distracted her. She did not dare touch it, but she spent five minutes at a time contemplating it, and we must confess, with her tongue stuck out. While sweeping the stairs, she stopped and stood still, forgetting her broom and the whole world, totally engrossed in looking at the shining star at the bottom of her pocket.

It was in one of these reveries that the Thénardiess found her.

At her husband's command, she had gone to look for her. She did not give her the usual slap or even call her names.

"Cosette," she said, almost gently, "come quick."

An instant later, Cosette entered the barroom.

The stranger took the bundle he had brought and untied it. This bundle contained a little wool dress, an apron, a coarse cotton undergarment, a petticoat, a scarf, wool stockings, and shoes—a complete outfit for a girl of seven. It was all black.

"My dear," said the man, "take this and go and dress yourself quickly."

The day was breaking when the inhabitants of Montfermeil who were beginning to open their doors saw going by on the road to Paris a poorly dressed man leading a little girl in mourning carrying a large pink doll. They were going toward Livry. It was the stranger and Cosette.

No one knew the man; as Cosette was no longer in tatters, few recognized her.

Cosette was going away. With whom? She did not know. Where? She had no idea. All she understood was that she was leaving behind the Thénardiers' inn. Nobody had thought to bid her goodby, and she did not say goodby to anybody. She went out of that house, hated and hating.

Poor gentle thing, whose heart had been only and always crushed up to then.

Cosette walked along seriously, opening her large eyes and looking at the sky. She had put her coin in the pocket of her new apron. From time to time she bent over and glanced at it, and then looked at the man. She felt almost as though she were near God.

X

IF YOU SEEK THE BEST, YOU MAY FIND THE WORST

The Thénardiess, as was her custom, had left her husband alone. She was expecting great events. When the man and Cosette were gone, Thénardier, after a good quarter of an hour, took her aside, and showed her the fifteen hundred francs.

"No more than that?" she said.

It was the first time, since the beginning of their ménage, that she had dared criticize the actions of her master.

The blow struck home.

"As a matter of fact, you're right," he said. "I'm a fool. Give me my hat."

He folded the three bank bills, thrust them into his pocket, and hurriedly started off, but he made a mistake and turned right. Some neighbors whom he asked put him in the correct direction: The lark and the man had been seen going toward Livry. He followed this information, walking rapidly and talking to himself.

"This man is obviously a millionaire, and me, I'm a fool. First he gave twenty sous, then five francs, then fifty francs, then fifteen hundred francs, just like that. He would have given fifteen thousand francs. But I'll catch up with him."

And then this bundle of clothes, packed beforehand for the little girl; all that was strange, there was a good deal of mystery behind it. It's hard to let go of a mystery once you catch hold of it. The secrets of the rich are sponges full of gold; one has to know how to squeeze them. All these thoughts were whirling around in his brain. "I'm a fool," he said.

When you leave Montfermeil and reach the turn made by the road to Livry, the way can be seen stretching a long distance along the plateau. Arriving at this point, he counted on being able to see the man and the little girl. He looked as far as he could but saw nothing. He inquired again. Meanwhile he was losing time. The passersby told him that the man and child whom he sought had traveled toward the woods in the direction of Gagny. He hurried that way.

They had the start on him, but a child walks slowly, and he was moving rapidly. And then he knew the country well.

Suddenly he stopped and struck his forehead like a man who has forgotten the main thing, and who is about to retrace his steps.

"I ought to have taken my gun!" he said.

Thénardier was one of those double natures who sometimes appear among us without our knowledge, and disappear without ever being known, because destiny has shown only one side of them. Many men are fated to live half submerged this way. In an ordinary situation, Thénardier had all that is necessary to make—we do not say to be—what passes for an honest tradesman, a good citizen. At the same time, under certain circumstances, under the operation of certain occurrences exciting his baser nature, he had in him all that was necessary to be a villain. He was a shopkeeper, in which a monster lay hidden. Satan must have squatted for a moment in some corner of the hole in which Thénardier lived and studied this hideous masterpiece.

After a moment's hesitation, he thought, "But then they'd have time to escape!"

And he continued on his way, moving rapidly, almost certain, with the wisdom of the fox scenting a flock of partridges.

In fact, when he had passed the ponds and obliquely crossed the large meadow to the right of the Avenue de Bellevue, as he reached the grassy path that nearly circles the hill and borders the arches of the old aqueduct of the abbey of Chelles, above a bush, he caught sight of the hat on which he had already built so many conjectures. The bushes were low. Thénardier realized that the man and Cosette were sitting there. The child could not be seen, she was so short, but he could see the head of the doll.

Thénardier was not mistaken. The man had sat down there to give Cosette a little rest. The innkeeper went around the bushes and suddenly appeared before the eyes of those he had been seeking.

"Pardon me, excuse me, monsieur," he said, out of breath; "but here's your fifteen hundred francs back."

So saying, he held out the three banknotes to the stranger.

The man raised his eyes: "What do you mean?"

Thénardier answered respectfully, "Monsieur, it means that I am taking Cosette back."

Cosette shuddered and moved closer to the man.

He answered, looking Thénardier straight in the eye and spacing his syllables: "You—take—Cosette—back?"

"Yes, monsieur, I am taking her back. I've thought it over. In fact, I have no right to give her to you. I am an honest man, you see. This little girl is not mine. She belongs to her mother. Her mother has entrusted her to me; I can only give her up to her mother. You will say: But her mother is dead. All right. In that case, I can only give up the child to a person who brings me a written order, signed by the mother, stating that I should deliver the child to him. That is clear."

Without answering, the man groped in his pocket, and Thénardier saw the billfold containing the bank bills reappear.

The tavern keeper felt a thrill of joy.

"Good!" he thought. "Calm down. He's going to corrupt me!"

Before opening the billfold, the traveler took a look around him. The place was absolutely deserted. There was not a soul either in the woods or in the valley. The man opened the billfold, and took out of it, not the handful of bankbills that Thénardier expected, but a little piece of paper, which he unfolded and presented to the innkeeper, saying, "You are quite right. Read that!"

Thénardier took the paper and read.

"Montreuil-sur-mer, March 25, 1823.

"Monsieur Thénardier:

You will deliver Cosette to the bearer.

He will settle all small debts.

I have the honor of greeting you with kind regards.

FANTINE"

"You know that signature?" the man asked.

It was indeed Fantine's signature, and Thénardier recognized it.

There was nothing he could say. He felt doubly enraged, enraged at being compelled to give up the bribe he had hoped for and enraged at being beaten. The man added, "You can keep this note as your receipt."

Thénardier retreated in good order.

"This signature is very well imitated," he grumbled between his teeth. "Well, so be it!"

Then he made a desperate effort.

"Monsieur," said he, "it is all right. Then you are the person. But you must settle 'all small debts.' There is a large amount due me."

The man rose to his feet, and said, while flipping some dust off his threadbare sleeve, "Monsieur Thénardier, in January the mother calculated that she owed you a hundred and twenty francs; in February you sent her a memorandum for five hundred francs; you received three hundred francs at the end of February, and three hundred at the beginning of March. Since then nine months have elapsed, which, at fifteen francs per month, the price agreed upon, amounts to a hundred and thirty-five francs. You had received a hundred francs extra. A remainder of thirty-five francs was due you. I have just given you fifteen hundred francs."

Thénardier felt like the wolf the instant he is being seized and crushed by the steel jaws of the trap.

"What is this devil of a man?" he thought.

He did what the wolf does, he sprang. Audacity had succeeded with him once already.

"Monsieur-I-don't-know-your-name," he said resolutely, this time dropping all show of respect. "I will take back Cosette or you must give me a thousand crowns."

The stranger said quietly, "Come, Cosette."

He took Cosette with his left hand and with the right picked up his staff, which was on the ground.

Thénardier noted the enormous size of the cudgel and the solitude of the place.

The man disappeared into the woods with the child, leaving the innkeeper stock-still and speechless.

As they walked away, Thénardier noted his broad shoulders, a little rounded, and his big fists.

Then his eyes swung back to his own puny arms and thin hands. "I must be a complete idiot," he thought, "not to have brought my gun, since I was going hunting."

However, the innkeeper did not abandon the pursuit.

"I want to know where he's going," he said; and he began to follow them at a distance. Two things remained in his possession, one a bitter mockery, the piece of paper signed "Fantine," and the other a consolation, the fifteen hundred francs.

The man was leading Cosette toward Livry and Bondy. He was walking slowly, his head bent down, in an attitude of reflection and sadness. The winter had stripped the woods of foliage, so Thénardier did not lose sight of them, though staying quite far behind. From time to time the man turned around and looked to see if he were being followed. Suddenly he saw Thénardier. He immediately went into the underbrush with Cosette, and both disappeared from sight. "What the devil!" said Thénardier. And he quickened his pace.

The density of the thicket compelled him to come closer to them. When the man reached the thickest part of the wood, he turned around again. In vain, Thénardier tried to hide among the branches, but he could not prevent the man from seeing him. The man glanced at him uneasily, then shrugged, and went on. Again the innkeeper took up the pursuit. They walked this way two or three hundred paces. Suddenly the man turned around once more. He saw the innkeeper. This time he looked at him so forbiddingly that Thénardier judged it "unprofitable" to go farther and went home.

XI

NUMBER 9430 COMES UP AGAIN, AND COSETTE DRAWS IT

Jean Valjean was not dead.

When he fell into the sea, or rather threw himself in, he was, as we have seen, free from his irons. He swam underwater to a ship at anchor to which a boat was fastened.

He found a way to hide in the boat until evening. At night he again took to the water, and reached shore a short way from Cap Brun.

There, as he did not lack for money, he was able to procure clothes. A little public house in the environs of Balaguier was haberdasher to escaped convicts, a lucrative business. Then Jean Valjean, like all those joyless fugitives trying to evade the eyes of the law and social morality, followed an obscure and wandering path. He found asylum first in Pradeaux, near Beausset. Then he went toward Grand Villard, near Briançon, in the Hautes Alpes. Groping and restless flight, threading the unknown mazes of the mole. Later some traces of his wanderings were found in Ain, on the territory of Civrieux, in the Pyrenees at Accons, at a place called the Grange-de-Doumecq, near the hamlet of Chavailles, and in the area around Périgueux, at Brunies, a canton of Chapelle Gonaguet. He finally reached Paris. We have just seen him at Montfermeil.

His first concern, on reaching Paris, had been to purchase mourning clothes for a little girl of seven, then to find lodgings. That done, he had gone to Montfermeil.

It will be remembered that, at the time of his former

escape, or near that time, he had made a mysterious journey of which the law had caught some glimpse.

Moreover, he was believed to be dead, and this deepened the obscurity surrounding him. In Paris he happened onto one of the papers that chronicled the event. He felt reassured, and almost as much at peace as if he really had been dead.

On the very evening of the day that Jean Valjean had rescued Cosette from the clutches of the Thénardiess, he went back to Paris again. He entered the city at nightfall, with the child, by the Barrière de Monceaux. There he took a cabriolet, which carried him as far as the Esplanade of the Observatory, where he got out, paid the driver, took Cosette by the hand, and, both of them in the dark night, walked through the deserted streets near l'Ourcine and la Glacière, toward the Boulevard de l'Hôpital.

The day had been strange and filled with emotion for Cosette; behind hedges, they had eaten bread and cheese bought at isolated taverns; they had often changed carriages and traveled short distances on foot. She did not complain, but she was tired, and Jean Valjean knew it from her pulling more heavily at his hand while they walked. He took her in his arms; Cosette, without letting go of Catherine, laid her head on Jean Valjean's shoulder and went to sleep.

Book Four

THE OLD GORBEAU HOUSE

I

MASTER GORBEAU

Forty years ago, the solitary pedestrian who ventured into the unfrequented regions of La Salpêtrière and went up along the boulevard as far as the Barrière d'Italie reached certain points where it could be said that Paris disappeared. It was no longer empty, there were people going by; it was not the country, there were houses and streets; it was not a city, the streets had ruts in them, like the highways, and grass grew in them; it was not a village, the houses were too tall. What was it then? It was an inhabited place with nobody to be seen, it was a deserted spot with someone in it; it was a boulevard of the big city, a street in Paris, wilder at night than a forest and gloomier by day than a graveyard.

It was the old sector of the Horse Market.

Our pedestrian, if he trusted himself beyond the four tumbling walls of this Horse Market, if willing to go even beyond the Rue du Petit-Banquier, leaving to the right a courtyard enclosed by high walls, then a meadow studded with stacks of tanbark that looked like gigantic beaver dams, then an enclosure half filled with lumber and piles of logs, sawdust, and shavings, from the top of which a huge dog was baying, then a long, low, completely ruined wall with a small dark and decrepit gate, covered with moss, that filled up with flowers in spring, then, in the loneliest spot, a hideous broken-down structure on which could be read in large letters, POST NO

BILLS; this bold adventurer would reach the corner of the Rue des Vignes-Saint-Marcel, a little-known area. There, near a factory and between two garden walls, could be seen at that time an old ruined hovel that, at first sight, seemed as small as a cottage and was, in fact, as large as a cathedral. It stood with its gable end toward the highway, hence its apparent small size. Almost the entire house was hidden. Only the door and one window could be seen.

This old dwelling had only two floors.

On close examination, the most striking feature was that the door could never have been anything but the door of a hovel, while the window, if it had been cut from stone instead of rough material, might have been the casement of a lordly residence.

The door was merely a collection of worm-eaten boards crudely held together by cross ties that looked like rough-cut logs of firewood. It opened directly onto a steep staircase with high steps covered with mud, plaster, and dust, and of the same breadth as the door, and which from the street seemed to rise straight as a ladder and disappear in the shadows between two walls. The top of the shapeless opening that this door closed upon was screened by narrow boards with a triangular opening that served as both skylight and ventilator when the door was shut. On the inside of the door a brush dipped in ink had traced with a couple of strokes the number 52, and above the door the same brush had daubed the number 50, so that a newcomer would hesitate, asking, "Where am I?"

The top of the entrance says, Number 50; the inside, however, replies, No! Number 52! We won't attempt to describe the dust-colored rags that served as curtains around the triangular ventilator.

The window was wide and quite high, with large panes in the sashes, and shutters; the panes had withstood a variety of wounds that were both concealed and revealed by ingenious strips and bandages of paper, and the shutters were so broken and disjointed that they endangered the passersby more than they shielded the occupants. Some horizontal slats were missing and had been crudely replaced by boards nailed horizontally, so that what had started as a Venetian blind ended as a solid shutter. This door with its dirty look and this window with its decent though dilapidated appearance, seen together in one and the same building, produced the effect of two mismatched beggars bound in the same direction and walking side by side, but with different attitudes under the same rags, one having always been a pauper while the other having once been a gentleman.

The staircase led up to a very spacious interior, which looked like a shed converted into a house. This structure had for its main channel of communication a long hall, off which opened, on either side, compartments of sorts in different dimensions, just barely habitable, more like booths than cells. These rooms looked out on the vacant lots of the neighborhood. Altogether, it was dark, dull, and dreary, even melancholic and sepulchral, and it was reached, either by the dim, cold rays of the sun or by icy draughts, according to whether the cracks were in the roof or the door. One interesting and picturesque feature of this kind of housing is the monstrous size of the spiders.

To the left of the front door, on the boulevard side, a small window that had been walled up formed a square niche some six feet from the ground, filled with stones that passing chldren had thrown into it.

Part of the building has recently been torn down, but what remains still conveys an idea of what it once was. The structure, taken as a whole, is not more than a hundred years old. A hundred years is youth to a church, but old age to a private house. It would seem that Man's dwelling shares the brevity of his existence and God's dwelling, His eternity.

The mailmen called the house No. 50–52, but it was known around the neighborhood as Gorbeau House.

Let us see how it came by that name.

The trivia collectors, who gather anecdotes as the herbalist his specimens, and prick the fleeting dates into their memories with a pin, know that in Paris during the last century, about 1770, there were two attorneys at the courts of Le Châtelet, one named Corbeau and the other Renard—two names anticipated by La Fontaine. The opportunity was altogether too inviting to be passed up by the fraternity of lawyers' clerks. So, very soon, the galleries of the courtrooms rang with the following parody, in rather lame verse:

> Maître Corbeau, sur un dossier perché,
> Tenait dans son bec une saisie executoire;

Maître Renard, par l'odeur alléché,
Lui fit à peu près cette histoire:
"Hé! bonjour!" etc.[1]

The two honest practitioners, annoyed by these shafts of wit, their dignity ruffled by the roars of laughter that followed them, decided to change their names and with that in mind applied to the king. The petition was presented to Louis XV on the very day on which the Pope's Nuncio and the Cardinal de La Roche-Aymon in the presence of his Majesty, devoutly kneeling, one on each side of Madame Du Barry, put her slippers on her naked feet, as she was getting out of bed. The king, who was laughing, kept it up; he proceeded gaily from the two bishops to the two attorneys, and absolved these gentlemen of the law from their names, or almost. It was granted to Master Corbeau, by the king's good pleasure, to add a flourish to the first letter of his name, making it Gorbeau; Master Renard was less fortunate, as he only got permission to put a *P* before the *R*, which made the word Prenard, or "grasping fellow," a name no less appropriate than the first.

Now, according to local tradition, this Master Gorbeau was the proprietor of the structure numbered 50–52 Boulevard de l'Hôpital. He was even the creator of the monumental window.

Hence, this building got its name of Maison Gorbeau.

Opposite No. 50–52 stands, among the shade trees lining the Boulevard, a tall elm, three quarters dead, and almost directly opposite, opens the Rue de la Barrière des Gobelins—at that time a street without houses, unpaved, bordered with scrubby trees, grass-grown or muddy, according to the season and running squarely up to the wall enclosing Paris. A smell of sulfur ascended in puffs from the roofs of a neighboring factory.

The Barrière was quite near. In 1832, the city wall still existed.

On its own, this city gate conjured up gloomy images.

[1] Master Crow, on a document perched,
In his beak held a fat execution,
Master Fox, with his jaws well besmirched,
Thus spoke up, to his neighbor's confusion.
"Good day! My fine fellow," said he, etc.

It was on the way to Bicêtre. It was there that under the Empire and the Restoration condemned criminals re-entered Paris on the day of their execution. It was there that, about the year 1829, was committed the mysterious assassination known as "the murder of the Barrière de Fontainebleau," whose perpetrators have never been discovered—a sinister problem not yet solved, a terrible enigma not yet unraveled. A few steps farther, and you find that fatal Rue Croulebarbe, where Ulbach stabbed the shepherdess of Ivry, melodramatically, in a thunderstorm. A few steps more, and you come to those awful clipped elm trees of the Barrière Saint-Jacques, that philanthropic expedient to hide the scaffold, that shabby and shameful Place de Grève of a shopkeeping society that recoils from capital punishment yet dares neither to abolish it with dignity nor maintain it with firm authority.

Thirty-seven years ago, except for this Place Saint-Jacques, which seemed foredoomed and always was horrible, perhaps the gloomiest of all this gloomy boulevard was the spot, still so unattractive, where the old building 50–52 stood.

The bourgeois houses did not begin to appear there till some twenty-five years later. The place was dreary. Added to the melancholic atmosphere, you were conscious of being between La Salpêtrière, whose dome was just in sight, and Bicêtre, whose gate was nearby—that is to say, between the madness of woman and that of man. As far as the eye could see, there was nothing but the slaughterhouses, the city wall, and there a factory façade, resembling a barracks or a monastery; everywhere hovels and heaps of trash, old walls as black as widows' clothes, and new walls as white as shrouds; everywhere, parallel rows of trees, buildings in rigid lines, low, flat structures, long, cold perspectives, and the dreary sameness of right angles. No variation in the terrain, not a caprice of architecture, not a wrinkle. Altogether, it was chilly, regular, and hideous. Nothing is so stifling as symmetry. Symmetry is boredom, the quintessence of mourning. Despair yawns. There is something more terrible than a hell of suffering—a hell of boredom. If such a hell existed, this section of the Boulevard de l'Hôpital might well serve as its approach.

Then, at nightfall, the moment when daylight is dying,

particularly in winter, at that hour when the evening breeze tears the last withered leaves off the elms, when the darkness is deep and starless, or when the moon and wind make holes in the clouds, this boulevard became positively terrifying. The dark outlines shrank together and dissolved in the obscurity like stumps of infinity. The passerby could not help thinking of the locality's innumerable gallows traditions. The solitude of this neighborhood in which so many crimes had been committed was fearful. One sensed snares in this obscurity, all the confused outlines seemed suspect in the gloom, and the rectangular cavities between the trees seemed like graves. By day, it was ugly; in the evening, it was dismal; at night, it was ominous. In summer at twilight, a few old women might be seen sitting under the elms on benches mouldy from the rain. These good women were given to begging.

Actually the neighborhood, which seemed more outdated than ancient, began to undergo a transformation after that. From then on anyone wanting to see it had to hurry. Every day, some detail was gone. Now, and for the last twenty years, the terminus of the railroad to Orleans lies just beside the old suburb and keeps it changing. Wherever you locate, on the outskirts of a capital, a railroad depot, it is the death of a suburb and the birth of a city. It seems that around these great centers of population movement, to the rumble of the mighty engines, to the snorting of the giant workhorses of civilization, devouring coal and spitting fire, the earth, teeming with seeds, trembles and opens to swallow down old habitations of men and to bring forth new ones. Old houses crumble, new houses spring up.

Since the depot of the Orleans railway invaded the grounds of La Salpêtrière, the narrow old streets adjoining the Fossés Saint-Victor and the Jardin des Plantes are giving way, violently crossed, as they are, three or four times a day, by those streams of stagecoaches, carts, and buses, which, in due course, push back the houses right and left; for there are things that sound strange, and yet are precisely corect; and, just as it is true that, in large cities, the sun makes the south-facing house façades vegetate and grow, it is equally undeniable that the frequent passage of vehicles widens the streets. The symptoms of a new life are clear. In that old provincial neighborhood, in its wildest corners, paving stone is beginning to appear, sidewalks are inching along, stretching to greater and greater distances, even in those parts where there are not yet any pedestrians. One morning, a memorable one in July 1845, black kettles filled with bitumen were seen smoking there; on that day, one could exclaim that civilization had reached the Rue de l'Ourcine and Paris had stepped across into the Faubourg Saint-Marceau.

II

A NEST FOR OWL AND WREN

It was in front of the Gorbeau structure that Jean Valjean came to a halt. Like the birds of prey, he had chosen the loneliest place to make his nest.

He fumbled in his waistcoat and took out a sort of pass key, opened the door, entered, then carefully closed it again and ascended the stairway, still carrying Cosette.

At the top of the stairs he took out another key, with which he opened another door. The room he entered and closed again immediately was a garret of sorts, rather spacious, furnished only with a mattress spread on the floor, a table, and a few chairs. A stove containing a fire, its hot coals visible, stood in one corner. The streetlamp shed a dim light across this poor interior. At the far end was a little room containing a cot bed. On this Jean Valjean lay the child without waking her.

He struck a light with a flint and steel and lit a candle, which, with his tinderbox, stood readied on the table; and, as he had done on the night before, he began to gaze at Cosette with a look of ecstasy in which the expression of kindness and tenderness verged on madness. The little girl, with that tranquil confidence that belongs only to extreme strength or extreme weakness, had fallen asleep without knowing with whom she was and went on sleeping without knowing where she was.

Jean Valjean bent down and kissed the child's hand.

Nine months before, he had kissed the hand of the mother, who had also just fallen asleep.

The same painful, pious, agonizing feeling now filled his heart.

He knelt down beside Cosette's bed.

The dawn turned to day, and still the child slept on. A pale ray from the December sun struggled through the garret window and traced long streaks of light and shade on the ceiling. Suddenly a quarrier's wagon, heavily laden, trundling over the cobblestones of the boulevard, shook the old building like the rumble of thunder, jarring it from the ground up.

"Yes, madame!" cried Cosette, starting up out of sleep. "Here I am! Here I am!"

And she threw herself out of the bed, her eyes still half closed with sleep, stretching out her hand toward the corner of the room.

"Oh! What shall I do? Where's my broom?" she said.

Her eyes opened fully, and she saw the smiling face of Jean Valjean.

"Oh! I forgot," she said. "Good morning, monsieur."

Children instantly accept joy and happiness with quick familiarity, being happy and joyful by nature.

Cosette noticed Catherine at the foot of the bed, picked her up at once, and, still playing, asked Jean Valjean a thousand questions. Where was she? Was Paris a big place? Was Madame Thénardier really very far away? Wouldn't she ever come back again, etc., etc. All at once she exclaimed, "How pretty it is here!"

It was an awful hovel, but she felt free.

"Shouldn't I sweep?" she finally asked.

"Play!" Jean Valjean answered.

And so the day went by. Cosette, without bothering to understand anything, was inexpressibly happy with her doll and her good friend.

III

TWO MISFORTUNES EQUAL ONE HAPPINESS

Dawn the next day found Jean Valjean again near Cosette's bed. He was waiting there, motionless, to see her wake up.

Something new was entering his soul.

Jean Valjean had never loved anything. For twenty-five years he had been alone in the world. He had never been a father, lover, husband, or friend. In prison he was cross, sullen, chaste, ignorant, and intractable. The heart of the former convict was like a virgin's. His sister and her children were only a vague distant memory, almost totally vanished. He had bent every effort to find them again and, not succeeding, had forgotten them. Human nature is that way. The other tender emotions of his youth, if he had any, were lost in oblivion.

When he saw Cosette, when he had rescued her, he felt his heart move again. Everything within him, all feeling and affection, was aroused and poured out on this child. He approached the bed where she slept and trembled there with delight; he felt inward yearnings, like a mother, and did not know what they were, since the strange and great motion of a heart beginning to love is incomprehensibly sweet.

Poor old heart, so new at it!

But, as he was fifty-five and Cosette only eight, all the love he might have felt through his whole life melted into a sort of ineffable glow.

This was the second white vision he had met. The bishop had caused the dawn of virtue on his horizon; Cosette invoked the dawn of love.

The first few days rolled by in this radiance.

As for her, Cosette, too, unconsciously underwent a change, poor little creature! She was so small when her mother left her, that she could not remember her now. As all children do, like the vine's young shoots that cling to everything, she had tried to love. She had not succeeded. Everybody had repelled her—the Thénardiers, their children, other children. She had loved the dog; it died, and after that no one and nothing would have anything to do with her. Mournful thing to say, and one that we have already hinted, at the age of eight her heart was cold. This was not her fault; it was not the faculty of love that she lacked, alas! It was the possibility. And so, from the very first day, everything that thought and felt in her began to love this kind old friend. She now felt something utterly new—a sensation of budding and of growth.

Her kind friend no longer impressed her as old and poor. In her eyes Jean Valjean was handsome, just as the garret seemed pretty.

Such are the effects of the dawn, of childhood, youth, and joy. The novelty of earth and life has something to do with it. Nothing is so charming as the ruddy tints that happiness can shed around a garret room. In the course of our lives, we have all had our rosy garret.

Nature had placed a wide separation—a fifty years' interval—between Jean Valjean and Cosette. This gulf was filled to the brim by fate. Fate abruptly brought together, and wedded with its irresistible power, these two shattered lives, dissimilar in years, but similar in sorrow. The one, in fact, complemented the other. Cosette's instinct sought a father, as Jean Valjean's instinct sought a child. To meet was to find one another. In that mysterious moment when their hands touched, they were welded together. When their two souls saw each other, they recognized mutual need, and they embraced.

If we take the words in their most comprehensive and absolute sense, it might be said that, separated from everything by the walls of the tomb, Jean Valjean was the bereaved husband, as Cosette was the orphan. This position made Jean Valjean, in a celestial sense, Cosette's father.

And, in truth, the mysterious impression worked on Cosette, in the deep woods at Chelles, by Jean Valjean's hand grasping her own in the darkness, was not an illusion but a reality. The coming of this man and his participation in this child's destiny had been the coming of God.

Meanwhile, Jean Valjean had chosen his hiding place well. There he felt completely secure.

The apartment that they occupied, with the side room for Cosette, was the one whose window looked out on the boulevard. This window being the only one in the house, there was no neighbor's prying eye to fear, either from that side or the opposite.

The ground floor of No. 50–52, a sort of dilapidated shed, served as a warehouse for market gardeners and was not connected to the upper floor. It was separated from it by the flooring, which had neither stairway nor trap door and was, as it were, the diaphragm of the old building. The upper floor contained, as we have said, several rooms and a few lofts, only one of which was occupied—by an old woman, who cleaned for Jean Valjean. All the rest was uninhabited.

It was this old woman, honored with the title of landlady but actually entrusted with the functions of concierge, who had rented him these lodgings on Christmas Day. He had passed himself off to her as a gentleman of means, ruined by the Spanish Bonds, who was going to live there with his granddaughter. He had paid her six months in advance, and requested the old dame to furnish the bedroom and the little side room, as we have described them. It was this old woman who had kindled the fire in the stove and readied everything for them on the evening of their arrival.

Weeks rolled by. In that meager shelter these two beings led a happy life.

From dawn on, Cosette laughed, chattered, and sang. Children have their morning song, like birds.

Sometimes Jean Valjean would take her little red hand, all chapped and frostbitten as it was, and kiss it. The poor child, accustomed only to blows, had no idea what this meant, and would draw back ashamed.

At times, she grew serious and looked thoughtfully at her little black dress. Cosette was no longer in rags; she was in mourning. She was issuing from utter poverty and was entering on life.

Jean Valjean had begun to teach her to read. Sometimes, while teaching the child to spell, he would remember that it was with the intention of doing evil that he had learned to read in prison. That intention had now changed into teaching a child to read. Then the former convict would smile with the pensive smile of angels.

He felt it in a preordination from on high, a will of some greater power than man, and he would drift off in reverie. Good thoughts as well as bad have their distant realms.

To teach Cosette to read and watch her playing was

practically all of Jean Valjean's life. And then, he would talk to her about her mother and teach her to pray.

She called him "Father," and knew him by no other name.

He spent hours watching her dress and undress her doll and listening to her chatter. Life seemed full of promise to him, men seemed good and just; in his thoughts he no longer reproached anyone with any wrong; he saw no reason now why he should not live to a very old age, since this child loved him. He looked forward to a whole future illuminated by Cosette as if with charmed light. The very best of us are not altogether exempt from some tinge of egotism. At times, with a sort of quiet satisfaction, he reflected that she would be by no means pretty.

This is only personal opinion; but to express our views completely, at the point Jean Valjean had reached when he began to love Cosette, it is not entirely clear that he did not need this fresh supply of goodness to keep him on the straight and narrow. He had just seen the wickedness of men and the misery of society in new ways—incomplete aspects and, unfortunately, showing only one side of the truth—the lot of woman summed up in Fantine, public authority personified in Javert. This time he had been sent back to prison for doing good; new waves of bitterness had swept over him; disgust and weariness had once more seized him; even memories of the bishop might occasionally fade, to reappear afterward, luminous and triumphant; but with time this blessed remembrance was growing fainter. Who can tell whether Jean Valjean was on the verge of discouragement and falling back on evil ways? He loved, and he grew strong again. Alas, he was as frail as Cosette. He protected her, and she gave him strength. Thanks to him, she could walk upright in life; thanks to her, he could persist in virtue. He was this child's support, and she was his prop and staff. Oh, divine unfathomable mystery of Destiny's compensations.

IV

WHAT THE LANDLADY DISCOVERED

Jean Valjean was prudent enough never to go out in the daytime. Every evening, however, around twilight, he would walk for an hour or two, sometimes alone, often with Cosette, selecting the most untraveled side alleys off the boulevards and going into the churches at nightfall. He was fond of going to Saint-Médard, the closest one. When he did not take Cosette, she stayed with the old woman; but it was the child's greatest joy to go out with her kind old friend. She even preferred an hour with him to her lovely tête-à-têtes with Catherine. He would walk along holding her by the hand and telling her pleasant things.

It turned out that Cosette was very playful.

The old woman was housekeeper and cook, and did the marketing.

They lived frugally, never without a small fire in the stove, but like people in reduced circumstances. Jean Valjean made no change in the furniture described on the first day, except that he had a solid door put up in place of the glass door to Cosette's little bedroom.

He still wore his yellow coat, his black trousers, and his old hat. On the street he was taken for a poor man. It sometimes happened that kind-hearted ladies would turn as they went by and hand him a penny. Jean Valjean accepted the penny and bowed humbly. Sometimes he would also meet some wretched creature begging alms, and then, glancing about him to be sure no one was looking, he would stealthily approach the beggar, slip a coin, often silver, into his hand, and rapidly walk away. This had its drawbacks. He began to be known in the neighborhood as "the beggar who gives alms."

The old landlady, a crabby individual, possessed with a keen observation of everything concerning her neighbors peculiar to the faubourgs, watched Jean Valjean closely without arousing his suspicion. She was a little deaf, which made her talkative. She had only two teeth left, one in the upper and one in the lower jaw, and she was continually clicking them together. She had questioned Cosette, who, knowing nothing, could tell nothing except that she came from Montfermeil. One morning the old sneak saw Jean Valjean go, with a look that seemed odd to her, into one of the uninhabited apartments of the building. She followed him with an old cat's steps, and could see him without herself being seen, through the chink of the door directly opposite. Undoubtedly for greater caution, Jean Valjean had turned his back to the door. The old woman saw him fumble in his pocket, and take out a needle case, scissors, and thread, and then proceed to rip open the lining of one of his coattails and draw out a piece of yellowish paper, which he unfolded. The old woman noted with dismay that it was a bank bill for a thousand francs. It was only the second or third she had ever seen. She slipped away quite frightened.

A moment later Jean Valjean accosted her, and asked her politely to get this thousand-franc bill changed for him, adding that it was the half-yearly interest on his property, which he had received the previous day. "Where?" thought the old woman. He did not go out until six o'clock, and the government treasury is certainly not open at that hour. The old woman got the note changed, all the while conjecturing. This thousand-franc bill, commented upon and multiplied, gave rise to a flock of breathless conferences among the gossips of the Rue des Vignes-Saint-Marcel.

A few days later, Jean Valjean, in his shirtsleeves, happened to be sawing wood in the entry. The old woman was in his room doing the housework. She was alone. Cosette was intent on the wood he was sawing. The woman saw the coat hanging on a nail and examined it. The lining had been sewn up. She felt it carefully and thought she could detect in the lapels and hems some wads of paper. Other thousand-franc bills no doubt!

She noticed, besides, that there were all sorts of things in the pockets. Not only were there the needles, scissors, and thread, which she had already seen, but a large pocketbook, a very big knife, and, still more suspect, several wigs of different colours. Every pocket of this coat seemed to contain something for sudden emergencies.

Thus, the occupants of the old building reached the closing days of winter.

V

A FIVE-FRANC PIECE FALLING TO THE FLOOR MAKES A NOISE

Near Saint-Médard was a beggar who sat crouching on the curbs around a condemned public well and to whom Jean Valjean often gave alms. He never passed this man without giving him a few pennies. Sometimes he would speak to him. Those who were envious of this poor creature said he was in the pay of the police. He was an old church beadle of seventy-five, always mumbling prayers.

One evening, as Jean Valjean was passing that way, unaccompanied by Cosette, he noticed the beggar sitting in his usual place, under the streetlamp, which had just been lit. The man, as usual, seemed to be bent over in prayer. Jean Valjean walked up to him and put a coin in his hand, as usual. The beggar suddenly looked up, gazed intently at Jean Valjean, and then quickly dropped his head. This movement was like a flash; Jean Valjean shuddered. It seemed to him that he had just seen by the light of the streetlamp not the calm, sanctified face of the aged beadle, but a terrible and familiar countenance. He experienced the sensation of someone suddenly face to face in the dark with a tiger. He recoiled, horror-stricken and petrified, not daring either to breathe or speak, to stay or flee, but gazing at the beggar who had once more bent down his head, with its tattered covering, and seemed to be no longer conscious of his presence. Some momentary instinct—perhaps the mysterious instinct of self-preservation—prevented Jean Valjean from uttering a word. The beggar had the same form, the same rags, the same general appearance as usual. "Come on," Jean Valjean said to himself. "I'm going crazy! I'm dreaming! It can't be!" And he went home, anxious and uneasy.

He scarcely dared admit, even to himself, that the face he thought he had seen was Javert's.

That night, on reflection, he regretted that he had not questioned the man so as to make him raise his head a second time. The next day at nightfall, he went back. The beggar was in his place. "Good evening!" Jean Valjean said firmly, as he gave him the accustomed alms. The beggar raised his head and answered in a whining voice, "Thanks, kind sir, thanks!" It was, indeed, only the old beadle.

Jean Valjean felt fully reassured. He even began to laugh. "Why the devil was I imagining I saw Javert," he thought; "is my sight already failing?" And he thought no more about it.

Some days later, around eight in the evening, he was in his room, giving Cosette her spelling lesson, which the child was repeating in a loud voice, when he heard the door of the building open and close again. That seemed odd to him. The old woman, the only occupant of the house besides himself and Cosette, always went to bed at dark to save candles. Jean Valjean signaled to Cosette to be silent. He heard someone coming up the stairs. It could just be the old woman who might have felt sick and gone out to the druggist's. Jean Valjean listened. The footstep was heavy and sounded like a man's, but the old woman wore heavy shoes, and there is nothing so much like a man's footstep as the tread of an old woman. However, Jean Valjean blew out his candle.

He sent Cosette to bed, whispering to her to lie down very quietly—and, as he kissed her forehead, the footsteps stopped. Jean Valjean sat stock-still, his back turned toward the door, still on the chair from which he had not moved, holding his breath in the dark. After a considerable time, not hearing anything more, he turned around without making any noise, and as he raised his eyes toward the door of his room, he saw a light through the keyhole. This ray of light was an evil star in the black background of the door and the wall. Obviously, there was somebody outside with a candle, listening.

A few minutes later, the light disappeared. But he heard no sound of footsteps, which seemed to indicate that whoever had been listening at the door had removed his shoes.

Jean Valjean threw himself on his bed without undressing but could not shut his eyes that night.

At daybreak, as he was sinking into an exhausted slumber, he was aroused by the creaking of the door to some room at the end of the hall, and then he heard the same footstep that had ascended the stairs on the preceding night. The step approached. He leaped out of bed and put his eye to the keyhole, which was quite a large one, hoping to get a glimpse of the person, whoever it might be, who had made his way into the building during the night and had listened at his door. It was indeed a man who passed by Jean Valjean's room, this time without stopping. The hall was still too dark for him to make out his features; but, when the man reached the stairs, a ray of light from outside made his figure stand out like a silhouette, and Jean Valjean had a full view of his back. The man was tall, wore a long frock coat and had a cudgel under his arm. It was the appalling figure of Javert.

Jean Valjean might have tried to get another look at him through his window that opened on the boulevard, but he would have had to raise the sash, and that he did not dare.

It was clear the man had entered by means of a key, as if at home. Who, then, had given him the key?—and what did it mean?

At seven in the morning, when the old lady came to do the rooms, Jean Valjean eyed her sharply, but did not question her. The old woman seemed the same as usual.

While she was doing her sweeping, she said, "Perhaps monsieur heard someone come in last night?"

At her age and on that boulevard, eight in the evening is the very darkest of the night.

"As a matter of fact, I did," he answered in the most natural tone. "Who was it?"

"It's a new lodger," said the old woman, "who has come to the house."

"And his name—?"

"Well, I don't quite recall. Dumont, or Daumont. Something like that."

"And what is this M. Daumont?"

The old woman studied him a moment with her shrewd little eyes, and answered, "A gentleman living on his income like you."

She may have intended nothing by this, but Jean Valjean thought he could make out that she did.

When the old woman was gone, he made a roll of a hundred francs he had in a drawer and put it into his pocket. Do as he might so the clinking of the silver would not be heard, a five-franc piece slipped from his grasp and rolled jingling away across the floor.

At dusk, he went to the street door and looked carefully up and down the boulevard. There was no one to be seen. The boulevard seemed utterly deserted. It is true that someone could have been hidden behind a tree.

He went upstairs again.

"Come," he said to Cosette.

He took her by the hand and they both went out.

Book Five

A DARK CHASE REQUIRES A SILENT HOUND

I

STRATEGY'S ZIGZAGS

In order to understand the pages immediately following, and others that will be found further on, an observation is necessary here.

For many years now, the author of this book, who is reluctantly compelled to speak of himself, has been away from Paris. Meanwhile Paris has been transformed. A new city has sprung up which is in some sense unknown to him. It is unnecessary for him to say that he loves Paris; Paris is his heart's birthplace. Through demolition and reconstruction, the Paris of his youth, that Paris he devoutly treasures in memory, has become a Paris of former times. Let him be permitted to speak of that Paris as though it still existed. It is possible that where the author is about to lead his readers, saying, "In such a street there is such a house," there is now no longer either house or street. The reader may verify it, if he chooses to take the trouble. As for himself, the author does not know the new Paris and writes with the old Paris before his eyes in an illusion that is precious to him. It is comforting for him to imagine that something still remains of what he saw when he was in his own country, and that all is not vanished. While we come and go in our native land, we imagine that we are indifferent to these streets, that these windows, roofs, and doors mean nothing to us, that these walls are strangers to us, that these trees are like any other trees, that these houses we never enter are of no use to us, that the pavement where we walk is no more than stone blocks. Later, when we are no longer there, we find that those streets are very dear to us, that we miss the roofs, windows, and doors, that the walls are essential to us, that the trees are beloved, that every day we did enter those houses we never entered, and that we have left something of our affections, our life, and our heart on those paving stones. All those places that we no longer see, which perhaps we shall never see again, but whose image we have preserved, assume a painful charm, return to us with the sadness of a ghost, make the holy land visible to us, and are, so to speak, the true shape of France; and we love them and call them up such as they are, such as they were, and hold onto them, unwilling to change a thing, for one clings to the form of the fatherland as to the face of the mother.

So permit us to speak of the past as the present. Having said this, we beg the reader to take note of it, and we will then continue.

Jean Valjean had immediately left the boulevard and begun to thread the streets, making as many turns as he could, sometimes doubling back on his tracks to make sure he was not followed.

This maneuver is characteristic of the hunted stag. On ground where the foot leaves a print, it has, among other advantages, that of deceiving the hunters and the dogs by reversing tracks. It is what is called in hunting terms, "a false return to cover."

There was a full moon. Jean Valjean was not sorry for that. Still near the horizon, the moon cut the streets into large prisms of light and shade. Jean Valjean could glide along the houses and the walls on the dark side and watch the light side. Perhaps he was not paying enough attention to the fact that the dark side was lost to him. However, through all the deserted little streets in the neighborhood of the Rue de Poliveau, he felt sure that no one was behind him.

Cosette walked along without asking any questions. The sufferings of the first six years of her life had introduced something passive into her nature. Besides—and this is a remark to which we will return more than once

—she had become familiar, without being fully aware of it, with the peculiarities of her good friend and the eccentricities of destiny. And then, she felt safe, being with him.

No more than Cosette did Jean Valjean know where he was going. He trusted God, and she trusted him. It was as though he too were holding someone greater than himself by the hand; he believed he felt some invisible being leading him. Ultimately, he had no definite idea, no plan. He was not even absolutely sure that this was Javert, and then it might be Javert, without Javert knowing that he was Jean Valjean. Wasn't he disguised? Wasn't he supposed to be dead? Nevertheless, strange things had been happening within the last few days. He wanted no more of them. He was determined to not enter Gorbeau House again. Like the animal driven from his den, he was looking for a hole to hide in till he could find one to stay in.

Jean Valjean traced many and varied labyrinths in the Quartier Mouffetard, which was asleep already as if still under the discipline of the Middle Ages and the yoke of the curfew; he produced diverse combinations, a clever stratagem, using the Rue Censier and the Rue Copeau, the Rue du Battoir-Saint-Victor and the Rue du Puits-l'Ermite. There are rooms in that area, but he did not even inquire, seeing nothing that suited him. He had no doubt whatever that if by any chance they had followed his track, they had now lost it.

As eleven o'clock struck in the tower of Saint-Etienne du Mont, he crossed the Rue de Pontoise in front of the headquarters of the commissioner of police, which is at No. 14. A few moments later, the instinct we have already mentioned made him turn around. At that moment he distinctly saw—thanks to the commissioner's lamp, which revealed them—three men following quite closely, as they passed one after another under this lamp on the dark side of the street. One of these men entered the alley leading to the commissioner's post. The one in the lead seemed to him decidedly suspicious.

"Come along, dear," he said to Cosette, and he hurried to leave the Rue de Pontoise.

He circled around the Arcade des Patriarches, which was closed because of the late hour, walked rapidly through the Rue de l'Epée-de-Bois and the Rue de l'Arbalète, and plunged into the Rue des Postes.

There was a square there, where the Collège Rollin now is, and from there the Rue Neuve-Sainte-Geneviève branches off.

(We do not have to add that the Rue Neuve-Sainte-Geneviève is an old street and that a carriage did not pass once in ten years through the Rue des Postes. In the thirteenth century this Rue des Postes was inhabited by potters, and its true name is Rue des Pots.)

The square was brightly lit by the moon. Jean Valjean concealed himself in a doorway, figuring that if these men were still following him, he could not fail to get a good view of them when they crossed the lighted area.

In fact, three minutes had not elapsed when the men appeared. There were four of them now, all tall, dressed in long brown coats, with round hats, and great clubs in their hands. They were no less forbidding for their size and large fists than their stealthy tread in the darkness. One would have taken them for four specters in civilian clothing.

They stopped in the center of the square and formed a knot like people conferring. They appeared undecided. The man who seemed to be the leader turned and pointed energetically in the direction Jean Valjean had taken; one of the others seemed to insist with some obstinacy on the opposite direction. At the instant when the leader turned, the moon shone full in his face. Jean Valjean recognized Javert perfectly.

II

IT IS FORTUNATE THAT VEHICLES CAN CROSS THE PONT D'AUSTERLITZ

Uncertainty was over for Jean Valjean; fortunately, it continued for the men. He took advantage of their hesitation; it was time lost for them, gained for him. He came out of the doorway in which he was concealed and made his way into the Rue des Postes toward the Jardin des Plantes. Cosette began to tire; he took her up in his arms and carried her. There was nobody in the streets, and the lamps had not been lit because of the moon.

He speeded up.

In a few steps, he reached the Goblet Pottery, on whose façade the old inscription stood out clearly legible by the light of the moon:

> De Goblet fils c'est ici la fabrique;
> Venez choisir des cruches et des brocs,
> Des pots à fleurs, des tuyaux, de la brique.
> A tout venant le Coeur vend des Carreaux.[1]

He passed by the Rue de la Clef, went past the Fontaine de Saint-Victor along the Jardin des Plantes by the lower streets, and reached the quay. There he looked around. The quay was deserted. The streets were deserted. Nobody behind him. He took a deep breath.

He reached the Pont d'Austerlitz.

It was still a toll bridge at that time.

He stepped up to the tollhouse and gave a sous.

"It is two sous," said the toll keeper. "You are carrying a child who can walk. Pay for two."

He paid, annoyed that his passing should have attracted any notice at all. Such flight should be an easy glide.

A large cart was crossing the Seine at the same time and like him was going toward the right bank. This was useful. He could go the whole length of the bridge in the shadow of this cart.

Toward the middle of the bridge, Cosette, her feet becoming numb, wanted to walk. He put her down and took her by the hand.

With the bridge behind them, he noted some lumberyards a little to the right and walked in that direction. To get there, he had to venture into a large clear open space. He did not hesitate. Those who followed him were evidently thrown off his track, and Jean Valjean believed

[1] Here's the Goblet and Sons Factory
Get your pitchers and jars,
Flowerpots, pipes, and bricks.
Big sale. All welcome.

himself out of danger. Sought for he might be, but followed he was not.

A little street, the Rue de Chemin-Vert-Saint-Antoine, opened between two lumberyards enclosed by walls. The street was narrow, obscure, and seemed made expressly for him. Before taking it, he looked back.

From the point where he was, he could see the whole length of the Pont d'Austerlitz.

Four shadows had just started over the bridge.

The shadows were coming from the Jardin des Plantes toward the right bank.

These four shadows were the four men.

Jean Valjean felt a tremor like that of the deer seeing the hounds again on its track.

One hope was left him; it was that these men had not started over the bridge, and had not seen him as he crossed the large square clear space leading Cosette by the hand.

In that case, by plunging into the little street in front of him, if he managed to reach the lumberyards, the marshes, the fields, the open grounds, he could escape.

It seemed to him that he might entrust himself to this silent little street. He turned into it.

III

SEE THE MAP OF PARIS OF 1727

Some three hundred paces on, he reached a point where the street forked. It divided into two streets, one turning off obliquely to the left, the other to the right. Jean Valjean was facing the two branches of a *Y*. Which should he choose?

He did not hesitate, but took the right one.

Why?

Because the left branch led toward the faubourg—that is to say, toward the inhabited region, and this right branch toward the country—that is, toward the uninhabited areas.

But now, they were no longer walking very quickly. Cosette's short stride slackened Jean Valjean's pace.

He picked her up and carried her again. Cosette rested her head upon the man's shoulder and did not say a word.

From time to time he turned and looked back. He was careful to stay on the dark side of the street. The street ran straight behind him. The two or three first times he turned, he saw nothing; the silence was total, and he kept on his way somewhat reassured. Suddenly, on turning around again, he thought he could see in the section of the street he had just passed, far off in the darkness, something moving.

He hurtled forward rather than walking, hoping to find some side street, to slip away and once more elude his pursuers.

He came to a wall.

But this wall did not prevent him from going farther; it was a wall forming the side of a cross alley, where the street Jean Valjean was then in came to an end.

Here again he had to decide: Should he take the right or the left?

He looked to the right. The alley ran on to a space between some buildings that were mere sheds or barns, then cut off. The end of this blind alley could clearly be seen—a great white wall.

He looked to the left. The alley on this side was open and, about two hundred paces farther on, ran into a wider street. That way lay safety.

The instant Jean Valjean decided to turn left, to try to reach the street he saw at the end of the alley, he noticed at the corner of the alley and the street he was about to head for what seemed a black statue.

It was a man, who had evidently just been posted there and who was waiting for him, guarding the passage.

Jean Valjean was startled.

The part of Paris where Jean Valjean was, between the Faubourg Saint-Antoine and La Râpée is one of those entirely transformed by recent construction—a change for the worse in the opinion of some, a transfiguration according to others. The vegetable gardens, the lumber-yards, and the old buildings are gone. There are new broad streets, amphitheaters, circuses, hippodromes, railroad stations, a prison, Mazas—progress, as we see, with its corrective.

Half a century ago, in the traditional popular language, which obstinately calls l'Institut *Les Quatre Nations* and l'Opera Comique *Feydeau*, the precise spot Jean Valjean had reached was called the Petit-Picpus. The Porte Saint-Jacques, the Porte Paris, the Barrière des Sergents, the Porcherons, the Galiote, the Célestins, the Capuchins, the Mail, the Bourbe, the Arbre-de-Cracovie, the Petite-Pologne, the Petit-Picpus, these are names of the old Paris floating on the surface of the new. The memory of the people sustains these waifs from the past.

The Petit-Picpus, which in fact hardly had a real existence and was never more than a rough sketch of a neighborhood, had almost the monastic look of a Spanish city. The roads were poorly paved, the streets were sparsely built up. Beyond the two or three streets we are about to mention, there was nothing but walls and solitude. Not a shop, not a vehicle, hardly a light here and there in the windows; every candle put out after ten o'clock. Gardens, convents, lumberyards, market gardens, marshes, a few scattered low houses, and great walls as high as the houses.

Such was the quarter in the last century. The Revolution had already very much altered it. The republican administration had demolished it, pierced it, run holes through it. Trash dumps had been established there. Thirty years ago, this neighborhood was disappearing, erased by new construction. It is now completely blotted out. The Petit-Picpus, of which no present map retains a trace, is shown clearly enough on the map of 1727, published in Paris by Denis Thierry, Rue Saint-Jacques, opposite the Rue du Plâtre, and in Lyons by Jean Girin, Rue Mercière, à la Prudence. The Petit-Picpus made what we have just called a *Y* of streets, formed by the forking of the Rue du Chemin-Vert-Saint-Antoine, the left branch taking the name Petite Rue Picpus and the right the name of the Rue Polonceau. The two branches of the *Y* were joined at the top as by a bar. This bar was called the Rue Droit-Mur. The Rue Polonceau ended there; the Petite Rue Picpus went on beyond, rising toward the Marché Lenoir. Anyone coming up from the Seine and reaching the end of the Rue Polonceau had on his left the Rue Droit-Mur turning abruptly at a right angle, in front of him the side wall of that street, and on his right a truncated prolongation of the Rue Droit-Mur, a dead end called the Cul-de-sac Genrot.

Jean Valjean was there.

As we just said, on perceiving the black form standing sentry at the corner of the Rue Droit-Mur and the Petite Rue Picpus, he was startled. There was no doubt about it. He was being watched by this shadow.

What should he do?

It was too late to turn back. What he had seen moving in the darkness some distance behind him a moment earlier was undoubtedly Javert and his squad. Probably Javert had already reached the beginning of the street of which Jean Valjean was at the end. To all appearances, Javert was acquainted with this little trap and had taken his precautions by sending one of his men to guard the exit. These conjectures, like certainties, whirled about wildly in Jean Valjean's troubled brain, as a handful of dust takes off in a sudden gust. He scrutinized the Cul-de-sac Genrot: high walls. He scrutinized the Petite Rue Picpus: a sentinel. He saw the dark form repeated in black on the white pavement flooded with moonlight. To advance was to come upon that man. To retreat was to throw himself into Javert's hands. Jean Valjean felt caught in a net that was slowly closing in. He looked up at the sky in despair.

IV

GROPING FOR ESCAPE

To understand what follows, we must form an exact image of the little Rue Droit-Mur, particularly the corner you leave on your left as you come out of the Rue Polonceau to enter this alley. The little Rue Droit-Mur was almost entirely lined on the right, as far as the Petite Rue Picpus, by shabby houses; on the left by a single building of severe outline, composed of several structures that gradually rose by a floor or two, one after the other, as they approached the Petite Rue Picpus, so that the building, very tall on the Petite Rue Picpus end, was quite low on the Rue Polonceau side. There, at the corner already mentioned, it was so low as to be merely a wall. This wall did not square up with the corner, but cut off diagonally, leaving a considerable space shielded by the two angles thus formed from observers in either the Rue Polonceau or the Rue Droit-Mur.

From these two angles of the truncated corner, the wall extended along the Rue Polonceau as far as a house numbered 49, and a shorter span along the Rue Droit-Mur, to the somber-looking building just mentioned, cutting past its gable end and thus making a new re-entry angle to the street. This façade looked rather gloomy; there was only one window to be seen, or rather two shutters covered with a sheet of zinc, and always closed.

The description offered here is rigorously exact and will certainly awaken precise memories in the minds of former inhabitants of the area.

This truncated corner was entirely filled by a thing that seemed like a colossal door in miserable condition. It was a vast shapeless assembly of perpendicular planks, broader above than below, bound together by long transverse iron bands. At the side there was a porte cochère of ordinary dimensions, which had evidently been cut within the last fifty years.

A linden tree lifted its branches above this corner, and the wall was covered with ivy on the Rue Polonceau side.

In Jean Valjean's immediate peril, this somber building had a solitary and uninhabited appearance that attracted him. He rapidly glanced over it. He thought if he could only manage to get into it, he might be safe. Hope came to him with the idea.

Midway along the front of this building on the Rue Droit-Mur, there were at every window of the various floors leaden waste pipes. The branchings of the tubing, which continued up from a central conduit to each of these waste pipes, formed a sort of tree against the façade. These pipe branches with their hundred elbows seemed like those old closely pruned grapevines that twist across the front of venerable farmhouses.

This grotesque espalier, with its sheet-iron branches, was the first object Jean Valjean noticed. He seated Cosette with her back against a stone post and, telling her to be quiet, ran to the spot where the conduit reached the pavement. Perhaps it would provide some means of scaling the wall and entering the house. But the conduit was dilapidated, no longer in use, and scarcely holding on. Besides, all the windows of this silent house were protected by thick iron bars, even the dormer windows. And then the moon was shining directly onto this façade, and the man watching from the end of the street would have seen Jean Valjean as he climbed. And then what should he do with Cosette? How could he lift her to the top of a four-story house?

He gave up climbing the conduit and crept along the wall to the Rue Polonceau.

When he reached this flattened corner where he had left Cosette, he noticed that no one could see him there. As we have just explained, he would be sheltered from all observation from every side. Besides, he was in the shadows. Finally, there were two doors. Perhaps they might be forced. The wall, across which he saw the linden and the ivy, evidently surrounded a garden, where he could at least conceal himself, though there were no leaves on the trees yet, and spend the rest of the night.

Time was running out. He must act quickly.

He tried the carriage door and found at once that it was fastened inside and out.

He approached the other large door with more hope. It was in extreme disrepair, its immense size making it even less secure; the planks were rotten; there were only three iron bands left, and these quite rusted. It might be possible to force this worm-eaten structure.

On examining it closely, he saw that this door was not a door. It had neither hinges, braces, lock, nor opening in the middle. The iron bands crossed it from one side to the other without a break. Through the crevices of the planks he saw the rubble work and stones, roughly cemented, which passersby could still have seen ten years ago. He had to admit with dismay that this apparent door was simply a wooden ornamentation of the wall against which it was placed. He could easily tear off a board, but then he would find himself face to face with a wall.

V

WHICH WOULD BE IMPOSSIBLE IF THE STREETS WERE LIT WITH GAS

At that moment a muffled and regular sound began to be heard some distance away. Jean Valjean ventured to peer around the street corner. Seven or eight soldiers, formed in platoon, had just turned into the Rue Polonceau. He saw the gleam of their bayonets. They were coming toward him.

The soldiers, at whose head he could make out the tall form of Javert, advanced slowly and cautiously. They stopped frequently. It was clear that they were exploring all recesses of walls and all entrances of doors and alleys.

It was—and here conjecture could not be mistaken—some patrol that Javert had met and requisitioned.

Javert's two assistants marched within the ranks.

At the rate at which they were going, and the stops they were making, it would take them about a quarter of an hour to reach the spot where Jean Valjean was. It was a frightening moment. A few minutes separated Jean Valjean from that awful precipice opening before him for the third time. And prison now was no longer simply prison; it was Cosette lost forever—a living death.

Now one thing alone was possible.

Jean Valjean had this trait, that he might be said to carry two knapsacks—in one he had the thoughts of a saint, in the other the impressive talents of a convict. He helped himself from one or the other as occasion required.

Among other resources, thanks to his numerous escapes from the galleys at Toulon, it will be remembered, he had become a master of that incredible art of climbing in the right angle of a wall, if need be to a six-story height; a feat achieved without ladders or crampons, by sheer muscular strength, supporting himself by the back of his neck, his shoulders, his hips, and his knees, scarcely making use of the few projections of the stone—the same feat that gave the corner of the yard of the Conciergerie of Paris its terrible renown some twenty years ago, after the convict Battemolle made his escape across it.

With his eye Jean Valjean measured the wall above which he saw the linden tree. It was about eighteen feet high. The angle it formed with the gable end of the large building was filled in its lower section with a triangular pile of masonry, probably intended to preserve this all too convenient recess from all too public use. This preventive filling-in of the nooks in a wall is very common in Paris.

This mass was about five feet high. From there on the distance left to climb to get up on the wall was scarcely more than fourteen feet.

The wall was capped by a flat stone without any projection.

The difficulty was Cosette. Cosette did not know how to scale a wall. Abandon her? Jean Valjean did not even think of it. To carry her was impossible. The whole strength of a man is necessary to accomplish these strange ascents. The slightest burden would make him lose his center of gravity, and he would fall.

He needed a rope. Jean Valjean had none. Where could he find a rope, at midnight, in the Rue Polonceau? Truly at that instant, if Jean Valjean had had a kingdom, he would have given it for a rope.

All extreme situations have their flashes that sometimes blind us, sometimes illuminate us.

Jean Valjean's desperate gaze encountered the lamppost in the Cul-de-sac Genrot.

At this period there were no gaslights in the streets of Paris. At nightfall they lit the streetlamps, which were placed at regular intervals and were raised and lowered by means of a rope running the whole length of the street and adjusted through the grooves of posts. The reel on which this rope was wound was enclosed below the lantern in a little iron box, whose key was kept by the lamplighter, and the rope itself was protected by a metal casing.

With the energy of an ultimate struggle, Jean Valjean crossed the street at a bound, entered the cul-de-sac, sprang the bolt of the little box with the point of his knife, and an instant later was back beside Cosette. He had a rope. They act quickly, these desperate inventors of expedients, in their struggles with destiny.

We explained that the streetlights had not been lit that night. So the lamp in the Cul-de-sac Genrot was naturally off like the rest, and a person might pass by without even noticing that it was not in place.

Meanwhile the time, the place, the darkness, Jean Valjean's preoccupation, his peculiar actions, his going to and fro, all this began to disturb Cosette. Any other child would have cried out long before. She contented herself with pulling Jean Valjean by his coattails. The sound of the approaching patrol was steadily becoming more distinct.

"Father," she whispered. "I'm scared. Who is coming up the street?"

"Shhh!" answered the unhappy man. "The Thénardiess!"

Cosette shuddered. He added, "Don't say a word; I'll take care of her. If you cry, if you make any noise, the Thénardiess will hear you. She's coming to catch you."

Then, with neither haste nor waste, with firm and rapid precision, so much the more remarkable at such a moment when the patrol and Javert might suddenly come upon him, he took off his tie, passed it around Cosette's body under the arms, taking care so it would not hurt the child, attached this tie to an end of the rope by means of the knot seamen call a sheet bend, took the other end of the rope in his teeth, removed his shoes and stockings and threw them over the wall, climbed upon the pile of masonry and began to pull himself up in the angle of the wall and the gable end with as much solidity and certainty as if he had the rungs of a ladder under his heels and elbows. Less than a half minute had passed before he was kneeling on the wall.

Cosette watched him, stupefied, without saying a word. Jean Valjean's instructions and the name of the Thénardiess had frozen her.

All at once, she heard Jean Valjean's voice calling to her in a whisper, "Put your back against the wall."

She obeyed.

"Don't say a word, and don't be afraid," added Jean Valjean.

And she felt herself lifted from the ground.

Before she had time to think, she was at the top of the wall.

Jean Valjean grabbed her, put her on his back, and took her two little hands in his left hand, lay down flat, and inched along the top of wall as far as the cut-off corner. As he had supposed, there was a building there, whose roof sloped from the top of the aforementioned wooden sheathing very nearly to the ground, with a gentle inclination, and just reaching the linden tree.

A fortunate circumstance, for the wall was much higher on this side than on the street. Jean Valjean could see the ground far below him.

He had just reached the inclined plane of the roof and had not yet left the crest of the wall, when a violent uproar announced the patrol's arrival. He heard Javert's thundering voice: "Search the cul-de-sac! The Rue Droit-Mur is guarded, the Petite Rue Picpus, too. I'll answer for it if he's in the cul-de-sac."

The soldiers rushed into the Cul-de-sac Genrot.

Jean Valjean slid down the roof, keeping hold of Cosette, reached the linden tree, and jumped to the ground. Whether from terror or courage, Cosette had not even whispered. Her hands were a bit scraped.

VI

BEGINNING OF AN ENIGMA

Jean Valjean found himself in a sort of garden, very large and strange-looking, one of those gloomy gardens that seem made to be seen on a winter's night. It was oblong, with a row of tall poplars at the far end, some clumps of rather tall trees in the corners, and a clear space in the center, where he could make out a very large isolated tree, then a few fruit trees, contorted and shaggy, like big bushes, some vegetable beds, a melon patch whose glass covers gleamed in the moonlight, and an old well. Here and there were stone benches that seemed black with moss. The walks were bordered with sad little shrubs, perfectly straight. Grass covered half of it, and a green moss covered the rest.

On one side of Jean Valjean were the building whose roof had been his access, and a woodpile, behind which, against the wall, was a stone statue, whose mutilated face was now a shapeless mask dimly visible in the darkness.

The building was in ruins, but some dismantled rooms

could be made out, one of which was filled up and seemed to be used as a shed.

The large building on the Rue Droit-Mur, which ran back down the Petite Rue Picpus, faced this garden with two façades at right angles. These inside façades were still gloomier than those on the outside. All the windows were barred. Not a light could be seen. On the upper stories there were shutters as in prisons. The shadow of one of these façades fell across the other, and down to the garden like an immense black pall.

No other house could be seen. The far end of the garden was lost in mist and darkness. Still, he could make out intersecting walls, as if there were other cultivated grounds beyond, as well as the low roofs of the Rue Polonceau.

One could not imagine anything as wild and solitary as this garden. No one was there, which was natural, given the hour; but it did not seem as though the place were made for anybody to walk in, even at noon.

Jean Valjean's first concern had been to find his shoes and put them on; then he went into the shed with Cosette. A man trying to escape never believes himself sufficiently concealed. The child, thinking constantly of the Thénardiess, shared his instinct, and crouched as low as she could.

Cosette trembled, and pressed close to his side. They heard the racket of the patrol poking around the cul-de-sac and the street, the clatter of their muskets against the stones, Javert's calls to the guards he had stationed, and his curses mingled with words they could not quite hear.

After a quarter of an hour, it seemed as though this stormy rumble began to recede. Jean Valjean did not breathe.

He had placed his hand gently on Cosette's mouth.

But the solitude around him was so strangely calm that the frightening noise, so furious and close, did not even cast over it a shadow of disturbance. It seemed as though the walls were built of the deaf stones spoken about in the Bible.

Suddenly, in the midst of this deep calm, a new sound rose; a celestial, divine, ineffable sound, as rapturous as the other was horrible. It was a hymn emerging from the darkness, a bewildering mingling of prayer and harmony in the fearful, shadowy silence of the night; women's voices, but with the pure accents of virgins, artless accents of children; voices not of this earth resembling those that the newborn still hear, and the dying hear already. This song came from the building overlooking the garden. As the uproar of the demons receded, one would have said, it was a choir of angels approaching in the shadows.

Cosette and Jean Valjean fell to their knees.

They did not know what it was; they did not know where they were; but they both felt, the man and the child, the penitent and the innocent, that they ought to be on their knees.

These voices had a strange effect: They did not prevent the building from seeming deserted. It was like a supernatural song in an uninhabited dwelling.

While the voices were singing, Jean Valjean was entirely absorbed in them. He no longer saw the night; he saw a blue sky. He seemed to feel the spreading of the wings we all have within us.

The chant broke off. Perhaps it had lasted a long time. Jean Valjean could not have said. Hours of ecstasy are never more than a moment.

Everything had relapsed into silence. There was nothing more in the street, nothing more in the garden. Everything that threatened, everything that reassured, all of it had vanished. The wind rattled the dry grass on top of the wall, which made a low, soft, and mournful noise.

VII

THE ENIGMA CONTINUED

The night wind had risen, which indicated that it must be between one and two in the morning. Poor Cosette was quiet. As she had sat down beside him and leaned her head on him, Jean Valjean thought that she was asleep. He bent over and looked at her. Her eyes were wide open, and she had a pensive look that pained Jean Valjean.

She was still trembling.

"Are you sleepy?" said Jean Valjean.

"I'm very cold," she answered.

A moment later she added, "Is she still there?"

"Who?" said Jean Valjean.

"Madame Thénardier."

Jean Valjean had already forgotten the means he had used to assure Cosette's silence.

"Oh!" he said. "She's gone. Don't be frightened."

The child sighed as if a weight had been lifted from her.

The ground was damp, the shed open on all sides, the wind constantly stronger. The man took off his coat and wrapped Cosette up in it.

"Are you warmer, now?"

"Oh! Yes, Father!"

"Well, wait here a moment. I'll be back soon."

He went out of the ruin and walked along the large building in search of some better shelter. He found doors, but they were all closed. All the ground-floor windows were barred.

As he passed the inner angle of the building, he noticed several arched windows in front of him, and he could see some light. He rose on tiptoe and looked in one of these windows. They all opened into a large hall paved with stone slabs and intersected by arches and pillars, where he could distinguish nothing beyond a slight glow and deep shadows. This glow came from a nightlamp burning in a corner. The hall was deserted, and not a thing moved. However, looking more carefully, he thought he saw something stretched out on the pavement, which appeared to be covered with a shroud and resembled a human form. It was lying face down, with arms outstretched in a cross, in the stillness of death. One would have said, because of a sort of serpent trailing along the pavement, that this sinister figure had a rope around its neck.

The whole hall was enveloped in that haze peculiar to dimly lit places, adding to the horror.

Jean Valjean often said afterwards that although in the course of his life he had seen many funereal sights, never had he seen anything more chilling and more terrible than that enigmatic figure fulfilling some strange mystery in that gloomy place, and glimpsed that way in the night. It was terrifying to suppose that perhaps it was dead, and still more terrifying to think that it might be alive.

He had the courage to press his forehead against the

glass and watch to see if the thing would move. Though he remained for what seemed a long time, the prostrate form made no movement. Suddenly he was seized with an inexpressible horror and fled. He ran toward the shed without daring to look behind him. It seemed to him that if he turned his head he would see the figure walking behind him with rapid strides, waving its arms.

He reached the ruin breathless; his knees gave way; a cold sweat oozed out of every pore.

Where was he? Who would ever have imagined anything equal to this sepulcher in the midst of Paris? What was this strange house? A building full of nocturnal mystery, calling to souls in the shadows with the voice of angels, and, when they came, abruptly presenting them with this frightening vision—promising to open the radiant gate of Heaven and opening the horrible door of the tomb. And that was in fact a building, a house with a street number? It was not all a dream? He had to touch the stone walls to believe it.

The cold, the anxiety, the night's anguish were giving him a fever, and all these thoughts were jostling in his brain.

He went over to Cosette. She was sleeping.

VIII

THE ENIGMA GROWS

The child had laid her head on a stone and gone to sleep.

He sat down near her and looked at her. Little by little, as he gazed at her, he calmed down and regained possession of his own free thoughts.

He plainly perceived the truth: from then on she would be the basis of his life, so long as she were there, so long as he had her with him, he would need nothing except her and fear nothing except on her account. He did not even feel cold, even though he had taken off his coat to cover her.

Meanwhile, through the reverie into which he had fallen, he had for some time been hearing a strange noise. It sounded like a little bell that someone was ringing. The sound came from the garden. It could be heard distinctly, though faintly. It was like the dimly heard tinkling of cowbells in the pastures at night.

This noise made Jean Valjean turn around.

He looked and saw that there was someone in the garden.

Something resembling a man was walking among the glass bells in the melon patch, rising up, bending over, stopping, with a regular motion, as if he were drawing or stretching something along the ground. This being seemed to limp.

Jean Valjean shook with the continual shiver of outcasts, to whom everything seems hostile and suspicious. They distrust the day because it helps to reveal them and the night because it helps to surprise them. Just then he had shuddered because the garden was empty, now he shuddered because there was someone in it.

From chimeric terrors he fell into real terrors. He said to himself that perhaps Javert and his spies had not gone away, that they had undoubtedly left somebody on watch in the street; that, if this man should discover him in the garden, he would cry thief, and would turn him in. He took the sleeping Cosette gently in his arms and carried her into the farthest corner of the shed behind a heap of old furniture. Cosette did not stir.

From there he watched the strange motions of the man in the melon patch. It seemed very odd, but the sound of the bell followed the man's every movement. When the man approached, the sound approached; when he moved away, the sound moved away; if he made some sudden motion, a trill accompanied the motion; when he stopped, the noise ceased. It seemed clear that the bell was attached to this man; but what could that mean? Who was this man on whom a bell was hung as on a ram or a cow?

While he was mulling over these questions, he touched Cosette's hands. They were icy.

"Oh! God!" he said.

He called to her softly, "Cosette!"

She did not open her eyes.

He shook her hard.

She did not wake up.

"Could she be dead?" he wondered, and he sprang up, trembling from head to foot.

The most terrible thoughts raced through his mind in

confusion. There are moments when hideous possibilities besiege us like a throng of furies and break down the doors of our brain. When those we love are in danger, our solicitude invents all sorts of follies. He remembered that sleep may be fatal in the open air on a cold night.

Cosette was pallid; she had fallen back to the ground at his feet, without making any response.

He listened for her breathing; she was breathing, but with a respiration that seemed faint and about to stop.

How could he warm her up again? How to rouse her? Everything else vanished from his thoughts. He rushed desperately out of the shed.

It was absolutely necessary for Cosette to be in bed and near a fire in less than a quarter of an hour.

IX

THE MAN WITH THE BELL

He walked straight up to the man he saw in the garden. He had taken out the roll of money from his vest pocket.

The man had his head down and did not see him coming. In a few strides, Jean Valjean was at his side.

Jean Valjean approached him, exclaiming, "A hundred francs!"

The man gave a start and looked up.

"A hundred francs for you," Jean Valjean repeated, "if you'll give me refuge for the night."

The moon shone full in Jean Valjean's dazed face.

"Welcome, Father Madeleine!" the man said.

This name, pronounced this way, at this dark hour, in this unknown place, by this unknown man, made Jean Valjean recoil.

He was ready for anything but that. The speaker was an old man, bent and lame, dressed something like a peasant, and he had on his left knee a leather knee-strap from which hung a bell. His face was in shadows and could not be clearly seen.

Meanwhile the old man had taken off his cap and was exclaiming nervously, "Oh heavens! How did you get here, Father Madeleine? However did you get in? Did you fall from heaven? There's no doubt, if you ever fall, that's where you'll fall from. And what's happened to you? No tie, no hat, no coat? You know, you'd have frightened anybody who didn't know you. No coat? Merciful heavens! Are the saints all crazy now? But how did you get in here?"

One word did not wait for another. The old man spoke with a calming rustic loquacity with a mixture of surprise and openness.

"Who are you? And what's this house?" asked Jean Valjean.

"Now that's a good one!" the old man exclaimed. "I'm the one you got the position for here, and this house is the one you got me the position in. And you don't remember me?"

"No," said Jean Valjean. "And how do you happen to know me?"

"You saved my life," said the man.

He turned, a ray of the moon lit up his profile, and Jean Valjean recognized old Fauchelevent.

"Ah!" said Jean Valjean. "You. Yes, I remember you."

"That's good!" the old man said reproachfully.

"What are you doing here?" added Jean Valjean.

"Oh, I'm covering my melons."

Indeed, at the moment when Jean Valjean accosted him, old Fauchelevent had in his hand the end of a piece of awning, which he was stretching out across the melon patch. He had already spread out several in this way during the hour he had been in the garden. It was this work that put him through the peculiar motions Jean Valjean observed from the shed.

He went on, "I said to myself: The moon is bright, there's going to be a frost. Suppose I put jackets on my melons? And," he added, looking at Jean Valjean, with a loud laugh, "you should have done as much for yourself! But what are you doing here?"

Knowing this man knew him, at least as Madeleine, Jean Valjean proceeded cautiously. He plied the old man with questions. Oddly enough their roles seemed reversed. It was he, the intruder, who interrogated.

"And what is this bell on your knee?"

"That's so they can keep away from me," answered Fauchelevent.

"How do you mean, keep away from you?"

Old Fauchelevent winked enigmatically.

"Ah! Bless me! There's only women in this house; plenty of young girls. It seems that I am dangerous to meet. The bell warns them. When I come, they go away."

"What is this house?"

"Why, you know quite well."

"No, I don't."

"Why, you got me this position here as gardener."

"Answer me as if I didn't know."

"Well, it is the Convent of the Petit-Picpus, then."

Jean Valjean remembered. Chance, that is to say, Providence, had dropped him precisely into this convent in the Quartier Saint-Antoine, to which old Fauchelevent, crippled by the fall under the cart, had been admitted on his recommendation two years earlier. He repeated as if he were talking to himself, "The Convent of the Petit-Picpus!"

"But now, really," resumed Fauchelevent, "how the devil did you manage to get in, you, Father Madeleine? No matter if you're a saint, you are still a man; and no men come in here."

"But you're here."

"I'm the only one."

"But," resumed Jean Valjean, "I have to stay here."

"Oh! My God," exclaimed Fauchelevent.

Jean Valjean went right up to the old man, and said to him gravely, "Father Fauchelevent, I saved your life."

"I was first to remember it," answered Fauchelevent.

"Well, now you can do for me what I once did for you."

Fauchelevent grasped in his old wrinkled trembling hands the robust hands of Jean Valjean, and it was some few seconds before he could speak; at last he exclaimed, "Oh! That would be a blessing from God if I could do something for you in return for that! Me, save your life! Monsieur Mayor, this old man is at your disposal."

It was as though a wonderful joy had transfigured the old gardener.

Radiance poured from his face.

"What do you want me to do?" he asked.

"I'll explain. You have a room?"

"I have a lone shanty, over there, behind the ruins of

the old convent, in a corner nobody ever sees. There are three rooms."

The hut was in fact so well concealed behind the ruins and so well placed that no one should see it, that Jean Valjean had not seen it.

"Good," said Jean Valjean. "Now I ask you for two things."

"What are they, Monsieur Madeleine?"

"First, that you won't tell anybody what you know about me. Second, that you won't try to learn anything more."

"All right. I know that you cannot do anything dishonest, and that you have always been a man of God. And then, besides, it was you who put me here. I am yours."

"Very well. But now come with me. We will go for the child."

"Ah!" said Fauchelevent. "There is a child!"

He said no more but followed Jean Valjean as a dog follows his master.

In half an hour Cosette, turned rosy again near a good fire, was asleep in the old gardener's bed. Jean Valjean had put on his tie and coat; his hat, which he had thrown over the wall, had been found and brought in. While Jean Valjean was putting on his coat, Fauchelevent had taken off his kneestrap with the bell attached, which now, hung on a nail near the fire, decorated the wall. The two men were warming themselves, with their elbows on a table, on which Fauchelevent had set a piece of cheese, some brown bread, a bottle of wine, and two glasses, and the old man said to Jean Valjean, putting his hand on his knee, "Ah! Father Madeleine! You didn't know me at first? You save people's lives and then you forget them? Oh! That's bad; they remember you. You're ungrateful!"

X

IN WHICH IT IS EXPLAINED HOW JAVERT LOST THE GAME

The events, the inverse of which, so to speak, we have just seen, had been brought about quite simply.

When Jean Valjean, on the night of the day that Javert

arrested him at Fantine's deathbed, escaped from the municipal prison of Montreuil-sur-mer, the police supposed that the escaped convict would start for Paris. Paris is a maelstrom in which everything is lost; and everything disappears in this whirlpool of the world as in the whirlpool of the sea. No forest conceals a man like this throng. Fugitives of all kinds know this. They go to Paris to drown; these are drownings that save. The police know it, too, and it is in Paris that they search for what they have lost elsewhere. They searched there for the ex-mayor of Montreuil-sur-mer. Javert was summoned to Paris to aid in the investigation. Javert, in fact, was of great help in the recapture of Jean Valjean. Javert's zeal and intelligence on this occasion were noted by M. Chabouillet, Secretary of the Prefecture under Comte Anglès. M. Chabouillet, who had already interested himself in Javert, secured the transfer of the inspector of Montreuil-sur-mer to the police of Paris. There Javert, in various ways, made himself—and, let us say, although the word seems unusual for such service, honorably—useful.

He thought no more of Jean Valjean—for these hounds always on the scent, today's wolf banishes the memory of yesterday's—when, in December 1823, he read a newspaper, he who never read the newspapers; but Javert, as a monarchist, made a point of knowing the details of the triumphal entry of the "Prince generalissimo" into Bayonne. Just as he finished the article that interested him, a name—Jean Valjean—at the bottom of the page attracted his attention. The newspaper announced that the convict Jean Valjean was dead and published the fact in terms so explicit that Javert had no doubt of it. He simply said, "That's that," then threw the paper aside and thought no more of it.

Sometime later a police notice was transmitted by the Prefecture of Seine-et-Oise to the Prefecture of Police of Paris concerning the kidnaping of a child, which had taken place, it was said, under peculiar circumstances, in the commune of Montfermeil. A little girl, seven or eight years old, the notice said, who had been entrusted by her mother to an innkeeper of the country, had been stolen by an unknown man; this little girl answered to the name of Cosette and was the child of a young woman named Fantine, who had died in a hospital, nobody knew when or where. This notice came to Javert's attention and set him thinking.

Fantine's name was well known to him. He remembered that Jean Valjean had actually made him—Javert—laugh aloud by requesting a respite of three days, in order to go for this creature's child. He recalled the fact that Jean Valjean had been arrested in Paris, as he was getting into the Montfermeil stagecoach. Some facts had even led him to think then that it was the second time he was entering this coach, and that he had already, the previous night, made another excursion to the environs of this village, for he had not been seen in the village itself. What was he doing in this region of Montfermeil? No one could guess. Javert understood it. Fantine's daughter was there. Jean Valjean was going after her. Now this child had been stolen by an unknown man! Who could this man be? Could it be Jean Valjean? But Jean Valjean was dead. Javert, without saying a word to anyone, caught the coach at the Plat d'Etain, Impasse de la Planchette, and took a trip to Monfermeil.

He expected to find enlightenment there; instead, he found mystery.

For the first few days the Thénardiers, in their spite, had spread the story all around. The Lark's disappearance had caused some talk in the village. Soon there were several versions of the story, which ended up as a case of kidnaping. Hence the police notice. However, when the first commotion was over, Thénardier, with his admirable instinct, soon arrived at the conclusion that it is never useful to attract the attention of the King's prosecutor; that the first result of his complaints in regard to the *kidnaping* of Cosette would be to train on himself, and on his many business problems, the sharp eye of justice. The last thing owls want is a candle. And first of all, how would he explain the fifteen hundred francs he had received? He stopped short, muzzled his wife, and professed to be astonished when anybody spoke to him of the stolen child. He knew nothing about it; undoubtedly he had made some complaint at the time that the dear little girl should be "taken away" so suddenly; he would have liked, for affection's sake, to keep her two or three days longer; but it was her "grandfather" who had come for her, the most natural thing in the world. He had added the part about the grandfather, for plausibility's sake. It was this story Javert heard on reaching Montfermeil. The grandfather put an end to Jean Valjean.

Javert, however, dropped a few questions like plummets into Thénardier's story. Who was this grandfather, and what was his name? Thénardier answered with simplicity: "He is a rich farmer, I saw his passport. I believe his name is M. Guillaume Lambert."

Lambert is a very respectable, reassuring name. Javert returned to Paris.

"Jean Valjean is really dead," he said, "and I am a fool."

Once more he had begun to forget the whole story, when, in the month of March 1824, he heard of an odd person who lived in the parish of Saint-Médard, called "the beggar who gives alms." This person was, so they said, a man living on his income, whose name nobody knew exactly, and who lived alone with a little girl eight years old, who knew nothing about herself except that she came from Montfermeil. Montfermeil! This constantly recurring name caught Javert's attention. An old beggar, a police informer and former beadle, to whom this person had extended his charity, added some further details. "This man was very unsociable, never going out except at night, speaking to nobody, except sometimes to the poor, and allowing nobody to get to know him. He wore a horrible old yellow coat which was worth millions, being lined all over with bank bills." This decidedly piqued Javert's curiosity. In order to get a close view of this fantastic rich man without frightening him away, one day he borrowed the beadle's old cloak and the place where the old informer would squat every night droning out his orisons and playing the spy as he prayed.

"The suspicious individual" did indeed come to Javert thus disguised and gave him alms; at that moment Javert raised his head, and the shock Jean Valjean received, on thinking that he recognized Javert, Javert received, on thinking that he recognized Jean Valjean.

However, the obscurity might have deceived him; Jean Valjean's death was officially certified; Javert still had serious doubts; and in case of doubt, Javert, a scrupulous man, never collared any man.

He followed the old man to Gorbeau House and got the old woman to talk, which was not at all difficult. She confirmed the story of the coat lined with millions, and told him the episode of the thousand-franc note. She had seen it! She had touched it! Javert hired a room. That very night he installed himself in it. He listened at the mysterious tenant's door, hoping to hear the sound of his voice, but Jean Valjean saw his candle through the keyhole and foiled the spy by keeping silent.

The next day Jean Valjean took off. But the noise of the five-franc piece he had dropped was noticed by the old woman, who, hearing money in motion, suspected that he was going to move out and hurried to warn Javert. At night, when Jean Valjean went out, Javert was waiting for him behind the trees on the boulevard with two men.

Javert had called for assistance from the Prefecture, but he had not given the name of the person he hoped to sieze. That was his secret; and he kept it for three reasons; first, because the least indiscretion might give the alarm to Jean Valjean; next, because the arrest of an escaped convict who was reputed dead, a criminal whom the records of justice had already classified forever as "among malefactors of the most dangerous kind," would be a magnificent success, which the old members of the Parisian police would certainly never leave to a newcomer like Javert, and he feared they would take his convict away from him; finally, because Javert, being an artist, liked surprises. He hated those vaunted successes that are deflowered by talking of them long in advance. He liked to develop his masterpieces in the shadows, and then unveil them suddenly afterward.

Javert had followed Jean Valjean from tree to tree, then from street corner to street corner, and had not lost sight of him a single instant; even in the moments when Jean Valjean felt himself most secure, Javert had his eye on him. Why didn't Javert arrest Jean Valjean? Because he was still in doubt.

It must be remembered that in those days, the police were not exactly able to act with impunity; they were hampered by a free press. Some arbitrary arrests, denounced by the newspapers, had reverberated even as far as the Chamber of Deputies, and made the Prefecture timid. To attack individual liberty was a serious thing. The officers were afraid of making mistakes; the Prefect held them responsible; an error was tantamount to dismissal. Imagine the effect that this brief paragraph, repeated in twenty papers, would have produced in Paris: "Yesterday, an old white-haired grandfather, a respectable person living on his income, who was taking a walk with his eight-year-old granddaughter, was arrested and taken to the Station of the Prefecture as an escaped convict!"

Let us add that Javert had his own personal scruples; the injunctions of his conscience were added to the injunctions of the Prefect. He really was in doubt.

Jean Valjean turned and walked away in the darkness.

Sadness, trouble, anxiety, weight of cares, this new calamity of being obliged to flee by night and to seek a chance asylum in Paris for Cosette and himself, the necessity of adapting his pace to that of a child, all this, even without his knowing it, had changed Jean Valjean's gait, and impressed on his bearing such an appearance of old age that the police, incarnate in Javert, could be deceived, and were. The impossibility of coming too close, his clothing of an old tutor back from exile, Thénardier's statement making him a grandfather; finally, the belief he had died at Toulon, added still more to the growing uncertainty in Javert's mind.

For a moment he had the idea of asking him abruptly for his papers. But if the man were not Jean Valjean, and if the man were not a good old honest man of means, he was probably some sharp customer deeply and skillfully involved in the obscure web of Parisian crime, some dangerous gang leader, who gave alms to conceal his other talents, an old trick. He had comrades, accomplices, emergency lodging in which he would surely hide out. All these detours he was taking in the streets seemed to indicate that he was no simple honest man. To arrest him too soon would be "to kill the goose that laid the golden eggs." What problem could there be in waiting? Javert was very sure that he would not escape.

So he walked on somewhat perplexed, continually pondering this mysterious character.

It was not until quite late, in the Rue de Pontoise, that, thanks to the bright light streaming from a bar, he distinctly recognized Jean Valjean.

In this world there are two beings that shudder to their core: the mother finding her child, and the tiger finding his prey. Javert felt this profound thrill.

As soon as he had positively recognized Jean Valjean,

the intimidating convict, he perceived that they were only three and sent to the commissioner of police on the Rue de Pontoise for reinforcements. Before grabbing a thorny stick, one puts on gloves.

This delay and stopping at the Carrefour Rollin to coordinate with his men made him lose the scent. However, he had very soon guessed that Jean Valjean's first wish would be to put the river between his pursuers and himself. He bowed his head and reflected, like a hound putting his nose to the ground to be sure of the way. Javert, with the integrity of his powerful instinct, went straight to the Pont d'Austerlitz. A word to the toll keeper set him right. "Have you seen a man with a little girl?" "I made him pay two sous," answered the tollman. Javert reached the bridge in time to see Jean Valjean on the other side of the river leading Cosette across the space lit by the moon. He saw him enter the Rue de Chemin-Vert-Saint-Antoine, he thought of the Cul-de-sac Genrot placed there like a trap, and of the only outlet from the Rue Droit-Mur into the Petite Rue Picpus. He put out beaters, as hunters say; he sent one of his men quickly by a detour to guard that outlet. Since a patrol was passing on its way back to its station at the Arsenal, he requisitioned it and took it along with him. In such games soldiers are trumps. Moreover, it is a maxim that to take the boar requires the knowledge of the hunter and the strength of the dogs. With these combinations arranged, feeling that Jean Valjean was caught between the Cul-de-sac Genrot on the right, his officer on the left, and himself, Javert, in the rear, he took a pinch of snuff.

Then he began to play. He enjoyed a ravishing and infernal moment; he let his man get ahead of him, knowing he had him, but wishing to put off as long as possible the moment of arrest, delighting to feel him caught and see him at liberty, fondly gazing at him with the rapture of the spider that lets the fly buzz, or the cat that lets the mouse run. The paw and the talon find a monstrous pleasure in the quivering of the animal imprisoned in their grasp. What delight there is in this suffocation!

Javert was rejoicing. The links of his chain were solidly welded. He was sure of success; now all he had to do was close his hand.

Accompanied as he was, the mere idea of resistance

was impossible, no matter how energetic, how vigorous, and how desperate Jean Valjean might be.

Javert advanced slowly, sounding and poking into all the recesses of the street on his way as he would the pockets of a thief.

When he reached the center of the web, the fly was no longer there.

His exasperation can be imagined.

He questioned his sentinel at the corner of the Rue Droit-Mur and Rue Picpus; this officer, who had remained stock-still at his post, had not seen the man pass.

It sometimes happens that a stag escapes though the hounds are after him; then the oldest hunters do not know what to say. Duvivier, Ligniville, and Desprez are at fault. At a setback like this, Artonge exclaimed, "It is not a stag, it is a sorcerer."

Javert would willingly have said the same.

His disappointment held a moment of despair and fury.

It is certain that Napoleon blundered in the Russian campaign, that Alexander blundered in the war in India, that Caesar blundered in the African war, that Cyrus blundered in the war in Scythia, and that Javert blundered in this campaign against Jean Valjean. He was wrong perhaps to hesitate in recognizing the former convict. The first glance should have been enough for him. He was wrong not to seize him pure and simple in the old wreck of a building. He did wrong in not arresting him when he positively recognized him in the Rue de Pontoise. He was wrong to hold a council with his aides, in full moonlight, in the Carrefour Rollin. Certainly advice is useful, and it is good to know and question those of the dogs that are worthy of credence; but the hunter cannot take too many precautions when he is chasing restless animals, like the wolf and the convict. Javert, through too much forethought in setting his bloodhounds on the track, alarmed his prey by giving him wind of the pursuit and made him start out. He was wrong, above all, when he had regained the scent at the Pont d'Austerlitz, to play the puerile game of holding such a man at the end of a thread. He thought himself stronger than he was and believed he could play mouse with a lion. At the same time, he thought himself too weak when he deemed it necessary to obtain reinforcements. Fatal caution, loss of precious time. Javert made all these blunders, and yet he was nonetheless one of the wisest and most thorough detectives who ever existed. He was, in the full force of the term, what in the hunt is called "a manageable dog." But who is perfect?

Great strategists sometimes nod.

Great blunders are often made, like large ropes, of a multitude of fibers. Take the cable thread by thread, take all the little determining motives separately, you break them one after another, and you say: That is all it is. Braid them and twist them together, they become an enormity; Attila hesitating between Marcian in the East and Valentinian in the West; Hannibal delaying at Capua; Danton falling asleep at Arcis-sur-Aube.

However this may be, even at the moment when he realized that Jean Valjean had escaped him, Javert did not lose his presence of mind. Sure that the convict who had broken out could not be far away, he set watches, arranged traps and ambushes, and searched the neighborhood all night long. The first thing he saw was the tampering with the lamp whose rope was cut. Precious clue, which led him astray, however, by directing his search toward the Cul-de-sac Genrot. In that cul-de-sac there are some rather low walls facing gardens whose limits include some very large uncultivated tracts. Jean Valjean evidently must have fled that way. The fact is that if he had gone down the Cul-de-sac Genrot a bit farther, he would have done so, and would have been lost. Javert explored those gardens and those grounds, as if he were searching for a needle.

At daybreak, he left two intelligent men on watch and returned to the Prefecture of Police, crestfallen as a spy who has been caught by a thief.

Book Six

PETIT-PICPUS

I

PETITE RUE PICPUS, NO. 62.

Half a century ago, nothing was more typical of the ordinary carriage door of the time than that of No. 62 Petite Rue Picpus. This door, usually half open in the most attractive manner, revealed two things that have nothing particularly funereal about them—a court surrounded by vine-covered walls, and the face of a lounging porter. Large trees could be seen over the rear wall. When a beam of sunshine enlivened the court, when a glass of wine enlivened the porter, it was difficult to pass by No. 62 Petite Rue Picpus without carrying away a pleasant memory. It was, however, a somber place you had glimpsed.

The door smiled; the house prayed and wept.

If you succeeded in getting past the porter, which was not easy—which for almost everybody was in fact impossible, since there was an "open-sesame" you had to know—if, having passed the porter, you entered a little vestibule on the right, which led to a stairway squeezed in between two walls, and so narrow that only one person could go by at a time; if you did not allow yourself to be frightened by the canary yellow paint with the chocolate dado extending along the stair wall, if you ventured up, you would pass a first landing, then a second, and reach the second story and a hall where the yellow hue and the chocolate plinth followed you with a calm persistence. Staircase and hall were lit by two handsome windows. The hall rounded a sudden corner and turned dark. If you went around that bend, you came, in a few steps, to a door, all the more mysterious in that it was not quite closed. You pushed it open and found yourself in a little room about six feet square, the floor tiled, washed, neat, and cold, and the walls hung with green-flowered nankeen paper, which cost fifteen cents a roll. A dull white light came from a large window with small panes to the left, which took up the whole width of the room. You looked, you saw no one; you listened, you heard neither a footstep nor any other human sound. The walls were bare; the room had no furniture, not even a chair.

You looked again, and you saw in the wall opposite the door a rectangular opening about a foot square, covered with a grate of crisscrossed iron bars, black, knotted, solid, that formed squares, I almost said meshes, less than an inch across. The little green flowers on the nankeen paper came up calmly and in good order to these iron bars, without being alarmed or scattered by the dismal contact. In case any living being had been so marvelously slim as to attempt to get in or out by the square hole, this grate would have prevented it. It did not let the body through, but it did let the eyes through, that is to say the mind. This seemed to have been thought of, for it had been backed up by a sheet of tin inserted in the wall a little behind it and pierced with a thousand holes more microscopic than those of a sieve. At the bottom of this plate there was an opening cut exactly like the mouth of a letterbox. A metal cord attached to a bell hung to the right of the grated opening.

If you pulled this cord, a bell tinkled and a voice was heard, very close to you, which startled you.

"Who is there?" asked the voice.

It was a woman's voice, a gentle voice, so gentle that it was mournful.

Here again there was a magic word you had to know. If you did not know it, the voice fell mute, and the wall turned silent again as if the startled obscurity of the sepulcher were on the other side.

If you knew the word, the voice replied, "Enter on the right."

Then to your right you noticed, opposite the window, a glazed door topped by a glass panel painted gray. You lifted the latch, you went through the door, and you felt precisely the same impression as when entering an enclosed box at the theater before the grate is lowered and the lights are lit. You were in fact in a sort of theater box, barely visible by the dim light from the glass door, narrow, furnished with two old chairs and a piece of tattered straw matting—a genuine box with its waist-high front bearing a tablet of black wood. This box was grated, but it was not a grate of gilt wood as at the Opera; it was a monstrous trellis of tangled iron bars, fastened to the wall by enormous bolts resembling clenched fists.

After a few minutes, when your eyes began to grow accustomed to the cavernous light, you tried to look through the grate, but could not see more than six inches beyond. There you saw a barrier of black shutters, secured and strengthened by wooden crossbars painted gingerbread-brown. These shutters were hinged, broken into long slender strips, and screened the whole length of the grate. They were always closed.

In a few moments, you heard a voice calling to you from behind these shutters, "I am here. What do you want from me?"

It was a beloved voice, sometimes an adored one. You saw nobody. You hardly heard a breath. It seemed a ghostly voice speaking to you across the portal of the tomb.

If you appeared under certain specific conditions, very rare, the narrow strip of one of these shutters opened in front of you, and the ghostly voice became an apparition. Behind the grate, behind the shutter, you glimpsed, insofar as the grate permitted, a head, of which you saw only the mouth and chin; the rest was covered with a black veil. You would catch a glimpse of a black guimpe and an ill-defined form covered with a black shroud. The head spoke to you, but did not look at you and never smiled at you.

The light coming from behind you was arranged so that you saw her in daylight, and she saw you in darkness. This light was symbolic.

Meantime your eyes gazed eagerly, through the fleeting aperture, into this place closed against all observation.

A profound haze cloaked this form clad in mourning. Your eyes strained into this obscurity, and sought to distinguish things around the apparition. After a little you perceived that you could see nothing. What you saw was night, the void, darkness, a wintry mist mingled with a sepulchral vapor, a sort of terrifying calm, a silence in which you distinguished nothing, not even sighs—a shadow in which you discerned nothing, not even phantoms.

What you saw was the interior of a cloister.

It was the interior of that stern and gloomy house that was called the convent of the Bernardines of the Perpetual Adoration. This box where you were was the locutory. That voice, the first that spoke to you, was the voice of the extern sister, who was always seated, motionless and silent, on the other side of the wall, near the square opening protected by the iron grate and the plate with the thousand holes, as though by a double visor.

The darkness in which the grated box was plunged arose from the fact that the locutory, which had a window toward the outside world, had none on the convent side. Profane eyes must see nothing of this sacred place.

Beyond this shade, however, there was something; there was a light; there was a life within this death. Although this convent was more cloistered than any other, we shall try to penetrate it, to take the reader with us and to relate, as fully as we may, something that storytellers have never seen and consequently never told.

II

THE OBEDIENCE OF MARTIN VERGA

This convent, which in 1824 had existed for many long years in the Petite Rue Picpus, was a community of Bernardines of the Obedience of Martin Verga.

These Bernardines, consequently, were attached, not to Clairvaux, like other Bernardines, but to Cîteaux, like the Benedictines. In other words, they were subjects of Saint Benedict rather than Saint Bernard.

Anyone at all familiar with old folios knows that in 1425 Martin Verga founded a congregation of Bernardine-Benedictines, with their chief convent at Salamanca and a subsidiary at Alcalá.

This congregation had branches in all the Catholic countries of Europe.

These grafts of one order on another are not unusual in

the Roman church. To speak of only a single order of Saint Benedict, the one in question—without counting the Obedience of Martin Verga, this order has four congregations attached to it: two in Italy, Monte Cassino and Santa Giustina of Padua; two in France, Cluny and Saint-Maur; and nine orders, Vallombrosa, Grammont, the Coelestines, the Camaldules, the Carthusians, the Humiliati, the Olivetans, the Sylvestrines, and finally Cîteaux; for Cîteaux itself, the trunk of other orders, is only an offshoot of Saint Benedict. Cîteaux dates back to Saint-Robert, the Abbé of Molesme, in the diocese of Langres in 1098. It was in 529 that the devil, who had retreated to the desert of Subiaco (he was old; had he become a hermit?), was driven from the ancient temple of Apollo, where he was living with Saint Benedict, then seventeen years old.

Next to the rules of the Carmelites, who go barefoot, wear a willow twig around the throat, and never sit down, the most severe rules are those of the Bernardine-Benedictines of Martin Verga. They are clothed in black with a guimpe, which, according to Saint Benedict's specific command, comes up to the chin. A serge dress with wide sleeves, a large woolen veil, the guimpe that rises to the chin, cut square across the breast, and the fillet, which comes down to the eyes, this is their dress. It is all black, except the fillet, which is white. The novices wear the same dress, all in white. The professed nuns also have a rosary by their side.

The Bernardine-Benedictines of Martin Verga perform the devotion of the Perpetual Adoration, as do the Benedictines called Ladies of the Holy Sacrament, who, at the beginning of this century, had two houses in Paris, one at the Temple, the other in the Rue Neuve-Sainte-Geneviève. In other respects the Bernardine-Benedictines of the Petit-Picpus, of whom we are speaking, were an order completely apart from the Ladies of the Holy Sacrament, whose cloisters were in the Rue Neuve-Sainte-Geneviève and at the Temple. There were many differences in their rules, some in their costume. The Bernardine-Benedictines of the Petit-Picpus wore a black guimpe, and the Benedictines of the Holy Sacrament and of the Rue Neuve-Sainte-Geneviève wore a white one and also wore on the chest a crucifix about three inches long in silver or copper gilt. The nuns of the Petit-Picpus did not wear this crucifix. The devotion of the Perpetual Adoration, common to the house of the Petit-Picpus and to the house of the Temple, left the two orders perfectly distinct. There is a similarity only in this respect between the Ladies of the Holy Sacrament and the Bernardines of Martin Verga, even as there is a similarity—in the study and the glorification of all the mysteries related to the infancy, life, and death of Jesus Christ, and to the Virgin—between two other orders widely differing and occasionally inimical: the Oratory of Italy, established in Florence by Philip di Neri, and the Oratory of France, established in Paris by Pierre de Bérulle. The Oratory of Paris claims the precedence, Philip di Neri being only a saint and Bérulle a cardinal.

Let us return to the severe Spanish rules of Martin Verga.

The Bernardine-Benedictines of this Obedience abstain from meat all year, fast during Lent and many other days special to them, rise out of their first sleep at one in the morning to read their breviary and chant matins until three, sleep on straw and in coarse woolen sheets in all seasons, never take baths, never light a fire, scourge themselves every Friday, observe the rule of silence, speak to one another only at recesses, which are very short, and wear a hair shirt for six months, from the fourteenth of September, the Exaltation of the Holy Cross, until Easter. These six months are a modification—the rules say all the year, but this haircloth chemise, intolerable in the heat of summer, produced fevers and nervous spasms. It became necessary to limit its use. Even with this mitigation, after the fourteenth of September, when the nuns put on this chemise, they have three or four days of fever. Obedience, poverty, chastity, permanence in the cloister; such are their vows, rendered much more difficult to fulfill by the rules.

The prioress is elected for three years by the mothers, who are called "vocal mothers," because they have a voice in the chapter. A prioress can be re-elected only twice, which limits the longest possible reign of a prioress to nine years.

They never see the officiating priest, who is always concealed from them by a wool curtain nine feet high. During the sermon, when the celebrating priest is in the chapel, they drop the veil over their faces; they must always speak softly, walk with their eyes on the ground and their head bowed. Only one man may enter the convent; the archbishop of the diocese.

In fact, there is one other, the gardener; but he is always an old man, and so that he is alone in the garden and the nuns may be warned and avoid him, a bell is attached to his knee.

They are subject to the prioress in absolute and passive submission. It is canonical subjection in its full abnegation. As at the voice of Christ, *ut voci Christi,* at a nod, at the first signal, *ad nutum, ad primum signum,* promptly, with pleasure, with perseverance, with a certain blind obedience, *prompte, hilariter, perseveranter, et caeca quadam obedientia,* like the file in the workman's hands, *quasi limam in manibus fabri,* forbidden to read or write without express permission, *legere vel scribere non addiscerit sine expressa superioris licentia.*

Each one of them in turn performed what they call the reparation, a prayer for all sins, for all faults, for all disorders, for all violations, for all iniquities, for all the crimes committed on earth. During twelve consecutive hours, from four o'clock in the afternoon till four o'clock in the morning, or from four o'clock in the morning till four o'clock in the afternoon, the sister who performs the reparation stays on her knees on the stone facing the Holy Sacrament, her hands clasped and a rope around her neck. When fatigue becomes insupportable, she prostrates herself, her face against the ground and her arms stretched out in a cross; this is her only relief. In this attitude, she prays for all the guilty in the universe. This is greatness touching on the sublime.

As this act is performed in front of a post bearing a burning taper they say interchangeably, "to perform the reparation" or "to be at the post." The nuns even prefer, out of humility, this latter expression, which involves an idea of torture and abasement.

"The performance of the reparation" is a process in which the whole soul is absorbed. The sister at the post would not turn around if a thunderbolt were to crash behind her.

In addition, there is always a nun on her knees before the Holy Sacrament. This duty lasts one hour. They are relieved like soldiers standing sentry. That is the Perpetual Adoration.

The prioresses and the mothers almost always have names of particular solemnity, recalling not the saints and the martyrs, but moments in the life of Christ, like Mother Nativity, Mother Conception, Mother Presentation, Mother Passion. The names of saints, however, are not prohibited.

When you see them, you see only the mouth.

They all have yellow teeth. Never did a toothbrush enter the convent. To brush the teeth is the top rung of a ladder whose bottom rung is—to lose the soul.

They never say about anything "my" or "mine." They have nothing of their own and must cherish nothing. They say "our" of everything; thus: "our veil," "our chaplet"; if they speak of their chemise, they say "our chemise." Sometimes they become attached to some little object, to a prayerbook, a relic, or a sacred medal. As soon as they notice that they are beginning to cherish the object, they give it up. They remember the reply of Saint Theresa, to whom a great lady, at the moment of entering her order, said, "Permit me, mother, to send for a holy Bible that I cherish very much." "Ah! you cherish something! In that case, do not enter our house."

None are allowed to shut themselves up and to have a home, a room. They live in open cells. When they meet one another, one says, "Praise and adoration to the Most Holy Sacrament of the altar!" The other responds, "Forever." The same ceremony when one knocks at another's door. Hardly is the door touched when a gentle voice is heard from the other side quickly saying, "Forever." Like all rituals, this becomes mechanical from habit; and one sometimes says "Forever" before the other has had time to say, what is actually rather long, "Praise and adoration to the Most Holy Sacrament of the altar!"

Among the Visitandines, the one who comes in says, "Ave Maria," and the one to whose cell she comes says, "Gratia plena." This is their good morning, which is, in fact, "full of grace."

At each hour of the day, three supplementary strokes sound from the bell of the convent church. At this signal, prioress, mothers, professed nuns, sister servants, novices, postulants, all break off from what they are saying, doing, or thinking, and say at once, if it is five o'clock, for example, "At five o'clock and at all times, praise and adoration to the Most Holy Sacrament of the altar!" If it is eight o'clock, "At eight and at all times," etc., and so on, according to whatever hour it may be.

This custom, intended to interrupt the thoughts and lead them back constantly to God, exists in many communities; only the formula varies. Thus, at the Infant Jesus, they say: "At the present hour and at all hours may the love of Jesus kindle my heart!"

The Benedictine-Bernardines of Martin Verga, cloistered fifty years ago in the Petit-Picpus, chant the offices in a grave psalmody, pure plain song, and always in full voice for the duration of the office. Wherever there is an asterisk in the missal, they pause and say in a low tone, "Jesus—Mary—Joseph." For the office for the dead, they take a pitch so low it is difficult for female voices to reach it. The effect is gripping and tragic.

The nuns of the Petit-Picpus had had a vault made under their high altar for the burial of their community. The "government," as they call it, did not permit corpses to be deposited in this vault. Therefore they were taken from the convent when they died. This distressed and horrified them, violating their sanctity.

They had obtained—small consolation—the privilege of being buried at a special hour and in a special place in the old Vaugirard Cemetery, located in ground formerly belonging to the Community.

On Thursday these nuns heard high mass, vespers, and all the offices as on Sunday. In addition they scrupulously observed all the little feast days, almost unknown to the people of the outer world, but which used to abound within the church in France and still do in Spain and Italy. Their hours in chapel are interminable. As to the number and duration of their prayers, we cannot give a better idea than by quoting the candid words of one of them: "The prayers of the postulants are frightful, the prayers of the novices worse, and the prayers of the professed nuns still worse."

Once a week the chapter assembles; the prioress presides, the vocal mothers attend. Each sister comes in turn, kneels on the stone, and confesses aloud, before everyone, the faults and sins she has committed during the week. The mothers consult together after each confession and announce the penalty aloud.

In addition to open confession, for which they reserve all somewhat serious faults, they have for venial faults what they call the *culpa*. To perform the *culpa* is to prostrate yourself face down during the service, before the prioress until she, who is never spoken of except as "our mother," indicates to the sinner, by a gentle rap on the side of your stall, that you may rise. The *culpa* is performed for very petty things; a broken glass, a torn veil, an involuntary delay of a few seconds at a service, a false note in church, etc.,—they are enough for the *culpa*. The *culpa* is entirely spontaneous; it is the *culpable* herself (this word is here etymologically correct) who judges herself and inflicts it on herself. On feast days and Sundays there are four chorister mothers who sing the offices in front of a large lectern with four music stands. One day a mother chorister intoned a psalm that began with *Ecce,* and, instead of *Ecce,* she pronounced out loud these three notes: *do, si, sol;* for this lapse she underwent a *culpa* that lasted through the whole service. What made the fault particularly egregious was that the chapter had laughed.

When a nun is called to the locutory, be it even the prioress, she drops her veil, it will be remembered, in such a way as to show nothing but her mouth.

The prioress alone can communicate with strangers. The others can see only their immediate family, and that very rarely. If by chance persons from the outside seek admission to see a nun whom they knew or loved in the world, formal negotiations are necessary. If it is a woman, permission may sometimes be granted; the nun comes and is spoken to through the shutters, which are never opened except for a mother or sister. It goes without saying that permission is always refused to men.

Such are the rules of Saint Benedict, intensified by Martin Verga.

These nuns are not joyous, rosy, and cheerful, as the daughters of the other orders often are. They are pale and serious. Between 1825 and 1830 three went insane.

III

SEVERITIES

A postulancy of at least two years is required, often four; a novitiate of four years. It is rare that the final vows can be pronounced under the age of twenty-three or twenty-four. The Bernardine-Benedictines of Martin Verga admit no widows into their order.

In their cells they subject themselves to many self-mortifications of which they must never speak.

The day on which a novice makes her profession she is dressed in her finest attire, her head decked with white roses, her hair glossy and curled; then she prostrates herself; a great black veil is spread over her, and the office for the dead is chanted. The nuns then divide into two files; one passes near her, saying in plaintive accents, "Our sister is dead," and the other responds in ringing tones, "Living in Jesus Christ!"

At the time of this story, a boarding school was attached to the convent. A school for young nobility, for the most part rich, among whom were noticeable Mesdemoiselles De Sainte-Aulaire and De Bélissen, and an English girl bearing the illustrious Catholic name of Talbot. These young girls, reared by the nuns between four walls, grew up in horror of the world and of the age. One of them said to us one day, "Seeing the open street made me shiver from head to foot." They were dressed in blue with a white cap and a Holy Spirit, in silver or copper gilt, on their breast. On certain high feast days, particularly on Saint Martha's day, they were allowed, as a great favor and supreme pleasure, to dress as nuns and perform the offices and the ritual of Saint Benedict for a whole day. At first the professed nuns lent them their black garments. That appeared profane, and the prioress forbade it. The loan was permitted only to novices. It is remarkable that these representations, undoubtedly tolerated and encouraged in the convent by a secret spirit of proselytism, and to give these children some foretaste of the holy habit, were a real pleasure and genuine recreation for the students. They were simply having fun. "It was new; it was a change." Candid thinking of childhood, which fails, however, to help us worldly ones understand the joy of holding a holy aspergillum in hand, and remaining standing hours at a time singing with three others in front of a lectern.

The pupils, austerities excepted, conformed to all the rituals of the convent. There are young women like this who, back in the world and after several years of marriage, have still not managed to break off the habit of quickly saying, to any knock at the door, "Forever!" Like the nuns, the boarders saw their relatives only in the locutory. Not even their mothers were permitted to embrace them. Strictness on this point was carried to the following extreme: One day a young girl was visited by her mother accompanied by a little sister three years old. The young girl wept, for she wanted very much to kiss her sister. Impossible. She begged that the child at least be permitted to pass her little hand through the bars so she might kiss it. This was refused almost with indignation.

IV

GAIETIES

The young girls have nonetheless filled the solemn house with charming memories.

At certain hours, childhood sparkled in this cloister. The recess bell would ring. A door swung on its hinges. The birds said, Good! Here come the children! An eruption of youth flooded the garden, which was cut by walks in the form of a cross, like a shroud. Radiant faces, white foreheads, frank eyes full of cheerful light, auroras of all sorts scattered through this darkness. After the chants, the bell ringing, the knells, and the offices, all at once this hum of little girls burst forth sweeter than the hum of bees. The hive of joy opened, and each one brought her honey. They played, they called to one another, they formed into groups, they ran; pretty little white teeth chatted in the corners; from a distance veils watched over the laughter, shadows spying the sunshine, but no matter! They sparkled, they laughed. These four dismal walls had their dazzling moments dimly lit by the reflection of so much joy; they too shared in this sweetly swarming whirlwind. It was like a spray of roses at a funeral. The young girls frolicked under the eyes of the nuns; the gaze of sinlessness does not disturb innocence. Thanks to these children, among so many hours of austerity, there was this one hour of artlessness. The little girls skipped, the larger ones danced. In this cloister, play was mingled with heaven. Nothing was so entrancing and exquisite as all these fresh, blooming souls. Homer might have laughed there with Perrault, and in this dark garden there were enough of youth, health, noise, cries, uproar, pleasure, happiness to smooth the wrinkles off all the old ladies from epics to fairy tales, palaces and huts, Hecuba to Mother Goose.

In this house, more than anywhere else, perhaps, have been heard those charming children's sayings that provoke a pensive laugh. It was within these four forbidding walls that a child of five years exclaimed one day, "Mother, a big girl has just told me I have only nine years and ten months more here. How wonderful!"

It was here, too, that this memorable dialogue occurred:

A MOTHER—"What are you crying for, dear?"

THE CHILD (six years old), sobbing—"I told Alice I knew my French history. She says I don't know it, but I do."

ALICE, older (nine years)—"No, she doesn't."

THE MOTHER—"Why, dear?"

ALICE—"She told me to open the book anywhere and ask her any question there was in the book, and she could answer it."

"Well?"

"She didn't answer it."

"Let's see. What did you ask her?"

"I opened the book anywhere, just as I said, and I asked her the first question I found."

"And what was the question?"

"It was: What happened next?"

And it was here that this profound observation was made about a rather dainty parrot, belonging to a lady boarder, "Isn't she nice! She picks off the top of her tart, just like a lady."

From one of the cloister flagstones, the following

confession was picked up, written beforehand, so as not to be forgotten, by a little seven-year-old sinner.

"Father, I accuse myself of having been avaricious.

"Father, I accuse myself of having been adulterous.

"Father, I accuse myself of having raised my eyes toward the gentlemen."

On one of the grassy banks of this garden, the following story was improvised by a rosy six-year-old mouth and listened to by blue eyes four and five years old:

"There were three little chickens who lived in a country where there were many, many flowers. They picked the flowers and they put them in their pockets. After that, they picked the leaves, and they put them with their toys. There was a wolf in the country, and there were many many woods; and the wolf was in the woods; and he ate up the little chickens."

And again, this other poem:

"Once something was hit with a stick.
It was Punch batting the cat.
It did him no good and hurt her a lot.
Then a lady put Punch into prison."

It was there, too, that these sweet and heartrending words were said by a little foundling whom the convent was rearing through charity. She heard the others talking about their mothers, and in her little nook she whispered, "As for me, my mother wasn't there when I was born."

There was a fat extern, Sister Agatha, always hurrying through the corridors with her bunch of keys. The very old girls—over ten, called her Agathokeys.

The refectory, a large rectangular room, which received light only from a cloister window with a fluted arch at garden level, was dark and damp, and, as the children said, full of beasts. All the surroundings bequeathed it their contingents of insects. Because of this each of its corners had been given in the pupils' language a peculiar and expressive name. There was the spiders' corner, the caterpillars' corner, the wood lice's corner, and the crickets' corner. The crickets' corner was near the kitchen and was highly desirable. It was not as cold as the others. From the refectory the names had moved over to the school room and served to distinguish there, as at the old Mazarin College, four nations. Each pupil belonged to one of these four nations according to the corner of the refectory in which she sat at meals. One day, the archbishop, making his pastoral visit, saw a pretty little blushing girl with beautiful fair hair going into a classroom, and he asked another student, a charming fresh-cheeked brunette, who was near him, "What is that little girl?"

"She's a spider, Monseigneur."

"Well, now, and that other one?"

"A cricket."

"And that one?"

"A caterpillar."

"Well now! And what might you be?"

"I'm a wood louse, Monseigneur."

Every house like this has its peculiarities. Early in this century, Ecouen was one of those serene and graceful places where, in an aura that was almost noble, young girls spent their childhood. At Ecouen, by way of ranking the procession of the Holy Sacrament, they made a distinction between the "virgins" and the "florists." There were also the "canopies" and the "censers," the former carrying the cords of the canopy, the latter swinging censers before the Holy Sacrament. The flowers came back by right to the florists. Four "virgins" walked at the head of the procession. On the morning of the great day, it was not uncommon to hear the question in the dormitory.

"Who here is a virgin?"

Madame Campan reports that a "little girl" seven years old said to a "big girl" of sixteen who was leading the procession, while she, the little one, remained in the rear, "You're a virgin, but not me."

V

DISTRACTIONS

Above the refectory door was written in large black letters this prayer, which was called "the white Paternoster," and which possessed the virtue of leading people straight to Paradise:

"Little white paternoster, which God made, which God said, which God put in Paradise. Going to bed at night, I finded [*sic*] three angels lying on my bed, one at the foot, two at the head, the good Virgin Mary in the middle, who told me I should go to bed, that nothing be bad. The good Lord is my father, the Holy Virgin is my mother, the three apostles are my brothers, the three virgins are my sisters. The shirt in which our God was born is the one that I have worn; the cross of Saint Marguerite is written on my breast, Madame the Virgin goes off through the fields, weeping for God, meeting Monsieur Saint John. Monsieur Saint John, where have you come from? I come from *Ave Salus*. You have not seen the good Lord, have you? He is on the tree of the cross, his feet hanging, his hands nailing, a little hat of white thorns on his head. Whoever shall say this three times at night, three times in the morning, will win Paradise at last."

In 1827, this distinctive orison had disappeared from the wall under a triple layer of paint. Today, it is fading away in the memory of a few young girls of that day, old ladies now.

A large crucifix hanging on the wall completed the decoration of this refectory, whose only door, as we believe we said, opened onto the garden. Two narrow tables, each with two wooden benches down their sides, extended from one end to the other of the refectory in two long parallel lines. The walls were white, and the tables black; these two colors of mourning are the only variety in convents. The meals were coarse, and the diet of even the children strict. A single plate, meat and vegetables together, or salt fish, constituted the fare. This brief meal was, however, an exception, reserved for the students alone. The children ate in silence, under the watchful eyes of the mother for the week, who if a fly now and then ventured to buzz against the rules, opened and clapped shut a wooden book. This silence was seasoned with the Lives of the Saints, read aloud from a little reading desk placed at the foot of the crucifix. The reader was an older pupil, selected for the week. At intervals along the bare table, there were glazed pottery bowls, in which each pupil washed her cup and dish herself, and sometimes threw in bits of refuse, tough meat or tainted fish, and was punished. These bowls were called "water basins."

A child who broke the silence made a "tongue cross." Where? On the floor. She licked the tiles. Dust, that end to all joys, was chastising poor little rosebuds guilty of chatter.

In the convent there was the only copy ever printed of a book no one was allowed to read. It was the Rules of Saint Benedict, arcana that no profane eye might see. *Nemo regulas, seu constitutiones nostras, externis communicabit.*

One day the students succeeded in filching the book and began eagerly reading it, a process frequently interrupted by fears of being caught, which made them hastily close the volume. But from this huge risk they derived small pleasure. A few unintelligible pages about the sins of young boys were what they found "most interesting."

They played in a garden walk bordered by several puny fruit trees. Despite the close watch and severe punishments, when the wind had shaken the trees, they sometimes succeeded in furtively picking up a green apple, a half-rotten apricot, or a worm-eaten pear. But I will turn to a letter I have in hand, written twenty-five years ago by a former pupil, now Madame la Duchesse ——, one of the most elegant women of Paris. I quote verbatim: "We hide our pear or our apple any way we can. When we go up to spread the covers on our beds before supper, we put them under our pillows, and at night eat them in bed, and when we cannot do that, we eat them in the lavatories." This was one of their liveliest pleasures.

Another time, also on the occasion of a visit of the archbishop to the convent, one of the young girls, Mademoiselle Bouchard, related to the Montmorencies, bet she would ask leave of absence for a day, a dreadful thing in such an austere community. The bet was accepted, but not one of those who took it up believed she would dare do it. When the moment came, as the archbishop was walking past the scholars, Mademoiselle Bouchard, to the indescribable dismay of her companions, left the ranks and said, "Monseigneur, leave of absence for a day." Mademoiselle Bouchard was tall and fresh-looking, with the prettiest little rosy face in the world. M. De Quélen smiled and said, "My dear child, leave of absence for a day! Three days, if you like. I grant you three days." The prioress could do nothing; the archbishop had spoken. A scandal to the convent but joy for the school. Imagine the effect.

This rigid cloister was not, however, so completely walled in that the passions of the outside world—drama, romance even—did not penetrate. To prove this, we will merely state briefly an actual, incontestable fact, though it has no intrinsic relationship to our story, not being attached by so much as a thread. We mention this merely to complete the picture of the convent in the mind of the reader.

There was about that time, then, in the convent, a mysterious person, not a nun, who was treated with great respect, known as Madame Albertine. Nothing was known about her, except that she was insane and that in the outside world she was thought to be dead. There were, it was said, involved in her story, some financial arrangements necessary for a great marriage.

This woman, a scant thirty years old, a beautiful brunette, stared hazily out of large black eyes. Was she looking at anything? No one knew. She would glide along rather than walk; she never spoke; it was not quite certain that she breathed. Her nostrils were thin and pale as though she had sighed her last. To touch her hand was touching snow. She had a strange ghostly grace. Wherever she went, people felt cold. One day, a sister seeing her go by, said to another, "She passes for dead." "Perhaps she is," answered the other.

Hundreds of stories were told about Madame Albertine. She was the eternal subject of curiosity among the boarders. In the chapel there was a gallery, which was called *l'Oeil-de-Boeuf*. In this gallery, which had only one circular opening, an *oeil-de-boeuf,* Madame Albertine attended the services. She was usually alone there, because from this gallery, which was elevated, the preacher or the officiating priest could be seen, which was forbidden to the nuns. One day, the pulpit was occupied by a young priest of high rank, the Duc de Rohan, a peer of France, who had been an officer of the Mousquetaires Rouges in 1815 when he was Prince de Léon, and who died afterward in 1830, a cardinal and Archbishop of Besançon. This was the first time that M. de Rohan had preached in the convent of the Petit-Picpus. Madame Albertine ordinarily attended the sermons and the offices with perfect calm and complete silence. That day, as soon as she saw M. de Rohan, she half rose, and in the stillness of the chapel, exclaimed out loud: "What? Auguste?" Astounded, the whole community turned their heads; the preacher raised his eyes, but Madame Albertine had fallen back into her motionless silence. A breath from the world outside, a glimmer of life, had passed for a moment across that dead and icy form, then all had vanished, and the lunatic had again become a corpse.

These two words, however, set everybody in the convent who could speak to chattering. How much there was in that "What? Auguste?" How many revelations! M. de Rohan's name was, in fact, Auguste. It was clear that Madame Albertine came from the highest society, since she knew M. de Rohan; that she had occupied a high position herself, since she spoke of so great a noble with such familiarity; and that she had some connection with him, of relationship perhaps, but beyond all doubt very intimate, since she knew his first name.

Two very strict duchesses, Mesdames de Choiseul and de Sérent, often visited the community, undoubtedly admitted by virtue of the privilege of *Magnates mulieres,* to the great terror of the school. When the two old ladies went by, all the poor young girls trembled and lowered their eyes.

M. de Rohan was, moreover, without knowing it, the object of the attention of the schoolgirls. At that time he had just been made, while waiting for the episcopacy, vicar-general of the Archbishop of Paris. He was in the habit of coming quite often to chant the offices in the chapel of the nuns of the Petit-Picpus. None of the young recluses could see him, because of the serge curtain, but he had a gentle, penetrating voice, which they came to recognize and distinguish. He had been a musketeer; and then he was very attractive, with beautiful chestnut hair, which he wore in curls, and a magnificent wide black sash, while his black cassock was of the most elegant cut imaginable. He loomed large in these sixteen-year-old imaginations.

No sound from outside penetrated the convent. There was, however, one year when the sound of a flute was heard, an event still remembered by the pupils of the time.

It was a flute played by somebody in the neighborhood,

always the same tune, one long since forgotten: "My Zétulbé, Come Reign o'er My Soul," and they heard it two or three times a day.

The young girls spent hours listening, the mothers were distracted, heads were spinning, punishments rained down. This lasted for several months. The pupils were all more or less in love with the unknown musician. Each one imagined herself Zétulbé. The sound of the flute came from the direction of the Rue Droit-Mur; they would have given anything, sacrificed everything, dared all to see, if only for a second, to catch a glimpse of the "young man" who played so deliciously on that flute and who, completely unaware, was playing at the same time on all their hearts. There were some who escaped by a service entrance, and climbed up to the fourth floor on the Rue Droit-Mur during leisure time, in the attempt to see him. Impossible. One went so far as to reach her arm above her head through the grate and wave her white handkerchief. Two were bolder still. They found a way to climb to the top of a roof at some risk, and finally succeeded in seeing the young man, who was in fact an old gentleman back from exile, ruined and blind, who was playing on the flute in his garret to wile away the time.

VI

THE LITTLE CONVENT

Within this enclosure of the Petit-Picpus there were three distinct buildings, the Great Convent in which the nuns lived, the school building in which the pupils lodged, and finally what was called the Little Convent. This was a separate building with a garden, in which many old nuns of various orders, remnants of cloisters destroyed by the Revolution, lived in common; a medley of all shades, black, gray, and white, from all the communities and of all possible varieties—what might be called, if such a coupling of names were not disrespectful, a motley convent.

From the time of the Empire, all these poor scattered and desolate maidens had been permitted to take shelter under the wings of the Benedictine-Bernardines. The government paid them a small pension; the ladies of the Petit-Picpus had received them eagerly. It was a bizarre mixture. Each followed her own rules. Sometimes the schoolgirls were permitted, as a special treat, to pay them a visit, so the young retained a recollection, among others, of Holy Mother Bazile, of Holy Mother Scholastique, and of Mother Jacob.

One of these refugees found herself virtually back in her own home. She was a nun of Sainte-Aure, the only one of her order who survived. At the beginning of the eighteenth century, the former convent of the Ladies of Sainte-Aure occupied this same house of the Petit-Picpus, which afterward belonged to the Benedictines of Martin Verga. This holy maiden, too poor to wear the magnificent dress of her order, which was a white robe with a scarlet scapular, had piously clothed a little image with it, which she willingly showed, and which she bequeathed to the house. In 1824, there remained of this order only one nun; today there remains only a doll.

In addition to these worthy mothers, a few old women of high society had obtained the prioress's permission, as had Madame Albertine, to retire to the Little Convent. Among the number were Madame de Beaufort d'Hautpoul, and Madame la Marquise Dufresne. Another was known in the convent only by the tremendous noise she made blowing her nose. The pupils called her Racketini.

About 1820 or 1821, Madame de Genlis, who at that time was editing a little magazine called *l'Intrépide*, asked permission to occupy a room at the convent of the Petit-Picpus. Monsieur the Duc d'Orléans recommended her. A buzzing in the hive; the mothers were all aquiver; Madame de Genlis had written novels, but she declared that she was the first to despise them, and then she had reached her phase of fierce devotion. God willing, and the prince as well, she entered.

After six or eight months she left, giving as a reason that the garden had no shade. The nuns were delighted. Though very old, she still played on the harp, and that very well.

On her departure, she left her mark on her cell. Madame de Genlis was superstitious and fond of Latin. These two traits give a rather good notion of her. A few years ago there could still be seen pasted up in a little wardrobe in her cell, where she locked up her money and jewelry, these five Latin lines written in her hand with red ink on yellow paper, and which, in her view, possessed the virtue of frightening away thieves:

> Imparibus meritis pendent tria corpora ramis:
> Dismas et Gesmas, media est divina potestas;
> Alta petit Dismas, infelix, infima, Gesmas;
> Nos et res nostras conservet summa potestas,
> Hos versus dicas, ne tu furto tua perdas.

These lines in sixth-century Latin, raise the question as to whether the names of the two thieves of Calvary were, as is commonly believed, Dimas and Gestas, or Dismas and Gesmas. This latter spelling would work against the Vicomte de Gestas' claim, in the last century, to be a descendant of the unrepentant thief. The useful virtue attributed to these lines was an article of faith in the order of the Hospitallers.

The church of the convent, built in such a way as to truly separate the Great Convent from the school, was, of course, common to the school, the Great Convent, and the Little Convent. The public was even admitted by an isolated entrance opening off the street. But everything was arranged so that none of the cloister inmates could see any face from the outside. Imagine a church, whose choir is seized by a gigantic hand and bent around to form, not, as in ordinary churches, a prolongation behind the altar, but a sort of room or dark cavern to the right of the priest; imagine this room closed off by the curtain seven feet high already mentioned; gather together in the shadow of this curtain on wooden stalls the nuns of the choir on the left, the pupils on the right, the sister servants and novices in the rear, and you will have some idea of the nuns of the Petit-Picpus attending divine service. This cavern, which was called the choir, communicated with the cloister by a narrow passage. The church received daylight from the garden. When the nuns were attending services in which their rules ordered silence, the public was advised of their presence only by the sound of the rising and falling stall-seats.

VII

A FEW OUTLINES AMONG THE SHADOWS

From 1819 to 1825, the prioress of the Petit-Picpus was Mademoiselle de Blemeur, whose religious name was Mother Innocent. She came from the family of Marguerite de Blemeur, author of the *Lives of the Saints of the Order of Saint Benedict*. She had been re-elected. A woman about sixty, short, fat, "chanting like a cracked kettle," says the letter from which we have already quoted, but an excellent woman, the only cheerful one in the whole convent, and on that account adored.

Mother Innocent was like her ancestor Marguerite, the Dacier of the Order. She was well-read, erudite, learned, skillful, curious about history, stuffed with Latin, crammed with Greek, full of Hebrew, and rather more a monk than a nun.

The subprioress was an old Spanish nun who was almost blind, named Mother Cineres.

Notable among the mothers were Mother Sainte-Honorine, the treasurer; Mother Sainte-Gertrude, first mistress of the novices; Mother Sainte-Ange, second mistress; Mother Annunciation, sacristan; Mother Sainte-Augustin, nurse, the only nun in the convent who was bad-humored; then Mother Sainte-Mechthilde (Mlle. Gauvain), quite young and with a wonderful voice; Mother des-Anges (Mlle. Drouet), who had been in the convent of the Filles-Dieu and in the convent of the Trésor, between Gisors and Magny; Mother Saint-Joseph (Mlle. de Cogolludo), Mother Sainte-Adelaide (Mlle. d'Auverney), Mother Miséricorde (Mlle. de Cifuentes, who had difficulty enduring the austerities), Mother Compassion (Mlle. de la Miltière, received at sixty in spite of the rules, very rich); Mother Providence (Mlle. de Laudinière), Mother Présentation (Mlle. de Siguenza), who was prioress in 1847; finally, Mother Sainte-Céligne (sister of the sculptor Ceracchi), who went insane; Mother Sainte-Chantal (Mlle. de Suzon), who also went mad.

Among the prettiest there was a charming girl of twenty-three from the Isle of Bourbon, a descendant of the Chevalier Roze, who was called in the outside world Mlle. Roze and who called herself Mother Assumption.

Mother Sainte-Mechthilde, who had charge of the singing and the choir, gladly made use of the pupils. She usually took the full scale of them, that is to say, seven, from ten years old to sixteen inclusive, of graduated voice and size, and had them sing, standing in a row, arranged according to their age from the smallest to the tallest. To the eye this offered something like a harp of young girls, a sort of Pan pipe made of angels.

Those of the servant sisters whom the pupils liked best were Sister Sainte-Euphrasie, Sister Sainte-Marguerite, Sister Sainte-Marthe, who was in her dotage, and Sister Sainte-Michael, whose long nose made them laugh.

All these women were gentle with all the children. The nuns were severe only with themselves. The only fires were in the school building; and the food, compared with that of the convent, was choice. Besides that, they received a thousand little attentions. Except that when a child went past a nun and spoke to her, the nun never answered.

This rule of silence had had the effect that, throughout the convent, speech was taken from human creatures and given to inanimate objects. Sometimes it was the church-bell that spoke, sometimes the gardener's knee bell. A deep-sounding bell, placed beside the extern sister and heard all over the house, indicated by its variations, which were a kind of acoustic telegraph, all the acts of material life to be performed, and it called to the locutory, if need be, this or that inhabitant of the house. Each person and each thing had its special ring. The prioress had one and one; the subprioress one and two. Six-five announced class time, so the pupils never said "going to class" but "going to six-five." Four-four was Madame de Genlis's signal. It was heard very often. "It's the four of hearts," said the uncharitable. Nineteen strokes announced a great event. It was the opening of the enclosure door, a fearful iron plank bristling with bolts that swung open only for the archbishop.

Except for him and the gardener, as we have said, no man ever entered the convent. The pupils saw two others; one, the chaplain, the Abbé Banès, old and ugly, whom they had the privilege of contemplating through a grate in the choir; the other, the art teacher, M. Ansiaux, whom the letter already quoted calls M. Anciot, and describes as a "horrid old hunchback."

We can see that all the men were carefully selected.

Such was this odd house.

VIII

POST CORDA LAPIDES

After sketching its moral features, it might be useful to give a few words to its material configuration. The reader already has some idea of it.

The convent of the Petit-Picpus-Saint-Antoine almost entirely filled up the large trapezoid formed by the intersection of the Rue Polonceau, the Rue Droit-Mur, the Petite Rue Picpus, and the dead end alley called Rue Aumarais on the old maps. These four streets surrounded this trapezoid like a moat. The convent was composed of several buildings and a garden. The principal building, taken as a whole, was an aggregation of hybrid constructions, which, from a bird's-eye view, presented quite accurately the shape of a gallows laid down on the ground.

The long arm of the gallows extended all along the Rue Droit-Mur between the Petite Rue Picpus and the Rue Polonceau; the short arm was a tall, gray, severe façade with barred windows overlooking the Petite Rue Picpus; the carriage door, No. 62, marked the end of it. Toward the middle of this façade, dust and ashes had whitened an old low-arched door (spiders made their webs there), which was opened only for an hour or two on Sunday and on the rare occasions when a nun's coffin was taken out of the convent. It was the public entrance of the church. The elbow of the gallows was a square hall, which served as pantry and which the nuns called the dispensary. In the long arm were the cells of the mothers, sisters, and novices. In the short arm were the kitchens, the refectory, with the cloister alongside it, and the church. Between door No. 62 and the corner of the closed Ruelle Aumarais was the school, which could not be seen from the outside. The rest of the trapezoid was the garden, much lower than the level of the Rue Aumarais, so the walls were considerably higher on the inside than on the outside. The garden, slightly convex, had on top of a center knoll a beautiful fir, pointed and conical, from which, as from the center of a shield, four broad walks fanned out and, arranged two by two between the broad walks, eight narrow ones, so that if the enclosure had been circular, the geometrical plan of the walks would have looked like a cross placed over a wheel. The walks, all extending to the very irregular garden walls, were of unequal length. They were bordered with gooseberry bushes. At the far end of the garden a row of tall poplars extended from the ruins of the old convent, which was at the corner of the Rue Droit-Mur, to the house of the Little Convent, which was at the corner of the Ruelle Aumarais. In front of the Little Convent was what was called the Little Garden. Add to this outline a courtyard, all sorts of angles made by interior buildings, prison walls, no view, and no neighborhood except for the long line of black roofs that ran along the other side of the Rue Polonceau, and you can form a complete image of the house of the Bernardines of the Petit-Picpus forty-five years ago. This holy house had been built on the exact site of a famous tennis court, which existed from the fourteenth to the sixteenth century, and which was called "the court of the eleven thousand devils."

All these streets, moreover, were among the oldest in Paris. These names, Droit-Mur and Aumarais, are very old; the streets bearing them are much older still. The Ruelle Aumarais was called the Ruelle Maugout; the Rue Droit-Mur was called the Rue des Eglantiers, because God opened the flowers before man cut the paving blocks.

IX

A CENTURY UNDER A GUIMPE

Since we are dealing with details of what was formerly the convent of the Petit-Picpus and have ventured to open a window on that secluded refuge, the reader will pardon us another little digression; foreign to the object of this book but characteristic and useful, it teaches us that the cloister itself has spawned unique characters.

In the Little Convent there was a centenarian who came from the Abbey of Fontevrault. Before the Revolution she had even been in society. She often spoke of M. de Miromesnil, keeper of the seals under Louis XVI, and of the lady of a Judge Duplat, whom she had known very well. It was her pleasure and her vanity to bring up these names on every possible occasion. She told wonders of the Abbey of Fontevrault, that it was like a city and that there were streets within the convent.

She spoke with a Picardy accent that delighted the pupils. Every year she solemnly renewed her vows, and, at the moment of taking the oath, she would say to the priest, "Monseigneur Saint Francis ceded it to Monseigneur Saint Julian, Monseigneur Saint Julian ceded it to Monseigneur Saint Eusebius, Monseigneur Saint Eusebius ceded it to Monseigneur Saint Procopius, etc., etc.; so I cede it to you, my father." And the pupils would laugh at what sounded a bit like a series of sneezes, charming little stifled laughs that made the mothers frown.

Another time, the centenarian was telling stories. She said that in her youth the Bernardins lived as freely as the Musketeers. It was a century that was speaking, but it was the eighteenth century. She told of the custom in Champagne and Burgundy, before the Revolution, of the four wines. When a great figure, a marshal of France, a prince, a duke, or peer, passed through a city of Burgundy or Champagne, the corporation of the city turned out to deliver an address and present him with four silver goblets in which were four different wines. On the first goblet he read the inscription "monkey wine," on the second "lion wine," on the third "sheep wine," on the fourth "swine wine." These four inscriptions expressed the four descending degrees of drunkenness: the first, which enlivens; the second, which irritates; the third, which stupefies; finally the last, which brutalizes.

In a cupboard under lock and key she had a mysterious object, which she cherished. The rules of Fontevrault did not prohibit it. She would not show this object to anybody. She shut herself in, which her rules permitted, and hid whenever she wanted to look at it. If she heard a step in the hall, she would shut the cupboard as quickly as her old hands would allow. The moment anybody spoke to her about this, she was silent, although she was so fond of talking. The most curious were foiled by her silence, and the most persevering by her obstinacy. This also was a topic of comment for all who were idle or listless in the convent. What on earth could this thing be, so secret and so precious, the centenarian's treasure? Undoubtedly, some sacred book, some unique chaplet or some proven relic? They were lost in conjecture. On the poor old woman's death they ran to the cupboard, sooner, perhaps, than was seemly, and opened it. The object of their curiosity was found under triple cloths, like a blessed paten. It was a faience plate, representing cupids in flight, pursued by apothecaries' boys, armed with enormous syringes. The pursuit is full of grimaces and comic postures. One of the charming little cupids is already spitted. He struggles, shakes his little wings, and still tries to fly away, but the buffoon responds with satanic laughter. Moral: love conquered by colic. This plate, actually very strange, may have had the distinction of giving an idea to Molière. The plate still existed in September 1845; it was for sale in a secondhand store in the Boulevard Beaumarchais.

This good old woman would accept no visit from the outside world, "Because," she said, "the locutory is too gloomy."

X

ORIGIN OF THE PERPETUAL ADORATION

That almost sepulchral locutory, which we have tried to sketch, is an entirely local feature, not duplicated with the same severity in other convents. At the convent of the Rue du Temple in particular, which to be sure belonged to another order, the black shutters were replaced by brown curtains and the locutory itself was a nicely parqueted parlor, whose windows were graciously draped with white muslin, while the walls displayed a variety of pictures, a portrait of a Benedictine nun with uncovered face, paintings of flowers, and even a Turk's head.

It was in the garden of the convent of the Rue du Temple that the horse chestnut tree stood that was considered the most beautiful and the largest in France and, among the good people of the eighteenth century, was called "the father of all the horse chestnuts in the kingdom."

As we have said, this convent of the Temple was occupied by the Benedictines of the Perpetual Adoration, quite distinct from the Benedictines who spring from Citeaux. That order of the Perpetual Adoration is not very old and does not date back more than two hundred years. In 1649, the Holy Sacrament was profaned twice, within a few days, in two churches in Paris—at Saint-Sulpice, and at Saint-Jean en Grève—a rare and terrible sacrilege that shocked the whole city. The Prior Vicar General of Saint-Germain-des-Prés ordered a solémn procession of all his clergy, in which la Papal Nuncio officiated. But this expiation was not sufficient for two noblewomen, Mme. Courtin, Marquise de Boucs, and la Comtess de Châteauvieux. This outrage, committed before the "most august sacrament of the altar," although transient, did not leave these two holy souls, and it seemed to them that it could be atoned for only by a "perpetual Adoration" in some convent. They both, one in 1652, the other in 1653, made donations of considerable sums to Mother Catherine de Bar, surnamed du Saint-Sacrement, a Benedictine nun, for her to found, with that pious aim, a monastery of the order of Saint-Benedict; the first permission for this foundation was given to Mothe Catherine de Bar, by M. de Metz, Abbé of Saint-Germain, "with the stipulation that no maiden shall be received unless she brings three hundred livres of income, which is six thousand livres of principal." After the Abbé of Saint-Germain, the king granted letters patent, and the whole, abbatial charter and letters royal, was confirmed in 1654, by the Chamber of Accounts and by the High Judicial Court.

Such is the origin and the legal consecration of the establishment of Benedictines of the Perpetual Adoration of the Holy Sacrament in Paris. Their first convent was "built new," on the Rue Cassette, with the funds of Mmes. de Boucs and de Châteauvieux.

This order, as we see, was not connected to the Benedictines called Cistercians. It sprang from the Abbé of Saint-Germain-des-Prés, in the same manner as the ladies of the Sacré-Coeur spring from the General of the Jesuits and the Soeurs de Charité from the General of the Lazarists.

It is also entirely different from the Bernardines of the Petit-Picpus, whose interior life we have just described. In 1657, Pope Alexander VII specially authorized the Bernardines of the Petit-Picpus to practice the Perpetual Adoration like the Benedictines of the Holy Sacrament. But the two orders, nonetheless, remained distinct.

XI

END OF THE PETIT-PICPUS

From the time of the Restoration, the convent of the Petit-Picpus had been dwindling; this was part of the general decline of the order, which, since the eighteenth century, has been going the way of all religious orders. Meditation is, as much as prayer, a necessity of humanity, but, like everything the Revolution has touched, it is undergoing transformation, and, from being hostile to social progress, will become favorable to it.

The house of the Petit-Picpus dwindled rapidly. In 1840, the little convent had disappeared; the school had disappeared. There were no longer either the old women or the young girls; the former were dead, the latter had gone away. *Volaverunt*.

The rules of the Perpetual Adoration are so rigid they inspire horror; those called to the religious life are repelled, and recruits go elsewhere. In 1845, it still gathered a few sister servants here and there, but no nuns of the choir. Forty years ago there were nearly a hundred nuns, fifteen years ago there were only twenty-eight. How many are there today? In 1847 the prioress was young, a sign that the choice was limited. She was not forty. As the number diminishes, the fatigue increases; service for each one becomes more difficult; they could see the moment approaching when there would be only a dozen sorrowful, bowed shoulders to bear the hard rules of Saint

Benedict. The burden is inflexible and remains the same for the few as for the many. It used to weigh down, now it crushes. So they die. Since the author of this book lived in Paris, two have died. One was twenty-five, the other twenty-three. The latter might say with Julia Alpinula, *Hic jaceo, Vixi annos viginti et tres.* It was because of this decay that the convent gave up the education of girls.

We could not go by this extraordinary, unknown, obscure house without entering and leading in those who accompany us, and who listen as we relate, perhaps for the benefit of some, the sad story of Jean Valjean. We have glimpsed that community full of its old practices, which seem so novel today. It is the closed garden. *Hortus conclusus.* We have spoken of this strange place in detail, but with respect, or as much as respect and detail are reconcilable. We do not understand everything, but we do not insult anything. We are equally distant from the hosannahs of Joseph de Maistre, who ultimately sanctifies the executioner, and the mockery of Voltaire, who goes so far as to mock the crucifix.

An illogicality of Voltaire, be it said by the way; for Voltaire would have defended Jesus as he defended Calas; and, even for those who deny the superhuman incarnation, what does the crucifix represent? The wise man assassinated.

In the nineteenth century religion is undergoing a crisis. We are unlearning certain things, and that is good, provided that while unlearning one thing we are learning another. No vacuum in the human heart! Certain forms are torn down, and so they should be, but on condition that they are followed by reconstructions.

In the meantime let us study things that are no more. It is necessary to understand them, if only to avoid them. The counterfeits of the past take assumed names, and are fond of calling themselves the future. That eternally returning specter, the past, not infrequently falsifies its passport. Let us be ready for the snare. Let us beware. The past has a face, superstition, and a mask, hypocrisy. Let us denounce the face and tear off the mask.

As to convents, they present a complex question. A question of civilization, which condemns them; a question of liberty, which protects them.

Book Seven

A PARENTHESIS

I

THE CONVENT AS AN ABSTRACT IDEA

This book is a drama whose first character is the Infinite.

Man is the second.

This being the case, since a convent happened to be on our path, we had to go in. Why? Because the convent, which is common to the East as well as to the West, to ancient as well as modern times, to Paganism as well as to Buddhism, to Islam as well as to Christianity, is one of the optical appliances man turns on the Infinite.

This is not the place for an inordinate development of certain ideas; however, while absolutely maintaining our reservations, our restrictions, and even our indignation, we must admit, whenever we meet the Infinite in man, whether well or poorly understood, we react with respect. There is in the synagogue, in the mosque, in the pagoda, and in the wigwam, a hideous side that we detest and a sublime aspect that we adore. What a subject of meditation, and what a limitless source of reverie is this reflection of God upon the human wall!

II

THE CONVENT AS A HISTORIC FACT

In the light of history, reason, and truth, monastic life stands condemned.

When they are plentiful in a country, monasteries are clots in the circulation, encumbrances, centers of indolence where there should be centers of industry. Monastic communities are to the great social community, what the ivy is to the oak, what the wart is to the human body. Their prosperity and corpulence are the impoverishment of the country. The monastic system, useful as it is in the dawn of civilization, in effecting the abatement of brutality by the development of the spiritual, is injurious in the adulthood of nations. Especially when it relaxes and enters upon its period of disorganization, as we now see it, it becomes bad for every reason that made it useful in its period of purity.

Withdrawals into convents and monasteries have had their day. Cloisters, though beneficial in the first training of modern civilization, cramp its growth and hinder its development. Taken as an institution and as a formative mode for man, monasteries, good in the tenth century, arguable in the fifteenth, are detestable in the nineteenth. The leprosy of monasticism has gnawed down, almost to skeletons, two admirable nations, Italy and Spain—one the light and the other the glory of Europe—for centuries; and, in our time, these two illustrious peoples are beginning to recover thanks only to the sound and vigorous hygiene of 1789.

The convent, the old-style convent particularly, such as appeared on the threshold of this century, in Italy, Austria, and Spain, is one of the gloomiest concretions of the Middle Ages. The cloister was the intersecting point of horrors. The Catholic cloister, properly speaking, is filled with the black radiance of death.

The Spanish convent is particularly dismal. There in the obscurity, below vaults filled with mist, below domes dense with shadow, rise massive Babel-like altars, lofty as cathedrals; there, in the deep gloom, immense white emblems of the crucifixion hang by chains; there, naked on ebony wood, huge ivory images of Christ are suspended—more than bloody, bleeding—hideous and magnificent, their bones protruding from the elbows, their kneecaps showing the integuments, their wounds revealing the flesh—crowned with silver thorns, nailed with gold nails, with drops of blood in rubies on their brows, and tears of diamonds in their eyes. The diamonds and the rubies seem wet, and down below there in the shadows, make veiled beings weep, their loins scratched and torn by the haircloth and by scourges with iron points, their breasts bruised by wicker pads, their knees lacerated by prayer; women do think themselves wives; specters that fancy themselves seraphim. Do these women think? No. Do they have a will? No. Do they love? No. Do they live? No. Their nerves have turned to bone, their bones to rock. Their veil is the woven night. Under that veil their breath is like some indescribable, tragic respiration of death. The abbess, a phantom, sanctifies and terrifies them. The immaculate one is there, austere. Such are the old convents of Spain—dens of terrible devotion, lairs inhabited by virgins, wild and savage places.

Catholic Spain was more Roman than Rome itself. The Spanish convent was the ideal of the Catholic convent. One could feel the East in it. The archbishop, as officiating kislaraga of heaven, locked in and zealously watched this harem of souls set apart for God. The nun was the odalisque, the priest was the eunuch. In their dreams the fervently devout were the chosen ones possessed of Christ. At night, the lovely naked youth descended from the cross and became the rapture of the cell. Lofty walls guarded from all the distractions of real life the mystic Sultana, who had the Crucified for Sultan. A single glance outside was an act of infidelity. The *in pace* took the place of the leather sack. What they threw into the sea in the East they threw into the earth in the West. On both sides, poor women wrung their hands; the waves for some—for the others the pit; there the drowned and here the buried alive. Monstrous parallel!

In our day, the champions of the past, unable to deny these things, have adopted the alternative of smiling at them. It has become the fashion, a convenient and a strange one, to suppress the revelations of history, to invalidate the comments of philosophy, and to elide all unpleasant facts and all gloomy inquiries. "Topics for declamation," say the skillful. "Declamation," echo the idiotic. Jean-Jacques, a declaimer; Diderot, a declaimer; Voltaire on Calas, Labarre, and Sirven, a declaimer! I forget who it is who has recently discovered Tacitus, too, as a declaimer, Nero a victim, and Holophernes a man really to be pitied.

Facts, however, are stubborn, and hard to baffle. The author of this book has seen, with his own eyes, about twenty miles from Brussels, and there since the Middle Ages, within everybody's reach, at the Abbey of Villars—the openings of the secret dungeons in the middle of the meadow that was once the courtyard of the cloister, and, on the banks of the Dyle, four stone cells, half underground and half underwater. These were *in pace*. Each of these dungeons has a remnant of an iron wicket, a latrine, and a barred skylight, which, on the outside, is two feet above the surface of the river, and from the inside is six feet above the ground. Four feet in depth, the river flows along the outer face of the wall; the ground is constantly wet. This saturated soil was the only bed of the *in pace* occupant. In one of these dungeons there remains the stump of an iron collar attached to the wall; in another may be seen a kind of square box, formed of four slabs of granite, too short for a human being to lie down in, too low to stand in erect. In this was placed a creature like ourselves and then a lid of stone was closed above her head. There it is. You can see it; you can touch it. These *in pace;* these dungeons; these iron hinges; these metal collars; this high skylight, on a level with the river's surface; this box of stone, covered by its lid of granite, like a sepulcher, with this difference, that it shut in the living and not the dead; this soil of mud, this cesspool; these oozing walls, how they declaim!

III

ON WHAT CONDITIONS WE CAN RESPECT THE PAST

Monasticism, as it was in Spain, as it is in Tibet, is a disease to civilization. It cuts off life. In a word, it depopulates. Incarceration, castration. In Europe, it has been a scourge. Add to that, the violence so often done to conscience; the vocations so frequently compulsory; the feudal system leaning on the cloister; primogeniture emptying into the monastery the family surplus; the cruelties we have just described; the *in pace;* mouths closed, brains walled-up, so many unfortunate intellects incarcerated in the dungeon of eternal vows; the assumption of the veil, the live burial of souls. Add these individual torments to the national degradation, and, whoever you may be, you will find yourself shuddering at the sight of the frock and the veil, those two winding sheets of human invention.

However, on certain points and in certain places, in spite of philosophy and progress, the monastic spirit persists in the middle of the nineteenth century, and at this very moment, a strange revival of asceticism amazes the civilized world. The persistence of superannuated institutions in striving to perpetuate themselves is like the obstinacy of a rancid perfume clinging to the hair, to the pretension of spoiled fish that insists on being eaten, the tenacious folly of a child's garment trying to clothe a man, or the tenderness of a corpse returning to embrace the living.

"Ungrateful!" exclaims the garment. "I shielded you in weakness. Why do you reject me now?" "I come from the depths of the sea," says the fish. "I was once a rose," cries the perfume. "I loved you," murmurs the corpse. "I civilized you," says the convent.

To this there is only one reply: "That was long ago."

To dream of the indefinite prolongation of things dead and the government of mankind by embalming; to restore dilapidated dogmas, regild the shrines, replaster the cloisters, reconsecrate the reliquaries, revamp old superstitions, replenish fading fanaticism, put new handles in worn-out aspergillums and sabers, reconstitute monasticism and militarism; to believe in the salvation of society by the multiplication of parasites; to impose the past on the present, all this seems strange. However, there are advocates for such theories as these. These theorists, thinking men, too, have a very simple process: They apply to the past a coating of what they term social order, divine right, morality, respect for our forefathers, time-honored authority, sacred tradition, legitimacy; and they go around, shouting, "Here, take this, my good people!" This kind of logic was familiar to the ancients; their soothsayers practiced it. Rubbing a black heifer with chalk, they would exclaim, "She is white." *Bos cretatus*.

As for ourselves, we distribute our respect here and there, and spare the past entirely, provided it consents to be dead. But, if it insists on being alive, we attack and try to kill it.

Superstitions, bigotries, hypocrisies, prejudices, these phantoms, phantoms though they be, cling to life; they have teeth and nails in their shadowy substance, and we must grapple with them individually and make war on them without truce; for it is one of humanity's inevitabilities to be condemned to eternal struggle with phantoms. A shadow is hard to seize by the throat and dash to the ground.

A convent in France, in the high noon of the nineteenth century, is a college of owls confronting the day. A cloister in the open act of asceticism right in the middle of the city, in '89, in 1830, and in 1848, Rome blossoming in Paris, is an anachronism. In ordinary times, to dispel an anachronism and make it vanish, one has only to determine the date. But, we do not live in ordinary times.

Let us attack, then.

Let us attack, but let us distinguish. The characteristic of truth is never to run to excess. What need has she of exaggeration? Some things must be destroyed, and some things must be merely cleared up and investigated. What power there is in courteous and serious examination! Let us not carry flame where light alone will suffice.

Well, then, assuming we are in the nineteenth century, we are opposed, as a general proposition, and in every nation, in Asia as well as in Europe, in India as well as in Turkey, to ascetic seclusion in monasteries. He who says "convent" says "marsh." Their putrescence is apparent, their stagnation is unhealthy, their fermentation fevers and sickens the nations, and their increase becomes an Egyptian plague. We cannot think without a shudder of those countries where fakirs, bonzes, santons, caloyers, marabouts, talapoins, and dervishes multiply in swarms, like vermin.

Having said this much, the religious question still remains. The question has some mysterious aspects, and we must ask leave to look at it closely.

IV

THE CONVENT VIEWED IN THE LIGHT OF PRINCIPLES

Men come together and live in common. By what right? By virtue of the right of association.

They shut themselves up. By what right? By virtue of the right of privacy.

They do not go out. By what right? By virtue of the right to come and go, which implies the right to stay at home.

And what are they doing there, at home?

They speak in low tones; they keep their eyes fixed on the ground; they work. They give up the world, cities, sensual enjoyments, pleasures, vanities, pride, interest. They are clad in coarse wool or linen. Not one of them possesses any property whatever. On entering, anyone who was rich becomes poor. What he had, he gives to everyone. He who was what is called a nobleman, a man of rank, a lord, is the equal of a peasant. The cell is identical for all. All undergo the same tonsure, wear the same frock, eat the same black bread, sleep on the same straw, and die on the same ashes. The same sackcloth is on every back, the same rope around every waist. If it is the rule to go barefoot, none wear shoes. There may be a prince among them; the prince is a shadow like all the rest. Titles no longer exist. Even family names have disappeared. They answer only to Christian names. All are bowed beneath the equality of their baptismal names. They have dissolved the family of the flesh and have formed in their community the family of the spirit. They have no other relatives than all mankind. They comfort the poor, they tend the sick. They elect those whom they are to obey, and they call one another brother.

You stop me, exclaiming, "But, that is the ideal monastery!"

It is enough that it is a possible monastery for me to take it into consideration.

That is why, in the preceding book, I spoke of a convent with respect. The Middle Ages aside, Asia aside, and the historical and political questions reserved, from the purely philosophical point of view, beyond the necessities of militant polemics, on condition that the monastery be absolutely voluntary and contain none but willing devotees, I should always consider the monastic community with a certain serious, and, in some respects deferential, attention. Where community exists, there likewise exists the true body politic, and where the latter is, there too is justice. The monastery is the product of the formula "Equality, Fraternity." Oh! How great is liberty! And how glorious the transfiguration! Liberty is enough to transform the monastery into a republic!

Let us proceed.

These men or women who live within those four walls and dress in haircloth are equals and call each other brother and sister. That is good, but is there anything else they do?

Yes.

What?

They look into the shadows, they kneel, and they clasp their hands.

What does that mean?

V

PRAYER

They pray.

To whom?

To God.

Pray to God, what is meant by that?

Is there an infinite outside of us? Is this infinite, one, immanent, permanent; necessarily substantial, since it is infinite, and because, if matter were lacking in it, it would in that respect be limited; necessarily intelligent, because it is infinite, and since if it lacked intelligence, it would be to that extent, finite? Does this infinite awaken in us the idea of essence, while we are able to attribute to ourselves the idea of existence only? In other words, is it not the absolute of which we are the relative?

At the same time, while there is an infinite outside of us, is there not an infinite within us? These two infinites (frightening plural!), do they not rest superimposed on one another? Does the second infinite not underlie the first, so to speak? Is it not the mirror, the reflection, the echo of the first, an abyss concentric with another abyss? Is this second infinite intelligent, also? Does it think? Does it love? Does it will? If the two infinites are intelligent, each one of them has a principle of will, and there is a "me" in the infinite above, as there is a "me" in the infinite below. The "me" below is the soul; the "me" above is God.

To place, by process of thought, the infinite below in contact with the infinite above is called "prayer."

Let us not take anything away from the human mind; suppression is evil. We just reform and transform. Certain faculties of man are directed toward the Unknown: thought, meditation, prayer. The Unknown is an ocean. What is conscience? It is the compass of the Unknown. Thought, meditation, prayer, these are the great mysterious directions of the needle. Let us respect them. Where do these majestic irradiations of the soul go? Into the shadow, that is, toward the light.

The greatness of democracy is that it denies nothing and renounces nothing of humanity. Next to the rights of Man, side by side with them, at least, are the rights of the Soul.

To crush out fanaticisms and revere the Infinite, such is the law. Let us not confine ourselves to falling prostrate beneath the tree of Creation and contemplating its vast ramifications full of stars. We have a duty to perform, to cultivate the human soul, to defend mystery against miracle, to adore the incomprehensible and reject the absurd; to admit nothing that is inexplicable excepting what is necessary, to purify faith and obliterate superstition from the face of religion, to remove the vermin from the garden of God.

VI

ABSOLUTE VIRTUE OF PRAYER

As for methods of prayer, all are good, as long as they are sincere. Turn your book facedown and you are in the infinite.

There is, we are aware, a philosophy that denies the infinite. There is also a philosophy, classified as pathologic, that denies the sun; this philosophy is called blindness.

To set up a theory that lacks a source of truth is an excellent example of blind assurance.

And the odd part of it is the haughty air of superiority and compassion assumed toward the philosophy that sees God, by this philosophy that has to grope its way. It makes one think of a mole exclaiming, "How I pity them with their sun!"

There are, we know, illustrious and powerful atheists. These men, in fact, led back again toward truth by their own power, are not absolutely sure of being atheists; with them, the matter is nothing but a question of definitions, and, at all events, even if they do not believe in God, they prove God, because they are great minds.

We hail, in them, the philosophers, while, at the same time, inexorably disputing their philosophy.

But, let us continue.

An admirable thing, too, is the facility of settling everything to one's satisfaction with words. A metaphysical school in the North, slightly impregnated with fogs, imagined that it effected a revolution in human understanding by substituting for the word "force" the word "will."

To say, "The plant wills," instead of "The plant grows," would be pregnant with meaning if you were to add, "The universe wills." Why? Because this would flow from it: The plant wills, so it has a "me"; the universe wills, so it has a God.

As for us, however, who, in direct opposition to this school, reject nothing *a priori*, a will in the plant, which is accepted by this school, seems more difficult to admit than a will in the universe, which it denies.

To deny the will of the infinite, that is to say God, can be done only on condition of denying the infinite itself. We have demonstrated that.

Denial of the infinite leads directly to nihilism. Everything becomes "a conception of the mind."

With nihilism no argument is possible. For the logical nihilist doubts the existence of his interlocutor and is not quite sure he exists himself.

From his point of view it is possible that to himself he may be only a "conception of his mind."

However, he does not notice that everything he has denied he admits wholesale by merely pronouncing the word "mind."

To sum up, no path is left open for thought by a philosophy that reduces everything to one conclusion, the monosyllable "No."

To "No," there is only one reply: "Yes."

Nihilism has no scope. There is no nothing. Zero does not exist. Everything is something. Nothing is nothing.

Man lives by affirmation even more than he does by bread.

To see and to show, even these are not enough. Philosophy should be energy; it should find its aim and effect in the improvement of mankind. Socrates should enter into Adam and produce Marcus Aurelius—in other words, bring forth from the man of enjoyment the man of wisdom—and change Eden into the Lyceum. Science should be a cordial. Enjoyment! Miserable goal, pitiful ambition! The brute enjoys. Thought is the true triumph of the soul. To offer thought to men's thirst, to give everyone, as an elixir, the idea of God, to make conscience and science fraternize in them, and to make them good men by this mysterious confrontation—such is the province of true philosophy. Morality is truth in full bloom. Contemplation leads to action. The absolute must be practical. The ideal must be made air and food and drink to the human mind. It is the ideal that has the right to say, *Take of it, this is my flesh, this is my blood.* Wisdom is a sacred communion. It is upon that condition that it ceases to be a sterile love of science and becomes the one and supreme method by which to rally humanity; from philosophy it is promoted to religion.

Philosophy must not be a mere watchtower built on mystery, from which to gaze on it at ease, with no other result than to be a convenience for the curious.

As for us, postponing the development of our thought to some other occasion, we will merely say that we do not comprehend either man as a starting point or progress as the goal, without the two great driving forces, faith and love.

Progress is the aim, the ideal is the model.

What is the ideal? It is God.

Ideal, absolute, perfection, the infinite—these are identical words.

VII

PRECAUTIONS TO BE TAKEN IN CENSURE

History and philosophy have eternal duties, which are at the same time simple duties—to oppose Caiaphas as bishop, Draco as judge, Trimalcio as legislator, and Tiberius as emperor. This is clear, direct, and limpid and presents no obscurity. But the right to live apart, even with its inconveniences and abuses, must be verified and dealt with carefully. The life of the cenobite is a human problem.

When we speak of convents, those seats of error but innocence, of mistaken views but good intentions, of ignorance but devotion, of torment but martyrdom, we must nearly always say yes or no.

A convent is a contradiction—its object salvation, its means self-sacrifice. The convent is supreme egotism resulting in supreme self-denial.

"Abdicate so you may reign" seems to be the motto of monasticism.

In the cloister they suffer to enjoy—they draw a bill of exchange on death—they discount the celestial splendor in terrestrial night. In the cloister, hell is accepted as the charge made in advance on the future inheritance of heaven.

The assumption of the veil or the cowl is a suicide reimbursed by an eternity.

It seems to us that in treating such a subject mockery would be quite out of place. Everything relating to it is serious, the good as well as the evil.

The upright man frowns but never smiles with an evil smile. We can understand anger but not malignity.

VIII

FAITH AND LAW

A few words more.

We blame the Church when it is saturated with intrigues; we despise the spiritual when it is harshly austere to the temporal; but always we honor the thoughtful man.

We bow to the man who kneels.

A faith is a necessity to man. Woe to him who believes in nothing.

A man is not idle because he is absorbed in thought. There is a visible labor and there is an invisible labor.

To meditate is to labor; to think is to act.

Folded arms work, clasped hands perform, a gaze fixed on heaven work.

Thales remained motionless for four years. He founded philosophy.

In our eyes, cenobites are not idlers, nor is the recluse a do-nothing.

To think of shadows is a serious thing.

Without at all invalidating what we have just said, we believe that a perpetual remembrance of the tomb is proper for the living. On this point, the priest and the philosopher agree, "We must die." The Abbé of La Trappe responds to Horace.

To mingle with one's life a certain awareness of the sepulcher is the law of the wise man, and it is the law of the ascetic. In this relation, the ascetic and the sage converge.

There is a material growth; we desire it. There is also a moral grandeur; we hold fast to it.

Unreflecting, headlong minds say, "What good are those motionless figures on the side of mystery? What purpose do they serve? What do they achieve?"

Alas! in the presence of the obscurity that surrounds and awaits us, not knowing what the vast dispersion of all things will do with us, we answer, There is, perhaps, no work more sublime than that done by these souls; and we add, There is no labor, perhaps, more useful.

Those who pray always are necessary to those who never pray.

In our view, the whole question is in the amount of thought that is mingled with the prayer.

Leibnitz praying is great; Voltaire worshiping is beautiful. *Deo erexit Voltaire.*

We are for religion, against the religions.

We are among those who believe in the pitifulness of orisons and in the sublimity of prayer.

Besides, in this moment through which we are passing, a moment that fortunately will not leave its stamp on the nineteenth century; in this hour, which finds so many with their foreheads bowed but their souls so little uplifted, among so many of the living whose motto is pleasure, and who are occupied with the brief, misshapen things of matter, whoever is self-exiled seems venerable to us. The monastery is a renunciation. Self-sacrifice, even when misdirected, is still self-sacrifice. To assume as duty a strict error has its peculiar grandeur.

Considered in itself, ideally, and holding it up to truth, until it is impartially and exhaustively examined from all points of view, the monastery and particularly the convent—for woman suffers most under our system of society, and in this exile of the cloister there is an element of protest—the convent, we repeat, unquestionably has a certain majesty.

This monastic existence, austere and gloomy as it is, of which we have indicated a few characteristics, is not life, for it is not liberty; it is not the grave, for it is not completion; it is that strange place from which, as from the summit of a lofty mountain, we see, on one side, the abyss in which we are, and, on the other, the abyss where we are to be; it is a narrow and misty boundary separating two worlds, at once illuminated and obscured by both, where the faint ray of life mingles with the uncertain ray of death; it is the twilight of the tomb.

As for us, we who do not believe what these women believe, but live like them by faith, never could look without a sort of tender and religious awe, a kind of pity full of envy, at those devoted beings, trembling yet confident—those humble yet august souls, who dare to live on the brink of the great mystery, waiting between the world closed to them and heaven not yet opened; turned toward the daylight not yet seen, with only the happiness of thinking that they know where it is; their aspirations directed toward the abyss and the unknown, their gaze fixed on the motionless obscurity, kneeling, dismayed, stupefied, shuddering, and half carried off sometimes by the deep breath of Eternity.

Book Eight

CEMETERIES TAKE WHAT IS GIVEN THEM

I

WHICH TELLS THE WAY TO ENTER A CONVENT

It was into this house that Jean Valjean had, as Fauchelevent said, "fallen from heaven."

He had crossed the garden wall at the corner of the Rue Polonceau. That angels' hymn he had heard in the middle of the night was the nuns chanting matins; that hall he had glimpsed in the darkness was the chapel; that phantom he had seen extended on the floor was the sister performing the reparation; that bell which had so strangely surprised him was the gardener's bell fastened to old Fauchelevent's knee.

When Cosette had been put to bed, Jean Valjean and Fauchelevent, as we have seen, took a glass of wine and a piece of cheese before a blazing fire; then, the only bed in the shanty being occupied by Cosette, they had each lain down on a bundle of straw. Before closing his eyes, Jean Valjean had said; "From now on I must stay here." These words chased one another through Fauchelevent's head all night long.

To tell the truth, neither of them had slept.

Jean Valjean, feeling that he was discovered and Javert was on his track, knew very well that he and Cosette were lost if they returned to the city. Since the new blast of wind that had burst on him had thrown him into this cloister, Jean Valjean had only one thought, to remain there. Now, for one in his unfortunate position, this convent was at once the safest and the most dangerous place; the most dangerous, because, no man being allowed to enter, if he should be discovered, it was a flagrant crime, and for Jean Valjean a single step from the convent to prison; the safest, because if he succeeded in getting permission to remain, who would come there to look for him? To live in an impossible place, that would be safety.

As for him, Fauchelevent was racking his brains. He began by deciding that he was utterly bewildered. How did Monsieur Madeleine get in there, with such walls! Nobody simply steps over the walls of a cloister. How did he happen to have a child with him? A man doesn't scale a steep wall with a child in his arms. Who was this child? Where did they both come from? Since Fauchelevent had been in the convent, he had not heard a word from Montreuil-sur-mer, and knew nothing of what had taken place. Father Madeleine wore that look which discourages questions; and moreover Fauchelevent said to himself, "One does not question a saint." To him Monsieur Madeleine had preserved all his prestige. From some words that had escaped Jean Valjean, however, the gardener thought he might conclude that Monsieur Madeleine had probably failed on account of the hard times and that he was pursued by his creditors; or it might be that he was compromised in some political affair and was hiding out; which did not at all displease Fauchelevent, who, like many of our peasants of the north, had an old Bonapartist heart. Being in hiding, Monsieur Madeleine had taken the convent for an asylum, and it was natural that he should wish to remain there. But the mystery to which Fauchelevent constantly returned and over which he was racking his brains was that Monsieur Madeleine should be there and that this little girl should be with him. Fauchelevent saw them, touched them, spoke to them, and yet did not believe it. The incomprehensible had made its way into Fauchelevent's hut. Fauchelevent was groping among conjectures, but saw nothing clearly except this: Monsieur Madeleine has saved my life. This single certainty was enough, and convinced him. He said to himself, "It's my turn now." He added in his conscience, "Monsieur Madeleine did not deliberate so long when it was a question of squeezing himself under the wagon to drag me out." He decided to save Monsieur Madeleine.

However, he asked himself several questions and gave several answers: "After what he has done for me, if he were a thief, would I save him? I would anyway. If he were an assassin, would I save him? I would anyway. Since he is a saint, shall I save him? Absolutely."

But to have him stay in the convent, what a problem! Before such a fantastic challenge, Fauchelevent did not recoil; this poor Picardy peasant, with no other ladder than his devotion, his goodwill, a little of that old-country cunning, engaged for once in the service of a generous intention, undertook to scale the impossibilities of the cloister and the craggy escarpments of the rules of Saint Benedict. Fauchelevent was an old man who had been selfish throughout his life and who, near the end of his days, crippled, infirm, having no remaining interest in the world, found it sweet to be grateful, and seeing a virtuous action to be done, threw himself into it like a man who, at the moment of death, finding at hand a glass of some good wine he had never tasted, would drink avidly. We might add that the air he had been breathing now for several years in the convent had destroyed his personality, and had finally made it necessary for him to do some good deed.

So, he resolved to devote himself to Monsieur Madeleine.

We have just described him as a "poor Picardy peasant." The description is true but incomplete. At this point in the story a closer look at Fauchelevent's psychology would be useful. He was a peasant, but he had been a notary, which added craft to his cunning and incisiveness to his simplicity. Having, for various reasons, failed in his business, from a notary he had fallen to a cartman and laborer. But, in spite of the oaths and blows that seem necessary with horses, he had retained something of the notary. He had some natural wit; he said neither "I is" nor "I has"; he could carry on a conversation, a rare thing in a village; and the other peasants said of him, "He talks almost like a gentleman." Fauchelevent belonged in fact to that class that the flippant and impertinent vocabulary of the last century termed "half-yeoman, half-yokel"; and which metaphors, falling from castle to hovel, label in the pigeonholes of the commonality "half-country, half-city, pepper-and-salt." Fauchelevent, though sorely tried and used by Fortune, a sort of poor old soul worn threadbare, was nevertheless impulsive and had a very willing heart, a precious quality, which prevents a man from ever being wicked. His faults and vices, for such he had, were superficial; and finally, his physical makeup was one that attracts the observer. That old face had none of those ugly wrinkles in the upper part of the forehead that indicate viciousness or stupidity.

At daybreak, having dreamed copiously, old Fauchelevent opened his eyes and saw Monsieur Madeleine, who, seated on his bunch of straw, was looking at Cosette as she slept. Fauchelevent half rose, and said, "Now that you're here, how will you manage to get in?"

This question summed up the situation and wakened Jean Valjean from his reverie.

The two men talked it over.

"To begin with," said Fauchelevent, "you must not set foot outside of this room, neither the little girl nor you. One step in the garden, and we are ruined."

"That's true."

"Monsieur Madeleine," Fauchelevent resumed, "you have arrived at a very good time; I mean to say very bad; one of these ladies is gravely ill. Because of that, they don't look this way much. She must be dying. They are saying the forty-hour prayers. The whole community is up in the air. It takes up their attention. The one who is departing is a saint. In fact, we are all saints here; the whole difference between them and me is that they say "our cell," and I say "my shanty." They're going to have the orison for the dying and then the orison for the dead. Today will be quiet here, but I cannot answer for tomorrow."

"However," Jean Valjean observed, "this shanty is under the corner of the wall; it is hidden by a sort of ruin; there are trees; they can't see it from the convent."

"And the nuns never come near it."

"Well?" said Jean Valjean.

The question mark following that "well" meant, "It seems to me we can stay here in hiding." This question mark is what Fauchelevent answered: "There are the little girls."

"What little girls?" asked Jean Valjean.

As Fauchelevent opened his mouth to explain the words he had just uttered, a single stroke of a bell was heard.

"The nun is dead," he said. "There is the knell."

And he motioned to Jean Valjean to listen.

The bell sounded a second time.

"It is the knell, Monsieur Madeleine. The bell will strike every minute, for twenty-four hours, until the body leaves the church. You see, they play. In their recess, if a ball rolls this way, that's enough: they'll come after it, in spite of the rules, and rummage all around here. Those cherubs are little devils."

"Who?" asked Jean Valjean.

"The little girls. You would be discovered very quickly. They would cry out, 'Look! A man!' But there's no danger today. There won't be any recess. The day will be all prayers. You can hear the bell. As I told you, a stroke every minute. It's the knell."

"I understand, Father Fauchelevent. There are boarding students."

And Jean Valjean thought to himself, "Then here's Cosette's education too, ready and waiting."

Fauchelevent exclaimed, "Good Lord! Are there little girls! They would scream at the sight of you! They would run off! Here, to be a man, is to have the plague. You see how they fasten a bell to my leg, as if I were some wild beast."

Jean Valjean was more and more lost in thought. "The convent would save us," he murmured. Then he raised his voice: "Yes, the difficulty is how to stay."

"No," said Fauchelevent, "it is how to get out."

Jean Valjean felt his blood run cold.

"To get out?"

"Yes, Monsieur Madeleine, in order to come in, you have to get out."

And, after waiting for a stroke of the tolling bell to die away, Fauchelevent went on, "It wouldn't be right to have you found here like this. Where have you come from? For me you fell from heaven, because I know you; but for the nuns, you have to come in at the door."

Suddenly they heard a complicated ringing on another bell.

"Oh!" said Fauchelevent. "That's the bell for the mothers. They are going to the chapter. They always hold a chapter when anybody dies. She died at daybreak. It's usually at daybreak that people die. But can't you go out the way you came in? Let's see; I don't mean to question you, but where did you come in?"

Jean Valjean turned pale; the mere idea of climbing down again into that intimidating street made him shudder. Make your way out of a forest full of tigers, and when out, imagine yourself advised by a friend to return. Jean Valjean imagined all the police still swarming over the area, officers on the watch, sentries everywhere, terrifying fists stretched out toward his collar, Javert, perhaps, at the corner of the square.

"Impossible," he said. "Father Fauchelevent, let's leave it that I fell from heaven."

"Ah! I believe it, I believe it," replied Fauchelevent. "You don't have to tell me. God must have taken you into his hand, to have a close look at you, and then put you down. Only he meant to put you into a monastery; he made a mistake. Listen! Another ring; that's to warn the porter to go and notify the municipality, so that they can notify the doctor, so he can come and see there really is a dead woman. All that is the ceremony of dying. The good ladies are not too fond of this visit. A doctor believes in nothing. He lifts the veil. Sometimes he even lifts something else. How quickly they notified the inspector, this time! What can the matter be? Your little one is still asleep. What's her name?"

"Cosette."

"She's your girl? Or I mean, you must be her grandfather?"

"Yes."

"For her, to get out will be easy. I have my door, which opens into the court. I knock; the porter opens. I have my basket on my back; the little girl is inside; I go out. Father Fauchelevent goes out with his basket—it's quite simple. You'll tell the little girl to keep very still. She'll be under cover. I'll leave her as soon as I can, with a good old friend of mine. She sells fruit on the Rue du Chemin-Vert. She's deaf and has a little bed. I'll scream into the fruit vender's ear that she's my niece and she must keep her for me till tomorrow. Then the little girl will come back in with you; for I'll bring you back. It has to be. But what are you going to do to get out?"

Jean Valjean shook his head.

"Just let nobody see me, that's all, Father Fauchelevent. Find some way to get me out, like Cosette, in a basket and under cover."

Fauchelevent scratched the tip of his ear with the middle finger of his left hand—a sign of serious perplexity.

A third ringing provided a diversion.

"That's the doctor going away," said Fauchelevent. "He has looked and said she's dead, good. When the inspector has stamped the passport to paradise, the undertaker sends a coffin. If it is a mother, the mothers lay her out; if it is a sister, the sisters lay her out. After which, I nail it up. That's a part of my gardening. A gardener is something of a gravedigger. They put her in a low room in the church that communicates with the street, and where no man can enter except the doctor. I don't count the pallbearers and myself as men. In that room I nail the coffin. The bearers come and take her, and giddyap, driver: That's the way they go to heaven. They bring in a box with nothing in it, they carry it away with something inside. That's what a burial is. *De profundis.*"

A ray of the rising sun beamed on the face of the sleeping Cosette, who half-opened her mouth dreamily, looking like an angel drinking in the light. Jean Valjean was gazing at her. He had stopped listening to Fauchelevent.

Not being heard is no reason for silence. The brave old gardener calmly went on with his garrulous recital.

"They dig the grave at the Vaugirard cemetery. They claim this Vaugirard cemetery is going to be eliminated. It's an old cemetery, not according to the regulations, it doesn't wear the uniform, and it's going to be retired. I'm sorry about that, it's convenient. I have a friend there—Father Mestienne, the gravedigger. The nuns here have the privilege of being carried to that cemetery at nightfall. There's a special order of the Prefecture, just for them. But what a lot of happenings since yesterday? Mother Crucifixion is dead, and Father Madeleine—"

"Is buried," said Jean Valjean, sadly smiling.

Fauchelevent echoed the word.

"You're quite right, if you were here for good, it would be a real burial."

For a fourth time the bell rang. Fauchelevent quickly took down the knee-strap and bell from the nail and buckled it on his knee.

"This time, it's for me. The mother prioress wants me.

Well! I'll bite my tongue. Monsieur Madeleine, don't budge, just wait for me. There's something new going on. If you're hungry, there is the wine, and bread and cheese."

And he went out of the hut, saying, "I'm coming, I'm coming."

Jean Valjean saw him hurry across the garden, as fast as his crooked leg would take him, glancing at his melons all the way.

In less than ten minutes, Father Fauchelevent, whose bell put the nuns to flight as he went along, rapped softly at a door and a gentle voice answered, "Forever, Forever!" that is to say, "Come in."

This was the parlor door allotted to the gardener, for use when it was necessary to communicate with him. This parlor was next to the chapter hall. The prioress, seated in the only chair in the parlor, was waiting for Fauchelevent.

II

FAUCHELEVENT CONFRONTING DIFFICULTY

A serious and troubled bearing is peculiar, on critical occasions, to certain characters and certain professions, particularly priests and monastics. As Fauchelevent entered, this double sign of preoccupation marked the countenance of the prioress, the charming and learned Mlle. de Blemeur, Mother Innocent, who was ordinarily cheerful.

The gardener made a timid bow and stopped at the threshold of the cell. The prioress, who was saying her rosary, raised her eyes and said, "Ah! It's you, Father Fauvent."

This abbreviation had been adopted in the convent.

Fauchelevent again began his bow.

"Father Fauvent, I had you called."

"I am here, Reverend Mother."

"I wish to speak to you."

"And as for me," said Fauchelevent, with a boldness

that inwardly alarmed him, "I have something to say to the most Reverend Mother."

The prioress looked at him.

"Ah, you have a communication to make to me."

"A petition!"

"Well, what is it?"

This good ex-notary Fauchelevent belonged to that class of peasants who are never disconcerted. A certain combination of ignorance and skill is very effective; you do not suspect it, and you accede to it. Within the little more than two years that he had lived in the convent, Fauchelevent had achieved a success in the community. Always alone, and even while attending to his garden, he had hardly anything to do but be curious. Distant as he was from all these veiled women going to and fro, he saw before him scarcely more than a fluttering of shadows. Through attention and acute observation, he had succeeded in clothing all the phantoms with flesh, and these dead were alive to him. He was like a deaf man whose sight is extended, like a blind man whose hearing is sharpened. He had applied himself to unraveling the meaning of the various ringings, and had deciphered them, so that in this enigmatic and taciturn cloister, nothing was hidden from him; this sphinx blabbed all her secrets in his ear. Knowing everything, Fauchelevent concealed everything. That was his art. The whole convent thought he was stupid—a great merit in religion. The mothers prized Fauchelevent. He was a rare mute. He inspired confidence. Moreover, he was regular in his habits, and never went out except when it was clearly necessary on account of the orchard and the garden. This discretion in his conduct was counted to his credit. He had, nevertheless, learned the secrets of two men: the convent porter, who knew the peculiarities of the interlocutory, and the gravedigger of the cemetery, who knew the singularities of burial; in this way, he had a double light on to these nuns—one on their life, the other on their death. But he did not abuse it. The convent thought well of him, old, lame, seeing nothing, probably a little deaf—so many good qualities! It would have been difficult to replace him.

The good man, with the assurance of one who feels he is appreciated, launched into a rustic harangue in front of the reverend prioress, quite diffuse and very profound. He spoke at length of his age, his infirmities, the weight of years henceforth doubly heavy on him, the growing demands of his work, the size of the garden, the nights to be spent—like last night, for example, when he had to put awnings over the melons on account of the moon—and finally ended with this: That he had a brother—(the prioress gave a start)—a brother no longer young—(second start of the prioress, but a reassured start)—that if they were willing, this brother could come live with him and help him; that he was an excellent gardener; that the community would get good services from him, better than his own; that, otherwise, if his brother were not admitted, as he, the oldest, felt that he was broken down and unequal to the labor, he would be obliged to leave, though with much regret; and that his brother had a granddaughter that he would bring with him, who would be reared under God in the house, and who, perhaps—who knows?—would someday become a nun.

When he had finished,the prioress stopped the sliding of her rosary through her fingers, and said, "Between now and nightfall, can you procure a strong iron bar?"

"For what sort of work?"

"To be used as a lever."

"Yes, reverend mother," answered Fauchelevent.

The prioress, without adding a word, rose, and went into the next room, which was the chapter hall, where the vocal mothers were probably assembled. Fauchelevent remained alone.

III

MOTHER INNOCENT

About a quarter of an hour elapsed. The prioress returned and sat down again.

Both seemed preoccupied. As well as we can, we report the dialogue that followed.

"Father Fauvent?"

"Reverend Mother?"

"You are familiar with the chapel?"

"I have a little box there for going to mass and the offices."

"And you have been into the choir for your work?"

"Two or three times."

"A stone has to be raised."

"Heavy?"

"The paving slab beside the altar."

"The stone that covers the vault?"

"Yes."

"That's a piece of work that would take two men."

"Mother Ascension, who is as strong as a man, will help you."

"A woman is never a man."

"We have only a woman to help you. Everybody does what he can. Because Dom Mabillon gives four hundred and seventeen epistles of Saint Bernard, and Merlonus Horstius gives only three hundred and sixty-seven, I do not think any the less of Merlonus Horstius."

"Nor do I."

"Merit consists in working according to our strength. A cloister is not a shipyard."

"And a woman is not a man. My brother is very strong."

"And then you will have a lever."

"That is the only kind of key that fits that kind of door."

"There is a ring in the stone."

"I will slip the lever through it."

"And the stone is arranged to pivot around."

"Very well, Reverend Mother, I will open the vault."

"And the four mother choristers will assist you."

"And when the vault is opened?"

"It must be shut again."

"Is that all?"

"No."

"Give me your orders, Most Reverend Mother."

"Fauvent, we have confidence in you."

"I am here to do everything."

"And to keep silent about everything."

"Yes, Reverend Mother."

"When the vault is opened—"

"I will shut it again."

"But before—"

"What, Reverend Mother?"

"Something must be lowered."

There was silence. The prioress, after a quivering of the underlip that resembled hesitation, spoke again. "Father Fauvent?"

"Reverend Mother?"

"You know that a mother died this morning."

"No."

"Then you did not hear the bell?"

"I don't hear anything at the far end of the garden."

"Really?"

"I can hardly catch my ring."

"She died at daybreak."

"And then, this morning, the wind didn't blow my way."

"It is Mother Crucifixion. One of the blessed."

The prioress was silent, moved her lips a moment as in a mental orison, and went on: "Three years ago, merely from having seen Mother Crucifixion at prayer, a Jansenist, Madame de Béthune, became orthodox."

"Ah! Yes, now I hear the knell, Reverend Mother."

"The mothers have carried her into the room of the dead, which opens into the church."

"I know."

"No other man than you can or must enter that room. See to it. Now wouldn't it look well for a man to enter the room of the dead!"

"More often!"

"What?"

"More often!"

"What did you say?"

"I said more often."

"More often than what?"

"Reverend Mother, I didn't say more often than what; I said more often."

"I do not understand you. Why do you say more often?"

"To agree with you, Reverend Mother."

"But I did not say more often."

"No; I said it to agree with you."

The clock struck nine.

"At nine in the morning, and at all hours, praise and adoration to the most holy sacrament of the altar," said the prioress.

"Amen!" said Fauchelevent.

The clock struck in good time. It cut short those "more oftens." Without it the prioress and Fauchelevent might never have untangled their snarl.

Fauchelevent wiped his forehead.

The prioress again made a little low murmur, probably sacred, then raised her voice. "During her lifetime Mother Crucifixion made many conversions; after her death, she will work miracles."

"Yes, she will!" answered Fauchelevent, correcting his misstep and trying not to blunder again.

"Father Fauvent, the community has been blessed in Mother Crucifixion. Undoubtedly we do not all have the good fortune to die like Cardinal de Bérulle, saying the holy mass, and to breathe out his soul to God, pronouncing the words, *Hanc igitur oblationem*. But without attaining so great a happiness, Mother Crucifixion had a very precious death. She was conscious right to the end. She spoke to us, then she spoke to the angels. She gave us her last commands. If you had a little more faith and if you could have been in her cell, she would have cured your leg by touching it. She smiled. We felt that she was returning to life in God. There was a touch of Paradise in that death."

Fauchelevent thought he had been listening to a prayer.

"Amen!" he said.

"Father Fauvent, we must do what the dead wish."

The prioress counted a few beads on her chaplet. Fauchelevent was silent. She continued, "On this question I have consulted several ecclesiastics laboring in the vineyards of Our Lord, who are engaged in clerical functions, and with admirable results."

"Reverend Mother, we hear the knell much better here than in the garden."

"Furthermore, she is more than a departed one; she is a saint."

"Like you, Reverend Mother."

"She had slept in her coffin for twenty years, by the express permission of our Holy Father, Pius VII."

"He who crowned the Emp—— Buonaparte."

For a shrewd man like Fauchelevent, the reminiscence was unintentional. Luckily the prioress, absorbed in her thoughts, did not hear him. She continued, "Father Fauvent?"

"Reverend Mother?"

"Saint-Diodorus, Archbishop of Cappadocia, wanted this single word written on his tomb: *Acarus,* which signifies an earthworm; that was done. Is it true?"

"Yes, Reverend Mother."

"The blessed Mezzoçane, Abbé of Aquila, wished to be buried under the gibbet; it was done."

"That is true."

"Saint-Terence, Bishop of Ostia, at the mouth of the Tiber, asked to have engraved on his tomb the mark put on the graves of parricides, in the hope that travelers would spit on his grave. It was done. We must obey the dead."

"So be it."

"The body of Bernard Guidonis, born in France near Roche Abeille, was, as he ordered, despite the king of Castile, brought to the church of the Dominicans of Limoges, although Bernard Guidonis was Bishop of Tuy, in Spain. Can this be denied?"

"No, indeed, Reverend Mother."

"The fact is sworn by Plantavit de la Fosse."

A few beads of her chaplet were said silently. The prioress went on, "Father Fauvent, Mother Crucifixion will be buried in the coffin she slept in for twenty years."

"That is right."

"It is a continuation of sleep."

"I'll have to nail her up then in that coffin?"

"Yes."

"And we'll put aside the undertaker's coffin?"

"Precisely."

"I am at the disposal of the most reverend community."

"The four mother choristers will help you."

"To nail up the coffin I don't need them."

"No. To lower it."

"Where?"

"Into the vault."

"What vault?"

"Under the altar."

Fauchelevent gave a start.

"The vault under the altar!"

"Under the altar."

"But—"

"You will have an iron bar."

"Yes, but—"

"You will lift the stone with the bar using the ring."

"But—"

"We must obey the dead. To be buried in the vault under the altar of the chapel, not to go into profane ground, to remain in death where she prayed in life; this was Mother Crucifixion's last request. She has asked it, that is to say, commanded it."

"But it is forbidden."

"Forbidden by men, commanded by God."

"If it should come out?"

"We have confidence in you."

"Oh! Me, I'm like a stone in your wall."

"The chapter has assembled. The vocal mothers, whom I have just consulted again and who are now deliberating, have decided that Mother Crucifixion should be, according to her desire, buried in her coffin under our altar. Think, Father Fauvent, if there should be miracles performed here, what glory to God for the community! Miracles spring from tombs."

"But, Reverend Mother, if the agent of the Health Commission—"

"Saint Benedict II, in the matter of burial, resisted Constantine Pogonatus."

"However, the Commissioner of Police—"

"Chonodemaire, one of the seven German kings who entered Gaul in the reign of Constantius, expressly recognized the right of those in orders to be buried in religion, that is to say, under the altar."

"But the Inspector of the Prefecture—"

"The world is nothing before the cross. Martin, eleventh general of the Carthusians, gave this motto to his order: *Stat crux dum volvitur orbis*."

"Amen," said Fauchelevent, imperturbable in this method of extricating himself whenever he heard any Latin.

Any audience whatever is sufficient for one who has been too long silent. The day the rhetorician Gymnastoras came out of prison, full of suppressed dilemmas and syllogisms, he stopped in front of the first tree he encountered, harangued it, and made very great efforts to convince it. The prioress, habitually subject to the constraint of silence, and having a surplus in her reservoir, rose, and exclaimed with the loquacity of an opened mill-sluice:

"I have on my right Benedict, and on my left Bernard. What is Bernard? He is the first Abbott of Clairvaux. Fontaine in Burgundy is blessed for having been his birthplace. His father's name was Tecelin, and his mother's Alethe. He began at Cîteaux, and ended at Clairvaux; he was ordained abbot by the Bishop of Chalons-sur-Saône, Guillaume de Champeaux; he had seven hundred novices, and founded a hundred and sixty monasteries; he overthrew Abelard at the Council of Sens in 1140, and Peter de Bruys and Henry his disciple, and another heterodox set called the Apostolicals; he confused Arnold of Brescia, struck monk Ralph dumb, the slayer of the Jews, presided in 1148 over the Council of Rheims, had Gilbert de la Porée, Bishop of Poitiers, condemned, had Eon de l'Etoile condemned, arranged the disputes of princes, advised the King, Louis le Jeune, counseled Pope Eugenius III, set the Temple to rights, preached the Crusade, performed two hundred and fifty miracles in his lifetime, and as many as thirty-nine in one day. What is Benedict? He is the patriarch of Monte Cassino; he is the second founder of the Claustral Holiness, he is the Basil of the West. His order has produced forty popes, two hundred cardinals, fifty patriarchs, sixteen hundred archbishops, four thousand six hundred bishops, four emperors, twelve empresses, forty-six kings, forty-one queens, three thousand six hundred canonized saints, and has endured fourteen hundred years. On one side, Saint Bernard; on the other the agent of the health commission! On one side, Saint Benedict; on the other the sanitary inspector! The state, Health Department, funeral regulations, rules, the administration, do we recognize these things? Anybody would be indignant to see how we are treated. We have not even the right to give our dust to Jesus Christ! Your sanitary commission is an invention of the Revolution. God subordinated to the Commissioner of Police; such is this age. Silence, Fauvent!"

Beneath this downpour, Fauchelevent was not entirely at ease. The prioress continued, "Nobody can doubt the convent's right to the sepulcher. Only fanatics and those who have gone astray could deny it. We live in times of terrible confusion. People are ignorant of things they ought to know, and know things of which they ought to be ignorant. They are crude and impious. These days there are people who do not distinguish between the great Saint Bernard and the so-called Bernard des Pauvres Catholiques, a certain good ecclesiastic who lived in the thirteenth century. Others blaspheme so far as to couple the scaffold of Louis the Sixteenth with the cross of Jesus Christ. Louis the Sixteenth was only a king. So let us watch out for God! Neither the just nor the unjust exist anymore. Voltaire's name is known, and the name of Caesar de Bus is not. Yet Caesar de Bus is in bliss and Voltaire is in hell. The last archbishop, the Cardinal of Perigord, did not even know that Charles de Gondren was successor to Bérulle, and François Bourgoin to Gondren, and Jean- François Senault to Bourgoin, and Father de Sainte-Marthe to Jean-François Senault. The name of Father Cotton is known, not because he was one of the three who pushed for the foundation of the Oratory, but because he was the subject of an oath for the Huguenot King Henry the Fourth. Saint François de Sales is popular with the world, because he cheated at gambling. And then religion is attacked. Why? Because there have been bad priests, because Sagittaire, Bishop of Gap, was a brother of Salone, Bishop of Embrun, and both were followers of Mammon. What does that matter? Does that prevent Martin de Tours from being a saint and having given half his cloak to a poor man? The saints are persecuted. Men shut their eyes to the truth. Darkness becomes habit. The most savage beasts are blind beasts. Nobody thinks of hell in earnest. Oh! The wicked people! 'By the king' now means 'By the Revolution.' Men no longer know what is due to the living or the dead. Holy death is forbidden. The sepulcher is a civil affair. This is horrible. Saint Leo the Second wrote two letters, one to Peter Notaire, the other to the King of the Visigoths, to combat and overthrow, on questions concerning the dead, the authority of the exarch and the supremacy of the emperor. Gautier, Bishop of Châlons, opposed Otho, Duke of Burgundy in this matter. The ancient magistracy agreed to it. Formerly we had votes in the chapter even concerning secular affairs. The Abbot of Cîteaux, general of the order, was hereditary counselor of the High Judicial Court of Burgundy. We do with our dead as we please. Why, the body of Saint Benedict himself is in France in the Abbey of Fleury, called Saint-Benedict-sur-Loire, though he died in Italy, at Monte Cassino, on a Saturday, the twenty-first of the month of March in the year 543! All this is incontestable. I abhor the psalm sayers, I hate the priors, I execrate heretics, but I should detest still more anyone who might maintain the contrary of what I have said. You have only to read Arnold Wion, Gabriel Bucelin, Trithemius, Maurolicus, and Dom Luke d'Achery."

The prioress took a deep breath, then turned toward Fauchelevent.

"Father Fauvent, is it settled?"

"It is settled, Reverend Mother."

"Can we count on you?"

"I shall obey."

"Good."

"I am entirely devoted to the convent."

"Done. You will close the coffin. The sisters will carry it into the chapel. The office of the dead will be said. Then they will return to the cloister. Between eleven o'clock and midnight, you will come with your iron bar. Everything will be done with the greatest secrecy. Only the four mother choristers, Mother Ascension, and you will be in the chapel."

"And the sister who will be at the post."

"She will not turn."

"But she will hear."

"She will not listen. Besides, what the cloister knows the world does not know."

Again there was a pause. The prioress continued. "You will take off your bell. It is unnecessary for the sister at the post to realize that you are there."

"Reverend Mother?"

"What, Father Fauvent?"

"Has the coroner made his visit?"

"He is going to come at four o'clock today. The bell has been rung to summon the coroner. But you do not hear any bells then?"

"I only pay attention to my own."

"That is good, Father Fauvent."

"Reverend Mother, I'll need a lever at least six feet long."

"Where will you get it?"

"Where there are gratings there are always iron bars. I have my heap of old iron at the back of the garden."

"About three quarters of an hour before midnight; do not forget."

"Reverend Mother?"

"What?"

"If you ever had any other work like this, my brother is very strong. A Turk."

"You will do it as quickly as possible."

"I cannot go very fast. I am infirm; it is on that account I need help. I limp."

"Limping is no crime, and it may be a blessing. The Emperor Henry the Second, who fought the Antipope Gregory, and reestablished Benedict the Eighth, has two surnames: the Saint and the Lame."

"Two surtouts are very good," murmured Fauchelevent, who was in fact a little hard of hearing.

"Father Fauvent, now that I think of it, we will take a whole hour. That is not too much. Be at the high altar with the iron bar at eleven o'clock. The office begins at midnight. It must all be finished a good quarter of an hour before."

"I will do everything to prove my zeal for the community. This is the arrangement. I'll nail up the coffin. At eleven o'clock precisely I'll be in the chapel. The mother choristers will be there. Mother Ascension will be there. Two men would be better. But no matter! I'll have my lever. We'll open the vault, lower the coffin, and close the vault again. After which, not a trace of anything. The government will suspect nothing. Reverend Mother, is that everything?"

"No."

"Then what else is there?"

"There is still the empty coffin."

This brought them to a standstill. Fauchelevent pondered. The prioress pondered.

"Father Fauvent, what should we do with the coffin?"

"It will be put in the ground."

"Empty?"

Another silence. With his left hand Fauchelevent made the sort of gesture that dismisses an unpleasant question.

"Reverend Mother, I nail up the coffin in the lower

room in the church, and nobody can come in there except me, and I'll cover the coffin with the pall."

"Yes, but the bearers, when they put it into the hearse and lower it into the grave, will surely notice that there is nothing inside."

"Ah! the de—!" exclaimed Fauchelevent.

The prioress began to cross herself, and looked fixedly at the gardener. "Vil" stuck in his throat.

He hurried to think up an expedient to wipe out the oath.

"Reverend Mother, I'll put some earth into the coffin. It will seem like a body."

"You are right. Earth is the same thing as man. So you will prepare the empty coffin?"

"I will attend to it.

The prioress' face, till then dark and anxious, became serene once more. She gave him the sign of a superior dismissing an inferior. Fauchelevent moved toward the door. As he was going out, the prioress gently raised her voice.

"Father Fauvent, I am pleased with you; tomorrow after the burial, bring your brother to me and have him bring his granddaughter."

IV

IN WHICH JEAN VALJEAN LOOKS AS THOUGH HE HAS READ AUSTIN CASTILLEJO

A lame man's stride is like the glance of a one-eyed man: They are slow to reach their mark. Furthermore, Fauchelevent was perplexed. It took him nearly a quarter of an hour to get back to the shanty in the garden. Cosette was awake. Jean Valjean had sat her down near the fire. As Fauchelevent entered, Jean Valjean was showing her the gardener's basket hanging on the wall and saying to her, "Listen carefully, my little Cosette. We must leave this house, but we'll come back, and we'll be very well off here. The fellow here will carry you out on his back inside that basket. You'll wait for me at a lady's house. I'll come and get you there. Above all, if you don't want the Thénardiess to take you back, obey and don't say a thing."

Cosette nodded seriously.

At the sound of Fauchelevent opening the door, Jean Valjean turned.

"Well?"

"Everything is arranged, and nothing is," said Fauchelevent. "I have permission to bring you in; but before bringing you in, we have to get you out. There's the snag. For the little girl, it's easy enough."

"You'll carry her out?"

"And she'll keep quiet?"

"She will."

"But you, Father Madeleine?"

And, after an anxious pause, Fauchelevent said, "But why not go out the way you came in?"

As before, Jean Valjean merely answered, "Impossible."

Fauchelevent, talking more to himself than to Jean Valjean, grumbled, "There's another thing that plagues me. I said I'd put some dirt in it. The thing is, I think that dirt, instead of a body, won't be the same, it won't do, it'll shake around, it'll move. The men will feel it. You understand, Father Madeleine, the government will find out."

Jean Valjean stared at him and thought he was raving.

Fauchelevent went on, "How the devil are you going to get out? The whole thing has to be done tomorrow. Tomorrow I'm supposed to bring you in. The prioress is expecting you."

Then he explained to Jean Valjean that this was a reward for a service that he, Fauchelevent, was rendering to the community. That it was a part of his duties to assist in burials, that he nailed up the coffins, and helped out the gravedigger at the cemetery. That the nun who died that morning had requested to be buried in the coffin she had used as a bed, and buried in the vault under the altar chapel. That this was forbidden by the police regulations, but that she was one of those departed ones to whom nothing is refused. That the prioress and the vocal mothers intended to carry out the will of the deceased. So much the worse for the government. That he, Fauchelevent, would nail up the coffin in the cell, raise the stone in the chapel, and lower the body into the vault. And that, in return for this, the prioress would admit his brother into the house as gardener and his niece as boarder. That his brother was M. Madeleine, and that his niece was Cosette. That the prioress had told him to bring his brother the next evening, after the fictitious burial at the cemetery. But that he couldn't bring M. Madeleine from the outside, if M. Madeleine wasn't outside. That that was the first difficulty. And then that he had another difficulty; the empty coffin.

"What is the empty coffin?" asked Jean Valjean.

Fauchelevent responded:

"The administration coffin."

"What coffin? What administration?"

"A nun dies. The municipality physician comes and says: There is a dead nun. The government sends a coffin. The next day it sends a hearse and some pall bearers to pick up the coffin and carry it to the cemetery. The bearers will come and take up the coffin; there won't be anything in it."

"Put somebody in it."

"A dead body? I don't have one."

"No."

"What then?"

"A live body."

"What live body?"

"Me," said Jean Valjean.

Fauchelevent, who had sat down, sprang up as if a cracker had burst under his chair.

"You!"

"Why not?"

Jean Valjean had one of those rare smiles that came over him like a sunrise in winter.

"You know, Fauchelevent, that you said: Mother Crucifixion is dead, and that I added: And Father Madeleine is buried. So it will be."

"Ah! Fine, you're laughing, you're not talking seriously."

"Very seriously, I have to get out!"

"No doubt about it."

"And I told you to find a basket and a cover for me, too."

"Well!"

"The basket will be of pine, and the cover will be black cloth."

"In the first place, a white cloth. The nuns are buried in white."

"All right, a white cloth."

"You aren't like other men, Father Madeleine."

To see such devices, which are nothing more than the wild and daring inventions of prison, appear in the midst of the peaceful things that surrounded him and mingled with what he called the "little humdrum doings of the convent," was to Fauchelevent as astonishing as seeing a seagull fishing in the gutter of the Rue Saint-Denis.

Jean Valjean continued, "The question is how to get out of here without being seen. This is the way. But in the first place, tell me, how is it done? Where is this coffin?"

"The empty one?"

"Yes."

"Down in what is called the dead room. It's on two trestles and under the pall."

"How long is the coffin?"

"Six feet."

"What is the dead room?"

"It's a room on the ground floor, with a grated window toward the garden that they close on the outside with a shutter, and two doors; one leading to the convent, the other to the church."

"What church?"

"The church on the street, the church for everybody."

"Do you have the keys to those two doors?"

"No. I have the key to the door into the convent; the porter has the key of the door into the church."

"When does the porter open that door?"

"Only to let in the pallbearers, who come to get the coffin; as soon as the coffin goes out, the door is closed again."

"Who nails up the coffin?"

"I do."

"Who puts the cloth on it?"

"I do."

"Are you alone?"

"No other man, except the police physician, can enter the dead room. That's even written on the wall."

"Tonight, when everyone is asleep in the convent, could you hide me in that room?"

"No. But I can hide you in a dark little closet that opens into the dead room. It's where I keep my burial tools, and I have the key, and responsibility for it."

"When will the hearse come for the coffin?"

"About three tomorrow afternoon. The burial takes place at the Vaugirard cemetery, a little before nightfall. It's not exactly nearby."

"I'll stay hidden in your tool closet, all night and all the next morning. And what about food? I'll be hungry."

"I'll bring you something."

"You can come and nail me up in the coffin at two o'clock."

Fauchelevent recoiled, and began to crack his finger joints.

"But it's impossible!"

"Not at all. To take a hammer and drive some nails into a board?"

What seemed unheard-of to Fauchelevent was, we repeat, simple to Jean Valjean. Jean Valjean had been in worse straits. Anyone who has been a prisoner knows the art of making himself small to match the diameter of the escape hatch. The prisoner is subject to flight as the sick man is to the crisis that cures or kills him. An escape is a cure. What would one not undergo to be cured? To be nailed up and carried out in a chest like a bundle, to live a long time in a box, to find air where there is none, to hoard his breath for hours at a time, to know how to be stifled without dying—that was one of Jean Valjean's saddest talents.

Besides, a coffin containing a living being, that convict's expedient, is also an emperor's expedient. If we are to believe the monk Austin Castillejo, this was the means that Charles V, wanting, after his abdication, to see La Plombes again one last time, used to bring her into the monastery of Saint-Just and to take her out again.

Fauchelevent, recovering a little, exclaimed, "But how will you manage to breathe?"

"I'll breathe."

"In that box? Only to think of it suffocates me."

"Surely you have a gimlet, you can make a few little holes around the mouth here and there, and you can nail it without drawing the upper board tight."

"Good! But if you happen to cough or sneeze?"

"No one escaping ever coughs or sneezes."

And Jean Valjean added, "Father Fauchelevent, I have to decide: Either I'm discovered here, or I agree to go out in the coffin."

Everybody has noticed the way cats stop and loiter in a half-open door. Hasn't everyone said to a cat: For heaven's sake why don't you come in? With opportunity half-open in front of them, there are men who have a similar tendency to remain undecided between two solutions, at the risk of being crushed by fate abruptly closing the opportunity. The overprudent, cats as they are, and because they are cats, sometimes run more danger than the bold. Fauchelevent was of this hesitating nature. However, Jean Valjean's coolness won him over in spite of himself. He grumbled, "It's true. There's no other way."

Jean Valjean went on, "The only thing that worries me is what will happen at the cemetery."

"That's just what doesn't bother me," exclaimed Fauchelevent. "If you're sure of getting yourself out of the coffin, I'm sure of getting you out of the grave. The gravedigger is a drunkard and friend of mine. He is Father Mestienne. An old son of the old vine. The gravedigger puts the dead in the grave, but I put the gravedigger in my pocket. I'll tell you what will happen. We'll get there a bit before dusk, three quarters of an hour before the cemetery gates are closed. The hearse will go to the grave. I'll follow; that's my business. I'll have a hammer, a chisel, and some pliers in my pocket. The hearse stops, the pallbearers tie a rope around your coffin and lower you. The priest says the prayers, makes the sign of the cross, sprinkles the holy water, and he's off. I stay on alone with Father Mestienne. He's my friend, I tell you. One of two things; either he'll be drunk or he won't be. If he isn't drunk, I say to him, Come have a drink before the Good Quince closes. I take him away, I get him drunk; It doesn't take long to get Father Mestienne befuddled; he's always halfway there. I lay him under the table, I take his card from him to get back into the cemetery, and I return without him. You'll have only me to deal with. If he's drunk, I say to him: Go home, I'll do your work. He goes away, and I pull you out of the hole."

Jean Valjean reached out his hand, and Fauchelevent grabbed it with a rustic outburst of touching devotion.

"It's settled, Father Fauchelevent. Everything will turn out all right."

"Provided nothing goes wrong," thought Fauchelevent. "How terrible that would be!"

V

IT IS NOT ENOUGH TO BE A DRUNKARD TO BE IMMORTAL

Next day, as the sun was setting, the scattered pedestrians on the Boulevard du Maine took off their hats as an old-fashioned hearse, adorned with death's-heads, crossbones, and teardrops drove by. In this hearse was a coffin covered with a white cloth, on which was displayed a large black cross like a large body with dangling arms. A draped carriage, in which they could see a priest in a surplice, and an altar boy in a red skull cap, followed. Two pallbearers in gray uniform with black trimmings walked on the right and left of the hearse. Bringing up the rear was an old man with a limp and dressed like a laborer. The procession moved toward the Vaugirard cemetery.

Sticking out of the man's pocket were the handle of a hammer, the blade of a cold chisel, and the double handles of a pair of pliers.

The Vaugirard cemetery was an exception among the cemeteries of Paris. It had its peculiar uses, including its carriage door, and its small door, which, in the neighborhood, old people who hung onto old words called the horse gate and the pedestrian gate. The Bernardine-Benedictines of the Petit-Picpus had obtained the right, as we have said, to be buried in a separate corner and in the evening, this ground having formerly belonged to their community. So the gravediggers, having to work in the cemetery in the evening in summer and at night in winter, were subject to special rules. In those days the gates of the Paris cemeteries closed at sunset, by municipal order, and the Vaugirard cemetery was no exception. The vehicle gate and the pedestrian gate were two contiguous gates beside a pavilion built by the architect Perronet, in which the gatekeeper of the cemetery lived. So these gates inexorably swung shut the instant the sun disappeared behind the dome of the Invalides. If at that moment any gravedigger was delayed in the cemetery his only resource for getting out was his gravedigger's card, given him by the administration for cemeteries. A sort of letterbox was arranged in the shutter of the gatekeeper's window. The gravedigger dropped his card into this box, the gatekeeper heard it fall, pulled the string, and the pedestrian door opened. If the gravedigger did not have his card, he gave his name; the gatekeeper, sometimes in bed and asleep, got up, went to identify the gravedigger, and open the door with the key; the gravedigger went out, but paid fifteen francs fine.

This cemetery, with its exceptions to the general rules, disturbed the symmetry of the administration. Soon after 1830 it was closed. The Montparnasse Cemetery, called the Cimetière de l'Est, has succeeded it, and has inherited this famous tavern near the Vaugirard cemetery, which was topped by a quince painted on a board, which on one side overlooked the customer's tables and on the other, the graves. It bore the inscription "The Good Quince."

The Vaugirard cemetery was what might be called a cemetery in decline. Mildew was taking over, flowers were dying. The well-to-do citizens cared little for burial at Vaugirard; it had a poor sound to it. Père Lachaise, now that's more like it. To be buried in Père Lachaise is like having mahogany furniture—inherent elegance. The Vaugirard cemetery was a venerable enclosure, laid out like an old French garden. Straight walks, boxwood, evergreens, hollies, old tombs under old yews, very tall grass. Night there was tragic, with dismal outlines.

The sun had not yet set when the hearse with the white pall and the black cross entered the drive of the Vaugirard cemetery. The lame man following it was our Fauchelevent.

The Mother Crucifixion's burial in the vault under the altar, Cosette's departure, Jean Valjean's entry into the dead room, all had been carried out without a hitch.

Let us say in passing that Mother Crucifixion's burial under the convent altar is, to us, perfectly forgivable. It is one of those faults that comes from a duty. The nuns had carried it off, not only without concern, but with approving conscience. In the cloister, the "government" is only an interference with authority and is always questionable. First the rules; as to the code, we will see. Men, make as many laws as you like, but keep them for yourselves. The tribute to Caesar is never more than the remnant of the tribute to God. A prince is nothing beside a principle.

Fauchelevent limped along behind the hearse, very pleased. His two schemes, one with the nuns, the other with M. Madeleine, one for the convent, the other against it, had succeeded equally well. Jean Valjean's calm had that powerful tranquillity that is contagious. Fauchelevent now had no doubt of success. What remained to be done was nothing. Within two years he had gotten the gravedigger drunk ten times, good Father Mestienne, a chubby old fellow. Father Mestienne was child's play for him. He did what he liked with him. He got him drunk at will and at leisure. Mestienne generally went along with Fauchelevent. Fauchelevent's security was complete.

As the convoy entered the avenue leading to the cemetery, Fauchelevent, happy, looked at the hearse and rubbed his large hands together, saying in an undertone, "What a farce!"

Suddenly the hearse stopped; they were at the gate. It was time to exhibit the burial permit. The undertaker whispered with the cemetery gatekeeer. During this colloquy, which always causes a delay of a minute or two, somebody, a stranger, came and stood behind the hearse at Fauchelevent's side. He was a workman wearing a vest with large pockets, and he had a pick under his arm.

Fauchelevent looked at this stranger.

"Who are you?" he asked.

The man answered, "The gravedigger."

If a man were to survive a cannon shot through the breast, he would look as Fauchelevent did.

"The gravedigger?"

"Yes."

"You!"

"Me."

"The gravedigger is Father Mestienne."

"He was."

"What do you mean, he was?"

"He's dead."

Fauchelevent was ready for anything but this, that a gravedigger could die. However, it is true; even gravediggers must die. By dint of digging graves for others, they open their own.

Fauchelevent remained speechless. He had hardly the strength to stammer, "But that's not possible!"

"That's the way it is."

"But," he repeated feebly, "the gravedigger is Father Mestienne."

"After Napoleon, Louis the Eighteenth. After Mestienne, Gribier. Friend, my name is Gribier."

Fauchelevent turned pale; he stared at Gribier.

He was a long, thin, sallow man, perfectly funereal. He looked like a would-be doctor turned gravedigger.

Fauchelevent burst out laughing.

"Ah! What odd things happen! Father Mestienne is dead. Little Father Mestienne is dead, but hurrah for little Father Lenoir! You know what little Father Lenoir is? It's the mug of red for a six spot. It's the mug of Surêne, ye gods! Real Paris Surêne. So he's dead, old Mestienne! I'm sorry about that; he was a good fellow. But so are you, you're a bon vivant. Isn't that so, comrade? We'll go and have a drink together, right away."

The man answered: "I've studied, I've graduated, I never drink."

The hearse had started up and was rolling along the main avenue of the cemetery.

Fauchelevent had slackened his pace. He was limping still more out of anxiety than infirmity.

The gravedigger walked in front of him.

Again Fauchelevent scrutinized the unexpected Gribier.

He was one of those men who, though young, look old, and, though thin, are very strong.

"Comrade!" cried Fauchelevent.

The man turned.

"I am the convent gravedigger."

"My colleague," said the man.

Fauchelevent, illiterate but clever, understood he was dealing with a very formidable species, a good talker.

He muttered, "So, Father Mestienne is dead?"

The man answered, "Absolutely. The good Lord consulted his list of outstanding debts. It was Father Mestienne's turn. Father Mestienne is dead."

Fauchelevent repeated mechanically, "The good Lord . . ."

"The good Lord," the man said authoritatively. "What the philosophers call the Eternal Father; the Jacobins, the Supreme Being."

"Aren't we going to get acquainted?" Fauchelevent stammered.

"We have. You're from the country, I'm a Parisian."

"We aren't acquainted as long as we haven't had a drink together. Empty your glass and open your heart. Come drink with me. You can't refuse."

"Business first."

Fauchelevent said to himself: I'm lost.

They were now only a few steps from the path leading to the nuns's corner.

The gravedigger went on, "I have seven youngsters to feed. They have to eat, so I cannot drink."

And he added with the satisfaction of a sober-minded citizen making a sententious phrase, "Their hunger is the enemy of my thirst."

The hearse turned at a huge cypress, left the main path, took a little one, rolled onto the grass, and headed into a thicket, indicating that the grave was nearby. Fauchelevent slackened his pace, but could not slacken the hearse's. Luckily the loose soil, wet by the winter rains, stuck to the wheels and slowed progress.

He approached the gravedigger.

"They have such a good little Argenteuil wine," suggested Fauchelevent.

"Villager," the man replied, "I shouldn't be a gravedigger. My father was doorkepper at the Prytanée. He intended me for literature. But he was unfortunate, he had losses on the stock market and I had to renounce the condition of an author. However, I'm still a public scribe."

"But then aren't you the gravedigger?" Fauchelevent replied, catching at a straw, feeble as it was.

"The one doesn't prevent the other. I cumulate."

Fauchelevent did not understand this last word.

"Let's go have a drink," he said.

Here an observation is necessary. Fauchelevent, whatever his anguish, proposed to drink, but did not explain himself on one point; who would pay? Ordinarily Fauchelevent proposed, and Father Mestienne paid. An offer to have a drink clearly resulted from the new situation produced by the new gravedigger, and he had to make this offer; but, not unintentionally, the old gardener left some aspects unclear. Fauchelevent, excited as he was, did not think about paying for the drinks.

The gravedigger went on, with a smile of superiority: "We must live. I accepted Father Mestienne's succession. Any student almost through his education is a philosopher. To the labor of my head, I've added the labor of my arm. I have my little writer's shop at the Market in the Rue de Sèvre. You know the place? the Marché des Parapluies. All the cooks of the Croix Rouge come to me; I dash off their declarations of true love. In the morning I write love letters; in the evening I dig graves. Such is life, comrade."

The hearse moved on; Fauchelevent, full of anxiety, looked all around. Huge drops of sweat were falling from his forehead.

"However," the gravedigger continued, "one cannot serve two mistresses; I'll have to choose between the pen and the pick. The pick hurts my hand."

The hearse stopped.

The altar boy got out of the mourning carriage, then the priest.

One of the front wheels of the hearse rode up on a little heap of earth, beyond which was an open grave.

"What a farce!" repeated Fauchelevent in consternation.

VI

IN HIS NARROW BOX

Who was in the coffin? We know. Jean Valjean.

Jean Valjean had arranged it so he could live in it, just managing to breathe.

It is strange how a clear conscience results in a general serenity. The entire plan prearranged by Jean Valjean had been working, and working well, since the night before. Like Fauchelevent, he was counting on Father Mestienne. He had no doubt at all of the outcome. Never was a situation more critical, never the serenity more total.

The coffin's four boards gave off a kind of terrible peacefulness. It seemed as if something of the repose of the dead had entered into Jean Valjean's tranquility.

From within that coffin he had been able to follow, and did, all phases of the fearful drama he was playing out with Death.

Soon after Fauchelevent had finished nailing down the top board, Jean Valjean had felt himself carried out, then wheeled along. With the diminished jolting, he had sensed he was passing from the paving stones to hard-packed ground; that is to say, leaving the streets and entering the boulevards. At a deep rumbling sound, he had guessed they were crossing the Pont d'Austerlitz. At the first stop he had realized they were entering the cemetery; at the second stop he had said to himself, "Here is the grave."

He felt hands hastily seizing the coffin, then a harsh scraping on the boards; he concluded they were tying rope around the coffin to lower it into the excavation.

Then he felt a sort of dizziness.

Probably the pallbearer and gravedigger had tipped the coffin and let the head down before the feet. He returned fully to himself on feeling that he was horizontal and motionless. He had touched bottom.

He felt a certain chill.

A voice rose above him, ice-cold and solemn. He heard some Latin words, which he did not understand, pronounced so slowly he could catch each one: "*Qui dormiunt in terrae pulvere, evigilabunt; alii in vitam aeternam, et alli in opprobrium, ut videant semper.*"

A child's voice said, "*De profundis.*"

The deep voice continued, "*Requiem aeternam dona ei, Domine.*"

The child's voice responded, "*Et lux perpetua luceat ei.*"

On the board that covered him he heard something like the gentle patter of a few raindrops—probably holy water.

He thought, "This will soon be over. A little more patience. The priest will go away. Fauchelevent will take

Mestienne away for a drink. They'll leave me. Then Fauchelevent will come back alone, and I'll get out. All that will take a good hour."

The deep voice resumed. "*Requiescat in pace.*"

And the child's voice said, "*Amen.*"

Jean Valjean, listening intently, made out something like receding footsteps.

"Now they've gone," he thought. "I am alone."

All at once, like a clap of thunder, he heard a sound above his head.

It was a spadeful of earth falling on the coffin.

A second spadeful of earth fell.

One of the breathing holes was stopped up.

A third spadeful of earth fell.

Then a fourth.

There are things stronger than the strongest man. Jean Valjean lost consciousness.

VII

IN WHICH WE LEARN THE ORIGIN OF THE SAYING "KEEP YOUR EYE ON YOUR CARD"

Here is what happened above the coffin in which Jean Valjean lay.

When the hearse had departed and the priest and the altar boy had gotten into the carriage and left, Fauchelevent, who had never taken his eyes off the gravedigger, saw him stoop and pick up his spade, which was standing in the heap of earth.

Hereupon, Fauchelevent formed a supreme resolve.

Placing himself between the grave and the gravedigger, and folding his arms, he said, "Let me pay."

The gravedigger eyed him with amazement, and replied, "What do you mean?"

Fauchelevent repeated, "Let me pay!"

"For what?"

"For the wine."

"What wine?"

"The Argenteuil."

"Where's the Argenteuil?"

"At The Good Quince."

"Go to hell!" said the gravedigger.

And he threw a spadeful of earth onto the coffin.

The coffin gave back a hollow sound. Fauchelevent staggered, and nearly fell into the grave himself. His voice touched with fear of death, he cried:

"Come on, friend, before The Good Quince closes!"

The gravedigger took up another spadeful of earth. Fauchelevent persisted:

"Let me pay," and he grabbed the gravedigger's arm.

"Listen, friend," he said, "I'm the gravedigger at the convent, and I've come to help you. It's a job we can do at night, so let's have a drink first."

And as he spoke, clinging desperately to this urgent plan, he asked himself, with some misgivings, "And even if he does have a drink—will he get drunk?"

"My good fellow," said the gravedigger, "if you insist, we'll have a drink, but only after work, never before."

And he heaved his spade again. Fauchelevent held him back.

"It's Argenteuil at six sous the pint!"

"Now," growled the gravedigger, "you're getting to be a nuisance. Ding-dong, ding-dong, the same thing over and over. Is that all you can say? Get a move on and mind your own business."

And he threw in the second spadeful.

Fauchelevent had reached the point when a man no longer knows what he is saying.

"Oh! Come on, have a drink, since I'm the one who's paying," he again repeated.

"When we've put the child to bed," said the gravedigger.

He tossed in the third spadeful, then, plunging his spade into the earth, he added, "You see now, it's going to be cold tonight, and the corpse would cry out after us, if we just dumped her there without nice warm blankets."

At this moment, in the act of filling his spade, the gravedigger bent over, and the pocket of his vest gaped open.

Fauchelevent's distracted glance fell on this pocket and remained there.

The sun was not yet hidden behind the horizon, and there was still enough light to distinguish something white in the gaping pocket.

All the lightning that the eye of a Picardy peasant can hold flashed into Fauchelevent's pupils. A new idea had just occurred to him.

Unbeknownst to the gravedigger, who was engrossed with his spadeful of earth, Fauchelevent slipped his hand from behind into the pocket, and drew out the white object.

The gravedigger flung the fourth spadeful into the open trench.

Just as he was turning for the fifth, Fauchelevent, gazing at him with imperturbable calm, asked, "By the way, my friend, do you have your card?"

The gravedigger stopped.

"What card?"

"The sun is setting."

"Well, let him put on his nightcap."

"The cemetery gate will be closed."

"Well, and so?"

"Do you have your card?"

"Oh! My card!" said the gravedigger, and he felt in his pocket.

After rummaging through one trouser pocket, he tried another. From these, he proceeded to try his watch fobs, exploring the first and turning the second inside out.

"No!" he said. "No! It's not here. I must have forgotten it."

"Fifteen francs fine!" said Fauchelevent.

The gravedigger turned green. Green is the pallor of the ashen-faced.

"Oh, my God, what an ass I am!" he exclaimed. "Fifteen francs fine!"

"Three hundred sou pieces," said Fauchelevent.

The gravedigger dropped his spade.

Fauchelevent's turn had come.

"Come on, soldier!" said Fauchelevent, "never give up. No need to kill yourself and feed the worms. Fifteen francs are fifteen francs, and besides, you might not have to pay. I'm an old hand, and you're not. I know all the tricks and traps and turns and twists of the business. I'll give you some friendly advice. One thing is sure, the sun is setting—touching the dome of the Invalides—and the graveyard will close in five minutes."

"That's true," replied the gravedigger.

"Five minutes is not enough time for you to fill the

grave—which is as deep as hell—and get out of here before the gate shuts."

"You're right."

"In which case, there's the fine of fifteen francs."

"Fifteen francs!"

"But you have time. . . . Where do you live?"

"Just beyond the gate. Fifteen minutes away. Number Eighty-seven Rue de Vaugirard."

"You do have time, if you pick up your heels and get moving."

"That's true."

"Once beyond the gate, scurry home, get your card, come back, and the gatekeeper will let you in again. When you have your card, there's nothing to pay. Then you can bury your corpse. I'll stay here and watch him while you're gone, to see he doesn't run away."

"I owe you my life, friend!"

"Off you go, quick!" said Fauchelevent.

The gravedigger, beside himself with gratitude, shook his hands and dashed off.

When the gravedigger had disappeared through the bushes, Fauchelevent listened until his footsteps died away, and then, bending over the grave, called out in a low voice: "Father Madeleine!"

No answer.

Fauchelevent shuddered. He dropped rather than climbed down into the grave, threw himself at the head of the coffin, and cried out, "Are you there?"

Silence in the coffin.

Fauchelevent, no longer able to breathe for the shivering, took his cold chisel and hammer, and wrenched off the top board. Jean Valjean's face could be seen in the twilight, his eyes closed and cheeks colorless.

Fauchelevent's hair stood on end with alarm; he rose to his feet, then tottered back against the side of the grave, ready to collapse on the coffin. He looked at Jean Valjean.

Jean Valjean lay there pallid and motionless.

Fauchelevent murmured in a voice low as a whisper, "He's dead!"

Then straightening up and crossing his arms so violently that his clenched fists beat against his shoulders, he exclaimed, "This is the way I've saved him!"

Then the poor old man began to sob, talking to himself

out loud—it is a mistake to think that talking to oneself is not natural; powerful emotions often speak aloud.

"It's Father Mestienne's fault. What did he go and die for, the fool? What was the use of going off that way, just when no one expected it? He's the one that killed poor Monsieur Madeleine. Father Madeleine! He's in the coffin. It's over. Now what's the sense of these things? Good God! He's dead! Yes, and his little girl—what am I to do with her? What will the fruit seller say? That a man like that could die like this. My Lord, is it possible! When I think that he got down under my cart! . . . Father Madeleine! Father Madeleine! Mercy, he's suffocated, I said so—but he wouldn't believe me. Now, here's a pretty piece of business! He's dead—the best of the very best men God ever made; the very best! And his little girl! I'm not going back there again. I'm going to stay here. To have done such a thing! Fine lot of good to be two old graybeards, in order to be two old fools. But, to begin with, how did he ever get into the convent—that's where it all started. Things like that shouldn't be. Father Madeleine! Father Madeleine! Father Madeleine! Madeleine! Monsieur Madeleine! Monsieur Mayor! He doesn't hear me. Get yourself out of this one now."

And he tore his hair.

From far off, through the trees, came a harsh grating sound. It was the cemetery gate swinging shut.

Fauchelevent again bent over Jean Valjean, but suddenly shot back with all the recoil possible in a grave. Jean Valjean's eyes were open, and gazing at him.

To observe death is terrifying, and to see a resurrection is nearly as much so. Fauchelevent turned cold and white as a stone, haggard and utterly disconcerted by all the excess emotion and, not knowing whether he was dealing with the dead or the living, stared at Jean Valjean, who in turn stared at him.

"I was falling asleep," said Jean Valjean.

And he sat up.

Fauchelevent dropped on his knees.

"Oh, blessed Virgin! How you frightened me!"

Then, springing again to his feet, he cried, "Thank you, Father Madeleine!"

Jean Valjean had merely fainted. The open air had revived him.

Joy is the reflex of terror. Fauchelevent had nearly as much difficulty as Jean Valjean in coming to his senses.

"Then you're not dead! Oh, what good sense you have! I called you so hard you came back. When I saw you with your eyes shut, I said, 'Oh no! He's suffocated!' I'd have gone stark raving mad—mad enough for a strait-jacket. They'd have put me in the Bicêtre. What do you think I'd have done, if you'd been dead? And your little girl! The fruit woman wouldn't have understood a thing about it! A child dumped into her lap, and its grandfather dead! That's a fine how-de-do. By all the saints in heaven, what a fix! Ah! But you're alive—that takes the cake!"

"I'm cold," said Jean Valjean.

These words called Fauchelevent right back to reality, which was urgent. Even when restored, these two men unconsciously felt a peculiar agitation and a strange inner uneasiness from the sinister disorientation of the place.

"Let's get out of here right away," said Fauchelevent.

He groped in his pocket and drew out a flask he had thought to bring along. "But first a drop of this!" he said.

The flask completed what the open air had begun. Jean Valjean took a swallow of brandy and felt thoroughly restored.

He got out of the coffin, and helped Fauchelevent nail down the lid again. Three minutes later they were out of the grave.

Fauchelevent was calm enough. He took his time. The cemetery was closed. There was no need to fear the return of Gribier, the new gravedigger, who was at home, hunting his card, and rather unlikely to find it, as it was in Fauchelevent's pocket. Without his card, he could not get back into the cemetery.

Fauchelevent took the spade and Jean Valjean the pick, and together they buried the empty coffin.

When the grave was filled, Fauchelevent said to Jean Valjean, "Come on, let's go; I'll keep the spade, and you take the pick."

Night was coming on.

Jean Valjean found it hard to move and walk. In the coffin he had stiffened considerably, become something of a corpse himself. The anchylosis of death had gripped him in his narrow wooden box, and, in a sense, he had to thaw himself out of the sepulcher.

"You're numb," said Fauchelevent; "and what a pity I'm bandy-legged, or we'd run a bit."

"No matter!" Jean Valjean replied. "A few steps will put my legs back in walking order."

They left by the avenues the hearse had taken. When they reached the closed gate and the porter's lodge, Fauchelevent, who had the gravedigger's card in his hand, dropped it into the box, the porter drew the cord, the gate opened, and they went through.

"How well it's going!" said Fauchelevent; "what a good plan you had, Father Madeleine!"

They passed the Vaugirard Gate with the greatest of ease. Near a graveyard, a pick and spade are your passports.

The Rue de Vaugirard was deserted.

"Father Madeleine," said Fauchelevent, as he went along, looking up at the houses, "you have better eyes than mine—which is Number Eighty-seven?"

"It's this one right here," said Jean Valjean.

"There's no one in the street," resumed Fauchelevent. "Give me the pick and wait a couple minutes."

Fauchelevent went into No. 87, climbed to the top floor, guided by the instinct that always leads the poor to the garret, and knocked, in the dark, at the door of a little attic room. A voice called out, "Come in!"

It was Gribier's voice.

Fauchelevent opened the door. The gravedigger's home was, like all shelters of the needy, an unfurnished but much-littered loft. A packing case of some kind—a coffin, perhaps—took the place of a bureau, a straw pallet the place of a bed, and the floor was both chairs and table. In one corner, on a ragged old scrap of carpet, was a haggard woman, and a number of children were huddled together. The whole of the wretched interior bore traces of recent upheaval. One would have said that there had been a highly localized earthquake. The lids were out of place, the ragged garments scattered about, the pitcher broken, the mother had been weeping, and the children probably beaten—all traces of a wild and disruptive search. It was plain the gravedigger had been looking wildly for his card and had made everything in the attic, from his pitcher to his wife, responsible for the loss. He looked desperate.

But Fauchelevent was in too great a hurry to end his adventure to notice this sad side of his triumph.

As he came in, he said, "I've brought your spade and pick."

Gribier looked at him dazedly. "Oh, it's you?"

"And, tomorrow morning, you'll find your card with the gatekeeper of the cemetery."

And he set down the pick and spade on the floor.

"What does all this mean?" asked Gribier.

"Why, it means that you let your card fall out of your pocket; that I found it on the ground when you had gone; that I buried the corpse; that I filled in the grave; that I finished your job; that the gatekeeper will give you your card, and that you won't have to pay the fifteen francs. That's what it means, soldier!"

"Thanks, friend!" exclaimed Gribier, in amazement. "Next time I treat."

VIII

SUCCESSFUL INTERROGATION

An hour later, in the middle of the night, two men and a child stood in front of No. 62, Petite Rue Picpus. The older man lifted the knocker and rapped.

It was Fauchelevent, Jean Valjean, and Cosette.

The two men had gone for Cosette to the shop of the fruit seller of the Rue du Chemin-Vert, where Fauchelevent had left her the evening before. Cosette had spent the twenty-four hours wondering what it all meant and trembling in silence. She trembled so much that she had not wept, nor had she eaten or slept. The worthy fruit woman had asked her a thousand questions without obtaining any answer beyond an unvarying sad look. Cosette did not let out a word of all she had heard and seen in the last two days. She guessed that they were going through a crisis. She felt, deep down, that she had to be "good." Who has not experienced the powerful effect of four words pronounced a certain way in the ear of some little frightened creature, "Don't say a thing!" Fear is mute. Besides, no one ever keeps a secret as well as a child.

But when, after those mournful twenty-four hours, she again saw Jean Valjean, she uttered such a cry of joy that any thoughtful person hearing her would have detected in it an escape from the brink of some abyss.

Fauchelevent belonged to the convent and knew all the passwords. Every door opened before him.

Thus had that doubly fearful problem been solved: getting out and getting back in.

The doorkeeper, who had his instructions, opened the little side door, which served to communicate between the court and the garden, and which, twenty years ago, could still be seen from the street, in the wall at the far end of the court, facing the carriage entrance. The porter admitted all three by this door, and from that point they went to the private inner parlor, where Fauchelevent had, on the previous evening, received the orders of the prioress.

The prioress, rosary in hand, was waiting for them. A mother, her veil down, stood near her. A modest taper lit, or really, pretended to light up, the parlor.

The prioress scrutinized Jean Valjean. Nothing scans so carefully as a downcast eye.

Then she proceeded to question him: "You are the brother?"

"Yes, Reverend Mother," replied Fauchelevent.

"What is your name?"

Fauchelevent replied, "Ultimus Fauchelevent!"

He had actually had a brother named Ultimus, who was dead.

"From what part of the country are you?"

Fauchelevent answered, "From Picquigny, near Amiens."

"How old are you?"

Fauchelevent answered, "Fifty."

"What work do you do?"

Fauchelevent answered, "Gardener."

"Are you a true Christian?"

Fauchelevent answered, "All of our family is."

"Is this your little girl?"

Fauchelevent answered, "Yes, Reverend Mother."

"You are her father?"

Fauchelevent answered, "Her grandfather."

The mother said to the prioress in an undertone, "He answers well."

Jean Valjean had not spoken a word.

The prioress looked at Cosette attentively, and then said, as an aside to the mother, "She will be homely."

The two mothers talked together very softly for a few minutes in a corner of the parlor, then the prioress turned and said, "Father Fauvent, you will have another knee-strap and bell. We need two, now."

So, next morning, two little bells were heard tinkling in the garden, and the nuns could not resist lifting a corner of their veils. They saw two men digging side by side, in the lower part of the garden under the trees—Fauvent and another. Great event! The silence was broken so far as to say, "It's an assistant gardener!"

The mothers added, "He is Father Fauvent's brother."

Jean Valjean was now installed; he had the leather knee-strap and bell; from then on it was official: His name was Ultimus Fauchelevent.

The strongest recommendation for Cosette's admission had been the prioress's remark, "She will be homely."

Having uttered this prediction, the prioress immediately took Cosette into her friendship and gave her a place in the school building as a charity pupil.

There is nothing but logic in this. Although they have no mirrors in convents, women are conscious of their own appearance; young girls who know they are pretty do not readily become nuns; the inclination to the calling being generally in inverse proportion to good looks, more is expected from the homely than from the attractive ones. Hence a marked preference for the homely.

This whole affair elevated old Fauchelevent; he had achieved a triple success; in the eyes of Jean Valjean whom he had rescued and sheltered; with the gravedigger, Gribier, whom he had saved from a fine; and, at the convent, which, thanks to him, in retaining Mother Crucifixion's coffin under the altar, eluded Caesar and satisfied God. There was a coffin with a body in it at the Petit-Picpus, and a coffin without a body in the Vaugirard cemetery. Public order was greatly disturbed by this, undoubtedly, but nobody was aware of it. As for the convent, its gratitude to Fauchelevent was deep. Fauchelevent became the best of servants and the most precious of gardeners.

At the next visit of the archbishop the prioress related the affair to His Grace, half by way of a confession and half as a boast.

The archbishop, on leaving the convent, spoke of it with commendation and very quietly to M. de Latil, the confessor of the King's brother and subsequently Archbishop of Rheims and a cardinal. This praise and admiration for Fauchelevent traveled far, for it went to Rome. We have seen a note addressed by the then reigning pope, Leo XII, to one of his relatives, Monsignore of the Papal Nuncio in Paris, who bore the same name as his own, Della Genga. It contained these lines: "It seems that in a convent in Paris, there is an excellent gardener who is a saintly man, named Fauvan." Not a whisper of all this fame reached Fauchelevent in his shanty; he continued to weed and graft and cover his melon-beds without being in the least aware of his excellence and holiness. He had no more inkling of his splendid reputation than any Durham or Surrey ox whose picture is published in the *London Illustrated News* with this inscription: "The ox that won the blue ribbon at the cattle show."

IX

ENCLOSURE

At the convent Cosette still kept quiet. She very naturally thought herself Jean Valjean's daughter. Moreover, knowing nothing, there was nothing she could tell, and then, in any case, she would not have told anything. As we have noted, nothing accustoms children to silence like misfortune. Cosette had suffered so much that she was afraid of everything, even speaking, even breathing. A single word had so often brought down an avalanche on her head! She had scarcely begun to feel reassured since she had been with Jean Valjean. She soon became accustomed to the convent. Still, she longed for Catherine, but didn't dare say so. One day, however, she said to Jean

Valjean, "If I'd known, Father, I would have brought her, too."

In becoming a pupil at the convent, Cosette had to wear the uniform of the schoolgirls. Jean Valjean succeeded in having the clothes she gave up given to him. It was the same mourning outfit he had her put on when she left the Thénardiers. It was not yet very worn. Jean Valjean rolled up the clothes, as well as the wool stockings and shoes, with a great deal of camphor and other aromatic things that convents are full of, and packed them in a small suitcase that he managed to procure. He put this suitcase on a chair near his bed, and always kept the key to it in his pocket.

"Father," Cosette asked him one day, "what is in that box there that smells so good?"

Father Fauchelevent, besides the "glory" we have just described, of which he was unconscious, was recompensed for his good deed; in the first place it made him happy, and then he had less work to do, as it was divided. Finally, as he was very fond of tobacco, he found the presence of M. Madeleine advantageous in another point of view; he used three times as much tobacco as before, and infinitely more voluptuously, since M. Madeleine paid for it. The nuns did not adopt the name of Ultimus; they called Jean Valjean "the other Fauvent."

If the holy women had possessed the slightest trace of Javert's discriminating keen eyesight, they might have noticed in course of time that when there was any little errand to do outside on account of the garden, it was always the elder Fauchelevent, old, infirm, and lame as he was, who went, and never the other; but, whether eyes continually fixed on God cannot play the spy, or whether they preferred constantly watching one another, they noticed nothing.

However, Jean Valjean was quite satisfied to keep quiet and still. Javert watched the neighborhood for a good long month.

For Jean Valjean the convent was like an island surrounded by wide waters. Henceforth these four walls were the world to him. Within them he could see enough of the sky to be serene, and enough of Cosette to be happy.

A very pleasant life began again for him.

He lived with Fauchelevent in the outbuilding at the

foot of the garden. This simple structure, built of scraps, which was still standing in 1845, consisted, as we have already stated, of three rooms, bare to the walls. The main one had been forcibly pressed upon M. Madeleine by Fauchelevent, for Jean Valjean had resisted in vain. The wall of this room, besides the two nails used for hanging up the knee-strap and the hoe, was decorated with a royalist specimen of paper money of '93, pasted above the fireplace, of which the following is a rendering:

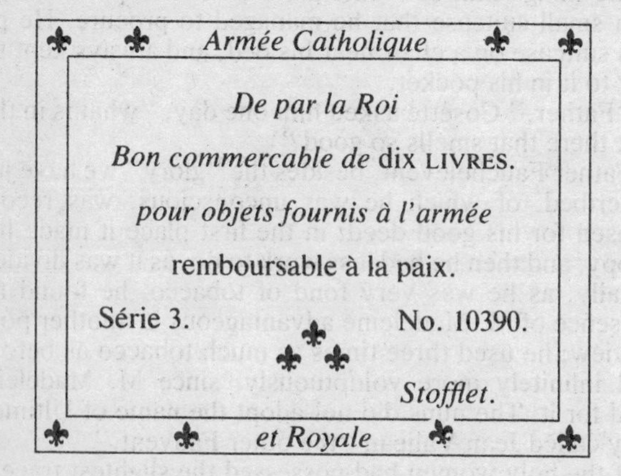
Armée Catholique

De par la Roi

Bon commercable de DIX LIVRES.

pour objets fournis à l'armée

remboursable à la paix.

Série 3. No. 10390.

Stofflet.

et Royale

This Vendean promissory note had been tacked to the wall by the preceding gardener, a former member of the Chouan, or Royalist, party, who had died at the convent and whom Fauchelevent had succeeded.

Jean Valjean worked all day in the garden and was very useful there. He had formerly been a pruner and was now quite pleased to be a gardener. The reader may recall that he was a veritable horticultural encyclopedia. His knowledge he turned to good account. Nearly all the orchard trees were wild stock; he grafted them and made them bear excellent fruit.

Cosette was allowed to come every day and spend an hour with him. As the sisters were sad, and he was kind, the child compared him with them, and worshiped him. Every day, at the appointed hour, she would hurry to the little shed. When she entered the old place, she filled it with paradise. Jean Valjean basked in her presence and felt his own happiness increase by reason of the happiness he conferred on Cosette. The delight we inspire in others has this enchanting peculiarity that, far from being diminished like every other reflection, it returns to us more radiant than ever. During recess, Jean Valjean would watch her from a distance as she played and romped, and he could distinguish her laughter among all the rest.

For now Cosette laughed.

Even her face had, in some measure, changed. The gloomy cast had disappeared. Laughter is sunshine; it chases winter from the human face.

When the recess was over and Cosette went in, Jean Valjean watched the windows of her schoolroom and at night he would get out of bed to take a look at the windows of the room in which she slept.

God has his own ways. The convent contributed, like Cosette, to confirm and complete in Jean Valjean the bishop's work. It cannot be denied that one of virtue's phases ends in pride. That way lies a bridge built by the Devil. Perhaps Jean Valjean was, without knowing it, near that very phase of virtue and that very bridge, when Providence flung him into the convent of the Petit-Picpus. So long as he compared himself only with the bishop, he had found himself unworthy and remained humble; but, for some time now, he had been comparing himself with the rest of men, and pride was springing up in him. Who knows? He might have finished by going gradually back to hatred.

The convent stopped him in this descent.

It was the second place of captivity he had seen. In his youth, in what had been for him the beginning of life, and later, quite recently too, he had seen another, a frightful place, a terrible place, whose severities had always seemed to him the iniquity of public justice and the crime of the law. Now, after having seen prison, he saw the cloister, and reflecting that he had been a convict, and that he now was, so to speak, a spectator of the cloister, he anxiously compared them in thought.

Sometimes he would lean on his spade and descend slowly along the endless spirals of reverie.

He thought of his former companions, and how miserable they were. They rose at dawn and toiled till nightfall. Scarcely allowed to sleep, they lay on cots and were allowed only mattresses two inches thick in halls that were warmed only during the harshest months. They were dressed in hideous red shirts and were favored with a pair of canvas pants in the heat of midsummer, and a wool jacket on their backs during the bitterest cold. They had no wine to drink, no meat except when sent on "extra hard labor." They lived without names, identified solely by numbers, and reduced, as it were, to ciphers, lowering their eyes, lowering their voices, with their hair cropped short, under the rod, in shame.

Then his thoughts reverted to the beings before his eyes.

These beings, too, lived with their hair close cut, their eyes bent down, their voices hushed, not in shame, but amid the world's scoffing; not with their backs bruised by the jailers stick, but with shoulders lacerated by self-inflicted penance. Their worldly names had perished, too, and they now existed under austere designations alone. They never ate meat and never drank wine; they often went until evening without food. They were not dressed in red shirts, but in black wool habits heavy in summer, light in winter, unable to increase or diminish them, without even the privilege, according to the season, of substituting a linen dress or a wool cloak, and then, for six months of the year, they wore underclothing of serge which gave them fevers. They lived not in dormitories warmed only in the bitterest frost of winter, but in cells where fire was never kindled. They slept not on mattresses two inches thick, but on straw. Finally, they were not even allowed to sleep, since every night after a day of labor, when first surrendering to rest, at the moment when they were just falling asleep, and barely feeling a little warmth, they were required to waken, get up and assemble for prayers in a freezing gloomy chapel, kneeling on the cold stone pavement.

On certain days, each one of these beings in turn had to stay for twelve hours at a time kneeling on the flagstones, or prostrate on her face, with her arms stretched out in a cross.

The others were men, these were women. What had these men done? They had robbed, ravished, plundered, killed, assassinated. They were highwaymen, forgers, poisoners, incendiaries, murderers, parricides. What had these women done? They had done nothing.

On one side, robbery, fraud, violence, lust, homicide,

every sort of sacrilege, every variety of offense; on the other, one thing only—innocence.

A perfect innocence almost raised aloft in a mysterious Assumption, still clinging to earth through virtue, already touching heaven through holiness.

On the one hand, the mutual admission of crimes detailed with bated breath; on the other, faults confessed aloud. And oh, what crimes! And oh, what faults!

On one side foul miasma, on the other ineffable perfume. On the one side, a moral pestilence, watched day and night, held in subjection by the cannon, and slowly consuming its infected victims; on the other, chaste kindling of every soul near the same hearth. There, utter gloom; here, the shadow, but a shadow full of light, and the light full of glowing radiations.

Two seats of slavery; but, in the former, rescue possible, a legal limit always in view, and also escape. In the second, perpetuity, the only hope at the furthest reaches of the future, that gleam of liberty which men call death.

In the first, the captives were chained by chains alone; in the other, chained by faith.

What resulted from the first? One vast curse, the gnashing of teeth, hatred, desperate depravity, a cry of rage against human society, sarcasm against heaven. What issued from the second? Benediction and love. And, in these two places, so alike, so different, these two species of beings so dissimilar were performing the same work, expiation.

Jean Valjean thoroughly understood the expiation of the first; personal expiation, expiation for oneself. But, he did not understand the other, of these blameless, spotless creatures, and he wondered tremulously: "Expiation of what? What expiation?"

A voice replied within his conscience: the most divine of all human generosity, expiation for others.

Here we withhold all theories of our own, we are merely the narrator; we place ourselves at Jean Valjean's point of view and merely reproduce his impressions.

Before him, he had the sublime summit of self-denial, the peak of virtue; innocence forgiving men their sins and expiating them in their stead; servitude endured, torture accepted, chastisement and misery sought by souls that had not sinned to save souls that had; the love of humanity losing itself in the love of God, but remaining there, distinct and supplicating; sweet, frail beings bearing the torments of those who are punished and the smile of those who are rewarded. And then he remembered he had dared to complain.

Often, in the middle of the night, he would get out of bed to listen to the grateful anthem of these innocent beings overwhelmed with austerities, and he felt the blood run cold in his veins as he reflected that those who were justly punished never raised their voices toward Heaven except to blaspheme, and that he, wretch that he was, had lifted his clenched fist against God.

Another strange thing that made him meditate profoundly seemed like an intimation whispered in his ear by Providence itself: the scaling of walls, the climbing over enclosures, the risk taken in defiance of danger or death, the difficult and painful ascent—those very efforts he had made to escape from the other place of expiation, he had made to enter this one. Was this a symbol of his destiny?

This house, also, was a prison, and dismally similar to the other from which he had fled, and yet he had never conceived anything like it.

Once more he was seeing grates, bolts, and bars of iron—to shut in whom? Angels. Those lofty walls he had seen surrounding lions were now encircling lambs.

It was a place of expiation, not of punishment; and yet it was still more austere, more somber, and more pitiless than the other. These virgins were more harshly bent than the convicts. The harsh, cold wind that had frozen his youth careened across that grated moat and manacled the vultures; but a blast still more biting and cruel beat upon the dove cote.

And why?

When he thought of these things, everything in him gave way before this mystery of sublimity. In these meditations, pride vanished. Again and again he reverted to himself; he felt his own pitiful unworthiness, and often wept. Everything that had occurred in his life during the last six months led him back toward the holy injunctions of the bishop—Cosette through love, the convent through humility.

Sometimes, in the evening, about dusk, at the hour when the garden was deserted, he was seen kneeling in the middle of the walk that ran beside the chapel, in front of the window through which he had looked, on the night of his first arrival, turned toward the spot where he knew that the sister performing the reparation was prostrate in prayer. Thus he prayed kneeling before the sister. It was as though he did not dare kneel directly before God.

Everything around him, this quiet garden, the balmy flowers, the children shouting with joy, the meek and simple women, the silent cloister, gradually entered into all his being, and gradually his soul subsided into silence like the cloister, into fragrance like the flowers, into peace like the garden, into simplicity like the women, into joy like the children. And then he reflected that two houses of God had received him in succession at the two critical moments of his life, the first when every door was closed and human society rejected him; the second, when human society was once more howling on his track, and prison once more gaped for him; and that, had it not been for the first, he would have fallen back into crime, and had it not been for the second, into punishment.

His whole heart melted in gratitude and he loved more and more.

Several years went by like this. Cosette was growing up.

of his first arrival, turned toward the spot where he knew that the sister performing the reparation was prostrate in prayer. Thus he prayed kneeling before the sister. It was as though he did not dare kneel directly before God.

Everything around him, this quiet garden, the balmy flowers, the children shouting with joy, the meek and simple women, the silent cloister, gradually entered into all his being, and gradually his soul subsided into silence like the cloister, into fragrance like the flowers, into peace like the garden, into simplicity like the women, into joy like the children. And then he reflected that two houses of God had received him in succession at the two critical moments of his life, the first when every door was closed and human society rejected him; the second, when human society was once more howling on his track, and prison once more gaped for him; and that, had it not been for the first, he would have fallen back into crime, and had it not been for the second, into punishment.

His whole heart melted in gratitude and he loved more and more.

Several years went by like this. Cosette was growing up.

MARIUS

Book One

PARIS ATOMIZED

I

PARVULUS

Paris has a child, and the forest has a bird; the bird is called the sparrow; the child is called the *gamin*.

Couple these two ideas, the one containing all the heat of the furnace, the other all the light of dawn; strike together these two sparks, Paris and infancy; and from them leaps forth a little creature. *Homuncio,* Plautus would say.

This little creature is full of joy. He does not have food every day, yet he goes to the theater every evening, if he wants to. He has no shirt on his back, no shoes on his feet, no roof over his head; he is like the flies in the air who lack all these things. He is from seven to thirteen years of age, lives in gangs, roams the streets, sleeps in the open air, wears an old pair of his father's pants that come down to his heels, an old hat from some other father that covers his ears, and a single suspender of yellow selvage, runs around, is always on the lookout, kills time, puffs a pipe, swears like an imp, hangs around the bistros, knows the thieves and robbers, is cozy with the street girls, rattles off slang, sings dirty songs, and is not at all bad at heart. This is because he has a pearl in his soul, innocence, and pearls do not dissolve in mud. So long as man is a child, God wills him to be innocent.

If one asked this vast city, "What is this creature?" it would answer, "It is my cub."

II

SOME OF HIS DISTINGUISHING MARKS

The *gamin* of Paris is the dwarf of the giantess.

We will not exaggerate; sometimes this cherub of the gutter does have a shirt, but then only one; sometimes he has shoes, but then they have no soles; sometimes he has shelter, and he loves it, because there he finds his mother; but he prefers the street, because there he finds his liberty. He has games of his own, devilish tricks of his own based on a hearty hatred of the bourgeoisie; he has his own metaphors; to be dead he calls "eating dandelions by the root"; he has his own occupations such as running for hacks, letting down carriage steps, sweeping toll crossings in rainy weather from one side of the street to the other, which he terms making *ponts des arts,* shouting out the speeches often made by the authorities on behalf of the French people, and dredging the cracks between the paving blocks; he has his own kind of money, consisting of all the little bits of wrought copper to be found on the public thoroughfares. This curious coin, which takes the name of loques, has an unvarying and well-regulated value throughout this little bohemia of children.

He has a fauna all his own, which he studies carefully in the corners; the good Lord's bug, the death's head grub, the mower, the devil, a black insect that threatens you by twisting around its tail armed with two horns. He has his fabulous monster with scales on its belly though not a lizard, has warts on its back though not a toad, that lives in the crevices of old lime-kilns and dry cisterns, a black, velvety, slimy, crawling creature, sometimes swift and sometimes slow, silent, staring, and so terrible that nobody has ever seen it; this monster he calls the "deaf thing." Searching for deaf things among the stones is an intimidating pleasure. Another joy is to raise a paving stone suddenly and see the wood lice. Every region of Paris is known for the finds that can be made there. There are earwigs in the lumber yards of the Ursulines, there are wood lice in the Pantheon, and tadpoles in the ditches of the Champ-de-Mars.

As for repartee, this youngster is Talleyrand's equal. He is no less cynical but more sincere. He is gifted with an odd kind of unpremeditated joviality; he stuns the shopkeeper with his wild laughter. His gaiety runs the gamut from high comedy to farce.

A funeral is passing. There is a doctor in the procession. "Hey," shouts a *gamin,* "since when do doctors take their work home?"

Another happens to be in a crowd. A grave-looking man, wearing spectacles and brass, turns on him indignantly, "You scamp, you've just been grabbing my wife's waist!"

"Me, sir! Search me!"

III

HE IS AGREEABLE

In the evening, by means of the few pennies he always manages to scrape together, the *homuncio* sees some theater. Merely by crossing that magic threshold, he is transfigured; he was a *gamin,* he becomes a *titi*. Theaters are a sort of ship turned upside down with the bilges at the top; the *titi* pile into this hold. The *titi* is to the *gamin* what the butterfly is to the grub; the same creature, but soaring on high. It is enough for him to be there with his radiant delight, his power of enthusiasm and joy, and his applause like the beating of wings, to make those bilges —close, dark, fetid, filthy, unwholesome, hideous, and detestable—a real paradise.

Give a creature the useless, deprive him of the necessary, and you have the *gamin*.

The *gamin* is not without a certain inclination toward literature. His tendency, however—we say it with a suitable degree of regret—would not be considered classic. By nature, he is only slightly academic. For instance, the popularity of Mlle. Mars among this little audience of children was laced with a touch of irony. The *gamin* called her Mademoiselle *Muche,* Lady Hide.

This creature jeers, wrangles, sneers, jangles, has frippery like a baby and rags like a philosopher, fishes and hunts in the sewer, extracts gaiety from trash, lashes the street corners with his wit, sneers and bites, hisses and sings, applauds and hoots, tempers Hallelujah with turalura, chants all sorts of rhythms from De Profundis to the *Chie-en-lit,* finds without searching, knows what he does not know, is Spartan to the point of flimflam, witless to the point of wisdom, lyric even to impurity, would squat on Olympus, wallows in the dung heap, and comes out covered with stars. The *gamin* of Paris is an urchin Rabelais.

He is never satisfied with his trousers unless they have a watch fob.

He is seldom astonished, still less often frightened, turns superstitions into doggerel and sings them, deflates exaggerations, makes light of mysteries, sticks out his tongue at ghosts, takes the poetry out of anything on stilts, and introduces caricature into all epic pomposities. This is not because he is prosaic, far from it; but he substitutes the phantasmagoria of farce for solemn dreams. If Adamastor appeared, he would holler, "Hey there! old goblin!"

IV

HE CAN BE USEFUL

Paris begins with the idly curious and ends with the *gamin,* two beings no other city achieves; passive acceptance satisfied with merely looking on, and tireless enterprise; Prudhomme and Fouillou. Paris alone has this in its natural history. All monarchy is summarized in the bystander; all anarchy in the *gamin.*

This pale child of the Paris faubourgs lives, grows, and gets into and out of scrapes, in the midst of suffering, a thoughtful witness of our social realities and our human problems. He think himself carefree, but he is not. He looks on, ready to laugh; ready, too, for something else. Whoever you may be who call yourselves Prejudice, Abuse, Ignominy, Oppression, Iniquity, Despotism, Injustice, Fanaticism, Tyranny, beware of the open-mouthed *gamin*.

This little fellow will grow.

What clay is he made of? Ordinary mud. A handful of common soil, a breath and, behold, Adam! A God merely has to pass by. A God has always passed by the *gamin*. Fortune works on this little creature. By this word fortune we mean, to some degree, chance. Now this pygmy—thoroughly kneaded with the coarse common earth, ignorant, illiterate, wild, vulgar, riffraff as he is—will he become an Ionian or a Boeotian? Wait; wheels turn, the life of Paris, the demon that creates children of chance and men of destiny, reversing the work of the Latin potter, makes the jug into an amphora.

V

HIS FRONTIERS

The *gamin* loves the city, he loves solitude, too, having something of the wise man in him. *Urbis amator,* like Fuscus; *ruris amator,* like Flaccus.

To wander about, musing, that is to say strolling, is for a philosopher a good way to pass time; particularly in that kind of mock countryside, ugly and strange, made up of two natures, that surrounds certain large cities, particularly Paris. To study the suburb is to study the amphibious. End of trees, beginning of houses, end of grass, beginning of pavement, end of furrows, beginning of shops, end of ruts, beginning of passions, end of the divine murmur, beginning of human hubbub; in all of this, an extraordinary level of interest.

Because of this, in these rather uninviting spots eternally classified as "gloomy," the dreamer selects his apparently aimless walks.

The writer of these lines has long been a wanderer

around the gates of Paris, and to him they are a moving source of memories. That close-clipped grass, the stony walks, the chalk, the clay and gypsum, the harsh monotony of open lots and fallow land, those plants of the market gardeners suddenly glimpsed in the background, that mixture of wild nature and urban landscape, those vast empty patches where the drummers of the garrison hold their noisy school and stammer out a sort of tentative battle, those solitudes by day and ambushes by night, the tottering old mill turning in the breeze, the hoists of the stone quarries, the wine shops at the cemetery corners, the mysterious charm of the high dark walls that slice right across vast stretches of vacant land, bathed in sunshine and alive with butterflies—all this attracted him.

Hardly anyone knows those strange places, the Glacière, the Cunette, the hideous wall of Grenelle, pockmarked by bullets, the Montparnasse, the Fosse-aux-Loups, the white hazel trees on the banks of the Marne, Montsouris, the Tombe-Issoire, the Pierre-Plate de Chatillon where there is an old exhausted quarry no longer good for anything but raising mushrooms, closed at ground level by a trapdoor of rotten boards. The Campagna of Rome is one idea; the suburb of Paris is another; to see nothing in an inviting landscape but fields, houses, or trees, is superficial; all aspects of things are thoughts of God. The place where an open plain meets a city is always marked by some indescribable, penetrating melancholy. There, nature and humanity address you at the same time. There, the originalities of place show up.

Anyone who, like ourselves, has rambled through these solitudes next to our suburbs, which one might call the limbo of Paris, has noticed, here and there, in the most deserted spot and at the most unexpected moment, beside some straggling hedge or in the corner of some dismal wall, little helter-skelter groups of children, filthy, muddy, dusty, uncombed, disheveled, playing mumbledy peg, crowned with violets. These are all the runaways of poor families. The outer boulevard is their breathing space, and the suburb belongs to them. There they play truant, continually. There they sing, ingenuously, their collection of dirty songs. They are there, or rather, they live there, far from all eyes, in the soft radiance of May or June, kneeling around a hole in the ground, flicking marbles with their thumbs, squabbling over pennies, irresponsible, birds flown, let loose and happy; and, the moment they see you, remembering that they have a trade and must make their living, they offer to sell you an old wool stocking full of June bugs, or a bunch of lilacs. These meetings with strange children are among the seductive but at the same time saddening charms of the Paris environs.

Sometimes among this crowd of boys, there are a few little girls—are they their sisters?—almost young women, thin, feverish, freckled, tanned, wreathed in rye-straw and poppies, gay, wild, barefoot. Some of them are seen eating cherries among the growing grain. In the evening, their laughter can be heard. These groups, warmly lit by the full noonday sun, or dimly seen in the twilight, linger in the dreamer's mind, and these visions mingle with his reveries.

Paris, the center; the banlieue, the circumference; to these children, this is the whole earth. They never venture beyond it. They can no more live outside of the Paris atmosphere than fish can live out of water. To them, beyond six miles from the city gates there is nothing more. Ivry, Gentilly, Arcueil, Belleville, Aubervilliers, Ménilmontant, Choisy-le-Roi, Billancourt, Meudon, Issy, Vanvre, Sèvres, Puteaux, Neuilly, Gennevilliers, Colombes, Romainville, Chatou, Asnières, Bougival, Nanterre, Enghien, Noisy-le-Sec, Nogent, Gournay, Drancy, Gonesse; these are the ends of the universe.

VI

A BIT OF HISTORY

At the time, though it is almost contemporary, in which the action of this story is laid, there was not, as there now is, a police officer at every street corner (an advantage we have no time to discuss); truant children abounded in Paris. The statistics gave an average of two hundred and sixty homeless children, picked up annually by the police on their rounds, in open lots, in houses under construction, and under the arches of bridges. One of these nests, still well-known, produced "the swallows of the Pont d'Arcole?" This is actually the most disastrous of social symptoms. All the crimes of man begin with the vagrancy of childhood.

We must make an exception of Paris, however. To a considerable degree, and notwithstanding the scenes we have just recalled, the exception is just. While in every other city the truant boy is the lost man; while almost everywhere the boy on his own is, in some way, dedicated and abandoned to a sort of fatal immersion in public vices which eat out of him all honesty, and conscience itself, the *gamin* of Paris, we must insist, unpolished and spotted as he is on the surface, is almost intact within. A marvelous thing to note, and one that shines forth in the glorious probity of our popular revolutions; a certain incorruptibility results from the mental tone that is to the air of Paris what salt is to the water of the ocean. To breathe the air of Paris preserves the soul.

What we say here in no way alleviates that pang we feel whenever we meet one of these children, around whom we seem to see torn and drifting ties of the disrupted family. In our present civilization, still so incomplete, it is not very abnormal to find these family ruptures separating in the darkness, scarcely knowing what has become of their children—dropping fragments of their life on the public highway. This produces confused destinies. It is called, for the sad event has its own expression, "being thrown onto the streets of Paris."

This abandoning of children, it must be said in passing, was not discouraged by the old monarchy. A little of Egypt and of Bohemia in the lower strata accommodated the higher spheres, and answered the purpose of the powerful. A hatred for educating the children of the people was dogma. What good was "a little learning"? Such was the password. Now, the truant child is the corollary of the ignorant child. Besides, the monarchy sometimes needed children, and then it skimmed the street.

Under Louis XIV, not to go any further back, the king very wisely wanted to build up a navy. The idea was a good one. But let us look at the means. There could be no navy if, side by side with the sailing vessel, the plaything of the wind, there were not another vessel capable of going where it pleased, to tow it along in case of need, either by oar or steam; the galleys were to the navy then, what steamers now are. So there had to be galleys, but galleys could be moved only by oarsmen, and therefore there must be galley slaves. Through the provincial administrators and the high judicial courts, Colbert made as many galley-slaves as possible. The bench set about the work with good heart. A man kept his hat on in front of a procession, a Huguenot attitude; he was sent to the galleys. A boy was found in the street; if he had no place to sleep, and was fifteen years old, he was sent to the galleys. Great reign, great age.

Under Louis XV, children disappeared in Paris; the police carried them off—nobody knows for what mysterious use. With horror, people whispered monstrous conjectures about the king's crimson baths. Barbier speaks ingenuously of these things. It sometimes happened that the officers, running short of children, took some who had fathers. In despair, the fathers went for the officers. In such cases, the court interfered and hung—whom? The officers? No. The fathers.

VII

THE GAMIN WILL HAVE HIS PLACE AMONG THE INDIAN CASTES

The Parisian order of *gamins* is almost a caste. One might say: Nobody wants anything to do with them.

This word *gamin* was printed for the first time, and passed from popular language into literature, in 1834. It was in a little work called *Claude Gueux* that the word first appeared. It created an uproar. The word was adopted.

The elements that go to make up respect among the *gamins* are very varied. We knew and had to do with one who was greatly respected and admired because he had seen a man fall from the towers of Notre Dame; another, because he had managed to get into the rear enclosure where the statues intended for the dome of the Invalides were deposited, and had swiped some of the lead; a third, because he had seen a coach turned over; and still another, because he knew a soldier who had almost knocked out a bourgeois's eye.

This explains that odd exclamation of a Parisian *gamin,* a deep lament that the people laugh at without comprehending. "Oh, Lordy, Lordy! ain't I unlucky! only think I never even saw anybody fall from a fifth floor"—the words pronounced with an inexpressible twang of his own.

And here was a fine saying for a peasant: "Father so-and-so, your wife's illness has killed her; why didn't you send for a doctor?" "What d'you expect, monsieur?" says the other. "Why, we poor people, *we have to die ourselves.*" But, if all the passiveness of the peasant is found in this saying, all the free-thinking anarchy of the urchin of the suburbs is contained in the following: A poor wretch on his way to the gallows was listening to his confessor, sitting beside him in the cart. A Paris boy hooted, "He's talking to his long-gown. Oh, the sniveler!"

A certain audacity in religious matters enhances the *gamin.* It is a great thing to have a lively wit.

Attending executions is a positive duty. These imps point to the guillotine and laugh. They give it all kinds of nicknames: "End of the Soup"—"Old Growler"—"Sky-Mother"—"The Last Mouthful," etc., etc. To miss nothing of the spectacle, they scale walls, hoist themselves onto balconies, climb trees, hang from window bars, cling to chimneys. The *gamin* is a born roofer as he is a born sailor. A roof frightens him no more than a mast. No festival comes up to the execution ground—La Grève. Samson and the Abbé Montes are the really popular names. They shout to the victim to encourage him. Sometimes, they admire him. Lacenaire, as a *gamin,* seeing the horrible Dautun die bravely, used an expression full of portent: "I was jealous of him!" In the order of *gamins* Voltaire is unknown, but they do know Papavoine. In the same tales, they mingle "the politicals" with murderers. They have traditions about the last clothes worn by all of them. They know that Tolleron had on a stoker's cap, and that Avril wore one of otter skin; that Louvel had on a round hat, that old Delaporte was bald and bare-headed, that Castaing was ruddy and good-looking, that Bories had a romantic beard, that Jean Martin kept on his suspenders, and that Lecouffé and his mother quarreled. "Now don't be finding fault with your basket," shouted a *gamin* to those two. Another, to see

Debacker pass, being too short for the crowd, began to climb a lamppost on the quay. A gendarme on that beat scowled at him. "Let me get up, Mister Gendarme," said the gamin. And then, to soften authority, he added, "I won't fall." "It's nothing to me whether or not you fall," replied the gendarme.

In the order of *gamins*, a memorable accident is greatly prized. A *gamin* reaches the very pinnacle of distinction if he happens to cut himself badly, "right to the bone."

The fist is no mean element of respect. One of the things the *gamin* is fondest of saying is, "I'm real strong!" To be left-handed makes you an object of envy. Squinting is highly esteemed.

VIII

IN WHICH WILL BE FOUND A CHARMING SAYING OF THE LATE KING

In summer, he metamorphoses into a frog; and in the evening, at nightfall, by the bridges of Austerlitz and Jena, from the coal rafts and washerwomen's boats, he plunges headfirst into the Seine, and into total infraction of the laws of modesty and the police. However, the policemen are on the lookout, and this can lead to a highly dramatic situation, which, on one occasion, gave rise to a memorable fraternal cry. This cry, which was quite famous around 1830, is a strategic signal from *gamin* to *gamin;* it is scanned like a verse of Homer, with a style of notation almost as inexplicable as the Eleusinian chant of the Panatheneans, recalling the ancient "Evohé!" It is as follows: "Watch out, Titi! Ohé-é-é! Bad stuff around the corner, beatings on the way! Grab yer duds and cut for the sewer!"

Sometimes this gnat—that's what he calls himself—can read; sometimes he can write; he always knows how to scrawl. By some unknown mysterious mutual instruction, he never hesitates to pick up all talents that may be useful in public things; from 1815 to 1830, he imitated the call of the turkey; from 1830 to 1848, he would scratch a pear on the walls. One summer evening, Louis-Philippe returning to the palace on foot, saw one of them, a little fellow so high, sweating and stretching up on tiptoe, sketching a gigantic pear on one of the pillars of the Neuilly gateway; the king, with that easy nature inherited from Henry IV, helped the boy, completed the pear, and gave the youngster a gold Louis, saying, "The pear's on that too!" The *gamin* loves uproar. A certain excess pleases him. He execrates "the curés." One day, in the Rue de l'Université, one of these young scamps was thumbing his nose at the carriage door of No. 69. "Why are you doing that at this door?" asked a passerby. The boy replied, "There's a curé there." It was, in fact, the residence of the Papal Nuncio. Nevertheless, whatever may be the Voltairian tendencies of the *gamin*, should an occasion present itself to become an altar boy, he might accept, and in that case would serve the mass properly. There are two things that tantalize him but he never attains—to overthrow the government, and to get his trousers sewn up.

The *gamin*, in his perfect state, possesses all the policemen of Paris and invariably on meeting one, can put a name to the face. He counts them off on his fingers. He studies their habits, and has special notes of his own on each one of them. He reads their souls like an open book. He will tell you offhand and without hesitating—this one is a traitor; this one is very mean; this one is tall, this one is ridiculous; (all these expressions, traitor, mean, tall, and ridiculous, have for him, a particular meaning)—"That guy thinks the Pont Neuf belongs to him, and keeps people from walking on the cornice outside of the parapets; that other one has a habit of bullying a person"; etc. etc.

IX

THE ANCIENT SOUL OF GAUL

There was something of this urchin in Poquelin, the son of the marketplace; there was something of him in Beaumarchais. The *gamin* style of life is a nuance of the Gallic mind. Mingled with good sense, it sometimes gives it added strength, as alcohol does to wine. Sometimes, it is a defect; Homer nods, agreed; one might say Voltaire plays the *gamin*. Camille Desmoulins was a faubourien. Championnet, who mistreated miracles, was a child of the Paris streets; as a small boy he had watered the porticoes of Saint-Jean-de-Beauvais and Saint-Etienne-du-Mont; he was familiar enough with the reliquary of Saint-Geneviève to command Saint Januarius's sacred vial.

The Paris *gamin* is respectful, ironic, and insolent. He has bad teeth because he is poorly fed, and his stomach suffers, and handsome eyes because he has wit. In the very presence of Jehovah, he would go hopping up the steps of Paradise. He is very good at boxing with hands and feet. Every manner of growth is possible to him. He plays in the gutter and rises up from it in riot; his effrontery is not cured by grapeshot; he was a scamp, he is a hero! Like the little Theban, he shakes the lion's skin; Barra the drummer was a Paris *gamin;* he shouts "Forward!" as the charger of Holy Writ says "Aha!" And in an instant, he goes from urchin to giant.

This child of the gutter is also the child of the ideal. Measure this span that reaches from Molière to Barra.

All in all, and to put it briefly, the *gamin* is a being who amuses himself because he is unfortunate.

X

ECCE PARIS, ECCE HOMO

To sum it all up once more, the Paris *gamin* nowadays is as the *graeculus* of Rome in ancient times, the people as a child, with the wrinkles of the old on its brow.

The *gamin* is a beauty and, at the same time, a disease of the nation—a disease that must be cured. How? By light.

Light makes whole.

Light enlightens.

All the generous sunrays of society spring from science, letters, the arts, and education. Make men, make men. Give them light, so they can give you warmth.

Sooner or later, the splendid question of universal education will take its position with the irresistible authority of absolute truth; and then those who govern under the French idea will have to make this choice: the children of France or the *gamins* of Paris; flames in the light or will o' the wisps in the gloom.

The *gamin* expresses Paris, and Paris expresses the world.

For Paris is a sum total. Paris is the ceiling of the human race. This whole prodigious city is an epitome of dead and living manners and customs. Anyone who sees Paris, seems to see the underside of all history with sky and constellations showing through. Paris has a Campidoglio, the Hôtel de Ville; a Parthenon, Notre-Dame; a Mount Aventine, the Faubourg Saint-Antoine; an Asinarium, the Sorbonne; a Pantheon, the Pantheon; a Via Sacra, the Boulevard des Italiens; a tower of the Winds, public opinion—and replaces the Gemoniae by ridicule. Its *majo* is the "faraud," its *Trasteverino* is the faubourien; its *hammal* is the strong man of the marketplace; its *lazzarone* is called the pègre; its cockney is the *gandin*. Everything that can be found anywhere is in Paris. The fishwoman of Dumarsais can hold her own with the herbwoman of Euripides, the discobolus Vejanus lives again in Forioso the tightrope-dancer, Therapontigonus Miles would go arm in arm with the grenadier Vadeboncoeur, Damasippus the curiosity dealer would be happy among the old junk shops, Vincennes would lay hold of Socrates just as the whole Agora would clap Diderot into a strong box; Grimod de la Reynière discovered roast beef cooked with its own fat as Curtillus had invented roast hedgehog; we see, again, under the balloon of the Arc de l'Etoile the trapeze mentioned in Plautus; the sword-eater of the Poecilium met by Apuleius is the saber swallower on the Pont-Neuf; the nephew of Rameau and Curculion the parasite make a pair; Ergasilus would get himself presented to Cambacérès by d'Aigrefeuille; the four dandies of Rome, Alcesimarchus, Phoedromus, Diabolus, and Argyrippe, can be seen going down la Courtille in the Labutat mail-coach; Aulus Gellius did not stay longer in front of Congrio than Charles Nodier before Punch and Judy; Marton is not a tigress, but Pardalisca was not a dragon; Pantolabus the buffoon chaffs Nomentanus the high-liver at the Café Anglais; Hermogenus is a tenor in the Champs Elysées and, around him, Thrasius the beggar dressed as Bobèche plies his trade; the bore who buttonholes you in the Tuileries makes you repeat, after a lapse of two thousand years, the apostrophe of Thesprion: *quis properantem me prehendit pallio?* The wine of Surêne parodies the wine of Alba; the red rim of Desaugiers balances the huge goblet of Balatron, Père Lachaise exhales, under nightly showers, the same glow seen in the Esquilies, and the grave of the poor purchased for five years is about the equivalent of the slave's hired coffin.

Ransack your memory for something Paris does not have. Trophonious's vat contains nothing that is not in Mesmer's tub; Ergaphilas is revived in Cagliostro; the Brahmin Vâsaphantâ is reincarnated in the Comte Saint-Germain; the cemetery of Saint-Médard turns out quite as good miracles as the Oumoumié mosque at Damascus.

Paris has an Aesop in Mayeux, and a Canidia in Mlle. Lenormand. It is alarmed like Delphi by the blinding realities of visions; it tips tables as Dodona did tripods. It puts the grisette on a throne as Rome did the courtesan; and if Louis XV is on the whole worse than Claudius, Madame Dubarry is better than Messalina. Paris combines in one wonderful type which has really lived, and is actually at our elbow now, Greek nudity, Hebrew ulcer, Gascon jest. It mingles Diogenes, Job, and Paillasse, dresses up a ghost in old numbers of the *Constitutionnel,* and looks as eccentric as Shodruc Duclos.

Though Plutarch may say, "The tyrant never grows old," Rome, under Sylla as well as under Domitian, gave in and meekly watered her wine. The Tiber was a Lethe, if we are to believe the somewhat doctrinaire eulogy pronounced on it by Varus Vibiscus: *Contra Gracchos Tiberim habemus. Bibere Tiberim, id est seditionem oblivisci*. Paris drinks a quarter of a million gallons of water per day, but that does not prevent it on occasion from sounding the alarm and ringing the tocsin.

Barring that, Paris is a good soul. It accepts everything royally; it is lenient in the realm of Venus; its Callipyge is Hottentot; as long as it laughs, it pardons; ugliness makes it merry, deformity puts it in good humor, vice distracts it; be amusing and you can be a scamp; even hypocrisy, that sublimity of cynicism, does not revolt it; it is so literary that it does not hold its nose over Basilius and is no more shocked at Tartuffe's prayer than Horace was at the petard of Priapus. No feature of the universal face is lacking in the profile of Paris. The Bal Mabile is not the polyhymnian dance of the Janiculum, but the wardrobe concessionaire there ogles the prostitute exactly as the procuress Staphyla watched the virgin Planesium. The Barrière du Combat is not a Coliseum, but there is as much ferocity as though Caesar were a spectator. The Syrian hostess has more grace than Mother Saguet, but if Virgil haunted the Roman tavern, David d'Angers, Balzac, and Charlet have sat down in the bistros of Paris. Paris is supreme. Geniuses flare up on all sides, and histrionics flourish. Adonaïs passes by in his twelve-wheeled chariot of thunder and lightning; Silenus makes his entry on his nag. For Silenus, read Ramponneau.

Paris is the synonym of Cosmos. Paris is Athens, Rome, Sybaris, Jerusalem, Pantin. All civilizations are there in abridged edition, all barbaric eras too. Paris would be annoyed to lose its guillotine.

A touch of the Place de Grève is good. What would all this continual merrymaking be without that seasoning? Our laws have wisely provided for this, and, thanks to them, the blade drips onto the mardi gras.

XI

RIDICULE AND REIGN

Of bounds and limits, Paris has none. No other city ever enjoyed this supreme control, which sometimes derides those it subjugates. *To please you, O Athenians!* cried Alexander. Paris does more than lay down the law; it lays down the fashion; Paris does more than lay down the fashion; it lays down the routine. Paris can be stupid if it likes; sometimes it indulges in this luxury, and the whole universe is stupid along with it. Then Paris wakes up, rubs its eyes, and says, "Am I ever stupid!" and bursts out laughing in the face of mankind. What a marvel, this city! How strange that all this mass of grandeur and burlesque could be so harmonious, that all this majesty is not disturbed by all the parody, and that the same mouth can blow the trump of the final judgment today and tomorrow a penny whistle; Paris has an all-commanding joviality. Its gaiety comes with thunder and its humor holds a scepter. Its hurricanes can spring from a grimace. Its outbursts, its great days, its masterpieces, its prodigies, its epics carry to the ends of the universe, and so do its cock-and-bull stories. Its laughter is a volcano that spatters the whole earth. Its jeers are sparks that catch fire. It forces on nations its caricatures along with its ideal; the loftiest monuments of human civilization accepts its sarcasms and lend their eternity to its japes. It is superb; it has a prodigious July Fourteenth that liberates the globe; it makes all nations take the oath; its night of August Fourth dispels a thousand years of feudalism in three hours; from its logic it makes the muscle of the unanimous will; it multiplies under all the forms of the sublime; its radiance touches Washington. Kosciusko, Bolivar, Botzaris, Riego, Bem, Manin, Lopez, John Brown, Garibaldi; it is every place where the future is kindling, at Boston in 1779, at l'Ile de Lèon in 1820, at Pesth in 1848, at Palermo in 1860; it whispers the mighty watchword *Liberty* in the ears of the American abolitionists gathered at Harper's Ferry, and also in the ears of the patriots of Ancona assembled in the shadows at the Archi, in front of the Gozzi tavern, by the sea; it creates Canaris; it creates Quiroga; it creates Pisacane; it radiates greatness across the earth; impelled by its breath, Byron dies at Missolonghi and Mazet at Barcelona; it is a rostrum beneath the feet of Mirabeau, and a crater beneath the feet of Robespierre; its books, its stage, its art, science, literature, and philosophy are the textbooks of the human race; Pascal belongs to it, Regnier, Corneille, Descartes, Jean-Jacques; Voltaire for every moment, Molière for every century; it makes the universal mouth speak its language, and that language becomes the Word; it builds up in every mind the idea of progress; the liberating dogmas it forges are swords by the pillows of the generations, and since 1789 all heroes of all nations have been made from the soul of its thinkers and poets; but that does not prevent it from playing the *gamin;* and even while transfiguring the world with its radiance, this enormous genius called Paris, draws Bouginier's nose in charcoal on the wall of the Temple of Theseus, and writes *Crédeville the robber* on the Pyramids.

Paris always bares its teeth; when not scolding, it is laughing.

Such is Paris. The smoke of its rooftops is the thought of the universe. A heap of mud and stone if you like, but above all, a moral being. It is more than great, it is immense. Why? Because it dares.

To dare; progress comes at this price.

All sublime conquests are, more or less, the rewards of daring. For Revolution to exist, it was not enough that Montesquieu should foresee it, that Diderot should preach it, that Beaumarchais should announce it, that Condorcet should calculate it, that Arouet should prepare it, that Rousseau should premeditate it; Danton had to dare it.

That cry of boldness is a *Fiat Lux!* The onward march of the human race requires that the heights around it constantly blaze with noble lessons of courage. Deeds of daring dazzle history and form one of man's guiding lights. The dawn dares when it rises. To strive, to brave all risks, to persist, to persevere, to be faithful to oneself, to grapple hand to hand with destiny, to surprise defeat by the slight terror it inspires, at one time to confront unjust power, at another to defy drunken triumph, to hold fast, to hold hard—such is the example nations need, and the light that electrifies them. The same powerful lightning darts from the torch of Prometheus and Cambronne's clay pipe.

XII

THE FUTURE LATENT IN THE PEOPLE

As for the people of Paris, even full grown, they are still the *gamins;* to depict the child is to depict the city, and therefore it is that we have studied this eagle through the outspoken sparrow.

It is in the faubourgs particularly, we insist, that the

Parisian race is found; there is the pure blood; there are the true features; there this population works and suffers, and suffering and toil are the two faces of men. There are vast numbers of unknown beings teeming with the strangest types of humanity, from the stevedore of the Rapée to the horse-slaughterer of Montfaucon. *Fex urbis*, cries Cicero; *mob*, adds the indignant Burke; the herd, the multitude, the populace. Those words are quickly said. But if so, what does it matter? What difference does it make if they go barefoot? They cannot read; never mind. Would you abandon them for that? Would you make their misfortune their curse? Can't the light penetrate these masses? Let us return to that cry: Light! And let us persist in it! Light! Light! Who knows but that these opacities will become transparent? Are revolutions not transfigurations? Go on, philosophers—teach, enlighten, kindle, think aloud, speak up, run joyfully toward broad daylight, fraternize in the public squares, announce the glad tidings, lavish your alphabets, proclaim human rights, sing your Marseillaises, sow enthusiasms, tear off green branches from the oak trees. Make thought a whirlwind. This multitude can be sublimated. Let us learn to avail ourselves of this vast conflagration of principles and virtues, which occasionally sparkles, bursts, and shudders. These bare feet, these naked arms, these rags, these shades of ignorance, depths of despair, the gloom can be used for the conquest of the ideal. Look through the medium of the people, and you will discern the truth. This lowly sand that you trample underfoot, if you throw it into the furnace and let it melt and seethe, will become sparkling crystal; and thanks to such as this a Galileo and a Newton will discover the stars.

XIII

LITTLE GAVROCHE

About eight or nine years after the events told in the second part of this story, on the Boulevard du Temple, and in the neighborhood of the Château d'Eau, there could be seen a little boy of eleven or twelve, who would have quite accurately realized the ideal of the *gamin* previously sketched, if, with the laughter of youth on his lips, his heart had not been absolutely dark and empty. This child was well decked out in a man's pair of pants, but he did not get them from his father, and in a woman's jacket, which was not from his mother. Strangers had clothed him in these rags out of charity. Yet he did have a father and a mother. But his father never thought of him, and his mother did not love him. He was one of those children so deserving of pity above all others, who have fathers and mothers and yet are orphans.

This little boy never felt so happy as when in the street. For him the pavement was not so hard as the heart of his mother.

His parents had kicked him out into life. He had simply taken flight.

He was a boisterous, pallid, nimble, wide-awake, roguish urchin, who looked both lively and sickly. He would come and go, sing, play pitch and toss, scrape the gutters, steal a little, but he did it cheerfully, like the cats and the sparrows, laughed when people called him a brat, and got angry when they called him a guttersnipe. He had no shelter, no food, no fire, no love, but he was lighthearted because he was free.

When these poor creatures become men, the millstone of our social system almost always reaches them, and grinds them down, but while they are children they escape because they are little. The slightest hole saves them.

However, deserted as this lad was, it sometimes happened every two or three months that he would say to himself, "Well, I think I'll go see my mother!" Then he would leave the Boulevard, the Cirque, the Porte Saint-Martin, go down along the quays, cross the bridges, reach the faubourgs, walk as far as the Salpêtrière, and arrive—where? Precisely at that double number, 50–52, known to the reader, the Gorbeau building.

At the time, the structure No. 50–52, usually empty and permanently decorated with the placard "Rooms to let," was, for a wonder, tenanted by several individuals who, as is always the case at Paris, had no other relation to or connection with each other. They all belonged to that indigent class which begins with the petty bourgeois in embarrassed circumstances and descends through levels of misery past the lowest strata of society until it reaches those two creatures with whom all the material things of civilization end, the sewer sweeper and the rag-picker.

The "landlady" of Jean Valjean's time was dead and had been replaced by another exactly like her. I do not remember what philosopher it was who said, "There is never a dearth of old women."

The new old woman was named Mme. Burgon, and her life had been remarkable for nothing except a dynasty of three parakeets, which had successively dominated her affections.

Among those who lived in the building, the most wretched of all were a family of four persons, father, mother, and two daughters nearly grown, all four lodging in the same garret room, one of those cells we have already described.

At first sight this family offered nothing in particular beyond its extreme destitution; in renting the room, the father had given his name as Jondrette. Some time after his moving in, which had, to borrow the memorable expression of the landlady, "strangely resembled the entry of nothing at all," this Jondrette said to the old woman, who, like her predecessor, was both concierge and charwoman, "Mother So-and-So, if anybody should come asking for a Pole or an Italian or perhaps a Spaniard, that would be for me."

This family was the family of our sprightly little barefoot urchin. When he came there, he found poverty and distress and, sadder still, no smile; a cold hearth and cold hearts. When he came in, they would ask, "Where have you come from?" He would answer, "From the streets." When he went away they would ask him, "Where are you going?" He would answer, "To the streets." His mother would say to him, "What have you come here for?"

In this absence of affection, the child lived like those pale plants that spring up in cellars. He felt no suffering from this mode of existence, and bore no ill will to anybody. He did not exactly know how a father and mother ought to be.

Yet his mother loved his sisters.

We forgot to say that on the Boulevard du Temple this boy went by the name of little Gavroche. Why was his name Gavroche? Probably because his father's name was Jondrette.

To break all links seems to be the instinct of some wretched families.

The room occupied by the Jondrettes in the Gorbeau tenement was the last at the end of the hall. The adjoining cell was occupied by a very poor young man called M. Marius.

Let us see who and what M. Marius was.

Book Two

THE GRAND BOURGEOIS

I

OVER NINETY YEARS OLD WITH THIRTY-TWO TEETH

In the Rue Boucherat, Rue de Normandie, and Rue de Saintonge, there still remain a few old inhabitants who remember a fine old man named M. Gillenormand, and who like to talk about him. This man was old when they were young. To those who look back sadly at that vague swarm of shadows they call the past, this figure has not yet entirely disappeared from the labyrinth of streets near the Temple, to which, under Louis XIV, were given the names of all the provinces of France, precisely as the names of all the capitals of Europe have been given in our day to the streets in the new Quartier Tivoli; an advance, by the way, in which progress is visible.

M. Gillenormand, who was as much alive as any man can be in 1831, was one of those men who become curiosities simply because they have lived a long time, and are strange because formerly they were like everybody else, and now they are no longer like anybody else. He was a peculiar old man, very truly a man of another age—the genuine bourgeois of the eighteenth century, a very perfect specimen, somewhat haughty, wearing his good old bourgeoisie as marquises wear their marquisates. He had passed his ninetieth year, walked erect, spoke distinctly, saw clearly, drank hard, ate, slept, and snored. He had every one of his thirty-two teeth. He wore glasses only for reading. He was of an amorous bent but said that for ten years past he had decidedly and entirely renounced women. He was no longer appealing, he said; he did not add, "I am too old," but, "I am too poor." He would say, "If I were not ruined, heehee!" His remaining income in fact was only about fifteen thousand livres. He dreamt of receiving a windfall, and having an income of a hundred thousand francs, in order to keep mistresses. He did not belong, as we see, to the sickly variety of octogenarians who, like M. de Voltaire, are dying men all through life; it was not a milk-and-water longevity; this jovial old man was always in good health. He was superficial, hasty, easily angered. He flew into a rage on every occasion, most frequently when wrong. When anybody contradicted him he raised his cane; he beat people as in the time of Louis XIV. He had an unmarried daughter over fifty years old, whom he belabored severely when he was angry, and whom he would gladly have horsewhipped. She seemed to him about eight years old. He vigorously cuffed his servants and would say, "Slut!" One of his oaths was "By the big slippers of big slipperdom!" In some respects he was of a singular tranquility: He was shaved every day by a barber who had been crazy and who hated him, being jealous of M. Gillenormand because of his wife, a pretty coquettish hairdresser. M. Gillenormand admired his own discernment in everything and pronounced himself very sagacious; this is one of his sayings: "I am truly perceptive; when a flea bites me, I can tell what woman it comes from." The terms he most often used were: *sympathetic men* and *nature*. He did not give to this last word the broad use our era has assigned it. But he twisted it into his own use in his little chimney-corner satires: "For civilization to have a little of everything," he would say, "Nature even gives it some specimens of amusing barbarism. Europe has samples of Asia and Africa, in miniature. The cat is a drawing-room tiger, the lizard is a pocket crocodile. The ballerinas at the opera are rosy savages. They do not eat men, they feed off them. Or rather, the little magicians change them into oysters, and swallow them. The Caribs leave nothing but the bones, they leave nothing but the shells. Such are our customs. We do not devour, we gnaw; we do not exterminate, we clutch."

II

LIKE MASTER, LIKE DWELLING

He lived in the Marais, Rue des Filles-du-Calvaire, No. 6. The house was his own. The house has been torn down and rebuilt since, and its number has probably been changed in the revolutions of numbering that Paris streets undergo. He occupied a large old apartment on the second floor, between the street and the gardens, covered to the ceiling with fine Gobelin and Beauvais tapestries of pastoral scenes; the subjects of the ceiling and the panels were repeated in miniature on the armchairs. He surrounded his bed with a large coromandel screen with nine leaves. Long, full curtains hung at the windows, making great, magnificent broken folds. The garden right below his windows was reached where two walls made an angle by means of a staircase of twelve or fifteen steps, which the old man ascended and descended very blithely. Aside from a library adjoining his room, he had a prized boudoir, an elegant retreat, surrounded by magnificent straw hangings covered with fleurs-de-lis and flowers, made on Louis XIV's galleys and ordered by M. de Vivonne from his convicts for his mistress. M. Gillenormand had inherited this from a ferocious maternal great-aunt, who died at the age of a hundred. He had had two wives. His manners were halfway between the courtier he had never been and the counselor he might have been. He was cheerful and affectionate when he wished to be. In his youth, he had been one of those men who are always deceived by their wives and never by their mistresses, because they are at the same time the most disagreeable husbands and the most charming lovers in the world. He was a connoisseur of painting. In his room he had a wonderful portrait of nobody knows whom, painted by Jordaens, done in broad brushstrokes, with millions of details, in a confused, spontaneous style. M. Gillenormand's clothing was not in the style of Louis XV, nor even in the style worn under Louis XVI; he wore the costume of the *incroyables* of the Directory. He had thought himself quite young until then and had kept up with the fashions. His coat was of light cloth, with broad facings, a long swallowtail, and large steel buttons. Add to this short breeches and shoe buckles. His hands were always in his pockets. He would say with authority: "The French Revolution was a bunch of rogues."

III

LUC-ESPIRIT

At sixteen, one evening at the opera, he had had the honor of being stared at simultaneously by two beauties then mature, their praises sung by Voltaire, La Camargo and La Sallé. Caught between two fires, he had made a heroic retreat toward a little dancer, a young girl named Nahenry, who was sixteen years old like himself, obscure as a cat, and with whom he fell in love. He was full of memories. He would exclaim, "How pretty she was, that Guimard-Guimardin-Guimardinette, the last time I saw her at Longchamps, done up in lofty sentiments, with her curious baubles in turquoise, her dress the color of a parvenu, and her fluttering muff!" In his youth he had worn a vest of Londrin from Provence, of which he talked frequently and fluently. "I was dressed like a Turk of the Levantine Levant," he would say. Mme. de Boufflers, having seen him by chance when he was twenty years old, described him as a "mad charmer." He ridiculed all the names he saw in politics or in power, finding them low and vulgar. He read the newspapers, "the news sheets, the gazettes," as he said, stifling with laughter. "Oh!" he said, "what are these people! Corbière! Humann! Casimir Périer! Those are ministers for you. I imagine this in a newspaper: M. Gillenormand, Minister; that would be a joke. Well, they are so stupid it might work!" He called everything freely by its name, proper or improper, and was never embarrassed by the presence of women. He would say coarse, obscene, and indecent things with an air of tranquility and imperturbability that was elegant. It was the offhand way of his time. One should note that the age of periphrases in verse was the age of crudities in prose. His godfather had predicted he would be a man of genius and gave him these two significant names: Luc-Esprit.

IV

AN ASPIRING CENTENARIAN

He had won several prizes in his youth at the secondary school in Moulins, where he was born, and had been crowned by the hands of the Duc de Nivernais, whom he called the Duke de Nevers. Neither the Convention, nor the death of Louis XVI, nor Napoleon, nor the return of the Bourbons, had been able to erase the memory of this coronation. For him the Duke de Nevers was the great figure of the century. "What a noble, great Lord," he said, "and how well he looked with his blue sash!" In M. Gillenormand's eyes, Catherine II had atoned for the crime of Poland's partition by buying the secret of the golden elixir from Bestuchef, for three thousand rubles. He would wax eloquent about it. "The elixir of gold," he exclaimed, "Bestuchef's yellow dye, General Lamotte's drops, in the eighteenth century, at a louis for a half-ounce flask, these were the great remedy for catastrophes in love, the panacea against Venus. Louis XV sent two hundred flasks to the Pope." He would have been greatly exasperated and thrown off his balance if anybody had told him that the elixir of gold was nothing but perchloride of iron. M. Gillenormand worshiped the Bourbons and held 1789 in horror; he was constantly relating how he saved himself during the Reign of Terror, and how, if he had not had a good deal of gaiety and wit, he would have been beheaded. If any young man ventured to eulogize the Republic in his presence, he turned black in the face and was angry enough to faint. Sometimes he would allude to his ninety years of age, and say, "I really hope that I shall not see ninety twice." At other times he intimated to his people that he intended to live a hundred years.

V

BASQUE AND NICOLETTE

He had his theories. Here is one of them: "When a man passionately loves women and has a wife of his own he cares for only a little, ugly, cross, legitimate, fond of asserting her rights, roosting on the Napoleonic Code and often jealous, he has only one way to get out of it and keep the peace, and, that is to let his wife have the purse strings. This abdication makes him free. The wife keeps herself busy, devotes herself to handling coin, verdigrising her fingers, the raising of tenants, the training of the farmers, convenes lawyers, presides over notaries, harangues justices, follows up lawsuits, draws up leases, dictates contracts, feels sovereign, sells, buys, regulates, promises and compromises, binds and cancels, cedes, concedes, and retrocedes, arranges, deranges, hoards, wastes; she does foolish things, a magisterial and personal pleasure, and this consoles her. While her husband disdains her, she has the satisfaction of ruining her husband." This theory M. Gillenormand had applied to himself, and it became his story. His wife, the second one, had administered his fortune in such a way that M. Gillenormand still had, when one fine day he found himself a widower, just enough to obtain, by turning almost everything into an annuity, an income of fifteen thousand francs, three quarters of which would expire with himself. He did not worry about leaving an inheritance. Moreover, he had seen that patrimonies met with misadventures and, for example, became *national property;* he had been present at examples of the requisitioned thirds, and he had little faith in the Ledger. "Rue Quincampoix for all that!" he said. His house in Rue des Filles-du-Calvaire, as we said, belonged to him. He had two servants, "a male and a female." When a servant entered his service, Monsieur G. rebaptized him. He gave to the men the name of their province: Nîmois, Comtois, Poitevin, Picard. His last valet was a big, dog-tired, wheezy man of fifty-five, incapable of running twenty steps, but as he was born in Bayonne, M. Gillenormand called him Basque. As for female servants, in his house they were all called Nicolette (even Magnon, who will reappear further on). One day a proud cook, a *cordon bleu* of the lofty race of concièrges, applied. "How much do you want a month?" asked M. Gillenormand. "Thirty francs." "What is your name?" "Olympie." "You'll have fifty francs, and your name will be Nicolette."

VI

IN WHICH WE SEE LA MAGNON AND HER TWO LITTLE ONES

With M. Gillenormand, grief was translated into anger; he was furious at being in despair. He had every prejudice and took every license. One of the things that made up his external relief and his internal satisfaction was, we just indicated, that he was still a youthful gallant and that he passed for such with dash. He called this having "royal renown." His royal renown sometimes attracted strange windfalls. One day there was brought to his house in a basket, something like an oyster basket, a big newborn baby boy, crying at the top of his lungs, and duly wrapped in swaddling clothes, which a servant girl turned away six months before attributed to him. At the time M. Gillenormand was fully eighty-four years old. Indignation and clamor on the part of the bystanders. And who did this bold hussy think would believe this? What effrontery! What abominable calumny! M. Gillenormand, however, displayed no anger. He looked at the bundle with the amiable smile of a man flattered by calumny, and said to the assembled, "Well, now, what is all this? What's the matter? What have we here? You are all agog, and acting like ignorant folk. At eighty-five, the Duke d'Angoulême, natural son of his majesty Charles IX, married a little hussy of fifteen; at eighty-three Monsieur Virginal, Marquis d'Alhuye and brother of Cardinal de Sourdis, Archbishop of Bordeaux, had, by a chambermaid of the wife of President Jacquin, a son, a true lovechild, who became a Knight of Malta and a knighted Councilor of State; one of the great men of this century, Abbé Tabarand, was the son of a man eighty-seven years old. These things are anything but uncommon. And then the Bible! With that, I declare that this little gentleman is not mine. But take care of him. It is not his fault.'' This process was easygoing. The creature, she who was called Magnon, sent him a second present the year after. Again it was a boy. This time Monsieur Gillenormand capitulated. He sent the two brats back to the mother, engaging to pay eighty francs a month for their support, on condition that the said mother should not begin again. He added, "I want the mother to treat them well. I will come to see them from time to time.'' Which he did. He had had a brother, a priest, who had been for thirty-three years rector of the Academy of Poitiers and who died at seventy-nine. "I lost him young,'' he said. This brother, of whom hardly a memory is left, was a quiet miser, who, being a priest, felt obliged to give alms to the poor whom he met, but never gave them anything more than coppers or worn-out sous, finding thus the means of going to Hell by the road to Paradise. As for M. Gillenormand, the elder, he was not hesitant about alms giving but gave willingly and nobly. He was benevolent, abrupt, charitable, and had he been rich, his inclination would have been to be magnificent. He wanted everything he cared about to be done on a grand scale, even improbities. One day, having been swindled in an inheritance by a businessman, in a gross and visible way, he uttered this solemn exclamation: "For shame! This is badly done! I'm really ashamed of these sniveling cheats. Everything is degenerating in this century, even the villains. Good Lord! This is no way to rob a man like me. I have been robbed as though in the woods, but stupidly robbed. *Silvae sint consul digna!*''

He had had, as we said, two wives; by the first a daughter, who remained unmarried, and by the second another daughter, who died at about thirty and who had married for love, by chance or otherwise, a soldier of fortune, who had served in the armies of the Republic and the Empire, had won the cross at Austerlitz, and been made colonel at Waterloo. "This is the disgrace of my family,'' said the old bourgeois. He took a great deal of snuff, and had a particularly graceful way of dusting his lace jabot with the back of his hand. He had very little belief in God.

VII

RULE: NEVER RECEIVE ANYBODY EXCEPT IN THE EVENING

Such was M. Luc-Esprit Gillenormand, who had not lost his hair, rather more gray than white, and always combed in waves. On the whole, and with all of this, a venerable man.

He was a man of the eighteenth century, frivolous and great.

In 1814, and in the early years of the Restoration, M. Gillenormand, who was still young—only seventy-four—had lived in the Faubourg Saint-Germain, Rue Servandoni, near Saint-Sulpice. He had retired to the Marais only on withdrawing from society, well after his eighty years were done.

And in retiring from society, he had walled himself in with his habits; the principal one, in which he was invariable, was to keep his door absolutely closed by day and never to receive anybody whatsoever, on any matter whatever, except in the evening. He dined at five o'clock, then his door was open. This was the custom of his century, and he would not swerve from it. "The day is vulgar," he said, "and deserves only closed shutters. Proper people light up their wit when the zenith lights up its stars." And he barricaded himself against everybody, even if it were the king. The old elegance of his time.

VIII

TWO DO NOT MAKE A PAIR

As for M. Gillenormand's two daughters, we have just mentioned them. They were born ten years apart. In their youth they had been very different and, in character as well as in countenance, were as far from being sisters as possible. The younger was a cheerful soul, attracted toward everything bright, loved flowers, poetry, and music, afloat in glorious spaces, enthusiastic, ethereal, in her dreams since childhood engaged to a dim heroic figure. The elder had also her fantasy; in the deep blue sky she saw a contractor, some good, coarse munitions maker, very rich, a splendidly stupid husband, a self-made millionaire, or even a prefect; receptions at the prefecture, an usher of the antechamber, with the chain at his neck, official balls, speeches at the mayor's, to be "Madame la Préfète," all this whirled in her imagination. When the two were young, the two sisters drifted thus, each in her own fantasy. Both had wings, one like an angel, the other like a goose.

No ambition is fully realized, here below at least. No paradise comes to earth in our day. The younger one had married the man of her dreams, but she was dead. The elder was not married.

At the moment when she makes her entry into this story, she was an aging figure of virtue, an incombustible prude with one of the sharpest noses and one of the most obtuse minds to be found. A characteristic detail: Outside of the immediate family nobody had ever known her first name. She was called Mademoiselle Gillenormand the elder.

In cant, Mlle. Gillenormand the elder could have put to shame any English miss. She was immodestly modest. She had one frightful reminiscence in her life: One day a man had seen her garter.

Age had only increased this pitiless modesty. Her dress front was never thick enough, never came up high enough. She piled on hooks and pins where nobody thought of looking. The characteristic of prudery is to increase the sentinels, as the fortress becomes less threatened.

However, explain who can these ancient mysteries of innocence, she allowed herself to be kissed without displeasure by an officer of the lancers who was her great-nephew and whose name was Théodule.

In spite of this favored lancer, the title "Prude," under which we have classed her, suited her absolutely. Mlle. Gillenormand was a kind of twilight soul. Prudery is half a virtue and half a vice.

To prudery she added bigotry, a suitable lining. She was of the fraternity of the Virgin, wore a white veil on certain feast days, murmured special prayers, revered "the holy blood," venerated "the sacred heart," stayed for hours in contemplation before a rococo-Jesuit altar in a chapel closed to the vulgar faithful, and let her soul soar there among the little marble clouds and along the rays of gilded wood.

She had a chapel friend, an old maid like herself, called Mlle. Vaubois, who was perfectly stupid, and in comparison with whom Mlle. Gillenormand had the happiness of being an eagle. Beyond her Agnus Deis and her Ave Marias, Mlle. Vaubois had no understanding except on the different ways of making preserves. Mlle. Vaubois, perfect in her way, was the ermine of stupidity without a single stain of intelligence.

We must say that in growing old, Mlle. Gillenormand had gained on the whole more than lost. This is the case with passive natures. She had never been mean, which is a relative virtue; and then, years wear off sharp corners, and the softening of time had come over her. She was sad with an obscure sadness whose secret even she did not possess. In her whole person there was the torpor of a life ended that had never begun.

She kept her father's house. M. Gillenormand had his daughter with him as we have seen M. Bienvenu had his sister with him. These households of an old man and an old maid are not rare, and always have the touching aspect of two frailties leaning on each other.

Between this old maid and this old man, there was besides in the house a child, a little boy, always trembling and mute before M. Gillenormand. M. Gillenormand never spoke to this child except sternly, and sometimes with a raised cane: "Here! Monsieur—rascal, scamp, come here! Answer me, rogue! Let me see you, good-for-nothing!" etc. etc. He idolized him.

It was his grandson. We will see this child again.

Book Three

THE GRANDFATHER AND THE GRANDSON

I

AN OLD SALON

When M. Gillenormand lived in the Rue Servandoni, he haunted several very fine and very noble salons. Though a bourgeois, M. Gillenormand was welcome. As he was witty twice over—first with his own wit, then with the wit that was attributed to him—he was even sought after and lionized. He went nowhere except on condition of dominating. There are men who desire influence at any price and to attract the attention of the others; where they cannot be oracles, they make themselves laughingstocks. M. Gillenormand was not like that; his dominance in the royalist salons he frequented cost him none of his self-respect. He was an oracle everywhere. He found himself facing off against M. de Bonald and even M. Bengy-Puy-Vallée.

Around 1817, he would always spend two afternoons a week at a house in his neighborhood, on the Rue Férou, that of the Baronne de T., a worthy and venerable lady whose husband had been, under Louis XVI, ambassador to Berlin. The Baron de T., who, during his lifetime, had been fascinated by ecstasies and magnetic visions, died as an emigré, ruined, leaving no fortune but ten manuscript volumes bound in red morocco with gilt edges, very strange accounts of Mesmer and his tub. Mme. de T., had not published the volumes for reasons of discretion, and supported herself on a small income, which had somehow survived the disaster. Mme. de T. lived far from the court—"A very mixed society," as she said—in noble, proud, and impoverished isolation. A few friends would gather about her widow's hearth twice a week, and this constituted a pure royalist salon. They had tea and, following the drift toward either staid elegy or wild enthusiasm, uttered groans or cries of horror over the century, over the charter, over the Buonapartists, over the prostitution of the blue sash among the bourgeoisie, over the Jacobinism of Louis XVIII; and they discussed in whispers the hopes resting on Monsieur, later Charles X.

They gleefully hailed the vulgar songs in which Napoleon was called "Nicolas." Duchesses, the most refined and charming women in the world, went into ecstasies over couplets like this addressed "to the federals":

Renfoncez dans vos culottes
Le bout d'chemis' qui vous pend.
Qu'on n' dis' pas qu' les patriotes
Ont arboré l'drapeau blanc!

They amused themselves with puns, which they thought terrible, with innocent play on words, which they considered venomous, with quatrains and even distiches; thus on the Dessolles ministry, a moderate cabinet of which MM. Decazes and Deserre were members:

Pour raffermir le trône ébranlé sur sa base,
Il faut changer de sol, et de serre et de case.

Or sometimes they drew up the list of the Chamber of Peers, "an abominably Jacobin Chamber," and in this list they arranged the names, so as to make royalist phrases like "Damas, Sabran, Gouvion Saint-Cyr." All of this done quite cheerfully.

In this closed little world they parodied the Revolution. For fun they parried the original rage, wielding it in the inverse direction. They sang their own little *ça ira:*

Ah! ça ira! ça ira! ça ira!
Les buonapartist' à la lanterne!

Songs are like the guillotine; they cut indifferently, today this head, tomorrow that one. It is only a variation.

In the Fualdès affair, which happened about that time, 1816, they took sides with Bastide and Jausion, because Fualdès was a "Buonapartist." They called the liberals "brothers and friends"; this was the highest degree of insult.

Like some menageries, the Baronne de T.'s salon had two lions. One was M. Gillenormand, the other was the Comte de Lamothe-Valois, of whom it was whispered, with a sort of consideration, "Do you know? He is the Lamothe of the necklace affair." Partisans do have such strange amnesties as these.

We will also add: Among the bourgeois, positions of honor are lowered by too easy access; you must be careful about whom you receive; just as there is a caloric loss in the vicinity of those who are cold, there is less consideration in contact with people who are scorned. The old high society held itself above this law as it did above all others. Marigny, La Pompadour's brother, is received by the Prince de Soubise. Despite? No, because of. Du Barry, godfather of La Vaubernier, is very welcome at the Marshal de Richelieu's. That society is Olympus. Mercury and the Prince de Geuménée are at home there. A thief is admitted, provided he is also a god.

The Count de Lamothe who, in 1815, was a man of seventy-five, was remarkable for nothing except his silent, sententious air, his cold, angular face, his perfectly polished manners, his coat buttoned up to his tie, and his long legs, always crossed in long, loose trousers of burnt sienna. His face was the color of his pants.

This M. de Lamothe was "esteemed" in this salon because of his "celebrity" and, strange to say but true, because of the name of Valois.

As for M. Gillenormand, his judgment was absolutely sound. He appeared authoritative because he had authority. Sprightly as he was, he had, and without loss of gaiety, a certain manner that was imposing, worthy, honorable, and genteelly haughty; and his great age added to it. A man is not nearly a century for nothing. Years ultimately crown a head with venerable disarray.

Moreover, he delivered some repartees certainly bearing the genuine sparkle. Thus when the King of Prussia, after restoring Louis XVIII, came to pay him a visit under the name of Comte de Ruppin, he was received by the descendant of Louis XIV somewhat like a Marquis of Brandenburg, and with the most delicate impertinence. M. Gillenormand approved this. "All kings who are not the King of France," he said, "are kings of some province." The following question and answer were spoken one day in his presence: "What is the sentence for the editor of the *Courier Français?*" "To be hung up for awhile." "*Up* is superfluous," observed M. Gillenormand. Quips like this create a position for a man.

At an anniversary Te Deum for the return of the Bourbons, seeing M. de Talleyrand go by, he said, "There goes His Excellency the Bour-bad."

M. Gillenormand was usually accompanied by his daughter, this long mademoiselle, then past forty, and seeming fifty, and by a beautiful little boy of seven, white, rosy, fresh-looking, with happy and trustful eyes, who never appeared in this salon without hearing a buzz around him: "How pretty he is! What a pity! Poor child!" This child was the boy to whom we alluded. They called him "poor child" because his father was "a brigand of the Loire," of the trap that refused royal authority.

This brigand of the Loire was M. Gillenormand's son-in-law, already mentioned, and whom M. Gillenormand called the disgrace of his family.

II

ONE OF THE RED SPECTERS OF THAT TIME

In those days, whoever passed through the little city of Vernon, and walked over that beautiful monumental bridge which we can soon expect to see replaced by some hideous metal arch, would have noticed, looking down from the top of the parapet, a man about fifty with a leather cap on his head, dressed in pants and jacket of coarse gray cloth, to which something yellow was stitched that had been a red ribbon, wearing wooden shoes, tanned by the sun, his face almost black, his hair almost white, a large scar on his forehead extending down his cheek, bent, bowed down, older than his years. He spent most of the day with a spade and a pruning knife in his hand, in one of those walled plots near the bridge, which run like a chain of terraces along the left bank of the Seine—charming enclosures full of flowers which if they were much larger one would call gardens, and if they were a little smaller, bouquets. All these enclosures are bounded by the river on one side and a house on the other. The man in the jacket and wooden shoes whom we have just mentioned lived, around 1817, in the smallest of these enclosures and the humblest of the houses. He lived there alone, solitary, in silence and in poverty, with a woman neither young nor old, neither beautiful nor ugly, neither peasant nor bourgeois, who served him. The square of ground he called his garden was well known in the town for the beauty of the flowers he cultivated in it. Flowers were his occupation.

By dint of labor, perseverance, attention, and pails of water, he had succeeded in creating after the Creator, and had invented certain tulips and dahlias that seemed to have been forgotten by Nature. He was ingenious; he anticipated Soulange Bodin in the formation of little clumps of peaty soil for the culture of rare and precious shrubs from America and China. By dawn in summer he was in his walks, digging, pruning, weeding, watering, walking in the midst of his flowers with an air of kindness, sadness, and gentleness, sometimes dreamy and motionless for hours at a time, listening to the song of a bird in a tree, the chatter of a child in a house, or more often with his eyes fixed on some dewdrop at the end of a blade of grass that the sun was turning into a gem. His fare was very frugal, and he drank more milk than wine. An urchin could make him yield, his servant scolded him. He was shy to the point of seeming unsociable, rarely went out, and saw nobody but the poor who rapped at his window, and his curé, Abbé Mabeuf, a good old man. Still, if anyone from the town or any stranger curious to see his tulips and roses knocked at his little house, he would open his door with a smile. This was the brigand of the Loire.

At the same time, anyone who had read the military memoirs, the biographies, the *Moniteur,* and the bulletins of the Grand Army, would have been struck by a name that appears quite often, Georges Pontmercy. As a young man, this Georges Pontmercy was a soldier in the regiment of Saintonge. The Revolution broke out. The Saintonge regiment was with the Army of the Rhine, for the old regiments of the monarchy kept their province names even after the fall of the monarchy and were not brigaded until 1794. Pontmercy fought at Spires, at Worms, at Neustadt, at Turkheim, at Alzey, at Mayence, where he was one of the two hunded who formed Houchard's rearguard. With eleven others he fought off the Prince of Hesse's corps behind the old rampart of Andernach, and only fell back to the bulk of the army when the enemy's cannon had effected a breach and clear shot from the top of the parapet to the slope below. He was under Kléber at Marchiennes and at the battle of Mont-Palissel, where he had his arm broken by a musket ball. Then he crossed the Italian frontier, and he was one of the thirty grenadiers who defended the Col di Tende with Joubert. Joubert was made adjutant-general, and Pontmercy second-lieutenant. Pontmercy was beside Berthier in the midst of the hail of bullets on that day at Lodi of which Bonaparte said: "Berthier was cannoneer, cavalier, and grenadier." He saw his old general, Joubert, fall at Novi, at the moment when, his sword raised, he was crying: "Forward!" Embarked with his company, through the needs of the campaign, on a small ship on the way from Genoa to some little port along the coast, he fell into a wasp's-nest of seven or eight English vessels. The Genoese captain wanted to shove the guns into the sea, hide the soldiers between decks, and slip through in the dark like a merchantman. Pontmercy had the colors raised on the halyards of the ensign staff, and sailed proudly under the guns of the British frigates. Fifty miles farther on, his boldness increasing, he attacked with his pinnace and captured a large English transport carrying troops to Sicily, so loaded with men and horses that the vessel was full to the hatches. In 1805, he was in that Malher division that captured Günzburg from the Archduke Ferdinand. At Wettingen under a shower of musket balls he held in his arms Colonel Maupetit, who was mortally wounded leading the 9th Dragoons. He distinguished himself at Austerlitz in that wonderful march in echelon under the enemy fire. When the cavalry of the Russian Imperial Guard crushed a battalion of the 4th of the Line, Pontmercy was one of those who counterattacked and overthrew the Guard. The emperor gave him the cross. Pontmercy successively saw Wurmser taken prisoner in Mantua, Melas in Alexandria, and Mack in Ulm. He was in the eighth corps of the Grand Army, which Mortier commanded, and which took Hamburg. Then he transferred to the 55th of the Line, which was the old Flanders regiment. At Eylau, he was in the churchyard where the heroic captain Louis Hugo, uncle of the author of this book, sustained alone with his company of eighty-three men, for two hours, the entire force of the enemy's army. Pontmercy was one of the three who came out of that churchyard alive. He was at Friedland. Then he saw Moscow, then the Beresina, then Lutzen, Bautzen, Dresden, Wachau, Leipsig, and the defiles of Glenhausen, then Montmirail, Chateau-Thierry, Caron, the banks of the Marne, the banks of the Aisne, and the formidable position at Laon. At Arney-le-Duc, as a captain, he cut down ten cossacks, and saved, not his general, but his corporal. He was wounded on that occasion, and twenty-seven splinters were extracted from his left arm alone. Eight days before the capitulation of Paris, he had exchanged with a comrade, and entered the cavalry. He had what was called under the old régime "the double-hand," that is to say equal skill as a soldier with the saber or the musket, as an officer with a squadron or a battalion. It is this skill, perfected by military education, that leads to certain special groups—the dragoons, for instance, who are both cavalry and infantry. He accompanied Napoleon to the island of Elba. At Waterloo he led a squadron of cuirassiers in Dubois's brigade. It was he who took the colors from the Lunenburg battalion. He carried the colors to the emperor's feet. He was covered with blood from a saber stroke across his face received while seizing the banner. The emperor, well pleased, cried out "You are a colonel, you are a baron, you are an officer of the Legion of Honor!" Pontmercy answered, "Sire, I thank you for my widow." An hour later, he fell into the ravine of Ohain. Now who was this Georges Pontmercy? He was that very brigand of the Loire.

We have already seen something of his story. After Waterloo, Pontmercy, dragged, as will be remembered, from the sunken road of Ohain, succeeded in rejoining the army, and was passed along from one ambulance to the next to the cantonments of the Loire.

The Restoration put him on half pay, then sent him to a residence, that is to say under surveillance at Vernon. The king, Louis XVIII, ignoring all that had been done in the Hundred Days, recognized neither his position as officer of the Legion of Honor, nor his rank of colonel, nor his title of baron. He, on the other hand, neglected no opportunity to sign "Colonel Baron Pontmercy." He had only one old blue coat, and he never went out without putting on the rosette of an officer of the Legion of Honor. The king's prosecutor notified him that he would be prosecuted for "illegally" wearing this decoration. When this notice was delivered to him by a friendly intermediary, Pontmercy answered with a bitter smile, "I do not know whether it is that I no longer understand French, or that you no longer speak it; but the fact is I do not understand you." Then he went out every day for a week with his rosette. Nobody dared disturb him. Two or three times the minister of war or the general commanding the Département wrote to him with this address: "Monsieur Commandant Pontmercy." He returned the letters unopened. At the same time, Napoleon at Saint Helena was treating Sir Hudson Lowe's missives addressed to *General Bonaparte* in the same way. Ultimately Pontmercy, excuse the word, had in his mouth the same sour saliva as his emperor.

So too, there were in Rome a few Carthaginian soldiers, taken prisoners, who refused to bow to Flaminius and who had a little of Hannibal's spirit.

One morning, he met the king's prosecutor in one of Vernon's streets, went up to him, and said, "Monsieur Prosecutor, am I allowed to wear my scar?"

He had nothing but his very scanty half pay as chief of squadron. He rented the smallest house he could find in Vernon. He lived there alone, as we have just seen. Under the Empire, between two wars, he had found time to marry Mlle. Gillenormand. The old bourgeois, who really felt outraged, consented with a sigh, saying, "The greatest families are forced to it." In 1815, Mme. Pontmercy, a splendid woman in every respect, noble and exceptional, and worthy of her husband, died, leaving a child. This child would have been the colonel's joy in his solitude, but the grandfather had imperiously demanded his grandson, declaring that unless he were turned over to him, he would disinherit him. The father yielded for the sake of the little boy, and not being able to have his child he set about loving flowers.

Actually, he had given up everything, not stirring or conspiring with others. He divided his thoughts between the innocent things he was doing and the great things he had done. He passed his time waiting for a carnation or remembering Austerlitz.

M. Gillenormand had no communication with his son-in-law. The colonel was to him "a bandit," and he was to the colonel "a blockhead." M. Gillenormand never spoke of the colonel, unless sometimes to make mocking allusions to "his barony." It was expressly understood that Pontmercy should never attempt to see his son or speak to him, under pain of the boy being turned away and disinherited. To the Gillenormands, Pontmercy was infectious. They intended to bring up the child to their liking. The colonel did wrong perhaps to accept these conditions, but he submitted to them, thinking that he was doing right and was sacrificing himself alone.

The inheritance from the grandfather Gillenormand was a small affair, but the inheritance from Mlle. Gillenormand the elder was considerable. This aunt, who had remained single, was very rich from the maternal side, and the son of her sister was her natural heir. The child, whose name was Marius, knew that he had a father, but nothing more. Nobody breathed a word about him. However, into the society into which his grandfather took him, the whisperings, the hints, the winks, eventually dawned on the little boy's mind; he finally understood something, and as he naturally absorbed by a sort of infiltration and slow penetration the ideas and opinions that formed the air he breathed, so to speak, he came little by little to think of his father only with shame and with a closed heart.

While he was growing up this way, every two or three months the colonel would escape, come furtively to Paris like a fugitive from justice breaking his ban, and go to Saint-Sulpice, at the time when Aunt Gillenormand took Marius to mass. There, trembling lest the aunt might turn around, concealed behind a pillar, motionless, not daring to breathe, he saw his child. The scarred veteran was afraid of the old maid.

From this, in fact, came his connection with the curé of Vernon, Abbé Mabeuf.

This worthy priest was the brother of a warden of Saint-Sulpice, who had several times noticed this man gazing upon his child, and the scar on his cheek, and the tears in his eyes. This man, clearly manly, but who wept like a woman, had attracted the warden's attention. This face remained in his memory. One day, having gone to Vernon to see his brother, he met Colonel Pontmercy on the bridge and recognized the man of Saint-Sulpice. The warden spoke of it to the curé, and the two, under some pretext, paid the colonel a visit. This visit led to others. The colonel, who at first was very reserved, finally unburdened himself, and the curé and the warden came to know the whole story, and how Pontmercy was sacrificing his own happiness for the future of his child. The result was that the curé felt a veneration and tenderness for him, and as for the colonel, he felt an affection for the curé. And, actually, when both are sincere and good, nothing mixes and amalgamates more easily than an old priest and an old soldier. They are really the same kind of man. One has devoted himself to his country on earth, the other to his country in heaven; there is no other difference.

Twice a year, on the first of January and on Saint George's Day, Marius wrote filial letters to his father, which his aunt dictated, and which, one would have thought, were copied from some manual; this was all that M. Gillenormand allowed; and the father would answer with very tender letters, which the grandfather shoved into his pocket without reading.

III

REQUIESCANT

Madame de T.'s salon was all that Marius Pontmercy knew of the world. It was the only opening by which he could look out into life. This opening was somber, and more cold than warmth, more night than day came through this porthole. The child, who was nothing but joy and light on entering this strange world, quickly became sad there and, more unusual at his age, grave. Surrounded by all these strange and imposing persons, he looked around with a serious astonishment. Everything combined to increase his amazement. In Madame de T.'s salon there were some very venerable noble old ladies, whose names were Mathan, Noah, Lévis, which was pronounced Lévi, Cambis, which was pronounced Cambyse. These antique faces and biblical names mingled in the child's mind with his Old Testament, which he was learning by heart, and when they were all present, seated in a circle around a dying fire, dimly lit by a green-shaded lamp, with their stern profiles, their gray or white hair, their long dresses from another age, whose mournful colors alone could be distinguished, at rare intervals dropping a few words that were both majestic and austere, the little Marius looked at them startled, thinking that he saw, not women, but patriarchs and magi, not real beings, but phantoms.

Among the phantoms was a scattering of priests who often attended this old salon, and a few gentlemen: the Marquis de Sassenay, executive secretary to Madame de Berry; the Viscomte de Valory, who published some monorhymed odes under the pseudonym of Charles Antoine; the Prince de Beauffremont who, quite young, was turning gray and had a pretty, witty wife whose scarlet velvet dresses with gold fringe, worn very low at the neck, startled this dark assembly; the Marquis de Coriolis d'Espinouse, in all of France the man who best understood "politeness in proportion"; the Count d'Amendre with his kindly chin; and the Chevalier de Port de Guy, a pillar of the Louvre library dubbed the king's study. M. de Port de Guy, bald and aged rather than old, would tell how in 1793, at sixteen, he was sent to prison as "refractory" and chained beside an octogenarian, the Bishop of Mirepoix, refractory too, but as a priest, while he was so as a soldier. This was at Toulon. Their job was to go to the scaffold at night and gather up the heads and bodies of those that had been guillotined during the day; they carried these dripping bodies on their backs, and behind the neck their red galley capes were crusted with blood, dry in the morning, wet at night. These tragic anecdotes were often heard in Madame de T.'s salon; and by dint of cursing Marat, they came to applaud Trestaillon. A few of the less visible deputies played their whist there, M. Thibord du Chalard, M. Lemarchant de Gomicourt, and the well-known jester of the Right, M. Cornet-Dincourt. The Judge de Ferrette, with his knee breeches and his thin legs, would sometimes pass through this salon on the way to M. de Talleyrand's. He had been the companion of the Comte Artois's leisure—the opposite of Aristotle cowering before Campaspe—he had made La Guimard walk on all fours, and thereby shown posterity a philosopher avenged by a judge.

As for the priests, there was Abbé Halma, the one to whom M. Larose, his assistant on *La Foudre,* said, "Come now! Who is not fifty years old? A few greenhorns perhaps?" Abbé Letourneur, the king's chaplain, Abbé Frayssinous, not yet either a count, or bishop, or minister, or peer, and who wore an old cassock missing some buttons, and Abbé Keravenant, curé of Saint-Germain-des-Prés; besides these the Papal Nuncio, at that time Monsignor Macchi, Archbishop of Nisibi, later a cardinal, remarkable for his long pensive nose, and another monsignor with the following titles: Abbate Palmieri, Domestic Prelate, one of the seven participating prothonotaries of the Holy See, canon of the Insignia of the Liberian Basilicate, advocate of the Saints, *postulatore di santi,* which has to do with the business of canonization and is tantamount to "master of requests on behalf of the paradise section." Finally, two cardinals, M. de la Luzerne and M. de Clermont-Tonnerre. The Cardinal de la Luzerne was a writer, and was to have the honor some years later of signing articles in the *Conservateur* side by side with Chateaubriand; M. de Clermont-Tonnerre was Archbishop of Toulouse and often came to rusticate at Paris with his nephew the Marquis of Tonnerre, who was Minister of Marine and of War. The Cardinal de Clermont-Tonnerre was a little, lively old man, who showed off his red stockings under a turned-up cassock; his peculiarities were a hatred of the Encyclopedia and a passionate enthusiasm for billiards; at that time, people walking on summer evenings along the Rue Madame, past the Hotel de Clermont-Tonnerre, would stop to hear the clicking of the balls and the cardinal's piercing crying out to his colleague in the conclave, Monseigneur Cottret, Bishop *in partibus* of Carysta: "Mark, Abbé, I have caromed." The Cardinal de Clermont-Tonnerre had been brought to Madame de T.'s by his most intimate friend, M. de Roquelaure, formerly Bishop of Senlis and one of the Forty. M. de Roquelaure was remarkably tall and known for his diligence at the Academy; through the glass door of the hall near the Library where the Académie Française then held its sessions, the curious could gaze at the old Bishop of Senlis every Friday, usually on his feet, freshly powdered, with violet stockings, and turning his back to the door, apparently to show his little collar to its best advantage. All these ecclesiastics, though most of them were courtiers as well as churchmen, added gravity to Madame de T.'s salon, whose lordly tone was enhanced by five peers of France, the Marquis de Vibraye, the Marquis de Talaru, the Marquis d'Herbouville, the Viscomte Dambray, and the Duc de Valentinois. This Duc de Valentinois, although Prince de Monaco, that is to say, a foreign sovereign prince, had such an exalted idea of France and the peerage that he saw everything through them. It was he who said, "The cardinals are the French peers of Rome; the Lords are the French peers of England." Finally, since in this century the Revolution must pervade, this feudal salon was, as we said, dominated by a bourgeois. M. Gillenormand reigned there.

That was the essence and the quintessence of Parisian reactionary society. Notables, even though royalists, were held in quarantine. In renown there is always anarchy. If he had been there, Chateaubriand would have had the same effect as Père Duchêne. However, a few repentant backsliders were tolerated in this orthodox world. The Comte Beugnot was conditionally there.

The "noble" salons of the present bear no resemblance to those salons. The Faubourg Saint-Germain of our day smells of heresy. Royalists today are demagogues, we should say in their favor.

At Madame de T.'s, in a superior society, there was exquisite and refined taste under an etiquette in full bloom. Their manners comprised all sorts of obligatory refinements that were the *ancien régime* itself, buried, but living. Some of these customs, particularly in language, seemed grotesque. A superficial observer would have taken as provincial what was only obsolete. They called a woman *madame la générale*. *Madame la colonelle* was not entirely unheard of. It was undoubtedly in memory of the Duchesses de Longueville and de Chevreuse, that the charming Madame de Léon preferred this form of address to her title of Princess. The Marquise de Créquy also called herself *madame la colonelle*.

It was this little elite that invented the affectation of always saying, when speaking to the king at the Tuileries, "the king" in the third person, and never "Your Majesty," since the title "Your Majesty" was "sullied by the usurper," Napoleon.

Facts and men were judged there. They ridiculed the century, which did away with the need to understand it. They supported one another in astonishment. Each communicated to the rest the quantity of light he possessed. Methuselah instructed Epimenides. The deaf kept the blind informed. They declared that the time since Coblentz had not occurred. Just as Louis XVIII was, by the grace of God, in the twenty-fifth year of his reign, the émigrés were, rightfully, in the twenty-fifth year of their youth.

Everything was harmonious; nothing was too vibrant; speech was hardly a whisper; matching the salon, the newspaper seemed a papyrus. Young people existed, but they seemed somewhat dead. In the entrance halls, the liveries were old-fashioned. Completely superannuated masters were waited on by similar servants. Altogether they had the appearance of having lived a long time earlier, and of resisting the tomb. Conserve, Conservatism, Conservative, was nearly their entire dictionary; "to be in good odor," was the point. There was in fact something aromatic about the opinions of these venerable groups, and their ideas smelled of Indian herbs. It was a mummified world. The masters were embalmed, the valets were stuffed.

A worthy old marquise, a ruined émigrée, left with only one servant, continued to say: "My people."

What did they do in Madame de T.'s salon? They were ultra.

To be ultra; though the things it represents have perhaps not disappeared, this word has lost its meaning. Let us define it.

To be ultra is to go beyond. It is to attack the scepter in the name of the throne, and the miter in the name of the altar; it is to mistreat the thing you support; it is to kick in the traces; it is to cavil at the stake for undercooking heretics; it is to reproach the idol for a lack of idolatry; it is to insult through an excess of respect; it is to find too little papistry in the pope, in the king too little royalty, and too much light in the night; it is to be dissatisfied with the albatross, with snow, with the swan, and the lily for not being white enough; it is to champion things to the point of becoming their enemy; it is to be so pro you become con.

The ultra spirit is a peculiar characteristic of the first phase of the Restoration.

There was never anything in history like this little span, beginning in 1814 and ending around 1820, with the advent of M. de Villèle, the practical man of the Right. These six years were an extraordinary moment, both brilliant and gloomy, smiling and somber, bright with the radiance of dawn, and at the same time wrapped in the darkness of the great catastrophes that still filled the horizon, though they were slowly sinking in the past. There, in that light and that shade, was a little world by itself, new and old, merry and sad, juvenile and senile, rubbing its eyes; nothing resembles an awaking so much as a return; a group that looked at France whimsically, and that France looked at with irony; streets full of good old owl marquises returned and returning, "ci-devants," astounded at everything, brave and noble gentlemen smiling at being back in France, and weeping over it too; delighted to see their country again, in despair at finding their monarchy gone; the nobility of the crusades spitting on the nobility of the empire, that is to say the nobility of the sword; historic races losing the meaning of history; sons of Charlemagne's comrades disdaining the companions of Napoleon. Swords, as we have said, insulted each other; the sword of Fontenoy was laughable, and nothing but rust; the sword of Marengo was hateful, and only a saber. Formerly disowned Yesterday. The sense of the grand was lost, as well as the sense of the ridiculous. There was somebody who called Bonaparte Scapin. That world no longer exists. None of it, we repeat, remains. When we draw some form out of it by chance and try to bring it alive again through thought, it seems as strange to us as an antediluvian world. The fact is, it too has been swallowed up by a deluge. It has disappeared under two revolutions. What floods ideas are! How quickly they cover all that they are commissioned to destroy and bury, and how rapidly they create frightful abysses!

Such was the character of the salons in those far-off

honest ages when M. Martainville was wittier than Voltaire.

The salons had a literature and politics all their own. They believed in Fiévée. M. Agier pronounced the law. They criticized M. Colnet, the publicist of the bookstall of the Quai Malaquais. Napoleon was nothing but the Corsican Ogre. Later, the introduction into history of M. the Marquis de Buonaparté, lieutenant-general of the king's armies, was a concession to the spirit of the century.

These salons did not stay pure for long. As early as 1818, doctrinaires, a troublesome species, began to appear in them. Their style was to be royalists and to apologize for it. Just where the ultras were proudest, the doctrinaires were slightly ashamed. They were witty; they were silent; their political dogmas were suitably starched with pride; they should have been successful. They indulged, rather conveniently, in an excess of white cravat and buttoned coat. The misfortune of the doctrinaire party was the creation of an aging youth. They assumed the pose of sages. Their dream was to graft a limited power onto an absolute and excessive principle. They opposed—and sometimes with a rare intelligence—a destructive liberalism with a conservative liberalism. They were heard to say, "Be considerate of royalism; it has done a great deal of real service. It has brought us back tradition, worship, religion, respect. It is faithful, brave, chivalric, loving, devoted. Though grudgingly, it brings the old grandeur of the monarchy to the new grandeur of the nation. It is wrong not to understand the Revolution, the Empire, glory, liberty, new ideas, new generations, the century. But have we not sometimes done it the same wrong it does us? The Revolution, whose heirs we are, ought to understand everything. To attack royalism is a misconception of liberalism. What a blunder, and what blindness! Revolutionary France lacks respect for historic France, that is to say for her mother, or for herself. After the 5th of September, the nobility of the monarchy is treated as the nobility of the empire was treated after the 8th of July. They were unjust toward the eagle, we are unjust toward the fleur-de-lis. Do we always need something to condemn? What use is it to deface the crown of Louis XIV or to scratch off the escutcheon of Henry IV? We rail at Monsieur de Vaublanc who erased the N's from the Pont d'Iéna. But what did he do? The same thing we are doing. Bouvines belongs to us as well as Marengo. The fleurs-de-lis are ours as well as the N's. They are our patrimony. What is gained by diminishing it? We must not disown our country in the past anymore than in the present. Why not want our whole history? Why not love all of France?"

That is the way the doctrinaires criticized and patronized royalism, which was displeased at being criticized and furious at being patronized.

The ultras marked the first period of royalism; the congregation represented the second. Skill succeeded fervor. Let us end this sketch here.

In the course of the narrative, the author of this book came upon this strange moment in contemporary history; he had to glance at it in passing and retrace some of the stranger features of that society now unknown. But it is done rapidly and with no bitter or derisive intention. Reminiscences, affectionate and respectful, for they relate to his mother, draw him to that past. Besides, we have to say, that same little world has its own greatness. We may smile at it, but we can neither despise nor hate it. It was the France of former times.

Like all children, Marius Pontmercy went through some sort of education. When he left the care of Aunt Gillenormand, his grandfather entrusted him to a worthy professor with the purest classic innocence. This young awakening soul passed from a prude to a pedant. Marius went through secondary education, then entered the law school. He was royalist, fanatical, and austere. He had little love for his grandfather, whose gaiety and cynicism wounded him, and the place of his father was a dark void.

Otherwise, he was an ardent but cool lad, noble, generous, proud, religious; honorable to the point of harshness, pure to the point of unsociability.

IV

THE BANDIT'S END

The completion of Marius's classical studies coincided with M. Gillenormand's retirement from the world. The old man bade farewell to the Faubourg Saint-Germain and to Madame de T.'s salon, and settled in the Marais, at his house in the Rue des Filles-du-Calvaire. In addition to the porter, his household consisted of the chambermaid Nicolette, who had succeeded Magnon, and the wheezy and short-winded Basque we already mentioned.

In 1827, Marius had just reached eighteen. On coming in one evening, he saw his grandfather with a letter in his hand.

"Marius," said M. Gillenormand, "you will set out tomorrow for Vernon."

"What for?" Marius said.

"To see your father."

Marius shuddered. He had thought of everything but this, that one day he might have to see his father. Nothing could have been more unexpected, more surprising, and, let us admit, disagreeable. It was aversion brought to intimacy. It was not sorrow; no, it was simple drudgery.

Besides his feelings of political antipathy, Marius was convinced that his father, the swordsman, as M. Gillenormand called him in gentler moments, did not love him; that was clear, since he had abandoned him and left him to others. Sensing he was not loved, he felt no love. Nothing could be more natural, he said to himself.

He was so astonished that he did not question M. Gillenormand. The grandfather continued, "It appears he is sick. He is asking for you."

And after a moment of silence he added, "Start out tomorrow morning. At the Cour des Fontaines I think there is a carriage that leaves at six o'clock and arrives at night. Take it. He says you should come quickly."

Then he crumpled up the letter and put it in his pocket. Marius could have left that evening and been with his father the next morning. At that time a stagecoach made the trip to Rouen from the Rue du Bouloi by night, passing through Vernon. Neither M. Gillenormand nor Marius thought of asking.

The next day at dusk, Marius arrived at Vernon. Candles were just beginning to light up. He asked the first person he met for "the house of Monsieur Pontmercy." For he agreed with the Restoration, and he, too, recognized his father neither as baron nor as colonel.

The house was pointed out to him. He rang; a woman came and opened the door with a small lamp in her hand.

"Monsieur Pontmercy?" Marius said.

The woman remained motionless.

"Is this the place?" Marius asked.

The woman gave an affirmative nod of the head.

"Can I speak with him?"

The woman gave a negative sign.

"But I am his son!" Marius replied. "He is expecting me."

"He isn't expecting you anymore," said the woman.

Then he noticed that she was in tears.

She pointed to the door of a low room. He went in.

In this room, which was lit by a tallow candle on the mantel, there were three men, one of them standing, one on his keees, and one in his nightshirt, lying flat on the floor. The one on the floor was the colonel.

The two others were a physician and a priest who was praying.

Three days before, the colonel had come down with a brain fever. When he first fell ill, feeling some foreboding, he had written to M. Gillenormand to ask for his son. He had grown worse. On the very evening of Marius's arrival at Vernon, the colonel had suffered a fit of delirium; he sprang out of his bed despite the servant, crying, "My son hasn't come! I am going out to meet him!" Then he had left his room and fallen to the floor in the hall. He had only just died.

The doctor and the curé had been called. The doctor had come too late, the curé had come too late. The son too had come too late.

By the dim candlelight, they could see on the colonel's pale cheek a large tear, fallen from his lifeless eye. The eye was glazed, but the tear was not dry. The tear was for his son's delay.

Marius looked at this man, whom he was seeing for the

first time, and for the last—this venerable and manly face, the open eyes that did not see, the white hair, the robust limbs on which he could see occasional brown lines which were saber wounds, and marks like species of red stars which were bullet holes. He looked at the gigantic scar that stamped heroism on this face where God had imprinted goodness. He thought that this man was his father and that the man was dead, and he felt nothing.

The sorrow he experienced was the sorrow he would have felt seeing any other man stretched out in death.

There was mourning, poignant mourning in that room. The servant was lamenting by herself in a corner, the curé was praying and sobbing audibly; the doctor was wiping his eyes; the corpse itself was weeping.

The doctor, the priest, and the woman looked at Marius through their affliction without saying a word. He was the stranger. Marius, too little moved, felt ashamed and embarrassed by his attitude; he had his hat in his hand, he let it drop to the floor to make them believe that grief left him without the strength to hold it.

At the same time he felt something like remorse, and he despised himself for acting this way. But was it his fault? He did not love his father, and that was all there was to it.

The colonel had left nothing. The sale of his furniture hardly paid for his burial. The servant found a scrap of paper which she handed to Marius. It contained this, in the colonel's handwriting.

"*For my Son.*—The emperor made me a baron on the battlefield of Waterloo. Since the Restoration contests this title I bought with my blood, my son will take it and bear it. I need not say that he will be worthy of it."

On the back, the colonel had added:

"At this same battle of Waterloo, a sergeant saved my life. The man's name is Thénardier. Not long ago, I believe he had a little tavern in a village near Paris, at Chelles or at Montfermeil. If my son should meet him, he will do Thénardier all the service he can."

Not from duty toward his father, but because of that vague respect for death that man feels so imperiously, Marius took this paper and kept it.

No trace remained of the colonel. M. Gillenormand had his sword and uniform sold to a secondhand dealer. The neighbors stripped the garden and carried off the rare flowers. The other plants turned to briars and scrub, or they died.

Marius stayed only forty-eight hours in Vernon. After the burial, he returned to Paris and went back to his law, thinking no more of his father than if he had never lived. In two days the colonel had been buried, and in three days forgotten.

Marius wore a mourning band on his hat. That was all.

V

THE ADVANTAGE OF GOING TO MASS IN BECOMING REVOLUTIONARY

Marius had kept up the religious habits of his childhood. One Sunday he had gone to hear mass at Saint-Sulpice, to the same chapel of the Virgin where his aunt took him when he was a little boy. That day being more absent-minded and dreamy than usual, he took his place behind a pillar and knelt down, without noticing it, at a Utrecht velvet chair, on the back of which this name was written: "Monsieur Mabeuf, churchwarden." The mass had hardly begun when an old man came up and said to Marius, "Monsieur, this is my place."

Marius moved away willingly, and the old man took his chair.

After mass, Marius remained absorbed in thought a few steps away; the old man approached him again and said, "I beg your pardon, monsieur, for disturbing you a little while ago, and again now; but you must have thought me impertinent, and I have to explain myself."

"Monsieur," said Marius, "it is unnecessary."

"Yes!" resumed the old man. "I don't want you to have a bad impression of me. You see I think a great deal of that place. The mass seems better to me there. Why? I'll tell you why. For ten years, regularly, every two or three months, I would see a poor, brave father come to that spot; he had no other opportunity and no other way of seeing his child, as he was prevented through some family agreement. He came at the hour when he knew his son was brought to mass. The little one never suspected that his father was here. Perhaps he did not even know that he had a father, the innocent child! The father would stay behind a pillar, so that nobody would see him. He looked at his child, and he wept. This poor man worshiped the little boy. I could see that. This place has become sanctified for me somehow, and I have acquired the habit of coming here to hear mass. I prefer it to the bench, where I have a right to be as a warden. I even knew this unfortunate gentleman slightly. He had a father-in-law, a rich aunt, relatives, I do not quite remember, who threatened to disinherit the child if he, the father, saw him. He had sacrificed himself so that his son might some day be rich and happy. They were kept apart by political opinions. Certainly I approve of political opinions, but there are people who do not know where to stop. Good Lord! Just because a man was at Waterloo doesn't make him a monster; a father is not separated from his child for that. He was one of Bonaparte's colonels. He is dead, I believe. He lived at Vernon, where my brother is curé, and his name is something like Pontmarie, Montpercy. He had a handsome saber scar."

"Pontmercy," said Marius, turning pale.

"Exactly; Pontmercy. Did you know him?"

"Monsieur," said Marius, "he was my father."

The old churchwarden clasped his hands, and exclaimed, "Ah! You are the child! Yes, that is it; he ought to be a man by now. Well! Poor child, you can say you had a father who loved you dearly."

Marius gave his arm to the old man and walked him to his house. Next day he said to M. Gillenormand, "We have set up a hunting party with a few friends. Will you allow me to be away for three days?"

"Four," answered the grandfather. "Go on; have a good time."

And, with a wink he whispered to his daughter, "Some love affair!"

VI

WHAT IT MEANS TO HAVE MET A CHURCHWARDEN

A little farther on we shall see where Marius went.

He was away for three days, then he returned to Paris, went straight to the library of the law school, and asked for the file of the *Moniteur*.

He read the *Moniteur;* he read all the histories of the Republic and the Empire; the *Mémorial de Sainte-Hélène;* all the memoirs, newspapers, bulletins, proclamations; he devoured everything. The first time he came across his father's name in the bulletins of the Grand Army he had a fever for a whole week. He went to see the generals under whom George Pontmercy had served—among others, Comte H. The churchwarden, Mabeuf, whom he had gone to see again, gave him an account of the life in Vernon, the colonel's retreat, his flowers and his solitude. Marius came to fully understand this rare, sublime, and gentle man, this lion-lamb who was his father.

In the meantime, engrossed in this study, which took up all his time, as well as all his thoughts, he hardly saw the Gillenormands anymore. He would appear at mealtimes; then when they looked for him, he was gone. The aunt grumbled. The grandfather smiled. "Now, now! It's the age for the lasses!" Sometimes the old man added: "The devil! I thought it was some gallantry. It seems to be a passion."

It was a passion, indeed. Marius was in the process of idolizing his father.

At the same time an extraordinary change took place in his ideas, a metamorphosis that occurred in gradual phases. Since this was the case with many minds of our time, we believe it useful to follow these phases step by step, and to indicate them all.

This story he had just discovered amazed him.

The first effect was bewilderment. Until then, the Republic, the Empire, had been nothing but monstrous words to him. The Republic, a guillotine in a twilight; the

Empire, a saber in the night. He had just looked into them, and there, where he expected to find only darkness and chaos, he had seen, with a sort of fearful wonder and joy, shining stars—Mirabeau, Vergniaud, Saint-Just, Robespierre, Camille Desmoulins, Danton—and a rising sun, Napoleon. He felt lost. He recoiled blinded by the splendors. Little by little, the astonishment gone, he grew accustomed to this radiance; he could study events without recoiling, he examined individuals without terror; the Revolution and the Empire fell into luminous perspective before his straining eyes; he saw each of these two groups of events and men moved into two enormous feats: the Republic into the sovereignty of civic rights restored to the masses, the Empire into the sovereignty of the French idea imposed upon Europe; he saw the great figure of the people spring out of the Revolution, and the great form of France out of the Empire. He felt in his conscience that all of it had been good.

It's probably unnecessary to indicate here what his amazement overlooked in this first far too synthetic appreciation. We are describing the state of a mind on the march. Progress is not accomplished at a bound. Having stated this, once and for all, for what precedes as well as for what is to follow, we continue.

He then realized that up to that time he had understood his country no better than he had his father. He had known neither one and had allowed a sort of voluntary night to screen his eyes. Now he could see; and on the one hand he admired, and on the other he worshiped.

He was filled with regret and remorse, and he reflected with despair that he could not divulge all his inmost thoughts except to a tomb. Oh! If only his father were living, if he still had him, if God in his mercy and goodness had allowed his father to be still alive, how he would have run, how he would have hurtled, how he would have cried out to his father, "Father! I'm here! My beliefs are the same as yours! I am your son!" How he would have embraced his white head, wet his hair with tears, gazed at his scar, taken him by the hand, admired his clothing, kissed his feet! Oh! Why had this father died so soon, so young, before justice was rendered, before the love of his son! Marius felt a continual pang in his heart, a constant "Alas!" At the same time he was becoming more truly dedicated, more truly grave, surer of his faith and his beliefs. Gleams of truth kept appearing to fill in his reasoning. It was like an interior growth. He felt a sort of natural broadening produced by these two new things, his father and his country.

As if with a new key, everything opened; he understood things he had hated, he delved into what he had abhorred; with a lasting clarity, he saw the providential, divine, and human meaning of the great things he had been taught to detest, and the great men he had been instructed to scorn. When he thought of his former opinions, which already seemed so old, though they were only yesterday's, he was cross at himself, but he smiled. From his father's rehabilitation he had naturally gone on to the rehabilitation of Napoleon.

However, we must admit that this last was not accomplished without a struggle.

From childhood on he had been indoctrinated with the views of the party of 1814 in regard to Bonaparte. All the prejudices of the Restoration, all its interests, all its instincts, tended to distort Napoleon. It execrated him still more than it did Robespierre. It made skillful use of the nation's weariness and the hatred of mothers. Bonaparte had become a sort of almost fabulous monster, and to portray him for the imagination of the people, which, as we have already said, is a childish imagination, the opinion of 1814 produces every terrifying mask in succession, from the terrible though still grand to the terrible tending to grotesque, from Tiberius to goblin. So, in speaking of Bonaparte, you might either weep, or burst out laughing, provided hatred was the basis. Marius had never had—about that man, as he was called—any other ideas in mind. They had grown together with the tenacity of his nature. There was within him a complete creature who was stubborn in his hatred of Napoleon.

On reading his history, particularly through studying it in documents, and materials, the veil that hid Napoleon from Marius's eyes gradually fell away. He perceived something immense, and suspected that he had been deceiving himself up to that moment about Bonaparte as well as about everything else; each day he saw more clearly; and he began to mount slowly, step by step, in the beginning almost with regret, afterward with rapture, and as though drawn by an irresistible fascination, through the somber stages first, then the dimly lit stages, finally the luminous and gleaming stages of enthusiasm.

One night he was alone in his little room under the eaves. His candle was burning; he was reading, leaning on his table by the open window. All sorts of reveries came to him from the expanse of space and mingled with his thought. What a spectacle night is! We hear dull sounds, not knowing where they come from; we see Jupiter, twelve hundred times larger than the earth, glowing like an ember, the sky is black, the stars sparkle, it is awe-inspiring.

He was reading the bulletins of the Grand Army, those Homeric strophes written on the battlefield; he saw there at times his father's name, the emperor's name everywhere; the whole of the great Empire appeared before him; he felt as if a tide were swelling and rising within him; it sometimes seemed his father was passing by him like a breath and whispering in his ear; gradually, strange things happened; he thought he heard the drums, the cannon, the trumpets, the measured tread of the battalions, the dull and distant gallop of the cavalry; from time to time he lifted his eyes to the sky and saw the colossal constellations shining in the limitless tracts, then they fell back to the book, and saw other vast things moving about confusedly. His heart was full. He was transported, trembling, breathless; suddenly, without knowing what moved him, or what he was obeying, he rose, stretched his arms out the window, stared into the darkness, the silence, the infinite, the eternal immensity and cried out: "Vive l'empereur!"

From that moment it was all over. The Corsican Ogre—the usurper—the tyrant—the monster who had been the lover of his sisters—the mountebank who took lessons from Talma—the poisoner of Jaffa—the tiger—Buonaparté—all this vanished, and gave way in his mind to a suffused and brilliant radiance in which from an inaccessible height the pale marble phantom of Caesar shone out. The emperor had been to his father only the beloved captain, recipient of admiration and devotion; to Marius he was something more. He was the predestined builder of the French, succeeding the Romans in the mastery of the world. He was the stupendous architect of a downfall, the successor of Charlemagne, of Louis XI, of

Henry IV, of Richelieu, of Louis XIV, and of the Committee of Public Safety, undoubtedly with his blemishes, his faults, and even his crimes—that is to say, being human—but noble in his faults, brilliant in his blemishes, mighty in his crimes.

He was the preordained man who had forced all nations to say "the Great Nation." He was better still; he was the very incarnation of France, conquering Europe by the sword that he held, and the world by the light that he shed. In Bonaparte Marius saw the flashing specter that will always rise over the frontier, that will guard the future. Despot, but dictator; despot resulting from a republic and summing up a revolution. Napoleon became to him the people-man as Jesus is the God-man.

We see that, like all new converts to a religion, his conversion intoxicated him, he plunged headlong into adhesion, and he went too far. His nature was such; once launched, it was almost impossible for him to hold back. Fanaticism for the sword took possession of him and mentally complicated his enthusiasm for the idea. He did not realize that along with genius, and indiscriminately, he was admiring power, that is to say he was installing in the two compartments of his idolatry, on one side what is divine, and on the other what is brutal. In several respects he began to deceive himself in other matters. He accepted everything. There is a way of falling into error while on the road of truth. He had a sort of willful implicit faith that swallowed everything whole. On entering his new path, he neglected the attenuating circumstances both in judging the crimes of the ancient *régime* and in measuring Napoleon's glory.

However this might be, a great step had been taken. Where he had formerly seen the fall of the monarchy, he now saw the rise of France. His orientation was changed. What had been the setting was now the rising of the sun. He had turned around.

All these revolutions came about in him without a hint of it to his family.

When, in this mysterious labor, he had entirely cast off his old Bourbon and ultra skin, when he had shed the aristocrat, the jacobite, and the royalist, when he was fully revolutionary, thoroughly democratic, and almost republican, he went to an engraver on the Quai des Orfévres, and ordered a hundred cards bearing the name: *Baron Marius Pontmercy*.

This was simply a logical consequence of the change that had taken place in him, a change in which everything gravitated around his father. However, since he knew nobody, and could not leave his cards at anybody's door, he put them in his pocket.

Through another natural consequence, as he drew nearer to his father, his memory, and the things for which the colonel had fought for twenty-five years, he drew away from his grandfather. As we have mentioned, for a long time he had found M. Gillenormand's capriciousness disagreeable. There was already between them all the distaste of a serious young man for a frivolous old man. Geront's gaiety shocks and exasperates Werther's melancholy. So long as the same political opinions and the same ideas had been common to them, Marius had met M. Gillenormand by means of them as though on a bridge. When this bridge fell, the abyss appeared. And then, above all, Marius felt inexpressibly revolted by the thought that M. Gillenormand, out of stupid motives, had pitilessly kept him away from the colonel, thus depriving the father of the child, and the child of the father.

Through affection and veneration for his father, Marius had almost reached an aversion for his grandfather.

Nothing of this, however, as we have said, was betrayed externally. Except that he was more and more unmoved—laconic at meals and scarcely ever at home. When his aunt scolded him for it, he was very sweet, and gave as an excuse his studies, courses, examinations, dissertations, etc. The grandfather did not change his infallible diagnosis: "In love? I know something about that."

Marius was continually away for short periods.

"Where can he be?" asked the aunt.

On one of the trips, which were always very short, he went to Montfermeil in obedience to the instruction his father had left him, and looked for the former sergeant of Waterloo, the innkeeper Thénardier. Thénardier had failed, the inn was closed, and nobody knew what had become of him. While doing these researches, Marius was away from the house four days.

"Decidedly," said the grandfather, "he is going astray."

They thought they noticed that he was wearing something, against his chest and under his shirt, hung from his neck by a black ribbon.

VII

SOME PETTICOAT

We have spoken of a lancer.

He was a great-nephew of M. Gillenormand's on the paternal side, who lived away from his family, and far from all domestic hearths, in an army garrison. Lieutenant Théodule Gillenormand fulfilled all the conditions required for what is called a handsome officer. He had "the waist of a girl," a way of rattling his saber, and an upcurled mustache. He came to Paris very rarely, so rarely that Marius had never seen him. The two cousins knew each other only by name. Théodule was, we think we mentioned, the favorite of Aunt Gillenormand, who preferred him because she did not see him. Not seeing people permits us to imagine them with every perfection.

One morning, Mlle. Gillenormand the elder had retired to her room as excited as her placid spirit allowed. Marius had asked his grandfather again for permission to make a short trip, adding that he intended to set out that evening. "Go!" the grandfather had answered, and M. Gillenormand had added aside, raising his eyebrows, "He is getting to be a recidivist." Mlle. Gillenormand had returned to her room very much perplexed, dropping this exclamation point on the stairs: "That's a bit much!" and this interrogation point: "But where *can* he be going?" She imagined some more or less illicit love affair, a woman in the shadows, a rendezvous, a mystery, and she would not have been sorry to take a closer look. The taste of a mystery is like the first hint of scandal; saintly souls never hate that. In the secret compartments of bigotry there is some curiosity for scandal.

She was thus prey to a blind desire to hear out a story.

As a diversion from this curiosity, which was stirring her up a little more than usual, she took refuge in her talents and began to stitch, cotton on cotton, in one of those embroideries of the Empire and Restoration periods with a great many carriage wheels. Clumsy work, crabbed worker. She had been sitting in her chair for some hours when the door opened. Mlle. Gillenormand raised her eyes; Lieutenant Théodule was facing her, in the regulation bow. She gave a cry of pleasure. You may be old, you may be a prude, you may be a bigot, you may be his aunt, but it is always pleasant to see a lancer enter your room.

"You, Théodule!" she exclaimed.

"Passing through, aunt."

"Then give me a kiss."

"Here you are!" said Théodule.

And he embraced her. Aunt Gillenormand went to her desk and opened it. "You will stay with us all week at least?"

"Aunt, I have to leave this evening."

"Impossible!"

"Inevitable."

"Stay, my dear Théodule, please."

"The heart says yes, but my orders say no. It is a simple story. We are changing stations; we were at Melun, we are going to Gaillon. To get from the old station to the new, we have to pass through Paris. I said, I'll go and see my aunt."

"Take this for your pains."

She put ten Louis into his hand.

"You mean for my pleasure, dear aunt."

Théodule kissed her a second time, and she had the joy of having her neck a little chafed by the braid of his uniform.

"Are you making the trip on horseback with your regiment?" she asked.

"No, aunt. I wanted to see you. I have a special permit. My orderly is taking my horse; I am going by stagecoach. And, speaking of that, I have a question to ask you."

"What is it?"

"My cousin, Marius Pontmercy, is traveling too, is he?"

"How do you know that?" exclaimed the aunt, her curiosity suddenly pricked.

"On arriving, I went right to the office to reserve my place inside."

"Well?"

"A traveler had already reserved an outside seat. I saw his name in the book."

"What name?"

"Marius Pontmercy."

"The wicked fellow!" exclaimed the aunt. "Ah! Your cousin is not a steady boy like you. To think that he's going to spend the night on a stagecoach."

"Like me."

"But for you, it is out of duty; for him, it is from dissipation."

"And so?" said Théodule.

Here, an event occurred in the life of Mlle. Gillenormand the elder; she had an idea. If she had been a man, she would have slapped her forehead. She queried Théodule: "Are you sure your cousin does not know you?"

"Yes. I have seen him; but he has never deigned to notice me."

"And so you are going to be traveling together?"

"He on the top, I inside."

"Where does this coach go?"

"To Les Andelys."

"Is that where Marius is going?"

"Unless, like me, he stops partway. I'll get off at Vernon to take the connecting coach for Gaillon. I don't know anything about Marius's route."

"Marius! What an ugly name! What an idea it was to name him Marius! But you at least—your name is Théodule!"

"I'd rather it were Alfred," said the officer.

"Listen, Théodule."

"I am listening, aunt."

"Pay attention."

"I am paying attention."

"Are you ready?"

"Yes."

"Well, Marius often goes away."

"Mmm!"

"He travels."

"Ah!"

"He sleeps away from home."

"Oh!"

"We want to know what's at the bottom of it all."

Théodule answered with the calm of a bronze figure: "Some petticoat."

And with the stifled chuckle that reveals certainty, he added, "A lass."

"That much is clear," exclaimed the aunt, who felt she was hearing M. Gillenormand's voice, and who felt her conviction spring irresistibly from this word "lass," said in almost the same tone by the grand-uncle and the grand-nephew. She went on, "Do us a kindness. Follow Marius a little way. Since he does not know you, it will be easy. Since there is a lass, try to see the lass. You can write us the tale. It will amuse Grandfather."

Théodule had no particular taste for this sort of spying; but he was very touched by the ten Louis, and thought he saw a possible succession of them. He accepted the task and said, "As you please, aunt." And he muttered, "So there I am, a duenna."

Mlle. Gillenormand kissed him.

"You would not play such pranks, Théodule. You are obedient to discipline, you are the slave of your orders, you are a scrupulous and dutiful man, and you would not leave your family to go and see such a creature."

The lancer put on the satisfied smirk of a bandit praised for his honesty.

Marius, on the evening following this dialogue, climbed onto the stagecoach without suspecting he was being watched. As to the watchman, the first thing that he did was fall asleep. His slumber was deep, the sign of a clear conscience. Argus snored all night.

At daybreak, the coach driver shouted: "Vernon! Vernon relay! Passengers for Vernon?" And Lieutenant Théodule woke up.

"Good," he growled, still half asleep, "I get off here."

Then his memory clearing by degrees, an effect of waking, he remembered his aunt, the ten Louis, and the account he was to render of Marius's acts and deeds. It made him laugh.

"Perhaps he got off the coach," he thought, while he buttoned up his uniform jacket. "Maybe he stopped at Poissy; he may have stopped at Triel; if he didn't get off at Meulan, he may have gotten off at Mantes, unless he got off at Rolleboise, or unless he only came as far as Pacy, with the choice of turning to the left toward

Evreux, or to the right toward Laroche Guyon. You chase him, aunt. What the devil shall I write to her, the good old woman?"

At this moment a pair of black trousers getting down from the top showed at the window of the coupé.

"Can that be Marius?" said the lieutenant.

It was Marius.

A little peasant girl, beside the coach, among the horses and postilions, was offering flowers to the passengers. "Flowers for your ladies," she cried.

Marius went up to her and bought the most beautiful flowers in her basket.

"Now," said Théodule leaping down from the coach, "there's something that interests me. Who the devil is he going to carry those flowers to? It ought to be a mighty pretty woman for such a fine bouquet. I'd like to see her."

And, no longer now by command, but out of personal curiosity, like those dogs that hunt on their own account, he began to follow Marius.

Marius paid no attention to Théodule. Some elegant women got out of the coach; he did not look at them. He seemed to see nothing around him.

"Is he in love?" thought Théodule.

Marius walked toward the church.

"All right," said Théodule to himself. "The church! That's it. These rendezvous spiced with a touch of mass are the best of all. Nothing is so exquisite as a glance that slips past the good Lord."

On reaching the church, Marius did not go in, but went behind the building. He disappeared around the corner of a buttress of the apse.

"The rendezvous is outside," said Théodule. "Now let's see the lass."

And he tiptoed toward the corner where Marius had turned.

On reaching it, he stopped, astounded.

Marius, his face hidden in his hands, was kneeling in the grass, on a grave. He had scattered his flowers. At the end of the grave, at a rise marking the head, there was a black wooden cross with this name in white letters: COLONEL BARON PONTMERCY. He heard Marius sobbing.

The lass was a grave.

VIII

MARBLE AGAINST GRANITE

This was where Marius had come the first time he left Paris. It was here that he returned every time M. Gillenormand said, "He is sleeping out."

Lieutenant Théodule was absolutely disconcerted by this unexpected encounter with a sepulcher; he felt a strange and disagreeable sensation that he was incapable of analyzing, made up of respect for a tomb mingled with respect for a colonel. He retreated, leaving Marius alone in the churchyard, and there was discipline in this retreat. Death appeared to him with huge epaulets, and he almost gave him a military salute. Not knowing what to write to his aunt, he decided to write nothing at all; and probably nothing would have come of Théodule's discovery regarding Marius's amours if, by one of those mysterious chance arrangements that so often happen, the scene at Vernon had not almost immediately been followed by a sort of counterblow in Paris.

Marius returned from Vernon early in the morning of the third day, was set down at his grandfather's, and, tired from the two nights spent in the coach, feeling the need of making up for his lack of sleep by an hour at the swimming school, dashed up to his room, took only time enough to lay down his traveling coat and the black ribbon he wore around his neck, and went away to the bath.

M. Gillenormand, who had risen early like all the elderly who are in good health, had heard him come in, and hurried as fast as he could with his old legs, to climb to the top of the stairs where Marius's room was, to give him a kiss, question him while embracing him, and find out something about where he had come from.

But the youth had taken less time to go down than the old man to go up, and when Grandfather Gillenormand went into the garret room, Marius was no longer there.

The bed had not been disturbed, and on it were trustingly laid the coat and the black ribbon.

"I like that better," said M. Gillenormand.

And a moment later he entered the drawing room

where Mlle. Gillenormand the elder was already seated, embroidering her carriage wheels.

The entrance was triumphant.

In one hand M. Gillenormand held the coat and in the other the neck ribbon, and cried out, "Victory! We are about to penetrate the mystery! We shall know the end of the mystery, unravel the wanton ways of our rascal! Here we are right to the core of the romance. I have the portrait!"

In fact, a black shagreen box, rather like a medallion, was fastened to the ribbon.

The old man took this box and looked at it for some time without opening it, with that air of desire, delight, and anger, with which a poor, hungry devil sees an excellent dinner pass right under his nose, when it is not for him.

"For it is clearly a portrait. I know all about these things. They are worn tenderly against the heart. What fools they are! Some abominable floozy, probably enough to bring on the shudders! Young people have such bad taste nowadays!"

"Let's see, father," said the old maid.

The box opened by pressing a spring. They found nothing in it but a piece of paper carefully folded.

"More and more predictable," said M. Gillenormand, bursting with laughter. "I know what that is. A love letter!"

"Ah! Then let's read it!" said the aunt.

And she put on her spectacles. They unfolded the paper and read this:

"*For my Son.*—The emperor made me a baron on the battlefield of Waterloo. Since the Restoration contests this title I have bought with my blood, my son will take it and bear it. I need not say that he will be worthy of it."

The feelings of the father and daughter are beyond description. They felt chilled as by the breath of a death's head. They did not exchange a word. M. Gillenormand, however, said in a low voice, and as if talking to himself, "It is the handwriting of that bandit."

The aunt examined the paper, turned it over every which way, then put it back in the box.

At that very moment, a little rectangular package wrapped in blue paper fell out of the coat pocket. Mademoiselle Gillenormand picked it up and unwrapped the blue paper. It was Marius's hundred cards. She passed one of them to M. Gillenormand, who read: *Baron Marius Pontmercy.*

The old man rang. Nicolette came. M. Gillenormand took the ribbon, the box, and the coat, threw them all on the floor in the middle of the drawing room, and said:

"Take those things away."

A full hour passed in complete silence. The old man and the old maid sat with their backs turned to one another, and were probably each individually thinking over the same things. At the end of that hour, Aunt Gillenormand said, "Pretty!"

A few minutes later, Marius appeared. He was just coming home. Even before crossing the threshold of the drawing room, he saw his grandfather holding one of his cards in his hand; the old man, on seeing him, exclaimed with his crushing air of sneering bourgeois superiority, "Well! Well! Well! Well! Well! So you are a baron now. My compliments. What does this mean?"

Marius blushed slightly, and answered, "It means I am my father's son."

M. Gillenormand stopped laughing, and said harshly, "Your father; I am your father."

"My father," resumed Marius with downcast eyes and stern manner, "was a humble and heroic man, who served the Republic and France gloriously, who was great in the greatest history that men have ever made, who lived a quarter of a century in the camps, under fire by day, and by night in the snow, in the mud, and the rain, who captured colors, who was twenty times wounded, who died forgotten and abandoned, and who had but one fault; that was to have too dearly loved two ingrates, his country and me."

This was more than M. Gillenormand could bear. At the word, "Republic," he rose, or rather, sprang to his feet. Every one of the words Marius had just spoken, produced on the old royalist's face the effect of a blast from a bellows on a burning coal. From dark he had turned red, from red to purple, and from purple to flaming.

"Marius!" he exclaimed, "abominable child! I don't know what your father was! I don't want to know! I know nothing about him and I don't know him! But what I do know is that there was never anything but miserable wretches among them! That they were all beggars, assassins, thieves, rabble in their red bonnets! I say all of them! I say all of them! I don't know anybody! I say all of them! Do you hear, Marius? Look here, you are as much a baron as my slipper! They were all bandits, those who served Robespierre! All brigands who served Bu-o-na-parté! All traitors who betrayed, betrayed, betrayed! Their legitimate king! All cowards who ran from the Prussians and English at Waterloo! That's what I know. If your father is among them I don't know him, I'm sorry, so much the worse. Your humble servant, sir!"

In turn, it was Marius who now became the coal, and M. Gillenormand the bellows. Marius shuddered in every limb, he had no idea what to do, his head was burning. He was the priest who sees all his wafers thrown to the winds, the fakir seeing a passerby spit on his idol. He could not allow such things to be said before him. But what could he do? His father had just been trodden underfoot and stamped on in his presence, but by whom? By his grandfather. How could he avenge the one without outraging the other? It was impossible for him to insult his grandfather, and it was equally impossible for him not to avenge his father. On one hand a sacred tomb, on the other a white head. For a few moments he felt dizzy and staggering with all this whirlwind in his head; then he raised his eyes, looked straight at his grandfather, and cried in a thundering voice: "Down with the Bourbons, and that great hog Louis XVIII!"

Louis XVIII had been dead for four years; but that made no difference to him.

Scarlet as he was, the old man suddenly turned whiter than his hair. He turned toward a bust of the Duc de Berry that stood on the mantel and bowed to it profoundly with a sort of peculiar majesty. Then he walked twice, slowly and in silence, from the fireplace to the window and from the window to the fireplace, covering the whole length of the room and making the parquet creak as if an image of stone were walking over it. The second time, he bent toward his daughter, who was enduring the shock with the stupor of an aged sheep, and said to her with a smile that was almost calm, "A baron like Monsieur and a bourgeois like myself cannot remain under the same roof."

And all at once straightening up, pallid, trembling, terrible, his forehead swelling with the fearful radiance of anger, he stretched his arm towards Marius and cried out, "Be off!"

Marius left the house.

The next day, M. Gillenormand said to his daughter, "You will send sixty pistoles every six months to that blood drinker, and never speak of him to me again."

Having an immense residue of fury to expend, and not knowing what to do with it, he spoke to his daughter coldly for more than three months.

Marius, for his part, left in indignation. We must mention a circumstance that aggravated his exasperation still further. There are always such inevitable little details complicating domestic dramas. Feelings are embittered by them, though in reality the faults are none the greater. In hurriedly carrying away Marius's "things" to his room at the old man's command, Nicolette had inadvertently dropped, probably on the garret stairs, which were dark, the black shagreen medallion containing the paper written by the colonel. Neither the piece of paper nor the medallion could be found. Marius was convinced that "Monsieur Gillenormand"—from that day forth he never named him otherwise—had thrown "his father's will" into the fire. He knew by heart the few lines written by the colonel, and consequently nothing was lost. But the paper, the writing, that sacred relic, all of that was his heart itself. What had been done with it?

Marius went away without saying where he was going and without knowing where he was going, with thirty francs, his watch, and a few clothes in a small bag. He hired a cabriolet by the hour, jumped in, and drove at random toward the Latin quarter.

What was Marius to do?

Book Four

THE FRIENDS OF THE A B C

I

A GROUP THAT ALMOST BECAME HISTORIC

During that seemingly indifferent time, a vague revolutionary thrill was noticeable. Gusts from the depths of '89 and '92 were in the air. Young Paris was, excuse the expression, in the process of moulting. People were transformed almost without suspecting it, by the very movement of the time. The hand that sweeps around the dial also moves among souls. Each individual took the next step forward. Royalists became liberals, liberals became democrats.

It was like a rising tide, complicated by a thousand ebbs; the peculiarity of the ebb is to make mixtures; thereby very singular combinations of ideas; at the same time men venerated Napoleon and liberty. Now we are writing history. Then, it was all mirage. Opinions pass through phases. Voltairian royalism, a strange variety, had a less strange counterpart, Bonapartist liberalism.

Other groups of thinkers were more serious. Here they fathomed principle; there they attached themselves to right. They longed for the absolute, they glimpsed the infinite realizations; by its very rigidity, the absolute pushes the mind toward the boundless and sets it afloat in the limitless. There is nothing like dogma to produce the dream. There is nothing like dream to create the future. Utopia today, flesh and blood tomorrow.

Advanced opinions had double foundations. A mere hint of mystery threatened "the established order of things," which was sullen and suspicious—a sign revolutionary in the highest degree. The ulterior motives of power meet the ulterior motives of the people under ground. The incubation of insurrections replies to the plotting of coups d'état.

At that time there were not yet in France any of those huge underlying organizations like the German Tugenbund and the Italian Carbonari; but here and there obscure excavations were branching out. La Cougourde was taking shape at Aix; in Paris, there was, among other affiliations of this kind, the Society of the Friends of the A B C.

Who were the Friends of the A B C? A society seeming to have as its aim the education of children; in reality, the remaking of men.

They declared themselves the Friends of the A B C [pronounced ah-bay-say]. The *abaissé* [the abased] were the people. They wished to raise them up. One pun that is not funny. Puns can be serious in politics, witness the *Castratus ad castra,* which made Narses a general of an army; witness *Barbari et Barbarini;* witness *Fueros y Fuegos;* witness *Tu es Petrus et super hanc Petram,* etc., etc.

The Friends of the A B C were few. It was a secret society in the embryonic state; we should almost say a coterie if coteries produced heroes. They met in Paris, at two places, near the Halles in a bistro called Corinth, which will be referred to hereafter, and near the Pantheon in a little café on the Place Saint-Michel, called Le Café Musain, now torn down; the first of these two meeting places was near the workingmen, the second near the students.

The usual secret meetings of the Friends of the A B C were held in a back room of the Café Musain.

This room, quite far from the café, to which it was connected by a very long corridor, had two windows, and an exit by a private stairway onto the little Rue des Grès. They smoked, drank, played, and laughed there. They talked very loud about everything, and in whispers about something else. Nailed to the wall, sufficient indication to awaken the suspicion of a police officer, was an old map of France under the Republic.

Most of the Friends of the A B C were students, in close association with a few workingmen. The names of the principals are as follows. To a certain extent they belong to history: Enjolras, Combeferre, Jean Prouvaire, Feuilly, Courfeyrac, Bahorel, Lesgle or Laigle, Joly, Grantaire.

These young men constituted a sort of family among themselves, through friendship. All except Laigle were from the South.

It was a remarkable group, vanished into the invisible depths behind us. At this point of the drama, it may be useful to throw a ray of light onto these young heads before the reader sees them sink into the shadow of a tragic adventure.

Enjolras, named first—later we will see why—was an only son and was rich. He was a charming young man, capable of being intimidating. He was angelically beautiful. He was Antinoüs, wild. You would have said, seeing the thoughtful reflection of his eye, that he had already, in some preceding existence, been through the revolutionary apocalypse. He knew its tradition like an eyewitness. He knew every little detail of that great thing. A pontifical and warrior nature, strange in a youth. He was officiating and militant; from the immediate point of view, a soldier of democracy; above the movement of the time, a priest of the ideal. He had a deep eye, slightly red lids, thick underlip, readily disdainful, and a high forehead. Much forehead in a face is like much sky in a horizon. Like certain young men early in this century and late in the last, who became illustrious in early life, he had an exceedingly youthful look, as fresh as a young girl's, though he had moments of pallor. Already a man, he still seemed a child. His twenty-two years appeared as seventeen; he was serious, he did not seem to know that there was a being on earth called woman. He had one passion only, justice; one thought only, to remove all obstacles. On Mount Aventine, he would have been Gracchus; in the Convention, he would have been Saint-Just. He hardly saw a rose, he ignored the spring, he did not hear the birds sing; Evadne's bare bosom would have moved him no more than Aristogeiton; to him, as to Harmodius, flowers were good only for hiding the sword. He was severe in his pleasures. Before anything but the Republic, he chastely dropped his eyes. He was the marble lover of liberty. His speech was roughly inspired and had the tremor of a hymn. He would spread his wings unexpectedly and astonish you by his soaring. Woe to the love affair that should venture to intrude on him! Had any grisette of the Place Cambrai or the Rue Saint-Jean-de-Beauvais, seeing this college boy's face, the body of a page, long fair lashes, blue eyes, that hair flying in the wind, rosy cheeks, pure lips, exquisite teeth, felt a desire to taste all this dawn, and tried her beauty on Enjolras, a surprising and terrible look would have suddenly shown her the great gulf, and taught her not to confuse Beaumarchais's dashing cherubino with this fearsome cherubim of Ezekiel.

Beside Enjolras who represented the logic of the Revolution, Combeferre represented its philosophy. Between the logic of the Revolution and its philosophy, there is this difference—that its logic could conclude in war, while its philosophy could only end in peace. Combeferre completed and corrected Enjolras. He was lower and broader. His desire was to instill into all minds the broad principles of general ideas; his motto was "Revolution, but civilization"; and he spread the vast blue horizon around the steep mountain. Hence, in all Combeferre's views, there was something attainable and practicable. Revolution with Combeferre was more possible than with Enjolras. Enjolras expressed its divine right and Combeferre its natural right. The first sprang from Robespierre; the second stopped at Condorcet. More than Enjolras, Combeferre lived the life of the world in general. Had it been given to these two young men to take a place in history, one would have been the upright man, the other the wise man. Enjolras was more virile, Combeferre was more humane. *Homo* and *Vir* indeed express the exact shade of difference. Combeferre was gentle, as Enjolras was severe, from natural purity. He loved the word "citizen," but he preferred the word "man." He would gladly have said *Hombre* like the Spaniards. He read everything, went to the theater, followed the public courts, learned the polarization of light from Arago, was intrigued by a lecture in which Geoffroy Saint-Hilaire had explained the double function of the exterior carotid artery and the interior carotid artery, one of which supplies the face, the other the brain; he kept pace with the times, followed science step by step, confronted Saint-Simon with Fourier, deciphered hieroglyphics, broke the pebbles that he found and talked about geology, drew a moth from memory, pointed out the mistakes in French in the Dictionnaire de l'Académie, studied Puységur and Deleuze, affirmed nothing, not even miracles; denied nothing, not even ghosts; looked over the files of the *Moniteur,* reflected. He declared that the future was in the hands of the schoolmaster and busied himself with questions of education. He wanted society to work relentlessly at the raising of the intellectual and moral level; at the coming of knowledge, at bringing ideas into circulation, at the growth of the mind in youth; and he feared that the poverty of the methods then in vogue, the meagerness of a literary world limited to two or three centuries, called classical, the tyrannic dogmatism of official pedants, scholastic prejudices, and routine, would result in making artificial oyster beds of our colleges. He was learned, purist, precise, polytechnical, a hard student, and at the same time given to musing, "even chimeric," said his friends. He believed in all the dreams: railroads, the suppression of suffering in surgical operations, the fixing of the image in the camera oscura, the electric telegraph, the steering of balloons. Little dismayed, on the whole, by the citadels built up on all sides against the human race by superstitions, despotisms, and prejudices, he was one of those who think that science will at last turn the position. Enjolras was a chief; Combeferre was a guide. You would have preferred to fight with the one and march with the other. Not that Combeferre was incapable of fighting; he did not refuse to grapple with an obstacle, and to attack it by main strength and by explosion, but gradually, by the teaching of axioms and the promulgation of positive laws, to put the human race in harmony with its destinies, pleased him better; and of the two lights, his inclination was rather toward illumination than conflagration. A fire would cause a dawn, undoubtedly, but why not wait for the break of day? A volcano illuminates, but the morning enlightens still better. Combeferre, perhaps, preferred the pure radiance of the beautiful to the flaming glory of the sublime. A light disturbed by smoke, an advance purchased by violence, only half satisfied this tender and serious mind. A headlong plunge of a nation into the truth, a 1793, startled him; but stagnation repelled him still more, he felt putrefaction in it and death; on the whole, he liked foam better than miasma, and he preferred the sewer to the cesspool, and Niagara Falls to the Lac de Montfaucon. In short, he wanted neither halt nor haste. While his tumultuous friends, chivalrously devoted to the absolute, adored and asked for splendid revolutionary adventures, Combeferre inclined to let progress do her work—the good progress, cold, perhaps, but pure; methodical, but irreproachable; phlegmatic, but imperturbable. Combeferre would have knelt down and clasped his hands, asking for the future to come in all its radiant purity and for nothing to disturb the immense virtuous evolution of the people. "The good must be innocent," he repeated incessantly. And in fact, if it is the grandeur of the Revolution to stare at the dazzling ideal, and to fly to it through the lightning, with blood and fire in the talons, then it is the beauty of progress to be without stain; and there is between Washington, who represents the one, and Danton, who incarnates the other, the same difference that separates the angel with the wings of a swan, from the angel with the wings of an eagle.

Jean Prouvaire was still a shade more subdued than Combeferre. He called himself Jehan, from that momentary little fancy that mingled with the deep and powerful movement giving rise to the study of the Middle Ages, then so necessary. Jean Prouvaire was addicted to love; he cultivated a pot of flowers, played the flute, wrote poetry, loved the people, pitied woman, wept over childhood, confused the future and God in the same faith, and blamed the Revolution for having cut off a royal head, that of André Chénier. His voice was usually delicate, but at times suddenly masculine. He was well read, to the point of erudition, and almost an orientalist. Above all, he was good, and, a very natural thing to one who knows how near goodness comes to grandeur, in poetry he preferred the grand. He knew Italian, Latin, Greek, and Hebrew; and he found them useful for reading only four poets: Dante, Juvenal, Aeschylus, and Isaiah. In French, he preferred Corneille to Racine, and Agrippa d'Aubigné to Corneille. He was fond of strolling in fields of wild oats and bluebells and paid almost as much attention to the clouds as to passing events. His mind had two aspects—one facing man, the other, God; he studied, or he contemplated. All day he pondered over social questions: wages, capital credit, marriage, religion, liberty of thought, liberty of love, education, punishment, misery, association, property, production and distribution, the lower enigma that covers the human anthill with a shadow; and at night he gazed at the stars, those enormous beings. Like Enjolras, he was rich, and an only son. He spoke gently, bowed his head, cast down his eyes, smiled with embarrassment, dressed badly, had an awkward air, blushed at nothing, was very timid. Still, intrepid.

Feuilly was a fan-maker, an orphan, who arduously earned three francs a day, and who had one thought only, to deliver the world from its bonds. He had still another preoccupation—to teach himself, which he also called deliverance. He had taught himself to read and write; all that he knew, he had learned on his own. Feuilly had a generous heart. He had a wide embrace. This orphan had adopted the people. Being without a mother, he had meditated on his mother country. He was not willing for there to be any man on earth without a country. Within himself he nurtured, with the deep instinct of the man of the people, what we now call *the idea of nationality*. He had learned history expressly to base his indignation on a knowledge of its cause. In this youthful group of utopians particularly interested in France, he represented the outside. His specialty was Greece, Poland, Hungary, Rumania, and Italy. He spoke these names incessantly, to the point and beside the point, with the tenacity of the just cause. Turkey against Greece and Thessaly, Russia against Warsaw, Austria against Venice, these violations exasperated him. The great highway robbery of 1772 excited him above all. There is no more sovereign eloquence than the truth in indignation; that was his eloquence. He could never dismiss that infamous date, 1772, that noble and valiant people blotted out by treachery, that threefold crime, that monstrous ambush, prototype and pattern of all the terrible suppressions of states that have stricken several noble nations since then and have, so to speak, erased the record of their birth. All the contemporary assaults on society date from that partition of Poland. The partition of Poland is a theorem with all the present political crimes for corollaries. There is no despot, no traitor, through almost a century, who has not stamped, confirmed, countersigned, and set his initials, *ne varietur,* to the partition of Poland. When you examine the list of modern treasons, that one appears at the head. The Congress of Vienna studied this crime before consummating its own. The halloo was sounded by 1772; 1815 is the quarry. Such was Feuilly's usual text. This poor workingman had made himself the teacher of justice, and she rewarded him by making him great. For in fact there is eternity in just causes. Warsaw cannot be Tartar any more than Venice can be Teutonic. The kings waste effort over this, as well as their honor. Sooner or later, the submerged country floats to the surface and reappears. Greece becomes Greece again, Italy becomes Italy again. The protest of the right against the fact persists forever. The robbery of a nation never becomes prescriptive. These lofty swindles have no future. You cannot remove the identifying mark from a nation as you can from a handkerchief.

Courfeyrac had a father whose name was M. de Courfeyrac. One of the false ideas of the Restoration in point of aristocracy and nobility was its faith in the particle. The particle, we know, has no significance. But the bourgeois of the time of *La Minerve* considered this poor *de* so highly that men thought themselves obliged to renounce it. M. de Chauvelin became M. Chauvelin, M. de Caumartin was M. Caumartin, M. de Constant de Rebecque simply Benjamin Constant, M. de Lafayette just M. Lafayette. Courfeyrac did not wish to be backward, and called himself simply Courfeyrac.

Concerning Courfeyrac, we might almost stop here, and merely say: for Courfeyrac, see Tholomyès.

Courfeyrac did have that youthful animation that we might call a diabolic beauty of mind. In later life, this dies out, like the playfulness of the kitten, and all that grace ends, on two feet in the bourgeois, and on four paws in the mouser.

This type of mind is transmitted from generation to generation of students, passed from hand to hand by the successive crops of youth, *quasi cursores,* nearly always alike, so that, as we have just indicated, any person who has listened to Courfeyrac in 1828 would have thought he was hearing Tholomyès in 1817. Except that Courfeyrac was a splendid fellow. Beneath the apparent similarities of the outer vivacity, there was great dissimilarity between Tholomyès and him. The latent man existing in each was in the first altogether different from what it was in the second. There was in Tholomyès an attorney, and in Courfeyrac a knight-errant.

Enjolras was the chief, Combeferre was the guide, Courfeyrac was the center. The others gave more light, he gave more heat; the truth is that he had all the qualities of a center—roundness and radiance.

Bahorel had figured in the bloody tumult of June 1822, at the time of young Lallemand's burial.

Bahorel was a creature of good humor and bad company, brave, a spendthrift, prodigal almost to the point of generosity, talkative almost to eloquence, bold almost to insolence; the best possible stock for the devil; with rash waistcoats and scarlet opinions; a wholesale blusterer, that is to say, enjoying nothing so much as a quarrel unless it were a riot, and nothing so well as a riot unless it were a revolution; always ready to break a flagstone, then tear up a street, then demolish a government, to see the effect it made; a student of the eleventh year. He had taken a sniff at the law but was not studying it. He had adopted for his motto "Never a lawyer," and for his coat of arms a bedroom table on which you might glimpse a square doctor's cap. Whenever he passed by the law school, which rarely happened, he buttoned up his overcoat, the short paletot was not yet invented, and took hygienic precautions. He said of the school portal, "What a fine old man!" and of the dean, M. Delvincourt, "What a monument!" In his studies he saw subjects for ditties, and in his professors opportunities for caricatures. Doing nothing, he ate up rather a large allowance, something like three thousand francs. His parents were country people, in whom he had succeeded in instilling a respect for their son.

He said of them, "They are peasants and not bourgeois, which explains their intelligence."

Bahorel, a capricious man, was very partial to several cafés; the others had habits, he had none. He loafed. To err is human, to loaf is Parisian. Ultimately, a penetrating turn of mind and more of a thinker than he seemed.

He served as a bond between the Friends of the A B C

and some other groups that were still formless, but were to take shape later.

In this conclave of young heads there was one bald member.

The Marquis d'Avaray, whom Louis XVIII made a duke for having helped him into a cab the day he emigrated, related that in 1814, as the king landed at Calais on his return to France, a man presented a petition to him.

"What do you want?" said the king.

"Sire, a post office."

"What is your name?"

"L'Aigle."[1]

The king scowled, looked at the signature of the petition, and saw the name written as LESGLE. This spelling, anything but Bonapartist, pleased the king, and he began to smile. "Sire," resumed the man with the petition, "my ancestor was a dog-trainer surnamed Lesgueules [The Maw]. This name has come down to me. My name is Lesgueules, by contraction Lesgle, and by corruption L'Aigle." This topped off the king's smile. He later gave the man the post office at Meaux, either intentionally or inadvertently.

The bald member of the club was son of this Lesgle, or Lègle, and signed his name Lègle (de Meaux). His comrades, for the sake of brevity, called him Bossuet.

Bossuet was a cheery fellow who was unlucky. His specialty was to succeed at nothing. On the other hand, he laughed at everything. At twenty-five he was bald. His father had died owning a house and some land; but he, the son, had found nothing more urgent than to lose this house and land in bad speculation. He had nothing left. He had considerable knowledge and wit, but he always miscarried. Everything failed him, everything deceived him; whatever he built up collapsed on him. If he split wood, he cut his finger. If he had a mistress, he soon discovered that he had also a friend. Some misfortune was constantly happening to him; hence his joviality. He would say, "I live under the roof of the falling tiles." Rarely astonished, since he was always expecting some accident, he took bad luck with serenity and smiled at the vexations of fate like one who hears a jest. He was poor, but his fund of good humor was inexhaustible. He

[1] The eagle.

soon reached his last sou, never his last burst of laughter. Met by adversity, he would greet that old acquaintance cordially, had a pat on the back for catastrophe; he was familiar enough with fate to call it by its nickname. "Good morning, evil Genius," he would say.

These persecutions of fortune had made him inventive. He was very resourceful. He had no money but found means, when it pleased him, to go to "reckless expense." One night, he even spent a hundred francs dining with a dim-witted girl, which inspired him in the midst of the orgy with this calculating line: "Daughter of five Louis, pull off my boots."

Bossuet was slowly making his way toward the legal profession; he was doing his law, à la Bahorel. Bossuet never had much lodging, sometimes none at all. He sometimes stayed with one, sometimes another, most often with Joly. Joly was studying medicine. He was two years younger than Bossuet.

Joly was a young hypochondriac. What he had learned from medicine was to be a patient rather than a physician. At twenty-three, he thought himself in poor health and spent his time looking at his tongue in a mirror. He declared that man is a magnet, like the needle, and in his room he placed his bed with the head to the south and the foot to the north, so that at night his circulatory system would not be counteracted by the global magnetic current. In stormy weather, he took his pulse. Nonetheless, the gayest of all. All these inconsistencies, young, finicky, sickly, joyful, got along very well together, and the result was an eccentric agreeable person whom his comrades, prodigal with consonants, called Jollly. "You can soar on four L's," [*ailes,* wings] said Jean Prouvaire.

Joly had the habit of rubbing his nose with the end of his cane, an indication of a sagacious mind.

All these young men, diverse as they were, and of whom as a whole we should only speak seriously, had the same religion: Progress.

All were legitimate sons of the French Revolution. The flightiest became solemn when pronouncing the date '89. According to the flesh, their fathers were, or had been Feuillants, Royalists, Doctrinaires; it hardly mattered, this earlier hurlyburly had nothing to do with them; they were young; the pure blood of principles flowed in their veins. They attached themselves with no intermediate shadings to incorruptible right and absolute duty.

Affiliated and initiated, they secretly sketched out their ideas.

Among all these passionate hearts and all these undoubting minds there was one skeptic. How did he happen to be there? Through juxtaposition. The name of this skeptic was Grantaire, and he usually signed with the rebus: R [*grand-R,* capital R]. Grantaire was a man who took great care not to believe anything. He was actually one of the students who had learned most during their stay in Paris; he knew that the best coffee was at the Café Lemblin, and the best billiard table at the Café Voltaire; that you could find good rolls and good girls at the hermitage on the Boulevard du Maine, broiled chicken at Mother Saguet's, excellent chowders at the Barrière de la Cunette, and a special light white wine at the Barrière du Combat. He knew the good places for everything; beyond that, boxing, tennis, some dances, and he was a knowledgeable cudgel player. To top it off, a great drinker. He was particularly ugly; the prettiest shoe-stitcher of that time, Irma Boissy, annoyed by his ugliness, had declared, "Grantaire is impossible"; but Grantaire's self-esteem was not disconcerted. He stared tenderly at every woman, appearing to say about all of them: *If only I wanted to;* and trying to make his comrades believe that he was in general demand.

All those words—rights of the people, rights of man, social contract, French Revolution, republic, democracy, humanity, civilization, religion, progress—were very nearly meaningless to Grantaire. He smiled at them. Skepticism, that dry rot of the intellect, had not left one entire idea in his mind. He lived in irony. This was his axiom: The one certainty is a full glass. He ridiculed all dedication under all circumstances, in the brother as well as the father, in Robespierre the younger as well as Loizerolles. "They're no further forward being dead," he exclaimed. He said of the cross: "A gallows that made good!" A rover, a gambler, a libertine, and often drunk, he annoyed these young thinkers by incessantly singing "I loves the girls and I loves good wine" to the tune of "Vive Henri IV."

Still, this skeptic had fanatacism. This fanaticism was

not for an idea, nor a dogma, nor an art, nor a science; it was for a man: Enjolras. Grantaire admired, loved, venerated Enjolras. To whom did this anarchical doubter ally himself in this phalanx of absolute minds? To the most absolute. In what way did Enjolras subjugate him? By ideas? No. Through character. A phenomenon often seen. A skeptic adhering to a believer is as simple as law of complementary colors. What we lack attracts Nobody loves the light like the blind man. The dwarf adores the drum major. The toad is always looking up at the sky. Why? To see the bird fly. Grantaire, crawling with doubt, loved to see faith soaring in Enjolras. He needed Enjolras. Without understanding it clearly, and without trying to explain it to himself, that chaste, healthy, firm, direct, hard, honest nature charmed him. Instinctively, he admired his opposite. His soft, wavering, disjointed, diseased, deformed ideas hitched onto Enjolras as to a backbone. His moral spine leaned on that firmness. Beside Enjolras Grantaire became somebody again. On his own, he was actually composed of two apparently incompatible elements. He was ironic and cordial. His indifference was loving. His mind dispensed with belief, yet his heart could not dispense with friendship. A thorough contradiction; for an affection is a conviction. This was his nature. There are men who seem born to be the opposite, the reverse, the counterpart. They are Pollux, Patroclus, Nisus, Eudamidas, Ephestion, Pechméja. They live only on condition of leaning on another; their names are sequels, only written preceded by the conjunction "and"; their existence is not their own; it is the other side of a destiny not their own. Grantaire was one of these men. He was the reverse of Enjolras.

We might almost say that affinities begin with the letters of the alphabet. In the series *O* and *P* are inseparable. You can, as you choose, pronounce *O* and *P*, or Orestes and Pylades.

Grantaire, a true satellite of Enjolras, lived in this circle of young people; he existed within it; he took pleasure only in it; he followed them everywhere. His delight was to see these forms coming and going in the haze of wine. He was tolerated for his good humor.

Enjolras, being a believer, disdained this skeptic, and being sober, scorned this drunkard. He granted him a bit of haughty pity. Grantaire was an unaccepted Pylades. Always treated rudely by Enjolras, harshly repelled, rejected, yet returning, he said of Enjolras, "What a fine statue!"

II

FUNERAL ORATION ON BLONDEAU, BY BOSSUET

On a certain afternoon, which had, as we shall see, some coincidence with events related before, Laigle de Meaux was leaning back lazily against the doorway of the Café Musain. He looked like a caryatid on vacation; he was supporting nothing but his daydreams. He was looking at the Place Saint-Michel. Leaning back is a way of lying down upright that is not disliked by dreamers. Laigle de Meaux was thinking, without sadness, of a little mishap that had happened to him the day before at the law school and that modified his personal plans for the future—plans that were actually rather hazy.

Reverie does not hinder a cabriolet from going by, nor the dreamer from noticing the cabriolet. Laigle de Meaux, whose eyes were wandering in a sort of general stroll, glimpsed through his somnambulism a two-wheeled vehicle turning into the square, which was moving at a walk, as if undecided. What did this cabriolet want? Why was it moving at a walk? Laigle looked at it. Inside, beside the driver, there was a young man, and in front of the young man, a large overnight bag. To passers-by, the bag displayed this name, written in big black letters on a card sewn to the cloth: MARIUS PONTMERCY.

This name changed Laigle's attitude. He straightened up and addressed this apostrophe to the young man in the cabriolet.

"Monsieur Marius Pontmercy?"

The cabriolet, thus hailed, stopped.

The young man, who also seemed to be lost in thought raised his eyes.

"Yes?" he said.

"You are Monsieur Marius Pontmercy?"

"Certainly."

"I was looking for you," said Laigle de Meaux.

"What do you mean?" inquired Marius; for in fact he had just left his grandfather's and was confronting a face he was seeing for the first time. "I don't know you."

"I don't know you, either," answered Laigle.

Marius thought he had met a buffoon, and that this was the beginning of a midstreet mystery. He was not in a pleasant humor just then. He frowned; Laigle de Meaux, imperturbable, continued; "You weren't at school the day before yesterday."

"Possibly."

"Definitely."

"You're a student?" asked Marius.

"Yes, monsieur. Like you. The day before yesterday I happened to go into the school. You know, it can happen. The professor was calling the roll. You know how ridiculous they are just now. If you miss the third call, they strike off your name. Sixty francs gone."

Marius began to listen. Laigle continued, "It was Blondeau who was calling the roll. You know Blondeau; he has a very pointed and malicious nose, and delights in smelling out the absent. He cannily began with the letter *P*. I wasn't listening, not being concerned with that letter. The roll wasn't going badly. No erasure, the universe was present, Blondeau was sad. I said to myself, Blondeau, my love, you won't have the slightest little execution today. Suddenly, Blondeau calls *Marius Pontmercy;* nobody answers. Blondeau, full of hope, repeats louder: *Marius Pontmercy?* And he seizes his pen. Monsieur, I have tender mercy. I quickly said to myself, here's a fine fellow who is going to be struck. Watch out. This is a real live fellow who isn't punctual. He's not a good boy. He's not a bookworm, a student who studies, a white-billed pedant, strong on science, letters, theology, and wisdom, one of those pristine idiots stretched smooth with four pins; a pin to a faculty. He's an honorable idler who loafs, who likes to rusticate, who cultivates the grisette, who pays his court to beauty, who is perhaps, at this very moment, with my mistress. Let us save him. Death to Blondeau! At that moment Blondeau dipped his pen, black from his marking, into the ink, cast his tawny eye over the room, and repeated for the third time: *Marius*

Pontmercy! I answered: *Present!* In that way you were not struck off."

"Monsieur!—" said Marius.

"And I was," added Laigle de Meaux.

"I don't understand," said Marius.

Laigle went on, "Nothing simpler. I was near the rostrum to answer, and near the door to escape. The professor was looking at me with a certain deliberation. Suddenly, Blondeau, who must be the malignant nose Boileau mentions, leaps to the letter *L. L* is my letter, I am from Meaux, and my name is Lesgle."

"L'Aigle!" interrupted Marius, "what a fine name."

"Monsieur, the Blondeau reaches this fine name and cries: '*Laigle!*' I answer: *Present!* Then Blondeau looks at me with the gentleness of a tiger, smiles, and says: If you are Pontmercy, you are not Laigle. A phrase that might seem ungracious to you, but which brought only grief to me. So saying, he erases me."

Marius exclaimed, "Monsieur, I'm mortified—"

"First of all," interrupted Laigle, "I beg leave to embalm Blondeau in a few words of feeling eulogy. I suppose him dead. It wouldn't take much change in his thinness, his paleness, his coldness, his stiffness, and his odor. And I say: *Erudimini qui judicatis terram.* Here lies Blondeau, Blondeau the Nose, Blondeau Nasica, the ox of discipline, *bos disciplinae,* the watchdog of orders, the angel of the roll, who was straight, square, exact, rigid, honest, and hideous. God has erased him as he erased me."

Marius replied, "I am very sorry—"

"Young man," said Laigle de Meaux, "let this be a lesson to you. In future, be punctual."

"I owe you a thousand apologies."

"Never again expose yourself to having your neighbor erased."

"I'm desperately sorry."

Laigle burst out laughing. "And I, delighted; I was on the verge of becoming a lawyer. This rupture saves me. I renounce the triumphs of the bar. I will not defend the widow, and I will not attack the orphan. No more toga, no more probation. Here is my release obtained. It is to you that I owe it, Monsieur Pontmercy. I intend to pay you a solemn visit of thanks. Where do you live?"

"In this cabriolet," said Marius.

"A sign of opulence," replied Laigle calmly. "I congratulate you. There you are, with a rent of nine thousand francs a year."

Just then Courfeyrac came out of the café.

Marius smiled sadly.

"I have been paying this rent for two hours, and I hope to get out of it; but, it's the usual story, I do not know where to go."

"Monsieur," said Courfeyrac, "come home with me."

"I should have priority," observed Laigle, "but I have no home."

"Silence, Bossuet," replied Courfeyrac.

"Bossuet," said Marius, "but I thought you called yourself Laigle."

"Of Meaux," answered Laigle; "metaphorically, Bossuet."

Courfeyrac got into the cabriolet.

"Driver," he said, "Hotel de la Porte-Saint-Jacques."

And that same evening, Marius was settled in a room at the Hotel de la Porte-Saint-Jacques, next door to Courfeyrac.

III
MARIUS AMAZED

Within a few days, Marius was Courfeyrac's friend. Youth is the season of prompt weldings and rapid healing. In Courfeyrac's presence, Marius breathed freely, a new thing for him. Courfeyrac asked him no questions, did not even think to. At that age, the countenance tells everything at once. Speech is unnecessary. Of some young men we might say that their faces are talkative. They look at one another, they know one another.

One morning, however, Courfeyrac abruptly put this question to him.

"By the way, do you have any political opinions?"

"What do you mean?" said Marius, almost offended at the question.

"What are you?"

"Bonapartist democrat."

"Gray shade of quiet mouse color," said Courfeyrac.

The next day, Courfeyrac introduced Marius to the Café Musain. Then he whispered in his ear with a smile, "I must see you into the Revolution." And he took him to the room of the Friends of the A B C. He presented him to the other members, saying in an undertone a simple introduction that Marius did not understand: "A pupil."

Marius had fallen into a wasps' nest of wits. Still, though silent and serious, he was neither the less winged, nor the less armed.

Up to this time solitary and inclined to soliloquy and privacy by habit and by preference, Marius was a little bewildered by this flock of young men about him. The various progressives attacked him all at once, perplexing him. The turbulent seesawing of all these minds at liberty and at work set his thoughts in a whirl. Sometimes, in the confusion, they roamed so far he had some difficulty finding them again. He heard talk of philosophy, of literature, of art, of history, of religion, in an unexpected way. He caught glimpses of strange notions, and, as he was not putting them into perspective, he was not sure it was not all chaos. On abandoning his grandfather's opinions for his father's, he had thought himself settled; he now suspected, anxiously and without daring to confess it to himself, that he was not. The angle from which he saw everything was beginning to shift again. A vague oscillation jarred his whole mental horizon. A strange internal hubbub, almost painful.

It seemed that to these young men there was nothing sacred. On every subject Marius heard a strange language annoying to his still-timid mind.

A theater poster appeared, bearing the title of a tragedy from the old classic repertory: "Down with tragedy, dear to the bourgeois!" cried Bahorel. And Marius heard Combeferre reply.

"You're wrong, Bahorel. The bourgeoisie love tragedy, and on that point we must leave the bourgeoisie alone. Tragedy in a wig has its reason for being, and I am not one of those who, in the name of Aeschylus, deny it the right to exist. There are rough drafts in nature; in creation there are ready-made parodies; a beak that isn't a beak, wings that aren't wings, fins that aren't fins, claws that aren't claws, a mournful cry that makes us want to laugh, there you have the duck. Now, since fowl exists alongside bird, I don't see why classic tragedy shouldn't exist opposite ancient tragedy."

Another time Marius happened to be passing through the Rue Jean-Jacques-Rousseau between Enjolras and Courfeyrac.

Courfeyrac took his arm.

"Listen to me. This is the Rue Plâtrière, now called Rue Jean-Jacques Rousseau, because of a singular household that lived on it sixty years ago. It consisted of Jean-Jacques and Thérèse. From time to time, little creatures were born there. Thérèse brought them forth. Jean-Jacques turned them out."

And Enjolras answered sternly, "Silence before Jean-Jacques! I admire that man. He disowned his children; very well; but he adopted the people."

Not one of these young men ever uttered the word "emperor." Jean Prouvaire alone sometimes said Napoleon; all the rest said Bonaparte. Enjolras pronounced it *Buonaparte*.

Marius was vaguely surprised. *Initium sapientiae*.

IV

THE BACK ROOM OF THE CAFÉ MUSAIN

Of the conversations among these young men that Marius listened to and in which he sometimes took part, one shocked him to the core.

This was held in the back room of the Café Musain. Nearly all the Friends of the A B C were together that evening. The large lamp was ceremoniously lit. They loudly talked of one thing and another, but without passion. Except for Enjolras and Marius, who were silent, each one harangued a little at random. Conversations among comrades sometimes include such good-natured uproar. It was a game and a fracas as much as a conversation. One threw out words that another caught. They were talking in each of the four corners.

No woman was admitted to this back room, except Louison, the café dishwasher, who passed through it from time to time to go from the washroom to the "laboratory."

Grantaire, slightly tipsy, was deafening the corner he had taken over, talking sense and nonsense at the top of his lungs. He cried, "I'm thirsty. Mortals, I have a dream: that the cask of Heidelberg has an attack of apoplexy, and that I am among the dozen leeches applied to it. I'd like a drink. I desire to forget life. Life is a hideous invention of somebody I don't know. It doesn't last, and it's good for nothing. You break your neck simply living. Life is a stage set in which there's little that's workable. Happiness is an old sash painted on one side. The Ecclesiast says, All is vanity; I agree with that good man who perhaps never existed. Zero, not wanting to go around entirely naked, has clothed himself in vanity. O vanity! The patching up of everything with big words! A kitchen is a laboratory, a dancer is a professor, a tumbler is a gymnast, a boxer is a pugilist, an apothecary is a chemist, a wig maker is an artist, a hod carrier is an architect, a jockey is a sportsman, a wood louse is a pterygobranchiate. Vanity has a right side and a wrong side; the right side is stupid, it is the native with his beads; the wrong side is silly, it is the philosopher with his rags. I weep over one and I laugh over the other. What is called honors and dignities, and even honor and dignity, is generally fool's gold. Kings make playthings of human pride. Caligula made a horse consul; Charles II made a sirloin a knight. So parade along between the consul Incitatus and the baronet Roastbeef. As for the intrinsic value of people, it is hardly more respectable. Listen to the panegyric that neighbors deliver on each other. White on white is ferocious; if the lily spoke, how it would fix the dove! A bigot gossiping about a devotee is more venomous than the asp and the blue viper. Such a pity I'm ignorant or I'd quote you a mass of things, but I don't know anything. For instance, I was always bright; when I was a pupil with Gros, instead of daubing pictures, I spent my time pilfering apples. So much for myself; as for the rest of you, you're just as good as I am. I don't give a damn about your perfections, excellences, and good qualities. Every good quality runs into a defect; economy borders on avarice, the generous are not far from the prodigal, the brave man is close to the bully; he who is very pious is slightly sanctimonious; there are just as many vices in virtue as there are holes in the mantle of Diogenes. Which do you admire, the slain or the slayer, Caesar or Brutus? Generally people are for the slayer. Hurrah for Brutus! He slew. That's virtue. Virtue, but folly, too. There are some odd stains on these great men. The Brutus who slew Caesar was in love with a statue of a little boy. This statue was by the Greek sculptor Strongylion, who also designed that statue of an Amazon called the "beautiful-limbed," Euknemos, which Nero carried with him on his journeys. This Strongylion left nothing but two statues which put Brutus and Nero in harmony. Brutus was in love with one and Nero with the other. The whole of history is merely one long repetition. One century plagiarizes another. The battle of Marengo copies the battle of Pydna; the Tolbach of Clovis and the Austerlitz of Napoleon are as like as two drops of blood. I make little of the victory. Nothing is so stupid as to be invincible; the real glory is to convince. But try to prove something! You're satisfied with success, what mediocrity! And with conquering, what misery! Alas, vanity and cowardice everywhere. Everything obeys success, even grammar. *Si volet usus*, says Horace. So I scorn the human race. Shall we descend from the whole to a part? Would you have me set about admiring the peoples? What people, if you please? Greece? The Athenians, those Parisians of old, killed Phocion, or perhaps we should say Coligny, and fawned on the tyrants to such a degree that Anacephoras said of Pisistratus, 'His urine attracts the bees.' The most eminent man in Greece for fifty years was that grammarian Philetas, who was so small and so thin that he had to put lead on his shoes so as not to be blown away by the wind. In the largest square of Corinth there was a statue by the sculptor Silanion, catalogued by Pliny; this statue represented Episthates. What did Episathates do? He invented the leg-trip in wrestling. That sums up Greece and glory. Let's go on to others. Shall I admire England? Shall I admire France? France? What for? Because of Paris? I've just told you my opinion of Athens. England? Why? Because of London? I hate Carthage. And then, London, the metropolis of luxury, is the capital of misery. In the single parish of Charing Cross, there are a hundred deaths a year from starvation. Such is Albion. I add, to complete, that I've seen an English girl dance with a crown of roses and blue spectacles. A groan then for England. If I don't admire John Bull, would I admire Brother Jonathan? I have little taste for this brother with his slaves. Take away *time is money,* and what is left of England? Take away *cotton is king,* and what is left of America? Germany is the lymph; Italy is the bile. Shall we go into ecstasies over Russia? Voltaire admired her. He also admired China. I confess that Russia has her beauties, among others a strong despotism; but I'm sorry for the despots. They have very delicate health. An Alexei decapitated, a Peter stabbed, a Paul strangled, another Paul flattened by blows from a boot heel, diverse Ivans butchered, several Nicholases and Basils poisoned, all that indicates that the palace of the Emperors of Russia is in an alarmingly unwholesome condition. All civilized nations offer the thinker this circumstance for his admiration: war; but war, civilized war, exhausts and sums up every form of banditry, from the brigandage of the Trabucaires in the gorges of Mount Jaxa to the maurading of the Comanche Indians in the Doubtful Pass. Would you tell me Europe is better than Asia? I admit that Asia is farcical, but I do not quite see what right you have to laugh at the Grand Lama, you people of the Occident who have incorporated into your fashions and your elegance all the multifarious ordures of majesty, from Queen Isabella's dirty chemise to the dauphin's commode. Gentlemen, humans, I tell you, rubbish! It's in Brussels that they consume the most beer, in Stockholm the most brandy, in Madrid the most chocolate, in Amsterdam the most gin, in London the most wine, in Constantinople the most coffee, in Paris the most absinthe; those are the most useful statistics. Paris wins hands down. In Paris, even the ragpickers are sybarites; Diogenes would have much rather been a ragpicker in the Place Maubert than a philosopher in Piraeus. Learn this also: the wineshops of the ragpickers are called *bibines;* the most celebrated are the Saucepan and the Slaughterhouse. Therefore, O drinking shops, eating shops, tavern signs, barrooms, tea parties, meat markets, dance houses, brothels, ragpickers' tipling shops, caravanserai of the caliphs, I swear to you, I am a voluptuary, I eat at

Richard's at forty sous a head, I must have Persian carpets for rolling Cleopatra naked! Where's Cleopatra? Ah! It's you, Louison! Good evening."

Thus Grantaire, more than drunk, unreeled his words, grabbing the dishwasher on her way by, in his corner of the back room at Musain.

Bossuet, reaching out a hand, tried to silence him, and Grantaire started in again louder then ever: "Eagle of Meaux, down with your claws. You have no effect on me with your gesture of Hippocrates refusing bric-a-brac from Artaxerxes. I dispense you from quieting me. Anyway, I'm sad. What would you have me tell you? Man is wicked, man is deformed; the butterfly has succeeded, man has missed. God failed on this animal. A crowd gives you nothing but choice of ugliness. The first man you meet will be a wretch. *Femme* rhymes with *infâme*, woman is infamous. Yes, I have the spleen, in addition to melancholy, with nostalgia, plus hypochondria, and I sneer, and I rage, and I yawn, and I'm tired, and I'm bored, and I'm tormented! Let God go to the Devil!"

"Silence, capital R!" broke in Bossuet, who was discussing a point of law and was more than half buried in a string of judicial argot, of which here is the conclusion: "—And as for me, though I'm barely a jurist and at best an amateur attorney, I maintain this: that by the terms of the common law of Normandy, at Saint Michael's, and for every year, an equivalent must be paid for the benefit of the seigneur, saving the rights of others, by each and every of them, as much proprietaries as those seized by inheritance, and this for all terms of years, leases, freeholds, contracts domainiary and domainial, of mortgagees and mortgagors—"

"Echo, plaintive nymph," muttered Grantaire.

Close beside Grantaire, at a table that was almost silent, a sheet of paper, an inkstand, and a pen between two wine glasses proclaimed that a farce was being drawn up. This important business was carried on in a whisper, and the two heads at work touched each other.

"Let's begin by finding the names. When we have them, we'll find a subject."

"That's good. Dictate: I'll write."

"Monsieur Dorimon?"

"Wealthy?"

"Of course."

"His daughter Celestine."

'—tine. What next?"

"Colonel Sainval."

"Sainval is old. I'd say Valsin."

Beside these would-be vaudevillians, another group, also taking advantage of the confusion to talk privately, were discussing a duel. An old man, thirty, was advising a young one, eighteen, and explaining to him what sort of an adversary he had to deal with. "The devil! Look out for yourself. He's a beautiful swordsman. His play is neat. He comes to the attack, no lost feints, good wrist, sparkling play, a flash, accurate step, and mathematic ripostes. My God! And he's left-handed, too."

In the corner opposite Grantaire, Joly and Bahorel were playing dominoes and talking of love.

"You are lucky," said Joly. "You have a mistress who's always laughing."

"That's a fault of hers," answered Bahorel. "Any mistress you have is wrong to laugh. It encourages you to deceive her. Seeing her happy takes away your remorse; if you see she's sad, your conscience bothers you."

"Ingrate! A laughing woman is a good thing! And you never quarrel!"

"That's part of the treaty we have made. When we made our little Holy Alliance, we each assigned our own boundary that we'd never cross. The part to the north belongs to Vaud, the south to Gex. Hence our peace."

"Peace is happiness digesting."

"And you, Jollllly, how is it coming, your falling out with Mamselle—you know who I mean?"

"She's sulking with cruel patience."

"But you're a lover pining away."

"Alas!"

"If I were in your place, I'd get rid of her."

"Easily said."

"And done. Isn't Musichetta her name?"

"Yes. Ah! Poor Bahorel, she's a superb girl, very literary, with small feet, small hands, dresses well, fair, plump, with eyes like a fortune-teller. I'm crazy about her."

"My dear friend, then you have to please her, be fashionable, show a bit more of your legs. Buy a pair of doeskin trousers at Staub's. They help."

"How much?" cried Grantaire.

The third corner was in the grips of a poetic discussion. Pagan mythology was wrestling with Christian mythology. The subject was Olympus, which Jean Prouvaire, by sheer romanticism, was supporting. Jean Prouvaire was timid only in repose. Once excited, he burst forth, a sort of gaiety characterized his enthusiasm, both laughing and lyric.

"Let's not insult the gods," he said. "The gods have perhaps not left us. Jupiter doesn't strike me as dead. The gods are dreams, you say. Well, even in nature, such as it now is, we find all the great old pagan myths again. To me a mountain like the Vignemarle, for instance, with the profile of a citadel, is still the headdress of Cybele; prove that Pan doesn't come at night to blow into the hollow trunks of the willows, stopping the holes with his fingers one after another; and I've always believed that Io had something to do with the cascade of Pissevache."

In the last corner, politics was the subject. They were denigrating the Charter of Louis XVIII. Combeferre defended it mildly, Courfeyrac was energetically battering it. On the table was an unfortunate copy of the famous Touquet Charter. Courfeyrac grabbed it and shook it, mingling with his arguments the rustling of that sheet of paper.

"First, I want no kings. If it were only from the economic point of view, I don't want them; a king is a parasite. You don't have kings gratis. Listen to this: cost of kings. At the death of Francis I, the public debt of France was thirty thousand livres; at the death of Louis XIV, it was two million six hundred thousand at twenty-eight livres the mark, which in 1760, was equivalent according to Desmarest, to four billion five hundred million, and which is equivalent today to twelve billion. Secondly, no offense to Combeferre, a charter granted is a vicious expedient of civilization. To avoid the transition, to smooth the passage, to deaden the shock, to make the nation move unawares from monarchy to democracy by the practice of constitutional fictions, these are all detestable arguments! No! No! Never give the people a false light. Principles wither and grow pale in your constitutional cellar. No half measures, no compromises, no grant from the king to the people. In all these grants, there is an Article 14. Along with the hand that gives there is the claw that takes back. I wholly refuse your charter. A charter is a mask; the lie is under it. A people who accept a charter, abdicate. Right is right only when entire. No! No charter!"

It was winter; two logs were crackling in the fireplace. It was tempting, and Courfeyrac could not resist. He crushed the poor Touquet Charter in his hand and threw it into the fire. The paper blazed up. Combeferre looked philosophically at the burning of Louis XVIII's masterpiece, and contented himself with saying; "The charter metamorphosed in flames."

And the sarcasms, the sallies, the jests, French dash, English humor, good taste and bad, good and bad reasoning, all the mingled follies of dialogue, rising at once and crossing from all points of the room, made a sort of joyous bombardment above their heads.

V

BROADENING THE HORIZON

The jostling of young minds against each other has this wonderful attribute, that one can never foresee the spark, nor predict the flash. What will spring up in a moment? Nobody knows. A burst of laughter starts from a scene of emotion. In a moment of buffoonery, the serious enters. Impulses depend on a chance word. The spirit of each is sovereign. A jest suffices to open the door to the unexpected. They are conferences with sharp turns, where the perspective suddenly changes. Chance is the director of these conversations.

A stern thought, oddly sprung from a clatter of words, suddenly crossed the melee in which Grantaire, Bahorel, Prouvaire, Bossuet, Combeferre and Courfeyrac were verbally fencing.

How does a phrase turn up in a dialogue? How does it happen that it makes its mark all at once on those who hear it? As we just said, nobody knows. In the midst of the uproar Bossuet suddenly ended some apostrophe to Combeferre with this date: "The eighteenth of June 1815: Waterloo."

At this name, Waterloo, Marius, who was leaning on a

table with a glass of water beside him, took his hand away from under his chin and began to look earnestly around the room.

"Pardieu," exlaimed Courfeyrac (*Parbleu*, at that period, was falling into disuse), "That number eighteen is strange, and impresses me. It is Bonaparte's fatal number. Put Louis before and Brumaire behind, you have the whole destiny of the man, with this expressive peculiarity, that the beginning is hard pressed by the end."

Enjolras, till then mute, broke the silence, and said to Courfeyrac, "You mean the crime by the expiation."

This word "crime" went beyond the endurance of Marius, already much excited by the abrupt evocation of Waterloo.

He rose, he walked slowly toward the map of France spread out on the wall, at the bottom of which could be seen an island in a separate compartment; he laid his finger on this compartment and said, "Corsica. A small island that has made France truly great."

This was a breath of chilling air. Everyone was silent. Clearly something was about to be said.

Bahorel, replying to Bossuet, was just assuming a favorite attitude. He gave it up to listen.

Enjolras, whose blue eye was not fixed on anybody and seemed staring into space, answered without looking at Marius, "France needs no Corsica to be great. France is great because she is France. *Quia nominor leo*."

Marius felt no desire to retreat; he turned toward Enjolras, and his voice rang with the vibration of his nerves, "God forbid I should lessen France! But it is not lessening her to join her with Napoleon. So let's talk then. I'm a newcomer among you, but I confess you astound me. Where are we? Who are we? Who are you? Who am I? Let's say what we believe about the emperor. I hear you say Buonaparte, accenting the *u* like the royalists. I can tell you that my grandfather does better yet; he says Buonaparté. I thought you were young men. But where is your enthusiasm? And what do you do with it? Whom do you admire if you don't admire the emperor? And what more do you need? If you don't like that great man, what great men would you want? He had everything. He was complete. He had in his brain the cube of human faculties. He made codes like Justinian, he ruled like Caesar, his conversation combined the lightning of Pascal with the thunderbolt of Tacitus, he made history and he wrote it, his bulletins are Iliads, he joined the figures of Newton with the metaphors of Muhammad, he left behind him in the Orient words as great as the pyramids; at Tilsit he taught majesty to emperors, at the Academy of Sciences he replied to Laplace, in the Council of State he held his ground with Merlin, he gave a soul to the geometry of some and to the trickery of others, he was legal with the attorneys and heavenly with the astronomers; like Cromwell blowing out one candle when two were lit, he went to the Temple to bargain over a curtain tassel; he saw everything; he knew everything; which did not prevent him from having a simple laugh by his child's cradle and all at once, a startled Europe listened, armies went into motion, artillery rolled along, bridges of boats stretched across the rivers, clouds of cavalry galloped in the hurricane, cries, trumpets, a trembling of thrones everywhere, the frontiers of the kingdoms wavered on the map, the sound of a superhuman blade was heard leaping from its sheath, men saw him, him, standing erect on the horizon with a flame in his hands and a resplendence in his eyes, unfolding in thunder his two wings, the Grand Army and the Old Guard, and they saw the archangel of war!"

Everyone was silent, and Enjolras looked down. Silence always has a slight effect of acquiescence or in some way of backing a person to the wall. Marius, almost without taking breath, continued in a burst of enthusiasm: "Be fair, my friends! To be the empire of such an emperor, what a splendid destiny for a nation, when that nation is France, and when it adds its genius to the genius of such a man! To appear and to reign, to march and to triumph, to have every capital for a staging area, to take his grenadiers and make kings of them, to decree the downfall of dynasties, to transfigure Europe at a double quickstep, so men feel, when you threaten, that you are laying your hand on the hilt of God's sword, to follow in one man Hannibal, Caesar, and Charlemagne, to be the people of a man who mingles with your every dawn the glorious announcement of a battle won, to be wakened in the morning by the cannon of the Invalides, to hurl into the vault of day mighty words that blaze forever, Marengo, Arcola, Austerlitz, Ièna, Wagram! To repeatedly call forth constellations of victories at the zenith of the centuries, to make the French Empire the successor of the Roman Empire, to be the grand nation and to bring forth the Grand Army, to send your legions flying across the whole earth as a mountain sends out its eagles, to vanquish, to rule, to strike thunder, to be for Europe a kind of golden people through glory, to sound through history a Titan's fanfare, to conquer the world twice, by conquest and by resplendence, that is sublime. What could be greater?"

"To be free," said Combeferre.

Marius in his turn bowed his head. These cold and simple words had pierced his epic effusion like a blade of steel, and he felt it vanish within him. When he raised his eyes, Combeferre was gone. Satisfied probably with his reply to the apotheosis, he had gone out, and all except Enjolras had followed him. The room was empty. Alone with Marius, Enjolras was looking at him gravely. Marius, meanwhile, having rallied his thoughts somewhat, did not consider himself beaten; there was still something simmering within him, which undoubtedly was about to find expression in syllogisms marshaled against Enjolras, when suddenly they heard somebody singing on the way downstairs. It was Combeferre:

> Si César m'avait donné
> La gloire et la guerre,
> Et qu'il me fallût quitter
>   L'amour de ma mère,
> Je dirais au grand César:
> Reprends ton sceptre et ton char,
>   J'aime mieux ma mère, ô gué!
>   J'aime mieux ma mère.[1]

The wild and tender tone with which Combeferre sang gave this stanza a strange grandeur. Marius, thoughtful

[1] If Caesar had given me
  Glory and war,
And if I must abandon
  The love of my mother,
I would say to great Caesar:
Take your scepter and chariot
  I love my mother more, alas!
  I love my mother more.

and with his eyes to the ceiling, repeated almost mechanically, "my mother—"

At that moment, he felt Enjolras's hand on his shoulder.

"Citizen," said Enjolras to him, "my mother is the Republic."

VI

RES ANGUSTA

That evening left Marius profoundly disturbed, with a dark inner sadness. He was experiencing what the earth may experience at the moment when it is opened by the plow so wheat may be sown; it feels only the wound; the thrill of the seed and joy of the fruit do not come until later.

Marius was gloomy. He had just achieved a faith; could he reject it so soon? He decided he could not. He declared to himself that he would not doubt, and he began to doubt in spite of himself. To be between two religions, one you have not yet abandoned and another you have not yet adopted, is intolerable; this twilight is pleasant only to batlike souls. Marius was an open eye, and he needed a true light. To him the dusk of doubt was harmful. Whatever his desire to stop where he was and hold fast there, he was irresistibly compelled to continue, to advance, to examine, to think, to go forward. Where was that going to lead him? After having taken so many steps that had brought him closer to his father, he now feared to take steps that would separate them. His dejection increased with every reflection. Steep cliffs rose around him. He was on good terms neither with his grandfather nor with his friends, rash for the former, backward for the others; and he felt doubly isolated, from old age and also from youth. He stopped going to the Café Musain.

In this mental turmoil he scarcely gave a thought to certain serious aspects of existence. The realities of life do not allow themselves to be forgotten. They came and abruptly jogged his memory.

One morning, the keeper of the house entered Marius's

room, and said to him, "Monsieur Courfeyrac is responsible for you."

"Yes."

"But I need money."

"Ask Courfeyrac to come and speak to me," said Marius.

Courfeyrac came; the host left them. Marius told him what he had not thought of saying before, that he was, so to speak, alone in the world, without any relatives.

"What will become of you?" said Courfeyrac.

"I have no idea," answered Marius.

"What are you going to do?"

"I have no idea."

"Do you have any money?"

"Fifteen francs."

"Do you want me to lend you some?"

"Never."

"Do you have any clothes?"

"What you see."

"Have you any jewelry?"

"A watch."

"A silver one?"

"Gold, here it is."

"I know an old-clothes dealer who'll take your overcoat and a pair of trousers."

"That's good."

"You'll then have only one pair of trousers, a waistcoat, a hat, and a coat."

"And my boots."

"What? You won't go barefoot? What opulence!"

"That will be enough."

"I know a watchmaker who'll buy your watch."

"That's good."

"No, it's not good. What will you do after that?"

"Whatever I have to. Anything honorable at least."

"Do you know English?"

"No."

"Do you know German?"

"No."

"Too bad."

"Why?"

"Because a friend of mine, a bookseller, is doing a sort of encyclopedia and you could have translated German or English articles. It's poor pay, but it's a living."

"I'll learn English and German."

"And in the meantime?"

"In the meantime I'll eat my coats and my watch."

The clothes dealer was sent for. He gave twenty francs for the clothes. They went to the watchmaker. He paid forty-five francs for the watch.

"Not bad," said Marius to Courfeyrac, on returning to the house. "With my fifteen francs, this makes eighty francs."

"The hotel bill?" observed Courfeyrac.

"Ah! I forgot,"said Marius.

The host presented his bill, to be paid on the spot. It amounted to seventy francs.

"I have ten francs left," said Marius.

"The devil," said Courfeyrac, "you'll have five francs to eat while you learn English, and five francs while you learn German. That will be swallowing a language very quickly or a hundred-sous piece very slowly."

Meanwhile Aunt Gillenormand, who was really a kind person on sad occasions, had finally tracked down Marius's lodgings.

One morning when Marius came home from school, he found a letter from his aunt, and the sixty pistoles, that is to say, six hundred francs in gold, in a sealed box.

Marius sent the thirty louis back to his aunt, with a respectful letter, in which he told her that he had the means to get by and from here on he could provide for all his necessities. At that time he had three francs left.

The aunt did not inform the grandfather of this refusal, for fear of exasperating him. Had he not said, "Nobody must ever speak to me of that bloodsucker"?

Marius left the Porte-Saint-Jacques Hotel, unwilling to run up a debt.

Book Five

THE EXCELLENCE OF MISFORTUNE

I

MARIUS INDIGENT

Life became harsh for Marius. To eat his coats and watch was nothing. He chewed the inexpressible cud of bitterness—a horrible thing, which includes days without bread, sleepless nights, evenings without a candle, a hearth without a fire, weeks without labor, a future without hope, a coat out at the elbows, an old hat that makes young girls laugh, the door found shut in your face at night because you have not paid your rent, the insolence of the porter and the landlord, the jibes of neighbors, humiliations, outraged self-respect, any drudgery acceptable, disgust, bitterness, prostration—Marius learned how one swallows all these things and how they are often the only things one has to swallow. At that time of life, when man has need of pride, because he has need of love, he felt mocked because he was badly dressed and ridiculed because he was poor. At the age when youth swells the heart with an imperial pride, he more than once dropped his eyes to his wornout boots, and experienced the undeserved shame and poignant blushes of poverty. Wonderful and terrible trial, from which the feeble come out infamous, from which the strong come out sublime. Crucible into which destiny casts a man whenever she desires a scoundrel or a demigod.

For there are many great deeds done in the small struggles of life. There is a determined though unseen bravery that defends itself foot by foot in the darkness against the fatal invasions of necessity and dishonesty. Noble and mysterious triumphs that no eye sees and no fame rewards, and no flourish of triumph salutes. Life, misfortunes, isolation, abandonment, poverty, are battlefields that have their heroes; obscure heroes, sometimes greater than the illustrious heroes.

Strong and rare natures are created this way; misery, almost always a stepmother, is sometimes a mother; privation gives birth to power of soul and mind; distress is the nurse of self-respect; misfortune gives good milk for great souls.

In Marius's life, there was a period when he swept his own hall, when he bought a pennyworth of Brie in the market, when he waited for nightfall to make his way to the baker's and buy a loaf of bread, which he carried furtively to his garret, as if he had stolen it. Sometimes there was seen slipping into the corner meatmarket, in the midst of jeering cooks who elbowed him, an awkward young man with books under his arm, who had a timid and frightened appearance, and who on entering took his hat off his forehead, which was dripping with sweat, made a low bow to the astonished butcher, another bow to the butcher's boy, asked for a lamb chop, paid six or seven sous for it, wrapped it up in paper, put it under his arm between two books, and went away. It was Marius. On this cutlet, which he cooked himself, he lived three days.

The first day he ate the meat; the second day he ate the fat; the third day he gnawed the bone. On several occasions, Aunt Gillenormand made overtures, and sent him the sixty pistoles. Marius always sent them back, saying he had no need of anything.

He was still in mourning for his father when the revolution described was achieved in his mind. Since then, he had never left off wearing black. His clothes were slowly leaving him, however. A day came, at last, when he had no coat. His trousers were going also. What could he do? Courfeyrac, for whom he also had done some good turns, gave him an old coat. For thirty sous, Marius had it turned by some porter or other, and it was like new. But this coat was green. Marius did not go out till after nightfall, which made his coat black. Still wishing to be in mourning, he clothed himself with night.

Through all this, he achieved admission to the bar. He was supposedly occupying Courfeyrac's room, which was decent, and where a certain number of law books, supported and filled out by some odd volumes of novels, made up the library required by the rules. He had his mail sent to Courfeyrac.

When Marius became a lawyer, he informed his grandfather of it, in a letter that was icy but full of submission and respect. M. Gillenormand took up the letter with trembling hands, read it, and threw it, torn in four pieces, into the wastebasket. Two or three days later, Mlle. Gillenormand overheard her father, who was alone in his room, talking aloud. This always happened when he was very excited. She listened; the old man said; "If you were not a fool, you would know that a man cannot be a baron and a lawyer at the same time."

II

MARIUS POOR

Poverty is like everything else. It gradually becomes endurable. It ends by taking shape and becoming fixed. You vegetate, that is to say you develop in some squalid way, sufficient for existence. This is how Marius Pontmercy's life was arranged.

He had left the narrowest place behind; the pass widened a little in front of him. By dint of hard work, courage, perseverance, and will, he had succeeded in earning from his labor about seven hundred francs a year. He had learned German and English; thanks to Courfeyrac, who introduced him to his friend the publisher, Marius filled, in the literary department of the bookhouse, the modest role of utility. He made out prospectuses, translated articles, annotated editions, compiled biographies, etc., net result, year in and year out, seven hundred francs. He lived on this. How? Not badly. We will spell it out.

At an annual rent of thirty francs, Marius occupied a wretched little room in the Gorbeau building, with no fireplace, called a cabinet, furnished with no more than the indispensable. The furniture was his own. He gave three francs a month to the old woman who had charge of the building, for sweeping his room and bringing him every morning a little warm water, a fresh egg, and a penny loaf of bread. On this loaf and this egg he would breakfast. His breakfast varied from two to four sous, depending on the price of eggs. At six in the evening he went down into the Rue Saint-Jacques, to dine at Rousseau's, opposite Basset the print dealer's, at the corner of the Rue des Mathurins. He ate no soup. He took a sixpenny plate of meat, a threepenny half-plate of vegetables, and a threepenny dessert. For three sous, as much bread as he liked. As for wine, he drank water. On paying at the counter, where Madame Rousseau was majestically seated, still plump and fresh in those days, he gave a sou to the waiter, and Madame Rousseau gave him a smile. Then he would leave. For sixteen sous, he had a smile and a dinner.

This Rousseau restaurant, where so few bottles and so many pitchers were emptied, was more an appeasant than a restorant. It no longer exists. The master had a fine title; he was called Rousseau the Aquatic.

Thus, breakfast four sous, dinner sixteen sous, his food cost him twenty sous a day, which was three hundred and sixty-five francs a year. Add the thirty francs for his room, and the thirty-six francs to the old woman, and a few other trifling expenses, and for four hundred and fifty francs, Marius was fed, lodged, and waited upon. His clothes cost him a hundred francs, his linen fifty francs, his laundry fifty francs. The whole did not exceed six hundred and fifty francs. This left him fifty francs. He was rich. He would occasionally lend ten francs to a friend. Courfeyrac borrowed sixty francs from him once. As for fire, having no fireplace, Marius had "simplified" it.

Marius always had two complete suits, one old "for every day," the other quite new for special occasions. Both were black. He had only three shirts, one he had on, another in the drawer, the third with the laundress. He replaced them as they wore out. They were usually ragged, so he buttoned his coat to the chin.

For Marius to arrive at this flourishing condition had taken years. Hard years, and difficult ones; those to get through, these to climb. Marius had never given up for a single day. He had undergone everything by way of privation; he had done everything except go into debt. He gave himself this credit, that he had never owed a sou to anybody. For him a debt was the beginning of slavery. He even felt that a creditor is worse than a master; for a master owns only your person, a creditor owns your dignity and can belabor that. Rather than borrow, he did not eat. He had spent many days of fasting. Feeling that all extremes meet, and that if we do not take care, abasement of fortune may lead to baseness of soul, he watched jealously over his pride. Such a habit or such an action as, in any other condition, would have appeared deferential, seemed humiliating, and he braced himself against it. He risked nothing, not wishing to take a backward step. His face had a kind of ruddy severity. He was timid to the point of rudeness.

In all his trials he felt encouraged and sometimes even upheld by a secret force within. The soul helps the body, and at certain moments raises it. It is the only bird that sustains its cage.

Beside his father's name, another name was graven on Marius's heart, the name of Thénardier. In his enthusiastic yet serious nature, Marius, surrounded with a sort of halo the man to whom he thought he owed his father's life, that brave sergeant who had saved the colonel in the midst of the cannonballs and bullets of Waterloo. He never separated the memory of this man from the memory of his father, and he associated them in his veneration. It was a sort of worship with two gradations, the high altar for the colonel, the low one for Thénardier. The idea of the misfortune into which he knew that Thénardier had fallen intensified his feeling of gratitude. In Montfermeil Marius had learned of the ruin and bankruptcy of the unlucky innkeeper. Since then, he had made untold efforts to track him down, and to try to reach him, in that dark abyss of misery in which Thénardier had disappeared. Marius had scoured the countryside; he had been to Chelles, to Bondy, to Gournay, to Nogent, to Lagny. For three years he had devoted himself to this, spending what little money he could spare in these explorations. Nobody could give him any news of Thénardier; it was thought he had gone abroad. His creditors had sought him, also, with less love than Marius, but with as much zeal, and had not been able to lay their hands on him. Marius blamed and almost hated himself for not succeeding in his searches. This was the only debt the colonel had left him, and Marius made it a point of honor to pay it. "How could it be," he thought, "that when my father lay dying on the battlefield, Thénardier could find him through smoke and the grapeshot and carry him off on his shoulders, and yet he owed him nothing, while I, who owe so much to Thénardier, cannot reach him in the darkness where he is suffering, and restore him, in turn, from death to life. Oh! I will find him!" Indeed, to find Thénardier, Marius would have given one of his arms, and to save him from his wretchedness, all his blood. To see Thénardier, to render some service to Thénardier, to say to him, "You do not know me, but I do know you. Here I am, make what you will of me!" This was Marius's sweetest and most magnificent dream.

III

MARIUS A MAN

Marius was now twenty. It was three years since he had left his grandfather. They remained on the same terms on both sides, without attempting a reconciliation, and without trying to meet. And, indeed, what was the use of meeting? To renew the conflict? Which one would have had the best of it? Marius was a vase of brass, but M. Gillenormand was an iron pot.

To tell the truth, Marius was mistaken as to his grandfather's heart. He imagined that M. Gillenormand had never loved him, and that this crusty and harsh yet smiling old man, who swore, screamed, stormed, and waved his cane, felt for him at most only the affection, both slight and severe, of the old men in comedies. Marius was deceived. There are fathers who do not love their children; there is no grandfather who does not adore his grandson. In reality, as we said, M. Gillenormand worshiped Marius. He worshiped him in his own way, with an accompaniment of cuffs and even blows; but, when the child was gone, he felt a dark void in his heart. He gave orders that nobody should speak of him again and regretted he was so well obeyed. At first he hoped that this Buonapartist, this Jacobin, this terrorist, this Septembrist, would return. But weeks, months, years passed; to the great despair of M. Gillenormand, the bloodsucker did not reappear! "But I could not do anything else than turn him away," said the grandfather, and he asked himself, "If it were to be done again, would I do it?" His pride promptly answered Yes, but his old head, which he shook in silence, sadly answered No. He had his hours of dejection. He missed Marius. Old men need affection as they do sunshine. It is warmth. However strong his nature might be, the absence of Marius had changed something in him. For nothing in the world would he have taken a step toward the "little rogue"; but he suffered. He never asked after him, but he thought of him constantly. He lived more and more withdrawn in the Marais. He was still just as gay and forceful, but his gaiety had a convulsive harshness as if it contained grief and anger, and his bursts of violence always ended in a sort of placid and gloomy exhaustion. He would sometimes say, "Oh! If he would only come back, what a good box on the ear I would give him."

As for the aunt, she thought too little to love very much; Marius was no longer anything to her but a sort of dim, dark outline; and she finally busied herself a good deal less about him than with the cat or the parakeet she probably had. What increased Grandfather Gillenormand's secret suffering was that he shut her entirely out, and let her suspect none of it. His chagrin was like those newly invented furnaces that consume their own smoke. Sometimes it happened that some blundering, officious body would speak to him of Marius, and ask, "What is your grandson doing?" or "What has become of him?" The old bourgeois would answer, with a sigh, if he was too sad, or giving his ruffle a tap, if he wished to seem gay, "Monsieur the Baron Pontmercy is grinding out his trifling cases in some hole."

While the old man was regretting, Marius was rejoicing. As with all good hearts, suffering had taken away his bitterness. He thought of M. Gillenormand only with kindness, but he had determined to receive nothing more from the man *who had been cruel to his father*. This was now the softened translation of his first indignation.

Moreover, he was happy in having suffered, and in suffering still. It was for his father. His hard life satisfied him and pleased him. He said to himself with a sort of joy that it was the least pain, that it was an expiation; that, except for this, he would have been punished otherwise and later, for his unnatural indifference toward his father, and toward such a father; that it would not have been just that his father should have had all the suffering, and himself none; what were his efforts and his privation, moreover, compared to the heroic life of the colonel? That finally his only way of drawing near his father, and becoming like him, was to be valiant against indigence as he had been brave against the enemy; and that this was doubtless what the colonel meant by the words *"He will be worthy of it."* Words that Marius continued to bear, not on his breast, the colonel's paper having disappeared, but in his heart.

And then, the day his grandfather drove him away, he was only a child; now he was a man. He felt it. Misery, we must insist, had been good to him. Poverty in youth, when it succeeds, is magnificent in that it turns the whole will toward effort and the whole soul toward aspiration. Poverty strips the material life entirely bare, and makes it hideous; from this arise inexpressible yearnings toward the ideal life. The rich young man has a hundred brilliant and coarse amusements, racing, hunting, dogs, cigars, gambling, banqueting, and the rest; busying the lower portions of the soul at the expense of its higher, more delicate ones. The poor young man must work for his bread; he eats; when he has eaten, he has nothing left but reverie. He enters God's theater free; he sees the sky, space, the stars, the flowers, the children, the humanity in which he suffers, the creation in which he shines. He looks at humanity so much that he sees the soul, he looks at creation so much that he sees God. He dreams, he feels that he is great; he dreams some more, and he feels that he is tender. From the egotism of the suffering man, he passes to the compassion of the contemplating man. A wonderful feeling springs up within him, forgetfulness of self, and pity for all. In thinking of the countless enjoyments nature offers, gives, and gives lavishly to open souls and refuses to closed souls, he, a millionaire of intelligence, comes to grieve for the millionaires of money. All hatred leaves his heart as all light enters his mind. And is he unhappy? No. The poverty of a young man is never miserable. Any lad at all, poor as he may be, with his health, his strength, his quick step, his shining eyes, his blood circulating warmly, his black locks, his fresh cheeks, his rosy lips, his white teeth, his pure breath, will always be envied by an old emperor. And then every morning he sets about earning his bread; and while his hands are earning his living, his backbone is gaining pride, his brain is gaining ideas. When his work is done, he returns to drifting reveries, to contemplation, to joy; he lives with his feet tangled in obstacles, on the pavement, in thorns, sometimes in the mire, his head in the light. He is firm, serene, gentle, peaceful, attentive, serious, content with little, benevolent; and he blesses God for having given him the two gifts that many of the wealthy lack: labor which makes him free, and thought, which makes him noble.

This is what had taken place in Marius. To tell the truth, he had even gone a little too far toward contemplation. The day when he reached the point of almost certainly earning his living, he stopped there, preferring to be poor, and curtailing labor to give to thought. That is to say, he sometimes spent whole days like a visionary, thinking, deep in the mute joys of contemplation and inner radiance. He had posed the problem of his life thus: to work the least possible at material labor, so he could work as much as possible at intangible labor; in other words, to give a few hours to real life, and cast the rest into the infinite. He did not realize, thinking that he lacked nothing, that contemplation thus obtained comes to be one of the forms of sloth, that he had settled for subduing the primary necessities of life and was resting too soon.

It was clear that, for his energetic and generous nature, this could only be a transitory state, and that at the first shock against the inevitable complications of destiny, Marius would awaken.

Meanwhile, though he was a lawyer, and whatever Grandfather Gillenormand might think, he was not practicing, not even on a petty scale. Reverie had turned him away from the law. To consort with attorneys, to attend courts, to track down cases was boring. Why should he do it? He saw no reason for changing his way of earning a living. This cheap, obscure publishing had eventually given him steady work, work with little labor, which, as we have explained, was just sufficient for him.

One of the booksellers for whom he worked, M. Magimel, I think, had offered to take him home, give him a good room, furnish him regular work, and pay him fifteen hundred francs a year. To have a good room! Fifteen hundred francs! Very well. But to give up his liberty! To work for a salary, to be a kind of literary clerk! In Marius's opinion, to accept would make his position better and worse at the same time; he would gain in comfort and lose in dignity; it was a total and beautiful misfortune given up for ugly and ridiculous constraint; something like a blind man gaining one eye. He refused.

Marius's life was solitary. From his taste for remaining outside of everything, and also from having been thoroughly startled by its excesses, he had decided not to enter the group presided over by Enjolras. They had remained good friends; they were ready to help one another, if need be, in all possible ways, but nothing more. Marius had two friends, one young, Courfeyrac, and one old, M. Mabeuf. He inclined toward the old one. First he was indebted to him for the revolution he had undergone; he was indebted to him for having known and loved his father. "He removed my cataract," he said.

Certainly the churchwarden had been decisive.

However, M. Mabeuf was not in that event anything more than the calm and passive agent of providence. He had enlightened Marius accidentally and unwittingly, like a candle somebody happens to bring; he had been the candle and not the somebody.

As to the interior political revolution in Marius, M. Mabeuf was entirely incapable of understanding it, desiring it, or directing it.

Since we will meet M. Mabeuf later, a few words would not be out of place.

IV

M. MABEUF

The day that M. Mabeuf said to Marius, "Certainly, I approve of political opinions," he expressed the real condition of his mind. All political opinions were alike to him, and he approved them all without distinction, provided they left him alone, as the Greeks called the Furies, "the beautiful, the good, the charming," the *Eumenides*. M. Mabeuf's political opinion was a passionate fondness for plants, and a still greater one for books. He had, like everybody else, his suffix *ist*, without which nobody could have lived in those days, but he was neither a royalist, nor a Bonapartist, nor a chartist, nor an Orléanist, nor an anarchist; he was an old-bookist.

He did not understand how men could occupy themselves hating one another about such nonsense as the charter, democracy, legitimacy, the monarchy, the republic, etc. when the world was filled with all sorts of mosses, herbs and shrubs, which they could look at and piles of folios and even thirty-twomos that they could pore over. He took good care not to be useless; having books did not prevent him from reading, being a botanist did not prevent him from being a gardener. When he met Pontmercy, there was this bond between the colonel and himself, that what the colonel did for flowers, he did for fruits. M. Mabeuf had succeeded in producing seedling pears as highly flavored as the pears of Saint-Germain; to one of his combinations, so it appears, we owe the October Mirabelle, now famous, and no less fragrant than the Summer Mirabelle. He went to mass rather from good feeling than from devotion, and because he loved men's faces but hated their noise, and only at church he found them gathered together and silent. Feeling that one ought to be something in the state, he had chosen the career of a churchwarden. Actually, he had never managed to love any woman as much as a tulip bulb, or any man as much as an Elzevir. He had long passed his sixtieth year, when one day somebody asked him, "Were you never married?" "I forget," he said. When he sometimes happened to say—and who doesn't—"Oh! If I were rich," it was not, like M. Gillenormand, on noticing a pretty girl, but on seeing an old book. He lived alone, with an old housekeeper. He was a little gouty, and when he slept, his old fingers, stiffened with rheumatism, clenched the folds of the sheets. He had written and published a *Flora of the Environs of Cauteretz* with colored illustrations, a highly esteemed work, whose plates he owned and which he sold himself. People came two or three times a day and rang his bell, in the Rue Mézières, for it. He earned fully two thousand francs a year from it; that was nearly all his income. Though poor, he had succeeded in gathering together, through patience, self-denial, and time, a valuable collection of rare volumes of every genre. He never went out without a book under his arm, and he often came back with two. The only decoration of the four ground-floor rooms which, with a small garden, made up his apartment, were some framed displays of herbs and a few engravings of the old masters. The sight of a sword or a gun chilled him. In his whole life, he had never been near a cannon, even at the Invalides. He had a passable stomach, a brother who was a curé, hair entirely white, no teeth left either in his mouth or in his mind, a tremor of the whole body, a Picard accent, a childlike laugh, weak nerves, and the appearance of an old sheep. With all that, no other friend nor any other intimate acquaintance among the living, beyond an old bookseller at the Porte Saint-Jacque named Royol. His dream was to naturalize the indigo plant in France.

His servant also had a peculiar quality of innocence. The poor good old woman was a spinster. Sultan, her cat, who could have meowed the Allegri's Miserere at the Sistine Chapel, had filled her heart and provided all the passion she needed. None of her dreams went so far as man. She had never got beyond her cat. Like him, she had whiskers. Her glory was her collection of white caps. She spent her time on Sunday after mass counting her linen in her trunk, and spreading out on her bed the dresses which she had bought in the piece and never had made up. She could read. M. Mabeuf had given her the name of *Mother Plutarch*.

M. Mabeuf took Marius into favor because Marius, being young and gentle, warmed his old age without arousing his timidity. With gentleness, youth has the effect on old men of sunshine without wind. When Marius was full of military glory, gunpowder, marches, and countermarches, and all those wonderful battles in which his father had given and received such mighty saber strokes, he would go to see M. Mabeuf, and M. Mabeuf talked with him about the hero from the floricultural point of view.

Toward 1830 his brother the curé died, and almost immediately, as with the coming of night, M. Mabeuf's whole horizon was darkened. By the failure of a notary, he lost ten thousand francs, which was all the money he possessed in his brother's name and his own. The revolution of July brought on a crisis in bookselling. In hard times, the first thing that does not sell is a *Flora*. *The Flora of the Environs of Cauteretz* stopped dead. Weeks went by without a purchaser. Sometimes M. Mabeuf would start up at the sound of the bell. "Monsieur," Mother Plutarch would say sadly, "it is the water bearer." In short, M. Mabeuf left the Rue Mézières one day, resigned his place as churchwarden, gave up Saint-Sulpice, sold a part, not of his books, but of his prints—what he prized the least—and went to live in a little house on the Boulevard Montparnasse, where however he remained only three months, for two reasons; first, the ground floor and the garden cost three hundred francs, and he did not dare to spend more than two hundred francs for his rent; secondly, being near the Fatou shooting gallery, he heard pistol shots, which he found unbearable.

He took his *Flora,* his plates, his herbariums, his portfolios, and his books, and settled near La Saltpêtrière in a sort of cottage in the village of Austerlitz, where for fifty crowns a year he had three rooms, a garden enclosed by a hedge, and a well. He took advantage of this change to sell nearly all his furniture. The day of his move into this new dwelling, he was very cheerful, and drove in nails himself to hang the engravings and the herb displays. The rest of the day he dug in his garden, and in the evening, seeing Mother Plutarch looking gloomy and thoughtful, he tapped her on the shoulder and said with a smile, "We still have the indigo."

Only two visitors, the bookseller from the Porte Saint-Jacque and Marius, were admitted to his cottage at Austerlitz, a rather bellicose name, which he found, to tell the truth, rather disagreeable.

However, as we have just indicated, brains absorbed in wisdom, in folly, or, as often happens, in both at once, are permeated only slowly by the affairs of life. Their own destiny is far from them. From such concentrations of mind comes a passivity which, if due to reason, would resemble philosophy. We decline, we descend, we fall, we are even overthrown, and we hardly notice it. This always ends, it is true, in an awakening, but a tardy one. In the meantime, we seem neutrals in the game being played between our good and our ill fortune. We are the stake, yet we look on the contest with indifference.

So it was that amid this darkness gathering around him, all his hopes dimming one after another, M. Mabeuf had remained serene, somewhat childishly, but very deeply. His state of mind had the swing of a pendulum. Once wound up by an illusion, he went on a long time, even when the illusion had disappeared. A clock does not stop at the very moment you lose the key.

M. Mabeuf had some innocent pleasures. These pleasures were cheap and unexpected; the least chance furnished them. One day Mother Plutarch was reading a romance novel in one corner of the room. She read aloud, as she understood better that way. In reading aloud you assume authority for what you are reading. There are people who read very loudly, and who appear to be giving their word of honor for what they are reading.

It was with that kind of energy that Mother Plutarch was reading the romance she held in her hand. Monsieur Mabeuf heard, but was not listening.

As she read, Mother Plutarch came to this passage. It was about an officer of dragoons and a beauty: "The belle *bouda* [pouted], and the *dragon* [dragoon]—"

Here she stopped to wipe her spectacles.

"Buddha and the Dragon," said M. Mabeuf in an undertone. "Yes, quite true, there was a dragon who, from the depth of his cave, belched flames from his jaws and was burning up the sky. Several stars had already been set on fire by this monster, who, besides, had claws like a tiger. Buddha went into his cave and succeeded in converting the dragon. That is a good book you are reading there, Mother Plutarch. There is no more beautiful legend."

And M. Mabeuf fell into a delicious reverie.

V

POVERTY A GOOD NEIGHBOR OF MISERY

Marius had a liking for this kind-hearted old man, who was slowly being seized by poverty, and who had gradually come to be astonished by it, without, however, as yet becoming sad. Marius met Courfeyrac, and sought out M. Mabeuf. Very rarely, however; once or twice a month, at most.

Marius enjoyed taking long walks alone on the outer boulevards, or at the Champ de Mars, or in the less popular paths of the Luxembourg Gardens. He would sometimes spend half a day looking at a vegetable garden, at the beds of salad greens, the chickens on the manure pile, and the horse turning the wheel of the pump. The passersby looked at him with surprise, and some thought that he had a suspicious appearance and an ominous manner. He was only a poor young man, dreaming aimlessly.

It was on one of these walks that he had discovered the Gorbeau house, and its isolation and cheapness being an attraction to him, he took a room in it. He was only known there by the name of M. Marius.

When they had met him, a few former generals or friends of his father's invited him to pay them a visit. Marius had not refused. They gave him the chance to talk about his father. So sometimes he went to see the Comte Pajol, to General Bellavesne, and to General Fririon at the Invalides. There would be music and dancing. On those evenings Marius put on his new suit. But he could go to the parties only when there was a hard freeze, because he could not afford a carriage and did not want to go at all unless his boots shone like mirrors.

Sometimes he would say, though without bitterness, "The customs of society are such that you can enter a drawing room filthy all over except for your shoes. A warm welcome requires one irreproachable feature: your conscience? No, your boots."

Even passion, except of the heart, dissipates in reverie. Marius's political fevers were over. The Revolution of

1830, by satisfying him and soothing him, had helped. His opinions remained unchanged, but without the fervor. Properly speaking, he no longer held opinions; he had sympathies. To what party did he belong? To the party of humanity. Among humanities he chose France; within the nation he chose the people; of the people he chose woman. His pity went out to her above all. He now preferred an idea to a fact, a poet to a hero, and he admired a book like Job still more than an event like Marengo. And then when returning at night along the boulevards after a day of meditation he saw through the branches of the trees the fathomless space, the nameless lights, the depths, the darkness, the mystery, everything that is only human seemed very petty.

Marius thought he had, and perhaps in fact he had, attained the truth of life and human philosophy, and in the end he had come to look at hardly anything but the sky, the only thing that truth can see from the bottom of her well.

This did not hinder him from piling up plans, schemes, frameworks, projects. In this state of reverie, an eye looking deep into Marius's soul would have been dazzled by its purity. In fact, were it given to our human eye to see into the consciences of others, we would judge a man much more surely from what he dreams than from what he thinks. There is will in the thought, there is none in the dream. Even in the gigantic and the ideal, the dream, which is completely spontaneous, takes and keeps the form of our mind. Nothing springs more directly and more sincerely from our innermost souls than our unreflected and indefinite aspirations toward the splendors of destiny. In these aspirations, much more than in ideas which are structured, studied, and compared, can we find the true character of each man. Our chimeras are most like us. Each of us dreams the unknown and the impossible according to his own nature.

Toward the middle of this year, 1831, the old woman who waited on Marius told him that his neighbors, the wretched Jondrette family, were about to be turned out into the street. Marius, who spent almost all his days away from the house, hardly knew he had any neighbors.

"Why are they being turned out?" he said.

"Because they do not pay their rent; they owe for two terms."

"How much is that?"

"Twenty francs," said the old woman.

Marius had thirty francs in reserve in a drawer.

"Here," he said to the old woman. "There are twenty-five francs. Pay for those poor people, give them five francs, and don't tell them that it's from me."

VI

THE REPLACEMENT

It happened that Lieutenant Théodule's regiment came to be stationed at Paris. This prompted a second idea from Aunt Gillenormand. Once she had thought she would have Marius watched by Théodule; now she schemed to have Théodule supplant Marius.

In any event, and in case the grandfather should feel a vague need of a young face in the house—these rays of dawn are sometimes comforting to ruins—it was expedient to find another Marius. "Yes," she thought, "this is merely an erratum such as I see in books; for Marius read Théodule."

A grandnephew is almost a grandson; for want of a lawyer a lancer will do.

One morning, as M. Gillenormand was reading something like *La Quotidienne*, his daughter entered and said in sweetest tones, for the matter concerned her favorite, "Father, Théodule is coming this morning to present his respects to you."

"Who is that—Théodule?"

"Your grandnephew."

"Ah!" said the grandfather.

Then he went back to his reading, thought no more of the grandnephew who was simply some Théodule, and soon got very agitated, as almost always happened when he read. The "sheet" which he had, royalist, as a matter of course, announced for the next day, without comment, one of the little daily occurrences in the Paris of that time. The students of the schools of Law and Medicine would meet in Place du Panthéon at noon—to debate. The question was one of the current topics: the artillery of the National Guard, and a conflict between the Minister of War and the "citizens' militia" on the subject of the cannon set down in the courtyard of the Louvre. The students were to "debate" this. It did not take much more to enrage M. Gillenormand.

He thought of Marius, who was a student, and who, probably, would go like the others to debate at noon, in the Place du Panthéon.

While he was dwelling on this painful thought, Lieutenant Théodule entered, wearing civilian clothes, an adroit touch, and was discreetly introduced by Mlle. Gillenormand. The lancer had thought it out this way: "The old druid hasn't put everything into an annuity. It's well worth my while to dress in civilian clothes occasionally."

Mlle. Gillenormand said aloud to her father, "Théodule, your grandnephew."

And, in a whisper, to the lieutenant, "Say yes to everything."

And she withdrew.

The lieutenant, little accustomed to such venerable encounters, stammered out with some timidity, "Good morning, Uncle," and made a mixed greeting composed of the involuntary and mechanical awkwardness of the military salute finished off with the bow of the bourgeois.

"Ah! It's you; very well, take a seat," said the old man.

And then, he entirely forgot the lancer.

Théodule sat down, and M. Gillenormand got up.

M. Gillenormand began to walk up and down with his hands in his pockets, talking aloud, and rubbing with his nervous old fingers the two watches he carried in his two waistcoat pockets.

"This pack of snivelers! They are gathering in the Place du Panthéon. As I live! Scapegraces hardly out of the nursery! Tweak their noses and the milk would run! And they will debate at noon tomorrow! What are we coming to? What are we coming to? It's clear that we're headed for the abyss. This is where the descamisados have led us! The civil artillery! To debate about the civil artillery! To go out and yammer in the open air about the flatulent barrage of the National Guard! And who will they find there with them? Just see where Jacobinism leads. I'll bet anything you please, a million to one, they'll all be fugitives from justice and discharged convicts. Republicans and convicts, like a nose and a handkerchief. Carnot said, 'Where would you have me go, traitor?' Fouché answered, 'Wherever you like, fool!' That is what you get with Republicans."

"That's true," said Théodule.

M. Gillenormand half turned his head, saw Théodule, and went on, "Just to think that this rogue has had the nerve to turn carbonaro! Why did you leave my house? To go out and be a Republican. Pish! In the first place the people don't want your Republic, they don't want it, they have good sense, they know very well that there have always been kings, and always will be, they know very well that the people, after all, are nothing but the people, they laugh at your Republic, do you understand, you idiot? Isn't your whimsy rather horrible? To fall for Père Duchesne, to cozy up to the guillotine, to sing ditties and play the guitar under the balcony of '93; it's enough to make us spit on all these young fools. They're all in a heap. Not one got away. It's enough to breathe the air of the street to make them go crazy. The nineteenth century is poison. The first whippersnapper you meet wears his goat's beard, thinks he is very clever, and tosses out his old relatives. That's republican, that's romantic. What does that mean, romantic? Be so kind as to tell me just what that means! Every possible folly. A year ago, you went to *Hernani*. I ask you, *Hernani!* Antitheses! Abominations that aren't ever written in French! And now they have cannon in the court of the Louvre. That's the highway robbery we've come to these days."

"You're quite right, Uncle," said Théodule.

M. Gillenormand started in again, "Cannon in the court of the Museum! Why? Cannon, what do you want? Do you want to shoot down the Apollo Belvedere? What have cartridges to do with Venus de Medici? Oh! These young folks nowadays, all scamps! He's not much, their Benjamin Constant! And those who aren't scoundrels are nitwits! They do all they can to be ugly, they're badly dressed, they're scared of women, they act like beggars when they get near a petticoat, and make the women burst out laughing; upon my word, you'd say the poor fellows are ashamed of love. They're homely, and they end up being stupid; they repeat Tiercelin's and Potier's puns, they have sackcoats, jockeys' waistcoats, coarse cotton shirts, coarse cloth trousers, coarse leather boots, and their chatter suits their feathers. Their jargon would do for their old shoes. And all these foolish brats have political opinions. They ought to be strictly forbidden to have any political opinions. They fabricate systems, they reform society, they demolish monarchy, they upset all laws, they put the attic in the cellar, and my doorkeeper in place of the king, they turn Europe topsy-turvy, they rebuild the world, and all the favors they get are sly peeps at washerwomen's legs as they climb into their carts! Oh! Marius! Oh! You beggar! Going to vociferate in a public square, to discuss, debate, take measures! They call that measures! Disorder shrinks into stupidities. I've seen chaos, I see a jumble. Schoolboys deliberating about the National Guard, you wouldn't see that among the Ojibways or the Cadodaches! The naked savages with pates like shuttlecocks, with clubs in their paws, aren't as wild as these bachelors. Fourpenny monkeys! They pass for learned and capable! They deliberate and reason! It's the end of the world. It's clearly the end of this miserable terraqueous globe. It needed some final hiccup. France will do it. Deliberate, you rogues. Such things will happen as long as they go and read the newspapers under the arches of the Odéon. It costs them a sou, and their good sense, and their intelligence, and their heart, and their soul, and their mind. They come away from there, and they desert the parental hearth and home. Those newspapers are the plague; all of them, even the *Drapeau Blanc!* Basically Martainville was a Jacobin. Oh! Just heavens! You can be proud of being the despair of your old grandfather!"

"That is quite clear," said Théodule.

And taking advantage of M. Gillenormand's pause for breath, the lancer added portentously, "There ought to be no newspaper but the *Moniteur* and no book but the *Annuaire Militaire.*"

M. Gillenormand went on.

"It's like their Sieyès! A regicide ending up a senator; that's always the way they end. They lash themselves with thee-and-thouing, and 'Citizen this and that,' so that they can be called Monsieur le Comte. Monsieur le Comte, my eye! The butchers of September. The philosopher Sieyès! I'm happy to say I never paid any more attention to the philosophies of all these philosophers than to the spectacles of the Tivoli clown. I saw the senators one day passing along the Quai Malaquais in mantles of violet velvet sprinkled with bees, and Henri IV hats. They were hideous. You'd have said they were the monkeys of the tiger's court. Citizens, I tell you your progress is lunacy, your humanity is a dream, your Revolution is a crime, your Republic is a monster, your virgin France is right out of the brothel, and I say so to all of you, whoever you are, be you publicists, be you economists, be you in the law, be you greater connoisseurs of liberty, equality, and fraternity than the ax of the guillotine! I tell you that, my lads!"

"My God," cried the lieutenant, "that is wonderfully true."

M. Gillenormand broke off a gesture he had begun, turned, looked the lancer Théodule steadily in the eyes, and said, "You're a fool."

Book Six

THE CONJUNCTION OF TWO STARS

I

THE NICKNAME: FORMATION OF FAMILY NAMES

Marius was now a handsome young man, of medium height, with heavy jet black hair, a high intelligent brow, wide and passionate nostrils, a frank and calm expression, and an indescribable something radiating from every feature that was at once noble, thoughtful, and innocent. His profile, all the lines of which were rounded, without loss of strength, possessed that Germanic gentleness that has made its way into French facial features through Alsace and Lorraine, and that entire absence of angles that rendered the Sicambri so recognizable among the Romans, that distinguishes the leonine from the aquiline race. He was in the season of life at which the mind of thinking men is made up in nearly equal proportions of depth and simplicity. In a difficult situation he possessed all the essentials of stupidity; another turn of the screw, and he could become sublime. His manners were reserved, cold, polished, far from free. But as his mouth was very pleasant, his lips the reddest and his teeth the whitest imaginable, his smile corrected the severity of his features. At certain moments there was a strange contrast between the chaste brow and the voluptuous smile. His eyes were small, their outlook vast.

At the time of his most wretched poverty, he noticed that girls would turn when he passed, and with a deathly feeling in his heart he fled or hid himself. He thought they were looking at him because of his old clothes, and that they were laughing at him; the truth is, they looked at him because of his graceful appearance, and they dreamed about him.

This mute misunderstanding between him and the pretty girls he met had made him hostile to society. He attached himself to none, for the excellent reason that he fled all of them. Thus he lived aimlessly—stupidly, said Courfeyrac.

Courfeyrac said to him, too, "Don't try to be a sage my dear lad. A piece of advice. Don't read so much, take a little more time to look at the ladies. The little devils are good for thee, O Marius! If you keep on fleeing and blushing you'll become a brute."

At other times Courfeyrac met him with, "Good day, Monsieur l'Abbé."

When Courfeyrac said anything of this kind to him, for the next week Marius avoided women, old as well as young, more than ever, and Courfeyrac on top of that.

However, of the whole immense creation, there were two women Marius never fled, and with whom he was not at all guarded. Indeed he would have been very much astonished had anybody told him that they were women. One was the old woman with the beard, who swept his room, and who gave Courfeyrac an opportunity to say, "As his servant wears her beard, Marius does not wear his." The other was a little girl he saw very often and never looked at.

For more than a year Marius had noticed in a deserted path in Luxembourg, the walk that runs along the parapet of the Pépinière, a man and a rather young girl nearly always sitting side by side on the same seat, at the most deserted end of the path, near the Rue de l'Ouest. Whenever the chance that controls the wandering of men whose eye is turned inward led Marius to this walk, and that was almost every day, he would find this couple there. The man might be sixty years old; he seemed sad and serious; his whole person presented the robust but wearied appearance of a soldier retired from active service. Had he worn a decoration, Marius would have said, "It is a former officer." His expression was kind, but it did not invite approach, and he never returned a look. He wore a blue coat and trousers and a broad-brimmed hat, which always looked new; a black tie, and Quaker linen, that is to say, brilliantly white, though of coarse texture. A grisette passing near him one day said, "There's a very nice widower." His hair was completely white.

The first time the young girl that accompanied him sat down on the seat they seemed to have adopted, she looked like a girl of about thirteen or fourteen, puny to the point of being almost ugly, awkward, insignificant, yet promising, perhaps, to have rather fine eyes. But they were always looking about with a sort of unpleasant assurance. She wore the uniform, both aged and childish, peculiar to the convent boarders, an ill-fitting garment of coarse black merino. They appeared to be father and daughter.

For two or three days Marius scrutinized this man, who was not yet elderly, and this little girl, not yet a woman; then he paid no more attention to them. For their part they did not even seem to see him. They talked together peacefully, unconcerned. The girl chatted incessantly and gaily. The old man spoke seldom, and at times looked at her with an expression of fatherliness.

Marius had acquired a sort of unconscious habit of gravitating to this walk. He always found them there.

It usually went this way:

Marius would generally reach the walk from the end opposite their seat, stroll the whole length of it, passing in front of them, then return to the end where he entered, and so on. He did this circuit five or six times on his walk, and this walk five or six times a week, but they and he had never come to exchange bows. Though they seemed, and perhaps because they seemed, to be avoiding observation, this man and this young girl had naturally excited the attention of the five or six students, who, from time to time, went walking along the Pépinière; the studious ones after their lectures, the others after their game of billiards. Courfeyrac, who belonged to the latter, had noticed them at some time or other but, finding the girl homely, had very quickly and carefully avoided them. He had fled like a Parthian, unleashing a nickname behind him. Struck especially by the clothing of the little girl and the hair of the old man, he had named the daughter *Mademoiselle Lanoire* [Black] and the father *Monsieur Leblanc* [White]; and so, as nobody knew them otherwise, in the absence of a name, these had become set. The students would say, "Ah! Monsieur Leblanc is on this bench!" and Marius, like the rest, had found it convenient to call this unknown gentleman M. Leblanc.

We shall do as they did and say M. Leblanc for the convenience of this story.

Marius saw them nearly every day at the same hour during the first year. He found the man very much to his liking, but the girl rather depressing.

II

LUX FACTA EST

The second year, at the precise point in this story that the reader has reached, it so happened that Marius broke off this habit of going to the Luxembourg, without really knowing why himself, and there were nearly six months during which he did not set foot in his path. At last he went back there again one day; it was a serene summer morning, Marius was as happy as one always is when the weather is fine. It felt as though he had in his heart all the birdsongs he was hearing, and all the bits of blue sky he saw through the trees.

He went straight to "his path," and as soon as he reached it, he saw, still on the same seat, the well-known pair. When he drew closer, however, he saw that it was indeed the same man, but it seemed to him that it was no longer the same girl! The woman whom he now saw was a noble, beautiful creature, with all the most bewitching feminine outlines at the precise moment when they are still combined with all the most charming graces of childhood—that pure and fleeting moment that can only be translated by these two words: sweet fifteen. Beautiful chestnut hair shaded with veins of gold, a brow that seemed marble, cheeks like roses, a pale bloom, a flushed whiteness, an exquisite mouth that gave off a smile like a gleam of sunshine and a voice like music, a head that Raphael would have given to Mary, on a neck that Jean Goujon would have given to Venus. And so nothing be lacking to this ravishing form, the nose was not beautiful, it was pretty; neither straight nor curved, neither Italian nor Greek; it was the Parisian nose; that is, something sprightly, fine, irregular, and pure, the despair of painters and the charm of poets.

When Marius walked past her, he could not see her eyes, which were always lowered. He saw only her long chestnut lashes, full of mystery and modesty.

But that did not prevent the beautiful girl from smiling as she listened to the white-haired man who was speaking to her, and nothing was so ravishing as this maidenly smile with the downcast eyes.

At the first instant Marius thought it was another daughter of the same man, undoubtedly a sister of the one he had seen before. But when the unvarying pattern of his stroll led him for the second time past the bench, and he had looked at her attentively, he recognized that she was the same one. In six months the little girl had become a young woman; that was all. Nothing is more common than this phenomenon. There is a moment when girls bloom in a twinkling, and become roses all at once. Yesterday we left them children, today we find them disturbing.

She had not only grown; she had become idealized. As three April days are enough for certain trees to put on a covering of flowers, six months had been enough for her to put on a mantle of beauty. Her April had come.

We sometimes see people, poor and mean, who seem to awaken, pass suddenly from indigence to luxury, incur expenses of all sorts, and suddenly become splendid, prodigal, and magnificent. That comes from income received; yesterday was payday. The young girl had received her dividend.

And then she was no longer the schoolgirl with her plush hat, her merino dress, her shapeless shoes, and her red hands; taste had come to her with beauty. She was a well-dressed woman, with a sort of simple and rich elegance lacking affectation. She wore a dress of black damask, a shawl of the same, and a white crepe hat. Her white gloves showed the delicacy of her hand, which played with the Chinese ivory handle of her parasol, and her silk boot revealed a dainty foot. When you passed near her, her whole being exhaled the penetrating fragrance of youth.

As for the man, he was still the same.

The second time Marius came by, the young girl raised

her eyes; they were of a deep celestial blue, but in the veiled azure was nothing beyond the look of a child. She looked at Marius with indifference, as she would have looked at a little monkey playing under the sycamores, or the marble vase that cast its shadow over the bench; and Marius too went on with his walk thinking of other things.

Four or five times more he passed by the bench where the young girl was, without even looking her way.

On the following days he came as usual to the Luxembourg; as usual he found "the father and the daughter" there, but he paid no attention to them. He thought no more of this girl now that she was beautiful than he had thought of her when she was homely. He went by quite close to the bench where she was sitting because that was his habit.

III

EFFECT OF SPRING

One day the air was mild, the Luxembourg was flooded with sunshine and shadow, the sky was as clear as if the angels had washed it that morning, the sparrows were twittering in the depths of the chestnut trees, Marius had opened his whole soul to nature, he was thinking of nothing, he was living and breathing, he walked by close to the bench, the young girl raised her eyes, their glances met.

But that time what was there in the young girl's glance? Marius could not have said. There was nothing, and there was everything. It was a strange flash.

She looked down, and he continued on his way.

What he had seen was not the simple, artless eye of a child; it was a mysterious abyss, half opened, then suddenly closed.

There comes a day when every young girl has this look. Woe to him on whom she looks!

This first glance of a soul not yet aware of itself is like dawn. It is the awakening of something radiant and unknown. Nothing can express the dangerous charm of this unexpected gleam that lightly glances off delicate mysteries and is made of innocence and future passion. It is a kind of irresolute tenderness revealed by chance, waiting. It is a trap that Innocence unconsciously lays, where she catches hearts without intending to, and without knowing it. It is a virgin glancing like a woman.

It is rare that deep reverie is not born of this glance wherever it falls. All that is pure and vestal is concentrated in this celestial and fatal gleem which, more than the most meaningful looks of the coquette, has the magic power of suddenly forcing into bloom in the innermost depths of a heart, this somber flower full of perfumes and poisons that is called love.

At night, on returning to his garret, Marius looked at his clothes, and for the first time realized that he had the slovenly indecency, and the unheard-of stupidity, to go walking in the Luxembourg in his everyday suit, a hat broken near the band, coarse teamsters' boots, black trousers shiny at the knees, and a black coat threadbare at the elbows.

IV

BEGINNING OF A GRAVE ILLNESS

The next day, at the usual hour, Marius took from his closet his new coat, his new trousers, his new hat, and his new boots; he dressed himself in this panoply, put on his gloves, prodigious prodigality, and went to the Luxembourg.

On the way, he met Courfeyrac, and pretended not to see him. Courfeyrac said to his friends, "I have just met Marius's new hat and coat, with Marius in them. Probably he was going to take an examination. He looked completely idiotic."

On reaching the Luxembourg, Marius took a turn around the fountain and looked at the swans; then he stood for a long time comtemplating a statue, whose head was black with moss and lacked a hip. Near the pond was a potbellied bourgeois of forty, holding a little boy of five by the hand, to whom he was saying, "Beware of extremes, my son. Keep an equal distance from despotism and anarchy." Marius listened to this good bourgeois. Then he took another turn around the fountain. Finally, he went toward his path, slowly, and as if reluctantly. One would have said he was compelled to go and at the same time prevented from going. He was completely unconscious of all this, and thought he was doing just as he did every day.

When he reached the path he saw M. Leblanc and the young girl at the other end "on their bench." He buttoned his coat, stretched it down so there would be no wrinkles, noticed with some satisfaction the shine of his trousers, and marched on the bench. There was something of attack in this march, and certainly a desire for conquest. So I say he marched on the bench, as I would say, Hannibal marched on Rome.

Beyond this, there was nothing that was not unconscious in all his movements, and he had in no way interrupted the customary preoccupations of his mind and work. He was thinking at that moment that the *Manuel du Baccalauréat* was a stupid book, and it must have been compiled by total cretins, to include the assignment of analyzing masterpieces of the human mind, three tragedies by Racine, and only one of Molière's comedies. He had a sharp ringing in his ear. While approaching the bench, he smoothed the wrinkles out of his coat, and his eyes were fixed on the young girl. It seemed to him that she filled the whole far end of the walk with a pale, bluish light.

As he drew nearer, his pace became slower and slower. Still some way from the bench, long before reaching the end of the walk, he stopped, and he had no idea how it happened, but he turned back. He did not even say to himself that he would not go to the end. The young girl could hardly have seen him so far off and noticed his fine appearance in his new suit. However, he held himself very straight, to look well, in case anybody might happen to notice him.

He reached the opposite end and then turned back, and this time he got a little nearer to the bench. He even came to within about three trees of it, but there he felt an indescribable inability to go farther, and he hesitated. He thought he had seen the young girl's face turned toward him. Still he made a great and manly effort, conquered his hesitation, and continued his advance. In a few seconds, he was walking past the bench, erect and firm, blushing to his ears, without daring to look to the right or the left, and with his hand in his coat like a statesman. At the moment he was passing under the guns of the fortress, he felt a frightful palpitation of the heart. She was wearing, as on the previous day, her damask dress and crepe hat. He heard the sound of an ineffable voice, which had to be "her voice." She was talking quietly. She was very pretty. He felt it, though he made no effort to see her. "However, she could not," he thought, "fail to have some esteem and consideration for me, if she knew that I was the real author of the dissertation on Marcos Obregon de la Ronda, which Monsieur François de Neufchâteau has put, as his own, at the beginning of his edition of *Gil Blas!*"

He passed the bench, went to the end of the walk, which was quite near, then turned and passed by the beautiful girl again. This time he was very pale. In fact, everything he was experiencing was very disagreeable. He walked away from the bench and from the young girl, and although his back was turned, he imagined that she was looking at him, and that made him stumble.

He made no effort to approach the seat again, he stopped midway in the path, and sat down there—a thing he never did—casting many sidelong glances, and reflecting, in the most indistinct depths of his mind, that after all it must be difficult for persons whose white hat and black dress he admired to be absolutely insensible to his glossy trousers and new coat.

After a quarter of an hour he rose, as if to go back to his walking toward that bench encircled by a halo. However, he stood silent and motionless. For the first time in fifteen months, he said to himself, the gentleman who sat there every day with his daughter had undoubtedly noticed him and probably thought his persistence very strange.

For the first time, also, he felt a certain irreverence in designating this unknown man, even in the silence of his thought, by the nickname of M. Leblanc.

He stayed this way for some minutes with his head down, tracing designs on the ground with a little stick he had in his hand.

Then he abruptly turned away from the bench, away from M. Leblanc and his daughter, and went home.

That day he forgot to go out to dinner. At eight o'clock in the evening he realized it, and since it was too late to go down to the Rue Saint-Jacques, he said, "Oh well," and he ate a piece of bread.

He did not go to bed until he had carefully brushed and folded his coat.

V

VARIOUS THUNDERBOLTS FALL ON MA'AM BOUGON

The next day, Ma'am Bougon—that is how Courfeyrac referred to the old concierge-landlady of the Gorbeau tenement—Ma'am Bougon, her name was really Madame Bougon, as we have stated, but the terrible Courfeyrac respected nothing—Ma'am Bougon was astounded to see M. Marius go out again in his new suit.

He went back to the Luxembourg, but did not get beyond his bench midway down the path. He sat there as on the previous day, gazing from a distance and distinctly seeing the white hat, the black dress, and particularly the bluish light. He did not stir from the seat, and did not go home until the gates of the Luxembourg were shut. He did not see M. Leblanc and his daughter leave the park. He concluded from that that they left the garden by the gate on the Rue de l'Ouest. Afterwards, some weeks later, when he thought of it, he could not remember where he had dined that night.

The next day, for the third time, Ma'am Bougon was thunderstruck. Marius went out in his new suit. "Three days running!" she exclaimed.

She tried to follow him, but Marius walked briskly and with immense strides; it was a hippopotamus attempting to catch a chamois. In two minutes she lost sight of him and came back out of breath, three quarters choked by her asthma, and furious. "Silly," she grumbled, "putting on his handsome clothes every day and making people run like that!"

Marius had gone to the Luxembourg.

The young girl was there with M. Leblanc. Marius went as near as he could, pretending to read a book, but he was still far off, then turned back and sat down on his bench, where he spent four hours watching the artless little sparrows as they hopped along the walk; they seemed to be mocking him.

Two weeks rolled by this way. Marius went to the Luxembourg, no longer to walk back and forth, but to sit down, always in the same place, and without knowing why. Once there he did not stir. Every morning he put on his new suit, not to be conspicuous, and he did it again the next morning.

She was certainly marvelously beautiful. The only possible remark that would come close to criticism, is that the contradiction between her look, which was sad, and her smile, which was joyful, gave her face a slightly wild expression, with the result that at certain moments this sweet face turned a bit strange without ceasing to be charming.

VI

TAKEN PRISONER

On one of the last days of the second week, Marius was as usual sitting on his bench, holding in his hand an open book of which he had not turned a page for two hours. Suddenly he trembled. A great event was beginning at the far end of the path. M. Leblanc and his daughter had left their bench, the daughter had taken the father's arm, and they were coming slowly toward the middle of the walk where Marius was. Marius closed his book, then he opened it, then he made an attempt to read. He trembled. The halo was coming straight toward him. "O dear!" he thought, "I'll never have time to make myself look natural." Meanwhile, the man with the white hair and the young girl were advancing. It seemed to take all of a century and only a second. "What are they coming by here for?" he asked himself. "Is she going to go by right here? Are her feet going to walk across the gravel in this path, two steps away from me?" He was overwhelmed, he would like to have been very handsome, he would like to have worn the cross of the Legion of Honor. He heard the gentle measured sound of their steps approaching. He imagined that M. Leblanc was hurling angry looks at him. "Is he going to speak to me?" he wondered. He bowed his head; when he raised it they were quite near. The young girl went by, and in passing she looked at him. She looked at him steadily, with a sweet and thoughtful look that made Marius tremble from head to foot. It seemed to him that she was reproaching him for having taken so long without coming to her, and that she was saying, "I am the one coming to you." Marius was bewildered by the eyes full of flashing light and fathomless abysses.

He felt as though his brain were on fire. She had come to him, what joy! And then, how she had looked at him! She seemed more beautiful than ever before. Beautiful with a beauty that combined all of the woman with all of the angel, a beauty that would have made Petrarch sing and Dante kneel. He felt as though he were swimming in the deep blue sky. At the same time he was horribly disconcerted, because there was dust on his boots.

He felt sure that she had seen his boots in this condition.

He followed her with his eyes till she disappeared, then he began to walk the Luxembourg like a madman. It is likely that at times he laughed, alone as he was, and spoke aloud. He was so strange and dreamy near the children and their nurses that each one thought he was in love with her.

He left the Luxembourg hoping to find her again in some street. He met Courfeyrac under the arches of the Odéon, and said, "Come and have dinner with me." They went to Rousseau's and spent six francs. Marius ate like an ogre. He gave six sous to the waiter. At dessert he said to Courfeyrac, "Have you read the papers? What a fine speech Audry de Puyraveau made!"

He was desperately in love.

After dinner he said to Courfeyrac, "Come to the theater with me." They went to the Porte Saint-Martin to see Lemaître in *L'Auberge des Adrets*. Marius enjoyed himself tremendously.

At the same time he became more strange and incomprehensible still. On leaving the theater, he refused to look at the garter of a little milliner who was crossing a gutter, and when Courfeyrac said, "I would not object to putting that woman in my collection," it almost horrified him.

Courfeyrac invited him to lunch the next day at the Café Voltaire. Marius went and ate still more than the day before. He was quite thoughtful, yet very gay. One would have said that he used any pretext to burst out laughing. He warmly embraced a visitor from the country who was introduced to him. A circle of students gathered around the table, and there was talk of the stupidities paid for by the government that were doled out from the rostrum at the Sorbonne; then the conversation fell upon the faults and gaps in the dictionaries and prosodies of Quicherat. Marius interrupted the discussion by exclaiming, "But it's very pleasant to have the Cross."

"He's a funny one!" said Courfeyrac, aside to Jean Prouvaire.

"No," replied Jean Prouvaire, "it's serious."

Indeed, it was serious. Marius was in the first violently enthralled throes of a grand passion.

One glance was enough.

When the gun is loaded, and the match is ready, nothing is simpler. A glance is a spark.

Marius was done for. He loved a woman. His destiny was entering the unknown.

The glances of women are like certain seemingly peaceful but really formidable machines. Every day you pass them in peace, with impunity, and without suspicion of danger. There comes a moment when you forget even that they are there. You come and go, you muse, and talk, and laugh. Suddenly you feel caught up! It is all over. The wheels have you, the glance has captured you. It has caught you, no matter how or where, by some wandering of your thought, through a momentary distraction. You are lost. You will be drawn in entirely. A train of mysterious forces has gained possession of you. You struggle in vain. No human succor is possible. You will be drawn down from wheel to wheel, from anguish to anguish, from torture to torture. You, your mind, your fortune, your future, your soul; and you will not leave the awesome machine, until, depending on whether you are in the power of a malevolent creature, or a noble heart, you are disfigured by shame or transfigured by love.

VII

ADVENTURES OF THE LETTER *U* ABANDONED TO CONJECTURE

Isolation, separation from all things, pride, independence, a taste for nature, lack of everyday material activity, life in itself, the secret struggles of chastity, and an ecstasy of goodwill toward the whole of creation, had prepared Marius for this possession called love. His worship for his father had gradually become a religion, and, like all religion, had withdrawn to his innermost heart. He needed something in the foreground. Love came.

A whole long month passed while Marius went to the Luxembourg every day. When the hour came, nothing could keep him away. "He's on duty," said Courfeyrac. Marius was living in the clouds, certain that the young girl was looking at him.

He finally grew bolder, and went up closer to the bench. However, he no longer walked past it, obeying at once the instinct of timidity and the instinct of prudence peculiar to lovers. He thought it better not to attract the "attention of the father." He formed his worked-out positions behind trees and the pedestals of statues with consummate art, so as to be seen as much as possible by the young girl and as little as possible by the old gentleman. Sometimes he would stand for half an hour at a time motionless behind some Leonidas or Spartacus with a book in his hand, over which his eyes, timidly raised, were looking for the young girl, while she was turning her charming profile toward him, with a faint smile. While talking away quite naturally and easily with the white-haired man, she rested on Marius all the reverie of a young girl's passionate eye. Ancient and immemorial art known by Eve from the first day of the world and by every woman from the first day of her life! Her tongue replied to one and her eyes to the other.

We must, however, suppose that M. Leblanc perceived something of this at last, for often when Marius came, he would get up and begin to take a walk. He had left their usual spot and taken the bench at the other end of the walk, near the Gladiator, as though to see whether Marius would follow them. Marius did not understand it and committed that blunder. "The father" began to be less punctual and did not bring "his daughter" every day. Sometimes he came alone. Then Marius did not stay. Another blunder.

Marius took no note of these symptoms. From the timid phase he had gone, by natural, inevitable progress, to the phase of blindness. His love was growing. He dreamed of her every night. And then an unexpected stroke of luck came his way, oil upon the fire, double darkness on his eyes. One night, at dusk, he found on the seat, which "M. Leblanc and his daughter" had just left, a handkerchief, a plain handkerchief without embroidery, but white, fine, and seeming to exude ineffable perfume. He seized it in ecstasy. The handkerchief was marked with the letters U. F.: Marius knew nothing of this beautiful girl, neither her family, nor her name, nor her address; these two letters were the first thing he had caught of her, adorable initials on which he immediately began to build his castle. *U* was clearly her first initial. Ursula, he thought, what a sweet name! He kissed the handkerchief, inhaled its perfume, put it over his heart, against his flesh in the daytime, and at night went to sleep with it on his lips.

"I feel her whole soul in it!" he exclaimed.

The handkerchief belonged to the old gentleman, who had simply dropped it from his pocket.

For days and days after this piece of good fortune, he always appeared at the Luxembourg kissing this handkerchief and placing it on his heart. The beautiful child did not understand this at all, and told him so through imperceptible signs.

"Oh, modesty!" said Marius.

VIII

EVEN THE INVALIDES MAY BE LUCKY

Since we have pronounced the word "modesty," and since we conceal nothing, we must say that once, however, through all his ecstasy "his Ursula" gave him a very serious pang. It was one of the days when she prevailed on M. Leblanc to leave the bench and walk down the path. A brisk north wind was blowing, which swayed the tops of the plane trees. Father and daughter, arm in arm, had just passed Marius's bench. Marius had stood up behind them and was following them with his eyes, as was natural in this desperate situation of the heart.

Suddenly a gust of wind, rather more lively than the rest, and probably entrusted with the little affairs of spring, flew down from La Pépinière, rushed onto the walk, wrapped the young girl in a lovely tremor worthy of Virgil's nymphs and the fauns of Theocritus, and raised her skirt, this skirt more sacred than that of Isis, almost to the garter. An exquisite limb was seen. Marius saw it. He was exasperated and furious.

The young girl had quickly smoothed down her dress with a gracefully startled gesture, but he was outraged nonetheless. True, he was alone in the walk. But there could have been somebody there. And if anyone had been there! Who could conceive of such a thing? What she had done was horrible! Alas, the poor child had done nothing, the wind was the sole culprit and yet Marius in whom all the Bartholo concealed in Cherubino was dazedly trembling, was determined to be cross, and was jealous of his own shadow. For this is the way the strange, bitter jealousy of the flesh is awakened in the human heart and imposed on man, however unjustly. But aside from this jealousy, there was nothing agreeable to him in the sight of that beautiful limb; the white stocking of any other woman would have given him more pleasure.

When "his Ursula," after reaching the end of the walk, and turning back with M. Leblanc, passed the bench where Marius had sat down again, he threw at her an angry, ferocious look. The young girl recoiled slightly, with that raising of the eyelids that says, "What is the matter with him?"

That was their first quarrel.

Marius had hardly finished this scene with her when somebody came down the walk. It was a disabled veteran, very bent, wrinkled and pale with age, in his Louis XV uniform, bearing the small oval patch of red cloth with crossed swords on his back, the soldier's Cross of Saint-Louis, and decorated also by an empty coat sleeve, a silver chin, and a wooden leg. Marius thought he could detect a very contented air about this man. It even seemed to him that the old cynic, as he hobbled along nearby, had given him a merry fraternal wink, as if they had some chance understanding and had shared some happy bit of good fortune. What had this relic of Mars seen to be so pleased? What had gone on between this leg of wood and the other? Marius felt a paroxysm of jealousy. "Perhaps he was there!" he said. "Perhaps he saw!" And he would have gladly strangled the veteran.

Time lending its aid, every sharp point is blunted. Marius's anger against "Ursula," however just and proper it might be, passed away. He forgave her at last; but it took a great effort; he sulked for three days.

Meanwhile, in spite of all that, and because of all that, his passion was growing, was growing frenzied.

IX

AN ECLIPSE

We have seen how Marius discovered, or thought he discovered, that her name was Ursula.

Hunger comes with love. To know that her name was Ursula was already a good deal, but not enough. In three or four weeks Marius had digested this piece of good fortune. He wanted another. He wanted to know where she lived.

He had committed one blunder in falling into the snare of the seat near the Gladiator. He had committed a second by not staying at the Luxembourg when M. Leblanc came there alone. He committed a third, a monstrous one. He followed "Ursula."

She lived in the Rue de l'Ouest, in the least populated part of it, in a new, modest three-story house.

From that moment Marius added to the happiness of seeing her at the Luxembourg, the happiness of following her home.

His hunger increased. He knew her name, her first name, at least, the charming name, the real name of a woman; he knew where she lived; he wanted to know who she was.

One night after he had followed them home, and seen them disappear through the carriage door, he went in after them, and said boldly to the doorkeeper, "Is it the gentleman on the second floor who has just come in?"

"No. It is the gentleman on the third."

Another fact. This success made Marius still bolder.

"In front?" he asked.

"My God!" said the doorkeeper. "The house only looks out on the street."

"And what is this gentleman?"

"He lives on his income, monsieur. A very kind man, who does a great deal of good for the poor, though not rich."

"What is his name?" continued Marius.

The porter raised his head, and said, "Is monsieur a detective?"

Marius retired, much abashed, but still in great transports. This represented progress.

"Good," he thought. "I know that her name is Ursula, that she is the daughter of a retired gentleman, and that she lives there, on the third floor, on the Rue de l'Ouest."

Next day M. Leblanc and his daughter made only a short visit to the Luxembourg; they went away while it was still broad daylight. Marius followed them to the Rue de l'Ouest, as was his custom. On reaching the carriage door, M. Leblanc had his daughter go in, then stopped, and before entering himself, turned and stared at Marius. The day after that they did not come to the Luxembourg. Marius waited in vain all day.

At nightfall he went to the Rue de l'Ouest, and saw a light in the windows of the third story. He walked under the windows until the light was put out.

The next day, nobody at the Luxembourg. Marius waited all day and then went to perform his night duty under the windows. That took him till ten in the evening. His dinner took care of itself. Fever supports the sick man, and love the lover.

He spent a week this way. M. Leblanc and his daughter appeared at the Luxembourg no more. Marius made melancholy conjectures; he did not dare watch the carriage door during the day. He limited himself to going at night to gaze at the reddish light of the windows. At times he saw shadows moving, and his heart beat faster.

On the eighth day when he reached the house, there was no light in the windows. "Well now!" he said, "the lamp is not lit yet. Yet it's dark. Or have they gone out?" He waited till ten. Till midnight. Till one in the morning. No light appeared in the third-story windows, and nobody entered the house. He went away very gloomy.

The next day—he lived only for tomorrow; there was no today left, so to speak, for him—the next day, as he had expected, he found nobody at the Luxembourg; at dusk he went to the house. No light in the windows; the blinds were closed; the third story was entirely dark.

Marius knocked at the carriage door, went in, and said to the doorkeeper, "The gentleman of the third floor?"

"Moved."

Marius tottered, and said feebly, "Since when?"

"Yesterday."

"Where does he live now?"

"I have no idea."

"And he didn't leave his new address?"

"No."

And the doorkeeper, looking up, recognized Marius.

"So! It's you!" he said. "You definitely do keep a sharp lookout."

Book Seven

PATRON-MINETTE

I

MINES AND MINERS

Every human society has what is called in the theaters a "third substage." The social soil is mined everywhere, sometimes for good, sometimes for evil. These works happen in strata; there are upper and lower mines. There is a top and a bottom to this dark subsoil, which sometimes sinks beneath civilization, to be carelessly trampled underfoot by our indifference. In the last century, the Encyclopedia was almost a strip mine. The dark caverns, those gloomy incubators of primitive Christianity, were merely awaiting an opportunity to explode beneath the Caesars and to flood the human race with light. For in the sacred shadow there is latent light. Volcanoes are full of a darkness capable of flashing flames. All lava begins at midnight. The catacombs, where the first mass was said, were not merely Rome's cellar; they were the undermining of the world.

Beneath the social structure, that complex wonder of a mighty burrow, there are excavations of every kind. There is the religious mine, the philosophic mine, the political mine, the economic mine, the revolutionary mine. This pick is an idea, that pick is a figure, the other pick is a vengeance. They call and they answer from one catacomb to another. Utopias travel underground through these conduits. They branch out in every direction. They sometimes meet there and fraternize. Jean-Jacques lends his pick to Diogenes, who lends him his lantern. Sometimes they fight. Calvin grabs Socinius by the hair. But nothing checks or interrupts the tension of all these energies toward their object or the vast simultaneous activity that goes to and fro, and up and down, and up again in these murky regions, and slowly transforms the upper through the lower, and the outer through the inner; vast hidden swarming of workers. Society catches hardly a hint of this work of undermining, which, without touching the surface, changes its substance. So many subterranean stages, so many differing labors, so many varying excavations. What comes from all this deep delving? The future.

The deeper we sink, the more mysterious are the workers. To a degree that social philosophy can recognize, the work is good; beyond that degree, it is doubtful and mixed; below, it becomes terrible. At certain depths, the excavations become impenetrable to the soul of civilization, man's breathing limit surpassed; the existence of monsters becomes possible.

The descending ladder is a strange one; each of its rungs corresponds to a step where philosophy can set foot, and where we discover one of her workers, sometimes divine, sometimes monstrous. Below Jan Hus is Luther; below Luther is Descartes; below Descartes is Voltaire; below Voltaire is Condorcet; below Condorcet is Robespierre; below Robespierre is Marat; below Marat is Babeuf. And that keeps on. Lower still, at the confused limit separating the indistinct from the invisible, are glimpsed other somber men, who perhaps do not yet exist. Those of yesterday are specters; those of tomorrow are larvae. The mind's eye dimly makes them out. The embryonic work of the future is one of the philosopher's visions.

A fetus world in limbo, what an incredible silhouette!

Saint-Simon, Owen, Fourier, are there, too, in side galleries.

Indeed, though an invisible divine chain links all these subterranean pioneers, who almost always believe they are isolated, and yet are not, their labors are very diverse, and the glow of some men contrasts with the flame of others. Some are paradisaic, others are tragic. Nevertheless, whatever the contrast, all these workers from the highest to the deepest down, from the wisest to the craziest, have one thing in common, and that is disinterestedness. Marat, like Jesus, forgets about himself. They leave self aside; they omit it; they do not think of themselves. They see something other than themselves. They have a light in their eyes, and that light is searching for the absolute. The highest has all heaven in his eyes; the lowest, enigmatic as he may be, still has beneath his brows the pale glow of the infinite. Whatever he may do, venerate anyone who has this sign, the star-eye.

The shadow-eye is the other sign.

There begins evil. Before the one whose eye has no light, reflect and tremble. Social order has its dark miners.

There is a point where undermining becomes burial, and where light goes out.

Below all these mines we have mentioned, below all these galleries, below this immense underground venous system of progress and utopia, far deeper in the earth, lower than Marat, lower than Babeuf, lower, much lower, and without any connection with the upper galleries, is the ultimate hole. An awe-inspiring place. This is what we have called the third substage. It is the grave of shadows. It is the cave of the blind *Inferi*.

It gives onto the abyss.

II

THE LOWEST DEPTHS

There disinterestedness vanishes. The demon is dimly present; every man for himself. The eyeless self howls, searches, gropes, and gnaws. The social Ugolino is in this chasm.

The savage outlines prowling this trough, half brute, half phantom, have no thought for universal progress, they do not know the idea or the word, they merely care for individual glut. They are almost unconscious, and within them there is a horrible obliteration. They have two mothers, both stepmothers, ignorance and misery. They have one guide, want; and their only form of satisfaction is appetite. They are voracious as beasts, that is to say ferocious, not like the tyrant, but like the tiger. From suffering, these goblins go on to crime; fated filiation, giddy procreation, the logic of darkness. What creeps around the third substage is no longer the stifled demand for the absolute, it is the protest of matter. Man there becomes dragon. Hunger and thirst are the point of departure; Satan is the point of arrival. From this cave comes Lacenaire.

In the fourth book, we have just seen one of the compartments of the upper mine, the great political, revolutionary, and philosophic undermining. There, as we have said, all is noble, pure, worthy, and honorable. There, it is true, men may be mistaken, and do make mistakes, but there error is venerable, because it involves so much heroism. For the sum of all work done there, there is one name: Progress.

The time has come to open other depths, horrible ones.

Beneath society there is, we insist, and until the day when ignorance disappears, the great cavern of evil.

This cave below everything is the enemy of all. It is universal hatred. This cave knows no philosophers; its dagger has never sharpened a pen. Its blackness has no relation to the sublime blackness of handwriting. Never have the fingers of night, clenching beneath this asphyxiating vault, turned the leaves of a book or unfolded a journal. Babeuf is a mere precursor of Cartouche; Marat is an aristocrat to Schinderhannes. The object of this cave is the ruin of all things.

Of all things. Including the upper mines, which it execrates. In its teeming horror, it does not undermine only the social order of the time; it undermines philosophy, it undermines science, law, human thought, civilization, revolution, progress. It goes by the stark names of theft, prostitution, murder, and assassination. It is darkness, and it desires chaos. It is vaulted with ignorance.

All the others, those above it, have only one object—to eliminate it. To that end philosophy and progress work through all their organs at the same time, through amelioration of the real as well as through contemplation of the absolute. Destroy the cave Ignorance, and you destroy the mole Crime.

We will condense in a few words a portion of what we have just said. The only social peril is darkness.

Humanity is similarity. All men are of the same clay. No difference, here below at least, lies in predestination. The same darkness before, the same flesh during, the same ashes after life. But ignorance, mixed with the human composition, blackens it. This incurable ignorance possesses the heart of man, and there becomes Evil.

III

BABET, GUEULEMER CLAQUESOUS, AND MONTPARNASSE

A quartet of bandits, Claquesous, Gueulemer, Babet, and Montparnasse, from 1830 to 1835 ruled over the third substage of Paris.

Gueulemer was a Hercules without a pedestal. His lair was the Arche-Marion sewer. He was six feet tall, and had a chest of iron, brazen biceps, cavernous lungs, a colossus's body, and a bird's skull. You would think you were seeing the Farnese Hercules dressed in canvas trousers and a cotton-velvet waistcoat. Gueulemer, built on this sculptural frame, could have subdued monsters; he found it easier to become one. Low forehead, large temples with crow's feet at less than forty, coarse short hair, a bushy cheek, a wild boar's beard; you can picture the man. His muscles asked for work, his stupidity would have none of it. This was a huge lazy power. He was an assassin through nonchalance. He was thought to be a creole. Probably there was a little of Marshal Brune in him, he having been a porter at Avignon in 1815. After that he had become a bandit.

Babet's diaphanous quality contrasted with the meatiness of Gueulemer. Babet was thin and shrewd. He was transparent but impenetrable. You could see daylight through his bones, but nothing through his eye. He professed to be a chemist. He had been clown for Bobèche, and buffoon for Bobino. He had played vaudeville at Saint-Mihiel. He was an affected man, a great talker, who italicized his smiles and put quotation marks around his gestures. His business was to sell in the street plaster busts and portraits of the "head of the Government." In addition, he pulled teeth. He had exhibited monstrosities at fairs, and had a booth with a trumpet and this placard: "Babet, dental artist, member of the Academies, physical experimenter on metals and metalloids, extirpates teeth, removes stumps left by other dentists. Price: one tooth, one franc fifty centimes; two teeth, two francs; three teeth, two francs fifty centimes. Don't miss this opportunity" (which meant "Get as many pulled as possible"). He had been married and had had offspring. He did not know what had become of his wife and children. He had lost them the way he might have lost his handkerchief. A remarkable exception in the obscure world to which he belonged, Babet read the papers. One day, during the time he had his family with him in his traveling booth, he had read in the *Messager* that a woman had been delivered of a child, likely to live, which had the face of a calf, and had exclaimed, "A fortune! My wife doesn't have the sense to bear me a child like that." Since then, he had left everything, "to take Paris in hand." His own expression.

What was Claquesous? He was night. Before showing himself, he waited till the sky was daubed with black. At night he came out of a hole, to which he returned before day. Where was this hole? Nobody knew. In the most perfect darkness, and to his accomplices, he always turned his back when he spoke. Was his name Claquesous? No. He said, "My name is Nothing-at-all." If a candle was brought he put on a mask. He was a ventriloquist. Babet said, "Claquesous is a nightbird with two voices." Claquesous was restless, roving, terrible. It was not certain he had a name, Claquesous being a nickname; it was not certain he had a voice, his stomach speaking more often than his mouth; it was not certain he had a face, nobody having seen anything but this mask. He disappeared as if he melted into thin air; he came and went like an apparition.

A mournful sight, that was Montparnasse. Montparnasse was a child; less than twenty, with a pretty face, lips like cherries, charming black hair, the glow of spring in his eyes; he had all the vices and aspired to all the crimes. The digestion of what was bad gave him an appetite for what was worse. He was *gamin* turned hooligan, hooligan turned assassin. He was gentle, effeminate, graceful, robust, weak, and ferocious. He wore his hat turned up on the left side, to better show off a lock of hair, according to the fashion of 1829. He lived by violent robbery. His coat was of the most fashionable cut, but threadbare. Montparnasse was a fashionplate living in distress and committing murders. The cause of all this young man's crimes was his desire to be well dressed. The first grisette who had said to him, "You are handsome," had spattered a stain of darkness into his heart and had made a Cain of this Abel. Thinking he was handsome, he wanted to be elegant; now, the first of elegances is idleness; idleness for a poor man is crime. Few prowlers were so much feared as Montparnasse. At eighteen, he already had left several corpses in his wake. More than one traveler lay in this wretch's shadow with outstretched arms and with his face in a pool of blood. Frizzled, pomaded, pinched in at the waist, hips like a woman, the bust of a Prussian officer, a buzz of admiration about him from the girls of the boulevard, an elaborately knotted tie, a billystick in his pocket, a flower in his buttonhole; such was this charmer of the shadows.

IV

MAKEUP OF THE BAND

These four bandits formed a sort of Proteus, snaking right through the police and endeavoring to escape from the indiscreet glances of Vidocq "in various forms, tree, flame, and fountain," lending each other their names and their tricks, concealing themselves in their own shadow, each a refuge and a hiding place for the others, sloughing off their personalities, as one takes off a false nose at a masked ball, sometimes simplifying themselves down to one, sometimes multiplying themselves till Coco-Lacour himself took them for a mob.

These four men were not four men at all, but a sort of mysterious robber with four heads preying on Paris wholesale; they were a monstrous polyp of evil that inhabits the crypt of society.

By means of their ramifications and the underlying network of relationships, Babet, Gueulemer, Claquesous, and Montparnasse controlled the general ambush business of the Département of the Seine. Originators of ideas in this line, men of midnight imagination, came to them for the execution. When the four villains were furnished with the first draft they would take charge of staging it. They worked up a scenario. They were always in a position to furnish a company in proportion and suitable to any enterprise that stood in want and was sufficiently lucrative. If a crime was in need of strong arms, they supplied accomplices to it. They had a company of actors of darkness at the disposition of every cavern tragedy.

They usually met at nightfall, their waking hour, in the waste grounds near La Salpêtrière. There they conferred. They had the twelve dark hours before them; they alloted their use.

Patron-Minette, such was the name given in underworld society to the association of these four men. In the fantastic old popular language, rapidly dying out, *Patron-Minette* means "morning," just as *entre chien et loup*, between dog and wolf, means "night." This name, Patron-Minette, probably came from the hour when their work ended, the dawn being the moment for the disappearance of phantoms and the dispersal of bandits. These four were known by that title. When the chief judge of the superior court visited Lacenaire in prison, he questioned him regarding some crime, which Lacenaire denied. "Who did do it?" asked the judge. Lacenaire made this reply, enigmatic to the magistrate, but clear to the police, "Patron-Minette, perhaps."

Sometimes a play can be imagined from the cast of characters: So, too, we can almost understand a band from the listing of the criminals. Here, since the names are preserved in documents, are the names to which the principal subordinates of Patron-Minette responded:

Panchaud, alias Printanier, alias Bigrenaille.

Brujon. (There was a dynasty of Brujons; we shall say something about it later.)

Boulatruelle, the roadmender, already introduced.

Laveuve.

Finistère.

Homer Hogu, a black man.

Mardisoir.

Dépêche.
Fauntleroy, alias Bouquetière.
Glorieux, a freed convict.
Barrecarrosse, alias M. Dupont.
Lesplanade-du-Sud.
Poussagrive.
Carmagnolet.
Kruideniers, alias Bizarro.
Mangedentelle.
Les-pieds-en-l'air.
Demi-liard, alias Deux-milliards.
Etc., etc.

We will ship some of them and not the worst. These names have faces. They signify not only beings, but species. Each of the names answers to a variety of misshapen toadstools of civilization's substrata.

These beings, by no means free about showing their faces, were not like those we see passing in the streets. During the day, wearied by their savage nights, they would go away to sleep, sometimes in the plaster-kilns, sometimes in the abandoned quarries of Montmartre or Montrouge, sometimes in the sewers. They burrowed.

What has become of these men? They still exist. They have always existed. Horace speaks of them: *Ambubaiarum collegia, pharmacopoloe, mendici, mimoe;* and so long as society remains what it is, they will be what they are. Under the dark vault of their cave, they are forever reproduced from the seepage of society. They return, specters, always the same; but they no longer bear the same name, and they are no longer in the same skins.

The individuals exterminated, the tribe still exists.

They always have the same faculties. From beggar to prowler, the race preserves its purity. They divine purses in pockets, they scent watches in fobs. To them gold and silver have a scent. There are naive bourgeois of whom you might say that they look robbable. These men patiently follow these bourgeois. When a foreigner or a peasant passes by, they quiver like a spider.

When, toward midnight, on a lone boulevard, you meet such men, or catch a glimpse of them, they are terrifying. They do not seem like men, but forms fashioned of the living mist; you would say that they are generally an integral portion of the darkness, that they are not distinct from it, that they have no soul beyond the gloom, and that it is only temporarily, to live a monstrous life for a few minutes, that they broke away from the night.

What is required to exorcise these goblins? Light. Floods of light. No bat can resist the dawn. Throw light on the society below.

Book Eight

THE NOXIOUS POOR

I

MARIUS, LOOKING FOR A GIRL IN A HAT, MEETS A MAN IN A CAP

Summer went by, then autumn; winter came. Neither M. Leblanc nor the young girl had set foot in the Luxembourg. Marius had one thought only, to see that sweet adorable face again. He searched continually, he searched everywhere: He found nothing. He was no longer Marius the enthusiastic dreamer, the resolute man, ardent yet firm, the bold challenger of destiny, the brain that projected and built future upon future, the young heart full of plans, projects, prides, ideas, and desires; he was a lost dog. He fell into a melancholy. It was all over for him. Work disgusted him, walking fatigued him, solitude wearied him, vast nature, once so full of forms, of illuminations, of voices, of counsels, of perspectives, of horizons, of teachings, was now empty in front of him. It seemed to him that everything had disappeared.

He was still pensive, for he could not be otherwise; but he no longer found pleasure in his thoughts. To everything silently but persistently proposed, he gloomily answered, What's the use?

He reproached himself a hundred times over. "Why did I follow her? I was so happy simply seeing her! She looked at me; wasn't that a lot? She seemed to love me. Wasn't that everything? After that there is nothing more. I was a fool. It's my own fault," etc. etc. Courfeyrac, to whom he confided nothing, that was his nature, but who had some inkling of the whole thing—had begun by congratulating him on being in love, actually amazed about it; then seeing Marius fallen into this melancholy, he had finally said to him, "I see that you've been prey to the senses. I tell you what, come to the Chaumière.

Once, taking heart from a beautiful September sun, Marius went along to the Bal de Sceaux, with Courfeyrac, Bossuet, and Grantaire, hoping—what a dream! —that he might possibly find her there. Needless to say, he did not. "Yet it's here that all the lost women are found," muttered Grantaire. Marius left his friends at the ball, and went back on foot alone, tired, feverish, with eyes sad and troubled in the dark, overcome by the noise and dust of the joyous coaches full of singing parties who passed him on their way back from the dance, while he, discouraged, was breathing in the pungent odor of the walnut trees by the wayside, to clear his head.

He lived more and more alone, bewildered, overwhelmed, given up to his inward anguish, pacing in his grief like a wolf in a cage, everywhere seeking the absent, dazed with love.

Another time, an accidental meeting produced a strange effect on him. In one of the little streets near the Boulevard des Invalides, he saw a man dressed like a laborer, wearing a cap with a long visor, which left a few locks of very white hair showing. Marius was struck by the beauty of this white hair, and noticed the man, who was walking slowly and seemed absorbed in painful meditation. Strangely enough, he thought he recognized M. Leblanc. It was the same hair, the same profile, as far as the cap allowed him to see, the same manner, only sadder. But why these workingman's clothes? What did that mean? What did this disguise signify? Marius was astounded. When he came to himself, his first impulse was to follow the man; who knows if he had finally picked up the trail he was seeking? In any event, he had to see the man again nearer, and clear up the enigma. But this idea occurred to him too late, the man was gone. He had taken some little side street, and Marius could not find him again. This encounter haunted him for a few days, and then faded away. "After all," he said to himself, "it is probably only a similarity."

II

A WAIF

Marius was still living in the Gorbeau building. He paid no attention to anybody there.

At the time, it is true, there were no tenants left in the house but himself and those Jondrettes whose rent he had once paid, without having ever spoken, actually, to either the father, or the mother, or the daughters. The other tenants had moved away or died, or had been turned out for not paying their rent.

One day, in the course of that winter, the sun had come out for a while in the afternoon, but it was the second of February, that ancient Candlemas-day whose treacherous sun, the precursor of six weeks of cold, inspired Matthew Laensberg with the two lines, which have deservedly become classic:

Qu'il luise ou qu'il luiserne,
L'ours rentre en sa caverne.[1]

Marius had just left his; night was falling. It was his dinnertime, for he had simply had to return to the habit of dinner, alas! Oh, infirmity of the ideal passions.

He had just crossed his threshold, which Ma'am Bougon was sweeping at that very moment, muttering at the same time this memorable monologue:

"What is there that's cheap now? Everything's expensive. People's troubles, that's all that's cheap. That's free, people's troubles."

Marius went slowly up the boulevard toward the city gate, on the way to the Rue Saint-Jacques. He was walking thoughtfully, with his head down.

Suddenly he felt someone elbow him in the dusk; he turned, and saw two young girls in rags, one tall and slender, the other a little shorter, passing by rapidly, breathless, frightened, and apparently in flight; they had

[1] Let it gleam or let it glimmer,
The bear goes back into his cave.

been coming toward him, had not seen him, and had jostled him in passing. In the twilight Marius could see their pale faces, hair tangled and flying, dreadful bonnets, tattered skirts, and bare feet. As they ran they were talking to each other. The taller one said in a very low voice, "The cops came. They almost pinched me at the circle."

The other answered, "I saw them. I made tracks."

Marius understood through their breathless talk that the gendarmes had not managed to capture these two young girls.

They dashed in under the trees of the boulevard behind him, and for a few seconds made a kind of dim patch of light among the shadows.

Marius stopped for a moment.

He was about to go on his way when he noticed a little grayish packet on the ground at his feet. He stooped down and picked it up. It was a sort of envelope that appeared to contain papers.

"All right," he said, "those poor creatures must have dropped this!"

He retraced his steps, he called, he did not find them; he concluded they were already beyond hearing, put the packet in his pocket and went off to dinner.

On his way, in an alley on the Rue Mouffetard, he saw a child's coffin covered with a black cloth, placed on three chairs and lit by a candle. He thought again of the two girls in the twilight.

"Poor mothers," he thought. "There's one thing sadder than to see their children die—to see them lead evil lives."

Then these shadows that had varied his sadness left his mind, and he fell back into his customary train of thought. He began to think again of his six months of love and happiness in the open air and the broad daylight under the beautiful trees of the Luxembourg.

"How somber my life has become!" he said to himself. "Young girls still appear in front of me. Except that they used to be angels; now they are ghouls."

III

FOUR-FACED JANUS

In the evening, as he was undressing for bed, he happened to feel in his coat pocket the packet he had picked up on the boulevard. He had forgotten it. He thought it might be well to open it, that the packet might contain the address of the young girls, if it really did belong to them, or in any event the information necessary to restore it to the person who had lost it.

He opened the envelope.

It was unsealed and contained four letters, also unsealed.

The addresses were on them.

All four gave off an odor of awful tobacco.

The first letter was addressed: *To Madame la Marquise de Grucheray, Square opposite the Chamber of Deputies, No.———*

Marius said to himself that he would probably find in the letter the information he was looking for, and that anyway, since the letter was not sealed, it could probably be read without impropriety.

It was as follows:

"MADAME LA MARQUISE:

The virtue of kindness and piety is what binds sosiety most closely. Call up your christian sentiment, and cast a look of compassion upon this unfortunate Spanish victim of loyalty and attachment to the sacred cause of legitimacy, which he has paid for with his blood, devoted his fortune, wholy, to defend this cause, and today finds himself in the greatest missery. He has no doubt that your honorable self will furnish him assistance to preserve an existence extremely painful for a soldier of education and of honor full of wounds, reckons in advance on the humanity that animmates you and on the interest which Madame la Marquise feels to a nation so unfortunate. Their prayer will not be in vain, and their gratitude will keep herr charming memory.

"From my respectful sentiments with which I have the honor to be,

"Madame,

"DON ALVARES, Spanish captain of cabalry, royalist refugee in France, who finds himself traveling for his country and resources failing him to continue his travels."

No address was added to the signature. Marius hoped to find the address in the second letter, whose heading ran: *to Madame, Madame la Comtess de Montvernet, Rue Cassette, No. 9.* Marius read as follows:

"MADAME LA COMTESS: This is an unfortunate mothur of a family of six children the last of whom is only eight months old, sick since my last lying-in, abandoned by my husband for five months haveing no ressources in the world the most frightful poverty.

"In the hope of Madame la Comtesse, she has the honor to be, Madame, with a profound respect,

"MOTHER BALIZARD."

Marius went on to the third which, like those preceding, was a plea; it read:

"MONSIEUR PABOURGEOT, elector, wholesale milliner, Rue Saint-Denis, corner of the Rue aux Fers.

"I take the liberty to address you this letter to pray you to accord me the favor of your simpathies and to interest you in a man of letters who has just sent a drama to the Théatre Français. Its subject is historical, and the action takes place in Auvergne in the time of the empire: Its style, I believe, is natural, laconic, and perhaps has some merit. There are verses to be sung in four places. The comic, the serious, the unforeseen, mingle with the variety of the characters and with a tint of romance spread lightly over all the plot, which advances misteriously, and by striking terns, to an outcome in the midst of several splendid scenes.

"My principal object is to satisfy the desire which progressively animates the man of our century, that is to say, fashion, that caprisious and grotesque weathercock which changes almost with every new wind.

"In spite of these qualities I have reason to fear that jealousy, the selfishness of the privileged authors, may secure my exclusion from the theater, for I am not ignorant of the distaste with which newcomers are swallowed.

"Monsieur Pabourgeot, your just reputation as an enlightened protector of literary fokes emboldens me to send my daughter to you, who will expose to you our indignant situation, needing bread and fire in this winter season. To tell you that I pray you to accept the homage which I desire to offer you in my drama and in all those which I make, is to prove to you how ambicious I am of the honor of sheltering myself under your aegis, and of adorning my writings with your name. If you deign to honor me with the most modest offering, I shall occupy myself immediately with a piece of verse for you to pay my tribut of recognition. This piece, which I will try to render as perfect as possible, will be sent to you before being inserted in the beginning of the drama and given on the stage.

"To Monsieur and Madame Pabourgeot,
My most respectful homage,

GENFLOT, man of letters.

"P.S. Were it only forty sous.

"Excuse me for sending my daughter and for not presenting myself, but sad motives of dress do not permit me, alas! to go out . . ."

Marius finally opened the fourth letter. There was on the address: *To the beneficent gentleman of the church of Saint-Jaques-du-Haut-Pas*. It contained these few lines:

"BENEFICENT MAN.

"If you will deign to accompany my daughter, you will see a misserable calamity, and I will show you my certificates.

"At the sight of these writings your generous soul will be moved with a sentiment of lively benevolence, for true philosophers always experience vivid emotions.

"Agree, compassionate man, that one must experience the most cruel necessity, and that to obtain relief it is very painful to have it witnessed by authority, as if we were not free to suffer and to die of starvation while waiting for some one to relieve our missery. The fates are very cruel to some and too lavish or too protective to others.

"I await your presence or your offering, if you deign to make it, and I pray you to have the kindness to accept the respectful sentiments with which I am proud to be,

"truly magnanimous man,
"your very humble
and very obedient servant,
"P. FABANTOU, dramatic artist."

After reading these four letters, Marius did not find himself much wiser than before.

In the first place none of the signers gave his address.

Then they seemed to come from four different individuals, Don Alvarès, Mother Balizard, the poet Genflot, and the dramatic artist Fabantou; but, strangely enough, these letters were all four written in the same hand.

What could he conclude from that, unless that they came from the same person?

In addition, and this made the conjecture still more likely, the paper, coarse and yellowing, was the same in all four, the odor of tobacco was the same, and although there was an evident attempt to vary the style, the same spelling mistakes were reproduced with a quiet certainty, and Genflot, the man of letters, was no more free from them than the Spanish captain.

Any attempt to solve this little mystery would be useless. If it had not been a stray find, it would have seemed a mystification. Marius was too sad to take a chance joke kindly or to lend himself to the game that the pavement seemed to be playing with him. It was as though he was playing blind man's buff among the four letters, which were mocking him.

Nothing, however, indicated that these letters belonged to the girls whom Marius had met on the boulevard. After all, they were merely a bunch of old papers and clearly of no value.

Marius put them back into the envelope, threw it into a corner, and went to bed.

Around seven in the morning, he had gotten up and breakfasted, and was trying to set to work when there was a gentle knock at his door.

Since he had no possessions, he never removed the key

from his door, except very rarely, when he was doing some pressing piece of work. And, in fact, even when he was away, he left his key in the lock. "You will be robbed," said Ma'am Bougon. "Of what?" asked Marius. The fact is, however, that one day somebody had stolen an old pair of boots, to Ma'am Bougon's great triumph.

There was a second knock, very gentle like the first.

"Come in," said Marius.

The door opened.

"What do you want, Ma'am Bougon?" asked Marius, without raising his eyes from the books and papers he had on his table.

A voice, which was not Ma'am Bougon's, answered, "I beg your pardon, monsieur . . ."

It was a hollow, cracked, smothered, rasping voice, the voice of an old man, roughened by brandy and liquors.

Marius turned quickly and saw a young girl.

IV

A ROSE IN MISERY

A girl who was quite young was standing in the half-opened door. The little round window through which the light found its way into the garret was exactly opposite the door, and lit up this form with a pallid light. It was a pale, puny, meager creature, nothing but a blouse and a skirt covered her shivering, chilled nudity. A string for a belt, a string for a headdress, bony shoulders protruding from the blouse, a blond and lymphatic pallor, dirty shoulderblades, red hands, the mouth open and sickly, some teeth missing, the eyes dull, bold, and drooping, the form of a misshapen young girl and the stare of a corrupted old woman; fifty years joined to fifteen, one of those beings who are both frail and horrible, who make people shudder or weep.

Marius stood up and gazed with a kind of astonishment at this being, so much like the shadowy forms that pass across our dreams.

The most touching thing about it was that this young girl had not come into the world to be ugly. In her early childhood, she must have even been pretty. The grace of her youth was still struggling against the hideous old age brought on by debauchery and poverty. A remnant of beauty was dying out on this face of sixteen, like the pale sun extinguished by terrible clouds at the dawn of a winter's day.

The face was not absolutely unknown to Marius. He thought he remembered seeing it somewhere.

"What do you want, mademoiselle?" he asked.

The young girl answered with her voice like a drunken convict, "Here is a letter for you, Monsieur Marius."

She called Marius by his name; he could not doubt that her business was with him; but who was this girl? How did she know his name?

Without waiting for an invitation, she came in. She came in resolutely, looking at the whole room and the unmade bed with a sort of assurance that chilled the heart. She was barefoot. Great holes in her skirt revealed her long limbs and her sharp knees. She was shivering.

As it turned out, she had in her hand a letter, which she presented to Marius.

In opening this letter, Marius noticed that the enormously large seal was still wet. The message could not have come far. He read:

"My amiable neighbor, young man!

"I have lerned your kindness towards me, that you paid my rent six months ago. I bless you, young man. My eldest daughter will tell you that we have been without a morsel of bread for two days, four persons, and my spouse sick. If I am not desseived, I think I may hope that your generous heart will soften at this exposure and will incline you to be propitious to me by deigning to provide me with some slight gift.

"I am, with the distinguished considerations due to the benefactors of humanity,

JONDRETTE

"P. S. My daughter will await your orders, dear Marius."

This letter, in the midst of the hazy event that had occupied Marius's thoughts since the previous evening, was a candle in a cave. Everything suddenly cleared up.

This letter came from the same source as the other four. It was the same writing, the same style, the same spelling, the same paper, the same odor of tobacco.

There were five missives, five stories, five names, five signatures, and a single signer. The Spanish Captain Don Alvarès, the unfortunate Mother Balizard, the dramatic poet Genflot, the old comedy writer Fabantou, were all four named Jondrette, if indeed Jondrette was named Jondrette.

During the rather long time that Marius had lived in the building, he had had, as we have said, few opportunities to see, or even catch a glimpse of, his very poor neighbors. His mind was elsewhere, and where the mind is, there the eyes are directed. He must have met the Jondrettes in the passage and on the stairs more than once, but to him they were only shadows; he had taken so little notice that on the previous evening he had brushed against the Jondrette girls on the boulevard without recognizing them; for it was evidently they; and it was with great difficulty that this girl, who had just come into his room, had awakened in him, beneath his disgust and pity, a vague recollection of having met with her somewhere else.

Now he saw everything clearly. He understood that the occupation of his neighbor Jondrette in his distress was to work on the sympathies of benevolent persons; that he procured their addresses, and that under assumed names he wrote letters to people whom he considered rich and compassionate, which his daughters carried, at their risk and peril; for this father was one who risked his daughters; he was playing a game with destiny, and he added them to the stakes. Marius understood, to judge by their flight in the evening, by their breathlessness, by their terror, by those words of argot he had heard, that probably these unfortunate things were also carrying on some of the secret trades of darkness, and that from all this the result was, in the midst of human society constituted as it is, two miserable beings who were neither children, nor girls, nor women, a species of impure yet innocent monsters produced by misery.

Sad creatures without name, age, or sex, to whom neither good nor evil were any longer possible, and for whom, on leaving childhood, there is nothing more in this world, neither liberty, nor virtue, nor responsibility. Souls blooming yesterday, faded today, like those flowers that fall in the street and are spattered by the mud before a wheel crushes them.

Meantime, while Marius watched her with pained surprise, the young girl walked up and down the room with the boldness of a specter. She nosed about, heedless of her nakedness. At times, her blouse, unfastened and torn, fell almost to her waist. She moved the chairs, she disturbed the toilet articles on the bureau, she felt Marius's clothes, she rummaged through things in the corners.

"Ah," she said, "you have a mirror!"

And as if she were alone, she hummed snatches of vaudeville songs, light refrains made dismal by her harsh and guttural voice. An indescribable constraint, restlessness, and humility showed through this audacity. Effrontery is shame.

Nothing could be sadder than to see her frolicking and, so to speak, fluttering about the room with the movements of a bird that is startled by the light or has a broken wing. You feel that under other conditions of education and of fate, the gay, free manner of this young girl might have been something sweet and charming. Never among animals does the creature born to be a dove change into an osprey. That is only seen among men.

Marius was reflecting, and let her alone.

She went to the table.

"Ah!" she said, "books!"

A light flashed through her glassy eyes. She went on, and her tone expressed that happiness of being able to boast of something to which any human is susceptible: "I can read, I can."

She grabbed up the book that lay open on the table and rapidly read "—General Bauduin received the order to take five battalions of his brigade and carry the château of Hougomont, which is in the middle of the plain of Waterloo—"

She stopped.

"Ah, Waterloo! I know that. It is a battle in the old

days. My father was there; my father served in the armies. We are jolly good Bonapartists at home, we are. Against the English, Waterloo is."

She put down the book, took up a pen, and exclaimed, "And I can write, too!"

She dipped the pen in the ink, and turning toward Marius:

"Would you like to see? Here, I am going to write something to show you."

And before he had had time to answer, she wrote on a sheet of blank paper, which was on the middle of the table, "The cops are here."

Then, throwing down the pen, "There are no mistakes in spelling. You can look. We've had an education, my sister and I. We weren't always what we are now. We weren't made—"

Here she stopped, fixed her jaded eye on Marius, and burst out laughing, saying in a tone that contained complete anguish stifled by complete cynicism, "Shoo!"

And she began to hum these words, to a lively tune:

J'ai faim, mon père.
Pas de fricot.
J'ai froid, ma mère.
Pas de tricot.
Grelotte,
Lolotte!
Sanglote,
Jacquot[1]

Hardly had she finished this stanza when she exclaimed, "Do you ever go to the theater, Monsieur Marius? I do. I have a little brother who's a friend of some actors and gives me tickets sometimes. Now, I don't like

[1] I'm starving, Father,
No grub at all.
I'm freezing, Mother,
I've got no shawl.
Shiver,
Lolotte!
Snivel,
Jacquot!

the seats in the balconies. You're crowded, you're uncomfortable. Sometimes there are coarse people; there are people who smell bad, too."

Then she looked at Marius, put on a strange expression and said to him, "Do you know, Monsieur Marius, you're a very pretty boy?"

And at the same time the same thought occurred to both of them, which made her smile and made him blush.

She went to him and laid her hand on his shoulder: "You don't pay any attention to me, but I know you, Monsieur Marius. I pass you here on the stairs, and then I see you visiting a man named Father Mabeuf, who lives out by Austerlitz, sometimes, when I'm walking that way. That suits you very well, your tangled hair."

Her voice tried to be very soft but only managed to be very low. Part of her words were lost in going from the larynx to the lips, as on a keyboard where some notes are missing.

Marius had drawn back quietly.

"Mademoiselle," he said, with his cold gravity, "I have a packet here, which is yours, I think. Let me return it to you."

And he handed her the envelope, which contained the four letters.

She clapped her hands and exclaimed, "We have looked everywhere!"

Then she snatched the packet and opened the envelope: "Lordy, Lordy, haven't we looked, my sister and I? And you've found it! On the boulevard? It must've been on the boulevard? You see, this dropped when we ran. It was my brat of a sister who made the stupid blunder. When we got home, we couldn't find it. As we didn't want to be beaten, since that does no good, no good at all, absolutely no good at all, we said at home that we'd carried the letters to the persons, and that they said nix! Now here they are, these poor letters. And how did you know they were mine? Ah, yes! By the writing! It was you, then, that we bumped into last evening. We didn't see you, really! I said to my sister, Is that a gentleman? My sister said, I think it's a gentleman!"

Meanwhile she had unfolded the petition addressed "to the beneficent gentleman of the church Saint-Jacques-du-Haut-Pas."

"Here!" said she, "this is for the old fellow who goes to mass. And this is the right time, too. I'm going to take it to him. He'll give us something perhaps for lunch."

Then she began to laugh, and added, "Do you know what it will be if we have lunch today? It'll be our lunch for the day before yesterday, our dinner for the day before yesterday, our lunch for yesterday, our dinner for yesterday, all that at one time this morning. That's how it is! If you don't like it, you can feed the worms, dogs!"

This reminded Marius of what the poor girl had come to his room for.

He felt in his waistcoat; he found nothing there.

The young girl went on, seeming to talk as though she were no longer conscious that Marius was there.

"Sometimes I go away at night. Sometimes I don't come back. Before coming to this place, last winter, we lived under the arches of the bridges. We hugged close together so's not to freeze. My little sister cried. That water, how sad it is! When I thought of drowning myself, I said, No; it's too cold. I go all alone when I want to, I sleep in the ditches sometimes. You know, at night, when I walk the boulevards, the trees look like gallows, all the black houses look big as the towers of Notre-Dame, the white walls are like the river, I say to myself: Well now, there's water there! The stars are like Chinese lanterns: They smoke, and the wind blows them out, I'm confused, as if I had horses breathing in my ear; though it's night, I hear a hurdygurdy and spinning wheels, I don't know what. I think that somebody is throwing stones at me, I run off without knowing it, everything's in a whirl, a whirl. When you haven't eaten, it's very queer."

And she looked at him strangely.

After a thorough exploration of his pockets, Marius finally put together five francs and sixteen sous. At the time this was all that he had in the world. "That will do for my dinner today," he thought, "tomorrow we'll see." He took the sixteen sous and gave the five francs to the young girl.

She took the piece eagerly.

"Good," she said, "there's a little sunshine!"

And as if the sun had had the effect of loosening an avalanche of argot, she rattled on:

"Five francs! A shiner! A monarch! In this dump! It's dandy! You're a good guy. I blow you my ticket. Bravo for the boodle! Two days of the jug! And beefsteak! And the fixings! We'll wash it all down and have a high old time of it!''

She drew her blouse back up over her shoulders, made a low bow to Marius, then a friendly wave of the hand, and moved toward the door, saying, ''Good-by to you, monsieur. It doesn't matter. I'm going to find the old man.''

On her way by she saw on the bureau a dry crust of bread moulding there in the dust; she sprang on it, and bit in, muttering, ''That's good! It's hard! It'll break my teeth!''

And she was gone.

V

THE PEEPHOLE OF PROVIDENCE

For five years Marius had lived in poverty, deprivation, distress, but he realized that he had never known real misery. Real misery he had just seen. It was this sprite that had just passed before his eyes. In fact, to see the misery of man only is nothing, you must see the misery of woman; to see the misery of woman only is to see nothing, you must see the misery of childhood.

When man has reached the last extremity, at the same time he reaches the last expedients. Woe to the defenseless beings who surround him! Work, wages, bread, fire, courage, willingness, all fail him at once. The light of day seems to die away outside, the moral light dies out within; in this gloom, man meets the weakness of woman and childhood and compels them to disgraceful uses.

Then every horror is possible. Despair is surrounded by fragile walls, which all open into vice or crime.

Health, youth, honor, the holy and passionate delicacies of the still tender flesh, the heart, virginity, modesty, that epidermis of the soul, are fatally disposed of by the blind groping that seeks help, encounters disgrace, and yet accommodates itself. Fathers, mothers, children, brothers, sisters, men, women, girls, cling together, almost grow together like a mineral formation, in that dark promiscuity of sexes, of relationships, of ages, of infancy, of innocence. They crouch, back to back, in a hovel of destiny. They glance at one another sorrowfully. Oh, the unfortunate! How pallid they are! How cold they are! It seems as though they were on a planet much farther from the sun than we.

To Marius this young girl was a sort of messenger from the night.

She revealed to him a hideous aspect of the darkness.

Marius almost reproached himself for his preoccupation with his reveries and passion that until now had kept him from noticing his neighbors. Paying their rent was an impulse; everybody would have had that impulse; but he, Marius, should have done better. What! A mere wall separated him from these abandoned beings, who lived by groping in the night beyond the pale of the living; he came in contact with them, he was in some way the last link of the human race that they touched, he heard them live or rather breathe beside him, and he took no notice of them! Every day at every moment, he heard them through the wall, walking back and forth, and yet he did not hear! And between their words there was groaning, and he did not even listen, his thoughts were elsewhere, on dreams, on impossible glimmerings, on loves in the sky, on infatuations; and all the while human beings, his brothers in Jesus Christ, his brothers in the people, were suffering agonies beside him! Agonizing uselessly; he even caused a portion of their suffering and aggravated it. For if they had another neighbor, a less distracted, more observant neighbor, an ordinary charitable man, their poverty would have been noticed, their distress signals would have been seen, and long ago perhaps they would have been gathered up and saved! Undoubtedly they seemed very depraved, very corrupt, very vile, very hateful even, but people rarely fall without becoming degraded. Besides, there is a point when the unfortunate and the infamous are associated and confused in a word, a mortal word, *les misérables;* whose fault is it? And then, when the fall is furthest, is that not when charity should be greatest?

While he was preaching to himself this way, for there were times when Marius, like all truly honest hearts, was his own monitor, and scolded himself more than he deserved, he looked at the wall that separated him from the Jondrettes, as if he could send his pitying glance through that partition to warm the unfortunate beings. The wall was a thin layer of plaster, held up by lath and joists, through which, as we have just seen, voices and words could be perfectly distinguished. It took the dreamer, Marius, not to have noticed this before. There was no paper hung on this wall, either on the Jondrettes' side or on Marius's side; its coarse construction was bare to the eye. Almost unconsciously, Marius examined this partition; sometimes reverie examines, observes, and scrutinizes, as thought would do. Suddenly he stood up; he had just noticed toward the top, near the ceiling, a triangular hole, where three laths left a space between them. The plaster, which should have stopped up the hole, was gone, and by getting up on the bureau he could see through the hole into the Jondrettes' garret. Pity has and should have its curiosity. This hole was a kind of peephole. It is lawful to perfidiously spy on misfortune in order to relieve it. "Let's see what these people are," thought Marius, "and to what poverty they have fallen."

He climbed up on the bureau, put his eye to the crevice, and looked.

VI

THE SAVAGE IN HIS LAIR

Cities, like forests, have their dens in which all their vilest and most terrible monsters hide. But in cities, what hides this way is ferocious, unclean, and petty, that is to say, ugly; in forests, what hides is ferocious, savage, and great, that is to say beautiful. Den for den, those of beasts are preferable to those of men. Caverns are better than the wretched holes that shelter humanity.

What Marius saw was a hole.

Marius was poor and his room was poorly furnished, but even as his poverty was noble, his garret was clean. The den he was seeing at that moment was abject, filthy, fetid, revolting, dark, sordid. For furniture there was merely a straw chair, a rickety table, a few old broken dishes, and in two of the corners two indescribable pallets; all the light came from a garret window of four panes, curtained with spiders' webs. Just enough light came through that skylight to make a man's face seem the face of a phantom. The walls had a leprous look and were covered with seams and scars like a face disfigured by some horrible malady; a putrid moisture oozed from them. There were obscene pictures on them coarsely sketched in charcoal.

The room Marius occupied had a dilapidated brick tiling; this one was neither paved nor floored; the inmates walked directly on the old plastering of the building, which had grown black underfoot. On this uneven soil where the dust was almost caked, and which was virgin only with respect to the broom, were grouped random constellations of socks, old shoes, and hideous rags; however, this room had a fireplace; so it rented for forty francs a year. There was a little of everything on the hearth, a chafing dish, a kettle, some broken boards, rags hanging from nails, a birdcage, some ashes, and even a little fire. Two embers were smoking sadly.

The fact that this garret was large added still more to its horror. It had projections, angles, black holes, recesses under the roof, bays, and promontories. Beyond were hideous, unfathomable corners, which seemed as if they must be full of spiders as big as a fist, centipedes as large as a foot, and perhaps even some human monsters.

One of the pallets was near the door, the other near the window. Each had one end next to the fireplace and both were opposite Marius. In a corner near the opening through which Marius was looking, hanging upon the wall in a black wooden frame, was a colored engraving at the bottom of which was written in large letters: THE DREAM. It represented a sleeping woman and a sleeping child, the child on the woman's lap, an eagle in a cloud with a crown in his beak, and the woman keeping the crown away from the child's head, but without waking; in the background Napoleon in a halo, leaning against a bright blue column with a yellow capital adorned with this inscription:

MARINGO
AUSTERLITS
IENA
WAGRAMME
ELOT

Below this frame a sort of wooden panel longer than it was wide was standing on the floor and leaning at an angle against the wall. It looked like a picture turned to the wall, a frame probably smeared on the other side, of a panel taken down from a wall and forgotten, waiting to be hung again.

Near the table, on which Marius saw a pen, ink, and paper, was sitting a man about sixty, small, thin, pale, haggard, with a keen, cruel, and restless air: a hideous wretch.

If he could have studied this face, Lavater would have found in it a mixture of vulture and shyster, the bird of prey and the haggler rendering each other ugly and complete, the haggler making the bird of prey base, the bird of prey making the haggler horrible.

This man had a long gray beard. He was dressed in a woman's blouse, which showed his shaggy chest and his naked arms bristling with gray hairs. Below the blouse were a pair of muddy trousers and boots from which the toes stuck out.

He had a pipe in his mouth and was smoking. There was no more bread in the lair, but there was tobacco.

He was writing, probably some such letter as those Marius had read.

On one corner of the table was an old odd volume with a reddish cover, the size of which, the old twelvemo of book series, revealed that it was a novel. On the cover was displayed the following title, printed in huge capitals: GOD, THE KING, HONOR, AND THE LADIES, BY DUCRAY-DUMINIL, 1814.

As he wrote, the man talked aloud, and Marius heard his words.

"To think there's no equality even when we're dead! Just look at the Père-Lachaise! The great and the very rich are in the upper part, in the avenue of the acacias, which is paved. They can go there in a carriage. The lowly, the poor, the unfortunate, they're put in the lower part, where there's mud up to the knees, in holes, in the dampness. They're put there so they'll rot sooner! You can't go to see them without sinking into the ground."

Here he stopped, banged his fist on the table, and added, gnashing his teeth, "Oh! I could eat the world!"

A big woman, who might have been forty years old or a hundred, was squatting near the fireplace, on her bare feet.

She was dressed only in a blouse and a knit skirt patched with pieces of old cloth. A coarse flax apron covered half the skirt. Although this woman was bent and drawn up into herself, one could see she was very tall. She was a kind of giantess beside her husband. She had hideous hair, light red sprinkled with gray, which she pushed back from time to time with her huge shiny hand with their flat nails.

Lying on the ground at her side, wide open, was a volume of the same format as the other, and probably part of the same novel.

On one of the pallets Marius could make out a slender, wan little girl sitting, almost naked, with her feet hanging down, seeming neither to listen nor see nor even live.

Undoubtedly the younger sister of the one who had come to his room.

She looked about eleven or twelve. On examining her more carefully, he saw she must be fourteen. It was the child who, on the boulevard the evening before had said, "I made tracks."

She was of the sickly species that stay back a long time then suddenly shoot up all at once. The poor creatures have neither childhood nor youth. At fifteen they look twelve; at sixteen they seem twenty. Today a little girl, tomorrow a woman. It is as though they leap through life, the better to get it over with sooner.

For the moment this creature looked like a child.

Nothing, moreover, indicated the performance of any work in this room; not a loom, not a wheel, not a tool. In one corner a few scraps of iron. It was all like the gloomy idle interlude between despair and death.

For some time Marius looked into that funereal interior, more frightening than a tomb, for the movements of a human soul and the palpitation of life could still be felt.

The garret, the cellar, the deep ditch, in which some of the wretched crawl at the bottom of the social edifice, are not the sepulcher itself, but its antechamber; yet like those rich men who display their greatest splendor at the entrance of their palace, death, so close at hand, seems to display his deepest misery in such vestibules.

The man fell silent, the woman did not speak, the girl

seemed not to breathe. Marius could hear the pen scratching over the paper.

The man grumbled, as he wrote, "Rabble! Rabble! Everything is rabble!"

This variation on Solomon's saying drew a sigh from the woman.

"My darling, be calm," she said. "Don't hurt yourself, dear. You are too good to write to all those people, my dear."

In poverty bodies cling close together, as in the cold, but hearts grow distant. This woman, to all appearances, must have loved this man with as much love as was in her; but probably from the repeated mutual reproaches growing out of the frightful distress that weighed on them all, the love had gone out. She now felt toward her husband nothing more than the ashes of affection. Still the words of endearment, as often happens, had survived. She said to him, "dear," "my darling," "my man," etc., with her lips, but her heart was silent.

The man returned to his writing.

VII

STRATEGY AND TACTICS

With a heavy heart, Marius was about to get down from the post of observation he had devised, when a sound attracted his attention and made him stay where he was.

The door of the garret was hastily opened. The eldest daughter appeared on the threshold. On her feet she had rough men's shoes, covered with mud, which had spattered as high as her red ankles, and she was wrapped in a ragged old cloak that Marius had not seen an hour before but that she had probably left at his door to inspire more pity and must have put on as she went out. She came in, closed the door behind her, stopped to catch her breath, for she was panting, then cried with an expression of joy and triumph, "He's coming!"

The father turned his eyes, the woman turned her head, the younger sister did not move.

"Who?" asked the father.

"The gentleman!"

"The philanthropist?"

"Yes."

"Of the church of Saint-Jacques?"

"Yes."

"The old man?"

"Yes."

"He's going to come?"

"He's right behind me."

"Are you sure?"

"Positive."

"He's really coming here?"

"In a fiacre."

"In a fiacre. It's a Rothschild!"

The father stood up.

"How can you be sure? If he's coming in a fiacre, how did you get here before him? You gave him the address, at least? You told him the last door at the end of the hall on the right? Provided he doesn't make a mistake? You found him at the church then? Did he read my letter? What did he say?"

"Slow down, slow down!" said the girl. "How you do run on, my good man! I'll tell you: I went into the church, he was at his usual place, I curtsied to him, and I gave him the letter, he read it and said to me: Where do you live, my child? I said: Monsieur, I will show you. He said to me: No, give me your address; my daughter has some purchases to make, I am going to take a carriage and I will get to your house as soon as you do. I gave him the address. When I told him the house number, he seemed surprised and hesitated for a moment, then he said: It doesn't matter, I'll come. When mass was over, I saw him leave the church with his daughter. I saw them get into a fiacre. And I plainly told him the last door at the end of the hall on the right."

"And how do you know he'll come?"

"I just saw the fiacre coming into the Rue du Petit-Banquier. That's what made me run."

"How do you know it is the same fiacre?"

"Because I had noticed the number."

"What is the number?"

"Four hundred and forty."

"Good, you're a clever girl."

The girl looked resolutely at her father, and pointing to

the shoes she had on, she said, "A clever girl, that may be. But I tell you I'll never put on these shoes again; I won't do it, for health first, and then for decency's sake. I don't know anything more provoking than soles that squeak and go ghee, ghee, ghee, all along the street. I'd rather go barefoot."

"You're right," answered the father, in a mild tone that contrasted with the young girl's rudeness, "but they wouldn't let you into the churches; the poor must have shoes. People don't go to God's house barefoot," he added bitterly. Then returning to the subject that occupied his thoughts, "And you are sure then, sure he is coming?"

"He is right on my heels," she said.

The man sprang up. There was a sort of illumination on his face.

"Wife!" he cried, "you hear. It's the philanthropist. Put out the fire."

The stupefied woman did not stir.

With the agility of an acrobat, the father grabbed a broken pot that stood on the mantel, and threw some water on the embers.

Then turning to his elder daughter: "Take the rush off the chair!"

His daughter did not understand him at all.

He grabbed the chair and with a kick ruined the seat. His leg went right through it.

As he was pulling out his leg, he asked his daughter, "Is it cold outside?"

"Very cold. It's snowing."

The father turned toward the younger girl, who was on the pallet near the window, and thundered at her, "Quick! Off the bed, good-for-nothing! Will you never do anything? Break a pane of glass!"

The little girl sprang off the bed trembling.

"Break a pane of glass!" he said again.

The child was speechless.

"Do you hear me?" repeated the father. "I told you to break a pane!"

With a sort of terrified obedience, the child stood up on tiptoe and punched a pane with her fist. The glass broke and fell with a crash.

"Good," said the father.

His eye ran hastily over all the nooks and crannies of

the garret. He was serious and brusque like a general making his final preparations as the battle was about to begin.

The mother, who had not yet said a word, got up and asked in a slow, muffled tone, her words seeming to come out as if curdled, "Dear, what do you want me to do?"

"Get into bed," the man answered.

His tone admitted of no deliberation. The mother obeyed and dropped heavily onto one of the pallets.

Meanwhile a sob was heard in a corner.

"What's that?" cried the father.

The younger daughter, coming out of the cranny she had retreated into, showed her bleeding fist. In breaking the glass she had cut herself; she went to her mother's bed, and was silently weeping.

It was the mother's turn to sit up and yell.

"What stupid things you're doing! Breaking that glass! She cut herself!"

"So much the better!" said the man. "I knew she would."

"What d'you mean, so much the better?" the woman asked.

"Silence!" replied the father. "I am suppressing the freedom of the press!"

Then tearing the blouse he had on, he made a bandage with which he hastily wrapped up the little girl's bleeding hand.

That done, his eye fell on the torn blouse with satisfaction.

"And the blouse, too," he said, "everything looks just right."

An icy wind whistled in at the window. The mist from outside entered and spread out like whitish cotton picked apart by invisible fingers. Through the broken pane the falling snow could be seen. The cold weather promised the day before by the Candlemas sun had come indeed.

The father cast a glance around him as if to assure himself that he had forgotten nothing. He took an old shovel and spread ashes over the moistened embers to hide them completely.

Then rising and standing with his back to the chimney, "Now," he said, "we can receive the philanthropist."

VIII

THE SUNBEAM IN THE HOLE

The older daughter went to her father and touched his hand.

"Feel how cold I am," she said.

"Pshaw!" answered the father. "I'm a good deal colder than that."

The mother cried impetuously, "You always have everything better than the rest, even pain."

"Enough!" said the man.

The mother, after a particularly significant look from the man, held her peace.

There was a moment of silence in the den. The eldest daughter was idly scraping the mud off the bottom of her dress, the young sister continued to sob; the mother had taken her head in both hands and was covering her with kisses, saying to her softly, "My treasure, please, it isn't serious, don't cry, you'll make your father angry."

"No!" cried the father, "on the contrary! Sob! Sob! That's just right."

Then, turning to the eldest, "Ah! But he isn't here yet! What if he doesn't come! I'll have put out my fire, knocked the bottom out of my chair, torn this blouse, and broken my window all for nothing."

"And cut the little girl!" murmured the mother.

"Do you know," resumed the father, "that it's as cold as a dog in this miserable garret? If the man does not come! Oh! That's it! He is making us wait for him! He's saying, Well! They'll just wait for me! That's what they're there for!—Oh! How I hate them, and how I'd strangle them with joy and rejoicing, enthusiasm and satisfaction, those rich men! All the rich! These supposedly charitable men, who go to mass, have a taste for the priesthood, preachy, preachy, who give in to the cowls, and think themselves better than us, who come to humiliate us, and to bring us clothes or so they call them! Rags not worth four sous, and bread! That's not what I want of the rabble! I want money! But money, never! Because they say that we'd go and drink it away, that we're drunks and do-nothings! And what've they been in their day? Thieves! They wouldn't have gotten rich without that! Oh! Somebody ought to take society by the four corners of the sheet and toss it all into the air! Everything would be broken, most likely, but at least nobody would have anything, there'd be that much gained! But what's he up to now, your mug of a benevolent gentleman? Is he coming? The brute may have forgotten the address! I'll bet that the old fool—"

Just then there was a light tap at the door, the man rushed forward and opened it, exclaiming with deep bows and fawning smiles, "Come in, monsieur! Do come in, noble benefactor, as well as your charming young lady."

A man of mature age and a young girl appeared at the door of the garret.

Marius had not left his place. What he felt at that moment escapes human language.

It was She.

Whoever has loved knows all the radiant meaning contained in the three letters of this word "she."

It certainly was she. Marius could hardly discern her through the luminous vapor that suddenly spread over his eyes. It was that sweet absent being, the star that had been his light for six months, it was the eye, the brow, the mouth, the beautiful vanished face that had brought him night by going away. The vision had been in an eclipse, it was reappearing.

She appeared again in this gloom, in this garret, in this misshapen den, in this horror!

Marius shuddered desperately. How could it be! It was she! The wild beating of his heart clouded his vision. He felt ready to dissolve in tears. How could it be! At last he was seeing her again after having sought for her so long! It seemed to him he had lost his soul and just found it again.

She was still the same, only a little paler; her delicate face was framed by a violet velvet hat, her figure was hidden under a black satin cape, below her long dress he caught a glimpse of her little foot squeezed into a silk boot.

She was still accompanied by M. Leblanc.

She stepped forward and laid a large package on the table.

The elder Jondrette girl had retreated behind the door and was glaring at that velvet hat, that silk dress, and that charming happy face.

IX

JONDRETTE ALMOST WEEPS

The room was so dark that people coming from outdoors felt as if they were entering a cellar. So the two newcomers moved with some hesitation, hardly discerning the dim forms around them, while they were seen and examined with perfect ease by the tenants of the garret, whose eyes were accustomed to this twilight.

M. Leblanc approached with his kind and compassionate look, and said to the father, "Monsieur, in this package you will find some new clothes, some stockings, and some blankets."

"Our angelic benefactor overwhelms us," said Jondrette, bowing down to the floor. Then, stooping to his eldest daughter's ear while the two visitors were examining the dreadful room, he added rapidly in a whisper, "See? What did I tell you? Rags! No money! They're all alike! Tell me, how was the letter to this old blubber-lip signed?"

"Fabantou," answered the daughter.

"The dramatic artist, good!"

This was lucky for Jondrette, for at that very moment M. Leblanc turned toward him and said, with the appearance of someone trying to remember a name, "I see that you are certainly to be pitied, Monsieur—"

"Fabantou," said Jondrette quickly.

"Monsieur Fabantou, yes, that's it. I remember."

"Dramatic artist, monsieur, with successful plays to his credit."

Here Jondrette evidently thought the moment had come to make an impression on the "philanthropist." In a tone of voice that belongs both to the braggadocio of the juggler at a fair and to the humility of a beggar on the highway, he proclaimed, "Pupil of Talma! Monsieur! I am a pupil of Talma! Fortune once smiled on me. Alas!

Now it is the turn of misfortune. Look, my benefactor, no bread, no fire. My poor darlings have no fire! My only chair unseated! A broken window! In such weather as this! My spouse in bed! Sick!"

"Poor woman!" said M. Leblanc.

"My child injured!" added Jondrette.

The child, her attention diverted by the arrival of the strangers, was staring at "the young lady," and had stopped her sobbing.

"Why don't you cry? Why don't you scream?" said Jondrette to her in a whisper.

At the same time he pinched her injured hand. All this with the skill of a juggler.

The little one shrieked.

The adorable young girl whom Marius in his heart called "his Ursula" went to her quickly.

"Poor, dear child!" she said.

"Look, my beautiful young lady," pursued Jondrette, "her bleeding wrist! It is an accident that happened on a machine where she worked for six sous a day. It may be necessary to cut off her arm."

"Really!" said the old gentleman in alarm.

The little girl, taking this seriously, began to sob again all the harder.

"Alas, yes, my benefactor!" answered the father.

For some moments, Jondrette had been looking at "the philanthropist" in a strange way. Even while speaking, he seemed to scrutinize him closely as if he were trying to recall something. Suddenly, taking advantage of a moment when the newcomers were anxiously questioning the smaller girl about her wounded hand, he passed over to his wife who was lying in her bed, looking overwhelmed and stupid, and whispered to her quickly, "Just look at that man!"

Then, turning toward M. Leblanc and continuing his lamentation, "You see, monsieur! For clothes I have nothing but a blouse of my wife's! And all torn at that. In deepest winter I cannot go out, for lack of a coat. If I had any sort of a coat, I'd go to see Mademoiselle Mars, who knows and likes me. She is still living in the Rue de la Tour-des-Dames, isn't she? You know, monsieur, we played together in the provinces. I shared her laurels. Célimène would come to my rescue, monsieur! Elmira would give alms to Belisarius! But no, nothing! And not a sou in the house! My wife sick and not a sou! My daughter dangerously injured and not a sou! My spouse has choking fits. It's her age, and then the nervous system has something to do with it. She needs help, and my daughter, too! But the doctor! The druggist! How can I pay them! Not a penny! I would fall on my knees before a penny, monsieur! You see how the arts have fallen! And do you know, my charming young lady, and you, my generous patron, do you know, you who breathe virtue and goodness, and who perfume that church where my daughter, in going to say her prayers, sees you every day? For I bring up my daughters religiously, monsieur. I have not allowed them to take to the theater. Ah! The rogues! That I should see them stumble! I do not jest! I fortify them with sermons about honor, about morals, about virtue! Ask them! They must walk straight. They have a father. They are none of those unfortunates who begin by having no family and end by marrying the public, who start as Mamselle Nobody and become Madame Everybody. Thank heavens! None of that in the Fabantou family! I mean to educate them virtuously, and so they can be honest and genteel and believe in God's sacred name! Well, monsieur, my worthy monsieur, do you know what is going to happen tomorrow? Tomorrow is the fourth of February, the fatal day, the last delay my landlord will give me; if I do not pay him this evening, tomorrow my eldest daughter, myself, my spouse with her fever, my child with her wound, we shall all four be turned out of doors, and driven off into the street, onto the boulevard, without shelter, into the rain, under the snow. You see, monsieur, I owe four quarters, a year! Sixty francs!"

Jondrette lied. Four quarters would have made only forty francs, and he could not have owed for four: It was not six months since Marius had paid for two.

M. Leblanc took five francs from his pocket and laid them on the table.

Jondrette had time to mutter into the ear of his elder daughter, "The beast! What does he think I'm going to do with five francs? It won't even pay for my chair and my window! I must cover my expenses!"

Meanwhile, M. Leblanc had taken off a large brown

overcoat that he was wearing over his blue surtout and hung it over the back of the chair.

"Monsieur Fabantou," he said, "I only have these five francs with me; but I am going to take my daughter home, and I will return this evening; it is this evening that you have to pay?"

Jondrette's face lit up with a strange expression. He answered quickly, "Yes, my noble monsieur. At eight o'clock, I must be at my landlord's."

"I'll be here at six o'clock, and I'll bring you the sixty francs."

"My benefactor!" cried Jondrette, distractedly.

And he added in an undertone, "Take a good look at him, wife!"

M. Leblanc took the arm of the beautiful young girl and turned toward the door. "Till this evening, my friends," he said.

"Six o'clock," said Jondrette.

"Six precisely."

Just then the overcoat on the chair caught the eye of the older daughter.

"Monsieur," she said, "you forgot your coat."

Jondrette threw a crushing glance at his daughter, accompanied by a huge shrug of the shoulders.

M. Leblanc turned and answered with a smile, "I did not forget it, I am leaving it."

"Oh, my patron," said Jondrette, "my noble benefactor, I'm dissolving in tears! Let me take you to your carriage."

"If you go out," replied M. Leblanc, "put on the overcoat. It is really very cold."

Jondrette did not have to be told twice. He quickly put on the brown overcoat.

And all three went out, Jondrette preceding the two strangers.

X

PRICE OF PUBLIC CONVEYANCE: TWO FRANCS AN HOUR

Marius had not missed a thing in this whole scene, and yet he had actually seen nothing of it. His eyes had remained on the young girl, his heart had, so to speak, seized on her and enveloped her entirely, from her first step into the garret. During the whole time she was there, he had lived that life of ecstasy that suspends material perceptions and precipitates the whole soul onto a single point. He did not contemplate the girl, but that light in a satin cloak and a velvet hat. Had the star Sirius entered the room he could not have been more dazzled.

While the young girl was opening the bundle, unfolding the clothes and the blankets, questioning the sick mother kindly and the little injured girl tenderly, he watched her every motion, endeavored to hear her words. He knew her eyes, her forehead, her beauty, her stature, her gait, he did not know the sound of her voice. He thought he had caught a few words of it once at the Luxembourg, but could not be absolutely sure. He would have given ten years of his life to hear it, to carry a little of that music in his soul. But all was lost in Jondrette's wretched displays and trumpeting. This added a real anger to Marius's transports. He looked at her lovingly. He could not imagine it really was that divine creature he was seeing in the midst of the misshapen beings of this monstrous lair. He seemed to see a hummingbird among toads.

When she went out, he had only one thought, to follow her, to cling to her traces, not to leave her without knowing where she lived, at least not to lose her again, after having so miraculously found her! He leaped down from the bureau and took his hat. As he was putting his hand on the bolt and was about to go out, he reflected and stopped. The hall was long, the stairs steep, Jondrette a great talker. Undoubtedly M. Leblanc had not yet gotten into his carriage; if he should turn around in the hallway, or on the stairs, or on the doorstep, and see him, Marius, in that house, he would certainly be alarmed and would find means to escape him again, and once more it would all be over. What could he do? Wait a little? But during the delay the carriage might leave. Marius was perplexed. At last he took the risk and left his room.

There was nobody in the hall. He ran to the stairs. There was nobody on the stairs. He hurried down, and reached the boulevard in time to see a fiacre turn the corner of the Rue du Petit-Banquier and return to the city.

Marius rushed in that direction. When he reached the corner of the boulevard, he saw the fiacre again going rapidly down the Rue Mouffetard; it was already far away, there was no way to catch up with it; what should he do? Run after it? Impossible; and anyway from the carriage they would certainly notice a man running after them at full speed and the father would recognize him. Just at this moment, incredible good fortune, Marius saw a public cab passing along the boulevard, empty. There was only one course to take—get into this cab and follow the fiacre. That was sure, effective, and safe.

Marius made a sign to the driver to stop, and cried out, "Just in time."

Marius had no tie, he had on his old working coat, with some of the buttons missing, and one of his shirt's front pleats was torn.

The driver stopped, winked, and reached his left hand toward Marius, rubbing his forefinger gently with his thumb.

"What?" said Marius.

"Pay in advance," said the driver.

Marius remembered that he had only sixteen sous with him.

"How much?" he asked.

"Forty sous."

"I'll pay when we get back."

The driver made no reply but to whistle an air from La Palisse, and whip his horse on.

Distraught, Marius watched the cab move off. For the want of twenty-four sous he was losing his joy, his happiness, his love! He was falling back into night! He had seen and was again going blind. He thought bitterly and with deep regret, one must admit, of the five francs he had given that very morning to that miserable girl. Had he had those five francs he would have been saved, he would have been born again, he would have come out of limbo and darkness, out of his isolation, his peevish humor, his bereavement; he would have again knotted the black thread of his destiny with that beautiful golden thread that had just floated before his eyes and broken off once more. He returned to the old building in despair.

It might have occurred to him that M. Leblanc had promised to return in the evening and that he had only to follow him then; but deep in contemplation, he had hardly heard it.

Just as he went up the stairs, on the other side of the boulevard, beside the deserted wall of the Rue de la Barrière des Gobelins, he noticed Jondrette in the "philanthropist's" overcoat, talking to one of those dangerous-looking men called "prowlers of the city gates," men with equivocal faces and suspicious speech, with an air of evil intentions, who usually sleep by day, which leads us to suppose they work by night.

These two men quietly talking while the snow was whirling about them made a picture a policeman certainly would have observed, but which Marius hardly noticed.

Nevertheless, however mournful his reflections, he could not help saying to himself that this prowler of the city gates with whom Jondrette was talking resembled a certain Panchaud, alias Printanier, alias Bigrenaille, whom Courfeyrac had once pointed out to him and who passed in the area for a very dangerous night-stalker. We have seen this man's name in the preceding book. This Panchaud, alias Printanier, alias Bigrenaille, figured afterward in several criminal trials and has since become a celebrated scoundrel. At that time he was still merely a notorious scoundrel. Nowadays, he is a matter of tradition among bandits and murderers. He had quite a following near the close of the last reign. And in the evening, at nightfall, at the hour when crowds gather and murmur; he was talked about at La Force in La Fosse-aux-Lions. In that prison, just at the spot where the latrine sewer that served for the astonishing escape of thirty prisoners in broad daylight in 1843 passes under the rampart walk, you might, above the flagging of those latrines, read his name, PANCHAUD, audaciously inscribed by him right on the rampart wall in one of his escape attempts. In 1832, the police already had their eye on him, but he had not yet really made his début.

XI

OFFERS OF SERVICE BY MISERY TO GRIEF

Marius slowly climbed the stairs of the old building; just as he was going into his cell, he saw in the hall behind him the elder Jondrette girl, who was following him. The sight of her was repellent: She had his five francs, it was too late to ask her for them, the cab was no longer there, the fiacre was far away. Besides, she would not give them back to him. As to questioning her about the address of the people who had just come, that was useless; it was plain that she did not know, since the letter signed Fabantou was addressed "to the beneficent gentleman of the Church Saint-Jacques-du-Haut-Pas."

Marius went into his room and shoved his door behind him.

It did not close; he turned and saw a hand holding the door partly open.

"What is it?" he asked. "Who's there?"

It was the Jondrette girl.

"Is it you?" said Marius almost harshly. "You again? What do you want?"

She seemed pensive and did not look at him. She had lost the assurance she had had in the morning. She did not come in but remained in the murky hall, where Marius could see her through the half-open door.

"So come now, are you going to answer?" asked Marius. "What do you want from me?"

She raised her mournful eyes, in which a sort of confused light seemed to shine dimly, and said to him, "Monsieur Marius, you look sad. What's the matter with you?"

"With me?"

"Yes, you."

"There's nothing the matter with me."

"Yes there is!"

"No."

"I tell you there is!"

"Leave me alone!"

Marius pushed the door again, but she still held it back.

"Listen," she said, "you're wrong. Though you may not be rich, you were good this morning. Be the same now. You gave me enough to eat, now tell me what's the matter. You're disturbed by something, that's obvious. I don't want you to be distressed. What can be done about it? Can I help you in some little way? Let me. I'm not asking for your secrets, you don't have to tell them to me, but still I might be useful. I can certainly help you, since I help my father. When he needs someone to deliver letters, go into houses, ask from door to door, find out an address, follow somebody, I do it. Now, you can certainly tell me what the matter is. I'll go and speak to the persons; sometimes if somebody speaks to the persons that's enough, and everything's all arranged. Use me."

An idea came into Marius's mind. What branch do we scorn when we feel we are sinking?

He went up to the girl.

"Listen," he said to her, gently.

She interrupted him with a flash of joy in her eyes.

"Oh! Yes, talk softly to me! I like that better."

"Well," he resumed, "you brought that old gentleman here with his daughter."

"Yes."

"Do you know their address?"

"No."

"Find it for me."

From gloomy, the girl's eyes had gone to joyful; they now turned dark.

"Is that what you want?" she asked.

"Yes."

"Do you know them?"

"No."

"You mean," she said hastily, "you don't know her, but you want to know her."

The girl's "them" changed to "her" with an indescribably bitter significance.

"Well, can you do it?" said Marius.

"Get you the beautiful young lady's address?"

Again, in these words "the beautiful young lady," there was a nuance that made Marius uneasy. He went on, "Well, no matter! The address of the father and daughter. Their address, yes!"

She looked steadily at him.

"What will you give me?"

"Anything you want!"

"Anything I want?"

"Yes."

"You'll get the address."

She looked down and then with a hasty movement closed the door.

Marius was alone.

He dropped into a chair, with his head and both elbows on the bed, lost in thoughts he could not grasp, and as if in a whirlpool. All that had happened since morning, the appearance of the angel, her disappearance, what this poor creature had just said to him, a gleam of hope floating in an ocean of despair, all this was teeming in his brain.

Suddenly he was violently torn from his reverie.

He heard the loud, harsh voice of Jondrette pronounce these words filled with strange interest for him:

"I tell you I'm sure I recognized him!"

Of whom was Jondrette talking? He had recognized whom? M. Leblanc? The father of "his Ursula"? What! Did Jondrette know him? In this sudden and unexpected way was Marius just about to get all the information whose lack made his own life seem hazy? Was he at last to know who it was he loved, who that young girl was? Who her father was? Was the dense shadow enveloping them about to be rolled away? Was the veil to be torn? Oh gods!

He sprang, rather than mounted, onto the bureau, and went back to his place near the little aperture in the partition.

Again he saw the interior of the Jondrette lair.

XII

USE OF M. LEBLANC'S FIVE-FRANC PIECE

Nothing had changed in the appearance of the family, except that the wife and daughters had opened the package and put on the wool stockings and underclothes. Two new blankets were thrown over the two beds.

Jondrette had evidently just come in. He was still out of breath. His daughters were sitting on the floor near the fireplace, the elder binding up the hand of the younger. His wife lay as if exhausted on the pallet near the fireplace, with a surprised expression on her face. Jondrette was walking up and down the garret with rapid strides. His eyes had an extraordinary look.

The woman, who seemed timid and stupefied in front of her husband, ventured to say to him, "What, really? You're sure?"

"Absolutely sure! It was eight years ago! But I recognize him! I spotted him immediately. What! It didn't strike you?"

"No."

"And yet I told you to pay attention. But it's the same height, the same face, hardly any older; there are some men who don't grow old; I don't know how they do it; it's the same tone of voice. He's better dressed, that's all! Mysterious old devil, I've got you where I want you!"

He checked himself, and said to his daughters, "Go on out, you two!" Then turning back to his wife, he added, "Strange it didn't strike you."

As they got up to obey, the mother stammered, "With her sore hand?"

"The air will do her good," said Jondrette. "Go along."

It was clear that this man was one of those who brook no reply. The two girls went out.

Just as they were passing the door, the father caught the elder by the arm and said with special emphasis,

"You be here at five o'clock precisely. Both of you. I'll need you."

Marius listened still more attentively.

Alone with his wife, Jondrette began to stalk the room again and took two or three turns in silence. Then he spent a few minutes in tucking the bottom of the blouse he was wearing inside the belt of his trousers.

Suddenly he turned toward the woman, folded his arms, and exclaimed, "And do you want me to tell you one thing? The young lady—"

"Well, what then?" said the woman. "About the young lady?"

Marius had no further doubt, it was indeed of her that they were talking. He listened with an intense anxiety. His whole life was concentrated in his ears.

But Jondrette stooped down and whispered to his wife. Then he straightened up and finished out loud, "It's her."

"That girl?" said the wife.

"That girl!" said the husband.

No words could express what was in the mother's reply of "that girl." It was surprise, rage, hatred, anger, mingled and combined in a monstrous intonation. The few words spoken, some name, undoubtedly, that her husband whispered in her ear, had been enough to rouse this huge drowsy woman and change her repulsiveness to hideousness.

"Impossible!" she exclaimed, "when I think that my daughters go barefoot and don't have a dress to put on! How could it be! A satin cloak, a velvet hat, silk boots, and all that! More than two hundred francs worth! One would think she was a lady! No, you're mistaken! Why, in the first place she was hideous, this one isn't bad! She's really not bad! She can't be the one!"

"I tell you she is. You'll see."

At this absolute affirmation, the woman raised her big red face and looked up at the ceiling with a hideous expression. At that moment she seemed to Marius even more intimidating than her husband. She was a sow with the stare of a tigress.

"What!" she went on. "Could that horrible beautiful young lady who looked at my girls with pity, actually be that beggar! Oh, would I like to stamp her heart out!"

She sprang off the bed and stood there for a moment,

her hair flying, nostrils flaring, mouth half open, fists clenched and held out behind her back. Then she fell back on the pallet. The man still walked up and down, paying no attention to his female.

After a pause, he approached her and stopped in front of her, his arms crossed, as before.

"And do you want me to tell you something else?"

"What?" she asked.

He answered rapidly in a low tone, "My fortune is made."

The woman stared at him with the look that means: Has he gone crazy?

He continued, "It's a good long time now that I've been a parishioner of the die-of-hunger-if-you-have-any-fire-and-die-of-cold-if-you-have-any-bread parish! I've had misery enough! My burden and other people's burdens, too! I'm not joking anymore, I don't find it comic any longer, enough puns, good God! No more farces, Father Eternal! I want food for my hunger, I want drink for my thirst! To gorge! To sleep! To do nothing! I want my turn, I do! Before I die! I want to be a bit of a millionaire!"

He took a turn around the garret and added, "Like other people."

"What do you mean?" asked the woman.

He shook his head, winked, and lifted his voice like a street doctor about to make a demonstration: "What do I mean? Listen!"

"Hush!" muttered the woman. "Not so loud! If it is business nobody should hear."

"Go on! Who is there to hear? Our neighbor? I saw him go out just now. Besides, what does he hear, that dunce? I tell you I saw him go out."

Nevertheless, by a sort of instinct, Jondrette lowered his voice, though not enough for his words to escape Marius. A favorable circumstance, and one that enabled Marius to lose nothing of this conversation, was that the fallen snow muffled the sound of the carriages on the boulevard.

Marius heard this: "Listen. He's caught, the Croesus! It's all right. It's already done. Everything's arranged. I've seen the men. He'll come this evening at six. To bring his sixty francs, my landlord, my fourth of February! It's not even a quarter! Wasn't that stupid! So he'll come at six! Our neighbor is out to dinner then. Mother Bougon is washing dishes in the city. There's nobody in the house. Our neighbor never comes back before eleven. The girls will stand watch. You'll help us. He'll pay up."

"And if he doesn't?" asked the wife.

Jondrette made a sinister gesture and said, "We'll execute him."

And he burst out laughing.

It was the first time that Marius had seen him laugh. The laugh was cold and faint and made him shudder.

Jondrette opened a closet near the chimney, took out an old cap, and put it on his head after brushing it with his sleeve.

"Now," he said, "I'm going out. I still have some men to see. Some good ones. You'll see how it's going to work out. I'll be back as soon as possible. It is a great hand to play. Look out for the house."

And with his two fists in the two pockets of his trousers, he stood a moment in thought, then exclaimed, "Do you know it's very lucky indeed that he didn't recognize me? If he had been the one to recognize me he would not have come back. He would escape us! It's my beard that saved me! My romantic beard! My pretty little romantic beard!"

And he began to laugh again.

He went to the window. The snow was still falling and blotted out the gray sky.

"What beastly weather!" he said.

Then, crossing one side of his coat over the other, he said, "This thing is too big. But no matter. He was wise to leave it for me, the old scoundrel! Without this I wouldn't have been able to go out and the whole thing would've been spoiled! But little things can make a difference!"

And pulling his cap over his eyes, he went out.

Hardly had he had time to take a few steps in the hall, when the door opened and his tawny and cunning face again appeared.

"I forgot," he said, "you'll have a charcoal fire."

And he threw into his wife's apron the five-franc piece the "philanthropist" had left him.

"A charcoal fire?" asked the woman.

"Yes."

"How many bushels?"

"Two good ones."

"That'll be thirty sous. With the rest, I'll buy something for dinner."

"The devil, no."

"Why?"

"Don't go spending the hundred-sous piece."

"Why?"

"Because I'll have something to buy."

"What?"

"Something."

"How much will you need?"

"Where's the nearest hardware store?"

"Rue Mouffetard."

"Oh! Yes, on a corner; I remember."

"But tell me now how much you'll need for what you have to buy?"

"Three francs and fifty sous."

"There won't be much left for dinner."

"Don't bother about eating today. There are better things to come."

"That's enough, my jewel."

At this word from his wife, Jondrette closed the door, and this time Marius heard his steps recede along the hall and go rapidly downstairs.

Just then the clock of Saint-Médard struck one.

XIII

SOLUS CUM SOLO, IN LOCO REMOTO, NON COGITABANTUR ORARE PATER NOSTER

Marius, dreamer though he was, as we have said, had a firm and energetic nature. His habits of solitary meditation, while developing sympathy and compassion in him, had perhaps diminished his ability to become irritated but left intact the faculty of indignation; he had the benevolence of a brahmin and the severity of a judge; he would have pitied a toad, but he would have crushed a viper. Now, it was into a viper's hole he had just been looking; he had a nest of monsters before his eyes.

"These wretches must be brought up short," he said.

None of the enigmas he hoped to see solved were yet cleared up; on the contrary, everything had perhaps become more puzzling; he knew nothing more about the beautiful child of the Luxembourg or the man whom he called M. Leblanc, except that Jondrette knew them. From the murky words that had been spoken, he distinctly saw one thing, that an ambush was being prepared, an obscure but terrible ambush; that they were both in great danger, she probably, her father certainly; that he must foil the Jondrettes' awful schemes and cut through the web of these spiders.

For a moment he looked at La Jondrette. She had pulled an old sheet-iron furnace out of a corner and was rummaging among scraps of iron.

He got down from the bureau as quietly as he could, careful not to make any noise.

In the midst of his dread at what was in preparation and the horror with which the Jondrettes had inspired him, he felt a sort of joy at the idea that perhaps he would be given the chance to be of great service to the one he loved.

But what should he do? Warn the persons threatened? Where could he find them? He didn't know their address. They had reappeared for an instant, then had plunged back into the bottomless depths of Paris. Wait at the door for M. Leblanc at six in the evening, the time when he would arrive and warn him of the trap? But Jondrette and his men would see him watching, the place was deserted, they would be stronger than he, they would find means to seize him or get him out of the way, and the person Marius wanted to save would be lost. One o'clock had just struck, the ambush was to be carried out at six. Marius had five hours before him.

There was only one thing to be done.

He put on his presentable coat, knotted a tie around his neck, took his hat, and went out, without making any more noise than if he had been walking barefoot on moss.

Besides, the Jondrette woman was still fumbling over her old iron scraps.

Once outside, he went to the Rue du Petit-Banquier.

He was about midway down that street near a very low wall that he could have stepped over in some places and that bordered a broad field, he was walking slowly, absorbed in his thoughts, and the snow deadened his steps; all at once he heard voices talking very near him. He turned his head, the street was empty, there was nobody in it, it was broad daylight, and yet he distinctly heard voices.

It occurred to him to look over this wall.

There were in fact two men there with their backs to the wall, seated in the snow, and talking softly.

These two were unknown to him. One was a bearded man in a tunic, and the other a long-haired man in tatters. The bearded man had on a Greek cap, the other was bareheaded, and there was snow in his hair.

By bending his head over above them, Marius could hear.

The long-haired one jogged the other with his elbow, and said, "With Patron-Minnette it can't fail."

"You think so?" asked the bearded one and the long-haired one replied, "It'll be a bankroll of five hundred for each of us, and the worst that can happen: five, six years, ten at most!"

The other answered hesitatingly, scratching under his Greek cap, "Yes, it's the real thing. We can't go against such things."

"I tell you the affair can't fail," replied the long-haired one. "We'll fix Father What's-His-Name's wagon."

Then they began to talk about a melodrama they had seen the evening before at La Gaîté.

Marius went on his way.

It seemed to him that the obscure words of these men, so strangely hidden behind that wall and crouching down in the snow, were perhaps not without some connection to Jondrette's terrible projects. That must be "the affair."

He went toward the Faubourg Saint-Marceau and asked at the first shop on his way where he could find a police inspector.

Number 14, Rue de Pontoise, was pointed out to him.

Marius went there.

Passing a bakery, he bought a two-sou loaf of bread and ate it, foreseeing he would have no dinner.

On his way he gave Providence its due. He reflected that if he had not given his five francs to the Jondrette girl in the morning, he would have followed M. Leblanc's fiacre and consequently known nothing, so that there would have been no obstacle to the Jondrettes' ambush, and M. Leblanc would have been lost, and his daughter undoubtedly with him.

XIV

IN WHICH A POLICE OFFICER GIVES A LAWYER TWO FISTICUFFS

On reaching Number 14, Rue de Pontoise, he went upstairs and asked for the superintendent.

"The superintendent isn't in," said one of the office boys, "but there is an inspector taking his place. Do you want to speak to him? Is it urgent?"

"Yes," said Marius.

The office boy took him into the superintendent's office. A tall man was standing there behind a railing, in front of a stove, holding up with both hands the flaps of a huge overcoat with a triple cape. He had a square face, a thin and firm mouth, very fierce, bushy grayish whiskers, and a stare that would turn your pockets inside out. You might have said of this stare, that it did not penetrate so much as ransack.

The man's appearance was not much less ferocious or intimidating than Jondrette's; occasionally the dog is no less startling than the wolf.

"What do you want?" he said to Marius, without adding "monsieur."

"The superintendent of police?"

"He is not here. I am here in his place."

"It is a very private matter."

"You can tell me."

"And very urgent."

"Then tell me quickly."

This man, calm and abrupt, was both alarming and reassuring. He inspired fear and confidence. Marius gave his account—that a person he only knew by sight was to be drawn into an ambush that very evening; that since he occupied the room next to the place, he Marius Pontmercy, attorney, had heard the whole plot through the partition; that the scoundrel who had contrived the plot was named Jondrette; that he had accomplices, probably prowlers of the city gates, among others a certain Panchaud, alias Printanier, alias Bigrenaille; that Jondrette's daughters would be lookouts; that there was no means of warning the threatened man, since not even his name was known; and finally, that all this was to be done at six that evening, at the most desolate spot on the Boulevard de l'Hôpital, in the house numbered 50–52.

At that number the inspector raised his head, and said coolly, "It is then in the room at the end of the hall?"

"Exactly," Marius said, and he added, "Do you know the house?"

The inspector remained silent a moment, then answered, warming the heel of his boot at the door of the stove, "So it seems."

He continued between his teeth, speaking less to Marius than to his necktie.

"There must be a dash of Patron-Minette in this."

That word struck Marius. "Patron-Minette," he said. "In fact I did hear that word."

And he told the inspector about the dialogue between the long-haired man and the bearded man in the snow behind the wall on the Rue du Petit-Banquier.

The inspector muttered, "The long-haired one must be Brujon, and the bearded one must be Demi-Liard, alias Deux-Milliards."

He had looked down again, and was thinking.

"As to the Father What's-His-Name, I have an inkling who he is. There, I have burned my coat. They always make the fire too big in these damn stoves. Number Fifty–Fifty-two. Old Gorbeau property."

Then he looked at Marius:

"You've seen only this bearded man and this long-haired man?"

"And Panchaud."

"You didn't see a sort of devilish little dandy prowling around there?"

"No."

"Nor a great, big, clumsy heap, like the elephant in the Jardin des Plantes?"

"No."

"Nor a wily one who looks like an old buffoon?"

"No."

"As to the fourth nobody sees him, not even his

helpers, clerks, and agents, so it's not very surprising that you didn't."

"No. Who are all those people?" inquired Marius.

The inspector answered, "And then it is not their time."

He relapsed into silence, then continued, "Number Fifty–Fifty-two. I know the shanty. Impossible for us to hide inside without the artists seeing us; then they would leave and break up the act. They're so modest! The public annoys them. None of that, none of that. I want to hear them sing and make them dance."

This monologue finished, he turned toward Marius, looked straight at him, and asked, "Will you be afraid?"

"Of what?" Marius said.

"Of these men?"

"No more than you!" Marius replied rudely, beginning to notice that this policeman had not yet called him monsieur.

The inspector looked at Marius still more steadily and continued with sententious solemnity, "Now you're talking like a brave and honest man. Courage does not fear crime, and honesty does not fear authority."

Marius interrupted him: "That's well and good; but what do you intend to do?"

The inspector merely answered, "The lodgers in that house have latchkeys to get in with at night. You must have one?"

"Yes," Marius said.

"Do you have it with you?"

"Yes."

"Give it to me," the inspector said.

Marius took his key from his waistcoat, handed it to the inspector, and added, "If you believe me, you will come in full force."

The inspector threw Marius a glance such as Voltaire would have thrown at a provincial academician who had proposed a rhyme to him; with a single movement he plunged both his hands, which were enormous, into the two immense pockets of his overcoat, and took out two small steel pistols, of the kind called fisticuffs. He presented them to Marius, saying hastily and curtly, "Take these. Go home. Hide in your room. Let them think you've gone out. They're loaded. Each with two balls. You will watch; there is a hole in the wall, as you have said. The men will come. Let them go on a little. When you feel the affair has come to a head, and that it is time to stop it, fire a pistol. Not too soon. The rest is my affair. A pistol shot in the air, into the ceiling, no matter where. Above all, not too soon. Wait till the consummation is begun; you're a lawyer, you know when that is."

Marius took the pistols and put them in the side pocket of his coat.

"They make a bunch that way, they show," said the inspector. "Put them in your fobs instead."

Marius hid the pistols in his fob pockets.

"Now," the inspector said, "there isn't a minute to be lost by anybody. What time is it? Half-past two. It is at seven?"

"Six o'clock," Marius said.

"I have enough time," continued the inspector, "but none to spare. Don't forget what I told you. Bang. A pistol shot."

"Don't worry," Marius answered.

And as Marius placed his hand on the latch of the door to go out, the inspector called to him, "By the way, if you need me between now and then, come or send word here. Ask for Inspector Javert."

XV

JONDRETTE MAKES HIS PURCHASE

A few moments later, toward three o'clock, Courfeyrac happened to pass along the Rue Mouffetard with Bossuet. The snow was falling still harder, filling the air. Bossuet was just saying to Courfeyrac, "Seeing all these snowflakes fall, it's like a swarm of white butterflies in the sky." All at once Bossuet saw Marius, who was going up the street toward the city gate with a strange look about him.

"Hold on, Marius," said Bossuet.

"I saw him," said Courfeyrac. "Don't let's speak to him."

"Why?"

"He's preoccupied."

"With what?"

"Don't you see that look on him?"

"What look?"

"Like a man following somebody."

"That's true," said Bossuet.

"And look at the eyes he's making!" added Courfeyrac.

"But who the devil is he following?"

"Some deary-sweety-flowery-bonnet! He's in love."

"But," observed Bossuet, "I don't see any deary, nor any sweety, nor any flowery bonnet in the street. There's not one woman."

Courfeyrac looked and exclaimed, "He's following a man!"

In fact a man with a cap on his head and whose gray beard they could make out, though only his back could be seen, was walking some twenty paces in front of Marius.

This man was dressed in a new overcoat, which was too large for him, and an awful pair of tattered and blackened trousers.

Bossuet burst out laughing.

"Who is that man?"

"That?" replied Courfeyrac. "A poet! Poets love wearing the pants of a rabbit-skin peddler and the coat of a peer of France."

"Let's see where Marius is going," Bossuet said. "Let's see where the man is going, let us follow them, eh?"

"Bossuet!" exclaimed Courfeyrac. "Eagle of Meaux! You're a prodigious fool. Follow a man following a man!"

They went on their way.

Marius had in fact seen Jondrette passing along the Rue Mouffetard and was watching him.

Jondrette went straight on without suspecting that there was now an eye trained on him.

He left the Rue Mouffetard, and Marius saw him go into one of the most wretched places on the Rue Gracieuse; he stayed there about a quarter of an hour, then returned to the Rue Mouffetard. He stopped at a hardware store, which then existed at the corner of the Rue Pierre-Lombard, and, a few minutes later, Marius saw him come out of the shop, holding in his hand a large cold chisel with a white wooden handle, which he concealed under his coat. At the upper end of the Rue du Petit-Gentilly, he turned to the left and walked rapidly to the Rue du Petit-Banquier. Night was falling; the snow, which had stopped for a moment, was beginning to fall again; Marius hid just at the corner of the Rue du Petit-Banquier, which was deserted as usual, and did not follow Jondrette farther. It was fortunate that he did, for on reaching the low wall where Marius had heard the long-haired man and the bearded man talking, Jondrette turned around, made sure that nobody was following him or saw him, then stepped over the wall, and disappeared.

The vacant lot bounded by this wall gave onto the rear court of a livery-stable-keeper of bad repute, who had failed but who had still a few old vehicles under his sheds.

Marius thought it best to take advantage of Jondrette's absence to go home; besides it was getting late; every evening, Ma'am Burgon, on going out to do her dish-washing in the city, would close the house door, which was always locked at dusk; Marius had given his key to the inspector of police, so it was important for him to hurry.

Evening had come; night had almost closed in; there was now only one spot in the horizon or in the whole sky lit by the sun—the moon.

It was rising red behind the low dome of La Salpêtrière.

Marius rapidly stode back to No. 50–52. The door was still open when he arrived. He went up the stairs on tiptoe and glided along the wall of the hall as far as his room. This hall, it will be remembered, was lined on both sides by garret rooms, which were all at that time empty and for rent. Ma'am Bourgon usually left the doors open. As he passed by one of these doors, Marius thought he glimpsed in the unoccupied cell four motionless heads, dimly visible in a remnant of daylight falling through the skylight. Not wishing to be seen Marius did not attempt to see. He managed to get into his room without being noticed and without a sound. It was just in time. A moment later he heard Ma'am Burgon going out and closing the door of the house.

XVI

IN WHICH WILL BE FOUND THE SONG TO AN ENGLISH TUNE POPULAR AROUND 1832

Marius sat down on his bed. It might have been half-past five. Only a half hour separated him from what was to come. He could hear his arteries beating as one hears the ticking of a watch in the dark. He thought of the double march going on that moment in the darkness, crime advancing on the one hand, justice coming on the other. He was not afraid but could not think without a sort of shudder of the things soon to take place. To him, as to all to whom some surprising adventure has suddenly occurred, the whole day seemed only a dream; and, to assure himself that he was not prey to a nightmare, he had to feel the chill of the two steel pistols in his fob pockets.

It had stopped snowing; the moon, brighter and brighter, was growing clear of the haze, and its light, mingled with the white reflection from the fallen snow, gave the room a twilight appearance.

There was a light in the Jondrette lair. Marius saw the hole in the partition shine with a gleam that seemed blood-red.

He was sure this glow could hardly be produced by a candle. However, there was no movement in their room, nobody was stirring there, nobody spoke, not a breath, only a deep icy stillness, and except for that light, he could have believed he was beside a tomb.

Marius quietly took off his boots and pushed them under his bed.

Some minutes passed. Marius heard the lower door turn on its hinges; a rapid, heavy step ascended the stairs and passed along the corridor, the latch of the garret room was noisily lifted; Jondrette had come in.

Several voices were immediately heard. The whole family was in the garret. Only they kept silent in the absence of the master, like cubs in the absence of the wolf.

"Here I am," he said.

"Good evening, Papa," yapped the daughters.

"Well then?" said the mother.

"It's going like a charm," answered Jondrette, "but my feet are cold as a dog's. Good, that's right, you're dressed up. You must inspire confidence."

"All ready to go out."

"You won't forget any of what I told you! You'll do all of it?"

"Don't worry about that."

"Because—" said Jondrette.

Marius heard him put something heavy on the table, probably the chisel he had bought.

"Ah, ha!" said Jondrette, "have you been eating here?"

"Yes," said the mother, "I've had three big potatoes and some salt. I took advantage of the fire to cook them."

"Well," replied Jondrette, "tomorrow we'll eat out. We'll have duck and all the trimmings. We'll eat like Charles the Tenth. Everything's going well."

Then he added, lowering his voice, "The mousetrap is set. The cats are ready."

He lowered his voice still more, and said, "Put that in the fire."

Marius heard a sound of charcoal, as if somebody was striking it with pincers or some iron tool, and Jondrette continued, "Have you greased the door hinges so that they won't make any noise?"

"Yes," answered the mother.

"What time is it?"

"Almost six. The half has just struck at Saint-Médard."

"The devil!" said Jondrette. "The girls must go and stand watch. Come here, you children, and listen to me."

There was a whispering.

Jondrette's voice rose again, "Has Burgon gone out?"

"Yes," said the mother.

"Are you sure there's nobody home in our neighbor's room?"

"He hasn't been back all day, and you know it's his dinnertime."

"You're sure?"

"Sure."

"All the same," replied Jondrette, "there's no harm in

going to see whether he's at home. Daughter, take the candle and go."

Marius dropped to his hands and knees and noiselessly crept under the bed.

Hardly had he concealed himself, when he saw a light through the cracks of his door.

"P'pa," cried a voice, "he's gone."

He recognized the voice of the older girl.

"Have you gone in?" asked the father.

"No," answered the girl, "but since his key's in the door, he's out."

The father called out, "Go in just the same."

The door opened, and Marius saw the girl come in with a candle. She looked the same as she had in the morning, except still more frightening in this light.

She walked straight toward the bed. Marius felt a momentary anxiety, but there was a mirror nailed on the wall near the bed; that was where she was going. She stretched up on tiptoe and looked at herself in it. A sound of old iron rattling came from the next room.

She smoothed her hair with the palm of her hand and smiled at the mirror, while singing in her broken sepulchral voice:

> Nos amours ont duré tout une semaine,
> Mais que du bonheur les instants sont courts!
> S'adorer huit jours, c'était bien la peine!
> Le temps des amours devrait durer toujours!
> Devrait durer toujours! devrait durer toujours![1]

Meanwhile Marius was trembling. It seemed impossible to him that she did not hear his breathing.

She went to the window and looked out, speaking aloud in her half-crazy way.

"How ugly Paris is in a white shirt!" she said.

She returned to the mirror and began her grimacing again, taking alternately front and side views of herself.

[1]A week of love, and gone again,
Such happiness so quickly over.
Eight days of bliss are worth the pain,
But hours of love should last forever,
Should last forever, last forever.

"Well," cried her father, "what are you doing now?"

"I'm looking under the bed and the furniture," she answered, continuing to arrange her hair; "there's nobody here."

"Ninny!" howled the father. "Here immediately, and let's not lose any time."

"Coming! Coming!" she said. "There's no time for anything in their shanty."

She hummed:

> Vous me quittez pour aller à la gloire,
> Mon triste coeur suivra partout vos pas.[1]

With a last glance at the mirror, she went out, shutting the door behind her.

A moment later, Marius heard the sound of the young girls' bare feet in the hall, and Jondrette's voice calling to them.

"Pay attention, now! One toward the city gate, the other at the corner of the Rue du Petit-Banquier. Don't lose sight of the house door a minute, and if you see the least thing, here right away! Hurry! You have a key to come in with."

The older daughter muttered, "Standing watch barefoot in the snow!"

"Tomorrow you'll have boots of brown silk!" said the father.

They went down the stairs, and a few seconds later the sound of the lower door shutting announced that they had gone out.

There was nobody left now in the house but Marius and the Jondrettes, and probably also the mysterious beings whom Marius had glimpsed in the twilight behind the door of the untenanted garret.

[1] You leave me for the paths of glory,
But my heart will follow you all the way.

XVII

USE OF MARIUS'S FIVE-FRANC PIECE

Marius decided that the time had come to take up his place at his observation point. In a twinkling, and with the agility of youth, he was at the hole in the partition.

He looked in.

The interior of the Jondrette apartment looked odd, and Marius found the explanation of the strange light he had noticed. A candle was burning in a verdigris candlestick, but that was not what really lit up the room. The whole room was, as it were, illuminated by the reflection of a large tin stove in the fireplace, filled with lighted charcoal—the fire the female Jondrette had readied during the day. The charcoal was burning and the stove red hot, a blue flame danced inside it and helped to show the shape of the chisel bought by Jondrette in the Rue Pierre-Lombard, which was turning red among the coals. In a corner near the door, and arranged as if for some anticipated use, were two heaps that appeared to be, one a heap of old iron pieces, the other a heap of ropes. All this would have made anyone, who knew nothing of what was coming, waver between a very sinister idea and a very simple one. The dingy room thus lit up seemed a smithy rather than a mouth of hell; but Jondrette, in that glare, looked more like a demon than a blacksmith.

The heat of the glowing coals was such that the candle on the table melted on the side toward the stove and was burning fastest on that side. An old shaded copper lantern, worthy of Diogenes turned Cartouche, stood on the mantel.

The furnace, which was set into the fireplace beside the almost extinguished embers, sent its smoke into the chimney flue and gave off no odor.

The moon, shining through the four panes of the window, threw its whiteness into the orange-flaming garret; and to Marius's poetic mind, a dreamer even in the moment of action, it was like a thought of heaven mingled with the misshapen nightmares of earth.

A breath of air, coming through the broken pane, helped dissipate the charcoal odor.

The Jondrette lair was, if the reader remembers what we have said of the Gorbeau house, admirably chosen as stage for a dark and violent deed and concealing crime. It was the farthest room of the most isolated house on the loneliest boulevard in Paris. If ambush had not existed, it would have been invented there.

The whole depth of a house and a multitude of untenanted rooms separated this hole from the boulevard, and its only window opened onto vacant lots surrounded by walls and palisade fences.

Jondrette had lit his pipe, sat down on the dismantled chair, and was smoking. His wife was speaking to him softly.

If Marius had been Courfeyrac, that is to say one of those men who laugh at every opportunity in life, he would have broken into laughter when his eye fell on this woman. She had on a black hat with plumes somewhat like the hats of the heralds-at-arms at the consecration of Charles X, an immense tartan shawl over her knit skirt, and the man's shoes her daughter had scorned in the morning. It was this outfit that had drawn from Jondrette the exclamation "Good, that's right! You're dressed up! You must inspire confidence!"

As to Jondrette, he had not taken off the new outsized overcoat that M. Leblanc had given him, and his clothing continued to offer that contrast between the coat and pants that constituted in Courfeyrac's eyes the ideal costume of a poet.

Suddenly Jondrette raised his voice. "By the way, now that I think of it. In this weather he'll come in a fiacre. Light the lantern, take it, and go downstairs. Stay there behind the lower door. The moment you hear the carriage stop, open the door immediately. He will come up. You will light him up the stairs and along the hall, and when he comes in here, go down again immediately, pay the driver, and send the fiacre away."

"And the money?" asked the woman.

Jondrette fumbled in his trousers, and handed her five francs.

"What's that?" she exclaimed.

Jondrette answered with dignity, "The monarch our neighbor gave us this morning."

And he added, "You know, we need two chairs here."

"What for?"

"To sit in."

Marius felt a shiver run down his back on hearing the woman's calm reply, "Oh, I'll just go snatch our neighbor's."

And with rapid movement she opened the door of the hovel, and went out into the hall.

Marius did not physically have the time to get down off the bureau and hide under the bed.

"Take the candle," cried Jondrette.

"No," she said, "that would get in my way; I have the two chairs to carry. There's moonlight."

Marius heard the heavy hand of Mother Jondrette groping for his key in the dark. The door opened. He stood nailed to his place in apprehension.

The woman came in.

The gable window let in a ray of moonlight between two great expanses of shadow, one of which entirely covered the wall against which Marius was leaning.

Mother Jondrette looked up, did not see Marius, took the two chairs, the only chairs Marius had, and went out, slamming the door noisily behind her.

She went back into the hovel.

"Here are the chairs."

"And here is the lantern," said the husband. "Go down quickly."

She hastily obeyed, and Jondrette was suddenly alone.

He arranged the two chairs on the two sides of the table, turned the chisel over in the fire, put an old screen in front of the fireplace, which concealed the stove, then went to the corner where the heap of ropes was, and stooped down, as if to examine something. Marius then saw that what he had taken for a shapeless heap was a rope ladder, very well made, with wooden rungs, and two large hooks to hang it by.

This ladder and a few big tools, actual bludgeons of iron, which were thrown on the pile of old iron heaped up behind the door, were not in the Jondrette room in the morning, and had evidently been brought there in the afternoon, during Marius's absence.

"Blacksmith's tools," thought Marius.

Had Marius been a little better informed in this line, he would have recognized, in what he took for smith's tools, certain instruments capable of picking a lock or forcing a door, and others capable of cutting or hacking—the two families of sinister tools that thieves call *cadets* and *fauchants*.

The fireplace and the table, with the two chairs, were exactly opposite Marius. The stove was hidden; the room was now lit only by the candle; the least scrap on the table or the mantel cast a huge shadow. A broken water pitcher masked half of one wall. In the room there was an unspeakably threatening dead calm. One could feel the approach of some horror.

Jondrette had let his pipe go out—a grave sign of preoccupation—and had come back and sat down. The candle brought out the savage sharp angles of his face. There were contractions of his brows, and abrupt spreadings of his right hand, as if he were replying to the last counsels of a dark interior monologue. In one of these obscure replies he was making to himself, he drew out the table drawer quickly, removed a long carving knife hidden there, and tried its edge on his nail. This done, he put the knife back into the drawer and shut it.

As for Marius, he grasped the pistol that was in his right fob pocket, took it out, and cocked it.

In cocking, the pistol gave a clear, sharp little sound.

Jondrette started and half rose from his chair.

"Who's there?" he cried.

Marius held his breath; Jondrette listened a moment, then began to laugh, saying, "What kind of a fool am I? It's the partition creaking."

Marius kept the pistol in his hand.

XVIII

MARIUS'S TWO CHAIRS FACE EACH OTHER

Just then the distant and melancholy vibration of a bell shook the windows. Six struck at Saint-Médard.

Jondrette marked each toll with a nod of his head. At the sixth, he snuffed the candle with his fingers.

Then he began to walk around the room, listened in the hall, walked, listened again: "Just so long as he comes!" he muttered; then he returned to his chair.

He had hardly sat down when the door opened.

Mother Jondrette had opened it and stood in the hall making a horrible, friendly grimace, which was lit up from beneath by one of the holes of the shaded lantern.

"Come in," she said.

"Come in, my benefactor," repeated Jondrette, rising precipitately.

M. Leblanc appeared.

He had an air of venerable serenity.

He laid four Louis on the table.

"Monsieur Fabantou," he said, "that's for your rent and your pressing needs. We will see about the rest."

"God reward you, my generous benefactor!" said Jondrette, and to his wife, "Send away the fiacre!"

She slipped away, while her husband was lavishing bows and offering a chair to M. Leblanc. A moment later she came back and whispered in his ear, "Done."

The snow that had been falling on and off since morning was so deep that they had not heard the fiacre arrive and did not hear it go away.

Meanwhile M. Leblanc had sat down.

Jondrette was in the chair opposite M. Leblanc.

Now, for an idea of the scene that follows, let the reader imagine the chilly night, the deserted streets near the Hôpital de La Salpêtrière covered with snow and white in the moonlight like immense shrouds, the flickering light of the streetlamps here and there casting a red glow on the tragic boulevards and the long rows of black elms, not a passerby perhaps within a mile around, the Gorbeau structure deep in silence, horror, and night, in that crumbling building, in the midst of this loneliness, in the midst of this darkness, the vast Jondrette garret lit by a candle, and in this den two men seated at a table, M. Leblanc calm, Jondrette smiling and cruel, his wife the she-wolf in a corner, and behind the partition, Marius, invisible, alert, missing not a word, not a movement, on watch, the pistol in his grasp.

Marius was experiencing horror, not fear. He clasped the butt of the pistol and felt reassured. "I shall stop this wretch when I please," he thought.

He felt the police were somewhere nearby, awaiting the agreed signal, all ready to stretch out an arm.

He hoped that from this terrible meeting between Jondrette and M. Leblanc some light would be thrown on all he wanted to know.

XIX

A CONCERN FOR DARK CORNERS

No sooner was M. Leblanc seated than he turned his eyes toward the empty pallets.

"How is the poor little injured one?" he asked.

"Not well," answered Jondrette with a doleful yet grateful smile, "not well at all, my worthy monsieur. Her older sister has taken her to the Bourbe to have her arm dressed. You will see them. They will be back directly."

"Madame Fabantou seems much better to me?" M. Leblanc went on, casting his eyes on the grotesque attire of La Jondrette, who, standing between him and the door, as though already guarding the exit, was looking at him in a threatening, almost defiant posture.

"She is dying," said Jondrette. "But you see, monsieur! She has so much courage, that woman! She is not a woman, she is an ox!"

The woman, touched by the compliment, retorted with the smirk of a flattered monster, "You are always too kind to me, Monsieur Jondrette."

"Jondrette!" said M. Leblanc. "I thought your name was Fabantou?"

"Fabantou or Jondrette!" replied the husband hastily. "Sobriquet as an artist!"

And, directing a shrug of the shoulders toward his wife, which M. Leblanc did not see, he continued with an emphatic and caressing tone of voice, "Ah! We have always gotten along together, this poor dear and I! What would be left us, if it were not for that? We are so unfortunate, my respected monsieur! We have arms, we have courage, but no work! I don't know how the government arranges it, but, on my word of honor, I am no Jacobin, monsieur, I am no rabble-rousing democrat, I wish them no harm, but if I were the ministers, on my most sacred word, things would be different. Now, for example, I wanted to have my girls learn the trade of making cardboard boxes. You will say, What! A trade? Yes, a trade! A simple trade! A living! What a downfall, my benefactor! What degradation, when one has been what we once were! Alas, we have nothing left from our days of prosperity! Nothing but one single thing, a painting, to which I cling, yet shall have to part with, for we must live! That's how it is, we must live!"

While Jondrette was talking, with an apparent disorder that detracted nothing from his crafty expression, Marius looked up and saw at the back of the room somebody he had not seen before. A man had come in so noiselessly that nobody had heard the door swing open. The man wore a violet knit waistcoat, old, worn-out, stained, cut, and showing gaps at all its folds, wide trousers of cotton velvet, socks on his feet, no shirt, his neck bare, his arms bare and tattooed, and his face stained black. He sat down in silence and with folded arms on the nearest bed, and as he stayed behind the woman, he could be made out only with difficulty.

That kind of magnetic instinct that warns the eye made M. Leblanc turn at almost the same time as Marius. He could not help a movement of surprise, which did not escape Jondrette.

"Ah! I see!" exclaimed Jondrette, buttoning up his coat complacently. "You're looking at your overcoat. It's a fine fit! Very fine!"

"Who is that man?" said M. Leblanc.

"That man?" said Jondrette. "A neighbor. Pay no attention to him."

This neighbor looked very strange. However, chemical factories abound in Faubourg Saint-Marceau. Many factory workers might get black faces. Actually, everything about M. Leblanc exuded a candid and intrepid confidence. He said, "Pardon me; you were saying Monsieur Fabantou?"

"I was telling you, monsieur and dear patron," replied Jondrette, leaning his elbows on the table, and gazing at M. Leblanc with staring and tender eyes, rather like a boa constrictor's, "I was telling you that I had a picture to sell."

There was a slight noise at the door. A second man entered and sat down on the bed behind Mother Jondrette. He had his arms bare, like the first, and a mask of ink or soot.

Although this man had, literally, slipped into the room, he could not prevent M. Leblanc from noticing him.

"Do not mind them," said Jondrette. "They live in this house. I was telling you, then, I have a valuable painting left. Here, monsieur, look."

He got up, went to the wall, at the foot of which stood the panel mentioned, and turned it around, still leaving it leaning against the wall. It looked like a painting, but the candle scarcely revealed it. Marius could not make out any of it, Jondrette being between him and the picture; he merely caught a glimpse of a coarse daub, with a sort of principal figure painted in the crude and glaring style of works by itinerant artists or of painted screens.

"What is that?" asked M. Leblanc.

Jondrette exclaimed, "A painting by a master; a high-priced picture, my benefactor! I cling to it as I do to my daughter, it brings back memories! But I have told you, and I cannot retract it, I am so unfortunate, I must part with it."

Whether by chance, or whether there was some beginning of distrust, while examining the picture, M. Leblanc glanced toward the back of the room. There were now four men there, three seated on the bed, one standing near the door frame, all four bare-armed, motionless, and with blackened faces. One of the three on the bed was leaning against the wall with his eyes closed, and one would have said he was asleep. That one was old; his white hair over his black face looked horrible. The two others seemed young; one was bearded, the other had long hair. None of them had shoes on; those who did not have socks were barefoot.

Jondrette noticed that M. Leblanc's eye had settled on the men.

"They are friends. They live nearby," he said. "They are dark because they work in charcoal. They are chimney menders. Don't concern yourself with them, my benefactor, but buy my picture. Take pity on my misery. I will not sell it to you at a high price. How much would you say it is worth?"

"But," said M. Leblanc, looking Jondrette full in the face like a man putting himself on his guard, "that is some tavern sign. It is worth about three francs."

Jondrette answered calmly, "Did you bring some money with you? I would settle for a thousand crowns."

M. Leblanc rose to his feet, backed up to the wall, and ran his eye rapidly over the room. He had Jondrette at his left on the side toward the window, and his wife and the four men at his right on the side toward the door. The four men did not budge, and did not even seem to see him; Jondrette had gone back to talking in a plaintive key, with his eyes so wild and his tones so mournful that M. Leblanc might have thought he was seeing no more nor less than a man crazed by misery.

"If you do not buy my picture, dear benefactor," said Jondrette, "I am without resources, I can only throw myself into the river. When I think that I wanted to have my two girls learn to work on medium-fine cardboard, cardboard for gift boxes. Well! They would need a table with a board at the bottom so the glasses don't fall to the ground, they must have a specially made stove, a pot with three compartments for the different degrees of strength that the glue must have according to whether it is used for wood, paper, or cloth, a knife to cut the cardboard, a gauge to adjust it, a hammer for tacking on the metal strips, brushes, what the devil, how do I know what else? And all this to earn four sous a day! And work fourteen hours! And every box passes through the girl's hands thirteen times! And wetting the paper! And without staining anything! And to keep the glue warm! The devil, I tell you! Four sous a day! How do you think one can live?"

While speaking, Jondrette did not look at M. Leblanc, who was watching him. M. Leblanc's eye was fixed on Jondrette, and Jondrette's eye on the door, Marius's breathless attention went from one to the other. M. Leblanc appeared to be asking himself, "Is this man an idiot?" Jondrette repeated two or three times with all sorts of varied inflections in the drawling and begging style, "I can only throw myself into the river! I went down three steps with that in mind the other day near the Pont d'Austerlitz!"

Suddenly his dull eye lit up with a hideous glare, this little man straightened up and turned horrifying, he took a step toward M. Leblanc and thundered at him, "But all this is not the point! Do you know me?"

XX

THE AMBUSH

The door of the garret had suddenly been flung open, disclosing three men in blue tunics with black paper masks. The first was spare and had a long iron-bound cudgel; the second, who was a sort of colossus, held by the middle of the handle, with the metal end down, a butcher's poleax. The third, a broad-shouldered man, not so thin as the first nor so heavy as the second, held in his clenched fist an enormous key stolen from some prison door.

It appeared that it was the arrival of these men for which Jondrette had been waiting. A rapid dialogue began between him and the man with the cudgel, the spare man.

"Is everything ready?" said Jondrette.

"Yes," answered the spare man.

"Then where is Montparnasse?"

"The young chief stopped to chat with your daughter."

"Which one?"

"The elder."

"Is there a fiacre below?"

"Yes."

"The cart is ready?"

"Ready."

"With two good horses?"

"Excellent."

"It's waiting where I said it should?"

"Yes."

"Good," said Jondrette.

M. Leblanc was very pale. He looked over everything around him in the room like a man who understands where he has landed, and his head, directed in turn toward all the heads surrounding him, moved on his neck with an attentive and astonished deliberation, but there was nothing in his manner resembling fear. He had made an improvised bulwark of the table; and this man who, the moment before, had the appearance merely of a kind old man, had suddenly become a sort of athlete, and placed his powerful fist on the back of his chair with a surprising and intimidating gesture.

This old man, so firm and so brave before so great a peril, seemed to be one of those natures who are courageous as they are good, simply and naturally. The father of someone we love is never a stranger to us. Marius felt proud of this unknown man.

Three of the men whom Jondrette had described as chimney menders had taken from the heap of old iron a large pair of shears, a crowbar, and a hammer, respectively, and placed themselves in front of the door without saying a word. The old man was still on the bed and had merely opened his eyes. Jondrette had sat down beside him.

Marius thought that in a few seconds more the time would come to interfere, and he raised his right hand toward the ceiling, in the direction of the hall, ready to fire off his pistol shot.

Jondrette, after his colloquy with the man who had the cudgel, turned back to M. Leblanc and repeated his question, accompanying it with that low, smothered, and terrible laugh of his: "You don't recognize me, then?"

M. Leblanc looked him in the face and answered, "No."

The Jondrette came up to the table. He leaned forward over the candle, folding his arms and thrusting his angular and ferocious jaws up toward M. Leblanc's calm face as nearly as he could without forcing him to draw back, and in that posture, like a wild beast just about to bite, he cried out, "My name is not Fabantou, my name is not Jondrette, my name is Thénardier! I am the innkeeper of Montfermeil! Do you understand? Thénardier! Now do you know me?"

An imperceptible flush passed over M. Leblanc's forehead, and he answered without a tremor or elevation of voice and with his usual calm, "No more than before."

Marius did not hear this answer. Anybody able to observe him at that moment in the darkness would have seen he was haggard, astounded, thunderstruck. When Jondrette had said, "My name is Thénardier," Marius had trembled in every limb and leaned against the wall as if he had felt the chill of a swordblade through his heart. Then his right arm, ready to fire the signal shot, dropped slowly, and at the moment that Jondrette had repeated,

"Do you understand? Thénardier!" Marius's unsteady fingers had almost dropped the pistol. Jondrette, in unveiling who he was, had not moved M. Leblanc, but he had completely unnerved Marius. That name of Thénardier, which M. Leblanc did not seem to know, Marius knew. Remember what that name was to him! That name he had worn on his heart, written in his father's will! He carried it in his innermost thought, in the holiest spot of his memory, in that sacred command "A man named Thénardier saved my life. If my son should meet him, he will do him all the good he can." That name, we remember, was one of the devotions of his heart; he mingled it with the name of his father in his worship. Could it be that here was Thénardier, here was that Thénardier, here was that innkeeper of Montfermeil, whom he had so long and vainly sought! He had found him at last, but how? This savior of his father was a criminal! This man, to whom Marius ardently wanted to devote himself was a monster! This deliverer of Colonel Pontmercy was in the actual commission of a crime whose nature Marius did not yet see very distinctly, but which looked like murder! And upon whom, Great God! What a stroke of destiny! What a bitter mockery of fate! From the depths of his coffin, his father commanded him to do all the good he could to Thénardier; for four years Marius had had no other thought than to pay this debt of his father's, and the moment when he was about to cause a criminal to be seized by justice in the midst of a crime, destiny said to him, That is Thénardier! His father's life, saved in a storm of grapeshot on the heroic field of Waterloo, at last he was about to reward this man for that, and to reward him with the scaffold! He had resolved, if ever he found this Thénardier, to accost him in no other way than by throwing himself at his feet, and now he found him indeed, but to deliver him to the executioner! His father said to him, Help Thénardier! And he was answering that voice by crushing Thénardier! Presenting, as a spectacle to his father in his grave, the man who had snatched him from death at the peril of his life, executed in the Place Saint-Jacques by the act of his son, this Marius to whom he had bequeathed this man! And what a mockery to have so long worn on his breast the last wishes of his father, written by his hand, only to act so frightfully contrary to them! But on the other hand, to watch this ambush and not prevent it! To condemn the victim and spare the assassin, could he be bound to any gratitude toward such a wretch? It was as though every idea Marius had had for the last four years was pierced through and through by this unexpected blow. He shuddered. Everything depended on him. Without their knowledge, he held in his hand those human beings moving there before his eyes. If he fired the pistol, M. Leblanc was saved and Thénardier was lost; if he did not, M. Leblanc was sacrificed, and, perhaps, Thénardier escaped. To hurl down the one or let the other fall! Remorse either way. What could he do? Which should he choose? To fail his most imperious memories, so many deep-seated resolutions, his most sacred duty, that most venerated paper! To fail his father's will, or allow a crime to be carried out? He seemed on the one hand to hear "his Ursula" entreating him for her father and on the other the colonel commending Thénardier to him. He felt crazed. His knees were giving way beneath him. And he did not even have time to deliberate, so furiously was the scene before his eyes rushing forward. It was like a whirlwind, which he had thought himself master of and which was carrying him away. He was on the point of fainting.

Meanwhile Thénardier, from here on we will call him by no other name, was walking to and fro before the table in a sort of wild and frenzied triumph.

He clutched the candle and put it on the mantel with such a shock that the flame almost went out and the tallow spattered on the wall.

Then he turned toward M. Leblanc and, with a frightful look, spit out this: "Singed! Smoked! Basted! On a spit!"

And he began to walk again, in full explosion.

"Ha!" he cried. "I've found you again at last, Monsieur philanthropist! Monsieur threadbare millionaire! Monsieur giver-of-dolls! Old marrow-bones! Ha! You don't recognize me? No, it wasn't you who came to Montfermeil, to my inn, eight years ago, on Christmas Eve 1823! It wasn't you who took away Fantine's child from my house! The Lark! It wasn't you who had a yellow overcoat! No! And a package of clothes in your hands just as when you came here this morning! What do you say now, wife! It's his mania, it appears, to carry packages of wool stockings into houses! Old benevolence, go on! Are you a hosier, Monsieur millionaire? You give the poor your shop sweepings, holy man! What a charlatan! Ha! You don't know me? Well, I recognized you! I knew you immediately as soon as you stuck your nose in here. Ah! You're going to find out at last that it's not all roses going into people's houses like that, under pretext that they are inns, with worn-out clothes, with the appearance of a pauper, to whom anybody would have given a sou, to deceive people, to act generous, take their servants away, and threaten them in the woods, and that you don't get out of it by bringing later, when people are ruined, an overcoat that's too large and two paltry hospital blankets, old beggar, child-stealer!"

He stopped, and appeared to be talking to himself for a moment. One would have said that his fury had dropped like the Rhône into some hole; then, as if he were finishing aloud something he had been saying to himself, he struck his fist on the table and cried, "With his honest look!"

And apostrophizing M. Leblanc: "My God! You mocked me once! You're the cause of all my misfortunes! For fifteen hundred francs you took away a girl I had and who certainly belonged to rich people and who had already brought me in a good deal of money, and from whom I ought to have gotten enough to live on all my life! A girl who would have made up all that I lost in that abominable inn where they had such royal sprees and where I ate up all my worldly goods like a fool! Oh! I wish that all the wine that was drunk in my house had been poison to those who drank it! But forget that! Say, now! You must have thought me a dupe when you went away with the Lark? You had your cudgel in the woods! You were the strongest! Revenge! The trumps are in my hand today. You're sunk, my good man! Oh! But don't I laugh! Indeed, I do! Didn't he fall into the trap? I told him I was an actor, that my name was Fabantou, that I acted comedy with Mamselle Mars, with Mamselle Muche, that my landlord must be paid tomorrow the fourth of February, and he did not even think that the fourth of January is quarter day and not the fourth of February! The ridiculous fool! And these four paltry coins he brings me! Wretch! He didn't even have the heart to go up to a hundred francs! And how he swallowed my platitudes! He amused me. I said to myself: Idiot! Go on, I've got you, I lick your paws this morning! I'll gnaw your heart tonight!"

Thénardier stopped. He was out of breath. His narrow little chest was panting like a blacksmith's bellows. His eye was filled with the base delight of a feeble, cruel, and cowardly animal, that can finally level what it has held in awe, and insult what it has flattered, the joy of a dwarf putting his heel on the head of Goliath, the joy of a jackal beginning to tear at a sick bull, dead enough not to be able to defend himself, still alive enough to suffer.

M. Leblanc did not interrupt him but said when he stopped, "I do not know what you mean. You are mistaken. I am a very poor man and anything but a millionaire. I do not know you; you are mistaking me for someone else."

"Ha!" screamed Thénardier. "What a clown! You still stick to that joke! You're floundering, old boy! Ah! You don't remember? You don't see who I am!"

"Pardon me, monsieur," answered M. Leblanc, with a tone of politeness that, at such a moment, had a peculiarly strange and powerful effect, "I see you are a bandit."

Who has not noticed that hateful people have their tender points; monsters are easily annoyed. At this word "bandit," the Thénardiess sprang off the bed. Thénardier seized his chair as if he were going to crush it in his hands: "Don't you stir," he shouted to his wife, and turning toward M. Leblanc: "Bandit! Yes, I know that you call us that, you rich people! Yes! It's true I've failed; I'm in hiding, I have no bread; I don't have even a sou, I am a bandit. For three days now I've eaten nothing, I am a bandit! Ah! You warm your feet; you have Sakoski shoes, you have padded overcoats like archbishops, you live on the second floor in houses with a concierge, you eat truffles, you eat forty-franc bunches of asparagus in January, and green peas, you gorge yourselves, and when you want to know if it's cold you look in the newspaper to see the degree registered on the thermometer of the inventor Chevalier. But we are our own thermometers! We don't need to go to the quay by the Tour de l'Horloge to see how many degrees below freezing it is; we feel the blood stiffen in our veins and the ice reach our hearts, and we say, 'There is no God!' And you come into our caves, yes, into our caves, and call us bandits. But we will eat you! We will devour you, poor little things! Monsieur millionaire, know this: I have been a man established in business, I have been licensed, I have been a voter, I am a citizen, I am! And you, perhaps, are not!"

Here Thénardier took a step toward the men in front of the door and added with a shudder, "When I think that he dares come and talk to me as if I were a cobbler!"

Then addressing M. Leblanc with a fresh burst of frenzy: "And know this, too, Monsieur philanthropist! I am no shifty man. I'm not a man whose name nobody knows, and who comes into houses to carry off children. I'm a former French solider; I should have been decorated. I was at Waterloo, I was, and in that battle I saved a general, Comte somebody or other. He told me his name, but his blasted voice was so weak I couldn't catch it. I only heard *thank you*. I would have preferred his name to his thanks. It would have helped me find him. This picture that you see, painted by David in Brussels, do you know who it represents? Me. David wanted to immortalize that feat of arms. I have the general on my back, and I am carrying him through the storm of grapeshot. That is history. He has never even done anything at all for me, that general; he's no better than the others. Nonetheless, I saved his life at the risk of my own, and I have my pockets full of certificates. I'm a soldier from Waterloo—name of a thousand names! And now that I've had the goodness to tell you all this, let's get down to business; I need money; I need a lot of money, I need an immense amount of money, and if I don't get it, I'll wipe you out, by God!"

Marius had regained some control over his feelings and was listening. The last trace of doubt had now vanished. It was indeed the Thénardier of the will. Marius shuddered at that reproach of ingratitude flung at his father and which he was on the point of justifying so fatally. His quandary increased. Moreover, there was in all these words of Thénardier's, in his tone, in his gestures, in his look that flashed out with every word, there was in this explosion of an evil nature completely exposing itself, in this mixture of braggadocio and abjectness, of pride and pettiness, of rage and folly in this chaos of real grievances and false sentiments, in this shamelessness of a vicious man tasting the sweetness of violence, in this brazen nakedness of a deformed soul, in this conflagration of every suffering combined with every hatred, something that was hideously evil and yet bitter as truth.

The masterpiece by David, whose purchase he had proposed to M. Leblanc, was, as the reader has guessed, nothing more than the sign of his shoddy inn, painted, as will be remembered, by himself, the only relic saved from his failure at Montfermeil.

As he had ceased to interfere with Marius's line of vision, Marius could now look at the thing, and in this daub he did make out a battle, a background of smoke, and one man carrying off another. It was the pair of Thénardier and Pontmercy; the savior sergeant, the colonel saved. Marius felt giddy; this picture in some way restored his father to life; it was no longer the sign of the Montfermeil inn, it was a resurrection; in it a tomb gaped open, from it a phantom arose. Marius felt his heart throb in his temples, he heard the cannon of Waterloo; his bleeding father dimly painted on this dusky panel startled him, and it seemed to him that that shapeless shadow was gazing steadily at him.

When Thénardier had taken breath, he trained his bloodshot eyes on M. Leblanc and said in a low and curt tone, "What do you have to say before we begin to make you dance?"

M. Leblanc said nothing. In the midst of this silence a hoarse voice threw in this ghastly sarcasm from the hall: "If there's any wood to split, I'm on hand!"

It was the man with the poleax, who was enjoying himself.

At the same time a huge face, bristly and dirty, appeared in the doorway, with a hideous laugh, which showed fangs rather than teeth.

It was the face of the man with the poleax.

"Why have you taken off your mask?" cried Thénardier, furiously.

"To laugh," replied the man.

For some moments, M. Leblanc had seemed to follow and to watch every movement of Thénardier, who, blinded and bewildered by his own rage, was walking back and forth in the lair with the confidence inspired by the feeling that the door was guarded, that he had armed possession of a disarmed man, and being nine to one, even if the Thénardiess was counted for one man only. In his apostrophe to the man with the poleax, he turned his back to M. Leblanc.

M. Leblanc seized this opportunity, pushed the chair away with his foot, the table with his hand, and at one bound, with a marvelous agility, before Thénardier had had time to turn around, he was at the window. To open it, climb onto the sill, and step through it took only a second. He was half outside when six strong hands seized him, and drew him forcibly back into the room. The three chimney menders had thrown themselves upon him. At the same time the Thénardiess had grabbed him by the hair.

Hearing the disturbance, the other criminals ran in from the hall. The old man on the bed, who seemed overcome with wine, got off the pallet, and came tottering along with a road mender's hammer in his hand.

One of the chimney menders, whose blackened face was lit up by the candle, and in whom Marius, in spite of this coloring, recognized Panchaud, alias Printanier, alias Bigrenaille, raised a sort of loaded club made of a bar of iron with a knob of lead at each end, over M. Leblanc's head.

Marius could not bear this sight. "Father," he thought, "pardon me!" And his finger sought the trigger of the pistol. The shot was just about to be fired when Thénardier's voice cried out, "Don't hurt him!"

This desperate attempt of the victim, far from exasperating Thénardier, had calmed him. There were two men in him, the ferocious man and the crafty man. Up to this moment, in the first flush of triumph, confronting his stricken and motionless prey, the ferocious man had been predominant; when the victim resisted and seemed to want a struggle, the crafty man reappeared and took over.

"Don't hurt him," he repeated. And without his slightest knowledge, the first result of this was to stop the pistol that was just about to go off, and to paralyze Marius, to whom the urgency seemed to disappear, and who, in view of this new phase of affairs, saw no impropriety in waiting longer. Who knows but some chance might arise that would save him from the fearful choice of letting Ursula's father perish or destroying the colonel's savior!

A herculean struggle had begun. With one blow square in the chest, M. Leblanc had sent the old man sprawling into the middle of the room, then with two strokes had knocked down two other assailants, whom he held one under each knee; the wretches screamed under the pressure as if they were under a granite millstone; but the four others had seized the formidable old man by the arms and the back and held him down over the two prostrate chimney menders. Thus, master of the latter and mastered by the former, crushing those below him and suffocating under those above him, vainly trying to shake off all the violence and blows being heaped on him, M. Leblanc disappeared under the horrible group of bandits, like a wild boar under a howling pack of hounds and mastiffs.

They succeeded in throwing him over on the bed nearest the window and held him there subdued. The Thénardiess had not let go of his hair.

"Here," said Thénardier, "leave it alone. You'll tear your shawl."

The Thénardiess obeyed, as the she-wolf obeys her mate, with a growl.

"Now, the rest of you," continued Thénardier, "search him."

M. Leblanc seemed to have given up all resistance. They searched him. There was nothing on him but a leather purse that contained six francs, and his handkerchief.

Thénardier put the handkerchief in his pocket.

"What, no billfold?" he asked.

"Nor any watch," answered one of the chimney menders.

"It doesn't matter," muttered the masked man with the big key, "he is an old rough." His voice had the timbre of a ventriloquist.

Thénardier went to the corner by the door and picked up a bundle of ropes, which he threw to them.

"Tie him to the foot of the bed," he said. And noticing the old fellow who was still lying motionless, stretched across the room from the blow of M. Leblanc's fist: "Is Boulatruelle dead?" he asked.

"No," answered Bigrenaille, "he's drunk."

"Sweep him into a corner," said Thénardier.

Two of the chimney menders shoved the drunkard over to the heap of old iron with their feet.

"Babet, what did you bring so many for?" said Thénardier softly to the man with the cudgel. "It wasn't necessary."

"What could I do?" replied the man with the cudgel, "they all wanted to be in on it. It's been a bad season. There's nothing going on."

The pallet on which M. Leblanc had been thrown was a sort of hospital bed supported by four big roughly squared wooden posts. M. Leblanc made no resistance. The thugs bound him firmly, standing, with his feet to the floor, by the bedpost farthest from the window and nearest to the chimney.

When the last knot was tied, Thénardier took a chair and came and sat down almost opposite M. Leblanc. Thénardier no longer looked like himself, in a few seconds his expression had gone from unbridled violence to tranquil and crafty mildness. Marius hardly recognized in that polite, bureaucratic smile, the almost bestial mouth that was foaming a moment before; he was astonished to see this fantastic and alarming metamorphosis and felt like a man seeing a tiger change into an attorney.

"Monsieur," said Thénardier.

And he dismissed with a gesture the men who were still holding M. Leblanc: "Stand back a little, and let me talk with monsieur."

They all moved away toward the door. He went on, "Monsieur, you were wrong in trying to jump out the window. You might have broken your leg. Now, if you please, we are going to have a quiet conversation. In the first place I must tell you of a circumstance I have noticed, which is that you have not yet made the least outcry."

Thénardier was right; this detail was accurate though it had escaped Marius in his anxiety. M. Leblanc had uttered only a few words without raising his voice and even in his struggle by the window with the six thugs, he had maintained the most profound and remarkable silence. Thénardier continued.

"My God! You could have cried 'thief' a little, and I wouldn't have found it out of order. 'Murder!' That's sometimes said, too, and, as far as I'm concerned, I wouldn't have minded. It's very natural for someone to make a little noise when he finds himself with people who don't inspire him with as much confidence as they might; you could have done it, and we wouldn't have disturbed you. We wouldn't even have gagged you. And I'll tell you why. It's because this room is very deaf. That's about all I can say for it, but I can say that much. It's a vault. We could fire off a bomb here, and at the nearest guardhouse it would sound like a drunken snore. A cannon could go boom here, and the thunder would go puff. It's a convenient apartment. But, in short, you didn't cry out, that was better, I compliment you for it, and I'll tell you what I conclude from it: My dear monsieur, when a man cries out, who comes? The police. And after the police? Justice. Well! You didn't cry out, because you were no more anxious than we to see justice and the police come. It's because—I suspected as much long ago—you have some interest in concealing something. As for us, we have the same interest. Now we can come to an understanding."

While he said this, it seemed as though Thénardier, with his gaze trained on M. Leblanc, was trying to thrust visual daggers into his prisoner's consciousness. Moreover, his language, marked by a sort of subdued and sullen insolence, was reserved and precise, and in this wretch who one moment before had been nothing but a crook, one could now detect the man who had studied to be a priest.

The prisoner's silence, this precaution he had maintained even to the point of endangering his life, this resistance to the first impulse of nature—to utter a cry—all this, it must be said since attention had been called to it, disturbed Marius and surprised him.

Thénardier's observation, well founded as it was, added in Marius's eyes still more to the mysterious cloud veiling this strange and serious figure whom Courfeyrac had dubbed M. Leblanc. But whatever he might be—bound with ropes, surrounded by cutthroats, half buried, so to speak, in a grave that was deepening every moment—this man remained impassive before Thénardier's fury and mildness; and at such a moment Marius could not repress his admiration for that superbly melancholy face.

Here was evidently a soul inaccessible to fear and ignorant of despair. Here was one of those men who rise above the terror of hopeless situations. However extreme the crisis, however inevitable the catastrophe, there was nothing there resembling the agony of the drowning man, staring horrified at the water closing over his head.

Thénardier quietly got up, went to the fireplace, took away the screen, which he leaned against the nearest pallet to reveal the stove full of glowing coals in which the prisoner could plainly see the chisel at a white heat, spotted here and there with little scarlet stars.

Then Thénardier came back and sat down by M. Leblanc.

"I will proceed," he said. "Now we can come to an understanding. Let's arrange this amicably. I was wrong to fly into a rage just now. I don't know what got into me, I went much too far, I exaggerated. For instance, because you are a millionaire, I told you I wanted money, a good deal of money, an immense amount of money. That would be unreasonable. My God, rich as you may be, you have your expenses; who doesn't? I don't want to ruin you, I'm not a bloodsucker, after all. I'm not one of those who, simply because they have the advantage, use the position to ridiculous ends. Here, I'm willing to go halfway and make some sacrifices. I only need two hundred thousand francs."

M. Leblanc did not breathe a word. Thénardier went on: "You see that I water my wine pretty well. I don't know the state of your fortune, but I know that you don't care much for money, and a benevolent man like you can certainly give two hundred thousand francs to a father of a family in bad straits. Certainly you are reasonable, too, you don't imagine that I would take the trouble I have today, that I would organize this evening's party, which is a very fine piece of work in the opinion of these gentlemen, only to end by asking you for enough to go and drink cheap red wine and eat a plate of veal at Desnoyers'. Two hundred thousand francs, it's worth it. Once that trifle is out of your pocket I assure you that all is said and done, and you need not fear in the least. You will say: But I don't have two hundred thousand francs with me. Oh! I'm not exacting. I don't require that. I only ask one thing. Be good enough to write what I dictate."

Here Thénardier paused, then he added, emphasizing each word and casting a smile toward the furnace, "I warn you that I won't admit that you cannot write."

A grand inquisitor might have envied that smile.

Thénardier pushed the table close to M. Leblanc and took the inkstand, a pen, and a sheet of paper from the drawer, which he left partly open, and from which gleamed the long blade of the knife.

He placed the sheet of paper in front of M. Leblanc.

"Write," he said.

The prisoner finally spoke: "How do you expect me to write? I am tied up."

"That's true, pardon me!" said Thénardier. "You're absolutely right."

And turning toward Bigrenaille: "Untie monsieur's right arm."

Panchaud, alias Printanier, alias Bigrenaille, carried out Thénardier's order. When the prisoner's right hand was free, Thénardier dipped the pen in the ink and presented it to him.

"Remember, monsieur, that you are in our power, absolutely at our discretion, that no human power can spirit you away from here, and that it would really grieve us to have to take unpleasant measures. I know neither your name nor your address, but I give you notice that you will remain tied until the person who will be instructed to deliver the letter you are about to write has returned. Now, kindly write."

"What?" asked the prisoner.

"I will dictate."

M. Leblanc took the pen.

Thénardier began to dictate: "My daughter—"

The prisoner shuddered and raised his eyes to Thénardier.

"Put 'my dear daughter,' " said Thénardier. M. Leblanc obeyed. Thénardier went on: "Come immediately—"

He stopped.

"You call her daughter, don't you?"

"Who?" asked M. Leblanc

"My God!" said Thénardier, "the little girl, the Lark."

M. Leblanc answered without the least apparent emotion, "I do not know what you mean."

"Well, go on," said Thénardier, and he began to dictate again.

"Come immediately, I absolutely need you. The person who will give you this note is directed to bring you to me. I am waiting for you. Come with confidence."

M. Leblanc had written everything down. Thénardier added, "Ah! Strike out 'come with confidence,' that might lead her to suppose that the thing is not quite clear and that distrust is possible."

M. Leblanc scratched out the three words.

"Now," continued Thénardier, "sign it. What's your name?"

The prisoner laid down the pen and asked, "Who is this letter for?"

"You know very well," answered Thénardier, "for the little girl, as I just told you."

It was obvious that Thénardier avoided naming the young girl in question. He said "the Lark," he said "the little girl," but he did not pronounce the name. The precaution of a shrewd man preserving his own secret before his accomplices. To speak the name would have been to give up the whole "affair" to them and to tell them more than they needed to know.

He resumed: "Sign it. What is your name?"

"Urbain Fabre," said the prisoner.

With a catlike gesture Thénlardier thrust his hand into his pocket and pulled out the handkerchief taken from M. Leblanc. He looked for the mark on it and held it up to the candle.

"U. F. That's it. Urbain Fabre. Well, sign U. F."

The prisoner signed.

"Since it takes two hands to fold the letter, give it to me, I'll fold it."

This done, Thénardier continued: "Put on the address, '*Mademoiselle Fabre,*' at your house. I know that you live not very far away, near Saint-Jacques-du-Haut-Pas, since you go there to mass every day, but I don't know the street. I see that you understand your situation. As you have not lied about your name, you will not lie about your address. Put it on yourself."

The prisoner paused pensively, then took the pen and wrote: "Mademoiselle Fabre, care of Monsieur Urbain Fabre, Rue Saint-Dominique-d'Enfer, No. 17."

Thénardier seized the letter with a convulsive movement.

"Wife!" he cried.

The Thénardiess sprang forward.

"Here is the letter! You know what you have to do. There's a fiacre below. Go right away, and come back immediately."

And addressing the man with the poleax: "Here, since you've taken off your nose-screen, go with the woman. Get up behind the fiacre. You know where you left the little carriage."

"Yes," said the man.

And, laying down his poleax in a corner, he followed the Thénardiess.

As they were going off, Thénardier put his head through the half-open door and screamed into the hall: "Above all don't lose the letter! Remember that it represents two hundred thousand francs."

The harsh voice of the Thénardiess answered, "Don't worry, I put it in my bosom."

Not a minute had passed when the snapping of a whip was heard, which grew fainter and rapidly died away.

"Good!" muttered Thénardier. "They are going at a good pace. At that speed the good housewife will be back in three quarters of an hour."

He drew a chair near the fireplace and sat down, crossing his arms and holding his muddy boots up to the stove.

"My feet are cold," he said.

By now there were only five bandits left in the hovel with Thénardier and the prisoner. Through the masks or the black varnish that covered their faces and made of them, as fear might choose, charcoal workers, Africans, or devils, these men had a dismal leaden appearance, and one felt that they would as soon commit a crime as any other drudgery, quietly, without anger or mercy, slightly bored. They were heaped together in a corner like brutes and were silent. Thénardier was warming his feet. The prisoner had relapsed into his silence. A gloomy stillness had succeeded the savage tumult that filled the garret a few moments before.

The candle, melted down by the heat of the stove, hardly lit up the enormous room, the fire had died down, and the monstrous heads cast looming shadows on the walls and ceiling.

No sound could be heard except the quiet breathing of the drunken old man, who was asleep.

Marius was waiting in an anxiety increasing on all

sides. The riddle was more impenetrable than ever. Who was this "little girl," whom Thénardier had also called the Lark? Was it his "Ursula"? The prisoner had not seemed to be moved by that word, the Lark, and answered in the most natural way in the world: I do not know what you mean. On the other hand, the two letters *U. F.* were explained; it was Urbain Fabre, and Ursula's name was no longer Ursula. That was what Marius could see most clearly. A sort of hideous fascination held him spellbound to the commanded position from which he observed the whole scene. There he was, almost incapable of reflection and motion, as if annihilated by such horrible things in such close proximity. He was waiting, hoping for some incident, no matter what, unable to collect his thoughts and not knowing what course to take.

"In any event," he thought, "if she is the Lark I'll surely see her, since the Thénardiess is going to bring her here. Then everything will be clear. I'll give my blood and my life if need be, but I'll rescue her. Nothing will stop me."

Nearly half an hour passed this way. Thénardier appeared absorbed in some dark meditation, the prisoner did not stir. Nevertheless, for some time, Marius thought he had occasionally heard a hushed dull noise from the prisoner's direction.

Suddenly Thénardier addressed the prisoner: "Monsieur Fabre, look here, I might as well tell you at once."

These few words seemed to promise a revelation. Marius listened closely. Thénardier continued, "My spouse is coming back, don't be impatient. I think the Lark really is your daughter, and I find it quite natural that you should keep her. But listen a moment; with your letter, my wife is going to find her. I told my wife to dress up, as you saw, so that your young lady would follow her without hesitation. They'll both get into the fiacre with my comrade behind. Somewhere outside one of the city gates, there is a little carriage with two very good horses in the traces. They will take your young lady there. She will get out of the fiacre. My comrade will get into the little carriage with her, and my wife will come back here to tell us 'It is done.' As for your young lady, no harm will be done her; the little carriage will take her to a place where she'll be safe, and as soon as you have given me the little two hundred thousand francs, she'll be sent back to you. If you have me arrested, my comrade will give the Lark a pinch, that's all."

The prisoner didn't utter a word. After a pause, Thénardier continued, "It's very simple, as you see. There will be no harm done unless you interfere. That's the whole story. I'm telling you in advance so you'll know."

He stopped; the prisoner did not break his silence, and Thénardier resumed, "As soon as my spouse is back and says, 'The Lark is on her way,' we'll release you, and you'll be free to go home to bed. You see we have no bad intentions."

Appalling images passed before Marius's mind. Was this possible! They were kidnapping the young girl, and were not going to bring her here? One of those monsters was going to carry her off into the gloom? Where? And if she were the one! And it was clear she was. Marius felt his heart stop. What should he do? Fire the pistol? Put all these wretches into the hands of justice? But the hideous man with the poleax would still be out of all reach with the young girl, and Marius remembered Thénardier's words, whose bloody meaning he guessed: "If you have me arrested, my comrade will give the Lark a pinch."

Now it was not merely by the colonel's will, it was by his love, by the peril of the one he loved, that he felt held back.

This appalling situation, which had gone on now more than an hour, changed at every moment. Marius had the strength to review successively all the more heartrending possibilities, seeking some hope and finding none. The tumult of his thoughts strangely contrasted with the deathly silence of the dingy room.

In the midst of this silence they heard the sound of the stairway door opening then closing.

The prisoner made a slight movement within his bonds.

"Here's the housewife," said Thénardier.

He had hardly said this, when in fact the Thénardiess burst into the room, red, breathless, panting, with glaring eyes, and cried, striking her large hands against her hips both at the same time: "False address!"

The outlaw whom she had taken with her came in behind her and picked up his poleax again.

"False address?" repeated Thénardier.

She responded: "Nobody! Rue Saint-Dominique, number seventeen, no Monsieur Urbain Fabre! They never heard of him!"

She stopped for lack of breath, then went on: "Monsieur Thénardier! This old boy has cheated you! You're too good, you see! Me, I'd have sliced that mug in four for you to begin with! And if he'd been ugly with you, I'd have cooked him alive! Then he'd have had to talk, and had to tell where the girl is, and had to tell where he's got the stash! That's how I would have done it! No wonder they say men are stupider than women! Nobody! Number seventeen! A large carriage gate! No Monsieur Fabre! Rue Saint-Dominique, full gallop, and tip for the driver, and all! I spoke to the porter and the concierge, a fine strong woman. They didn't know him."

Marius took a breath. She, Ursula or the Lark, whom he no longer knew what to call, was safe.

While his exasperated wife was vociferating, Thénardier had sat down on the table; he stayed there a few seconds without saying a word, swinging his right leg, which was hanging down, and gazing at the stove with a look of savage reverie.

Finally he said to the prisoner with a slow and singularly ferocious inflection, "A false address! What did you hope to accomplish by that?"

"To gain time!" cried the prisoner with a ringing voice.

And at the same moment he shook off his bonds; they were cut. The prisoner was no longer fastened to the bed except by one leg.

Before the seven men had had time to recover and spring at him, he had bent over to the fireplace, reached his hand toward the furnace, then rose up, and now Thénardier, the Thénardiess, and the bandits, recoiling from shock into the back part of the room, stared at him dumfounded, as he held above his head the glowing chisel, which gave off an ominous light. He stood almost free and in commanding position.

At the judicial inquest, to which the ambush in the Gorbeau structure subsequently gave rise, it appeared that a large coin, cut and worked in a special way, was found in the garret, when the police searched it; this coin was one of those marvels of labor that the patience of prison produces in the darkness and for the darkness, marvels that are nothing else than instruments of escape. These hideous and delicate products of a wonderful art are to jewelry what the metaphors of argot are to poetry. There are Benvenuto Cellinis in prisons, even as there are Villons in language. The unhappy man who aspires to freedom finds the means, sometimes without tools, with a folding knife, with an old case knife, to split a sou into two thin plates, to hollow out the two plates without touching the stamp of the face, and cut a screwthread along the edge of the sou, so as to make the plates adhere anew. This screws and unscrews at will; it is a box. In this box, they conceal a watch spring, and this watch spring, if properly used, severs shackles of some size and even iron bars. The unfortunate convict is believed to possess only a sou; no, he posseses liberty! A big coin of this kind, on later examination by the police, was found open and in two pieces in the room under the pallet near the window. A little saw of blue steel was also discovered, which could be concealed in the big sou. It is likely that when the cutthroats were searching the prisoner's pockets, he had this coin on him and managed to hide it in his hand; and that afterward, having his right hand free, he unscrewed it and used the saw to cut the ropes by which he was fastened, which would explain the slight noise and the imperceptible movements Marius had noticed.

Being unable to bend down for fear of betraying himself, he had not cut the cords on his left leg.

The bandits had recovered from their first surprise.

"Don't worry," said Bigrenaille to Thénardier. "He is still held by one leg, and he won't get away, I'll answer for that. I tied that shank for him."

The prisoner now raised his voice. "You are pitiful, but my life is not worth the trouble of so much coercion. As far as imagining that you could make me speak, that you could make me write what I don't want to write, that you could make me say what I don't want to say—"

He pulled up the sleeve of his left arm, and added, "Here."

At the same time he stretched out his arm and laid against the naked flesh the glowing chisel, which he held in his right hand by the wooden handle.

They heard the hissing of the burning flesh; the odor peculiar to chambers of torture spread through the garret room. Marius staggered in horror; the felons themselves shuddered; the strange old man scarcely winced, and while the red iron was sinking into the smoking wound, he turned, impassive and almost nobly, to Thénardier, his fine face showing no hatred, its suffering vanishing in serene majesty.

With great and lofty natures, the rebellion of the flesh and the senses against the assaults of physical pain brings out the soul and makes it appear on the countenance, in the same way that military mutinies force the captain to show himself.

"Miserable people," he said, "have no more fear of me than I have of you."

And drawing the chisel out of the wound, he threw it through the window, which was still open; the horrible glowing tool disappeared, whirling into the night, and fell in the distance and was quenched in the snow.

The prisoner resumed, "Do what you like."

He was disarmed.

"Grab him," said Thénardier.

Two of the outlaws laid their hands on his shoulders, and the masked man with the ventriloquist's voice stood in front of him, ready to knock out his brains with a blow of the huge key at the slightest movement.

At the same time Marius heard below him, at the foot of the partition, but so near that he could not see who was talking, this colloquy, exchanged in a low voice: "There is only one thing left to do."

"Kill him!"

"Right!"

It was the husband and wife holding counsel.

Thénardier walked slowly toward the table, opened the drawer, and took out the knife.

Marius was fingering the trigger of his pistol. Unparalleled perplexity! For an hour there had been two voices in his conscience, one telling him to respect the will of his father, the other crying out for him to help the prisoner. Uninterrupted, these two voices continued their struggle, which threw him into agony. Up to that moment he had vaguely hoped to find some means of reconciling these two duties, but no possible way had occurred. Meanwhile the danger was urgent, the last limit of delay was passed; a few steps away from the prisoner, Thénardier was reflecting, knife in hand.

Marius cast his eyes wildly about him; the last automatic resource of despair.

Suddenly he started.

At his feet, on the table, a bright ray of the full moon fell on a sheet of paper, seeming to point it out to him. On that sheet he read this line, printed in large letters that very morning, by the elder Thénardier girl:

"THE COPS ARE HERE."

An idea flashed across Marius's mind; there was the means he was seeking, the solution to this dreadful problem torturing him, to spare the assassin and to save the victim. He knelt down on his bureau, reached out and caught up the sheet of paper, quietly detached a bit of plaster from the partition, wrapped it in the paper, and threw the whole thing through the crevice into the middle of the room.

It was just in time. Thénardier had conquered his last fears, or his last scruples, and was moving toward the prisoner.

"Something fell!" cried the Thénardiess.

"What is it?" said the husband.

The woman had sprung forward and picked up the piece of plaster wrapped in the paper. She handed it to her husband.

"Where did this come from?" asked Thénardier.

"Good Lord!" said the woman. "How do you suppose it got in? It came through the window."

"I saw it go by," said Bigrenaille.

Thénardier hurriedly unfolded the paper and held it up to the candle.

"It's Eponine's writing! Hell!"

He signaled to his wife, who approached quickly, and he showed her the line written on the sheet of paper, then he added softly, "Quick! The ladder! Leave the meat in the trap, and clear out!"

"Without cutting the man's throat?" asked the Thénardiess.

"We don't have time."

"Which way?" inquired Bigrenaille.

"Through the window," answered Thénardier. "Since Ponine threw the stone through the window, that shows the house isn't watched on that side."

The mask with the ventriloquist's voice laid down his big key, lifted both arms into the air, and opened and shut his hands rapidly three times, without saying a word. This was like the signal to clear the decks on a ship. The outlaws holding the prisoner let go of him; in the twinkling of an eye, the rope ladder was unrolled out of the window and firmly fixed to the casing by the two iron hooks.

The prisoner paid no attention to what was going on around him. He seemed to be dreaming or praying.

As soon as the ladder was attached, Thénardier cried, "Come, spouse!"

And he rushed toward the window.

But as he was stepping out, Bigrenaille seized him roughly by the collar.

"No, you don't, old fox! After us."

"After us!" howled the bandits.

"You're children," said Thénardier. "We're wasting time. The cops are right on our heels."

"Well," said one of the thugs, "let's draw lots to see who goes out first."

Thénardier exclaimed, "Are you fools? Are you cracked? You're a pack of idiots! Losing time, are you? Drawing lots, are you? With a wet finger! For the short straw! Write our names, put 'em in a cap—"

"Would you like my hat?" cried a voice from the door.

They all turned round. It was Javert.

He had his hat in his hand and was holding it out with a smile.

XXI

THE VICTIMS SHOULD ALWAYS BE ARRESTED FIRST

At nightfall Javert had posted his men and hidden himself behind the trees on the Rue de la Barrière-des-Gobelins, which faces the Gorbeau house on the other side of the boulevard. He began by "opening his pocket," to put in the two young girls charged with watching the approaches to the house. But he only "bagged" Azelma. As for Eponine, she was not at her post; she had disappeared, and he had not been able to collar her. Then Javert put himself on watch and listened for the agreed signal. The going and coming of the fiacre had worried him very much. At last, he became impatient, and, sure that there was a nest there, sure of being in luck, having recognized several of the felons who had gone in, he finally decided to go up without waiting for the pistol shot.

It will be remembered that he had Marius's passkey.

He had come at the right time.

The frightened outlaws rushed for the arms they had thrown down anywhere in their attempt to escape. In less than a second, these seven appalling men were grouped in a posture of defense, one with his poleax, another with his key, a third with his club, the others with shears, pliers, and hammers, Thénardier grasping his knife. The Thénardiess seized a huge paving stone, which was in the corner by the window and which her daughters used as a stool.

Javert put on his hat again and stepped into the room, his arms folded, his cane under his arm, his sword in its sheath.

"Halt!" he said. "You will not leave by the window, you will leave by the door. It is healthier. There are seven of you, fifteen of us. Don't let's scuffle like a bunch of provincials. Let's be nice."

Bigrenaille took a pistol he had concealed under his blouse, and put it into Thénardier's hand, whispering in his ear, "It's Javert. I don't dare shoot at that man. Do you?"

"Good Lord!" Thénardier muttered.

"Well, then, shoot."

Thénardier took the pistol and aimed at Javert.

Javert, who was within three paces, looked at him steadily and merely said, "Don't go and shoot. It'll misfire."

Thénardier pulled the trigger. The pistol misfired.

"I told you so!" said Javert.

Bigrenaille threw down his cudgel at Javert's feet.

"You're the king of the devils! I give up."

"And you?" Javert asked the other cutthroats.

They answered, "Me too!"

Javert replied calmly, "That's it, that's good, just as I said, you're being nice."

"I ask one thing only," said Bigrenaille, "that's that I can have tobacco when I'm in solitary."

"Granted," said Javert.

And turning round and calling behind him, "Come in now!"

A squad of gendarmes with drawn swords and policemen armed with bludgeons rushed in. They tied up the thugs. This crowd of men, dimly lit by a candle, filled the den with shadow.

"Handcuffs on all of them!" cried Javert.

"Just you come close!" cried a voice that was not a man's voice but nobody would have dared identify as a woman's.

The Thénardiess had holed up in a corner of the window embrasure, and it was she who had just bellowed.

The policemen and officers fell back.

She had thrown off her shawl but kept on her hat; her husband, cowering behind her, was almost hidden under the fallen shawl, and she covered him with her body, holding the paving block in both hands above her head with the poise of an amazon about to hurl a rock.

"Watch out!" she cried.

They all crowded back toward the hall. A wide space was left in the middle of the room.

The Thénardiess cast a glance at the bandits who had allowed themselves to be tied and muttered in a harsh and guttural tone, "Cowards!"

Javert smiled and advanced into the open space that the Thénardiess had staked out with her eyes.

"Don't come any nearer! Get away," she cried, "or I'll crush you!"

"What a grenadier!" said Javert. "Mother, you have a beard like a man but claws like a woman."

And he kept walking toward her.

The Thénardiess, her hair disheveled, raving, braced her legs, bent backward, and heaved the paving stone wildly at Javert's head. Javert ducked, the stone passed over him, hit the wall behind, knocking down a large piece of the plaster, and returned, bounding across the room, which luckily was almost empty, finally stopping at Javert's heels.

At that moment Javert reached the Thénardier couple. One of his huge hands fell on the woman's shoulder and the other on her husband's head.

"Handcuffs!" he cried.

The policemen returned in a body, and in a few seconds Javert's order was executed.

The Thénardiess, completely crushed, looked at her manacled hands and those of her husband, dropped to the floor, and exclaimed, with tears in her eyes, "My daughters!"

"They have been taken care of," said Javert.

Meanwhile the officers had found the drunken fellow, who was asleep behind the door, and shook him. He woke up, sputtering.

"Is it over, Jondrette?"

"Yes," answered Javert.

The six manacled bandits were on their feet; however, they still retained their spectral appearance, three blackened, three masked.

"Keep on your masks," said Javert.

And, passing them in review with the eye of a Frederic II on parade at Potsdam, he said to the three chimney menders, "Good evening, Bigrenaille. Good evening, Brujon. Good evening, Deux Milliards."

Then, turning toward the three masks, he said to the poleax man, "Good evening, Gueulemer."

And to the man with the cudgel, "Good evening, Babet."

And to the ventriloquist, "Hello, Claquesous."

Just then he noticed the bandits' prisoner, who, since the entrance of the police, had not uttered a word, and had his head down.

"Untie monsieur!" said Javert, "and don't let anybody out."

So saying, he sat down with authority at the table still bearing the candle and the writing materials, drew a stamped sheet from his pocket, and began his report.

When he had written the first lines, purely formulaic and always identical, he raised his eyes: "Bring forward the gentleman whom these gentlemen had bound."

The offiers looked around.

"Well," asked Javert. "So where is he?"

The bandits' prisoner, M. Leblanc, M. Urbain Fabre, the father of Ursula, or the Lark, had disappeared.

The door was guarded, but the window was not. As soon as he was untied, and while Javert was writing, he had taken advantage of the disturbance, the tumult, the confusion, the darkness, and a moment where their attention was not fixed on him, to leap out the window.

An officer ran to the window and looked down. There was nobody to be seen outside.

The rope ladder was still trembling.

"The devil!" said Javert, between his teeth, "that was to be the best one."

XXII

THE LITTLE BOY WHO CRIED IN PART TWO

The day after the one in which these events took place in the house on the Boulevard de l'Hôpital, a child, who seemed to come from somewhere near the Pont d'Austerlitz, went along the side street toward the Barrière de Fontainebleau. Night had closed in. The child was pale, thin, dressed in rags, with summer trousers in the middle of February; he was singing at the top of his lungs.

At the corner of the Rue du Petit-Banquier, an old crone was fishing around in a heap of rubbish by the light of a street lamp; the child bumped into her as he passed, then backed off, exclaiming, "Why! Me, I just took that for an enormous, enormous dog!"

The second time he pronounced the word "enormous" with a facetious emphasis that capitals would best express: "an enormous, ENORMOUS dog!"

The old woman straightened up in a rage.

"Jailbait!" she muttered. "If I had not been bent over, I know where I'd have planted my foot!"

The child was already some distance away.

"Tsk, tsk!" he said. "Perhaps I wasn't wrong, after all."

Choking with indignation, the old woman straightened up all the way, the red glare of the lantern fully illuminating her gray face, deeply furrowed with wrinkles and sharp edges, with crows' feet down to the corners of her mouth. Her body was lost in the shadow, and only her head showed. One would have said it was the mask of Decrepitude cut out by a flash in the dark. The child studied her.

"Madame," he said, "is not my type."

He went on his way and began to sing again:

> Le roi Coupdesabot
> S'en allait à la chasse,
> A la chasse aux corbeaux—

At the end of these three lines he stopped. He had reached No. 50–52 and, finding the door locked, began to bang away at it with his foot, heroic echoing kicks that revealed the men's shoes he was wearing rather than the child's feet he still had.

Meantime, this same old woman he had met with at the corner of the Rue du Petit-Banquier was running after him, shrieking and gesticulating wildly. "What's the matter? What is the matter? Good Lord! They're staving in the door! They're breaking into the house."

The kicking kept up.

The old woman was breathless.

"Is that the way they use houses nowadays?"

Suddenly she stopped. She had recognized the *gamin*.

"What! It's that little devil!"

"Why hello, it's the old woman," said the child. "Good evening, Burgonmuche. I've come to see my ancestors."

The old woman responded with a composite grimace, a splendid grafting of hatred onto decay and ugliness, unfortunately lost in the dark: "There's nobody there, Nosey."

"Yeah?" said the child, "then where's my father?"

"At La Force."

"Well, well! And my mother?"

"At Saint-Lazare."

"Do tell! And my sisters?"

"At Les Madelonnettes."

The child scratched the back of his ear, looked at Ma'am Burgon and said, "Aha!"

Then he turned on his heel, and a moment later the old woman, still on the doorstep, heard him singing in his clear, fresh voice, as he disappeared under the black elms shivering in the wintry winds:

Le roi Coupdesabot
S'en allait à la chasse,
A la chasse aux corbeaux,
Monté sur des échasses.
Quand on passait dessous,
On lui payait deux sous.[1]

[1] The noble king Coupdesabot
A-hunting he would often go
To bag some game, perhaps a crow.
Atop a pair of stilts and hence
When ere his people passed below
They'd have to pay this king two cents.

SAINT-DENIS AND IDYLL OF THE RUE PLUMET

Book One

A FEW PAGES OF HISTORY

I

WELL CUT

The years 1831 and 1832, the two years immediately connected to the July Revolution, are one of the most peculiar and most striking periods in history. These years rise like two mountains between those before and after. They have revolutionary grandeur. We see precipices there. The social masses, the very foundation of civilization, the consolidated group of superimposed and cohering interests, the venerable profile of old France, constantly appear and disappear through the stormy clouds of systems, passions, and theories. These appearances and disappearances have been called resistance and momentum. Occasionally we see a gleam of truth, that daylight of the human soul.

This remarkable period is brief enough and is beginning to take on enough distance so that we can now grasp its principal outlines.

We will attempt to do that.

The Restoration had been one of those intermediate phases, difficult to define, composed of fatigue, murmurs, rumors, sleep, tumult—nothing more nor less than a great nation grinding to a halt. These periods are peculiar and deceive the politicians who would like to take advantage of them. At first, the nation only asks for a rest; men have one thirst alone, for peace; they have one ambition, to be inconspicuous. That is a translation of standing still. Great events, great fortunes, great ventures, great men, thank God, they have seen enough of them; they are fed up with them. They would exchange Caesar for Prusias, and Napoleon for the king of Yvetot. "What a good little king he was!" They have been walking since daybreak, it is the evening of a long, hard day; they did the first relay with Mirabeau, the second with Robespierre, the third with Bonaparte, they are thoroughly exhausted. Every one of them asks for a bed.

Wearied devotions, heroisms grown old, ambitions surfeited, fortunes made, all seek, demand, implore, solicit—what? A place to lie down. They have it. They take possession of peace, tranquility, leisure; they are satisfied. At the same time, however, certain facts rise up, demand recognition, and knock at the door on their own account. These facts have sprung from revolutions and wars; they exist, they live, they have a right to settle into society, and they do settle in; and most of the time the facts are pioneers and quartermasters that merely prepare the ground for principles.

Then, that is what appears to the political philosopher.

While weary men demand rest, faits accomplis demand guarantees. Guarantees to facts are the same thing as rest to men.

This is what England demanded of the Stuarts after the Protector; this is what France demanded of the Bourbons after the Empire.

These guarantees are a necessity of the times. They must be agreed to. The princes "grant" them, but in reality it is the force of circumstances that gives them. A profound truth, and a piece of useful knowledge, of which the Stuarts had no suspicion in 1662 and which the Bourbons did not even glimpse in 1814.

The predestined family that returned to France when Napoleon fell had the fatal simplicity to believe that it was they that gave, and that what they had given they could take back; that the house of Bourbon possessed the divine right, and France possessed nothing; and that the political rights conceded in the Charter of Louis XVIII were only a branch of the divine right, detached by the House of Bourbon and graciously given to the people until such day as the king would wish to take it back again. Still, from the regret that the gift cost them, the Bourbons should have sensed that it did not come from them.

They were surly with the nineteenth century. They made a sour face at every sign of thriving in the nation. To adopt a trivial word, that is to say, a popular and a true one, they looked glum. The people saw it.

The Bourbons believed they were strong, because the Empire had been swept away before them like a scene at a theater. They did not notice that they themselves had been brought on the same way. They did not see that they were in that same hand that had taken away Napoleon.

They believed they had taken root because they were the past. They were mistaken; they were part of the past, but the whole past was France. The roots of French society were not in the Bourbons but in the nation. These obscure and hardy roots constituted not the right of a family but the history of a people. These roots grew everywhere except beneath the throne.

To France, the house of Bourbon was the illustrious bloodstained center of her history, but it was not the principal element of her destiny or the essential basis of her politics. She could do without the Bourbons; she had done without them for twenty-two years; there had been a solution of continuity; they did not suspect it. And how could they suspect it, they who imagined that Louis XVII reigned on the 9th of Thermidor and that Louis XVIII reigned on the day of Marengo. Never, since the beginning of history, have princes been so blind in the presence of facts and the portion of divine authority that facts contain and promulgate. Never had that earthly pretension called the right of kings denied the divine right to such an extent.

A capital error that led that family to repossess the guarantees "granted" in 1814, the concessions, as it called them. Sad thing! What they called their concessions were our conquests; what they called our encroachments were our rights.

When its hour seemed to come, the Restoration, supposing itself victorious over Bonaparte, and thinking itself strong and deeply rooted, made its abrupt decision and risked its throw. One morning it stood up against France, and, raising its voice, denied the collective title and the individual title—sovereignty to the nation, liberty to the citizen. In others words, it denied the nation what made it a nation and the citizen what made him a citizen.

This is the essence of those famous acts called the July Ordinances.

The Restoration fell.

It fell justly. We must say, however, that it had not been absoulutely hostile to all forms of progress. Some great things were done while it stood by.

Under the Restoration the nation became accustomed to discussion with calm, which the Republic had lacked; and to grandeur in peace, which the Empire had lacked. Free and strong, France had been an encouraging spectacle to the other people of Europe. The Revolution had had its say under Robespierre; the cannon had had its say under Bonaparte; under Louis XVIII and Charles X, intelligence found a way to be heard. The wind let up, the torch was relit. The pure light of mind was seen trembling on serene peaks. A magnificent spectacle, full of usefulness and charm. For fifteen years, in complete peace, and openly in public places, these great principles, so old to the thinker, so new to the statesman, were seen at work: equality before the law, freedom of conscience, freedom of speech, freedom of the press, the accessibility of every function to every aptitude. This went on until 1830. The Bourbons were an instrument of civilization, which broke in the hands of Providence.

The fall of the Bourbons was full of grandeur, not on their part, but on the part of the nation. They left the throne with gravity, but without authority; their descent into the night was not one of those solemn disappearances that leave a somber feeling in history; it was neither the spectral calm of Charles I nor the eagle cry of Napoleon. They simply went away. They laid down the crown, and did not keep the halo. They were worthy, but they were not august. To some extent they fell short of the majesty of their misfortune. Charles X, during the voyage from Cherbourg, having a round table cut into a square table, appeared more solicitous of imperiled etiquette than of the falling monarchy. This pettiness saddened the devoted men who loved them and the serious men who honored their race. The people, on their side, were wonderfully noble. The nation, attacked one morning by armed force, by a sort of royal insurrection, knew itself so strong that it felt no anger. It defended itself, restrained itself, put things back in their places—the government into the hands of the law, the Bourbons into exile, and stopped, alas! It took the old king, Charles X from under that dais that had sheltered Louis XIV and placed him gently on the ground. It touched the royal individuals only sadly and with caution. It was not a man, it was not a few men, it was France, all France, France victorious and intoxicated with her victory, seeming to remember herself, and putting in practice before the eyes of the whole world the grave words of Guillaume du Vair after the day of the barricades: "It is easy for those who are accustomed to gathering the favors of the great, and to leap like a bird from branch to branch, from an afflicted to a floushing fortune, to demonstrate their daring against their prince in his adversity; but to me the fortune of my kings will always be venerated, particularly when they are in distress."

The Bourbons carried away with them respect but not regret. As we have said, their misfortune was greater than they. They faded away on the horizon.

The July Revolution immediately found friends and enemies throughout the world. The former rushed in with enthusiasm and joy, the latter turned away; each according to his own nature. At first the princes of Europe, owls in this dawn, closed their eyes, shocked and dumfounded, and opened them only to threaten. An understandable fear, an excusable anger. This strange revolution had scarcely been a shock; it did not even do vanquished royalty the honor of treating it as an enemy and shedding its blood. In the eyes of the despotic governments, always eager to have liberty slander itself, the July Revolution had the fault of being formidable and yet mild. Nothing, however, was attempted, or plotted against it. The most dissatisfied, the most irritated, the most horrified, bowed to it; whatever our selfishness and our prejudices, a mysterious respect springs from events in which we feel the collaboration of a hand higher than man's.

The July Revolution is the triumph of what is right over facts. A thing full of splendor.

The right prostrating the fact. Thence the glory of the Revolution of 1830, thence its mildness, also. What is right, when it triumphs, has no need to be violent.

Right is just and true.

The property of right is that it is always beautiful and pure. The fact, even the most necessary in appearance, even the most accepted by its contemporaries, if it exists only as fact, and if it contains too little of right, or none at all, is inevitably destined to become with time deformed, unclean, perhaps even monstrous. If you instantly want to establish the degree of ugliness that fact may reach, seen from the distance of centuries, look at Machiavelli. Machiavelli is not an evil genius, nor a demon, nor a cowardly and miserable writer; he is nothing but fact. And he is not merely the Italian fact, he is the European fact, the fact of the sixteenth century. He seems hideous, and he is so, in the presence of the moral idea of the nineteenth.

This conflict between right and fact has endured since the origins of society. To bring the duel to an end, to consolidate the pure ideal with the human reality, to make the right peacefully interpenetrate the fact, and the fact the right, this is the work of the wise.

II

BADLY SEWED

But the work of the wise is one thing, the work of the able another.

The Revolution of 1830 soon ground to a halt.

As soon as a revolution strikes the shore, the able carve up the wreck.

In our century, the able have decreed to themselves the title of statesmen, so that this word "statesman" has come to be somewhat a word of argot. Indeed, let no one forget that wherever there is ability alone, there is necessarily pettiness. To say "able" amounts to saying "mediocre."

Just as saying "statesmen" is sometimes tantamount to saying "traitors."

According to the able, therefore, revolutions such as the July Revolution, are arteries cut; a prompt ligature is needed. Right, too grandly proclaimed, is disquieting. So, with right once affirmed, the state must be reaffirmed. Liberty being assured, we must think about power.

Thus far the wise do not separate from the able, but they do begin to distrust. Power, very well. But, first, what is power? Secondly, where does it come from?

The able do not seem to hear the murmurs of objection, and they go on with their work.

According to these politicians, ingenious in masking profitable fictions with necessity, the first need of a people after a revolution, if this people form part of a monarchical continent, is to procure a dynasty. In this way, they say, the people can have peace after their revolution, that is to say, time to stanch their wounds and put their house in order. The dynasty hides the scaffolding and covers the ambulance.

Now, it is not alway easy to procure a dynasty.

In case of necessity, the first man of genius, or even the first adventurer you meet, will do for a king. In the first place you have Bonaparte, and in the second Iturbide.

But the first family you meet is not enough to make a dynasty. There must be a certain amount of antiquity in a race, and the wrinkles of centuries cannot be improvised.

If, after a revolution, we assume the statesman's perspective, of course with every necessary reservation, what are the qualities of the king who springs from the revolution? He may be, and it is well that he should be, revolutionary, that is to say, an actual participant in this revolution, that he have had a hand in it, that he be compromised in it or made illustrious, that he have touched the ax or handled the sword.

What are the qualities of a dynasty? It should be national; that is to say, revolutionary at a distance, not through acts performed, but through ideas accepted. It should be composed of the past and be historic, of the future and be sympathetic.

All this explains why the first revolutions content themselves with finding a man, Cromwell or Napoleon; and why the second absolutely insists on finding a family, the house of Brunswick or the house of Orléans.

Royal houses are like those Indian banyan trees in which each branch, by bending to the ground, takes root there and becomes another banyan. Each branch may become a dynasty. On the sole condition that it bends to the people.

Such is the theory of the able.

This, then, is the great art, to give a success something of the sound of catastrophe, so that those who profit by it may tremble, too, to moderate a step forward with fear, to enlarge the curve of transition to the extent of retarding progress, to tame this work, to denounce and restrain the asperities of enthusiasm, to cut off the corners and the claws, to muffle triumph, to swaddle the upright, to wrap up the people-giant in flannel and hurry him to bed, to impose a diet on this excess of health, to put Hercules under convalescent treatment, to dilute the event with the expedient, to offer to minds thirsting for the ideal this nectar cut with barley water, to take precautions against too much success, to furnish the revolution with a lampshade.

The year 1830 carried out this theory, already applied to England by 1688.

The year 1830 is a revolution arrested midway. Half progress, quasi-right. Now, logic ignores the Almost, just as the sun ignores the candle.

Who stops revolutions halfway? The bourgeoisie.

Why?

Because the bourgeoisie is the self-interest that has attained satisfaction. Yesterday it was appetite, today it is plenitude, tomorrow it will be satiety.

The phenomenon of 1814 after Napoleon was reproduced in 1830 after Charles X.

There has been an erroneous attempt to make a special class of the bourgeoisie. The bourgeoisie is simply the contented portion of the people. The bourgeois is the man who now has time to sit down. A chair is not a caste.

But, by wishing to sit down too soon, we may stop the progress of even the human race. That has often been the fault of the bourgeois.

The commission of a fault does not constitute a class. Egotism is not one of the divisions of the social order.

Moreover, we must be just, even toward egotism. After the shock of 1830, the condition to which that part of the nation called the bourgeoisie aspired was not inertia, which is complicated by indifference and idleness and contains some shame; it was not slumber, which supposes a momentary forgetfulness accessible to dreams; it was a halt.

Halt is a word formed with a singular and almost contradictory double meaning: a troop on the march, that is to say, movement; a stopping, that is to say, repose.

A halt is the regaining of strength, it is armed and watchful repose; it is the accomplished fact that stations sentinels and keeps on guard. A halt supposes battle yesterday and battle tomorrow.

This is the interval between 1830 and 1848.

What we here call battle may also be called progress.

So the bourgeoisie, as well as the statesmen, felt the need for a man who would say "Halt!" An Although-Because. A composite individuality signifying both revolution and stability; in other words, assuring the present through the evident compatibility of the past with the future.

This man was found ready-made. His name was Louis-Philippe d'Orléans.

The 221 made Louis-Philippe king. Lafayette undertook the coronation. He called it "the best of republics."

The Hôtel de Ville of Paris replaced the Cathedral of Rheims.

This substitution of a demi-throne for the complete throne was "the work of 1830."

When the able had finished their work, the immense flaw of their solution became apparent. All this was done without reference to absolute right. The absolute right cried out, "I protest!" then faded into obscurity.

III

LOUIS-PHILIPPE

Revolutions have a terrible arm and a fortunate hand; they strike hard and choose well. Even when incomplete, even degenerate and abused, and reduced to the condition of junior revolution, like the Revolution of 1830, they almost always retain enough providential light to prevent a fatal fall. Their eclipse is never an abdication.

Still, let us not boast too loudly; even revolutions can be deceived and disclose grave mistakes.

Let us return to 1830. The year 1830 was fortunate in its deviation. In the establishment that called itself order after the abbreviated Revolution, the king was better than royalty. Louis-Philippe was an exceptional man.

Son of a father to whom history will certainly allow attenuating circumstances, but as worthy of esteem as that father had been worthy of blame; having all private virtues and many public virtues; careful of his health, his fortune, his person, his business, knowing the value of a minute, though not always of a year; sober, serene, peaceful, patient; good man and good prince; sleeping with his wife and having lackeys in his palace whose business it was to exhibit the conjugal bed to the bourgeoisie, an ostentation of domestic regularity that had its use after the illegitimate displays of the elder branch; knowing all the languages of Europe, and, what is rarer, all the languages of all interests, and speaking them; admirable representative of "the middle class," but surpassing it, and in every way greater than it; having the excellent sense, even while appreciating the blood from which he sprang, to esteem himself above all for his own intrinsic worth, and, about the question of his descendance even, very particular, declaring himself Orléans and not Bourbon; very much first Prince of the Blood, while he was only Most Serene Highness, but a *franc bourgeois* when addressed as Majesty; diffuse in public, concise in private; a declared, but not proven, miser; in reality one of those economical persons who are prodigal in matters of their fancies or their duty; well read, but not very appreciative of letters; a gentleman, but not chivalrous; simple, calm, and strong; worshiped by his family and by his house; a seductive talker, an undeceived statesman, internally cold, ruled by the present interest, governing always by the nearest convenience, incapable of malice or gratitude, pitilessly wearing out superiors on mediocrities, able in opposing through parliamentary majorities those mysterious unanimities that mutter almost inaudibly beneath thrones; expansive, sometimes imprudent in his expansion, but with marvelous skill in that imprudence; fertile in expedients, in faces, in masks, making France afraid of Europe and Europe of France; loving his country incontestably, but preferring his family; prizing domination more than authority, and authority more than dignity; a disposition to this extent fatal, that, turning everything toward success, it admits of ruse, and does not absolutely repudiate baseness; but which is profitable to this extent, that it preserves politics from violent shocks, the state from fractures, and society from catastrophes; minute, correct, vigilant, attentive, sagacious, indefatigable; contradicting himself sometimes, and going back on his word; bold against Austria at Ancona, obstinate against England in Spain, bombarding Antwerp and paying Pritchard; singing the Marseillaise with conviction; inaccessible to depression, to weariness, to taste for the beautiful and the ideal, to foolhardy generosity, to Utopia, to chimeras, to anger, to vanity, to fear; having every form of personal bravery; general at Valmy, soldier at Jemappes, his life threatened eight times by regicides, yet always smiling; brave as a grenadier, courageous as a thinker; anxious merely before the chances of a European disturbance and unfit for great political adventures; always ready to risk his life, never his work; disguising his will as influence so as to be obeyed as an intelligence rather than as king; endowed with observation and not with divination, paying little attention to minds, but able to read the character of men, that is to say, needing to see in order to judge; prompt and penetrating good sense, practical wisdom, ready speech, prodigious memory; digging incessantly into that memory, his only point of resemblance with Caesar, Alexander, and Napoleon; knowing facts, details, dates, proper names; ignorant of tendencies, passions, the diverse spirits of the mob, interior aspirations, the hidden and obscure upheavals of souls, in a word, all that might be called the invisible current of conscience; accepted by the surface, but little in accord with the inner France; making his way by shrewdness; governing too much and not reigning enough; his own prime minister; excelling in making the pettiness of realities into an obstacle to the immensity of ideas; adding to a true creative faculty for civilization, order, and organization an indescribable spirit of routine and chicanery; founder and proxy of a dynasty; possessing something of Charlemagne and something of a lawyer; when all is said and done, a lofty, original figure, a prince who knew how to gain power in spite of France's anxiety and jealousy. Louis-Philippe will be classed among the eminent men of his century and would be ranked among the most illustrious rulers of history if he had had a little love of glory and had appreciated what is great to the same extent that he appreciated what is useful.

Louis-Philippe had been handsome and, when old, was still fine looking; not always agreeable to the nation, he always was to the multitude; he pleased. He had this gift, charm. Majesty he lacked; he neither wore the crown, though king, nor white hair, though an old man. His manners were of the old régime, and his habits of the new, a mixture of the noble and the bourgeois that suited 1830; Louis-Philippe was regnant transistion; he had preserved the older pronunciation and the older spelling which he put to the service of modern opinions; he loved Poland and Hungary, but he wrote *les polonois,* and pronounced *les hongrais*. He wore the dress of the National Guard like Charles X, and the ribbon of the Legion of Honor like Napoleon.

He rarely went to chapel, not at all to the hunt, never to the opera—he was incorruptible by priests, dog-keepers, and danseuses, which affected his popularity with the bourgeoisie. He had no court. He went out with his umbrella under his arm, and this umbrella for a long time was part of his aura. He was something of a mason, something of a gardener, and something of a doctor; he once bled a postilion who fell off his horse; Louis-Philippe no more went without his lancet than Henry III without his dagger. The royalists laughed at this ridiculous king, the first who had spilled blood to heal.

In historic complaints against Louis-Philippe, there are subtractions to be made; there is what is to be charged to the royalty, what is to be charged to the reign, and what is to be charged to the king; three columns, each of which gives a different total. The right of democracy confiscated, progress made the second interest, the protests of the street violently repressed, the military execution of insurrections, riots cleared by arms, the Rue Transnonain, the councils of war, the absorption of the real country by the legal country, the governing shared jointly by three hundred thousand privileged persons—these are acts of the royalty. Belgium refused, Algeria too harshly conquered, and, like India by the English, with more barbarism than civilization, the breach of faith with Abd-el-Kader, Blaye, Deutz bought, Pritchard paid—these are acts of the reign. His policies, which looked rather to the family than to the nation, are the acts of the king.

As we see, when the deduction is made, the charge against the king is diminished.

His major fault was this: He was modest in the name of France.

Where does this fault come from?

Louis-Philippe was too fatherly as a king; this incubation of a family that is to be hatched into a dynasty is afraid of everything, and cannot brook interference; hence excessive timidity, annoying to a people who have July 14 in their civil traditions and Austerlitz in their military traditions.

Moreover, if we throw aside public duties, which demand to be fulfilled first, this deep tenderness of Louis-Philippe for his family the family deserved. This domestic group was wonderful. Their virtues rubbed shoulders with their talents. One of Louis-Philippe's daughters, Maria d'Orléans, put the name of her descent among artists as Charles d'Orléans had put it among poets. Out of her soul she made a statue she called Jeanne d'Arc. Two of Louis-Philippe's sons drew from Metternich this demagogic eulogy: "They are young men such as we rarely see, and princes such as we never see."

This, without withholding, but also without exaggerating, is the truth about Louis-Philippe.

To be Prince Egalité, to bear within himself the contradiction of the Restoration and the Revolution, to have the threatening aspect of the revolutionary that becomes reassuring in the ruler, such was the fortune of Louis-Philippe in 1830; never was there a more complete adaptation of a man to an event; the one entered into the other, and there was an incarnation. Louis-Philippe is 1830 made man. Moreover, he had in his favor that grand designation for the throne, exile. He had been proscribed, a wanderer, poor. He had lived by his labor. In Switzerland, this heir to the richest princely domains in France had sold an old horse to procure food. At Reichenau he had given lessons in mathematics, while his sister Adelaide did sewing and embroidery. These memories associated with a king fired the bourgeoisie's enthusiasm. With his own hands he had demolished the last iron cage of Mont-Saint-Michel, built by Louis XI and used by Louis XV. He was the companion of Dumouriez, he was the friend of Lafayette; he had belonged to the Jacobin Club; Mirabeau had slapped him on the shoulder; Danton had said to him, "Young man!" At twenty-four, in '93, as M. de Chartres, from the back of an obscure bench in the Convention, he had been present at the trial of Louis XVI, so aptly named "that poor tyrant." The blind clairvoyance of the Revolution, crushing royalty in the king, and the king with the royalty, almost without noticing the man in the savage overthrow of the idea, the vast tempest of the tribunal assembly, the public wrath questioning, Capet not knowing what to answer, the fearful stupefied vacillation of this royal head under that somber blast, the relative innocence of all in that catastrophe, of those who condemned as well as of the one who was condemned—he had seen these things, had observed this maelstrom; he had seen the centuries appear at the bar of the Convention; he had seen behind Louis XVI, that hapless, responsible bystander, rising up in the darkness, the fear-inspiring criminal, the monarchy; and there was still in his soul a respectful fear before this limitless justice of the people, almost as impersonal as the justice of God.

The effect that the Revolution produced on him was tremendous. His memory was like a living impression of those great years, minute by minute. One day, before a witness whom it is impossible for us to doubt, he accurately ran through by heart the whole letter A of the alphabetic list of the constituent assembly.

Louis-Philippe was a king of broad daylight. While he reigned, the press was free, the tribune was free, conscience and speech were free. The laws of September are clear and open. Though well knowing the corroding power of light on privileges, he left his throne exposed to the light. History will acknowledge this loyalty.

Like all men of history who have left the scene, Louis-Philippe is now to be put on trial by the human conscience. As yet he is only before the grand jury.

The hour in which history speaks with its free and venerable accent has not yet struck for him; the time has not come to pronounce final judgment on this king; even that austere and illustrious historian, Louis Blanc, has recently modified his first verdict: Louis-Philippe was the elect of those two almosts that are called the 221 and 1830, that is to say, of a demi-parliament and a demi-revolution; and in any event, from the superior point of view in which philosophy ought to be placed, we could judge him here, as we have intimated before, only under certain reservations in the name of the absolute democratic principle; in the eyes of the absolute, beyond these rights—the rights of man first, the rights of the people afterward—all is usurpation. But we can say at present, having made these reservations, that to sum up and in whatever way he is considered, Louis-Philippe, taken by himself and from the point of view of human goodness, will remain, to use the age-old language of history, one of the best princes who ever sat upon a throne.

What is held against him? That throne. Take the king away from Louis-Philippe, there remains the man. And the man is good. He is sometimes so good as to be admirable. Often, in the midst of the gravest cares, after a day of struggle against the entire diplomacy of the continent, he went home in the evening to his apartment, and there, exhausted with fatigue, bowed down with sleep, what did he do? He took a bundle of documents and spent the night reviewing a criminal prosecution, feeling that it was something to stand up against Europe, but that it was much greater still to save a man from the executioner. He was obstinate against his keeper of the seals; inch by inch he disputed the terrain of the guillotine with the attorneys-general, "those babblers of the law," as he called them. Sometimes the heaped-up documents covered his table; he examined them all; it anguished him to give up those wretched condemned heads. One day he said to the same witness whom we have just now referred to, "Last night I saved seven." During the early years of his reign, the death penalty was abolished, and the re-erected scaffold was a severe blow to the king. La Grève having disappeared with the elder branch, a bourgeois Grève was instituted under the name of la Barrière Saint-Jacques; "practical men" felt the need of a quasilegitimate guillotine; and this was one of the victories of Casimir Perier, who represented the more conservative portions of the bourgeoisie, over Louis-Philippe, who represented its more liberal portions. Louis-Philippe had annotated Beccaria with his own hand. After the attempted assassination through the Fieschi's mechanical device, he exclaimed, "What a pity that I wasn't wounded! I could have pardoned him." At another time, alluding to the resistance of his ministers, he wrote concerning a political convict, who is one of the noblest figures of our times: "His pardon is granted; it only remains for me to obtain it." Louis-Philippe was as gentle as Louis IX, and as good as Henry IV.

Now, for us, in history where goodness is the pearl of great price, he who has been good stands almost above him who has been great.

Since Louis-Philippe has been considered with severity by some, harshly, perhaps, by others, it is very natural that a man, himself now a phantom, who knew this king, should come forward to testify for him before history; this testimony, whatever it may be, is obviously and above all disinterested; an epitaph written by a dead man is sincere; one shade may console another; the sharing of the same darkness gives the right to praise; and there is little fear that it will ever be said of two tombs in exile: This one flattered the other.

IV

CRACKS IN THE FOUNDATION

At the moment when the drama we are relating is about to penetrate into the depths of one of the tragic clouds that cover the first years of Louis-Philippe's reign, we could not be ambiguous, and this book had to be explicit in regard to this king.

Louis-Philippe entered into royal authority without violence, without direct action on his part, by the action of a revolutionary transfer, clearly very distinct from the real aim of the revolution, but in which he, the Duc d'Orléans, had no personal initiative. He was born a prince and believed himself elected king. He had not given himself this command; he had not taken it; it had been offered to him and he had accepted it, convinced—wrongly in our opinion, but convinced—that the offer was consistent with right and that the acceptance was consistent with duty. Hence a possession in good faith. Now, we say it in all conscience, with Louis-Philippe possessing in good faith, and democracy attacking in good faith, the terror that arises from social struggles is chargeable neither to the king nor to the democracy. A clash of principles resembles a clash of the elements. The ocean defends the water, the hurricane defends the air; the king defends royalty, the democracy defends the people; the relative, which is the monarchy, resists the absolute, which is the republic; society bleeds under this struggle, but its suffering of today will be its safety hereafter; and, in any event, there is no censure due to those who struggle; one of the two parties is obviously mistaken; right is not like the colossus of Rhodes, on two shores at once, one foot in the republic, one foot in royalty; it is indivisible, and all on one side; but those who are mistaken are sincerely mistaken; a blind man is no more a guilty party than a Vendéen is a bandit. So let us impute these terrible collisions only to the fatality of things. Whatever these tempests may be, human responsibility is not involved.

Let us conclude this exegesis.

Right from the start, the government of 1830 had a hard life. Born yesterday, it was obliged to fight today.

It was barely installed when it began to feel on all sides vague movements directed against the apparatus of July, still so newly set up, and so far from secure.

Resistance was born on the day after, perhaps even on the eve.

From month to month the hostility increased, and from mute it became outspoken.

The July Revolution, tardily accepted outside of France by the kings, had been diversely interpreted in France.

God makes his will visible to men in events, an obscure text written in a mysterious language. Men make their translations of it instantly; hasty translations, incorrect, full of mistakes, omissions, and misreadings. Very few minds understand the divine language. The wisest and calmest, the most profound, decipher slowly, and, when they arrive with their text, the need has long since gone by; there are already twenty translations in the public square. From each translation a party is born, and from each misreading a faction; and each party believes it has the only true text, and each faction believes it possesses the light.

Often the government itself is a faction.

In revolutions there are some swimmers going against the current; they are the old parties.

The old parties, attached to hereditary right by the grace of God, since revolutions rose from the right of revolt, think they in turn have a right of revolt. An error. For in revolutions the revolted party is not the people, it is the king. Revolution is precisely the opposite of revolt. Every revolution, being a normal accomplishment, contains in itself its own legitimacy, which false revolutionists sometimes dishonor, but which persists even when sullied, which survives even when stained with blood. Revolutions spring, not from an accident, but from necessity. A revolution is a return from the factitious to the real. It is, because it must be.

The old legitimist parties none the less assailed the Revolution of 1830 with all the violence that springs from false reasoning. Errors are excellent projectiles. They struck it skillfully just where it was vulnerable, at the defect in its armor, its lack of logic; they attacked this revolution in its royalty. They cried out to it: Revolution, why this king? Factions are blind men who aim straight.

This cry was uttered by the republicans, too. But, coming from them, the cry was logical. What was blindness with the legitimists was clear-sightedness with the democrats. The year 1830 had gone bankrupt for the people. The democracy indignantly reproached it with its failure.

Between attacks from the past and attacks from the future, the July establishment was struggling on. It represented the moment, in conflict on the one hand with the monarchical centuries, on the other hand with the eternal right.

Beyond French borders, moreover, no longer being revolution but becoming the monarchy, 1830 was obliged to keep in step with Europe. To preserve peace, additional complications. A harmony required in the wrong way is often more onerous than a war. From this hidden conflict, always muzzled but always muttering, came an armed peace, that ruinous expedient of civilization always suspicious of itself. The royalty of July reared, in spite of the lash, in the harness of the European cabinets. Metternich would gladly have reined it in. Pushed around in France by progress, it pushed the reactionary monarchies of Europe. Towed, it towed.

Meanwhile, within the country, pauperism, the proletariat, wages, education, the penal system, prostitution, the lot of woman, riches, misery, production, consumption, distribution, exchange, money, credit, rights of capital, rights of labor, all these questions built up above society, an awesome overhang.

Outside of the political parties properly speaking, another movement was showing up. The philosophic ferment responded to the democratic ferment. The élite felt disturbed, as did the masses; differently, but just as much.

Thinkers were meditating, while the soil, that is to say, the people, traversed by the revolutionary currents, trembled beneath them with mysterious epileptic shocks. These thinkers, some isolated, others gathered into families and almost into communion, were turning over social questions, peacefully, but profoundly; impassive miners, who were quietly digging their galleries into the depths of a volcano, scarcely disturbed by the muffled commotions and the half-seen glow of lava.

This tranquility was not the least beautiful spectacle of that agitated period.

These men left the question of rights to political parties; they busied themselves with the question of happiness.

The well-being of man was what they wished to extract from society.

They elevated the material questions, questions of agriculture, of industry, of commerce, almost to the dignity of a religion. In civilization such as it is constituted to some small extent by God, to a greater by man, interests are combined, aggregated, and amalgamated in such a way as to form actual hard rock, according to a dynamic law patiently studied by the economists, those geologists of politics.

These men who grouped themselves under different rubrics, but who may all be designated by the generic title of socialists, tried to pierce this rock and to make the living waters of human happiness rush out of it.

From the question of the scaffold to the question of war, their labors embraced everything. To the rights of man, proclaimed by the French Revolution, they added the rights of woman and the rights of the child.

It will surprise no one that here, for various reasons, we do not exhaustively deal with the theoretical questions raised by socialism. We merely indicate them.

All the problems the socialists raised aside from cosmogonic visions, dreams, and mysticism, can be reduced to two principal problems.

First problem:

To produce wealth.

Second problem:

To distribute it.

The first problem contains the question of labor.

The second contains the question of wages.

In the first problem the question is of the employment of force.

In the second, of the distribution of enjoyment.

From the good use of force results public power.

From the good distribution of enjoyment results individual happiness.

By good distribution, we must understand not equal distribution, but equitable distribution. The highest equality is equity.

From these two things combined, public power and individual happiness, social prosperity results.

Social prosperity means happy men, the citizen free, the nation great.

England solves the first of these two problems. She

creates wealth admirably; she distributes it badly. This solution, which is complete only on one side, leads her inevitably to two extremes: monstrous opulence, monstrous misery. All the enjoyment to a few, all the privation to the rest, that is to say, to the people; privilege, exception, monopoly, feudality, springing from labor itself. A false and dangerous situation that founds public power upon private misery, which plants the grandeur of the state in the suffering of the individual. A grandeur ill constituted, in which all the material elements are combined, and into which no moral element enters.

Communism and agrarian law think they have solved the second problem. They are mistaken. Their distribution kills production. Equal partition abolishes emulation. And consequently labor. It is a distribution made by the butcher, who kills what he divides. It is therefore impossible to stop at these professed solutions. To kill wealth is not to distribute it.

The two problems must be solved together to be well solved. The two solutions must be combined to form only one.

Solve merely the first of the two problems, you will be Venice or England. Like Venice you will have an artificial power, or like England material power; you will be the evil rich. You will perish by violence, as Venice died, or by bankruptcy, as England will. And the world will let you die and fall, because the world lets everything fall and die that is nothing but selfishness, everything that does not represent a virtue or an idea for the human race.

Of course, it is understood that by these words, Venice, England, we do not mean the people, but the social constructions; the oligarchies superimposed on the nations, not the nations themselves. The nations always have our respect and our sympathy. Venice, the people, will be reborn; England, the aristocracy, will fall, but England, the nation, is immortal. With this said, we proceed.

Solve the two problems, encourage the rich, and protect the poor, suppress misery, put an end to the unjust speculation on the weak by the strong, put a bridle on the iniquitous jealousy of the one who is on the road, against the one who has reached his goal, adjust wages to labor mathematically and fraternally, join free and compulsory education to the growth of childhood, and make science the basis of manhood, develop the intelligence while you occupy the arm, be at the same time a powerful people and a happy family, democratize property, not by abolishing it but by universalizing it, in such a way that every citizen without exception may be a proprietor, an easier thing than it is believed to be; in two words, learn to produce wealth and learn to distribute it, and you will have material grandeur and moral grandeur combined; and you shall be worthy of calling yourselves France.

This, above and beyond a few stray sects, is what socialism said; that is what it sought to realize; this is what it outlined in men's minds.

Admirable efforts! Sacred attempts!

These doctrines, these theories, these resistances, the unforeseen necessity for the statesman to consult with the philosopher, confused evidences half seen, a new politics to create, in accord with the old world, and yet not too discordant with the ideal of the revolution; a state of affairs in which Lafayette had to be used to oppose Polignac, the intuition of progress glimpsed through the riots, the chambers, and the street, rivalries to balance around him, his faith in the Revolution, perhaps some uncertain eventual resignation arising from the vague acceptance of a definitive superior right, his desire to remain in his lineage, his family pride, his sincere respect for the people, his own honesty—all of this preoccupied Louis-Philippe almost painfully, and at times strong and as courageous as he was, overwhelmed him under the difficulties of being king.

He felt beneath his feet a terrible disintegration, which was not, however, a crumbling into dust—France being more France than ever.

Dark drifts covered the horizon. A strange shadow coming nearer and nearer was spreading over men little by little, over things, over ideas; a shadow that came from indignation and systems. All that had been hurriedly stifled was stirring and fermenting. Sometimes the conscience of the honest man caught its breath, so great was the confusion in that air in which sophisms mingled with truths. Minds trembled in the social anxiety like leaves at the approach of the storm. The electric tension was so great that at certain moments any chance comer, though unknown, gave off light. Then the twilight obscurity would fall again. At intervals, deep and half-smothered mutterings enabled men to judge the amount of lightning in the cloud.

Hardly twenty months had rolled by since the July Revolution; the year 1832 had opened with a menacing atmosphere. The distress of the people; laborers without bread; the last Prince de Condé lost in the darkness; Brussels driving away the Nassaus as Paris had driven away the Bourbons; Belgium offering herself to a French prince, and given to an English prince; the Russian hatred of Nicholas; at our back two demons of the south, Ferdinand in Spain, Miguel in Portugal; the earth quaking in Italy; Metternich extending his hand over Bologna; France bluntly opposing Austria at Ancona; in the north some ill-omened sound of a hammer once more nailing Poland into its coffin; throughout Europe angry looks peering at France; England a suspicious ally, ready to push over anyone leaning and throw herself on anyone fallen; the peerage sheltering itself behind Beccaria to deny four heads to the law; the fleur-de-lis erased from the king's carriage; the cross torn down from Notre-Dame; Lafayette weakened; Lafitte ruined; Benjamin Constant dead in poverty; Casimir Perier dead from loss of power; the political disease and the social disease breaking out in the two capitals of the realm, one the city of thought, the other the city of labor; in Paris civil war, in Lyons servile war; in the two cities the same furnace glare; the flush of the crater on the forehead of the people; the South fanaticized, the West uneasy; the Duchesse de Berry in La Vendée; plots, conspiracies, uprising, cholera, added to the dismal mutter of ideas, the dismal uproar of events.

V

FACTS FROM WHICH HISTORY SPRINGS AND WHICH HISTORY IGNORES

Toward the end of April everything was worse. The fermentation turned into a boiling. Since 1830, there had been here and there a few small riots, quickly repressed, but breaking out again, signs of a vast underlying conflagration. Something terrible was brooding. Glimpses were caught of the features, still indistinct and scarcely visible, of a possible revolution. France looked to Paris; Paris looked to the Faubourg Saint-Antoine.

The Faubourg Saint-Antoine, secretly heated, was coming to a boil.

The bistros of the Rue de Charonne, although the junction of the two epithets seems odd when applied to bistros, were serious and stormy.

There the government, pure and simple, was brought into question. There men publicly discussed whether to fight or to stay quiet. There were back rooms where an oath was administered to workingmen, that they would be in the streets at the first alarm, and "that they would fight without counting the enemy." The agreement once made, a man seated in the corner of the bistro said in a ringing voice, "You understand it! You have sworn it!" Sometimes they went upstairs to a closed room, and there scenes occurred that were almost masonic. Oaths were administered to the initiated "to render service to them as they would to their own fathers." That was the formula.

In the lower rooms they read "subversive" pamphlets. "They pelted the government," says a secret report of the times.

Such words as these were heard: "I don't know the names of the leaders. As for us, we'll only know the day two hours beforehand." A workingman said, "There are three hundred of us, let's put in ten sous each, that will total a hundred and fifty francs for making powder and ball." Another said, "I don't ask six months, I don't ask two. In less than two weeks we'll meet the government face to face. With twenty-five thousand men we can make our stand." Another said, "I don't go to bed, because I'm busy making cartridges all night." From time to time, men "like bourgeois in fine coats" came, "causing embarrassment," and with an air "of command," shook hands with the most important, and went away. They never stayed more than ten minutes. Words of deep significance were exchanged in a low voice: "The plot is ripe, the thing is complete." "This was whispered by everyone there," to borrow the actual expression of one of the participants. The exaltation was such that one day, right in a bistro, a workingman exclaimed, "We have no arms!" One of his comrades answered, "The soldiers have!" thus parodying, without suspecting it, Bonaparte's proclamation to the army of Italy. "When they had anything more secret," adds a report, "they did not communicate it there." One can hardly understand what they could conceal after saying what they said.

The meetings were sometimes regularly scheduled. At some, there were never more than eight or ten people, and always the same ones. In others, anybody who chose entered, and the room was so full they were forced to stand. Some were there out of enthusiasm and passion; others because it was on their way to work. As in the time of the revolution, there were in these bistros some female patriots, who embraced the newcomers.

Other revealing facts were coming to light.

A man entered a bistro, drank, and went out, saying, "Wine merchant, whatever we owe, the Revolution will pay."

At another, opposite the Rue de Charonne, revolutionary officers were elected. The ballots were gathered in caps.

Some workingmen met at a fencing master's, who gave lessons in the Rue de Cotte. There was a trophy of arms there, made of wooden swords, canes, clubs, and foils. One day they took the buttons off the foils. A workingman said, "We are twenty-five; but they don't count on me, because they consider me a machine." This machine was afterward Quénisset.

Little ordinary things that were premeditated gradually took on a strange notoriety. A woman sweeping her doorstep said to another woman, "For a long time they have been hard at work making cartridges." Proclamations were read in the open street, addressed to the National Guards of the Départements. One of these proclamations was signed: "Burtot, wine merchant."

One day at a liquor dealer's door in the Lenoir market, a man with a heavy beard and an Italian accent climbed on a block and read aloud a singular piece of writing that seemed to emanate from an occult power. Groups formed around him and applauded. Passages that most stirred the crowd were gathered and noted down. ". . . Our doctrines are trammeled, our proclamations are torn down, our people posting notices are watched and thrown into prison . . ." "The recent fall in cottons has converted many moderates . . ." "The future of the peoples is being worked out in our obscure ranks." ". . . Here are the terms laid down: action or reaction, revolution or counterrevolution. For, in our times, we no longer believe in inertia or immobility. For the people or against the people, that is the question. There is no other." ". . . The day that we no longer suit you crush us, but until then help us go forward." All this in broad daylight.

Other acts, bolder still, were suspected by the people because of their very audacity. On April 4, 1832, a passerby mounted the block at the corner of the Rue Saint-Marguerite and cried, "I am a Babouvist!" But under Babeuf the people scented Gisquet.

Among other things, this man said, "Down with property! The leftist opposition are cowards and traitors. When they want to be right, they preach revolution. They are democrats so they won't be beaten, and royalists so they won't have to fight. The republicans are feathered beasts. Don't trust the republicans, citizen laborers."

"Silence, citizen spy!" cried a workingman.

This put an end to the speech.

Mysterious incidents occurred.

At nightfall, a workingman met "a well-dressed man" near the canal, who said to him, "Where are you going, citizen?" "Monsieur," said the workingman, "I do not have the honor of knowing you." "But I know you very well." And the man added, "Don't be afraid. I am an agent of the Committee. They suspect that you are not very sure. You know that if you reveal anything, we have an eye on you." Then he gave the workingman a handshake and went away, saying, "We will meet again soon."

The police, on the lookout, overheard, not merely in the bistros, but in the street, notable dialogues: "Get yourself admitted immediately," said a weaver to a cabinetmaker.

"Why?"

"There'll be some shooting to do."

Two people in rags exchanged these remarkable phrases, stuffed with apparent Jacquerie.

"Who governs us?"

"Monsieur Philippe."

"No, it's the bourgeoisie."

One would be mistaken to suppose that we used the word Jacquerie in bad part. The Jacques were the poor. Those who are hungry have just cause.

Another time, two men were heard passing by, one of whom said to the other, "We have a good plan of attack."

Of a private conversation between four men crouching in a ditch at the fork of the road by the Barrière du Trône, was caught only this, "Everything possible will be done so he'll no longer walk the streets of Paris."

Who was *he?* Obscurely threatening.

"The principal leaders," as they said in the Faubourg, kept out of sight. They were believed to meet to put their heads together, in a bistro near Point Saint-Eustache. One named Aug———, chief of the Tailors' Benevolent Society, Rue Mondétour, was thought to act as principal intermediary between the chiefs and the Faubourg Saint-Antoine. Nevertheless, there was always great obscurity concerning these chiefs, and no actual fact could weaken the singularly bold response given later by a prisoner before the Court of Peers.

"Who was your leader?"

"I knew none, and I recognized none."

It was all hardly more than words, yet transparent, vague; sometimes rumors in the air, thirdhand reports, hearsay. Other hints would crop up.

A carpenter, working on the Rue de Reuilly, nailing boards to a fence around a lot where a house was being built, found in the lot a fragment of a letter, on which the following lines were still legible.

". . . The Committee must take measures to prevent recruiting in the sections for the different societies . . ."

And in a postscript:

"We have learned that there are muskets at No. 5 (bis) Rue du Faubourg-Poissonière, totaling five or six thousand, at an armorer's in that court. The section has no arms."

What excited the carpenter and made him show the thing to his neighbors was that a few steps farther on he picked up another paper also torn, but still more significant, whose form we reproduce here because of the historic interest of these strange documents:

Q	C	D	S	
				Learn this list by heart. *Afterward, tear it up. Men* *who are admitted will do the* *same when you have trans-* *mitted their orders to them.* *Health and fraternity.* *u og á fe.* L.

Those who were in on the secret at the time of this discovery did not know until later the meaning of the four capitals: *quint*, *urions*, *centurions*, *decurions*, *scouts*, and the sense of those letters: *u og á fe*, which was a date, and which meant *this* 15*th April*, 1832. Under each capital were inscribed names followed by very characteristic indications. Thus: Q. *Bannerel*. 8 muskets. 83 cartridges. Sure man. C. *Boubière*. 1 pistol. 40 cartridges. D. *Rollet*. 1 foil. 1 pistol. 1 pound of powder. S. *Teissier*. 1 saber. 1 cartridge box. Exact. *Terreur*. 8 muskets. Brave, etc.

Finally, this carpenter found, in the same enclosure, too, a third paper on which was written in pencil, but very legibly, this enigmatic list:

Unity. Blanchard. Arbre-sec. 6.
Barra. Soize. Salle-au-Comte.
Kosciusko. Aubry the butcher?
J. J. R.
Caius Gracchus.
Right of revision. Dufond. Four.
Fall of the Girondins. Derbac. Maubuée.
Washington. Pinson. 1 pist. 86 cart.
Marseillaise.
Sover. of the people. Michel. Quincampoix. Saber.
Hoche.
Marceau. Plato. Arbre-sec.
Warsaw. Tilly, crier of *Le Populaire*.

The honest bourgeois who finally came into possession of this list knew its significance. It appeared that this list gave the complete nomenclature of the sections of the Fourth Arrondissement of the Society of the Rights of Man, with the names and residences of the chiefs of sections. Today, when all these facts then unknown are simply a matter of history, they can be published. It should be added that the founding of the Society of the Rights of Man seems to have come after the time when this paper was found. Perhaps it was merely a draft.

Meanwhile, after rumors and speeches, after written indications, material facts began to leak out.

In the Rue Popincourt, in a junk shop, in a bureau drawer, seven sheets of gray paper all evenly folded in quarto were seized; these sheets enclosed twenty-six squares of the same gray paper folded in the shape of cartridges, and a card on which was written:

Saltpeter,	12 ounces.
Sulphur,	2 ounces.
Charcoal,	2 ounces and a half.
Water,	2 ounces.

The official report of the seizure stated that the drawer gave off a strong odor of powder.

A mason going home after his day's work forgot a little package on a bench near the Pont d'Austerlitz. This package was carried to the guardhouse. It was opened and disclosed two printed dialogues, signed *Lahautière,* a song entitled "Workingmen, Unite" and a tin box full of cartridges.

A workingman, drinking with a comrade, had him put his hand on him to see how warm he was; the other felt a pistol under his vest.

In a ditch on the boulevard, between Père-Lachaise and the Barrière du Trône, at the most solitary spot, some children at play discovered under a heap of chips and rubbish a bag that contained a bullet-mold, a wooden mandrel for making cartridges, a wooden mortar in which there were some grains of hunting powder, and a little melting pot whose interior showed unmistakable traces of melted lead.

At five in the morning, some policemen, unannounced, entered the house of a man named Pardon, later a member of the section of the Barricade-Merry, and still later killed in the insurrection of April 1834, found him standing not far from his bed, with cartridges in his hands, caught in the act.

About the time of day when workingmen are relaxing, two men were seen to meet between the Barrière Picpus and the Barrière Charenton in a little cross alley between two walls near a wine dealer's who had a card table in front of his door. One took a pistol from under his shirt and handed it to the other. As he was handing it to him he noticed that the perspiration from his chest had transmitted some moisture to the powder. He primed the pistol and added some powder to what was already in the pan. Then the two men went their ways.

A man named Gallais, later killed in the Rue Beaubourg in the April uprising, boasted he had seven hundred cartridges and twenty-four gunflints at home.

The government received word one day that arms and two hundred thousand cartridges had just been distributed in the Faubourg. The next week, thirty thousand cartridges were distributed. Remarkably, the police could not seize one. An intercepted letter stated, "The day is not distant when eighty thousand patriots will be under arms."

All this ferment was public, we might almost say tranquil. The imminent insurrection gathered its storm calmly in the face of the government. No singularity was lacking in this crisis, still subterranean, but already perceptible. The middle class talked quietly with workingmen about the preparations. They would say, "How is the uprising coming along?" in the same tone in which they would have said, "How's your wife?"

A furniture dealer, Rue Moreau, asked, "Well, when are you going to attack?"

Another shopkeeper said, "You'll attack very soon, I know. A month ago there were fifteen thousand of you, now there are twenty-five thousand." He offered his gun and a neighbor offered a little pistol, which he wanted to sell for seven francs.

All in all, the revolutionary fervor was increasing. No place in Paris or in France was exempt from it. The artery was throbbing everywhere. Like those membranes born of certain inflammations and formed in the human body, the network of secret societies began to spread over the country. From the association of the Friends of the People, public and secret at the same time, sprang the Society of the Rights of Man, which dated one of its orders of the day *Pluviôse, year* 40 *of the Republican Era*, which was to survive even the decrees of the superior court pronouncing its dissolution, and which had no hesitation in giving its sections such significant names as these:

The Pikes	*The Vagrants*
Tocsin	*Forward March*
Alarm Gun	*Robespierre*
Phrygian Cap	*Level*
January 21	*Ça ira*
The Beggars	

The Society of the Rights of Man spawned the Society of Action. These were the more impatient who left it and ran forward. Other associations sought to recruit from the large mother societies. The section chiefs complained of being pestered by this. Thus arose The Gallic Society and the Organizing Committee of the Municipalities. Thus the associations for the Freedom of the Press, for Individual Freedom, for the Education of the People, against Direct Taxes. Then the society of the Egalitarian Workingmen, which divided into three factions, the Egalitarians, the Communists, and the Reformers. Then the Army of the Bastilles, a sort of cohort with a military organization, four men commanded by a corporal, ten by a sergeant, twenty by a second lieutenant, forty by a lieutenant; there were never more than five hundred men who knew each other. A creation in which precaution was combined with boldness and seemingly marked with the genius of Venice. The central committee, which was the head, had two arms, the Society of Action and the Army of the Bastilles. A legitimist association, the Chevaliers of Fidelity, moved among these republican affiliations. But it was denounced and repudiated.

The Parisian societies spread to the principal cities. Lyons, Nantes, Lisle, and Marseilles had their Society of the Rights of Man, the Carbonari, the Free Men. Aix had a revolutionary society called the Cougourde. We have already written that word.

In Paris the Faubourg Saint-Marceau was hardly less seething than the Fauborug Saint-Antoine, and the schools no less excited than the faubourgs. A café on the Rue Saint-Hyacinthe, and the drinking and smoking room of the Seven Billiards, Rue des Mathurin-Saint-Jacques, served as rallying places for the students. The Society of the Friends of the A B C, affiliated with the Mutualists of Angers and with the Cougourde of Aix, met, as we have seen, at the Café Musain. These same young people also gathered, as we have said, in Corinthe, a bistro near the

Rue Mondétour. These meetings were secret, others were as public as possible, and we may judge their boldness by this fragment of an interrogation during one of the subsequent trials: "Where was this meeting held?" "Rue de la Paix." "In whose house?" "In the street." "What sections were there?" "Only one." "Which one?" "The Manuel section." "Who was the leader?" "I was." "You are too young to have reached alone the grave decision to attack the government. Where did your instructions come from?" "From the central committee."

The army was undermined at the same time as the population, as was later proven by the movements of Béford, Lunéville, and Epinal. They counted on the fifty-second regiment, the fifth, the eighth, the thirty-seventh, and the twentieth light. In Burgundy and in the cities of the South the tree of Liberty was planted. That is to say, a pole topped by the revolutionary red bonnet.

Such was the situation.

This situation was, as we said in the beginning, made tangible and emphatic by the Faubourg Saint-Antoine more than by any other portion of the population. There was the stitch in the side.

This old faubourg, populous as an anthill, industrious, courageous, and choleric as a hive, was trembling with the expectation and the desire for a commotion. Everything was in turmoil, and yet labor was not interrupted on that account. Nothing can give an idea of that vivid yet somber state of affairs. In that faubourg there is bitter distress hidden under garret roofs; there are also ardent and unusual minds. And it is particularly in regard to distress and intelligence that it is dangerous for extremes to meet.

The Faubourg Saint-Antoine had still other causes of excitement, for it felt the rebound of the commercial crises, of the failures, strikes, and unemployment inherent in great political disturbances. In time of revolution, misery is at once cause and effect. The blow it strikes rebounds. This population, full of proud virtue, filled with a hidden heat to the boiling point, always ready for an armed contest, prompt to explode, irritated, deep, laid with mines, seemed only in wait for the fall of a spark. Whenever certain sparks are floating over the horizon, driven by the wind of events, we cannot help thinking of the Faubourg Saint-Antoine and the terrible chance that placed that powderkeg of sufferings and ideas at the gates of Paris.

The bistros of the Faubourg-Antoine, more than once referred to in the preceding sketch, have a historic notoriety. In times of trouble their words are more intoxicating than their wine. A sort of prophetic spirit and a whiff of the future circulates among them, swelling hearts and enlarging souls. The bistros of the Faubourg-Antoine are like those taverns of Mount Aventine, over the Sybil's cave, and communicating with the deep and sacred afflatus; taverns whose tables were almost tripods, and where men drank what Ennius calls "*the sibylline wine*."

The Fauborg Saint-Antoine is a reservoir of people. Revolutionary agitation makes fissures in it through which popular sovereignty flows. This sovereignty may do harm; it makes mistakes like everything else; but, even when led astray, it is still great. We may say of it as of the blind Cyclops, *Ingens*.

In '93, according to whether the mood in the air was good or bad, according to whether it was the day of fanaticism or of enthusiasm, from the Faubourg Saint-Antoine would come sometimes savage legions, sometimes heroic bands.

Savage. We must explain this word. What was the aim of those bristling men who in the demiurgic days of revolutionary chaos, tattered, howling, wild, with cudgel raised and pike aloft, rushed over old overturned Paris? They wanted the end of oppressions, the end of tyrannies, the end of the sword, work for man, education for children, an amenable social climate for women, liberty, equality, fraternity, bread for all, ideas for all; the Edenization of the world, Progress. Pushed to the limit and beside themselves, terrible, half-naked, a club in their hands and a roar in their mouths, they demanded this holy, good, and gentle thing, progress. They were savages, yes, but the savages of civilization.

They proclaimed the right furiously; they wanted, even if through fear and trembling, to force the human race into paradise. They seemed barbarians, and they were saviors. With the mask of night they demanded the light.

In contrast with these men, wild, we admit, and terrible, but wild and terrible for the good, there are other men, smiling, embroidered, gilded, beribboned, in silk stockings, in white feathers, in yellow gloves, in polished shoes, who, leaning on a velvet table beside a marble mantel, softly insist on the maintenance and preservation of the past, the Middle Ages, divine right, fanaticism, ignorance, slavery, the death penalty, and war, glorifying politely and in mild tones the saber, the stake, and the scaffold. As for us, if we were compelled to choose between the barbarians of civilization and the civil advocates of barbarism, we would choose the barbarians.

But, thank heaven, another choice is possible. No sheer fall is necessary, forward no more than backward. Neither despotism, nor terrorism. We desire progress on a gentle slope.

God provides for this. The smoothing of slopes, this is God's whole policy.

VI

ENJOLRAS AND HIS LIEUTENANTS

At about this period, Enjolras, in view of possible events, took a sort of mysterious account of things.

Everyone was in secret assembly at the Café Musain.

Mingling a few semi-enigmatic but significant metaphors with his words, Enjolras said, "We must know where we are and who we can rely on. If we want fighting men, we must make them. Have the wherewithal to strike. That can do no harm. Travelers have a better chance of a goring when there are bulls in the road than when there are none. So let's take a little count of the herd. How many of us are there? We cannot put this work off till tomorrow. Revolutionaries should always be ready; progress has no time to lose. Beware the unexpected. We have to go over all the seams we've made, and see if they hold. This business should be probed clear to the bottom today. Courfeyrac, you'll see the Polytechnicians. It's their day off. Today, Wednesday. Feuilly, will you see the men of la Glacière? Combeferre has promised me to go to Picpus. There's really an excellent swarm there. Bahorel will visit the Estrapade. Prouvaire, the masons are growing lukewarm; you'll bring us news from the lodge in the Rue de Grenelle-Saint-Honoré. Joly will go to Dupuytren's clinic, and take the pulse of the Medical School. Bossuet will make a little tour of the Palais de Justice and chat with the young lawyers. I'll take charge of the Cougourde."

"Then everything's settled," said Courfeyrac.

"No."

"What else is there then?"

"Something very important."

"What?" inquired Combeferre.

"The Barrière du Maine," answered Enjolras.

For a moment, Enjolras seemed lost in his reflections, then he went on. "At the Barrière du Maine there are marble cutters, painters, assistants in sculptors' studios. It is an enthusiastic family, but subject to cooling off. I don't know what's been ailing them lately. They're thinking of other things. They're fading out. They spend their time playing dominoes. Somebody must go talk to them a bit, firmly, too. They meet at Richefeu's. They can be found there between noon and one. We'll have to blow on those embers. I had counted on that absentminded Marius for this, since he's good on the whole, but he doesn't come anymore. I have to have somebody for the Barrière du Maine. There's nobody left."

"Me," said Grantaire, "I'm here."

"You?"

"Me."

"You to indoctrinate republicans! You, to warm up, in the name of principles, hearts that have grown cold!"

"Why not?"

"Can you be good for something?"

"But I have a vague ambition in that direction," said Grantaire.

"You don't believe in anything."

"I believe in you."

"Grantaire, do you want to do me a favor?"

"Anything. Polish your boots."

"Well, don't meddle in our affairs. Sleep off your absinthe."

"You're an ingrate, Enjolras."

"You'd be a fine man to go to the Barrière du Maine! You'd be capable of that!"

"I'm capable of going down the Rue des Grès, of crossing the Place Saint-Michel, of striking off through the Rue Monsieur-le-Prince, of taking the Rue de Vaugirard, of passing the Carmelites, of turning into the Rue d'Assas, of reaching the Rue du Cherche-Midi, of leaving behind me the War Ministry, of hurrying through the Rue des Vieilles-Tuileries, of striding through the Boulevard, of following the Chaussée du Maine, of crossing over the Barrière, and of entering Richefeu's. I am capable of that. My shoes are capable of it."

"Do you know anything about those comrades at Richefeu's?"

"Not much. We're on good terms, though."

"What will you say to them?"

"I'll talk about Robespierre, by God. About Danton, about principles."

"You!"

"Me! You don't do me justice. When I get going, I'm formidable. I've read Prudhomme, I know the Contrat Social, I know my constitution of the year Two by heart. 'The Liberty of the citizen ends where the Liberty of another citizen begins.' Do you take me for a brute? I have an old assignat in my drawer. The Rights of Man, the sovereignty of the people, ye gods! I'm even a bit of a Hébertist. I can repeat, for six hours at a time, watch in hand, superb things."

"Be serious," said Enjolras.

"I'm fierce," answered Grantaire.

Enjolras thought for a few seconds and gestured like a man making up his mind.

"Grantaire," he said gravely. "I agree to try you. You'll go to the Barrière du Maine."

Grantaire lived in a furnished room quite near the Café Musain. He went out and came back in five minutes. He had gone home to put on a Robespierre waistcoat.

"Red," he said as he came in, looking straight at Enjolras.

Then, with the flat of his huge hand, he smoothed the two scarlet points of his waistcoat over his breast.

And, going up to Enjolras, he whispered in his ear, "Don't worry."

He jammed down his hat resolutely and went out.

A quarter of an hour later, the back room of the Café Musain was deserted. All the Friends of the A B C had gone, each his own way, about their business. Enjolras, who had reserved the Cougourde for himself, went out last.

Those of the Courgourde of Aix who were in Paris met in those days on the Plain of Issy, in one of the abandoned quarries so numerous on that side of the city.

On his way toward that place of rendezvous, Enjolras reviewed the situation. The gravity of events was obvious. When events, premonitory of some latent social ill, are moving heavily along, the slightest complication stops them and shackles them. A phenomenon that brings on collapses and rebirths. Enjolras caught glimpses of a luminous uprising under the dark skirts of the future. Who knows? Perhaps the moment was approaching. The people seizing their rights again, what a glorious spectacle! The Revolution majestically resuming possession of France and saying to the world: Tomorrow! Enjolras was pleased. The furnace was heating up. At that very instant, he had a powder train of friends spread across Paris. He was inwardly composing, with the philosophical and penetrating eloquence of Combeferre, the cosmopolitan enthusiasm of Feuilly, Courfeyrac's animation, Bahorel's laughter, Jean Prouvaire's melancholy, Joly's science, and Bossuet's sarcasms, a sort of electric spark to catch fire in all directions at once. All of them put to work. Surely, the result would answer the effort. This led him to think of Grantaire. "Well now," he said to himself, "the Barrière du Maine isn't far out of my way. Suppose I go as far as Richefeu's? Let's take a little look at what Grantaire is doing, how he's coming along."

One o'clock sounded from the belfry of Vaugirard when Enjolras reached the Richefeu smoking den. He opened the door, went in, crossed his arms, letting the door go so it swung and hit his shoulders, and looked into the room full of tables, men and smoke.

A voice was ringing out in the mist, sharply answered by another voice. It was Grantaire talking with an adversary whom he had found.

Grantaire was seated opposite another figure, at a table of Saint Anne marble strewn with bran and dotted with dominoes; he was rapping the marble with his fist, and what Enjolras heard was this:

"Double six."

"Four."

"The beast! I can't play."

"You're done for. Two."

"Six."

"Three."

"Ace."

"It's my turn."

"Four points."

"Hardly."

"Your turn."

"I made an awful blunder."

"You're doing well."

"Fifteen."

"Seven more."

"That makes me twenty-two." Musing. "Twenty-two!"

"You didn't expect the double six. If I had played it in the beginning, it would have changed the whole game."

"Two again."

"Ace."

"Ace! Well, five."

"I haven't any."

"You just played, I believe?"

"Yes."

"Blank."

"Does he ever have the luck! Ah! You are lucky!" Long pause. "Two."

"Ace."

"Neither a five nor an ace. That's a nuisance for you."

"Domino."

"Bitch!"

Book Two

EPONINE

I

THE FIELD OF THE LARK

Marius had observed the unexpected dénouement of the ambush for which he had tipped off Javert; but hardly had Javert left the old ruin, carrying away his prisoners in three carriages, when Marius also slipped out of the house. It was only nine in the evening. Marius went to Courfeyrac's. Courfeyrac was no longer the imperturbable inhabitant of the Latin Quarter; he had gone to live in the Rue de la Verrerie "for political reasons"; this quarter was one where the insurrection migrated in those days. Marius said to Courfeyrac, "I've come to sleep at your place." Courfeyrac drew a mattress off his bed, where there were two, laid it on the floor, and said, "There you are."

The next day, by seven in the morning, Marius went back to the tenement, paid his rent, and what was due to Ma'am Bougon, had his books, bed, table, bureau, and his two chairs loaded onto a handcart, and went off without leaving his address, so that when Javert came back later in the morning to question Marius about the previous evening's events, he found only Ma'am Bougon, who answered him, "moved out!"

Ma'am Bougon became convinced that Marius was somehow an accomplice of the robbers seized the night before. "Who would have thought it?" she exclaimed among the concierges of the neighborhood. "A young man who looked almost like a girl!"

Marius had two reasons for his prompt departure. The first was that he now had a horror of that house, where he had seen, so near at hand and in all its most repulsive and most ferocious development, a social deformity perhaps still more hideous than the evil rich: the evil poor. The second was that he had no wish to figure in the trial that would probably follow and be brought forward to testify against Thénardier.

Javert thought that the young man, whose name he had not remembered, had been frightened and had escaped, or had perhaps not even returned home at the time of the ambush; still he made some effort to find him, but without success.

A month rolled by, then another. Marius was still with Courfeyrac. He knew from a young attorney, a habitué of the court anterooms, that Thénardier was in solitary confinement. Every Monday Marius sent to the clerk of La Force five francs for Thénardier.

Having no money left, Marius borrowed the five francs from Courfeyrac. It was the first time in his life he had borrowed money. This periodic five francs was a double enigma, to Courfeyrac who furnished them and to Thénardier who received them. "Who can it be going to?" thought Courfeyrac. "Where can it be coming from?" Thénardier asked himself.

Marius, moreover, was woebegone. Everything had relapsed into gloom. He didn't see anything ahead of him anymore; his life was again plunged into that mystery in which he had been blindly groping. For a moment he had again seen close at hand in that obscurity the young girl whom he loved, the old man who seemed her father, these unknown beings who were his only interest and his only hope in all the world; and at the very moment he had thought to hold on to them, a gust had swept all the shadows away. Not a spark of certainty or truth had escaped even from that most fearful shock. No conjecture was possible. He did not even know the name he had thought he knew. Certainly it was no longer Ursula. And the Lark was a nickname. And what should he think about the old man? Was he really hiding from the police? The white-haired workingman whom Marius had met near the Invalides suddenly came back to mind. It now seemed probable that the workingman and M. Leblanc were the same. He had disguised himself then? This man had heroic sides and equivocal sides. Why had he not called for help? Why had he escaped? Was he, yes or no, the father of the young girl? Finally, was he really the man whom Thénardier thought he recognized? Thénardier could have been mistaken. So many problems without a solution. All this, it's true, detracted nothing from the angelic charms of the young girl of the Luxembourg. Poignant misery; Marius had passion in his heart and night over his eyes. He was pushed, he was drawn, and he could not stir. All had vanished, except love. Even of love, he had lost the instincts and the sudden illuminations. Ordinarily, this flame that consumes us illumines us also a little and sheds some useful light. Marius no longer even heard those vague promptings of passion. Never did he say to himself, "Suppose I go there?" "Suppose I try this?" The one he could no longer call Ursula was clearly somewhere; nothing told Marius which way to look. His whole life could now be summed up as an absolute uncertainty in an impenetrable mist. To see her again, Her; he yearned for it continually; he no longer hoped for it.

On top of everything, his poverty returned. Close to him, right behind him, he could feel its icy breath. During all these torments, and for a long time now, he had stopped his work, and nothing is more dangerous than discontinued labor; it is habit lost. A habit easy to abandon, difficult to resume.

A certain amount of reverie is good, like a narcotic in discreet doses. It soothes the fever, occasionally high, of the brain at work, and produces in the mind a soft, fresh vapor that corrects the all too angular contours of pure thought, fills up the gaps and intervals here and there, binds them together, and dulls the sharp corners of ideas. But too much reverie submerges and drowns. Woe to the intellectual who lets himseff fall completely from thought into reverie! He thinks he will rise again easily, and he says that, after all, it is the same thing. An error!

Thought is the labor of the intellect, reverie its pleasure. To replace thought with reverie is to confound poison with nourishment.

Marius, we remember, had begun this way. Passion arrived unexpectedly and had eventually flung him headlong into bottomless and aimless chimeras. There was no more going out of the house except to walk and dream.

A sluggish creation. A tumultuous and stagnant gulf. And, as work diminishes, necessities increase. This is the law. Man, in the dreamy state, is naturally prodigal and luxurious; the relaxed mind cannot lead a disciplined life. In this mode of life, there is some good mingled with the evil, for if the softening is fatal, the generosity is wholesome and good. But the poor man who is generous and noble, and who does not work, is lost. His resources dry up, his needs mount up.

Fatal slope, down which the firmest and the noblest are drawn, as well as the weakest and most vicious, and which leads to one of these two pits, suicide or crime.

By continually going out for reverie, a day comes when you go out to drown yourself.

Excess reverie produces men like Escousse and Lebras. Marius was slowly heading down this slope, his eyes fixed on the one he no longer saw. What we have just written here seems strange, but it is true. The memory of an absent being grows bright in the darkness of the heart; the more it has disappeared the more radiant it is; the despairing gloomy soul sees that light in its horizon; star of the interior night. She—this was Marius's entire thought. He dreamed of nothing else; he felt confusedly that his old coat was becoming an impossible coat and that his new coat was becoming an old coat, that his shirts were wearing out, that his hat was wearing out, that his boots were wearing out, that is to say, that his life was wearing out, and he said to himself, "If I could only see her again before I die."

A single sweet idea remained to him, that she had loved him, that her eyes had told him so, that she did not know his name but that she knew his soul, and that, perhaps, wherever she was, whatever that mysterious place might be, she still loved him. Who knows but that she was dreaming of him as he was dreaming of her? Sometimes in the inexplicable hours, known to every heart that loves, with reasons to be sad, yet feeling a vague thrill of joy, he said to himself, It is her thoughts that are coming to me! Then he added, Perhaps my thoughts reach her, too.

This illusion, which made him shake his head moments later, still managed to cast into his soul some ray that sometimes seemed like hope. From time to time, particularly at the evening hour that saddens dreamers most of all, he would leave on the pages of a notebook that he devoted to that purpose the purest, the most impersonal, the most ideal of the reveries with which love filled his brain. He called that "writing to her."

We must not suppose that his reason was disoriented. Quite the contrary. He had lost the capacity to work and move firmly toward a definite end, but he was more lucid and correct than ever. In a calm and real light, though a strange one, Marius saw what was going on around him, even the most ordinary events or men; he had the right word to say about everything with a sort of honest languor and disinterested candor. His judgment, almost detached from hope, soared.

In this state of mind nothing escaped him, nothing deceived him, and he constantly saw the basis of life, humanity, and destiny. Happy, even in anguish, is he to whom God has given a soul worthy of love and grief! He who has not seen the things of this world, and the hearts of men in this double light, has seen nothing, and knows nothing of the truth.

The soul that loves and suffers is in the sublime state.

The days went by, however, one after another, and nothing new showed up. It merely seemed to him that the dreary space that remained for him to travel was contracting with every instant. He thought that he was already distinctly seeing the brink of the bottomless precipice.

"Can it be," he repeated to himself, "that I'll never see her again?"

If you go up the Rue Saint-Jacques, pass the city gate, and follow the old interior boulevard to the left for some distance, you come to the Rue de la Santé, then La Glacière, and, a little before reaching the small stream of the Gobelins, you find a sort of field, which, in the long monotonous circuit of the Paris boulevards, is the only spot where Ruisdael would be tempted to sit down.

The indescribable something from which grace springs is there, a green meadow crossed by tight-drawn lines, on which rags are drying in the wind, an old market-garden farmhouse built in the time of Louis XIII, with its large roof grotesquely pierced by dormer windows, broken fences, a small pond between the poplars, women, laughter, voices; on the horizon the Panthéon, the tree of the Deaf-Mutes, the Val-de-Grâce, black, squat, fantastic, amusing, magnificent, and in the background the severe square summits of the towers of Notre-Dame.

As the place is worth seeing, nobody goes there. Hardly a cart or a wagon in a quarter of an hour.

It happened one day that Marius's solitary walks brought him to this spot near the pond. That day there was a rarity on the boulevard, a pedestrian. Vaguely struck with the almost sylvan charm of the spot, Marius asked this traveler, "What is the name of this place?"

The traveler answered, "It is the Field of the Lark."

And he added, "It was here that Ulbach killed the shepherdess from Ivry."

But after that word "lark," Marius had heard nothing more. There are such sudden constellations in the dream state that a single word can produce. The whole mind abruptly condenses around one idea, and cannot take in another thing.

In the depths of Marius's melancholy, the Lark was the name that had replaced Ursula. "Yes," he said in the kind of unreasoning stupor peculiar to these mysterious asides, "this is her field. Here I shall learn where she lives."

It was absurd, but irresistible.

And every day he returned to this Field of the Lark.

II

EMBRYONIC FORMATION OF CRIMES IN THE INCUBATION OF PRISONS

Javert's triumph in the Gorbeau house had seemed complete, but it was not so.

In the first place, and this was his principal regret, Javert had not made the prisoner prisoner. The victim who slips away is more suspect than the assassin; and it was likely that this person, so precious a capture to the bandits, would be a no less valuable prize to the authorities.

And then, Montparnasse had escaped Javert.

He would have to wait for another occasion to lay his hand on "that devilish dandy." Montparnasse, in fact, having met Eponine, who was standing guard under the trees of the boulevard, had led her away, preferring to be Némorin with the daugher than Schinderhannes with the father. Well for him that he did. He was free. As for Eponine, Javert nabbed her; trifling consolation. Eponine had joined Azelma at Les Madelonnettes.

Finally, on the trip from the Gorbeau place to La Force, one of the principal prisoners, Claquesous, had been lost. Nobody knew how it happened, the officers and sergeants "couldn't understand it," he had changed into vapor, he had slid out of the handcuffs, he had slipped through the cracks of the carriage, the fiacre was leaky, and had fled; nothing could be said, except that on reaching the prison there was no Claquesous. There were either fairies or police in the matter. Had Claquesous melted away into the darkness like a snowflake in the water? Was there some secret connivance of the officers? Did this man belong to the double enigma of disorder and of order? Was he concentric with infraction and repression? Did this sphinx have forepaws in crime and hindpaws in authority? Javert refused to accept such schemes, and his hair rose on end in view of such compromising situations; but his squad contained other inspectors besides himself, perhaps more deeply initiated than himself, although his subordinates, in the secrets of the prefecture, and Claquesous was so great a scoundrel that he might be a very good officer. To be on such intimate juggling relations with darkness is excellent for crime and admirable for the police. There are such double agents. However that might be, Claquesous was lost and was not found again. Javert appeared more irritated than surprised by it.

As for Marius, "that dolt of a lawyer," who was "probably frightened," and whose name Javert had forgotten, Javert did not worry much about him. Besides, he was a lawyer; they always turn up again. But was he merely a lawyer?

The inquiry began.

The police judge thought it best not to put one member of the Patron-Minette band into solitary confinement, hoping for a little informing, perhaps. This was Brujon, the long-haired man of the Rue du Petit-Banquier. He was left in the Cour Charlemagne, and the watchmen kept their eyes on him.

This name, Brujon, is one of the traditions of La Force. In the hideous courtyard of the so-called Bâtiment Neuf, which the administration named Cour Saint-Bernard, and which the robbers named La Fosse-aux-Lions, on that wall covered with filth and mold, that rises on the left to the height of the roofs, near an old rusty iron door leading into the former chapel of the ducal hotel of La Force, now a dormitory for prisoners, a dozen years ago there could still be seen a sketch of a fortress coarsely carved in the stone with a nail, and below it this signature:

BRUJON, 1811.

The Brujon of 1811 was the father of the Brujon of 1832.

This last, of whom only a glimpse was caught in the Gorbeau ambush, was a sprightly young fellow, very cunning and clever, with a flurried, plaintive look. It was because of this flurried air that the judge had selected him, thinking that he would be of more use in the Cour Charlemagne than in solitary.

Robbers do not cease operations because they are in the hands of justice. They are not so easily disconcerted. Being in prison for one crime does not prevent the inception of another. They are artists who simultaneously have a picture on exhibit in the salon, while painting a new one in their studio.

Brujon seemed dazed by the prison. He was sometimes seen for hours at a time in the Cour Charlemagne, standing near the canteen window, staring like an idiot at that dirty list of prices of supplies which began with *garlic*, 62 *centimes*, and ended with *cigars, cinq centimes*. Or instead, he would spend his time trembling and making his teeth chatter, saying he had a fever and asking if one of the twenty-eight beds in the fever ward was free.

Suddenly, around mid-February 1832, it was discovered that Brujon, that sleepy fellow, had sent out, through the agents of the house, not in his own name, but in the name of three of his comrades, three different errands, which had cost him in all fifty sous, a tremendous expense that caught the attention of the prison warden.

He looked into it and by consulting the price list of orders hung up in the convicts' waiting room, found that the fifty sous were made up thus: three requests, one to the Panthéon, ten sous; one to the Val-de-Grâce, fifteen sous; and one to the Barrière de Grenelle, twenty-five sous. This was the most expensive of the whole list. Now the Panthéon, the Val-de-Grâce, and the Barrière de Grenelle happened to be the residences of three of the most dreaded prowlers of the city gates, Kruideniers alias Bizarro, Glorieux, a liberated convict, and Barrecarosse, onto whom this incident drew the eyes of the police. They guessed that these men were affiliated with Patron-Minette, two of whose chiefs, Babet and Gueulemer, were locked up. It was supposed that Brujon's messages sent, not to any houses, but to persons who were awaiting them in the street, must have been notices of some projected crime. There were still other indications; they arrested the three prowlers and thought they had foiled Brujon's machination, whatever it was.

About a week after these measures were taken, one night, a watchman, who was checking the dormitory in the lower part of the New Building, just as he put his chestnut into the chestnut-box—this is the means used to make sure that the watchmen carried out their duty exactly; every hour a chestnut had to fall into every box nailed on the doors of the dormitories—a watchman then saw through the peephole of the dormitory Brujon sitting up in his bed and writing something by the light of the sconce. The warden entered, Brujon was put into the dungeon for a month, but they could not find what he had written. The police learned nothing more.

It is certain, however, that the next day a "postilion" was thrown from the Cour Charlemagne into La Fosse-aux-Lions, over the five-story building that separates the two courts.

Prisoners call a ball of bread artistically kneaded, which is sent "into Ireland," that is to say, over a prison roof, from one court to the other, a postilion. Etymology: over England; from one county to the other; "into Ireland." This ball falls in the courtyard. Whoever picks it up opens it and finds a letter in it addressed to some prisoner in the court. If it is a convict who finds it, he sends the letter along to its destination; if it is a warden, or one of those secretly bribed prisoners who are called sheep in the prisons and foxes in the galleys, the letter is carried to the office and delivered to the police.

This time the postilion reached its address, although

the one for whom the message was destined was then in solitary. Its recipient was none other than Babet, one of the four heads of Patron-Minette.

The postilion contained a paper rolled up, on which there were only these two lines:

"Babet, there is an affair on the Rue Plumet. A grating in a garden."

This was the thing that Brujon had written during the night.

In spite of spies, both male and female, Babet found means to send the letter from La Force to La Salpêtrière to "a good friend" of his shut up there. This girl in turn transmitted the letter to another whom she knew, named Magnon, who was closely watched by the police, but not yet arrested. This Magnon, whose name the reader has already seen, had some relations with the Thénardiers that will be related later, and could, by going to see Eponine, serve as a bridge between La Salpêtrière and Les Madelonnettes.

Just at that very moment, the evidence in Thénardier's prosecution failing in respect to his daughters, it happened that Eponine and Azelma were released.

When Eponine came out, Magnon, who was watching for her at the door of Les Madelonnettes, handed her Brujon's note to Babet, charging her to find out about the affair.

Eponine went to the Rue Plumet, reconnoitered the iron gate and the garden, looked at the house, spied, watched, and, a few days later, carried to Magnon, who lived in the Rue Clocheperce, a biscuit, which Magnon transmitted to Babet's mistress at La Salpêtrière. In the dark symbolism of the prisons, a biscuit signifies, "No go."

So that less than a week after that, Babet and Brujon, meeting on the La Force watchpath, as one was going "to inquiry," and the other was returning from it, "Well," asked Brujon, "Rue P?" "Biscuit," answered Babet.

This was the end of that fetus of crime, engendered by Brujon in La Force.

This abortion, however, led to results entirely foreign to Brujon's program, as we shall see.

Often, thinking to knot one thread, we tie another.

III

AN APPARITION TO FATHER MABEUF

Marius no longer visited anybody, but sometimes he happened to meet Father Mabeuf.

While Marius was slowly descending those dismal steps, which might be called cellar stairs, leading into places without light where we hear the fortunate walking above us, M. Mabeuf was descending, too.

The *Flora of Cauteretz* was absolutely not selling anymore. The experiments on indigo had not succeeded in the little garden of Austerlitz, which had poor exposure. M. Mabeuf could only cultivate a few rare plants that like moisture and shade. He was not discouraged, however. He had obtained a bit of ground in the Jardin des Plantes, with good light, to carry on "at his own cost," his experiments with indigo. For this he had pawned the plates of his *Flora*. He had reduced his lunch to two eggs, and he left one of them for his old servant, whose wages he had not paid for fifteen months. And often lunch was his only meal. He didn't laugh his childlike laugh anymore, he had become morose, and he now received no visits. Marius was right in not thinking to go there. Sometimes, when M. Mabeuf went to the Jardin des Plantes, the old man and the young man would meet on the Boulevard de l'Hôpital. They did not speak, but sadly nodded their heads. It is a bitter thing that there should be a moment when misery separates! They had been two friends; now they were two passersby.

The bookseller, Royol, was dead. M. Mabeuf now had only his books, his garden, and his indigo; to him those were the three forms that happiness, pleasure, and hope had taken. It was enough to live on. He said to himself, "When I have made my blue seeds, I shall be rich, I'll take my plates out of the pawnship, I'll bring my *Flora* into vogue through charlatanism, by big payments and advertisements in the newspapers, and I'll buy that copy of Pierre de Médine's *Art de Naviguer*, with woodcuts, edition 1559." In the meantime he worked all day on his indigo bed, and at night went back home to water his garden and read his books. M. Mabeuf was at this time very nearly eighty years old.

One night he saw a singular apparition.

He had come home while it was still broad daylight. Mother Plutarch, whose health was poor, was sick and had gone to bed. His dinner was a bone with a little meat still on it, and a bit of bread that he had found on the kitchen table. He sat down on a block of stone, which he used as a garden bench.

Near this bench, as with most old orchard gardens, there stood a dilapidated hut made of joists and boards, a warren on the ground floor, a fruit house above. There were no rabbits in the warren, but there were a few apples in the fruit house. A remnant of the winter's store.

With the aid of his spectacles, M. Mabeuf had begun to leaf through and read two books that fascinated him, and even absorbed him, a more serious thing at his age. His natural timidity inclined him, to a certain extent, to accept superstitions. The first of these books was the famous treatise of President Delancre, *On the Inconstancy of Demons;* the other was the quarto of Mutor de la Rubaudière, *On the Devils of Vauvert and the Goblins of La Bièvé*. This last book interested him more, since his garden was one of the spots formerly haunted by goblins. Twilight was beginning to whiten everything above and blacken everything below. As he read, Father Mabeuf was looking across the book in his hand at his plants, and among others at a magnificent rhododendron, which was one of his consolations; there had been four days of drought, wind, and sun, without a drop of rain; the stalks wilted, the buds hung down, the leaves were falling, they all needed to be watered; the rhododendron particularly was a sad sight. Father Mabeuf was one of those to whom plants have souls. The old man had worked all day on his indigo bed, he was exhausted, nonetheless he got up, put his books on the bench, and walked, bent over and with tottering steps, to the well, but when he had grasped the chain, he could not even draw it far enough to unhook it. Then he turned and looked with anguish toward the sky, which was filling with stars.

The evening had that serenity that buries the sorrows of man under a strangely dreary yet eternal joy. The night promised to be as dry as the day had been.

"Stars everywhere!" thought the old man. "Not the smallest cloud! Not a teardrop of water."

And his head, which had been raised for a moment, fell back on his breast.

He raised it again and looked at the sky, murmuring, "A drop of dew! A little pity!"

He endeavored once more to unhook the well-chain, but he could not.

At that moment he heard a voice, which said, "Father Mabeuf, would you like to have me water your garden?"

At the same time he heard a sound like a passing deer in the hedge, and he saw springing out of the shrubbery a sort of tall, slender girl, who came and stood before him, looking at him boldly. She had less the appearance of a human being than of a form that had just been born of the twilight.

Before Father Mabeuf, who was easily startled and who was, as we have said, subject to fear, could answer a word, this being, whose motions seemed grotesquely abrupt in the twilight, had unhooked the chain, plunged in and drawn out the bucket, and filled the watering pot, and the good man saw this apparition with bare feet and a ragged skirt running along the beds, distributing life around her. The sound of the water on the leaves filled Father Mabeuf's soul with joy. It seemed to him that now the rhododendron was happy.

When the first bucket was emptied, the girl drew a second, then a third. She watered the whole garden.

Moving along the walks, her silhouette appearing entirely black, shaking her torn shawl over her long angular arms, she looked rather like a bat.

When she had finished, Father Mabeuf approached her with tears in his eyes and laid his hand on her forehead.

"God will bless you," he said, "you are an angel, since you care for flowers."

"No," she answered, "I'm the devil, but that's all the same to me."

Without waiting for and without hearing her answer, the old man exclaimed, "What a pity that I am so unfortunate and so poor, and cannot do anything for you!"

"You can do something," she said.

"What?"

"Tell me where Monsieur Marius lives."

The old man did not understand.

"What Monsieur Marius?"

He raised his glassy eyes and seemed to be looking for something that had vanished.

"A young man who used to come here."

Meanwhile M. Mabeuf had fumbled in his memory.

"Ah! yes—" he exclaimed, "I know what you mean. Wait a minute! Monsieur Marius—the Baron Marius Pontmercy, yes! He lives—or rather he does not live there now—Ah! Well, I don't know."

While he spoke, he had bent over to tie up a branch of the rhododendron, and went on,

"Ah! I remember now. He walks along the boulevard very often, and goes toward La Glacière. Rue Croulebarbe. The Field of the Lark. Go that way. He isn't hard to find."

When M. Mabeuf rose up, there was nobody there; the girl had disappeared.

He was not a little frightened.

"Really," he thought, "if my garden was not watered, I might think it had been a spirit."

An hour later, when he had gone to bed, this came back to him, and, as he was falling asleep, at that blurred moment when thought, like the fabulous bird that changes itself into fish to pass through the sea, gradually takes the form of dream to pass through sleep, he said to himself confusedly, "Indeed, this is very much like what Rubaudière tells about the goblins. Could it be a goblin?"

IV

AN APPARITION TO MARIUS

A few days after this visit of a "spirit" to Father Mabeuf, one morning—it was Monday, the day Marius borrowed the hundred-sous piece from Courfeyrac for Thénardier—Marius had put this hundred-sous piece in his pocket, and before carrying it to the prison office, he had gone "to take a little walk," hoping it would enable him to work on his return. It was everlastingly so. As soon as he got up in the morning, he would sit down in front of a book and a sheet of paper to work on some translation; the work he had on hand at that time was the translation into French of a well-known quarrel between two Germans, the controversy between Gans and Savigny; he took up Savigny, he took up Gans, read four lines, tried to write one of them, could not, saw a star between the paper and his eyes, and rose from his chair, saying, "I'll go out. That will loosen me up."

And he would go to the Field of the Lark.

There he saw the star more than ever, and Savigny and Gans less than ever.

He returned, tried to get back to work, and failed; he found no way to tie a single one of the broken threads in his brain; then he would say, "I won't go out tomorrow. It prevents me from working." Yet he went out every day.

He lived in the Field of the Lark rather than in Courfeyrac's room. That was his real address: Boulevard de la Santé, seventh tree from the Rue Croulebarbe.

That morning, he had left this seventh tree and sat down on the bank of the brook of the Gobelins. The bright sun was gleaming through the new and glossy leaves.

He was thinking of "Her!" And his dreaminess, becoming reproachful, fell back on himself; he thought sadly of the idleness, the paralysis of the soul growing within him, and of that night that was becoming denser in front of him hour by hour to the point where he had already stopped seeing the sun.

Meanwhile, through this painful evolution of hazy ideas that were not even a soliloquy, action had so diminished within him that he was left without even the strength to pour out his grief; it was through this melancholy distraction that the sensations of the outside world reached him. Behind and below him, on both banks of the stream, he heard the washerwomen of the Gobelins beating their linen; and over his head, the birds chattering and singing in the elms. On the one hand the sound of liberty, of carefree happiness, of winged leisure; on the other, the sound of labor. A thing that plunged him into deep reverie, almost reflection, these two joyful sounds.

All at once, in the midst of his lethargic ecstasy, he heard a familiar voice say, "Ah, there he is!"

He looked up and recognized the unfortunate child

who had come to his room one morning, the older of the Thénardier girls, Eponine; he now knew her name. Strangely, she had become more impoverished and more beautiful, two further steps that seemed impossible. She had accomplished a double progress, toward the light and toward distress. She was barefoot and in rags, as when she had so resolutely come into his room, only her rags were two months older; the holes were larger, the tatters dirtier. It was the same rough voice, the same forehead tanned and wrinkled by exposure; the same free, wild, and wandering gaze. Added to her earlier expression, she had that mixture of fear and sorrow that a prison experience adds to misery.

She had spears of straw and grass in her hair, not like Ophelia gone mad through contact with Hamlet's madness, but because she had slept in some stable loft.

And with all of this, she was beautiful. What a star, O youth!

She had stopped in front of Marius, an expression of pleasure on her pale face, and something close to a smile.

For a few seconds she stood there as though she could not speak.

"I've found you, then?" she said at last. "Father Mabeuf was right; it was on this boulevard. How I've looked for you! If you only knew! Do you know that? I've been in the jug. Two weeks. They let me go, seeing there was nothing against me. And then I'm still a minor. Two months to go. Oh, how I've looked for you! Six weeks now. You don't live down there any longer?"

"No," said Marius.

"Oh, I understand. Because of the affair. A ruckus like that is disagreeable. You've moved. Hey, look! Why are you wearing such an old hat? A young man like you must have fine clothes. D'you know, Monsieur Marius, Father Mabeuf calls you Baron Marius, I forget what else. It's not true that you're a baron? Barons are old, they go to the Luxembourg in front of the château where it is sunniest, they read the *Quotidienne* for a sou. Once I took a letter to a baron's like that. He was more than a hundred years old. But tell me, where d'you live now?"

Marius did not answer.

"Ah!" she continued, "you have a hole in your shirt. I must mend it for you."

She went on with an expression that gradually grew darker, "You don't seem glad to see me?"

Marius said nothing; she paused herself for a moment, then exclaimed, "But if I wanted to I could easily make you look happy!"

"How?" inquired Marius. "What do you mean?"

She bit her lip; she seemed to hesitate, as if going through a kind of interior struggle. At last, she appeared to decide on her course.

"Who cares, it makes no difference. You look sad, I want you to be glad. But promise me that you'll laugh, I want to see you laugh and hear you say, Ah, well! That's good. Poor Monsieur Marius! You know, you promised me you would give me whatever I should ask—"

"Yes! But tell me!"

She looked straight into Marius's eyes and said, "I have the address."

Marius turned pale. All his blood flowed back to his heart.

"What address?"

"The address you asked me for."

She added as if she were making an effort, "The address—you know well enough!"

"Yes!" stammered Marius.

"The young lady's!"

Having pronounced this word, she sighed deeply.

Marius sprang off the wall where he was sitting and grabbed her wildly by the hand.

"Oh! Come! Show me the way, tell me! Ask me for anything you like! Where is it?"

"Come with me," she answered. "I'm not sure of the street and the number; it's all the way on the other side, but I know the house very well. I'll show you."

She withdrew her hand and added in a tone that would have pierced the heart of an observer, but which did not even touch the giddy and ecstatic Marius, "Oh! How pleased you are!"

A cloud crossed Marius's brow. He grabbed Eponine by the arm: "Swear to me one thing!"

"Swear?" she said. "What does that mean? So now you want me to swear?"

And she laughed.

"Your father! Promise me, Eponine! Swear to me that you won't give this address to your father!"

She turned to him, astounded.

"Eponine! How d'you know my name is Eponine?"

"Promise what I ask you!"

But she did not seem to hear him.

"That's nice! You called me Eponine!"

Marius caught her by both arms at once.

"But answer me now, for heaven's sake! Pay attention to what I'm saying, swear that you won't give the address you know to your father!"

"My father?" she said. "Oh! Yes, my father! Don't worry about him. He's in solitary. Besides, I don't concern myself with my father!"

"But you aren't promising me!" exclaimed Marius.

"Let me go then!" she said, bursting into laughter. "How you do shake me! Yes, yes! I promise you that! I swear it! What do I care? I won't give the address to my father. There, will that do? Is that it?"

"Nor to anybody?" said Marius.

"Nor to anybody."

"Now," added Marius, "take me there."

"Right away?"

"Right away."

"Come on. Oh! How pleased he is!" she said.

After a few steps, she stopped.

"You're following me too closely, Monsieur Marius. Let me go on ahead, and follow me like that, without seeming to. It won't do for a fine young man like you to be seen with a woman like me."

No tongue could say all that there was in that word "woman" thus uttered by this child.

She went on a few steps and stopped again; Marius caught up with her. She spoke to him without turning: "By the way, you know you've promised me something?"

Marius fumbled in his pocket. He had nothing in the world but the five francs intended for Thénardier. He took it and put it into Eponine's hand.

She opened her fingers and let the coin fall to the ground, then, looking at him glumly, "I don't want your money," she said.

Book Three

THE HOUSE ON THE RUE PLUMET

I

THE SECRET HOUSE

Toward the middle of the last century, a velvet-capped presiding judge of the High Judicial Court of Paris having a mistress, but on the quiet—for in those days the great lords displayed their mistresses and the bourgeois concealed theirs—had a little house built in the Faubourg Saint-Germain, in the deserted Rue de Blomet, now called the Rue Plumet, not far from the spot that then went by the name of the Combat des Animaux.

This was a detached two-story house; two rooms on the ground floor, two bedrooms on the second, a kitchen below, a boudoir above, a garret under the roof, the whole fronted by a garden with a large iron gate opening onto the street. This garden covered about an acre. It was all that the passersby could see; but in back of the house there was a small yard with a low building at the far end, two rooms only and a cellar, a convenience intended to conceal a child and nurse in case of need. Through a secret door at the rear, this building opened onto a long narrow passage, paved, winding, open to the sky, artfully concealed between two high walls, and as though lost between the enclosures of the gardens and fields, following all the corners and turnings. This corridor came to an end at another door, also concealed, that opened a third of a mile away, almost in another quarter, on the unbuilt end of the Rue de Babylone.

The judge used to come in this way, so that those even who might have watched and followed him, and those who might have observed that the judge went somewhere mysteriously every day, could not have suspected that going to the Rue de Babylone was going to the Rue Blomet. By skillful purchases of land, the ingenious magistrate was able to have this secret route to his house made on his own ground, and thus without being detected. He had later sold off small lots bordering on the passage for flower and vegetable gardens, and the proprietors of these lots of ground supposed on both sides that what they saw was a partition wall and did not even suspect the existence of that long ribbon of pavement winding between two walls among their beds and fruit trees. The birds alone saw this curiosity. It is probable that the larks and the sparrows of the last century did a good deal of gossiping about the presiding judge.

The house, built of stone in the Mansard style, wainscoted, and furnished in the Watteau style, stonework inside, smoke-tree outside, walled with a triple flowering hedge, had a discreet, coquettish, and solemn appearance about it, as befits a caprice of love and the judiciary.

This house and this passage, since disappeared, were still in existence fifteen years ago. In '93, a coppersmith bought the house to pull it down, but he being unable to pay for its demolition, the nation sent him into bankruptcy. So it was the house that demolished the coppersmith. Thereafter the house remained empty, and slowly fell into ruin, like all dwellings no longer enlivened by human presence. So it remained, furnished with its old furniture, and always for sale or rent, and the ten or twelve persons who passed through the Rue Plumet in the course of a year were notified of this by a yellow illegible piece of paper that had hung on the garden gate since 1810.

Toward the end of the Restoration, these same passersby might have noticed that the paper had disappeared, and also that the shutters of the upper story were open. The house was indeed occupied. The windows had "little curtains," a sign that there was a woman there.

In October 1829, a man of a certain age had appeared and rented the house as it stood, including of course the building in the rear and the passage that ran out to the Rue de Babylone. He had the secret openings of the two doors of this passage repaired. The house, as we have just said, was still more or less furnished with the judge's old furniture. The new tenant had ordered a few repairs, added here and there what was lacking, replaced a few flagstones in the yard, a few bricks in the basement, a few treads in the staircase, a few boards in the floors, a few panes in the windows, and finally came and settled in with a young girl and an aged servant, without any noise, more like somebody stealing in than like a man entering his own house. The neighbors did not gossip about it, for the simple reason that there were no neighbors.

This scarcely noticeable tenant was Jean Valjean; the young girl was Cosette. The servant was a spinster named Toussaint, whom Jean Valjean had saved from the hospital and misery and who was old, stuttering, and provincial, three qualities that had convinced Jean Valjean to take her with him. He hired the house under the name of M. Fauchelevent, gentleman. In what has been related before, the reader was undoubtedly still quicker than Thénardier to recognize Jean Valjean.

Why had Jean Valjean left the convent of the Petit-Picpus? What had happened?

Nothing had happened.

As we recall, Jean Valjean was happy in the convent, so happy that his conscience at last began to be troubled. He saw Cosette every day, he felt fatherhood sprouting and growing within him more and more, he cherished this child in his soul, he said to himself that she was his, that nothing could take her from him, that this would last indefinitely, that certainly she would become a nun, since every day she was gently led on toward it, that this way the convent was henceforth her universe as well as his, that he would grow old there and she would grow up there, that she would grow old there and he would die there; that finally, a dazzling hope, no separation was possible. In reflecting on this, he at last began to see difficulties. He questioned himself. He asked himself whether all this happiness was really his own, if it were not made up of the happiness of another, of the happiness of this child whom he was appropriating and plundering, he, an old man; if this was not a robbery? He said to himself that this child had a right to know what life was before renouncing it; that to cut her off, in advance, and, in some sense without consulting her, from all pleasures, under pretense of saving her from all trials, taking advantage of her ignorance and isolation to give her an artificial vocation, was an outrage to a human creature and a lie to God. And who knows but, thinking all this over someday, and being a nun reluctantly, Cosette might come to hate him? A final thought, which was almost selfish and less hero than the others, but one he could not bear. He resolved to leave the convent.

He made up his mind, recognizing with despair that it had to be done. As for objections, there were none. Five years between those four walls, and away from the world had necessarily destroyed or dispersed his causes of concern. He could calmly return to the life outside. He had grown old, and everything had changed. Who would recognize him now? And then, to look at the worst, there was no danger except for himself, and he had no right to condemn Cosette to the cloister for the reason that he had been condemned to prison. Besides, what is danger in the presence of duty? Actually, nothing prevented him from being careful and taking proper precautions.

As for Cosette's education, it was almost complete.

Once he had reached the decision, he waited for an opportunity. It was not slow to arise. Old Fauchelevent died.

Jean Valjean requested an audience with the reverend prioress, and told her that with a small inheritance he had received on the death of his brother, which would enable him to live without working, he would leave the service of the convent and take away his daughter; but that since it was not fair that Cosette, not taking her vows, had been educated gratuitously, he humbly begged the reverend prioress to allow him to offer the community, as indemnity for the five years Cosette had passed there, the sum of five thousand francs.

Thus Jean Valjean left the Convent of the Perpetual Adoration.

On leaving, he took in his own hands, and would not entrust to any assistant, the little box whose key he always had with him. This box puzzled Cosette, because of the smell of embalming that it gave off.

Let us say at once that this box never left him again.

He always had it in his room. It was the first and sometimes the only thing that he carried away in his changes of residence. Cosette laughed about it and called this box "the inseparable," saying, "I'm jealous of it."

However, Jean Valjean did not appear again in the open city without deep anxiety.

He discovered the house in the Rue Plumet and buried himself in it. He was provided from then on with the name of Ultimus Fauchelevent.

At the same time he rented two other lodgings in Paris, in order to attract less attention than if he always stayed in the same neighborhood, to be able to change his lodging if need be, at the slightest anxiety, and finally, so as never again to find himself in such straits as on the night when he had so miraculously escaped from Javert. These two apartments were both very simple and shabby, in two neighborhoods far apart from each other, one in the Rue de l'Ouest, the other in the Rue de l'Homme-Armé.

From time to time he would go off, either to the Rue de l'Homme-Armé, or to the Rue de l'Ouest, to spend a month or six weeks with Cosette, without taking Toussaint. He was waited on by the porters, and posed as a man of some means from the suburbs, with a pied-à-terre in the city. This man of lofty virtue had three addresses in Paris in order to escape from the police.

II

JEAN VALJEAN A NATIONAL GUARD

Still, properly speaking, he lived in the Rue Plumet, and he had ordered his life there in the following way:

Cosette lived in the house with the servant; she had the large bedroom with painted woodwork, the boudoir with gilded moldings, the judge's salon furnished with tapestries and huge armchairs; she had the garden. Jean Valjean had a bed put into Cosette's room with a canopy of antique damask in three colors, and an old and beautiful Persian rug, bought at Mother Gaucher's in the Rue du Figuier-Saint-Paul, and, to soften the severity of these magnificent old things, he had added to this medley all the little lively and graceful furnishings used by young girls, a set of shelves, a bookcase and gilt-stamped books, a writing case, a desk blotter, a worktable inlaid with pearl, a silver vanity case, a dressing table in Japanese porcelain. Long damask curtains of three colors, on a red ground, matching those of the bed, hung at the second-story windows. On the first floor, tapestry curtains. All winter Cosette's Petite Maison was warmed from top to bottom. As for him, he lived in the sort of porter's lodge in the backyard, with a mattress on a cot bedstead, a white wood table, two rush chairs, a china water pitcher, a few books on a board, his dear box in a corner, never any fire. He ate dinner with Cosette, and there was whole wheat bread on the table for him. He said to Toussaint, when she entered their service, "Mademoiselle is the mistress of the house." "And you, m-monsieur?" replied Toussaint, astounded. "Me, I am much better than the master, I am the father."

Cosette had been trained in housekeeping at the convent, and she budgeted the expenses, which were very moderate. Every day Jean Valjean took Cosette's arm and went out for a walk with her. They would go to the least frequented walk of the Luxembourg, and every Sunday to mass, always at Saint Jacques-du-Haut-Pas, because it was quite far away. As that is a very poor neighborhood, he gave a great deal of alms there, and the unfortunate would surround him in the church. Thus, the addressee of Thénardier's letter was "the benevolent gentleman of the church of Saint Jacques-du-Haut-Pas." He was fond of taking Cosette to visit the needy and the sick. No stranger came into the house in the Rue Plumet. Toussaint brought the provisions, and Jean Valjean himself went for the water to a tap nearby on the boulevard. They kept the wood and the wine in a kind of half-sunken vault faced with rocks, which was near the gate on the Rue de Babylone and which had been the judge's grotto; for, in the time of the Folies and the Petites Maisons, there was no love without a grotto.

On the Rue de Babylone door there was a box for letters and papers; but since the three occupants of the house on the Rue Plumet received neither papers nor letters, the box, formerly the go-between for the affair and the confidante of a legal dandy, was now entirely limited to notices from the receiver of taxes and the Guard announcements. For M. Fauchelevent belonged to the National Guard: He had not been able to slip through the close mesh of the enrollment of 1831. The municipal investigation made at that time had extended even to the convent of the Petit-Picpus, a sort of impenetrable and holy cloud from which Jean Valjean had issued, venerable in the eyes of his magistracy and consequently worthy of defending it.

Three or four times a year, Jean Valjean donned his uniform and performed his duties; very willingly in fact; it was a good disguise, which let him mix with everybody else while leaving him alone. Jean Valjean had reached his sixtieth year, the age of legal exemption; but he did not seem more than fifty; moreover, he had no desire to hide from his sergeant-major and to cavil with the Comte de Lobau; he had no civil standing; he was concealing his name, he was concealing his identity, he was concealing his age, he was concealing everything; and, as we have just said, he was very willingly a National Guard. To look like all the rest in the crowd of taxpayers, this was his whole ambition. This man's ideal was to have the soul of an angel and a bourgeois façade.

We must note one detail, however. When Jean Valjean went out with Cosette, he dressed as we have seen, and looked rather like an old officer. When he went out alone, and this was usually in the evening, he always wore the jacket and pants of a laborer, and wore a cap that hid his face. Was this precaution, or humility? Both at once. Cosette was used to the enigmatic side of her destiny, and hardly noticed her father's peculiarities. As for Toussaint, she venerated Jean Valjean, and thought everything he did was good. One day, her butcher, who had caught sight of Jean Valjean, said to her; "That's a funny one."

She answered, "He's a s-saint!"

Neither Jean Valjean nor Cosette nor Toussaint ever came in or went out except by the gate on the Rue de Babylone. Unless one had seen them through the bars of the garden gate, it would have been difficult to guess that they lived on the Rue Plumet. This gate was always shut. Jean Valjean had left the garden uncultivated, so it would not attract attention.

In this, he was mistaken, perhaps.

III

FOLIIS AC FRONDIBUS

The garden, left untended this way for more than half a century, had taken on a strange charm. Forty years ago pedestrians would stop in the street to look at it, without suspecting the secrets it concealed behind its fresh green thickets. At that time more than one dreamer often allowed his eyes and thoughts to wander indiscreetly through the bars of the ancient gate, which was padlocked, twisted, tottering, attached to two green mossy pillars, and oddly crowned with a pediment of indistinct arabesques.

There was a stone seat in a corner, one or two moldy statues, some trellises loosened by time and rotting against the wall; no walks or lawn; grass everywhere. Horticulture had left, and nature returned. Weeds were abundant, a wonderful chance for a poor bit of earth. The wallflowers had a heyday. Nothing in the garden opposed the sacred urge toward life; unhampered growth was at home there. The trees bent down to the briers, the briers rose to the trees, the shrub had climbed, the branch had bowed, what runs along the ground had tried to find things that bloom in the air, what floats in the wind had stooped toward plants that trail in the moss; trunks, branches, leaves, twigs, tufts, tendrils, shoots, thorns were mingled, crossed, married, confused; vegetation, in a close and strong embrace, had celebrated and accomplished there under the satisfied eye of the Creator, in this enclosure of three hundred square feet, the sacred mystery of its fraternity, a symbol of human fraternity. The garden was no longer a garden; it was a colossal underbrush, that is to say, something as impenetrable as a forest, populous as a city, tremulous as a nest, dark as a cathedral, scented as a bouquet, solitary as a tomb, teeming as a throng.

In Floréal, this enormous shrubbery, at liberty behind its grating and within its four walls, entered the rutting season, the secret labor of universal germination, thrilled at the rising sun almost like a stag inhaling the breath of universal love and feeling the April sap mounting and boiling in his veins, and shaking his immense green antlers in the wind, scattered over the moist ground, over the broken statues, over the sinking staircase of the little house, and even over the pavement of the deserted street, starry flowers, pearling dew, fecundity, beauty, life, joy, perfume. At noon, a thousand white butterflies took refuge there, and it was a heavenly sight to see these living snowflakes of summer whirling in the shade. There, in this sweet darkness of greenery, a multitude of innocent voices spoke softly to the soul, and what the warbling had forgotten to say, the humming completed. In the evening, a dreamy vapor rose from the garden and swathed it; a shroud of mist, a calm celestial sadness, covered it; the intoxicating odor of honeysuckle and bindweed rose on all sides like an exquisite subtle poison; you heard the last calls of the woodpecker, and the wagtails drowsing under the branches; you felt the sacred intimacy of bird and tree; by day the wings delighted the leaves; by night the leaves protected the wings.

In winter, the underbrush was black, wet, bristling, shivering, and allowed a partial view of the house. Instead of flowers in the branches and dew on the flowers, you perceived the snail's long silver ribbons on the thick, cold carpet of yellow leaves; but in any case, in every aspect, in every season, spring, winter, summer, autumn, this little enclosure exhaled melancholy, contemplation, solitude, liberty, the absence of man, the presence of God, and the old rusty grating seemed to say, "This garden is mine!"

Although the pavement of Paris was all around, the classic and splendid residences of the Rue de Varennes were a few steps away, the dome of the Invalides was quite near and the Chamber of Deputies not far off; although the carriages of the Rue de Bourgogne and the Rue Saint-Dominique rolled pompously through its neighborhood, and the yellow, brown, white, and red buses passed each other in the adjoining square—the Rue Plumet was a solitude; and the death of the old proprietors, the passing of a revolution, the downfall of ancient fortunes, absence, oblivion, forty years of abandon and widowhood, had been enough to call back into this privileged place the ferns, mulleins, hemlocks, milfoils, the tall weeds, the big flaunting plants with large leaves of pale greenish material, the lizards, beetles, restless, rapid insects; to bring out of the depths of the earth, and display within these four walls, an indescribably wild, savage grandeur; and for nature, which frustrates the paltry arrangements of man and always gives its whole self where it gives itself at all, as much in the ant as the eagle, to come and display itself in a poor little Parisian garden with as much asperity and majesty as in a virgin forest of the New World.

Nothing is really small; anyone open to the deep penetration of nature knows this. Although no absolute satisfaction may be granted to philosophy, no more in circumscribing the cause than in limiting the effect, the contemplator falls into unfathomable ecstasies because of all this decay of forces resulting in unity. Everything works for everything.

Algebra applies to the clouds; the radiance of the star benefits the rose; no thinker would dare to say that the perfume of the hawthorn is useless to the constellations. Who could ever calculate the path of a molecule? How do we know that the creations of worlds are not determined by falling grains of sand? Who can understand the reciprocal ebb and flow of the infinitely great and the infinitely small, the echoing of causes in the abyss of being and the avalanches of creation? A mite has value; the small is great, the great is small; all is balanced in necessity: frightening vision for the mind. There are marvelous relations between beings and things; in this inexhaustible whole, from sun to grub, there is no scorn; each needs the other. Light does not carry terrestrial perfumes into the azure depths without knowing what it does with them; night distributes the stellar essence to the sleeping plants. Every bird that flies has the thread of the infinite in its claw. Germination includes the hatching of a meteor and the tap of a swallow's beak breaking the egg, and it guides the birth of an earthworm and the advent of Socrates. Where the telescope ends, the microscope begins. Which of the two has the greater view? Choose. A bit of mold is a pleiad of flowers; a nebula is an anthill of stars. The same promiscuity, and still more wonderful, between the things of the intellect and material things. Elements and principles are mingled, combined, espoused, multiplied one by another, to the point that the material world and the moral world are brought into the same light. Phenomena are perpetually folded back on themselves. In the vast cosmic changes, universal life comes and goes in unknown quantities, rolling everything up in the invisible mystery of the emanations, using everything, losing no dream from any single sleep, sowing a microscopic animal here, crumbling a star there, oscillating and gyrating, making a force of light and an element of thought, disseminated and indivisible, dissolving all, save that geometric point, the self; reducing everything to the soul-atom; making everything blossom into God; entangling, from the highest to the lowest, all activities in the obscurity of a dizzying mechanism, linking the flight of an insect to the movement of the earth, subordinating—who knows, if only by the identity of the law—the evolutions of the comet in the firmament to the circling of the protozoa in the drop of water. A machine made of mind. Enormous gearing, whose first motor is the gnat and whose last is the zodiac.

IV

CHANGE OF GRATING

It seemed as though this garden, first made to conceal licentious mysteries, had been transformed and rendered fit for the shelter of chaste mysteries. It no longer had either bowers, lawns, arbors, or grottoes; a magnificent disheveled obscurity fell like a veil on all sides; Paphos had become Eden again. Some secret repentance had purified this retreat. This flowergirl now offered her flowers to the soul. This coquettish garden, once so compromised, had returned to virginity and modesty. A judge assisted by a gardener, a man who thought he was a second Lamoignon, and another man who thought he was a second Lenôtre, had distorted it, pruned it, crumpled it, bedizened it, fashioned it for gallantry; nature had taken it over again, had filled it with shade and arranged it for love.

In this solitude there was also a heart that was all ready. Love had only to show its face; there was a temple there composed of greenery, of grass, of moss, of bird sighs, of soft shade, of agitated branches, and a soul made of gentleness, of faith, of candor, of hope, of aspiration, and of illusion.

Cosette had left the convent, still almost a child; she was a little more than fourteen years old, and she was "at the awkward age"; as we have said, aside from her eyes, she seemed more homely than pretty; she had no ungraceful features, but she was gawky, thin, timid and bold at the same time, a big child, in short.

Her education was finished; that is to say, she had been taught religion and also, and above all, devotion; then "history," that is, the thing that goes by that name in the convent, geography, grammar, the participles, the kings of France, a little music, to draw profiles, etc., but beyond this she was ignorant of everything, which is a charm and a peril. The soul of a young girl should not be left in obscurity; in later life, all too sudden and vivid mirages spring up, as in a camera oscura. She should be gently and discreetly enlightened, rather by the reflection of realities than by their direct harsh light. A useful and graciously severe half-light that dissipates puerile fear and prevents a fall. Nothing but the maternal instinct, a wonderful intuition combining the memories of the maiden and the experience of the woman, knows how this half-light should be applied, and of what it should be formed. Nothing can make up for this instinct. To form the mind of a young girl, all the nuns in the world are not equal to one mother.

Cosette had had no mother. She had only had many mothers.

As for Jean Valjean, he certainly had in him all sorts of tenderness and solicitude, but he was only an old man who knew nothing at all about matters maternal.

Now, in this work of education, in this serious question of the preparing a woman for life, what a quantity of knowledge is needed to struggle against that ignorance we call innocence.

There is nothing like a convent to prepare a young girl for passions. The convent turns her thoughts in the direction of the unknown. Her heart, thrown back on itself, makes itself a channel, being unable to overflow, and deepens, being unable to expand. Thence visions, suppositions, conjectures, romances sketched out, longings for adventures, fantastic constructions, whole castles built in the interior obscurity of the mind, dark and secret dwellings where the passions find an immediate lodging as soon as the grating is crossed and they are permitted to enter. The convent is a repression which, in order to triumph over the human heart, must continue throughout life.

On leaving the convent, Cosette could have found nothing sweeter and more dangerous than the house on the Rue Plumet. It was the continuation of solitude with the beginning of liberty; an enclosed garden, but a sharp, rich, voluptuous, and odorous nature; the same dreams as in the convent, but with glimpses of young men; a grating, but onto the street.

Still, we repeat, when she came there she was only a child. Jean Valjean gave her this uncultivated garden. "Do whatever you like with it," he said to her. It delighted Cosette; she ransacked every thicket and turned over every stone, she looked for "animals"; she played while waiting to dream; she loved this garden for the insects she found in the grass under her feet, until she would love it for the stars she could see in the branches over her head.

And then she loved her father, that is to say, Jean Valjean, with all her heart, with a frank filial passion that made the good man a welcome and very pleasant companion for her. We remember that M. Madeleine was a great reader; Jean Valjean continued that; through it he had come to talk very well; he had the secret wealth and eloquence of a humble, earnest intellect that has come into its own culture. He retained just enough harshness to flavor his goodness; he had a rough mind and a gentle heart. At the Luxembourg in their conversations, he gave long explanations of everything, drawing on what he had read, drawing also on what he had suffered. As she listened, Cosette's eyes wandered dreamily.

This simple man was enough for Cosette's thoughts, even as the wild garden was for her eyes. When she had had a good chase after the butterflies, she would come up to him breathless and say, "Oh! How I have run!" He would kiss her forehead.

Cosette adored the good man. She was always running after him. Wherever Jean Valjean was, was happiness. Since Jean Valjean did not live in the house or the garden, she found more pleasure in the paved backyard than in the enclosure full of flowers, and in the little bedroom furnished with rush chairs than in the large parlor hung with tapestry, where she could recline on silk armchairs. Jean Valjean sometimes said to her, smiling with the happiness of being put upon, "Why don't you go home? Why don't you leave me alone?"

She would give him those charming rebuffs that are so graceful coming from the daugher to the father.

"Father, I am very cold in your house; why don't you put in a carpet and stove here?"

"Dear child, there are many people better than I, who do not even have a roof over their heads."

"Then why do I have a fire and things like that?"

"Because you are a woman and a child."

"Pooh! Then men ought to be cold and uncomfortable?"

"Some men."

"Well, all right, I'll come here so often that you'll have to have a fire."

Again she said to him, "Father, why do you eat miserable bread like that?"

"Because, my daughter."

"Well, if you eat it, I'll eat it."

Then, so that Cosette would not eat whole wheat bread, Jean Valjean ate white bread.

Cosette had only vague memories of her childhood. She prayed morning and evening for her mother, whom she had never known. The Thénardiers remained as two hideous faces out of some nightmare. She remembered that "one day, at night," she had been sent into the woods for water. She thought that that was very far from Paris. It seemed to her that she had begun life in a pit and Jean Valjean had lifted her out of it. Her childhood impressed her as a time when there were only centipedes, spiders, and snakes around her. When she was dozing at night, before going to sleep, since she had no very clear idea of being Jean Valjean's daughter, and that he was her father, she imagined that her mother's soul had passed into this good man and come to live with her.

When he sat down, she would rest her cheek on his white hair and silently drop a tear, saying to herself, "This is perhaps my mother, this man!"

Although this may be a strange statement, in her profound ignorance as a girl brought up in a convent, maternity moreover being absolutely unintelligible to virginity,

Cosette had come to imagine that she had had as little of a mother as possible. She did not even know her name. Whenever she asked Jean Valjean what it was, Jean Valjean was silent. If she repeated her question, he answered by a smile. Once she insisted; the smile ended with a tear.

Jean Valjean's silence veiled Fantine with night.

Was this prudence? Was it respect? Was it a fear of giving up that name to the chances of another memory than his own?

While Cosette was a little girl, Jean Valjean had been fond of talking with her about her mother; when she was older, he found it impossible. It seemed to him he no longer dared. Was this on account of Cosette? Was it because of Fantine? He felt a sort of religious horror at introducing that shade into Cosette's thoughts and at bringing in the dead as a party to their destiny. The more sacred that shade was to him, the more intimidating it seemed to him. He thought of Fantine and felt overwhelmed with silence. He could dimly see in the darkness something like a finger raised to lips. Had all that modesty that had once been Fantine's and, during her life, had been forced out of her by violence, returned after her death to take its place over her, to watch, indignant, over the peace of the dead woman, and to guard her fiercely in her tomb? Did Jean Valjean, without knowing it, feel its influence? We who believe in death are not among those who would reject his mysterious explanation. Hence the impossibility of pronouncing, even for Cosette that name, "Fantine."

One day Cosette said to him, "Father, I saw my mother in a dream last night. She had two great wings. My mother must have been close to sanctity in her life."

"Through martyrdom," answered Jean Valjean.

Still, Jean Valjean was happy.

When Cosette went out with him, she leaned on his arm, proud, happy, her heart brimming with pleasure. At all these indications of a tenderness so exclusive and so fully satisfied with him alone, Jean Valjean inwardly melted with delight. The poor man shuddered, flooded with an angelic joy; he said to himself that he really had not suffered enough to deserve such radiant happiness, and he thanked God, in the depths of his soul, for having permitted him, a miserable man, to be so loved by this innocent creature.

V

THE ROSE DISCOVERS SHE IS AN INSTRUMENT OF WAR

One day Cosette happened to look in her mirror, and she said to herself, "Well, now!" It almost seemed to her that she was pretty. This threw her into strange anxiety. Up to this moment she had never thought of her face. She had seen herself in her mirror, but she had not looked at herself. And then, she had often been told that she was homely; Jean Valjean alone would quietly say, "Not at all! Not at all!" However that might be, Cosette had always thought herself unappealing and had grown up in that idea with the pliant resignation of childhood. And now suddenly her mirror was saying like Jean Valjean, "Not at all!" She did not sleep at all that night. "Could I be pretty?" she thought. "How funny it would be if I were pretty!" And she recalled those companions whose beauty had made an impression in the convent and said, "Really? Could I be like Mademoiselle So-and-So?"

The next day she looked at herself, but not by chance, and she had her doubts. "How could I have thought that?" she said. "No, I am homely." She had merely slept badly, she had rings under her eyes, and she was pale. She had not felt too happy the night before, thinking she was beautiful, but she was sad at no longer thinking so. She did not look at herself again, and for more than two weeks, she tried to comb her hair with her back to the mirror.

In the evening after dinner, she usually did needlepoint or some convent work in the salon, while Jean Valjean read by her side. Once, on raising her eyes from her work, she was very much surprised at the anxious way her father was looking at her.

At another time, she was passing along the street, and it seemed to her that somebody behind her, whom she did not see, said, "Pretty woman, badly dressed." "Nonsense!" she thought. "That's not me. I'm well dressed and homely." At the time she had on her plush hat and merino dress.

At last, she was in the garden one day, and heard poor old Toussaint saying, "Monsieur, do you notice how pretty mademoiselle is getting?" Cosette did not hear what her father answered. Toussaint's words threw her into a sort of commotion. She ran out of the garden, went up to her room, hurried to the mirror, it was three months since she had looked at herself, and let out a cry. She was dazzled by herself.

She was beautiful and pretty; she could not help agreeing with Toussaint and her mirror. Her figure had filled out, her skin had become fair, her hair had grown lustrous, an unknown splendor was alight in her blue eyes. The consciousness of her beauty came to her complete, in a moment, like broad daylight when it bursts on us; others noticed it, Toussaint said so, it was clearly of her that the passersby had spoken, there was no more doubt; she went down into the garden again, thinking herself a queen, hearing the birds sing, it was in winter, seeing the sky golden, the sunshine in the trees, flowers among the shrubbery, wild, mad, in an inexpressible rapture.

As for him, Jean Valjean felt a deep indefinable pang in his heart.

For some time, he had in fact been contemplating with terror that beauty appearing more radiant every day on Cosette's sweet face. A dawn, charming to all others, dreary to him.

Cosette had been beautiful for some time before she noticed it. But, from the first day, this unexpected light that rose slowly and by degrees enveloped the young girl's whole person wounded Jean Valjean's gloomy eyes. He felt it as a change in a happy life, so happy that he dared not stir for fear of disturbing something. This man who had passed through every distress, who was still all bleeding from the lacerations of his destiny, who had been almost evil and had become almost holy, who, after dragging the chain of the work gang, now bore the invisible but heavy chain of indefinite infamy, this man whom the law had not released, and who might at any moment be retaken and led back from the obscurity of his virtue to the broad light of public shame, this man accepted all, excused all, pardoned all, blessed all, wished well to all, and only asked of Providence, of men, of the laws, of society, of nature, of the world, this one thing, that Cosette love him!

That Cosette continue to love him! That God would not prevent the heart of his child from turning to him, and remaining his! Loved by Cosette, he felt healed, refreshed, soothed, satisfied, rewarded, crowned. Loved by Cosette, he was content! He asked nothing more. Had anybody said to him, "Do you wish for anything better?" he would have answered, "No." Had God said to him, "Do you want heaven?" he would have answered, "I would be the loser."

Anything that could affect this condition, be it only on the surface, made him shudder as if it were the beginning of change. He had never known very clearly what the beauty of a woman was; but by instinct he understood that it was terrible.

This beauty blooming more and more triumphant and superb beside him, under his very eyes, on the naïve and intimidating brow of this child—he looked at it, from the depths of his ugliness, his old age, his misery, his reprobation, and his dejection, with dismay.

He said to himself, "How beautiful she is! What will become of me?"

Here in fact was the difference between his tenderness and the tenderness of a mother. What he saw with anguish, a mother would have seen with delight.

The first symptoms were not slow to manifest themselves.

From the day after the one on which she had said, "Really, I am beautiful!" Cosette gave attention to her clothing. She remembered the words of the passersby: "Pretty, but badly dressed," breath of an oracle that had passed her and vanished after depositing in her heart one of the two germs which must afterward fill the whole life of the woman, coquetry. Love is the other.

With faith in her beauty, the entire feminine soul blossomed within her. She was horrified at the merino and ashamed of the plush. Her father had never refused her anything. Suddenly she knew the whole science of the hat, the dress, the cloak, the boot, the cuff, the material that hangs well, the becoming color, that science which makes the Parisian woman something so charming, so deep, and so dangerous. The phrase "alluring woman" was invented for her.

In less than a month little Cosette was, in that Thébaid of the Rue de Babylone, not only one of the prettiest women, which is something, but one of the "best dressed" in Paris, which is much more. She would have liked to meet her passerby to hear what he would say, and "to show him!" The truth is that she was ravishing on all scores, and could perfectly distinguish between a Gérard hat and an Herbaut hat.

Jean Valjean watched these ravages with anxiety. He, who felt that he could never do better than creep, or walk at the most, saw wings growing on Cosette.

Still, merely by simple inspection of Cosette's clothes, a woman would have recognized that she had no mother. Certain little proprieties, certain special conventions, had not been observed. A mother, for instance, would have told her that a young girl does not wear damask.

The first day Cosette went out with her dress and cloak of black damask and her white crepe hat she came to take Jean Valjean's arm, gay, radiant, rosy, proud, and gleaming. "Father," she said, "how do you like this?" Jean Valjean answered in a tone that resembled the bitter voice of envy, "Charming!" He seemed the same as usual during the walk. When they came back he asked Cosette, "Aren't you going to wear your dress and hat anymore, you know the ones?"

This occurred in Cosette's room. Cosette turned toward the wardrobe where her boarding school dress was hanging.

"That get-up!" she said. "Father, what would you have me do with it? Oh, I'll never wear those awful things again. With that object on my head, I look like Madame Mad-Poodle."

Jean Valjean sighed deeply.

From that day on, he noticed that Cosette, who previously was always asking to stay in, saying, "Father, I have a much better time here with you," was now always asking to go out. Indeed, what is the use of having a pretty face and a delightful dress, if you do not show them?

He also noticed that Cosette no longer had the same preference for the backyard. She now preferred to stay in the garden, not even avoiding the iron gate. Jean Valjean, grim, did not set his foot in the garden. He stayed in his backyard, like a dog.

In learning that she was beautiful, Cosette lost the grace of not knowing it; an exquisite grace, for beauty heightened by artlessness is ineffable, and nothing is so adorable as dazzling innocence, going about her business and holding in her hand, quite unconsciously, the key to a paradise. But what she lost in ingenuous grace, she gained in pensive and serious charm. Her whole person, pervaded by the joys of youth, innocence, and beauty, breathed a splendid melancholy.

It was at this time that Marius, after the lapse of six months, saw her again at the Luxembourg.

VI

THE BATTLE COMMENCES

In her seclusion, Cosette, like Marius in his, was all ready to catch fire. Destiny, with its mysterious and fatal patience, was slowly bringing these two beings closer, fully charged and languishing with the stormy electricities of passion, these two souls holding love as two clouds hold lightning, which were to meet and mingle in a glance like clouds in a flash.

The power of a glance has been so much abused in love stories that it has come to be disbelieved. Few people dare say nowadays that two beings have fallen in love because they have looked at each other. Yet that is the way love begins, and only that way. The rest is only the rest, and comes afterwards. Nothing is more real than the great shocks that two souls give each other in exchanging this spark.

At that particular moment when Cosette unconsciously turned with a glance that so affected Marius, Marius had no suspicion that he also had a glance that affected Cosette.

She received from him the same harm and the same blessing.

For a long time she had seen and scrutinized him as young girls scrutinize and see, while looking the other way. Marius still thought Cosette ugly, while Cosette already began to think Marius beautiful. But as he paid no attention to her, this young man meant nothing to her.

Still she could not help saying to herself that he had

beautiful hair, beautiful eyes, beautiful teeth, a charming voice, when she heard him talking with his comrades; that he walked with an awkward gait, if you will, but with a grace of his own; that he did not at all appear stupid; that his whole person was noble, gentle, natural, and proud, and finally that though he seemed poor he looked handsome.

On the day their eyes met and finally said abruptly to each of them those first obscure ineffable things that the glance stammers out, Cosette did not immediately understand. She went back pensively to the house in the Rue de l'Ouest to which Jean Valjean, according to his custom, had gone to spend six weeks. The next day, on waking, she thought of this unknown young man, so long indifferent and icy, who now seemed to be paying some attention to her, and it did not seem to her that this attention was pleasant in the least. She was rather a little angry at this disdainful beau. An undercurrent of war was rumbling within her. It seemed to her, and she felt a still altogether childish pleasure in it, that at last she should be avenged.

Knowing that she was beautiful, she felt convinced though in an indistinct way, that she had a weapon. Women play with their beauty as children do with their knives. They wound themselves with it.

We remember Marius's hesitations, his palpitations, his terrors. He remained at his bench and did not approach, which vexed Cosette. One day she said to Jean Valjean; "Father, let's walk a little this way." Seeing that Marius was not coming to her, she went to him. In a case like this, every woman is like Muhammad. And then, oddly enough, the first symptom of true love in a man is timidity, in a young woman, boldness. This is surprising, and yet nothing is more natural. It is the two sexes tending to unite, and each acquiring the qualities of the other.

That day Cosette's glance maddened Marius, Marius's glance made Cosette tremble. Marius went away confident, and Cosette anxious. From that day on, they adored each other.

The first thing Cosette felt was a vague yet deep sadness. It seemed to her that since yesterday her soul had turned black. She no longer recognized herself. The purity of soul of young girls composed of coldness and gaiety, is like snow. It melts in the face of love, which is its sun.

Cosette did not know what love was. She had never heard the word uttered in its earthy sense. In the books of profane music that came into the convent, *amour* was replaced by *tambour*, or *Pandour*. This created enigmas to exercise the imaginations of the girls, such as "Oh! How delightful is tambour!" or "Pity is not a Pandour!" But Cosette had left while still too young to have paid much attention to "tambour." She did not know, therefore, a name to give to what she was feeling. Is one the less sick for not knowing the name of the disease?

Loving in ignorance, she loved with all the more passion. She did not know whether it was good or evil, beneficent or dangerous, necessary or accidental, eternal or transitory, permitted or prohibited: She loved. She would have been astonished if anyone had said, "You can't sleep? But that's forbidden! You can't eat? That's wrong! You have sinking spells and palpitations! That's not right. You blush and turn pale when a certain being dressed in black appears at the end of a certain green walk! Why, that's abominable!" She would not have understood and would have answered: "How can I be blamed for something I can't help and about which I know nothing?"

It so happens that this particular love was precisely the sort best suited to the state of her soul. It was a sort of remote worship, a mute contemplation, a deification by an unknown votary. It was the apprehension of adolescence by adolescence, her dreams becoming romance and remaining dream, the wished-for phantom realized at last and made flesh, but still without name or wrong or fault or need or defect; in a word, a lover distant and ideal, a chimera having form. Any closer and more palpable encounter at this first stage would have terrified Cosette, still half buried in the magnifying mirage of the cloister. She had all the terrors of children and all the terrors of nuns mingled. The spirit of the convent, in which she had been steeped for five years, was still slowly evaporating from her whole person and made everything tremulous around her. In this condition, it was not a lover she needed, it was not even an admirer, it was a vision. She began to adore Marius as something charming, luminous, and impossible.

Since extreme artlessness borders on extreme coquetry, she smiled at him, very frankly.

Every day she waited impatiently for the hour to take their walk, she found Marius there, she felt inexpressibly happy, and sincerely believed that she was telling everything that was on her mind when she said to Jean Valjean, "What a delightful garden the Luxembourg is!"

Marius and Cosette were in the dark in regard to each other. They did not speak, they did not exchange greetings, they saw each other; and, like the stars in the sky separated by million of miles, they lived by gazing at each other.

Thus it was that Cosette gradually became a woman, and beautiful and loving, grew with a consciousness of her beauty, and in ignorance of her love. Coquettish on top of all that, through innocence.

VII

TO SADNESS, SADNESS AND A HALF

Every condition has its instinct. The old eternal mother, Nature, silently warned Jean Valjean of Marius's presence. Jean Valjean shuddered in his innermost being. Seeing nothing, knowing nothing, he still gazed persistently at the darkness surrounding him, as if he perceived on one side something being built, and on the other something collapsing. Marius, also warned, and according to the deep law of God, by this same mother, Nature, did all that he could to hide himself from the "father." It sometimes happened, however, that Jean Valjean did catch sight of him. Marius's ways became quite unnatural. He had a suspicious caution and an awkward boldness. He no longer came near them; he would sit some distance away, and remained there in an ecstasy; he had a book and pretended to be reading; why did he pretend? He used to wear his old suit, now he had on his new suit every day; it was not entirely certain that he did not curl his hair, he had strange eyes, he wore gloves; in short, Jean Valjean cordially detested this young man.

Cosette gave no ground for suspicion. Without knowing exactly what was happening, she felt very definitely that it was something and that it must be concealed.

Between Cosette's new interest in clothes and the habit of wearing new suits that had grown on this unknown man, there was a parallel that worried Jean Valjean. It was a coincidence perhaps, doubtless, certainly, but a dangerous one.

He never opened his mouth to Cosette about the unknown man. One day, however, he could not contain himself, and with that uncertain despair that plummets to the core of its unhappiness, he said to her, "What a pedantic air that young man has!"

A year before, as an unconcerned little girl, Cosette would have answered, "Why no, he's charming." Ten years later, with the love of Marius in her heart, she would have answered, "Pedantic and insupportable superficially, you're quite right!" At this particular stage of life and feeling, she merely answered with supreme calm, "That young man!"

As if she were seeing him for the first time in her life.

"How stupid I am!" thought Jean Valjean. "She hadn't even noticed him. I've shown him to her myself."

O simplicity of the old, profundity of the young!

There is another law of these young years of suffering and concern, of these acute struggles of first love against first obstacles, that the young girl does not allow herself to be caught in any trap, the young mans falls into all of them. Jean Valjean had begun a veiled war against Marius, which Marius, with the sublime folly of his passion and his age, did not detect. Jean Valjean set a hundred snares; he changed his hours, he changed his seat, he forgot his handkerchief, he went to the Luxembourg alone; Marius barged headlong into every trap; and to all these questions left on his path by Jean Valjean he answered ingenuously, yes. Meanwhile Cosette was still walled in behind her apparent unconcern and her imperturbable tranquility, so that Jean Valjean came to this conclusion: "This booby is madly in love with Cosette, but Cosette doesn't even know he exists!"

There was nevertheless a pang in his heart. The instant when Cosette would fall in love might come at any moment. Doesn't everything begin by indifference?

Only once did Cosette make a mistake and startle him. He got up from the bench to go, after sitting there three hours, and she said, "So soon!"

Jean Valjean had not discontinued the strolls in the Luxembourg, not wishing to do anything strange, and above all dreading to arouse any suspicion in Cosette; but during those hours so sweet to the two lovers, while Cosette was sending her smile to the intoxicated Marius, who noticed nothing but that, and now saw nothing in the world except one radiant, adored face, Jean Valjean glared pointedly at Marius. He who had come to believe that he was no longer capable of a malevolent feeling had moments in which, when Marius was there, he thought he was once more becoming savage and ferocious, and felt those old depths of his soul, once so wrathful, reawakening and rising against the young man. It seemed to him almost as if the unknown craters were forming within him again.

So now he was there, this creature? What had he come for? He came to pry, to sniff, to examine, to test; he came to say, "Now, why not?" He had come to prowl around his, Jean Valjean's, life! To prowl around his happiness, to grab it and carry it off!

Jean Valjean added, "Yes, that's it! What's he looking for? An adventure? What does he want? A flirtation!—and as for me! What! After first being the most miserable of men, I'll be the most unfortunate; I'll have spent sixty years of life on my knees; I'll have suffered all a man can suffer; I'll have grown old without having been young, have lived with no family, no relatives, no friends, no wife, no children! I'll have left my blood on every stone, on every thorn, on every post, along every wall; I'll have been gentle, although the world was harsh to me, and good, though it was evil; I'll have become an honest man in spite of all; I'll have repented the wrongs I've done, and pardoned the wrongs done to me, and the moment I'm rewarded, the moment it's over, the moment I'm reaching the end, the moment I have what I desire, rightfully and justly, I have paid for it, I have earned it—it will all disappear, and I'll lose Cosette, and I'll lose my life, my joy, my soul, because this booby has seen fit to come and loiter at the Luxembourg."

Then his eyes filled with a strange and dismal light. It

was no longer a man looking at a man; it was not an enemy sizing up an enemy. It was a dog looking at a robber.

We know the rest. Marius's madness kept up. One day he followed Cosette to the Rue de l'Ouest. Another he spoke to the porter; the porter in turn said to Jean Valjean, "Monsieur, who is that curious young man who has been asking for you?" The next day, Jean Valjean cast the glance at Marius that Marius finally noticed. A week later, Jean Valjean had moved. He resolved never to set foot again either in the Luxembourg, or in the Rue de l'Ouest. He returned to the Rue Plumet.

Cosette did not complain, she said nothing, she asked no questions, she did not look for any reason; she had already reached the point when one fears discovery and self-betrayal. Jean Valjean had not experienced this misery, the only sort with charm, and the only misery he did not know; for this reason, he did not understand the deep significance of Cosette's silence. He noticed only that she had become sad, and he became gloomy. On either side there was conflicting inexperience.

Once he made an attempt. He asked Cosette, "Would you like to go to the Luxembourg?"

A ray brightened Cosette's pale face.

"Yes," she said.

They went. Three months had passed. Marius no longer went there. Marius was not there.

The next day, Jean Valjean asked Cosette again, "Would you like to go to the Luxembourg?"

Sadly and quietly, she answered, "No!"

Jean Valjean was hurt by this sadness and harrowed by this gentleness.

What was taking place in this spirit so young, and already so impenetrable? What was going on there? What was happening to Cosette's soul? Sometimes, instead of going to bed, Jean Valjean sat by his cot with his head in his hands and spent whole nights asking himself, "What is in Cosette's mind?" and wondering what she could be thinking about.

Oh! In those hours, what mournful looks he turned toward the cloister, that chaste summit, that abode of angels, that inaccessible glacier of virtue! With what despairing rapture he contemplated that convent garden, full of unknown flowers and secluded maidens, where all perfumes and all souls rose straight toward Heaven! How he worshiped that Eden, now closed forever, from which he had voluntarily left and foolishly descended! How he regretted his self-denial, his madness in having brought Cosette back to the world, poor hero of sacrifice, caught and thrown by his very devotion. How he repeated to himself, "What have I done?"

Still nothing of this was revealed to Cosette—neither bad humor nor severity. Always the same serene, kind face. Jean Valjean's manner was more tender and paternal than ever. If anything could have suggested less happiness, it was this greater gentleness.

As for her, Cosette was pining. She suffered from Marius's absence, as she had rejoiced in his presence, strangely, without really knowing it. When Jean Valjean broke off their usual walks, her woman's instinct whispered confusedly in the depths of her heart that she must not appear to cling to the Luxembourg; and that if it didn't matter to her, her father would take her back there. But days, weeks, and months went by. Jean Valjean had tacitly accepted Cosette's tacit consent. She regretted it. It was too late. The day she returned to the Luxembourg, Marius was no longer there. So Marius had disappeared; it was all over; what could she do? Would she ever find him again? She felt a constriction of her heart, which nothing relaxed, increasing every day; she no longer knew whether it was winter or summer, sunshine or rain, whether the birds sang, whether it was the season for dahlias or daisies, whether the Luxembourg was more charming than the Tuileries, whether the linen the washerwoman brought home was starched too much, or not enough, whether Toussaint did her marketing well or badly; and she became dejected, absorbed, intent on a single thought, her eye vaguely staring, as when one looks into the night at the deep black place where an apparition has vanished.

Still she did not let Jean Valjean see a thing, except her pallor. She kept her face sweet for him.

This pallor was more than enough to make Jean Valjean anxious. Sometimes he would ask, "What's the matter?"

She would answer, "Nothing."

And after a pause, because she felt he was sad, too, she would add, "And you, Father, isn't something the matter with you?"

"Me? Nothing," he said.

These two beings, who had loved each other so exclusively, and with so touching a love, and who had lived so long for each other, were now suffering beside one another and through one another; without speaking of it, without harsh feeling, and smiling all the while.

VIII

THE CHAIN

The more unhappy of the two was Jean Valjean. Youth, even in its sorrows, always has a glimmer all its own.

At certain moments, Jean Valjean suffered so much that he became puerile. It is the peculiarity of grief to bring out the childish side of a man. He felt irresistibly that Cosette was slipping away from him. He would have been glad to struggle, to hold her back, to rouse her enthusiasm by something external and striking. These ideas —puerile, as we have just said, and at the same time senile—gave him by their very childishness a just idea of the influence of gold braid over young girls' imaginations. Once he happened to see a general ride by on horseback in full uniform, Comte Coutard, Commandant of Paris. He envied this gilded man, he thought what happiness it would be to be able to put on that coat, which was an incontestable thing, that if Cosette could see him that way it would dazzle her, that when he gave her his arm and walked past the Tuileries gate, they would present arms to him, and that that would so satisfy Cosette that it would destroy her inclination to look at young men.

An unexpected shock came to him in the midst of these sad thoughts.

In the isolated life which they were leading, and since they had come to live in the Rue Plumet, they had fallen into a habit. They sometimes made a pleasure excursion to go and watch the sun rise, a gentle joy suited to those who are entering life and those who are leaving it.

A walk at early dawn, to anyone who loves solitude, is equivalent to a walk at night, with the gaiety of nature added. The streets are empty and the birds are singing. Cosette, herself a bird, usually woke up early. These morning excursions were arranged the evening before. He proposed, she accepted. They were planned as a conspiracy, they went out before daybreak, and these were so many pleasant hours for Cosette. Such innocent eccentricities have a charm for the young.

Jean Valjean's inclination was, as we know, to go to untraveled spots, to solitary nooks, to neglected places. At that time near the city gates of Paris, there were some poor fields, almost in the city, where in summer a scanty crop of wheat would grow, and which in autumn, after this was gathered, seemed not to have been harvested, but rather stripped. Jean Valjean had a predilection for these fields. Cosette did not dislike them. To him it was solitude, to her it was liberty. There she became a little girl again, she could run and almost play, she took off her hat, laid it on Jean Valjean's knees, and gathered flowers. She looked at the butterflies on the blossoms, but did not catch them; gentleness and tenderness are born with love, and the young girl with a trembling, fragile idea in her heart feels pity for a butterfly's wing. She wove garlands of wild poppies, which she put upon her head, and which, lit up and illuminated in the sunshine, and blazing like a flame, made a crown of fire for her fresh, rosy face.

Even after their life had turned sad, they continued their habit of morning walks.

So one October morning, tempted by the deep serenity of the autumn of 1831, they had gone out, and found themselves at daybreak near the Barrière du Maine. It was not day, it was dawn: a wild and ravishing moment. A few constellations here and there in the deep pale heavens, the earth all black, the sky all white, a shivering in the blades of grass, everywhere the mysterious thrill of the twilight. A lark, which seemed mixed in with the stars, was singing at an enormous height, and one would have said that this hymn from minutia to infinite was calming the immensity. In the east, against the steely-sharp clarity of the horizon, the Val-de-Grâce stood out in its obscure mass; Venus was rising in splendor behind that dome like a soul escaping from a dark edifice.

All was peace and silence; nobody on the highway; on

the footpaths a few scattered workmen, hardly visible, going to their work.

Jean Valjean was seated in the sidewalk, on some timbers lying by the gate of a lumberyard. He had his face turned toward the road, and his back toward the light; he had forgotten the sun, which was just rising; he had fallen into one of those deep meditations that absorb the whole mind, and even imprison the senses, an equivalent to four walls. There are some meditations that can be called vertical; when one is at the bottom it takes time to return to the earth's surface. Jean Valjean had sunk into one of these reveries. He was thinking of Cosette, of the happiness possible if nothing came between her and him, of that light with which she filled his life, providing the climate for his soul. He was almost happy in his reverie. Cosette, standing near him, was watching the clouds turning pink.

Suddenly, Cosette exclaimed, "Father, I think somebody is coming, over there." Jean Valjean looked up.

Cosette was right.

The highway leading to the former Barrière du Maine is a prolongation, as everybody knows, of the Rue de Sèvres and is intersected at a right angle by the interior boulevard. At the corner of the highway and the boulevard, at the point where they diverge, a sound was heard, difficult to explain at such an hour, and a kind of moving confusion appeared. Some shapeless thing coming from the boulevard was entering the highway.

It grew larger, it seemed to move in order, still it was bristling and quivering; it looked like a wagon, but they could not make out the load. There were horses, wheels, cries; whips were cracking. By degrees the features became definite, although enveloped in the darkness. It was in fact a wagon that had just turned out of the boulevard onto the road, and was making its way toward the city gate, near Jean Valjean; a second, similar one followed it, then a third, then a fourth; seven vehicles rounded the turn in succession, the horses' heads touching the rear of the wagons. Dark forms were moving on these wagons, flashes showed in the twilight, like drawn swords, something clanked like the rattling of chains; it kept coming, the voices grew louder, and it was as terrible as something from the cavern of dreams.

As it approached it took form hazily behind the trees

with the pallor of an apparition; the mass whitened; daylight, rising little by little, spread a wan glow over this crawling thing, both sepulchral and alive, the heads of the shadows became the faces of the corpses, and it was this:

Seven wagons were moving in a line down the road. The first six were oddly constructed. They were like coopers' drays, a sort of long ladder placed on two wheels, forming shafts at the forward end. Each dray, or better, each ladder, was drawn by four horses in tandem. Strange clusters of men were being carried on these ladders. In the little light that there was, these men were not seen, only guessed. Twenty-four on each wagon, twelve on each side, back to back, their faces toward the passersby, their legs hanging down, these men were traveling this way; and they had something behind them that clanked, a chain, and at their necks something that gleamed, an iron collar. Each had his own collar, but the chain was for all; so that these twenty-four men, if they should happen to get down from the dray and walk, would be subject to a sort of inexorable unity, and have to snake across the ground with the chain for a backbone, rather like centipedes. In the front and rear of each wagon, stood two men armed with muskets, each with an end of the chain under his foot. The collars were square. The seventh wagon, a huge cart with racks, but without a cover, had four wheels and six horses, and carried a resounding heap of iron kettles, melting pots, stoves, and chains, among which were scattered a number of men, who were bound and lying at full length, and who seemed to be sick. This cart, entirely exposed to view, was furnished with broken grids that seemed to have played a part in ancient punishments.

These wagons kept to the middle of the street. At either side marched a row of sordid-looking guards, wearing tricornered hats like the soldiers of the Directory, stained, torn, filthy, muffled up in Invalides' uniforms and hearse-boys' trousers, half gray and half blue, almost in tatters, with red epaulets, yellow bandoleers, sheath knives, muskets, and clubs: a species of servant-soldiers. These henchmen seemed a compound of the depravity of the beggar and the authority of the executioner. The one who appeared to be their chief had a horsewhip in his hand. All these details, blurred by the twilight, were coming clearer and clearer in the growing light. At the head and the rear of the convoy, gendarmes marched on horseback, solemn, and with drawn swords.

This cortège was so long that when the first wagon reached the city gates, the last had hardly turned out of the boulevard.

A crowd, appearing out of nowhere and gathered in a twinkling, as often happens in Paris, was crowding in on both sides of the highway and looking on. In the neighboring lanes people could be heard shouting and calling to each other and the wooden shoes of the market gardeners running over for a look contributed to this cacophonous sunrise symphony.

The men heaped on the drays were silent as they were jolted along. They were blue with the chill of the morning. They all had on coarse cotton trousers, and their bare feet were in wooden shoes. The rest of their attire was according to the fancy of misery. Their clothing was hideously disparate: Nothing is more dismal than the harlequin of rags. Felt hats jammed out of shape, glazed caps, hideous cloth caps, and beside the workman's smock, the black coat out at the elbows; several had women's hats; others had baskets on their heads; hairy chests could be seen, and through the holes in their clothing tattos, temples of love, burning hearts, cupids. Rashes and red sores were also visible. Two or three had a straw rope attached to the bars of the dray and hanging beneath them like a stirrup, to secure their feet. One of them held in his hand and lifted to his mouth something like a black stone, which he seemed to be gnawing; it was bread. There were none but dry eyes among them, dulled or lit with an evil light. The escort troop was cursing, the prisoners did not whisper; from time to time came the thud of a club on their shoulders or their heads; some of the men were yawning; their rags were terrible; their feet hung down, their shoulders rocked, their heads banged together, their irons rattled, their eyes glared fiercely, their fists were clenched or open inertly like the hands of the dead; behind the convoy a troop of children were bursting with laughter.

This file of wagons, whatever it was, was dismal. It was obvious that tomorrow, that in an hour, a shower might spring up, that it would be followed by another, and another, and that the worn-out clothing would be soaked through, that once wet, these men would never get dry, that once chilled, they would never get warm again, that their trousers would be stuck to their skin by the rain, that water would fill their wooden shoes, that blows of the whip could not prevent the chattering of their teeth, that the chain would continue to hold them by the neck, that their feet would continue to swing; and it was impossible not to shudder at seeing these human beings thus bound and passive under the chilling clouds of autumn, and given up to the rain, to the wind, to all the fury of the elements, like trees and stones.

The clubs did not spare even the sick, who lay roped and motionless in the seventh wagon, seeming to have been thrown there like sacks filled with misery.

Suddenly, the sun appeared; the immense radiance of the Orient burst forth, and one would have said that it set all these savage heads on fire. Their tongues were loosed, a conflagration of sneers, of oaths, and songs burst out. The broad horizontal light cut the whole file in two, illuminating their heads and their bodies, leaving their feet and the wheels in the dark. Their thoughts appeared on their faces; the moment was appalling; demons visible with their masks dropped, ferocious souls laid bare. Lit up, this group was still dark. Some, who seemed cheery, had quills in their mouths and were blowing vermin onto the crowd, selecting the women; the dawn intensified the mournful profiles through dark shadows; every one of these beings was deformed by misery; and it was so monstrous that it seemed to change the sunbeams into the glare of lightning. The wagonload at the head of the cortège were singing at the top of their lungs with ghastly joviality, a medley by Desaugiers, then famous, *La Vestale;* the trees fluttered mournfully on the sidewalks, the bourgeois listened with faces of idiotic bliss to these obscenities chanted by specters.

Every form of distress was present in this chaos of a cortège; there were the facial angles of every beast, old men, youths, bald heads, gray beards, cynical monstrosities, dogged resignation, savage grimaces, insane attitudes, snouts set off with caps, heads like young girls with corkscrew curls over their temples, faces childish and therefore horrifying, thin skeleton faces that lacked only death. On the first wagon was a Negro, who had, perhaps, been a slave and could compare chains. The fearful leveler, disgrace, had passed over these brows; at this abased degree the utmost transformation had taken place in all of them; and ignorance, changed to stupidity, was the equal of intelligence changed to despair. No possible choice among these men who seemed the élite of the mire. It was clear that the marshal, whoever he was, of this foul procession had not classified them. These beings had been bound and coupled pell-mell, probably in alphabetical disorder, and loaded haphazardly onto the wagons. The aggregation of horrors, however, always produces a result; every addition of misfortune gives a total; from each chain came a common soul, and each cartload had its own features. Beside the one that was singing was one that was howling; a third was begging; one was seen gnashing its teeth; another was threatening the bystanders, another blaspheming God; the last was silent as the tomb. Dante would have thought he saw the seven circles of Hell on their way.

A march from condemnation toward punishment, made ominously, not on the intimidating flashing chariot of the Apocalypse but more dismal still on a hangman's cart.

One of the guard, who had a hook on the end of his club, from time to time pretended to stir up this heap of human ordure. An old woman in the crowd pointed them out with her finger to a little boy five years old, and said "Little wretch, that'll teach you!"

As the songs and the blasphemy increased, the one who seemed the captain of the escort cracked his whip, and at that signal, a fearful, dull, and unselective cudgeling, which sounded like hail, fell on the seven wagons; many roared and foamed; which increased the glee of the gamins who had gathered, a swarm of flies on these wounds.

Jean Valjean's eyes had become frightening. They were no longer eyes; they were the deep windows that take the place of seeing in certain unfortunate creatures, that seem unconscious of reality, reflecting dazzling horrors and catastrophes. He was not looking at a sight; he was experiencing a vision. He endeavored to get up, to flee, to escape; he could not move a limb. Sometimes things that you see grab and hold you. He was spellbound, dazed, petrified, asking himself, through a vague unutterable anguish, the meaning of this sepulchral persecution, and the source of this pandemonium pursuing him. All at once he raised his hand to his forehead, a common gesture with those to whom memory suddenly returns; he remembered that this really was the route, that this detour was usual to avoid meeting the king, which was always possible on the Fontainebleau road, and that, thirty-five years before, he had passed through this city gate.

Cosette, though from another cause, was equally terrified. She did not understand; what she saw did not seem possible to her; at last she exclaimed, "Father! What can that be in those wagons?"

Jean Valjean answered: "Convicts."

"And where are they going?"

"To prison."

At this moment the cudgeling, multiplied by a hundred hands, reached its climax; blows with the flat of the sword joined in; it was a fury of whips and clubs; the prisoners crouched, a hideous obedience was produced by the torture, and all fell silent with the look of chained wolves. Cosette trembled all over; she asked, "Father, are they still men?"

"Sometimes," said the man of misery.

It was in fact the chain that, setting out before daybreak from Bicêtre, took the Mans road to avoid Fontainebleau, where the king was at the time. This detour made the terrible journey last three or four days longer; but to spare the royal person the sight of the torture, it could well be prolonged.

Jean Valjean returned home overwhelmed. Such encounters are shocks, and the memory they leave resembles a convulsion.

Jean Valjean, however, on the way back to the Rue de Babylone with Cosette, did not notice that she asked him other questions regarding what they had just seen; perhaps he was himself too much absorbed in his own dejection to heed her words or answer them. But at night, as Cosette was leaving him to go to bed, he heard her say in an undertone, and as if talking to herself, "It seems to me that if I should meet one of those men in my path, O my God, I would die just from seeing him near me!"

Fortunately it happened that on the day following this tragic sight, there were, connected with some official celebration, festivities in Paris, a review in the Champ de Mars, rowing matches on the Seine, theatricals on the Champs-Elysées, fireworks at l'Etoile, illuminations everywhere. Jean Valjean, doing violence to his habits, took Cosette to these festivities, to divert her mind from the memories of the day before, and to efface under the laughing tumult of all Paris the abominable thing that had passed in front of her. The review, which enlivened the fête, made the wearing of uniforms quite natural; Jean Valjean put on his National Guard uniform with the vague inner feeling of a man who is taking refuge. Yet the object of this walk seemed attained. Cosette, whose law was to please her father, and for whom, moreover, every sight was new, accepted the diversion with the easy, blithe grace of youth, and did not look too disdainfully on that promiscuous bowl of joy called a public fête; so Jean Valjean believed that he had succeeded, and that no trace remained of the hideous vision.

Some days later, one morning, when the sun was bright, and they were both on the garden steps—another infraction of the rules that Jean Valjean seemed to have imposed on himself, and of the habit of staying in her room that sadness had imposed on Cosette, she, in her dressing gown, was standing in that early morning undress which is so charmingly becoming to young girls, and looks like a cloud on a star; and, with her head in the sunlight, rosy from having slept well, under the tender gaze of the gentle man, she was picking a daisy to pieces. Cosette was ignorant of the enchanting game of chance, "I love thee, a little, a lot, passionately," etc.; who could have taught it to her? She was fingering this flower, by instinct, innocently, without suspecting that to pick a daisy to pieces is to pluck a heart. If there were a fourth Grace named Melancholy, and if it were smiling, she would have seemed that Grace.

Jean Valjean was fascinated by the contemplation of her slender fingers on that flower, forgetting everything in the radiance of this child. A robin was twittering in the shrubbery beside them. White clouds were crossing the sky so gaily that one would have said they had just been set free. Cosette went on plucking the petals off her flower attentively; she seemed to be thinking of something; but it must have been pleasant. Suddenly she turned her head over her shoulder with the delicate motion of the swan, and said to Jean Valjean, "Father, what are they then, the convicts?"

Book Four

AID FROM BELOW OR FROM ABOVE

I

WOUND OUTSIDE, CURE WITHIN

Thus their life gradually grew darker.

Only one distraction was left to them, and this had formerly been a pleasure, to take bread to those who were hungry and clothing to those who were cold. In these visits to the poor, in which Cosette often accompanied Jean Valjean, they found some remnant of their former lightheartedness; and, sometimes, when they had had a good day, when a great deal of distress had been relieved and many little children revived and made warm, in the evening, Cosette was a bit cheerful. It was during this time that they visited the Jondrettes.

The day after that visit, Jean Valjean appeared in the house in the morning, with his ordinary calm, but with a large wound on his left arm, very much inflamed and infected, which looked like a burn and which he explained away. This wound kept him indoors for more than a month with fever. He would not see a doctor. When Cosette urged it, he replied, "Call for the veterinarian."

Cosette dressed it night and morning with such grace and angelic pleasure in being useful to him that Jean Valjean felt all his old happiness return, his fears and his anxieties dissipate, and he looked at Cosette, saying, "Oh! The good wound! Oh! The kind injury!"

Seeing that her father was sick, Cosette had deserted the little house and renewed her interest in the little lodge and backyard. She spent almost all her time with Jean Valjean, and read to him from the books he liked. In general, travel books. Jean Valjean was coming alive again; his happiness revived with inexpressible radiance; the Luxembourg, the unknown young prowler, Cosette's coldness, all these clouds over his soul faded away. He now said to himself, "I imagined all that. I'm an old fool."

His happiness was so great that the horrible discovery of the Thénardiers, made in the Jondrette den, and so unexpectedly, had in some sort coasted over him. He had managed to escape; his trace was lost, what did he care about the rest? He thought of it only to grieve over those wretches. "They are now in prison and can do no more harm," he thought. "Pitiful family!"

As to the hideous vision of the Barrière du Maine, Cosette never mentioned it again.

At the convent, Sister Sainte-Mechthilde had taught Cosette music. Cosette had the voice of a soulful songbird, and sometimes in the evening, in the humble lodging of the wounded man, she sang plaintive songs that cheered Jean Valjean.

Spring came, the garden was so wonderful at that season, that Jean Valjean said to Cosette, "You never go there, I wish you would walk in it." "As you like, Father," said Cosette.

And, out of obedience to her father, she went back to her walks in the garden, usually alone, for, as we have noted, Jean Valjean, who probably dreaded being seen through the gate, hardly ever went there.

Jean Valjean's wound had been a diversion.

When Cosette saw that her father was suffering less, and that he was getting well, and that he seemed happy, she felt a contentment that she did not even notice, so gently and naturally did it come. It was then March, the days were growing longer, winter was leaving, winter always carries with it something of our sadness; then April came, that daybreak of summer, fresh as every dawn, gay as every childhood; weeping a little sometimes like the infant it is. Nature in this month has charming glimmers that pass from the sky, the clouds, the trees, the fields, and the flowers, into the heart of man.

Cosette was still too young for this April joy, which resembled her, not to find its way to her heart. Unconsciously, without any suspicion on her part, the darkness passed away from her mind. In the spring it grows light in sad souls, as at noon it is light in cellars. And Cosette was not very sad now. That is the way things stood, but she did not notice it. In the morning, about ten, after breakfast, when she had managed to entice her father into the garden for a quarter of an hour, and while she was walking in the sun in front of the steps, supporting his wounded arm, she did not notice that she was constantly laughing and that she was happy.

Overjoyed, Jean Valjean saw her become fresh and rosy again.

"Oh! The blessed wound!" he repeated in a whisper.

And he was grateful to the Thénardiers.

As soon as his wound had healed, he resumed his solitary twilight walks.

It would be a mistake to believe that one can walk in this way alone in the uninhabited regions of Paris, and not meet with some adventure.

II

MOTHER PLUTARCH IS NOT EMBARRASSED BY THE EXPLANATION OF A PHENOMENON

One evening, little Gavroche had had no dinner; he remembered that he had had no dinner the day before either; this was becoming tiresome. He decided to try for some supper. He went wandering beyond La Salpêtrière, in the deserted spots; those are the places for good luck; where there is nobody, something can be found. He came to a settlement that seemd to him to be the village of Austerlitz.

In one of his preceding strolls, he had noticed an old garden there haunted by an old man and an old woman, and in this garden a passable apple tree. Beside the apple tree, there was a sort of fruit shed, poorly enclosed, where an apple might be acquired. An apple is a supper; an apple is life. What ruined Adam might save Gavroche. The garden was on a lonely lane unpaved and bordered with bushes for lack of houses; a hedge separated it from the lane.

Gavroche headed for the garden; he found the lane, he recognized the apple tree, he verified the fruit shed, he examined the hedge; a hedge is one stride. The sun was sinking, not a cat in the lane, the time was good. Gavroche prepared for his entry, then suddenly stopped. Somebody was talking in the garden. Gavroche looked through one of the openings in the hedge.

Within two steps of him, at the foot of the hedge on the other side, precisely at the point where the hole he was eyeing would have taken him, lay a stone which made a kind of seat, and on this seat the old man of the garden was sitting, with the old woman standing in front of him. The old woman was grumbling. Gavroche, who was anything but discreet, listened.

"Monsieur Mabeuf!" said the old woman.

"Mabeuf!" thought Gavroche, "that's an odd name."

The old man who was addressed did not budge. The old woman repeated, "Monsieur Mabeuf."

Without raising his eyes from the ground, the old man decided to answer:

"What, Mother Plutarch?"

"Mother Plutarch!" thought Gavroche, "another odd name."

Mother Plutarch resumed, and the old man was forced to enter into the conversation: "The landlord is dissatisfied."

"Why so?"

"Three quarters due."

"In three months there will be four."

"He says he will turn you out on the street."

"I shall go."

"The grocery woman wants to be paid. She's holding onto her firewood. What will you use to keep warm this winter? We won't have any wood."

"There is the sun."

"The butcher is refusing credit, he won't give us any more meat."

"That's all right. I don't digest meat well. It is too heavy."

"What will we have for dinner?"

"Bread."

"The baker is demanding something on account, and says no money, no bread."

"Very well."

"What will you eat?"

"We have apples from the apple tree."

"But, monsieur, we can't just live like that without money."

"I don't have any."

The old woman went away, the old man stayed alone. He began to reflect. Gavroche was reflecting on his side. It was almost dark.

The first result of Gavroche's reflection was that instead of climbing over the hedge he crept under. The branches separated a little at the bottom of the bushes.

"Heigh-ho," exclaimed Gavroche internally, "an alcove!" And he hid in it. He was almost touching Father Mabeuf's seat. He heard the octogenarian breathe.

Then, for dinner, he tried to sleep.

Sleep of a cat, sleep with one eye. Even while dozing off, Gavroche kept watch.

The white of the twilight sky blanched the earth, and the lane made a livid line between two rows of dusky bushes.

Suddenly, two dim forms appeared on that whitened band. One came in the lead, the other some distance behind.

"There are two interlopers," growled Gavroche.

The first form seemed some old bourgeois, bent and thoughtful, dressed more than simply, walking with the slow pace of an aged man, and taking his ease in the starry evening.

The second was straight, firm, and slight. It regulated its step by the step of the first; but in the unusual slowness of the gait, dexterity and agility were evident. In addition to something wild and startling, this form had the total appearance of what was then called a dandy; the hat was of the latest style, the coat was black, well cut, probably of fine cloth, and closely fitted at the waist. The head was held up with a robust grace, and, under the hat, could be seen in the twilight the pale profile of a young man. This profile had a rose in its mouth. The second form was familiar to Gavroche: It was Montparnasse.

As to the other, he could have said nothing about it, except that it was some old man.

Gavroche immediately applied himself to observation.

One of these two clearly had designs on the other. Gavroche was well situated to see the outcome. The alcove had very conveniently become a hiding place.

Montparnasse on the prowl, at such an hour, in such a place—it was threatening. Gavroche felt his gamin's heart moved with pity for the old man.

What could he do? Intervene? One weakness in aid of another? That would be ludicrous to Montparnasse. Gavroche could not avoid the fact that, to this formidable bandit of eighteen, first the old man, then the child, would be simply two mouthfuls.

While Gavroche was deliberating, the attack was made, sharp and hideous. The attack of a tiger on a wild ass, a spider on a fly. Without notice, Montparnasse threw away the rose, sprang on the old man, collared him, grasped him and hung on, and Gavroche could hardly restrain a cry. A moment later, one of these men was under the other, exhausted, panting, struggling, with a knee of marble on his breast. Only it was not altogether as Gavroche had expected. The one on the ground was Montparnasse; the one above was the older man. All this happened a few steps away from Gavroche.

The old man had taken the blow and returned it, and returned it so terribly that in the twinkling of an eye the assailant and assailed had changed roles.

"There is a brave veteran!" thought Gavroche.

And he could not help clapping his hands. But the applause was lost. It did not reach the two combatants, absorbed and deafened by each other, and mingling their breath in the struggle.

There was silence. Montparnasse stopped struggling. Gavroche said under his breath, "Can he be dead?"

The man had not spoken a word nor uttered a cry. He got to his feet, and Gavroche heard him say to Montparnasse, "Get up."

Montparnasse got up, but the man held on to him. Montparnasse had the humiliated and furious attitude of a wolf caught by a sheep.

Gavroche looked and listened, trying to back up his eyes with his ears. He was having a marvelous time.

He was rewarded for his conscientious concern as a spectator. He was able to seize on the wing the following dialogue, which took on a strangely tragic tone from the darkness. The old man questioned. Montparnasse replied.

"How old are you?"

"Nineteen."

"You are strong and healthy. Why don't you work?"

"It's boring."

"What is your business?"

"Loafer."

"Talk seriously. Can I do anything for you? What would you like to be?"

"A thief."

There was a silence. The old man seemed deeply pensive. He was motionless, yet did not release Montparnasse.

From time to time the young bandit, vigorous and nimble, made the efforts of a beast caught in a snare. He gave a shake, attempted a trip, twisted his limbs desperately, tried to escape. The old man did not appear to notice, and with a single hand held his two arms with the sovereign indifference of absolute strength.

The old man's reverie continued for some time, then, looking steadily at Montparnasse, he gently raised his voice and spoke to him, in that darkness where they were, a sort of solemn allocution of which Gavroche did not lose a syllable:

"My child, through laziness you are entering into the most laborious of existences. Ah! You declare yourself a loafer! Prepare to labor. Have you seen a terrible machine called the rolling mill? Beware of it, it is a clever, fierce thing. If it catches your coattail, you're entirely drawn in. This machine is idleness. Stop, while there's still time, and save yourself! Otherwise, it is all over; you'll soon be between the gears. Once caught, give up hope for anything more. On to fatigue, idler! No more rest. The implacable iron hand of labor has seized you. Earn a living, have a task, accomplish a duty, you don't want that! To be like others is tiresome! Well then! You'll be different. Work is the law; whoever spurns it as tiresome will have it as punishment. You're unwilling to be a workingman, you will be a slave. Work releases you on the one hand only to retake you on the other; you're unwilling to be its friend, you'll be its slave. Ah! You have refused the honest weariness of men, you'll have the sweat of the damned. While others sing, you'll rave. You will see from far away, from below, other men at work; it will seem to you that they are at rest. The laborer, the reaper, the sailor, the blacksmith, will appear to you in the light like the blessed in some paradise. What a radiance in the anvil! To drive the plough, to bind the sheaf, is happiness. The bark running free before the wind, what a festival! You, idler, dig, draw, roll, march! Drag your halter, you're a beast of burden in hell's train. Ah! To do nothing, that's your aim. Well, not a week, not a day, not an hour, without crushing exhaustion. You won't be able to lift a thing except with anguish. Every minute that elapses will make your muscles crack. What will be a feather for others will be a rock for you. The simplest things will become steep. Life will become a monster around you. Coming, going, breathing, so many terrible labors. Your lungs will feel like a hundred-pound weight. To go here rather than there will become a problem to solve. Any other man who wants to go out opens his door, it's done, he's out of doors. You, if you wish to go out, have to pierce your wall. To go out in the street, what does everybody do? Everybody goes down the staircase! But you, you'll tear up your bed clothes, you'll make a rope of them strip by strip, then you'll go through your window and you'll hang on that thread over an abyss, and it will be at night, in a storm, in the rain, in a hurricane, and, if the rope is too short, you'll have one way left to go down, to fall. To fall as chance would have it, into the abyss, from whatever height, onto what? Onto whatever is below, to the unknown. Or you'll climb through the chimney flue, at the risk of burning yourself; or you'll crawl through a sewer, at the risk of being drowned. I'm not talking about the holes you have to conceal, the stones you must take out and put back twenty times a day, the mortar you have to hide in your mattress. A lock shows up; in his pocket the bourgeois has his key, made by a locksmith. You, if you want to go out, are condemned to make a frightful masterpiece; you'll take a big sou, you'll cut it into two slices; with what tools? You'll invent them. That's your business.

Then you'll hollow out the interior of these two slices, preserving the outside carefully, and all around the edge you'll cut a screw thread, so they'll fit closely together, like a bottom and a cover. The bottom and the top screwed together that way, nobody will suspect anything. To the watchmen, for you will be watched, it will be a big sou; to you, it will be a box. What will you put in this box? A little bit of steel. A watch spring in which you'll cut teeth, which will be a saw. With this saw, as long as a pin, and hidden in this sou, you'll have to cut the bolt of the lock, the slide of the bolt, the clasp of the padlock, and the bar at your window, and the iron ring that you'll have on your leg. With this masterpiece finished, this prodigy accomplished, all those miracles of art, of cunning, of skill, of patience, executed, if it comes to be known that you are the author, what will be your reward? The dungeon. There is your future. Idleness, pleasure, what pits! To do nothing is a dreary course to take, do you know that? To live idle on the substance of society! To be useless, that is to say, noxious! That leads straight to the lowest depth of misery.

"Woe to anyone who aspires to be a parasite! He'll be vermin. Ah! You don't enjoy working? Ah! You will have one thought only; to eat, and drink, and sleep in luxury. You'll drink water, you'll eat black bread, you'll sleep on a board, with irons riveted to your limbs, whose chill you'll feel at night against your flesh! You'll break those irons, you'll run off. Fine. You'll drag yourself on your belly in the bushes, and eat grass like the beasts of the forest. And you'll be picked up again. And then you'll spend years in a dungeon, fastened to a wall, groping for a drink from your pitcher, gnawing a frightful loaf of darkness that the dogs wouldn't touch, eating beans the worms have eaten before you. You'll be a wood louse in a cellar. Oh! Take pity on yourself, miserable child, young thing, a suckling not twenty years ago, who undoubtedly has a mother still alive! I beg you, listen to me. You want fine black clothes, shining pumps, to curl your hair, to put sweet-scented oil on your locks, to please your women, to be handsome. You'll be close-shaven, with a red tunic and wooden shoes. You want a ring on your finger, you'll have an iron collar on your neck. And if you look at a woman, a blow of the club. And you'll go in there at twenty, and you'll come out at fifty! You'll enter young, rosy, fresh, with your eyes bright and all your teeth white, and your beautiful youthful hair; you'll come out broken, bent, wrinkled, toothless, horrible, with white hair! Oh! My poor child, you're taking the wrong road, laziness is giving you bad advice; the hardest of all labor is robbery. Trust me, don't undertake this dreadful drudgery of being an idler. Becoming a rascal isn't practical. It's not so hard to be an honest man. Go, now, and think of what I have said to you. And now, what did you want from me? My purse? Here it is."

And the old man, releasing Montparnasse, put his purse in his hand, which Montparnasse weighed for a moment; after which, with the same automatic precaution as if he had stolen it, Montparnasse let it glide gently into the back pocket of his coat.

All this said and done, the good man turned his back and quietly resumed his walk.

"Blockhead!" murmured Montparnasse.

Who was this man? The reader has doubtless guessed.

Montparnasse, dazed, watched him till he disappeared in the twilight. This contemplation was fatal to him.

While the old man was moving away, Gavroche was approaching.

With a side glance, Gavroche made sure that Father Mabeuf, perhaps asleep, was still sitting on the seat. Then the urchin came out of his bushes and began to creep along in the shade, behind the motionless Montparnasse. He reached Montparnasse without being seen or heard, gently slipped his hand into the back pocket of the fine black cloth coat, took the purse, withdrew his hand, and, creeping off again, slid away like an adder into the darkness. Montparnasse, who had no reason to be on his guard, and who was reflecting for the first time in his life, noticed nothing. When he had reached the point where Father Mabeuf was, Gavroche threw the purse over the hedge, and fled at full speed.

The purse fell on Father Mabeuf's foot. This shock woke him up. He stooped down, and picked up the purse. He did not understand it at all, and he opened it. It was a purse with two compartments; in one there were some small coins; in the other, there were six napoleons.

M. Mabeuf, extremely startled, carried the thing to his housekeeper.

"It fell from heaven," said Mother Plutarch.

Book Five

AN END UNLIKE THE BEGINNING

I

SOLITUDE AND THE BARRACKS

Cosette's grief, still so poignant and so acute four or five months before, had, without her knowledge, entered convalescence. Nature, spring, her youth, her love for her father, the gaiety of the birds and the flowers, were filtering little by little, day by day, drop by drop, into this soul so pure and so young, something that almost resembled oblivion. Was the fire dying out entirely? Or was a bed of embers merely building up? The truth is that she had scarcely anything left of that sad, burning feeling.

One day she suddenly thought of Marius. "Well, now," she said, "I don't think of him anymore."

In the course of that very week she noticed, as he went past the iron garden gate, a very handsome officer of lancers, waist like a wasp, ravishing uniform, cheeks like a young girl's, saber under his arm, waxed mustache, polished chapska on his head. Moreover, fair hair, full blue eyes, plump, vain, insolent and pretty face; the very opposite of Marius. A cigar in his mouth. Cosette thought that this officer undoubtedly belonged to the regiment in barracks on the Rue de Babylone.

The next day, she saw him pass again. She noticed the time.

After that—was it chance?—she saw him pass almost every day.

The officer's comrades noted that there was, in this garden so "badly kept up," behind that wretched rococo grating, a pretty creature that almost always happened to be there at the passing of the handsome lieutenant, who is not unknown to the reader, and whose name was Théodule Gillenormand.

"Well, now," they said to him. "There's a little girl who has her eye on you; why don't you look at her?"

"Do you suppose I have the time," answered the lancer, "to look at all the girls who look at me?"

This was the very moment when Marius was sinking gradually toward death and saying, "If I could only see her again before I die!" Had his wish been realized; had he seen Cosette at that moment looking at a lancer, he would have been unable to utter a word and would have expired from grief.

Whose fault was it? Nobody's.

Marius was of the temperament that sinks into grief and remains there; Cosette was of the sort that plunges in and comes out again.

Indeed Cosette was passing through that dangerous moment, the inevitable phase of feminine reverie abandoned to itself, when the heart of an isolated young girl is like the tendrils of a vine that take hold, as chance determines, of the capital of a column or a tavern signpost. A hurried and decisive moment, critical for every orphan, whether poor or rich, for riches do not defend against a bad choice; misalliances are formed very high up; the real misalliance is that of souls; and, just as more than one unknown young man, without name, or birth, or fortune, is a marble column that sustains a temple of great sentiments and broad ideas, so too you may find a satisfied and opulent man of the world, with well-shined boots and varnished speech, who, if you look not at the exterior but the interior, that is to say, at what is reserved for the wife, is nothing but a stupid nonentity, obscurely haunted by violent, impure, and debauched passions; a tavern signpost.

What was there in Cosette's soul? A soothed or sleeping passion; love in a wavering state; something limpid, shining, disturbed to a certain depth, murky below. The image of the handsome officer was reflected from the surface. Was there a memory at the bottom? Deep down? Perhaps. Cosette did not know.

A singular incident followed.

II

COSETTE'S FEARS

In early April, Jean Valjean went on a trip. This, we know, happened with him from time to time, at very long intervals. He would be away for one or two days at most. Where did he go? Nobody knew, not even Cosette. Once only, on one of these trips, she had accompanied him in a fiacre as far as the corner of a little cul-de-sac, on which she read *Impasse de la Planchette*. There he got out, and the fiacre took Cosette back to the Rue de Babylone. It was generally when money was needed for the household expenses that Jean Valjean made these little journeys.

So Jean Valjean was away. He had said, "I'll be back in three days."

In the evening, Cosette was alone in the drawing room. To amuse herself, she had opened her piano and began to sing, playing an accompaniment, the chorus from *Euryanthe,* "Hunters wandering in the woods!" perhaps the most beautiful piece of music ever written.

All at once it seemed to her that she heard footsteps in the garden.

It could not be her father, he was away; it could not be Toussaint, she was in bed. It was ten o'clock at night.

She went to the window shutter, which was closed and put her ear to it.

It seemed to her it was a man's step, that he was walking very softly.

She immediately ran up to the second floor, into her room, opened a slide in her blind, and looked into the garden. The moon was full. She could see as plainly as in broad daylight.

There was nobody there.

She opened the window. The garden was absolutely still and all she could see of the street was as deserted as it always was.

Cosette thought she had been mistaken. She had imagined she heard this noise. It was a hallucination produced by Weber's somber and majestic chorus, which opens startling depths to the mind, which trembles visibly like a bewildering forest, and in which we hear the crackling of the dead branches beneath the anxious step of the hunters dimly seen in the twilight.

She thought no more about it.

Actually, by nature Cosette was not easily startled. There was in her veins the blood of the gypsy and the barefoot adventuress. It must be remembered she was more a lark than a dove. She was wild and brave at heart.

The next day, not so late, at nightfall, she was walking in the garden. In the midst of her confused and engrossing thoughts, she thought she heard a momentary sound like the sound of the evening before, as if somebody were walking in the darkness under the trees, not very far from her, but she said to herself that nothing is more like a step in the grass than the rustling of two limbs against each other, and she paid no attention to it. Besides, she could not see anything.

She left the underbrush; she still had to cross a little green plot of grass to reach the steps. As Cosette came out of the shrubbery the moon, which had just risen behind her, projected her shadow onto this grassy plot in front of her.

Cosette stood still, terrified.

Beside her shadow, the moon clearly projected onto the grass another shadow, strangely frightening and terrifying, a shadow with a round hat.

It was like the shadow of a man who might have been standing in the edge of the shrubbery, a few steps behind Cosette.

For a moment she was unable to speak, or cry, or call, or stir, or turn her head.

At last she summoned up all her courage and resolutely turned around.

There was nobody there.

She looked at the ground. The shadow had disappeared.

She went back into the shrubbery, boldly searched through the corners, went as far as the gate, and found nothing.

She felt her blood run cold. Was this too a hallucination? Was it? Two days in succession? One hallucination can be overlooked, but two hallucinations? What made her most anxious was that the shadow was certainly not a phantom. Phantoms hardly wear round hats.

The next day Jean Valjean returned. Cosette told him what she thought she had heard and seen. She expected to be reassured, and that her father would shrug his shoulders and say, "You're a foolish little girl."

Jean Valjean became anxious.

"It may be nothing," he said to her.

He left her under some pretext and went into the garden, and she saw him examining the gate very closely.

During the night she woke up; now she was certain she distinctly heard somebody walking very near the steps under her window. She ran to her slide and opened it. There was in fact a man in the garden with a big club in his hand. Just as she was about to cry out, the moon lit up the man's face. It was her father.

She went back to bed, saying, "So he really is anxious!"

Jean Valjean spent that night in the garden and the two following nights. Cosette saw him through the hole in her shutter.

The third night the moon was smaller and rose later, it might have been one in the morning, she heard a loud burst of laughter and her father's voice calling her, "Cosette!"

She sprang out of bed, threw on her dressing-gown, and opened her window.

Her father was below on the grass.

"I woke you up to show you," he said. "Look, here is your shadow in a round hat."

And he pointed to a shadow on the grass made by the moon, and which really did look rather like a man in a round hat. It was a figure produced by a sheet-iron stovepipe with a cap that rose above a neighboring roof.

Cosette began to laugh too, all her gloomy suppositions disappeared, and the next day, while breakfasting with her father, she joked about the mysterious garden haunted by shadows of stovepipes.

Jean Valjean became completely calm again; as for Cosette, she did not pay much attention to whether the stovepipe was really in the same direction as the shadow she had seen or thought she saw, and whether the moon was in the same part of the sky. She did not wonder about the oddity of a stovepipe that is afraid of being caught in the act and leaves when you look at its shadow, for the shadow had disappeared when Cosette turned around, and Cosette had really believed she was certain of that. She was fully reassured. The evidence appeared complete, and the idea that there could have been anybody walking in the garden that evening, or that night, no longer entered her head.

A few days later, however, a new incident occurred.

III

ENRICHED BY THE COMMENTARIES OF TOUSSAINT

In the garden, near the iron gate onto the street, there was a stone bench protected from the gaze of the curious by a hedge which, with some effort, the arm of a passerby could reach through.

One evening in this same month of April, Jean Valjean had gone out; after sunset Cosette had sat down on the bench. The wind was freshening in the trees, Cosette was musing; a vague sadness was coming over her little by little, that invincible sadness brought on by evening which comes perhaps, who knows, from the mystery of the tomb half-opened at that hour.

Perhaps Fantine was in that shadow.

Cosette stood up, slowly made the round of the garden, walking in the grass, which was wet with dew, and saying to herself through the kind of melancholy somnambulism in which she was enveloped, "I really should have wooden shoes for the garden at this time of day. I'll catch a cold."

She returned to the bench.

Just as she was sitting down, she noticed in the space she had just left a rather large stone that clearly was not there the moment before.

Cosette thought about this stone, asking herself what it meant. Suddenly, the idea that the stone did not reach the bench by itself, that somebody had put it there, that an arm had passed through that grating, this idea occurred to her and scared her. It was a genuine fear this time; there was the stone. No doubt was possible, she did not touch it, fled without daring to look behind her, took refuge in the house, and immediately shut the glass door to the front steps with shutter, bar, and bolt. She asked Toussaint, "Has my father come in?"

"Not yet, mademoiselle."

(We have noted once and for all Toussaint's stammering. Allow us to stop indicating it. We are reluctant to keep up the musical notation of an infirmity.)

Jean Valjean, a man given to thought and a night walker, often came home only quite late at night.

"Toussaint," said Cosette, "you are careful in the evening to bar the shutters well, onto the garden at least, and to really put the little iron things into the little rings which fasten them?"

"Oh! Don't worry, mademoiselle."

Toussaint did not fail, and Cosette knew it very well, but she could not help adding, "Because it's so deserted around here!"

"For that matter," said Toussaint, "it's true. We would be assassinated before we'd have time to say Boo! And then, since Monsieur doesn't sleep in the house. But don't be afraid, mademoiselle, I fasten the windows like Bastilles. Women alone! I'm sure that's enough to make us shudder! Just imagine! To see men come into the room at night and say Hush! to you and set themselves about cutting your throat. It isn't so much the dying, people die, that's all right, we know very well that we have to die, but it is the horror of having such people touch you. And then their knives, they must cut badly! O God!"

"Be still," said Cosette. "Close everything securely."

Cosette, horrified by the melodrama Toussaint improvised, and perhaps also by the recurring memory of the previous week's apparitions, did not even dare to say, "Go and look at the stone somebody laid on the seat!" for fear of opening the garden door again, and lest "the men" would come in. She had all the doors and windows carefully closed, made Toussaint go over the whole house from cellar to garret, shut herself up in her room, drew her bolts, looked under her bed, lay down, and slept badly. All night long she saw the stone big as a mountain and full of caves.

At sunrise—the peculiarity of sunrise is to make us laugh at all our night terrors, and our laughter is always proportioned to the fear we have had—at sunrise Cosette, on waking, looked at her fright as a nightmare, and said to herself, "What have I been dreaming about? This is like those steps I thought I heard at night last week in the garden! It's like the shadow of the stovepipe! Am I going to be a coward now?"

The sun, gleaming through the cracks of her shutters, and turning the damask curtains crimson, reassured her to such an extent that it all vanished from her thought, even the stone.

"There was no stone on the bench, any more than there was a man with a round hat in the garden; I dreamed the stone as I did the rest."

She got dressed, went down to the garden, and ran to the bench. She was in a cold sweat. The stone was still there.

But this was only for a moment. What is fear by night turns to curiosity by day.

"Oh my," she said, "now let's see."

She lifted the stone, which was rather large. There was something underneath that looked like a letter.

It was a white paper envelope. Cosette seized it; there was no address on the one side, no seal on the other. Still the envelope, though open, was not empty. There were sheets of paper inside.

Cosette examined it. She felt no more fright or curiosity; there was a beginning of anxiety.

Cosette took out the contents of the envelope, a small notebook, each page of which was numbered and contained a few lines written in a rather pretty handwriting, thought Cosette, and very fine.

Cosette looked for a name—there was none; a signature—none. To whom was it addressed? To her probably, since a hand had placed the packet on her bench. From whom did it come? An irresistible fascination took possession of her, she tried to lift her eyes from these pages that trembled in her hand, she looked at the sky, the street, the acacias all steeped in light, some pigeons flying around a neighboring roof, then all at once her eye eagerly dropped to the manuscript, and she said to herself that she must know what there was in it.

This is what she read.

IV

A HEART BENEATH A STONE

The reduction of the universe to a single being, the expansion of a single being into God, this is love.

Love is the salutation of the angel to the stars.

How sad the soul when it is sad from love!

What a void is the absence of the being who alone fills the world! Oh! How true that the beloved becomes God! One would understand that God might be jealous if the Father of all had not clearly made creation for the soul, and the soul for love!

One glimpse of a smile under a white crepe hat with lilac veil is enough for the soul to enter the palace of dreams.

God is behind everything, but everything hides God. Things are black, creatures are opaque. To love a human being is to make her transparent.

Certain thoughts are prayers. There are moments when, whatever the attitude of the body, the soul is on its knees.

Separated lovers belie absence by a thousand chimeric things that have their own reality. They are prevented from seeing each other, they cannot write to each other; they find a host of mysterious ways to correspond. They exchange the song of the birds, the perfume of flowers, children's laughter, sunlight, the sighs of the wind, the starlight, the whole of creation. And why not? All of God's works were made to serve love. Love is powerful enough to charge all nature with its messages.

O Spring! You are a letter that I write to her.

The future belongs still more to the heart than the mind. To love is the only thing that can occupy and fill up eternity. The infinite requires the inexhaustible.

Love partakes of the soul itself. It is of the same nature. Like the soul, it is a divine spark; it is incorruptible, indivisible, imperishable. It is a point of fire within us, which is immortal and infinite, which nothing can limit and nothing can extinguish. We feel it burning even in the marrow of our bones, and we see it radiate even to the depths of the sky.

O love! Adorations! Light of two minds that understand each other, of two hearts interchanged, of two glances that interpenetrate! You will come to me, won't you, happiness? Walks together in the solitudes! Blessed, radiant days! Occasionally I have dreamed that from time to time hours detached themselves from the life of the angels and came down to pass through the destiny of men.

God can add nothing to the happiness of those who love one another, but to give them unending duration. After a life of love, an eternity of love is a superabundance, indeed; but to intensify the ineffable felicity that love gives to the soul in this world is impossible, even for God. God is the plenitude of heaven; love is the plenitude of man.

You look at a star for two reasons, because it is luminous and because it is impenetrable. You have at your side a softer radiance and a greater mystery, woman.

Whoever we may be, we all have our living, breathing beings. If they fail us, the air fails us, we stifle, then we die. To die for lack of love is horrible. The asphyxia of the soul.

When love has dissolved and mingled two beings into an angelic sacred unity, the secret of life is found for them; they are then but the two terms of a single destiny; they are then but the two wings of a single spirit. Love, soar!

The day that a woman walking past sheds a light on you as she goes, you are lost, you love. You have then only one thing left to do: to think of her so earnestly that she will be compelled to think of you.

What love begins can only be finished by God.

True love is in despair and in raptures over a lost glove or a handkerchief found, and it requires eternity for its devotion and its hopes. It is composed at the same time of the infinitely great and the infinitely small.

If you are stone, be loadstone, if you are plant, be sensitive, if you are man, be love.

Nothing is enough for love. We have happiness, we wish for paradise; we have paradise, we wish for Heaven.

O ye who love each other, all this is in love. Be wise enough to find it. As much as Heaven, love has contemplation, and more than Heaven, passionate delight.

"Does she still come to the Luxembourg?" "No, monsieur." "She hears mass in this church, doesn't she?" "She no longer comes here." "Does she still live in this house?" "She has moved away!" "Where has she gone to live?" "She did not say!"

What a somber thing, not to know the address of one's soul!

Love has its childishness, the other passions have their pettiness. Shame on the passions that make man little! Honor to what makes him a child!

There is a strange thing—do you know what? I am in the night. There is a being who has gone away and carried the heavens with her.

Oh, to be laid side by side in the same tomb, hand clasped in hand, and from time to time, in the darkness, to caress a finger gently, that would be enough for my eternity.

You who suffer because you love, love still more. To die of love is to live by it.

Love. A somber starry transfiguration is mingled with this torture. There is ecstasy in the agony.

O joy of the birds! It is because they have their nest that they have their song.

Love is a celestial breathing of the air of paradise.

Deep hearts, wise minds take life as God has made it; it is a long trial, an unintelligible preparation for the unknown destiny. This destiny, the true one, begins for man with the first step inside the tomb. Then something appears to him, and he begins to discern the definite. The definite, think about this word. The living see the infinite; the definite reveals itself only to the dead. Meantime, love and suffer, hope and contemplate. Woe, alas, to the one who shall have loved bodies, forms, appearances only. Death will take everything from him. Try to love souls, you shall find them again.

In the street I met a very poor young man who was in love. His hat was old, his coat was threadbare—there were holes at his elbows; the water seeped through his shoes and the stars through his soul.

What a great thing, to be loved! What a greater thing still, to love! The heart becomes heroic through passion. It is no longer composed of anything but what is pure; it no longer rests on anything but what is elevated and great. An unworthy thought can no more spring up in it than a nettle on a glacier. The lofty and serene soul, inaccessible to common passions and common emotions, rising above the clouds and shadows of this world, its follies, its falsehoods, its hatreds, its vanities, its miseries, inhabits the blue of the skies, and no longer feels anything but the deep subterranean commotions of destiny, as the summit of the mountains feels the quaking of the earth.

If no one loved, the sun would go out.

V

COSETTE AFTER THE LETTER

During the reading, Cosette gradually fell into reverie. At the very moment she raised her eyes from the last line of the last page, the handsome officer, it was his time, was passing triumphant before the grating. Cosette thought him hideous.

She turned back to contemplate the letter. It was written in a gorgeous handwriting, Cosette thought; in the same hand, but with different inks, sometimes very black, sometimes pale, as when ink is added to the inkwell, and consequently on different days. So it was a thought pouring itself out sigh by sigh, intermittently, without order, without choice, without aim, as chance would have it. Cosette had never read anything like it. This manuscript, in which she found still more clarity than obscurity, seemed to her like a half-opened sanctuary. To her eyes, each of these mysterious lines was resplendent and flooded her heart with a strange glow. The education she had received had always spoken to her of the soul and never of love, almost like speaking of the log and not the flame. This manuscript of fifteen pages suddenly and sweetly revealed to her the whole of love, the sorrow, the destiny, the life, the eternity, the beginning, the end. It was like a hand that had opened and suddenly thrown her a handful of sunbeams. In these few lines she felt a passionate, ardent, generous, honest nature, a consecrated will, an immense pain and a boundless hope, an oppressed heart, a joyful ecstasy. What was this manuscript? A letter. A letter with no address, no name, no date, no signature, intense and disinterested, an enigma composed of truths, a message of love made to be brought by an angel and read by a virgin, a rendezvous given beyond the earth, a love letter from a phantom to a shade. He was a calm yet despairing absence, who seemed ready to take refuge in death, and who sent to his absent one the secret of destiny, the key of life, love. It had been written with one foot in the grave and one finger in Heaven. These lines, fallen one by one onto the paper, were what might be called drops of a living soul.

Now these pages, from whom could they come? Who could have written them?

Cosette did not hesitate for a single moment. One single man.

He!

Daylight had revived in her mind. Everything had reappeared. She felt a wonderful joy and deep anguish. It was he! He who had written to her! He who was there! He the one whose arm had passed through that gate! While she was forgetting him, he had found her again! But had she forgotten him? No, never! She was mad to have thought so for even a moment. She had always loved him, always adored him. The fire had been banked and had smoldered for a while, but she clearly saw it had only sunk in the deeper, and now it burst out anew and fired her whole being. This letter was like a spark dropped from that other soul into hers. She felt the conflagration rekindling. She was pierced by every word of the manuscript: "Oh, yes!" she said. "How I recognize all this! This is what I had already read in his eyes."

As she finished it for the third time, Lieutenant Théodule came back past the iron gate, rattling his spurs on the pavement. Cosette automatically raised her eyes. She thought him flat, stupid, silly, useless, conceited, odious, impertinent, and very ugly. The officer thought it his duty to smile. She turned away insulted and indignant. She would have gladly thrown something at his head.

She fled, went back to the house again, and shut herself up in her room to read over the manuscript again, to learn it by heart, and to muse. When she had read it well, she kissed it, and tucked it into the front of her dress.

It was done. Cosette had fallen back into profound seraphic love. The abyss of Eden had reopened.

All that day Cosette was in a sort of daze. She could

hardly think, her ideas were like a tangled skein in her brain. She could not manage to put her thoughts together, she was hoping while she trembled; what were they? Vague things. She dared promise herself nothing, and wanted to refuse herself nothing. Pallors swept over her face and chills over her body. It seemed to her at times that she was entering the chimeric; she asked herself, "Is it real?" Then she felt the precious letter under her dress, she pressed it against her heart, she felt its corners against her flesh, and if Jean Valjean had seen her at that moment, he would have shuddered before the luminous unknown joy that flashed from her eyes. "Oh, yes!" she thought, "It certainly is he! This came from him for me!"

And she said to herself that an intervention of angels, a celestial chance, had restored him to her.

O transfigurations of love! O dreams! This celestial chance, this intervention of angels, was that bullet of bread thrown by one robber to another, from the Cour Charlemagne to La Fosse-aux-Lions, over the roofs of La Force.

VI

THE ELDERLY ARE MADE TO GO OUT WHEN CONVENIENT

When evening came, Jean Valjean went out; Cosette got dressed. She arranged her hair in the most becoming way, and she put on a dress whose neckline, as it had been given one snip of the scissors too many, thereby exposing the chest a bit lower, was, as young girls say, "a little indecent." It was not in the least indecent but it was prettier than otherwise. She did all this without knowing why.

Did she intend to go out? No.

Was she expecting a visit? No.

At dusk, she went down to the garden. Toussaint was busy in her kitchen, which looked out on the backyard.

She began to walk under the branches, brushing them aside with her hand from time to time, because some of them were very low.

She reached the bench.

The stone was still there.

She sat down, and laid her soft white hand on that stone as though to caress it and thank it.

All at once, she had that indefinable impression we feel, though we see nothing, when there is somebody standing behind us.

She turned her head and stood up.

It was he.

He was bareheaded. He looked pale and thin. She could hardly see his black clothes. The twilight dimmed his fine forehead and screened his eyes with darkness. Under a veil of incomparable sweetness, he wore something of death and of night. His face was lit by the light of a dying day, and by the thought of a departing soul.

It seemed as though he was not yet a phantom and no longer a man.

His hat was lying a few steps away in the shrubbery.

Cosette, ready to faint, did not utter a cry. She drew back slowly, for she felt herself attracted forward. He did not stir. Through the sad and ineffable something that cloaked him, she felt the look of his eyes, which she did not see.

In retreating, Cosette encountered a tree and leaned back against it. Without the tree, she would have fallen.

Then she heard his voice, the voice she had never really heard, scarcely rising above the rustle of the leaves, and murmuring; "Pardon me, I am here. My heart is bursting, I couldn't live as I was, so I've come. Have you read what I put there, on the bench? Do you recognize me at all? Don't be afraid of me. It has been a long time now; do you remember the day when you looked at me? It was at the Luxembourg, near the Gladiator. And the day you walked past me? It was the sixteenth of June and the second of July. It will soon be a year. For a very long time now, I haven't seen you at all. I asked the woman who collects for the chairs, she told me that she never saw you anymore. You used to live on the Rue de l'Ouest, on the third floor front, in a new house, you see, I know! I followed you. What was I to do? And then you disappeared. I thought I saw you pass once when I was reading the papers under the arches of the Odéon. I ran. But no. It was a person who had a hat like yours. At night, I come here. Do not be afraid, nobody sees me. I come to look up at your windows from nearby. I walk very softly so you won't hear, because you might be scared. The other evening I was behind you, you turned around, I fled. Once I heard you sing. I was happy. Does it disturb you that I listen to you sing through the shutter? It cannot harm you. Can it? You see, you are my angel, let me come sometimes; I think I am going to die. If you only knew! I adore you! Pardon me, I'm talking to you, I don't know what I'm saying to you, perhaps I annoy you, am I annoying you?"

"Oh!" she said.

And she collapsed as though she were dying.

He caught her, she fell, he caught her in his arms, he held her tightly, unconscious of what he was doing. He held her up though tottering himself. He felt as if his head were filled with smoke; flashes of light slipped through his eyelids; his thoughts vanished; it seemed to him that he was performing a religious act, and that he was committing a profanation. Moreover, he did not feel one passionate desire for this ravishing woman, whose form he felt against his heart. He was lost in love.

She took his hand and laid it on her heart. He felt the paper there, and stammered, "You love me, then?"

She answered in a voice so low it was no more than a breath, "Hush! You know it!"

And she hid her blushing head against the proud and dazed young man.

He fell to the seat, she by his side. There were no more words. The stars were beginning to shine. How was it that their lips met? How is it that the birds sing, that the snow melts, that the rose opens, that May blooms, that the dawn whitens behind the black trees on the shivering summit of the hills?

One kiss, and that was all.

Both trembled, and they looked at each other in the darkness with brilliant eyes.

They felt neither the cool night nor the cold stone nor the damp ground nor the wet grass; they looked at each other, and their hearts were full of thought. They had clasped hands, without knowing it.

She did not ask him; did not even think where and how he had managed to get into the garden. It seemed so natural to her that he should be there.

From time to time Marius's knee touched Cosette's, a touch that thrilled.

At times, Cosette faltered out a word. Her soul trembled on her lips like a drop of dew on a flower.

Gradually they began to talk. Overflow succeeded to silence, which is fullness. The night was serene and glorious above their heads. These two beings, pure as spirits, told each other everything, their dreams, their frenzies, their ecstasies, their chimeras, their despondencies, how they had adored each other from afar, how they had longed for each other, their despair when they had ceased to see each other. They confided to each other in an intimacy of the ideal, which already nothing could have increased, all that was most hidden and most mysterious in themselves. They told each other, with a candid faith in their illusions, all that love, youth, and the remnant of childhood that was theirs, brought to mind. These two hearts poured themselves out to each other, so that at the end of an hour, it was the young man who had the young girl's soul and the young girl who had the soul of the young man. They interpenetrated, they enchanted, they dazzled each other.

When they had finished, when they had told each other everything, she laid her head on his shoulder, and asked him: "What is your name?"

"My name is Marius," he said. "And yours?"

"My name is Cosette."

Book Six

LITTLE GAVROCHE

I

A MALEVOLENT TRICK OF THE WIND

Since 1823, while the Montfermeil inn was gradually foundering and being swallowed up, not in the abyss of a bankruptcy, but in the sewer of petty debts, the Thénardier couple had had two more children; both male. This made five; two girls and three boys. It was a lot.

The Thénardiess had relieved herself of the last two, at an early age and still quite small, with remarkable good fortune.

Relieved is the word. In this woman there was only a fragment of human nature. A phenomenon, actually, of which there is more than one example. Like Madame de la Maréchale de La Mothe-Houdancourt, the Thénardiess was a mother only to her daughters. Her maternity ended there. Her hatred of the human race began with her boys. On the side toward her sons, her malign quality was precipitous, and at that spot her heart had a fearful escarpment. As we have seen, she detested the eldest; she execrated the two others. Why? Because. The most terrible of motives and the most unanswerable of responses: Because. "I have no use for a squalling pack of children," said this mother.

We must explain how the Thénardiers had succeeded in disencumbering themselves of their two youngest children, and even in deriving a profit from them.

The Magnon girl, spoken of some pages back, was the

one who had succeeded in getting her two children endowed by the good Gillenormand. She lived on the Quai des Célestins, at the corner of that very old Rue du Petit-Musc that has done what it could to change its evil renown into good odor. Many will remember that great epidemic of croup thirty-five years ago that devastated the neighborhoods bordering on the Seine in Paris, and of which science took advantage to experiment on a large scale as to the efficacy of inhalations of alum, now so happily replaced by the tincture of iodine externally applied. In that epidemic, Magnon lost her two boys, still very young, on the same day, one in the morning, the other at night. This was a blow. These children were precious to their mother; they represented eighty francs a month. These eighty francs were paid with great exactness, in the name of M. Gillenormand, by his agent, M. Barge, a retired constable, Rue du Roi-de-Sicile. With the children dead, the income was buried. Magnon looked for an expedient. In that dark masonry of evil of which she was a part, everything is known, secrets are kept, and each aids the other. Magnon needed two children! The Thénardiess had two. Same sex, same age. Good arrangement for one, good investment for the other. The little Thénardiers became the little Magnons. Magnon left the Quai des Célestins and went to live in the Rue Clocheperce. In Paris, the identity that binds an individual to himself is broken from one street to the next.

The government, not being notified, did not object, and the substitution took place in the most natural way in the world. Only Thénardier demanded, for this loan of children, ten francs a month, which Magnon promised, and even paid. It goes without saying that M. Gillenormand continued to pay. Twice a year he would come to see the little ones. He did not notice the change. "Monsieur," said Magnon to him, "how they do look like you."

Thénardier, to whom identities came easily, took this opportunity to become Jondrette. His two girls and Gavroche had hardly had time to perceive that they had two little brothers. At a certain depth of misery, people are possessed by a sort of spectral indifference, and look at their fellow beings as at ghosts. Your nearest relatives are often merely vague shadowy forms for you, hardly distinct from the nebulous background of life, and easily blended with the invisible.

On the evening of the day she had delivered her two little ones to Magnon, expressing her willingness to freely renounce them forever, the Thénardiess had, or feigned to have, a scruple. She said to her husband, "But this amounts to abandoning one's children!" Thénardier, magisterial and phlegmatic, cauterized the scruple with this phrase: "Jean-Jacques Rousseau did better!" From scruple the mother passed to anxiety: "But suppose the police come to bother us? What we've done here, Monsieur Thénardier, tell me, is it legal?" Thénardier answered, "Everything is legal. Nobody will see anything but the sky. Besides, with children who don't have a sou, nobody cares to look into it closely."

Magnon had a kind of elegance in crime. She liked to dress up. She shared her rooms, furnished in a gaudy and appalling style, with a shrewd Frenchified English thief. This naturalized Parisian Englishwoman, recommendable for very rich connections, intimately acquainted with the medals of the Bibliothèque and the diamonds of Mademoiselle Mars, afterward became famous in the judicial records. She was called *Mamselle Miss*.

The two little ones fallen to Magnon had nothing to complain about. Well endowed by the eighty francs, they were cared for, like everything that is a matter of business; not badly clothed, not badly fed, treated almost like "little gentlemen," better with the false mother than with the true. Magnon acted the lady and did not talk argot in their presence.

They spent some years thus: Thénardier foresaw good things to come. It occurred to him one day to say to Magnon who was bringing him his monthly ten francs, "*The father* must give them an education."

Suddenly, these two poor children, till then well cared for, even by their bad luck, were abruptly thrown out into life, and compelled to begin it.

A mass arrest of malefactors like that at the Jondrette garrett, necessarily complicated with subsequent searches and seizures, is truly a disaster for this hideous occult counter-society living beneath the public society; an event like this brings on all manner of collapse in that gloomy world. The catastrophe of the Thénardiers produced the catastrophe of Magnon.

One day, a short time after Magnon handed Eponine the note relative to the Rue Plumet, there was a sudden police raid on the Rue Clocheperce. Magnon was arrested as well as Mamselle Miss, and the whole household, which was suspect, was included in the haul. The two little boys were playing at the time in a backyard, and saw nothing of the raid. When they wanted to go in, they found the door closed and the house empty. A cobbler, whose shop was across the street, called them and handed them a piece of paper "their mother" had left for them. On the paper there was an address: M. Barge, rent-agent, Rue du Roi-de-Sicile, No. 8. The man of the shop said to them, "You don't live here anymore. Go there—it's nearby—the first street on the left. Ask your way with this paper."

The children set off, the older leading the younger, and holding in his hand the paper that was to be their guide. He was cold, and his numb little fingers had only an awkward grasp, and held the paper loosely. As they were turning out of the Rue Clocheperce, a gust of wind snatched it from him, and, as the night was coming on, the child could not find it again.

They began to wander aimlessly in the streets

II

IN WHICH LITTLE GAVROCHE TAKES ADVANTAGE OF NAPOLEON THE GREAT

Spring in Paris is often accompanied by keen and sharp north winds, that do not exactly freeze, but do produce frostbite; these winds, which mar the most beautiful days, have precisely the effect of those cold drafts that sneak into a warm room through the cracks around a window or a poorly closed door. It seemed as though the dreary door of winter were partly open and the wind coming that way. In the spring of 1832, the time when the first great epidemic of this century broke out in Europe, these winds were sharper and more piercing than ever. A door still more icy than that of winter was ajar. The door of the sepulcher. The breath of cholera was felt in those winds.

From the meteorological point of view, these cold winds had this peculiarity, that they did not exclude a strong electric tension. Storms accompanied by thunder and lighting often occurred during this time.

One evening when the winds were blowing harshly, so much so that January seemed to have returned and the bourgeois had put on their coats again, little Gavroche, always shivering cheerfully under his rags, was standing as if in ecstasy, before a wig-maker's shop near the carrefour de l'Orme-Saint-Gervais. He was sporting a woman's wool shawl, picked up who knows where, worn as a muffler. Little Gavroche seemed to be intensely admiring a wax bride, with a deep décolletage and a headdress of orange flowers, that was revolving behind the showcase window, between two lamps, exhibiting its smile to the passersby; but in reality he was watching the shop to see if he could swipe a cake of soap from the display, which he would sell for a sou to a hairdresser in the suburbs. Often he managed to lunch off one of these cakes. He called this kind of work, for which he had some talent, "shaving the barbers."

As he was contemplating the bride and squinting at the cake of soap, he muttered between his teeth: "Tuesday. It isn't Tuesday. Is it Tuesday? Perhaps it's Tuesday. Yes, it's Tuesday."

Nobody ever discovered what this monologue referred to.

If, by any chance, the soliloquy referred to the last time he had eaten, that was three days earlier, as it was then Friday.

Warmed by a good stove, the barber in his shop was shaving a customer and from time to time glancing toward this enemy, this frozen brazen gamin, who had both hands in his pockets but his wits clearly unsheathed.

While Gavroche was examining the bride, the windows, and the Windsor soap, two children of unequal height, rather neatly dressed, and still smaller than he, one about seven years old, the other five, timidly turned the knob of the door and entered the shop, asking for something, charity, perhaps, in a plaintive manner that resembled a groan more than a prayer. They both spoke at once and their words were unintelligible because sobs choked the younger one, and the cold made the other's teeth chatter. The barber turned with a furious expression, and without leaving his razor, shoving back the older one with his left hand and the little one with his knee, pushed them into the street and shut the door saying, "Coming to freeze people for nothing!"

The two children trudged on, crying. Meanwhile a cloud had come up; it began to rain.

Little Gavroche ran after them and accosted them, "What's the matter with you, little brats?"

"We don't know where to sleep," answered the older one.

"Is that all?" said Gavroche. "That's nothing. Does anybody cry for a thing like that? Are these a couple of canaries?"

And assuming, through his slightly bantering superiority, a tone of softened authority and gentle protection, "Kiddos, come with me."

"Yes, monsieur," said the first.

And the two children followed him as they would have followed an archbishop. They had stopped crying.

Gavroche led them up the Rue Saint-Antoine toward the Bastille.

Gavroche, as he left, cast an indignant glance back at the barber's shop.

"He has no heart that mackerel," he muttered. "He's an *Angliche*."

A girl, seeing them all three marching in a row, Gavroche at the head, broke into loud, disrespectful laughter.

"Good day, Mamselle Omnibus," said Gavroche to her.

A moment later, the barber recurring to him, he added, "I'm wrong about the animal; he's no mackerel, he's a snake. Wigpicker, I'm going after a locksmith, and I'll have a rattle put on your tail."

This barber had raised his ire. As he leaped across a running gutter, he sassed a concierge with a beard fit to meet Faust on the Brocken, who had her broom in her hand.

"Madame," he said to her, "you've come out with your horse, I see."

Then he splattered a pedestrian's polished boots with mud.

"Beast!" cried the man, furious.

Gavroche poked his nose above his shawl.

"Monsieur complains?"

"About you!" said the pedestrian.

"The bureau is closed," said Gavroche. "I'm receiving no more complaints."

Meanwhile, further up the street he saw, quite frozen under a carriage entrance, a beggar girl of thirteen or fourteen, whose clothes were so short that they bared her knees. The little girl was getting too old for that. Growth plays you such tricks. The skirt becomes short at the moment that nudity becomes indecent.

"Poor girl!" said Gavroche. "Doesn't even have any undies. But here, take this."

And, unfurling all that good wool he had around his neck, he threw it onto her bony, purple shoulders, and muffler became shawl.

The little girl looked at him, astonished, and took the shawl in silence. At a certain depth of distress, the poor in their stupor no longer groan over evil, and are no longer thankful for good.

This done, "Brrr!" said Gavroche, shivering worse than Saint Martin, who, at least, kept half his cloak.

At this *brrr!* the storm, doubling its fury, turned violent. The malignant skies punish good actions.

"Ah," exclaimed Gavroche, "what's the meaning of this? Rain again! Good God, if this continues, I cancel my subscription!"

And he set off again.

"Never mind," he added, glancing back at the beggar girl who was cuddling into the shawl, "There's someone with a first-rate peel."

And, looking up at the clouds, he cried: "Caught!"

The two children were limping along behind him.

As they passed one of those thick lattices that indicate a bakery, for bread, like gold, is kept behind iron gratings, Gavroche turned, "Ah ha, kiddos, have we dined?"

"Monsieur," answered the elder, "we haven't eaten since early this morning."

"So you don't have a father or mother?" replied Gavroche, majestically.

"Excuse us, monsieur, we do have a papa and mama, but we don't know where they are."

"Sometimes that's better than knowing," said Gavroche, who was a thinker.

"For two hours now," continued the taller one, "we've been walking; we've been looking for things at every corner, but we haven't found anything."

"I know," said Gavroche. "The dogs eat everything up."

After a moment's silence, he went on, "Ah! we've lost our authors. We don't know now what we've done with them. That won't do, gamins. It's stupid to lose track of folk like them, of a reasonable age. Oh, yes, we'll need to swill regardless."

Still he did not question them. To lack a home, what could be more natural?

The elder of the two *mômes,* almost entirely restored to the ready unconcern of childhood, made this exclamation: "Still, it's strange. And Mama, who promised to take us to look for some blessed boxwood on Palm Sunday."

"I see," answered Gavroche.

"Mama," added the boy, "is a lady who lives with Mamselle Miss."

"Indeed," replied Gavroche.

Meanwhile he had stopped, and for a few minutes he had been groping and fumbling in all sorts of recesses in his rags.

Finally he raised his head with an air intended only to convey satisfaction, but was actually triumphant.

"Let's be calm, kiddos. Here's enough for supper for three."

And he took a sou from one of his pockets.

Without giving the two little boys time for amazement, he pushed them both into the baker's shop, and laid his sou on the counter, crying, "Boy! Five centimes' worth of bread."

The baker, who was the owner himself, took a loaf and a knife.

"In three pieces, boy!" resumed Gavroche, and he added with dignity, "There are three of us."

And seeing that the baker, after having examined the three costumes, had taken a black loaf, he poked his finger deep into his nose with a sniff as imperious as if he had had the great Frederick's pinch of snuff at the end of his thumb, and hurled in the baker's face this indignant comment: "Whazzachuaver?"

Those of our readers who may be tempted to see in this

summons of Gavroche to the baker a Russian or Polish word, or one of those savage cries which the Iowas and the Botocudos hurl at each other from one bank of a stream to the other in their solitudes, are informed that it is a phrase they use every day (they, our readers), and which takes the place of this phrase: what is that you have there? The baker understood perfectly well, and answered:

"Why! It is bread, very good bread of the second quality."

"You mean *larton brutal,*" replied Gavroche, with calm, cold disdain. "None of your black bread! We want white bread, boy! *Larton savonné!* I'm treating."

The baker could not help smiling, and while he was cutting the white bread, he looked at them in a compassionate way that offended Gavroche.

"Come on, paper cap!" he said, "what are you fathoming us like that for?"

All three placed end to end would hardly have made a fathom.

When the bread was cut, the baker put the sou in his drawer, and Gavroche said to the children, "*Morfilez.*"

The little boys looked at him confused.

Gavroche began to laugh: "Ah! Yes, that's true, they don't know yet, they're so small."

And he added, "Eat."

At the same time he handed each of them a piece of bread.

And, thinking that the elder, who seemed to him more worthy of his conversation, deserved some special encouragement and ought to be relieved of all hesitation in regard to satisyfing his appetitie, he added, giving him the largest piece, "Pop that in your gun."

There was one piece smaller than the other two; he took it for himself.

The poor children were starving, Gavroche included. While they were tearing the bread with their fine teeth, they were cluttering the shop of the baker, who, now that he had received his pay, was regarding them testily.

"Let's go back to the street," said Gavroche.

They went on toward the Bastille.

From time to time when they were passing in front of a lighted shop, the smaller one stopped to look at the time on a lead watch suspended from his neck by a string.

"This decidedly is a real brat," said Gavroche.

Then he thoughtfully muttered between his teeth: "All the same, if I had any kids, I'd hug them tighter than this."

As they finished their pieces of bread and reached the corner of that gloomy Rue des Ballets, from which the low and forbidding wicket gate of La Force can be seen: "Hello, is that you, Gavroche?" said somebody.

"Hello, that you, Montparnasse?" said Gavroche.

A man had just accosted the gamin, and this man was none other than Montparnasse, disguised behind blue eyeglasses, but recognizable by Gavroche.

"You sly one!" continued Gavroche. "You have a hide the color of a mustard poultice and blue specs like a doctor. You're right in style, old man."

"Shhh!" said Montparnasse. "Not so loud."

And he hastily drew Gavroche out of the light of the shops.

The two little boys followed automatically, holding each other by the hand.

When they were under the black arch of a carriage gate, sheltered from sight and from the rain, "Do you know where I'm going?" inquired Montparnasse.

"To the Abbey of Monte à Regret,"[1] said Gavroche.

"Joker!"

And Montparnasse added, "I'm going to find Babet."

"Ah!" said Gavroche. "Her name is Babet."

Montparnasse lowered his voice.

"Not her, his."

"Ah, Babet!"

"Yes, Babet."

"I thought he was locked up."

"He slipped through the keyhole," answered Montparnasse.

And he rapidly told the gamin how, on that very morning, Babet, transferred to the Conciergerie, had escaped by turning left instead of right in "the vestibule of the examination hall."

Gavroche praised his skill.

"Quite some dentist!" he said.

Montparnasse added a few particulars regarding Babet's escape and finished with, "Oh! That's not all!"

[1] To the scaffold. (V.H.)

While listening, Gavroche had caught hold of a cane Montparnasse had in his hand, had unconsciously pulled on the upper part, and the blade of a dagger appeared.

"Ah!" he said, hastily pushing the dagger away, "you've brought your gendarme disguised as a bourgeois."

Montparnasse gave him a wink.

"The devil!" resumed Gavroche, "then you're going to have a tussle with the cops?"

"One never knows," answered Montparnasse with an air of indifference. "It's always smart to have a pin on you."

Gavroche persisted, "What are you up to tonight?"

Montparnasse resumed the serious note again and said, biting off his syllables, "A thing or two."

And abruptly changing the conversation, "By the way!"

"What?"

"A tale of yesterday. Just imagine. I met a bourgeois. He makes me a present of a sermon and his purse. I put that in my pocket. A minute later, I feel in my pocket. There's nothing there."

"Except the sermon," said Gavroche.

"But you," resumed Montparnasse, "where are you off to?"

Gavroche showed his two protégés and said, "I'm going to bed down these children."

"Where do they sleep?"

"At my house."

"Your house. Where's that?"

"At my house."

"So you've got a room?"

"Yes, I've got a room."

"And where's your room?"

"In the elephant," said Gavroche.

Montparnasse, although by nature not easily surprised, could not restrain an exclamation: "In the elephant?"

"Well, yes, in the elephant!" replied Gavroche. "Whazzematruthat?"

This is also a word in the language that nobody writes and everybody speaks. Whazzematruthat signifies "What is the matter with that?"

The profound observation of the gamin recalled Montparnasse to calm and good sense. He seemed to return to more respectful sentiments for Gavroche's lodging.

"Oh, I see!" he said. "Yes, the elephant. Is it nice there?"

"Very nice," said Gavroche. "Really first-rate. It's less drafty than under the bridges."

"How do you get in?"

"I get in."

"There's a hole then?" asked Montparnasse.

"Damn it! But you musn't tell. It's between the forelegs. The cops haven't seen it."

"And you climb up? Yes, I see."

"A flick of the wrist, crick, crack, it's done, gone."

After a moment, Gavroche added, "For these kids I'll have a ladder."

Montparnasse began to laugh: "Where the devil did you get these brats?"

Gavroche simply answered, "These kiddos came as a present from a wig-maker."

Meanwhile Montparnasse had turned thoughtful.

"You recognized me very easily," he murmured.

He took from his pocket two little objects that were nothing but two quill tubes wrapped in cotton and put one in each nostril. This gave him a new nose.

"That changes you," said Gavroche, "you're not so ugly, you should keep them in all the time."

Montparnasse was a handsome fellow, but Gavroche was a scoffer.

"Joking aside," asked Montparnasse, "how d'you like it?"

He had also assumed another voice. In the twinkling of an eye, Montparnasse had become unrecognizable.

"Oh! Play Punch!" exclaimed Gavroche.

The two little ones, who had not been listening till now, so busy themselves picking their noses, were attracted by this name and looked at Montparnasse with dawning joy and admiration.

Unfortunately Montparnasse was anxious.

He laid a hand on Gavroche's shoulder and said to him, dwelling on his words, "Listen to this, boy, if I were on the Square, with my *dogue*, my *dague*, and my *digue*, and if you were so prodigal as to offer me twenty fat sous, I wouldn't refuse to work for them, but this isn't Mardi Gras."

This grotesque phrase produced a singular effect on the

gamin. He turned hastily, swept his small keen eyes around him with intense attention, and noticed, a few steps away, a policeman, whose back was turned to them. Gavroche let an "Ah, yes!" escape him, which he suppressed on the spot, and shaking Montparnasse's hand, "Well, good night," he said, "I'm off to my elephant with my kids. On the supposition that you should need me some night, you'll find me there. I live on the second floor. There is no doorman. You should ask for Monsieur Gavroche."

"Fine," said Montparnasse.

And they separated, Montparnasse making his way toward the Grève and Gavroche toward the Bastille. The little five-year-old dragged along by his brother, whom Gavroche was dragging, turned around several times to watch Punch departing.

The unintelligent phrase by which Montparnasse had warned Gavroche of the presence of the policeman contained no other talisman than the consonance *dig* repeated five or six times under various forms. This syllable *dig*, not pronounced in isolation, but artfully mingled with the words of a phrase, means "Watch out, we can't talk freely." In Montparnasse's phrase there was furthermore a literary beauty that escaped Gavroche, that is my dogue, my dague, and my digue, an expression of the argot of the Temple, signifying "my dog, my knife, and my wife," very much in use among the clowns and the Queues Rouges in the golden age, when Molière was writing and Callot was drawing.

Twenty years ago, there could still be seen in the southeast corner of the Place de la Bastille, near the canal siding dug in the former moat of the prison citadel, a grotesque monument that has now faded from the memory of Parisians and is worthy of leaving some trace, for it was an idea from the "member of the Institute, General-in-Chief of the Army of Egypt."

We say monument, although it was only a rough model. But this rough model itself, a huge sketch, a vast carcass of an idea of Napoleon's which two or three successive gusts of wind had carried off and tossed farther away from us each time, had become historic and acquired a permanence in contrast with its provisional aspect. It was an elephant, forty feet high, constructed of framework and masonry, bearing on its back a tower like a house, formerly painted green by some housepainter, now painted black by the sun, the rain, and the weather. In that open and deserted corner of the Square, the broad front of the colossus, his trunk, his tusks, his size, his enormous rump, his four feet like columns, produced at night, under the starry sky, a startling and terrible outline. One couldn't tell what it meant. It was a sort of symbol of the force of the people. It was gloomy, enigmatic, and immense. It was a mysterious and mighty phantom, visibly standing by the side of the invisible specter of the Bastille.

Few strangers visited this edifice, no passerby looked at it. It was falling to ruins; every season the mortar coming loose from its sides opened hideous wounds on it. The city officials had forgotten it since 1814. It was there in its corner, gloomy, diseased, crumbling, surrounded by a rotten railing, continually sullied by drunken coachmen; crevices zigzagging across the belly, a lath was sticking out of the tail, the tall grass grew far up between its legs; and as the level of the square had been rising for thirty years all around it, by that slow continuous movement that imperceptibly raises the soil of great cities, it was in a hollow, and it seemed as if the earth had sunk beneath it. It was filthy, scorned, repulsive, superb, ugly to the eye of the bourgeois, melancholy to the eye of the thinker. To some extent, it partook of filth about to be swept away, and to some extent of a majesty soon to be decapitated.

As we have said, at night it looked changed. Night is the true medium for everything shadowy. As soon as twilight fell, the old elephant was transfigured; it assumed a tranquil, intimidating form in the fearful serenity of the darkness. Being of the past, it was of the night; and this obscurity suited its greatness.

This monument, rude, squat, clumsy, harsh, severe, almost deformed, but certainly majestic, and marked by a sort of magnificent savage gravity, has disappeared, leaving to a peaceable reign the sort of gigantic stove, adorned with its stovepipe, which has taken the place of the forbidding nine-towered fortress, almost as the bourgeoisie replaces feudality. It is very natural that a stove should be the symbol of an epoch when a teakettle contains power. This period will pass, it is already on its way out; we are beginning to understand that, if there can be force in a boiler, there can only be power in a brain; in other words, what leads and controls the world is not locomotives but ideas. Harness the locomotives to the ideas, yes, but do not mistake the horse for the horseman.

However this may be, to return to the Place de la Bastille, the architect of the elephant had succeeded in making something grand out of plaster; the architect of the stovepipe has succeeded in making something petty with bronze.

This stovepipe, baptized with a ringing name, the Column of July, this would-be monument of an abortive revolution, was still, in 1832, wrapped in an immense scaffolding, which we for our part still miss, and by a large board enclosure, which completed the elephant's isolation.

It was toward this corner of the square, dimly lit by the reflection of a distant lamp, that the gamin led his two *mômes*.

We must be allowed to stop here long enough to state that we are within simple reality and that twenty years ago the police tribunals had to condemn on a complaint for vagrancy and breach of a public monument a child who had been caught sleeping in this very interior of the elephant of the Bastille. This fact stated, we go on.

As they neared the colossus, Gavroche understood the effect that the infinitely great may produce on the infinitely small, and said, "Brats, don't be frightened."

Then through a gap in the fence he entered the elephant's enclosure and helped the kids to crawl through the breach. Somewhat timorously, the two children followed Gavroche without saying a word, and trusted themselves to that little Providence in rags who had given them bread and promised them a lodging.

Lying alongside the fence was a ladder, which in the daytime was used by the workmen of the neighboring lumberyard. Gavroche lifted it with unusual vigor and set it up against one of the elephant's forelegs. About the point where the ladder ended, a sort of black hole could be made out in the belly of the colossus.

Gavroche showed the ladder and the hole to his guests and said to them, "Up and in."

The two little fellows looked at each other in terror.

"You're afraid, *mômes!*" exclaimed Gavroche.

And he added, "You'll see."

He clasped the elephant's wrinkled foot, and in a twinkling, without deigning to make use of the ladder, he reached the crevice. He entered it as an adder glides into a hole, and disappeared, and a moment later the two children saw his pallid face at the edge of the black hole.

"Well," he cried, "why don't you come up, kids? You'll see how nice it is! Come on up," he said, to the older one, "I'll give you a hand."

The little ones urged each other forward. The gamin scared them and reassured them at the same time, and then it was raining very hard. The older one ventured. The younger one, seeing his brother go up, and himself left all alone between the paws of this huge beast, felt very much like crying, but he did not dare.

The older one clambered up the rungs of the ladder, tottering badly. While he was on his way Gavroche encouraged him with the exclamations of a fencing master to his pupils, or of a mule driver to his mules: "Don't be afraid!"

"That's it!"

"Keep coming!"

"Put your foot there!"

"Your hand here!"

"Courage!"

And when he came within reach he caught him quickly and vigorously by the arm and pulled him up.

"Gobbled!" he said.

The boy had gone through the crevice.

"Now," said Gavroche, "wait for me. Monsieur, be so kind as to sit down."

And, going out by the crevice as he entered, he let himself slide with the agility of a monkey along the elephant's leg, he dropped on his feet in the grass, caught the little five-year-old by the waist and set him halfway up the ladder, then he began to climb up behind him, crying to the older one, "I'll push; you pull."

In an instant the little fellow was lifted, pushed, dragged, pulled, stuffed, crammed into the hole with no time to realize what was going on. And Gavroche, coming in after him, pushing back the ladder with a kick so it fell onto the grass, began to clap his hands, and cried,

"Here we are! Hurrah for General Lafayette! Brats, my home!"

Gavroche was in fact at home.

O unexpected utility of the useless! Charity of the great! Goodness of the giants! This monstrous monument that had contained an emperor's thought had become the box of a gamin. The kid had been accepted and sheltered by the colossus. The bourgeois in their Sunday clothes, who passed by the elephant of the Bastille, often said, eyeing it scornfully with their bulging eyes, "What's the use of that?" It's use was to save from the cold, the frost, the hail, the rain, to protect from the wintry wind, to spare from sleeping in the mud, which breeds fever and from sleeping in the snow, which breeds death, a little being with no father or mother, with no bread, no clothing, no sanctuary. Its use was to receive the innocent whom society repelled. Its use was to diminish public error. It was a den open for the one to whom all doors were closed. It seemed as if the miserable old mastodon, invaded by vermin and oblivion, covered with warts, mold, and scars, tottering, worm-eaten, abandoned, condemned, a sort of colossal beggar vainly seeking the alms of a benevolent glance in the middle of the Square, had taken pity on this other beggar, the poor pygmy who went around with no shoes on his feet, no roof over his head, blowing on his fingers, clothed in rags, fed on what is thrown away. This was the use of the elephant of the Bastille. This idea of Napoleon's, disdained by men, had been taken up by God. What had been merely illustrious had become august. To realize what he conceived, the emperor needed porphyry, brass, iron, gold, marble; for God the old assemblage of boards, joists, and plaster was enough. The emperor had had a dream of genius; in this titanic elephant, armed, prodigious, brandishing his trunk, bearing his tower and making the joyous and vivifying waters gush out on all sides around him, he wanted to incarnate the people. God had done a grander thing with it, he sheltered a child.

The hole by which Gavroche had entered was a break hardly visible from the outside, concealed as it was, and as we have said, under the elephant's belly, and so narrow that hardly anything but cats and *mômes* could have skinned through.

"Let's start," said Gavroche, "by telling the doorkeeper we aren't in."

And plunging into the obscurity with certainty, like someone familiar with his room, he took a board and blocked the hole.

Gavroche dove again into the darkness. The children heard the sputtering of the taper plunged into the phosphoric bottle. The chemical match did not yet exist; the Fumade tinderbox represented progress at that period.

A sudden light made them blink; Gavroche had just lit one of those bits of string soaked in resin that are known as cellar-rats. The cellar-rats, which made more smoke than flame, dimly illuminated the inside of the elephant.

Gavroche's two guests looked around and felt something like what one would feel shut up inside the great cask of Heidelberg, or better still, what Jonah must have felt in the Biblical belly of the whale. A complete and gigantic skeleton appeared and enveloped them. Above, a long dusky beam, projecting at regular intervals massive encircling timbers, represented the vertebral column with its ribs, stalactites of plaster hung down like the viscera, and from one side to the other huge spiderwebs made dusty diaphragms. Here and there in the corners great blackish spots could be seen, which looked almost alive and rapidly moved around with a wild and startled motion.

The debris fallen from the elephant's back onto his belly had filled up the concavity, so they could walk on it as on a floor.

The smaller one clung close to his brother and whispered, "It's dark!"

This word made Gavroche cry out. The petrified look of the two *mômes* necessitated a shock.

"What are you driving at?" he exclaimed. "Are we the snivelers? Are we being squeamish? Must you have the Tuileries? Are you idiots? Speak up! I warn you I don't belong to the regiment of dopes. Do you think you're the brats of the pope's headwaiter?"

A little roughness is good in cases of fear. It is reassuring. The two children moved in close to Gavroche.

Gavroche, paternally softened by this confidence, turned "from the grave to the gentle" and spoke to the little one. "Little idiot," he said to him, accenting the insult with a caressing tone, "it's outside that it's dark. Outside it is raining, in here it isn't raining; outside it's cold, in here there isn't a speck of wind; outside there are heaps of folks, here there isn't anybody; outside there isn't even a moon, here there's my candle!"

The two children began to look at the apartment with less fear, but Gavroche did not allow them much leisure for contemplation.

"Quick," he said.

And he pushed them toward what we are very happy to be able to call the bottom of the room.

His bed was there.

Gavroche's bed was complete. That is to say, there was a mattress, a covering, and an alcove with curtains.

The mattress was a straw mat, the covering a large blanket of coarse gray wool, very warm and almost new. The alcove was like this: three rather long laths, sunk and firmly settled into the rubbish of the floor, that is to say of the belly of the elephant, two in front and one behind; and tied together by a string at the top, so as to form a pyramidal frame. This frame supported a fine trellis of brass wire that was simply hung over it, but artfully applied and kept in place by wire fastenings in such a way that it entirely enveloped the three laths. A row of large stones were firmly placed on the ground all around this trellis so as to let nothing through. This trellis was nothing more or less than a fragment of those copper nettings used to enclose the birdhouses in menageries. Gavroche's bed under this netting was as if in a cage. Altogether it was like an Eskimo tent.

It was this netting that took the place of curtains.

Gavroche barely moved the stones that kept down the netting in front, and the two folds of the trellis, which lay one over the other, opened.

"Down on your hands and knees!" said Gavroche.

He made his guests enter the cage carefully, then he crept in after them, pulled back the stones, and hermetically closed the opening.

They were all three stretched on the straw.

Small as they were, none of them could have stood up in the alcove. Gavroche was still holding the cellar-rat in his hand.

"Now," he said, "snooze! I am going to extinguish the candelabra."

"Monsieur," inquired the older brother of Gavroche, pointing to the netting, "what is that?"

"That," said Gavroche, "is for the rats. Now snooze!"

However, he felt it incumbent to add a few words for the instruction of these beings of a tender age, and he added: "They are things from the Jardin des Plantes. They're used for ferocious animals. Therz a 'ole room full of 'em. Jiss climb a wall, skin in a window, and slip under a door. You get as much as you want."

While he was talking, he wrapped a fold of the cover around the smaller one, who murmured, "Oh! that's nice! It's warm!"

Gavroche looked with satisfaction at the cover.

"That's also from the Jardin des Plantes," said he. "I got that from the monkeys."

And, showing the older one the mat where he was lying, a very thick mat and well made, he added, "That was the giraffe's."

After a pause, he went on, "The animals had all this. I took it from them. They didn't mind. I told them: It's for the elephant."

He paused before adding, "We go over the walls and we don't give a damn about the government. That's all."

The two children studied with a timid, stupefied respect this intrepid, inventive being, a vagabond like them, isolated like them, wretched like them, who was something wonderful and all-powerful, who seemed supernatural, and whose countenance was made up of all the grimaces of an old clown mingled with the most natural and pleasant smile.

"Monsieur," said the elder timidly, "so you're not afraid of the gendarmes?"

Gavroche merely answered, "Youngster! we don't say gendarmes, we say cops."

The smaller boy had his eyes open, but he said nothing. As he was on the edge of the mat, the elder being in the middle, Gavroche tucked the cover under him as a mother would have done, and raised the mat under his head with some old rags in such a way as to make a pillow. Then he turned toward the older one.

"Eh! We're pretty well off here!"

"Oh, yes," answered the boy, looking at Gavroche with the expression of a rescued angel.

The two poor little soaked children were beginning to warm up.

"Ah, now," continued Gavroche, "what in the world were you crying for?"

And pointing out the little one to his brother:

"A youngster like that, that's one thing, but a big boy like you crying, that's stupid; makes you look like a calf."

"Well," said the child. "We had no room, no place to go."

"Brat!" replied Gavroche, "we don't say a room, we say digs."

"And then, we were afraid to be all alone like that in the night."

"We don't say night, we say devil's pit."

"Thank you, monsieur," said the child.

"Listen to me" continued Gavroche, "you must never whine anymore for anything. I'll take care of you. You'll see what fun we have. In summer we'll go to the Glacière with Navet, a comrade of mine, we'll go swimming in the Basin, we'll run on the tracks in front of the Pont d'Austerlitz completely naked, that makes the washerwomen mad. They scream, those grouches, if you only knew how batty they are! We'll go see the skeleton man. He's alive. On the Champs-Elysées. That parishioner is as thin as anything. And then I'll take you to the theater. I'll take you to Frederick Lemaître's. I get tickets, I know the actors, I even acted once in a play. We were shrimps just so high, we ran around under a cloth that made the sea. I'll get you hired at my theater. We'll go see the savages. They're not real, those savages. They have red tights that wrinkle, and you can see their elbows darned with white thread. After that, we'll go to the Opera. We'll go in with the claque. The claque at the Opera is very select. I wouldn't go with the claque on the boulevards. At the opera, just think, some pay twenty sous, but they're fools. They call them dishrags. And then we'll go see the guillotining. I'll show you the executioner. He lives in the Rue des Marais. Monsieur Sanson. There is a mailbox on his door. Oh, we have great fun!"

At this moment, a drop of wax fell on Gavroche's finger, and recalled him to the realities of life.

"Damn!" he said, "there's the wick used up. Watch out! I can't spend more than a sou a month for my illumination. When we go to bed, we have to go to sleep. We don't have time to read Monsieur Paul de Kock's novels. Besides, the light might show through the cracks of the carriage door, and the cops couldn't help seeing."

"And then," timidly observed the older boy, who alone dared talk with Gavroche and answer back, "a spark might fall into the straw, we have to be careful not to burn the house up."

"We don't say burn the house," said Gavroche, "we say torch the place."

The storm had picked up. Between claps of thunder they heard the downpour beating against the back of the colossus.

"Pour away, old rain!" said Gavroche. "I do like to hear the decanter emptying along the house's legs. Winter is a fool; it throws away its goods, it's a waste of good time, it can't wet us, and it just grumbles, the old bucket brigade!"

This allusion to thunder, whose every consequence Gavroche accepted as a philosopher of the nineteenth century, was followed by a very vivid flash, so blinding that a trace of it came in by the crevice in the elephant's belly. Almost at the same instant the thunder burst furiously. The two little boys let out a cry and rose so quickly that the trellis was almost thrown out of place; but Gavroche turned his bold face toward them, and took advantage of the clap of thunder to burst out laughing.

"Calm down, children. Don't let's upset the edifice. That was superb thunder; give us some more. That was no chickenfeed lightning! Bravo, God! That's almost as good as at the theater."

This said, he restored order in the trellis, gently pushed the two children back down onto the bed, pressed their knees to stretch them out full length, and exclaimed, "As God is lighting his candle, I can blow out mine. Children, we must sleep, my young humans. It's very bad not to sleep. It would make you wobbly in your insides, or, as the big bugs say, stink in your jaws. Wind yourselves up well in the peel! I'm going to extinguish. Everybody set?"

"Yes," murmured the first, "I'm fine. It's as if I had feathers under my head."

"We don't say head," cried Gavroche. "We say attic."

The two children squeezed close to each other. Gavroche finished arranging them on the mat, and pulled the cover up to their ears, then repeated for the third time the injunction in hieratic language, "*Pioncez,* snooze!"

And he blew out the taper.

Hardly was the light out when a strange tremor began to agitate the trellis under which the three children were lying. It was a mass of dull rubbings, which gave a metallic sound, as if claws and teeth were grinding the copper wire. This was accompanied by all sorts of little sharp cries.

The little boy of five, hearing this racket over his head, and shivering with fear, dug the older brother with his elbow, but the older one had already "*pioncé,*" according to Gavroche's order. Then the little boy, no longer capable of fearing him, ventured to accost Gavroche, but very low, and holding his breath:

"Monsieur?"

"Yeah?" said Gavroche, who had just closed his eyes.

"What's that?"

"It is the rats," answered Gavroche.

And he laid his head back on the mat.

In fact the rats, which swarmed by the thousands in the carcass of the elephant, and were those living black spots we mentioned, had been held in awe by the candle as long as it burned, but as soon as this cavern, virtually their city, had been restored to night, smelling there what the good storyteller Perrault calls "some fresh meat," they had rushed in en masse on Gavroche's tent, climbed to the top, and were biting its mesh as if trying to get through this new-fashioned mosquito netting.

The little boy still did not go to sleep.

"Monsieur!" he said again.

"Yeah?" said Gavroche.

"What are the rats?"

"They're mice."

This explanation reassured the child somewhat. He had seen some white mice in the course of his life, and he was not afraid of them. However, he spoke up again:

"Monsieur?"

"Yeah?" replied Gavroche.

"Why don't you have a cat?"

"I had one," answered Gavroche, "I brought one here, but they ate her up for me."

This second explanation undid the work of the first, and the little fellow began to tremble again. The dialogue between him and Gavroche was resumed for the fourth time.

"Monsieur!"

"Yeah?"

"Who was it that was eaten up?"

"The cat."

"Who was it that ate the cat?"

"The rats."

"The mice?"

"Yes, the rats."

The child, dismayed by these mice who ate cats, went on. "Monsieur, would the mice eat us?"

"You bet!" said Gavroche.

The child's terror was complete. But Gavroche added, "Don't be 'fraid! They can't get in. And then I'm here. Here, hold my hand. Be still and *pioncez!*"

At the same time Gavroche took hold of the little fellow's hand across his brother. The child clasped his hand against his body, and felt safe. Courage and strength have such mysterious communications. Once more it was silent around them, the sound of voices had startled and driven away the rats; in a few minutes they might have returned and done their worst in vain, the three lads, sound asleep, heard nothing more.

The night hours went by. Darkness covered the immense Place de la Bastille; a wintry wind mingled with the rain, blew in gusts, the patrolmen poked around in the doors, alleys, yards, and dark corners, and, looking for nocturnal vagabonds, passed silently by the elephant; the monster upright, motionless, with open eyes in the darkness, appeared to be in reverie and well satisfied with his good deeds, and he sheltered from the heavens and from men the three poor sleeping children.

To understand what follows, we must remember that at that time the guardhouse of the Bastille was at the far end of the Square, and that what occurred near the elephant could neither be seen nor heard by the sentinel.

Toward the end of the hour that immediately precedes daybreak, a man turned out of the Rue Saint-Antoine, running, crossed the Square, rounded the great enclosure of the July Column, and slipped between the slats and under the belly of the elephant. Had any light whatever shone on this man, from his thoroughly wet clothing, one would have guessed he had spent the night in the rain. When under the elephant, he let out a strange call belonging to no human language and which a parrot alone could reproduce. He twice repeated this call, of which the following gives only an imperfect idea: "Kirikikiou!"

At the second call, a clear, cheerful young voice answered from the belly of the elephant, "Yes!"

Almost immediately the board that closed the hole moved away, and let out a child, who slid along the elephant's leg and dropped lightly near the man. It was Gavroche. The man was Montparnasse.

As for this call *kirikikiou*, it was undoubtedly what the child meant by "Ask for Monsieur Gavroche."

On hearing it, he woke with a start, crawled out of his "alcove," separating the netting a little, which he afterward carefully closed again, then he had opened the trap and went down.

The man and the child recognized each other silently in the dark; Montparnasse merely said, "We need you. Come give us a hand."

The gamin did not ask for any other explanation.

"Here I am," he said.

And they both headed for the Rue Saint-Antoine, which Montparnasse had just left, winding their way rapidly through the long file of wagons that go down at that time toward the markets.

The market gardeners, crouching among the salads and vegetables, half asleep, buried up to the eyes in the hoods of their wagons on account of the driving rain, did not even notice these strange pedestrians.

III

THE FORTUNES AND MISFORTUNES OF ESCAPE

What had taken place that same night at La Force was this:

An escape had been concocted between Babet, Brujon, Gueulemer, and Thénardier, though Thénardier was in solitary. Babet had done the job for himself during the day, as we know from Montparnasse's account to Gavroche. Montparnasse was to help them from outside.

Having spent a month in a punishment cell, Brujon had had time, first to braid a rope, secondly, to perfect a plan. Formerly these harsh cells in which the discipline of the prison leaves the condemned to himself were composed of four stone walls, a ceiling of stone, a pavement of tiles, a camp bed, a grated air-hole, a double iron door, and were called "dungeons"; but the dungeon has been thought too horrible; now it is composed of an iron door, a grated air-hole, a camp bed, a pavement of tiles, a ceiling of stone, four stone walls, and it is called "punishment cell." There is a little light in them around noon. The inconvenience of these cells, which, as we see, are not dungeons, is that they allow beings to reflect, who should be made to work.

So Brujon had reflected, and he had gotten out of the punishment cell with a rope. As he was reputed very dangerous in the Cour Charlemagne, he was put into the Bâtiment Neuf. The first thing he found in the Bâtiment Neuf was Gueulemer, the second was a nail; Gueulemer, that is to say crime, a nail, that is to say liberty.

Brujon, of whom the time has come to give a full description, was, with an appearance of delicate complexion and a profoundly premeditated languor, a polished, gallant, intelligent robber, with an enticing look and an atrocious smile. His look was a result of his will and his smile of his nature. His first studies in his art were directed toward roofs; he had made great improvements in the business of the lead strippers who plunder roofing and skin eave gutters by the process called "the double fat."

What made the moment particularly favorable for an escape attempt, was that at that very time some workmen were taking off and relaying part of the prison's slate roofing. The Cour Saint-Bernard was not entirely isolated from the Cour Charlemagne and the Cour Saint-Louis. There were scaffoldings and ladders aloft; in other words, bridges and stairways leading to deliverance.

Bâtiment-Neuf, the most decrepit affair in the world, was the weak point of the prison. The walls were so much corroded by saltpeter that they had been obliged to put a wood facing over the arches of the dormitories, because the stones came loose and fell onto the prisoners' beds.

Notwithstanding this decay, the blunder was committed of shutting up in the Bâtiment-Neuf the most dangerous of the accused, of putting the "hardened criminals" in there, as they say in prison language.

The Bâtiment-Neuf contained four dormitories, one above the other, and an attic called the Bel-Air. A large chimney, probably of some ancient kitchen of the Ducs de La Force, started from the ground floor, passed through the four stories, cutting in two all the dormitories, where it appeared as a kind of flattened pillar, and went out through the roof.

Gueulemer and Brujon were in the same dormitory. As a precaution, they had been put on the lower floor. It happened that the heads of their beds rested against the chimney flue.

Thénardier was right above them in the attic known as the Bel-Air.

The pedestrian who stops in the Rue Culture-Sainte-Catherine beyond the barracks of the firemen, in front of the carriage gate of the bathhouse, sees a yard full of flowers and shrubs in boxes, at whose far end is a little white rotunda with two wings enlivened by green blinds, the bucolic dream of Jean-Jacques. Not more than ten years ago, above this rotunda rose a black wall, enormous, hideous, and bare, against which it was built. This was the encircling wall of La Force.

This wall, behind the rotunda, was Milton seen behind Berquin.

High as it was, this wall was topped by a still blacker roof which could be seen beyond. This was the roof of the Bâtiment-Neuf. You noticed in it four dormer windows with gratings; these were the windows of the Bel-Air. A chimney pierced the roof, the chimney that passed through the dormitories.

The Bel-Air, this attic of the Bâtiment-Neuf, was a kind of large garret hall, secured with triple gratings and double sheet iron doors studded with monstrous nails. Entering at the north end, you had on your left the four windows, and on your right, opposite the windows, four large square cages, with spaces between, separated by narrow passages, built breast-high of masonry with iron bars to the roof.

Thénardier had been in solitary in one of these cages since the night of February 3. Nobody has ever discovered how, or by what contrivance, he had succeeded in procuring and hiding a bottle of that wine invented, it is said, by Desrues, with which a narcotic is mixed, and which the band of the *Endormeurs* has made famous.

In many prisons there are perfidious employees, half jailers and half thieves, who aid in escapes, who sell a treacherous servility to the police, and make a little on the side.

On this same night, then, on which little Gavroche had picked up the two wandering children, Brujon and Gueulemer, knowing that Babet, who had escaped that very morning, was waiting for them in the street as well as Montparnasse, got up softly and began to pierce the flue of the chimney touching their beds with the nail Brujon had found. The fragments fell onto Brujon's bed, so nobody heard them. The hailstorm and the thunder shook the doors on their hinges and made a frightful and convenient uproar in the prison. Those of the prisoners who woke up pretended to go back to sleep again and left Gueulemer and Brujon alone. Brujon was adroit; Gueulemer was vigorous. Before any sound had reached the watchman, who was lying in the grated cell with a window opening into the sleeping room, the wall was pierced, the chimney scaled, the iron trellis that closed the upper opening of the flue forced, and the two formidable bandits were on the roof. The rain and wind increased, the roof was slippery.

"What a good *sorgue* for a *crampe,*"[1] said Brujon.

A gulf six feet wide and eighty feet deep separated them from the parapet. At the bottom of this gulf they could see a sentinel's musket gleaming in the darkness. They fastened one end of the rope that Brujon had made in his cell to the stumps of the chimney bars they had just twisted off, threw the other end over the encircling wall, cleared the gulf at a bound, clung to the coping of the wall, swung their legs over it, let themselves one after the other slip down the rope onto a little roof adjoining the bathhouse, pulled down their rope, dropped into the bathhouse yard, crossed it, pushed open the porter's slide, pulled the cord hanging nearby, opened the carriage door, and were in the street.

It was not three quarters of an hour since they had

[1] What a good night for an escape. [V.H.]

stood up on their beds in the darkness, their nail in hand and their plan in their heads.

A few moments later, they had rejoined Babet and Montparnasse, who were prowling the neighborhood.

In pulling down their rope they had broken it, and there was a piece still fastened to the chimney on the roof. They had suffered no damage beyond having pretty thoroughly skinned their hands.

That night Thénardier had received a tip—it never could be ascertained how—and did not go to sleep.

About one in the morning, the night being very dark, he saw two shadows going by on the roof, in the rain and the raging wind, in front of the window opposite his cage. One stopped at the window long enough for a look. It was Brujon. Thénardier recognized him and understood. That was enough for him.

Thénardier, described as an assassin, and detained under the charge of setting an ambush by night with force and arms, was kept in constant sight. A sentry, who was relieved every two hours, marched with loaded gun past his cage. The Bel-Air was lit by a reflector. The prisoner had irons on his feet weighing fifty pounds. Every afternoon at four, a warden, escorted by two dogs—this was customary at that period—entered his cage, laid down near his bed a two-pound loaf of black bread, a jug of water, and a dish full of very thin soup with a few beans afloat in it, examined his irons, and struck against the bars. This man, with his dogs, returned twice in the night.

Thénardier had obtained permission to keep a kind of iron spike, which he used to nail his bread into a crack in the wall, "in order," he said, "to keep it from the rats." As Thénardier was under constant surveillance, they anticipated no difficulty from this spike. However, it was remembered afterward that a warden had said, "It would be better to just let him have a wooden pike."

At two in the morning, the sentry, who was an old soldier, was relieved, and his place was taken by a new recruit. A few moments later, the man with the dogs made his visit and went away without noticing anything, except the extreme youth and the "peasant look" of the "greenhorn." Two hours later, at four, when they came to relieve the conscript, they found him asleep, lying on the ground like a log near Thénardier's cage. As for Thénardier, he was not there. His broken irons were on the floor. There was a hole in the ceiling of his cage, and above that, another hole in the roof. A board had been torn off his bed, and undoubtedly carried off, as it was not found again. There was also seized in the cell a half-empty bottle, containing the rest of the drugged wine that had put the soldier to sleep. The soldier's bayonet had disappeared.

At the time of this discovery, it was supposed that Thénardier was well out of all reach. The reality is that he was no longer in the Bâtiment-Neuf, but was still in great danger.

On reaching the roof of the Bâtiment-Neuf, Thénardier found the remnant of Brujon's cord hanging from the bars of the upper trap of the chimney, but this broken end being much too short, he was unable to escape over the sentry's path, as Brujon and Gueulemer had done.

Turning from the Rue des Ballets into the Rue du Roi-de-Sicile, on the right you almost immediately encounter a dirty indentation. In the last century a house stood there, of which only the rear wall remains, a genuine wall of ruins that rises to the height of the third story among the neighboring buildings. This ruin is recognizable by two large square windows that are still visible; the one in the middle, nearer the right gable, is crossed by a worm-eaten joist fitted like a cap-piece for a shoring. Through these windows could formerly be glimpsed a dreary, high wall, a part of the battlement wall of La Force.

The void that the demolished house left on the street is half filled by a palisade fence of rotten boards, supported by five stone posts. Hidden in this enclosure is a little shanty built against the part of the ruin that remains standing. The fence has a gate, which a few years ago was fastened by only a latch.

Thénardier was on the crest of this ruin a little after three in the morning.

How had he gotten there? Nobody has ever been able to explain or understand. The lightning must have both confused and helped him. Did he use the ladders and the scaffoldings of the roofers to get from roof to roof, enclosure to enclosure, compartment to compartment, to the buildings of the Cour Charlemagne, then the buildings of the Cour Saint-Louis, the encircling wall, and from there to the ruin on the Rue du Roi-de-Sicile? But there were gaps in this route that would seem to make it impossible.

Did he lay down the plank from his bed as a bridge from the roof of the Bel-Air to the encircling wall, and did he crawl on his belly along the coping of the wall, all around the prison as far as the ruin? But the battlement wall of La Force followed a crenelated and uneven line, it rose and fell, it sank down at the barracks of the firemen, it rose at the bathhouse, it was cut by buildings, it was not of the same height on the Hotel Lamoignon as on the Rue Pavée, it had slopes and right angles everywhere; and then the sentries would have seen the dark outline of the fugitive; for these considerations too, the route taken by Thénardier is still almost inexplicable. Either way, an impossible flight. Had Thénardier, illuminated by that fearful thirst for liberty that changes precipices into ditches, iron gratings into caned screens, a cripple into an athlete, an old gimpy into a bird, stupidity into instinct, instinct into intelligence, and intelligence into genius, had Thénardier invented and improvised a third method? It has never been known.

One cannot always grasp the marvels of escape. The man escaping, let us repeat, is inspired; there is something of star and lightning in the mysterious gleam of flight; the effort toward liberation is no less surprising than the flight toward the sublime; and we say of an escaped robber, How did he manage to scale that roof? Just as it is said of Corneille, Where did he learn *that he would die?*

However this may be, dripping with sweat, soaked through by the rain, his clothes in shreds, his hands skinned, his elbows bleeding, his knees torn, Thénardier had reached what children, in their figurative language, call the cut of the ruin wall, he had stretched himself out on it at full length, and there his strength failed him. A steep escarpment, three stories high, separated him from the pavement of the street.

The rope he had was too short.

He was waiting there, pale, exhausted, having lost all the hope he had had, still covered by night, but saying to himself that day was just about to dawn, dismayed at the idea of hearing in a few moments the neighboring clock of Saint-Paul strike four, the hour when they would come to relieve the sentry and would find him asleep under the open roof, and find him too, staring humbly through the fearful depth, by the glimmer of the lamps, at the damp and black pavement, that longed-for yet terrible pavement that meant death or liberty.

He wondered whether his three accomplices in escape had succeeded, if they had heard him, and if they would come to his aid. He listened. Except for a patrolman, nobody had passed through the street since he had been there. Nearly all the farmers driving down from Montreuil, Charonne, Vincennes, and Bercy to Les Halles go through the Rue Saint-Antoine.

The clock struck four. Thénardier shuddered. A few moments later, that wild and confused noise that follows the discovery of an escape broke out in the prison. The sounds of doors opening and shutting, the squeak of grates on their hinges, the tumult in the guardhouse, the harsh calls of the gatekeepers, the sound of the musket butts on the pavement of the courtyards reached him. Lights moved up and down in the grated windows of the dormitories, a torch ran along the attic of the Bâtiment-Neuf, the firemen of the barracks alongside had been called. Their helmets, which the torches lit up in the rain, were going to and fro along the roofs. At the same time Thénardier saw toward the Bastille a whitish cloud throwing a dismal pallor over the lower part of the sky.

He was on the top of a wall ten inches wide, stretched out beneath the storm, with two precipices, to the right and left, unable to stir, giddy at the prospect of falling, and horrified at the certain prospect of arrest, and his thoughts, like the pendulum of a clock, went back and forth from one of these ideas to the other: "Dead if I fall, taken if I stay."

In this anguish, he suddenly saw, the street being still wrapped in obscurity, a man gliding along the walls, and coming from the direction of the Rue Pavée, stop in the indentation above which Thénardier was suspended. This man was joined by a second, who was walking with the same precaution, then by a third, then by a fourth. When these men were together, one of them lifted the latch of the gate in the fence, and they all four entered the enclosure of the shanty. They were right under Thénardier. These men had evidently selected this recess so as to be able to talk without being seen by passersby or by the sentry who guards the gate of La Force a few steps beyond. It must also be stated that the rain kept this sentinel in his sentry box. Thénardier, not being able to distinguish their faces, listened to their words with the desperate attention of a wretch who feels he is lost.

Something resembling hope passed across Thénardier's eyes; these men were talking argot.

The first said, in a low voice, but distinctly, "*Décarrons*. Why're we *maquillons icigo?*"[1]

The second answered, "*Il lansquine* enough to put out the *riffe* of the *rabouin*. And then the *coqueurs* are all around, there's a *grivier* carrying a *gaffe,* shall we let them *emballer* us *icicaille?*"[2]

These are two words, *icigo* and *icicaille,* both meaning *ici* [here] and belonging, the first to the argot of the city gates, the second to the argot of the Temple, were glimmers of light to Thénardier. By *icigo* he recognized Brujon, who was a prowler of the city gates, and by *icicaille* Babet, who, among all his other trades, had been a secondhand dealer at the Temple.

The old argot from the golden age of Louis XIV is now spoken only at the Temple, and Babet was the only one there who spoke it quite purely. Without *icicaille,* Thénardier would not have recognized him, for he had entirely disguised his voice.

Meanwhile the third put in a word: "No emergency yet, let's wait a little. How do we know he doesn't need our help?"

By this, which was only French, Thénardier recognized Montparnasse, whose elegance consisted in understanding all argots and speaking none.

As to the fourth, he was silent, but his huge shoulders gave him away. Thénardier had no doubts. It was Gueulemer.

Brujon replied almost impetuously, but still in a low voice, "What's this you *bonnez* us? The *tapissier* couldn't draw his *crampe*. He don't even know the *trus! Bouliner* his *limace* and *faucher* his *empaffes, maquiller* a *tortouse, caler boulins* in the *lourdes, braser* the *taffes, maquiller caroubles, faucher* the Bards, drop his *tor-*

[1] Let's go, what're we doing here? (V.H.)

[2] It's raining enough to put out the devil's fire. And then the police are all around. There's a soldier standing guard. Are we going to let them pick us up here? (V.H.)

touse, panquer himself, *camoufler,* one must be a *mariol!* That old man couldn't do it, he don't know how to *goupiner!*"[1]

Babet added, still in that prudent, classic argot spoken by Poulailler and Cartouche, which is to the bold, new, strongly colored, and risqué argot Brujon used, what the language of Racine is to the language of André Chénier, "Your *orgue tapissier* must have been *marroné* on the stairs. You have to be *arcasien*. He's a *galifard*. He's been played the *harnache* by a *roussin,* or even a *roussi,* who's beaten him *comtois*. Use your *oche,* Montparnasse, d'you hear those *criblements* in the *collège?* You've seen all the *camoufles*. He's *tombé,* come on! He's gotta be left to his twenty *longes*. I have no *taf,* I'm no *taffeur,* that's *colombé,* but there is nothing more but to make the *lezards,* or they'll make us *gambiller* for it. Don't *renauder,* come with *nousiergue*. Let's go *picter* a *rouillarde encible*."[2]

"You don't leave friends in difficulty," muttered Montparnasse.

"I *bonnis* you he's *malade,*" replied Brujon. "At the moment, the *tapissier* isn't worth a *broque!* We can't do a thing. *Décarrons*. Every moment I expect a *cogne* to *cintrer* me in *pogne!*"[3]

Montparnasse still resisted, but feebly; the truth is, these four men, with that loyalty criminals show in never abandoning each other, had been prowling all night around La Force at whatever risk, in hope of seeing

[1] What's this you're telling us? The innkeeper couldn't give the slip. He don't even know the trade! Tear up his shirt and cut up his sheets for rope, make holes in the doors, forge papers, make keys, cut his irons, hang his rope, hide, disguise himself, you gotta be a devil! That old man couldn't do it, he don't know how. (V.H.)

[2] Your innkeeper must've been nabbed in the act. You gotta be a devil. He's an apprentice. He's been duped by a stool pigeon, or even a sheep, who got him to talk. Listen, Montparnasse, d'you hear those cries in the prison? You've seen all those lights. They've got him, come on! He's gotta be left to his twenty years. I have no fear, I'm no coward, that's known, but there's nothing more to be done, or otherwise they'll make us dance. Don't be angry, come with us. Let's go drink a bottle of old wine together. (V. H.)

[3] I tell you he's nabbed. At this moment, the innkeeper isn't worth a penny. We can't do a thing. Let's go. Anytime now, I expect a cop to grab me. (V. H.)

Thénardier rise above some wall. But the night, which was really becoming too light, storming enough to keep all the streets empty, the growing cold, their soaked clothing, their inadequate shoes, the alarming uproar that had just broken out in the prison, the passing hours, the patrolmen they had met, fleeting hope, fear returning, all this impelled them to retreat. Montparnasse himself, who was, perhaps, to some slight extent a son-in-law of Thénardier, yielded. A moment more, and they would be gone. Thénardier gasped on his wall like the shipwrecked sailors of the *Medusa* on their raft when they saw the ship that had appeared vanish over the horizon.

He did not dare call them, a cry overheard might destroy everything; he had an idea, a final one, a flash of light; he took out of his pocket the end of Brujon's rope, which he had detached from the chimney of the Bâtiment Neuf, and threw it into the enclosure.

The rope fell at their feet.

"A widow!"[1] said Babet.

"My *tortouse!*"[2] said Brujon.

"There's the innkeeper," said Montparnasse.

They looked up. Thénardier inched his head out.

"Quick!" said Montparnasse, "do you have the other end of the rope, Brujon?"

"Yes."

"Tie the two ends together, we'll throw him the rope, he'll fasten it to the wall, he'll have enough to get down."

Thénardier ventured to speak: "I'm numb."

"We'll warm you."

"I can't move."

"Slide down, we'll catch you."

"My hands are stiff."

"Just tie the rope to the wall."

"I can't."

"One of us has to get up there," said Montparnasse.

"Three stories!" said Brujon.

An old plaster flue for a stove that had formerly been used in the shanty crept along the wall, rising almost to the spot where they saw Thénardier. This flue, then very cracked and full of seams, has since fallen, but its traces can still be seen. It was very narrow.

[1] A rope (argot of the Temple). (V. H.)

[2] My rope (argot of the Barrières). (V. H.)

"We could get up by that," said Montparnasse.

"By that flue!" exclaimed Babet, "an *orgue*,[1] never! It would take a *mion*."[2]

"It would take a *môme*,"[3] added Brujon.

"Where can we find a brat?" said Gueulemer.

"Wait," said Montparnasse, "I've got the answer."

He softly opened the gate in the fence, made sure nobody was passing in the street, went out carefully, shut the door behind him, and started at a run toward the Bastille.

Seven or eight minutes elapsed, seven or eight thousand centuries to Thénardier; Babet, Brujon, and Gueulemer kept their teeth clenched; at last the door opened again, and Montparnasse appeared, out of breath, with Gavroche. The rain still kept the street entirely empty.

Little Gavroche entered the enclosure and calmly looked at these cutthroats. The water was dripping from his hair. Gueulemer spoke to him, "Brat, are you a man?"

Gavroche shrugged and answered, "A *môme* like *mézig* is an *orgue*, and *orgues* like *vousailles* are *mômes*."[4]

"How the *mion* plays with the spittoon!"[5] exclaimed Babet.

"The *môme pantinois* isn't *maquillé* of *fertille lansquinée*,"[6] added Brujon.

"What do you want?" said Gavroche.

Montparnasse answered, "To climb up this flue."

"With this widow,"[7] said Babet.

"And *ligoter* the *tortouse*,"[8] continued Brujon.

"To the *monté* of the *montant*"[9] resumed Babet.

"To the *pieu* of the *vanterne*,"[10] added Brujon.

"And then?" said Gavroche.

[1] A man. (V. H.)
[2] A child (argot of the Temple). (V. H.)
[3] A child (argot of the Barrières). (V. H.)
[4] A kid like me is a man, and men like you are kids. (V. H.)
[5] The kid's tongue is well-hinged! (V. H.)
[6] The Parisian child isn't made of wet straw. (V. H.)
[7] This rope. (V. H.)
[8] Fasten the rope. (V. H.)
[9] To the top of the wall. (V. H.)
[10] To the cross bar of the window. (V. H.)

"That's all!" said Gueulemer.

The *gamin* examined the rope, the flue, the wall, the windows, and made that inexpressible and disdainful sound with the lips that signifies, "That's all?"

"There's a man up there we want you to save," replied Montparnasse.

"Will you?" added Brujon.

"Ass!" answered the child, as if the question seemed absurd; and he took off his shoes.

Gueulemer caught up Gavroche with one hand, put him on the roof of the shanty, whose wormeaten boards bent beneath the child's weight, and handed him the rope that Brujon had tied together during Montparnasse's absence. The *gamin* went toward the flue, which was easy to enter, thanks to a large hole at the roof level. Just as he was about to start, Thénardier, who saw safety and life approaching, bent over the edge of the wall; the first gleam of day lit up his forehead running with sweat, his livid cheeks, his thin savage nose, his gray bristly beard, and Gavroche recognized him.

"Wait a minute!" he said, "that's my father!—Well, never mind!"

And taking the rope in his teeth, he resolutely began the ascent.

He reached the top of the ruin, straddled the old wall like a horse, and tied the rope firmly to the upper crossbar of the window.

A moment later Thénardier was in the street.

As soon as he had touched the pavement, as soon as he felt himself out of danger, he was no longer either fatigued, benumbed, or trembling; the terrible things he had undergone vanished like a whiff of smoke, all that strange and ferocious intellect awoke, and found itself bristling and free, ready to march on. The man's first words were these: "Now, who're we going to eat?"

It is needless to explain the meaning of this frightfully transparent word, which signifies all together to kill, assassinate, and plunder. *Eat,* real meaning: *devour*.

"First, let's hide," said Brujon, "wind it up in three words and we'll separate immediately. There was an affair with some promise in the Rue Plumet, a deserted street, an isolated house, an old rusty gate onto a garden, some lone women."

"Well, why not?" inquired Thénardier.

"Your *fée*[1] Eponine went to see it," answered Babet.

"And she brought a biscuit to Magnon," added Gueulemer, "nothing to *maquiller* there."[2]

"The *fée* isn't *loffe*,"[3] said Thénardier. "Still we'll have to see."

"Yes, yes," said Brujon, "we'll have to see."

Meanwhile none of these men seemed to notice Gavroche, who, during this colloquy, had seated himself on one of the stone supports of the fence; he waited a few minutes, perhaps for his father to turn toward him, then put on his shoes, and said, "It's all over? You have no more use for me? Men! You are out of trouble. I'm off. I've got to go and get my *mômes* up."

And he left.

The five men went out of the enclosure one after another.

When Gavroche had disappeared at the turn of the Rue des Ballets, Babet took Thénardier aside.

"Did you notice that *mion?*" he asked him.

"What *mion?*"

"The *mion* who climbed the wall and brought you the rope."

"Not much."

"Well, I don't know, but it seems to me it's your son."

"What?" said Thénardier. "You think so?"

And he left.

[1] Your daughter. (V. H.)
[2] Nothing doing there. (V. H.)
[3] Stupid. (V. H.)

Book Seven

ARGOT

I

ORIGIN

Pigritia is a terrible word.

It engenders a world: *la pègre,* read robbery, and a hell; *la pègrenne,* read hunger.

So idleness is a mother.

She has a son, robbery, and a daughter, hunger.

Where are we now? In argot.

What is argot? It is at the same time the nation and the idiom, it is robbery under its two aspects: people and language.

Thirty-four years ago, the narrator of this grave and gloomy story introduced into a work written with the same aim as the present one,[1] a robber who talked argot, and there was amazement and shock. "What! Argot! But argot is hideous! Why, it's the language of convicts, of the galleys, of prison, of all that is most abominable in society!" etc., etc., etc.

We never understood this sort of objection.

Since then two powerful novelists, one of whom is a profound observer of the human heart, the other an intrepid friend of the people, Balzac and Eugène Sue, having made bandits talk in their natural tongue as the author of *Le dernier jour d'un condamné* had done in 1828, the same outcry was made. It was repeated: "What do these

[1] *Le dernier jour d'un condamné, Last Day of a Condemned Man.*

writers mean by this revolting patois? Argot is appalling! Argot makes us shudder!

Who would deny it?

Where the purpose is to probe a wound, an abyss, or a society, since when has it been a crime to descend too far, to plumb it to the bottom? We had always thought it was sometimes an act of courage, and at the very least a simple and useful act, worthy of the sympathetic attention merited by a duty accepted and accomplished. Not explore the whole, not study the whole, stop halfway, why? To stop is the job of the plumb and not of the sounder.

Certainly, to go to the lowest depths of the social order, where the earth ends and the mire begins, to search in those thick waters, to pursue, seize, and cast up still throbbing onto the pavement this abject idiom streaming with filth as it is dredged up into the light this way, this pustulous vocabulary in which each word seems a huge ring from some monster of the slime and darkness, is neither an attractive nor an easy task. Nothing is gloomier than contemplating the teeming horror of argot, thus bared by the light of thought. It seems, in fact, like a species of horrible beast made for the night, just wrenched out of its cesspool. We seem to be seeing a frightful living and bristling underbrush that trembles, moves, quivers, demands its darkness again, threatens, and stares. This word is like a fang, that one a quenched and bleeding eye; this phrase seems to move like the claw of a crab. All of it is alive with the hideous vitality of things organized in disorganization.

Now, since when has horror excluded study? Since when has the sickness driven away the physician? Imagine a naturalist who refused to study the viper, the bat, the scorpion, the scolopendra, the tarantula, and who cast them back into their darkness, saying: Oh! how ugly they are! The thinker who turned away from argot would be like a surgeon who turned away from an ulcer or a wart. He would be a philologist hesitating to examine a fact of language, a philosopher hesitating to scrutinize a fact of humanity. For, it must certainly be said to those who do not know it, argot is both a literary phenomenon and a social result. What is argot, properly speaking? Argot is the language of misery.

Here we may be stopped; facts may be generalized,

which is sometimes a method of extenuating them; it may be said that all trades, all professions—one might almost add all the accidents of the social hierarchy and all forms of the intellect—have their argot. The merchant who says: *Available Montpellier, fine-quality Marseilles,* the stockbroker who says: *Seller sixty, dividend off,* the gambler who says: *I'll see you a ten better, spades are trump,* the huissier of the Norman Isles who says: *The enfeoffor restricted to his lands cannot claim the fruits of these grounds during the heritable seizure of the renouncer's fixtures,* the actor who says: *We laid an egg,* the whale hunter who says: *There she blows, there she breaches,* the phrenologist who says: *Amativeness, combativeness, secretiveness,* the fencing master who says: *Tierce, quartre, retreat,* the typesetter who says: *A piece of pie,* everyone, typesetter, fencing master, phrenologist, whale hunter, actor, gambler, stockbroker, merchant, speaks argot. The cobbler who says: *my kid,* the shopkeeper who says: *my counter-jumper,* the barber who says: *my clerk,* the printer who says: *my devil,* speak argot. In strictness, and if we will be absolute, all the various methods of saying right and left, the sailor's *port* and *starboard,* the stagehand's *court side* and *garden side,* the beadle's *Epistle side* and *Gospel side,* are argot. There is an argot of the affected as there was the argot of the *Précieuses.* The Hôtel de Rambouillet bordered to some extent on the Cour des Miracles. There is an argot of duchesses, witness this phrase written in a love letter by a very great lady and a very pretty woman of the Restoration: *You will find in these postings a mobitude of rations why I should libertize.*[1] Diplomatic ciphers are argot; the Pontifical Chancellory, in saying 26 for *Rome, grkztntgzyal* for *packet,* and *abfxustgrnogrkzu tu* xi for *Duke of Modena,* is speaking argot. The physicians of the Middle Ages who, to say carrot, radish, and turnip, said: *opoponach, perfroschinum, reptitalmus, dracatholicum angelorum, postmegorum,* spoke argot. The sugar manufacturer who says: *Rectified, loaf, clarified, crushed, lump, molasses, mixed common, burned, caked,* this honest manufacturer talks argot. A certain critical school of twenty years ago which said: *Half of Shakespeare is*

[1] You will find in this gossip a multitude of reasons why I should be so bold. (V. H.)

plays on words and puns spoke argot. The poet and the artist who, with deep significance, described M. de Montmorency as "bourgeois," if he is not familiar with poetry and statues, speak argot. The classical scholar who calls flowers *Flora,* fruits *Pomona,* the sea *Neptune,* love *the fires,* beauty *the attractions,* a horse a *courser,* the white or the tricolored cockade *the rose of Bellona,* the three-cornered hat *the triangle of Mars,* the classical scholar speaks argot. Algebra, medicine, botany, have their argot. The wonderful language of seafaring, so complete and picturesque, spoken by Jean Bart, Duquesne, Suffren, and Duperré, which mingles with the whistling in the rigging, with the sound of the loudspeaking trumpet, with the clash of the boarding-ax, with the rolling, with the wind, with the squall, with the cannon, is all a heroic and splendid argot which is to the savage argot of crime what the lion is to the jackal.

No doubt. But, whatever may be said about it, not everyone will agree with this understanding of the word "argot." As for us, we continue to apply to this word its old acceptation, precise, circumscribed, and definite and we limit argot to argot. The real argot, the argot *par excellence,* if these words can be joined, the immemorial argot, which was a realm, is nothing more nor less, we repeat, than the ugly, restless, sly, treacherous, venomous, cruel, crooked, vile, deep, deadly language of misery. At the extremity of all debasements and all misfortunes, there is an ultimate misery that revolts and determines to enter into a struggle against the whole mass of fortunate things and reigning rights; a hideous struggle in which, sometimes by fraud, sometimes by force, sickly and fierce alike, it attacks social order with pinpricks through vice and club strokes through crime. For the needs of this struggle, misery has invented a language of combat, which is argot.

To buoy up and sustain above oblivion, above the abyss, a mere fragment of any language whatsoever that man has spoken and would otherwise be lost, that is to say one of the elements, good or evil, of which civilization is composed or with which it is involved, is to extend the data of social observation; it is to serve civilization itself. This service Plautus rendered, intentionally or unintentionally, by making two Carthaginian soldiers speak Phoenician; this service Molière rendered by making so many of his personages speak Levantine and all manner of patois. Here objections arise again: the Phoenician, perfectly right! The Levantine, well and good! Even patois, so be it! These are languages that have belonged to nations or provinces; but argot? What is the use of preserving argot? What is the use of "buoying up" argot?

For this we have a brief answer. Certainly, if the language that a nation or a province has spoken is worthy of interest, there is something still more worthy of attention and study in the language that misery has spoken.

It is the language spoken in France, for example, for more than four centuries, not merely by a particular form of misery, but by misery, every possible human misery.

And then, we insist, the study of social deformities and infirmities and attention drawn to them in order to cure them, is not a work in which choice is permissible. The historian of morals and ideas had a mission no less austere than that of the historian of events. The latter has the surface of civilization, the struggles of the crowns, the births of princes, the marriages of kings, the battles, the assemblies, the great public men, the revolutions in the sunlight, all the exterior; the other historian has the interior, the foundation, the people who work, who suffer, and who wait, overburdened woman, agonizing childhood, the secret wars of man against man, the obscure ferocities, the prejudices, the established iniquities, the subterranean reactions of the law, the secret evolutions of souls, the vague shudderings of the multitudes, the starvation, the barefoot, the bare-armed, the disinherited, the orphans, the unfortunate and the infamous, all the specters that wander in darkness. He must descend with a heart filled with charity and severity, as a brother and as a judge, to those impenetrable pillboxes and the confused groveling, to those who bleed and those who strike, those who weep and those who curse, those who fast and those who devour, those who suffer wrong and those who commit it. Have these historians of hearts and souls lesser duties than the historians of exterior facts? Do you think that Dante has fewer things to say than Machiavelli? Is the underworld of civilization, because it is deeper and gloomier, less important than the upper? Do we really know the mountain when we do not know the cavern?

However, we must say in passing that, from some

words of what precedes, a decided separation between the two classes of historians might be inferred, which does not exist in our mind. No man is a good historian of the open, visible, signal, and public life of the nations, if he is not, at the same time to a certain extent the historian of their deeper and hidden life; and no man is a good historian of the interior if he does not know how to be, whenever there is need, the historian of the exterior. The history of morals and ideas penetrates the history of events, and vice versa. They are two orders of different facts that answer to each other, that are always linked together and often produce each other. All the lineaments that Providence traces on the surface of a nation have their dark but distinct parallels underneath, and all the convulsions of the underside produce upheavals at the surface. Since true history deals with everything, the true historian deals with everything.

Man is not a circle with a single center; he is an ellipse with two focii. Facts are one, ideas are the other.

Argot is nothing more nor less than a wardrobe in which language, having some bad deed to do, disguises itself. It puts on word-masks and metaphoric rags.

In this way it becomes horrible.

We can hardly recognize it. Is it really the French tongue, the great human tongue? There it is, ready to enter on the scene and give the cue to crime, and fitted for all the uses of the repertory of evil. It no longer walks, it hobbles; it limps on the crutch of the Cour des Miracles, a crutch that can be metamorphosed into a club; it gives itself the name of vagrancy; all the specters, its valets, have sullied it; it drags itself along and rears its head, the two characteristics of the reptile. It is apt for all roles, made squint-eyed by the forger, verdigrised by the poisoner, charcoaled by the incendiary's soot, and the murderer applies his red.

When we listen, on the side of honest people, at the door of society, we overhear the dialogue of those who are outside. We distinguish questions and answers. We notice, without understanding, a hideous murmur, sounding almost like human tones, but nearer a howling than speech. This is argot. The words are uncouth and marked by an indescribably fantastic bestiality. We think we hear hydras talking.

It is the unintelligible in the dark. It gnashes and it

whispers, completing twilight with enigma. It grows black in misfortune, it grows blacker still in crime; these two blacknesses amalgamated make Argot. Darkness in the atmosphere, darkness in the deeds, darkness in the voices. Appalling toad language, which comes and goes, hops, crawls, drivels, and moves monstrously in that boundless gray mist made up of rain, night, hunger, vice, lying, injustice, nakedness, asphyxia, and winter, the high noon of the miserable.

Let us have compassion for the chastened. Who, alas! are we ourselves? Who am I who speak to you? Who are you who listen to me? Whence do we come? And is it quite certain that we did nothing before we were born? The earth is not without resemblance to a jail. Who knows whether man is a prisoner of Divine Justice?

Look closely at life. It is so constituted that we feel punishment everywhere.

Are you what is called a lucky man? Well, you are sad every day. Each day has its great grief or its little care. Yesterday you were trembling for the health of one who is dear to you, today you fear for your own; tomorrow it will be an anxiety about money, the next day the slanders of a calumniator, the day after the misfortune of a friend; then the weather, then something broken or lost, then a pleasure for which you are reproached by your conscience or your vertebral column; another time, the course of public affairs. Not to mention heartaches. And so on. One cloud is dissipated, another gathers. Hardly one day in a hundred of unbroken joy and sunshine. And you are of that small number who are lucky! As for other men, stagnant night is upon them.

Thoughtful minds make little use of this expression: the happy and the unhappy. In this world, clearly the vestibule of another, no one is happy.

The true division of humanity is this: the luminous and the dark.

To diminish the number of the dark, to increase the number of the luminous, there is the aim. That is why we cry: education, knowledge! To learn to read is to kindle a fire; every syllable spelled sparkles.

But whoever says light does not necessarily say joy. There is suffering in the light; an excess burns. Flame is hostile to the wing. To burn and yet to fly, this is the miracle of genius.

When you know and when you love you will still suffer. The day dawns in tears. The luminous weep, be it only over the dark ones.

II

ROOTS

Argot is the language of the dark.

Thought is stimulated to its most somber depths, social philosophy is provoked to its most poignant meditations, in the presence of this enigmatic dialect, which is both withered and rebellious. Here there is visible chastisement. Each syllable looks branded. The words of the common language here appear as if wrinkled and shriveled under the red-hot iron of the executioner. Some seem to be still smoking. A phrase affects you like the branded shoulder of a robber suddenly laid bare. Ideas almost refuse to be expressed by these substantives condemned by justice. Its metaphor is sometimes so shameless we feel it has worn the iron collar.

Still, in spite of and because of all that, this strange dialect has a right to its compartment in that great impartial collection in which there is place for the rusty farthing as well as for the gold medal, and which is called literature. Argot, whether we consent to it or not, has its syntax and its poetry. It is a language. If, by the deformity of certain terms, we recognize that it was mumbled by Mandrin, by the splendor of certain metonomies, we feel that it was spoken by Villon.

This verse so exquisite and so famous:

Mais où sont les neiges d'antan?[1]

is a verse of argot. *Antan—ante annum*—is a word of the argot of Thunes, which signifies "the past year," and by extension "*formerly.*" There could still be read thirty-five years ago, at the time of the departure of the great chain in 1827, in one of the dungeons of Bicêtre, this

[1] But where are the snows of yesteryear? (V. H.)

maxim engraved on the wall with a nail by a king of Thunes condemned to prison: *Les dabs d'antan trimaient siempre pour la pierre du Cöesre.* Which means: "The kings of old always went to be consecrated." In the mind of that king, consecration was prison.

The word *decarade*, which expresses the departure of a heavy wagon at a gallop, is attributed to Villon, and it is worthy of him. This word, which strikes fire with four feet, resumes in a masterly onomatopoeia the whole of La Fontaine's admirable line:

Six forts chevaux tiraient un coche.[1]

From a purely literary point of view, few studies would be more curious and more fruitful than that of argot. It is a complete language within a language, a sort of diseased excrescence, a sickly graft that has produced a vegetation, a parasite that has its roots in the old Gallic trunk, whose sinister foliage creeps over an entire side of the language. This is what might be called the primary aspect, the vulgar aspect of argot. But to those who study language as it should be studied, that is to say as geologists study the earth, argot appears, as it were, a true alluvium. According to whether we dig more or less deeply, we find in argot, under the old popular French, either Provençal, Spanish, Italian, Levantine, that language of the Mediterranean ports, or English and German, Romance in its three varieties, French Romance, Italian Romance, Romance Romance, Latin, and finally Basque and Celtic. A deep and strange formation. A subterranean edifice built in common by all the miserable. Each accursed race has deposited its stratum, each suffering has dropped its stone, each heart has given its pebble. A multitude of evil, low, or embittered souls, who have passed through life and vanished into eternity, are preserved here almost entire and in some way still visible under the form of a monstrous word.

Look at Spanish. The old Gothic argot swarms with it. Here is *boffette*, blow, which comes from *bofeton; vantane*, window (afterward *vanterne*), which comes from *vantana; gat*, cat, which comes from *gato; acite*, oil,

[1] Six sturdy horses pulled a coach.

which comes from *aceyte*. Look at Italian. Here is *spade*, sword, which comes from *spada; carvel*, boat, which comes from *caravella*. Look at English. Here is *bichot*, bishop; *raille*, spy, which comes from *rascal, rapscallion; pilche*, box, which comes from *pilcher*, sheath. Look at German. Here is *caleur*, waiter, *kellner; hers*, master, *herzog* (duke). Look at Latin. Here is *frangir*, to break, *frangere; affurer*, to rob, *fur; cadène*, chain, *catena*. There is a word that appears in all the languages of the continent with a sort of mysterious power and authority, the word *magnus;* the Scotchman makes of it his *mac*, which designates the chief of the clan, Mac Farlane, Mac Callummore, the great Farlane, the great Callummore;[1] argot makes of it the *meck*, and afterwards, the *meg*, that is to say God. Look at Basque. Here is *gahisto*, the devil, which comes from *gaïztoa*, evil; *sorgabon*, a good night, which comes from *gabon*, good evening. Look at Celtic. Here is *blavin*, handkerchief, which comes from *blavet*, gushing water; *mènesse*, woman (in a bad sense), which comes from *meinec*, full of stones; *barant*, brook, from *baranton*, fountain; *goffeur*, locksmith, from *goff*, blacksmith; *guedouze*, death, which comes from *guenn-du*, white-black. Finally, look at history. Argot calls crowns *maltèses*, a reminiscence of the coins that circulated on the galleys of Malta.

Besides the philological origins we have just pointed out, argot has other still more natural roots, which spring, so to speak, from the mind of man itself.

First, the direct creation of words. In this lies the mystery of languages. To paint with words that have forms, we do not know how or why. This is the primitive foundation of all human language—what might be called the granite. Argot swarms with words of this variety, rootwords, made out of whole cloth, we do not know where or by whom, without etymology, without analogy, without derivation, solitary words, barbarous, sometimes hideous words, which have a singular power of expression, and which are all alive. The executioner, *taule;* the forest, *sabri;* fear, flight, *taf;* the lackey, *larbin;* the general, the préfet, the minister, *pharos;* the devil, *rabouin*. There

[1] It should, however, be observed that *mac* in Celtic means son. (V. H.)

is nothing stranger than these words, which mask and yet reveal. Some of them, *rabouin*, for example, are at the same time grotesque and terrible and produce the effect of a cyclopian grimace.

Secondly, metaphor. It is the peculiarity of a language, the object of which is to tell everything and conceal everything, to abound in figures. Metaphor is an enigma that offers itself as a refuge to the robber plotting a strike, to the prisoner planning an escape. No idiom is more metaphoric than argot, *to unscrew the coco,* to wring the neck; *to wind up,* to eat; *to be sheaved,* to be judged; *a rat,* a bread thief; *il lansquine,* it rains, an old and striking figure, that somehow carries its date with it, assimilating the long slanting lines of the rain with the thick and driving pikes of the lansquenets, or German foot soldiers, and which includes in a single word the popular metonomy, *it is raining pitchforks*. Sometimes, as argot passes from the first period to the second, words pass from the savage and primitive state to the metaphoric sense. The devil ceases to be *the rabouin* and becomes *the baker,* the one who fills the ovens. This is wittier, but less grand; something like Racine after Corneille, like Euripedes after Aeschylus. Certain phrases of argot which partake of both periods, with both the barbaric and the metaphorical character, are like phantasmagorias. *Les sorgueurs vont sollicer des gails à la lune* (the prowlers are going to steal some horses tonight). This sweeps past the mind like a flock of specters. We do not know what we are seeing.

Thirdly, expedience. Argot lives on the language. It uses it as it fancies, it takes from it by chance, and contents itself often, when the necessity arises, with summarily and grossly distorting it. Sometimes with common words thus deformed, and merged with words of pure argot, it forms picturesque expressions in which we feel the mixture of the two preceding elements, direct creation and metaphor: *Le cab jaspine, je marronne que la roulotte de Pantin trime dans la sabri,* the dog barks, I suspect that the Paris coach is going by in the woods. *Le dab est sinve, la dabuge est merloussière, la fée est bative,* the bourgeois is stupid, the bourgeoise is cunning, the daughter is pretty. Most commonly, in order to mislead listeners, argot contents itself with indiscriminately adding to all the words of the language a sort of ignoble tail, a suffix of *aille*, of *orgue*, of *iergue*, or of *uche*. Thus: *Vouziergue trouvaille bonorgue ce gigotmuche?*[1] Do you like this leg of mutton? A phrase addressed by Cartouche to a turnkey, to know whether the amount offered for an escape satisfied him. The suffix of *mar* was added fairly recently.

Being the idiom of corruption, argot is easily corrupted. Moreover, as it always seeks disguise as soon as it feels understood, it transforms itself. Unlike all other vegetation, every ray of light on it kills what it touches. Thus argot goes on decomposing and recomposing incessantly; an obscure and rapid process that never ceases. It changes more in ten years than the language in ten centuries. Thus the *larton*[2] becomes the *lartif;* the *gail*[3] becomes the *gaye;* the *fertanche*,[4] the *fertille;* the *momignard*, the *momacque;* the *fiques*,[5] the *frusques;* the *chique*,[6] the *égrugeoir;* the *colabre*,[7] the *colas*. The devil is first *gahisto*, then the *rabouin*, then the baker; the priest is the *ratichon*, then the boar; the dagger is the twenty-two, then the *surin*, then the *lingre;* police officers are *railles*, then *roussins*, then *rousses*, then lacing merchants, then *couqueurs*, then *cognes;* the executioner is the *Taule*, then *Charlot*, then the *atigeur*, then the *becquilard*. In the seventeenth century, to fight was *to take some tobacco;* in the nineteenth it is *to chaw the jaws*. Twenty different expressions have passed between these two extremes. Cartouche would be speaking Hebrew to Lacenaire. All the words of this language are in perpetual flight like the men who use them.

From time to time, however, and because of this very change, the ancient argot reappears and again becomes new. It has its headquarters where it is continuous. The temple preserves the argot of the seventeenth century; Bicêtre, when it was a prison, preserved the argot of Thunes. There one heard the suffix *anche* of the old Thuners. *Boyanches tu?*[8] (do you drink?) *Il croyanche*[9] (he

[1] *Trouvez-vous ce gigot bon?*
[2] Bread.
[3] Horse.
[4] Straw.
[5] Clothes.
[6] The church.
[7] The neck.
[8] *Bois-tu.*
[9] *Il croit.*

believes). But perpetual movement is the law, nonetheless.

If the philosopher succeeds in arresting for one moment, for the observer, this incessantly evaporating language, he falls into painful yet useful meditations. No study is more efficacious and more prolific in instruction. Not a metaphor, not an etymology of argot that does not contain its lesson. Among these men, *to beat* means *to feign;* they beat a sickness; craft is their strength.

To them the idea of man is inseparable from the idea of shade. The night is called *sorgue;* man, *orgue*. Man is a derivative of night.

They have acquired the habit of considering society as an atmosphere that kills them, as a fatal force, and they speak of their liberty as one would of his health. A man arrested is *sick;* a man condemned is *dead*.

What is most terrible to the prisoner entombed within the four stone walls is a sort of icy chastity; he calls the dungeon the *castus*. In this funereal place, life outside always appears at its most cheerful. The prisoner has irons on his feet; you might suppose he would be thinking that people walk with their feet? No, he is thinking that people dance with their feet; so, let him succeed in sawing through his irons, his first idea is that now he can dance, and he calls the saw a *fandango*. A *name* is a *center,* a deep assimilation. The thug has two heads, one that regulates his actions and controls him during his whole life, another that he has on his shoulders on the day of his death; he calls the head that counsels him to crime the *sorbonne,* and the head that expiates it the *tronche*. When a man has nothing but rags on his body and vice in his heart, when he has reached that double degradation, material as well as moral, that characterizes, in its two acceptations, the word "beggarly," he is ready for crime; he is like a well-whetted knife; he has two edges, his distress and his wickedness; so argot does not say "a tramp"; it says a *réguisé*. What is prison? A brazier of damnation, a Hell. The convict calls himself a *fagot*. Finally, what name do the malefactors give to the prison? *The college*. A whole penitentiary system might spring from this word.

The robber too has his cannon fodder, his material for plunder, you, me, whoever: the *pantre* (*pan,* everyone).

Would you like to know where most of the prison songs

originated, those refrains called in the special vocabulary the *lirlonfa?* Listen to this.

At the Châtelet de Paris there was a long, wide cellar, which was eight feet below the level of the Seine. It had neither windows nor ventilators, the only opening was the door; men could enter, but not air. For a ceiling the cellar had a stone arch, and for a floor, ten inches of mud. It had been paved with tiles, but, under the oozing of the waters, the pavement had rotted and broken up. Eight feet above the floor, a long massive beam crossed this vault from side to side; from this beam there hung, at intervals, chains three feet in length, and at the end of these chains there were iron collars. Men condemned to the galleys were put into this cellar until the day of their departure for Toulon. They were pushed under this beam, where each had his irons swinging in the darkness, waiting for him. The chains, those pendent arms, and the collars, those open hands, seized these wretches by the neck. They were riveted, and they were left there. The chain being too short, they could not lie down. They remained motionless in this cave, in this blackness, under this timber, almost hung, forced to monstrous exertions to reach their bread or their pitcher, the arch above their heads, the mud up to their knees, their excrement running down their legs, collapsing with fatigue, their hips and knees giving way, hanging by their hands to the chain to rest, unable to sleep except standing, and constantly woken up by the strangling of the collar: some did not wake up. In order to eat, they had to drag their bread, which was thrown into the mud, up the leg with a heel, to within reach of the hand. How long did they stay this way? A month, two months, six months sometimes; one remained a year. It was the antechamber to the galleys. Men were put there for stealing a hare from the king. In this hell-sepulcher what did they do? What can be done in a sepulcher? They died. What can be done in a hell? They sang. For where there is no more hope, song remains. In the waters near Malta, when a galley was approaching, the song was heard before the oars. The poor poacher Survincent, who had passed through the cellar-prison of the Châtelet, said "It was the rhymes that sustained me." Uselessness of poetry. What is the use of rhyme? In this cellar almost all the argot songs were born. It is from the dungeon of the Grand Châtelet de

Paris that the melancholy refrain of Montgomery's galley comes: *Timaloumisaine, timoulamison.* Most of these songs are abject; some are cheerful; one is tender:

Icicaille est le théâtre
Du petit dardant.[1]

Try as you will, you cannot annihilate that eternal relic of the human heart, love.

In this world of dark deeds, secrecy is preserved. Secrecy is everyone's interest. Secrecy to these wretches is the unity that serves as a basis of union. To violate secrecy is to tear from each member of this savage community something of himself. To inform in the energetic language of argot, is called *Manger le morceau.*[2] As if the informer seized a bit of everyone's substance, and fed on a morsel of the flesh of each.

What is receiving a blow? The hackneyed metaphor replies, *C'est voir trente-six chandelles.*[3] Here argot intervenes and says: *chandelle, camoufle.* Hence, the common language gives as a synomym for a blow, *camouflet.* Thus, by a sort of upward penetration, through the aid of a metaphor, that incalculable trajectory, argot rises from the cavern to the Academy; and Poulailler saying: "I light my *camoufle,*" has Voltaire write: "Langleviel La Beaumelle deserves a hundred *camouflets!*"

A search into argot is a discovery at every step. Study and research into this strange idiom lead to the mysterious intersection between popular society and outcast society.

Argot is speech turned convict.

That the thinking principle of man can be trampled down so low, that it can be bound and dragged there by the obscure tyrannies of fate, that it can be tied to who knows what support on that precipice, this is appalling.

Oh, pitiful thoughts of the miserable!

Alas! Will no one come to the aid of the human soul in this gloom? Is it its destiny forever to await the spirit, the liberator, the immense rider of Pegasus and the hippo-

[1] Here we have the theater
Of the little archer (Cupid).

[2] To eat the morsel.

[3] It is to see thirty-six candles; English, to see stars.

griffs, the aurora-hued combatant who descends from the skies with wings, the radiant Knight of the future? Will it always call to its aid the gleaming lance of the ideal in vain? Is it condemned to hear the Evil coming horribly through the depths of the abyss, and to see nearer and nearer at hand, under the hideous water, that dragon-head, those jaws reeking with foam, that serpentine waving of claws, distensions, and rings? Must it remain there, with no ray of light, no hope, abandoned to that horrible approach, vaguely scented by the monster, shuddering, disheveled, wringing its hands, forever chained to the rock of night, hopeless Andromeda, white and naked in the darkness?

III

ARGOT THAT WEEPS AND ARGOT THAT LAUGHS

As we see, all argot, the argot of four hundred years ago and today, is pervaded with that somber spirit of symbolism that gives to its every word sometimes an appearance of grief, sometimes an air of menace. We feel in it the old, savage gloom of those vagrants of the Cour des Miracles who played cards with packs peculiar to themselves, some of which have been preserved. The eight of clubs, for instance, represented a large tree bearing eight enormous cloverleafs, a sort of fantastic personification of the forest. At the foot of this tree a fire was seen where three hares were roasting a hunter on a spit, and in the background, over another fire, was a steaming pot from which the head of a dog projected. Nothing can be more mournful than these pictured reprisals, on a pack of cards, in the days of the stake for roasting contrabandists, and the cauldron for boiling counterfeiters. The various forms that thought assumed in the realm of argot, even song, even raillery, even menace, all had this impotent and exhausted character. All the songs, some melodies of which have been preserved, were humble and sad to the point of tears. The underworld calls itself *the poor pègre*, and it is always the hare in hiding, the mouse escaping, the bird flying off. It scarcely complains, it merely sighs; one of its groans has come down to us: "*Je n'entrave que le dail comment meck, le daron des orgues, peut atiger ses mômes et ses momignards et les locher criblant sans être agité lui-même.*"[1] The miserable being, whenever he has time to reflect, imagines himself insignificant before the law and wretched before society; he prostrates himself, he begs, he turns toward pity; we feel that he sees himself in the wrong.

Toward the middle of the last century, there was a change. The prison songs, the robbers' ritornels, took on an insolent and jovial expression. The plaintive *maluré* was supplanted by the *larifla*. In the eighteenth century, we find in almost all the songs of the galleys, the chain gangs, and the prisons, a diabolic enigmatic gaiety. We hear this boisterous and strident refrain, which seems lit with a phosphorescent gleam, as if tossed at the forest by a will-o'-the-wisp playing the fife:

Mirlababi surlababo
Mirliton ribon ribette
Surlababi mirlababo
Mirliton ribon ribo.

This was sung while cutting a man's throat in a cave or forest.

A serious symptom. In the eighteenth century the old melancholy of these gloomy classes was dissipating. They began to laugh. They ridicule the great *meg* and the great *dab*. Speaking of Louis XV, they call the King of France "the Marquis of Pantin." There they are almost cheerful. A sort of flickering light is given off by these wretches, as if conscience ceased to weigh on them. These pitiful tribes of the darkness no longer have merely a desperate audacity of deeds, they have the reckless audacity of mind. A sign that they are losing a perception of their criminality and that they feel some mysterious support unconsciously given, even among thinkers and dreamers. A sign that pillage and robbery are beginning to infiltrate even doctrines and sophisms, in such a way

[1] I do not understand how God, the father of men, can torture his children and his grandchildren, and hear them cry without being tortured himself. (V. H.)

as to lose something of their ugliness by giving much of it to the sophisms and the doctrines. A sign in short, if no diversion arises, of some prodigious imminent outburst.

Let us pause a moment. Whom are we accusing here? Is it the eighteenth century? Is it its philosophy? Certainly not. The work of the eighteenth century is sound and good. The Encyclopedists, Diderot at their head; the physiocrats, Turgot at their head; the philosophers, Voltaire at their head; the utopians, Rousseau at their head: These are four sacred legions. To them we owe the immense advance of humanity toward the light. They are the four vanguards of the human race going to the four cardinal points of progress, Diderot toward the beautiful, Turgot toward the useful, Voltaire toward the true, Rousseau toward the just. But beside and beneath the philosophers, there were the sophists, a poisonous vegetation mingled with the healthy growth, hemlock in the virgin forest. While on the main staircase of the Palais de Justice the executioner was burning the great liberating books of the century, writers now forgotten were publishing, with the privilege of the king, many strangely disorganizing writings greedily read by the outcast. Some of these publications, strange to say, patronized by a prince, are still in the *Bibliothèque Secrète*. These facts, deep rooted though ignored, were unperceived on the surface. Sometimes the very obscurity of a fact is its danger. It is obscure because it is subterranean. Of all the writers, the one perhaps who dug the most unwholesome tunnel through the masses was Restif de La Bretonne.

This work, adapted to all Europe, caused greater ravages in Germany than anywhere else. In Germany, during a certain period, summed up by Schiller in his famous drama *The Robbers*, robbery and plunder, elevated to a protest against property and labor, appropriated certain elementary, specious, and false ideas, seemingly just, absurd in reality, wrapped themselves in these ideas, somehow disappeared with them, took an abstract name, and passed into the state of theory, and in this way circulated among the laboring, suffering, and honest multitudes, unknown even to the imprudent chemists who had prepared the mixture, unknown even to the masses who accepted it. Whenever a thing of this sort occurs, it is serious. Suffering engenders wrath; and while the prosperous classes blind themselves, or fall asleep, which also closes the eyes, the hatred of the unfortunate classes lights its torch at some morose or ill-formed mind dreaming in a corner, and begins to examine society. Examination by hatred, a terrible thing.

Hence, if the misfortune of the time so wills, those frightful commotions that were formerly called *Jacqueries*, in comparison to which purely political agitations are child's play, and which are not merely the struggle of the oppressed against the oppressor but the revolt of discomfort against well-being. Then, everything collapses.

Jacqueries are people-quakes.

This danger, imminent perhaps in Europe toward the end of the eighteenth century, was cut short by the French Revolution, that immense act of probity.

The French Revolution, which is nothing more nor less than the ideal armed with the sword, rose abruptly, and by that very movement, closed the door of evil and opened the door of good.

It released the question, promulgated truth, drove away miasma, purified the century, crowned the people.

We can say that it created man a second time, in giving him a second soul, his rights.

The nineteenth century inherits and profits by its work, and today the social catastrophe we just now indicated is simply impossible. Blind is he who prophesies it! Idiotic is he who dreads it! Revolution is vaccination against Jacquerie, or peasant revolt.

Thanks to the Revolution, social conditions have changed. The feudal and monarchical diseases are no longer in our blood. There is nothing more of the Middle Ages in our constitution. We no longer live in the times when frightful interior swarming erupted, when men heard beneath their feet the obscure course of a muffled sound, when some mysterious uprising of molehills appeared on the surface of civilization, when the earth fissured, the mouths of caverns opened, and men saw monstrous heads spring suddenly from the earth.

The revolutionary sense is a moral sense. The sentiment of rights, once developed, develops the sentiment of duty. The law of all is liberty, which ends where the liberty of others begins, according to Robespierre's admirable definition. Since '89, the entire people has been expanding in the sublimated individual; there is no poor man who, having his rights, lacks his ray of light; the starving man feels within him the honor of France; the dignity of the citizen is an interior armor; he who is free is scrupulous; he who votes reigns. Hence incorruptibility; hence the abortion of unwholesome lusts; hence the eyes heroically averted from temptations. The revolutionary purification is such that on a day of deliverance, a 14th of July or 10th of August, there is no longer a mob. The first cry of the enlightened and enlarging multitudes is, Death to robbers! Progress is an honest man; the ideal and the absolute pick no pockets. In 1848 who escorted the chests containing the wealth of the Tuileries? The ragpickers of the Faubourg Saint-Antoine. The rag mounted guard over the treasure. Virtue made these tatters resplendent. There, in those wagons, in chests hardly closed, some even half open, amid a hundred glittering jewel cases, there was that old crown of France all in diamonds, topped by the regent's carbuncle of royalty, which was worth thirty millions. Barefoot, they guarded that crown.

No more Jacquerie. I regret it on account of the able. That is the old terror which has had its last effect, and which can never be used again in politics. The mainspring of the red specter is broken. Everybody knows it now. The scarecrow no longer scares. The birds take liberties with the puppet, the beetles make free with it, the bourgeois laugh at it.

IV

THE TWO DUTIES: TO WATCH AND TO HOPE

This being so, is all social danger dissipated? Certainly not. No Jacquerie. Society may be reassured on that account; the blood will no longer rush to its head, but let it devote some attention to its breathing. Apoplexy is no longer to be feared, but consumption is there. Society's consumption is called misery.

We die undermined as well as blasted away.

Let us not weary of repeating it, to think first of all of the outcast and sorrowful multitudes, to solace them, give them air, enlighten them, love them, enlarge their horizon magnificently, spare nothing on education in all its forms, offer them the example of labor, never the example of idleness, diminish the weight of the individual burden by intensifying the idea of the universal object, limit poverty without limiting wealth, create vast fields of public and popular activity, have, like Briareus, a hundred hands to stretch out on all sides to the exhausted and the feeble, employ the collective power in the great duty of opening workshops for all hands, schools for all aptitudes and laboratories for all intelligences, increase wages, diminish suffering, balance the ought and the have, that is to say, proportion enjoyment to effort and gratification to need, in a word, evolve from the social structure, for the benefit of those who suffer and those who are ignorant, more light and more comfort; this is, as sympathetic souls should not forget, the first of fraternal obligations; this is, as selfish hearts should know, the first of political necessities.

And, we must say, all that is only a beginning. The real point is this: Labor cannot be a law without being a right.

We will not dwell on it; this is not the place.

If nature is called providence, society should be called foresight.

Intellectual and moral growth is no less indispensable than material amelioration. Knowledge is a viaticum, thought is of primary necessity, not only grain but truth is nourishment. Through fasting from knowledge and wisdom, reason becomes emaciated. As with stomachs, we should pity minds that do not eat. If there is anything more poignant than a body agonizing for want of bread, it is a soul dying of hunger for light.

All progress tends toward the solution. Someday we will be surprised. With the human race rising, the lower strata will quite naturally leave the zone of distress. The abolition of misery will be brought about by a simple elevation of level.

We would do wrong to doubt this blessed solution.

The past, it is true, is very strong right now. It is reviving. This revivification of a corpse is surprising. Here it is walking and advancing. It seems victorious; this dead man is a conqueror. He comes with his legion, superstitions, with his sword, despotism, with his banner, ignorance; within a little time he has won ten battles. He advances, he threatens, he laughs, he is at our doors. As for us, we will not despair. Let us sell the field where Hannibal is camped.

We who believe, what can we fear?

There is no backward flow of ideas any more than of rivers.

But those who do not want the future should think it over. In saying no to progress, it is not the future that they condemn, but themselves. They are giving themselves a melancholy disease; they are inoculating themselves with the past. There is only one way of refusing tomorrow, and that is to die.

Now, no death—that of the body as late as possible, never that of the soul—is what we desire.

Yes, the enigma will say its word, the sphinx will speak, the problem will be solved. Yes, the people, rough-hewn by the eighteenth century, shall be completed by the nineteenth. An idiot is any who doubts it! The future birth, the speedy birth of universal well-being, is a divinely inevitable phenomenon.

Immense combined thrusts rule human affairs and lead them all in a given time to the logical condition, that is to say, to equilibrium; that is to say, to equity. A force composed of earth and Heaven results from humanity and governs it; this force is a worker of miracles; miraculous outcomes are not more difficult for it than extraordinary changes. Aided by science, which comes from man, and by the event, which comes from Another, it is scarcely dismayed by those contradictions in the posing of problems that seem impossibilities to the vulgar. It is no less capable of making a solution emerge from the rapprochement of ideas than a lesson from the rapprochement of facts; and we may expect everything from this mysterious power of progress, which one fine day confronts the Orient with the Occident in the depths of a sepulcher, and makes the Imams talk with Bonaparte in the interior of the great pyramid.

In the meantime, no halt, no hesitation, no interruption in the grand march of minds. Social philosophy is essentially science and peace. Its aim is, and its result must be, to dissolve angers by the study of antagonisms. It examines, it scrutinizes, it analyzes; then it recomposes. It proceeds by way of reduction, eliminating hatred.

That a society may be swamped in a gale that breaks

loose over men, this has been seen more than once; history is full of shipwrecks of peoples and empires; customs, laws, religions, some fine day, the mysterious hurricane passes by and sweeps them all away. The civilizations of India, Chaldea, Persia, Assyria, Egypt, have disappeared, one after the other. Why? We do not know. What are the causes of these disasters? We do not know. Could these societies have been saved? Was it their own fault? Did they persist in some fatal vice that destroyed them? How much of suicide is there in these terrible deaths of a nation and of a race? Questions without an answer. Darkness covers the condemned civilizations. They were not seaworthy, for they were sinking; we have nothing more to say; and it is with a sort of bewilderment that, far back in that ocean called the past, behind those colossal billows, the centuries, the foundering of those huge ships, Babylon, Nineveh, Tarsus, Thebes, Rome, under the terrible blast that comes from all the mouths of darkness. But darkness there, light here. We do not know the diseases of the ancient civilizations, we know the infirmities of our own. Everywhere across it we have the rights of light; we contemplate its beauties and lay bare its deformities. Where it is unsound we probe; and, once the disease is determined, the study of the cause leads to the discovery of the remedy. Our civilization, the work of twenty centuries, is at once their monster and their prodigy; it is worth saving. It will be saved. To relieve it is already a great deal; to enlighten it is something more. All the labors of modern social philosophy should converge toward this end. Today's thinker has a great duty, to auscultate civilization.

We repeat, this auscultation encourages; and it is by this insistence on encouragement that we would finish these few pages, an austere interlude of a sorrowful drama. Beneath the mortality of society we feel the imperishability of humanity. Because here and there it has those wounds, craters, and those ringworms, solfataras, because of a volcano that erupts and hurls out its pus, the globe does not die. The diseases of a people do not kill man.

Nevertheless, anyone who follows the social clinic's progress shakes his head at times. The strongest, the tenderest, the most logical have their moments of doubt.

Will the future come? We can almost ask this question,

it seems, when we see such terrible shadows. Sullen face-to-face encounter of the selfish and the miserable. On the side of the selfish, prejudices, the darkness of the education of wealth, appetite increasing through intoxication, a stultifying of prosperity, which deafens, a dread of suffering taken, for some, as far as an aversion to sufferers, an implacable satisfaction, the self so puffed up it closes the soul; on the side of the miserable, covetousness, envy, hatred of seeing others enjoy, the deep yearnings of the human animal toward gratification, hearts filled with gloom, sadness, want, inevitability, ignorance impure and simple.

Must we continue to lift our eyes toward heaven? Does the luminous point we discern there come from those being quenched? The ideal is terrible to see, thus lost in the depths—minute, isolated, imperceptible, shining, but surrounded by all those great black menaces monstrously amassed around it, yet no more in danger than a star in the jaws of the clouds.

Book Eight

ENCHANTMENTS AND DESOLATIONS

I

SUNSHINE

The reader will remember that Eponine, having recognized through the grating the inhabitant of that Rue Plumet, to which Magnon had sent her, had begun by diverting the bandits from the Rue Plumet, had then taken Marius there, and that after several days of ecstasy in front of that iron gate, Marius, drawn by the force that propels iron toward the magnet and the lover toward the stones of his loved one's house, had finally entered Cosette's garden as Romeo did Juliet's. It had even been easier for him than for Romeo; Romeo was obliged to scale a wall, Marius had only to slightly push aside one of the bars of the decrepit gate, which was loose in its rusty socket, like the teeth of old people. Marius was slender and easily slipped through.

As there was never anybody in the street, and as, moreover, Marius entered the garden only at night, he ran no risk of being seen.

From that blessed holy moment when a kiss betrothed these two souls, Marius came every evening. If, at this period of her life, Cosette had fallen in love with an unscrupulous man, a libertine, she would have been ruined; for there are generous natures that give themselves, and Cosette was one. One of the generosities of woman is to yield. Love, at that height where it is absolute, is associated with an inexpressibly celestial blindness of modesty. But what risks you run, O noble souls! Often, you give the heart, we take the body. Your heart remains to you, and you look at it in the darkness, and shudder. Love has no middle term; either it destroys, or it saves. All human destiny is this dilemma. This dilemma, destruction or salvation, no fate proposes more inexorably than love. Love is life, if it is not death. Cradle; coffin, too. The same sentiment says yes and no in the human heart. Of all the things God has made, the human heart is the one that sheds most light, and, alas! most night.

God willed that the love Cosette met should be one of those loves that save.

Throughout the month of May of that year 1832, every night, in that poor, wild garden, under that shrubbery each day more perfumed and dense, two human beings composed of every chastity and every innocence, overflowing with all the felicities of Heaven, closer to archangels than men, pure, honest, intoxicated, radiant, glowed for each other in the darkness. It seemed to Cosette that Marius had a crown, and to Marius that Cosette had a halo. They touched, they gazed at each other, they clasped hands, they pressed close together; but there was a distance they did not pass. Not that they respected it; they were ignorant of it. Marius felt a barrier, Cosette's purity, and Cosette felt a support, Marius's loyalty. The first kiss was also the last. Since then, Marius had not gone beyond touching Cosette's hand, or her scarf, or her curls, with his lips. Cosette was to him a perfume, and not a woman. He breathed her. She refused nothing and he asked nothing. Cosette was happy, and Marius was satisfied. They were living in that ravishing condition that might be called the dazzling of one soul by another. It was that ineffable first embrace of two virginities within the ideal. Two swans meeting on the Jungfrau.

At that moment of love, a moment when passion is absolutely silent under omnipotence of ecstasy, Marius, pure seraphic Marius, would have been more capable of visiting a woman of the streets than of raising Cosette's dress above the ankle. Once, on a moonlit night, Cosette stooped to pick up something from the ground, her dress loosened and revealed the swelling of her breasts. Marius averted his eyes.

What happened between these two beings? Nothing. They were adoring one another.

At night, when they were there, this garden seemed a living, sacred place. All the flowers opened around them and offered them their incense; they too opened their souls and poured them out to the flowers: The lusty vigorous vegetation trembled full of sap and intoxication around these two innocent creatures, and they spoke words of love at which the trees thrilled.

What were these words? Whispers, nothing more. These whispers were enough to arouse and excite all this nature. A magic power, which one could hardly understand on reading in some book this light talk made to be borne away and dissipated like whiffs of smoke by the wind beneath the leaves. Take from these whispers of two lovers the melody that springs from the soul and accompanies them like a lyre, what remains is only a shadow. You say, What! Is that all? Yes, childish things, repetitions, laughter about nothing, useless things, absurdities, all that is deepest and most sublime in the world! The only things worth being said and listened to.

These absurdities, these poverties, the man who has never heard them, the man who has never uttered them, is an imbecile and a sorry man.

Cosette said to Marius, "Do you know my name is Euphrasie?"

"Euphrasie? Why no, your name is Cosette."

"Oh! Cosette is such an ugly name that they gave me somehow when I was little. But my real name is Euphrasie. Don't you like that name, Euphrasie?"

"Yes—but Cosette is not ugly."

"Do you like it better than Euphrasie?"

"Why—yes."

"Then I like it better, too. It's true, it is pretty, Cosette. Call me Cosette."

And the smile she added made of this dialogue an idyl worthy of a celestial grove.

At another time she looked at him steadily and exclaimed, "Monsieur, you are handsome, you are beautiful, you are witty, you are not stupid in the least, you are much wiser than I, but I defy you with this word: I love you!"

And Marius, in a boundless blue sky, thought he heard a verse sung by a star.

Or again, she gave him a little tap because he coughed, and said to him, "Don't cough, sir. I don't allow coughing here without my permission. It's very bad to cough and disturb me. I want you to be well, because, in the first place, if you weren't well, I'd be very unhappy. What can I do?"

And that was all purely divine.

Once Marius said to Cosette, "Just think, at one time I thought your name was Ursula."

This made them laugh for a whole evening.

In the midst of another conversation, he happened to exclaim, "Oh! One day at the Luxembourg I would have been glad to break the last bones of a veteran!"

But stopped short. To go further, he would have been obliged to speak to Cosette of her garter, and that he could not do. There was an unknown coast there, the flesh, before which this immense innocent love recoiled with a kind of sacred awe.

Marius imagined life with Cosette like this, without anything else: coming every evening to the Rue Plumet, pushing aside the willing old bar of the judge's gate, sitting side by side on the bench, watching through the trees the sparkle of the coming night, having the fold of his trouser knee intimate with the fullness of Cosette's dress, caressing her thumbnail, saying dearest to her, each in turn inhaling the scent of the same flower, forever. During this time clouds were scudding over their heads. Every breath of wind bears away more of man's dreams than clouds from the sky.

That this chaste, almost severe, love was absolutely without gallantry, we will not say. "To pay compliments" to the one we love is the first method of caressing, a demi-audacity venturing. A compliment is something like a kiss through a veil. Pleasure sets her soft seal there, while still in hiding. The heart recoils before pleasure, the better to love. Marius's soft words, all saturated as they were with chimera, were, so to speak, sky-blue. Birds, when they are flying on high beside the angels, must hear such words. Mingled with them, however, there was life, humanity, all the positiveness of which Marius was capable. It was what is said in the grotto, a prelude to what will be said in the alcove: a lyrical effusion, the strophe and the sonnet mingled, the gentle hyperboles, all the refinements of adoration arranged in a bouquet and exhaling a subtle celestial perfume, an ineffable warbling of heart to heart.

"Oh!" murmured Marius, "how beautiful you are! I don't dare look at you. That's why I'm staring at you. You are a grace. I don't know what's the matter with me. When the tip of your shoe appears, the hem of your dress completely overwhelms me. And then what an enchanting glow when I catch a glimpse of your thoughts. You reason amazingly. At times you seem to me a dream. Speak, I'm listening to you, I'm admiring you. O Cosette! How strange and charming it is! I'm really mad. You're adorable, mademoiselle. I study your feet with a microscope and your soul with a telescope."

And Cosette answered, "I've been loving you a little more every minute since this morning."

Questions and answers fared as they might in this dialogue, always coming around naturally at last to love, like those weighted toys that always fall upright.

Cosette's whole person was naïvete, innocence, transparency, whiteness, honesty, radiance. One could say of Cosette that she was pellucid. She gave anyone who saw her a sensation of April and of dawn. There was dew in her eyes. Cosette was a condensation of auroral light in womanly form.

It was quite natural that Marius, adoring her, should admire her. But the truth is that this little schoolgirl, fresh from the convent, talked with an exquisite perception and at times made all sorts of true and delicate observations. Her chatter was conversation. She made no mistakes and saw clearly. Woman feels and speaks with the tender instinct of the heart, that infallibility. Nobody knows like a woman how to say things that are both sweet and profound. Sweetness and depth, this is all of woman; this is all of Heaven.

In this fullness of felicity, tears constantly came to their eyes. A smashed insect, a feather falling from a nest, a twig of hawthorn broken, moved them to pity, and their ecstasy, gently drowned in melancholy, seemed to ask nothing better than to weep. The most sovereign symptom of love is a tenderness that is sometimes almost insupportable.

And, beside this—all these contradictions are the lightning play of love—they laughed easily and with a charming freedom, and so familiarly that they sometimes seemed almost like two boys. Nevertheless, though hearts intoxicated with chastity may be all unconscious, nature, which can never be forgotten, is always present. There she is, with her aim, animal yet sublime; and whatever may be the innocence of souls, we feel, in the most modest meetings, the adorable and mysterious nuance that differentiates a pair of lovers from two friends.

They worshiped each other.

The permanent and the immutable endure. There is loving, there is smiling and laughing and pouts and interlacing fingers and fondling speech, yet that does not hinder eternity. Two lovers hide in the evening, in the twilight, in the invisible with the birds, with roses, they fascinate one another in the shadow with their hearts that speak through their eyes, they murmur, they whisper, and during all this time, sweeping orbits of stars fill up infinity.

II

THE WONDER OF TOTAL HAPPINESS

Their existence was vague, bewildered with happiness. They did not notice the cholera that decimated Paris that same month. They had been as open with each other as they could be, but this had not gone very far beyond their names. Marius had told Cosette that he was an orphan, that his name was Marius Pontmercy, that he was a lawyer, that he lived by writing things for publishers, that his father was a colonel, a hero, and that he, Marius, had quarreled with his grandfather, who was rich. He had also said something about being a baron; but that had produced no effect upon Cosette. Marius a baron! She did not understand. She did not know what the word meant. Marius was Marius. As for her, she had confided to him that she had been brought up at the Convent of the Petit-Picpus, that her mother was dead, as was his, that her father's name was M. Fauchelevent, that he was very kind, that he gave a great deal to the poor, but that he was poor himself, and that he deprived himself of everything while he deprived her of nothing.

Strange to say, in the sort of symphony Marius had been living since he had seen Cosette, the past, even the most recent past, had become so confused and distant to him that what Cosette told him satisfied him completely. He did not even think to speak to her of the nocturnal adventure at the Gorbeau house, the Thénardiers, the wound burning, and the strange attitude and singular flight of her father. Marius had temporarily forgotten all that; he did not even know at night what he had done in the morning, nor where he had had lunch, nor who had spoken to him; he had songs in his ear that made him deaf to every other thought; he existed only during the hours in which he saw Cosette. Then, since he was in Heaven, it was quite natural he should forget the earth. They were both languidly supporting the indefinable burden of immaterial pleasures. Thus live these sleepwalkers called lovers.

Alas! Who has not experienced all these things? Why does there come an hour when we leave this azure, and why does life continue afterward?

Love almost replaces thought. Love is a burning forgetfulness of everything else. There is no more an absolute logical chain in the human heart than there is a perfect geometrical figure in the celestial mechanics. To Cosette and Marius there was nothing in existence beyond Marius and Cosette. The universe around them had fallen out of sight. They lived in a golden moment. There was nothing before, nothing after. Marius scarcely thought whether Cosette had a father. He was so dazzled that his brain was wiped clean. So what did they talk about, these lovers?—As we have seen, of the flowers, the swallows, the setting sun, the rising moon, of everything important. They had said everything, except everything. The everything of lovers is nothing. But the father, the realities, the garret, those thugs, that adventure, what was the use? And was he quite certain that that nightmare was real? They were two, they adored each other, there was nothing but that. Everything else was not. Probably this erasure of the hell behind us is a part of reaching paradise. Have we seen demons? Are there any? Have we trembled? Have we suffered? We know nothing now about that. A rosy cloud settles onto it.

These two beings, then, were living this way, way up, with all the improbability of nature; neither at the nadir nor the zenith, between man and seraph, above earth, below the ether, in the clouds; scarcely flesh and bone, soul and ecstasy from head to foot; too sublimated already to walk on the earth, and still too weighed down with humanity to disappear in the sky, in suspension like atoms awaiting precipitation; apparently outside of destiny; ignoring that beaten track yesterday, today, tomorrow; astounded, swooping, floating; at times, light enough to soar into infinity; almost ready for eternal flight.

They were sleeping awake in this rocking cradle. O splendid lethargy of the real overwhelmed by the ideal!

Sometimes, because Cosette was so beautiful, Marius closed his eyes before her. With eyes closed is the best way to look at the soul.

Marius and Cosette did not ask where this would lead them. They looked at themselves as arrived. It is a strange pretension for men to ask that love should lead them somewhere.

III

SHADOW COMMENCES

Jean Valjean suspected nothing.

A little less dreamy than Marius, Cosette was cheerful, and that was enough to make Jean Valjean happy. Cosette's thoughts, her tender preoccupations, the image of Marius that filled her soul, detracted nothing from the incomparable purity of her beautiful, chaste, and smiling forehead. She was at the age when the maiden bears her love as the angel bears her lily. So Jean Valjean was reassured. And then when two lovers have an understanding, they always get along well; any third person who might disturb their love is kept in perfect blindness by a very few precautions, always the same for all lovers. So Cosette never made any objections to Jean Valjean's proposals. Did he wish to stay home? Very well. Would he like to spend the evening with Cosette? She was delighted. As he always went to bed at ten o'clock, on those occasions Marius would not come to the garden till after that time, when from the street he would hear Cosette open the glass door leading out onto the steps. It goes without saying that Marius was never met by day. Jean Valjean no longer even thought that Marius was in existence. Once, only, one morning, he happened to say to Cosette, "Why, you have something white on your back!" The evening before, Marius in transport, had pressed Cosette against the wall.

Old Toussaint, who went to bed early, thought of nothing but going to sleep, once her work was done, and was unaware of everything, like Jean Valjean.

Never did Marius set foot in the house. When he was with Cosette, they hid in a recess near the steps, so they could neither be seen nor heard from the street, and they would sit there, contenting themselves often, by way of conversation, with pressing each other's hands twenty times a minute while looking into the branches of the trees. At such moments, a thunderbolt might have fallen within thirty paces of them, and they would not have suspected it, so deeply was the reverie of the one absorbed by the reverie of the other.

Limpid purities. Hours all white, almost all alike. Such loves as these are a collection of lily leaves and dove-down.

The whole garden was between them and the street. Whenever Marius came in and went out, he carefully replaced the bar of the grating in such a way that nothing out of order would be seen.

He went away around midnight, returning to Courfeyrac's. Courfeyrac said to Bahorel, "Would you believe it? Marius comes home nowadays at one o'clock in the morning."

Bahorel answered, "What do you expect? Sowing his wild oats."

At times Courfeyrac folded his arms, put on a serious air, and said to Marius, "You're getting dissipated, young man!"

Courfeyrac, a practical man, was not pleased at this reflection of an invisible paradise on Marius; he had little taste for unpublished passions, he was impatient with them and would occasionally serve Marius with a summons to return to reality.

One morning, he threw out this admonition, "My dear fellow, you strike me at present as being situated in the moon, kingdom of dream, province of illusion, capital: Soap-Bubble. Come, be a good boy, what's her name?"

But nothing could make Marius "confess." You might have torn out his nails sooner than one of the two sacred syllables that composed that ineffable name, *Cosette*. True love is luminous as the dawn, and silent as the grave. Except that there was, to Courfeyrac, this change in Marius, that his taciturnity was radiant.

During this sweet month of May, Marius and Cosette knew these transcendent joys:

To quarrel and to say monsieur and mademoiselle, merely to say Marius and Cosette better afterwards;

To talk at length, and with most minute detail, of people who did not interest them in the least; a further proof that, in this ravishing opera called love, the libretto is almost nothing;

For Marius, to listen to Cosette talking clothes;

For Cosette, to listen to Marius talking politics;

To hear, knee to knee, the wagons roll along the Rue de Babylone;

To gaze at the same planet in space, or the same worm glowing in the grass;

To keep silent together; a pleasure still greater than to talk;

Etc., etc.

Meanwhile various complications were approaching.

One evening Marius was making his way to the rendezvous by the Boulevard des Invalides; he usually walked with his head down; as he was just turning the corner of the Rue Plumet, he heard someone saying very near him, "Good evening, Monsieur Marius."

He looked up and recognized Eponine.

This produced a strange effect on him. He had not thought even once of this girl since the day she brought him to the Rue Plumet, he had not seen her again, and she had completely gone out of his mind. He had grounds for gratitude toward her; he owed his present happiness to her, and yet it annoyed him to meet her.

It is a mistake to suppose that passion, when it is fortunate and pure, leads man to a state of perfection; it leads him simply as we have said, to a state of forgetfulness. In this situation man forgets to be bad, but he also forgets to be good. Gratitude, duty, necessary and troublesome memories, vanish. At any other time Marius would have felt very differently toward Eponine. Absorbed in Cosette, he had not even clearly realized that this Eponine's name was Eponine Thénardier, and that she bore a name written in his father's will, that name to which he would have been, a few months earlier, so ardently devoted. We show Marius just as he was. Even his father was disappearing somewhat from his soul beneath the splendor of his love.

With some embarrassment, he answered, "Ah, you, Eponine!"

"Why do you speak to me so sternly? Have I done anything to you?"

"No," he answered.

Certainly, he had nothing against her. Far from it. Except, he felt that he could not do otherwise, now that he had whispered to Cosette, than speak coldly to Eponine.

As he was silent, she exclaimed, "So tell me—"

Then she stopped. It seemed as if words failed this creature, once so reckless and bold. She attempted to smile and could not. She began again, "Well?"

Then she was silent again, and stood with her eyes cast down.

"Good evening, Monsieur Marius," she said all at once abruptly, and she went off.

IV

CAB ROLLS IN ENGLISH AND YELPS IN ARGOT

The next day, it was the 3rd of June, the 3rd of June, 1832, a date that must be noted because of the grave events then hanging over the Paris horizon like thunderclouds. At nightfall, Marius was following the same path as the evening before, with the same rapturous thoughts in his heart, when he perceived, under the trees of the boulevard, Eponine approaching him. Two days in succession, this was too much. He turned hastily, left the boulevard, changed his route, and went to the Rue Plumet through the Rue Monsieur.

This caused Eponine to follow him to the Rue Plumet, a thing she had not done before. She had been content until then to see him on his way through the boulevard without even seeking to meet him. On the previous evening only, had she tried to speak to him.

So Eponine followed him without a suspicion on his part. She saw him push aside the bar of the gate, and slip into the garden.

"Why!" she said. "He's going into the house."

She went up to the gate, felt the bars one after another, and easily recognized the one Marius had moved.

In an undertone she murmured mournfully, "None of that, Lisette!"

She sat down on the base of the gate, close to the grating, as if she were guarding it. It was just at the point where the grating joined the neighboring wall. There was a dark nook, in which Eponine was entirely hidden.

She remained this way for more than an hour, without stirring or breathing, a prey to her own thoughts.

Around ten in the evening, one of the two or three passersby in the Rue Plumet, a belated old bourgeois who was hurrying through this deserted, ill-reputed place, staying close to the garden grating, on reaching the angle between the gate and the wall, heard a sullen and threatening voice saying, "I wouldn't be surprised if he comes every evening!"

He glanced around him, saw nobody, did not dare look into that dark corner, and was very much frightened. He doubled his pace.

This person had reason to hurry, for a very few moments later, six men, who were walking separately and at some distance from each other along the wall, and who might have been taken for a slightly drunk patrol, entered the Rue Plumet.

The first to arrive at the garden gate stopped and waited for the others; in a second they were all six together.

These men began to talk in a low voice.

"It's *icicaille,*" said one of them.

"Is there a *cab*[1] in the garden?" asked another.

"I don't know. In any case I've *levé*[2] a bullet which we'll make him *morfiler*."[3]

"Do you have some mastic to *frangir* the *vanterne?*"[4]

"Yes."

"The grating is old," added a fifth, who had a voice like a ventriloquist.

"So much the better," said the second to have spoken. "It will not *cribler*[5] under the *bastringue*,[6] and won't be so hard to *faucher*.[7]"

The sixth, who had not yet opened his mouth, began examining the grating as Eponine had done an hour before, grasping each bar successively and shaking it carefully. In this way he came to the bar Marius had loosened. Just as he was about to lay hold of this bar, a hand, starting abruptly from the shadow, fell upon his arm, he felt himself pushed sharply back by the middle of his breast, and a roughened voice said to him without crying out, "There's a *cab*."

At the same time he saw a pale girl standing in front of him.

The man felt that commotion that always follows the unexpected. He bristled up hideously; nothing is so frightful to see as ferocious beasts which are startled, their appearance when terrified is terrifying. He recoiled, and stammered, "What is this creature?"

"Your daughter."

It was indeed Eponine who was speaking to Thénardier.

On the appearance of Eponine the five others, that is to say, Claquesous, Gueulemer, Babet, Montparnasse, and Brujon, approached without a sound, without haste, without saying a word, with the ominous slowness peculiar to these men of the night.

In their hands could be seen fiendish tools. Gueulemer

[1] Dog. (V. H.)

[2] Brought. From the Spanish *llevar*. (V. H.)

[3] Eat. (V.H.)

[4] *To break a pane* by means of an adhesive tape, which, sticking to the window, holds the glass and prevents noise. (V. H.)

[5] Squeak. (V.H.)

[6] Saw. (V. H.)

[7] Cut. (V. H.)

had one of those crooked crowbars the prowlers call *fanchons*.

"Ah, there, what are you doing here? What do you want from us? Are you crazy?" exclaimed Thénardier, as much as one can exclaim in a whisper. "Why do you come and get in our way?"

Eponine began to laugh and sprang at his neck.

"I'm here, my darling father, because I'm here. Is there any law against sitting on the stones these days? It's you who shouldn't be here. Why are you coming here, since it's a biscuit? I told Magnon so. There's nothing to do here. But give me a kiss now, my dear good father! What a long time since I've seen you! You're out then?"

Thénardier tried to free himself from Eponine's arms, and muttered, "Very well. You've kissed me. Yes, I'm out. I'm not in. Now, go."

But Eponine did not loose her hold and redoubled her caresses.

"My darling father, how did you do it? You must've been pretty clever to get out of that one! Tell me! And my mother? Where's my mother? Give me some news of Mamma."

Thénardier answered, "She's well, I don't know, let me alone, I told you to go."

"I don't want to go away just now," said Eponine, with the pettishness of a spoiled child, "you send me away when here it's four months since I've seen you, and I've hardly had time to kiss you."

And she caught her father again by the neck.

"Ah! Come on now, this is foolish," said Babet.

"Let's hurry!" said Gueulemer, "the *coqueurs* may come along."

The ventriloquist sang this distich:

> Nous n' sommes pas le jour de l'an,
> A bécoter papa maman.[1]

Eponine turned toward the five thugs.

"Why, that is Monsieur Brujon. Good evening, Mon-

[1] 'Tis not the first of the new year,
To hug papa and mamma dear. (V. H.)

sieur Babet. Good evening, Monsieur Claquesous. Don't you remember me, Monsieur Gueulemer? How goes it, Montparnasse?"

"Yes, they recognize you," said Thénardier. "But good evening, good night, good-by! Don't bother us!"

"It's the hour for foxes, not pullets," said Montparnasse.

"You see well enough that we're trying to *goupiner icigo*,"[1] added Babet.

Eponine took Montparnasse's hand.

"Watch out," he said, "you'll cut yourself, I have a *lingre*[2] open."

"My darling Montparnasse," answered Eponine very gently, "we must have confidence in people. I am my father's daughter, perhaps. Monsieur Babet, Monsieur Gueulemer, it's I who was charged with finding out about this affair."

It is remarkable that Eponine was not speaking argot. Since she had known Marius, that awful language had become impossible to her.

She pressed in her little hand, as bony and weak as the hand of a corpse, the great rough fingers of Gueulemer, and continued, "You know very well I'm no fool. Usually, you believe me. I've done you service at various times. Well, I've learned all about this one, you'd expose yourself uselessly, you see. I swear to you that there's nothing to be done in that house."

"There are lone women," said Gueulemer.

"No. The people have moved away."

"The candles haven't, anyhow!" said Babet.

And he showed Eponine, through the top of the trees, a light that was moving about in the garret of the cottage. It was Toussaint, who had stayed up to hang out her clothes to dry.

Eponine made a final effort.

"Well," she said, "they are very poor, and it's a shanty where there isn't a sou."

"Go to the devil!" cried Thénardier. "When we've turned the house upside down, put the cellar at the top and the garret at the bottom, we'll tell you what

[1] To work here. (V. H.)
[2] Knife. (V.H.)

there is inside, and whether it is *balles, ronds,* or *broques*."[1]

And he pushed her to pass by.

"My good friend Monsieur Montparnasse," said Eponine, "I beg you, you're a good boy, don't go in!"

"Watch out, you'll cut yourself," replied Montparnasse.

Thénardier added, with his decisive tone, "Clear out, *fée,* and let men do their work!"

Eponine let go of Montparnasse's hand, which she had taken again, and said, "So you want to go into that house?"

"Just a little!" said the ventriloquist, with a sneer.

Then she placed her back against the grating, faced the six bandits who were armed to the teeth, and to whom the night gave faces of demons, and said in a low, firm voice, "Well, I don't want you to."

They stopped, astonished. The ventriloquist cut off his sneer. She resumed.

"Friends! Listen to me. Now I'll tell you. In the first place, if you go into the garden, if you touch this grating, I'll cry out, I'll rap on doors, I'll wake everybody up, I'll have all six of you arrested, I'll call the police!"

"She would do it," said Thénardier in a low tone to Brujon and the ventriloquist.

She shook her head and added, "Beginning with my father!"

Thénardier approached.

"Not so close!" she said.

He drew back, muttering between his teeth, "Why, what is the matter with her?" and he added, "Slut!"

She began to laugh derisively.

"You can try all you like, you won't go in, I'm not the daughter of a dog, I'm the daughter of a wolf. There are six of you, what's that to me? You're men. Well, I'm a woman. I'm not afraid of you, not one bit. I tell you that you won't go into this house, because I don't like the idea. If you come near, I'll bark. I told you I'm the *cab,* I don't care about you. Go on about your business, you annoy me. Go wherever you like, but don't come back here, I forbid it! You have knives, I have feet and hands. That makes no difference to me, so come ahead!"

[1] Francs, sous or farthings.

She took a step toward the cutthroats; she was frightening, she began to laugh.

"What the devil! I'm not afraid. This summer, I'll be hungry; this winter, I'll be cold. Are they some fools, these geese, to think they can scare a girl! Scared? I spit on it! Because you have hussies for mistresses who hide under the bed when you raise your voice, it won't do here! Me, I'm not afraid of anything!"

She kept her eye fixed on Thénardier and said, "Not even you, Father!"

Then she went on, skimming her ghastly bloodshot eyes over the bandits, "What is it to me whether somebody picks me up tomorrow on the pavement of the Rue Plumet, beaten to death with a club by my own father, or whether they find me in a year in the ditches of Saint-Cloud, or on the Ile de Cygnes, with the rotting garbage and the dead dogs?"

She had to stop; a dry cough seized her, her breath wheezed out of her narrow, feeble chest.

She started again, "I just cry out. They come, bang! You're six; but I'm everybody."

Thénardier made a movement toward her.

"No you don't!" she cried.

He stopped and said to her mildly, "Well, no; I won't touch you, but don't speak so loud. Daughter, you want to hinder us in our work? We still have to earn our keep. You don't love your father anymore?"

"You irritate me," said Eponine.

"Still, we have to live, we have to eat—"

"Die."

Saying which, she sat down against the gatepost, humming:

> Mon bras si dodu,
> Ma jambe bien faite,
> Et le temps perdu.[1]

She had her elbow on her knee and her chin in her hand, and she was casually swinging her foot. Her dress was full of holes and showed her sharp shoulder blades.

[1] So plump my arm,
My leg well made,
And time, time flies. (V. H.)

The neighboring lamp lit up her profile and her pose. Nothing could be more resolute or more surprising.

The six thugs, sullen and abashed at being held in check by a girl, moved under the protecting shade of the lantern and conferred, their shoulders hunched in fury and humiliation.

She watched them with a quiet, indomitable look.

"Something's the matter with her," said Babet. "Some reason. Is she in love with the *cab?* But it is a pity to miss out on this. Two women, an old fellow who lives in a back court, there are pretty good curtains at the windows. The old fellow must be a *guinal.*[1] Very promising."

"Well, you go in, the rest of you," exclaimed Montparnasse. "Do it. I'll stay here with the girl, and if she makes one false move . . ."

He made the open knife in his hand glint by the light of the lantern.

Thénardier said nothing and seemed ready for anything.

Brujon, who was something of an oracle and who had, as we know, "put the thing together," had not yet spoken. He appeared thoughtful. He had a reputation for recoiling from nothing, and they knew that one time from sheer bravado he had plundered a police station. Besides, he wrote verses and songs, which gave him great authority.

Babet questioned him.

"You're not saying anything, Brujon?"

Brujon stayed silent a minute longer, then he shook his head in several different ways, and at last decided to speak.

"Here you are: this morning I met two sparrows fighting; tonight, I run into a woman squawking. All this is bad business. Let's go."

They went away.

As they went, Montparnasse muttered, "Even so, if they'd let me, I'd have made her feel the weight of my hand."

Babet answered, "Not me. I don't hit ladies."

At the street corner they stopped and exchanged this enigmatic dialogue in smothered tones:

[1] A Jew.

"Where're we going to sleep tonight?"

"Under Pantin."[1]

"Do you have the key to the grate with you, Thénardier?"

"What do you expect?"

Eponine, who had not taken her eyes off them, saw them turn back the way they had come. She rose and began to creep along the walls and houses behind them. She followed them as far as the boulevard. There, they separated, and she saw the men slink into the dark and seem to melt away.

V

THINGS OF THE NIGHT

After the bandits left, the Rue Plumet resumed its calm nocturnal air.

What had just taken place in this street would not have surprised a forest. The clumps of trees, underbrush, briars, the branches roughly intertwined, the tall grass, have a darkly mysterious existence; this wild teeming mass has sudden glimpses of the invisible; there, what is below man distinguishes through the dark what is above man; and things unknown to us the living confront one another in the night. Nature, bristling and untamed, takes fright at certain approaches in which she suspects the supernatural. The forces of the shadows know each other and have mysterious equilibrium among them. Teeth and claws dread the intangible. Bloodthirsty brutality, voracious and starving appetites in quest of prey, instincts armed with claws and jaws, which find in the belly their origin and their object, anxiously watch and sniff the impassive spectral figure prowling beneath a shroud, standing in its hazy trembling robe, and seeming to them to live with a dead and terrible life. These brutalities, nothing more than matter, confusedly dread having anything to do with the boundless darkness condensed into an unknown being. A black figure barring the passage stops the

[1] Paris. (V. H.)

wild beast dead. What comes from the graveyard intimidates and disconcerts what comes from the den; the ferocious is afraid of the sinister: Wolves recoil before a ghoul.

VI

MARIUS BECOMES REAL ENOUGH TO GIVE COSETTE HIS ADDRESS

While this sort of dog in human form was mounting guard over the iron gate, and the six were skulking away from a girl, Marius was with Cosette.

Never had the sky been more studded with stars, or more charming, the trees more tremulous, the odor of the shrubs more penetrating; never had the birds gone to sleep in the leaves with a more hushed sound; never had all the harmonies of the universal serenity better responded to the interior music of love; never had Marius been more in love, happier, more in ecstasy. But he had found Cosette sad. Cosette had been weeping. Her eyes were red.

It was the first cloud in this wonderful dream.

Marius's first greeting was, "What's the matter?"

"I'll tell you."

Then she sat down on the bench near the doorsteps, and as he took his place beside her, trembling, she continued, "This morning, my father told me to get ready, that he had business to attend to, and perhaps we would go away."

A shudder wracked Marius from head to foot.

When we are at the end of life, to die means to go away; when we are at the beginning, to go away means to die.

Each day for six weeks, Marius gradually, slowly, by degrees, had been taking possession of Cosette. A possession entirely ideal, but thorough. As we have explained, in first love the soul is taken long before the body; later, the body is taken long before the soul; sometimes the soul is not taken at all. Because there is none, the Faublas and the Prudhommes would add; but fortunately the sarcasm is a blasphemy. So Marius possessed Cosette, as minds possess; but he wrapped her in his whole soul and clutched her jealously with an incredible conviction. He possessed her smile, her breath, her perfume, the deep radiance of her blue eyes, the softness of her skin when he touched her hand, the charming mark she had on her neck, all her thoughts. They had agreed never to go to sleep without dreaming of each other, and they had kept their word. He possessed all Cosette's dreams. He untiringly watched, and sometimes brushed with his breath the short hairs at the back of her neck, and he declared to himself that there was not one of those little hairs that did not belong to him, Marius. He gazed at and adored the things she wore, her bow, her gloves, her cuffs, her slippers, as sacred objects of which he was master. He thought he was lord of those pretty tortoise-shell combs in her hair, and he even said to himself, dim and confused stammerings of dawning desire, that there was not a thread of her dress, not a mesh in her stockings, not a fold of her underthings, that was not his. At Cosette's side, he felt near his wealth, near his property, near his despot, and near his slave. It seemed they so completely mingled their souls, that if they wanted to take them back again, it would have been impossible to identify them. "This one is mine." "No, it's mine." "I assure you that you're mistaken. This is really me." "What you take for you, is me." Marius was something that was a part of Cosette, and Cosette was something that was a part of Marius. Marius felt Cosette living within him. To have Cosette, to possess Cosette, was not separable from breathing. Into the midst of this faith, of this intoxication, of this virginal possession, marvelous and absolute, of this sovereignty, the words "We are going away" fell all at once, and the sharp voice of reality cried to him, "Cosette is not yours!"

Marius woke up. For six weeks he had lived, as we have said, outside of life; this phrase "going away" brought him roughly back.

He could not find a word. It was her turn to say, "What is the matter?"

He answered so softly that Cosette hardly heard him, "I don't understand what you said."

"This morning my father told me to arrange all my things and be ready, that he would give me his clothes to pack, that he had to take a trip, that we were going away, that we must have a large trunk for me and a small one for him, to get all that ready within a week, and that perhaps we would go to England."

"But that's monstrous!" exclaimed Marius.

It is certain that at that moment, in Marius's mind, no abuse of power, no violence, no abomination of the cruelest tyrants, no action of Busiris, Tiberius, or Henry VIII, was equal in ferocity to this: M. Fauchelevent taking his daughter to England because he has business to do.

He asked in a feeble voice, "And when would you leave?"

"He didn't say when."

"And when will you return?"

"He didn't say when."

Marius arose and said coldly, "Cosette, are you going?"

Cosette raised her beautiful eyes full of anguish and answered in a sort of daze, "Where?"

"To England? Will you go?"

"Why are you speaking to me this way?"

"I am asking you if you will be going?"

"What would you have me do?" she said, clasping her hands.

"So, you are going?"

"If my father goes?"

"So, you are going?"

Cosette took Marius's hand and pressed it without answering.

"Very well," said Marius. "Then I shall go somewhere else."

Cosette felt the meaning of this word still more than she understood it. She turned so pale that her face became white in the darkness. She stammered, "What do you mean?"

Marius looked at her, then slowly raised his eyes to heaven and answered, "Nothing."

When he lowered his eyes, he saw Cosette smiling at him. The smile of the woman we love has a brilliance that shows by night.

"How stupid we are! Marius, I have an idea."

"What?"

"Go if we go! I'll tell you where! Come and join me where I am!"

Marius was now a man entirely awake. He had fallen back into reality. He cried to Cosette, "Go with you? Are you mad? But it takes money, and I have none! Go to England? Why, I owe now, I don't know, more than ten Louis to Courfeyrac, one of my friends whom you don't know! I have an old hat that isn't worth three francs, I have a coat missing some buttons in front, my shirt is all torn, my elbows are out, my boots let in the water; for six weeks I haven't given it a thought and I haven't told you about it. Cosette! I'm a miserable wretch. You only see me at night, and you give me your love; if you should see me by day, you would give me a sou! Go to England? I can't even pay for a passport!"

He threw himself against a nearby tree, standing with his arms above his head, his forehead against the bark, feeling neither the tree, which was chafing his skin, nor the fever that was pounding his temples, motionless, and ready to fall, like a statue of Despair.

He stood like that a long time. One could remain through eternity in such abysses. At last he turned. Behind him he heard a little stifled sound, soft and sad.

It was Cosette sobbing.

She had been weeping for more than two hours while Marius had been thinking.

He came to her, fell on his knees, and slowly prostrating himself, he took the tip of her foot, which peeped from under her dress and kissed it.

She let him do it in silence. There are moments when woman accepts, like a somber and resigned goddess, the religion of love.

"Don't weep," he said.

She murmured, "But perhaps I'm going away, and you can't come!"

He continued, "Do you love me?"

She answered him by sobbing out those words of paradise that are never more enrapturing than when they come through tears, "I adore you."

He went on in a tone of voice that was an inexpressible caress, "Don't cry. Tell me, can you do that for me, not cry?"

"Do you love me, too?" she said.

He caught her hand.

"Cosette, I have never given my word of honor to anybody, because I stand in awe of my word of honor. I feel that my father is at my side. Now, I give you my most sacred word of honor that, if you go away, I will die."

There was in the tone in which he pronounced these words a melancholy so solemn and so quiet that Cosette trembled. She felt that chill that is produced by something dark and true passing over us. From the shock she stopped crying.

"Now listen," he said, "don't expect me tomorrow."

"Why not?"

"Don't expect me till the day after tomorrow!"

"Oh! Why not?"

"You'll see."

"A day without seeing you! That's impossible."

"Let us sacrifice one day to gain perhaps a whole life."

And Marius added in an undertone, and aside, "He is a man who changes none of his habits, and he has never received anybody till evening."

"What man are you speaking of?" inquired Cosette.

"Me? I didn't say anything."

"What is it you hope for, then?"

"Wait till the day after tomorrow."

"You want that?"

"Yes, Cosette."

She took his head in both her hands, rising on tiptoe to reach his height and trying to see his hope in his eyes.

Marius went on, "It occurs to me you have to know my address, something may happen, we don't know; I live with that friend named Courfeyrac, Rue de la Verrerie, number sixteen."

He put his hand in his pocket, took out a penknife, and wrote with the blade on the plaster of the wall:

16, *Rue de la Verrerie.*

Cosette, meanwhile, began to look into his eyes again.

"Tell me your idea. Marius, you have an idea. Tell me. Oh! Tell me, so I won't worry tonight!"

"My idea is this, that it is impossible for God to have wanted to separate us. Expect me the day after tomorrow."

"What shall I do till then?" said Cosette. "You, you are out doors, you come and go! How happy men are. I have to stay alone. Oh! How sad I will be! What is it you are going to do tomorrow evening, tell me?"

"I'll try something."

"Then I'll pray, and I'll think of you from now till then,

so you'll succeed. I won't ask any more questions, since you don't want me to. You are my master. I'll spend my evening tomorrow singing that music from *Euryanthe* that you love, you came to hear it one evening under my shutter. But day after tomorrow you will come early; I'll expect you at night, at nine precisely. I'm telling you now. Oh, dear! How sad that the days are so long! You understand—when the clock strikes nine, I'll be in the garden."

"And I will too."

And without saying it, moved by the same thought, drawn on by those electric currents that put two lovers in continual communication, both intoxicated with pleasure even in their grief, they fell into each other's arms, without perceiving that their lips were joined, while their eyes, overflowing with ecstasy and full of tears, were fixed on the stars.

When Marius left, the street was empty. It was the moment when Eponine was following the robbers to the boulevard.

While Marius was thinking with his head against the tree, an idea had passed through his mind, an idea, alas, that he himself considered senseless and impossible. He had made a desperate decision.

VII

OLD HEART AND YOUNG TOGETHER

Grandfather Gillenormand had passed his ninety-first year. He still lived with Mlle. Gillenormand, Rue des Filles-du-Calvaire, No. 6, in his old house. He was, as we remember, one of those venerable old men who await death still erect, whom age loads without making them stoop, and whom grief does not bend.

Still, for some time, his daughter had said, "My father is failing." He no longer beat the servants; he struck his cane with less animation on the top doorstep, when Basque was slow in opening the door. The July Revolution had scarcely exasperated him for six months. He had seen almost tranquilly in the *Moniteur* this coupling of words: M. Humblot Conté, peer of France. The fact is, the old man was filled with dejection. He did not bend, he did not yield; that was no more a part of his physical than his moral nature; but he felt an inner failing. Four years he had been waiting for Marius, convinced that the wayward little scapegrace would ring at his door some day or other: Now, in certain gloomy hours, he had come to say to himself that if Marius should delay even a little longer . . . It was not death that was insupportable to him; it was the idea that perhaps he would never see Marius again. Never see Marius again—that had not, even for an instant, entered his thoughts until then; now the idea began to appear to him, and it chilled him. Absence, as always happens when feelings are natural and true, had only increased his grandfather's love for the ungrateful child who had gone away like that. It is on December nights, with the thermometer at zero, that we think most of the sun. M. Gillenormand was or thought himself, in any event, incapable of taking a step, he the grandfather, toward his grandson; "I would sooner die," he said. He acknowledged no fault on his side; but he thought of Marius only with a deep tenderness and the mute despair of an old man heading away into the darkness.

He was beginning to lose his teeth, which added to his sadness.

M. Gillenormand, without however acknowledging it to himself, for he would have been furious and ashamed at it, had never loved a mistress as he loved Marius.

He had had hung in his room, at the foot of his bed, as the first thing which he wished to see on awaking, an old portrait of his other daughter, who was dead, Mme. Pontmercy, a portrait done when she was eighteen. He looked at this portrait incessantly. He happened to say one day while looking at it, "I think it looks like the child."

"Like my sister?" replied Mlle. Gillenormand. "Why yes."

The old man added, "And like him, too."

Once, as he was sitting, dejected, his knees pressed together and his eyes almost closed, his daughter ventured to say to him, "Father, are you still so angry with him?"

She stopped, not daring to go further.

"With whom?" he asked.

"With that poor Marius?"

He raised his old head, laid his thin and wrinkled fist upon the table, and cried in his most irritated and quivering tone, "Poor Marius, you say? That gentleman is a rascal, a worthless knave, vain, ungrateful, with no heart, no soul, a proud, wicked boy!"

And he turned away so his daughter would not see the tear in his eyes.

Three days later, after a silence that had lasted for four hours, he said to his daughter snappishly, "I had had the honor to beg Mademoiselle Gillenormand never to speak of him to me."

Aunt Gillenormand gave up all attempts and came to this profound diagnosis: "My father never loved my sister very much after her folly. It is clear that he detests Marius."

"After her folly," meant after she married the colonel.

Still, as may have been conjectured, Mlle. Gillenormand had failed in her attempt to substitute her favorite, the officer of lancers, for Marius. The supplanter Théodule had not succeeded in the least. M. Gillenormand had not accepted the *quid pro quo*. The void in the heart does not accommodate itself to a proxy. As for Théodule, though suspecting an inheritance, he rebelled at the drudgery of pleasing. The old man wearied the lancer, and the lancer shocked the old man. Lieutenant Théodule was undoubtedly lively, but a babbler; frivolous, but vulgar; a good liver, but of bad company; he had mistresses, it is true, and he talked about them a good deal, that is also true; but he talked about them badly. All his qualities had a defect. M. Gillenormand had wearied of hearing him tell of all the favors he had won in the neighborhood of his barracks, on the Rue de Babylone. And then Lieutenant Théodule sometimes came in his uniform with the tricolor cockade. This made him simply insupportable. Finally Grandfather Gillenormand said to his daughter, "I've had enough of him, your Théodule. I have little taste for warriors in time of peace. Entertain him yourself, if you like. The clashing of blades in battle is not so awful, after all, as the rattle of the sheaths against the pavement. And then, to harness himself like a bully and strap himself up like a flirt, to wear a corset under a cuirass, is to be ridiculous twice over. A real man keeps an equal distance from swagger and roguery. Neither hector, nor heartless. Keep your Théodule for yourself."

It was no use for his daughter to say, "Still, he is your grandnephew," it turned out that M. Gillenormand, who was a grandfather to the tips of his fingers, was not a granduncle at all.

Actually, since he had good judgment and made the comparison, Théodule only served to increase his regret for Marius.

One evening, it was June 4, which did not prevent M. Gillenormand from having a blazing fire in his fireplace, he had said goodnight to his daughter, who was sewing in the adjoining room. He was alone in his room with the rural scenery, his feet up on the andirons, half enveloped in his vast coromandel screen with nine folds, leaning on his table on which two candles were burning under a green shade, buried in his tapestried armchair, a book in his hand, but not reading. He was dressed as usual and looked like an antique portrait of Garat. This would have caused him to be followed in the streets, but his daughter always covered him when he went out in a huge bishop's overcoat, which hid his clothes. At home, except for getting up and going to bed, he never wore a dressing gown. "It makes one look old," he said.

M. Gillenormand thought of Marius lovingly and bitterly, and, as usual, the bitterness predominated. An increase of tenderness always ended by boiling over and turning to indignation. He was at the point where we seek to adopt a course, and to accept what tears us apart. He was just explaining to himself that now there was no longer any reason for Marius to return, that if he had been going to return, he would have done so already, that he must give him up. He tried to bring himself around to the idea that it was over, that he would die without seeing "that gentleman" again. But his whole nature revolted; his old paternity could not consent to it. "Well, there it is," he said, this was his sorrowful refrain. "He will not come back!" His bald head had fallen onto his breast, and he was vaguely training a lamentable and irritated look on the embers of his hearth.

He was in just such a reverie, when his old servant, Basque, came in and asked, "Can monsieur receive Monsieur Marius?"

The old man straightened up, pallid and like a corpse

that rises under a galvanic shock. All his blood had flown back to his heart. He faltered. "Monsieur Marius what?"

"I don't know," answered Basque, intimidated and disconcerted by his master's appearance. "I have not seen him. Nicolette just told me there is a young man here, and to say that it is Monsieur Marius."

M. Gillenormand stammered out in a whisper, "Show him in."

And he remained in the same attitude, his head shaking, his eyes fixed on the door. It opened. A young man entered. It was Marius.

Marius stopped at the door, as if waiting to be asked to come in.

His almost shabby clothing was not perceived in the obscurity produced by the green shade. Only his face could be distinguished, calm and grave, but strangely sad.

As if choked with astonishment and joy, M. Gillenormand sat for some moments without seeing anything but a light, as though in the presence of an apparition. He was almost fainting; he saw Marius through a blinding haze. It was he, it was really Marius!

At last! After four years! He took him all in, so to speak, all at a glance. He thought him beautiful, noble, striking, adult, a mature man, with graceful attitude and pleasing air. He would gladly have opened his arms, called him, rushed to him, his heart melted in rapture, affectionate words welled up and overflowed in his breast; indeed, all his tenderness rose to his lips and, through the contrast that was the basis of his nature, harsh words came out. He said abruptly, "What has brought you here?"

Marius answered, embarrassed, "Monsieur—"

M. Gillenormand would have liked Marius to throw himself into his arms. He was displeased with Marius and with himself. He felt that he was rough and Marius was cold. To the old man it was an insupportable and irritating anguish, to feel so tender and so tearful inside, while he could only be outwardly harsh. The bitterness returned. He interrupted Marius sharply, "Then what did you come for?"

This *then* signified: *If you didn't come to embrace me.* Marius looked at his grandfather, whose pallor had changed to marble.

"Monsieur—"

The old man went on, sternly, "Have you come to ask my pardon? Have you seen the error of your ways?"

He thought to put Marius on the track, that "the child" would bend. Marius shuddered; it was the disavowal of his father that was being asked of him; he looked down and answered, "No, monsieur."

"Well then," exclaimed the old man impetuously, with grief that was bitter and angry, "what do you want from me?"

Marius clasped his hands, took a step, and said in a feeble, trembling voice, "Monsieur, have pity on me."

This word moved M. Gillenormand; spoken sooner, it would have softened him, but it came too late. The grandfather stood up; he supported himself on his cane with both hands, his lips were white, his forehead quivered, but his tall stature commanded the stooping Marius.

"Pity on you, monsieur! The youth asks pity from the old man of ninety-two! You are entering life, I am leaving it; you go to the theater, the ball, the café, the billiard room; you have wit, you please the women, you are a handsome fellow, while I cannot leave my chimney corner in midsummer; you are rich with the only riches there are, while I have all the poverties of old age: infirmity, isolation. You have your thirty-two teeth, a good stomach, a keen eye, strength, appetite, health, cheer, a forest of black hair, while I do not even have white hair left; I have lost my teeth, I am losing my legs, I am losing my memory, there are three names of streets that I am always confusing, the Rue Charlot, the Rue du Chaume, and the Rue Saint-Claude, that is where I am. You have the whole future before you full of sunshine, I am beginning to see none of it, so far am I gone into the night; you are in love, of course, I am not loved by anybody in the world, and you ask pity of me. Great heavens, Molière missed that. If that is the way you jest at the Palais, Messieurs Lawyers, I offer you my sincere compliments. You are funny fellows."

And the nonagenarian repeated in a low, angry tone, "Come now, what do you want of me?"

"Monsieur," said Marius, "I know that my presence is displeasing to you, but I have only come to ask one thing of you, and then I will go away immediately."

"You are a fool!" said the old man. "Who is telling you to go away?"

This was the translation of those loving words he had deep in his heart: *Come, ask my pardon now! Throw yourself at my neck!* M. Gillenormand felt that Marius was going to leave him in a few moments, that his unkind reception repelled him, that his harshness was driving him away; he said all this to himself, and his anguish increased; and since his anguish immediately turned to anger, his harshness increased. He would have liked for Marius to understand, and Marius did not, which enraged the old man. He continued, "What! You have left me! Me, your grandfather, you left my house to go who knows where; you have pained your aunt, you have been leading the life of a bachelor, that much is clear, it's more convenient playing the elegant, going home at all hours, amusing yourself; you have not given me one sign of life; you have run up debts without even telling me to pay them; you have made yourself a breaker of windows and a rioter, and, at the end of four years, you come to my house and have nothing to say but that!"

This violent method of pushing the grandson to tenderness produced only silence from Marius. M. Gillenormand folded his arms, a posture that with him was particularly imperious, and apostrophized Marius bitterly.

"Let us be brief. You have come to ask me for something you say? Well what? What is it? Speak up!"

"Monsieur," said Marius, with the look of a man who feels he is about to fall into an abyss, "I have come to ask your permission to get married."

M. Gillenormand rang. Basque half-opened the door.

"Send my daughter in."

A second later—the door opened again. Mlle. Gillenormand did not come in, but showed herself. Marius was standing, mute, his arms hanging down, with the look of a criminal. M. Gillenormand was coming and going, stalking up and down the room. He turned toward his daughter and said, "Nothing. It is Monsieur Marius. Say good evening to him. Monsieur wishes to marry. That is all. Go."

The crisp, harsh tones of the old man's voice betrayed a strange depth of feeling. The aunt gave Marius a bewildered glance, appeared hardly to recognize him, allowed neither a motion nor a syllable to escape her, and disappeared at a breath from her father, quicker than a dry leaf before a hurricane.

Meanwhile Grandfather Gillenormand had come back to stand with his back to the fireplace.

"You marry! At twenty-one! You have arranged that! You have nothing but a permission to ask! A formality. Sit down, monsieur. Well, you have had a revolution since I last had the honor of seeing you. The Jacobins have had the upper hand. You ought to be satisfied. You are a republican, are you not, since you are a baron? You can reconcile the two. The Republic is sauce to the barony. Are you decorated by July? Did you take a bit of the Louvre, monsieur? Near here, in the Rue Saint-Antoine, opposite the Rue des Nonaindières, there is a bullet stuck in the wall of a house, two stories up, with this inscription: July 18th, 1830. Go see that. It makes a good impression. Ah! Pretty things those friends of yours do. By the way, aren't they making a fountain in place of the monument to Monsieur the Duc de Berry? So you want to marry? Whom? Can the question be asked without indiscretion?"

He stopped, and, before Marius had time to answer, he added violently, "Come now, you have a business? Your fortune made? How much do you earn at your lawyer's trade?"

"Nothing," said Marius, with a steadfastness and resolution that were almost savage.

"Nothing? You have nothing to live on but the twelve hundred livres I send you?"

Marius made no answer. M. Gillenormand continued, "Then I understand the girl is rich?"

"As I am."

"What! No dowry?"

"No."

"Some expectations?"

"I believe not."

"With nothing to her back! And what is the father?"

"I do not know."

"What is her name?"

"Mademoiselle Fauchelevent."

"Fauche-what?"

"Fauchelevent."

"Pftt!" said the old man.

"Monsieur!" exclaimed Marius.

M. Gillenormand interrupted him in the tone of a man who is talking to himself.

"There it is, twenty-one, no business, twelve hundred livres a year, Madame the Baroness Pontmercy will go to market to buy two sous' worth of parsley."

"Monsieur," said Marius, in the desperation of a last vanishing hope, "I implore you, in the name of heaven, with clasped hands, monsieur, I throw myself at your feet, allow me to marry her!"

The old man burst into a shrill, dreary laugh, through which he coughed and spoke.

"Ha, ha, ha! You said to yourself, 'The devil! I'll go and find that old wig, that silly dolt! What a pity I am not twenty-five! How I would toss him a good respectful notice! How I would give him the runaround. Never mind, I'll say to him: Old idiot, you are too happy to see me, I feel like getting married, I feel like wedding Mamselle Whoever, daughter of Monsieur Whatever, I have no shoes, she has no chemise, all right; I feel like throwing my career to the dogs, my future, my youth, my life; I feel like taking a plunge into misery with a wife at my neck, that is my idea, you must consent to it! And the old fossil will consent.' Go, my boy, as you please, tie yourself to your paving block, espouse your Pousselevent, your Couplevent—Never, monsieur! Never!"

"Father!"

"Never!"

At the tone in which this "never" was pronounced, Marius lost all hope. He paced the room with slow steps, his head bowed, tottering, more like a man who is dying than like one who is going away. M. Gillenormand followed him with his eyes, and, at the moment the door opened and Marius was leaving, he took four steps with the senile vivacity of impetuous and self-willed old men, seized Marius by the collar, drew him back forcibly into the room, threw him into an armchair, and said to him, "Tell me about it!"

It was the single word, "father," dropped by Marius, that had caused this turnabout.

Marius looked at him bewildered. M. Gillenormand's changing countenance expressed nothing now but a rough and ineffable good nature. The watchdog had been replaced by the grandfather.

"Come on, let's see, speak up, tell me about your love

scrapes, jabber, tell me everything! Lord! How foolish these young folks are!"

"Father," Marius resumed.

The old man's whole face shone with an ineffable radiance.

"Yes! That is it! Call me father, and you shall see!"

Now there was something so kind, so sweet, so open, so paternal, in this abruptness, that in this sudden passage from discouragement to hope, Marius was as though intoxicated, stupefied. He was sitting near the tables, the light of the candle made the shabbiness of his clothing apparent, and the grandfather gazed at it in surprise.

"Well, Father," said Marius.

"Come now," interrupted M. Gillenormand, "then you really haven't a sou? You are dressed like a thief."

He fumbled in a drawer and took out a purse, which he laid on the table: "Here, there is a hundred Louis, buy yourself a hat."

"Father," pursued Marius, "my good father, if you knew. I love her. You don't realize; the first time I saw her was at the Luxembourg, she used to come there; in the beginning I didn't pay much attention to her, and then I don't know how it happened, I fell in love with her. Oh! How wretched it has made me! Now at last I see her every day, at her own house, her father does not know it, just think they're going away, we see each other in the garden in the evening, her father wants to take her to England, so I said to myself: I'll go and see my grandfather and tell him about it. I could go crazy, I'd die, I'd get sick, I'd throw myself into the river. I absolutely have to marry her because I'd go crazy. Now, that's the whole truth, I don't believe I've forgotten anything. She lives in a garden where there is an iron grate, in the Rue Plumet. It's near the Invalides."

Grandfather Gillenormand, radiant with joy, had sat down by Marius's side. While listening to him and enjoying the sound of his voice, he enjoyed at the same time a long pinch of snuff. At that word, Rue Plumet, he stopped in mid-sniff and let the rest of his snuff fall on his knees.

"Rue Plumet! You say Rue Plumet? Let's see now! Aren't there some barracks down there? Why yes, that's it. Your cousin Théodule has told me about her. The lancer, the officer. A lassie, my good friend, a lassie! Lord yes, Rue Plumet. That's what used to be called Rue

Blomet. It comes back to me now. I have heard about this little girl of the gate on the Rue Plumet. In a garden, a Pamela. Your taste is not bad. They say she's nice. Between ourselves, I believe that ninny of a lancer has paid her a little attention. I don't know how far it went. After all, that doesn't matter. And then, we must not believe him. He is a boaster. Marius! I think it is very well for a young man like you to be in love. That goes with your age. I like you better in love than as a Jacobin. I like you better taken by a petticoat, Lord! By twenty petticoats, than by Monsieur de Robespierre. As for me, I do myself this justice that in the matter of *sansculottes,* I have never liked anything but women. Pretty women are pretty women, what the devil! There is no objection to that. As for the little girl, she receives you unknown to papa. That's all right. I've had adventures like that myself. More than one. Do you know what we do? We don't exaggerate the thing; we don't rush to the tragic; we don't conclude with marriage and with Monsieur the Mayor and his sash. We are quite simply a bit shrewd about it. We use good common sense. Slip over it, mortals; don't marry. We come and find Grandfather, who is a good man at heart, and who almost always has a few rolls of Louis in an old drawer; we say to him, 'Grandfather, this is the way it is.' And grandfather says, 'That's entirely natural. Youth must fare and old age must wear. I've been young, you'll be old. Go on, my boy, you will repay this to your grandson. There are two hundred pistoles. Have a good time, lad! Nothing better! That's the way the thing should be done. We don't marry, but that doesn't stop us.' You understand me?"

Marius, petrified and unable to say a word, shook his head.

The good man burst into laughter, winked his old eye, gave him a tap on the knee, looked straight into his eyes with a significant and sparkling expression, and said to him with the most affectionate shrug of the shoulders, "Ninny! Make her your mistress."

Marius turned pale. He had understood nothing of all that his grandfather had been saying. This rigmarole of Rue Blomet, of Pamela, of barracks, of a lancer, had gone past Marius like a phantasmagoria. None of it could relate to Cosette, who was a lily. The old man was wandering from the point. But this wandering had terminated on a word that Marius did understand, and which was a deadly insult to Cosette. That phrase "make her your mistress," entered the heart of the chaste young man like a sword.

He rose, picked up his hat, which was on the floor, and strode firmly toward the door. There he turned, bowed profoundly before his grandfather, raised his head again, and said, "Five years ago you outraged my father; today you have outraged my wife. I ask nothing more of you, monsieur. Adieu."

Grandfather Gillenormand, astounded, opened his mouth, stretched out his arms, attempted to rise, but before he could utter a word, the door closed and Marius had disappeared.

For a few moments the old man was motionless, and as though dumfounded, unable to speak or breathe, as if a hand were clutching his throat. At last he tore himself from his chair, ran to the door as fast as a man past ninety can run, opened it and cried, "Help, help!"

His daughter appeared, then the servants. He continued with a pitifully hoarse voice, "Run after him! Catch him! What have I done to him! He's mad! He's going! Oh! My God! Oh! My God! This time he won't come back!"

He went to the window that looked on the street, opened it with his tremulous old hands, hung more than halfway out, while Basque and Nicolette held on to him from behind, and cried, "Marius! Marius! Marius! Marius!"

But Marius was already out of hearing and was at that very moment turning the corner of the Rue Saint-Louis.

The nonagenarian raised his hands to his temples two or three times, with an expression of anguish, drew back tottering, and sank into an armchair, pulseless, voiceless, tearless, shaking his head, and moving his lips, stunned, with no more left in his eyes or heart than something deep and mournful, resembling night.

Book Nine

WHERE ARE THEY GOING?

I

JEAN VALJEAN

That very day, toward four in the afternoon, Jean Valjean was sitting alone on an outer slope of the most solitary embankment of the Champ de Mars. Whether from prudence, or a need for reflection, or simply as a result of one of those unconscious changes of habits that creep into all lives little by little, he now rarely went out with Cosette. He was wearing his workingman's smock, brown linen trousers, and his cap with the long visor hid his face. He was now calm and happy concerning Cosette; his earlier alarm had disappeared; but for a week or two he had felt anxieties of a different nature. One day, walking on the boulevard, he had seen Thénardier; thanks to his disguise, Thénardier had not recognized him; but since then Jean Valjean had seen him again several times, and he was now certain that Thénardier was prowling the neighborhood. This alone was enough to make him take serious steps. Thénardier meant every danger at once. Moreover, Paris was not calm; for any man with anything in his life to conceal, the political troubles had the inconvenience of making the police very active and very secretive, and in seeking to track a man like Pépin or Morey, they would very likely discover a man like Jean Valjean. Jean Valjean had decided to leave Paris, and even France, and to cross over to England. He had told Cosette. In less than a week he wanted to be gone. He was sitting on the embankment in the Champ de Mars, mulling over a variety of thoughts, Thénardier, the police, the journey, and the difficulty of procuring a passport.

On all these points he was anxious.

Finally, an inexplicable circumstance that had just erupted and was still alarming had put him even more on the alert. That very morning, awake before the others and walking in the garden before Cosette's shutters opened, he had suddenly come upon this line scratched on the wall, probably with a nail.

16, *Rue de la Verrerie.*

It was quite recent, the lines were white against the old black mortar, a tuft of nettles at the foot of the wall was powdered with fresh fine plaster. It had probably been done during the night. What was it? An address? A signal for others? A warning for him? In any case, it was clear that the garden had been violated, that strangers had been there. He recalled the strange incidents that had already alarmed the house. His mind worked away on this canvas. He took care not to speak to Cosette about the line written on the wall, for fear of frightening her.

In the midst of these meditations, he noticed, from a shadow cast by the sun, that somebody had just stopped on the crest of the embankment right behind him. He was about to turn around, when a sheet of folded paper fell onto his knees, as if a hand had dropped it from above his head. He took the paper, unfolded it, and read on it the following, in large letters written with a pencil:

MOVE OUT.

Jean Valjean rose hastily, there was nobody left on the embankment; he looked around and caught sight of a creature larger than a child, smaller than a man, dressed in a gray shirt and trousers of dirt-colored corduroy, who jumped over the parapet and slid into the gully of the Champ de Mars.

Jean Valjean returned home immediately, deep in thought.

II

MARIUS

Marius had left M. Gillenormand's house desolated. He had entered with very small hope; he came out with immense despair.

Still, and those who have observed the stirrings of the human heart will understand it, the lancer, the officer, the ninny, the cousin Théodule, had left no shadow in his mind. Not the slightest. The dramatic poet might apparently hope for some complication due to this revelation, made point-blank to the grandson by the grandfather. But what the drama would gain, the truth would lose. Marius was at that age when we believe no evil; later the age comes when we believe everything. Suspicions are nothing more nor less than wrinkles. Early youth has none. What overwhelms Othello glides over Candide. Suspect Cosette! There are a mass of crimes that Marius could have more easily committed.

He began to walk the streets, the resource of those who are suffering. He could never remember what he thought about. At two in the morning he returned to Courfeyrac's and threw himself, fully dressed, on his mattress. It was broad daylight when he fell asleep, with that awful, heavy slumber when ideas pulse in the brain. When he woke up, he saw Courfeyrac, Enjolras, Feuilly, and Combeferre standing in the room, hats on their heads, all ready to go out, and engrossed in preparations.

Courfeyrac said to him, "Are you coming to General Lamarque's funeral?"

It was as though Courfeyrac were speaking Chinese.

He went out some time after them. He put into his pocket the pistols that Javert had confided to him for the adventure of February 3, and which were still in his possession, still loaded. It would be difficult to say what obscure thought had prompted him to take them with him.

He rambled about all day without knowing where; it rained at times; he did not notice; for his dinner he bought a penny roll at a baker's, put it in his pocket, and forgot it. He looked as if he had bathed in the Seine without being aware of it. There are moments when a man has a furnace in his brain. Marius was in one of those moments. He had no hopes left, he had no fears left; he had reached that state since the evening before. He waited for night with feverish impatience, and only one clear idea; it was that at nine o'clock he would see Cosette. This last happiness was now his whole future; afterward, darkness. At intervals, walking along the most deserted boulevards, he seemed to hear strange sounds in Paris. He roused himself from his reverie, and said, "Are they fighting?"

At nightfall, at precisely nine o'clock, as he had promised Cosette, he was in the Rue Plumet. As he approached the iron gate he forgot everything else. It was forty-eight hours since he had seen Cosette, he was going to see her again, every other thought faded away, and he felt only a deep and wonderful joy. Those minutes in which we live centuries always have this sovereign and wonderful peculiarity, that while they are going by, they entirely fill the heart.

Marius moved the bar and hurried into the garden. Cosette was not at the spot where she usually waited for him. He crossed the thicket and went to the recess near the steps. "She is waiting for me there," he said. Cosette was not there. Looking up, he saw that the house shutters were closed. He took a turn around the garden; the garden was deserted. Then he returned to the house, and, mad with love, intoxicated, dismayed, exasperated with grief and anxiety, like a master who returns home at an untoward hour, he rapped on the shutters. He rapped, he rapped again, at the risk of seeing the window open and the forbidding face of the father appear and ask him, "What do you want?" This would be nothing compared with what he now began to see. When he had rapped, he raised his voice and called Cosette. "Cosette!" he cried. "Cosette!" he repeated imperiously. There was no answer. It was all over. Nobody in the garden; nobody in the house.

Marius fixed his despairing eyes on that dismal house, as black, as silent, and emptier than a tomb. He looked at the stone bench where he had spent so many loving hours with Cosette. Then he sat down on the steps, his heart full of tenderness and determination, he blessed his love in the depths of his thoughts, and said to himself that since Cosette was gone, there was nothing more for him but to die.

Suddenly he heard a voice that seemed to come from the street, hollering through the trees, "Monsieur Marius!"

He stood up.

"What?" he said.

"Monsieur Marius, is it you?"

"Yes."

"Monsieur Marius," added the voice, "your friends are expecting you at the barricade on the Rue de la Chanvrerie."

This voice was not entirely unknown to him. It was something like Eponine's hoarse voice. Marius ran to the gate, pushed aside the movable bar, poked his head through, and saw somebody who seemed like a young man rapidly disappearing in the twilight.

III

M. MABEUF

Jean Valjean's purse was useless to M. Mabeuf. M. Mabeuf, in his venerable childlike austerity, had not accepted the gift of the stars; he did not admit that a star could coin itself into gold Louis. He did not guess that what fell from the sky came from Gavroche. He carried the purse to the commissioner of police of the quarter, as a lost article, returned by the finder for the claimants. The purse was lost, in fact. It goes without saying that nobody reclaimed it, and it did not help M. Mabeuf.

M. Mabeuf continued to sink.

The experiments with indigo had succeeded no better at the Jardin des Plantes than in his garden at Austerlitz. The year before, he owed his housekeeper her wages; now, we have seen, he owed three quarters of his rent. After the term of thirteen months, the pawnbroker had sold the plates of his *Flora*. A coppersmith had made saucepans of them. His plates gone, no longer being able even to complete the broken sets of his *Flora* he still possessed, he had given up engravings and text at a ridiculous price to a secondhand bookseller, as odd copies. Now he had nothing left of his whole life's work. He began to eat up the money from these copies. When he saw that this slender resource was failing him, he gave up his garden and left it uncultivated. Before that, long before, he had given up the two eggs and bit of beef he occasionally used to eat. He dined on bread and potatoes. He had sold his last furniture, then all his spare bedding and clothing, then his collections of plants and his prints; but he still had his most precious books, several of which were extremely rare, including *Les Quadrains Historiques de la Bible*, edition of 1560, *La Concordance des Bibles* by Pierre de Besse, *Les Marguerites de la Marguerite* by Jean de la Haye with a dedication to the Queen of Navarre, the book *On the Charge and Dignity of the Ambassador* by the Sieur de Villiers Hotman, a *Florilegium Rabbinicum* of 1644, a Tibullus of 1567 with this splendid inscription: *Venetiis, in aedibus Manutianis;* finally a Diogenes Laertius, printed at Lyons in 1644, containing the famous variations of the manuscript 411, of the thirteenth century in the Vatican, and those of the two manuscripts of Venice, 393 and 394, so profitably studied by Henry Estienne, and all the passages in the Doric dialect that are found only in the celebrated twelfth-century manuscript of the library of Naples. M. Mabeuf never made a fire in his room and went to bed by daylight so as not to burn a candle. It seemed that he had now no neighbors, he was shunned when he went out and was aware of it. A child's misery is of concern to a mother, a young man's misery is of concern to a young woman, an old man's misery is of concern to nobody. Of all miseries this is the coldest. Still Father Mabeuf had not entirely lost his childlike serenity. His eye regained some vivacity when it alighted on his books, and he smiled when he thought of the Diogenes Laertius, which was the only copy in all the world. His glassfront bookcase was the only piece of furniture beyond the indispensable that he had preserved.

One day Mother Plutarch said to him, "I have nothing to buy dinner with."

What she called dinner was a loaf of bread and four or five potatoes.

"On credit?" said M. Mabeuf.

"You know well enough that they refuse me."

M. Mabeuf opened his bookcase, looked for a long time at all his books, one after another, as a father, forced to decimate his children, would look at them before choosing, then grabbed one of them, put it under his arm, and went out. He returned two hours later with nothing under his arm, laid thirty sous on the table, and said, "Buy something for dinner."

From that moment on, Mother Plutarch saw settling over the old man's white face a dark veil that never lifted again.

The next day, the day after, every day, he had to begin again. M. Mabeuf went out with a book and came back with a little money. As the secondhand bookstall keepers saw that he was forced to sell, they bought from him for twenty sous what he had paid twenty francs for. Sometimes to the same booksellers. Volume by volume, the whole library disappeared. At times he would say, "But I am eighty years old," as if he had some lingering hope of reaching the end of his days before reaching the end of his books. His sadness deepened. One event, however, gave him pleasure. He went out with a Robert Estienne, which he sold for thirty-five sous on the Quai Malaquais, and returned with an Aldine that he had bought for forty sous in the Rue des Grès. "I owe five sous," said he to Mother Plutarch, glowing with joy.

That day he had no dinner.

He belonged to the Horticultural Society. His poverty was known there. The president of this society came to see him, promised to speak to the Minister of Agriculture and Commerce about him, and did so. "Why, how can we let that happen?" exclaimed the minister. "I should think so! An old philosopher! A botanist! An inoffensive man! We must do something for him!" The next day M. Mabeuf received an invitation to dine at the minister's. Trembling with joy, he showed the letter to Mother Plutarch. "We are saved!" he said. On the appointed day, he went to the minister's. He noticed that his ragged necktie, his large, old, square coat, and his shoes polished with egg, surprised the waiters. Nobody spoke to him, not even the minister. About ten in the evening, as he was still expecting some word, he heard the minister's wife, a beautiful lady in a low-necked dress whom he had not dared approach, asking, "Who could that old gentleman be?" He went home on foot, at midnight, in a driving rain. He had sold an Elzevir to pay for the fiacre to go there.

He had acquired the habit, every evening before going to bed, of reading a few pages in his Diogenes Laertius. He knew enough Greek to enjoy the details of the text he possessed. Now he had no other joy. Some weeks went by. Suddenly Mother Plutarch fell sick. There is one thing sadder than having no money to buy bread; that is having nothing with which to buy medicine. One night, the doctor had ordered a very expensive potion. And then the illness grew worse, and a nurse was needed. M. Mabeuf opened his bookcase; there was nothing left. The last volume was gone. Only the Diogenes Laertius remained.

He put the only copy under his arm and went out; it was June 4, 1832; he went to the Porte Saint-Jacques to Royol's successor and returned with a hundred francs. He laid the pile of five-franc pieces on the old servant's bedroom table, and went back to his room without saying a word.

The next day, by dawn, he was sitting on the stone post that lay on its side in the garden, and all morning he could be seen from across the hedge with his head bowed down, motionless, vaguely staring at the withered beds. Occasionally he wept; the old man did not seem to notice. In the afternoon, extraordinary noises broke out in Paris. They sounded like musket shots, and the clamor of a mob.

Father Mabeuf raised his head. He saw a gardener going by and asked, "What is that?"

The gardener answered, his spade on his shoulder and in the calmest tone, "It's a riot."

"What, a riot?"

"Yes. They are fighting."

"What are they fighting about?"

"No idea!" said the gardener.

"Where is it?" continued M. Mabeuf.

"Near the Arsenal."

Father Mabeuf went into the house, picked up his hat, automatically looked for a book to put under his arm, did not find any, said, "Ah, yes, I forgot," and dazedly wandered off.

Book Ten

JUNE 5, 1832

I

THE SURFACE OF THE QUESTION

What constitutes an émeute, a riot? Nothing and everything. An electricity gradually released, a flame suddenly leaping forth, a drifting force, a passing wind. This wind brushes heads that think, dreaming minds, suffering souls, burning passions, howling miseries, and sweeps them away.

Where?

Almost anywhere. Across the state, across laws, across the prosperity and the insolence of others.

Irritated convictions, sharpened enthusiasms, aroused indignations, repressed instincts of war, exalted young courage, noble impulses, curiosity, the taste for change, a thirst for the unexpected, that feeling of pleasure in reading the poster for a new play, and hearing the welcome ringing of the prompter's bell at the theater; vague hatreds, spites, disappointments, every vanity that blames destiny for its failure; discomforts, empty dreams, ambitions shut in by high walls, anyone hoping for a way out of a downfall; finally, at the very bottom, the rabble, that mud which catches fire—such are the elements of the riot.

The greatest and the smallest; the creatures who prowl around outside of everything, waiting for any opportunity, bohemians, people without an occupation, street-corner idlers, those who sleep at night in the open, with no other roof than the cold clouds of the sky, those who seek their bread each day by chance and not by labor, the anonymous ones of misery and vacancy, the barefoot—they belong to the riot.

Whoever harbors in his soul some secret revolt against any act whatsoever of the state, of life or of fate, borders on the riot, and as soon as it appears, begins to quiver, and feel lifted up by the whirlwind.

The émeute is a sort of waterspout in the social atmosphere that suddenly takes form under certain thermal conditions, and in its whirling rises, runs, thunders, tears up, razes, crushes, demolishes, uproots, dragging with it the great spirits and the paltry, the strong man and the feeble mind, tree trunk and straw.

Woe to those it sweeps along, as well as to those it strikes! It shatters them one against the other.

It communicates to those it seizes a mysterious, extraordinary power. It fills the first comer with the force of events; it makes projectiles of everything. It makes a bullet of a pebble and a general of a dockhand.

If we may believe certain oracles of crafty politics, from the governmental point of view, a modicum of émeute is desirable. Theorem: The émeute strengthens those governments it does not overthrow. It tests the army; it concentrates the bourgeoisie; it stretches the muscles of the police; it determines the strength of the social framework. It is a gymnastic training; it is almost hygienic. Power is healthier after a riot, like a man after a rubdown.

Thirty years ago, the émeute was seen from still other points of view.

For everything there is a theory that proclaims itself "common sense"; Philinte against Alceste; mediation offered between the true and the false; explanation, admonition, a somewhat haughty extenuation, which because it is a mixture of blame and excuse, thinks itself wisdom and is often mere pedantry. An entire political school, called the school of compromise, has sprung from this. Between cold and warm water, this is the party of tepid water. This school, with its pretended depth, wholly superficial, that dissects effect without going back to the causes, chides the agitations of the public square from the heights of a demi-science.

To hear this school: "The riots that complicated the

achievement of 1830 robbed that great event of a portion of its purity. The revolution of July had been a fine popular gust of wind, quickly followed by blue sky. They brought back the cloudy sky. They degraded that revolution, at first so remarkable for its unanimity, to the level of a quarrel. In the July Revolution, as in all sudden progress, there were some secret fractures; the riots brought them to light. One could say, 'Ah! This is broken.' After the July Revolution, only the deliverance was felt; after the riots, the catastrophe was felt.

"Every riot closes shops, depresses the economy, terrifies the stock market, suspends commerce, hobbles business, precipitates failures; no more money, private fortunes shaken, public credit disturbed, industry disconcerted, capital hoarded, jobs reduced, fear everywhere; counteractions in all the cities, hence yawning gulfs. It has been calculated that the first day of a riot costs France twenty million, the second forty, the third sixty. A three-day riot costs a hundred and twenty million, which, looking only at the financial result, is equivalent to a disaster, a shipwreck, or the loss of a battle that annihilated a fleet of sixty vessels of the line.

"Beyond a doubt, historically, émeutes had their beauty; the paving-block war is no less grand and no less pathetic than the war of the thickets; in the one there is the spirit of forests; in the other the heart of cities; one has Jean Chouan, the other has Jeanne. The émeutes illuminated, with red light, but splendidly, all the most original outgrowths of the Parisian character, generosity, devotion, tempestuous gaiety, students proving that bravery is part of intelligence, the National Guard unwavering, bivouacs of shopkeepers, fortresses of *gamins,* scorn of death among the people on the street. Schools and legions came into conflict. After all, between the combatants, there was only a difference of age; they were the same race; they are the same stoical men who die at twenty for their ideas, at forty for their families. The army, always sad in civil wars, opposed audacity with prudence. At the same time that they demonstrated the intrepidity of the people, the riots brought about the education of bourgeois courage.

"Very well. But is it all worth the bloodshed? And to the bloodshed add the future darkened, progress compromised, anxiety among the best men, honest liberals despairing, foreign absolutism delighted with these wounds inflicted on the revolution by itself, the vanquished of 1830 triumphantly saying, 'We told you so!' Add Paris enlarged perhaps, but France surely diminished. Add, for we must tell it all, the massacres that too often dishonored the victory of order grown ferocious over liberty gone mad. Taken altogether, émeutes have been disastrous.

Thus speaks this quasi-wisdom with which the bourgeoisie, that quasi-people, so gladly contents itself.

As for us, we reject this too broad and consequently too convenient word, émeute. Between a popular movement and a popular movement, we draw a distinction. We do not ask whether an émeute cost as much as a battle. In the first place why a battle? Here the question of war arises. Is war less a scourge than the émeute a calamity? And then, are all émeutes calamities? And what if the 14th of July did cost a hundred and twenty million? The establishment of Philip V in Spain cost France two billion. Even at the same price, we would prefer the 14th of July. Moreover, we reject these figures, which seem to be reasons, and are only words. Given an émeute, we examine it for itself. In everything said in the theoretical objection just presented, only the effect is questioned, but we seek the cause.

We will be specific.

II

THE ESSENTIAL QUESTION

There is émeute, there is insurrection; they are two different angers; one is wrong, the other right. In democratic states, the only governments founded on justice, it sometimes happens that a faction usurps power; then the whole rises up, and the necessary vindication of its right may go so far as armed conflict. In all questions springing from the collective sovereignty, the war of the whole against the faction I will call insurrection; the attack of the faction against the whole is émeute; according to whether the Tuileries contain the King or the Convention, they are justly or unjustly attacked. The same cannon pointed against the crowd is wrong the 10th of August, and right the 14th of Vendémiaire. Similar in appearance, but fundamentally different; the Swiss defend the false, Bonaparte defends the true. What universal suffrage has done in its freedom and its sovereignty cannot be undone by the street. The same goes for affairs of pure civilization; the instinct of the masses, clear-sighted yesterday, may be clouded tomorrow. The same fury is lawful against Terray, and absurd against Turgot. The destruction of machines, the pillage of storehouses, the tearing up of rails, the demolition of docks, the mistaken acts of the multitudes, the denial of justice to progress by the people, Ramus assassinated by the students, Rousseau driven out of Switzerland with stones, is émeute. Israel against Moses, Athens against Phocion, Rome against Scipio, is the émeute; Paris against the Bastille is insurrection. The soldiers against Alexander, the sailors against Christopher Columbus, this is the same revolt; an impious revolt; why? Because Alexander does for Asia with the sword what Christopher Columbus does for America with the compass; Alexander, like Columbus, finds a world. These gifts of a world to civilization are such extensions of light that all resistance to them is criminal. Sometimes the people counterfeits fidelity to itself. The mob is traitor to the people. Is there, for instance, anything stranger than that long and bloody protest of the contraband saltmakers, a legitimate chronic revolt, which, at the decisive moment, on the day of salvation, at the hour of the people's victory, espouses the throne, turns Chouan, and from insurrection against makes itself a riot for! Dreary masterpieces of ignorance! The contraband saltmaker escapes the royal gallows, and, with a bit of rope at his neck, displays the white cockade. "Death to the salt tax" turns into "Vive le Roi." Saint Bartholomew assassins, September murderers, Avignon massacres, assassins of Coligny, assassins of Madame de Lamballe, assassins of Brune, Miquelets, Verdets, Cadenettes, companions of Jéhu, Chevaliers du Brassard—this is riot. La Vendée is a great Catholic émeute.

The sound of the advancing right is recognizable, it does not always come from the quaking of the overthrown masses; there are foolish rages, there are cracked bells; every tocsin does not sound with the ring of bronze. The clash of passions and ignorances is different from the shock of progress. Rise, if you will, but to grow. Show me which way you are going. There is no insurrection but forward. Every other uprising is evil; every violent step backward is an émeute; to retreat is an act of violence against the human race. Insurrection is the truth's outburst of rage; the paving stones that insurrection tears up throw off the spark of right. These stones leave only their mud to riot. Danton against Louis XVI is insurrection, Hébert against Danton is riot.

Hence, if insurrection in given cases may be, as Lafayette said, the most sacred of duties, émeute may be the most deadly of crimes.

There is also some difference in the thermal intensity; the insurrection is often a volcano, the émeute is often a straw fire.

The revolt, as we have said, is sometimes on the side of power. Polignac is a rioter; Camille Desmoulins is a governor.

Insurrection is sometimes resurrection.

Since the solution of everything by universal suffrage is an entirely modern occurrence, and all history, for four thousand years before that, filled with violated rights and the suffering of the people, each period of history brings with it such protest as it can. Under the Caesars there was no insurrection, but there was Juvenal.

The *facit indignatio* replaces the Gracchi.

Under the Caesars there is the exile of Syene; there is also the man of the *Annales*.

We do not speak of the sublime exile of Patmos, who also bears down on the real world with a protest in the name of the ideal, makes a tremendous satire of a vision, and throws on Nineveh-Rome, on Babylon-Rome, on Sodom-Rome, the flaming reverberations of the Apocalypse.

John on his rock is the Sphinx on her pedestal; we cannot understand him; he is a Jew, and it is Hebrew; but the man who wrote the *Annales* is a Latin; let us rather say he is a Roman.

As the Neros reign darkly, they should be pictured so. Engraving with the burin alone would be pale; a concentrated biting prose should be poured into the grooves.

Despots make their contribution to thinkers. Speech in chains is terrible speech. The writer doubles and triples his style when silence is imposed by a master over the people. From this silence springs a certain mysterious fullness that filters and congeals into brass in the thoughts. Compression in history produces concision in the historian. The granite solidity of some celebrated prose is only a condensation produced by the tyrant.

Tyranny constrains the writer to shortenings of diameter that are increases of force. The Ciceronian period, hardly sufficient on Verres, would lose its edge on Caligula. Less breadth in the phrase, more intensity in the blow. Tacitus thinks with his arm drawn back.

The nobility of a great heart, condensed into justice and truth, strikes like a thunderbolt.

Be it said in passing, one should note that Tacitus was not historically superimposed on Caesar. The Tiberii were reserved for him. Caesar and Tacitus are two successive phenomena whose meeting seems mysteriously avoided by Him who, in staging the centuries, regulates the entrances and exits. Caesar is great, Tacitus is great; God spares these two grandeurs by not hurling them at each other. The judge, striking Caesar, might strike too hard, and be unjust. God did not will it. The great wars of Africa and Spain, the destruction of the Cilician pirates, civilization introduced into Gaul, into Britain, into Germany, all this glory covers the Rubicon. There is a delicacy of divine justice here, hesitating to let loose the terrible historian on the illustrious usurper, saving Caesar from Tacitus, and granting the genius some extenuating circumstances.

Certainly, despotism is always despotism, even under a despot of genius. There is corruption under illustrious tyrants, but the moral pestilence is still more appalling under infamous tyrants. In those reigns nothing veils the shame; and makers of examples, Tacitus as well as Juvenal, belabor this inexcusable ignominy most profitably in full view of the human race.

Rome smells worse under Vitellius than under Sylla. Under Claudius and under Domitian, there is a depravity to match the ugliness of the tyrant. The debasement of the slaves is a direct result of the despot; a miasma is given off by these crouching consciences that reflects the master; the public powers are unclean; hearts are small, consciences are dull; souls are puny; this is so under Caracalla, this is so under Commodus, this is so under Heliogabalus, while under Caesar only the rank odor peculiar to the eagle's eyrie comes from the Roman Senate.

Hence the arrival, apparently late, of the Tacituses and Juvenals; when the hour of evidence is in, then the professor appears.

But Juvenal and Tacitus, like Isaiah in biblical times, like Dante in the Middle Ages, are men; riot and insurrection are the multitude, sometimes wrong, sometimes right.

In the most usual cases rioting springs from a material fact; insurrection is always a moral phenomenon. The riot is Masaniello; the insurrection is Spartacus. Insurrection borders on the mind, riot on the stomach; Gaster is irritated; but Gaster, certainly, is not always wrong. In cases of famine, riot, Buzançais, for instance, has a true, pathetic, and just point of departure. Still it remains riot. Why? Because fundamentally right, it was wrong in form. Savage though right, violent though strong, it struck haphazardly; it walked like the blind elephant, crushing; it left behind it the corpses of old men, women, and children; without knowing why, it poured out the blood of the inoffensive and the innocent. To nurture the people is a good aim; to massacre it is an evil means.

Every armed protest, even the most legitimate, even the 10th of August, even the 14th of July, begins with the same trouble. Before right emerges, there is tumult and froth. In the beginning insurrection is a riot, even as the river is a torrent. Ordinarily it ends in that ocean, revolution. Sometimes, however, coming from the high mountains that loom over the moral horizon, justice, wisdom, reason, right, made of the purest snow of the ideal, after a long fall from rock to rock, after having reflected the sky in its transparency and been swollen by a hundred affluents in the majestic aura of triumph, insurrection suddenly loses itself in some bourgeois quagmire, like the Rhine in a marsh.

All this is the past; the future is different. Universal suffrage is admirable in that it dissolves the riot in its principle and, by giving a vote to insurrection, disarms it. The vanishing of war, street war as well as the war of the frontiers, such is inevitable progress. Whatever today may be, peace is tomorrow.

However, insurrection, riot—in what way the first differs from the second—the bourgeois, properly speaking, knows little of these nuances. To him, everything is sedition, rebellion pure and simple, revolt of the dog against the master, attempt to bite that must be punished by chain and kennel, barking, yelping, till the day when the dog's head, suddenly enlarged, stands out dimly in the darkness with a lion's face.

Then the bourgeois cries, *Vive le peuple!*

With this explanation given, what for history is the movement of June 1832? Is it a riot? Is it an insurrection?

It is an insurrection.

We may, in this presentation of a fearful event, sometimes say the émeute, or the riot, but only to denote the surface facts, and always maintaining the distinction between the form émeute and the substance insurrection.

This movement of 1832, in its rapid explosion and in its dismal extinction, had so much grandeur that even those who see in it only a riot do not speak of it without respect. To them it is like a remnant of 1830. "Aroused imaginations," they say, "do not calm down in a day." A revolution is not stopped dead. It always has some necessary undulations before returning to the condition of peace like a mountain descending toward the plain. There are no Alps without their Jura, nor Pyrenees without Asturias.

This pathetic crisis of contemporary history, which Parisians remember as "the time of the riots," is surely a characteristic moment amid the tempestuous periods of this century. A last word before resuming the narrative.

The events we are about to relate belong to that dramatic and living reality that the historian sometimes neglects, for lack of time and space. Yet in them, we insist, is the life, the heartbeat, the tremor of humanity. Little incidents, we believe we have said, are, so to speak, the foliage of great events and are lost in the great span of history. The era known as "the time of the riots" abounds in details of this kind. The judicial investigations, for reasons other than history, did not reveal everything, nor perhaps get to the bottom of everything. So we will bring to light, among the known and public circumstances, some things that have never been known, deeds passed over by the forgetfulness of some, the death of others. Most of the actors in those gigantic scenes have disappeared; from the next day on they were silent; but what we will relate, we can say that we saw. We will change some names, for history relates and does not inform against, but we will paint reality. From the nature of the book we are writing, we only show one side and one episode, and that certainly the least known, of the days of the 5th and 6th of June, 1832; but we shall do it in such a way that the reader may glimpse, under the gloomy veil we are about to lift, the real countenance of that fearful public tragedy.

III

A BURIAL: OPPORTUNITY FOR REBIRTH

In the spring of 1832, though for three months cholera had chilled all hearts and dampened their agitation with an inexpressibly mournful calm, Paris had for a long time been ready for a commotion. As we have said, the great city is like a piece of artillery; when it is loaded the falling of one spark is enough, the shot goes off. In June 1832, the spark was the death of General Lamarque.

Lamarque was a man of renown and action. Under the Empire and under the Restoration, he had successively shown the two forms of bravery necessary to the two eras, the bravery of the battlefield and the bravery of the rostrum. He was eloquent as he had been valiant; men felt a sword in his speech. Like Foy, his predecessor, after having upheld command, he upheld liberty. He sat between the left and the extreme left, loved by the people because he accepted the chances of the future, loved by the masses because he had served the Emperor well. He was, with Counts Gérard and Drouet, one of Napoleon's marshals *in petto*. The treaties of 1815 angered him like a personal offense. He hated Wellington with a direct hatred that pleased the multitude; and for seventeen years, hardly noticing intervening events, he had majestically preserved the sadness of Waterloo. On his deathbed, he had pressed to his breast a sword presented to him by the officers of the Hundred Days. Napoleon died pronouncing the word *armée*, Lamarque pronouncing the word *patrie*. His death, which had been anticipated, was dreaded by the people as a loss and by the government as a pretext. This death brought a mourning. Like everything bitter, mourning may turn into revolt. That is what happened.

On the eve and the morning of the 5th of June, the day set for Lamarque's funeral, the Faubourg Saint-Antoine, which the procession was to skirt, took on an intimidating aura. That tumultuous network of streets was teeming with rumors. Men armed themselves as best they could. Some carpenters carried their bench claw "to smash in the doors." One of them had made a dagger out of a buttonhook by breaking off the tip and sharpening the stump. In the fever "to attack," another had slept for three nights fully dressed. A carpenter named Lombier met a comrade who asked him, "Where are you going?" "Well, I have no weapon." "What then?" "I'm going to my yard to look for my compasses." "What for?" "I don't know," said Lombier. A certain Jacqueline, an energetic man, hailed every worker who passed by with, "Come on, you there!" He bought ten sous' worth of wine, and said, "Do you have any work?" "No." "Go to Filspierre's, between the Barrière Montreuil and the Barrière Charonne, you'll find work." At Filspierre's they found cartridges and arms. Certain known leaders ran from house to house gathering their people. At Barthélemy's, near the Barrière du Trone, and at Capet's, at the Petit-Chapeau, the drinkers accosted each other seriously. They were heard to say, "Where's your pistol?" "Under my tunic." "And yours?" "Under my shirt." On the Rue Traversière, in front of the Roland workshop, and in the Cour de la Maison-Brûlée, in front of Bernier's machine shop, groups were whispering. Among the most ardent was noticed a certain Mavot, who never worked more than a week in one shop, before the masters sent him away, "because they had to argue with him every day." Mavot was killed the next day at the barricade in the Rue Ménilmontant. Pretot, who was also to die in the conflict, seconded Mavot, and to the question "What is your aim?" answered, "*Insurrection.*" Some workingmen, gathered at the corner of the Rue de Bercy, were waiting for a man named Lemarin, revolutionary officer for the Faubourg Saint-Marceau. Orders were passed around almost openly.

On the 5th of June, then, a day of mingled rain and sunshine, General Lamarque's procession passed through Paris with official military pomp, somewhat increased by way of precaution. Two battalions, drums muffled, muskets reversed, ten thousand National

Guardsmen, their sabers at their sides, the batteries of artillery of the National Guard, escorted the coffin. The hearse was drawn by young men. The officers of the Invalides followed immediately behind, bearing branches of laurel. Then came a multitude, strangely agitated, the section chiefs of the Friends of the People, the Law School, the Medical School, refugees from all nations, Spanish, Italian, German, Polish flags, horizontal tricolored flags, every possible banner, children waving green branches, stonecutters and carpenters, who were on a strike at that moment, printers recognizable by their paper caps, walking two by two, three by three, uttering cries, almost all brandishing clubs, a few of them swords, without order, and yet with a single soul, now a rout, now a column. Some platoons chose chiefs; a man, quite openly armed with a pair of pistols, seemed to be passing others in review as they filed off before him. On the cross alleys of the boulevards, in the branches of the trees, on the balconies, at the windows, on the roofs, were swarms of heads, men, women, children; their eyes were full of anxiety. An armed multitude was passing by, a terrified multitude was looking on.

The government too was observing. It was observing, with its hand on the hilt of the sword. One could see, all ready to march, with full cartridge boxes, guns and muskets loaded, in the Place Louis XV, four squadrons of cavalry, in the saddle, trumpets in the lead; in the Latin Quarter and at the Jardin des Plantes, the Municipal Guard spread out from street to street; at the Halle aux Vins a squadron of dragoons, at La Grève half of the 12th Light, the other half at the Bastille, the 6th dragoons at the Célestins, the Court of the Louvre full of artillery. The rest of the troops were stationed in the barracks, without counting the regiments on the outskirts of Paris. Anxious authority held suspended over the threatening multitude twenty-four thousand soldiers in the city, and thirty thousand in the suburbs.

Various rumors circulated through the cortège. They talked of legitimist intrigues; they talked of the Duke of Reichstadt, whom God was marking for death at the very moment the populace was designating him for empire. A personage unknown to this day announced that at the appointed hour two foremen who had been won over would open to the people the doors of an arms factory.

The dominant expression on the uncovered foreheads of most of those present was one of subdued enthusiasm. Here and there in this multitude, a prey to so many violent but noble emotions, could also be seen some faces of malefactors and vile mouths that said "Pillage!" There is a certain turmoil that stirs up the bottom of the marsh, and raises clouds of mud in the water. A phenomenon not unknown to "well-run" police forces.

The cortège made its way, with a feverish slowness, from the house of the deceased, along the boulevards as far as the Bastille. It rained sporadically; the rain had no effect on that throng. Several incidents, the coffin taken around the Vendôme column, the stones thrown at the Duc de Fitz-James who was seen on a balcony with his hat on, the Gallic cock torn from a popular flag and dragged in the mud, a police officer wounded by a sword at the Porte Saint-Martin, an officer of the 12th Light saying out loud, "I am a republican"; the Polytechnic School arriving unexpectedly after the students forced the issue, cries of "Vive l'école polytechnique! Vive la république!" marked the progress of the procession. At the Bastille, long and formidable files of the curious from the Faubourg Saint-Antoine met up with the cortège and a terrible simmering began to rouse the multitude.

One man was heard saying to another, "Do you see that man with the red beard? He is the one who will say when we must fire." It seems that the same red beard was found later with the same function in another riot, the Quénisset affair.

The hearse passed the Bastille, followed the canal, crossed the little bridge, and reached the esplanade of the Pont d'Austerlitz. There it stopped. At that moment a bird's-eye view of this multitude would have suggested a comet, whose head was at the esplanade, while the tail, spreading over the Quai Bourdon, covered the Bastille, and stretched along the boulevard as far as the Porte Saint-Martin. A circle was drawn up around the hearse. The vast assemblage fell silent. Lafayette spoke and bade farewell to Lamarque. It was a touching and noble moment, all heads uncovered, all hearts throbbed. Suddenly a man on horseback, dressed in black, appeared in the midst of the throng with a red flag, others say with a pike surmounted by a red cap. Lafayette looked away. Exelmans left the cortège.

This red flag raised a storm and disappeared in it. From the Boulevard Bourdon to the Pont d'Austerlitz a roar like a surging billow stirred the multitude. Two prodigious shouts arose: "Lamarque to the Panthéon! Lafayette to the Hôtel de Ville!" Some young men, amid the cheers of the throng, took up the harness and began to pull Lamarque in the hearse over the Pont d'Austerlitz, and Lafayette in a fiacre along the Quai Morland.

In the cheering crowd that surrounded Lafayette, a German was noticed and pointed out, named Ludwig Snyder, who later died a centenarian, who had also been in the war of 1776, and who had fought at Trenton under Washington and under Lafayette at Brandywine.

Meanwhile, on the left bank, the municipal cavalry was in motion and had just barred the bridge; on the right bank the dragoons left the Célestins and deployed along the Quai Morland. The men who were pulling Lafayette suddenly saw them at the bend of the Quai, and cried, "The dragoons!" The dragoons were advancing at a walk, in silence, their pistols in their holsters, their sabers in their sheaths, their muskets at rest, with an air of gloomy expectation.

At two hundred paces from the little bridge, they halted. The fiacre bearing Lafayette made its way up to them, they opened their ranks, let it pass, and closed again behind it. At that moment the dragoons and the multitude came together. The women fled in terror.

What took place in that fatal moment? Nobody could tell. It was the dark moment when two clouds mingle. Some say that a trumpet flourish sounding the charge was heard from the direction of the Arsenal, others that a child thrust a dagger at a dragoon. The fact is that three shots were suddenly fired, the first killed the leader of the squadron, Cholet, the second killed an old deaf woman who was closing her window in the Rue Contrescarpe, the third nicked the epaulet of an officer; a woman cried, "They're beginning too soon!" and all at once was seen, from the side opposite the Quai Morland, a squadron of dragoons that had remained in barracks turning out at a gallop, with swords drawn, from the Rue Bassompierre and the Boulevard Bourdon, sweeping everything in their way.

Then the last word has been said, the tempest breaks loose; stones fall like hail; musket-fire bursts out, many rush headlong down the bank and cross the little branch of the Seine that is now filled in; the lumberyards of the Ile Louviers, that vast ready-made citadel, bristle with combatants; they tear up stakes, they fire pistol shots; a barricade begins to rise; the young men crowded back cross the Pont d'Austerlitz with the hearse at a run and charge the Municipal Guard; the carbineers rush up; the dragoons ply the saber; the crowd scatters in every direction; a rumor of war flies to the four corners of Paris; men cry "To arms!" They run, they tumble, they fly, they resist. Wrath sweeps the riot along as the wind does with a fire.

IV

OUTBURSTS OF FORMER TIMES

Nothing is more extraordinary than the first swarming of a riot. Everything bursts out everywhere at once. Was it foreseen? Yes. Was it prepared? No. Where does it spring from? From the pavements. Where does it fall from? From the clouds. Here the insurrection has the characteristics of a plot; there of an improvisation. The first comer takes possession of a current in the multitude and leads it wherever he wants. A beginning full of terror mingled with a sort of frightful gaiety. At first there is shouting, the shops close, the displays of the merchants disappear; then some isolated shots; people flee; gun butts strike against carriage doors; you hear the servant girls laughing in the yards of the houses and saying, "There's going to be a real ruckus!"

Before a quarter of an hour had elapsed, here is what had taken place at practically the same time at twenty different points in Paris.

In the Rue Sainte-Croix-de-la-Bretonnerie, some twenty young men, with beards and long hair, entered a smoking room and came out again a moment later, bearing a horizontal tricolor flag covered with crepe and having at their head three armed men, one with a sword, another with a gun, the third with a pike.

In the Rue des Nonnains-d'Hyères, a well-dressed potbellied bourgeois, with a ringing voice, a bald head, a high forehead, a black beard, and one of those rough mustaches that cannot be smoothed down, publicly offered cartridges to passersby.

In the Rue Saint-Pierre-Montmartre, some men with bare arms paraded a black flag on which these words could be read in white letters: "Republic or death." In the Rue des Jeûneurs, the Rue du Cadran, the Rue Montorgueil, and the Rue Mandar, groups appeared waving flags on which the word "section" with a number could be seen in gold letters. One of these flags was red and blue with an imperceptible white stripe between.

An arms factory was plundered on the Boulevard Saint-Martin, as were three armorer's shops, the first in the Rue Beaubourg, the second in the Rue Michel-le-Comte, the third in the Rue du Temple. In a few minutes the thousand hands of the multitude seized and carried off two hundred and thirty muskets, nearly all double-barreled, sixty-four swords, eighty-three pistols. To arm more people, one took the gun, another the bayonet.

Opposite the Quai de la Grève, young men armed with muskets installed themselves in women's apartments to shoot. One of them had a musket with a matchlock. They rang, entered, and set to making cartridges. One of these women said, "I did not know what cartridges were; my husband told me to."

A throng broke into a junk shop on the Rue des Vieilles-Haudriettes and took some yataghans and Turkish arms.

The corpse of a mason killed by a musket shot was lying in the Rue de la Perle.

And then, right bank, left bank, on the quays, on the boulevards, in the Latin Quarter, in the market area, breathless men, workingmen, students, section chiefs, read proclamations, cried, "To arms!" broke the streetlamps, unharnessed wagons, tore up the pavements, smashed in house doors, uprooted the trees, ransacked the cellars, rolled kegs, heaped up paving stones, pebbles, pieces of furniture, boards, made barricades.

They forced the bourgeois to help them. They went into the women's houses, they made them give up their absent husbands' sword and gun, and wrote over the door in white: "Weapons surrendered." Some signed "with their names" receipts for the gun and sword, and said, "Send for them tomorrow to the mairie." They disarmed the solitary sentinels in the streets and National Guards going to their assignments. They tore off the officers' epaulets. In the Rue du Cimetière-Saint-Nicolas, an officer of the National Guard, pursued by a troop armed with clubs and foils, took refuge with great difficulty in a house he was able to leave only at night and in disguise.

In the Quartier Saint-Jacques, the students came out of their houses in swarms and went up the Rue Saint-Hyacinthe to the café Du Progrès or down to the café Des Sept-Billards, on the Rue des Mathurins. There, in front of the doors, some young men standing on the posts distributed arms. They pillaged the lumberyard on the Rue Transnonain to make barricades. At a single location, the inhabitants resisted, at the corner of the Rues Sainte-Avoye and Simon-le-Franc where they destroyed the barricade themselves. At a single location, the insurgents gave way; they abandoned a barricade begun in the Rue du Temple after having fired on a detachment of the National Guard, and fled through the Rue de la Corderie. In the barricade the detachment picked up a red flag, a package of cartridges, and three hundred pistol balls. The National Guards tore up the flag and carried the shreds on the point of their bayonets.

Everything we are relating here slowly and successively took place simultaneously in all parts of the city in the midst of vast tumult, like a myriad of flashes in a single peal of thunder.

In less than an hour twenty-seven barricades rose from the ground in the market quarter. At the center was that famous house, No. 50, which was the fortress of Jeanne and his hundred and six companions, and which, flanked on one side by a barricade at Saint-Merry and on the other by a barricade on the Rue Maubuée, commanded three streets, the Rue des Arcis, the Rue Saint-Martin, and the Rue Aubry-le-Boucher on which it fronted. Two barricades at right angles ran back, one from the Rue Montorgueil to the Grande Truanderie, the other from the Rue Geoffroy Langevin to the Rue Sainte-Avoye. Without counting innumerable barricades in twenty other quarters of Paris, in the Marais, at Mount Sainte-Geneviève, there was one, on the Rue Ménilmontant, featuring a carriage door torn off its hinges; another near the little bridge of the Hôtel Dieu made with a small carriage unhitched and overturned, within three hundred yards of the prefecture of police.

At the barricade on the Rue des Ménétriers, a well-dressed man distributed money to the laborers. At the barricade on the Rue Grenétat a horseman appeared and handed to the one who seemed to be the leader of the barricade a roll that looked like a roll of money. "This," said he, "is to pay the expenses, wine, etcetera." A young man of fair complexion, without a tie, went from one barricade to another carrying orders. Another, with drawn sword and a blue police cap on his head, was stationing sentinels. Within the barricades, wineshops and porters' lodges were converted into guardhouses. Moreover, the uprising was conducted according to the soundest military tactics. The narrow, uneven, sinuous streets, full of turns and corners, were admirably chosen—the area near Les Halles in particular, a network of streets more intricate than a forest. The Society of the Friends of the People, so it was said, had assumed the direction of the insurrection in the Quartier Sainte-Avoye. A man, killed in Rue du Ponceau, who was searched, had a map of Paris on him.

What had really assumed the direction of the émeute was a sort of unknown impetuosity in the atmosphere. The insurrection had abruptly built the barricades with one hand, and with the other seized nearly all the posts of the garrison. In less than three hours, like a trail of powder catching fire, the insurgents had invaded and occupied on the right bank the Arsenal, the mayor's office of the Place Royale, all the Marais, the Popincourt arms factory, the Galiote, the Château d'Eau, all of the streets near the markets; on the left bank, the barracks of the Vétérans, Sainte-Pélagie, the Place Maubert, the powder mill of the Deux Moulins, all the city gates. At five in the afternoon they were masters of the Bastille, the Lingerie, the Blancs-Manteaux; their scouts touched the Place des Victoires, and threatened the Bank, the barracks of the Petits-Pères, and the Hôtel des Postes. A third of Paris was involved.

At all points the struggle had begun on a gigantic scale; and from the disarmings, from the domiciliary visits, from the armorers' shops hastily invaded, there was the result that the combat, begun by throwing stones, was continued by rifle fire.

Around six in the evening, the arcade Du Saumon became a battlefield. The rioters were at one end, the troops at the opposite. They fired from one gate to the other. One observer, a dreamer, the author of this book, who had gone to get a close view of the volcano, found himself caught in the arcade between the two fires. He had nothing but the protection of the pilasters that separate the shops to protect him from the bullets; he spent close to an hour in this delicate situation.

Meanwhile the drums beat the long roll, the National Guards hurriedly dressed and armed themselves, the legions left the town halls, the regiments left their barracks. Opposite the arcade De l'Ancre, a drummer was struck by a dagger. Another, on the Rue du Cygne, was assailed by some thirty young men, who destroyed his drum and took away his sword. Another was killed in the Rue Grenier-Saint-Lazare. In the Rue Michel-le-Comte three officers fell dead one after another. Several Municipal Guards, wounded in the Rue des Lombards, turned back.

In front of the Cour Batave, a detachment of National Guards found a red flag bearing this inscription: "Republican revolution, No. 127." Was it a revolution, in fact?

The insurrection had made the center of Paris a sort of inextricable, tortuous, colossal citadel.

There was the focus, there the clear center of combat. All the rest were only skirmishes. What proved that all would be decided there was that they were not yet fighting.

In some regiments, the soldiers were hesitant, which added to the frightening obscurity of the crisis. They remembered the popular ovation, which in July 1830 had greeted the neutrality of the 53rd of the line. Two intrepid men, who had been proven by the great wars, Marshal de Lobau and General Bugeaud, were in command, Bugeaud under Lobau. Enormous patrols, composed of battalions of the line surrounded by entire companies of the National Guard, and preceded by a commissioner of police with his badge, went out reconnoitering the insurgent streets. On their side, the insurgents placed pickets at the street corners and boldly sent patrols outside the barricades. They kept watch on both sides. The government, with an army in its hand, hesitated; night was coming on, and the tocsin of Saint-Merry began to be heard. The Minister of War of the time, Marshal Soult, who had seen Austerlitz, observed this with gloomy countenance.

These old hands, accustomed to correct maneuvering, and having no resource or guide except tactics, that compass of battles, are completely lost in the presence of that vast foam called the wrath of the people. The wind of revolutions is not tractable.

The National Guard of the suburbs hurried together in disorder. A battalion of the 12th Light ran down from Saint-Denis, the 14th of the Line arrived from Courbevoie, the batteries of the Military School had taken up position at the Carrousel; artillery came from Vincennes.

Solitude reigned at the Tuileries. Louis-Philippe was full of serenity.

V

ORIGINALITY OF PARIS

For two years, as we have said, Paris had seen more than one insurrection. Outside of the insurgent quarters, nothing is usually more strangely calm than the physiognomy of Paris during an uprising. Paris grows accustomed to everything very quickly—it's only an émeute—and Paris is so busy that it does not get worked up over such a trifle. These colossal cities alone can contain such spectacles. These immense precincts alone can contain at the same time a civil war and an indescribably eerie tranquillity. Usually, when the insurrection begins, when the drum, the long roll, the call to arms are heard, the shopkeeper merely says, "It seems there's some squabble in the Rue Saint-Martin."

Or: "Faubourg Saint-Antoine."

Often he adds coolly, "Somewhere down that way."

Afterward, when he distinguishes the dismal and harrowing uproar of musketry and the platoons firing, the shopkeeper says, "So, it's warming up. Well now, it's really warming up!"

A moment later, if the uprising approaches and swells, he precipitately shuts up his shop, and hastily dons his uniform; which is to say, places his goods in safety and risks his person.

They fire at each other on the street corners, in an

arcade, in a cul-de-sac; barricades are taken, lost, retaken; blood flows, the fronts of the houses are riddled with grapeshot, bullets kill people in their beds, corpses litter the pavement. A few streets away, you hear the clicking of billiard balls in the cafés.

The theaters open their doors and play comedies; the curious chat and laugh two steps from these streets full of war. The fiacres jog along; passersby are going to dine in the city, sometimes in the very area where there is fighting. In 1831 a fusillade was suspended to let a wedding party pass by.

During the insurrection of the 12th of May 1839, in the Rue Saint-Martin, a sickly little old man, pulling a handcart topped by a tricolored rag, in which there were decanters filled with some liquid, went back and forth from the barricade to the troops and the troops to the barricade, offering glasses of cocoa impartially—now to government, now to anarchy.

Nothing is stranger; and this is the peculiar property of the Paris riots, not found in any other capital. Two things are needed for it, the greatness of Paris and its gaiety. It requires the city of Voltaire and of Napoleon.

This time, however, in the armed contest of the 5th of June 1832, the great city felt something that was, perhaps, stronger than herself. She was afraid. Everywhere, in the most distant and the most "disinterested" quarters, you saw doors, windows, and shutters closed in broad daylight. The courageous were armed, the cowards hid. The careless and busy wayfarer disappeared. Many streets were as empty as at four in the morning. Alarming stories went the rounds, ominous rumors were spread. "That *they* had taken the Bank"; "that, merely at the cloisters of Saint-Merry, there were six hundred, entrenched and fortified in the church"; "that the line was doubtful"; "that Armand Carrel had been to see Marshal Clausel and that the marshal had said, 'Have one regiment in place first,' "; "that Lafayette was sick, but that he had said to them, 'I am with you. I will follow you anywhere that there is room for a chair' "; "that it was necessary to keep on their guard; that at night people would pillage the isolated houses in the deserted neighborhoods of Paris (the imagination of the police was recognized here, that Anne Radcliffe element in government)"; "that a battery had been set up in the Rue

Aubry-le-Boucher"; "that Lobau and Bugeaud were conferring; and that at midnight, or daybreak at the latest, four columns would march at once on the center of the émeute, the first coming from the Bastille, the second from the Porte Saint-Martin, the third from La Grève, the fourth from Les Halles"; "that perhaps the troops would evacuate Paris and fall back on the Champ de Mars"; "that nobody knew what might happen, but that certainly, this time, it was serious." They were concerned about Marshal Soult's hesitation. "Why doesn't he attack right away?" It is certain he was deeply absorbed. The old lion seemed to scent in that darkness some unknown monster.

Evening came on, the theaters did not open; the patrols made their rounds spitefully; pedestrians were searched; the suspicious were arrested. At nine there were more than eight hundred persons under arrest; the prefecture of police was crowded, the Conciergerie was crowded, La Force was crowded. At the Conciergerie, in particular, the long vault called the Rue de Paris was strewn with bundles of straw, on which lay a throng of prisoners, harangued valiantly by the man of Lyons, Lagrange. The rustling of all this straw, stirred by all these men, was like the sound of a downpour. Elsewhere the prisoners lay in the open air in the prison yards, piled one on top of another. Anxiety was widespread, a certain nervousness, little known to Paris.

People barricaded themselves in their houses; wives and mothers were terrified; you heard only this: "Oh, my God! He hasn't come home!" One scarcely heard even a distant rumbling of a wagon. On their doorsteps, people listened to the rumors, the cries, the tumult, the faint and indistinct sounds, things that prompted them to say, "That's the cavalry," or "Those are the ammunition wagons galloping in," the trumpets, the drums, the musket fire, and above all, that mournful tocsin of Saint-Merry. They waited for the first cannon shot. Armed men appeared at the street corners and disappeared, crying, "Go home!" And people hastened to bolt their doors. They said, "How will it turn out?" Progressively, night fell, Paris seemed more and more ominously lit by the stupendous flame of the uprising.

Book Eleven

THE ATOM FRATERNIZES WITH THE HURRICANE

I

SOME INSIGHTS INTO THE ORIGIN OF GAVROCHE'S POETRY—

AN ACADEMICIAN'S INFLUENCE ON THAT POETRY

The moment the insurrection erupted from the impact of the people against the troops in front of the Arsenal, causing a repercussion from the front to the rear of the throng following the hearse, which, for the whole length of the boulevard, was pushing toward the head of the procession, there was a terrible back surge. The mass wavered, the ranks broke, everyone ran, darted, slipped away, some with cries of attack, others with the pallor of flight. The great river covering the boulevards divided in a twinkling, overflowed to the right and the left, and poured in torrents into two hundred streets at once with the rushing of an opened mill-sluice. At that moment a ragged child who was coming down the Rue Ménilmontant, holding in his hand a branch of blooming laburnum, which he had just gathered on the heights of Belleville, noticed in the display of a secondhand dealer's shop an old horse pistol. He threw his flowering branch onto the pavement, and cried out, "Mother Whatziss, I'm borrowing your gadget."

And he ran off with the pistol.

Two minutes later, a flood of terrified bourgeois who were fleeing through the Rue Amelot and the Rue Basse met the child brandishing his pistol and singing:

> La nuit on ne voit rien,
> Le jour on voit très-bien,
> D'un écrit apocryphe
> Le bourgeois s'ébouriffe,
> Pratique la vertu,
> Tutu chapeau pointu![1]

It was little Gavroche off to war.

On the boulevard he noticed that the pistol had no hammer.

Who wrote this refrain that gave him the beat for his marching, and all the other songs he liked to sing from time to time? We do not know. Who knows? They were his own, perhaps. Actually, Gavroche kept up with all the current popular tunes, and mixed in his own warbling with them. A sprite and a devil, he made a medley of the voices of nature and the voices of Paris. He combined the repertory of the birds with the repertory of the workshops. He knew some painter's boys, a tribe close to his own; it seems that for three months he had been a printer's apprentice. He had run an errand one day for M. Baour-Lormian, one of the Forty. Gavroche was a gamin of letters.

Gavroche had no idea that on that wretched rainy night when he had offered the hospitality of his elephant to two brats, it was for his own brothers he had played Providence. His brothers in the evening, his father in the morning; such had been his night. On leaving the Rue des Ballets at early dawn, he had returned in haste to the elephant, artfully extracted the two *mômes*, shared with

[1] If night is a pall,
In the day you see all,
By an apocryphal text,
The bourgeois is most vexed,
Nurture virtue,
Bottom-pointed hat!

them such breakfast as he could invent, then went off, entrusting them to that good mother, the streets, who had almost brought him up, too. On leaving them, he had set up a rendezvous for that evening at the same place and left them this discourse as a farewell: "I'm cutting, in other words, I decamp, or, as they say at the court, I haul off; brats, if you don't find papa and mamma, come back here tonight. I'll chuck you some supper and give you a bed." The two children, picked up by some policeman and put in the lockup, or stolen by some traveling circus, or simply lost in the immense Parisian turmoil, had not returned. The lower strata of the existing social world are full of such lost traces. Gavroche had not seen them since. Ten or twelve weeks had gone by since that night. More than once he had scratched the top of his head and said, "Where the devil are my two children?"

Meanwhile he had reached, pistol in hand, the Rue du Pont-aux-Choux. He noticed that there was only one shop in the street left open, and that one, a matter worthy of reflection, a pastry shop. This was a providential opportunity to eat one more apple turnover before embarking on the unknown. Gavroche stopped, fumbled in his trousers, felt in his fob, turned out his pockets, found nothing in them, not a sou, and began to cry, "Help!"

It is hard to just miss out on the ultimate cake.

Gavroche nonetheless continued on his way.

Two minutes later, he was in the Rue Saint-Louis. While passing through the Rue du Parc-Royal he felt the need of some compensation for the impossible apple turnover, and he gave himself the immense pleasure of tearing down the theater posters in broad daylight.

A bit farther along, seeing a group of well-to-do individuals go by, who appeared to be men of property, he shrugged his shoulders, and spit out at random this mouthful of philosophic bile: "These rich men, how fat they are! They stuff themselves. They wallow in good dinners. Ask them what they do with their money. They have no idea. They eat it, that's all! Gone with the belly."

II

GAVROCHE ON THE MARCH

The brandishing of a pistol without a hammer, holding it in one's hand in the open street, is such public behavior that Gavroche felt his spirits rise with every step. Between the snatches of the Marseillaise he was singing, he cried, "All's going well. I'm suffering a good deal in my left paw, I'm broken with my rheumatism, but I'm content, citizens. The bourgeois have nothing to do but behave; I'm going to sneeze subversive couplets at them. What are the detectives? They're dogs. By jinks! Don't let's fail in respect for dogs. Though that's what my pistol is, without a hammer. I've just come from the boulevard, my friends, it's getting hot, it's coming to a boil, it's simmering. It's time to skim the pot. Forward, men! Let their impure blood water the furrows! I give my days for my country. I'll never see my concubine again, n-e-ver, done, yes. Never! But no matter, let's be joyful! Let's fight, ye gods and little fishes! I've had enough of despotism."

At that moment, as the horse of a passing lancer of the National Guard had fallen, Gavroche laid his pistol on the pavement, helped the man up, then he helped get the horse on his feet. After which he picked up the pistol and went on his way.

In the Rue de Thorigny, all was peace and silence. This apathy, inherent to the Marais, contrasted with the vast surrounding uproar. Four gossips were chatting on a doorstep. Scotland has her trios of witches, but Paris has her quartet of gossips; and the "Thou shalt be king" would be cast just as ominously at Bonaparte in the Baudoyer Square as at Macbeth in the heath of Armuyr. It would come in almost the same croak.

The gossips of the Rue de Thorigny were interested only in their own affairs. They were three concierges and a ragpicker with her basket and hook.

The four semed to be standing at the four corners of old age, which are decay, decrepitude, ruin, and sorrow.

The ragpicker was humble. In this outdoor society, the ragpicker bows, the concierge patronizes. That is a result of the sweepings, which are, as the concierges would have it, fat or lean, according to the fancy of the one who makes the heap. There may be kindness in the broom.

This ragpicker was a grateful recipient, and she smiled, such a smile, at the three concierges. Things such as this were said: "Ah, now, so your cat is still mean, is she?"

"Luddy! Cats, you know, are nat'rally the enemies of dogs. It's the dogs that complain."

"And folks, too."

"Still, cats' fleas don't get on folks."

"That's not the trouble, dogs are dangerous. I remember one year there was so many dogs they had to put it in the papers. It was the time they had the big sheep at the Tuileries who pulled the King of Rome's little wagon. Do you remember the King of Rome?"

"Me, I liked the Duc de Bourdeaux better."

"As for me, I knew Louis XVII. I like Louis XVII better."

"It's meat that's expensive, Ma'am Patagon!"

"Oh! Don't speak of it, the stuff is a horror. Horrible horror. You get nothing but the bones, nowadays."

Here the ragpicker intervened: "Ladies, business is very dull. The garbage heaps are shabby. Folks don't throw anything away these days. They eat everything."

"There are poorer people than you, Vargoulême."

"Oh, that's true!" replied the ragpicker, with deference. "As for me, I have an occupation."

There was a pause, and the ragpicker, yielding to that necessity for display that lies deepest in the human heart, added, "In the morning when I get home, I pick over the basketful, I make my sorties [probably sortings]. It makes heaps in my room. I put the rags in a basket, the cores in a tub, the linens in my closet, the woolens in my bureau, the old papers by the window, the things good to eat into my bowl, the bits of glass in the fireplace, the old shoes behind the door, and the bones under my bed."

Gavroche, who had stopped behind, was listening.

"Old women," he said, "now what business do you have talking politics?"

A volley came back at him, composed of a quadruple hoot.

"Now there's another scoundrel!"

"What's he got in his stump? A pistol."

"Now I ask you, that beggar of a *môme!*"

"They're never quiet if they're not upsetting authority."

Gavroche, in disdain, made no reply beyond merely lifting the tip of his nose with his thumb while opening his hand wide.

The ragpicker cried out, "Nasty bare-paws!"

The one who answered to the name of Ma'am Patagon clapped her hands in horror.

"There's going to be troubles, that's sure. That rascal next door with his beard, I used to see him go by every morning arm in arm with a young thing in a pink cap; today I see him go by, he was giving his arm to a musket. Ma'am Bacheux says that there was a revolution last week in . . . in . . . in . . . where's the place? In Pontoise. And then do you see him with his pistol, that horrible tramp? It seems the Célestins are all full of cannon. What would you have the government do with the layabouts who do nothing but invent ways to bother people, when we're beginning to be a little quiet, after all the troubles we've had, good Lord, and that poor queen I saw going by in the tumbril! And all this will raise the price of snuff again. It's an outrage! And surely I'll go to see you guillotined, you scoundrel."

"You're sniffling, you antique," said Gavroche. "Blow your promontory."

And he passed on.

When he reached the Rue Pavée, the ragpicker came back to mind, and he soliloquized in these terms: "You're wrong to insult the revolutionaries, Mother Heap-o'-dust. This pistol is your interest. It's so you'll have more good things to eat in your basket."

Suddenly he heard a noise behind him; it was the concierge Patagon who had followed him, and was shaking her fist at him from a distance, hollering, "You're nothing but a bastard!"

"On that score," said Gavroche, "I'm profoundly indifferent."

Soon after, he passed the Hôtel Lamoignon. There he shouted out his appeal: "En route for battle!"

And he was seized by a fit of melancholy. He looked at his pistol with a reproachful air that seemed an attempt at endearment.

"I go off," he said to it, "but you don't!"

One dog may distract attention from another. A skinny mongrel was going by. Gavroche was moved to pity.

"My poor bowwow," he said, "have you swallowed a barrel? All the hoops are showing."

Then he bent his steps toward the Orme-Saint-Gervais.

III

JUST INDIGNATION OF A BARBER

The worthy barber who drove away the two little boys to whom Gavroche had opened the paternal intestines of the elephant was in his shop, busy shaving an old legionary who had served under the Empire. They were chatting. The barber had naturally spoken of the uprising, then of General Lamarque, and from Lamarque they had turned to the emperor. Hence a conversation between a barber and a soldier, which Prudhomme, had he been present, would have enriched with arabesques, and which he would have called *Dialogue of the Razor and the Saber*.

"Monsieur," said the barber, "how did the emperor ride?"

"Badly. He didn't know how to fall. So he never fell."

"Did he have fine horses? He must have had fine horses!"

"The day he gave me the cross, I noticed his animal. She was a racing mare, perfectly white. Her ears were very wide apart, deep saddle, fine head, marked with a black star, very long neck, knees strongly jointed, protruding ribs, sloping shoulders, powerful hindquarters. A little more than fifteen hands high."

"A pretty horse," said the barber.

"It was His Majesty's animal."

The barber felt that after this a little silence was proper; he conformed to it, then went on, "The emperor was only wounded once, wasn't he, monsieur?"

The old soldier answered with the calm and sovereign tone of a man who was there, "In the heel. At Ratisbon. I never saw him so well dressed as he was that day. He was as neat as a pin."

"And you, Monsieur Veteran, you must have been wounded often?"

"I?" said the soldier. "Nothing much. I got two saber

slashes in my neck at Marengo, a ball in my right arm at Austerlitz, another in my left hip at Jena, at Friedland a bayonet thrust—there—at Moscow seven or eight lancings, no matter where, at Lutzen a shell burst that crushed my finger—Ah! And then at Waterloo a bullet in my leg. That's all."

"How beautiful," exclaimed the barber with a pindaric accent, "to die on the battlefield! Upon my word, rather than die in my bed of sickness, slowly, a little every day, with drugs, poultices, syringes, and medicine, I would prefer a cannonball in my belly."

"You're not very fastidious," said the soldier.

He had hardly finished when a frightful crash shook the shop. A pane of the store window had suddenly shattered.

The barber turned pale.

"O God!" he cried, "there is one!"

"What?"

"A cannonball."

"Here it is," said the soldier.

And he picked up something rolling on the floor. It was a stone.

The barber ran to the broken window and saw Gavroche, who was running with all his might toward the Marché Saint-Jean. On passing the barber shop, Gavroche, who had the two *mômes* on his mind, could not resist the desire to bid him good day and had tossed a stone through his window.

"See!" screamed the barber, who from white had turned blue. "He makes mischief for the sake of mischief. What has anybody done to him, that gamin?"

IV

THE CHILD WONDERS AT THE OLD MAN

Meanwhile at the Marché Saint-Jean where the guard was already disarmed, Gavroche had just joined forces with a band led by Enjolras, Courfeyrac, Combeferre, and Feuilly. They were more or less armed. Bahorel and Jean

Prouvaire had joined them and enlarged the group. Enjolras had a double-barreled shotgun, Combeferre a National Guard's musket bearing the number of the legion, and stuck in his belt two pistols that could be seen through his unbuttoned coat, Jean Prouvaire an old cavalry musket, Bahorel a carbine; Courfeyrac was brandishing an unsheathed sword-cane. Feuilly, a drawn saber in his hand, marched in the van, crying, "Poland forever!"

They were coming from the Quai Morland tieless, hatless, breathless, soaked by the rain, lightning in their eyes. Gavroche approached them calmly: "Where are we going?"

"Come on," said Courfeyrac.

Behind Feuilly marched, or rather bounded, Bahorel, a fish in the water of the uprising. He had on a crimson waistcoat, and words to crush everything. His waistcoat unsettled a pedestrian, who cried out in desperation, "There are the reds!"

"The reds, the reds!" replied Bahorel. "An odd fear, bourgeois. As for me, I don't tremble before a red poppy, little red riding hood gives me no dismay. Bourgeois, believe me, let's leave the fear of red to horned cattle."

He caught sight of a piece of wall placarded with the most peaceful sheet of paper in the world, a permission to eat eggs, a charge for Lent, addressed by the Archbishop of Paris to his "flock."

Bahorel exclaimed, "Polite way of saying geese."

And he tore the permission off the wall. This conquered Gavroche. From that moment, Gavroche studied Bahorel.

"Bahorel," observed Enjolras, "you're wrong. You should have left those instructions alone, it has nothing to do with what we're after. You're spending your wrath uselessly. Economize your ammunition. We don't fire out of rank—not with the soul any more than the gun."

"Each in his own way, Enjolras," retorted Bahorel. "This bishop's prose annoys me, I want to eat eggs without anybody's permission. You have the cold burning style; I have a good time. Besides, I'm not exhausting myself, I'm gaining new energy; and if I tore down that pastoral letter, by Hercules, it was to whet my appetite."

This word "Hercules" struck Gavroche. He sought every opportunity to instruct himself, and this tearerdown of posters had his esteem. He asked him, "What does that mean, 'Hercules'?"

Bahorel replied, "It means holy name of a dog in Latin."

Here Bahorel recognized a pale young man with a black beard, who was looking at them from a window as they went by, probably a Friend of the A B C. He cried out to him, "Quick, cartridges! *Para bellum.*"

"*Bel homme!* [Handsome man!] That's true," said Gavroche, who now understood Latin.

A rowdy cortège followed them, students, artists, young men affiliated to the Cougourde d'Aix, workingmen, rivermen, armed with clubs and bayonets; a few, like Combeferre, with pistols stuck into their waistbands. A man who seemed very old was marching with this band. He was not armed, and he was hurrying, so as not to be left behind, although he had a thoughtful expression. Gavroche noticed him.

"Whoossat?" he said to Courfeyrac.

"That's an old man."

It was M. Mabeuf.

V

THE OLD MAN

We should say what had happened.

Enjolras and his friends were on the Boulevard Bourdon, near the warehouses, when the dragoons charged. Enjolras, Courfeyrac, and Combeferre were among those who took to the Rue Bassompierre, crying, "To the barricades!" In the Rue Lesdiguières they met an old man trudging along. What attracted their attention was that this good man was walking zigzag, as if he were drunk. Moreover, he had his hat in his hand, although it had been raining all morning, and was raining hard at that very moment. Courfeyrac recognized Father Mabeuf. He knew him from having many times accompanied Marius to his door. Knowing the peaceful and more-than-timid habits of the old church-warden–bookworm, and astonished to see him in the midst of this tumult, within two steps of the cavalry charges, almost in the midst of a fusillade, bareheaded in the rain, and walking among the bullets, he went up to him, and the émeuter of twenty-five and the old man exchanged this dialogue:

"Monsieur Mabeuf, go home."

"What for?"

"There's going to be a row."

"Good."

"Sabers, musket fire, Monsieur Mabeuf."

"Good."

"Cannon."

"Good. Where are you going, you boys?"

"We are going to overthrow the government."

"Good."

And he followed them. From that moment on he had not uttered a word. His step had suddenly become firm; some workmen had offered him an arm, he refused with a shake of the head. He moved up almost to the front rank of the column, with both the motion of a man who is walking and the countenance of a man who is asleep.

"What a desperate old man!" murmured the students. The rumor ran through the assemblage that he was—a former Conventionist—an old regicide. The company had turned into the Rue de la Verrerie.

Little Gavroche marched on singing at the top of his lungs, which made him a sort of clarion. He sang:

Voici la lune qui paraît,
Quand irons-nous dans la forêt?
Demandait Charlot à Charlotte.
Tou tou tou
Pour Chatou.
Je n'ai qu'un Dieu, qu'un roi, qu'un liard et qu'une botte.

Pour avoir bu de grand matin
La rosée à même le thym,
Deux moineaux étaient en ribote.
Zi zi zi
Pour Passy
Je n'ai qu'un Dieu, qu'un roi, qu'un liard et qu'une botte.

Et ces deux pauvres petits loups
Comme deux grives étaient soûls;
Un tigre en riait dans sa grotte.
Don don don
Pour Meudon.

Je n'ai qu'un Dieu, qu'un roi, qu'un liard et qu'une botte.
L'un jurait et l'autre sacrait
Quand irons-nous dans la forêt?
Demandait Charlot à Charlotte.
Tin tin tin
Pour Pantin.
Je n'ai qu'un Dieu, qu'un roi, qu'un liard et qu'une botte.[1]

They made their way toward Saint-Merry.

VI

RECRUITS

The band grew by the minute. Toward the Rue des Billettes they were joined by a tall man, who was turning gray, whose rough and bold bearing Courfeyrac, Enjolras, and Combeferre noticed, but whom none of them knew. Gavroche, busy singing, whistling, humming, leading off, rapping on the shutters of the shops with the butt of his hammerless pistol, paid no attention to this man.

As it happened, in the Rue de la Verrerie they passed by Courfeyrac's door.

"That's lucky," said Courfeyrac, "I've forgotten my purse, and I've lost my hat." He left the company and went up to his room, four stairs at a time. He grabbed an old hat and his purse. He also picked up a large square box, the size of a big suitcase, which was hidden among his dirty clothes. As he was running down again, the concierge hailed him: "Monsieur de Courfeyrac?"

1. See how the moon is shining, when do we go to the woods? Charlot asked Charlotte/Too, too, too, for Chatou. I have only one of everything: God, king, sou, boot./For having drunk in early morning, of the dew and thyme. Two sparrows were boozing./Zi, zi, zi, for Passy. I have one God, king, sou, boot./And these poor little wolves were as drunk as two thrushes; a tiger laughed away in his cave./Don, don, don, for Meudon. I have one God, king, sou, boot./One of them swore and the other one cursed. When do we go to the woods? Charlot asked Charlotte./Tin, tin, tin, for Pantin. I have one God, king, sou, boot.

"Concierge, what's your name?" responded Courfeyrac.

The concierge stood aghast.

"Why, you know it very well; I'm the concierge, my name is Mother Veuvain."

"Well, if you call me Monsieur de Courfeyrac again, I'll call you Mother de Veuvain. Now, speak up, what is it? What do you want?"

"There is somebody who wants to speak to you."

"Who?"

"I don't know."

"Where is he?"

"In my lodge."

"The devil!" said Courfeyrac.

"But he has been waiting more than an hour for you to come home!" replied the concièrge.

At the same time, a sort of young workingman, thin, pale, small, freckled, dressed in a torn workshirt, and patched corduroy pants, and who looked more like a girl in boy's clothes than a man, came out of the lodge and said to Courfeyrac in a voice which, to be sure, was not the least like a woman's voice, "Monsieur Marius, if you please?"

"He's not in."

"Will he be in this evening?"

"I don't know anything about it."

And Courfeyrac added, "As for myself, I won't be in."

The young man stared at him, and asked him, "Why?'

"Because."

"Where are you going?"

"What's that to you?"

"Do you want me to carry your box?"

"I'm going to the barricades."

"Do you want me to go with you?"

"If you like," answered Courfeyrac. "The road is free; the streets belong to everybody."

And he ran off to rejoin his friends. When he had reached them, he gave the box to one of them to carry. It was not until a quarter of an hour later that he noticed that the young man had in fact followed them.

A mob does not go precisely where it wants to. We have explained that a gust of wind carries it along. They went beyond Saint-Merry and found themselves, without really knowing how, in the Rue Saint-Denis.

Book Twelve

CORINTH

I

HISTORY OF CORINTH SINCE ITS FOUNDATION

Parisians who, today, on entering the Rue Rambuteau from the side of Les Halles, notice on their right, opposite the Rue Mondétour, a basket maker's shop, with a basket for a sign, in the shape of the emperor Napoleon the Great, with this inscription:

NAPOLÉON EST FAIT
TOUT EN OSIER,[1]

do not suspect the terrible scenes that this very place saw thirty years ago.

Here were the Rue de la Chanvrerie, which the old signs spelled Chanverrerie, and the celebrated bistro called Corinth.

The reader will remember all that has been said about the barricade erected on this spot, actually eclipsed by the barricade of Saint-Merry. We are about to throw some little light onto this famous barricade of the Rue de la Chanvrerie, now fallen into deep obscurity.

Permit us to return, for the sake of clarity, to the simple means already used for Waterloo. Those who would like to accurately picture the confused blocks of houses

[1] Napoleon is made
All of willow braid.

standing at that time near the Pointe Saint-Eustache, at the northeast corner of the markets of Paris, Les Halles, where the Rue Rambuteau now begins, only have to imagine touching the Rue Saint-Denis at its summit, and the markets at its base, an *N*, of which the two vertical strokes would be the Rue de la Grande Truanderie and the Rue de la Chanvrerie, and the Rue de la Petite Truanderie would make the transverse stroke. The old Rue Mondétour cut the three strokes at the most awkward angles. With the result that the labyrinthine web of these four streets, within a space of four hundred square yards, between the markets and the Rue Saint-Denis, in one direction, and between the Rue du Cygne and the Rue des Prêcheurs in the other direction, made seven little islands of houses, oddly intersecting, of various sizes, placed crosswise and as if by chance, only slightly separated, like blocks of stone in a stone yard, by narrow crevices.

We say narrow crevices, and we cannot give a more apt idea of those obscure, closely packed, angular lanes, bordered by hovels eight stories high. These houses were so dilapidated that in the Rues de la Chanvrerie and de la Petite Truanderie, the fronts were shored up with beams, reaching from one house to another. The street was narrow and the gutter wide, the pedestrian walked along a pavement that was always wet, beside shops like cellars, great stone blocks banded with iron, immense garbage heaps, and alley gates fortified by huge old gratings. The Rue Rambuteau has devastated all this.

The name Mondétour gives a marvelous image of this whole twisting route. A little farther along you found it still better expressed by the Rue Pirouette, which ran into the Rue Mondétour.

The pedestrian coming from the Rue Saint-Denis into the Rue de la Chanvrerie saw it gradually narrow away in front of him as if he had entered an elongated funnel. At the end of the street, he found the passage barred on the market side and would have thought himself in a cul-de-sac, if he had not noticed to the right and left two black openings by which he could escape. These were the Rue Mondétour, which joined the Rue des Prêcheurs on one side, and the Rues du Cygne and Petite Truanderie on the other. At the end of this sort of cul-de-sac, at the corner of the opening on the right, could be seen a house lower than the rest, and forming a kind of promontory on the street.

In this house, only three stories high, an illustrious wineshop had been festively located for three hundred years. This bistro raised a joyful sound on the very spot that old Théophile has made famous in these two lines:

> Là branle le squelette horrible
> D'un pauvre amant qui se pendit.[1]

It was a good location. The proprietorship was handed down from father to son.

In the days of Mathurin Régnier, this wineshop was called the *Pot aux Roses* [the Pot of Roses], and as rebuses were in fashion, its sign was a post *[poteau]* painted rose color. In the last century, the worthy Natoire, one of the whimsical masters, now held in disdain by the traditionalists, after a bit too much to drink several times in this wineshop at the same table where Régnier had gotten drunk, gratefully painted a bunch of Corinth grapes on the rose-colored post. The landlord, overjoyed, changed his sign and added below the bunch these words in gold letters: *The Grape of Corinth*. Hence the name Corinth. Nothing is more natural to drinkers than an ellipsis. The ellipsis is the zigzag of a phrase. Corinth gradually dethroned the *Pot aux Roses*. The last landlord of the dynasty, Father Hucheloup, not even aware of the tradition, had the post painted blue.

A ground-floor room containing the counter, a room on the second floor with the billiard table, a spiral wooden staircase piercing the ceiling, wine on the tables, smoke on the walls, candles in midday, such was the wineshop. A stairway with a trapdoor in the ground-floor room led to the cellar. On the third floor were the rooms of the Hucheloups. It was reached by a stairway, actually a ladder rather than a stairway, whose only entrance was by a back door in the large room on the first floor. In the attic were two garret rooms with dormer windows, nests for servants. The kitchen shared the ground floor with the barroom.

Perhaps Father Hucheloup was a born chemist, he was

[1] There rattles the horrible skeleton/Of a poor lover who hung himself.

certainly a cook; people not only drank in his bistro, they ate there. Hucheloup had invented an excellent dish found only at his house; it was stuffed carp, which he called *carpes au gras*. This was eaten by the light of a tallow candle, or a lamp from the days of Louis XVI, on tables to which an oilcloth was tacked for a tablecloth. Men would come there from some distance. One fine morning, Hucheloup thought proper to advise passersby of his "specialty"; he dipped a brush in a pot of blacking, and as he had a spelling all his own, just as he had a cuisine of his own, he improvised on his wall this remarkable inscription:

CARPES HO GRAS.

One winter, the showers and the storms decided to erase the *S* at the end of the first word and the *G* that began the third, and it was left like this:

CARPE HO RAS.

Time and rain contributing, a humble gastronomic advertisement had become a profound piece of advice that paraphrased Horace, Seize the hours.

So it happened that, without knowing French, Father Hucheloup had known Latin, that he had brought philosophy out of his kitchen and that, desiring simply to eclipse Carême, he had equaled Horace. And what was striking was that this also meant: Enter my wineshop.

Nothing of all this exists today. The Mondétour labyrinth was ripped up and opened wide in 1847, and is probably gone by now. The Rue de la Chanvrerie and Corinth have disappeared under the pavements of the Rue Rambuteau.

As we have said, Corinth was one of the meeting places, if not rallying points, of Courfeyrac and his friends. It was Grantaire who had discovered Corinth. He had gone in because of *Carpe Horas*, and he returned because of *Carpes au Gras*. They drank there, they ate there, they shouted there; they paid little, they paid poorly, they did not pay at all, they were always welcome. Father Hucheloup was a good man.

Hucheloup, a good man, as we have just said, was a cook with a mustache of an amusing variety. He always looked cross, seemed to want to intimidate his customers, grumbled at people who came to his house, and appeared more disposed to pick a quarrel with them than serve them their soup. And still, we maintain, they were always welcome. This oddity had brought trade to his shop, and led young men to him who would say to each other, "Come and hear Father Hucheloup grouse." He had been a fencing master. He would suddenly burst out laughing. Coarse voice, good devil. His was a comic heart, with a tragic face; he asked nothing better than to frighten you, rather like those snuffboxes in the shape of a pistol. The discharge is a sneeze.

His wife was Mother Hucheloup, a bearded creature, very ugly.

Around 1830 Father Hucheloup died. With him the secret of the *carpes au gras* was lost. His widow, scarcely consolable, kept up the bistro. But the cuisine degenerated and became execrable, the wine, which had always been bad, became frightful. Courfeyrac and his friends continued to go to Corinth, however—"out of pity," said Bossuet.

Widow Hucheloup was short-winded and shapeless, with memories of the country. She relieved their pointlessness by her pronunciation. She had her own way of saying things that spiced up her village and the springtime reminiscences. It had once been her good fortune, she declared, to hear "the leadbreasts sing in the hawkthorns."

The second-floor room, containing "the restaurant," was a long, wide room, cluttered with stools, chairs, benches, and tables, and a rickety old billiard-table. It was reached by the spiral staircase that ended at the corner of the room in a square hole like the hatchway of a ship.

This room, lit by a single narrow window and a lamp that was always burning, looked like a garret. All the four-legged pieces of furniture behaved as if they had only three. The whitewashed walls had no ornament except this quatrain in honor of Ma'am Hucheloup:

Elle étonne à dix pas, elle épouvante à deux,
Une verrue habite en son nez hasardeux;

On tremble à chaque instant qu'elle ne vous la mouche,
Et qu'un beau jour son nez ne tombe dans a bouche.[1]

This was written in charcoal on the wall.

Ma'am Hucheloup, the original, went back and forth from morning till night before this likeness in quatrain perfectly at ease. Two servants, called Chowder and Fricassée, and for whom nobody had ever known any other names, helped Ma'am Hucheloup put on the tables the carafes of bluish and the various broths that were served to the hungry in earthen dishes. Chowder, fat, round, red, and boisterous, former favorite sultana of the defunct Hucheloup, was uglier than any mythological monster; still, since it is fitting for the servant to stay behind the mistress, she was less ugly than Ma'am Hucheloup. Fricassée, long, delicate, pale with a lymphatic whiteness, rings around her eyes, drooping eyelids, always exhausted and dejected, subject to what might be called chronic weariness, first up, last to bed, served everybody, even the other servant, mildly and in silence, smiling through fatigue with a sort of vague sleepy smile.

There was a mirror above the counter. Before entering the restaurant room, you might read on the door this line written in chalk by Courfeyrac:

Feast if you can and eat if you dare.

II

PRELIMINARY GAIETY

Laigle de Meaux, as we know, lived more with Joly than elsewhere. He had a place to lay his head as the bird has a branch. The two friends shared everything, even to some degree Musichetta. They were what, among the Chapeau Brothers, are called *bini*. On the morning of the

[1] She astounds at ten paces, terrifies at three; a large wart inhabits her perilous beak; you constantly tremble lest she blow it your way, and lest her nose slip in her mouth some fine day.

5th of June, they went to breakfast at Corinth. Joly, whose head was stopped up, had a bad cold that Laigle was beginning to share. Laigle's coat was threadbare, but Joly was well dressed.

It was about nine o'clock in the morning when they opened the door to the Corinth.

They went up to the second floor.

Chowder and Fricassée received them. "Oysters, cheese, and ham," said Laigle.

And they sat down at a table.

The bistro was empty; only two of them were there.

Fricassée, recognizing Joly and Laigle, put a bottle of wine on the table.

As they were at their first oysters, a head appeared at the hatchway of the stairs, and a voice said, "I was passing. In the street I smelled a delicious odor of Brie. I have come in."

It was Grantaire.

Grantaire took a stool and sat down at the table.

Seeing Grantaire, Fricassée put two bottles of wine on the table.

That made three.

"Are you going to drink those two bottles?" Laigle asked Grantaire.

Grantaire answered, "Everyone is ingenious; you alone are ingenuous. Two bottles never sank a man."

The others had begun by eating. Grantaire began by drinking. A half bottle was quickly downed.

"Do you have a hole in your stomach?" resumed Laigle.

"You've surely got one in your elbow," said Grantaire.

And, after emptying his glass, he added, "Ah, now, Laigle of the funeral orations, your coat is old."

"I hope so," replied Laigle. "That makes us get along well, my coat and I. It has adopted all my wrinkles, it doesn't bind me anywhere, it has adapted to all my deformities, it is complaisant to all my motions; I feel it only because it keeps me warm. Old coats are the same thing as old friends."

"That's true," exclaimed Joly, joining in the dialogue, "an old *habit* [coat] is an old *abi* [friend]."

"Particularly," said Grantaire, "in the mouth of a man with a cold id his doze."

"Grantaire," asked Laigle, "have you just come from the boulevard?"

"No."

"We saw the head of the procession go by, Joly and I."

"It is a barvelous spectacle," said Joly.

"How quiet this street is!" exclaimed Laigle. "Who would suspect that Paris is all topsy-turvy? You see this used to be all monasteries around here! Du Breul and Sauval give the list of them, and the Abbé Lebeuf. They were all around, they swarmed, the shod, the unshod, the shaven, the bearded, the grays, the blacks, the whites, the Franciscans, the Minimi, the Capuchins, the Carmelites, the Lesser Augustines, the Greater Augustines, the Old Augustines. Droves of them."

"Don't talk about monks," interrupted Grantaire, "it makes me want to scratch."

Then he exclaimed, "Ugh! I just swallowed a bad oyster. And now here's hypochondria claiming me again. The oysters are spoiled, the servants are ugly. I hate humankind. Just now in the Rue Richelieu I passed by the great public library. The heap of oyster shells they call a library disgusts me to think of. What a lot of paper! What a lot of ink! What a lot of scribbling! Somebody has written all that! What idiot was it who said that man is a featherless biped? And then, I met a pretty girl whom I knew, beautiful as spring, worthy to be called Floréal, and delighted, transported, happy, in seventh heaven, the poor creature, because yesterday a hideous banker pitted with smallpox deigned to fancy her. Alas! Woman watches the publican no less than the fop; cats chase mice as well as birds. This damsel, less than two months ago, was a good girl in a garret, she attached the little copper rings in the eyelets of corsets, how do you say it? She sewed, she had a cot, she lived beside a flowerpot, she was contented. Now she is a bankeress. This transformation was wrought last night. I met the victim this morning, full of joy. The hideous part of it is that the wench was just as pretty today as yesterday. Her financier didn't appear on her face. Roses have this much more or less than women, that the traces pests leave on them are visible! Ah! There's no morality on the earth; I call to witness the myrtle, symbol of love, the laurel, symbol of war, the olive, that goose, symbol of peace, the apple, which almost choked Adam with its seed, and the fig, the grandfather of petticoats. As for rights, do you want to know what rights are? The Gauls covet Clusium, Rome protects Clusium and asks them what Clusium has done to them. Brennus answers, 'What Alba did to you, what Fidenae did to you, what the Aequi, the Volsci, and the Sabines did to you. They were your neighbors. The Clusians are ours. We understand neighborhood as you do. You stole Alba, we take Clusium.' Rome says, 'You will not take Clusium.' Brennus took Rome. Then he cried, '*Vae victis!*' That's what rights are. Ah! In this world, what beasts of prey! What eagles! It makes me crawl all over."

He held out his glass to Joly, who filled it again, then he drank and proceeded, almost without interruption by this glass of wine which nobody noticed, not even himself.

"Brennus, who takes Rome, is an eagle; the banker, who takes the grisette, is an eagle. No greater shame here than there. So let's believe in nothing. There is one reality alone: to drink. Whatever may be your opinion, whether you're for the lean cock, like the Canton of Uri, or for the fat cock, like the Canton of Glaris, it hardly matters, drink. You talk to me of the boulevard, of the procession, et cetera. Ah, now, there's going to be a revolution again, is there? This poverty of means on the part of God astonishes me. He has to keep greasing the grooves of events continually. It hitches, it doesn't go. Quick, a revolution. God has his hands black with that nasty cart-grease all the time. In his place, I'd work more simply, I wouldn't be winding up my machine every moment, I'd lead the human race smoothly, I'd knit events stitch by stich, without breaking the thread, I'd have no emergency, I'd have no extraordinary repertory. What you fellows call progress moves by two motors, men and events. But sad to say, from time to time the exceptional is necessary. For events as well as for men, the stock company is not enough; you need a few geniuses among men, and revolutions among events. Great accidents are the law; the order of things cannot get along without them; and, seeing a comet, one would be tempted to believe that Heaven itself is in need of star actors. At the moment you least expect it, God placards a meteor on the wall of the firmament. Some strange star comes along, underlined by an enormous tail. And that makes Caesar die. Brutus strikes him with a knife, and God with a comet. Snap, there's an aurora borealis, there's a revolution, there's a great man; 'Ninety-three in big letters. Starring Napoleon, the comet of 1811 at the top of the poster. Ah! The beautiful blue poster, all studded with unexpected flourishes! Boom! Boom! Extraordinary spectacle. Look up, loungers. Everything's disheveled, the star as well as the drama. Good God, it's too much, and it's not enough. These emergency resources seem magnificence and are poverty. My friends, Providence is down to dubious means. A revolution, what does that prove? That God is hard up. He makes a coup d'état, because there is a solution of continuity between the present and the future, and because he, God, is unable to join the two ends. In fact, that confirms my conjectures about the condition of Jehovah's fortune; and to see so much discomfort above and below, so much pettiness and meanness and stinginess and distress in the heavens and on the earth, from the bird without a grain of millet to me who haven't a hundred thousand livres of income, to see human destiny, much worn out, and even royal destiny, which is showing through to the warp, witness the Prince of Condé hung, to see winter, which is nothing but a rip in the zenith with the wind blowing through, to see so many tatters even in the brand-new purple of the morning on the tops of the hills, to see the dewdrops, those fake pearls, to see the frost, that paste, to see humanity ripped, and events patched, and so many spots on the sun, and so many holes in the moon, to see so much misery everywhere, I suspect that God is not rich. He keeps up appearances, it is true, but I sense the pinch. He gives a revolution as a merchant whose credit is low gives a ball. We mustn't judge the gods by appearances. Beneath the gilding of the sky I catch a glimpse of a poor universe. Creation is bankrupt. That's why I am a malcontent. See, it's the fifth of June, it's very dark; since morning I've been waiting for daybreak. It hasn't come, and I'll bet it won't come all day. It's the negligence of a badly paid clerk. Yes, everything's badly arranged, nothing fits anything, this old world is all rickety, I side with the opposition. Everything's going across the grain; the universe is a tease. It's like children, those who want it haven't, those who don't want it have. Sum total: I scoff.

Besides, Laigle de Meaux, that baldhead, afflicts my sight. It humiliates me to think I'm the same age as that bare knee. Still, I criticize, but I don't insult. The universe is what it is. I'm speaking here without malice and to ease my conscience. Receive, Father Eternal, the assurance of my distinguished respects. Oh! By all saints of Olympus and by all the gods of Paradise, I was not made to be a Parisian, that is to say, to ricochet forever, like a shuttlecock between two rackets, from the company of loafers to the company of rioters! I was made to be a Turk looking on all day long at Oriental hussies performing those exquisite Egyptian dances, as lascivious as the dreams of a chaste man, or a Beauce peasant, or a Venetian gentleman surrounded by gentlewomen, or a little German prince, furnishing half a foot soldier to the Germanic Confederation, and spending his leisure hours drying his socks on his hedge, that is to say, on his frontier! There's the destiny for which I was born! Yes, I said Turk, and I don't deny it. I don't understand why the Turks are commonly held in bad repute; there is some good in Muhammad; respect for the inventor of seraglios with houris, and paradises with odalisques! Let us not insult Islam, the only religion adorned with a hen roost! To that, I insist on a drink. The earth is a great folly. And it appears that they're going to fight, these idiots, to get their heads broken, to massacre one another, in midsummer, in the verdant month of June, when they might go off with some creature on their arm, to inhale in the fields the huge cup of tea of the new mown hay! Really, they are too silly. An old broken lamp that I saw just now at a junk shop gives rise to a reflection. It's time to enlighten the human race. Yes, here I am sad again. What a pain it is to swallow an oyster or a revolution the wrong way! I'm growing dismal. Oh! The frightful old world! They mutually strive, and plunder, and prostitute one another, they kill one another, and they get used to it all!"

And Grantaire, after this fit of eloquence, had a fit of coughing, well deserved.

"Speakig of revolutiod," said Joly, "it appears that Barius is decidedly aborous."

"Does anybody know who it is?" inquired Laigle.

"Do."

"No?"

"Do! I tell you."

"Marius's amours!" exclaimed Grantaire. "I see them now. Marius is a fog, and he must have found a vapor. Marius is of the poets' race. He who says poet says fool. *Tymbraeus Apollo*. Marius and his Mary, or his Maria, or his Marietta, or his Marion, they must make odd lovers. I can imagine how it is. Ecstasies where they forget to kiss. Chaste on earth, but coupling in the infinite. They are souls that have senses. They sleep together in the stars."

Grantaire was broaching his second bottle, and perhaps his second harangue, when a new actor emerged from the square hole of the stairway. It was a boy of less than ten years, ragged, very small, yellow, a mug of a face, a keen eye, monstrous long hair, wet to the skin, a complacent look.

The child, choosing without hesitation among the three, although he evidently knew none of them, addressed himself to Laigle de Meaux.

"Are you Monsieur Bossuet?" he asked.

"That is my nickname," answered Laigle. "What do you want?"

"This is it. A big fellow with blond hair on the boulevard said to me: Do you know Mother Hucheloup? I said, Yes, Rue Chanvrerie, the old man's widow. He said to me, Go there. You'll find Monsieur Bossuet there, and you'll tell him from me: A—B—C. It's a joke somebody's playing on you, isn't it? He gave me ten sous."

"Joly, lend me ten sous," said Laigle, and turning toward Grantaire, "Grantaire, lend me ten sous."

This made twenty sous Laigle gave the child.

"Thank you, monsieur," said the little fellow.

"What's your name?" asked Laigle.

"Navet, Gavroche's friend."

"Stay with us," said Laigle.

"Have breakfast with us," said Grantaire.

The child answered, "I can't, I am with the procession, I'm the one hollering, 'Down with Polignac!' "

And dragging his foot in a long scrape behind him, which is the most respectful of all possible bows, he went off.

The child gone, Grantaire went on.

"That is the pure gamin. There are many varieties of gamin genus. The notary gamin is called *saute-ruisseau,* the cook gamin is called *marmiton,* the baker gamin is called *mitron,* the lackey gamin is called *groom,* the sailor gamin is called *mousse,* the soldier gamin is called *tapin,* the painter gamin is called *rapin,* the trader gamin is called *trottin,* the courtier gamin is called *menin,* the king gamin is called *dauphin,* the god gamin is called *bambino.*"

Meanwhile Laigle was meditating; he said in an undertone, "A—B—C, meaning Lamarque's funeral."

"The big blond man," observed Grantaire, "is Enjolras, who sent to let you know."

"Shall we go?" said Bossuet.

"It's raidig," said Joly. "I swore to go through fire, dot water. I don't wadt to catch cold."

"I'm staying here," said Grantaire. "I prefer breakfast to a hearse."

"Conclusion: We stay," resumed Laigle. "Well, let's drink then. Besides we can miss the funeral, without missing the émeute."

"Ah! The ébeute, I'm id for that," exclaimed Joly.

Laigle rubbed his hands together: "Now they're going to let out the Revolution of 1830. True, it's been getting tight in the armholes."

"It don't make much difference with me, your revolution," said Grantaire. "I don't loathe this government. It's the crown tempered with the nightcap. It is a scepter terminating in an umbrella. In fact, today, come to think of it, in this weather Louis-Philippe could make good use of his royalty at both ends, extend the scepter end against the people, and open the umbrella end against the sky."

The room was dark, great clouds were capping off the suppression of the daylight. There was nobody in the bistro, nor in the street, everybody having gone "to see the events."

"Is it noon or midnight?" cried Bossuet. "We can't see a speck. Fricassée, a light."

Grantaire, melancholy, was drinking.

"Enjolras despises me," he murmured. "Enjolras said: Joly's sick. Grantaire's drunk. It was to Bossuet that he sent Navet. If he'd come for me I'd have followed him. So much the worse for Enjolras! I won't go to his funeral."

With this decision reached, Bossuet, Joly, and Grantaire did not stir from the wineshop. Around two in the afternoon, the table on which they were leaning was covered with empty bottles. Two candles were burning, one in a perfectly green copper candlestick, the other in the neck of a cracked decanter. Grantaire had drawn Joly and Bossuet toward wine; Bossuet and Joly had led Grantaire toward joy.

As for Grantaire, since noon, he had gone beyond wine, an indifferent source of dreams. Wine, for serious drunks, enjoys only a limited success. There is, concerning inebriation, black magic and white magic; wine is only white magic. Grantaire was a daring drinker of dreams. The blackness of a fearful drunkenness yawning before him, far from checking him, drew him on. He had left the bottle behind and taken to the jug. The jug is the abyss. Having at hand neither opium nor hashish, and wanting to fill his brain with mist, he had taken recourse to the frightful mixture of brandy, stout, and absinthe which produces such terrible lethargy. It is from these three vapors, beer, brandy, and absinthe, that the lead of the soul is formed. They are three shades of night; the celestial butterfly is drowned in them; and there arise, in a membranous smoke vaguely condensed into bat wings, three mute furies—Nightmare, Night, Death—flitting above the sleeping Psyche.

Grantaire was not yet to this dreary phase; far from it. He was extravagantly gay, and Bossuet and Joly kept pace with him. They clinked glasses. To the eccentric emphasis of his words and ideas Grantaire added incoherency of gesture; he rested his left wrist on his knee with dignity, his elbow at a right angle, and his tie untied, astride a stool, his full glass in his right hand, and he threw out to the fat servant Chowder these solemn words: "Let the palace doors be opened! Let everybody belong to the Académie Française and have the right to embrace Madame Hucheloup! Let's drink."

And turning toward Ma'am Hucheloup he added, "Antique woman consecrated by use, approach that I may gaze upon thee!"

And Joly exclaimed, "Chowder add Fricassée, dod't give Gradtaire ady bore to drigk. He spedds his bodey foolishly. Sidce this bordigg he's already devoured id desperate prodigality two fragcs didety-five cedtibes."

And Grantaire replied, "Who's been unhooking the stars without my permission to put them on the table in the shape of candles?"

Bossuet, very drunk, had preserved his calm.

He sat in the open window, wetting his back with the falling rain, and gazed at his two friends.

Suddenly he heard a tumult behind him, hurried steps, cries of "To arms!" He turned and in the Rue Saint-Denis, at the end of the Rue de la Chanvrerie, caught sight of Enjolras going by, carbine in hand, and Gavroche with his pistol, Feuilly with his saber, Courfeyrac with his sword, Jean Prouvaire, Combeferre and Bahorel with their muskets, and all the armed and stormy gathering that was following them.

The Rue de la Chanvrerie was hardly as long as the range of a carbine. Bossuet improvised a speaking trumpet with his two hands, and shouted, "Courfeyrac! Courfeyrac! Ahoy!"

Courfeyrac heard the call, saw Bossuet, and came a few steps into the Rue de la Chanvrerie, crying a "What do you want?" that was met on the way by a "Where are you going?"

"To make a barricade," answered Courfeyrac.

"Well then, here! This is a good place! Make it here!"

"That's true, Eagle," said Courfeyrac.

And at a sign from Courfeyrac, the band rushed into the Rue de la Chanvrerie.

III

NIGHT BEGINS TO GATHER OVER GRANTAIRE

The place was indeed admirably chosen, the entrance to the street wide, the far end narrowed and like a cul-de-sac, with Corinth choking it off, Rue Mondétour easy to close to the right and left, no attack possible except from the Rue Saint-Denis, that is from the front, and without cover. Bossuet, slightly drunk, had the sharp vision of Hannibal fasting.

As the mob burst in, the whole street was seized with terror. All pedestrians vanished. In a flash, at the end, to right and left, shops, stalls, alley gates, windows, blinds, dormer windows, shutters of every size, were closed from the ground to the rooftops. One frightened old woman had attached a mattress in front of her window on two clothes poles, as a shield against the bullets. The bistro was the only house that stayed open; and that for good reason, because the band had rushed into it. "Oh my God! Oh my God!" sighed Ma'am Hucheloup.

Bossuet had gone down to meet Courfeyrac.

Joly, who had come to the window, cried out, "Courfeyrac, you should take ad ubbrella. You'll catch code."

Meanwhile, in a few minutes, twenty iron bars had been wrested from the grated front of the wineshop, twenty yards of pavement had been torn up; as it went by, Gavroche and Bahorel had seized and tipped over the dray of a lime merchant named Anceau; this dray contained three barrels full of lime, which they placed under the piles of paving stones; Enjolras had opened the trapdoor of the cellar, and all the widow Hucheloup's empty casks had gone to flank the lime barrels; Feuilly, with his fingers accustomed to painting the delicate folds of fans, had buttressed the barrels and the dray with two massive heaps of rubble: stuff improvised like the rest of it, taken from anywhere. Some shoring beams had been pulled down from the front of a neighboring house and laid across the casks. When Bossuet and Courfeyrac looked back, half the street was already barred by a rampart higher than a man. There is nothing like the hand of the people to build whatever can be built by demolishing.

Chowder and Fricassée had joined the laborers. Fricassée went back and forth loaded with rubbish. Her weariness contributed to the barricade. She served paving stones, as she would have served wine, sleepily.

An omnibus with two white horses passed by the end of the street.

Bossuet stepped over the paving blocks, ran, stopped the driver, made the passengers get down, gave his hand "to the ladies," dismissed the conductor, and came back with the vehicle, leading the horses by the bridle.

"An omnibus," he said, "doesn't pass by Corinth. *Non licet omnibus adire Corinthum.*"

A moment later the horses were unhitched and going off on their own through the Rue Mondétour, and the omnibus, lying on its side, completed the barring of the street.

Ma'am Hucheloup, completely upset, had taken refuge on the second floor.

Her eyes were glazed, and she looked without seeing, crying in a whisper. Her shrieks of horror didn't leave her throat.

"It's the end of the world," she murmured.

Joly deposited a kiss on Ma'am Hucheloup's coarse, red, wrinkled neck, and said to Grantaire, "My dear fellow, I've always considered a woman's neck an infinitely delicate thing."

But Grantaire was attaining the peak of dithyramb. As Chowder came up to the first floor, Grantaire seized her by the waist and pulled her toward the window with wild bursts of laughter.

"Chowder is ugly!" he cried; "Chowder is the dream of ugliness! Chowder is a chimera. Listen to the secret of her birth: a Gothic Pygmalion making cathedral gargoyles fell in love with one of them one fine morning, the most horrible of all. He implored Love to animate her, and that made Chowder. Behold her, citizens! Her hair is the color of chromate of lead, like that of Titian's mistress, and she is a good girl. I warrant you she'll fight well. Every good girl contains a hero. As for Mother Hucheloup, she's a brave old woman. Look at her mustache! She inherited it from her husband. A hussaress, mark my words, she'll fight too. They two by themselves will frighten the suburbs. Comrades, we will overthrow the government, as sure as there are fifteen acids intermediate between margaric acid and formic acid. Basically, I don't care a fig about any of it. Messieurs, my father always detested me, because I couldn't understand mathematics. I only understand love and liberty. I'm Grantaire, a good boy. Never having had any money, I never got used to it, and therefore I've never felt the need of it; but if I'd been rich, there would have been no more poor! You would have seen. Oh, if the good hearts had the fat purses, how much better everything would be! I imagine Jesus Christ with Rothschild's fortune! How much good he would have done! Chowder, embrace me! You are voluptuous and timid! You have cheeks that call for the kiss of a sister, and lips that demand the kiss of a lover."

"Be still, wine cask!" said Courfeyrac.

Grantaire answered, "I am Capitoul and Master of Floral Games!"

Enjolras, who was standing on the crest of the barricade, musket in hand, raised his fine austere face. Enjolras, we know, had something of the Spartan and the Puritan. He would have died at Thermopylae with Leonidas, and would have burned Drogheda with Cromwell.

"Grantaire," he cried, "go sleep it off somewhere else. This is the place for intoxication, not drunkenness. Don't dishonor the barricade!"

This angry speech produced a singular effect on Grantaire. It was as though he had received a glass of cold water in the face. He suddenly appeared sober. He sat down, leaned on a table near the window, looked at Enjolras with an inexpressible gentleness, and said to him, "Let me sleep here."

"Go sleep somewhere else," cried Enjolras.

But Grantaire, keeping his tender, troubled eyes fixed on him answered, "Let me sleep here—until I die here."

Enjolras stared at him disdainfully.

"Grantaire, you're incapable of belief, of thought, of will, of life, and of death."

Grantaire replied gravely, "You'll see."

He stammered out a few more unintelligible words, then his head fell heavily on the table, and, a common effect of the second stage of inebriety into which Enjolras had rudely and suddenly pushed him, a moment later he was asleep.

IV

ATTEMPT AT CONSOLING THE WIDOW HUCHELOUP

In ecstasies with the barricade, Bahorel cried out, "The street's bare-chested! How well it looks!"

Even while helping to demolish the wineshop, Courfeyrac tried to console the widowed landlady.

"Mother Hucheloup, weren't you complaining the other day that you'd been summoned and fined because Fricassée had shaken a rug out your window?"

"Yes, my good Monsieur Courfeyrac. Oh! My God! Are you going to put that table into your horror too? And besides that, for the rug, and also for a flowerpot that fell from the attic to the street, the government fined me a hundred francs. If that isn't an abomination!"

"Well, Mother Hucheloup, we're avenging you."

Mother Hucheloup, in this reparation they were making her, did not seem to understand her advantage very clearly. She was satisfied after the manner of that Arab woman who, having been struck by her husband, went to complain to her father, crying for vengeance and saying; "Father, you owe my husband a blow for a blow." The father asked, "Which cheek did he strike?" "The left." The father struck the right cheek and said, "Now you're satisfied. Go tell your husband he struck my daughter, but I've struck his wife."

The rain had let up. Recruits had arrived. Under their workshirts some workingmen had brought a keg of powder, a hamper containing bottles of vitriol, two or three carnival torches, and a basket full of torches, "leftovers from the king's fête," which fête was quite recent, having taken place on May Day. It was said that these supplies came from a grocer of the Faubourg Saint-Antoine, named Pépin. They broke the only lamp in the Rue de la Chanvrerie, the lamp opposite the Rue Saint-Denis, and all the lamps in the surrounding streets, Mondétour, du Cygne, des Prêcheurs, and de la Grande and de la Petite Truanderie.

Enjolras, Combeferre, and Courfeyrac directed everything. Two barricades were being built at the same time, both touching the house of Corinth and making a right angle; the larger one closed the Rue de la Chanvrerie, the other closed the Rue Mondétour in the direction of the Rue du Cygne. This last barricade, very narrow, was constructed only of casks and paving stones. There were about fifty laborers there, some thirty armed with muskets, for, on their way they had effected a wholesale loan from an armorer's shop.

Nothing could have been more fantastic and more motley than this band. One had a short jacket, a cavalry saber, and two horse pistols; another was in shirt sleeves, with a round hat, and a powderhorn hung at his side; a third had a breastplate of nine sheets of brown paper and was armed with a saddler's awl. There was one of them crying out, "Let's exterminate to the last man, and die on the point of our bayonets!" This man had no bayonet.

Another displayed over his coat a cross-belt and cartridge-box of the National Guard, its box cover adorned with this inscription in red cloth: *Public Order*. Countless muskets bearing the numbers of their regiments, few hats, no ties, many bare arms, some pikes. Add to this all ages, all faces, small pale young men, bronzed stevedores. Everyone was hurrying, and, while helping each other, they talked about the possible chances—that they would have help by three o'clock in the morning—that they were sure of one regiment—that Paris would rise. Terrible subjects, mingled with a sort of cordial joviality. One would have said they were brothers, they did not know each other's names. Great perils share this beauty, that they bring to light the fraternity of strangers.

A fire had been lit in the kitchen, and they were melting pitchers, dishes, forks, all the pewterware of the wineshop into bullets. They drank through all of it. Percussion caps and buckshot rolled pell-mell on the tables among glasses of wine. In the billiard room, Ma'am Hucheloup, Chowder, and Fricassée, variously modified by terror, one stupefied, another breathless, the third alert, were tearing up old linen and making lint; three insurgents were helping them, three long-haired, bearded, and mustached wags who raveled the cloth with the fingers of a linen draper, and made them tremble.

The tall man whom Courfeyrac, Combeferre, and Enjolras had noticed as he joined the company at the corner of the Rue des Billettes was working on the little barricade, and making himself useful there. Gavroche worked on the large one. As for the young man who had waited for Courfeyrac at his house and had asked him for Monsieur Marius, he had disappeared about the time the bus was overturned.

Gavroche, completely carried away and radiant, had taken responsibility for getting everything ready. He came and went, upstairs and down, up again, bustled, sparkled. He seemed to be there for everyone's encouragement. Was he spurred on? Yes, certainly, by his misery. Did he have wings? Yes, certainly, his joy. Gavroche was a whirlwind. They saw him incessantly, they heard him constantly. He filled the air, being everywhere at once. He was a kind of almost irritating ubiquity; no stop possible with him. The enormous barricade felt him on its back. He vexed the loungers, he excited the idle, he revived the weary, he provoked the thoughtful, kept some cheerful, others breathing, others angry, all in motion, piqued a student, was biting to a workingman; took position, stopped, started up again, flitted above the tumult and the effort, leaped from these to those, whispered, hummed, and stirred up the whole team; the fly on the revolutionary coach.

Perpetual motion was in his little arms, and perpetual clamor in his little lungs.

"Cheerly! More paving stones! More barrels! More machines? Where can we get some? A basket of plaster, to stop up that hole. It's too small, your barricade. It has to go higher. Pile on everything, brace it with everything. Break up the house. A barricade is Mother Gibou's tea party. Hold on, there's a glass door."

This made the laborers shout, "A glass door? What d'you expect us to do with a glass door, tubercle?"

"Hercules yourselves!" retorted Gavroche. "A glass door in a barricade, that's excellent. It doesn't stop them from attacking, but it bothers them in taking it. Then you've never swiped apples over a wall with broken bottles on it? A glass door, it'll cut the corns of the National Guards, when they try to climb over the barricade. Glass is the devil. Ah, now, you must have an unbridled imagination, my comrades."

Still, he was furious at his hammerless pistol. He went from one to the next demanding, "A musket! I want a musket! Why don't you give me a musket?"

"A musket for you?" said Combeferre.

"Well?" replied Gavroche. "Why not? I had one in 1830, in the argument with Charles X."

Enjolras shrugged his shoulders.

"When there are enough for the men, we'll give them to the children."

Gavroche turned fiercely, and answered him, "If you're killed before me, I'll take yours."

"Gamin!" said Enjolras.

"Smooth-face!" said Gavroche.

A stray dandy who was lounging at the end of the street provided a diversion.

Gavroche hollered to him, "Come with us, young man! Well now, this poor old country—aren't you going to do anything for her?"

The dandy fled.

V

THE PREPARATIONS

The journals of the time that said that the barricade of the Rue de la Chanvrerie—that "almost impregnable construction," as they call it—reached a third-story level, were mistaken. The fact is that it did not exceed an average height of six or seven feet. It was built in such a manner that the combatants could, at will, either disappear behind the wall or look over it, and even scale the crest of it by means of a quadruple row of paving stones superimposed and arranged like steps on the inner side. The front of the barricade on the outside, composed of piles of paving stones and barrels bound together by timbers and boards interlocked in the wheels of the Anceau cart and the overturned omnibus, had a bristling and inextricable look about it.

An opening wide enough for a man to pass through had been left between the wall of the houses and the end of the barricade farthest from the wineshop, so that a sortie would be possible. The pole of the omnibus was turned upright and held with ropes, and a red flag, fixed to this pole, floated over the barricade.

The little Mondétour barricade, hidden behind the wineshop, was not very noticeable. The two barricades united formed a staunch redoubt. Enjolras and Courfeyrac had not thought it right to barricade the other end of the Rue Mondétour which opens a passage to the markets through the Rue des Prêcheurs, no doubt wanting to preserve a possible link with the outside, and having little dread of being attacked from the dangerous and difficult alley des Prêcheurs.

Except for this passage remaining open, which constituted what Folard, in his strategic style, would have called a communications trench, and bearing in mind also the narrow opening arranged on the Rue de la Chanvrerie, the interior of the barricade, where the wineshop made a salient angle, presented an irregular quadrilateral closed on all sides. There was an interval of about twenty paces between the larger barricade and the tall houses forming the end of the street, so that we might say the barricade backed up against these houses all inhabited, but closed from top to bottom.

All this labor was accomplished without hindrance in less than an hour, and without this handful of bold men seeing a bearskin hat or a bayonet. The few bourgeois who still ventured into the Rue Sant-Denis at that period of the émeute cast a glance down the Rue de la Chanvrerie, perceived the barricade, and hurried on.

The two barricades finished, the flag run up, a table was dragged out of the wineshop, and Courfeyrac climbed onto the table. Enjolras brought the square box and Courfeyrac opened it. This box was filled with cartridges. When they saw the cartridges, there was a shudder among the bravest, and a moment of silence.

Courfeyrac distributed them with a smile.

Each received thirty cartridges. Many had powder and set about making others with the balls they were molding. As for the keg of powder, it was on a table by itself near the door, and was being held in reserve.

The long roll that was running throughout Paris did not let up, but it had gotten to be only a monotonous sound to which no one paid any more attention. At times it would come close, then move away with gloomy modulations.

They loaded their muskets and their carbines all together, without haste, with solemn gravity. Enjolras placed three sentinels outside the barricades, one in the Rue de la Chanvrerie, the second in the Rue des Prêcheurs, the third at the corner of la Petite Truanderie.

Then, with the barricades complete, the posts assigned, the muskets loaded, the lookouts placed, alone in these fearful streets in which there were now no pedestrians, surrounded by these dumb, and seemingly dead houses, which throbbed with no human motion, wrapped in the deepening shadows of the twilight, which was beginning to fall, in the midst of this obscurity and silence, through which they felt the advance of something inexpressibly tragic and terrifying, isolated, armed, determined, tranquil, they waited.

VI

WHILE WAITING

In these hours of waiting what did they do? This we have to tell, for this is history.

While the men were making cartridges and the women lint, while a large pot, full of melted pewter and lead destined for the bullet mold was smoking over a hot stove, while the lookouts were watching the barricades with weapons in hand, while Enjolras, whom nothing could distract, was watching the lookouts, Combeferre, Courfeyrac, Jean Prouvaire, Feuilly, Bossuet, Joly, Bahorel, a few others besides, sought each other out and got together, as in the most peaceful days of their student conversations, and in a corner of this bistro turned into a pillbox, within two steps of the redoubt they had thrown up, their carbines primed and loaded resting on the backs of their chairs, these gallant young men, so near their last hour, began to recite a love poem.

What poem? Here it is:

Vous rappelez-vous notre douce vie,
Lorsque nous étions si jeunes tous deux,
Et que nous n'avions au coeur d'autre envie
Que d'être bien mis et d'être amoureux.

Lorsqu'en ajoutant votre âge à mon âge,
Nous ne comptions pas à deux quarante ans,
Et que, dans notre humble et petit ménage,
Tout, même l'hiver, nous était printemps?

Beaux jours! Manuel était fier et sage,
Paris s'asseyait à de saints banquets,
Foy lançait la foudre, et votre corsage
Avait une épingle où je me piquais.

Tout vous contemplait. Avocat sans causes,
Quand je vous menais au Prado dîner,
Vous étiez jolie au point que les roses
Me faisaient l'effet de se retourner.

Je les entendais dire: Est-elle belle!
Comme elle sent bon! quels cheveux à flots!
Sous son mantelet elle cache une aile;
Son bonnet charmant est à peine éclos.

J'errais avec toi, pressant ton bras souple.
Les passants croyaient que l'amour charmé
Avait marié, dans notre heureux couple,
Le doux mois d'avril au beau mois de mai.

Nous vivions cachés, contents, porte close,
Dévorant l'amour, bon fruit défendu;
Ma bouche n'avait pas dit une chose
Que déja ton coeur avait répondu.

La Sorbonne était l'endroit bucolique
Où je t'adorais du soir au matin.
C'est ainsi qu'une âme amoureuse applique
La carte du Tendre au pays latin.

O place Maubert! O place Dauphine!
Quand, dans le taudis frais et printanier,
Tu tirais ton bas sur ta jambe fine,
Je voyais un astre au fond du grenier.

J'ai fort lu Platon, mais rien ne m'en reste
Mieux que Malebranche et que Lamennais;
Tu me démontrais la bonté céleste
Avec une fleur que tu me donnais.

Je t'obéissais, tu m'étais soumise.
O grenier doré! te lacer! te voir!
Aller et venir dès l'aube en chemise,
Mirant ton front jeune à ton vieux miroir!

Et qui donc pourrait perdre la mémoire
De ces temps d'aurore et de firmament,
De rubans, de fleurs, de gaze et de moire,
Où l'amour bégaye un argot charmant?

Nos jardins étaient un pot de tulipe;
Tu masquais la vitre avec un jupon;
Je prenais le bol de terre de pipe,
Et je te donnais la tasse en japon.

Et ces grands malheurs qui nous faisaient rire!
Ton manchon brûlé, ton boa perdu!
Et ce cher portrait du divin Shakspeare
Qu'un soir pour souper nous avons vendu!

J'étais mendiant, et toi charitable;
Je baisais au vol tes bras frais et ronds.
Dante in-folio nous servait de table
Pour manger gaîment un cent de marrons.

Le première fois qu'en mon joyeux bouge
Je pris un baiser à ta lèvre en feu,
Quand tu t'en allas décoiffée et rouge,
Je restai tout pâle et je crus en Dieu!

Te rappeles-tu nos bonheurs sans nombre,
Et tous ces fichus changés en chiffons?
Oh! que de soupirs, de nos coeurs pleins d'ombre,
Se sont envolés dans les cieux profonds![1]

Do you remember our sweet life
When we were so young, we two,
And had in our hearts no other desire
Than to be well dressed and be in love.

When by adding your age to mine,
We couldn't reach forty years between us,
And, in our humble little home,
Everything, even in winter, seemed spring?

Beautiful days! Manuel was proud and wise,
Paris sat down to incredible banquets,
Foy was waxing eloquent, and your blouse
Had a pin that pricked me.

Everyone gazed at you. A lawyer without a case,
When I took you to The Prado for dinner,
You were so pretty that the roses
Seemed to turn away.

I heard them say: Isn't she beautiful!
How lovely she smells! What flowing hair!

Under her cape she's hiding wings;
Her charming hat has scarcely bloomed.

I wandered with you, squeezing your lissome arm.
People passing thought that charmed love
Had married in us, the happy couple,
The sweet month of April with the handsome month of May.

We lived hidden away, happy, the door closed,
Devouring love, good forbidden fruit;
My mouth had not said one thing
When already your heart had answered.

The Sorbonne was the bucolic spot
Where I adored you from dusk to dawn.
That is how a loving soul applies
The map of Tenderness to the Quartier Latin.

O Place Maubert! O Place Dauphine!
When, in the meager springlike room,
You drew your stocking up over your slim leg,
I saw a star in a garret nook.

I've read a lot of Plato, but remember nothing
Better than Malebranche and Lammenais;
You showed me celestial kindness
With the flower you gave me.

I obeyed you, you were in my power.
O gilded garret! To lace you up! To see you
Coming and going from daybreak in a chemise,
Gazing at your young forehead in your old mirror!

And who could ever lose the memory
Of those times of dawn and sky,
Of ribbons, of flowers, of muslin and watered silk,
When love stammers a charmed argot?

Our gardens were a pot of tulips;
You screened the window with your slip;
I would take the pipe clay bowl,
And I gave you the porcelain cup.

And those great calamities that made us laugh!
Your muff burnt, your boa lost!
And that beloved portrait of the divine Shakespeare
That we sold one evening for our supper!

The hour, the place, these memories of youth recalled, the few stars beginning to shine in the sky, the funereal repose of these deserted streets, the imminence of the inexorable event, gave a pathetic charm to these verses, murmured in a low tone in the twilight by Jean Prouvaire, who, as we have said, was a gentle poet.

Meanwhile they had lit a lamp at the little barricade, and at the larger one, one of those wax torches seen on Mardi Gras in front of the wagons loaded with masks, on their way to the Comtille. These torches, as we have seen, came from the Faubourg Saint-Antoine.

The torch had been placed in a kind of cage, closed in with paving stones on three sides, to shelter it from the wind, and placed in such a manner that all the light fell on the flag. The street and the barricade remained plunged in obscurity, and nothing could be seen but the red flag, fearfully lit up, as if by an enormous dark lantern.

This light tinged the scarlet of the flag an indescribably terrible purple.

VII

THE MAN RECRUITED IN THE RUE DES BILLETTES

By now night had closed in, nothing was coming. There were only confused sounds, and at intervals musket volleys, infrequent, poorly sustained, and distant. This pro-

---

I was a beggar, and you charitable;
I gave fleeting kisses to your cool round arms.
Dante in-folio was our table
For gaily consuming a hundred chestnuts.

The first time, in my joyful hovel,
I stole a kiss from your fiery lips,
When you went off disheveled and pink,
I stayed there pale and believed in God!

Do you remember our countless joys,
And all those shawls turned to rags?
Oh! From our shadow-filled hearts what sighs
Flew off into the limitless skies!

longed respite was a sign that the government was taking its time and massing its forces. These fifty men were waiting for sixty thousand.

Enjolras felt himself caught up by the impatience that seizes strong souls on the threshold of important events. He went to find Gavroche, who had set himself to making cartridges in the lower room by the doubtful light of two candles, placed on the counter because of the powder scattered over the tables. These two candles threw no rays outside. The insurgents moreover had taken care not to have any lights in the upper stories.

At this moment Gavroche was very busy, though not exactly with his cartridges.

The man from the Rue des Billettes had just entered the low-ceilinged room and had taken a seat at the table with the least light. A large infantry musket had fallen to his lot, and he held it between his knees. Gavroche, hitherto, distracted by a hundred "amusing" things, had not even seen this man.

When he came in, Gavroche mechanically followed him with his eyes, admiring his musket, then, suddenly, when the man had sat down the gamin arose. Had anyone watched this man up to this time, he would have seen him observe everything about the barricade and the band of insurgents with strange attention; but since he had come into the room, he had fallen into a kind of meditation and appeared to see nothing more of what was going on. The gamin approached this thoughtful character, and began to tiptoe around him the way one walks near somebody he fears to awake. At the same time, over his childish face, at once so saucy and so serious, so carefree and so profound, so cheerful and so touching, there passed all those grimaces of the old that signify, "Oh, no! Impossible! I'm seeing things! I'm dreaming! Could it be? No, it isn't! Why yes! Why no!" etc. Gavroche rocked back and forth on his heels, clenched both fists in his pockets, twisted his neck like a bird, invested in one outsized pout all the sagacity of his lower lip. He was dazed, uncertain, credulous, convinced, bewildered. He had the appearance of the chief of the eunuchs in the slave market discovering a Venus among frumps, and the air of an amateur recognizing a Raphael in a heap of daubs. Every part of him was at work, the instinct that scents and the intellect that combines. It was clear that an event had occurred for Gavroche.

It was in the depths of this meditation that Enjolras accosted him.

"You're small," said Enjolras, "nobody will see you. Go out of the barricades, slip along by the houses, look around the streets a little, and come and tell me what's going on."

Gavroche straightened up.

"Little folks are good for something then! That's very lucky! I'll go! Meantime, trust the little folks, distrust the big—" And Gavroche, raising his head and lowering his voice, added, pointing to the man of the Rue des Billettes, "You see that big fellow there?"

"Well?"

"He's an informer."

"You're sure?"

"It wasn't two weeks ago he pulled me by the ear off the cornice of the Pont-Royal where I was taking the air."

Enjolras hastily left the gamin and murmured a few words very low to a workingman from the wine docks who was nearby. The worker went out of the room and returned almost immediately, accompanied by three others. The four men, four broad-shouldered dockhands, without doing anything that could attract his attention, placed themselves behind the table on which the man of the Rue des Billettes was leaning. They were obviously ready to throw themselves on him.

Then Enjolras approached the man and asked him, "Who are you?"

At this abrupt question, the man gave a start. He looked straight to the depths of Enjolras's frank eyes and appeared to catch his thought. He smiled a smile that was the most disdainful, the most energetic, and the most resolute imaginable and answered with a haughty gravity, "I see how it is—Well, yes!"

"You're an informer?"

"I am a government officer."

"Your name is?"

"Javert."

Enjolras made a sign to the four men. In a twinkling, before Javert had time to turn around, he was collared, thrown down, bound, searched.

They found on him a little round card framed between two pieces of glass and bearing on one side the arms of France, engraved with this legend: *Surveillance et vigilance,* and on the other side this endorsement: "JAVERT, inspector of police, aged fifty-two," and the signature of the prefect of police of the time, M. Gisquet.

Besides that he had his watch and his purse, which contained a few gold pieces. They left him his purse and his watch. Under the watch, at the bottom of his fob, they felt and took a sheet of paper in an envelope, which Enjolras opened, and on which he read these lines, written in the prefect's own hand.

"As soon as his political mission is fulfilled, Inspector Javert will ascertain, by a special examination, whether it is true that malefactors have promising enterprises on the slope of the right bank of the Seine, near the Pont d'Iéna."

The search finished, they stood Javert up, tied his arms behind his back, fastened him in the middle of the lower room to that celebrated post that had formerly given its name to the wineshop.

Gavroche, who had witnessed the whole scene and approved the whole by silent nods of the head, approached Javert and said to him, "The mouse has caught the cat."

All this was executed so rapidly that it was finished as soon as it was noticed in the wineshop. Javert had not uttered a cry. Seeing Javert tied to the post, Courfeyrac, Bossuet, Joly, Combeferre, and the men scattered around the two barricades, ran in.

Backed up against the post, and tied with ropes so he could make no movement, Javert held up his head with the intrepid serenity of the man who has never lied.

"It's an informer," said Enjolras.

And turning toward Javert, "You will be shot ten minutes before the barricade is taken."

Javert replied in his most imperious tone, "Why not immediately?"

"We're economizing on powder."

"Then do it with a knife."

"Spy," said the handsome Enjolras, "we are judges, not assassins."

Then he called Gavroche.

"You! Go on about your business! Do what I told you."

"I'm going," cried Gavroche.

And pausing just as he was starting, "By the way, you'll give me his musket? I leave you the musician, but I want the clarinet."

The gamin gave a military salute and sprang gaily through the opening in the large barricade.

VIII

SEVERAL INTERROGATION POINTS CONCERNING ONE LE CABUC, WHO PERHAPS WAS NOT LE CABUC

The tragic picture we have begun would not be complete, the reader would not see in their exact and true relief these great moments of social parturition and revolutionary birth in which convulsion mingled with effort, if we were to omit in the outline sketched here an incident full of epic and savage horror that occurred almost immediately after Gavroche's departure.

Mobs, as we know, are like snowballs, and gather a mass of tumultuous men as they roll. These men do not ask one another where they come from. Among the passersby who had joined themselves to the company led by Enjolras, Combeferre, and Courfeyrac there was a person wearing a dockhand's jacket worn out at the shoulders, who gesticulated and vociferated and had the look of a sort of savage drunkard. This man, who was named or nicknamed Le Cabuc and was entirely unknown, in fact, to those who claimed to recognize him, very drunk, or feigning to be, was seated with a few others at a table they had dragged outside the bistro. This Cabuc, while inciting those to drink who were with him, seemed to gaze with an air of reflection at the large house behind the barricade, whose five stories overlooked the whole street and faced toward the Rue Saint-Denis. Suddenly he exclaimed, "Comrades, do you know what? It's from that house that we have to shoot. If we're at the windows, if anyone comes into the street, we'll give them hell."

"Yes, but the house is shut up," said one of the drinkers.

"Knock!"

"They won't open."

"Bash the door in!"

Le Cabuc runs to the door, which had a very massive knocker, and raps. The door does not open. He raps a second time. Nobody answers. A third rap. The same silence.

"Is there anybody there?" cries Le Cabuc.

Nothing stirs.

Then he seizes a musket and begins to beat the door with the butt. It was an old alley door, arched, low, narrow, solid, entirely of oak, lined on the inside with sheet-iron and with iron braces, a genuine fortress postern. The blows made the house tremble, but did not shake the door.

Nevertheless it is likely that the inhabitants were alarmed, for they finally saw a little square window on the fourth floor light up and open, and at this window appeared a candle, and the pious and frightened face of a gray-haired man, the doorkeeper.

The man who was knocking stopped.

"Messieurs," asked the doorkeeper, "what do you want?"

"Open!" said Le Cabuc.

"Messieurs, I cannot."

"Open, I'm warning you!"

"Impossible, messieurs!"

Le Cabuc took his musket and aimed at the doorkeeper's head; but as he was below and it was very dark, the doorkeeper did not see him.

"Yes, or no, will you open?"

"No, messieurs!"

"You say no?"

"I say no, my good—"

The porter did not finish. The musket went off; the ball entered under his chin and passed out at the back of the neck, passing through the jugular. The old man sank without a sigh. The candle fell and was extinguished, and nothing could now be seen but an immovable head lying on the edge of the window, and a little whitish smoke floating toward the roof.

"That's it!" said Le Cabuc, letting the butt of his musket drop on the pavement.

Hardly had he uttered these words when he felt a hand

grab his shoulder with the weight of an eagle's talons and heard a voice say, "On your knees!"

The murderer turned and saw before him the white cold face of Enjolras. Enjolras had a pistol in his hand.

At the gunfire, he had come over.

With his left hand he had grasped Le Cabuc's collar, blouse, shirt, and suspenders.

"On your knees," he repeated.

And with a majestic movement the slender young man of twenty bent the broad-shouldered and robust stevedore like a reed and made him kneel in the mud. Le Cabuc tried to resist, but he seemed to have been seized by a superhuman grasp.

Pale, his neck bare, his hair flying, Enjolras, with his woman's face, had at that moment some inexpressible quality of the ancient Themis. His flaring nostrils, his downcast eyes, gave to his implacable Greek profile that expression of wrath and chastity which from the point of view of the ancient world belonged to justice.

The whole barricade ran over, then all stood in a circle at some distance, feeling that it was impossible to utter a word in the presence of the act they were about to witness.

Le Cabuc, vanquished, no longer attempted to defend himself, but trembled in every limb. Enjolras let go of him and took out his watch.

"Collect your thoughts," said he. "Pray or think. You have one minute."

"Pardon!" murmured the murderer, then he bowed his head and mumbled some inarticulate oaths.

Enjolras did not take his eyes off his watch; he let the minute pass, then he put his watch back into his fob. This done, he took Le Cabuc, who was writhing against his knees and howling, by the hair, and placed the muzzle of his pistol at his ear. Many of those intrepid men, who had so tranquilly entered upon the most terrible of enterprises, looked away.

They heard the explosion, the assassin fell face forward on the pavement, and Enjolras straightened up and looked around the circle, determined and severe.

Then he pushed the body away with his foot, and said, "Throw that outside."

Three men lifted the wretch's body, which was quivering with the last reflex convulsions of the life that had flown, and threw it over the small barricade into the little Rue Mondétour.

Enjolras had remained thoughtful. Shadow, mysterious and grand, was slowly spreading across his fearful serenity. He suddenly raised his voice. There was a silence.

"Citizens," said Enjolras, "what that man did is horrible, and what I have done is terrible. He killed, that is why I killed him. I was forced to do it, for the insurrection must have its discipline. Assassination is still a greater crime here than elsewhere; we are under the eyes of the Revolution, we are the priests of the Republic, we are the sacramental host of duty, and no one can defame our combat. I therefore judged and condemned that man to death. As for myself, compelled to do what I have done, but abhorring it, I have judged myself also, and you shall soon see to what I have sentenced myself."

Those who heard shuddered.

"We will share your fate," cried Combeferre.

"So be it," added Enjolras. "One word more. In executing that man, I obeyed necessity; but necessity is a monster of the old world, the name of necessity is Fatality. Now the law of progress is that monsters disappear before angels, and that Fatality vanish before Fraternity. This is a bad time to pronounce the word 'love.' No matter, I pronounce it, and I glorify it. Love, yours is the future. Death, I use you, but I hate you. Citizens, in the future there shall be neither darkness nor thunderbolts, neither ferocious ignorance nor blood for blood. As Satan shall be no more, so Michael shall be no more. In the future no man will slay his fellow, the earth will be radiant, the human race will love. It will come, citizens, that day when all shall be concord, harmony, light, joy, and life; it will come, and it is so that it may come that we are going to die."

Enjolras was silent. His virgin lips closed; and he remained some time standing on the spot where he had spilled blood, in marble immobility. His staring eye made everyone around him speak low.

Jean Prouvaire and Combeferre silently shook hands and, leaning against one another in the corner of the barricade, considered, with an admiration not unmingled with compassion, this severe young man, executioner and priest, luminous like the crystal and rock also.

Let us say right here that later, after the action, when

the corpses were carried to the morgue and searched, there was a police officer's card found on Le Cabuc. In 1848, the author of this book had in his own hands the special report made on the subject to the prefect of police in 1832.

Let us add that, if we are to believe a police tradition, strange but probably well founded, Le Cabuc was Claquesous. The fact is that after the death of Le Cabuc, nothing more was heard of Claquesous. Claquesous left no trace on his disappearance. He would seem to have been amalgamated with the invisible. His life had been darkness, his end was night.

The whole insurgent group were still under the emotion of this tragic trial, so quickly instituted and terminated, when once more Courfeyrac saw in the barricade the small youth who had called at his house for Marius that morning.

This boy, who had a bold and reckless air, had come at night to join the insurgents.

Book Thirteen

MARIUS ENTERS THE SHADOW

I

FROM THE RUE PLUMET TO THE QUARTIER SAINT-DENIS

That voice which through the twilight had called Marius to the barricade of the Rue de la Chanvrerie sounded to him like the voice of destiny. He wanted to die, the opportunity presented itself; he was knocking at the door of the tomb, a hand in the shadow held out the key. These dreary clefts in the darkness facing despair are tempting. Marius pushed aside the bar that had let him pass so many times, came out of the garden, and said, "Let's go!"

Mad with grief, no longer feeling anything fixed or solid in his brain, incapable of accepting anything henceforth from fate, after these two months passed in the intoxications of youth and of love, overwhelmed by all the reveries of despair, he had now one desire alone: to make a quick end of it.

He began to walk rapidly. It happened that he was armed, having Javert's pistols with him.

In the streets he lost sight of the young man he thought he had seen.

Marius, who had left the Rue Plumet by the boulevard, crossed the Esplanade and the Pont des Invalides, the Champs-Elysées, the Place Louis XV, and entered the Rue de Rivoli. The stores were open, the gas was burning under the arches, women were buying in the shops, people were spooning up ice cream at the Café Laiter, they were eating little cakes at the Pâtisserie Anglaise. However, a few post-chaises were setting off at a gallop from the Hôtel des Princes and the Hôtel Meurice.

Marius entered through the Delorme arcade into the Rue Saint-Honoré. The shops here were closed, the merchants were chatting in front of their half-open doors, people were moving around, street lamps were burning, above the first floors all the windows showed lights as usual. There was cavalry in the Place du Palais-Royal.

Marius followed the Rue Saint-Honoré. As he receded from the Palais-Royal, there were fewer lighted windows; the shops were entirely closed, nobody was chatting in the doorways, the streets grew gloomy, and at the same time the throng grew denser. For the pedestrians were now a throng. Nobody was seen to speak in this throng, and yet a deep, dull hum rose from it.

Toward the Fontaine de l'Arbre-Sec, there were "gatherings," still and somber groups, among those coming and going, like stones in the middle of a running stream.

At the entrance of the Rue des Prouvaires, the throng no longer moved. It was a resisting, massive, solid, compact, almost impenetrable block of people, heaped together and talking in whispers. Black coats and round hats had almost disappeared. Overalls, workshirts, caps, bristly, dirty faces prevailed. This crowd wavered confusedly in the misty night. Its whispering had the harsh sound of a roar. Although nobody was walking, a trampling could be heard in the mud. Beyond this dense mass, in the Rue du Roule, in the Rue des Prouvaires, and in the extension of the Rue Saint-Honoré, there was not a single window in which a candle was burning. In those streets the rows of lamps were seen stretching away solitary and decreasing. The lamps of those days were like great red stars hanging from ropes, and they threw a shadow on the pavement like a huge spider. These streets were not empty. Rifles could be seen in stacks, bayonets moving and troops bivouacking. The curious did not pass this boundary. There, traffic came to a halt. There, the crowd ended and the army began.

Marius willed with the will of a man who no longer hopes. He had been called; he had to go. He found a way to pass through the crowd and through the bivouac of troops, avoiding patrols and sentinels. He made a detour, reached the Rue de Béthisy, and worked his way toward the markets. At the corner of the Rue des Bourdonnais the street lamps ended.

After having crossed the zone of the crowd and passed the outer fringe of troops, he found himself in the midst of something terrible. Not another pedestrian, not a soldier, not a light; nobody. Solitude, silence, night; a mysterious chill gripped him. To turn down a street was like entering a cellar.

He continued on.

He took a few steps. Somebody passed near him at a run. Was it a man? A woman? Were there several? He could not tell. It had gone by and vanished.

By a circuitous route, he came to a little street that he judged to be the Rue de la Poterie; around the middle of this alley he ran into some obstacle. He put out his hands. It was an overturned cart; his foot recognized puddles, mudholes, paving stones, scattered and heaped up. A barricade had been planned there and abandoned. He climbed over the stones and found himself on the other side of the obstruction. He walked very close to the posts and guided himself by the walls of the houses. A bit beyond the barricade, he seemed to catch a glimpse of something white in front of him. He approached, it took form. It was two white horses, the omnibus horses unhitched by Bossuet that morning, which had wandered haphazardly from street to street all day long, and had finally stopped there, with the exhausted paitence of brutes that no more understood the ways of man than man understands the ways of Providence.

Marius left the horses behind him. As he came to a street that felt like the Rue du Contrat Social, a musket shot coming from who knows where and passing at random through the darkness whistled by close to him, and the ball pierced a copper shaving bowl hanging in front of a barber's shop. This shaving bowl with the bullet hole could still be seen in 1846, in the Rue du Contrat Social, at the corner pillars of Les Halles.

This musket shot was still a sign of life. From that moment on he met not another thing.

The whole route was like a descent down a flight of dark stairs.

Marius went on nonetheless.

II

PARIS—AN OWL'S EYE VIEW

A creature who could have soared above Paris at that moment with the wings of the bat or the owl would have seen a gloomy spectacle.

All that old market district of Les Halles, which is like a city within the city, traversed by the Rues Saint-Denis and Saint-Martin, where a thousand little alleys cross each other and where the insurgents had made their stronghold and their assembly area, would have appeared to him like an enormous black hole dug out of the center of Paris. There the eye fell into an abyss. Thanks to the broken street lamps, thanks to the closed windows, all radiance ceased there, all life, all sound, all motion. The invisible police of the uprising watched everywhere and maintained order, that is to say, night. To drown the paucity of their number in a vast obscurity and to multiply each combatant by the possibilities that obscurity contains are the necessary tactics of insurrection. At nightfall, every window where a candle was lit had received a bullet. The light was extinguished, sometimes the inhabitant killed. Thus nothing stirred. There was nothing there but fright, mourning, stupor in the houses; in the streets a sort of sacred horror. Even the long lines of windows and of stories were not perceptible, the notching of the chimneys and the roofs, the dim reflections that gleam on the wet and muddy pavement. Any eye looking down from above into that mass of shade would have glimpsed here and there perhaps, at extended intervals, indistinct lights showing up broken and fantastic lines, outlines of singular constructions, something like ghostly glimmers coming and going among ruins; these were the barricades. The rest was a lake of obscurity, misty, heavy, funereal, above which rose, motionless and dismal silhouettes, the tower of Saint-Jacques, the church of Saint-Merry, and two or three others among those great buildings of which man makes giants and night makes phantoms.

All around this deserted, disquieting labyrinth, in the neighborhoods where the traffic of Paris was not stopped dead, and where a few rare lamps shone out, the aerial observer might have distinguished the metallic glint of sabers and bayonets, the dull rumbling of artillery, and the swarming of silent battalions steadily growing; a formidable girdle that was tightening and slowly closing around the émeute.

The beleaguered quarter was now only a sort of monstrous cavern; everything in it seemed to be sleeping or motionless, and, as we have just seen, none of the streets by which you might have entered offered anything but darkness.

A savage darkness, full of snares, full of startling and unknown encounters, where it was frightening to penetrate and ghastly to stay, where those who entered shuddered before those who were awaiting them, where those who waited trembled before those who were to come. Invisible combatants entrenched at every street corner; the ambush of the grave hidden in dense night. It was over. No further light to be hoped for there beyond the flash of rifles, no other encounter but the sudden rapid apparition of death. Where? How? When? Nobody knew; but it was certain and inevitable. There, in that place marked out for the contest, the government and the insurrection, the National Guard and the popular societies, the bourgeoisie and the émeute were to grope their way together. For men on each side, the necessity was the same. To leave that place slain or victors, the only possible issue henceforth. A situation so extreme, an obscurity so overpowering, that the most timid felt themselves filled with resolution and the boldest with terror.

Moreover, on both sides, fury, rancor, equal determination. For some, to advance was to die, and nobody thought of retreat; for others, to stay was to die, and nobody thought of flight.

Everything would have to be decided the next day, the triumph on this side or that one, the insurrection a revolution or a blunder. The government understood it as well as the rebels; every last bourgeois felt it. Hence a feeling of anguish that mingled with the impenetrable darkness of this quarter where all was to be decided; hence a redoubling of anxiety around this silence from which a catastrophe was to issue. One sound alone could be heard, a sound as heartrending as a death rattle, menacing as a malediction, the tocsin of Saint-Merry. Nothing was so blood-chilling as the din of this wild, desperate bell wailing in the darkness.

As often happens, nature seemed to have put herself in accord with what men were about to do. Nothing disturbed the funereal harmonies of that whole. The stars had disappeared, heavy clouds filled the whole horizon with their melancholy folds. There was a black sky over those dead streets, as if an immense pall had unfurled across that immense tomb.

While a battle still entirely political was preparing in this same place which had already seen so many revolutionary events, while the youth, the secret associations, the schools in the name of principles, and the middle class in the name of interests, were moving in to dash against each other, to grapple and overthrow each other, while each was hurrying and calling the final and decisive hour of the crisis, far off and outside of that fatal sector, in the deepest of the unfathomable caverns of that miserable old Paris which is disappearing under the splendor of the happy and opulent Paris, the gloomy voice of the people was heard dimly growling.

A fearful, sacred voice, composed of the roaring brute and the speech of God, which terrifies the feeble and warns the wise, which comes at the same time from below like the voice of the lion and from above like the voice of thunder.

III

THE FAR LIMIT

Marius had reached Les Halles.

There, all was quieter, darker, stiller than in the neighboring streets. One would have said that the icy peace of the grave had issued from the earth and spread over the sky.

Against this dark background, however, a red glare silhouetted the high roofs of the houses that barred the Rue de la Chanvrerie on the side toward Saint-Eustache. It was the reflection of the torch blazing away in the barricade of Corinth. Marius walked toward this glare. It led him to the Beet Market, and he dimly saw the dark mouth of the Rue des Prêcheurs. He turned into it. The insurgents' lookout on guard at the other end did not notice him. He felt that he was very near what he had come to seek, and he walked on tiptoe. This way he reached the bend of that short end of the Rue Mondétour, which was, as we remember, the only link Enjolras kept open to the outside. Around the corner of the last house on his left, cautiously advancing his head, he looked into this end of the Rue Mondétour.

A little beyond the black corner of the alley and the Rue de la Chanvrerie, which threw a broad shadow that hid him along with the rest, he noticed a glow on the pavement, a portion of the bistro, behind that a lamp flickering against a kind of shapeless wall, and men crouching with muskets on their knees. All this was within twenty yards of him. It was the interior of the barricade.

The houses on the right of the alley hid from him the rest of the bistro, the large barricade, and the flag.

Marius had only one step more to take.

Then the unhappy young man sat down on a stone, crossed his arms, and thought of his father.

He thought of that heroic Colonel Pontmercy who had been such a brave soldier, who had defended the frontier of France under the Republic, and reached the frontier of Asia under the emperor, who had seen Genoa, Alexandria, Milan, Turin, Madrid, Vienna, Dresden, Berlin, Moscow, who had left on every field of victory in Europe drops of that same blood that he, Marius, had in his veins, who had grown gray before his time in discipline and in command, who had lived with his sword belt buckled, his epaulets falling on his breast, his cockade blackened by powder, his forehead creased by the helmet, in barracks, in camp, on bivouac, in the ambulance, and who after twenty years had returned from the great wars with his cheek scarred, his face smiling, simple, tranquil, admirable, pure as a child, having done everything for France and nothing against her.

He said to himself that his day had come, too, that his hour had struck at last, that after his father, he too was to be brave, intrepid, bold, to face the bullets, bare his breast to the bayonets, pour out his blood, seek the enemy, seek death, that he was to wage war in his turn and to enter the field of battle, and that this field of battle he was about to enter was the street, and the war he was about to wage was civil war!

Civil war was yawning like an abyss before him, and he saw that this was where he was to fall.

Then he shuddered.

He thought of his father's sword that his grandfather had sold to a junk shop, and that he himself so painfully regretted. He said to himself that it was good that the chaste and valiant sword had escaped him and gone off angrily into the darkness; that if it had fled that way, it was because it was intelligent and because it foresaw the future; because it saw the émeute coming, the war of the gutters, the war of the pavements, the shots from cellar windows, blows given and received from behind; because, coming from Marengo and Friedland, it did not want to go to the Rue de la Chanvrerie, because after what it had done with the father, it would not do this with the son! He said to himself that if that sword were there, if having received it from the bedside of his dead father, he had dared bring it for this night combat between Frenchmen at a crossroads, most surely it would have burned his hands, and flared up in his face like the sword of the angel! He said to himself that it was fortunate that it was not there and that it had disappeared, that it was fine, that it was just, that his grandfather had been the true guardian of his father's glory, and that it was better that the colonel's sword had been sold at auction, sold to a junk man, thrown among scrap iron, than be used today to pierce the side of the country.

And then he began to weep bitterly.

It was horrible. But what could he do? Live without Cosette, he could not. Since she had gone away, he must surely die. Had he not given her his word of honor that he would die? She had gone away knowing that; therefore it pleased her that Marius should die. And then it was clear that she no longer loved him, since she had gone away like that, without notifying him, without a word, without a letter, and she knew his address! What use is life and why live any longer? And then, to have come so far, and recoil! To have approached the danger, and fled! To have come and looked into the barricade, and slinked away! To slink away all trembling, saying, "In fact, I've had enough of this, I've seen it, that's enough, it's civil war, I'm leaving!" To abandon his friends who were expecting him! Who needed him perhaps! Who were a handful against an army! To fail in all things at the same time, in his love, his friendship, his word! To give his cowardice the pretext of patriotism! But this was impossible, and if his father's ghost were there in the shadow and saw him recoil, he would strike him with the flat of his sword and cry out, "Advance, coward!"

A prey to the seesaw of his thoughts, he bowed his head.

Suddenly he straightened up. A sort of splendid rectification had come over him. There is an expansion of thought peculiar to the proximity of the grave; being near death makes us see the truth. A view of the act he felt himself perhaps on the verge of entering no longer appeared lamentable, but superb. In his mind's eye, the street war was suddenly transfigured by some indescribable inner working of the soul. All the tumultuous question marks of his reverie came flooding back, but without troubling him. He had an answer for each of them.

Now let's see, why should his father be indignant? Aren't there cases when insurrection rises to the dignity of duty? What shame could there be to the son of Colonel Pontmercy in the impending combat? It's no longer Montmirail or Champaubert; it's something else. It's no longer a question of a sacred territory, but of a holy idea. The country laments, but humanity applauds. Besides, is it true that the country is mourning? France is bleeding, but liberty smiles; and seeing the smile of liberty, France forgets her wound. And then, looking at the matter from a still higher standpoint, why do men talk of civil war?

Civil war? What does that mean? Is there any foreign war? Isn't every war fought between men, between brothers? War is modified only by its aim. There's neither foreign war nor civil war; there's only unjust war and just war. Until the day when the great human pact is concluded, war, at least the war which is the struggle of the hurrying future against the lingering past, may be necessary. Who can reproach such a war! War becomes shame, the sword becomes a dagger, only when it assassinates right, progress, reason, civilization, truth. Then, civil war or foreign war, it is iniquitous; its name is crime. Outside of that holy thing, justice, by what right does one form of war despise another? By what right does Washington's sword disown Camille Desmoulins's pike? Leonidas against the foreigner, Timoleon against the tyrant, which is the greater? One is the defender, the other is the liberator. Shall we brand, without troubling ourselves about the goal, every resort to arms in the interior of a city? Then mark with infamy Brutus, Marcel, Arnold of Blankenheim, Coligny. War of the thickets? War of the streets? Why not? It was the war of Ambiorix, of Artaveld, of Marnix, of Pelagius. But Ambiorix fought against Rome, Artaveld against France, Marnix against Spain, Pelagius against the Moors; all of them against the foreigner. Well, monarchy is the foreigner; oppression is the foreigner; divine right is the foreigner. Despotism violates the moral frontier, as invasion violates the geographical frontier. To drive out the tyrant or to drive out the English is, in either case, to regain your territory. There comes an hour when protest no longer suffices; after philosophy there must be action; the strong hand finishes what the idea has sketched; *Prometheus Bound* begins, Aristogeiton completes; the *Encyclopédie* enlightens souls, the 10th of August electrifies them. After Aeschylus, Thrasybulus; after Diderot, Danton. Mobs have a tendency to accept a master. Their mass deposits apathy. A mob easily becomes obedient. Men must be aroused, pushed, shocked by the very benefits of their deliverance, their eyes wounded with the truth, light thrown at them in terrible handfuls. They should be blinded a little for their own safety; this dazzling wakens them. Hence the necessity for tocsins and wars. Great warriors must rise, illuminate the nations by audacity, and shake free this sad humanity covered with shadow by divine right. Caesarean glory, force, fanaticism, irresponsible power, and absolute dominion, a mob stupidly occupied with gazing, in their twilight splendor, at these gloomy triumphs of the night. Down with the tyrant? But what is this? Of whom are you speaking? Are you calling Louis-Philippe the tyrant? No; no more than Louis XVI. They are both what history is accustomed to calling good kings; but principles cannot be parceled out, the logic of the true is rectilinear, the peculiarity of truth is to be without complacence; no compromise, then; all encroachment on man must be repressed; there is divine right in Louis XVI, there is *parce que Bourbon* in Louis-Philippe; both represent to a certain degree the confiscation of the right; and to wipe out the universal usurpation, it is necessary to fight them; when it is necessary, France always taking the initiative. When the master falls in France, he falls everywhere. In short, to re-establish social truth, to give back liberty her throne, to give back the people to the people, to give back sovereignty to man, to replace the purple on the head of France, to restore in their fullness reason and equity, to suppress every germ of antagonism by restoring every man to himself, to abolish royal obstacles to the immense universal concord, to replace the human race on a level with right—what cause is more just, and, consequently, what war greater? These wars construct peace. An enormous fortress of prejudices, privileges, superstitions, lies, exactions, abuses, violence, iniquity, darkness, is still standing on the world with its towers of hatred. It must be thrown down. This monstrous pile must be made to fall. To conquer at Austerlitz is great; to take the Bastille is immense.

There is nobody who has not noticed it in himself, the soul—and this is the marvel of its complicated unity and ubiquity—has the wonderful faculty of reasoning almost coolly in the most desperate extremities; and it often happens that disconsolate passion and deep despair, in the very agony of their darkest soliloquies, weigh subjects and discuss theses. Logic mingles with convulsion, and the thread of a syllogism floats unbroken in the dreary storm of thought. This was Marius's state of mind.

Even while thinking, overwhelmed but resolute, hesitating, however, and indeed shuddering in view of what he was about to do, his gaze wandered around the interior of the barricade. The insurgents were chatting in undertone, without moving around; and there was the quasi-silence which marks the last phase of waiting. Above them, at a fourth-story window, Marius made out a sort of spectator or witness who seemed strangely attentive. It was the doorkeeper killed by Le Cabuc. From below, by the reflection of the torch hidden among the paving stones, this head was dimly visible. Nothing was stranger in that gloomy and uncertain light than that livid, motionless, astonished face with its bristling hair, its staring eyes, and its gaping mouth, leaning over the street in an attitude of curiosity. One would have said that the one who was dead was gazing at those who were about to die. A long trail of blood that had flowed from his head ran down in ruddy streaks from the window to the height of the second story, where it stopped.

Book Fourteen

THE GRANDEUR OF DESPAIR

I

THE FLAG: ACT ONE

Nothing came yet. The clock of Saint-Merry had struck ten. Enjolras and Combeferre had sat down, carbine in hand, near the opening of the large barricade. They were not talking, they were listening; seeking to catch even the faintest, most distant sound of a march.

Suddenly, in the midst of this dismal calm, a clear, young, cheerful voice, seeming to come from the Rue Saint-Denis, rose and began to sing distinctly to the old popular tune, *"Au Clair de la Lune,"* these lines ending in a sort of cry similar to the crow of a cock:

Mon nez est en larmes,
Mon ami Bugeaud,
Prêt-moi tes gendarmes
Pour leur dire un mot.
En capote bleue,
La poule au shako,
Voici la banlieue!
Co-cocorico![1]

[1] My nose is in tears,
My good friend Bugeaud,
Just lend me your spears
To tell them my woe.

They grasped each other by the hand.

"It's Gavroche," said Enjolras.

"He's warning us," said Combeferre.

A headlong run startled the empty street; they saw a creature nimbler than a clown climb over the bus, and Gavroche bounded into the barricade all breathless, saying, "My musket! Here they are."

An electric thrill coursed through the whole barricade, and a moving of hands was heard, feeling for their muskets.

"Do you want my carbine?" said Enjolras to the gamin.

"I want the big musket," answered Gavroche.

And he took Javert's musket.

Two sentinels had been driven back and had come in almost at the same time as Gavroche. They were the sentry from the end of the street and the lookout from la Petite Truanderie. The vidette in the little Rue des Prêcheurs stayed at his post, which indicated that nothing was coming from the direction of the bridges and markets.

The Rue de la Chanvrerie, in which a few paving stones were dimly visible by the reflection of the light thrown onto the flag, offered to the insurgents the appearance of a great black porch opening into a cloud of smoke.

Every man had taken up his post for the combat.

Forty-three insurgents, among them Enjolras, Combeferre, Courfeyrac, Bossuet, Joly, Bahorel, and Gavroche, were on their knees in the large barricade, their heads even with the crest of the wall, the barrels of their muskets and their carbines pointed over the paving stones as through loopholes, watchful, silent, ready to fire. Six, commanded by Feuilly, were stationed with their muskets raised, in the windows of the two upper stories of Corinth.

A few moments more elapsed, then a sound of footsteps, measured, heavy, many, was distinctly heard coming from the direction of Saint-Leu. This sound, at first faint, then distinct, then heavy and resounding, ap-

---

In blue cassimere,
Hen on the shako,
The banlieue is here!
Co-cocorico!

proached slowly, without a halt, without interruption, with a tranquil and terrible continuity. Nothing but this could be heard. It was at once the silence and the sound of the statue of the Commendatore, but this stony tread was so indescribably enormous and so multiple that it called up at the same time the idea of a throng and a ghost. It was as though they were hearing the stride of the fearful statue Legion. The tread came closer; still closer, and stopped. They seemed to hear at the end of the street the breathing of many men. They could see nothing, however, except at the very end, in that dense obscurity, they made out a throng of metallic threads, as fine as needles and almost imperceptible, that moved about like those phosphoric networks we perceive under our closed eyelids at the moment of falling asleep, in the first mists of slumber. They were bayonets and musket barrels dimly lit up by the distant reflection of the torch.

There was still a pause, as if on both sides they were waiting. Suddenly, from the depth of that shadow, a voice, so much the more ominous, because nobody could be seen, and because it seemed as though it were the obscurity itself that was speaking, cried, "Who goes there?"

At the same time they heard the click of the leveled muskets.

Enjolras answered in a vibrant tone:

"The French Revolution!"

"Fire!" said the voice.

Crimson flashed across the façades on the street, as if the door of a furnace were opened and abruptly closed.

A fearful explosion burst over the barricade. The red flag fell. The volley had been so heavy and so dense that it had cut the staff, that is to say, the very point of the pole of the omnibus. Some bullets that had ricocheted off the cornices of the houses entered the barricade and wounded several men.

This first burst created a chilling impression. The attack was so harsh as to make the boldest ponder. It was evident that they were dealing with a whole regiment at least.

"Comrades," cried Courfeyrac, "don't waste the powder. Let's wait to reply till they come down the street."

"And first of all," said Enjolras, "let's hoist the flag again!"

He picked up the flag, which had fallen just at his feet.

They heard the rattling of the ramrods in the muskets outside; the troops were reloading.

Enjolras continued, "Who is there who has courage here? Who is going to raise the flag on the barricade?"

Nobody answered. To climb up onto the barricade at the moment when without a doubt it was targeted again, was sure death. The bravest hesitates to sentence himself. Enjolras himself shuddered. He repeated, "Nobody volunteers?"

II

THE FLAG: ACT TWO

Since they had arrived at Corinth and had begun building the barricade, hardly any attention had been paid to Father Mabeuf. M. Mabeuf, however, had not left the flock. He had gone into the ground floor of the bistro and sat down behind the counter. There he had been, so to speak, crumbling within himself. He no longer seemed to look or think. Courfeyrac and others had accosted him two or three times, warning him of the danger, begging him to go away, but he had not appeared to hear them. When nobody was speaking to him, his lips moved as if he were answering somebody, and as soon as anybody spoke to him, his lips became still and his eyes lost all semblance of life. Some hours before the barricade was attacked, he had assumed a pose that he had not left since, his hands on his knees and his head bent forward as if he were looking into an abyss. Nothing had been able to draw him out of this attitude; it seemed as though his mind were not in the barricade. When everybody had gone to take a place for combat, there remained in the lower room only Javert tied to the post, an insurgent with drawn saber watching Javert, and he, Mabeuf. At the moment of the attack, at the discharge, the physical shock reached him, and somehow woke him up; he suddenly got to his feet, crossed the room, and at the instant when Enjolras repeated his appeal, "Nobody volunteers?" they saw the old man appear in the doorway of the wineshop.

His presence produced some commotion in the group. A cry arose: "It's the Voter! It's the Conventionist! It's the Representative of the people!"

Probably he did not hear them.

He walked straight to Enjolras, the insurgents fell back before him with a religious awe, he snatched the flag from Enjolras, who drew back petrified, and then, nobody daring to stop him or aid him, this old man of eighty, with shaking head but firm foot, began to climb slowly up the stairway of paving stones built into the barricade. It seemed so somber and grand that everyone around him cried, "Hats off!" At each step it was terrifying; his white hair, his decrepit face, his large forehead bald and wrinkled, his hollow eyes, his quivering and open mouth, his old arm raising the red banner, surged up out of the shadow and loomed in the bloody light of the torch, and they seemed to see the ghost of '93 rising out of the earth, the flag of terror in its hand.

When he reached the top of the last step, when this trembling and terrible phantom, standing on that mound of rubbish before twelve hundred invisible muskets, rose up, in the face of death and as if he were stronger than it, the whole barricade in the darkness seemed a supernatural, colossal image.

There was one of those silences that occur only in the presence of wonders.

In the midst of this silence the old man waved the red flag and cried: "*Vive la révolution! Vive la république!* Fraternity! Equality! And death!"

From the barricade they heard a low and rapid muttering like the murmur of a hurried priest dispatching a prayer. It was probably the commissioner of police making the legal summons at the other end of the street.

Then the same ringing voice that had cried, "Who goes there?" cried, "Disperse!"

M. Mabeuf, pallid, haggard, his eyes illumined by the mournful fires of insanity, raised the flag above his head and repeated, *"Vive la république!"*

"Fire!" said the voice.

A second discharge, like a shower of grapeshot, beat against the barricade.

The old man fell to his knees, then rose up, let go of the flag and fell heavily backward onto the pavement inside, with his arms stretched out in a cross.

Streams of blood ran from under him. His old face, pale and sad, seemed to be gazing at the sky.

One of those emotions greater than man, which make us forget even to defend ourselves, seized the insurgents, and horror struck, they respectfully approached the corpse.

"What men these regicides are!" said Enjolras.

Courfeyrac bent over to Enjolras's ear.

"This is only for you, and I don't wish to diminish the enthusiasm. But he was anything but a regicide. I knew him. His name was Father Mabeuf. I don't know what got into him today. But he was a brave blockhead. Just look at that face."

"Blockhead and Brutus heart," answered Enjolras.

Then he raised his voice:

"Citizens! This is the example the old give the young. We hesitated, he came! We fell back, he advanced! This is what those who tremble with old age teach those who tremble with fear! This patriarch is noble in the sight of the country. He has had a long life and a magnificent death! Now let us protect his corpse, let everyone defend this old man dead as he would defend his father living, and let his presence among us make the barricade impregnable!"

A murmur of somber and determined solidarity followed these words.

Enjolras stooped down, raised the old man's head, and fiercely kissed him on the forehead, then, moving his arms and handling the dead with a tender care, as if he feared hurting him, he took off his coat, showed the bleeding holes to all of them, and said:

"There is our flag now."

III

GAVROCHE WOULD HAVE DONE BETTER TO ACCEPT ENJOLRAS'S CARBINE

They threw a long black shawl belonging to the widow Hucheloup over Father Mabeuf. Six men made a stretcher of their muskets, they laid the corpse on it, and they slowly bore it, bareheaded, with solemnity, to the large table in the low room.

These men, completely absorbed in the grave and sacred thing they were doing, were not thinking of their own perilous situation.

When the corpse passed by Javert, who was still impassive, Enjolras said to the spy, "You! Soon enough."

During this time little Gavroche, who alone had not left his post and had stayed on watch, thought he saw some men stealthily approaching the barricade. Suddenly he cried out, "Watch out!"

Courfeyrac, Enjolras, Jean Prouvaire, Combeferre, Joly, Bahorel, Bossuet, all sprang out of the wineshop. There was hardly a moment to spare. They caught sight of a glinting expanse of bayonets undulating above the barricade. Tall Municipal Guards were penetrating, some by climbing over the bus, others through the opening, pushing in front of the gamin, who retreated but did not run.

The moment was critical. It was that first fearful instant of inundation, when the stream rises to the level of the bank and the water begins to filter through the fissures in the dike. A second more, and the barricade would have been taken.

Bahorel sprang at the first Guard who entered, and killed him point-blank with his carbine; the second killed Bahorel with his bayonet. Another had already felled Courfeyrac, who was crying "Help!" The largest of all, a kind of colossus, marched on Gavroche with fixed bayonet. The gamin took Javert's enormous musket in his little arms, aimed it resolutely at the giant, and pulled the trigger. Nothing went off. Javert had not loaded his musket. The Municipal Guard burst out laughing and raised his bayonet over the child.

Before the bayonet touched Gavroche the musket dropped from the soldier's hands, a ball had struck the Municipal Guard in the middle of the forehead, and he fell on his back. A second ball struck the other Guard, who had assailed Courfeyrac, full in the breast and threw him onto the pavement.

It was Marius who had just entered the barricade.

IV

POWDER KEG

Still hidden in the bend of the Rue Mondétour, Marius had watched the first phase of the combat, irresolute and shuddering. However, he was not able for long to resist that mysterious and sovereign infatuation that could be called the appeal of the abyss. Faced with imminent peril, the death of M. Mabeuf, that fatal enigma, faced with Bahorel slain, Courfeyrac crying "Help!" that child threatened, his friends to succor or to avenge, all hesitation had vanished, and he had rushed into the conflict, his two pistols in hand. With the first shot he had saved Gavroche, and with the second freed Courfeyrac.

At the shots, at the cries of the wounded Guards, the attackers had scaled the bulwark, whose summit now bristled with Municipal Guards, soldiers of the Line, National Guards of the suburbs, at least half exposed, musket in hand. They already covered more than two thirds of the wall but did not leap into the enclosure; they seemed to hesitate, fearing some snare. They looked into the obscure barricade as one would look into a lion's den. The light of the torch only lit up their bayonets, their bearskin caps, and the upper part of their anxious and angry faces.

Marius now had no weapon, he had thrown down his discharged pistols, but he had noticed the powder keg in the low room near the door.

As he turned half around, looking in that direction, a soldier aimed at him. As the man made ready to fire at Marius, a hand was laid on the muzzle of the musket, and stopped it. It was somebody who had sprung forward, the young workingman with corduroy trousers. The shot went off, passed through the hand, and perhaps also through the workingman, for he fell, but the ball did not reach Marius. All this in the smoke, rather guessed than seen. Marius, who was entering the room, hardly noticed it. Still he had caught a dim glimpse of that musket aimed at him, and that hand which had stopped it, and he had heard the shot. But in moments like that the things we see waver and rush on, and we stop for nothing. We feel vaguely propelled toward still deeper shadow, and everything is cloud.

The insurgents, surprised but not terrified, had rallied. Enjolras had cried, "Wait! Don't fire at random!" In the first confusion, in fact, they might hit one another. Most of them had gone up to the window of the second story and to the dormer windows, from which they looked down on the assailants. The most determined, with Enjolras, Courfeyrac, Jean Prouvaire, and Combeferre, had haughtily placed their backs to the houses in the rear, openly facing the ranks of soldiers and guards crowning the barricade.

All this was accomplished without panic, with that strange and threatening gravity that precedes mêlées. On both sides they were aiming point-blank, so close that they could talk to each other in an ordinary tone. Just as the spark was about to fly, an officer in a gorget and huge epaulets raised his sword and said, "Surrender!"

"Fire!" said Enjolras.

The two explosions were simultaneous, and everything disappeared in the smoke.

A stinging, stifling smoke over the wounded and dying, who writhed, with dull and feeble groans.

When the smoke cleared away, the combatants on both sides could be seen, thinned out, but still in the same places, and reloading their weapons, in silence.

Suddenly, a thundering voice was heard crying, "Get back, or I'll blow up the barricade!"

All turned in the direction of the voice.

Marius had entered the ground-floor room, had taken the powder keg, and then he had taken advantage of the smoke and the sort of obscure fog filling the entrenched enclosure, to slip along the barricade as far as that cage of paving stones holding the torch. To pull out the torch, to put the keg of powder in its place, to push the pile of paving stones under the keg, which instantly stove in—all this with a sort of terrible self-control—had taken Marius only the effort of stooping down and rising up; and now all of them, National Guards, Municipal Guards, officers, soldiers, grouped at the other extremity of the barricade, looked at him with horror, his foot on the stones, the torch in his hand, his stern face lit by deadly resolution, lowering the flame of the torch toward that formidable pile in which they discerned the broken barrel of powder, and uttering that terrifying cry:

"Get back, or I'll blow up the barricade!"

Marius on this barricade, after the octogenarian, was a vision of the young revolution after the specter of the old.

"Blow up the barricade!" said a sergeant, "and yourself, too!"

Marius answered, "And myself, too."

And he brought down the torch toward the powder keg.

But there was no longer anybody on the wall. The assailants, leaving their dead and wounded, fled pell-mell and in disorder toward the far end of the street, and were once more lost in the night. It was a rout.

The barricade was cleared.

V

END OF JEAN PROUVAIRE'S RHYME

Everyone flocked around Marius. Courfeyrac sprang to his neck.

"There you are!"

"What luck!" said Combeferre.

"Just in time!" said Bossuet.

"Without you I'd have been dead!" continued Courfeyrac.

"Without you I'd have been gobbled up!" added Gavroche.

Marius inquired, "Where's the leader?"

"You're the leader," said Enjolras.

All day Marius had felt a furnace in his brain, now it was a whirlwind. This maelstrom within him affected him as if it were outside his body and sweeping him along. It seemed to him that he was already at an immense distance from life. His two luminous months of joy and of love, terminating abruptly on this frightful precipice, Cosette lost to him, this barricade, M. Mabeuf dying for the Republic, himself a chief of insurgents, all these things appeared as a monstrous nightmare. He was obliged to make a mental effort to assure himself that all this surrounding him was real. Marius had lived too little as yet to know that nothing is more imminent than the impossible, and that what we must always foresee is the unforeseen. He was a spectator of his own drama, as of a play one does not grasp.

In this mist in which his mind was struggling, he did not recognize Javert, who, bound to his post, had not moved his head during the attack on the barricade, and who watched the revolt going on about him with the resignation of a martyr and the majesty of a judge. Marius did not even notice him.

Meanwhile the assailants made no movement, they could be heard marching and swarming at the end of the street, but they did not venture forward, either because they were awaiting orders, or, before hurling themselves again at that impregnable redoubt, they were awaiting reinforcements. The insurgents had posted sentinels, and some who were students in medicine had set about dressing the wounded.

They had thrown the tables out of the bistro, with the exception of two reserved for lint and cartridges, and the one bearing Father Mabeuf; they added them to the barricade, and had replaced them in the lower room by the mattresses from the beds of the widow Hucheloup, and the servants. On these mattresses they had laid the wounded; as for the three poor creatures who lived in Corinth, nobody knew what had become of them. They found them at last, however, hidden in the cellar.

Bitter feelings darkened their joy over the regained barricade.

They called the roll. One of the insurgents was missing. And who? One of the dearest. One of the most valiant, Jean Prouvaire. They looked for him among the wounded, he was not there. They looked for him among the dead, he was not there. He was evidently a prisoner.

Combeferre said to Enjolras, "They have our friend; we have their officer. Have you set your heart on the death of this spy?"

"Yes," said Enjolras; "but less than on the life of Jean Prouvaire."

This took place in the basement room near Javert's post.

"Well," replied Combeferre, "I'm going to tie my

handkerchief to my cane, and go with a flag of truce to offer to give them their man for ours."

"Listen," said Enjolras, laying his hand on Combeferre's arm.

There was a significant clicking of weapons at the end of the street.

They heard a manly voice cry out, "*Vive la France!* Long live the future!"

They recognized Prouvaire's voice.

There was a flash and an explosion.

Silence reigned again.

"They've killed him," exclaimed Combeferre.

Enjolras looked at Javert and said to him, "Your friends have just shot you."

VI

THE AGONY OF DEATH AFTER THE AGONY OF LIFE

A peculiarity of this kind of war is that the attack on the barricades is almost always made head on, and in general the assailants abstain from turning the positions, whether it be that they dread ambush or are afraid of becoming entangled in the crooked streets. The whole attention of the insurgents therefore was directed to the main barricade, which was evidently the point still threatened, and where the struggle would infallibly have to resume. Marius, however, thought of the little barricade and went to it. It was deserted, guarded only by the lamp that flickered between the stones. The little Rue Mondétour, moreover, and the branch streets of la Petite-Truanderie and le Cygne were perfectly quiet.

As Marius, with the inspection done, was turning back, he heard his name faintly spoken in the darkness:

"Monsieur Marius!"

He shuddered, for he recognized the voice that had called him two hours before, through the gate in the Rue Plumet.

Only now this voice seemed no more than a breath.

He looked about him and saw nobody.

Marius thought he was mistaken, that it was an illusion added by his mind to the extraordinary realities colliding around him. He started to leave the recess in which the barricade was placed.

"Monsieur Marius!" repeated the voice.

This time he could not doubt, he had distinctly heard; he looked and saw nothing.

"At your feet," said the voice.

He stooped and saw a form in the shadows, dragging itself toward him. It was crawling along the pavement. It was this that had spoken to him.

By the lantern light he could just make out a blouse, a pair of torn corduroy trousers, bare feet, and something resembling a pool of blood. Marius caught a glimpse of a pale face that rose toward him and said, "You don't know me?"

"No."

"Eponine."

Marius bent down quickly. It was indeed that unhappy child. She was dressed as a man.

"How did you get here? What are you doing there?"

"I'm dying," she said.

There are words and incidents that rouse even those who are overwhelmed. Marius exclaimed with a start, "You're wounded! Wait, I'll carry you inside! They'll dress your wounds! Is it serious? How can I pick you up so as not to hurt you? Where are you hurt? Help! My God! But what did you come here for?"

And he tried to pass his arm under her to lift her.

In lifting her he touched her hand.

She gave a feeble cry.

"Have I hurt you?" asked Marius.

"A little."

"But I've only touched your hand."

She raised her hand into Marius's sight, and in the center of that hand Marius saw a black hole.

"What's the matter with your hand?" he asked.

"It's wounded."

"Wounded?"

"Yes."

"By what?"

"By a bullet."

"How?"

"Did you see a musket aimed at you?"

"Yes, and a hand that stopped it."

"That was mine."

Marius shuddered.

"What madness! Poor child! But that's not so bad, if that's all, it's nothing, let me carry you to a bed. They'll take care of you, people don't die from a shot in the hand."

She whispered, "The bullet went through my hand, but it also went out through my back. It's no use moving me from here. I'll tell you how you can take care of me, better than a surgeon. Sit down beside me on that stone."

He obeyed; she laid her head on Marius's knees, and without looking at him, she said, "Oh! That's so much better! How comfortable this is! That's it! I'm not suffering anymore!"

She stayed still for a moment, then turned her head with an effort and looked at Marius.

"Do you know, Monsieur Marius? It bothered me you went into that garden; it was silly, since I was the one who showed you the house, and then, well, I surely should have known that a young man like you—"

She stopped, and, leaping over the gloomy transitions that were undoubtedly in her mind, she added with a heartrending smile, "You thought me ugly, didn't you?"

She went on, "See, you're lost! Nobody will get out of the barricade, now. It was I who led you into this, it was! You're going to die, I'm sure. And still when I saw him aiming at you, I put my hand on the muzzle of the musket. How odd it is! But it was because I wanted to die before you. When that bullet hit me, I dragged myself over here, nobody saw me, nobody picked me up. I waited for you, I said, So, he won't come? Oh! If you knew, I bit on my blouse, I was suffering so! Now I'm fine. Do you remember the day I came to your room and looked at myself in your mirror, and the day I met you on the boulevard near some working women? How the birds sang! It wasn't so very long ago. You gave me five francs, and I said to you, I don't want your money. Did you pick up your coin? You're not rich. I didn't think to tell you to pick it up. The sun was shining, I wasn't cold. Do you remember, Monsieur Marius? Oh! I'm happy! We're all going to die."

She had a wandering, grave, and touching air. Her torn blouse showed her bare throat. While she was talking she rested her wounded hand on her breast where there was another hole, and with each pulsation there was a flow of blood like a jet of wine from an open cask.

Marius gazed at this unfortunate creature with profound compassion.

"Oh!" she exclaimed suddenly. "It's coming back. I'm choking!"

She grabbed her blouse and bit it, and her legs writhed on the pavement.

At this moment the bantam rooster voice of little Gavroche resounded through the barricade. The child had climbed up on a table to load his musket and was gaily singing the song then so popular:

En voyant Lafayette
Le gendarme répète
Sauvons-nous! Sauvons-nous! Sauvons-nous![1]

Eponine raised herself up and listened, then she murmured, "There he is!"

And turning toward Marius, "My brother's here. He mustn't see me. He would scold me."

"Your brother?" asked Marius, who thought in the bitterest, sorrowful depths of his heart, of the duties his father had bequeathed him toward the Thénardiers, "Who is your brother?"

"That little boy."

"The one singing?"

"Yes."

Marius started.

"Oh! Don't go away!" she said, "it won't be long now!"

She was sitting almost upright, but her voice was very faint and broken by hiccoughs and hoarse gasping. She brought her face as close as she could to Marius's. She added with a strange expression, "Listen, I don't want to deceive you. I have a letter in my pocket for you. Since yesterday. I was told to mail it. I kept it. I didn't want it to reach you. But you would hold it against me perhaps when we meet again so soon. We will meet again, won't we? Take your letter."

She grasped Marius's hand convulsively with her

[1] On seeing Lafayette, the policeman repeats, let's clear out!

wounded hand, but she no longer seemed to feel the pain. She put Marius's hand into the pocket of her blouse. Marius did feel a piece of paper there.

"Take it," she said.

Marius took the letter.

She made a sign of satisfaction and of consent.

"Now for my pains, promise me—"

And she hesitated.

"What?" asked Marius.

"Promise me!"

"I promise you."

"Promise to kiss me on the forehead when I'm dead. I'll feel it."

She let her head fall back on Marius's knees and her eyelids closed. He thought the poor soul had gone. Eponine lay motionless, but just when Marius supposed her forever asleep, she slowly opened her eyes, revealing the somber depths of death, and said to him with an accent whose sweetness already seemed to come from another world, "And then, do you know, Monsieur Marius, I believe I was a little in love with you."

She tried to smile again and died.

VII

GAVROCHE A PROFOUND CALCULATOR OF DISTANCES

Marius kept his promise. He kissed that livid forehead beaded with an icy sweat. This was not infidelity to Cosette; it was a thoughtful, gentle farewell to an unhappy soul.

It was not without a thrill that he had taken the letter Eponine had given him. He had felt at once that it was important. He was impatient to read it. The heart of man is made this way; the unfortunate child had hardly closed her eyes when Marius thought to unfold this paper. He laid her gently on the ground and went away. Something told him he could not read that letter in sight of this corpse.

He went to a candle in the lower room. It was a little

note, folded and sealed with a woman's elegant care. The address was in a woman's hand, and read:

"To M. Marius Pontmercy, care of M. Courfeyrac, Rue de la Verrerie, No. 16."

He broke the seal and read:

"My beloved, alas! My father wants us to leave immediately. Tonight we will be at the Rue de l'Homme-Armé, No. 7. In a week we will be in England. COSETTE. June 4th."

Such was the innocence of this love that Marius did not even know Cosette's handwriting.

What had happened can be told in a few words. Eponine had done it all. After the evening of the 3rd of June, she had had a double concern, to thwart the projects of her father and the cutthroats against the house in the Rue Plumet, and to separate Marius from Cosette. She had exchanged rags with the first young rogue she found who thought it fun to dress up as a woman while Eponine was disguised as a man. It was she who, in the Champ de Mars, had given Jean Valjean the expressive warning "Move out!" Jean Valjean returned home and said to Cosette, "We are leaving tonight, and going to the Rue de l'Homme-Armé with Toussaint. Next week we will be in London." Cosette, prostrated by this unexpected blow, had hastily written two lines to Marius. But how should she get the letter to the post? She did not go out alone, and Toussaint, surprised at such an errand, would surely show the letter to M. Fauchelevent. In this anxiety, Cosette saw, through the gate, Eponine in men's clothes, who was now continually prowling around the garden. Cosette called "the young workingman" and handed him five francs and the letter, saying to him, "Carry this letter to its address right away." Eponine put the letter in her pocket. The next day, June 5, she went to Courfeyrac's to ask for Marius, not to give him the letter, but, a thing that every jealous and loving soul will understand, "to see." She waited there for Marius, or at least for Courfeyrac—still to see. When Courfeyrac said to her, "We're going to the barricades," an idea flashed across her mind. To throw herself into that death as she would have thrown herself into any other, and to push Marius into it. She followed Courfeyrac, made sure of the spot where they were building the barricade; and, quite sure, since Marius had received no notice and she had intercepted the letter, that at nightfall he would be at his usual evening rendezvous, she went to the Rue Plumet, waited there for Marius, and sent him, in the name of his friends, that appeal that must, she thought, lead him to the barricade. She counted on Marius's despair when he did not find Cosette; she was not mistaken. She returned herself to the Rue de la Chanvrerie. We have seen what she did there. She died with that tragic joy of jealous hearts that drag the being they love into death with them, saying, "Nobody shall have him!"

Marius covered Cosette's letter with kisses. So she still loved him? For a moment he had the idea that now he need not die. Then he said to himself, "She's going away. Her father is taking her to England, and my grandfather refuses to consent to the marriage. Nothing is fated to change." Dreamers like Marius have these extreme depressions, and dire decisions come out of them. The weariness of living is unbearable; death is sooner over. Then he thought that there were two duties remaining for him to fulfill; to inform Cosette of his death and to send her a last farewell, and to save from the imminent catastrophe fast approaching this poor child, Eponine's brother and Thénardier's son.

He had a pocket notebook with him, the same one that had contained the pages on which he had written so many thoughts of love for Cosette. He tore out a leaf and wrote these few lines in pencil:

"Our marriage was impossible. I asked my grandfather, and he has refused; I have no funds, nor do you. I ran to your house, I did not find you, you know the promise I gave you? I am keeping it. I will die. I love you. When you read this, my soul will be near you, and will smile upon you."

Having nothing to seal this letter with, he merely folded the paper, and wrote on it this address:

"To Mlle. Cosette Fauchelevent, care of M. Fauchelevent, Rue de l'Homme-Armé, No. 7."

The letter folded, he remained a moment lost in thought, took out his notebook again, opened it, and wrote these four lines on the first page with the same pencil: "My name is Marius Pontmercy. Carry my corpse to my grandfather's, M. Gillenormand, Rue des Filles-du-Calvaire, No. 6, in the Marais."

He put the book into his coat pocket, then called Gavroche. The gamin, at the sound of Marius's voice, ran up with a joyful and devoted expression.

"Will you do something for me?"

"Anything," said Gavroche. "Good God! Without you, I'd have been cooked, for sure."

"You see this letter?"

"Yes."

"Take it. Get out of the barricade immediately"—worried, Gavroche began to scratch his ear—"and tomorrow morning you will carry it to its address, to Mademoiselle Cosette, at M. Fauchelevent's, Rue de l'Homme-Armé, No. 7."

The heroic boy answered, "Ah well, but meanwhile they'll take the barricade, and I won't be here."

"The barricade will not be attacked again before daybreak, according to all appearance, and won't be taken before tomorrow noon."

The new respite that the assailants were allowing the barricade was, in fact, stretching out. It was one of those intermissions, frequent in night battles, which are always followed by an increased fury.

"Well," said Gavroche, "suppose I go and carry your letter in the morning?"

"It will be too late. The barricade will probably be blockaded; all the streets will be guarded, and you won't be able to get out. Go, right away!"

Gavroche had nothing more to say; he stood there, undecided, and sadly scratching his ear. Suddenly, with one of his birdlike motions, he took the letter.

"All right," he said.

And he started off at a run by the little Rue Mondétour.

Gavroche had an idea which decided him, but which he did not tell, for fear that Marius would make some objection to it.

That idea was this:

"It's hardly midnight, the Rue de l'Homme-Armé is not far, I'll take the letter there right away, and I'll be back in time."

Book Fifteen

THE RUE DE L'HOMME-ARMÉ

I

THE BLOTTER TALKS

What are the convulsions of a city compared to the émeutes of the soul? Man is a depth still more profound than the people. At that very moment, Jean Valjean was prey to a frightful uprising. Every gulf had reopened within him. He too, like Paris, was shuddering on the threshold of a formidable and obscure revolution. A few hours had sufficed. His destiny and conscience were suddenly covered with shadow. Of him too, as of Paris, we could say that the two principles are face to face. The angel of light and the angel of darkness are to grapple on the bridge over the abyss. Which of the two will hurl down the other? Which will win out?

On the eve of that same day, June 5th, Jean Valjean, with Cosette and Toussaint, had moved into the Rue de l'Homme-Armé. A sudden turn of fortune was waiting for him there.

Cosette had not left the Rue Plumet without an attempt at resistance. For the first time since they had lived together, Cosette's will and Jean Valjean's will had shown themselves distinct; they had been, if not conflicting, at least contradictory. There was objection on one side and inflexibility on the other. The abrupt advice—move out —tossed to Jean Valjean by an unknown hand, had alarmed him to the point of making him absolute. He believed himself trailed and pursued. Cosette had to yield.

They both arrived in the Rue de l'Homme-Armé without opening their mouths or saying a word, absorbed in their personal preoccupations; Jean Valjean so anxious that he did not notice Cosette's sadness, Cosette so sad that she did not notice Jean Valjean's anxiety.

Jean Valjean had brought Toussaint, which he had never done in his earlier absences. He saw the possibility that he might not return to the Rue Plumet, and he could neither leave Toussaint behind, nor tell her his secret. Besides, he felt that she was devoted and safe. Between servant and master, betrayal begins with curiosity. But Toussaint, as if predestined to be Valjean's servant, was not curious. She said through her stuttering, in her Barneville peasant's speech, "I am as I am; I do my work, the rest is none of my business."

In this departure from the Rue Plumet, which was almost a flight, Jean Valjean took nothing along but the little embalmed case christened by Cosette "the inseparable." Full trunks would have required porters, and porters are witnesses. They summoned a coach to the door on the Rue Babylone, and they went away.

It was with great difficulty that Toussaint got permission to pack up a little linen and clothing and a few toilet articles. Cosette herself carried only her writing case and her blotter.

To increase the solitude and mystery of this disappearance, Jean Valjean had arranged not to leave the little house on the Rue Plumet till evening, which left Cosette time to write her note to Marius. They arrived at the Rue de l'Homme-Armé after nightfall.

They went to bed in virtual silence.

The apartment in the Rue de l'Homme-Armé was in a rear court, on the third floor, and consisted of two bedrooms, a living room, and a kitchen adjoining the dining table, with a loft, where there was a cot bed that fell to Toussaint. The living room was both the entrance hall and separation between the two bedrooms. The apartments contained all the necessary furnishings.

Human nature is so constituted that we are reassured almost as foolishly as we are alarmed. Hardly was Jean Valjean at the Rue de l'Homme-Armé before his anxiety decreased, and gradually disappeared. There are calming places that have some automatic effect on the mind. Obscure street, peaceful inhabitants. Jean Valjean felt a strange contagion of tranquility in that lane of the old Paris, so narrow that it was barred to carriages by a beam laid on two posts, deaf and dumb in the midst of the noisy city, twilight in broad day, and, so to speak, incapable of emotions between its two rows of tall, century-old houses that kept their silence like the patriarchs that they are. There is stagnant oblivion in this street. Jean Valjean could breathe in peace there. How could anybody find him there?

His first task was to place "the inseparable" by his side.

He slept well. Night lends counsel; we might add, night brings calm. The next morning he woke up almost cheerful. He thought the dining room charming, though it was hideous, furnished with an old round table, a low sideboard topped by a hanging mirror, a wormeaten armchair, and a few other chairs loaded down with Toussaint's bundles. Through an opening in one of these bundles, Jean Valjean's National Guard uniform could be seen.

As for Cosette, she had Toussaint bring a bowl of soup to her room and did not make her appearance till evening.

About five o'clock, Toussaint, who was coming and going, very busy with this little move, set some cold chicken on the dining room table, which Cosette, out of deference to her father, consented to look at.

This done, Cosette, on the pretext of a severe headache, said good night to Jean Valjean, and shut herself in her bedroom. Jean Valjean ate a chicken wing with a good appetite, and resting his elbows on the table, was gradually regaining his serenity and sense of security.

While he was eating this frugal dinner, he became confusedly aware, on two or three occasions, of some stammering from Toussaint, who said to him, "Monsieur, there is some row; they're fighting in Paris." But, absorbed in a swarm of inner schemes, he paid no attention to it. To tell the truth, he had not heard.

He got up and began to walk from the window to the door, and from the door to the window, growing calmer and calmer.

With the calm, Cosette, his single engrossing care, kept coming back to mind. Not that he was troubled about her headache, a petty case of nerves, a young girl's brooding, a passing cloud, in a day or two it would be gone; but he thought of the future, and, as usual, he thought of it pleasantly. After all, he could see no obstacle to their happy life resuming its course. At certain moments, everything seems impossible; at others, everything appears easy; Jean Valjean was in one of those happy moments. They usually follow after the bad ones, like day after night, by that law of succession and contrast that lies at the very foundation of nature, and which superficial minds call antithesis. In this peaceful street where he had taken refuge, Jean Valjean was relieved of all that had been troubling him for some time past. From the very fact that he had seen a good deal of darkness, he began to glimpse a little blue sky. To have left the Rue Plumet without complications or incidents was already a piece of good fortune.

Perhaps it would be prudent to leave the country, if only for a few months, and go to London. Well, they would go. To be in France, to be in England, what did that matter, as long as he had Cosette with him? Cosette was his nation. Cosette was enough for his happiness; the idea that perhaps he was not enough for Cosette's happiness, this idea, once cause of fever and insomnia, did not even occur to him. All his past griefs had disappeared, and he was in full flush of optimism. Cosette, being near him, seemed to belong to him; an optical effect that everybody has experienced. He settled in his own mind, and with great ease, the departure for England with Cosette, and he saw his happiness rebuilt, no matter where, in the landscape of his reverie.

While still walking up and down, with slow steps, his eye suddenly fell on something strange.

Facing him he saw, in the inclined mirror hanging above the sideboard, and clearly read the lines that follow:

"My beloved, alas! My father wants us to leave immediately. Tonight we will be at the Rue de L'Homme-Armé, No. 7. In a week we will be in London. COSETTE. June 4th."

Jean Valjean stood aghast.

On arriving, Cosette, had laid her blotter on the sideboard in front of the mirror, and, wholly absorbed in her anguish, had forgotten it there, without even noticing that she left it wide open, and open exactly to the page on which she had blotted the lines she had written and entrusted to the young workman passing through the Rue Plumet. The writing was printed on the blotter.

The mirror reflected the writing, resulting in what geometry calls the symmetric image, by which the writing reversed on the blotter was corrected by the mirror, and presented its original form; and Jean Valjean had beneath his eyes the letter Cosette had written Marius the evening before.

It was simple and devastating.

Jean Valjean went to the mirror. He read the five lines again, but believed none of it. They produced the effect on him of an apparition in a flash of lightning. It was a hallucination. It was impossible. It could not be.

Little by little his perception became more precise; looking at Cosette's blotter, the consciousness of the real fact returned. He picked up the blotter and said, "This is what it comes from." He feverishly examined the lines printed on the blotter, the reversal of the letters made a strange scrawl, and he made no sense of them. Then he said to himself: "But that doesn't mean anything, there's nothing written there." And he drew a deep breath, with an inexpressible sigh of relief. Who has not felt these silly joys in horrible moments? The soul does not give up to despair until it has exhausted all illusions.

He held the blotter in his hand and gazed at it, foolishly happy, almost laughing at the hallucination that had duped him. All at once his eyes fell on the mirror, and he saw the vision again. The lines were drawn there with inexorable clarity. This time it was no mirage. The repetition of a vision is reality, it was palpable, it was the writing restored by the mirror. He understood.

Jean Valjean staggered, dropped the blotter, and sank into the old armchair by the sideboard, his head drooping, his eye glassy, bewildered. He told himself that it was all clear, and that the light of the world was eclipsed forever, and that Cosette had written that to somebody. Then he heard his soul, turned terrible once more, give a stifled roar in the darkness. So go and take away from the lion the dog he has in his cage.

A strange, sad circumstance, at that moment Marius did not yet have Cosette's letter; chance had brought it, like a traitor, to Jean Valjean before delivering it to Marius.

Until that moment Jean Valjean had never been defeated when put to the test. He had been subjected to fearful trials; no violence or bad luck had been spared him; the ferocity of fate, armed with every vengeance and every social scorn, had taken him for subject and greedily pursued him. He had neither recoiled nor flinched before anything. When he had to, he had accepted every extremity; he had sacrificed his reconquered inviolability of manhood, given up his liberty, risked his head, lost all, suffered all, and had remained so disinterested and stoical that at times one could have believed him selfless, like a martyr. His conscience, inured to all possible assaults of adversity, might seem forever impregnable. Well, anyone able to see his inner core would have been compelled to admit that at this hour it was weakening.

For of all the tortures he had undergone in that long inquisition allotted to him by destiny, this was the most fearful. Never had such pincers seized him. He felt the mysterious quiver of every latent sensibility. He felt the laceration of the unknown fiber. Alas, the supreme ordeal, or let us say instead, the only ordeal, is the loss of the beloved being.

Poor old Jean Valjean did not, certainly, love Cosette otherwise than as a father; but, as we have already mentioned, into this paternity the very bereavement of his life had brought every love; he loved Cosette as his daughter, and he loved her as his mother, and he loved her as his sister; and, as he had never had either lover or wife, as nature is a creditor who accepts no protest, that sentiment, too, the most indestructible of all, was mingled with the others, vague, ignorant, pure with the purity of blindness, unconscious, celestial, angelic, divine; less like a sentiment than an instinct, less like an instinct than an attraction, imperceptible and invisible, but real; and love, properly speaking, existed in his enormous tenderness for Cosette as the vein of gold in the mountain, dark and virgin.

Remember that state of heart we have already pointed out. No marriage was possible between them, not even that of souls; and still it was certain that their destinies were espoused. Except for Cosette, that is to say, except for a childhood, Jean Valjean, in all his long life, had known nothing of those things man can love. The passions and the loves that succeed one another had not left on him those successive greens, a tender green over a somber green, that we notice on leaves that have lived through the winter, and on men who are past their forties. In short, and we have more than once insisted upon it, all that interior fusion, all that whole, whose result was a lofty virtue, ended in making of Jean Valjean a father for Cosette. A strange father forged out of the grandfather, the son, the brother, and the husband that existed in Jean Valjean; a father in whom there was even a mother; a father who loved Cosette, and who adored her, and to whom that child was light, family, homeland, paradise.

So, when he saw that it was positively ended, that she was escaping him, that she was slipping through his hands, eluding him, that it was cloud, water, when he had before his eyes this crushing evidence—another is the object of her heart, another is the desire of her life, there is a beloved; I am only the father; I no longer exist—when he could no longer doubt as he said to himself, "She's going off away from me!" his grief surpassed the possible. To have done all that he had done and come to this! And, how was it possible, to be nothing! Then, as we have just said, he felt a shudder of revolt from head to toe. Down to the roots of his hair he felt the immense awakening of selfishness, and the self howled in the abyss of his soul.

There are interior collapses. The penetration of a torturing certainty within man does not occur without breaking up and pulverizing certain deep elements that are sometimes the man himself. Grief, when it reaches this level, is a panic of all the forces of consciousness. These are fatal crises. Few among us come through them unchanged and firm in duty. When the limit of suffering is topped, the most imperturbable virtue is disconcerted. Jean Valjean took up the blotter, and convinced himself anew; he bent as if petrified over the undeniable lines, with staring eye; and such a cloud formed within him that one might have believed the whole interior of that soul was crumbling.

He examined this revelation, through the magnifying powers of reverie, with an apparent and frightful calm, for it is a terrible thing when man's calm reaches the rigidity of the statue.

He measured the appalling step his destiny had taken without an inkling on his part; he recalled his fears of the previous summer, so foolishly dissipated; he recognized the precipice; it was still the same; except that Jean Valjean was no longer on the brink, he was at the bottom.

An extraordinary and poignant thing, he had fallen without noticing. All the light of his life had gone, he still believing he was seeing the sun.

His instinct did not hesitate. He put together certain circumstances, certain dates, certain of Cosette's blushes and pallors, and he said to himself, "He is the one." The divination of despair is a sort of mysterious bow that never misses its target. With his first conjecture, he hit Marius. He did not know the name, but he found the man at once. He distinctly recognized, at the depths of the implacable evocation of memory, the unknown prowler of the Luxembourg, that wretched seeker of flirtations, that romantic idler, that imbecile, that coward, for it is cowardice to come and make eyes at girls who are beside their father who loves them.

After he had firmly established that that young man was at the bottom of this state of affairs, and that everything stemmed from him, he, Jean Valjean, the regenerated man, the man who had so labored on his soul, the man who had made so many efforts to resolve all life, all misery, and all misfortune into love; he looked within himself and saw a specter, Hatred.

Great griefs contain dejection. They discourage existence. The man they enter feels something go out of him. In youth, their visit is dismal; in later years it is ominous. Alas, when the blood is hot, when the hair is black, when the head is erect on the body like the flame on the torch, when the sheaf of destiny is still quite full, when the heart, filled with a fortunate love, still has pulsations that can be responded to, when we have before us the time to atone, when all women are there, and all smiles, and all the future, and all the horizon, when the strength of life is complete, if despair is a fearful thing, then what is it in old age, when the years rush along, growing bleaker and bleaker, at the twilight hour, when we begin to see the stars of the tomb!

While he was thinking, Toussaint entered. Jean Valjean stood up and asked her, "In what direction is it? Do you know?"

Toussaint, astonished, could only answer:

"If you please?"

Jean Valjean resumed: "Didn't you tell me just now that they were fighting?"

"Oh! yes, monsieur," answered Toussaint. "It's over by Saint-Merry."

There are some mechanical impulses that come over us, even without our knowledge, from our deepest thoughts. It was undoubtedly under the influence of just such an impulse, of which he was hardly conscious, that five minutes later Jean Valjean found himself in the street.

He was bare-headed, seated on the stone block by the door of his house. He seemed to be listening.

Night had fallen.

II

THE GAMIN AN ENEMY OF LIGHT

How much time did he spend this way? What were the ebbs and flows of that tragic meditation? Did he straighten up? Did he stay bowed? Had he been bent to the point of breaking? Could he still straighten up and regain a foothold in his conscience on something solid? He himself could probably not have said.

The street was empty. A few anxious bourgeois, rapidly returning home, hardly noticed him. Every man for himself in times of peril. The lamplighter came as usual to light the lamp that hung directly opposite the door of No. 7, and went away. To anyone who might have examined him in that shadow, Jean Valjean would not have seemed a living man. There he was, seated on the post beside his door, immovable as an icy specter. A congealing can take over in despair. The tocsin was audible, as were vague stormy sounds. In the midst of all this convulsive din of the bell mingled with the émeute, the clock of Saint-Paul struck eleven, gravely and without haste, for the tocsin is man, the hour is God. The passing of the hour had no effect on Jean Valjean; Jean Valjean did not stir. However,.almost at that very moment, there was a sharp explosion in the direction of Les Halles, a second followed, more violent still; it was probably that attack on the barricade of the Rue de la Chanvrerie we have just seen repulsed by Marius. At this double discharge, whose fury seemed increased by the stupor of the night, Jean Valjean shuddered; he looked up in the direction the sound came from; then he sank down on the block, crossed his arms, and his head drooped slowly onto his breast.

He went on with his dark inner dialogue.

Suddenly he raised his eyes, somebody was walking down the street, he heard steps near him, he looked, and, by the light of the lamp, in the direction of the Archives, he perceived a pale face, young and radiant.

Gavroche had just reached the Rue de l'Homme-Armé.

Gavroche was looking up and seemed to be searching for something. He saw Jean Valjean perfectly well, but he took no notice of him.

After looking up, Gavroche looked down; he rose on tiptoe and felt the doors and windows of the ground floors; they were all closed, bolted, and chained. After finding five or six houses barricaded in this way, the gamin shrugged his shoulders, and took counsel with himself in these terms: "Well, now . . ."

Then he began to look up again.

Jean Valjean, who a moment earlier in the state of mind in which he was, would not have spoken or even replied to anybody, felt irresistibly impelled to speak to this child.

"Little boy," he said, "what's the matter?"

"The matter is that I'm hungry," answered Gavroche tartly. And he added, "Little yourself."

Jean Valjean felt in his pocket and took out a five-franc piece.

But Gavroche, who was of the wagtail species and slipped quickly from one action to another, had picked up a stone. He had noticed a street lamp.

"Well, well," he said, "you still have your lamps here. That's not proper form, my friends. It's disorderly. Sorry, this will have to go!"

And he threw the stone into the lamp, whose glass fell with such a clatter that some bourgeois, hidden behind their curtains in the opposite house, cried out, "There's 'Ninety-three all over again!"

The lamp swung violently and went out. The street suddenly went dark.

"That's it, old street," said Gavroche, "put on your nightcap."

And turning toward Jean Valjean: "What do you call that gigantic monument you've got there at the end of the street? The Archives, right? They ought to chip off a bit of those big fool columns, and politely make a barricade of them."

Jean Valjean went up to Gavroche.

"Poor devil," he said, in an undertone, and speaking to himself, "he's hungry."

And he put the hundred-sous piece in his hand.

Gavroche cocked up his nose, astonished at the size of this big sou; he looked at it in the dark, and its whiteness dazzled him. He knew five-franc pieces by hearsay; their reputation was appealing; he was delighted to see one up close. He said, "Let's contemplate the tiger."

He gazed at it for a few moments in ecstasy; then, turning toward Jean Valjean, he handed him the piece, and said majestically, "Bourgeois, I prefer to break lamps. Take back your wild beast. I'm incorruptible. It has five claws but it don't scratch me."

"Do you have a mother?" inquired Jean Valjean.

Gavroche answered, "Perhaps more than you have."

"Well," replied Jean Valjean, "keep this money for your mother."

Gavroche felt softened. Besides he had just noticed that the man who was talking to him had no hat, and that inspired him with confidence.

"Really," he said, "it isn't to keep me from breaking the lamps?"

"Break all you like."

"You're a fine fellow," said Gavroche.

And he put the five-franc piece into one of his pockets.

His confidence increasing, he added, "Do you belong on this street?"

"Yes; why?"

"Could you show me number seven?"

"What do you want with number seven?"

Here the boy stopped; he feared that he had said too much; he plunged his nails vigorously into his hair, and merely answered, "Ah! That's it."

An idea flashed across Jean Valjean's mind. Anguish has such lucidities. He said to the child, "Are you the one who's bringing me the letter I'm waiting for?"

"You?" said Gavroche. "You're not a woman."

"The letter is for Mademoiselle Cosette; isn't it?"

"Cosette?" muttered Gavroche. "Yes, I think it's that funny name."

"Well," resumed Jean Valjean, "I'm to deliver the letter to her. Give it to me."

"In that case you must know that I'm sent from the barricade?"

"Of course," said Jean Valjean.

Gavroche thrust his hand into another of his pockets and drew out a folded paper.

Then he gave a military salute.

"Respect for the dispatch," he said. "It comes from the provisional government."

"Give it to me," said Jean Valjean.

Gavroche held the paper raised above his head.

"Don't imagine that this is a love letter. It's for a woman, but it's for the people. We men, we're fighting, and we respect the sex. We're not like folks in high life, where there are lions who send love letters to camels."

"Give it to me."

"The fact is," continued Gavroche, "you look to me like a fine fellow."

"Give it to me, quick."

"Take it."

And he handed the piece of paper to Jean Valjean.

"And be quick about it, Monsieur What's-your-name; Mamselle What's-her-name is waiting."

Jean Valjean asked, "Is it to Saint-Merry that the answer should be sent?"

"In that case," exclaimed Gavroche, "you would make one of those things vulgarly called blunders. That letter comes from the barricade in the Rue de la Chanvrerie, and I'm going back there. Good night, citizen."

This said, Gavroche went away, or rather, resumed his flight like an escaped bird toward the spot he came from. He plunged back into the obscurity as if making a hole in it, with the rapidity and precision of a projectile; the little Rue de l'Homme-Armé became silent and solitary; in a twinkling, this strange child, who had shadow and dream within him, was buried in the dusk of those rows of black houses, and was lost there like smoke in the darkness; and one might have thought him dissipated and vanished, if, a few minutes after his disappearance, a loud shattering of glass and the fine splintering crash of a lamp falling onto the pavement had not abruptly reawakened the indignant bourgeois. It was Gavroche passing along the Rue du Chaume.

III

WHILE COSETTE AND TOUSSAINT SLEEP

Jean Valjean went in with Marius's letter.

He groped his way upstairs, pleased with the darkness like an owl that holds his prey, opened and softly closed the door, listened to see if he heard any sound, established that, to all appearances, Cosette and Toussaint were asleep, plunged three or four matches into the bottle of the Fumade tinderbox before he managed to raise a spark, his hand was trembling so much; there was theft in what he had just done. At last his candle was lit, he leaned his elbows on the table, unfolded the paper, and read.

In violent emotions, we do not read, we prostrate the paper we hold, so to speak, we strangle it like a victim, we crush the paper, we bury the nails of our wrath or our delight in it; we race to the end, we leap to the beginning; attention is fevered; it understands the essentials wholesale, almost; it seizes a point, and all the rest disappears. In Marius's note to Cosette, Jean Valjean saw only these words.

"—I will die . . . When you read this, my soul will be near you."

Faced with these two lines, he was in horrible turmoil; he sat for a moment as if crushed by the change of emotion occurring within him, he looked at Marius's note with a sort of drunken surprise; he had before his eyes that marvel, the death of the hated being.

He uttered a hideous cry of inward joy. So, it was finished. The end was coming sooner than he had dared to hope. The being who encumbered his destiny was disappearing. He was going away on his own, freely, of his own accord. Without any intervention on his, Jean Valjean's, part, through no fault of his, "that man" was about to die. Perhaps even, he was already dead. Here his fever began to calculate. No. He is not dead yet. The letter was evidently written to be read by Cosette in the morning; since those two rounds of firing heard between eleven o'clock and midnight, there had been nothing; the barricade will not be seriously attacked till daybreak; but that makes no difference, for the moment "that man" got mixed up with this war, he was lost; he is caught in the net. Jean Valjean felt that he was delivered. So he would find himself alone once more with Cosette. Rivalry ceased; the future began again. He merely had to keep the note in his pocket. Cosette would never know what had become of "that man." "I merely have to let things take their course. That man cannot escape. If he isn't dead yet, he surely will die. How fortunate!"

When all this was said within him, he became gloomy.

Then he went down and awakened the doorkeeper.

About an hour later, Jean Valjean went out in the full dress of a National Guard, and armed. The doorkeeper had easily found in the neighborhood what was necessary to complete his equipment. He had a loaded musket and a cartridge box full of cartridges. He headed toward Les Halles.

IV

THE EXCESS OF GAVROCHE'S ZEAL

Meanwhile an adventure had just befallen Gavroche.

After having conscientiously stoned the lamp in the Rue du Chaume, Gavroche came to the Rue des Vieilles-Haudriettes, and, seeing not a living soul, thought it a good opportunity to strike up all the song of which he was capable. His pace, far from slackening from the singing, accelerated. He began to scatter along the sleeping or terrified houses these incendiary couplets:

L'oiseau médit dans les charmilles,
Et prétend qu'hier Atala
Avec un russe s'en alla.
  Où vont les belles filles,
    Lon la.
Mon ami pierrot, tu babilles,
Parce que l'autre jour Mila
Cogna sa vitre, et m'appela. Où vont, etc.
Les drôlesses sont fort gentilles;
Leur poison qui m'ensorcela
Griserait monsieur Orfila. Où vont, etc.
J'aime l'amour et ses bisbilles,
J'aime Agnès, j'aime Paméla,
Lise en m'allumant se brûla. Où vont, etc.
Jadis, quand je vis les mantilles
De Suzette et de Zéila,
Mon âme à leurs plis se mêla. Où vont, etc.
Amour, quand, dans l'ombre où tu brilles,
Tu coiffes de roses Lola,
Je me damnerais pour cela. Où vont, etc.
Jeanne, à ton miroir tu t'habilles!
Mon coeur un beau jour s'envola;
Je crois que c'est Jeanne qui l'a. Où vont, etc.
Le soir, en sortant des quadrilles,
Je montre aux étoiles Stella
Et je leur dis: regardez-la. Où vont, etc.[1]

[1] The bird gossips in the arbor
And pretends that yesterday Atala
Went off with a Russki.
Where the pretty girls are going, Lon la.
Friend Pierrot, you're babbling,
Because the other day Mila
Broke her window and called me.
The hussies are really nice;
Their poison that bewitched me
Would sozzle Monsieur Orfila.
I love love and its petty tiffs,

Gavroche, still singing, was lavish with pantomime. Action is the strong point of refrain. His face, an inexhaustible repertory of masks, made grimaces that were more convulsive and more fantastic than the mouths of a torn cloth in a heavy wind. Unfortunately, as he was alone and in the night, it was neither seen nor visible. Lost riches!

Suddenly he stopped short. "Let's interrupt the romance," he said.

His catlike eye had just made out in the recess of a carriage door what is called in painting a composition: that is to say, a being and a thing; the thing was a handcart, the being was an Auvergnat asleep in it.

The arms of the cart were resting on the pavement and the Auvergnat's head was resting on the tailboard of the cart. His body was curled up on the inclined plane and his feet touched the ground.

Gavroche, with his experience of the things of this world, recognized a drunk. It was some street porter who had drunk too much and was sleeping it off.

"This," thought Gavroche, "is what summer nights are good for. The Auvergnat is asleep in his cart. We take the cart for the Republic and we leave the Auvergnat to the monarchy."

His mind had just received this illumination: "That cart would go beautifully on our barricade."

The Auvergnat was snoring.

Gavroche dragged the cart gently by the back end and the Auvergnat by the forward end, that is to say, by the

---

I love Agnes, I love Pamela,
In kindling me, Lisa got burnt.
Of old, when I saw the mantillas
Of Suzette and of Zeila,
My soul got mixed up in their folds.
Love, when, in the shadows where you gleam,
You coif Lola with roses,
I would damn myself for that.
Jeanne, at your mirror you're getting dressed!
One fine day my heart took off;
I think it's Jeanne who has it.
In the evening, coming out of the dance,
I show Stella to the stars
And I say to them: just look at her.
Where the pretty girls are going.

feet, and, in a minute, the Auvergnat, imperturbable, was lying flat on the pavement. The cart was released.

Gavroche, accustomed to facing the unforeseen on all sides, always had everything on his person. He felt in one of his pockets, and took out a scrap of paper and a stub of a red pencil pilfered from some carpenter.

He wrote:

"*French Republic*

"Received your cart."

And he signed it, "GAVROCHE."

This done, he put the paper into the pocket of the still snoring Auvergnat's velvet waistcoat, seized the cross-piece with both hands, and started off toward Les Halles, pushing the cart before him at a full gallop with a glorious triumphal uproar.

This was perilous. There was a post at the Imprimerie Royale. Gavroche did not think of it. This post was occupied by the National Guards from the banlieue. A certain watchfulness began to excite the squad, and their heads lifted from their camp beds. Two lamps broken one after another, that song sung at the top of the lungs, it was a good bit for such cowardly streets, which long to go to sleep at sunset, and put their snuffer on the candle so early. For an hour in this peaceful district, the gamin had been making the uproar of a fly in a bottle. The sergeant from the banlieue listened. He waited. He was a prudent man.

The furious rolling of the cart filled the measure of possible delay, and induced the sergeant to attempt a reconnaissance.

"There is a whole band there," he said, "we must go softly."

It was clear that the hydra of anarchy had gotten out of its box, and was raging in the neighborhood.

And the sergeant ventured out of the post with stealthy tread.

Suddenly, Gavroche, pushing his cart, just as he was going to turn out of the Rue des Vieilles-Haudriettes, found himself face to face with a uniform, a shako, a plume, and a musket.

For the second time, he stopped short.

"Well, well," he said, "that's him. Good morning, public order."

Gavroche's astonishments were short and quickly thawed.

"Where are you going, vagabond?" cried the sergeant.

"Citizen," said Gavroche, "I haven't called you bourgeois yet. What do you insult me for?"

"Where are you going, rascal?"

"Monsieur," resumed Gavroche, "yesterday you may have been a man of wit, but you were discharged this morning."

"I want to know where you're going, scoundrel?"

Gavroche answered.

"You do talk nicely. Really, nobody would guess your age. You should sell all your teeth at a hundred francs apiece. That would give you five hundred francs."

"Where are you going? Where are you going? Where are you going, bandit?"

Gavroche replied, "Now there are naughty words. The first time they put you out to nurse, they should wipe your mouth better."

The sergeant crossed his bayonet.

"Will you tell me where you're going, finally, wretch?"

"My general," said Gavroche, "I'm going after the doctor for my wife, who is put to bed."

"To arms!" cried the sergeant.

To save yourself by means of what has ruined you, that is the masterpiece of great men; Gavroche measured the entire situation at a glance. It was the cart that had compromised him, it was up to the cart to protect him.

At the moment the sergeant was about to rush at Gavroche, the cart became a projectile and, hurled with all the gamin's might, ran into him furiously, and the sergeant, struck right in the stomach, fell backward into the gutter while his musket went off in the air.

At the sergeant's cry, the men of the post had rushed out pell-mell; the musket shot produced a general barrage at random, after which they reloaded and began again.

This musketry at blindman's buff lasted a full quarter of an hour and killed several panes of glass.

Meanwhile Gavroche, who had desperately doubled back, stopped five or six streets away and sat down breathless on the block at the corner of the Enfants-Rouges.

He listened attentively.

After catching his breath for a few moments, he turned in the direction where the firing was raging, raised his left hand to the level of his nose, and threw it forward three times, striking the back of his head with his right hand at the same time: a sovereign gesture in which the Parisian gamin has condensed French irony, and which is evidently effective, since it has already lasted a half century.

This cheerfulness was marred by a bitter reflection.

"Yes," he said, "I grin, I twist, I brim with joy; but I'm losing my way, I'll have to make a detour. If only I get to the barricade in time."

Thereupon, he resumed his course.

And, still running, "Ah, yes, where was I?" he said.

He picked up his song again, as he plunged rapidly through the streets and receded in the darkness.

Mais il reste encor des bastilles,
Et je vais mettre le holà
Dans l'ordre public que voilà
Où vont les belles filles.
Lon la.
Quelqu'un veut-il jouer aux quilles?
Tout l'ancien monde s'écroula
Quand la grosse boule roula. Où vont, etc.
Vieux bon peuple, a coups de béquilles,
Cassons ce Louvre où s'étala
La monarchie en falbala. Où vont, etc.
Nous en avons forcé les grilles,
Le roi Charles-Dix ce jour-là
Tenait mal et se décolla. Où vont, etc.[1]

[1] But there still are some bastilles,
And I'm going to put a halt
To public order there.
Where the pretty girls are going.
Anyone want a game of skittles?
All the old world crumbled
When the fat ball rolled.
Good old people, with a stroke of the crutch,
Let's break up the Louvre where they showed
The monarchy in furbelows.
We have forced their gates,
King Charles Ten that day

The call-to-arms at the post was not without results. The cart was conquered, the drunk was taken prisoner. One was put on the woodpile; the other afterward tried before a court-martial, as an accomplice. The public ministry of the time availed itself of this circumstance to show its indefatigable zeal for the defense of society.

Gavroche's adventure, preserved among the traditions of the quarter of the Temple, is one of the most terrible recollections of the old bourgeois of the Marais, and is entitled in their memory: "Nocturnal Attack on the Post of the Imprimerie Royale."

Held on poorly and came unstuck.
Where the pretty girls are going.

The call-to-arms at the post was not without results. The cart was conquered, the drunk was taken prisoner. One was put on the woodpile; the other afterward tried before a court martial, as an accomplice. The public ministry of the time availed itself of this circumstance to show its indefatigable zeal for the defense of society.

Gavroche's adventure, preserved among the traditions of the quarter of the Temple, is one of the most terrible recollections of the old bourgeois of the Marais, and is entitled in their memory: "Nocturnal Attack on the Post of the Imprimerie Royale."

Held on good, and came unstuck.

Where the pretty girls are gone.

JEAN VALJEAN

Book One

WAR BETWEEN FOUR WALLS

I

THE CHARYBDIS OF THE FAUBOURG SAINT-ANTOINE AND THE SCYLLA OF THE FAUBOURG DU TEMPLE

The two most memorable barricades that the observer of social diseases could mention do not belong to the period in which the action of this book is placed. These two barricades, both of them symbols in two different ways of a terrible situation, rose from the earth at the time of the fatal insurrection of June 1848, the biggest street war history has ever seen.

It sometimes happens that, even against principles, even against liberty, equality, and fraternity, even against universal suffrage, even against the government of all by all, from the depths of its anguish, of its discouragements, its privations, its fevers, its distresses, its miasmas, its ignorance, and its darkness, that great madman, the rabble, protests, and the populace gives battle to the people.

The vagabonds attack the common right; the ochlocracy rises against the demos.

Those are mournful days; for there is always a certain amount of right even in this madness, there is suicide in this duel, and these words, intended for insults—beggars, rabble, ochlocracy, populace—indicate, alas, rather the fault of those who reign than the fault of those who suffer; rather the fault of the privileged than the fault of the outcasts.

As for us, we never pronounce these words except with sorrow and respect, for when philosophy fathoms the facts to which they correspond, it often finds in them many grandeurs among the miseries. Athens was an ochlocracy; the impoverished made Holland; the populace more than once saved Rome; and the rabble followed Jesus Christ.

There is no thinker who has not sometimes contemplated the nether magnificences.

It was undoubtedly of this rabble that Saint Jerome thought, and of all those poor people, and of all those beggars, and of all those wretches, from which sprang the apostles and the martyrs, when he uttered those mysterious words: *Fex urbis, lex orbis*.

The exasperations of this multitude that suffers and bleeds, its misconstrued violences against the principles that are its life, its forcible resistance to the law, are popular coups d'état and must be repressed. The man of integrity devotes himself to it, and out of the very love for that multitude, he battles against it. But how excusable he feels it, even while opposing it; how he venerates it, even while resisting it! It is one of those rare moments when, in doing what we have to do, we feel something that disconcerts and almost dissuades from going further; we persist, we are compelled to; but the conscience, though satisfied, is sad, and the performance of the duty is marred by a pang.

June 1848 was, let us hasten to say, a thing apart, and almost impossible to classify in the philosophy of history. All that we have just said must be set aside when we consider that extraordinary émeute in which was felt the sacred anxiety of labor demanding its rights. It had to be put down, that was duty, for it was attacking the Republic. But what basically was June 1848? A revolt of the people against itself.

When the subject is not lost sight of, there is no digression; let us then be permitted to direct the reader's attention for a moment to the two absolutely unique barricades of which we have just spoken and which characterized that insurrection.

One obstructed the entrance to the Faubourg Saint-Antoine; the other defended the approaches of the Faubourg du Temple; those witnessing the construction, under the bright blue sky of June, of these two frightful masterpieces of civil war, will never forget them.

The Saint-Antoine barricade was monstrous; it was three stories high and seven hundred feet long. It barred from one corner to the other the vast opening of the Faubourg, that is to say, three streets; ravined, jagged, notched, abrupt, indented with an immense rent, buttressed with mounds that were themselves bastions, pushing out salients here and there, strongly backed up by the two great promontories of houses of the Faubourg, it rose like a cyclopean embankment at the far side of the intimidating square that saw the 14th of July. Nineteen barricades stood at intervals along the streets in the rear of this mother barricade. Merely from seeing it, you felt in the Faubourg the immense agonized suffering that had reached that extreme moment when troubles rush into catastrophe. Of what was this barricade made? Of the ruins of three seven-story houses, torn down for the purpose, said some. Of the wonders worked by all passions, said others. It had the woeful aspect of all the works of hatred: Ruin. You might say: Who built that? You might also say: Who destroyed that? It was the improvization of ferment. Here! That door! That grating! That shed! That casement! That broken stove! That cracked pot! Give everything! Throw on everything! Push, roll, dig, dismantle, overturn, tear down everything! It was the collaboration of the pavement, the pebble, the timber, the iron bar, the scrap, the broken windowpane, the stripped chair, the cabbage stump, the tatter, the rag, and the malediction. It was large and it was small. It was the bottomless pit parodied on the spot by chaos come again. The mass beside the atom; the stretch of wall torn down and the broken dish; a menacing fraternization of all rubbish. Sisyphus had tossed in his rock and Job his potsherd. On the whole, terrible. It was the acropolis of the ragamuffins. Overturned carts roughened the slope; an immense dray was laid out, crosswise, the axle pointing to the sky, and seemed a scar on that tumultuous façade; an omnibus, cheerily hoisted by main strength to the very top of the pile, as if the architects of that savagery wanted to add sauciness to terror, presented its unharnessed pole to unknown horses of the air. This gigantic mass, the aluvium of émeute, brought to mind an Ossa upon Pelion of all the revolutions; '93 upon '89, the 9th Thermidor upon the 10th of August, the 18th Brumaire upon the 21st of January, Vendémaire upon Prairial, 1848 upon 1830. The Place deserved the pains, and that barricade was worthy to appear on the very spot where the Bastille had disappeared. Were the ocean to make dikes, this is the way it would build them. The fury of the flood was imprinted on that misshapen obstruction. What flood? The mob. You would have thought you were seeing uproar petrified. You would have thought you heard, above that barricade, as though they were there on their hive, the humming of the enormous black bees of progress by force. Was it underbrush? Was it a Bacchanal? Was it a fortress? Vertigo seemed to have built it with the beat of its wings. There was something of the cloaca in this redoubt, and something of Olympus in the jumble. You saw there, in a chaos full of despair, rafters from roofs, sections of dormers with their wallpaper, window sashes with all their glass dumped in the debris, waiting for the artillery, disjointed chimneys, wardrobes, tables, benches, a howling upheaval, and those thousand beggarly things, the rejects of even the beggar, containing fury and nothingness alike. One would have said that it was the tatters of a people, tatters of wood, of iron, of bronze, of stone, and that the Faubourg Saint-Antoine had swept them there to its door with one colossal sweep of the broom, making its barricade of its misery. Logs shaped like chopping blocks, dismembered chains, wooden frames with brackets in the shape of gibbets, wheels projecting horizontally from the wreckage—all of these amalgamated to this edifice of anarchy the forbidding form of the old tortures suffered by the people. The barricade Saint-Antoine made a weapon of everything; all that civil war can throw at the head of society was hurled from it; it was not battle, it was paroxysm; the carbines that defended the stronghold, among them some blunderbusses, scattered bits of delftware, knucklebones, coat buttons, even table casters, dangerous projectiles because of the copper. This barricade was furious; it threw up to the clouds an inarticulate clamor; defying the army at times, it covered itself with mob and with tempest; a throng of flaming heads crowned it; a swarming filled it; its crest was thorny with muskets, with swords, with clubs, with axes, with pikes, and with bayonets; a huge red flag slapped in the wind; there were heard cries of command, battle songs, drum rolls, the sobbing of woman, and the dark wild laughter of the starving. It was gigantic and living; and, as from the back of an electric beast, there came from it a crackling of thunder. The spirit of revolution cloaked with its cloud that summit growling with the voice of the people which is like the voice of God; a strange majesty emanated from that titanic hodful of refuse. It was a garbage heap, and it was Sinai.

As we have said before, it attacked in the name of the Revolution—what? The Revolution. This barricade, chance, disorder, bewilderment, misunderstanding, the unknown, set itself against the Constituent Assembly, the sovereignty of the people, universal suffrage, the nation, the Republic; and it was the Carmagnole defying the Marseillaise.

An insane but heroic defiance, for this old Faubourg is a hero.

The Faubourg and its redoubt lent each other aid. The Faubourg put its shoulder to the redoubt, the redoubt braced itself on the Faubourg. The huge barricade extended like a cliff, and against it broke the strategy of Africa's generals. Its caverns, its excrescences, its warts, its humps, grimaced, so to speak, and sneered beneath the smoke. Grapeshot vanished there in the misshapen; shells sank in, were swallowed up, were engulfed; bullets only managed to bore holes; what use is it to cannonade chaos? And regiments, accustomed to the most savage sights of war, looked anxiously on this kind of wild beast redoubt, a wild boar through its bristling, a mountain through its enormity.

A mile from there, at the corner of the Rue du Temple, which runs into the boulevard near the Château d'Eau, if you boldly poke out your head beyond the point formed by the front of the Magasin Dallemagne, you would see in the distance, beyond the canal, in the street that climbs the slopes of Belleville, at the culminating point of the hill, a strange wall reaching the second story of the house fronts, a sort of hyphen between the houses on the right and the houses on the left, as if the street had folded back its highest wall, and abruptly shut itself in. This wall was built of paving stones. It was straight, correct, cold, perpendicular, leveled with the square, built on a line, aligned by the plummet. Cement was undoubtedly lacking, but as in certain Roman walls, that did not weaken its rigid architecture. From its height its depth could be guessed. The entablature was mathematically parallel to the base. Here and there could be distinguished on the gray surface almost invisible loopholes, which resembled black threads. These loopholes were separated from each other by equal intervals. The street was deserted as far as the eye could see. Every window and every door was shut. In the background rose this obstruction, which turned the street into a cul-de-sac; an immovable and quiet wall; nobody could be seen, nothing could be heard; not a cry, not a sound, not a breath. A sepulcher.

The dazzling June sun flooded this terrible thing with light.

This was the barricade of the Faubourg du Temple.

As soon as you reached the site and took it in, it was impossible, even for the boldest, not to turn thoughtful before this mysterious apparition. It was fitted, dovetailed, imbricated, rectilinear, symmetrical, and deathly. There was in it science and darkness. You felt that the chief of that barricade was a geometer or a specter. You beheld it and you spoke softly.

From time to time, if anybody—soldier, officer, or representative of the people—ventured to cross the solitary street, a sharp, low whistling was heard, and the pedestrian fell wounded or dead, or, if he escaped, a bullet would bury itself in some closed shutter, in a space between the stores, in the plaster of a wall. Sometimes a large canister shot. For the men of the barricade had made two small guns out of two pieces of cast-iron gas pipe, stopped up at one end with oakum and fire clay. No useless expenditure of powder. Almost every shot told. There were a few corpses here and there, and pools of blood on the pavement. I remember a white butterfly flying back and forth in the street. Summer does not abdicate.

In the vicinity, the pavement of carriage entrances was covered with wounded.

You felt yourself beneath the eye of somebody you did not see, that the whole length of the street was held in the line of fire.

Massed behind the sort of saddleback made by the narrow bridge over the canal at the entrance to the Faubourg du Temple, the soldiers of the attacking column, calm and collected, looked at this dismal redoubt, this immobility, this impassability, spewing death. Some crept along the ground as far as the summit of the bridge, taking care that their shakos did not show over it.

The valiant Colonel Monteynard admired this barricade with a shudder. "How well that's built!" he said to a representative. "Not one stone projects beyond another. It's porcelain." At that moment a ball broke the cross on his breast, and he fell.

"The cowards!" some said. "But let them show themselves! Let us see them! They don't dare! They're hiding!" The barricade of the Faubourg du Temple, defended by eighty men, attacked by ten thousand, held out for three days. On the fourth day, they did as at Zaatcha and at Constantine; they pierced through the houses, they went along the roofs, the barricade was taken. Not one of the eighty cowards thought of flight; all of them were killed, except the leader, Barthélemy, of whom we shall speak presently.

The barricade Saint-Antoine was the tumult of thunder; the barricade du Temple was silence. Between these two redoubts there was the difference between the terrible and the ominous. The one seemed a gaping mouth; the other a mask.

Admitting that the gloomy and gigantic insurrection of June was composed of an anger and an enigma, you felt in the first barricade the dragon, and behind the second the sphinx.

These two fortresses were built by two men, one named Cournet, the other Barthélemy. Cournet made the barricade Saint-Antoine; Barthélemy the barricade du Temple. Each was the image of the man who built it.

Cournet was a tall man; he had broad shoulders, a red face, a crushing fist, a bold heart, a loyal soul, a sincere and terrible eye. Intrepid, energetic, irascible, stormy, the most cordial of men, the most formidable of warriors.

War, conflict, the mêlée, were the air he breathed, and put him in good humor. He had been a naval officer, and from his carriage and voice you could guess he sprang from the ocean, he came from the tempest; he carried over the hurricane into battle. Save in genius, there was something of Danton in Cournet, as, save in divinity, there was something of Hercules in Danton.

Barthélemy, thin, puny, pale, taciturn, was a kind of tragic gamin who, struck by a policeman, watched for him, waited for him, and killed him, and at seventeen was sent to prison. He came out, and built this barricade.

Later, a terrible thing, in London, both outlaws, Barthélemy killed Cournet. It was a mournful duel. Some time later, caught in the meshes of one of those mysterious fatalities mingled with passion, catastrophes in which French justice sees extenuating circumstances, and in which English justice sees only death, Barthélemy was hung. The gloomy social edifice is so constructed that, thanks to material privation, thanks to moral darkness, this unfortunate being who contained an intelligence, certainly firm, perhaps great, began with the galleys in France and ended with the gallows in England. Barthélemy, for all occasions, hoisted but one flag: the black flag.

II

WHAT CAN YOU DO IN THE ABYSS BUT TALK?

Sixteen years tell in the subterranean education of the émeute, and June 1848 understood far better than June 1832. Thus the barricade of the Rue de la Chanvrerie was no more than a rough draft, an embryo, compared with the two colossal barricades we have just sketched; but for the period it was forbidding.

Under Enjolras's supervision, for Marius no longer looked to anything, the insurgents turned the night to their advantage. The barricade was not only repaired, but enlarged. They raised it two feet. Iron bars planted in the paving stones were like lances at rest. All sorts of rubbish added, and brought from all sides, increased the exterior intricacy. The redoubt was skillfully made over into a wall inside and a thicket outside.

They rebuilt the stairway of paving stones, which allowed them to climb up, as on a citadel wall.

They put the barricade in order, cleared up the lower room, took over the kitchen for a hospital, completed the dressing of the wounds; gathered up the powder scattered over the floor and the tables, cast bullets, made cartridges, scraped lint, distributed the weapons of the fallen, cleaned the interior of the redoubt, picked up the debris, carried away the corpses.

They deposited the dead in a heap in the little Rue Mondétour, of which they were still masters. The pavement was red for a long time at that spot. Among the dead were four National Guards from the suburbs. Enjolras had their uniforms laid aside.

Enjolras advised two hours of sleep. Advice from Enjolras was an order. Still, only three or four took advantage of it. Feuilly used these two hours to engrave this inscription on the wall facing the wineshop:

"VIVENT LES PEUPLES!"

The three words, graven in the stone with a nail, were still legible on that wall in 1848.

The three women took advantage of the night's respite to disappear for good, which made the insurgents breathe more freely.

They found refuge in some neighboring house.

Most of the wounded could and would still fight. But there were, on a straw mattress and some bunches of straw, in the kitchen now become a hospital, five severely wounded men, two of whom were Municipal Guards. The wounds of the Municipal Guards were dressed first.

Nothing now remained in the lower room but Mabeuf, under his black cloth, and Javert bound to the post.

"The is the room of the dead," said Enjolras.

Its entire far end faintly lit by a candle, with the mortuary table behind the post like a horizontal bar, a sort of large dim cross produced by Javert standing, and Mabeuf lying.

The pole of the omnibus, although maimed by the musket fire, was still high enough for them to hang a flag on it.

Enjolras, who had this quality of a leader, always to do as he said, fastened the pierced and bloody coat of the slain old man to this pole.

Meals had stopped. There was neither bread nor meat. The fifty men of the barricade, in the sixteen hours they had been there, had very soon exhausted the meager provisions of the bistro. In a given time, every barricade that holds out inevitably becomes the raft of *The Medusa*. They must resign themselves to hunger. They were in the early hours of that Spartan day of the 6th of June when, in the barricade Saint-Merry, Jeanne, surrounded by insurgents who were asking for bread, and faced with those warriors, crying, "Something to eat!" answered, "What for? It's three o'clock. At four o'clock we'll be dead."

As they could eat nothing, Enjolras forbade drinking. He prohibited wine, and rationed the brandy.

In the cellar they found some fifteen bottles, full and hermetically sealed. Enjolras and Combeferre examined them. As they were coming up Combeferre said, "It's some of the old stock of Father Hucheloup who began as a grocer."

"It ought to be splendid wine," observed Bossuet. "It's lucky Grantaire is asleep. If he were on his feet, we'd have a hard time saving those bottles." In spite of the murmurs, Enjolras put his veto on the fifteen bottles, and so that no one should touch them, and for them to be as it were consecrated, he had all the bottles placed under the table on which Father Mabeuf was lying.

Around two o'clock in the morning, they took a count. There were thirty-seven of them left.

Day was beginning to dawn. They had just extinguished the torch, which had been put back in its socket of paving stones. The interior of the barricade, that little court taken from the street, was drowned in darkness, and seemed, through the dim twilight horror, the deck of a disabled ship. Going back and forth, the combatants moved around in it like black forms. Above this terrible nest of shadow, the upper floors of the mute houses were outlined in red; at the very top the wan chimneys appeared. The sky had that charming undecided hue, which may be white, and may be blue. Some birds were flying about with their joyful songs. The tall house that formed the rear of the barricade, being toward the east, had a rosy reflection on its roof. At the fourth-floor window, the morning breeze played with the gray hairs on the dead man's head.

"I'm delighted that the torch is out," said Courfeyrac to Feuilly. "That torch, shuddering in the wind, annoyed me. It seemed afraid. The light of a torch is like the wisdom of a coward; it's not clear, because it trembles."

The dawn awakens minds as well as birds; everyone was chatting.

Seeing a cat prowling around a waterspout, Joly extracted some philosophy from it.

"What is the cat?" he exclaimed. "It is a corrective. God, having made the mouse, said, 'I've made a blunder.' And he made the cat. The cat is the erratum of the mouse. The mouse, plus the cat, is the revised and corrected proof of creation."

Combeferre, surrounded by students and workmen, spoke of the dead, of Jean Prouvaire, of Bahorel, of Mabeuf, and even of Le Cabuc, and of the stern sadness of Enjolras. He said, "Harmodius and Aristogeiton, Brutus, Chereas, Stephanus, Cromwell, Charlotte Corday, Sand —after the deed, all of them had their moment of anguish. Our hearts are so fluctuating, and human life is such a mystery that, even in a civic murder, even in a liberating murder, if there is such a thing, the remorse of having struck a man surpasses the joy of having served the human race."

And, such is the meandering course of conversation, a moment later, by a transition from Jean Prouvaire's poetry, Combeferre was comparing the translators of the Georgics, Raux with Cournand, Cournand with Delille, pointing out the few passages translated by Malfilâtre, particularly the omens at the death of Caesar; and from this word, Caesar, they came back to Brutus.

"Caesar," said Combeferre, "fell justly. Cicero was severe on Caesar, and he was right. That severity is not diatribe. When Zoïlus insults Homer, when Maevius insults Virgil, when Visé insults Molière, when Pope insults Shakespeare, when Fréron insults Voltaire, it's an old law of envy and hatred at work; genius attracts insult, great men are always barked at more or less. But Zoïlus and Cicero are two. Cicero is a judge through thought, even as Brutus is a judge through the sword. As for me,

I condemn that final justice, the sword; but antiquity admitted it. Caesar, the violator of the Rubicon—conferring, as coming from himself, the dignities that came from the people, not rising on the entrance of the senate—acted, as Eutropius says, the part of a king and almost a tyrant, *regia ac penè tyrannica*. He was a great man; so much the worse, or so much the better; the lesson is the greater. His twenty-three wounds touch me less than the spittle on the face of Jesus Christ. Caesar was stabbed by senators; Christ was slapped by lackeys. In the greater outrage, we feel the God."

Bossuet, overlooking the talkers from the top of the heap of paving stones, exclaimed, carbine in hand, "O Cydathenaeum, O Myrrhinus, O Probalinthe, O graces of Aeantides. Oh! Who will grant me to pronounce the verses of Homer like a Greek of Laurium or of Edapteon?"

III

LIGHT AND DARK

Enjolras had gone to make a reconnaissance. He went out by the little Rue Mondétour, creeping along next to the houses.

The insurgents, we must say, were full of hope. The manner in which they had repelled the attack during the night had led them almost to scorn in advance the daybreak attack. They waited for it and smiled at it. They had no more doubt of their success than of their cause. Moreover, help was evidently about to come. They counted on it. With that facility for triumphant prophecy that is part of the strength of the fighting Frenchman, they divided the coming day into three distinct phases: that at six in the morning a regiment, "which had been worked on," would join them. At noon, all Paris in revolt; at sundown, revolution.

They heard the tocsin of Saint-Merry, which had not let up a moment since the evening before, proof that the other barricade, the great one, that of Jeanne, was still holding out.

All these hopes were communicated from one to another in a sort of cheerful yet terrible whisper, like the buzz of a hive of bees at war.

Enjolras reappeared. He was returning from his gloomy eagle's walk in the obscurity beyond. He listened for a moment to all this joy with his arms crossed, one hand over his mouth. Then, fresh and rosy in the growing whiteness of the morning, he said, "The whole army of Paris is fighting. A third of that army is drawn up against the barricade where you are. Besides the National Guard, I can make out the shakos of the Fifth of the line and the colors of the Sixth Legion. You will be attacked in an hour. As for the people, they were boiling yesterday, but this morning they're not moving. Nothing to wait for, nothing to hope for. No more from a faubourg than from a regiment. You are abandoned."

These words fell on the buzzing of the groups, and had the effect the first drops of the storm produce on the swarm. All were struck dumb. There was a moment of inexpressible silence, in which one could have heard the flight of death.

This moment was brief.

A voice, from the most obscure depths of the groups, cried out to Enjolras, "All right there. Let's make the barricade twenty feet high, and let's all stand by it. Citizens, let's offer the protest of corpses. Let's show that, if the people abandon the republicans, the republicans do not abandon the people."

These words relieved the minds of all of them from the painful cloud of personal anxieties. They were greeted by an enthusiastic acclamation.

The name of the one who spoke these words was never known; it was some obscure man in his workshirt, an unknown, forgotten man, a passing hero, that great anonymous always found in human crises and in social advances, who, at the moment, speaks the decisive word supremely, and who vanishes into the darkness after having for a moment represented, in a flash of light, the people and God.

This inexorable resolution so filled the air of June 6, 1832, that, at almost the same moment, in the barricade of Saint-Merry, the insurgents raised this cry, which was recorded at the trial, and has come down in history: "Let them come to our aid or let them not come, what does it matter? Let us die here to the last man."

As we see, the two barricades, although essentially isolated, communicated.

IV

FIVE LESS, ONE MORE

After the man of the people had spoken, declaring "the protest of corpses," pronouncing the goal of the common soul, from every mouth there arose a cry that was strangely satisfied yet terrible, funereal in meaning and triumphant in tone:

"Long live death! Let's all stay!"

"Why all?" said Enjolras.

"All! All!"

Enjolras went on, "The position is good, the barricade is fine. Thirty men are enough. Why sacrifice forty?"

They replied, "Because nobody wants to leave."

"Citizens," cried Enjolras, and in his voice there was almost an angry tremor, "the Republic is not rich enough in men to incur useless expenditures. Vainglory is a waste. If it is the duty of some to leave, that duty should be performed as well as any other."

Enjolras, the man of principle, had over his coreligionists the sort of omnipotence that emanates from the absolute. Still, notwithstanding this omnipotence, there was a murmur.

Leader to the tips of his fingers, Enjolras, seeing that they murmured, insisted. He resumed with authority, "Let those who fear to be only thirty, say so."

The murmurs increased.

"Besides," observed a voice from one of the groups, "to leave is easy to say. The barricade is hemmed in."

"Not toward Les Halles," said Enjolras. "The Rue Mondétour is open, and by the Rue des Prêcheurs you can reach the Marché des Innocents."

"And there," put in another voice from the group, "he'll be taken. He'll fall upon some fine guard of the line or the suburb. They'll see a man going by in cap and blouse. 'Where are you coming from? You wouldn't belong to the barrricade, would you?' And they look at your hands. You smell of powder. Shot."

Enjolras, without answering, touched Combeferre's shoulder, and they both went into the lower room.

They came back a moment later. Enjolras held out in his hands the four uniforms he had kept in reserve. Combeferre followed him, bringing the cross belts and shakos.

"With this uniform," said Enjolras, "you can mingle with the ranks and escape. Here are enough for four."

And he threw them onto the unpaved ground.

Not a waver in the stoic audience. Combeferre spoke: "Come on. We must have a little pity. Do you know what we're talking about now? It's about women. Let's see. Are there any wives, yes or no? Are there any children, yes or no? Are there, yes or no, any mothers, who rock the cradle with their foot and who have heaps of little ones around them? Let any among you who have never seen the breast of a nursing woman hold up his hand. Ah! You want to die, I want that too, I who am speaking to you, but I don't want to feel the ghosts of women wringing their hands around me. Die, so be it, but don't make others die. Suicides like those that will be carried out here are sublime; but suicide is restricted, and can have no extension; and as soon as it touches those next to you, the name of suicide is murder. Think of little blond heads, and think of white hair. Listen, only a moment ago, Enjolras, he just told me about it, saw at the corner of the Rue du Cygne a casement lit up, a candle in a poor window, on the sixth floor, and on the glass the quivering shadow of the head of an old woman who appeared to have spent the night watching and to be still waiting. Perhaps she is the mother of one of you. Well, let that man leave, and let him hurry to say to his mother, 'Mother, here I am!' Let him feel at ease, the work here will be done just as well. When a man supports his relatives by his labor, he has no right to sacrifice himself. That is deserting his family. And those who have daughters, and those who have sisters! Have you thought about that? You get killed, there you are dead, very well, and tomorrow? Young girls who have no bread, that's terrible. Man begs, woman sells. Ah! Those charming beings, so graceful and sweet, who have flowered bonnets, who fill the house with chastity, who sing and chatter, who are like a living perfume, who prove the existence of angels in heaven by the purity of maidens on the earth, that Jeanne, that Lisa, that Mimi, those adorable and honest creatures who are your benediction and your pride, oh, God, they'll be hungry! What would you have me say to you? There's a market for human flesh; and it's not with your ghostly hands, fluttering about them, that you can prevent them from entering it! Think of the street, think of the pavement covered with pedestrians, think of the shops in front of which women walk to and fro with bare shoulders, through the mud. Those women also had been pure. Think of your sisters, those of you who have them. Misery, prostitution, the police, Saint-Lazare, that's where those delicate beautiful girls will fall, those fragile wonders of modesty, grace, and beauty, fresher than the lilacs of the month of May. Ah! You get yourselves killed! Ah! You're no longer with them! Very well; you wanted to deliver the people from monarchy, you give your young girls to the police. Friends, beware, have compassion. Women, unfortunate women, we're not used to giving them much thought. We boast that women have not received the education of men, we prevent them from reading, we prevent them from thinking, we prevent them from interesting themselves in politics; will you prevent them from going to the morgue tonight and identifying your corpses? Come, those who have families must be good fellows and give us a handshake and go away, and leave us to the business here all alone. I know well that it takes courage to leave, it's difficult; but the more difficult it is, the more praiseworthy. You say: I have a musket, I'm at the barricade, come the worst, I'm staying. Come the worst, that's easily said. My friends, there is a tomorrow; you won't be here on that tomorrow, but your families will. And what suffering! See, a pretty, healthy child with cheeks like an apple, that babbles, that chatters, that jabbers, that laughs, that smells sweet to the kiss, do you know what becomes of him when he is abandoned? I saw one, very small, no taller that that. His father was dead. Some poor people had taken him in out of charity, but they didn't have enough bread for themselves. The child was always hungry. It was winter. He didn't cry. They saw him go up to the stove where there was never any fire, whose pipe was plastered with yellow clay. The child picked off some of that clay with his little fingers and ate it. His breathing was harsh, his face gray, his legs weak, his belly big. He didn't say anything. They would speak to him, he didn't answer. He died. He was brought to the Necker Hospital to die, where I saw him. I was an intern at that hospital. Now, if there are any fathers among you, fathers whose delight it is to take a walk on Sunday holding in their great strong hand the little hand of their child, let each of those fathers imagine that that child is his own. That poor little bird, I remember him well, it seems to me I can see him now, when he lay naked on the dissecting table, his ribs projecting under his skin like graves under the grass of a churchyard. We found a kind of mud in his stomach. There were ashes in his teeth. Come, let's search our conscience and take counsel with out hearts. Statistics show that the mortality of abandoned children is fifty-five percent. I repeat it, it's a question of wives, it's a question of mothers, it's a question of young girls, it's a question of babies. Am I speaking to you for yourselves? We know very well what you are; we know very well that you're all brave, good heavens! We know very well that your souls are filled with joy and glory at giving your life for the great cause; we know very well that you feel elected to die usefully and magnificently, and that each of you clings to his share of the triumph. Well and good. But you're not alone in this world. There are other beings of whom we must think. We must not be selfish."

They all bowed their heads gloomily.

Strange contradictions of the human heart in its most sublime moments! Combeferre, who spoke this way, was not an orphan. He remembered the mothers of others, and he forgot his own. He was going to be killed. He was "selfish."

Marius, hungry, feverish, successively driven from every hope, stranded on grief, most dismal of shipwrecks, saturated with violent emotions and feeling the approaching end, was sinking deeper and deeper into that visionary stupor that always precedes the fatal hour when voluntarily accepted.

A doctor might have studied in him the growing symptoms of that febrile absorption known and classified by science, and which is to suffering what ecstasy is to pleasure. Despair too has its ecstasy. Marius had reached that point. He witnessed it all as from outside; as we have said, the things that were occurring before him seemed remote; he saw the whole, but did not notice the details. He saw the men going back and forth through a bewildering glare. He heard the voices speak as from the depth of an abyss.

Still this moved him. There was one point in this scene that pierced through to him, and woke him up. He had now only one idea, to die, and he would not be diverted from it; but he thought, in his funereal somnambulism, that while destroying oneself it is not forbidden to save another.

He raised his voice:

"Enjolras and Combeferre are right," he said. "No useless sacrifice. I'm adding my voice to theirs, and we must hurry. Combeferre has given the criteria. There are some among you who have families, mothers, sisters, wives, children. Let them leave the ranks."

Nobody stirred.

"Married men and supporters of families, out of the ranks!" repeated Marius.

His authority was great. Enjolras was indeed the leader of the barricade, but Marius was its savior.

"I order it," cried Enjolras.

"I beseech you," said Marius.

Then, roused by the words of Combeferre, shaken by Enjolras's order, moved by Marius's prayer, those heroic men began to inform against each other. "That's true," said a young man to a middle-aged man. "You are the head of a family. Go away." "It's actually you," answered the man, "you have two sisters you support." And an unparalled conflict broke out. It was as to which one should not allow himself to be laid at the door of the tomb.

"Hurry," said Courfeyrac, "in a quarter of an hour it will be too late."

"Citizens," continued Enjolras, "this is the Republic, and universal suffrage reigns. You yourselves choose those who ought to go."

They obeyed. In a few minutes five were unanimously designated and left the ranks.

"There are five!" exclaimed Marius.

There were only four uniforms.

"Well," resumed the five, "one must stay."

And it was a question of who should stay, and who should find reasons why the others should stay. The generous quarrel started up again.

"You, you have a wife who loves you." "But you, you have your old mother." "You have neither father nor mother, what will become of your three little brothers?" "You're the father of five children." "You have a right to live, you're seventeen, it's too soon."

These great revolutionary barricades were rendezvous of heroisms. There the improbable was natural. These men were not surprised at one another.

"Hurry!" repeated Courfeyrac.

Somebody cried out from the group to Marius, "You designate which one has to stay."

"Yes," said the five, "choose. We'll obey you."

Marius no longer believed any emotion was possible. Yet, at this idea, to select a man for death, all his blood flowed back toward his heart. He would have turned paler if that were possible.

He walked toward the five, who smiled at him, and each one, his eye full of the great flame seen in the depths of history over the Thermopylaes, shouted, "Me! Me! Me!"

And Marius, in a stupor, counted them; there were still five! Then his eyes fell on the four uniforms.

At this moment a fifth uniform dropped, as if from heaven, onto the four others.

The fifth man was saved.

Marius looked up and saw M. Fauchelevent.

Jean Valjean had just entered the barricade.

Whether by information obtained, or by instinct, or by chance, he had come through the little Rue Mondétour. Thanks to his National Guard uniform, he had easily gotten through.

The sentry placed by the insurgents on the Rue Mondétour had not given the signal of alarm for a lone National Guard. He allowed him to turn into the street, saying to himself, "He's a reinforcement, probably, and at the very worst a prisoner." The moment was too serious for the sentinel to be diverted from his duty and his observation post.

At the moment when Jean Valjean entered the redoubt, nobody had noticed him, all eyes being fixed on the five chosen men and on the four uniforms. Jean Valjean himself saw and understood, and silently he stripped off his coat and threw it onto the pile with the others.

The emotions were indescribable.

"Who is this man?" asked Bossuet.

"He," answered Combeferre, "is a man who saves others."

Marius added in a grave voice, "I know him."

This assurance was enough for all.

Enjolras turned toward Jean Valjean: "Citizen, you are welcome."

And he added, "You know that we are going to die."

Without answering, Jean Valjean helped the insurgent he was saving to put on his uniform.

V

WHAT HORIZON IS VISIBLE FROM THE TOP OF THE BARRICADE

Everyone's situation, in the hour of death in that implacable place, found its symbol and summit in the supreme melancholy of Enjolras.

Within himself Enjolras had the plenitude of revolution; he was incomplete notwithstanding, as much as the absolute can be; he clung too much to Saint-Just, not enough to Anacharsis Clootz; still his mind, in the society of the Friends of the A B C, had finally taken on a certain polarization from Combeferre's ideas; for some time, he had little by little been leaving the narrow forms of dogma, and allowing himself to tread the broad paths of progress, and he had come to accept, as its definitive and magnificent evolution, the transformation of the great French Republic into the immense human republic. As to the immediate means, in a condition of violence he wanted them to be violent; in that he had not varied; and he was still of that epic and formidable school summed up in the spirit of 1793.

Enjolras was standing on the paving-stone steps, his elbow on the muzzle of his carbine. He was thinking; he started, as if at a passing gust of wind; places where death is have this oracular effect. His eyes, filled with interior sight, gave off a kind of stifled fire. Suddenly he raised his head, his fair hair fell back like that of the angel on his somber chariot of stars, it was the mane of a startled lion with a flaming halo. And Enjolras exclaimed:

"Citizens, do you imagine the future? The streets of the cities flooded with light, green branches on the thresholds, the nations sisters, men just, the old blessing the children, the past loving the present, thinkers in full liberty, believers in full equality, for religion the heavens; God a direct priest, human conscience the altar, no more hatred, the fraternity of the workplace and the school, for reward and for penalty, notoriety; to all, labor; for all, law; over all, peace; no more bloodshed, no more war, mothers happy! To subdue matter is the first step; to realize the ideal is the second. Reflect on what progress has already done. Once the early human races looked with terror on the hydra, which blew on the waters, the dragon, which vomited fire, the griffin, monster of the air, which flew with the wings of an eagle and the claws of a tiger; fearful animals that were above man. Man, however, has laid his snares, the sacred snares of intelligence, and has at last caught the monsters.

"We have tamed the hydra, and he is called the steamship; we have tamed the dragon, and he is called the locomotive; we are on the point of taming the griffin, we already have him, and he is called the balloon. The day when this promethean work will be finished, and man will have definitely harnessed to his will the triple chimera of the ancients, the hydra, the dragon, and the griffin, he will be the master of water, fire, and air, and he will be to the rest of living creation what the ancient gods formerly were to him. Courage, and forward! Citizens, where are we headed? To science made government, to the force of things recognized as the only public force, to the natural law having its sanction and penalty in itself and spread by its own self-evidence, to a dawn of truth corresponding with the dawn of day. We are tending toward the union of the peoples; we are tending toward the unity of man. No more fictions; no more parasites. The real governed by the true, such is the aim. Civilization will hold its courts on the summit of Europe, and later in the middle of the continents, in a grand parliament of intelligence. Something like this has already been seen.

The Amphictyons had two sessions a year, one at Delphi, place of the gods, the other at Thermopylae, place of the heroes. Europe will have her Amphictyons; the globe will have its Amphictyons. France bears within her the sublime future. This is the gestation of the nineteenth century. What was sketched by Greece is worth being finished by France. Listen, my friend, Feuilly, valiant workingman, man of the people, man of all peoples. I venerate you. Yes, you clearly see future ages; you are right. You knew neither a father nor a mother, Feuilly; you have adopted humanity for your mother, and right for your father. You are going to die here, that is, to triumph. Citizens, whatever happens today, through our defeat as well as through our victory, we are going to effect a revolution. Just as fires light up the whole city, revolutions light up the whole human race. And what revolution shall we bring about? I've just said it, the revolution of the True. From the political point of view, there is one single principle: the sovereignty of man over himself. This sovereignty of myself over myself is called Liberty. Where two or more of these sovereignties associate the state begins. But in this association there is no abdication. Each sovereignty gives up a certain portion of itself to form the common right. That portion is the same for all. This identity of concession that each makes to all, is Equality. The common right is nothing more nor less than the protection of all radiating on the rights of each. This protection of all over each is called Fraternity. The point of intersection of these aggregated sovereignties is called Society. This intersection being a junction, this point is a knot. Hence what is called the social tie. Some say social contract, which is the same thing, the word contract being etymologically formed with the idea of tie. Let us understand each other in regard to equality; for, if liberty is the summit, equality is the base. Equality, citizens, is not all vegetation on one level, a society of big blades of grass and little oaks; a neighborhood of jealousies emasculating each other; civilly, it is all aptitudes having equal opportunity; politically, all votes having equal weight; religiously, all consciences having equal rights. Equality has an organ: free and compulsory education. The right to the alphabet, we must begin by that. The primary school obligatory for everyone, the higher school offered to everyone, such is the law. From identical schools spring an equal society. Yes, education! Light! Light! Everything comes from light, and everything returns to it. Citizens, the nineteenth century is great, but the twentieth century will be happy. Then there will be nothing more like the old history. Men will no longer have to fear, as they do now, a conquest, an invasion, a usurpation, a rivalry of nations with the armed hand, an interruption of civilization depending on a marriage of kings, a birth in the hereditary tyrannies, a partition of the peoples by a Congress, a dismembering through the downfall of a dynasty, a combat of two religions meeting head on, like two goats of darkness, on the bridge of infinity; they will no longer have to fear famine, exploitation, prostitution from distress, misery from lack of work, and the scaffold, and the sword, and the battle, and all the highway robberies of chance in the forest of events. We might almost say: There will be no more events. Men will be happy. The human race will fulfill its law as the terrestrial globe fulfills its own; harmony will be re-established between the soul and the star; the soul will gravitate about the truth like the star about the light. Friends, this hour we are living in, and in which I am speaking to you is a somber one, but such is the terrible price of the future. A revolution is a tollgate. Oh! The human race will be delivered, uplifted, and consoled! We are affirming it on this barricade. Where would the shout of love begin, if not from the summit of sacrifice? Oh my brothers, this is the junction between those who think and those who suffer; this barricade is made neither of paving stones, nor of timbers, nor of iron; it is made of two mounds, a mound of ideas and a mound of sorrows. Here misery encounters the ideal. Here day embraces night, and says: I will die with you and you will be born again with me. From the heavy embrace of all desolations springs faith. Sufferings bring their agony here, and ideas their immortality. This agony and immortality will mingle and make up our death. Brothers, whoever dies here dies in the radiance of the future, and we are entering a grave illuminated by the dawn."

Enjolras broke off rather than ceased, his lips moved noiselessly, as if he were continuing to speak to himself, and they kept on looking at him attentively, still trying to hear. There was no applause; but for a long time they whispered. Speech being breath, the rustling of intellects is like the rustling of leaves.

VI

MARIUS HAGGARD, JAVERT LACONIC

Let us describe what was happening in Marius's thoughts.

Remember the condition of his mind. As we have just mentioned, nothing seemed any more to him now than a dream. His understanding was troubled. Marius, we must insist, was under the shadow of the great black wings that open above the dying. He felt he had entered the tomb; it seemed to him that he was already on the other side of the wall, and he no longer saw the faces of the living except with the eyes of the dead.

How did M. Fauchelevent come to be there? Why was he there? What had he come to do? Marius asked himself none of these questions. Besides, since our despair has the peculiarity of including others as well as ourselves, it seemed logical to him that everybody should come to die.

Except that he thought of Cosette with a pang.

Anyway, M. Fauchelevent did not speak to him, did not look at him, and did not even seem to hear when Marius said: I know him.

As for Marius, M. Fauchelevent's attitude was a relief to him, and if we could use such a word for such impressions, we would say it pleased him. He had always felt it absolutely impossible to speak to that enigmatic man, who seemed to him both equivocal and imposing. It was also a long time since he had seen him; which, with Marius's timid and reserved nature, increased the impossibility still more.

The five designated men left the barricade by the little Rue Mondétour; they looked exactly like National Guards; one of them went away weeping. Before going, they embraced those who remained.

When the five sent away into life had gone, Enjolras

thought of the one condemned to death. He went into the lower room. Javert, tied to the pillar, was thinking.

"Do you need anything?" Enjolras asked him.

Javert answered, "When are you going to kill me?"

"Wait. Right now we need all our cartridges."

"Then give me a drink," said Javert.

Enjolras gave him a glass of water, and, since Javert was bound, he helped him to drink.

"Is that all?" asked Enjolras.

"I'm uncomfortable at this post," answered Javert. "It wasn't thoughtful to leave me to spend the night here. Tie me as you like, but please lay me on a table. Like the other."

And with a nod he indicated M. Mabeuf's body.

At the back of the room, there was, it will be remembered, a long wide table on which they had cast bullets and made cartridges. With all the cartridges made and all the powder used up, that table was free.

At Enjolras's order, four insurgents untied Javert from the post. While they were untying him, a fifth held a bayonet to his breast. They left his hands tied behind his back, they put a light, strong whipcord around his feet, which allowed him to take fifteen-inch steps like those who are mounting the scaffold, and they made him walk to the table at the back of the room, on which they extended him, tightly bound by the middle of his body.

For greater security, with a rope fixed to his neck, they added to the system of bonds that made all escape impossible, that type of ligature called in the prisons a martingale, which, starting from the back of the neck, divides across the stomach and is fastened to the hands after passing between the legs.

While they were binding Javert, a man, on the threshold of the door, gazed at him with singular attention. The shadow this man produced made Javert turn his head. He raised his eyes and recognized Jean Valjean. He did not even give a start; he haughtily dropped his eyelids and merely said, "Of course."

VII

THE SITUATION GROWS SERIOUS

It was rapidly growing light. But not a window was opened, not a door stood ajar; it was the dawn, not the hour of awakening. The far end of the Rue de la Chanvrerie opposite the barricade had been evacuated by the troops, as we have said; it seemed free, and with an ominous tranquility it lay open to wayfarers. The Rue Saint-Denis was as silent as the avenue of the Sphinxes at Thebes. Not a living being at the crossroads, which were whitening in a reflection of the sun. Nothing is so dismal as this brightness of deserted streets.

They saw nothing, but they could hear a mysterious movement taking place some distance away. It was clear that the critical moment was at hand. As in the evening, the sentries were driven in, but this time all of them.

The barricade was stronger than at the time of the first attack. Since the departure of the five, it had been raised still higher.

On the report of the sentry who had been watching the market area, Enjolras, for fear of a surprise from the rear, made an important decision. He had barricaded the little passage of the Rue Mondétour, which till then had been open. For this purpose they lifted the paving for the length of a few more houses. In this way, the barricade, walled in on three streets, in front on the Rue de la Chanvrerie, to the left on the Rue du Cygne and la Petite Truanderie, at the right upon the Rue Mondétour, was really almost impregnable; it is true that they were permanently shut in. It had three fronts, but no longer an outlet. "A fortess-mousetrap," said Courfeyrac with a laugh.

Near the door of the wineshop Enjolras had piled up some thirty paving stones, "torn up to spare," said Bossuet.

The silence was now so profound on the side from which the attack must come that Enjolras had each man return to his post for battle.

A ration of brandy was distributed to all.

Nothing is stranger than a barricade preparing for an assault. Each man chooses his place, as at a play. They lean on their sides, their elbows, their shoulders. There are some who make themselves stalls with paving stones. There is a corner of a wall that is annoying, they move away from it; here is a projection that might afford protection, they take shelter in it. The left-handed are precious; they take places that are inconvenient for the rest. Many make arrangements to fight sitting down. They wish to be at their ease for killing and comfortable for dying. In the deadly war of June 1848, an insurgent, who had perfect aim and who fought from the top of a terrace, on a roof, had a Voltaire armchair carried up there; a charge of grapeshot found him in it.

As soon as the leader has ordered the decks cleared for the fight, all disorderly movements cease; no more skirmishing with one another; no more coteries; no more asides; no more standing apart; everything that is in the various minds converges, and changes into waiting for the attacker. A barricade before danger, chaos; in danger, discipline. Peril produces order.

As soon as Enjolras had taken his double-barreled carbine, and placed himself on a kind of battlement he had reserved, everyone fell silent. A patter of dry little snapping sounds was confusedly heard along the wall of paving stones. They were cocking their muskets.

Their bearing was actually firmer and more confident than ever; an excess of sacrifice is a support; they no longer had any hope, but they had despair. Despair, the final weapon which sometimes gives victory; Virgil has said so. Supreme resources spring from extreme determination. To embark on death is sometimes the means of escaping a shipwreck; and the coffin lid becomes a life-saving plank.

As on the evening before, all attention was turned, and we might almost say boring in, on the end of the street, now light and visible.

They did not have long to wait. Activity distinctly started up again in the direction of Saint-Leu, but it was not like the movement of the first attack. A rattle of chains, the menacing jolt of a mass, a clicking of brass bounding over the pavement, a sort of solemn uproar, warned that an ominous body of iron was approaching. There was a shudder in the bowels of those peaceful old streets, cut through and built up for the fruitful circulation of interests and ideas, and which were not made for the monstrous rumbling of the wheels of war.

The stare of all the combatants on the far end of the street became savage.

A piece of artillery appeared.

The gunners were pushing the piece forward; the carriage was set for firing; the front wheels had been removed; two supported the carriage, four were at the wheels, others followed with the caisson. The smoke of the burning match was seen.

"Fire!" cried Enjolras.

The whole barricade fired, the explosion was terrible; an avalanche of smoke covered and effaced the gun and the men; in a few seconds the cloud dissipated, and the cannon and the men reappeared; those in charge of the piece finished placing it in position in front of the barricade, slowly, correctly, and without haste. Not a man had been touched. Then the gunner, bearing his weight on the breech, to elevate the range, began to point the cannon with the gravity of an astronomer adjusting a telescope.

"Bravo for the gunners!" cried Bossuet.

And the whole barricade applauded.

A moment later, placed squarely in the middle of the street, astride the gutter, the gun was in battery. A formidable mouth was open onto the barricade.

"Come on, be quick!" said Courfeyrac. "There's the brute. After the flick, the punch. The army is stretching out its big paw to us. The barricade is going to be seriously shaken. The muskets grope, but the artillery takes."

"It's a bronze eight-pounder, new model," added Combeferre. "Those pieces, if they exceed even slightly the proportion of ten parts of tin to a hundred of copper, may burst. The excess of tin makes them too tender. In that case they have hollows and chambers in the vent. To avoid this danger, and to be able to force out the load, it might be necessary to return to the process of the fourteenth century, hooping, and strengthening the piece on the exterior by a succession of unsoldered steel rings, from the breech to the trunnion. In the meantime, they remedy the defect as they can; they find out where the holes and the hollows in the bore of a cannon are by means of a searcher. But there's a better way, that's the movable star of Gribeauval."

"In the sixteenth century," observed Bossuet, "they rifled their cannon."

"Yes," answered Combeferre, "that increases the ballistic power, but diminishes the accuracy of the aim. Beyond that, over a short range, the trajectory does not have the desirable rigidity, the parabola is exaggerated, the path of the projectile is not direct enough to permit it to hit the intermediate objects, a necessity of combat, however, whose importance increases with the proximity of the enemy and the rapidity of the firing. This lack of tension in the curve of the projectile in the rifled cannon of the sixteenth century is due to the weakness of the charge; weak charges, for this kind of weapon, are required by the necessities of ballistics, such as, for instance, the preservation of the carriages. On the whole, artillery, that despot, cannot do all it would like; strength is a great weakness. A cannonball travels only two thousand miles an hour; light travels two hundred thousand miles a second. Such is the superiority of Jesus Christ over Napoleon."

"Reload arms," said Enjolras.

How was the facing of the barricade going to behave under fire? Would the shot make a breach? That was the question. While the insurgents were reloading their muskets, the gunners loaded the cannon.

There was intense anxiety in the redoubt.

The gun went off; the detonation burst.

"Present!" cried a cheerful voice.

And at the same time as the cannonball hit the outside, Gavroche tumbled into the barricade.

He came by way of the Rue du Cygne, and he had nimbly clambered over the secondary barricade, which fronted on the labyrinth of la Petite Truanderie.

Gavroche produced a greater effect in the barricade than the cannonball.

The ball lost itself in the rubble. At the most it broke a wheel of the omnibus, and finished off the old Anceau cart. Seeing which, the barricade began to laugh.

"Proceed," cried Bossuet to the gunners.

VIII

THE GUNNERS TAKEN SERIOUSLY

They surrounded Gavroche.

But he had no time to tell anything. Marius, shuddering, took him aside.

"What have you come here for?"

"Well, now," said the boy "And what have you come for?"

He looked straight at Marius with his epic effrontery. His eyes grew large with proud clarity.

Marius continued, sternly, "Who told you to come back? Did you at least deliver my letter to its address?"

Gavroche felt some little remorse in relation to that letter. In his haste to return to the barricade, he had gotten rid of it rather than delivered it. He had to admit to himself that he had entrusted it rather rashly to that stranger, whose face he could not even make out. True, this man was bareheaded, but that was not enough. On the whole he was giving himself some little interior remonstrances on this subject, and he feared Marius's reproaches. To get out of trouble, he took the simplest course: He lied abominably.

"Citizen, I carred the letter to the doorkeeper. The lady was asleep. She'll get the letter when she wakes up."

In sending this letter, Marius had two objects: to say farewell to Cosette, and to save Gavroche. He had to be content with half of what he intended.

Sending his letter and the presence of M. Fauchelevent in the barricade, this coincidence occurred to his mind. He pointed out M. Fauchelevent to Gavroche.

"Do you know that man?"

"No," said Gavroche.

In fact, as we have just mentioned, Gavroche had only seen Jean Valjean in the dark.

The troubled and sickly conjectures that had risen in Marius's mind were dispelled. Did he know M. Fauchelevent's opinions? M. Fauchelevent might be a republican. Hence his very natural presence in this conflict.

Meanwhile Gavroche was already at the other end of the barricade, crying, "My musket!"

Courfeyrac ordered it to be given him.

Gavroche warned his "comrades," as he called them, that the barricade was surrounded. He had had great difficulty getting through. A battalion of the line, whose muskets were stacked in la Petite Truanderie, were watching the side on the Rue du Cygne; on the opposite side the municipal guard was occupying the Rue des Prêcheurs. In front, they had the bulk of the army.

This information given, Gavroche added, "I authorize you to give them a dose of pills."

Meanwhile Enjolras, on his battlement, was watching, listening intently.

The assailants, undoubtedly dissatisfied with the effect of their fire, had not repeated it.

A company of infantry of the line had come in and occupied the far end of the street, behind the gun. The soldiers tore up the pavement, and with the stones constructed a little low wall, a sort of breastwork that was hardly more than eighteen inches high, and fronted on the barricade. At the corner on the left of this breastwork, they saw the head of the column of a battalion from the suburbs drawn up in the Rue Saint-Denis.

Enjolras, on the watch, thought he detected the particular sound that is made when canisters of grapeshot are taken from the caisson, and he saw the gunner change aim and incline the piece slightly to the left. Then the cannoneers began to load. The gunner seized the linstock himself and brought it near the touch-hole.

"Heads down, keep close to the wall!" cried Enjolras, "and all on your knees along the barricade!"

The insurgents, who were scattered in front of the bistro and had left their combat stations on Gavroche's arrival, rushed pell-mell toward the barricade; but before Enjolras's order was executed, the gun went off with a rattle like grapeshot.

The shot was directed at the opening of the redoubt, it richocheted against the wall, and this terrible richochet killed two men and wounded three.

If that continued, the barricade was no longer tenable. It was not proof against grapeshot.

There was a wave of consternation.

"Let's prevent the second shot, at any rate," said Enjolras.

And, lowering his carbine, he aimed at the gunner, who, at that moment, bending over the breech of the gun, was correcting and finally adjusting the aim.

This gunner was a fine-looking sergeant of artillery, quite young, blond, with a mild face, and the intelligent air suited to that awesome, ominous weapon, which, by perfecting itself in horror, must end in ending war.

Combeferre, standing near Enjolras, looked at this young man.

"What a pity!" said Combeferre. "What a hideous thing these bloodbaths are! I'm sure, when there are no more kings, there will be no more war. Enjolras, you're aiming at that sergeant, you're not looking at him. Just think that he's a charming young man; he's intrepid; you can see that he's a thinker; these young artillerymen are well educated; he has a father, a mother, a family; he's in love, probably; he's twenty-five at most; he might be your brother."

"He is," said Enjolras.

"Yes," said Combeferre, "and mine, too. Well, don't let's kill him."

"Leave me alone. We must do what we must."

And a tear rolled slowly down Enjolras's marble cheek.

At the same time he pressed the trigger of his carbine. The flash burst out. The artillery sergeant turned twice around, his arms stretched out in front of him, and his head raised as if to drink the air, then he fell over sideways onto the gun, and lay there motionless. His back could be seen, from the center of which a stream of blood gushed upward. The bullet had entered his breast and passed through his body. He was dead.

They had to carry him away and replace him. It did give those defending the barricade a few extra minutes.

IX

USE OF THAT OLD POACHER SKILL, AND THE INFALLIBLE SHOT THAT INFLUENCED THE CONDEMNATION OF 1796

Opinions were flying back and forth in the barricade. The gun was about to fire again. They could not hold out a quarter of an hour in that storm of grapeshot. It was absolutely necessary to deaden the blows.

Enjolras threw out his command: "We must put a mattress there."

"We don't have any," said Combeferre, "the wounded are on them."

Jean Valjean, seated out of the way on a block, at the corner of the wineshop, his musket between his knees, had up to that moment taken no part in what was going on. He seemed not to hear the combatants around him say, "There's a free musket."

At Enjolras's order, he got up.

It will be remembered that on the arrival of the company in the Rue de la Chanvrerie, an old woman, foreseeing bullets, had put her mattress up across her window. This window, a garret window, was on the roof of a house six stories high standing a little outside the barricade. The mattress, placed crosswise, was resting at the botton on two laundry poles, and held up at the top by two ropes, which, in the distance, seemed like threads and which were attached to nails driven into the window casing. These two ropes stood out clearly against the sky like hairs.

"Can somebody lend me a double-barreled carbine?" said Jean Valjean.

Enjolras, who had just reloaded his, handed it to him.

Jean Valjean aimed at the window and fired.

One of the two ropes of the mattress was severed.

The mattress was now hanging by only one thread.

Jean Valjean fired the second barrel. The second rope whipped the glass of the window. The mattress slid down between the two poles and fell into the street.

The barricade applauded.

They all shouted, "There's a mattress!"

"Yes," said Combeferre, "but who'll go out after it?"

The mattress had, in fact, fallen outside the barricade, between the besieged and the besiegers. Now, since the death of the gunner had enraged the troops, the soldiers had begun to lie flat on their stomachs behind the low wall of paving stones they had raised, and, to make up for the unavoidable silence of the artillery, which was stalled while its crew was being reorganized, they had opened fire on the barricade. The insurgents made no response to these volleys, to spare their ammunition. The fusillade was spent against the barricade; but the street, filled with bullets, was a nightmare.

Jean Valjean went out into the street through the opening, crossed through the hail of bullets, went to the mattress, picked it up, put it on his back, and returned to the barricade.

He shoved the mattress into the opening himself. He secured it against the wall in such a way that the artillerymen did not see it.

This done, they waited for the blast of grapeshot.

They did not have long to wait.

With a roar, the cannon vomited its package of shot. But there was no ricochet. The pellets miscarried against the mattress. The desired effect was obtained. The barricade was saved.

"Citizen," said Enjolras to Jean Valjean, "the Republic thanks you."

Bossuet laughed admiringly. He exclaimed, "It's immoral that a mattress should have so much power. Triumph of what yields over what thunders. Anyway, glory to the mattress that nullifies a cannon."

X

DAWN

At that moment Cosette awoke.

Her room was small, neat, modest, with a long window to the east, looking out on the back court of the house.

Cosette knew nothing of what was going on in Paris. She had not left her room all evening and had already been there when Toussaint had said, "It seems there's a row."

Cosette had slept only a few hours, but well. She had had sweet dreams, partly owing perhaps to her little bed being very white. Somebody who was Marius had appeared to her surrounded by a light. She awoke with the sun in her eyes, which at first gave the effect of a continuation of her dream.

Her first emotion, on coming out of this dream, was joyful. Cosette felt entirely reassured. Like Jean Valjean a few hours before, she was passing through that reaction of the soul which absolutely refuses unhappiness. She began to hope with all her might without knowing why. Then came a pang. It was three days now since she had seen Marius. But she said to herself that he must have received her letter, that he knew where she was, and that he had so many good ideas that he would find some means to reach her. "Today for sure, and perhaps this very morning." It was broad daylight, but the rays of light were very horizontal; she thought it was very early, that she should get up, however, to be ready for Marius.

She felt she could not live without Marius, and that consequently, that was enough, and that Marius would come. No objection was admissible. All of that was certain. It was monstrous enough already to have suffered through three days. Marius absent for three days, that was unfair of God. Now Heaven's cruel sport was an ordeal that was over. Marius was coming and would bring good news. Thus is youth constituted; it quickly dries its eyes; it believes sorrow useless and does not accept it. Youth is the smile of the future before an unknown being, which is itself. It is natural for it to be happy. It seems to breathe hope.

Besides, Cosette could not manage to recall what Marius had said to her on the subject of this absence, which was to last only one day, or what explanation he had given her about it. Everyone has noticed how cleverly a piece of money, dropped on the floor, runs and hides, and how artfully it makes itself undiscoverable. There are thoughts that play us the same trick; they hide in a corner of our brain; it is all over; they are lost; impossible to put the memory back in touch with them. Cosette was a little vexed at the senseless petty efforts her memory made. She said to herself that it was very bad of her and very wicked to have forgotten words uttered by Marius.

She got up and performed the two ablutions, of the soul and the body, prayer and dressing.

In extreme cases, we may introduce the reader into a nuptial chamber, but not into a virgin's bedroom. Verse would hardly dare, prose should not.

It is the interior of a flower still in the bud, it is a whiteness in the shade, it is the innermost cell of a closed lily that should not be seen by man, while it has not yet been looked upon by the sun. Woman in the bud is sacred. The innocent bed thrown open, the adorable seminudity that is afraid of itself, the white foot taking refuge in a slipper, the breast that veils itself before a mirror as if that mirror were an eye; the slip that hurries to hide the shoulder at the creaking of a piece of furniture or the passing of a wagon, the ribbons tied, the hooks done up, the lacings drawn, the starts, the shivers of cold and modesty, the exquisite shyness in every movement, the almost winged anxiety where there is no cause for fear; the successive phases of the clothing as charming as the clouds of the dawn; it is not fitting for all this to be described, and it is even too much to refer to it.

The eye of man should be still more reverent before the rising of a young maiden than before the rising of a star. The possibility of touch should increase respect. The down of the peach, the dust of the plum, the radiated crystal of snow, the butterfly's wing powdered with feathers, are gross things beside that chastity that does not even know it is chaste. The young maiden is only the glimmer of a dream and is not yet statue. Her alcove is hidden in the shadows of the ideal. The indiscreet touch of the eye desecrates this dim penumbra. Here, to gaze is to profane.

We will show nothing, then, of all that pleasant little confusion attendant on Cosette's waking.

An Eastern tale says that the rose was made white by God, but since Adam looked at it while it was half open, it was ashamed and blushed. We are among those who feel speechless in the presence of young maidens and flowers, finding them almost sacred.

Cosette dressed quickly, combed and arranged her hair, which was a simple thing at that time, when women did not puff out their ringlets and braids with cushions and rolls, and did not put crinoline in their hair. Then she opened the window and looked all around, hoping to discover something of the street, a corner of a house, a patch of pavement, and to be able to watch for Marius there. But she could see none of the street. The back courtyard was surrounded by high walls, and only a few gardens were visible. Cosette declared these gardens hideous; for the first time in her life she found flowers ugly. The least bit of a street gutter would have been more to her liking. She finally began to look at the sky, as if she thought that Marius might come that way, too.

Suddenly she dissolved into tears. Not that it was fickleness of soul, but, with hopes cut off by discouragement, she vaguely felt some indefinable horror. Things do float in the air. She said to herself that she was not sure of anything; that to lose sight of was to lose; and the idea that Marius might indeed return to her from the sky appeared no longer charming but morbid.

Then, such are these clouds, calm returned to her, and hope, and a sort of smile, unconscious but trusting in God.

Everyone was still in bed in the house. A rural silence reigned. Not a shutter had been opened. The doorkeeper's lodge was closed. Toussaint was not up, and Cosette very naturally thought her father was asleep. She must have suffered a great deal, and she must have been still suffering, for she said to herself her father had been unkind; but she was counting on Marius. The eclipse of such a light was entirely impossible. She prayed. At times she heard some distance away a kind of muffled slamming, and she said, "It's odd that people are opening and shutting carriage doors this early." It was the cannon battering the barricade.

A few feet below Cosette's window, there was, in the old black cornice of the wall, a nest of martins; the swelling of this nest projected a little beyond the cornice, so that the inside of this little paradise could be seen from above. The mother was there, opening her wings like a fan over her brood; the father flew about, went away, then returned, bringing food and kisses in his beak. The rising day gilded this happy thing, the great law Multiply was there, smiling and august, and this sweet mystery was blossoming in the glory of the morning. Cosette, her hair in the sunshine, her soul in fantasy, made luminous by inner love and the outer dawn, leaned out unconsciously, and, almost without daring to acknowledge to herself that she was thinking of Marius at the same time, began to look at these birds, this family, this male and this female, this mother and these little ones, with the deep restlessness which a nest gives to a young girl.

XI

THE SHOT THAT MISSES NOTHING AND KILLS NOBODY

The assailants' barrage kept up. The musket fire and grapeshot alternated, without causing much damage. The top of the façade of Corinth alone suffered; the window of the second floor and the dormer windows in the roof, riddled with buckshot and bullets, were slowly demolished. The combatants who were posted there had to retreat. Besides, this is one of the tactics of attacking barricades; to tease for a long time, in order to exhaust the ammunition of the insurgents, if they commit the blunder of replying. When it is noticed, from the slackening of their fire, that they have no more bullets or powder, the assault is made. Enjolras did not fall into this trap; the barricade did not reply.

With each platoon volley, Gavroche poked out his cheek with his tongue, a mark of lofty disdain.

"That's right," he said, "tear up the cloth. We need lint."

Courfeyrac taunted the grapeshot about its lack of effect, and said to the cannon, "You're stretching yourself thin, my good man."

In a battle, people plot and scheme, as at a dance. It is likely that this silence in the redoubt began to perplex the besiegers and make them fear some unanticipated accident, and that they felt the need to see through that heap of paving stones and know what was going on behind that impassable wall, which was taking their fire without answering it. The insurgents suddenly noticed a helmet shining in the sun on a neighboring roof. A sapper was backed up against a tall chimney and seemed to be there as a lookout. He could see directly into the barricade.

"There's a troublesome overseer," said Enjolras.

Jean Valjean had returned his carbine to Enjolras, but he had his musket.

Without saying a word, he aimed at the sapper and a second later the helmet, struck by a bullet, fell clattering into the street. The startled soldier disappeared hurriedly.

A second observer took his place. This was an officer. Jean Valjean, who had reloaded his musket, aimed at the newcomer, and sent the officer's helmet to keep company with the soldier's. The officer did not insist, and withdrew very quickly. This time the warning was understood. Nobody appeared on the roof again, and they gave up watching the barricade.

"Why didn't you kill the man?" asked Bossuet of Jean Valjean.

Jean Valjean did not answer.

XII

DISORDER THE PARTISAN OF ORDER

Bossuet murmured in Combeferre's ear, "He hasn't answered my question."

"He's a man with a kindly musket," said Combeferre.

Those who still recall some of that now distant period know that the National Guard of the suburbs fought valiantly against the insurrections. It was particularly eager and intrepid in the days of June 1832. Many a good bistrokeeper of Pantin, of Les Vertus, or of La Cunette, whose "establishment" lacked trade because of the uprising, turned ferocious on seeing his dancehall deserted, and died to preserve the order represented by the tavern. In those days, simultaneously bourgeois and heroic, in the presence of ideas that had their knights, interests had their champions. The prosaic motive detracted nothing from the bravery of the action. A decreasing pile of coins made bankers sing the *Marseillaise*. They poured out their blood lyrically for the counter; and with a Lacedemonian enthusiasm they defended the shop, that immense diminutive of one's nation.

Actually, we have to say that there was nothing in all this that was not extremely serious. It was the social elements entering conflict, while awaiting the day when they would enter equilibrium.

Another sign of that era was anarchy mingled with governmentalism (barbaric name of the correct party). Men were for order without discipline. The drums beat unexpectedly, at the command of some colonel of the National Guard, capricious rollcalls; many a captain went to the fire on impulse; many a National Guard fought on whim and on his own account. In the critical moments, on the "days," they took counsel less from their leaders than their instincts. In the regulation army there were genuine guerrillas, some of the sword, like Fannicot; others of the pen, like Henri Fonfrède.

Civilization, unfortunately represented at that period by an aggregation of interests rather than by a group of principles, was, or thought it was, in peril; it raised the alarm; every man making himself a center, defended it, aided it, and protected it in his own way; and anybody and everybody took it on himself to save society.

Zeal sometimes went to the extent of extermination. Such a platoon of National Guards constituted themselves, of their own private authority, a court-martial, and condemned and executed an insurgent prisoner in five minutes. It was an improvisation of this kind that had killed Jean Prouvaire. Ferocious lynch law—which no party has the right to reproach in others, for it is applied by the republic in America as well as by monarchy in Europe—this lynch law is liable to mistakes. During one uprising, a young poet, named Paul Aimé Garnier, was pursued in the Place Royale at the point of a bayonet, and only escaped by taking refuge under the carriage entrance of Number 6. The cry was "There is another Saint-Simonian!" And they wanted to kill him. Now, he had under his arm a volume of the memoirs of the Duc de Saint-Simon. A National Guard had read on the book the name "Saint-Simon," and cried, "Kill him!"

On June 6, 1832, a company of National Guards of the suburbs, commanded by Captain Fannicot, mentioned above, got themselves, through whim and a sense of fun, decimated in the Rue de la Chanvrerie. The fact, strange as it may seem, was proven by the judicial investigation carried out after the insurrection of 1832. Captain Fannicot, a bold and impatient bourgeois, a sort of soldier of fortune on the order of those we have just characterized, a fanatical and insubordinate governmentalist, could not resist the impulse to open fire before the given time and the ambition of taking the barricade all by himself, that is with his company. Exasperated by the successive appearance of the red flag and the old coat, which he took for the black flag, he loudly blamed the generals and corps leaders, who were holding counsel and did not feel that the moment for the decisive assault had come, and were leaving—according to a celebrated expression of one of them—"the insurrection to stew in its own juice." As for him, he thought the barricade ripe, and, as what is ripe ought to fall, he made the attempt.

He commanded men as resolute as himself, "madmen," said a witness. His company, the same that had shot the poet Jean Prouvaire, was the first of the battalion posted at the corner of the street. At the moment when it was least expected, the captain hurled his men against the barricade. This movement, executed with more zeal than strategy, cost the Fannicot company dearly. Before it had covered two thirds of the street, it was greeted by a general volley from the barricade. Four, the most daring, who were running in advance, were shot down point-blank at the very foot of the redoubt; and this courageous mob of National Guards, very brave men, but with no military tenacity, had to fall back, after some hesitation, leaving fifteen dead on the pavement. The moment of hesitation gave the insurgents time to reload, and a second volley, very murderous, reached the company before it was able to regain the corner of the street, its shelter. At one moment it was taken between two lines of fire, and it absorbed the volley of the gun in firing position, which, receiving no orders, had not discontinued its fire. The intrepid and imprudent Fannicot was one of those killed by this volley. He was slain by the cannon, that is to say, by order.

This attack, more furious than serious, irritated Enjolras.

"The fools!" he said. "They're getting their men killed and using up our ammunition for nothing."

Enjolras spoke like the true general of émeute that he

was. Insurrection and repression never contend with equal arms. Insurrection, readily exhaustible, has only a certain number of shots to fire and a certain number of combatants to expend. A cartridge box emptied, a man killed, are not replaced. Repression, having the army, does not count men and, having Vincennes, does not count shots. Repression has as many regiments as the barricade has men, and as many arsenals as the barricade has cartridge boxes. Thus they are struggles of one against a hundred, which always end in the destruction of the barricade; unless revolution, erupting suddenly, casts its flaming archangel's sword into the balance. That happens. Then everything rises, the pavements begin to ferment, the redoubts of the people swarm, Paris thrills sovereignly, the *quid divinum* is set free, a 10th of August is in the air, a 29th of July is in the air, a marvelous light appears, the yawning jaws of force recoil, and the army, that lion, sees before it, erect and tranquil, that prophet, France.

XIII

PASSING GLIMMERS

In the chaos of sentiments and passions that defend a barricade, there is some of everything: bravery, youth, honor, enthusiasm, the ideal, conviction, the eager fury of the gambler, and above all, intervals of hope.

One of those intervals, one of those vague thrills of hope, suddenly, at the most unexpected moment, crossed the barricade of the Rue de la Chanvrerie.

"Listen!" exclaimed Enjolras, constantly on the alert, "it seems to me that Paris is waking."

It is certain that for an hour or two on the morning of the 6th of June the insurrection had a certain revival. The obstinacy of the tocsin of Saint-Merry reanimated some dull hopes. In the Rue du Poirier, in the Rue des Gravilliers, barricades were starting up. In front of the Porte Saint-Martin, a lone young man armed with a carbine attacked a squadron of cavalry. Without shelter of any kind, in the open boulevard, he dropped on one knee, raised his weapon to his shoulder, fired, killed the chief of the squadron, and turned around, saying, "There's another who won't do us any more harm." He was cut down by a saber. In the Rue Saint-Denis, a woman fired on the Municipal Guard from behind a lowered blind. The slats of the blind were seen to tremble at each report. A boy of fourteen was arrested in the Rue de la Cossonerie with his pockets full of cartridges. Several posts were attacked. At the entrance of the Rue Bertin-Poirée, a very sharp and entirely unexpected volley greeted a regiment of cuirassiers, at whose head marched General Cavaignac de Baragne. In the Rue Planche-Mibray they threw down on the troops from the rooftops old fragments of pottery and household utensils, a bad sign; and when this fact was reported to Marshal Soult, Napoleon's old lieutenant grew thoughtful, remembering the saying of Suchet at Saragossa: "We're lost when the old women empty their chamber pots on our heads."

These general symptoms that broke out just when it was supposed the émeute was localized, this fever of wrath regaining the upper hand, these sparks that flew here and there above the deep masses of combustible material called the faubourgs of Paris, all taken together gave the military chiefs cause for anxiety. They hastened to snuff out these beginnings of conflagration. Until these sparks were quenched, they put off the attacks on the barricades of Maubuée, de la Chanvrerie, and Saint-Merry, so they would have them only to deal with and might be able to finish all at one blow. Columns were thrown into the rebellious streets, sweeping the large ones clear, probing the small ones to the right, to the left, sometimes slowly and with caution, sometimes at a double-quick step. The troops beat in the doors of the houses from which there had been firing; at the same time cavalry maneuvers dispersed the groups on the boulevards. This repression was not accomplished without noise nor without that tumultuous uproar peculiar to confrontations between the army and the people. This was what Enjolras inferred, in the intervals between the cannon and the musket volleys. Besides, he had seen some wounded passing the end of the street on litters and said to Courfeyrac, "Those wounded aren't our doing."

The hope did not last long; the gleam was soon eclipsed. In less than half an hour what was in the air vanished; it was like heat lightning, and the insurgents felt that kind of leaden pall fall on them that the indifference of the people casts over the obstinate when abandoned.

The general movement, which seemed to have been vaguely conceived, had miscarried; and the attention of the minister of war and the strategy of the generals could now be concentrated on the three or four barricades still standing.

The sun rose above the horizon.

An insurgent called to Enjolras, "We're hungry here. Are we really going to die like this without eating?"

Still leaning on his battlement, without taking his eyes off the far end of the street, Enjolras nodded.

XIV

IN WHICH WILL BE FOUND THE NAME OF ENJOLRAS'S MISTRESS

Seated on a paving stone beside Enjolras, Courfeyrac continued his insults to the cannon, and every time that that gloomy cloud of projectiles known as grapeshot passed by, with its monstrous sound, he received it with an outburst of irony.

"You're tiring your lungs, my poor old brute, I'm sorry for you, you're wasting your energy. That's not thunder; no, it's a cough."

And those around him laughed.

Courfeyrac and Bossuet, whose valiant good humor increased with the danger, like Madame Scarron, replaced food with joking, and, since they had no wine, poured out cheerfulness for all.

"I admire Enjolras," said Bossuet. "His impassive boldness astonishes me. He lives alone, which makes him perhaps a little sad. Enjolras suffers for his greatness, which binds him to celibacy. The rest of us more or less all have mistresses who make us mad, that is to say brave. When we're as amorous as a tiger, the least we can do is to fight like a lion. It's one way of avenging ourselves for the tricks that Mesdames our grisettes play us. Roland gets himself killed to spite Angelica; all our heroism comes from our women. A man without a woman is a pistol without a hammer; it's the woman who makes the man go off. Well, Enjolras has no woman. He's not in love, yet he finds a way to be intrepid. It is an incredible thing that a man can be as cold as ice and as bold as fire."

Enjolras did not seem to be listening, but had anyone been nearby, he would have heard him murmur in an undertone, "*Patria.*"

Bossuet was still laughing when Courfeyrac exclaimed, "Something new!"

And, assuming the manner of an usher announcing an arrival, he added, "The Honorable Eight-Pounder."

In fact, a new character had just entered the scene. It was a second piece of ordnance.

The artillerymen quickly executed the maneuvers, and placed this second piece in battery near the first.

This suggested the conclusion.

A few moments later, the two weapons, rapidly serviced, opened up directly on the redoubt; the platoon barrage of the line and the suburbs supported the artillery.

Another cannonade was heard at some distance. At the same time that two cannon were raging against the redoubt in the Rue de la Chanvrerie, two other pieces of ordnance, aimed, one on the Rue Saint-Denis, the other on the Rue Aubry-le-Boucher, were riddling the barricade Saint-Merry. The four cannon echoed one another gruesomely.

The baying of the dismal dogs of war answered each other.

Of the two pieces now battering the barricade in the Rue de la Chanvrerie, one fired grapeshot, the other cannonballs.

The gun that hurled cannonballs was elevated a little, and the range was calculated so that the ball struck the extreme edge of the upper ridge of the barricade, notched it, and crumbled the paving stones over the insurgents in showers.

This procedure was intended to drive the combatants from the summit of the redoubt and force them to crowd together in the interior, that is, it anticipated the assault.

Once the combatants were driven from the top of the barricade by the cannonballs and from the windows of the bistro by the grapeshot, the attacking columns could venture into the street without being watched, perhaps even without being under fire, suddenly scale the redoubt, as on the evening before, and—who knows?—take it by surprise.

"We absolutely must reduce the inconvenience of those pieces," said Enjolras, and he cried, "Fire on the cannoneers!"

Everyone was ready. The barricade, which had been silent for such a long time, opened fire desperately; seven or eight volleys succeeded each other with a sort of rage and joy; the street was filled with a blinding smoke, and after a few minutes, through this haze pierced by flame, they could confusedly make out two thirds of the cannoneers lying under the wheels of the guns. Those who remained standing continued to serve the pieces with rigid composure, but the fire was slackened.

"This works well," said Bossuet to Enjolras. "Success."

Enjolras shook his head and answered, "A quarter of an hour more of this success, and there won't be ten cartridges in the barricade."

It would seem that Gavroche heard this remark.

XV

GAVROCHE OUTSIDE

Courfeyrac suddenly noticed somebody at the foot of the barricade, outside in the street, under the line of fire.

Gavroche had taken a basket from the wineshop, had gone out through the opening, and was quietly occupied in emptying into his basket the full cartridge boxes of the National Guards who had been killed on the slope of the redoubt.

"What are you doing there?" said Courfeyrac.

Gavroche cocked up his nose.

"Citizen, I'm filling my basket."

"But don't you see the grapeshot?"

Gavroche answered, "So, it's raining. So what?"

Courfeyrac cried out, "Come back!"

"In a bit," said Gavroche.

And he sprang deeper into the street.

It will be remembered that the Fannicot company, on retiring, had left behind them a trail of corpses.

Some twenty dead lay scattered along the whole length of the street on the pavement. Twenty cartridge boxes for Gavroche, a supply of cartridges for the barricade.

The smoke in the street was like a fog. Anyone who has seen a cloud tumble into a mountain gorge between two steep cliffs can imagine this smoke concentrated and as if thickened by two gloomy lines of tall houses. It rose slowly and was constantly renewed; hence a gradual darkening that turned broad daylight dim. The combatants could hardly see each other from one end of the street to the other, although it was very short.

This haze, probably intentional and calculated by the leaders who were to direct the assault on the barricade, was useful to Gavroche.

Under the folds of this veil of smoke, and thanks to his small size, he could go quite far into the street without being seen. He emptied the first seven or eight cartridge boxes without much danger. He crawled on his belly, ran on his hands and feet, held his basket in his teeth, twisted, slid, writhed, wormed his way from one body to another, and emptied a cartridge box as a monkey opens a nut.

From the barricade, though he was still within hearing, they did not dare call him to return, for fear of attracting attention to him.

On one corpse, of a corporal, he found a powder flask.

"In case of thirst," he said as he put it into his pocket.

By successive advances, he reached a point where the fog from the firing became transparent.

So that the sharpshooters of the line drawn up and on the alert behind their wall of paving stones and the sharpshooters of the suburbs massed at the corner of the street suddenly discovered something moving in the smoke.

Just as Gavroche was relieving a sergeant who lay near a stone block of his cartridges, a ball struck the body.

"The devil!" said Gavroche. "There they go, killing my dead for me."

A second bullet splintered the pavement beside him. A third upset his basket.

Gavroche looked and saw that it came from the sharpshooters of the suburbs.

He stood up straight, on his feet, his hair in the wind, his hands on his hips, his eye bracketed on the National Guards who were firing, and he sang,

> On est laid à Nanterre,
> C'est la faute à Voltaire,
> Et bête à Palaiseau,
> C'est la faute à Rousseau.[1]

Then he picked up his basket, put back in, without losing a single one, the cartridges that had fallen out, and, advancing toward the barrage, began to empty another cartridge box. There a fourth bullet just missed him again. Gavroche sang,

> Je ne suis pas notaire,
> C'est la faute à Voltaire;
> Je suis petit oiseau,
> C'est la faute à Rousseau.[2]

A fifth bullet only managed to draw a third couplet from him.

> Joie est mon caractère,
> C'est la faute à Voltaire;
> Misère est mon trousseau,
> C'est la faute à Rousseau.[3]

This went on for some time.

The sight was appalling and fascinating. Gavroche,

[1] They're ugly in Nanterre
because of Voltaire,
and stupid in Palaiseau
because of Rousseau.

[2] I'm no notary
because of Voltaire;
I'm just a sparrow
because of Rousseau.

[3] Joy's my nature
because of Voltaire;
Misery's my trousseau
because of Rousseau.

under fire, was mocking the firing. He seemed to be very much amused. It was the sparrow pecking at the hunters. He replied to each volley with a verse. They aimed at him incessantly, they always missed him. The National Guards and the soldiers laughed as they aimed at him. He lay down, then stood up, hid in a doorway, then sprang out, disappeared, reappeared, escaped, returned, answered the volleys by thumbing his nose, and meanwhile pillaged cartridges, emptied cartridge boxes, and filled his basket. The insurgents, breathless with anxiety, followed him with their eyes. The barricade was trembling; he was singing. It was not a child; it was not a man; it was a strange mystic gamin, the invulnerable dwarf of the mêlée. The bullets ran after him, he was more nimble than they. He was playing an indescribably terrible game of hide-and-seek with death; every time the flat-nosed face of the specter approached, the gamin snapped his fingers.

One bullet, however, better aimed or more treacherous than the others, finally reached the will-o'-the-wisp child. They saw Gavroche totter, then fall. The whole barricade gave a cry; but there was an Antaeus in this pygmy; for the gamin to touch the pavement is like the giant touching the earth; Gavroche had fallen only to rise again; he sat up, a long stream of blood was streaking his face, he raised both arms in the air, looked in the direction the shot had come from, and began to sing,

> Je suis tombé par terre,
> C'est la faute à Voltaire,
> Le nez dans le ruisseau,
> C'est la faute à—[1]

He did not finish. A second bullet from the same marksman cut him short. This time he fell facedown on the pavement and did not stir again. That great little soul had taken flight.

[1] I dropped from the air
because of Voltaire,
to the gutter I go
because of . . .

XVI

HOW BROTHER BECOMES FATHER

At that very moment in the Luxembourg garden—for the eye of the drama should be present everywhere—two children were holding each other by the hand. One might have been seven years old, the other five. Soaked by the earlier rain, they were walking in the paths on the sunny side; the older one was leading the little one; they were pale and in rags; they looked like wild birds. The smaller one said; "I want something to eat."

The elder, already something of the protector, led his brother with his left hand and had a stick in his right.

They were alone in the garden. The garden was empty, the gates had been closed by order of the police on account of the insurrection. The troops that had bivouacked there had been called away because of the combat.

How had these children gotten there? Could they have escaped from some haff-open barracks; was there perhaps in the neighborhood, at the Barrière d'Enfer, or on the esplanade of the Observatoire, or in the neighboring square overlooked by the pediment with the inscription *invenerunt parvulum pannis involutum,* some traveling circus tent they had fled; had they perhaps the evening before evaded the eye of the garden keepers at closing time, and had they spent the night in some one of those nooks where people read the papers? The fact is that they were wandering and that they seemed free. To be wandering and to seem free is to be lost. These poor little ones were lost indeed.

These two children were the same ones Gavroche had worried about, and whom the reader will remember. Children of the Thénardiers, rented out to Magnon, attributed to M. Gillenormand, and now leaves fallen from all these rootless branches and whirled across the ground by the wind.

Their clothing—neat in Magnon's time and which served her as window dressing for M. Gillenormand—had become tatters.

These creatures belonged from then on to the statistics

of "abandoned children," whom the police report, collect, mislay, and find again on the streets of Paris.

It required the commotion of just such a day for these little outcasts to be in this garden. If the officers had noticed them, they would have driven away these rags. Poor children cannot enter the public gardens; still, one would think that, as children, they had a right to the flowers.

They were there thanks to the closed gates. They were in violation of the rules. They had slipped into the garden, and they had stayed there. Closed gates do not dismiss the watchmen; their job is supposed to continue, but it is relaxed and at its ease; and the watchmen, excited too by the public anxiety and busier with matters outside than inside, were no longer paying attention to the garden and had not seen the two delinquents.

It had rained the night before, and even a bit that morning. But in June showers are of no consequence. One can hardly realize, an hour after a storm, that the fine fair day had been rainy. The ground in summer is as quick to dry as a child's cheek.

At this time of the solstice, the light of the full moon is, so to speak, piercing. It seizes everything. It applies itself and spreads over the earth with a sort of suction. It is as though the sun were thirsty. A shower is a glass of water; a rain is immediately swallowed. In the morning everything was streaming, in the afternoon all was dusty.

Nothing is so beautiful as greenery washed by the rain and wiped by the sunbeam; it is warm freshness. The gardens and the meadows, having water at their roots and sunshine in their flowers, become vases of incense, and exhale all their perfumes at once. Everything laughs, sings, and proffers itself. We feel sweet intoxication. Spring is a provisional paradise; sunshine helps to make man patient.

There are people who ask nothing more—living beings who, having the blue sky, say, "That's enough!" Dreamers absorbed in marvel, drawing an indifference to good and evil from idolatry of nature, contemplators of the cosmos radiantly diverted from man, who do not understand how anybody can busy himself with the hunger of these, with the thirst of those, with the nakedness of the poor in winter, with the lymphatic curvature of a little backbone, with pallet, garret, dungeon, the rags of shivering little girls, when he could dream under the trees; peaceful and terrible souls, pitilessly content. Stangely, the infinite is enough for them. This great need of man, the finite, which admits of embrace, they ignore. The finite, which admits of progress, sublime toil, they do not think of. The indefinite, which is born of human and divine combination, of the infinite and the finite, escapes them. Provided they are face to face with immensity, they smile. Never joy, always ecstasy. To lose themselves is their life. To them the history of humanity is only a fragmentary plan. All is not there, the true All still lies beyond; what is the use of busying ourselves with that detail—man? Man suffers, that may be so; but look at Taurus rising! The mother has no milk, the newborn dies, I know nothing about that, but look at this marvelous rosette formed by a transverse section of the sapwood of the fir tree when examined under the microscope! Compare that with the most beautiful springtide! These thinkers forget to love. The zodiac has such success with them that it prevents them from seeing the weeping child. God eclipses the soul. There is a family of such minds, both petty and great. Horace belonged to it, Goethe belonged to it, La Fontaine perhaps; magnificent egotists of the infinite, tranquil spectators of grief, who do not see Nero if the weather is fine, from whom the sunshine hides the stake, who would watch the guillotine at work, looking for an effect of light, who hear neither the cry, nor the sob, nor the last breath, nor the tocsin, to whom all is well, since there is a month of May, who, so long as there are clouds of purple and gold above their heads, declare themselves content, and who are determined to be happy until the light of the stars and the song of the birds are exhausted.

They are of a dark radiance. They do not suspect that they are to be pitied. But they certainly are. He who does not weep does not see. We should admire and pity them, as we would pity and admire a being at once light and darkness, with no eyes under his brows and a star in the middle of his forehead.

In the indifference of these thinkers, according to some, lies a superior philosophy. So be it; but in this superiority there is some infirmity. One may be immortal and a cripple: Vulcan, for instance. One may be more than man and less than man. The immense incomplete exists in nature. Who knows that the sun is not blind?

But then, after all, in whom to trust? *Solem quis dicere falsum audeat?* Thus certain geniuses themselves, certain Most High mortals, men of stars, may have been deceived! What is on high, at the top, at the summit, in the zenith, what sends over the earth so much light, may see little, may see badly, may see nothing! Is that not disheartening? No. But what is there, then, above the sun? The God.

On June 6, 1832, toward eleven o'clock in the morning, the Luxembourg, solitary and unpeopled, was delightful. In the sunlight, the patterns of trees and flowers treated themselves to sweet smells and delights. The branches, wild with the noonday brilliance, seemed to be seeking to embrace each other. In the sycamores there was a chattering of linnets, the sparrows were jubilant, the woodpeckers climbed up the horse chestnuts, tapping with their beaks at the holes in the bark. The flowerbeds accepted the legitimate royalty of the lilies; the most august of perfumes is what comes from such whiteness. You inhaled the spicy odor of the pinks. The old rooks of Marie de Médicis were amorous in the great trees. The sun gilded, crimsoned, and kindled the tulips, which are nothing more nor less than all varieties of flame made flowers. All about the tulip beds whirled the bees, sparks from these flame-flowers. Everything was grace and gaiety, even the coming rain; that old offender, from whom the honeysuckles and lilies of the valley would profit, was not a worry; the swallows flew low, charming menace. Whoever was there breathed happiness; life was sweet; all this nature exhaled candor, help, assistance, paternity, caress, dawn. The thoughts that fell from the sky were as soft as the child's little hand that you kiss.

Under the trees, the statues, bare and white, had robes of shade torn by light; these goddesses were all tattered by the sunshine; it hung from them in shreds on all sides. Around the great basin, the earth was already so dry as to be almost baked. There was enough wind here and there to raise little riots of sand. A few yellow leaves, relics of the last autumn, chased one another joyfully, and seemed to be playing the gamin.

The abundance of light was inexpressibly comforting. Life, sap, warmth, odor, overflowed; beneath creation you felt the enormity of its source; in all these breezes saturated with love, in this coming and going of reflections and reverberations, in this prodigious expenditure of rays, in this indefinite outlay of fluid gold, you felt the prodigality of the inexhaustible; and behind this splendor, as behind a curtain of flame, you caught a glimpse of God, millionaire of the stars.

Thanks to the sand, there was not a trace of mud; thanks to the rain, there was not a speck of dust. The bouquets had just been washed; all the velvets, all the satins, all the enamels, all the golds that spring from the earth in the form of flowers, were irreproachable. This magnificence was tidy. The great silence of happy nature filled the garden. A celestial silence compatible with a thousand melodies, cooings of nests, hummings of swarms, palpitations of the wind. All the harmony of the season was accomplished in a graceful whole; the entrances and exits of spring took place in the desired order; the lilacs ended, the jasmine began; some flowers were belated, some insects in advance; the vanguard of the red butterflies of June fraternized with the rearguard of the white butterflies of May. The plane trees were getting a new skin. The breeze scooped out waves in the magnificent vastness of the horse chestnuts. It was resplendent. A veteran from the adjacent barracks, looking through the iron fence, said, "There is spring under arms, and in full dress."

All nature was breaking its fast; creation was at the table; it was the right time; the great blue cloth was spread in the sky, and the great green over the earth; the sun shone *à giorno*. God was serving up the universal repast. Every creature had its food or its fodder. The ringdove found hempseed, the chaffinch found millet, the goldfinch found chickweed, the redbreast found worms, the bee found flowers, the fly found infusoria, the grosbeak found flies. They ate one another a little, to be sure, which is the mystery of evil mingled with good; but not an animal had an empty stomach.

The two little abandoned creatures were near the great pool, and, slightly disturbed by all this light, they tried to hide, an instinct of the poor and feeble before magnificence, even though impersonal, and they kept behind the shelter for the swans.

Here and there, at intervals, when the wind fell, they

confusedly heard cries, a hum, a kind of tumultuous rattle, which was the musket fire, and dull thuds, which were cannon reports. There was smoke above the roofs in the direction of the markets. A bell, which seemed to be calling, sounded in the distance.

The children did not seem to notice these sounds. The smaller one repeated from time to time in an undertone, "I'm hungry."

At almost the same time as the two children, another couple approached the great basin. This was a man of fifty, who was leading by the hand a man of six. Doubtless a father with his son. The boy had a fat brioche in his hand.

At that time, certain nearby houses, in the Rue Madame and the Rue d'Enfer, had keys to the Luxembourg, which the occupants used when the gates were closed, a favor since discontinued. This father and this son probably came from one of those houses.

The two poor little fellows saw "this Monsieur" coming and hid a little more carefully.

He was a bourgeois. The same, perhaps, whom one day Marius, in spite of his feverish love, had heard near this same great pool, counseling his son to "beware of extremes." He had an affable and lofty manner, and a mouth which, never closed, was always smiling. This automatic smile, produced by too much jaw and too little skin, shows the teeth rather than the soul. The child, with his bitten brioche, which he did not finish, seemed stuffed. The boy was dressed as a National Guard, because of the émeute, and the father remained in civilian clothes for safety's sake.

The father and son had stopped near the pool in which the two swans were sporting. This bourgeois seemed to have a special admiration for the swans. He resembled them in this respect, that he walked like them.

For the moment, the swans were swimming, which is their principal talent, and they were superb.

If the two poor little fellows had listened, and had been of an age to understand, they might have gathered up the words of a grave man. The father said to the son, "The sage lives content with little. Look at me, my son. I do not love pomp. I am never seen in coats decked out with gold and gems; I leave that false splendor to badly organized minds."

Here deep sounds of shouting that came from the direction of the markets broke out with a redoubling of bells and uproar.

"What is that?" asked the child.

The father answered, "It is a saturnalia."

Just then he noticed the two ragamuffins standing motionless behind the green cottage of the swans.

"There is the beginning," he said.

And after a moment, he added, "Anarchy is entering this garden."

Meanwhile the son bit the brioche, spat it out, and suddenly began to cry.

"What are you crying for?" asked the father.

"I'm not hungry anymore,"said the child.

The father's smile broadened.

"You don't need to be hungry, to eat a cake."

"I am sick of my cake. It's stale."

"You don't want any more of it?"

"No."

The father showed him the swans.

"Throw it to those palmipeds."

The child hesitated. Not to want any more of one's cake is no reason for giving it away.

The father continued, "Be humane. We must take pity on the animals."

And, taking the cake from his son, he threw it into the pool.

The cake fell near the edge.

The swans were at some distance away in the center of the basin and busy with some prey. They had seen neither the bourgeois nor the brioche.

The bourgeois, feeling that the cake was in danger of being lost, and aroused by this useless shipwreck, devoted himself to a telegraphic agitation that finally attracted the swans' attention.

They noticed something floating, veered about like the ships they are, and moved slowly toward the bun with that serene majesty that is fitting to white animals.

"*Cygnes* [swans] understand *signes* [signs]," said the bourgeois, delighted at his own wit.

Just then the distant tumult in the city suddenly increased again. This time it was ominous. There are some gusts of wind that speak more distinctly than others. The one that blew at that moment clearly brought the roll of drums, shouts, musket volleys, and the dismal replies of the tocsin and the cannon. This was coincident with a black cloud that abruptly shut out the sun.

The swans had not yet reached the brioche.

"Let's go home," said the father, "they are attacking the Tuileries."

He took his son's hand again. Then he went on, "From the Tuileries to the Luxembourg, there is only the distance separating royalty from the peerage; it is not far. It is going to rain musket balls."

He looked at the cloud.

"And perhaps too the rain itself is going to rain; the heavens are joining in; the younger branch of the Bourbons is condemned. Come on home, quickly."

"I would like to see the swans eat the brioche," said the child.

The father answered, "That would be unwise."

And he led away his little bourgeois.

The son, regretting the swans, turned his head toward the water, until a bend in the rows of trees hid it from him.

Meanwhile, at the same time as the swans, the two little wanderers had approached the bun. It was floating on the water. The smaller one was looking at the brioche, the larger was watching the bourgeois who was going away.

The father and the son entered the labyrinth of walks leading to the grand stairway of the cluster of trees on the side toward the Rue Madame.

As soon as they were out of sight, the older boy quickly lay down with his face over the rounded edge of the pool, and, holding on with his left hand, hanging out over the water, almost falling in, with his right hand reached his stick out toward the cake. The swans, seeing the enemy, made haste, and in making haste produced an effect with their breasts that was useful to the little fisherman; the water flowed away from the swans, and one of those smooth concentric waves pushed the bun gently toward the child's stick. As the swans came up, the stick touched the cake. The child made a quick movement, drew in the brioche, frightened the swans, seized the cake, and got up. The cake was soaked; but they were hungry and thirsty. The eldest broke the brioche in two pieces, one large and one small, took the small one for himself, gave the large one to his little brother, and said to him, "Poke that in your gun."

XVII

MORTUUS PATER FILIUM MORITURUM EXPECTAT

Marius had sprung out of the barricade. Combeferre had followed him. But it was too late. Gavroche was dead. Combeferre brought back the basket of cartridges; Marius brought back the child.

"Alas!" he thought. What the father had done for his father he was returning to the son; only Thénardier had brought back his father alive, while he was bringing back the child dead.

When Marius re-entered the redoubt with Gavroche in his arms, his face, like the child's, was covered with blood.

Just as he had stooped down to pick up Gavroche, a ball grazed his skull; he did not notice it.

Courfeyrac took off his tie and bound up Marius's forehead.

They laid Gavroche on the same table as Mabeuf, and they stretched the black shawl over the two bodies. It was large enough for the old man and the child.

Combeferre distributed the cartridges from the basket he had brought back.

This gave each man fifteen shots.

Jean Valjean was still at the same place, motionless on his block. When Combeferre presented him his fifteen cartridges, he shook his head.

"There is a rare eccentric," said Combeferre softly to Enjolras. "He finds a way not to fight in this barricade."

"Which does not prevent him from defending it," answered Enjolras.

"Heroism has its originals," replied Combeferre.

And Courfeyrac, who had overheard, added, "He is a different kind from Father Mabeuf."

A notable fact: The shots battering the barricade hardly disturbed the interior. Those who have never undergone the whirlwind of this kind of war can have no idea of the strange moments of tranquility mingled with the convulsions. Men come and go, they chat, they joke, they lounge. An acquaintance of ours heard a combatant say to him in the midst of the grapeshot: "This is like a bachelor's breakfast." The redoubt in the Rue de la Chanvrerie, we repeat, seemed very calm inside. Every turn and phase of fortune had been or would soon be exhausted. From critical the position had become threatening, and from threatening it was probably becoming desperate. As the condition of affairs grew gloomy, the heroic glow colored the barricade more and more. Enjolras gravely commanded it, in the attitude of a young Spartan devoting his drawn sword to the somber genius Epidotas.

Combeferre, with an apron at his waist, was dressing the wounded; Bossuet and Feuilly were making cartridges with the flask of powder plucked by Gavroche from the dead corporal, and Bossuet was saying to Feuilly, "We will soon take the stagecoach to another planet"; Courfeyrac, on the few paving stones he had reserved for himself near Enjolras, was laying out and arranging a whole arsenal, his sword cane, his musket, two horse pistols, and a pocket pistol, with the care of a girl who is putting a little workbox in order. Jean Valjean was looking in silence at the opposite wall. A workingman was fastening on his head with a string a large straw hat belonging to Mother Hucheloup, "for fear of sunstroke," he said. The young men of the Cougourde d'Aix were chatting gaily with one another, as if they were anxious to talk patois for the last time. Joly, who had taken down the widow Huchleoup's mirror, was examining his tongue in it. A few combatants, having discovered some crusts of bread, almost moldy, in a drawer, were eating them greedily. Marius was anxious about what his father was going to say to him.

XVIII

THE VULTURE BECOMES PREY

We *must* dwell on a psychological fact, peculiar to barricades. Nothing that characterizes this surprising war of the streets should be omitted.

Whatever might be that strange interior tranquility we have just mentioned, the barricade, for those who are within it, is nonetheless a vision.

There is an apocalypse in civil war, all the mists of the unknown are mingled with these savage flames, revolutions are sphinxes, and whoever has been through a barricade believes he has passed through a dream.

What is felt in those places, as we have indicated in reference to Marius, and as we shall see in what follows, is more and is less than life. Once out of the barricade, a man no longer knows what he has seen inside it. He was mighty; he does not know it. He was surrounded by combating ideas that had human faces; he had his head in the light of the future. There were corpses lying down and phantoms standing up. The hours were colossal and seemed hours of eternity. He lived in death. Shadows passed by. What were they? He saw hands on which there was blood; it was an appalling uproar, it was also a hideous silence; there were open mouths that shouted and other open mouths that held their peace; he was in smoke, in the night, perhaps. He thinks he has touched the ominous ooze of the unknown depths; he sees something red in his nails. He remembers nothing more.

Let us return to the Rue de la Chanvrerie.

Suddenly between two volleys they heard the distant sound of a clock striking.

"It is noon," said Combeferre.

The twelfth stroke had not sounded when Enjolras sprang to his feet and flung down from the top of the barricade this thundering shout:

"Carry some paving stones into the house. Fortify the windows with them. Half the men to the muskets, the other half to the stones. Not a minute to lose."

A platoon of sappers, their axes on their shoulders, had just appeared in battle order at the end of the street.

This could only be the head of a column; and of what column? The column of attack, obviously. The sappers, responsible for demolishing the barricade, must always precede the soldiers whose duty it is to scale it.

They were evidently close to the moment that M. de Clermont-Tonnerre, in 1822, called "the twist of the necklace."

Enjolras's order was executed with the haste peculiar to ships and barricades, the only combat situations where escape is impossible. In less than a minute, two thirds of the paving stones Enjolras had had piled up at the door of Corinth were carried up to the second floor and the garret; and before a second minute had elapsed, these stones, artfully laid one on top of another, walled up half the window on the second floor and the dormer windows of the attic. A few openings, carefully arranged by Feuilly, chief builder, allowed musket barrels to poke through. This armament of the windows could be performed the more easily since the grapeshot had let up. The two cannon were now firing balls at the center of the wall, in order to make a hole, and if possible, a breach for the assault.

When the paving stones, destined for the last defense, were in position, Enjolras had them carry up to the second story the bottles he had placed under the table where Mabeuf was.

"Who will drink that?" Bossuet asked him.

"They will," answered Enjolras.

Then they barricaded the lower window and held in readiness the iron crosspieces used to bar the door of the bistro on the inside at night.

The fortress was complete. The barricade was the rampart, the wineshop was the dungeon keep.

With the remaining paving stones, they closed up the opening beside the barricade.

As the defenders of a barricade are always obliged to husband their ammunition, and as the besiegers know it, the besiegers perfect their arrangements with a sort of provoking leisure, expose themselves to fire ahead of time, but in appearance more than in reality, and relax. The preparations for the attack are always made with a certain methodical slowness, after which the thunderbolt.

This slowness allowed Enjolras to review the whole

picture, and to perfect it. He felt that since such men were to die, their death should be a masterpiece.

He said to Marius, "We're the two leaders; I'll give the last orders inside. You stay outside and watch."

Marius positioned himself for observation on the crest of the barricade.

Enjolras had the door of the kitchen, which, we remember, was the hospital, nailed up.

"No spattering on the wounded," he said.

He gave his last instructions in the lower room in a quick but profoundly calm voice; Feuilly listened, and answered for the rest of them.

"Second floor, keep your axes ready to cut the staircase. Do you have them?"

"Yes," said Feuilly.

"How many?"

"Two axes and a poleax."

"Good. There are twenty-six of us left on our feet."

"How many muskets are there?"

"Thirty-four."

"Eight extra. Keep those eight muskets loaded like the rest, and at hand. Swords and pistols in your belts. Twenty men to the barricade. Six in ambush at the dormer windows and at the second-story window to fire down on the assailants through the loopholes in the paving stones. There can't be a single wasted movement here. The moment the drum beats the charge, the twenty downstairs must rush to the barricade. The first there will get the best places."

With these orders carried out, he turned to Javert, and said, "I won't forget you."

And, laying a pistol on the table, he added, "The last man to leave this room will blow out the spy's brains!"

"Here?" inquired a voice.

"No, let's not leave this corpse with ours. You can climb over the little barricade on the Rue Mondétour. It's only four feet high. The man is well tied up. Take him there, and execute him there."

There was one man, at that moment, who was more impassive than Enjolras; it was Javert.

At this point, Jean Valjean appeared.

He was among the insurgents. He stepped forward, and said to Enjolras, "You are the commander?"

"Yes."

"You thanked me just now."

"In the name of the Republic. The barricade has two saviors, Marius Pontmercy and you."

"Do you think I deserve a reward?"

"Certainly."

"Well, I have one to ask."

"What?"

"To blow out that man's brains myself."

Javert raised his head, saw Jean Valjean, made an imperceptible movement, and said, "That is appropriate."

As for Enjolras, he had begun to reload his carbine; he glanced around him: "No objection."

And turning to Jean Valjean: "Take the informer."

Jean Valjean, in fact, took possession of Javert by sitting down on the end of the table. He caught up the pistol, and a slight click announced that he had cocked it.

Almost at that very moment, they heard a flourish of trumpets.

"Here they come!" shouted Marius, from the top of the barricade.

Javert began to laugh with that peculiar noiseless laugh of his, and, looking steadily at the insurgents, said to them, "You're not much healthier than I."

"Outside, everyone!" cried Enjolras.

The insurgents sprang forward in a cluster and on their way out they got in the back, allow us the expression, this final word from Javert: "We'll meet again soon!"

XIX

JEAN VALJEAN TAKES HIS REVENGE

When Jean Valjean was alone with Javert, he untied the rope holding the prisoner by the middle of the body, whose knot was under the table. Then he motioned to him to get up.

Javert obeyed, with that undefinable smile bearing the essence of supremacy of enchained authority.

Jean Valjean took Javert by the martingale as you would take a beast of burden by the harness, and, tugging him along after him, went out of the bistro slowly, for with his legs fettered, Javert could take only very short steps.

Jean Valjean had the pistol in his hand.

This way they crossed the interior trapezoid of the barricade. The insurgents, intent on the imminent attack, were looking the other way.

Marius alone, positioned at the left end of the wall, saw them go by. This group of victim and executioner took a light from the sepulchral gleam in his soul.

With some difficulty, bound as Javert was, but without letting go of him for a single instant, Jean Valjean made him scale the little barricade on the Rue Mondétour.

When they had climbed over this wall, they found themselves alone in the little street. Nobody could see them now. The corner of the house hid them from insurgents. A few steps away, the corpses carried out of the barricades made a terrible mound.

Among the heap of dead, they saw a livid face, a flowing head of hair, a wounded hand, and a woman's breast half naked. It was Eponine.

Javert glanced sidelong at this dead body and, perfectly calm, said in an undertone, "It seems to me I know that girl."

Then he turned toward Jean Valjean.

Jean Valjean put the pistol under his arm, and glared at Javert with a look that had no need of words to say, "Javert, it is I."

Javert answered.

"Take your revenge."

Jean Valjean took a knife out of his pocket, and opened it.

"A *surin!*" exclaimed Javert. "You're right. That suits you better."

Jean Valjean cut the martingale that Javert had about his neck, then he cut the ropes on his wrists, then, stooping down, he cut the cord on his feet; and standing up, he said to him, "You are free."

Javert was not easily astonished. Still, complete master of himself as he was, he could not escape an emotion. He stood aghast and motionless.

Jean Valjean continued. "I don't expect to leave this place. Still, if by any chance I do, I live, under the name of Fauchelevent, in the Rue de l'Homme-Armé, Number Seven."

Javert scowled like a tiger half opening the corner of his mouth, and he muttered between his teeth, "Take care."

"Go on," said Jean Valjean.

Javert went on, "You said Fauchelevent, Rue de l'Homme-Armé?"

"Number Seven."

Javert repeated in an undertone, "Number Seven." He buttoned his coat, resumed the military rigidity between his shoulderblades, turned half around, crossed his arms, supporting his chin with one hand, and walked off in the direction of the markets. Jean Valjean followed him with his eyes. After a few steps, Javert turned back, and shouted to Jean Valjean, "You irritate me. Kill me instead."

Javert did not notice that his tone was now more respectful toward Jean Valjean.

"Go away," said Jean Valjean.

Javert receded slowly. A moment later he turned the corner of the Rue des Prêcheurs.

When Javert was gone, Jean Valjean fired the pistol in the air.

The he re-entered the barricade and said, "Done."

Meanwhile what had taken place is this:

Busy with the street rather than the wineshop, Marius had not until then looked attentively at the spy bound in the dusky rear of the basement room.

When he saw him in broad daylight clambering over the barricade on his way to die, he recognized him. A sudden memory came to his mind. He remembered the inspector of the Rue de Pontoise, and the two pistols he had handed him and which he had used, he, Marius, in this very barricade; and not only did he recollect the face, he also recalled the name.

This memory, however, was misty and indistinct, like all his ideas. It was not an affirmation he was making to himself, it was a question: "Isn't this that police inspector who told me his name was Javert?"

Perhaps there was still time to intervene for this man? But he would first have to know if it were indeed that Javert.

Marius called to Enjolras, who had just taken his place at the other end of the barricade.

"Enjolras!"

"What?"

"What's that man's name?"

"Who?"

"The police officer. Do you know his name?"

"Of course. He told us."

"What is his name?"

"Javert."

Marius sprang up.

At that very moment they heard the pistol shot.

Jean Valjean reappeared and called out, "Done."

A dreary chill passed through Marius's heart.

XX

THE DEAD ARE RIGHT AND THE LIVING ARE NOT WRONG

The death throes of the barricade were approaching.

All things concurred in the tragic majesty of this supreme moment; a thousand mysterious clashes in the air, the breath of armed masses set in motion in streets they could not see, the intermittent gallop of cavalry, the heavy concussion of artillery on the march, the platoon volleys, and cannonades crisscrossing in the labyrinth of Paris, the smoke of battle rising all golden above the rooftops, mysterious cries, remote, vaguely terrible flashes of menace everywhere, the tocsin of Saint-Merry which had taken on the sound of sobbing, the sweetness of the season, the splendor of the sky full of sunshine and clouds, the beauty of the day, and the appalling silence of the houses.

For, since evening, the two rows of houses in the Rue de la Chanvrerie had become two walls; savage walls. Doors closed, windows closed, shutters closed.

In those days, so different from our own, when the time had come that the people wanted to make an end of a state of affairs that had lasted too long, of a granted charter or of a constitutional country, when universal anger was abroad in the atmosphere, when the city consented to the ripping up of its paving, when insurrection made the bourgeoisie smile by whispering its password, then the inhabitant filled with émeute, so to speak, was the auxiliary of the combatant, and the house fraternized with the impromptu fortress that leaned against it. When the condition of affairs was not ripe, when the insurrection was not decidedly accepted, when the mass disavowed the movement, it was all over for the combatants, the city changed into a desert around the revolt, souls were chilled, refuges were walled up, and the street became a corridor to help the army in taking the barricade.

A people cannot be surprised into more rapid progress than it wants. Woe to him who attempts to force its hand! A people cannot be pushed around. Then it abandons the insurrection to its own devices. The insurgents become pariahs. A house is an escarpment, a door is a refusal, a fuçade is a wall. This wall sees, hears, and does not want. It could open up and save you. No. This wall is a judge. It looks upon you and condemns you. How somber these closed houses are! They seem dead, they are living. Life, which is as if suspended in them, still exists. Nobody has come out of them for twenty-four hours, but nobody is missing. In the interior of this rock, people come and go, they go to bed, they get up; they are at home there; they eat and drink, they are afraid there, a terrifying thing! Fear excuses this terrible inhospitality; it tempers it with timidity, a mitigating circumstance. Sometimes even, and this has been seen, fear becomes passion; fright may change to fury, as prudence to rage; hence this saying so profound: "The extremists of moderation." There are conflagrations of supreme dismay giving off rage like a dismal smoke. "What do these people want? They are never pleased. They compromise peaceable men. As if there were not enough revolution as it is! What did they come here for? Let them get out of it themselves. So much the worse for them. It's their own fault. They only got what they deserve. It doesn't concern us. Here is our poor street riddled with bullets. They're a bunch of good-for-nothings. Above all, don't open the door." And the house takes on the look of a tomb. The insurgent in front of that door is breathing his last; he sees the grapeshot and drawn sabers coming; if he calls out, he knows that they hear him, but that they will not come; there are walls that might protect him, there are men who might save him; and those walls have ears of flesh, and those men have bowels of stone.

Whom shall he accuse?

Nobody, and everybody.

The imperfect age in which we live.

It is always at her own risk and peril that Utopia transforms herself into insurrection, and from a philosophic protest becomes an armed protest, from Minerva, Pallas. The Utopia that grows impatient and turns into riot knows what awaits her; almost always she is too soon. Then she resigns herself and stoically accepts, instead of triumph, catastrophe. She serves, without complaining, and even exonerating them, those who deny her, and it is her magnanimity to consent to desertion. She is indomitable against hindrance and gentle toward ingratitude.

But is it actually ingratitude?

Yes, from the point of view of the human race.

No, from the point of view of the individual.

Progress is the mode of man. The general life of the human race is called Progress; the collective advance of the human race is called Progress. Progress marches on; it makes the great human and terrestrial journey toward the celestial and divine; it has its halts where it rallies the belated flock; it has its pauses where it meditates, in sight of some splendid Canaan suddenly unveiling its horizon; it has its nights when it sleeps; and it is one of the bitter anxieties of the thinker to see the shadow over the human soul, and to feel progress asleep in the darkness, without being able to waken it.

"Perhaps God is dead," said Gérard de Nerval one day, to the writer of these lines, confusing progress with God, and mistaking the interruption of the movement for the death of the Being.

He who despairs is wrong. Progress infallibly wakes up, and, in short, we might say that it advances even in sleep, for it has grown. When we see it upright again, we find it taller. To be always peaceful belongs to progress no more than to the river; raise no obstruction, throw in no rocks; the obstacle makes water foam and humanity seethe. Hence troubles; but after these troubles, we recognize that there has been some ground gained. Until order, which is nothing more nor less than universal peace, is established, until harmony and unity reign, progress will have revolutions for way stations.

What then is progress? We have just said. The enduring life of the peoples.

Now, it sometimes happens that the momentary life of individuals offers resistance to the eternal life of the human race.

Let us acknowledge it without bitterness, the individual has his distinct interest and may without offense announce that interest and defend it: The present has its excusable quantum of selfishness; the life of the moment has its rights and is not bound to sacrifice itself continually to the future. The generation now having its passing turn on earth is not compelled to abridge it for the generations, its equals after all, that will have their turn afterward. "I exist," murmurs that somebody whose name is Everyone. "I'm young and I'm in love, I'm old and I want to rest, I'm the father of a family, I'm working, I'm prospering, I'm doing a good business, I have houses to rent, I have money in the government, I'm happy, I have a wife and children, I love all this, I desire to live, leave me alone." Hence, at certain periods, a deep chill on the magnanimous vanguard of the human race.

Utopia, moreover, we must admit, departs from its radiant sphere in making war. The truth of tomorrow, she borrows her process, battle, from yesterday's lie. She, the future, acts like the past. She, the pure idea, becomes an act of force. She compromises her heroism by a violence for which she should justly answer; a violence of opportunity and expediency, contrary to principles, and for which she is fatally punished. Utopia in revolt fights the old military code in her hand; she shoots spies, she executes traitors, she eliminates living beings and casts them into the unknown dark. She uses death, a solemn thing. It seems as though Utopia had lost faith in the radiation of light, her irresistible and incorruptible strength. She strikes with the sword. But no sword is simple. Every blade has two edges; he who wounds with one wounds himself with the other.

This reservation made, and made in all severity, it is impossible for us not to admire, successful or not, the glorious combatants of the future, the professors of Utopia. Even when they fail, they are venerable, and it is perhaps in failure that they have the greater majesty. Victory, when it is according to progress, deserves the applause of the peoples; but a heroic defeat deserves their compassion. One is magnificent, the other is sublime. For ourselves, who prefer martyrdom to success, John

Brown is greater than Washington, and Pisacane is greater than Garibaldi.

Surely some must be on the side of the vanquished.

Men are unjust toward these great pioneers of the future when they fail.

The revolutionaries are accused of striking terror. Every barricade seems an outrage. Their theories are incriminated, their aim is suspected, their afterthought is dreaded, their conscience is denounced. They are reproached with raising, building, and heaping up against the reigning social state a mound of miseries, of sorrows, of iniquities, of plaints, of despairs, and with tearing up blocks of darkness from the lower depths with which to entrench themselves and to fight. Men cry out to them, "You're unpaving hell!" They might answer, "That's why our barricade is made of good intentions."

The best, certainly, is the peaceable solution. On the whole, let us admit, when we see the paving block, we think of the bear, and his is a will about which society is not at ease. But the salvation of society depends on itself; to its own will, we appeal. No violent remedy is necessary. Study evil lovingly, verify it, then cure it. That is what we urge.

However that may be, even when fallen, particularly when fallen, august are the ones who, all around the world, with eyes fixed on France, struggle for the great work with the inflexible logic of the ideal; they give their life as a pure gift for progress; they accomplish the will of Providence; they perform a religious act. At the appointed hour, with all the disinterestedness of an actor reaching his cue, obedient to the divine scenario, they enter the tomb. And this hopeless combat, and this stoic disappearance, they accept in order to lead to its splendid and supreme universal consequences the magnificent movement of man, irresistibly begun on the 14th of July 1789; these soldiers are priests. The French Revolution is an act of God.

Still, there are—and it is proper to add this distinction to the distinctions already indicated in another chapter—there are accepted insurrections that are called revolutions; there are rejected revolutions that are called émeutes. An insurrection breaking out is an idea undergoing its examination before the people. If the people drops its black ball, the idea is withered fruit; the insurrection is a brawl.

To go to war at every summons and whenever Utopia desires it is not the part of the people. The nations do not have always and at every instant the temperament of heroes and martyrs.

They are positive. A priori, insurrection repels them: first, because it often results in catastrophe; second, because it always has an abstraction for its point of departure.

For, and this is beautiful, it is always for the ideal, and for the ideal alone, that those who dedicate themselves repeatedly do so. An insurrection is an enthusiasm. Enthusiasm may work itself into anger—hence the resort to arms. But every insurrection that takes aim at a government or a regime aims still higher. Thus, for instance, let us repeat that what the leaders of the insurrection of 1832, and particularly the young enthusiasts of the Rue de la Chanvrerie, fought against, was not exactly Louis-Philippe. Frankly, most of them honored the qualities of this king, midway between monarchy and revolution; none hated him. But they were attacking the younger branch of divine right in Louis-Philippe as they had attacked the elder branch in Charles X; and what they desired to stamp out in overthrowing royalty in France, as we have explained, was the usurpation of man over man, and of privilege over right, in the whole world. Paris without a king means, as a consequence, the world without despots. They reasoned in this way. Their aim was undoubtedly remote, vague perhaps, and receding before effort, but great.

That is the way it is. And men sacrifice themselves for these visions, which, to the sacrificed, are illusions almost always, but illusions with which, on the whole, all human certainty is mingled. The insurgent poetizes and gilds the insurrection. He throws himself into these tragic things, intoxicated with what he is going to do. Who knows? Perhaps they will succeed. They are few; they have against them a whole army; but they are defending right, natural law—that sovereignty of each over himself, that tolerates no abdication—justice, truth, and in case of need they die like the three hundred Spartans. This suggests not Don Quixote but Leonidas. And they go forward, and, once engaged, they never retreat, they hurl themselves headlong, hoping for unparalleled victory, consummated revolution, progress set free, the aggrandizement of the human race, universal deliverance; and seeing at worst a Thermopylae.

These jousts for progress often fail, and we have just said why. The throng is restive under the sway of the paladins. The heavy masses, the multitudes, fragile because of their very weight, dread uncertainties; and there is uncertainty in the ideal.

Moreover, let it not be forgotten, interests are there, scarcely friendly to the ideal and the emotional. Sometimes the stomach paralyzes the heart.

The grandeur and beauty of France are that she cares less for the belly than other peoples; she knots the rope about her loins more easily. She is first awake, last asleep. She marches in the lead. She is a pioneer.

That is because she is an artist.

The ideal is nothing more nor less than the culminating point of logic, even as the beautiful is nothing more nor less than the summit of the true. The artist people is therefore the consistent people. To love beauty is to see light. This is why the torch of Europe, that is to say, civilization, was first borne by Greece, who passed it to Italy, who passed it to France. Divine pioneer peoples! *Vitai lampada tradunt!*

An admirable thing, the poetry of a people is the gauge of its progress. The quantity of civilization is measured by the quantity of imagination. Except that a civilizing people must remain a manly people. Corinth, yes; Sybaris, no. He who becomes effeminate becomes corrupt. We must be neither dilettantes nor virtuosos; but we must be artists. In the matter of civilization, we must not refine, but we must attain to the sublime. On this condition, we give the human race the pattern of the ideal.

The modern ideal has its model in art, and its means in science. It is through science that we shall realize that august vision of the poets: social beauty. We shall reproduce Eden by A+B. At the point civilization has reached, the exact is a necessary element of the splendid, and the artistic sentiment is not merely served, but completed by the scientific organ; dream must calculate. Art, which is the conqueror, must bear on science, which is the mover. The solidity of the base is important. The modern spirit is the genius of Greece with the genius of India for its vehicle: Alexander on the elephant.

Races petrified in dogma or demoralized by lucre are unfit to lead civilization. Genuflection before the idol or the dollar atrophies the muscle which moves and the will which goes. Hieratic or mercantile absorption diminishes the radiance of a people, lowers its horizon by lowering its level, and deprives it of that intelligence of the universal aim, at the same time human and divine, which makes the missionary nations. Babylon has no ideal. Carthage has no ideal. Athens and Rome have and preserve, even through all the dense night of centuries, haloes of civilization.

France is of the same quality of people as Greece and Italy. She is Athenian via the beautiful, and Roman via the great. In addition she is good. She gives herself. She is more often than other peoples in the spirit of devotion and sacrifice. Except that this spirit takes her and leaves her. And here lies the great peril for those who run when she wishes to walk, or who walk when she wishes to stop. France has her relapses of materialism, and, at certain moments, the ideas that obstruct that sublime brain lack anything that recalls French greatness, and take on the dimensions of a Missouri or a South Carolina. What is to be done? The giantess is playing the dwarf; immense France has her childish whims. That is all.

To this nothing can be said. A people, like a star, has the right of eclipse. And all is well, provided the light returns and the eclipse does not degenerate into night. Dawn and resurrection are synonyms. The reappearance of the light is identical with the persistence of the self.

Let us admit these things calmly. Death on the barricade, or a grave in exile, are acceptable alternatives for dedication. The true name of dedication is disinterestedness. Let the abandoned submit to abandonment, let the exile submit to exile, and let us content ourselves with imploring the great peoples not to recede too far, when they do recede. They must not, under pretext of a return to reason, go too far in the descent.

Matter exists, the moment exists, interest exists, the belly exists, but the belly must not be the only wisdom. The momentary life has its rights, we admit, but the permanent life has its own as well. Alas! To have risen does not prevent falling. We see this in history more often than we would wish. A nation is illustrious; it tastes the ideal; then it bites the filth, and finds it good; and if we ask why it abandons Socrates for Falstaff, it answers, "Because I love statesmen."

One more word before returning to the fray.

A battle like the one we are now describing is nothing but a convulsive movement toward the ideal. Fettered progress is sickly, and it has these tragic epilepsies. The disease of progress, civil war, we have had to encounter along our way. It is one of the fatal phases, at once act and intermission, of this drama whose pivot is a social outcast, and whose true title is *Progress*.

Progress!

This frequent cry is our encompassing thought; and, at the present point of this drama, the idea that it contains still having more than one ordeal to undergo, we are perhaps permitted, if not to lift its veil, then at least to let the light clearly shine through it.

The book the reader has now before his eyes—from one end to the other, in its whole and in its details, whatever the omissions, the exceptions, or the faults—is the march from evil to good, from injustice to justice, from the false to the true, from night to day, from appetite to conscience, from rottenness to life, from brutality to duty, from Hell to Heaven, from nothingness to God. Starting point: matter; goal: the soul. Hydra at the beginning, angel at the end.

XXI

THE HEROES

Suddenly the drum beat the charge.

The attack was a hurricane. The evening before, in the dark, the barricade had been approached silently as if by a boa constrictor. Now, in broad daylight, in this open street, surprise was completely impossible; the strong hand, moreover, was unmasked, the cannon had started up the roar, the army rushed on the barricade. Fury was now skill. A powerful column of infantry of the line, intersected at equal intervals by National Guards and Municipal Guards on foot, and supported by deep masses heard but unseen, turned into the street at quick step, drums beating, trumpets sounding, bayonets fixed, sappers at their head, and, unswerving under the projectiles, came straight to the barricade with the weight of a bronze column against a wall.

The wall held well.

The insurgents fired impetuously. The barricade scaled had a mane of lightning flashes. The assault was so sudden that for a moment it was overflowing with assailants, but it shook off the soldiers as the lion does the dogs, and it was covered with besiegers only as a cliff with foam, to reappear, a moment later, steep, black, and imposing.

The column, compelled to fall back, remained massed in the street, unsheltered but awesome, and replied to the redoubt by a mighty fusillade. Whoever has seen fireworks remembers that sheaf made by a crossing of flashes that is called the bouquet. Imagine that bouquet, not vertical now, but horizontal, bearing a ball, a buckshot, or a bullet, at the tip of each of its jets of fire, and scattering death in its clusters of thunder. The barricade was faced with that.

Equal resolution on both sides. Bravery there was almost barbaric, and was mingled with a sort of heroic ferocity that began with the sacrifice of self. Those were the days when a National Guard fought like a Zouave. The troops wanted to make an end of it; the insurrection wanted to struggle on. The acceptance of death in full youth and in full health makes a frenzy of courage. Every man in this mêlée felt a magnitude bestowed by the supreme hour. The street was covered with dead.

Enjolras was at one end of the barricade and Marius at the other. Enjolras, who carried the whole barricade in his head, reserved and sheltered himself; three soldiers fell one after the other under his battlement, without even having noticed him; Marius fought without shelter. He provided a target, with more than half his body above the summit of the redoubt. There is no wilder prodigal than a miser who takes the bit in his teeth; there is no man more fearful in action than a dreamer. Marius was terrible and pensive. He was in the battle as in a dream. One would have thought him a phantom firing a musket.

The cartridges of the besieged were running low—not so their sarcasms. In this whirlwind of the sepulcher in which they were, they laughed.

Courfeyrac was bareheaded.

"Whatever have you done with your hat?" inquired Bossuet.

Courfeyrac answered, "They've knocked it off at last with their barrage."

Or else they said haughty things.

"Does anybody understand these men," exclaimed Feuilly bitterly (and he cited the names, well-known names, fumous even, some of the old army), "who promised to join us, and took an oath to help us, and who were bound to it in honor, and who are our generals, and who abandon us!"

And Combeferre simply answered with a grave smile, "There are people who observe the rules of honor as we observe the stars, from far off."

The interior of the barricade was so strewn with torn cartridges that one would have sald it had been snowing.

The assailants had the numbers; the insurgents the position. They were on the top of a wall, and they shot down the soldiers point-blank, as they stumbled over the dead and wounded and became entangled in the escarpment. This barricade, built as it was, and admirably buttressed, was really one of those positions in which a handful of men hold a legion in check. Still, constantly reinforced and increasing under the shower of cannonballs, the attacking column inexorably approached, and now, little by little, step by step, but with certainty, the army squeezed the barricade as the screw squeezes the winepress.

The assaults came one after the other. The horror continued to increase, then burst out over this pile of paving stones, in this Rue de la Chanvrerie, a struggle worthy of the walls of Troy. These men—wan, tattered, and exhausted, who had not eaten for twenty-four hours, who had not slept, who had only a few more shots left to fire, who felt their pockets empty of cartridges, nearly all wounded, their heads or arms bound with a smutty blackened cloth, with holes in their coats where the blood was flowing, scarcely armed with worthless muskets and old hacked swords—became Titans: The barricade was ten times approached, assaulted, scaled, and never taken.

To get some idea of this struggle, imagine fire applied

to a mass of awesome courage, and that you are witnessing the conflagration. It was not a combat, it was the interior of a furnace; mouths were breathing flame; their faces were extraordinary. There the human form seemed impossible, the combatants flashed flames, and it was terrible to see coming and going in that lurid smoke these salamanders of the fray. The successive simultaneous scenes of this grand slaughter, we won't attempt to paint. Only the epic has the right to fill twelve thousand lines with one battle.

One would have thought it was that hell of Brahminism, the most formidable of the seventeen abysses, which the Veda calls the Forest of Swords.

They fought hand to hand, tooth and nail, foot to foot, with pistols, with sabers, with fists, at a distance, close up, from above, from below, from everywhere, from the rooftops, from the windows of the bistro, from the gratings of the cellars into which some had slipped. They were one against sixty. The façade of Corinth, half demolished, was hideous. The window, riddled with grapeshot had lost glass and sash, reduced to nothing but a shapeless hole, confusedly blocked up with paving stones. Bossuet was killed; Feuilly was killed; Courfeyrac was killed; Joly was killed; Combeferre, pierced by three bayonet thrusts in the chest, just as he was lifting a wounded soldier, had only time to look to heaven, and expired.

Marius, still fighting, was so hacked with wounds, particularly about his head, that his features were lost in blood, and you would have said that he had his face covered with a red handkerchief.

Enjolras alone was untouched. When his weapon failed, he reached his hand to right or left, and an insurgent put whatever weapon he could in his grasp. Of four swords, one more than Francis I at Marignan, he was left with only one stump.

Homer says, "Diomed slays Axylus, son of Teuthras, who dwelt in happy Arisbe; Euryalus, son of Mecisteus, exterminates Dresos and Opheltios, Aesepus, and that Pedasus whom the Naiaid Abarbarea conceived by the irreproachable Bucolion; Ulysses overthrows Pidutes of Percote; Antilochus, Ablerus; Polypaetes, Astyalus; Polydamas, Otus of Cyllene; and Teucer, Aretaon. Meganthis dies beneath the spear of Euripylus. Agamemnon,

King of heroes, prostrates Elatus born in the lofty city that the sounding Satnois bathes." In our old poems of exploits, the *chansons de gestes,* Esplandian attacks the giant Marquis Swantibore with a two-edged flame, while he defends himself by stoning the knight with the towers that he tears up. Our ancient mural frescoes show us the two dukes of Brittany and of Bourbon, armed, mailed, and crested for war, on horseback, and meeting each other, battle-ax in hand, masked with iron, booted with iron, gloved with iron, one caparisoned with ermine, the other draped with azure; Brittany with his lion between the two horns of his crown, Bourbon with a monstrous fleur-de-lis on the visor of his casque. But to be superb, it is not necessary to bear, like Yvon, the ducal morion, to have in fist, like Esplandian, a living flame, or like Phyles, father of Polydamas, to have brought from Ephyrae a fine armor, a present from the king of men, Euphetes; it is enough to give life for a conviction or for a loyalty. That naïve little soldier, yesterday a peasant in Beauce or Limousin, who prowls, cabbage knife at his side, around the children's nurses in the Luxembourg, that pale young student bent over a piece of anatomy or a book, a fair-haired youth who trims his beard with scissors, take them both, breathe on them a breath of duty, place them opposite each other in the Boucherat Square or the Cul-de-sac Blanche-Mibray, and let the one fight for his flag, and the other for his ideal, and let them both imagine they are fighting for the country; the strife will be colossal; and the shadow that will be thrown on that great epic field where humanity is struggling, by this bluecoat and this sawbones at each other's throats, will equal the shadow cast by Megaryon, King of Lycia, full of tigers, wrestling body to body with the immense Ajax, equal of the gods.

XXII

STEP BY STEP

When none of the leaders were left except Enjolras and Marius, who were at the extreme ends of the barricade, the center, which Courfeyrac, Joly, Bossuet, Feuilly, and

Combeferre had so long sustained, gave way. Without making an actual breach, the artillery had deeply indented the center of the redoubt; there, the summit of the wall had disappeared under the bullet, and had tumbled down; and the debris that had fallen, sometimes on the inside, sometimes on the outside, had finally made, as it was heaped up on either side of the wall, a kind of slope, one on the inside, one on the outside. The exterior talus offered an inclined plane for attack.

A final assault was now attempted, and this one succeeded. The mass, bristling with bayonets and hurled at a double-quick step, came on irresistibly, and the dense battle front of the attacking column appeared in the smoke at the top of the escarpment. This time, it was over. The group of insurgents who defended the center fell back pell-mell.

Then grim love of life was roused in some. Covered by the aim of that forest of muskets, several were now unwilling to die. This is a moment when the instinct of self-preservation raises a howl, and the animal reappears in the man. They were pushed back to the tall six-story house that formed the rear of the redoubt. This house might be safety. This house was barricaded and, as it were, walled in from top to bottom. Before the troops of the line would be in the interior of the redoubt, there was time for a door to open and shut, a flash was enough for that, and the door of this house, suddenly half opened and immediately closed again, to these despairing men meant life. Behind this house, there were streets, possible flight, space. They began to strike this door with the butts of their muskets, and with kicks, calling, shouting, begging, wringing their hands. Nobody opened. From the window on the third story, the death's head looked at them.

But Enjolras and Marius, with seven or eight who had rallied around them, sprang forward and protected them. Enjolras shouted to the soldiers, "Keep back!" and, an officer not obeying, Enjolras killed him. He was now in the little interior court of the redoubt, with his back to the house of Corinth, his sword in one hand, his carbine in the other, keeping the door of the wineshop open while he barred it against the assailants. He cried to the despairing, "There is only one door open. This one." And, covering them with his body, alone facing a battalion, he had them pass in behind him. They all rushed in. Enjolras, executing with his carbine, which he was now using as a cane, what fencers call *la rose couverte,* beat down the bayonets around him and in front of him, and entered last of all; for an instant it was a nightmare, the soldiers struggling to get in, the insurgents struggling to close the door. The door was closed with such violence that, in jamming into its frame, it displayed—cut off, and adhering to the casement—the thumb and fingers of a soldier who had caught hold of it.

Marius had stayed outside. A shot had broken his shoulder blade; he felt that he was fainting, that he was falling. At that moment, his eyes already closed, he experienced the shock of a vigorous hand seizing him, and his fainting fit, in which he lost consciousness, left him hardly time for this thought, mingled with the last memory of Cosette: "I'm being taken prisoner. I am to be shot."

Enjolras, not seeing Marius among those who had taken refuge in the wineshop, had the same idea. But they had reached that moment when each has only time to think of his own death. Enjolras secured the bar of the door and bolted it, and fastened it with a double turn of lock and key, while they were beating furiously on the outside, the soldiers with the butts of their muskets, the sappers with their axes. The assailants were massed against this door. The siege of the bistro was now beginning.

The soldiers, we must say, were greatly irritated.

The death of the artillery sergeant had angered them; and then, a more deadly thing, during the few hours preceding the attack, it had been heard among them that the insurgents mutilated prisoners, and that in the bistro there was the body of a headless soldier. This sort of unfortunate rumor is the ordinary accompaniment of civil wars, and it was a false report of this kind that later caused the catastrophe of the Rue Transnonain.

When the door was barricaded, Enjolras said to the rest, "Let's sell ourselves dearly."

Then he went over to the table where Mabeuf and Gavroche were lying. Two straight and rigid forms could be seen under the black cloth, one large, the other small, and the two faces were vaguely outlined beneath the stiff folds of the shroud. A hand projected from below the pall and hung toward the floor. It was the old man's.

Enjolras bent down and kissed that venerable hand, as the evening before he had kissed the forehead.

They were the only kisses he had given in his life.

We must be brief. The barricade had struggled like a gate of Thebes; Corinth struggled like a house of Saragossa. Such resistance is dogged. No quarter. No parley possible. They are willing to die provided they kill. When Suchet says, "Capitulate," Palafox answers, "After the war with cannon, war with the knife." Nothing was lacking in the storming of the Hucheloup bistro: neither the paving stones raining from the window and the roof onto the besiegers, and exasperating the soldiers by their horrible mangling, nor the shots from the cellars and the garret windows, nor fury of attack, nor rage of defense; nor, finally, when the door yielded, the frenzied madness of extermination. The assailants, on rushing into the wineshop, their feet tangled in the panels of the door, which were beaten in and scattered over the floor, found no combatant there. The spiral stairway, which had been cut down with the ax, lay in the middle of the low room, a few wounded had just died, all who were not killed were on the second floor, and there, through the hole in the ceiling, which had been the entrance for the stairway, a terrific barrage broke out. It was the last of the cartridges. When they were gone, when these terrible men in their death agony had no more powder or ball, each took two of those bottles reserved by Enjolras, of which we have spoken, and they defended the ascent with these frightfully fragile clubs. They were bottles of nitric acid. We give these gloomy facts of the carnage just as they are. The besieged, alas, make a weapon of everything. Greek fire did not dishonor Archimedes, boiling pitch did not dishonor Bayard. All war is appalling, and there is nothing to choose in it. The fire of the besiegers, although difficult and from below upward, was murderous. The edge of the hole in the ceiling was very soon surrounded with the heads of the dead, flowing with long red and steaming streams. The uproar was inexpressible; a confined and burning smoke cast almost total darkness over the combat. Words fail to express horror when it reaches this degree. There were no men left in this now infernal conflict. They were no longer giants against colossi. It was more like Milton and Dante than Homer. Demons attacked, specters resisted.

It was the heroism of monsters.

XXIII

ORESTES FASTING AND PYLADES DRUNK

At last, climbing on each other's shoulders, helping themselves by the skeleton of the staircase, climbing up the walls, hanging to the ceiling, cutting to pieces at the very edge of the hatchway the last resistants, some twenty of the besiegers, soldiers, National Guards, Municipal Guards, pell-mell, most of them disfigured by wounds in the face in this terrible ascent, blinded with blood, furious, become savages, burst into the second-floor room. There was now only one single man there on his feet, Enjolras. Without cartridges, without a sword, he had remaining in his hand only the barrel of his carbine, whose stock he had broken over the heads of those coming in. He had put the billiard table between the assailants and himself; he had retreated to the corner of the room, and there, with proud eye, haughty head, and that stump of a weapon in his grasp, he was still so formidable that a large space was left around him. A cry went up: "This is the leader. He's the one who killed the artilleryman. Since he's put himself there, it's a good place. Let him stay. Let's shoot him on the spot."

"Shoot me," said Enjolras.

And, throwing away the stump of his carbine, and crossing his arms, he presented his breast.

The audacity to die well always moves men. The moment Enjolras had crossed his arms, accepting the end, the uproar of the conflict in the room and all that chaos suddenly hushed into a sort of sepulchral solemnity. It seemed as though the menacing majesty of Enjolras, disarmed and motionless, weighed on that tumult, and as though, merely by the authority of his tranquil eye, this young man, who alone had no wound, superb, bloody, fascinating, indifferent as if he were invulnerable, compelled that sinister mob to kill him respectfully. His beauty, augmented at that moment by his dignity, was resplendent, and, as if he could no more be fatigued than wounded, after the terrible twenty-four hours just elapsed, he was fresh and healthy. Perhaps it was of him that the witness spoke who said afterward before the court-martial, "There was one insurgent whom I heard called Apollo." A National Guard who was aiming at Enjolras dropped his weapon, saying, "It is as though I'm about to shoot a flower."

Twelve men formed in platoon in the corner opposite Enjolras and readied their muskets in silence.

Then a sergeant cried, "Take aim!"

An officer intervened.

"Wait."

And addressing Enjolras, "Do you wish your eyes bandaged?"

"No."

"Was it really you who killed the sergeant of artillery?"

"Yes."

A few seconds earlier Grantaire had woken up.

Grantaire, it will be remembered, had been asleep since the previous day in the upper room of the bistro, sitting in a chair, slouched forward on a table.

He embodied, in all its force, the old metaphor "dead drunk." The hideous potion, absinthe-stout-alcohol, had thrown him into a lethargy. His table was small and of no use in the barricade, so they had left it to him. He was still in the same posture, his breast doubled over the table, his head lying flat on his arms, surrounded by glasses, jugs, and bottles. He slept with that crushing sleep of the torpid bear and the overfed leech. Nothing had affected him, neither the musket fire, nor the cannonballs, nor the grapeshot, which penetrated through the casement into the room where he was. Nor the prodigious uproar of the assault. Except that he responded sometimes to the cannon with a snore. He seemed waiting there for a cannonball to come and save him the trouble of awaking. Several corpses lay around him; and, at the first glance, nothing distinguished him from those deep sleepers of death.

Noise does not waken a drunkard; silence wakens him.

This peculiarity has been observed more than once. The collapse of everything around him augmented Grantaire's oblivion; destruction was a lullaby to him. The sort of halt in the tumult surrounding Enjolras was a shock to his heavy slumber. As if from the sudden halt of a galloping coach, the sleeper awoke. Grantaire stood up with a start, stretched his arms, rubbed his eyes, looked, yawned, and understood.

Drunkenness ending is like a curtain torn away. We see altogether, and at a single glance, all that had been concealed. Everything is suddenly presented to the memory; and the drunkard who knows nothing of what has taken place for twenty-four hours has no sooner opened his eyes than he is aware of all that has happened. His ideas come back to him with an abrupt lucidity; the haze of drunkenness, a sort of vapor that blinds the brain, dissipates, and gives way to clear and precise impressions of the reality.

Relegated as he was to a corner and as though sheltered behind the billiard table, the soldiers, their eyes fixed upon Enjolras, had not even noticed Grantaire, and the sergeant was preparing to repeat the order: "Take aim!" when suddenly they heard a powerful voice cry out beside them, "*Vive la République!* Count me in."

Grantaire was on his feet.

The immense glare of the whole combat he had missed and in which he had not been, appeared in the flashing eye of the transfigured drunkard.

He repeated, "*Vive la République!*" crossed the room firmly, and took his place in front of the muskets beside Enjolras.

"Two at one shot," he said.

And, turning toward Enjolras gently, he said to him, "Will you permit it?"

Enjolras shook his hand with a smile.

The smile was not finished before the report was heard.

Enjolras, pierced by eight bullets, remained backed up against the wall as if the bullets had nailed him there. Except that his head was tilted.

Grantaire, struck down, collapsed at his feet.

A few moments later, the soldiers dislodged the last insurgents who had taken refuge in the top floors. They fired through a wooden lattice into the garret. They fought in the attic. They hurled the bodies out the windows, some still living. Two voltigeurs, who were trying to raise the shattered omnibus, were killed by two shots from a carbine fired from the dormer windows. A man in a workman's shirt was pitched out headlong, with a bayonet wound in his stomach, and his death throes ended on the ground. A soldier and an insurgent slipped together on the slope of the tiled roof and would not let go of each other, and fell, clasped in a wild embrace. Similar struggle in the cellar. Cries, shots, savage stamping. Then silence. The barricade was taken.

The soldiers commenced the search of the houses in the vicinity and the pursuit of fugitives.

XXIV

PRISONER

Marius was in fact a prisoner. Prisoner of Jean Valjean.

The hand that had seized him from behind as he was falling, and the grasp he had felt in losing consciousness, was Jean Valjean's hand.

Jean Valjean had taken no other part in the combat than to expose himself. Save for him, in that supreme phase of the death struggle, nobody would have thought of the wounded. Thanks to him, present everywhere in the carnage like a providence, those who fell were taken up, carried into the lower room, and their wounds dressed. In the intervals, he repaired the barricade. But nothing like a blow, an attack, or even a personal defense came from his hands. He was silent and gave aid. Moreover, he had only a few scratches. The bullets wanted no part of him. If suicide figured in what had occurred to him in coming to this sepulcher, in that respect he had not succeeded. But we doubt whether he had thought of suicide, an irreligious act.

In the dense cloud of the combat, Jean Valjean did not appear to see Marius; the fact is, he never took his eyes off him. When a shot struck Marius down, Jean Valjean bounded with the agility of a tiger, dropped on him as upon a prey, and carried him away.

At that moment the whirlwind of the attack concentrated so fiercely on Enjolras and the door of Corinth that nobody saw Jean Valjean cross the unpaved field of the barricade, holding the unconscious Marius in his arms, and disappear behind the corner of the house of Corinth.

It will be remembered that this corner formed a sort of promontory on the street; it sheltered from bullets and pellets, and from sight too, a few square feet of ground. Thus, in conflagrations there is sometimes a room that does not burn; and in the most furious seas, beyond a cape or at the end of a cul-de-sac of shoals, a placid little haven. It was in this recess of the interior trapezium of the barricade that Eponine had died.

There, Jean Valjean stopped; he let Marius slip to the ground, set his back to the wall, and cast his eyes about him.

The situation was appalling.

For the moment, for two or three minutes, perhaps, this stretch of wall was a shelter; but how escape from this massacre? He remembered his anguish in the Rue Polonceau, eight years before, and how he had managed to escape; that was difficult then, today it was impossible. Before him he had that deaf and implacable house of six stories, which seemed inhabited only by the dead man, leaning on his windowsill; on his right he had the low barricade that closed the Petite Truanderie; to clamber over this obstacle looked easy, but above the crest of the wall a row of bayonet points could be seen. A company of the line was posted beyond this barricade, on watch. It was obvious that to cross the barricade was to meet the fire of a platoon, and that any head that ventured to rise above the top of the wall of paving stones would serve as a target for sixty muskets. At his left he had the field of combat. Death was behind the corner of the wall.

What should he do?

A bird alone could have extricated himself from that place.

And he had to decide instantly, find an expedient, adopt his course. They were fighting a few steps away from him; by good luck, everyone was fiercely intent on a single point, the door of Corinth; but let one soldier, a single one, get the idea of going around the house, or flanking it, and it would be all over.

Jean Valjean looked at the house in front of him, he looked at the barricade beside him, then he looked at the ground, with the violence of last extremity, in desperation, as if he wanted to bore a hole in it with his eyes.

Because of his persistent stare, something vaguely tangible in such an agony outlined itself and took shape at his feet, as if there were a power in the eye to make the desired thing appear. A few steps away, at the foot of the little wall so pitilessly watched and guarded on the outside, under some fallen paving stones that partly hid it, he noticed an iron grating laid flat and level with the ground. This grating, made of strong transverse bars, was about two feet square. The stone frame that held it had been torn up, and it was unsecured. Through the bars there was a glimpse of an obscure opening, something like the flue of a chimney or the pipe of a cistern. Jean Valjean sprang forward. His old science of escape rose to his brain like a flash. To remove the stones, to lift the grating, to load up Marius, who was as inert as a corpse, on his shoulders, to climb down, with that burden on his back, with the help of his elbows and knees, into this kind of well, fortunately not very deep, to drop back over his head the heavy iron trapdoor on which the stones he had moved rolled back again, to find a foothold on a flagged surface ten feet below the ground, this was executed like things done in delirium, with the strength of a giant and the speed of an eagle; it took hardly a minute or two.

Jean Valjean found himself, with Marius still unconscious, in a sort of long underground passage.

There, deep peace, absolute silence, night.

The impression he had formerly felt in falling from the street into the convent came back to him. Only what he was now carrying away was not Cosette; it was Marius.

He could now just hear above him, like a vague murmur, the awesome tumult of the bistro being taken by assault.

Book Two

THE INTESTINE OF LEVIATHAN

I

THE EARTH IMPOVERISHED BY THE SEA

Paris throws five million a year into the sea. And this not metaphorically. How, and in what way? Day and night. With what purpose? None. With what thought? Without thinking about it. For what use? For nothing. By means of what organ? By means of its intestine. What is its intestine? Its sewer.

Five million is the most moderate of the approximate figures that the estimates of special science give.

After long experimentation, science now knows that the most fertilizing and the most effective of manures is that of man. The Chinese, we must say to our shame, knew it before us. No Chinese peasant, Eckeberg tells us, goes to the city without carrying back, at the two ends of his bamboo pole, two buckets full of what we call filth. Thanks to human fertilizer, the earth in China is still as young as in the days of Abraham. Chinese wheat yields a hundred and twenty fold. There is no guano comparable in fertility to the detritus of a capital. A great city is the most powerful of dung producers. To employ the city to enrich the plain would be a sure success. If our gold is manure, on the other hand, our manure is gold.

What is done with this gold, manure? It is swept into the abyss.

At great expense, we send out convoys of ships, to gather up at the South Pole the droppings of petrels and penguins, and the incalculable element of wealth that we have at hand, we send to the sea. All the human and animal manure that the world loses, if restored to the land instead of being thrown into the water, would suffice to nourish the world.

This garbage heaped up beside the stone blocks, the tumbrils of mire jolting through the streets at night, the awful scavengers' carts, the fetid streams of subterranean slime that the pavement hides from you, do you know what all this is? It is the flowering meadow, it is the green grass, it is marjoram and thyme and sage, it is game, it is cattle, it is the satisfied lowing of huge oxen in the evening, it is perfumed hay, it is golden wheat, it is bread on your table, it is warm blood in your veins, it is health, it is joy, it is life. So wills that mysterious creation, transformation on earth and transfiguration in heaven.

Put that into the great crucible; your abundance will spring from it. The nutrition of the plains makes the nourishment of men.

You have the power to throw away this wealth, and to think me ridiculous into the bargain. That will be the crowning glory of your ignorance.

Statistics show that France, alone, deposits effluent totaling a hundred million every year into the Atlantic from the mouths of her rivers. Note this: With that hundred million you might pay a quarter of the expenses of the government. The cleverness of man is such that he prefers to throw this hundred million into the gutter. It is the very substance of the people that is carried away, here drop by drop, there in floods, by our sewers' wretched vomiting into the rivers, and our rivers' into the ocean. Each hiccup of our cloaca costs us a thousand francs. From this two results: the land impoverished and the water contaminated. Hunger rising from the furrow and disease rising from the river.

It is well-known, for instance, that at this moment the Thames is poisoning London.

As for Paris, within the last few years it has been necessary to move most of the mouths of the sewers down stream below the last bridge.

A double tubular arrangement, provided with valves and sluiceways, sucking up and flowing back, a system of elementary drainage, as simple as man's lungs, and already in full operation in several villages in England, would suffice to bring into our cities the pure water of the fields and send back into our fields the rich water of the cities; and this easy seesaw, as simple as can be, would retain for us the hundred million thrown away. We are thinking about other things.

The present system does harm in attempting to do good. The intention is good, the result is sad. Men think they are purging the city; they are emaciating the population. A sewer is a mistake. When drainage everywhere, with its double function, restoring what it takes away, will have replaced the sewer, that simple impoverishing washing, then, this being combined with the givens of a new social economy, the products of the earth will be increased tenfold, and the problem of misery will be wonderfully diminished. Add the suppression of parasites and it will be solved.

In the meantime, the public wealth runs off into the river, and the leakage continues. Leakage is the word. Europe is ruining herself in this way by exhaustion.

As for France, we have just cited her figure. Now, since Paris contains a twenty-fifth of the total French population, and the Parisian guano is the richest of all, we are within the truth in estimating at five million the portion of Paris in the loss of the hundred million that France annually throws away. These five million, turned to aid and benefit, would double the splendor of Paris. The city expends them in sewers. So that we may say the great prodigality of Paris, her marvelous festivity, her Beaujon folly, her orgy, her outpouring of gold by the handful, her pageant, her luxury, her magnificence, is her sewer.

It is in this way that, in the blindness of a bad political economy, we drown and allow to float downstream and be lost in the depths the welfare of all. There should be Saint-Cloud nettings for the public fortune.

Economically, the fact can be summed up thus: Paris a leaky basket.

Paris, that model city, that pattern of well-made capitals that every nation tries to copy, that metropolis of the ideal, that august country of initiative, of impulse and enterprise, that center and abode of the mind, that nation city, that hive of the future, that marvelous compound of

Babylon and Corinth, from the point of view we have just indicated, would make a peasant of Fukien shrug his shoulders.

Imitate Paris, and you will be ruined.

Moreover, particularly in this immemorial and senseless waste, Paris also is an imitator.

These surprising ineptitudes are not new; there is no young folly in this. The ancients acted like the moderns. "The sewers of Rome," says Liebig, "absorbed all the well-being of the Roman peasant." When the Campagna of Rome was ruined by the Roman sewer, Rome exhausted Italy, and when she had put Italy into her cloaca, she poured in Sicily, then Sardinia, then Africa. The sewer of Rome engulfed the world. This cloaca offered its yawning depths to the city and to the globe. *Urbi et orbi*. Eternal city, unfathomable sewer.

In these things, as well as in others, Rome sets the example.

Paris follows this example with all the stupidity peculiar to cities of genius.

For the necessities of the operation we have just explained, Paris has another Paris under herself; a Paris of sewers, which has its streets, its crossroads, its squares, its blind alleys, its arteries, and its circulation, which is slime, minus the human form.

For we must flatter nothing, not even a great people; where there is everything, there is ignominy by the side of sublimity; and, if Paris contains Athens, the city of light, Tyre, the city of power, Sparta, the city of manhood, Nineveh, the city of prodigy, it also contains Lutetia, the city of mire.

Besides, the seal of her power is there too, and the titanic sinkhole of Paris realizes, among its monuments, that strange ideal realized in humanity by some men, such as Machiavelli, Bacon, and Mirabeau: the sublimely abject.

The subsoil of Paris, if the eye could penetrate the surface, would have the appearance of a colossal madrepore coral. A sponge hardly has more straits and passages than the clump of earth fifteen miles in circumference, on which rests the ancient great city. Without speaking of the catacombs, which are a cellar apart, without speaking of the inextricable trellis of the gas pipes, without counting the vast tubular system for the distribution of fresh water that ends in the hydrants, the sewers alone form a prodigious dark network under both banks; a labyrinth whose descent is its thread.

In the humid haze, the rat appears, seemingly the product of the accouchement of Paris.

II

THE ANCIENT HISTORY OF THE SEWER

Imagine Paris taken off like a bedcover, a bird's-eye view of the subterranean network of the sewers would sketch on both banks a sort of huge branch grafted onto the river. On the right bank, the belt-sewer is the trunk of this branch, the secondary conduits are the limbs, and the primary drains will be the twigs.

This figure is only general and half exact, since the right angle, which is the ordinary angle of this kind of underground ramification, is very rare in vegetation.

We can form a mental picture more closely resembling this strange geometric plan by imagining spread across a background of darkness some grotesque alphabet of the East jumbled together, their deformed letters joined to each other, apparently pell-mell and as if by chance, sometimes by their corners, sometimes by their ends.

The sinks and sewers played an important part in the Middle Ages, in the Later Byzantine Empire, and in the ancient East. Plagues were born in them, despots died in them. The multitudes looked with an almost religious awe at these beds of corruption, monstrous cradles of death. The vermin pit of Benares is no less bewildering than the Lion Pit of Babylon. Tiglath Pilezer, according to the rabbinical books, swore by the sinkhole of Nineveh. It was from the sewer of Münster that John of Leyden made his false moon rise, and it was from the cloaca pit of Kekhschab that his eastern Menaechmus, Mokannah, the veiled prophet of Khorassan, made his false sun rise.

The history of men is reflected in the history of cloacae. The Gemoniae describe Rome. The sewer of Paris has been a terrible thing in past times. It has been a sepulcher, it has been an asylum. Crime, intelligence, social protest, liberty of conscience, thought, theft, all that human laws pursue or have pursued, have hidden in this hole; the Maillotins in the fourteenth century, the Tire-laines in the fifteenth, the Huguenots in the sixteenth, the Illuminati of Morin in the seventeenth, the Chauffeurs in the eighteenth. A hundred years ago, the midnight dagger blow came from there, the pickpocket in danger ducked into it; the forest had its cave; Paris had its sewer. Vagrancy, that Gallic *picareria,* accepted the sewer as an affiliation of the Cour des Miracles, and at night, crafty and ferocious, returned to the Maubué conduit as into an alcove.

It was quite natural that those whose field of daily labor was the cul-de-sac Vide-Gousset, or the Rue Coupe-Gorge, should have for their nightly abode the culvert of the Chemin Vert or the Hurepoix kennel. Hence a swarm of traditions. All sorts of phantoms haunt these long solitary corridors, putrescence and miasma everywhere; here and there a breathing hole through which Villon inside chats with Rabelais outside.

In old Paris, the sewer is the rendezvous of all depletions and all attempts. Political economy sees in it a detritus, social philosophy sees in it a residuum.

The sewer is the conscience of the city. All things converge into it and are confronted with one another. In this lurid place there is darkness, but there are no secrets. Each thing has its real form, or at least its definitive form. It can be said for the garbage heap that it is no liar. Naïveté has taken refuge there. Basil's mask is found there, but we see the pasteboard, and the strings, and the inside as well as the outside, and it is emphasized with honest mud. Scapin's false nose is close by. All the uncleanliness of civilization, once it is out of service, falls into this pit of truth, where the immense social slippage is brought to an end. It is swallowed up, but it is displayed in it. This pell-mell is a confusion. Here, no more false appearances, no possible plastering, filth takes off its shirt, absolute nakedness, rout of illusions and mirages, nothing more but what is, wearing the sinister face of what is ending. Reality and disappearance. Here, the stump of a bottle confesses drunkenness, a basket handle tells of domestic life; here, the apple core that has had literary opinions becomes again an apple core; the face on the big sou freely coats itself with verdigris, the spittle of Caïaphas encounters Falstaff's vomit, the louis d'or that comes from the gambling house jostles the nail trailing the suicide's bit of a rope, a livid fetus rolls by wrapped in spangles that danced at the Opéra last Mardi Gras, a cap that has judged men wallows near a rottenness that was one of Peggy's petticoats; it is more than brotherhood, it is closest intimacy. All that used to be painted is besmirched. The last veil is rent. A sewer is a cynic. It tells all.

This sincerity of uncleanness pleases us, and is a relief to the soul. When a man has spent his time on earth enduring the spectacle of the grand airs assumed by reasons of state, oaths, political wisdom, human justice, professional honesty, the necessities of position, incorruptible robes, it is a consolation to enter a sewer and see the slime that befits it.

At the same time it is a lesson. As we have just said, history passes through the sewer. The Saint Bartholomew's Day massacres filter drop by drop through the pavements. The great public assassinations, the political and religious butcheries, traverse this vault of civilization, and push their dead into it. To the reflecting eye, all the historic murderers are there, in the hideous gloom, on their knees, with a little of their shroud for an apron, dolefully sponging up their work. Louis XI is there with Tristan, Francis I is there with Duprat, Charles IX is there with his mother, Richelieu is there with Louis XIII, Louvois is there, Letellier is there, Hébert and Maillard are there, scraping the stones, and trying to efface all trace of their deeds. Beneath these vaults we hear the broom of these specters. We breathe the enormous fetidness of social catastrophes. We see reddish reflections in the corners. There flows a terrible water, in which bloody hands have been washed.

The social observer should enter these shadows. They are part of his laboratory. Philosophy is the microscope of thought. Everything wants to flee from it, but nothing escapes it. Tergiversation is useless. What side of your character do you show in tergiversation? The shameful side. Philosophy pursues evil with its honest search, and does not permit it to slip away into nothingness. In the effacement of things that disappear, in the lessening of those that vanish, it recognizes everything. It reconstructs the royal from the rag and the woman from the tatter. With the sewer it reproduces the city; with the sludge it reproduces its customs. From a fragment it infers the amphora. From the print of a fingernail on a parchment it recognizes the difference between the Jewry of the Judengasse and the Jewry of the Ghetto. In what remains it finds what has been, the good, the ill, the false, the true, the bloodstain in the palace, the ink blot in the cavern, the drop of grease in the brothel, trials undergone, temptations welcomed, orgies spewed out, the wrinkles that characters have acquired in abasing themselves, the trace of prostitution in souls whose own grossness has made them capable of it, and, on the vest of the porters of Rome, the mark of Messalina's elbow.

III

BRUNESEAU

In the Middle Ages, the sewer of Paris was legendary. In the sixteenth century, Henry II attempted an exploration, which failed. Less than a hundred years ago, the cloaca, as Mercier testifies, was abandoned to itself, and became whatever it could.

Such was that ancient Paris, given up to quarrels, to indecisions, and to gropings. For a long time it was rather stupid. Later, '89 showed how cities come to their wits. But, in the good old days, the capital had little sense; she could not manage her affairs either morally or materially, nor sweep away her filth any better than her abuses. Everything was an obstacle, everything raised a question. The sewer, for instance, impeded any and all itinerary. Men could no more succeed in orienting themselves in its channels than in understanding themselves in the city; above, the unintelligible, below, the inextricable; beneath the confusion of tongues there was the confusion of cellars; Labyrinth underlay Babel.

Sometimes, the sewer of Paris took it into its head to overflow, as if that unappreciated Nile were suddenly seized with wrath. There were, a dreadful thing, floods from the sewer. At times this stomach of civilization had indigestion, the cloaca flowed back into the city's throat, and Paris had the aftertaste of its slime. These resemblances of the sewer to remorse had some good in them; they were warnings, very badly received, however; the city was indignant that its sludge should have so much audacity, and did not countenance the return of the excrement. Drive it away better.

The inundation of 1802 is live memory among Parisians of eighty. The mire spread out in a cross in the Place des Victoires, where the statue of Louis XIV is; it entered the Rue Saint-Honoré by the two mouths of the sewer of the Champs-Elysées, the Rue Saint-Florentin by the Saint-Florentin sewer, the Rue Pierre-à-Poisson by the sewer of the Sonnerie, the Rue Popincourt by the sewer of the Chemin-Vert, the Rue de la Roquette by the sewer of the Rue de Lappe; it covered the curbstones of the Rue des Champs-Elysées to the depth of some fourteen inches; and, on the south, by the conduit of the Seine performing its function in the inverse way, it entered the Rue Mazarine, the Rue de l'Echaudé, and the Rue des Marais, where it stopped, at a length of a hundred and twenty yards, just a few steps from the house where Racine had lived—respecting, in the seventeenth century, the poet more than the king. It attained its maximum depth in the Rue Saint-Pierre, where it rose three feet above the flagging of the waterspouts, and its maximum extent in the Rue Saint-Sabin, where it spread out over a length of two hundred and sixty-one yards.

At the beginning of this century, the sewer of Paris was still a mysterious place. Sludge can never be in good repute; but here ill fame degenerated to the point of horror. Paris dimly realized that she had a terrible cellar beneath her. People talked of it as of that monstrous bog of Thebes that swarmed with centipedes fifteen feet long and that might have served as a bathtub for Behemoth. The big boots of the sewer-men never ventured beyond certain known points. They were still very near the time when the scavengers' carts from one of which Sainte-Foix fraternized with the Marquis de Créqui, were simply emptied into the sewer. As for cleansing, that operation was left to the downpours, which obstructed more than they swept out. Rome still left some poetry to her cloaca, and called it Gemoniae; Paris insulted hers and called it the Stink-Hole. Science and superstitions were at one in regard to the horror. The Stink-Hole was no less revolting to hygiene than to legend. The Goblin Monk had appeared under the fetid arch of the Mouffetard sewer; the corpses of the Marmousets had been thrown into the sewer of the Barillerie; Fagon had attributed the fearful malignant fever of 1685 to the great gap in the sewer of the Marais which remained open until 1833, in the Rue Saint-Louis, almost in front of the sign of the Gallant Messenger. The mouth of the sewer of the Rue de la Mortellerie was famous for the pestilence that came from it; with its pointed iron grating that looked like a row of teeth, it lay in that fatal street like the jaws of a dragon breathing hell onto men. Popular imagination seasoned the gloomy Parisian sink with an indefinably hideous mixture of the infinite. The sewer was bottomless. The sewer was the barathrum. The idea of exploring those leprous regions never even occurred to the police. To tempt that unknown, to throw the lead into that darkness, to go on a voyage of discovery in that abyss, who would have dared? It was frightful. Somebody did come forward, however. The cloaca had its Christopher Columbus.

One day in 1805, on one of those rare visits that the emperor made to Paris, the minister of the interior came to the master's private audience. In the Place du Carrousel they could hear the clattering swords of all those marvelous soldiers of the Grand Republic and the Grand Empire; there was a multitude of heroes at Napoleon's door; men of the Rhine, of the Scheldt, of the Adige, and of the Nile; companions of Joubert, of Desaix, of Marceau, of Hoche, of Kléber; balloonists of Fleurus; grenadiers of Mayence, pontooneers of Genoa, hussars whom the Pyramids had gazed at, artillerymen whom Junot's bullet had spattered, cuirassiers who had taken the fleet at anchor in the Zuyder Zee; these had followed Bonaparte over the bridge of Lodi, those had been with Murat in the trenches of Mantua, others had preceded Lannes in the sunken road of Montebello. The whole army of that time was there, in the Court of the Tuileries, represented by a squad or a platoon, guarding Napoleon in repose; and it was the splendid era when the grand army had Marengo behind it and Austerlitz ahead. "Sire," said the minister of the interior to Napoleon, "Yesterday I saw the boldest man in your empire." "Who is the man," said the emperor quickly, "and what has he done?" "He wishes to do something, sire." "What?" "To visit the sewers of Paris."

That man existed, and his name was Bruneseau.

IV

UNKNOWN DETAILS

The visit was made. It was a formidable campaign; a night battle against pestilence and asphyxia. It was at the same time a voyage of discoveries. One of the survivors of this exploration, an intelligent workingman, then very young, was still telling a few years ago, the curious details that Bruneseau thought it his duty to omit in his report to the prefect of police, as unworthy of the administrative style. Disinfecting processes were very rudimentary at that time. Hardly had Bruneseau passed the first branchings of the subterranean network, than eight out of the twenty laborers refused to proceed any farther. The operation was complicated; the visit involved cleaning; it was necessary therefore to clean, and at the same time to measure; to note the water entrances, to count the gratings and the mouths, to verify the branchings in detail, to indicate the currents at the points of separation, to reconnoiter the respective borders of the various basins, to fathom the little sewers grafted onto the principal sewer, to measure the height of each corridor under the keystone, and the width at the spring of the arch as well as at the floor level, finally to determine the ordinates of the levelings at a right angle to each water entrance, either from the floor of the sewer or from the surface of the street. They progressed with difficulty. It was not uncommon for the stepladders to plunge into three feet of sludge. The lanterns flickered in the miasmas. From time to time, they brought out a sewerman who had fainted. At certain places, a precipice. The soil had sunk, the pavement had crumbled, the sewer had changed into a blind well; they found no solid ground; one man suddenly disappeared; they had great difficulty recovering him. On the advice of Fourcroy, they lit up from point to point, in the sufficiently purified places, great cages full of oakum and saturated with resin. In places, the wall was covered with shapeless fungi, and one would have said with tumors; the stone itself seemed diseased in this unbreatheable medium.

Bruneseau, in his exploration, proceeded from the head toward the mouth. At the point of separation of the two water conduits from the Grand-Hurleur, he deciphered on a projecting stone the date 1550; this stone indicated the limit reached by Philibert Delorme, who was charged by Henry II with visiting the subterranean canals of Paris. This stone was the mark of the sixteenth century on the sewer; Bruneseau also found the handiwork of the seventeenth century, in the conduit of the Ponceau and the conduit of the Rue Vieille du Temple, built between 1600 and 1650, and the handiwork of the eighteenth century in the western section of the collecting canal, banked up and arched in 1740. These two arches, especially the later one, from 1740, were more cracked and more dilapidated than the masonry of the belt sewer, which dated from 1412, the epoch when the fresh-water brook of Ménilmontant was raised to the dignity of Great Sewer of Paris, an advancement analogous to that of a peasant who should become first valet de chambre to the king; something like Gros Jean transformed into Lebel.

Here and there, chiefly under the Palais de Justice, they thought they recognized some cells of ancient dungeons built in the sewer itself. Hideous *in pace*. An iron collar hung in one of these cells. They walled them all up. Some odd things were found; among other things the skeleton of an orangutan that disappeared from the Jardin des Plantes in 1800, a disappearance probably connected with the famous and incontestable appearance of the devil in the Rue des Bernardins in the last year of the eighteenth century. The poor devil finally drowned himself in the sewer.

Under the long arched passage that ends at the Arche Marion, a ragpicker's basket, in perfect condition, was the admiration of connoisseurs. Everywhere, the mud, which the workmen had come to handle intrepidly, was rich in precious objects, gold and silver trinkets, precious stones, coins. Any giant who filtered this cloaca would have had the riches of centuries in his sieve. At the point of separation of the two branches of the Rue du Temple and the Rue Sainte-Avoye, they picked up a strange Huguenot medal in copper, bearing on one side a hog wearing a cardinal's hat, and on the other a wolf with the tiara on his head.

The most surprising discovery was at the entrance of the Great Sewer. This entrance had been formerly closed by a grating, of which only the hinges remained. Hanging from one of these hinges was a sort of shapeless filthy rag, which, undoubtedly caught there on its way by, had fluttered in the darkness, and was finally worn to tatters. Bruneseau brought his lantern to this strip and examined it. It was of very fine cambric, and on the least worn of the corners they made out a heraldic crown embroidered above these seven letters: LAVBESP. The crown was a marquis's crown, and the seven letters signified *Laubespine*. They recognized that what they had before their eyes was a piece of Marat's shroud. In his youth, Marat had had his amours. It was when he was part of the household of the Comte-d'Artois in the capacity of veterinarian of the stables. From these amours, a matter of history, with a great lady, he had preserved this sheet. Flotsam or souvenir. At the time of his death, since it was the only fine linen he had in the house, he was shrouded in it. In this linen that had seen pleasure, old women dressed out for the tomb the tragic Friend of the People.

Bruneseau moved on. They left the scrap where it was; they did not finish it off. Was this contempt or respect? Marat deserved both. And then, destiny was so imprinted on it that they might hesitate to touch it. Besides, we should leave the things of the grave in the place they choose. In short, the relic was strange. A marquise had slept on it; Marat had rotted in it; it had passed through the Panthéon to come at last to the sewer rats. This rag of the bedroom, whose every fold Watteau would once have gladly sketched, had at last become worthy of Dante's steady eye.

The complete tour of the subterranean sewer system of Paris took seven years, from 1805 to 1812. While he was still performing it, Bruneseau laid out, directed, and completed some considerable works; in 1808 he lowered the floor of the Ponceau, and, creating new lines everywhere, he extended the sewer, in 1809, under the Rue Saint-Denis as far as the Fontaine des Innocents; in 1810, under the Rue Froidmanteau and under La Salpêtrière; in 1811, under the Rue Neuve-des-Petits-Pères, the Rue du Mail, the Rue de l'Echarpe, and the Place Royale; in 1812, under the Rue de la Paix and the Chaussée d'Antin. At the same time, he disinfected and purified the whole network. After the second year, Bruneseau was assisted by his son-in-law Nargaud.

Thus, at the beginning of this century, the old society cleansed its lower depths and performed the ablutions on its sewer. At least it was cleaned somewhat.

Tortuous, fissured, unpaved, crackling, interrupted by quagmires, broken by fantastic bends, rising and falling illogically, fetid, savage, wild, submerged in obscurity, with scars on its pavements and gashes on its walls, appalling, seen retrospectively, such was the ancient sewer of Paris. Ramifications in every direction, crossings of trenches, branchings, multiple forkings, stars as if in mines, cul-de-sacs, arches covered with saltpeter, foul cesspools, a scabby ooze on the walls, drops falling from the ceiling, darkness; nothing equaled the horror of this old voiding crypt, Babylonian digestive apparatus, cavern, grave, gulf pierced with streets, titanic molehill in which the mind seems to see prowling through shadows, in the excrement that has been splendor, that enormous blind mole, the past.

This, we repeat, was the sewer of former times.

V

PRESENT PROGRESS

Today the sewer is neat, cold, straight, correct. It almost realizes the ideal of what is understood in England by the word "respectable." It is comely and sober; drawn by the line; we might almost say neat as a pin. It is like a contractor become a state councilor. We almost see clearly in it. The filth behaves decently. At first glance, one would readily take it for one of those underground passages formerly so common and useful for the flight of monarchs and princes, in the good old days "when the people loved their kings." The present sewer is a beautiful sewer; the pure style reigns in it; the classic rectilinear alexandrine, which, driven from poetry, appears to have taken refuge in architecture, seems mingled with every stone of that long darkish and whitish arch; each discharging mouth is an arcade; the Rue de Rivoli sets the fashion even in the cloaca. Ultimately, if the geometric line is in place anywhere, it surely is in the stercorary trenches of a great city. There, all should be subordinated to the shortest road. The sewer has now assumed a certain official aspect. Even the police reports of which it is sometimes the object are no longer lacking in respect for it. The words that characterize it in the administrative language are elevated and dignified. What was once called a gut is called a gallery; what was called a hole is called a vista. Villon would no longer recognize his old dwelling in case of need. This network of caves still has of course its immemorial population of rodents, swarming more than ever; from time to time, a rat, an old mustache, risks showing his head at the window of the sewer and examines the Parisians; but even these vermin have grown tame, content as they are with their subterranean palace. The cloaca has nothing left of its primitive ferocity. The rain, which fouled the sewer of former times, washes the sewer of the present day. Do not trust in it too much, however. Miasmas still inhabit it. It is more hypocritical than irreproachable. The prefecture of police and the health commission have labored in vain. In spite of all the processes of purification, it exhales a vague odor, suspect as Tartuffe after confession.

Let us admit, since, all things considered, sweeping up is an homage the sewer pays to civilization, and as, from this point of view, Tartuffe's conscience is an advance on Augeas's stable, it is certain that the sewer of Paris has been improved.

It is more than an advance; it is a transmutation. Between the ancient sewer and the present sewer, there is a revolution. Who has wrought this revolution?

The man whom everybody forgets, and whom we have named. Bruneseau.

VI

FUTURE PROGRESS

The excavation of the sewer of Paris has been no small task. The last ten centuries have labored on it, without being able to complete it any more than they have been able to finish Paris. In fact, the sewer receives all the repercussions of the growth of Paris. It is a species of dark underground polyp with a thousand antennae that grows below while the city grows above. Whenever the city opens a street, the sewer puts out an arm. The old monarchy had constructed only twenty-five thousand four hundred and eighty yards of sewers; Paris had reached that point on the 1st of January 1806. After that period, of which we shall speak again directly, the work was profitably and energetically resumed and continued; Napoleon built—the figures are interesting—five thousand two hundred and fifty-four yards; Louis XVIII, six thousand two hundred and forty-four; Charles X, eleven thousand eight hundred and fifty-one; Louis-Philippe, ninety-seven thousand three hundred and fifty-five; the Republic of 1848, twenty-five thousand five hundred and seventy; the existing régime, seventy-seven thousand one hundred; in all, at the present time, two hundred and forty-seven thousand eight hundred and twenty-eight yards; a hundred and forty miles of sewers; the enormous entrails of Paris. Obscure ramification always under construction; unnoticed and immense undertaking.

As we see, the subterranean labyrinth of Paris is today more than tenfold what it was at the beginning of the century. It is hard to realize all the perseverance and effort that were necessary to bring this cloaca to the point of relative perfection it has now reached. It was with great difficulty that the old monarchic establishment and, in the last ten years of the eighteenth century, the revolutionary mayoralty, had succeeded in piercing the thirteen miles of sewers that existed before 1806. All sorts of obstacles hindered this operation, some peculiar to the nature of the soil, others inherent in the very prejudices of the laboring population of Paris. Paris is built on a deposit strangely rebellious to the spade, the hoe, the drill, to human control. Nothing more difficult to pierce and penetrate than that geological formation on which is superimposed the wonderful historical formation called Paris; as soon as, under whatever form, work begins and ventures into that layer of alluvium, subterranean resistance abounds. There are liquid clays, living springs, hard rocks, those deep, soft mires that technical science calls "mustards." The pick moves forward laboriously in these calcareous strata alternating with seams of very fine clay and laminar schistose beds, encrusted with oyster shells contemporary to the preadamite oceans. Sometimes a stream suddenly splits apart an arch under construction, and swamps the laborers; or a slide of marl loosens and rushes down with the fury of a cataract, crushing the largest sustaining timbers like glass. Quite recently in Villette, when, without interrupting navigation and without emptying the canal, it was necessary to lead the collecting sewer under the Saint-Martin canal, a fissure opened in the bed of the canal; the water suddenly rose in the works underground, beyond all ability of the pumps; they had to send down a diver to find the fissure, which was in the neck of the great basin, and it was stopped only with great difficulty. Elsewhere, near the Seine, and even at some distance from the river, as, for instance, at Belleville, Grande Rue, and the Lunière arcade, there is quicksand where a man can be rapidly buried. Add asphyxia from the miasma, burial by cave-ins, sudden settlings of the bottom. Add typhus, with which the workers are slowly infected. In our lifetime, they excavated the gallery of Clichy, with a causeway to receive a water main from the Ourcq, work carried out in a trench over ten yards deep; they finished vaulting the Bièvre—in spite of mudslides, through excavations, often putrid, and using props, from the Boulevard de l'Hôpital to the Seine; to deliver Paris from the torrential runoff from Montmartre and to furnish an outlet for that fluvial sea of twenty-two acres stagnating near the Barrière des Martyrs, they constructed the line of sewers from the Barrière Blanche to the Aubervilliers road in four months, working day and night, at a depth of twelve yards; in a feat never seen before, they constructed a sewer in the Rue Barre-du-Bec, entirely underground, without a trench, twenty feet below the surface. And after all of this, they vaulted three thousand yards of sewers in all parts of the city, from the Rue Traversière–Saint-Antoine to the Rue de Lourcine; by branching the Arbalète, they relieved the Carrefour Censier-Mouffetard from inundation by the rain; they built the Saint-Georges sewer on stonework and concrete in the quicksand. After all this as well as directing the dangerous lowering of the floor of the Notre-Dame-de-Nazareth branch, Engineer Duleau died. There are no bulletins for these acts of bravery, more useful, however, than the stupid slaughter of the battlefield.

In 1832, the sewers of Paris were far from being what they are today. Bruneseau had made a beginning, but it took the cholera epidemic to bring about the vast reconstruction that has since taken place. It is surprising that, for instance, in 1821 a portion of the belt sewer, called the Grand Canal, as at Venice, was still stagnating in the open, in the Rue des Gourdes. It was only in 1823 that the city of Paris found in its pocket the forty-nine thousand eight hundred and ninety dollars and one cent necessary for the covering of this shame. The three cesspools of Le Combat, Le Cunette, and Saint-Mandé, with their discharging branches, their apparatus, their pits, and their purifying branches, only date from 1836. The intestinal canal of Paris has been rebuilt anew, and, as we have said, increased more than tenfold within a quarter of a century.

Thirty years ago, at the time of the insurrection of the 5th and 6th of June, it was still in many places almost the ancient sewer. A large number of streets, now cambered, were then open at the center. At the low point where the gutters of a street or a square terminated, you often saw large rectangular gratings with great bars, whose iron shone, polished by the feet of the multitude, dangerous and slippery for wagons, and making the horses stumble. The official language of roads and bridges gave these low points and gratings the expressive name of *Cassis*. In 1832, in many streets, the Rue de l'Etoile, the Rue Saint-Louis, the Rue du Temple, the Rue Vieille-du-Temple, the Rue Notre-Dame-de-Nazareth, the Rue Folie-Méricourt, the Quai aux Fleurs, the Rue du Petit-Musc, the Rue de Normandie, the Rue Pont-aux-Biches, the Rue des Marais, Faubourg Saint-Martin, the Rue Notre-Dame-des-Victoires, Faubourg Montmartre, the Rue Grange-Batelière, in the Champs-Elysées, the Rue Jacob, the Rue de Tournon, the old Gothic cloaca still cynically showed its jaws. They were enormous, sluggish gaps of stone, sometimes surrounded by stone blocks, with monumental effrontery.

Paris, in 1806, still had the same length of sewers established in May 1663: two thousand sixty-six yards. According to Bruneseau, on the 1st of January, 1832, there were forty-four thousand and seventy-three yards. From 1806 to 1831, there were built annually, on an average, eight hundred and twenty yards; since then there have been constructed every year eight, and even ten thousand yards of galleries, in masonry of small materials laid in hydraulic cement on a foundation of concrete.

At thirty-five dollárs a yard, the hundred and forty miles of sewers of the present Paris represent nine million.

Besides the economic progress we pointed out earlier, grave problems of public hygiene are linked with this immense question of the sewer of Paris.

Paris is between two sheets, a sheet of water and a sheet of air. The sheet of water lying at a considerable depth underground, but already tapped by two borings, is furnished by the bed of green sand lying between the chalk and the jurassic limestone; this bed can be represented by a disk with a radius of seventy miles; a multitude of rivers and brooks filter into it; we drink the Seine, the Marne, the Yonne, the Oise, the Aisne, the Cher, the Vienne, and the Loire, in a glass of water from the well of Grenelle. The sheet of water is healthy; it comes, first from heaven, then from the earth; the sheet of air is unwholesome, it comes from the sewer. All the miasmas of the cloaca are mingled with the breathing air of the city; hence that foul breath. The air taken from above a dunghill, it has been scientifically determined, is purer than the air taken from above Paris. In a given time, progress aiding, with mechanisms being perfected, and knowledge increasing, the sheet of water will be used to purify the sheet of air. That is to say, to wash the sewer. By washing the sewer, of course, we mean restitution of the mire to the land; return of the muck to the soil, and the manure to the fields. From this simple act will result, for the whole social community a reduction of misery and an improvement of health. At the present time, the radiation of the diseases of Paris extends a hundred and fifty miles out from the Louvre, taken as the hub of this pestilential wheel.

We might say that, for ten centuries, the cloaca has been the disease of Paris. The sewer is the taint the city has in her blood. The popular instinct is never mistaken. The trade of sewerman was formerly almost as perilous, and almost as repulsive to the people, as the trade of slaughterer, so long held in horror and left to the executioner. It took high wages to persuade a mason to disappear in that fetid ooze; the well-digger's ladder hesitated to plunge into it; it was said proverbially, "to descend into the sewer is to enter the grave"; and all manner of hideous legends, as we have said, covered this colossal drain with terror; awful sink, bearing the traces of the revolutions of the globe as well as of the revolutions of men, and in which we find vestiges of all the cataclysms from the shellfish of the deluge down to Marat's rag.

Book Three

MIRE, BUT SOUL

I

THE CLOACA AND ITS SURPRISES

It was in the sewer of Paris that Jean Valjean found himself.

Further resemblance between Paris and the sea: As in the ocean, the diver can disappear.

The transition was incredible. From the very center of the city, Jean Valjean had gone out of the city, and, in the twinkling of an eye, the time it took to lift a cover and close it again, he had passed from broad daylight to complete obscurity, from noon to midnight, from uproar to silence, from the whirlwind of thunder to the stagnation of the tomb, and, by a mutation much more prodigious still than that of the Rue Polonceau, from the most extreme peril to the most absolute security.

Sudden fall into a cave; disappearance in the dungeon of Paris; leaving that street in which death was everywhere for this kind of sepulcher in which there was life, it was a strange moment. He stood for some seconds as though stunned; listening, dazed. The trapdoor of safety had suddenly opened beneath him. Celestial goodness had in some way taken him by treachery. Adorable ambushes of Providence!

Except that the wounded man did not stir, and Jean Valjean did not know whether what he was carrying off in this grave were alive or dead.

His first sensation was blindness. Suddenly he could

not see a thing. It seemed also that in one minute he had become deaf. He could not hear a thing. The frenzied storm of murder raging a few feet above him only reached him, as we have said, thanks to the thickness of the earth that separated him from it, stifled and indistinct, and like a rumbling at a great depth. He felt that it was solid ground under his feet; that was all; but that was enough. He reached out one hand, then the other, touched the wall on both sides, and realized that the passage was narrow; he slipped, and realized that the pavement was wet. He advanced one foot with caution, fearing a hole, a pit, some gulf; he made sure that the stone flooring continued. A whiff of fetid odor told him where he was.

After a few moments, he was no longer blind. A little light fell from the air hole through which he had slipped in, and his eye grew accustomed to this cavern. He began to distinguish something. The passage in which he had come to earth, no other word better expresses the condition, was walled up behind him. It was one of those cul-de-sacs technically called branchments. In front of him, there was another wall, a wall of night. The light from the air hole died out ten or twelve paces from the point where Jean Valjean stood, and scarcely produced a pallid whiteness over a few yards of the damp wall of the sewer. Beyond, the opacity was massive; to enter it appeared horrible, like being swallowed up. He could, however, force his way into that wall of mist, and he must do it. He even had to hurry. Jean Valjean thought that the grating he had noticed under the paving stones might also be noticed by the soldiers, and that everything depended on that chance. They too could descend into the well and explore it. There was not a minute to be lost. He had laid Marius on the ground, he gathered him up, this is again the right word, replaced him on his shoulders, and began to walk. He resolutely entered that obscurity.

The truth is that they were not so safe as Jean Valjean supposed. Perils of another kind, and no less great, were perhaps ahead of them. After the flashing whirl of the combat, the cavern of miasmas and pitfalls; after chaos, the cloaca. Jean Valjean had fallen from one circle of Hell to another.

At the end of fifty paces he had to stop. A question arose. The passage terminated in another which it met transversely. These two roads were offered. Which should he take? Should he turn to the left or to the right? How should he guide himself in this black labyrinth? The labyrinth, as we have remarked, has a thread: its descent. To follow the descent is to go to the river.

Jean Valjean understood this at once.

He said to himself that he was probably in the sewer of Les Halles; that, if he chose the left fork and followed the descent, he would come in less than a quarter of an hour to some mouth on the Seine between the Pont-au-Change and the Pont Neuf, that is to say, he would reappear in broad day in the most populous portion of Paris. He might come out in some gathering of corner idlers. Amazement of the pedestrians at seeing two bloody men emerge from the ground under their feet. Arrival of policeman, call to arms in the next guardhouse. He would be seized before he got out. It was better to plunge into the labyrinth, to trust to this darkness, and to rely on Providence for the outcome.

He chose the right, and went up the ascent.

When he had turned the corner of the gallery, the distant gleam of the air hole disappeared, the curtain of obscurity fell back over him, and he was blind again. He went forward nonetheless, and as rapidly as he could. Marius's arms were around his neck, and his feet hung down behind him. With one hand he held both arms and groped for the wall with the other. Marius's cheek touched his and stuck to it, being bloody. He felt a warm stream, which came from Marius, flow over him and penetrate his clothing. Still, a moist warmth at his ear, which touched the wounded man's mouth, indicated breathing, and consequently life. The passage through which Jean Valjean was now moving was not so small as the first. He walked in it with difficulty. The rains of the previous day had not yet run off, and made a little stream in the center of the bed, and he was compelled to hug the wall, to keep his feet out of the water. He went on this way in the pitch black. He was like the creatures of night groping in the invisible, and lost underground in the veins of darkness.

However, little by little, whether some distant air holes sent a little floating light into this opaque mist or his eyes became accustomed to the obscurity, some dim vision came back to him, and he again began to get some confused perception, now of the wall he was touching, and now of the arch under which he was passing. The pupil dilates in the night, and at last finds day in it, even as the soul dilates in misfortune, and at last finds God in it.

To find his way was difficult.

The track of the sewers echoes, so to speak, the track of the streets that overlie them. In the Paris of that day there were two thousand two hundred streets. Picture to yourselves below them that forest of dark branches called the sewer. The sewers existing at that time, placed end to end, would have given a length of thirty miles. We have already said that the present network, thanks to the extraordinary activity of the last thirty years, is no less than a hundred and forty miles.

Jean Valjean began with a mistake. He thought he was under the Rue Saint-Denis, and it was unfortunate that he was not there. Beneath the Rue Saint-Denis there is an old stone sewer, which dates back to Louis XIII and goes straight to the collecting sewer, called the Great Sewer, with a single bend, on the right, at the level of the ancient Cour des Miracles, and a single branch, the Saint-Martin sewer, whose four arms meet in a cross. But the gallery of the Petite Truanderie, whose entrance was near the bistro of Corinth, never joined the underground passage in the Rue Saint-Denis; it runs into the Montmartre sewer, and it was there that Jean Valjean was headed. There, opportunities of losing the way abound. The Montmartre sewer is one of the most labyrinthine in the ancient network. Luckily Jean Valjean had left behind him the sewer of Les Halles, whose geometrical plan represents a multitude of interlocked topgallant masts; but he had ahead of him more than one awkward encounter and more than one street corner—for these are streets—showing up in the shadows like a question mark; first, to his left, the vast Plâtrière sewer, a kind of Chinese puzzle, shoving and jumbling its chaos of *T*'s and *Z*'s under the Hôtel des Postes and the rotunda of the grain market to the Seine, where it terminates in a *Y;* second, to his right, the crooked corridor of the Rue du Cadran, with its three teeth, which are so many blind alleys; third, to his left, the branch of the Mail, complicated almost at its entrance by a kind of fork, and after zigzag upon zigzag, terminating in the great voiding crypt of the Louvre, truncated and ramified in all directions; finally, to the right, the cul-de-sac passage of the Rue des Jeûneurs, with countless little reducts here and there, before arriving at the central sewer, which alone could lead him to some outlet distant enough to be secure.

If Jean Valjean had had any notion of what we have here pointed out, he would have quickly perceived, merely from feeling the wall, that he was not in the underground gallery of the Rue Saint-Denis. Instead of the old hewn stone, instead of the ancient architecture, haughty and royal even in the sewer, with floor and running courses of granite, and mortar of thick lime, which cost seventy-five dollars a yard, he would have felt beneath his hand the contemporary economy, the economical expedient, the millstone grit laid in hydraulic cement on a bed of concrete, which cost thirty-five dollars a yard, the bourgeois masonry known as "small materials"; but he knew nothing of all this.

He went on anxiously but calmly, seeing nothing, knowing nothing, plunged into chance, that is to say, swallowed up in Providence.

By degrees, we must say, some horror got to him. The shadow that surrounded him entered his mind. He was walking in an enigma. This aqueduct of the cloaca is intimidating; it is dizzily intertwined. It is indeed a dreary thing to be caught in this Paris of darkness. Jean Valjean was obliged to find and almost invent his route without seeing it. In that unknown region, each step he took might be the last. How would he get out? Would he find an outlet? Would he find it in time? Would this colossal subterranean sponge with cells of stone submit to being penetrated and pierced through? Would he meet with some unanticipated knot of obscurity? Would he encounter the inextricable and the insurmountable? Would Marius die of hemorrhage, and he of hunger? Would they both perish there at last, and become two skeletons in some niche of that night? He did not know. He asked himself all this, and he could not answer. The intestine of Paris is an abyss. Like the prophet, he was in the belly of the monster.

Suddenly he was surprised. At the most unexpected moment, and without having diverged from a straight line, he discovered he was no longer rising; the water of the brook lapped against his heels instead of the top of his feet. The sewer was now heading down. Why? Would he then soon reach the Seine? This danger was great, but the peril of retreat was still greater. He continued to advance.

It was not toward the Seine that he was going. The saddleback formed by the topography of Paris on the right bank empties one of its slopes into the Seine and the other into the Great Sewer. The crest of this saddleback which determines the division of the waters follows a very capricious line. The culminating point, which is the point of separation of the flow, is for the Saint-Avoye sewer beyond the Rue Michel-le-Comte, for the sewer of the Louvre near the boulevards, and for the Montmartre sewer, near Les Halles. It was at this culminating point that Jean Valjean had arrived. He was making his way toward the belt sewer; he was on the right road. But he knew none of that.

Whenever he came to a branch, he felt its angles, and if he found the opening not as wide as the corridor where he was, he did not enter, and kept on his route, judging correctly that every narrower way must terminate in a cul-de-sac and could only lead him away from his object, the outlet. Thus he evaded the quadruple snare spread for him in the darkness, by the four labyrinths we have just mentioned.

Eventually he felt he was getting away from under the Paris that was petrified by the émeute, in which the barricades had cut off traffic, and that he was coming under the Paris that was alive and normal. Above his head he suddenly heard a sound like thunder, distant, but continuous. It was the rumbling of carriages.

He had been walking for about half an hour, at least by his own calculation, and had not yet thought of resting, except that he had changed the hand that supported Marius. The darkness was deeper than ever, but this depth reassured him.

All at once he saw his shadow in from of him. It was outlined by an almost imperceptible red glow, which turned the floor at his feet and the arch above his head vaguely crimson and which glided along to his right and his left on the two slimy walls of the corridor. In amazement he turned around.

Behind him, in the portion of the passage through which he had passed, at what seemed to him an immense distance throwing its rays into the dense obscurity, burned a sort of horrible star that appeared to be looking at him.

It was the somber star of the police that was rising in the sewer.

Behind this star were moving in disorder eight or ten black forms, straight, indistinct, terrible.

II

EXPLANATION

During the day of the 6th of June, a search of the sewers had been ordered. It was feared that they would be taken as a refuge by the vanquished, and Prefect Gisquet was to ransack the occult Paris, while General Bugeaud was sweeping the public Paris; a linked double operation that demanded a double strategy of public power, represented above by the army and below by the police. Three platoons of officers and sewer men explored the subterranean streets of Paris, the first, the right bank, the second, the left bank, the third, under the Ile de la Cité.

The officers were armed with carbines, clubs, swords, and daggers.

What was at that moment headed toward Jean Valjean was the lantern of the right bank patrol.

This patrol had just visited the crooked gallery and the three blind alleys beneath the Rue du Cadran. While they were taking their candle to the end of these blind alleys, Jean Valjean had come to the entrance of the gallery on his way, had found it narrower than the principal passage, and had not entered it. He had gone on beyond. The policemen, on coming out of the Cadran gallery, had thought they heard the sound of feet in the direction of the belt sewer. It was in fact Jean Valjean's footsteps. The sergeant in command of the patrol lifted his lantern, and the squad began to look into the mist in the direction the sound came from.

This was an indescribable moment for Jean Valjean.

Luckily, if he could see the lantern well, the lantern saw him badly. It was light and he was shadow. He was far off and merged in the black of the place. He drew close to the side of the wall, and stopped.

Still, he did not realize what was moving there behind him. Lack of sleep and food, his emotions had thrown him, too, into the visionary state. He saw a flaring flame, and around it specters. What was it? He did not understand.

Since Jean Valjean had stopped, the noise ceased.

The men of the patrol listened and heard nothing, they looked and saw nothing. They consulted.

At that time there was a sort of service crossroads at this point of the Montmartre sewer, which has since been suppressed because of the little interior lake that formed in it, by the damming up in heavy storms of the torrents of rainwater. The patrol could gather in a group in this square.

Jean Valjean saw these goblins form a kind of circle. These mastiffs' heads bunched together and whispered.

The result of this council held by the watchdogs was that they had been mistaken, that there had been no noise, that there was nobody there, that it was useless to bother with the belt sewer, that it would be wasted time, but that they must hurry toward Saint-Merry, that if there were anything to do and any "bousingot," any wild democrat, to track down, it was in that quarter.

From time to time parties resole their old terms of insult. In 1832, the word "bousingot" filled the interim between the word "Jacobin," which was worn out, and the word "demagogue," then almost unused, but which has since done such excellent service.

The sergeant gave the order to file left toward the slope to the Seine. If they had thought of dividing into two squads and going in both directions, Jean Valjean would have been caught. It hung by this thread. Probably the instructions from the prefecture, foreseeing the possibility of a fight and that the insurgents might be numerous, forbade the patrol to separate. The patrol resumed its march, leaving Jean Valjean behind. Of all these movements, Jean Valjean perceived nothing except the eclipse of the lantern, which suddenly turned back.

Before going away, the sergeant, to ease the police conscience, discharged his carbine in the direction they were abandoning, toward Jean Valjean. The detonation rolled from echo to echo in the crypt like a rumbling of this titanic bowel. Some plaster that fell into the stream and spattered the water a few steps from Jean Valjean made him aware that the ball had struck the arch above his head.

Slow and measured steps resounded on the floor for some time, more and more deadened by the progressive increase of the distance, the group of black forms sank away, a glimmer oscillated and floated, making a ruddy circle in the vault, which decreased, then disappeared; the silence became deep again, the obscurity once more became complete, blindness and deafness resumed possession of the darkness; and Jean Valjean, not yet daring to stir, stood for a long time with his back to the wall, his ear intent and eye dilated, watching the vanishing of that phantom patrol.

III

THE STALKER AND THE STALKED

We must do the police of that period this justice that, even in the gravest public conjunctures, it imperturbably performed its duties of watch and ward. In its eyes an émeute was no pretext for giving malefactors a loose rein and for neglecting society because the government was in peril. The ordinary duty was performed correctly in addition to the extraordinary duty and was not disturbed by it. In the midst of an incalculable political event already begun, under the pressure of a possible revolution, and without allowing himself to be diverted by the insurrection and the barricade, an officer would "spin" a thief.

Something just like this occurred in the afternoon of the 6th of June beside the Seine, on the shore of the right bank, a little beyond the Pont des Invalides.

There is no shore there now. The place has changed in appearance. But on that bank, two men some distance apart seemed to be observing each other, one avoiding the other. The one in front was trying to increase the distance, the one behind to lessen it.

It was like a game of chess played at a distance and silently. Neither one seemed to hurry, and both walked slowly, as if each was afraid that by too much haste he would double his partner's pace.

One would have said it was an appetite following a prey, without appearing to do so on purpose. The prey was crafty and kept on its guard.

The requisite proportions between the tracked marten and the tracking hound were observed. The one trying to escape had a slight build and a sickly look; the one trying to seize, a tall individual, had a tough look and promised to be tough in any encounter.

The first, feeling himself the weaker, was avoiding the second; but he avoided him in a profoundly ferocious way; anyone observing him would have seen in his eyes the gloomy hostility of flight, and all the menace contained in fear.

The shore was deserted; there was no one there, not even a boatman nor a lighterman on the barges moored here and there.

These two men could not have been easily seen, except from the opposite quay and to anyone who might have examined them from that distance, the man in front would have seemed like a bristly creature, tattered and skulking, restless and shivering under a ragged workshirt, and the other, like a classic and official person, wearing the overcoat of authority buttoned to the chin.

The reader might recognize these two men, if he could see them closer.

What was the purpose of the second one?

Probably to put the first in warmer clothes.

When a man clad by the state pursues a man in rags, it is in order to make him also a man clad by the state. Except that the color is the whole question. To be clad in blue is glorious; to be clad in red is the opposite.

There is a crimson of the lower depths.

It was probably some annoyance and some crimson of this kind that the first wished to avoid.

If the other was allowing him to go on and had not yet seized him, it was, according to all appearances, in the hope of seeing him wind up at some significant rendezvous, with some group of lawful prizes. This delicate operation is called "spinning."

What makes this conjecture the more probable is that

the closely buttoned man, noticing from the shore a fiacre that was driving along the quay empty, beckoned to the driver; the driver understood, and evidently recognized with whom he was dealing, turned his horse, and began to follow the two men on the upper part of the quay at a walk. This was not noticed by the equivocal and ragged character in front.

The fiacre rolled along past the trees of the Pont des Champs-Elysées. Above the parapet, the bust of the driver could be seen moving along, whip in hand.

One of the secret instructions of the police to officers contains this article: "Always have a vehicle within call, in case of need."

While maneuvering, each on his own side with irreproachable strategy, these two men approached a ramp of the quay sloping down to the beach, which, at that time, allowed the coach-drivers coming from Passy to go to the river to water their horses. This ramp has since been removed, for the sake of symmetry; the horses perish with thirst, but the eye is satisfied.

It seemed likely that the man in the workshirt would go up by this ramp in order to attempt an escape into the Champs-Elysées, a place decorated with trees, but on the other hand much traveled by officers, and where his pursuer would have easily seized him by force.

This point of the quay is very near the house brought from Moret to Paris in 1824, by Colonel Brack, and called the house of Francis I. A guardhouse is quite nearby.

To the great surprise of his observer, the man pursued did not take the ramp from the watering place. He continued on down the shore along the quay.

His position was visibly becoming critical.

Unless it was to throw himself into the Seine, what was he going to do?

No way after that for getting up to the quay; no other ramp, and no staircase; and they were very near the spot, marked by the turn of the Seine toward the Pont d'Iéna, where the shore, narrowing more and more, terminates in a slender tongue, and is lost under water. There he would inevitably find himself caught between the steep wall on his right, the river on the left and in front, and authority on his heels.

It is true that this end of the shore was masked from

sight by a mound of rubbish from six to seven feet high, the product of some demolition. But did this man hope to hide effectively behind this heap of rubble, which the other one only had to walk around? The expedient would have been puerile. He certainly did not dream of it. The innocence of robbers does not go that far.

The heap of rubbish made a sort of rise at the edge of the water, which stretched out like a promontory, as far as the wall of the quay.

The man pursued reached this little hill and doubled around it, so that he was no longer seen by the other.

The latter, not seeing, was not seen; he took advantage of this to abandon all pretense and to walk very rapidly. In a few seconds he came to the mound of rubbish and walked around it. There, he stopped in amazement. The man whom he was hunting was gone.

Total eclipse of the man in the workshirt.

The beach beyond the mound of rubbish had scarcely a length of thirty yards, then it plunged below the water that beat against the wall of the quay.

The fugitive could not have thrown himself into the Seine nor scaled the quay without being seen by his stalker. What had become of him?

The man in the closely buttoned coat walked to the end of the bank, and paused there a moment pensively, his fists convulsive, his eyes ferreting. Suddenly he slapped his forehead. He had just noticed, at the point where the land ended and the water began, a wide, low iron grating, arched, with a heavy lock and three massive hinges. This grating, a sort of door cut into the bottom of the quay, opened onto the river as much as onto the beach. A blackish stream flowed from beneath it. This stream emptied into the Seine.

Beyond its heavy rusty bars could be distinguished a sort of vaulted, dark corridor.

The man crossed his arms and looked at the grating reproachfully.

This look not enough, he tried to push it; he shook it, it resisted firmly. Probably it had just been opened, although no sound had been heard, a strange circumstance with a grating so rusty; but certainly it had been closed again. That indicated that the one for whom this door had just opened, had used not a hook but a key.

This obvious fact immediately struck the mind of the man who was exerting himself, shaking the grating, and forced out of him this indignant reaction:

"That's a bit much! A government key!"

Then, immediately calming down, he expressed a whole world of inner ideas by this puff of monosyllables accented almost ironically: "Well! Well! Well! Well!"

So saying, hoping who knows what, either to see the man come out, or to see others go in, he posted himself on watch behind the heap of rubbish, with the patient rage of a pointer.

As for him, the cabby, who adapted to his every movement, had halted above him near the parapet. The driver, foreseeing a long stay, fitted the muzzles of his horses into the bag of oats wet at the bottom, so well known to Parisians, to whom the governments, be it said in parenthesis, sometimes apply it. The few passersby on the Pont d'Iéna, before going off, turned their heads to look for a moment at these two motionless features of the landscape, the man on the shore, the fiacre on the quay.

IV

HE ALSO BEARS HIS CROSS

Jean Valjean had resumed his advance and had not stopped again.

This progress became more and more laborious. The level of the arches varies; the medium height is about five feet six inches, and was calculated for the height of a man; Jean Valjean was compelled to bend so as not to hit Marius against the arch; he had to stoop constantly, then rise up, to grope incessantly for the wall. The moisture of the stones and the slime on the floor lent poor support, whether for hand or foot. He was wading in the hideous dunghill of the city. The occasional gleams from the air holes appeared only at infrequent intervals, and so wan that the noonday seemed only moonlight; all the rest was mist, miasma, opacity, blackness. Jean Valjean was hungry and thirsty; thirsty particularly; and this place, like the sea, is full of water you cannot drink. His strength, which was prodigious, and very little diminished by age, thanks to his chaste and sober life, began to give way notwithstanding. He was growing tired, and as his strength diminished the weight of his load increased. Marius, dead perhaps, weighed heavily on him as inert bodies do. Jean Valjean supported him in such a way that his chest was not compressed and his breathing could always be as free as possible. He could feel the rapid scurrying of the rats between his legs. One of them was so frightened as to bite him. From time to time through the aprons of the sewer openings came a breath of fresh air, which revived him.

It might have been three in the afternoon when he arrived at the belt sewer.

He was first astonished at this sudden widening. Abruptly he found himself in the gallery where his outstretched hands did not reach the two walls, and under an arch that his head did not touch. The Great Sewer is in fact eight feet wide and seven high.

At the point where the Montmartre sewer joins the Great Sewer, two other subterranean galleries, that of the Rue de Provence and that of the Abattoir, come in too, making a square. Between these four possible ways a less sagacious man would have been undecided. Jean Valjean took the widest, that is to say, the belt sewer. But there the old question came back: to go down, or up? He thought that their situation was urgent, and that he must, at whatever risk, now reach the Seine. In other words, descend. He turned to the left.

Well for him that he did so. For it would be an error to suppose that the belt sewer has two outlets, one toward Bercy, another toward Passy, and that it is, as its name indicates, the subterranean belt of the Paris of the right bank. The Great Sewer, which, it must be remembered, is nothing more nor less than the former brook of Ménilmontant, terminates upstream in a cul-de-sac, that is to say, its ancient starting point, which was its spring, at the foot of the hill of Ménilmontant. It has no direct access to the branch that gathers up the waters of Paris below the Popincourt quarter and empties into the Seine by the Amelot sewer above the ancient Ile Louviers. This branch, which completes the collecting sewer, is separated from it, under the Rue Ménilmontant itself, by a solid wall that marks the point of separation of the waters upstream and down. Had Jean Valjean gone up the gallery, he would have come, after extreme effort, exhausted, expiring, in the darkness, to a wall. He would have been lost.

Strictly speaking, by going back a little, entering the passage of the Filles-du-Calvaire, as long as he did not hesitate at the subterranean branchings of the Boucherat crossing, by taking the Saint-Louis corridor, then, on the left, the Saint-Gilles passage, then by turning to the right and avoiding the Saint-Sébastien gallery, he might have come to the Amelot sewer, and from there, provided he had not gone astray in the sort of *F* under the Bastille, reached the outlet on the Seine near the Arsenal. But, for that he would have to have been perfectly familiar with the huge madrepore of the sewer in all its ramifications and in all its tubes. Now, we must repeat, he knew nothing of this frightful system of paths along which he was making his way; and, had anybody asked him where he was, he would have answered: In the night.

His instinct served him well. To keep heading down was, in fact, possible safety.

To his right he left the two passages that spread in the form of a claw under the Rue Lafitte and the Rue Saint-Georges, and the long forked corridor of the Chaussée d'Antin.

A little beyond an effluent that was probably the branching of the Madeleine, he stopped. He was very tired. A large air hole, probably the manhole on the Rue d'Anjou, produced an almost vivid light. With all the gentleness of a brother for his wounded sibling, Jean Valjean laid Marius on the side bank of the sewer. Marius's bloody face appeared, under the white gleam from the air hole, as if at the bottom of a tomb. His eyes were closed, his hair adhered to his temples like brushes dried in red paint, his hands hung lifelessly, his limbs were cold, there was coagulated blood at the corners of his mouth. A clot of blood had gathered in the knot of his tie; his shirt was embedded in the wounds, the cloth of his coat chafed the gaping gashes in the living flesh. Jean Valjean, removing the garments with the ends of his fingers, laid his hand on his breast; the heart was still beating. Jean Valjean tore up his shirt, bandaged the wounds as best he could, and stanched the flowing blood; then, bending in the twilight over Marius, who was still unconscious and almost lifeless, he looked at him with an inexpressible hatred.

In opening Marius's clothes, he had found two things in his pockets, the bread that had been forgotten there since the previous day, and Marius's notebook. He ate the bread and opened the notebook. On the first page he found the four lines written by Marius. They will be remembered.

"My name is Marius Pontmercy. Carry my corpse to my grandfather's, M. Gillenormand, Rue des Filles du Calvaire, No. 6, in the Marais."

By the light of the air hole, Jean Valjean read these four lines, and stopped a moment as if self-absorbed, repeating in an undertone: "Rue des Filles du Calvaire, Number Six, Monsieur Gillenormand." He replaced the notebook in Marius's pocket. He had eaten, strength had returned to him: He put Marius on his back again, laid his head carefully on his right shoulder, and began to walk down the sewer.

The Great Sewer, following the course of the valley of Ménilmontant, is almost six miles long. It is paved for a considerable part of its course.

This guiding torch of the street names of Paris with which we are lighting Jean Valjean's subterranean progress for the reader, Jean Valjean did not have. Nothing told him what zone of the city he was passing through, nor what route he had followed. Only the growing pallor of the gleams of light which he saw from time to time, indicated that the sun was leaving the pavement, and that the day would soon be gone; and the rumblings of the wagons above his head, having gone from continuous to intermittent, then having almost ceased, he concluded that he was no longer under central Paris, and that he was approaching some solitary region, in the vicinity of the outer boulevards or the farthest quays. Where there are fewer houses and fewer streets, the sewer has fewer airholes. The darkness grew denser around Jean Valjean. He nonetheless continued to advance, groping in the obscurity.

This obscurity suddenly became terrible.

V

FOR SAND AS WELL AS WOMAN THERE IS A FINESSE THAT IS PERFIDY

He could feel that he was entering the water, and that under his feet, he had no longer pavement, but mud.

Along the coastline of Brittany or Scotland, it sometimes happens that a traveler or a fisherman, walking on the beach at low tide far from the bank, suddenly notices that for several minutes he has been walking with some difficulty. The beach beneath his feet is like pitch; his soles stick to it; it is no longer sand, it is glue. The beach is perfectly dry, but at every step he takes, as soon as he lifts his foot, the print fills up with water. The eye, however, has not noticed any change; the immense strand is smooth and tranquil, all the sand looks the same, nothing distinguishes the solid surface from the surface that is no longer so; the joyous little cloud of sand fleas continues to spring tumultuously over the wayfarer's feet. The man keeps on going forward, tending toward the land, endeavors to get nearer the upland. He is not anxious. Anxious about what? He somehow feels as if the weight of his feet increased with every step he takes. Suddenly he sinks in. He sinks in two or three inches. Decidedly he is not on the right path; he stops to take his bearings. All at once, he looks at his feet. His feet have disappeared. The sand covers them. He pulls his feet out of the sand, he wants to retrace his steps, he turns back, he sinks in deeper. The sand comes up to his ankles, he pulls out and lurches to the left, the sand is half a leg deep, he hurtles to the right, the sand comes up to his shins. Then he recognizes with unspeakable terror that he is caught in the quicksand, and that underneath him he has the terrifying medium in which man can no more walk than fish can swim. He throws off his load if he has one, he lightens himself like a ship in distress; it is already too late, the sand is above his knees.

He calls, he waves his hat or his handkerchief, the sand

keeps gaining on him; if the beach is deserted, if the land is too far off, if the sandbank has too poor a reputation, if there is no hero in sight, it is all over, he is condemned to sink in. He is condemned to that appalling burial, long, infallible, implacable, impossible to slacken or to hasten, that goes on for hours, that will not end, that seizes you erect, free and in full health, that sucks you down by the feet, that, with every attempted effort, at every shout, drags you a little deeper, that appears to punish you for your resistance by strengthening its grip, that pulls the man slowly into the earth while leaving him all the time to look at the horizon, the trees, the green fields, the smoke of the villages on the plain, the sails of the ships on the sea, the birds flying and singing, the sunshine, the sky. Enlizement is the grave turned into a tide, rising from the depths of the earth toward a living man. Each minute is an inexorable laying-out. The victim attempts to sit, to lie down, to creep; every movement he makes buries him; he straightens up, he sinks in; he feels that he is being swallowed up; he howls, implores, shrieks to the clouds, writhes, despairs. See him waist-deep in the sand; the sand reaches his breast, he is now only a bust. He raises his arms, utters furious groans, clutches the beach with his nails, wants to hold onto that straw, leans on his elbows to pull himself out of this soft sheath, sobs in a frenzy; the sand rises. The sand reaches his shoulders, the sand reaches his neck; the face alone is now visible. The mouth cries, the sand fills it; silence. The eyes still stare, the sand shuts them; night. Then the forehead decreases, a little hair flutters above the sand; a hand protrudes, comes through the surface of the beach, moves and shakes, and disappears. Sinister obliteration of a man.

Sometimes a horseman is dragged under with his horse, sometimes the cartman with his cart; everything sinks beneath the beach. It is a shipwreck other than in the water. It is the earth drowning man. The earth, filled with the ocean, becomes a trap. It presents itself as a plain and opens like a wave. The abyss is capable of such treachery.

This fatal mishap, always possible on one or another seacoast, was also possible thirty years ago in the Paris sewer.

Before the important works begun in 1833, the subterranean system of Paris was subject to suddenly giving way.

The water filtered into certain underlying particularly friable soils; the floor, which was of paving stones as in the old sewers, or of hydraulic cement on concrete as in the new galleries, its support lost, would buckle. A bend in a floor of that kind is a crack, a crumbling. The floor gave way over a certain length. This crevasse, a hiatus in a gulf of mud, was technically called *fontis*. What is a fontis? It is the seashore quicksand suddenly encountered underground; it is the beach of Mont-Saint-Michel in a sewer. The diluted soil is as though in fusion; all its molecules are in suspension in a soft medium; it is not land, and it is not water. Depth sometimes very great. Nothing more frightening than such an encounter. If the water predominates, death is prompt, there is swallowing up; if the earth predominates, death is slow, there is gradual sinking.

Can you imagine such a death? If enlizement is terrible on the shore of the sea, what is it in the cloaca? Instead of the open air, the full light, the broad day, that clear horizon, those vast sounds, those free clouds whence rains life, those boats seen in the distance, that hope under every form, probable passers, succor possible until the last moment; instead of all that, deafness, blindness, a black vault, a tomb interior already prepared, death in the mire under cover! The slow stifling by the excrement, a stone box in which asphyxia opens its claw in the slime and takes you by the throat; fetidness mingled with the dying breath; mire instead of sand, hydrogen sulfide instead of the hurricane, dung instead of the ocean? And to call, and to gnash your teeth, and writhe, and struggle, and agonize, with that huge city above your head knowing nothing about it at all.

Inexpressible horror of dying this way! Death sometimes redeems its atrocity by a certain terrible dignity. At the stake, in the shipwreck, man may be great; in the flame as in the foam, grace is possible; you are transfigured while falling into that abyss. But not here. Death is unclean. It is humiliating to expire. The last fleeting visions are abject. Filth is synonymous with shame. It is mean, ugly, infamous. To die in a butt of Malmsey, like Clarence, so be it; in the sewerman's pit, like d'Escoubleau, that is horrible. To struggle in it is hideous; at the very moment of your final agony, you are splashing. There is darkness enough for it to be Hell, and slime enough for it to be only a slough, and the dying man does not know whether he will become a specter or a toad.

Everywhere else the grave is gloomy; here it is deformed.

The depth of the fontis varied, as well as its length and its density, according to the more or less yielding character of the subsoil. Sometimes a fontis was three or four feet deep, sometimes eight or ten; sometimes no bottom could be found. Here the mire was almost solid, there almost liquid. In the Lunière fontis, it would have taken a man a day to disappear, while he would have been devoured in five minutes by the Phélippeaux slough. The mire supports weight more or less according to its greater or lesser density. A child escapes where a man is lost. The first law of safety is to divest yourself of every kind of burden. To throw away his bag of tools, or his basket, or his hod, is the first thing that every sewerman does when he feels the soil giving way beneath him.

The fontis had various causes: friability of the soil; some crevasse at a depth beyond the reach of man; the violent showers of summer; the incessant storms of winter; the long misty rains. Sometimes the weight of the neighboring houses on a marly or sandy soil pushed out the arches of the subterranean galleries and made them yield, or the floor would give way and crack under this crushing pressure. In this way a century ago the settling of the Panthéon obliterated part of the cellars on Mont-Sainte-Geneviève. When a sewer sank beneath the pressure of the houses, the difficulty was sometimes revealed above in the street by a kind of sawtooth separation between the paving blocks; this rent developed in a serpentine line along the whole length of the cracked vault, and then, since the evil was visible, the remedy could be prompt. It often happened too that the interior damage was not revealed by any exterior scar. And, in that case, woe to the sewermen. Entering into the sunken sewer without warning, they might perish. The old registers make mention of some workingmen who were buried in this way in the fontis. They list several names; among others that of the sewerman who was pulled under in a slough below the kennel on the Rue Carême-Prenant, whose name was Blaise Poutrain; this Blaise Poutrain was brother of Nicholas Poutrain, who was the last grave-digger of the cemetery called Charnier des Innocents in 1785, the date at which that cemetery died.

There was also that young and charming Vicomte d'Escoubleau, of whom we have spoken, one of the heroes of the siege of Lerida, where they mounted the assault in silk stockings, led by violins. D'Escoubleau, surprised one night with his cousin, the Duchesse de Sourdis, was drowned in a quagmire of the Beautreillis sewer, in which he had taken refuge to escape from the Duc. Mme. de Sourdis, when this death was described to her, called for her smelling salts, and forgot to weep through too much inhalation of salts. In such a case, there is no persisting love; the cloaca extinguishes it. Hero refuses to wash Leander's corpse. Thisbe stops her nose at sight of Pyramus.

VI

THE FONTIS

Jean Valjean found himself faced with a fontis.

This kind of settling often happened then in the subsoil of the Champs-Elysées, very unfavorable for hydraulic works, and giving poor support to underground constructions, due to its excess fluid. This fluidity surpasses even that of the sands of the Saint-Georges quarter, which could only be overcome by stonework over concrete, and the clay beds tainted with gas in the Quartier des Martyrs, so liquid that the corridor could be crossed below the gallery of the Martyrs only by means of a metallic tube. When, in 1836, they demolished, in order to rebuild, the old stone sewer under the Faubourg Saint-Honoré, in which we now find Jean Valjean caught, the quicksand, which is the subsoil from the Champs-Elysées to the Seine, was such an obstacle that the work lasted nearly six months, to the great outcry of the bordering proprietors, especially the proprietors of hotels and coaches. The work was more than difficult; it was dangerous. It is true that there were four months and a half of rain, and three risings of the Seine.

The fontis that Jean Valjean fell upon was caused by the showers of the previous day. A yielding of the pavement, imperfectly supported by the underlying sand, had dammed up the rainwater. After infiltration, came a sinking. The floor, broken up, had disappeared in the mire. What distance did it cover? Impossible to say. The obscurity was deeper than anywhere else. It was a mudhole in the cavern of night.

Jean Valjean felt the pavement slipping away under him. He entered this slime. It was water on the surface, mire at the bottom. He certainly had to cross it. To retrace his steps was impossible. Marius was dying, and Jean Valjean exhausted. Where else could he go? Jean Valjean kept on. Actually, the quagmire seemed not very deep for a few steps. But as he advanced, his feet sank in more. He soon had the mire halfway up to his knees, and water above his knees. He walked on, holding Marius, with both arms as high above the water as he could. Now the mud came up to his knees, and the water to his waist. He could no longer turn back. He sank in deeper and deeper. This mire, dense enough for one man's weight, clearly could not bear two. Marius and Jean Valjean might have had a chance to get out separately. Jean Valjean kept on going, supporting this dying man who might already be a corpse.

The water came up to his armpits; he felt that he was foundering; he could scarcely move in the deep mire. The density, which was the support, was also the obstacle. He still held Marius up, and, with an unparalleled outlay of strength, he kept moving; but he was sinking deeper. Now he had only his head out of the water, and his arms supporting Marius. In the old pictures of the deluge, there is a mother doing thus with her child.

He sank still deeper, he threw his face back to keep clear of the water, and to be able to breathe; anyone seeing him in this obscurity would have thought he saw a mask floating on the darkness; he was dimly aware of Marius's drooping head and livid face above him; he made a desperate effort, and shoved a foot forward; his foot struck something solid; a support. Just in time.

He rose up and writhed and rooted himself on this support with a sort of fury. It seemed like the first step of a staircase climbing back up toward life.

This support, found in the mire at the last moment, was

the beginning of the other slope of the flooring, which had bent without breaking, and had curved under the water like a board, and in a single piece. A well-constructed paving forms a vault, and has this firmness. This fragment of flooring, partly submerged, but solid, was a real slope, and, once up on this slope, they were saved. Jean Valjean ascended the inclined plane, and reached the other side of the quagmire.

On coming out of the water, he struck against a stone, and fell onto his knees. This seemed fitting, and he stayed there for some time, his soul lost in unspoken prayer to God.

He rose, shivering, chilled, filthy, bending beneath this dying man, whom he was dragging on, all dripping with slime, his soul filled with a strange light.

VII

SOMETIMES WE GO AGROUND WHEN WE EXPECT TO GET ASHORE

He started on his way once more.

However, if he had not left his life in the fontis, he seemed to have left his strength. This supreme effort had exhausted him. His exhaustion was so great that every three or four steps he had to pause for breath, and leaned against the wall. Once he had to sit down on the curb to change Marius's position and he thought he would stay there. But if his vigor were gone his energy was not. He got to his feet again. He walked desperately, almost rapidly, for a hundred paces without raising his head, almost without breathing, and suddenly struck against the wall. He had reached a bend in the sewer and, reaching the turn with his head down, he had bumped into the wall. He looked up, and at the far end of the passage, down there in front of him, far, far away, he saw a light. This time, it was not the terrible light; it was the clear white light. It was the light of day.

Jean Valjean saw the outlet.

A condemned soul who, from the midst of the furnace,

suddenly caught sight of an exit from Gehenna, would feel what Jean Valjean felt. It would fly frantically with the stumps of its burned wings toward the radiant door. Jean Valjean felt no more exhaustion, he no longer felt Marius's weight, he found his knees of steel again, he ran rather than walked. As he approached, the outline of the outlet appeared more and more distinctly. It was a rounded arch, not as high as the vault, which lowered by degrees, and not as wide as the gallery, which narrowed as the top grew lower. The tunnel ended on the inside in the form of a funnel; a vicious contraction, copied from the wickets of houses of detention, logical in a prison, illogical in a sewer, and which has since been corrected.

Jean Valjean reached the outlet.

There he stopped.

It was indeed the outlet, but it did not let him out.

The arch was closed off by a strong grating, and the gate which, according to all appearances, rarely swung on its rusty hinges, was held in its stone frame by a heavy lock which, red with rust, seemed like an enormous brick. He could see the keyhole, and the strong bolt deeply plunged into the iron catch. The lock was plainly a double lock. It was one of those Bastille locks common in old Paris.

Beyond the grating, the open air, the river, the daylight, the beach, very narrow, but enough to get away. The distant quays, Paris, that gulf where one is so easily lost, the wide horizon, liberty. He recognized to his right, downstream, the Pont d'Iéna, and to his left, upstream, the Pont des Invalides; the spot would have been propitious for waiting for night and escaping. It was one of the most deserted spots in Paris; the beach that faces the Gros Caillou. Flies came in and went out through the bars of the grating.

It might have been half-past eight in the evening. The daylight was fading.

Jean Valjean laid Marius along the wall on the dry part of the floor, then walked to the grating and clenched the bars with both hands; the shaking was frenzied, the movement nothing. The iron gate did not budge. Jean Valjean seized the bars one after another, hoping to be able to tear out the least solid one, and to make a lever of it to lift the door or break the lock. Not a bar would yield. A tiger's teeth are not more solid in their sockets. No lever; no possible purchase. The obstacle was invincible. No means of opening the door.

So would they have to die there? What should he do? What would become of them? To go back; start out again on the terrible road he had already traversed; he did not have the strength. Besides, how cross that quagmire again, from which he had escaped only by miracle? And after the quagmire, there was that police patrol from which, certainly, one would not escape twice. And then where should he go? Which direction should he follow? To follow the descent was not to reach the goal. If he came to another outlet, he would find it blocked by a door or a grating. All the outlets were undoubtedly closed in this way. Chance had unsealed the grating by which they had entered, but evidently all the other mouths of the sewer were fastened. He had only succeeded in escaping into a prison.

It was over. All that Jean Valjean had done was useless. God refused him.

They were both caught in the gloomy and immense web of death, and Jean Valjean could feel, running over those black threads trembling in the darkness, the appalling spider.

He turned his back on the gate, and dropped onto the pavement, collapsed rather than sitting, beside the still-motionless Marius, and his head sank between his knees. No exit. This was the last drop of anguish.

Of whom did he think in this overwhelming dejection? Neither of himself nor of Marius. He thought of Cosette.

VIII

THE TORN COATTAIL

In the midst of this prostration, a hand was laid on his shoulder, and a low voice said to him, "Go halves."

Somebody in that darkness? Nothing is so like a dream as despair, Jean Valjean thought he was dreaming. He had heard no footsteps. Was it possible? He raised his eyes.

A man was there in front of him.

This man was dressed in a workshirt; he was barefoot; he was holding his shoes in his left hand; he had evidently taken them off to be able to reach Jean Valjean without being heard.

Jean Valjean did not hesitate for a moment. Unforeseen as the encounter was, this man was known to him. This man was Thénardier.

Although woken up, so to speak, with a start, Jean Valjean, used to being on the alert and on the watch for unexpected blows that he must quickly parry, instantly regained possession of all his presence of mind. Besides, the state of affairs could not be worse, a certain degree of distress is incapable of any further crescendo, and Thénardier himself could not add to the blackness of this night.

There was a momentary pause.

Thénardier, lifting his right hand to his forehead, shaded his eyes with it, then knit his brows while he winked, which, with a slight pursing of the mouth, characterizes the sagacious attention of a man trying to recognize another. He did not succeed. Jean Valjean, we have just said, turned his back to the light, and was actually so disfigured, so muddy and bloodstained, that at high noon he would have been unrecognizable. On the other hand, with the light from the opening shining in his face, a cellar light, it is true, livid, but precise in its lividness, Thénardier struck Jean Valjean at once. This inequality of conditions was enough to ensure Jean Valjean some advantage in this mysterious duel which was about to open between the two conditions and the two men. The encounter took place between Jean Valjean veiled and Thénardier unmasked.

Jean Valjean immediately realized that Thénardier did not recognize him.

They gazed at each other for a moment in this penumbra, as if they were taking each other's measure. Thénardier was first to break the silence.

"How are you going to manage to get out?"

Jean Valjean did not answer.

Thénardier continued, "Impossible to pick the lock. Still you must get away from here."

"That's true," said Jean Valjean.

"Well, go halves."

"What do you mean?"

"You've killed the man; very well. As for me, I have the key."

Thénardier pointed to Marius. He went on, "I don't know you, but I'd like to help you. You must be a friend."

Jean Valjean began to understand. Thénardier took him for a murderer.

Thénardier went on, "Listen, my friend. You haven't killed that man without looking to see what he had in his pockets. Give me my half. I'll open the door for you."

And, taking a big key half out from under his shirt, which was full of holes, he added, "Would you like to see what the key to freedom looks like? There it is."

Jean Valjean stayed silent, doubting whether what he saw was real. It was Providence appearing in the guise of horror, and the good angel springing out of the ground in the form of Thénardier.

Thénardier plunged his fist into a huge pocket hidden under his shirt, pulled out a rope, and handed it to Jean Valjean.

"Here," said he, "I'll give you the rope to boot."

"A rope, what for?"

"You need a stone too, but you'll find one outside. There's a heap of rubbish there."

"A stone, what for?"

"Fool, since you're going to throw the Parisian into the river, you need a stone and a rope; without them it would float on the water."

Jean Valjean took the rope. Everybody has accepted things automatically.

Thénardier snapped his fingers as if a sudden idea had come to him.

"By the way, my friend, how did you manage to get out of the quagmire over there? I haven't dared try it. Pugh! You don't smell very good."

After a pause, he added, "I'm asking you questions, but you're right not to answer them. That's an apprenticeship for the examining judge. And then by not speaking at all, you run no risk of saying too much. It doesn't matter, just because I can't see your face, and I don't know your name, you'd do wrong to suppose that I don't know who you are and what you want. It's understood. You've bashed up this gentleman a little; now you want to tuck him in somewhere. You need the river, the great oubliette. I'm going to get you out of the scrape. To help a good fellow in trouble, that suits me just fine."

While commending Jean Valjean for keeping quiet, he was obviously trying to make him talk. He shoved his shoulders, to catch a glimpse of his profile, and exclaimed, without however rising above his moderate tone of voice, "Speaking of the quagmire, you're a first-rate brute. Why didn't you throw him in there?"

Jean Valjean kept his peace.

Thénardier resumed, raising the rag that served him as a tie up to his Adam's apple, a gesture that completes the sagacious air of a serious man.

"As a matter of fact, perhaps you did act wisely. When they come tomorrow to stop the hole, the workmen would certainly have found the *pantinois* forgotten there, and they would've been able, thread by thread, straw by straw, to nab the trace, and reach you. Something went through the sewer? Who? Where did he come out? Did anybody see him come out? The police have brains. The sewer is a traitor and informs against you. A discovery like that is rare, it attracts attention, few people use the sewer for their business, while the river belongs to everybody. The river is the true grave. After a month, they fish you up the man in the nets of Saint-Cloud. Well, and so what? It's a carcass, that's all! Who killed this man? Paris. And justice don't even inquire into it. You've done right."

The more loquacious Thénardier became, the more silent was Jean Valjean. Thénardier nudged his shoulder again.

"Now, let's finish the business. Let's share. You've seen my key, show me your money."

Thénardier was haggard, tawny, equivocal, a little threatening, though friendly.

There was one strange circumstance; Thénardier's manner was not natural; he did not seem entirely at his ease; while he did not put on an air of mystery, he talked softly; from time to time he laid his finger on his mouth, and whispered, "Hush!" It was hard to guess why. There was nobody there but them. Jean Valjean thought that perhaps some other cutthroats were hidden in some cranny not far off, and that Thénardier did not care to share with them.

Thénardier went on, "Let's be done. How much did the *pantre* have in his deeps?"

Jean Valjean groped in his own pockets.

It was, as will be remembered, his habit to have money on him. The gloomy life of expedience to which he was condemned made this a law for him. This time, however, he was caught short. On putting on his National Guard's uniform the evening before, he had forgotten, gloomily absorbed as he was, to take his billfold with him. He only had some coins in his waistcoat pocket. It came to about thirty francs. He turned out the pocket, soaked with filth, and laid out on the ledge of the sewer a louis d'or, two five-franc pieces, and five or six big sous.

Thénardier stuck out his lower lip with a significant twist of the neck.

"You didn't kill him for much," he said.

In all familiarity, he began to poke at the pockets of Jean Valjean and Marius. Jean Valjean, principally concerned in keeping his back to the light, did not interfere with him. While he was feeling Marius's coat, Thénardier, with the dexterity of a juggler, found means, without attracting Jean Valjean's attention, to tear off a strip, which he hid under his shirt, probably thinking that this scrap of cloth might help him later to identify the assassinated man and the assassin. He found, however, nothing more than the thirty francs.

"It's true," he said, "both together, you have no more than that."

And, forgetting his words, "go halves," he took the whole thing.

He hesitated a bit before the big sous. On reflection, he took them too, mumbling, "No matter! It's still knifing people too cheap."

So saying, he took the key out from under his shirt again.

"Now, friend, you've got to go out. This is like the fair, you pay as you leave. You've paid, get out."

And he began to laugh.

In extending to an unknown the help of the key, and in having someone besides himself go out by this gate, did he have the pure and disinterested intention of saving an assassin? We are entitled to doubt it.

Thénardier helped Jean Valjean put Marius back on his shoulders; then he tiptoed toward the grating in his bare feet, beckoning to Jean Valjean to follow him, he looked outside, laid his finger against his lips, and stood for a few seconds as if in suspense; with the inspection done, he put the key into the lock. The bolt slid and the door swung. There was neither creaking nor grinding. It was done very quietly. It was clear that this grating and its hinges, oiled with care, were opened more often than would have been supposed. This quiet was ominous; in it you could feel the furtive comings and goings, the silent entrances and exits of the men of the night, and the wolf-like tread of crime. The sewer was evidently in complicity with some myserious band. This taciturn grating was a receiver.

Thénardier half opened the gate, left just a passage for Jean Valjean, closed the grating again, turned the key twice in the lock, and plunged back into the obscurity, without making more noise than a breath. He seemed to walk with the velvet paws of a tiger. A moment later, this hideous providence had reentered the invisible.

Jean Valjean was outside.

IX

MARIUS SEEMS DEAD TO ONE WHO IS A GOOD JUDGE

He let Marius down onto the shore.

They were outside!

The miasmas, the obscurity, the horror, were behind him. The balmy air, pure, living, joyful, freely available, flowed around him. Everywhere about him silence, but the charming silence of a sunset in a clear sky. Twilight had fallen; night was coming, the great liberator, the friend of all those who need a mantle of darkness to escape from an anguish. The sky extended on all sides like an enormous calm. The river came to his feet with the sound of a kiss. He heard the airy dialogue of the nests bidding each other good night in the elms of the Champs-Elysées. A few stars, faintly piercing the pale blue of the zenith, and visible to reverie alone, produced their imperceptible little resplendences in the immensity. Evening was unfurling, over Jean Valjean's head all the caresses of the infinite.

It was the exquisite hour that says neither yes nor no. There was already night enough for one to be lost in it in a short distance, and still day enough for one to be recognized near at hand.

For a few seconds Jean Valjean was irresistibly overcome by all this august and caressing serenity; there are such moments of forgetfulness; suffering refuses to harass the wretched; everything is eclipsed in thought; peace covers the dreamer like a night; and, under the expansive twilight, and in imitation of the sky which is lighting up, the soul becomes starry. Jean Valjean could not but gaze at that vast clear shadow above him; pensive in the majestic silence of the eternal heavens, he took a bath of ecstasy and prayer. Then, hastily, as if a feeling of duty came back to him, he bent over Marius, and, dipping up some water in the hollow of his hand, he threw a few drops gently into his face. Marius's eyelids did not part; but his half-opened mouth was breathing.

Jean Valjean was plunging his hand into the river again, when suddenly he felt an indescribable uneasiness, such as we feel when we have somebody behind us, without seeing him.

We have already referred elsewhere to this impression, with which everybody is acquainted.

He turned around.

Just as earlier, somebody was indeed behind him.

A tall man, wrapped in a long overcoat, with crossed arms, and holding in his right hand a club whose leaden knob could be seen—stood erect a few steps behind Jean Valjean, who was stooping over Marius.

With the aid of the shadow, it was a sort of apparition. A simple man would have been afraid because of the twilight, and a reflective man because of the club.

Jean Valjean recognized Javert.

The reader has doubtless guessed that Thénardier's pursuer was none other than Javert. Javert, after his unanticipated departure from the barricade, had gone to the prefecture of police, had given an account verbally to the prefect in person in a short audience, had then immediately returned to his duty, which implied—the note found on him will be remembered—a certain surveillance of the shore on the right bank of the Champs-Elysées, which for some time had roused the attention of the police. There he had seen Thénardier and had followed him. The rest is known.

It is also understood that the opening of that gate so obligingly for Jean Valjean was a piece of sagacity on the part of Thénardier. Thénardier felt that Javert was still there; the man who is watched has a scent that does not deceive him; a bone had to be thrown to this hound. An assassin, what a godsend! Here was a scapegoat, which must never be refused. By putting Jean Valjean out instead of himself, Thénardier gave a victim to the police, threw them off his own track, had himself forgotten in a larger matter, rewarded Javert for his delay, which always flatters a spy, earned thirty francs, and counted surely, as for himself, on escaping with the help of this diversion.

Jean Valjean had passed from one shoal to another.

These two encounters blow on blow, to fall from Thénardier onto Javert—it was hard.

Javert did not recognize Jean Valjean, who, as we have said, no longer looked like himself. He did not uncross his arms, he secured his club in his grasp by an imperceptible movement, and said in a curt, calm tone, "Who are you?"

"Me."

"Who, you?"

"Jean Valjean."

Javert put the club between his teeth, bent his knees, bent down, laid his two powerful hands on Jean Valjean's shoulders, which they clamped like two vices, examined him, and recognized him. Their faces almost touched. Javert's look was terrible.

Jean Valjean stood inert under the grasp of Javert like a lion submitting to the claw of a lynx.

"Inspector Javert," he said, "you have me. Besides, since this morning, I have considered myself your prisoner. I did not give you my address to try to escape you. Take me. Only grant me one thing."

Javert did not seem to hear. He glared at Jean Valjean. His rising chin pushed his lips toward his nose, a sign of savage reverie. At last, he let go of Jean Valjean, rose up as straight as a stick, grasped his club firmly, as if in a dream, murmured rather than pronounced this question:

"What are you doing here? And who is this man?" As

he spoke to Jean Valjean, Javert's tone of voice continued to convey the recent suggestion of respect.

Jean Valjean answered, and the sound of his voice seemed to awaken Javert: "It is about him that I wanted to speak. Dispose of me as you like; but first help me carry him home. I only ask that of you."

Javert's face contracted, as happened to him whenever anybody seemed to consider him capable of a concession. Still he did not say no.

He stooped down again, took a handkerchief from his pocket, which he dipped in the water, and wiped Marius's bloodstained forehead.

"This man was in the barricade," he said in an undertone, and as if speaking to himself. "This is the one they called Marius."

A spy of the first quality, who had observed everything, listened to everything, heard everything, and recollected everything, believing he was about to die; who spied even in his death throes, and who, leaning on the first step of the grave, had taken notes.

He grabbed Marius's hand, trying to find a pulse.

"He is wounded," said Jean Valjean.

"He's dead," said Javert.

Jean Valjean answered, "No. Not yet."

"So, you have brought him here from the barricade?" observed Javert.

His preoccupation must have been great, as he did not dwell longer on this perplexing escape through the sewer, and did not even notice Jean Valjean's silence after his question.

As for Jean Valjean, he seemed to have only one idea. He resumed, "He lives in the Marais, Rue des Filles-du-Calvaire, at his grandfather's—I forget the name."

Jean Valjean felt in Marius's coat, took out the notebook, opened it to the page penciled by Marius, and handed it to Javert.

There was still enough light adrift in the air to enable one to read. Besides, Javert had in his eye the feline phosphorescence of the birds of the night. He deciphered the few lines written by Marius and muttered, "Gillenormand, Rue des Filles du Calvaire, No. 6."

Then he cried, "Driver?"

The reader will remember the fiacre that was waiting, in case of need.

Javert kept Marius's notebook.

A moment later, the carriage, arriving by the watering-place ramp, was on the beach. Marius was laid on the back seat, and Javert sat down beside Jean Valjean on the front seat.

When the door was shut, the fiacre moved off rapidly, going up the quay in the direction of the Bastille.

They left the quays and entered the streets. The driver, a black silhouette on his box, whipped up his bony horses. Glacial silence in the coach. Marius, motionless, his body braced in the corner of the carriage, his head dropping on his breast, his arms dangling, his legs rigid, seemed waiting for nothing now but a coffin; Jean Valjean seemed made of shadow, and Javert of stone; and in that carriage full of night, whose interior, whenever it passed a lamp, appeared to turn lividly pale as if from an intermittent flash, chance had grouped together and seemingly confronted the three tragic immobilities—the corpse, the specter, and the statue.

X

RETURN OF THE PRODIGAL SON—OF HIS LIFE

At every jolt over the pavement, a drop of blood fell from Marius's hair.

It was after nightfall when the fiacre arrived at No. 6, in the Rue des Filles-du-Calvaire.

Javert set foot on the ground first, verified by a glance the number above the carriage door, and, lifting the heavy wrought-iron knocker, decorated in the old fashion with a goat and a satyr defying each other, struck a violent blow. The door partly opened, and Javert pushed it. The doorkeeper half-showed himself, yawning and half-awake, a candle in his hand.

Everybody in the house was asleep. People go to bed early in the Marais, especially on days of émeute. That good old quarter, startled by the revolution, takes refuge in slumber, as children, when they hear the goblins coming, hide their heads very quickly under their covers.

Meanwhile Jean Valjean and the driver lifted Marius out of the coach, Jean Valjean supporting him by the armpits, and the coachman by the knees.

While he was carrying Marius in this way, Jean Valjean slipped his hand under his clothes, which were in tatters, felt his breast, and assured himself that the heart was still beating. It was even beating a little less feebly, as if the motion of the carriage had brought about a certain renewal of life.

Javert called out to the doorkeeper in the tone that befits the government, in confronting the doorkeeper of a factious man.

"Somebody whose name is Gillenormand?"

"It is here. What do you want with him?"

"His son is brought home."

"His son?" said the porter with amazement.

"He is dead."

Jean Valjean who, ragged and dirty, was coming up behind Javert, and whom the concierge beheld with some horror, motioned to him with his head that he was not.

The old man did not appear to understand either Javert's words or Jean Valjean's signs.

Javert continued, "He has been to the barricade, and here he is."

"To the barricade!" exclaimed the doorkeeper.

"He got himself killed. Go and wake his father."

The porter did not budge.

"Why aren't you going?" resumed Javert.

And he added: "There will be a funeral here tomorrow."

With Javert, the common incidents of the public thoroughfares were classed categorically, which is the foundation of prudence and vigilance, and each contingency had its compartment; the possible facts were somehow in the drawers, and they came out as the occasion demanded, in variable quantities; in the street there were racket, émeute, carnival, funeral.

The porter merely woke Basque. Basque woke Nicolette; Nicolette woke Aunt Gillenormand. As for the grandfather, they let him sleep, thinking he would know it soon enough in any event.

They carried Marius up to the second floor, without anybody, in fact being aware of it in the other parts of the house, and they laid him on an old couch in M. Gillenormand's anteroom; and, while Basque went for a doctor and Nicolette was opening the linen closets, Jean Valjean felt Javert touch him on the shoulder. He understood, and went downstairs, with Javert behind him.

The porter watched them leave as he had seen them arrive, with drowsy dismay.

They got into the fiacre again, and the driver mounted his box.

"Inspector Javert," said Jean Valjean, "grant me one thing more."

"What?" asked Javert roughly.

"Let me go home a moment. Then you will do with me whatever you like."

Javert remained silent for a few seconds, his chin drawn into the collar of his overcoat, then he let down the window in front.

"Driver," he said, "Rue de l'Homme-Armé, No. Seven."

XI

A SHAKE-UP IN THE ABSOLUTE

They did not open their mouths again for the whole distance.

What did Jean Valjean want? To finish what he had begun; to inform Cosette, to tell her where Marius was, to give her perhaps some other useful information, to make, if he could, certain final dispositions. As for himself, for what concerned him personally, it was all over; he had been seized by Javert and did not resist; another than he, in such a condition, would perhaps have thought vaguely of that rope that Thénardier had given him and of the bars of the first cell he might enter; but, since the bishop, there had been in Jean Valjean, in view of any violent attempt, even upon his own life, let us repeat, a deep religious hesitation.

Suicide, that mysterious assault on the unknown, which may contain in certain measure the death of the soul, was impossible for Jean Valjean.

At the entrance of the Rue de l'Homme-Armé, the fiacre stopped, this street being too narrow for carriages to enter. Javert and Jean Valjean got out.

The driver humbly represented to M. the Inspector that the Utrecht velvet of his carriage was all stained with the blood of the assassinated man and with the mud of the assassin. That was what he had understood. He added that an indemnity was due him. At the same time, taking his little book from his pocket, he begged M. the Inspector to have the goodness to write him "a little scrap of certificate to that effect."

Javert pushed back the little book the driver handed him, and said, "How much must you have, including your stop and your trip?"

"It is seven hours and a quarter," answered the driver, "and my velvet was brand new. Eighty francs, M. Inspector."

Javert took four napoleons from his pocket and dismissed the fiacre.

Jean Valjean thought that Javert's intention was to take him on foot to the post of the Blancs-Manteaux or to the post of the Archives, which are quite near by.

They entered the street. It was, as usual, empty. Javert followed Jean Valjean. They reached No. 7. Jean Valjean rapped. The door opened.

"Very well," said Javert. "Go on up."

With a strange expression on his face and as though it took him some effort to speak this way, he added, "I will wait for you here."

Jean Valjean looked at Javert. This way of doing things was hardly like him. However, the fact that Javert might now feel a sort of lordly confidence in him, the confidence of a cat granting a mouse liberty within the range of his paws, resolute as Jean Valjean was to give himself up and be done with it, the attitude could not hold much surprise for him. He opened the door, went into the house, called out to the doorkeeper who had gone off to sleep and simply pulled the release cord from his bed, "It is I," and went upstairs.

On reaching the second floor, he paused. Every via dolorosa has its stations. The window on the landing, which was a guillotine window, was open. As in many old houses, the staircase was on an exterior wall and had a view out on the street. The street lamp, directly across the way, cast some light on the steps, which provided savings on the lighting.

Either for a breath of fresh air or automatically, Jean Valjean stuck his head out of the window. He leaned out over the street. It is short, and the street lamp lit it from one end to the other. Jean Valjean was dumfounded; there was nobody at all in the street.

Javert had gone away.

XII

THE GRANDFATHER

Basque and the doorkeeper had carried Marius into the drawing room still stretched out motionless on the bench where they laid him on his arrival. The doctor, to whom they had sent word, arrived at a run. Aunt Gillenormand had gotten out of bed.

She walked up and down, beside herself, wringing her hands and incapable of doing anything but saying, "Good Lord, is it possible!" She occasionally added, "Everything will be messed up with blood!" When the first horror had passed, a certain philosophic attitude came over her, represented by the exclamation, "It had to end like this!" She never went so far as to add, "I told you so!" which is quite customary on occasions of this sort.

On the doctor's orders, a cot had been set up beside the bench. The doctor examined Marius and, after establishing that there was a steady pulse, that the wounded man had no penetrating chest wounds, and that the blood at the corners of his lips came from the nasal cavities, he had him placed flat on the bed, without a pillow, his head on a level with his body and even a bit lower, his chest bare so as to make breathing easier. Mlle. Gillenormand, seeing that they were taking off Marius's clothes, withdrew. She began to say her beads in her room.

The body had not received any interior lesion; a bullet, deadened by the notebook, had deflected, and grazed the ribs with a hideous gash, but not deep, and consequently not dangerous. The long walk underground had completed the dislocation of the broken shoulder blade, and there were serious difficulties there. There were sword cuts on the arms. No scar disfigured his face; the head, however, was as if covered with hacks; what would the result of these wounds be to the head? Did they stop at the scalp? Did they affect the skull? That could not yet be determined. A serious symptom was that they had caused the fainting, and people do not always wake from such faintings. The hemorrhage, moreover, had exhausted the wounded man. From the waist down, the lower part of the body had been protected by the barricade.

Basque and Nicolette tore up linen and made bandages; Nicolette sewed them, Basque folded them. There being no lint, the doctor stopped the flow of blood from the wounds temporarily with rolls of cotton. Beside the bed, three candles were burning on a table where the surgical instruments were spread out. The doctor washed Marius's face and hair with cold water. A bucketful was red in a moment. The porter, candle in hand, stood by.

The doctor seemed to reflect sadly. From time to time he shook his head, as if in some interior monologue. A bad sign for the patient, these mysterious dialogues of the physician with himself.

As the doctor was wiping the face and touching the still closed eyelids lightly with his finger, a door opened at the far end of the salon, and a long, pale figure approached.

It was the grandfather.

For two days the émeute had very much agitated, exasperated, and absorbed M. Gillenormand. He had not slept during the previous night, and he had had a fever all day. At night, he had gone to bed very early, recommending that everything in the house be bolted, and from fatigue, he had fallen asleep.

The slumbers of old men are easily broken; M. Gillenormand's room was next to the salon, and, in spite of the precautions they had taken, the noise had awakened him. Surprised by the light that he saw at the crack of his door, he had gotten out of bed, and groped his way to the next room.

He was on the threshold, one hand on the knob of the half-opened door, his head bent a little forward and shaking, his body wrapped in a white bathrobe, straight and without folds like a shroud; he was surprised and had the appearance of a phantom looking into a tomb.

He noticed the bed, and on the mattress that bleeding young man, white with a waxy whiteness, his eyes closed, his mouth open, his lips pallid, naked to the waist, gashed everywhere with red wounds, motionless, brightly lit.

From head to toe, the grandfather shook with as violent a shiver as ossified limbs can have; his eyes, whose cornea had become yellow from his great age, were veiled with a sort of glassy haze. In an instant his whole face assumed the cadaverous angles of a skeleton head, his arms drooped as if a spring were broken in them, and his astonishment was expressed by the separation of the fingers of his aged, tremulous hands; his knees bent forward, showing through the opening of his nightgown his poor naked legs bristling with white hairs, and he murmured, "Marius!"

"Monsieur," said Basque, "monsieur has just been brought home. He has been to the barricade, and—"

"He is dead!" cried the old man in a terrible voice. "Oh! The brigand."

Then a sort of sepulchral transfiguration pulled up this nonagenarian as straight as a young man.

"Monsieur," he said, "you are the doctor. Come, tell me one thing. He is dead, isn't he?"

The physician, at the peak of anxiety, kept his silence.

M. Gillenormand wrung his hands with a terrific burst of laughter.

"He is dead! He is dead! He got himself killed at the barricade! Out of hatred for me! It is against me that he did this! Ah, the bloodsucker! This is the way he comes back to me! Misery of my life, he is dead!"

He went to a window, opened it wide as if he were stifling, and, standing before the darkness, he began to talk into the street to the night: "Pierced, gashed, slaughtered, exterminated, slashed, cut to pieces! Do you see that, the vagabond! He knew very well I was waiting for him, and that I had had his room arranged for him, and that I had hung at the head of my bed his portrait at the time when he was a darling boy! He knew very well he had only to come back, and that for years I had been calling him, and that I sat at night in my chimney corner, with my hands on my knees, not knowing what to do, and that I was a fool because of him! You knew it very well, that you had only to come in and say, 'Here I am,' and that you would be the master of the house, and that I would obey you, and that you would do whatever you liked with your old booby of a grandfather. You knew it very very well, and you said, 'No, he is a royalist; I won't go!' And you went to the barricades, and you got yourself killed out of spite! To avenge yourself for what I said to you about Monsieur le Duc de Berry! That is unspeakable! Go to bed, then, and sleep quietly! He is dead! That is my waking."

The physician, who began to be anxious on two accounts, left Marius for a moment, and went to M. Gillenormand and took his arm. The grandfather turned around, looked at him with eyes that seemed swollen and bloody, and said quietly, "Monsieur, I thank you. I am calm, I am a man, I saw the death of Louis XVI, I know how to bear up under events. There is one thing which is terrible, to think that it is your newspapers that do all the harm. You will have scribblers, talkers, lawyers, orators, tribunes, discussions, progress, lights, rights of man, freedom of the press, and this is the way they bring home your children for you. Oh! Marius! It is abominable! Killed! Dead before me! A barricade! Oh! The bandit! Doctor, you live in the quarter, I believe? Oh! I know you well. I see your carriage pass below my window. I am going to tell you. You would be wrong to think I am angry. We don't get angry with a dead man; that would be stupid. That is a child I brought up. I was an old man when he was yet quite small. He played in the Tuileries with his little spade and his little chair, and, so that the keeper would not scold, with my cane I filled up the holes in the ground that he made with his spade. One day he cried, 'Down with Louis XVIII!' and went away. It is not my fault. He was all rosy and fair. His mother is dead. Have you noticed that all little children are fair? Why is that? He is the son of one of those brigands of the Loire; but children are innocent of the crimes of their fathers. I remember when he was this high. He could not pronounce the *d*'s. His talk was so soft and so indistinct that you would have thought it was a bird. I remember that once, in front of the Farnese Hercules, they made a circle to admire and wonder at him, that child was so beautiful!

It was a head such as you see in pictures. I spoke to him in my gruff voice, I frightened him with my cane, but he knew very well it was for fun. In the morning, when he came into my room, I scolded, but it seemed like sunshine to me. You can't defend yourself against these tykes. They take you, they hold on to you, they never let go of you. The truth is, there was never any amour like that child. Now, what do you say of your Lafayette, your Benjamin Constant, and of your Tirecuir de Corcelles, who kill him for me! It can't go on like this."

He approached Marius, who was still livid and motionless, and to whom the physician had returned, and he began to wring his hands. The old man's white lips moved as if automatically, and made way for almost indistinct words, like a last breath, which could scarcely be heard: "Oh, heartless! Oh, politics! Oh, scoundrel! Oh, Septembrist!" Reproaches whispered by a dying man to a corpse.

Little by little, as internal eruptions must always work their way out, the links between his words returned, but the grandfather appeared to have lost the strength to utter them, his voice was so dull and faint it seemed to come from the other side of an abyss:

"It is all the same to me, I am going to die too, myself. And to think that there's not one little hussy in Paris who wouldn't have been glad to make the wretch happy! A rascal who, instead of amusing himself and enjoying life, went to fight and got himself riddled like a brute! And for whom? For what? For the Republic! Instead of going to dance at the Chaumière, as young people should! It is well worth being twenty years old. The Republic, a deuced fine folly. Poor mothers, raise your pretty boys then. Come on, he is dead. That will make two funerals under the carriage gate. Then you fixed yourself out like that for the fine eyes of General Lamarque! What had he done for you, this General Lamarque? A swordsman! A babbler! To get killed for a dead man! If it isn't enough to drive a man crazy! Think of it! At twenty! And without turning his head to see if he was not leaving somebody behind him! Here now are the poor old men who have to die all alone. Perish in your corner, owl! Well, indeed, so much the better, it is what I was hoping, it is going to kill me dead. I am too old, I am a hundred, I am a hundred thousand; for a long time now I have had a right to be dead. With this blow, it is done. It is all over then, how lucky! What is the use of making him breathe ammonia and all this heap of drugs? You are wasting your efforts, idiot doctor! Go on, he is dead, stone dead. I understand it, I, who am dead, too. He hasn't done the thing halfway. Yes, these times are unspeakable, unspeakable, unspeakable, and that is what I think of you, of your ideas, of your systems, of your masters, of your oracles, of your doctors, of your scamps of writers, of your beggars of philosophers, and of all the revolutions that for sixty years have frightened the flocks of crows in the Tuileries! And as you had no pity in getting yourself killed like that, I will not have even any grief for your death, do you understand, murderer?"

At this moment, Marius slowly raised his lids, and his gaze, still veiled with the astonishment of lethargy, rested on M. Gillenormand.

"Marius!" cried the old man. "Marius! My darling Marius! My child! My dear son! You are opening your eyes, you are looking at me, you are alive, thank you!"

And he fainted.

Book Four

JAVERT OFF THE TRACK

I

JAVERT OFF THE TRACK

Javert made his way slowly away from the Rue de L'Homme-Armé.

He walked with his head down for the first time in his life, and, for the first time in his life as well, with his hands behind his back.

Until that day, of Napoleon's two attitudes, Javert had assumed one, the one that expresses resolution, arms folded across breast; the one that expresses uncertainty, hands behind back, was unknown to him. Now, a change had taken place; his whole person, slow and gloomy, bore the mark of anxiety.

He plunged into the silent streets.

But he kept to one direction.

He took the shortest route toward the Seine, reached the Quai des Ormes, went along the quai, passed the Grève, and stopped, a short way from the police station of the Place du Châtelet, at the corner of the Pont Notre-Dame. Between the Pont Notre-Dame and the Pont au Change on the one hand, and on the other between the Quai de la Mégisserie and the Quai aux Fleurs, there is a sort of square lake traversed by rapids.

This point of the Seine is dreaded by mariners. Nothing is more dangerous than this current, cramped at that time and troubled by the piles of the mill on the bridge, since removed. The two bridges, so close to each other, increase the danger, and the water races alarmingly under the arches. It rolls on with broad, terrible folds; it gathers and roils up; the flood strains at the piles of the bridge as if to tear them out with huge liquid ropes. Men who fall in there are never seen again; the best swimmers drown.

Javert leaned both elbows on the parapet, with his chin in his hands, and while his fingers were clenched mechanically in the thicket of his sideburns, he reflected.

A new thing, a revolution, a catastrophe had just taken place in the depths of his being; and there was matter for self-examination.

Javert was in torment.

For some hours Javert had ceased to be uncomplicated. He was troubled; this brain, so limpid in its blindness, had lost its transparency; there was a cloud in this crystal. Javert felt that the sense of duty was coming apart in his conscience, and he could not hide it from himself. When he had so unexpectedly met Jean Valjean on the shore of the Seine, there had been something in him of the wolf retaking his prey and of the dog that finds his master again.

Before him he saw two roads, both equally straight; but he did see two; and that terrified him—he who had never in his life known anything but one straight line. And, bitter anguish, these two roads were contradictory. One of these two straight lines excluded the other. Which of the two was the true one?

His situation was beyond words.

To owe life to a malefactor, to accept that debt and to pay it, to be, in spite of himself, on a level with a fugitive from justice, and to pay him for one service with another; to allow him to say, "Go away," and to say to him in turn "You are free"; to sacrifice duty, that general obligation, to personal motives, and to feel in these personal motives something general too, and perhaps superior; to betray society in order to be true to his own conscience; that all these absurdities should be realized and that they should accumulate on himself—this is what prostrated him.

One thing had astonished him, that Jean Valjean had spared him, and one thing had petrified him, that he, Javert, had spared Jean Valjean.

Where was he? He looked for but could no longer find himself.

What should he do now? To give up Jean Valjean, that was wrong; to leave Jean Valjean free, that was wrong. In the first case, the man of authority would fall lower than the convict; in the second, a convict rose higher than the law and set his foot on it. In both cases, dishonor to him, Javert. In every course open to him, there was a downfall. Destiny has certain extremities overhanging the impossible, beyond which life is no more than an abyss. Javert was at one of these extremities.

One of his causes for anxiety was that he was compelled to think. The very violence of all these contradictory emotions forced him to it. Thought, an uncommon thing for him, and singularly painful.

There is always a certain amount of internal rebellion in thought; and he was irritated at having it within him.

Thought, on any subject, no matter what, outside of the narrow circle of his functions, had been to him in any case a waste and a fatigue; but thought about the day that had just gone by was torture. However, he absolutely had to look into his conscience after such shocks and render an account of himself to himself.

What he had just done made him shudder. He had, he, Javert, thought good to decide, against all the police regulations, against the whole social and judicial organization, against the entire code, in favor of a release; that had pleased him; he had substituted his own affairs for the public affairs; could this be unjustifiable? Every time he set himself face to face with this nameless act he had committed, he trembled from head to toe. How could he resolve it? A single resource remained: to return immediately to the Rue de l'Homme-Armé, and have Jean Valjean arrested. It was clear that that was what he must do. He could not.

Something barred the way to him in that direction.

Something? What? Is there anything else in the world besides tribunals, sentences, police, and authority? Javert's thoughts were in upheaval.

A convict sacred! A convict not to be seized by justice! And that Javert's doing!

That Javert and Jean Valjean, the man made to be severe and the man made to be submissive, that these two men, each of them the object of the law, should come to this point of setting themselves above the law, could anything be more terrible?

What then! Enormities such as this can happen and nobody should be punished? Jean Valjean, stronger than the entire social order, should be free and he, Javert, continue to eat the bread of the government!

His reflections grew darker and more terrible.

Through these reflections he might also have reproached himself a little regarding the insurgent carried to the Rue des Filles-du-Calvaire; but he did not think of it. The lesser fault was lost in the greater. Besides, that insurgent was clearly a dead man, and legally, death extinguishes pursuit.

So Jean Valjean was the burden weighing on his mind.

Jean Valjean confused him. All the axioms that had served as the supports of his life crumbled away before this man. Jean Valjean's generosity toward him, Javert, overwhelmed him. Other acts, which he remembered and had hitherto treated as lies and follies, returned to him now as realities. M. Madeleine reappeared behind Jean Valjean, and the two figures overlaid each other so as to make one, which was venerable. Javert felt that something horrible was penetrating his soul, admiration for a convict. Respect for a man on the work gang, could that be possible? He shuddered at the thought yet could not shake it off. It was useless to struggle, he was reduced to confessing before his own inner tribunal the sublimity of the wretch. That was odious.

A beneficent malefactor, a compassionate convict, kind, helpful, clement, returning good for evil, returning pardon for hatred, loving pity rather than vengeance, preferring to destroy himself rather than destroy his enemy, saving the one who had struck him, kneeling on the heights of virtue, nearer angels than men. Javert was compelled to acknowledge that this monster existed.

This could not go on.

Certainly, and we repeat it, he had not given himself up without resisting this monster, this infamous angel, this hideous hero, who made him almost as indignant as astounded. Twenty times, while he was in that carriage face to face with Jean Valjean, the legal tiger had roared within him. Twenty times he had been tempted to throw himself on Jean Valjean, to seize and devour him, that is to say, arrest him. What in fact could be simpler? To cry out at the first police station they passed, "Here is a fugitive from justice!" To call the gendarmes and say to them, "This man is yours!" Then to go away, to leave the condemned man there, to ignore the rest, to have nothing more to do with it. The man is the prisoner of the law forever; the law will do what it will with him. What could be more just? Javert had said all this to himself; he had wanted to go further, to act, to arrest the man, and, then as now, he had not been able to; and every time his hand had been raised convulsively toward Jean Valjean's collar, the hand, as if under an enormous weight, had fallen back, and in the depths of his mind he had heard a voice, a strange voice crying out to him, "Very well. Give up your savior. Then have Pontius Pilate's basin brought, and wash your claws."

Then his reflections turned back to himself, and beside Jean Valjean exalted, he saw himself, him, Javert, degraded.

A convict was his benefactor!

But also why had he allowed this man to let him live? In that barricade he had the right to be killed. He should have availed himself of that right. To have called the other insurgents to his aid against Jean Valjean, to have forced them to shoot him, that would have been better.

His ultimate anguish was the loss of all certainty. He felt uprooted. The code was no longer anything but a stump in his hand. He was dealing with scruples of an unknown species. Within him there was a revelation of feeling entirely distinct from the declarations of the law, his only standard hitherto. To retain his old virtue, that no longer sufficed. An entire order of unexpected facts rose and took control of him. An entire new world appeared to his soul; favor accepted and returned, devotion, compassion, indulgence, acts of violence committed by pity on austerity, respect of persons, no more final condemnation, no more damnation, the possibility of a tear in the eye of the law, a mysterious justice according to God going counter to justice according to men. In the darkness he could see the fearful rising of an unknown moral sun; he was horrified and blinded by it. An owl compelled to an eagle's gaze.

He said to himself that it was true then, that there were exceptions, that authority might be taken aback, that rules might stop short before a fact, that everything was not framed in the text of the code, that the unforeseen might be obeyed, that the virtue of a convict might set a snare for the virtue of a functionary, that the monstrous might be divine, that destiny had such ambushes as these, and he thought with despair that even he had not been proof against surprise.

He was compelled to recognize the existence of kindness. This convict had been kind. And he himself, wonderful to tell, he had just been kind. Therefore he had become depraved.

He thought himself cowardly. He was a horror to himself.

Javert's ideal was not to be humane, not to be great, not to be sublime; it was to be irreproachable. Now he had just failed.

How had he reached that point? How had all this happened? He could not have said. He took his head in his hands, but it was in vain; he could not explain it to himself.

He had certainly always had the intention of returning Jean Valjean to the law, whose captive Jean Valjean was, and he, Javert, its slave. While he held him, he had not confessed to himself for a single moment that he had a thought of letting him go. It was in some sense without his knowledge that his hand had opened and released him.

All sorts of questions flashed before his eyes. He asked himself questions and gave answers, and his answers frightened him. He asked himself: "This convict, this desperate man, I have pursued to the point of persecution, and he has had me beneath his feet, and could have avenged himself, and ought to have done so both for his revenge and for his security; in granting me life, in sparing me, what has he done? His duty? No. Something more. And I, in sparing him in turn, what have I done? My duty? No. Something more. So is there something more than duty?" Here he was startled; his scale fell out of balance; one end slipped into the abyss, the other flew up into the sky, and Javert felt no less dismay from the one that was above than from the one that was below. He was not in the least what is called a Voltairean, or a philosopher, or a skeptic; on the contrary, respectful by instinct toward the established church, he knew it only as an august fragment of the social whole; order was his dogma and was enough for him; since he had reached the age of a man and an official, he had placed almost all his religion in the police. Being, and we employ the words here without the slightest irony and in their most serious sense, being, we have said, a spy as other men are priests. He had a superior, M. Gisquet; he had scarcely thought, until today, of that other superior, God.

This new chief, God, he was feeling unawares, and he was perplexed by that.

He had lost his bearings in this unexpected presence; he had no idea what to do with this superior; he who was not ignorant of the notion that the subordinate is bound always to yield, that he should neither disobey, nor blame, nor discuss, and that, in presence of a superior who astonishes him too much, the inferior has no resource but resignation.

But how manage to send in his resignation to God?

However this might be, and it was to this that he kept returning, one thing overruled everything else for him, that was, that he had just committed an appalling infraction. He had closed his eyes on a convicted second offender who was illegally at large. He had set a convict free. He had robbed the law of a man who belonged to it. He had done that. He could not understand himself. The very reasons for his action escaped him; he caught only the whirl of them. Up to this moment he had lived by the blind faith that a dark probity engenders. This faith was leaving him, this probity was failing him. All that he had believed in was dissipating. Truths he had no wish for besieged him inexorably. He must henceforth be another man. He suffered the strange pangs of a conscience suddenly operated on for a cataract. He could see what it revolted him to see. He felt that he was emptied, useless, broken off from his past life, destitute, dissolved. Authority was dead in him. He had no further reason for being.

Terrible situation! Moved to emotion.

To be granite, and to doubt! To be the statue of punishment cast whole in the mold of the law, and to suddenly see that you have under your breast of bronze something preposterous and disobedient that almost resembles a heart! To be led by it to render good for good, although you may have said until then that this good was evil! To be the watchdog, and to fawn! To be ice, and to melt! To be a vise, and to become a hand! To feel your fingers suddenly open! To lose your hold, appalling thing!

The projectile man no longer sure of his route, and recoiling!

To be obliged to acknowledge this: Infallibility is not infallible; there can be an error in the dogma; all is not said when a code has spoken; society is not perfect; authority is complicated with vacillation; a crack is possible in the immutable; judges are men; the law may be deceived; the tribunals may be mistaken! To see a flaw in the immense blue crystal of the firmament!

What was happening in Javert was the Fampoux of a rectilinear conscience, the derailment of a soul, the crushing of a probity irresistibly hurled in a straight line and breaking up against God. Certainly, it was strange, that the fireman of order, the engineer of authority, mounted on the blind iron horse of the rigid path, could be thrown off by a ray of light! That the incommutable, the direct, the correct, the geometrical, the passive, the perfect, could bend! That there should be a road to Damascus for the locomotive!

God, always interior to man, and unyielding—he the true conscience—to the false; prohibition to the spark to extinguish itself; an order to the ray to remember the sun; an injunction to the soul to recognize the real absolute when it is confronted with the fictitious absolute; humanity imperishable; the human heart inamissible—that splendid phenomenon, the most beautiful perhaps of our interior wonders, did Javert understand it? Did Javert penetrate it? Did Javert form any idea of it? Clearly not. But under the pressure of this incontestable incomprehensible, he felt that his head was bursting.

He was less the transfigured than the victim of this miracle. He endured it, exasperated. He saw in it only an immense difficulty of existence. It seemed to him that from then on his breathing would be restricted forever.

To have the unknown over his head, he was not accustomed to that.

Until now all that he had above him had been to his eyes a smooth, simple, limpid surface; nothing unknown there, nothing obscure; nothing that was not definite, coordinated, chained, precise, exact, circumscribed, limited, shut in, all foreseen; authority was a plane; no fall in it, no dizziness in confronting it. Javert had never seen the unknown except below. The irregular, the unexpected, the disorderly opening of chaos, the possible slipping into an abyss; all of that belonged to inferior regions, to the rebellious, the wicked, the miserable. Now Javert was thrown over backward, and he was startled by this monstrous apparition: a gulf above him.

What then! He was completely demolished! He was absolutely disconcerted! What could he trust? What he had been convinced of was giving way!

How could it be? The chink in society's armor could be found by a magnanimous wretch! An honest servant of the law could find himself suddenly caught between two crimes, the crime of letting a man escape, and the crime of arresting him! Everything was not certain in the order given by the state to the official! There might be blind alleys in duty! What then! Was all that real? Was it true that an old bandit, weighed down by convictions, could rise up and ultimately be right? Was that credible? Were there cases then when the law should, before a transfigured crime, withdraw, stammering excuses?

Yes, there were! And Javert saw that! And Javert realized it! And not only could he not deny it, but he was party to it. Those were realities. It was abominable that real facts could reach such deformity.

If facts did their duty, they would be content to be the proofs of the law; it is God who sends facts. So was anarchy about to descend from on high?

So—and beneath the magnifying power of anguish, and in the optical illusion of consternation, all that might have restrained and corrected his impression vanished, and society, and the human race, and the universe, were summed up in his eyes in one simple, terrible feature—so punishment, the thing judged, the force due to legislation, the decrees of the sovereign courts, the magistracy, the government, prevention and repression, official wisdom, legal infallibility, the principle of authority, all the dogmas on which rest political and civil security, sovereignty, justice, the logic flowing from the code, the social absolute, public truth—all of that became confusion, jumble, chaos; himself, Javert, the watchman of order, incorruptibility in the service of the police; the mastiff-providence of society vanquished and prostrated; and over all this ruin a man standing with a green cap on his head and a halo around his brow; such was the upheaval to which he had come; such was the frightful vision he had in his soul.

Could that be endurable? No.

Unnatural state, if ever there was one. There were only two ways to get out of it. One, to go resolutely to Jean Valjean, and to return the convict to the dungeon. The other . . .

Javert left the parapet, and, with his head erect this time, made his way resolutely toward the post indicated by a lamp at one of the corners of the Place du Châtelet.

On reaching it, he saw a sergeant through the window, and he entered. Merely from the way in which they push open the door of a guardhouse, policemen recognize each other. Javert gave his name, showed his card to the sergeant, and sat down at the table of the post, where a candle was burning. There was a pen on the table, a leaden inkstand, and some paper in readiness for possible reports and the orders of the night patrol.

This table, always accompanied by its rush-seated chair, is an institution; it exists in all the police stations; it is invariably adorned with a boxwood saucer, full of sawdust, and a pasteboard box full of red sealing wafers, and it is the lower stage of the official style. There the literature of the state begins.

Javert took the pen and a sheet of paper, and began to write. This is what he wrote:

SOME OBSERVATIONS
FOR THE BENEFIT OF THE SERVICE

"First: I beg Monsieur the Prefect to glance at this.

"Second: Prisoners, returning from interrogation, take off their shoes and remain barefoot on the pavement while they are being searched. Many cough on returning to the prison. This involves hospital expenses.

"Third: Spinning is good, with relays of officers at intervals; but on important occasions there should be two officers at least who do not lose sight of each other, so that, if, for any cause whatever, one officer weakens in the service, the other is watching him, and supplements him.

"Fourth: It is difficult to explain why the special regulation of the prison of the Madelonnettes forbids a prisoner to have a chair, even on paying for it.

"Fifth: At the Madelonnettes, there are only two bars to the sutler's window, which enables the sutler to let the prisoners touch her hand.

"Sixth: The prisoners, called barkers, who call the other prisoners to the parlor, make the prisoner pay them two sous for calling his name distinctly. This is a theft.

"Seventh: For a dropped thread, they hold back ten sous from the prisoner in the weaving shop; this is an abuse on the part of the contractor, since the cloth is just as good.

"Eighth: It is annoying that the visitors of La Force have to cross the Cour des Mômes to reach the parlor of Sainte-Marie l'Egyptienne.

"Ninth: It is certain that every day gendarmes are heard in the yard of the prefecture, relating the examinations of those brought before the magistrates. For a gendarme, who should hold such things sacred, to repeat what he has heard in the examining chamber is a serious breach.

"Tenth: Mme. Henry is an honest woman; her sutler's window is very neat; but it is wrong for a woman to keep the wicket of the trapdoor to the secret cells. It is not worthy of the conciergerie of a great civilization."

Javert wrote these lines in his calmest and most correct handwriting, not omitting a dot, and making the paper squeak resolutely under his pen. Beneath the last line he signed:

"JAVERT,
"Inspector, 1st class.

"At the station of the Place du Châtelet.
"June 7, 1832, about one o'clock in the morning."

Javert dried the fresh ink of the paper, folded it like a letter, sealed it, wrote on the back: "Note for the administration," left it on the table, and went out of the post. The glazed and grated door closed behind him.

He again crossed the Place du Châtelet diagonally, regained the quay, and returned with automatic precision to the very spot he had left a quarter of an hour before; he leaned on his elbows there, and found himself once more in the same attitude, on the same stone of the parapet. It seemed as if he had not stirred.

The darkness was total. It was the sepulchral moment that follows midnight. A ceiling of clouds concealed the stars. The sky was only an ominous depth. The houses in the city no longer showed a single light; nobody was going by; all that he could see of the streets and the quays was deserted; Notre-Dame and the towers of the Palais de Justice seemed like features of the night. A lamp reddened the curb of the quay. The silhouettes of the bridges were distorted in the mist, one behind the other. The rains had swelled the river.

The place where Javert was leaning was, it will be remembered, situated directly over the rapids of the Seine, perpendicularly above the formidable whirlpool that knots and unknots itself like an endless screw.

Javert leaned out and looked. Everything was black. He could make out nothing. He heard a frothing sound; but he did not see the river. At intervals, in that giddy depth, a gleam appeared in dim serpentine contortions, the water having this ability, in the most complete darkness, of taking light, nobody knows where, and changing it into a snake. The gleam vanished, and everything became indistinct once more. Immensity seemed to open there. What was beneath was not water, it was chasm. The wall of the quay, abrupt, confused, mingled with vapor, suddenly concealed, seemed an escarpment of the infinite.

He saw nothing, but he perceived the hostile chill of the water, and the insipid odor of the moist stones. A savage breath rose from that abyss. The swollen river guessed at rather than perceived the tragic whispering of the current, the dismal vastness of the arches of the bridge, the imaginable fall into that gloomy void, all that shadow was full of horror.

For some minutes Javert remained motionless, gazing into that opening of darkness; he contemplated the invisible with a fixedness resembling attention. The water gurgled. Suddenly he took off his hat and laid it on the edge of the quay. A moment later, a tall, black form, which from the distance some belated pedestrian might have taken for a phantom, appeared standing on the parapet, bent toward the Seine, then sprang up, and fell straight into the darkness; there was a dull splash; and the night alone was admitted to the secret convulsions of that obscure form which had disappeared under the water.

Book Five

GRANDSON AND GRANDFATHER

I

IN WHICH WE SEE THE TREE WITH THE PLATE OF ZINC ONCE MORE

Sometime after the events we have just related, the Sieur Boulatruelle had a vivid emotion.

The Sieur Boulatruelle is that road-laborer from Montfermeil we have already glimpsed in the dark portions of this book.

Boulatruelle, it will perhaps be remembered, was a man occupied with varied troubling things. He broke stones and damaged travelers on the highway. Digger and robber, he had one dream; he believed in treasures buried in the forest of Montfermeil. He hoped one day to find money in the ground at the foot of a tree; meanwhile, he was willing to search for it in the pockets of the passersby.

Nevertheless, for the moment, he was prudent. He had just had a narrow escape. As we know, he had been picked up in the Jondrette garret with the other bandits. Utility of a vice: His drunkenness had saved him. It could never be clearly determined whether he was there as a robber or as robbed. An order of no grounds, founded on his clearly proven state of drunkenness on the evening of the ambush, had set him at liberty. He regained the freedom of the woods. He returned to his road from Gagny to Lagny to break stones for the use of the state, under administrative surveillance, downcast, very thoughtful, a little cooled toward robbery, which had nearly ruined him, but turning with only the greater affection toward wine, which had just saved him.

As to the vivid emotion he had a short while after his return beneath the thatched roof of his road-laborer's hut, it was this:

One morning a little before daybreak, Boulatruelle, on the way to work according to his habit, and on the lookout, perhaps, noticed a man among the branches, whose back alone was visible, but whose form, it seemed to him through the distance and the twilight, was not altogether unknown to him. Boulatruelle, although a drunkard, had a correct and lucid memory, an indispensable defensive arm to anyone slightly in conflict with the legal order.

"Where the devil have I seen something like that man?" he asked himself.

But he could find no answer, except that it looked like somebody he confusedly remembered.

Boulatruelle, however, aside from the identity he did not manage to recall, made some comparisons and calculations. This man was not from the neighborhood. He had come there. On foot, evidently. No public carriage goes through Montfermeil at that hour. He had walked all night. Where had he come from? Not far off. For he had neither bag nor bundle. From Paris, undoubtedly. Why was he in the woods? Why was he there at such an hour? What had he come to do?

Boulatruelle thought of the treasure. By dint of digging into his memory he dimly recollected having already had, several years before, a similar alert concerning a man, who, it struck him, was very possibly the same man.

While he was meditating, under the sheer weight of his meditation he had bowed his head, which was natural but not very smart. When he raised it again there was nothing there anymore. The man had vanished in the forest and the twilight.

"The deuce," said Boulatruelle, "I'll find him again, I'll discover the parish of that parishioner. This Patron-Minette prowler has a why, and I'll find it out. Nobody has a secret in my woods without my cooperation."

He took his pickax, which was very sharp.

"Here is something," he muttered, "for prying into the ground or a man."

And, as one attaches one thread to another thread, doing his best to follow the path the man must have taken, he set off through the thicket.

When he had gone a hundred yards or so, daylight, which was beginning to break, helped him. Footsteps on the sand here and there, grass matted down, heath broken off, young branches bent into the bushes and rising again with a graceful slowness, like the arms of a pretty woman stretching herself on awaking, showed him a sort of track. He followed it, then he lost it. Time was passing. He pushed farther forward into the woods and reached a kind of rise. A morning hunter who was walking along a path in the distance, whistling the tune of Guillery, gave him the idea of climbing a tree. Though old, he was agile. Nearby there was a very tall beech tree worthy of Tityrus and Boulatruelle. Boulatruelle climbed the beech as high as he could.

The idea was a good one. In scanning the countryside in the direction where the woods were completely wild and tangled, Boulatruelle suddenly caught sight of the man.

Hardly had he noticed him when he lost sight of him.

The man entered, or rather glided, into a distant glade masked by tall trees, but which Boulatruelle knew very well from having noticed there, near a great heap of millstone, a wounded chestnut tree bandaged with a plate of zinc nailed to the bark. This glade is the one formerly called the Blaru ground. The heap of stones, intended for who knows what use, which could be seen there thirty years ago, is undoubtedly there still. Nothing equals the longevity of a heap of stones, unless it is that of a palisade fence; it is there provisionally. What a reason for enduring!

Boulatruelle, with the speed of joy, let himself fall from the tree rather than climbing down. The lair was found, the problem was to catch the game. That famous treasure of his dreams was probably there.

It was no easy matter to reach that glade. By the beaten paths, which take a thousand provoking zigzags, it required a good quarter of an hour. In a straight line, through the underbrush, which is singularly thick, very thorny, and very aggressive there, it took a good half hour. There was Boulatruelle's mistake. He believed in the straight line; a respectable optical illusion, but one that ruins many men. The underbrush, bristling as it was, appeared to him the best road.

"Let us take the wolves' Rue de Rivoli," he said.

Boulatruelle, accustomed to going astray committed the blunder this time of going straight.

He threw himself resolutely into the thick of the bushes.

He had to deal with hollies, with nettles, with hawthorns, with sweetbriers, with thistles, with exceedingly irascible brambles. He was considerably scratched.

At the bottom of a ravine he found a stream that had to be crossed.

He finally reached the Blaru glade after forty minutes, sweating, soaked, breathless, torn, ferocious.

Nobody in the glade.

Boulatruelle ran to the heap of stones. It was in place. Nobody had carried it away.

As for the man, he had vanished into the forest. He had escaped. Where? Which way? Into what thicket? Impossible to guess.

And, a bitter thing, behind the heap of stones, in front of the tree with the zinc plate, there was some fresh earth, a pick, forgotten or abandoned, and a hole.

The hole was empty.

"Robber!" cried Boulatruelle, shaking both fists at the horizon.

II

ESCAPING FROM CIVIL WAR, MARIUS PREPARES FOR DOMESTIC WAR

For a long time Marius was neither dead nor alive. For several weeks he had a fever accompanied by delirium and serious cerebral symptoms resulting rather from the concussion produced by the wounds in the head than from the wounds themselves.

He repeated the name of Cosette during entire nights

in the dismal loquacity of fever and with the gloomy obstinacy of agony. Some of the gashes gave serious concern, since the suppuration of large wounds is always liable to reabsorb and consequently to kill the patient, under certain atmospheric influences; at every change in the weather, at the slightest storm, the physician was anxious, "Above all, the wounded man must not have any excitement," he repeated. The dressings were complicated and difficult, since the fastening of bandages by adhesive tape was not yet invented. For lint Nicolette used a sheet "as big as a ceiling," she said. It was not without difficulty that the chlorinated lotions and the nitrate of silver overcame the gangrene. As long as there was danger, M. Gillenormand, in despair at the bedside of his grandson, was, like Marius, neither dead nor alive.

Every day, and sometimes twice a day, a very well-dressed gentleman with white hair, such was the description given by the doorkeeper, came to inquire after the wounded man, and left a large package of lint for the dressings.

At last, on the 7th of September, three months to the day after the sorrowful night when they had brought him home dying to his grandfather, the physician declared him out of danger. Convalescence began. However, Marius was still obliged to stay for more than two months stretched out on a chaise longue, because of the complications resulting from the fracture of the shoulder blade. There is always a last wound like this that will not close, that prolongs the dressings, to the great annoyance of the patient.

However, this long sickness and this long convalescence saved him from pursuit. In France, there is no anger, even governmental, that six months does not extinguish. Emeutes, in the present state of society, are to such a degree everybody's fault that they are followed by a certain need to close the eyes.

Let us add that the infamous Gisquet order, which enjoined physicians to inform against the wounded, had so outraged public opinion, and not only public opinion, but the king first of all, that the wounded were shielded and protected by this indignation; and, with the exception of those who had been taken prisoners in actual combat, the courts-martial dared not disturb any. Marius was therefore left in peace.

M. Gillenormand went through every anguish first, and then through every ecstasy. They had great difficulty in preventing him from spending every night with the wounded man; he had his large armchair brought to the side of Marius's bed; he insisted that his daughter should take the finest linen in the house for compresses and bandages. Mlle. Gillenormand, like a prudent and elder person, found means to spare the fine linen, while she let the grandfather suppose that he was obeyed. M. Gillenormand did not allow anybody to explain to him that for making lint, cambric is not as good as coarse linen, nor new linen as good as old. He superintended all the dressings, from which Mlle. Gillenormand modestly absented herself. When the dead flesh was cut away with scissors, he would say, "Ow! Ow!" Nothing was so touching as to see him hand a cup of herbal tea to the wounded man with his gentle senile trembling. He overwhelmed the doctor with questions. He did not realize that he always asked the same ones.

The day the physician announced to him that Marius was out of danger, the good man was in delirium. He gave his doorkeeper three Louis as a tip. In the evening, when he went to his room, he danced a gavotte, making castanets of his thumb and forefinger, and singing the following song:

Jeanne est née à Fougère,
Vrai nid d'une bergère;
J'adore son jupon,
Fripon.

Amour, tu vis en elle;
Car c'est dans sa prunelle
Que tu mets ton carquois,
Narquois!

Moi, je la chante et j'aime,
Plus que Diane même,
Jeanne et ses durs tetons
Bretons.[1]

[1] Joan was born in Fougère,
Best nest for a shepherdess;

Then he knelt on a chair, and Basque, who watched him through the half-open door, was certain he was praying.

Hitherto, he had hardly believed in God.

At each new phase of improvement, which continued to grow more and more visible, the grandfather raved. He unconsciously did a thousand cheerful things; he ran up and down stairs without knowing why. A neighbor, a pretty woman actually, was amazed to receive a large bouquet one morning; it was M. Gillenormand who sent it to her. The husband made a scene. M. Gillenormand attempted to take Nicolette on his knees. He called Marius Monsieur the Baron.

He shouted, *"Vive la République!"*

He would constantly ask the physician, "There's no more danger, is there?" He gazed at Marius with a grandmother's eyes. He looked at him tenderly when he ate. He no longer knew himself, he no longer counted on himself. Marius was the master of the house, there was abdication in his joy, he was the grandson of his grandson.

In this lightheartedness that possessed him, he was the most venerable of children. For fear of tiring or annoying the convalescent, he would step behind him to smile at him. He was contented, joyful, enraptured, delightful, young. His white hairs added a sweet majesty to the cheerful light upon his face. When grace is joined to wrinkles, it is adorable. There is something of the dawn in happy old age.

As for Marius, while he let them dress his wounds and care for him, he had one set idea: Cosette.

Since the fever and the delirium had left him, he had not uttered that name, and they might have supposed that he no longer thought of it. He held his peace, precisely because his soul was there.

I adore her petticoat,
Rascal.
Love, you live alone in her;
It's in her eye
You shoot your darts,
Jabbering!
Me, I sing of her and I love,
Even more than Diana,
Joan and her firm breasts
From Brittany.

He did not know what had become of Cosette; the whole affair of the Rue de la Chanvrerie was like a cloud in his memory; shadows, almost indistinct, were floating in his mind, Eponine, Gavroche, Mabeuf, The Thénardiers, all his friends mingled drearily with the smoke of the barricade; the strange fleeting appearance of M. Fauchelevent in that bloody drama produced on him the effect of an enigma in a tempest; he understood nothing about his own life; he knew neither how, nor by whom, he had been saved, and nobody about him knew; all that they could tell him was that he had been brought to the Rue des Filles-du-Calvaire in a fiacre by night; past, present, future, everything seemed now but the mist of a vague idea; but within this mist there was an immovable point, one clear and precise feature, something that was granite, a resolve, a will: to find Cosette again. To him the idea of life was not distinct from the idea of Cosette; he had decreed in his heart that he would not accept the one without the other, and he was unalterably determined to demand from anybody, no matter whom, who might wish to compel him to live, from his grandfather, from Fate, even from Hell, the restitution of his vanished Eden.

He did not hide the obstacles from himself.

Let us emphasize one point here: He was not won over and was little softened by all the solicitude and tenderness of his grandfather. In the first place, he was not in on the secret of it all; then, in his sick man's reveries, perhaps still feverish, he distrusted this gentleness as a strange new thing, whose aim was to subdue him. He remained cold to it. Marius said to himself it was all right so long as he, Marius, did not speak and offered no resistance; but that, when the question of Cosette was raised, he would find another approach, and his grandfather's real attitude would be unmasked. Then it would be harsh revival of family questions, a confrontation of views, every sarcasm and every objection at once: Fauchelevent, Coupelevent, fortune, poverty, misery, the stone at the neck, the future. Violent opposition, conclusion, refusal. Marius was bracing himself in advance.

And then, as he took new hold of life, his former griefs reappeared proportionately, the old ulcers of his memory reopened, he thought once more of the past. Colonel Pontmercy appeared again between M. Gillenormand and him, Marius; he said to himself that there was no real goodness to be hoped for from the one who had been so unjust and so hard to his father. And with health, there returned a sort of harshness toward his grandfather. The old man bore it gently.

Without showing it in any way, M. Gillenormand noticed that Marius, since he had been brought home and restored to consciousness, had not once said to him "Father." He did not say "monsieur," it is true; but he found means to say neither the one nor the other, by a certain turn of phrase.

A crisis was clearly approaching.

As almost always happens in similar cases, Marius, in order to test his strength, skirmished before battle. This is called feeling out the ground. One morning it happened that M. Gillenormand, over a newspaper that had fallen into his hands, spoke lightly of the Convention and let go with a royalist slur against Danton, Saint-Just, and Robespierre. "The men of ninety-three were giants," said Marius, sternly. The old man was silent, and did not let out a whisper for the rest of the day.

Marius, who still held in mind the inflexible grandfather of his early years, saw in this silence an intense concentration of anger, foresaw from that a sharp conflict, and increased his preparations for combat in the inner recesses of his thought.

He determined that in case of refusal he would tear off his bandages, dislocate his shoulder, lay bare and open his remaining wounds, and refuse all nourishment. His wounds were his ammunition. To have Cosette or to die.

He waited for the favorable moment with the crafty patience of the sick.

That moment came.

III

MARIUS ATTACKS

One day while his daughter was putting in order the vials and cups on the marble top of the bureau, M. Gillenormand bent over Marius and said to him in his tenderest tone, "You see, my darling Marius, in your place I would eat meat now rather than fish. A fried sole is excellent to begin a convalescence, but to put the sick man back on his legs, it takes a good veal cutlet."

Marius, whose strength had nearly all returned, gathered it together, sat up in bed, rested his clenched hands on the sheets, looked his grandfather in the face, assumed a terrible air, and said, "This leads me to say something to you."

"What is that?"

"It is that I wish to marry."

"Foreseen," said the grandfather. And he burst out laughing.

"How do you mean, foreseen?"

"Yes, foreseen. You will have her, your lassie."

Marius, astounded, and overwhelmed by the dazzling burst of happiness, trembled in every limb.

M. Gillenormand continued, "Yes you will have her, your handsome, pretty little girl. She comes every day in the guise of an old gentleman to inquire after you. Since you were wounded, she has spent her time in weeping and making lint. I have made inquiries. She lives in the Rue-de-l'Homme Armé, Number Seven. Ah, there we are! Ah, so you want her! Well, you shall have her. That catches you! You had arranged your little plot; you said to yourself: I'm going to make it known bluntly to that grandfather, to that mummy of the Regency and the Directory, to that old beau, to that Dorante become a Géronte; he has had his levities too, himself, and his love affairs, and his grisettes, and his Cosettes; he has had his day, his wings, he has eaten his spring bread; he must remember it. We'll see. Battle. Ah! You take the bull by the horns. That's good. I propose a cutlet, and you answer: 'A propos, I wish to marry.' That is what I call a transition. Ah! You had reckoned on some bickering. You didn't know that I was an old coward. What do you say to that? You are riled. To find your grandfather still more stupid than yourself, you didn't expect that, you lose the argument you were about to have with me, Monsieur the Lawyer; it's provoking. Well, too bad, rage on. I will do what you want, that cuts you out of it, idiot. Listen. I have made inquiries, I'm sly too; she is charming, she is modest, the thing about the lancer is not true, she has made heaps of lint, she is a jewel, she worships you; if you had died, there would have been three of us; her bier would have accompanied mine. I had a strong notion, as soon as you were better, to plant her squarely at your bedside, but it is only in romances that they introduce young girls unceremoniously beside the couch of the pretty wounded men who interest them. That does not do. What would your aunt have said? You have been quite naked three-quarters of the time, my good man. Ask Nicolette, who has not left you a minute, if it was possible for a woman to be here. And then what would the doctor have said? That doesn't cure a fever, a pretty girl. Well, at any rate, it is all right; don't let us talk anymore about it, it is said and done, it is settled; take her. There is my ferocity. Do you see, I saw that you did not love me; I said: What is there that I can do, then, to make this animal love me? I said: Hold on! I have my little Cosette under my hand; I'll give her to him, he must surely love me a little then, or let him say why. Ah! You thought that the old fellow was going to storm, to put on a gruff voice, to cry No, and to lift his cane against all this dawn. Not at all. Cosette, so be it; love, so be it; I ask nothing better. Monsieur, be so kind as to get married. Be happy, my dear child."

So saying, the old man burst into sobs.

And he took Marius's head, and he hugged it in both arms against his old breast, and they both began to weep. That is one of the forms of supreme happiness.

"Father!" exclaimed Marius.

"Ah! You love me then!" said the old man.

There was an ineffable moment. They choked and could not speak.

At last the old man stammered, "Come, come! The ice is broken. He has called me 'Father.' "

Marius released his head from his grandfather's arms and said softly, "But, Father, now that I am well, it seems to me that I could see her."

"Foreseen again, you will see her tomorrow."

"Father!"

"What?"

"Why not today?"

"Well, today. Here goes for today. You have called me 'Father,' three times, it is well worth that. I will see to it. She will be brought to you. Foreseen, I tell you. This has already been put into verse. It is the conclusion of André Chénier's elegy of the *Jeune malade,* André Chénier who was murdered by the scound——, by the giants of ninety-three."

M. Gillenormand thought he perceived a slight frown on Marius's brow, although, in truth, we should say, he was no longer listening to him, flown off as he was into ecstasy, and thinking far more of Cosette than of 1793. The grandfather, trembling at having introduced André Chénier so inopportunely, hastily went on, "Murdered is not the word. The fact is that the great revolutionary geniuses, who were not evilly disposed, that is incontestable, who were heroes, my God, found that André Chénier embarrassed them a little, and they had him guillot——. That is to say, those great men, on the seventh of Thermidor, in the interest of the public safety, begged André Chénier to have the kindness to go——"

M. Gillenormand, choked by his own sentence, could not continue; neither able to finish it nor to retract it, while his daughter was arranging the pillow behind Marius, the old man, overwhelmed by so many emotions, hurtled as quickly as his age permitted, out of the bedroom, pushed the door to behind him, and, purple, strangling, foaming, his eyes starting from his head, found himself face to face with honest Basque who was polishing boots in the hall. He seized Basque by the collar and cried full in his face with fury, "By the hundred thousand Javottes of the devil, those brigands assassinated him!"

"Who, monsieur?"

"André Chénier!"

"Yes, monsieur," said Basque in dismay.

IV

MADEMOISELLE GILLENORMAND AT LAST THINKS IT NOT IMPROPER THAT MONSIEUR FAUCHELEVENT SHOULD COME IN WITH SOMETHING UNDER HIS ARM

Cosette and Marius saw each other again.

What the interview was, we will not attempt to say. There are things we should not undertake to paint; the sun is among them.

The whole family, including Basque and Nicolette, were assembled in Marius's room when Cosette entered.

She appeared on the threshold; it seemed as if she were in a cloud.

Just at that instant the grandfather was about to blow his nose; he stopped short, holding his nose in his handkerchief, and looking at Cosette above it, "Adorable!" he exclaimed.

Then he blew his nose noisily.

Cosette was intoxicated, enraptured, startled, in Heaven. She was as frightened as one can be by happiness. She stammered, quite pale, quite red, wishing to throw herself into Marius's arms, and not daring to. Ashamed to show her love before all those people. We are pitiless toward happy lovers; we stay there when they have the greatest desire to be alone. Yet they have no need at all of society.

With Cosette and behind her had entered a man with white hair, grave, smiling nevertheless, but with a vague and poignant smile. This was "Monsieur Fauchelevent"; this was Jean Valjean.

He was very well dressed, as the porter had said, in a new black suit, with a white cravat.

The porter was a thousand miles from recognizing in this correct bourgeois, in this probable notary, the frightful corpse-bearer who had landed at his door on the night of the 7th of June, ragged, filthy, hideous, haggard, his face masked by blood and dirt, supporting the unconscious Marius in his arms; still his doorkeeper's flair was awakened. When M. Fauchelevent had arrived with Cosette, the porter could not help confiding this remark to his wife, "I don't know why I keep thinking I have seen that face somewhere before."

M. Fauchelevent, in Marius's room, stayed near the door, as if apart. He had under his arm a package similar in appearance to an octavo volume, wrapped in paper. The paper was greenish and seemed moldy.

"Does this gentleman always have books under his arm like that?" asked Mlle. Gillenormand, who did not like books, softly to Nicolette.

"Well," answered M. Gillenormand, who had heard her, in the same tone, "he is a scholar. What then? Is that his fault? Monsieur Boulard, whom I knew, never went out without a book, he neither, and always had an old volume against his heart, like that."

And bowing, he said, in a loud voice, "Monsieur Tranchelevent—"

Father Gillenormand did not do this on purpose, but inattention to proper names was an aristocratic way of his.

"Monsieur Tranchelevent, I have the honor of asking you for my grandson, Monsieur the Baron Marius Pontmercy, for the hand of mademoiselle."

Monsieur Tranchelevent bowed.

"It is done," said the grandfather.

And, turning toward Marius and Cosette, with arms extended and blessing, he cried, "Permission to adore each other."

They did not make him say it twice. Who cares? The endearments began. They talked softly, Marius reclining on his chaise longue, Cosette standing near him. "Oh, my God!" murmured Cosette, "I am seeing you again! It is you! It is you! To have gone off to fight like that! But why? It is horrible. For four months I have been dead. Oh, how bad of you it is to have been in that battle! What had I done to you? I pardon you, but you won't do it again. Just now, when they came to tell us to come, I thought again I would die, but it was from joy. I was so sad! I did not take time to dress myself; I must look a fright. What will your relatives say of me, to see me with a ragged collar? But speak now! You are letting me do all the talking. We're still on the Rue de l'Homme-Armé. They say your shoulder was terrible. They told me they could put a fist in it. And then that they've cut your flesh with scissors. That is frightful. I've cried, I have no eyes left. It's strange that anybody can suffer like that. Your grandfather looks very kind. Don't disturb yourself; don't rest on your elbow, do be careful, you'll hurt yourself. Oh, how happy I am! So our troubles are all over! I feel all mixed up. I wanted to say something to you and I've completely forgotten it. Do you love me still? We live on the Rue de l'Homme-Armé. There's no garden. I've been making lint all the time. Here, monsieur, look, it is your fault, my fingers are callused."

"Angel!" said Marius.

"Angel" is the only word in the language that cannot be worn out. No other word would resist the pitiless use lovers make of it.

Then, as there were spectators, they stopped, and did not say another word, contenting themselves with touching each other's hands very gently.

M. Gillenormand turned toward everyone in the room, and shouted, "Why don't you speak up, the rest of you? Make a lot of noise, behind the scenes. Come on, a little uproar, what the devil! So these children can chatter at their ease."

And, approaching Marius and Cosette, he said to them softly, "You just go ahead. Don't let us disturb you."

Aunt Gillenormand witnessed with amazement this burst of light into her aged interior. This amazement was not at all aggressive; it was not in the least the scandalized and envious look of an owl at two ringdoves; it was the dazed eye of a poor innocent girl of fifty-seven; it was incomplete life beholding that triumph, love.

"Mademoiselle Gillenormand the elder," said her father to her, "I told you plainly that this would happen."

He paused for a moment and added, "Behold the happiness of others."

Then he turned toward Cosette: "How pretty she is! How pretty she is! She is a Greuze. So you are going to have her all to yourself, rascal! Ah! My rogue, you have narrowly escaped me, you are lucky, if I weren't fifteen years too old, we would cross swords to decide who should have her. Well now! I'm in love with you, mademoiselle. That is very natural. It is your due. Ah! The sweet pretty charming little wedding that this is going to make! Saint-Denis du Saint-Sacrement is our parish, but

I will get a dispensation so you can be married at Saint-Paul. The church is better. It was built by the Jesuits. It has more flair. It is opposite the fountain of Cardinal de Birague. The masterpiece of Jesuit architecture is at Namur. It is called Saint-Loup. You must go there after you are married. It is worth the journey. Mademoiselle, I am altogether of your opinion, I want girls to marry, they are made for that. There is a certain Sainte-Catherine whom I would always like to see with her hair down. To be an old maid is fine, but it is cold. The Bible says: Multiply. To save the people, we need Jeanne d'Arc; but to make the people, we need Mother Gigogne. So, marry, my beauties. I really don't see the good of being an old maid. I know very well that they have a separate chapel in the church, and that they talk a good deal about the sisterhood of the Virgin; but, ye gods, a handsome husband, a fine fellow, and, at the end of the year, a big flaxen-haired boy who takes his milk merrily, and who has nice wrinkles of fat on his legs, and who squeezes your breast in his little rosy paws, while he laughs like the dawn, that is better after all than holding a taper at vespers and singing *Turris eburnea!*"

The grandfather executed a pirouette on his ninety-two-year-old heels, and began to talk again, like a spring released:

> Ainsi, bornant le cours de tes rêvasseries.
> Alcippe, il est donc vrai, dans peu tu te maries.[1]

"By the way!"

"What, father?"

"Didn't you have an intimate friend?"

"Yes, Courfeyrac."

"What has become of him?"

"He is dead."

"Very well."

He sat down near them, made Cosette sit down, and took their four hands in his old wrinkled hands. "She is exquisite, this darling. She is a masterpiece, this Cosette! She is a very little girl and a very great lady. She will be only a baroness, that is stooping; she was born a mar-

[1] So, curbing your reveries,
Alcippe, it's true you're nearly wed.

quise. Hasn't she the eyelashes? My children, fix it well in your noddles that you are on the right course. Love one another. Be foolish about it. Love is the foolishness of men, and the wisdom of God. Adore each other. Only," he added suddenly darkening, "what a misfortune! Now that I think of it! More than half of what I have is in annuity; as long as I live, it's all well enough, but after my death, twenty years or so from now, ah, my poor children, you will not have a sou. Your beautiful white hands, Madame the Baronne, will do the devil the honor to tweak him by the tail."

"Mademoiselle Euphrasie Fauchelevent has six hundred thousand francs."

It was Jean Valjean's voice.

He had not yet uttered a word, nobody seemed even to remember that he was there, and he stood erect and motionless behind all these happy people.

"How is Mademoiselle Euphrasie involved?" asked the grandfather, startled.

"That's me," answered Cosette.

"Six hundred thousand francs!" resumed M. Gillenormand.

"Less fourteen or fifteen thousand francs, perhaps," said Jean Valjean.

And he placed on the table the package Aunt Gillenormand had taken for a book.

Jean Valjean opened the package himself; it was a bundle of banknotes. They ran through them, and they counted them. There were five hundred bills of a thousand francs, and a hundred and sixty-eight of five hundred. In all, five hundred and eighty-four thousand francs.

"Now there is a good book," said M. Gillenormand.

"Five hundred and eighty-four thousand francs!" murmured the aunt.

"This settles things very well, doesn't it, Mademoiselle Gillenormand the elder?" resumed the grandfather. "This devil of a Marius, he has found you a grisette millionaire on the tree of dreams! So now trust in the lovemaking of young people! Students find studentesses with six hundred thousand francs. Cherubino works better than Rothschild."

"Five hundred and eighty-four thousand francs!" repeated Mlle. Gillenormand in an undertone. "Five hundred and eighty-four! You might say six hundred thousand, you know!"

As for Marius and Cosette, they were looking at each other during this time; they paid little attention to this detail.

V

DEPOSIT YOUR MONEY IN SOME FOREST RATHER THAN WITH SOME NOTARY

The reader has undoubtedly understood, without the need to explain at length, that Jean Valjean, thanks to his first escape of a few days after the Champmathieu affair, had been able to come to Paris and to withdraw from Lafitte's in good time the sum he had earned under the name of Monsieur Madeleine, at Montreuil-sur-mer; and that, in the fear of being retaken, which did in fact happen to him a short time later, he had concealed and buried that sum in the forest of Montfermeil, in the place called the Blaru grounds. The sum, six hundred and thirty thousand francs, all in banknotes, was of small bulk, and was contained in a box; but to preserve the box from moisture he had placed it in an oaken chest full of chestnut shavings. In the same chest, he had put his other treasure, the bishop's candlesticks. It will be remembered that he carried away these candlesticks when he escaped from Montreuil-sur-mer. The man glimpsed for the first time one evening by Boulatruelle was Jean Valjean. Afterward, whenever Jean Valjean was in need of money, he would go to the Blaru glade for it. Hence the absences which we mentioned. He had a pickax somewhere in the bushes, in a hiding place known only to himself. When he saw that Marius was convalescing, sensing that the hour was approaching when this money might be useful, he had gone after it; and again it was he that Boulatruelle saw in the woods, but this time in the morning, and not at night. Boulatruelle inherited the pickax.

The real sum was five hundred and eighty-four thousand five hundred francs. Jean Valjean took out five hundred francs for himself. "After that we will see," he thought.

The difference between this sum and the six hundred and thirty thousand francs withdrawn from Lafitte's represented the expenses of ten years, from 1823 to 1833. The five years spent in the convent had cost only five thousand francs.

Jean Valjean put the two silver candlesticks on the mantel, where they shone, to Toussaint's great admiration.

Moreover, Jean Valjean knew that he was free of Javert. It had been mentioned in his presence, and he had verified the fact in the *Moniteur,* which published it, that an inspector of police, named Javert, had been found drowned under a washerwoman's boat between the Pont au Change and Pont Neuf, and that a paper left by this man, otherwise irreproachable and highly esteemed by his chiefs, led to a belief that he had committed suicide during a fit of mental aberration. "In fact," thought Jean Valjean, "since once he had me in his power, he let me go, he must already have been crazy."

VI

EACH IN HIS OWN WAY, THE TWO OLD MEN DO EVERYTHING SO THAT COSETTE MAY BE HAPPY

All the preparations were made for the wedding. On consultation, the physician said that it might take place in February. This was December. Some ravishing weeks of perfect happiness flowed by.

Not the least happy was the grandfather. He would remain for a quarter of an hour at a time gazing at Cosette.

"The wonderful pretty girl!" he exclaimed. "And her manners are so sweet and so good. It is of no use to say anything else, she is the most charming young girl I have ever seen in my life. Besides, she will have virtues for you sweet as violets. She is a grace, that's all! You can only live nobly with such a creature. Marius, my boy, you are a baron, you are rich, don't do silly lawyering, I beg of you."

Cosette and Marius had abruptly gone from the grave to paradise. There had been little caution in the transition, and they would have been stunned if they had not been so dazzled.

"Do you understand anything at all about it?" Marius said to Cosette.

"No," answered Cosette, "but it seems to me that the good Lord is looking out for us."

Jean Valjean did everything, smoothed everything, conciliated everything, made it all easy. He hurried toward Cosette's happiness with as much eagerness, and apparently as much joy, as Cosette herself.

As he had been a mayor, he knew how to solve a delicate problem, the secret he alone knew: Cosette's civil state. To bluntly state her origin, who knows? That might prevent the marriage. He drew Cosette out of all difficulty. He arranged a family of dead people for her, a sure means of incurring no objection. Cosette was what remained of an extinct family; Cosette was not his daughter, but the daughter of another Fauchelevent. Two brothers Fauchelevent had been gardeners at the convent of the Petit-Picpus. They went to the convent, the best recommendations and the most respectable testimonials abounded; the good nuns, little apt and little inclined to fathom questions of paternity, and understanding no malice, had never known very exactly of which Fauchelevent little Cosette was the daughter. They said what was wanted of them, and said it with zeal. A notary's act was drawn up. Cosette became in the eyes of the law Mademoiselle Euphrasie Fauchelevent. She was declared an orphan. Jean Valjean arranged to be designated, under the name of Fauchelevent, as Cosette's guardian, with M. Gillenormand as overseeing guardian.

As for the five hundred and eighty-four thousand francs, that was a legacy left to Cosette by a dead person who had wished to remain anonymous. The original legacy had been five hundred and ninety-four thousand francs; but ten thousand francs had been expended for Mademoiselle Euphrasie's education, of which five thousand francs were paid to the convent itself. This legacy, deposited in the hands of a third party, was to be given to Cosette at her majority or at the time of her marriage.

Altogether this was very acceptable, as we see, especially with a basis of more than half a million. True, there were a few odd details here and there, but nobody saw them; one of the interested parties had his eyes bandaged by love, the other by the six hundred thousand francs.

Cosette learned that she was not the daughter of that old man whom she had so long called father. He was only a relative; another Fauchelevent was her real father. At any other time, this would have broken her heart. But at this ineffable hour, it was only a little shadow, a darkening, and she was so joyful that this cloud was quick to disappear. She had Marius. The young man came, the good old man faded away; such is life.

And then, for many long years Cosette had been used to seeing enigmas around her; everybody who has had a mysterious childhood is always ready for certain renunciations.

She continued, however, to say "father" to Jean Valjean.

Cosette, in raptures, was enthusiastic about Grandfather Gillenormand. It is true he loaded her with madrigals and presents. While Jean Valjean was building a normal situation in society for Cosette, and an unimpeachable estate, M. Gillenormand was watching over the wedding presents. Nothing amused him so much as being magnificent. He had given Cosette a dress of Binche lace that had come down to him from his own grandmother. "These fashions have come round again," he said, "old things are all the rage, and the young women of my old age dress like the old women of my childhood."

He rifled his respectable round-bellied bureaus of coromandel lacquer that had not been opened for years. "Let us put these dowagers to the confession," said he; "let us see what they have in them." He noisily stripped the deep drawers full of dressing table articles of all his wives, of all his mistresses, and of all his ancestresses. Pekins, damasks, lampas, painted moires, dresses of gros de Tours, Indian handkerchiefs embroidered with a gold that could be washed, dauphines in the piece finished on both sides, Genoa and Alençon lace, antique jewelry, candy boxes of ivory ornamented with microscopic battles, clothes, ribbons—he lavished everything on Cosette. Cosette, astonished, desperately in love with Marius and wild with gratitude toward M. Gillenormand, dreamed of a boundless happiness clad in satin and velvet. Her array of wedding presents seemed to her held aloft by seraphim. Her soul soared into the azure on wings of Mechlin lace.

The intoxication of the lovers was only equaled, as we have said, by the ecstasy of the grandfather. It was like a flourish of trumpets in the Rue des Filles-du-Calvaire.

Every morning, a new offering of finery from the grandfather to Cosette. Every possible furbelow blossomed out splendidly around her.

One day Marius, who was fond of talking gravely in the midst of his happiness, said in reference to some incident, "The men of the Revolution are so great that they already have the prestige of centuries, like Cato and like Phocion, and each of them seems a *mémoire antique* [antique memory]."

"Moire antique!" exclaimed the old man. "Thank you, Marius. That is precisely the idea I was searching for."

And the next day a magnificent dress of tea-colored moire antique was added to Cosette's wedding trousseau.

The grandfather extracted a wisdom from these rags: "Love, all very well; but it needs this with it. The useless is needed in happiness. Happiness is only the essential. Season it for me enormously with the superfluous. A palace and her heart. Her heart and the Louvre. Her heart and the great fountains of Versailles. Give me my shepherdess, and have her be a duchess if possible. Bring me Phillis crowned with bluebells, and add to her a hundred thousand francs a year. Open a bucolic nook out of sight under a marble colonnade. I consent to the bucolic, and also to the fairy work in marble and gold. Dry happiness is like dry bread. To eat, but never to dine. I wish for the superfluous, for the useless, for the extravagant, for the too much. I remember having seen in the cathedral of Strasbourg a clock as high as a three-story house, which marked the hour, which was good enough to mark the hour, but did not look as though it were made for that; and which, after having struck noon or midnight, noon, the hour of the sun, midnight, the hour of love, or any other hour that you please, gave you the moon and the stars, the earth and the sea, the birds and the fish, Phoebus and Phoebe, and a host of things that came out of a niche, and the twelve apostles, and the Emperor Charles the Fifth, Eponine and Sabinus, and a crowd of little gilded men who played on the trumpet, to boot. Not counting the ravishing chimes it flung into the air on all occasions without anybody knowing why. Is a paltry naked dial that only tells the time as good as that? As for me, I agree with the great clock of Strasbourg, and I prefer it to the cuckoo clock from the Black Forest."

M. Gillenormand raved particularly concerning the wedding, and every old dodderer of the eighteenth century passed pell-mell through his dithyrambs.

"You know nothing about the art of fêtes. You do not know how to put together a happy day in these times," he exclaimed. "Your nineteenth century is soft. It lacks excess. It ignores the rich, it ignores the noble. In everything, it is close-shaven. Your third estate is tasteless, colorless, odorless, and shapeless. Dreams of your bourgeoises who set up an establishment, as they put it: a pretty boudoir freshly decorated in palissandre and chintz. Stand back! The Sieur Hunks espouses the Lady Catchpenny. Magnificence and splendor. They have stuck a louis d'or to a taper. There you have the age. I beg to flee beyond the Sarmatians. Ah, in 1787, I predicted that all was lost, the day I saw the Duc de Rohan, Prince de Léon, Duc de Chabot, Duc de Montbazon, Marquis de Soubise, Vicomte de Thouars, peer of France, go to Longchamps in a rattletrap. That has borne its fruits. In this century, people do business, they gamble at the Bourse, they make money, and they are disagreeable. They care for and varnish their surface; they are spruced up, washed, soaped, scraped, shaved, combed, waxed, smoothed, rubbed, brushed, cleaned on the outside, irreproachable, polished like a pebble, prudent, nice, and at the same time, by the virtue of my mistress, they have in the depths of their conscience dung heaps and cloacas enough to disgust a cowgirl who blows her nose with her fingers. I grant these times this device: Nasty neatness. Marius, don't get angry; let me speak; I speak no evil of the people, you see; I have my mouth full of your people; but take it not amiss that I have my little fling at the bourgeoisie. I am one of them. Who loves well lashes well. On that, I say it boldly, people marry nowadays, but they don't know how to marry. Ah! It is true, I regret the pretty ways of the old times. I regret the whole of it. That elegance, that chivalry, those courtly dainty ways, the joyous luxury that everybody had, music making part of the wedding, symphony above, drumming below, dances, joyful faces at the table, far-fetched madrigals, songs, fireworks, free laughter, the devil and his entourage, big bows of ribbon. I miss the bride's garter. The bride's garter is cousin to the belt of Venus. On what does the Trojan war spin? By heaven, on Helen's garter. Why do they fight, why does Diomede the divine shatter that great bronze helmet with ten points on Meriones' head, why do Achilles and Hector pick at each other with great pike thrusts? Because Helen let Paris take her garter. With Cosette's garter, Homer would make the Iliad. He would put into his poem an old babbler like me, and he would call him Nestor. My friends, formerly, in that lovely formerly, people married knowingly; they made a good contract, then a good banquet. As soon as Cujas went out, Gamache came in. But, ye gods, the stomach is an agreeable animal that demands its due and wants its wedding too. They supped well, and they had a beautiful neighbor at table without a guimpe, who hid her chest only moderately! Oh! The wide laughing mouths, and how gay they were in those times! Youth was a bouquet; every young man terminated in a branch of lilac or a bunch of roses; if one was a warrior, he was a shepherd; and if, by chance, he was a captain of dragoons, he found some way to be called Florian. They thought everything of being pretty, they embroidered themselves, they laid on the crimson. A bourgeois looked like a flower, a marquis looked like a precious stone. They did not wear stirrups to their trousers, they did not wear boots. They were flaunting, glossy, moire, gorgeous, fluttering, dainty, coquettish, which did not prevent them from having a sword at their side. The hummingbird has beak and claws. That was the time of the *Indes galantes*. One aspect of the century was the delicate, the other was the magnificent; and—the devil!—they had a good time. Nowadays, they are serious. The bourgeois is miserly, the bourgeois is prudish; your century is unfortunate. People would drive away the Graces for their low necklines. Alas! They hide beauty as a deformity. Since the Revolution, everything has trousers, even the ballerinas; a danseuse must be grave; your rigadoons are doctrinaire. Better to be majestic. We would be quite shocked without our chin tucked in our cravat.

The ideal of a scapegrace of twenty who gets married is to be like Monsieur Royer-Collard. And do you know where we are going with that majesty? To being small. Learn this: Joy is not merely joyful; it is great. So be lovers gaily, what the devil! And marry, when you do marry, with the fever and dizziness and uproar and to-do of happiness. Gravity at the church, all right. But, as soon as mass is over, wham! We must make a dream whirl around the bride. A marriage should be royal and fantastical; it ought to walk in procession from the cathedral of Rheims to the pagoda of Chanteloup. I'm horrified by a cowardly wedding! Be in Olympus, at least for that day. Be gods. Ah! You might be sylphs, Games and Laughters, Argyraspides; you are elfs! My friends, every new husband ought to be the Prince Aldobrandini. Take advantage of this unique moment in your life to fly off into the empyrean with the swans and the eagles, free to fall back the next day into the bourgeoisie of the frogs. Don't economize on Hymen, don't strip him of his splendors; don't stint the day on which you shine. Wedding is not housekeeping. Oh, if I had my fancy, it would be gallant, you would hear violins in the trees. This is my program: sky-blue and silver. I would bring the rural divinities into the fête, I would convoke the dryads and the nereids. Nuptials of Amphitrite, a rosy cloud, nymphs with well-dressed heads and all naked, an academician offering quatrains to the goddess, a car drawn by marine monsters.

> Tritton trottait devant, et tirait de sa conque
> Des sons si ravissants qu'il ravissait quiconque.[1]

Now, there's a program for a fête that is one, or I don't know anything about it, my fine friends!"

While the grandfather, in full lyric effusion, was listening to himself, Cosette and Marius were intoxicated with looking at each other freely.

Aunt Gillenormand took it all in with her imperturbable placidity. Within five or six months she had had a certain number of emotions; Marius returned, Marius brought back bleeding, Marius brought back from a barricade,

[1] Triton trotted along in front and drew from his conch
Sounds so ravishing he'd ravish anyone.

Marius dead, then alive, Marius reconciled, Marius betrothed, Marius marrying a pauper, Marius marrying a millionaire. The six hundred thousand francs had been her last surprise. Then her first communicant indifference returned to her. She went regularly to church, said her rosary, read her prayerbook, whispered *Aves* in one part of the house, while they were whispering *I Love You's* in the other, and vaguely saw Marius and Cosette as two shadows. The shadow was herself.

There is a certain condition of inert asceticism in which the soul, neutralized by torpor, a stranger to what might be called the business of living, perceives, aside from earthquakes and catastrophes, no human impressions—neither pleasant impressions, nor painful impressions. "This devotion," said Grandfather Gillenormand to his daughter, "corresponds to a cold in the head. You smell nothing of life. No bad odor, but no good one."

Still, the six hundred thousand francs had resolved the old maid's hesitation. Her father had acquired the habit of counting on her so little that he had not consulted her about the consent to Marius's marriage. He had acted with impetuosity, according to his wont, having as a despot turned slave one thought alone, to satisfy Marius. As for the aunt, that the aunt existed, and that she might have an opinion had not even occurred to him; and, perfect sheep as she was, this had ruffled her. A little rebellious inwardly, but outwardly impassible, she said to herself, "My father settles the question of the marriage without me, I will settle the question of the inheritance without him." She was rich, in fact, and her father was not. She had therefore reserved her decision on that score. It is probable that, if the marriage had been poor, she would have left it poor. So much the worse for monsieur, my nephew! He marries a beggar, let him be a beggar. But Cosette's half-million pleased the aunt, and changed her feelings in regard to this pair of lovers. Some consideration is due to six hundred thousand francs, and it was clear that she could not do anything but leave her fortune to these young people, since they no longer needed it.

It was arranged that the couple should live with the grandfather. M. Gillenormand absolutely insisted on giving them his room, the finest in the house. "It will rejuvenate me," he declared. "It is an old project. I always had the idea of making it a bridal chamber." He filled the room with a profusion of gallant old things. He hung the walls and the ceiling with an extraordinary material that he had in the bolt, and that he believed to be from Utrecht, a satin background with golden immortelles, and velvet auriculas. "The Duchesse d'Anville's bed," he said, "was draped with this cloth at La Roche-Guyon." He put a little Saxony figure on the mantel, holding a muff over her naked stomach.

M. Gillenormand's library became the attorney's office that Marius needed; an office, it will be remembered, being rendered necessary by the rules of the order.

VII

THE EFFECTS OF DREAM MINGLED WITH HAPPINESS

The lovers saw each other every day. Cosette came with M. Fauchelevent. "It is reversing the order of things," said Mlle. Gillenormand, "that the intended should come to the house to be courted like this." But Marius's convalescence had led to the habit and the armchairs in the Rue des Filles-du-Calvaire, better for long talks than the straw-seated chairs of the Rue de l'Homme-Armé, had rooted it. Marius and M. Fauchelevent saw one another, but did not speak to each other. That seemed to be understood. Every girl needs a chaperone. Cosette could not have come without M. Fauchelevent. To Marius, M. Fauchelevent was the condition of Cosette. He accepted it. In laying on the carpet, vaguely and generally, matters of politics from the point of view of the improvement of the general lot, they managed to say a little more than yes and no to each other. Once, on the subject of education, which Marius wanted to see free and obligatory, spread over all forms, lavished on everyone like air and sunshine, in one word, available to all people, they fell into unison and almost into a conversation. Marius remarked on this occasion that M. Fauchelevent talked well, and even with a certain elevation of language. There was, however, something lacking. M. Fauchelevent was something less than a man of the world and something more.

Marius, inwardly and deep in his thoughts, surrounded this M. Fauchelevent, who seemed to him simply benevolent and cold, with all sorts of silent questions. At times doubts about his own recollections would come over him. In his memory there was a hole, a black place, an abyss scooped out by four months of agony. Many things were lost in it. He was led to ask himself if it were really true that he had seen M. Fauchelevent, such a man, so serious and so calm, in the barricade.

This was not, however, the only quandary that the appearances and the disappearances of the past had left in his mind. We must not suppose that he was released from all those obsessions of the memory that force us, even when happy, even when satisfied, to look back with melancholy. The head that does not turn toward past horizons contains neither thought nor love. At times Marius covered his face with his hands, and the vague past tumultuously crossed the twilight that filled his brain. He would see Mabeuf fall again, would hear Gavroche singing under the hale of bullets; he felt again the chill of Eponine's forehead against his lip; Enjolras, Courfeyrac, Jean Prouvaire, Combeferre, Bossuet, Grantaire, all his friends, would rise up in front of him, then dissipate. All these beings, dear, sorrowful, valiant, charming, or tragic—were they dreams? Had they really existed? The émeute had cloaked everything in its smoke. Great fevers have great dreams. He would question himself; he groped within himself; he was dizzy with all these vanished realities. Then where were they all? Was it really true that all were dead? A fall into the darkness had carried off everything, except himself. It all seemed to him to have disappeared as if behind a curtain at a theater. There are such curtains that drop in life. God is moving on to the next act.

And he, was he really the same man? He, the poor man, was rich; he, the abandoned, had a family; he, the despairing, was marrying Cosette. It seemed to him that he had passed through a tomb, that he had gone into it black and had come out white. And in this tomb, the others had remained. At certain moments, all these beings of the past, returned and present, formed a circle around him and made him gloomy; then he would think of Cosette, and became serene once more; but it required nothing less than this felicity to erase that catastrophe.

M. Fauchelevent almost had a place among the vanished human beings. Marius hesitated to believe that the Fauchelevent of the barricade was the same as this Fauchelevent in flesh and blood, so gravely seated near Cosette. The first was probably one of those nightmares coming and going with his hours of delirium. But, their two natures each showed a closed façade to the other, and no question was possible from Marius to M. Fauchelevent. The idea did not even occur to him. We have already indicated this characteristic circumstance.

Two men who have a common secret and who, by a sort of tacit agreement, do not exchange a word on the subject, such a thing is less rare than one would think.

Once only, Marius made an attempt. He brought the Rue de la Chanvrerie into the conversation, and, turning toward M. Fauchelevent, he said to him, "Do you know that street well?"

"What street?"

"The Rue de la Chanvrerie."

"The name of that street means nothing to me," answered M. Fauchelevent in the most natural tone in the world.

The answer, which bore on the name of the street, and not on the street itself, appeared to Marius more conclusive than it was.

"Decidedly," he thought, "I have been dreaming. I have had a hallucination. It was somebody who looked like him. M. Fauchelevent was not there."

VIII

TWO MEN IMPOSSIBLE TO FIND

The enchantment, great as it was, did not erase other preoccupations from Marius's mind.

During the preparations for the marriage, and while waiting for the appointed time, he had some difficult and careful retrospective researches made.

He owed gratitude on several sides, he owed some on his father's account, he owed some on his own.

There was Thénardier; there was the unknown man who had brought him, Marius, to M. Gillenormand's.

Marius persisted in trying to find these two men, not intending to marry, to be happy, and to forget them, and fearing that these debts of duty unpaid might cast a shadow over his life, so luminous ahead. It was impossible for him to leave all these arrears unsettled behind him; and before joyfully entering the future, he wanted to settle with the past.

The fact that Thénardier was a scoundrel took away nothing from the fact that he had saved Colonel Pontmercy. Thénardier was a criminal to everybody except Marius.

And not knowing the real scene of the Waterloo battlefield, Marius did not know this peculiarity, that with reference to Thénardier, his father was in the strange situation of owing his life to him without owing him any thanks.

None of the various agents whom Marius employed managed to find any trace of Thénardier. The disappearance seemed complete on that side. The Thénardiess had died in prison pending examination on the charge. Thénardier and his daughter Azelma, the only two remaining of that woeful group, had plunged back into the shadows. The gulf of the social Unknown had silently closed over these beings. On the surface there could no longer even be seen that quivering, that trembling, those obscure concentric circles that announce that something has fallen there, that we may cast in the lead.

With the Thénardiess dead, Boulatruelle put out of the case, Claquesous disappeared, the principal accused escaped from prison, the prosecution for the ambush at the Gorbeau house was almost abortive. The affair was left in deep obscurity. The superior court was obliged to settle for two subalterns, Panchaud, alias Printanier, alias Bigrenaille, and Demi-Liard, alias Deux-Milliards, who were tried and condemned to ten years in prison. Hard labor for life was pronounced against their accomplices who had escaped and did not appear. Also for nonappearance, Thénardier, chief and ringleader, was condemned to death. This condemnation was the only thing that remained in regard to Thénardier, casting its ominous glare on that buried name like a candle beside a bier.

Moreover, by crowding Thénardier back into the lowest depths, for fear of being retaken, this condemnation added to the thick darkness that covered the man.

As for the other, as for the unknown man who had saved Marius, the researches at first had some result, then stopped short. They succeeded in finding the fiacre that had brought Marius to the Rue des Filles-du-Calvaire on the evening of the 6th of June. The driver declared that on the 6th of June, by order of a police officer, he had been "stationed," from three in the afternoon until nightfall on the quay of the Champs-Elysées, above the outlet of the Great Sewer; that, about nine o'clock in the evening, the iron gate to the sewer, which overlooks the river beach, was opened; that a man came out, carrying another man on his shoulders, who seemed to be dead; that the officer, who was watching at that point, arrested the living man, and seized the dead man; that, on the order of the officer, he, the driver, received "all those people" into the fiacre; that they went first to the Rue des Filles-du-Calvaire; that they left the dead man there; that the dead man was Monsieur Marius, and that he, the driver, recognized him plainly, although he was alive "this time"; that they then got into his carriage again; that he whipped up his horses; that, within a few steps of the door to the Archives, he had been called to stop; that there, in the street, he had been paid and left, and that the officer took away the other man; that he knew nothing more, that the night was very dark.

Marius, we have said, remembered nothing. He merely remembered having been seized from behind by a vigorous hand at the moment he was falling backward in the barricade, then everything went blank. He had recovered consciousness only at M. Gillenormand's.

He was lost in conjectures.

He could not doubt his own identity. How did it come to be, however, that, falling in the Rue de la Chanvrerie, he had been picked up by the police officer on the banks of the Seine, near the Pont des Invalides? Somebody had carried him from Les Halles to the Champs-Elysées. And how? By the sewer. Unparalleled devotion!

Somebody? Who?

This was the man that Marius was seeking.

Of this man, who was his savior, nothing; no trace; not the least hint.

Although compelled to great reserve in this respect, Marius pushed his researches as far as the prefecture of police. There, no more than anywhere else, did the information obtained lead to any new light on the matter. The prefecture knew less than the driver of the fiacre. They had no knowledge of any arrest made on the 6th of June at the grating of the Great Sewer; they had received no officer's report about that fact, which, at the prefecture, was regarded as a fable. They attributed the invention of this fable to the driver. A driver who wants a tip is capable of anything, even of imagination. Nonetheless, the thing had certainly happened, and Marius could not doubt it, unless by doubting his own identity, as we have just said.

Everything about the strange enigma was inexplicable.

This man, this mysterious man, whom the driver had seen coming out of the Great Sewer gate carrying Marius unconscious on his back, and whom the police officer on the lookout had arrested in the very act of saving an insurgent, what had become of him? What had become of the officer himself? Why had this officer kept silent? Had the man succeeded in escaping? Had he bribed the officer? Why had this man given no sign of life to Marius, who owed everything to him? His disinterestedness was no less wonderful than his devotion. Why didn't this man reappear? Perhaps he was above recompense, but nobody is above gratitude. Was he dead? What kind of man was he? What did he look like? Nobody could say. The driver answered, "It was a very dark night." Basque and Nicolette, in their amazement, had only looked at their young master covered with blood. The doorkeeper, whose candle had lighted Marius's tragic arrival, alone had noticed the man in question, and this is the description he gave: "He was horrible."

In the hope of deriving some help in his research from them, Marius had kept the bloody clothes he was wearing when he was brought back to his grandfather's. On examining the coat, it was noticed that one part of the hem was oddly torn. A piece was missing.

One evening, Marius spoke to Cosette and Jean Valjean about this whole strange adventure, of the countless inquiries he had made, and of his lack of success. The cold countenance of "Monsieur Fauchelevent" made him impatient. He exclaimed with a vivacity that had almost the vibration of anger, "Yes, that man, whoever he may be, was sublime. Do you know what he did, monsieur? He intervened like the archangel. He must have thrown himself into the midst of the fighting, snatched me out of it, opened the sewer, dragged me into it, carried me through it! He must have made his way for more than four miles through hideous subterranean galleries, bent, stooping, in the darkness, in the cloaca, more than four miles, monsieur, with a corpse on his back! And with what aim? With the single aim of saving that corpse. And that corpse was I. He said to himself: 'Perhaps there is a glimmer of life still there; I'll risk my own life for that miserable spark!' And he did not risk his own life once but twenty times! And each step was a danger. The proof is that on coming out of the sewer he was arrested. Do you know, monsieur, that that man did all that? And he could be expecting a recompense. What was I? An insurgent. What was I? A defeated man. Oh! If Cosette's six hundred thousand francs were mine—"

"They are yours," interrupted Jean Valjean.

"Well," resumed Marius, "I would give them to find that man!"

Jean Valjean kept silent.

Book Six

THE WHITE NIGHT

I

THE 16TH OF FEBRUARY, 1833

The night of the 16th of February, 1833, was a blessed night. Above its darkness, the heavens were open. It was the wedding night of Marius and Cosette.

The day had been all one would wish for.

It had not been the sky-blue festival dreamed of by the grandfather, a fairy scene with a tangle of cherubs and cupids above the heads of the married pair, a marriage worthy a frieze; but it had been sweet and mirthful.

The fashions of marriage were not in 1833 what they are today. France had not yet borrowed from England that supreme delicacy of eloping with one's wife, of making one's escape on leaving the church, of hiding oneself ashamed of one's happiness, and of combining the behavior of a bankrupt with the transports of Solomon. They had not yet learned all that there is chaste, exquisite, and decent, in jolting one's paradise in a carriage, in intersecting one's mystery with click-clacks, in taking a tavern bed for a nuptial bed, and in leaving behind, in the common alcove at so much a night, the most sacred of life's memories pell-mell with the conversations with the stagecoach driver and the servant girl at the tavern.

In this second half of the nineteenth century in which we live, the mayor and his sash, the priest and his chasuble, the law and God, are not enough; we must complete them with the Longjumeau postilion; blue waistcoat with red facings and bell-buttons, an armband with plaque, breeches of green leather, oaths at Norman horses with knotted tails, imitation gold braid, patent leather hat, coarse powdered hair, enormous whip, and heavy boots. France does not yet push elegance as far as the English nobility, to have a hailstorm of down-at-the-heel slippers and old shoes beating on the bridal carriage, in memory of Churchill, afterward Marlborough, or Malbrouck, who was assailed on his marriage day by the anger of an aunt who brought him good luck. The old shoes and slippers are not yet part of our nuptial celebrations; but patience, good taste continuing to spread, we shall come to it.

In 1833, a hundred years ago, marriage was not performed at a full trot.

In that day, it was still supposed, strange to say, that a marriage is an intimate and social festival, that a patriarchal banquet does not spoil domestic solemnity, that gaiety, even excessive provided it be seemly, does no harm to happiness, and finally that it is venerable and good that the fusion of these two destinies from which a family is to rise should begin in the house, and that the household should have the nuptial chamber for a witness thereafter.

And they had the audacity to be married at home.

The marriage took place, therefore, according to that now obsolete fashion, at M. Gillenormand's.

Natural and ordinary as this matter of marriage may be, the banns to be published, the deeds to be drawn up, the mayor, the church, always make it somewhat complex. They could not be ready before the 16th of February.

Now, we mention this circumstance for the pure satisfaction of being exact, it happened that the 16th was Mardi Gras. Hesitations, scruples, particularly from Aunt Gillenormand.

"Mardi Gras!" exclaimed the grandfather. "So much the better. There is a proverb:

> Mariage un Mardi Gras,
> N'aura point d'enfants ingrats.[1]

[1] Marriages on Mardi Gras
Produce no ingrate brats.

Let's go on. Here goes for the sixteenth! Do you want to put it off, you, Marius?"

"Certainly not!" answered the lover.

"Let us get married," said the grandfather.

So the marriage took place on the 16th, notwithstanding the public gaiety. It rained that day, but there is always a little patch of blue in the sky of happiness, which lovers see, even though the rest of creation may be under an umbrella.

The previous evening, Jean Valjean had handed to Marius, in presence of M. Gillenormand, the five hundred and eighty-four thousand francs.

The marriage being performed under the law of community, the deeds were simple.

From then on Toussaint was of no use to Jean Valjean; Cosette inherited her and promoted her to rank of lady's maid.

As for Jean Valjean, there was a beautiful room in the Gillenormand house furnished expressly for him, and Cosette had said to him so irresistibly, "Father, I beg you," that she had made him almost promise he would come and occupy it.

A few days before the day set for the marriage, an accident happened to Jean Valjean; he slightly crushed the thumb of his right hand. It was not serious; and he had allowed nobody to take care of it, bandage or even to see it, not even Cosette. It forced him, however, to swathe his hand in a bandage, and to carry his arm in a sling, and prevented his signing anything. M. Gillenormand, as Cosette's overseeing guardian, took his place.

We shall take the reader neither to the municipal hall nor to the church. We hardly follow two lovers as far as that, and we generally turn our backs on the drama as soon as it puts the bridegroom's flower into his buttonhole. We shall merely mention an incident that, although unnoticed by the wedding party marked its progress from the Rue des Filles-du-Calvaire to Saint-Paul.

At that time, they were repaving the north end of the Rue Saint-Louis. It was fenced off where it leaves the Rue du Parc-Royal. It was impossible for the wedding carriages to go directly to Saint-Paul. They had to change route, and the simplest way was to turn off onto the boulevard. One of the guests observed that it was Mardi Gras, and that the boulevard would be cluttered with carriages. "Why?" asked M. Gillenormand. "Because of the masks." "Capital!" said the grandfather; "let's go that way. These young folks are marrying; they are going to enter on the serious things of life. It will prepare them for it to see a bit of masquerade."

They went by the boulevard. The first of the wedding carriages contained Cosette and Aunt Gillenormand, M. Gillenormand, and Jean Valjean. Marius, still separated from his betrothed, according to the custom, did not come till the second. On leaving the Rue des Filles-du-Calvaire, the nuptial cortège was involved in the long procession of carriages making an endless chain from the Madeleine to the Bastille and from the Bastille to the Madeleine.

Masks were everywhere on the boulevard. It made no difference that it rained at times; Pantaloon, Harlequin, and Gilles were obstinate. In the good humor of that winter of 1833, Paris had disguised herself as Venice. We no longer see such a Mardi Gras nowadays. Everything being a constant carnival, there is no carnival left.

The cross alleys were choked with passengers, and the windows with the curious. The terraces that crown the peristyles of the theaters were lined with spectators. Besides the masks, they could see that parade, peculiar to Mardi Gras as well as to Longchamps, of vehicles of all varieties, hackney coaches, spring carts, carrioles, cabriolets, moving in order, rigorously linked to one another by the police regulations, and, as it were, running in grooves. Anybody in one of these vehicles is both spectator and spectacle. Police sergeants kept those two interminable parallel files on the outer sides of the boulevard moving with opposite motion, and watched, so nothing hindered their double current, over those two streams of carriages flowing, the one down, the other up, the one toward the Chaussée d'Antin, the other toward the Faubourg Saint-Antoine. The carriages of the peers of France and ambassadors, decorated with coats of arms, kept to the middle of the roadway, coming and going freely. Certain magnificent and joyful cortèges, notably the Fat Ox, had the same privilege. In this Parisian gaiety, England cracked her whip; the postchaise of Lord Seymour, teased with a nickname by the populace, passed along with much ado.

In the double file, with some Municipal Guards galloping alongside like sheepdogs, honest family carryalls, loaded down with great-aunts and grandmothers, exhibited at their doors fresh groups of disguised children, clowns of seven, clownesses of six, enchanting little creatures, feeling that they were officially part of the public mirth imbued with the dignity of their harlequinade, and displaying the gravity of functionaries.

From time to time, there was a tie-up somewhere in the procession of vehicles; one of the two lateral files would stop until the knot was disentangled; one carriage obstructed was enough to paralyze the whole line. Then they would be on their way again.

The wedding carriages were in the line going toward the Bastille and moving along the right side of the boulevard. At the Rue du Pont-aux-Choux, there was a pause. At almost the same moment, on the other side, the other line, which was going toward the Madeleine, also stopped. At this point in that line, there was a carriage load of masked revelers.

These carriages, or to put it more correctly, these cartloads of masks, are well known to the Parisians. If they failed to show up on a Mardi Gras or a Mid-Lent, people would suspect something and would say: "There is something behind all that. Probably the ministry is going to change." A heaping up of Cassandras, Harlequins, and Columbines, jolting along above the passersby, every possible grotesquery from the Turk to the savage, Hercules supporting marquises, jades who would make Rabelais stop his ears even as the Bacchantes made Aristophanes lower his eyes; flax wigs, rosy tights, coxcombs' hats, crosseyed spectacles, Janot cocked hats teased by a butterfly, shouts thrown out to the pedestrians, arms akimbo, bold postures, naked shoulders, masked faces, unmuzzled shamelessness; a chaos of effrontery marshaled by a driver crowned with flowers; such is this institution.

Greece required the chariot of Thespis, France requires the vulgar fiacre of Vadé.

Everything can be parodied, even parody. The saturnalia, that grimace of the ancient beauty, has gradually swelled into Mardi Gras, and the bacchanal, formerly crowned with vine branches, inundated with sunlight, showing breasts of marble in a divine seminudity, today grown flabby under the soaking rags of the north, has ended in a vulgar masqueraded rabble.

The tradition of the carriages of masks goes back to the oldest times of the monarchy. The accounts of Louis XI allow the bailiff of the palace "twenty sous of Tours for three masquerade coaches at the street corners." In our day, these noisy crowds of creatures are commonly carted around by some ancient rattletrap, piling onto its open top, or else they overwhelm with their rowdy band an excise cart with a broken cover. Twenty of them load down a carriage for six. There are some on the bench, on the jumpseat, on the sides of the cover, on the shafts. They even ride on the carriage lanterns. They are standing, lying, sitting, feet curled up, legs dangling. The women occupy the men's knees. Their mad pyramid can be seen from a distance above the swarming heads. These carriage loads make mountains of mirth in the midst of the mob. Collé, Panard, and Piron flow from them, rich in argot. They spit the street catechism down on the people. This fiacre, become outsized from its load, has an air of conquest. Uproar is in front, Brouhaha in the back. They vociferate, they vocalize, they howl, they burst, they writhe with happiness; gaiety bellows, sarcasm flahes, joviality spreads itself in a crimson glow; two harridans lead on the farce, which expands into apotheosis; it is the triumphal chariot of Laughter.

Laughter too cynical to be frank. And, in fact, the laughter is suspect. This laughter has a mission: to show off the carnival to the Parisians.

These ribald wagons emitting an indefinable darkness make the philosopher think. There is a hint of government in them. We lay our finger there on a mysterious affinity between public men and public women.

That amassed depravities should add up to total gaiety, that by piling ignominy on opprobrium, a people are enticed; that serving as a caryatid to prostitution amuses the crowds while insulting them; that the mob loves to see passing by on the four wheels of a fiacre this monstrous living heap, rag-tinsel, half filth and half light, barking and singing; that people should applaud this glory made up of every shame; that there should be no festival for the hordes unless the police exhibit among them this sort of twenty-headed hydra of joy, certainly is sad! But what can be done? These tumbrils of beribboned, beflowered slime are insulted and forgiven by the public laughter. The laughter of all is the accomplice of universal degradation. Certain unwholesome festivals chip away at the people, and make it a rabble. And for rabbles as well as for tyrants, buffoons are needed. The king has Roquelaure, the people have Harlequin. Paris is the great foolish town, whenever she is not the great sublime city. The carnival is a part of her politics. Paris, we must admit, willingly accepts comedy through infamy. She demands of her masters—when she has masters—but one thing: "Dab a little makeup on the mud!" Rome was of the same humor. She loved Nero. Nero was a titanic lighterman.

Chance had it, as we have just said, that one of these misshapen bunches of masked women and men, jolted along in a huge calash, came to a halt on the left of the boulevard while the wedding cortège was stopping on the right. From one side of the boulevard to the other, the carriage with the masks looked at the carriage opposite, carrying the bride.

"Well now," said a mask, "a wedding."

"A sham wedding," replied another. "We're the real thing."

And, too far off to be able to accost the wedding party, fearing besides any undue attention from the police, the two masks looked at other things.

The whole carriage load of masks had enough to do a moment later when the crowd began to hoot at it, the mob caressing the maskers; and the two masks that had just spoken had to confront the crowd with their comrades; they had all too few of the projectiles available from Les Halles to answer the tremendous jibes from the people. A wild exchange of metaphors was carried on between masks and crowd.

Meanwhile, two other masks in the same carriage, an oldish giant-nosed Spaniard with an enormous black mustache, and a puny slut, a very young girl, with a black velvet mask, had also noticed the wedding party, and, while their companions and the passersby were lampooning one another, carried on a dialogue in undertones.

Their asides were covered by the tumult and lost in it. The gusts of rain had soaked the carriage, which was thrown wide open; the February wind is not warm; even while answering the Spaniard, the girl, with her low-necked dress, shivered, laughed, and coughed.

This was the dialogue:

"Look at that, will you?"

"What, *daron?*"[1]

"Do you see that old guy?"

"What old guy?"

"There, in the first *roulotte*[2] of the wedding party, on our side."

"Yes."

"Well?"

"I'm sure I know him."

"Ah!"

"I'd like somebody to slit my throat if I don't know that *pantinois*."

"Today's the day that Paris is Pantin."

"Can you see the bride if you lean across?"

"No."

"And the groom?"

"There's no groom in that *roulotte*."

"Well!"

"Unless it's the other old fellow."

"Really lean forward and try to see the bride."

"I can't."

"No matter, that old fellow who has something the matter with his paw, I'm sure I know him."

"And what good does it do you to know him?"

"Who knows? Sometimes!"

"I don't care much for old men, I don't."

"I know him."

"Know him to your heart's content."

"How the devil is he at the wedding?"

"We're at it, too, ourselves."

"Where's this wedding party from?"

"How do I know?"

"Listen."

"What?"

"You should do something."

"What?"

"Get out of our *roulotte* and *filer*[3] that wedding party."

[1] *Daron*, father.

[2] *Roulotte*, carriage.

[3] *Filer*, follow.

"What for?"

"To find out where it's going and what it is. Hurry and get out, run, my *fée*,[1] you're young."

"I can't leave the carriage."

"Why not?"

"I'm rented."

"Ah, the devil!"

"I owe my day to the prefecture."

"That's true."

"If I leave the carriage, the first officer to see me arrests me. You know very well."

"Yes, I know."

"Today I'm bought by *Pharos*."[2]

"Makes no difference. That old fellow worries me."

"Old men worry you. You're not a young girl, though."

"He's in the first carriage."

"Well?"

"In the bride's *roulotte*."

"What then?"

"So he is the father."

"What's that to me?"

"I tell you that he's the father."

"There isn't any other father."

"Listen."

"What?"

"As for me, I can hardly go out unless I'm masked. Here, I'm hidden, nobody knows I'm here. But tomorrow, there are no more masks. It's Ash Wednesday. I could *fall*.[3] I have to get back to my hole. You're free."

"Not so very."

"More than I am, anyway."

"Well, what then?"

"You have to try to find out where this wedding party has gone."

"Where it's going?"

"Yes."

"I know that."

"Where is it going, then?"

"To the Cadran Bleu."

[1] *Fée*, daughter.
[2] *Pharos*, the government.
[3] *Fall*, be arrested.

"In the first place, it's not in that direction."

"Well! To the Râpée."

"Or somewhere else."

"It's free. Weddings are free."

"That isn't all. I tell you, you must try to let me know about this wedding party that the old fellow belongs to, and where that wedding party lives."

"Not likely! You think it would be possible, one week later, to find a wedding party that passed by in Paris on Mardi Gras. A *tiquante*[1] in a haystack!"

"No matter, try. Understand, Azelma?"

The two lines started moving again in opposite directions on the two sides of the boulevard, and the carriage of the masks lost sight of the bride's roulotte.

II

JEAN VALJEAN STILL HAS HIS ARM IN A SLING

To realize one's dream. To whom is that given? There must be elections for that in heaven; we are all unconscious candidates; the angels vote. Cosette and Marius had been elected.

At the municipal hall and in the church, Cosette was luminous and touching. Toussaint, aided by Nicolette, had dressed her.

Cosette wore her dress of Binche lace over a skirt of white taffeta, a veil of English lace, a necklace of fine pearls, a crown of orange flowers; all this was white, and in this whiteness, she was radiant. It was an exquisite candor, dilating and transfiguring itself in clarity. One would have said she was a virgin in process of becoming a goddess.

Marius's beautiful hair was perfumed and gleaming; here and there, under the thick locks, pale lines could be glimpsed, the scars from the barricade.

The grandfather, superb, his head held high, uniting more than ever in his clothing and manner all the ele-

[1] *Tiquante*, pin.

gance of the time of Barras, escorted Cosette. He took the place of Jean Valjean, who, as his arm was in a sling, could not give his arm to the bride.

Jean Valjean, in black, followed and smiled.

"Monsieur Fauchelevent," said the grandfather to him, "this is a happy day. I vote for the end of affliction and sorrow. There must be no more sadness anywhere from now on. By Jove! I decree joy! Evil has no right to exist. That there are unfortunate men—that is truly a disgrace to the blue sky. Evil does not come from man, who is basically good. All human miseries have hell for their capital and headquarters, otherwise known as the Tuileries of the devil. Well, here am I making speeches again! As for me, I no longer have any political opinions; for men to be rich, that is to say, happy, that's all I ask."

When, with the ceremonies over, after pronouncing every possible yes before the mayor and the priest, after signing the registers at the municipality and the sacristy, after exchanging their rings, after kneeling elbow to elbow under the canopy of white moire in the smoke of the censer, hand in hand, admired and envied by all, Marius in black, she in white, preceded by the usher in colonel's epaulettes, striking the pavement with his halberd, between two hedges of marveling spectators, they reached the portal of the church where the doors were both opened wide, ready to get into the carriage again, and everything was over, Cosette could still not believe it. She looked at Marius, she looked at the throng, she looked at the sky; it seemed as if she were afraid of waking up. Her astonished and bewildered look added a touch of sorcery. To return, they got into the same carriage, Marius beside Cosette; M. Gillenormand and Jean Valjean sat opposite. Aunt Gillenormand had withdrawn one degree, and was in the second carriage. "My children," said the grandfather, "here you are Monsieur the Baron and Madame the Baronne, with thirty thousand francs a year." And Cosette, leaning close up to Marius, caressed his ear with this angelic whisper, "So it is true. My name is Marius. I am Madame You."

These two beings were resplendent. They were at the irrevocable, unattainable hour, at the dazzling point of intersection of all youth and joy. They realized Jean Prouvaire's verses; together they did not add up to forty years. It was marriage sublimated; these two children were two lilies. They did not see each other, they contemplated one another. Cosette beheld Marius in a glory; Marius beheld Cosette on an altar. And on that altar and in that glory, the two apotheoses mingling, in the background, mysteriously, behind a cloud to Cosette, in flashing flame to Marius, there was the ideal, the real, the rendezvous of kiss and dream, the nuptial pillow.

Every torment they had experienced was returned to them in intoxication. It seemed to them that the griefs, the sleeplessness, the tears, the anguish, the dismay, the despair, become caresses and radiance, rendered still more enchanting the magical moment that was approaching; and that their sorrows were so many servants preparing their joy. To have suffered, how good it is! Their grief made a halo around their happiness. The long agony of their love ended in an ascension.

In these two souls there was the same enchantment, shaded toward anticipation in Marius and modesty in Cosette. They said to each other in a whisper, "We will go and see our little garden in the Rue Plumet again." The folds of Cosette's dress covered his knee.

Such a day is an ineffable mixture of dream and certainty. You possess and you conjecture. You still have some time before you for imagination. It is an unspeakable emotion on that day to be at noon and to think of midnight. The delight of these two hearts overflowed on the throng and gave joy to the passersby.

People stopped in the Rue Saint-Antoine in front of the church of Saint-Paul to see, through the carriage window, the orange blossoms trembling on Cosette's head.

Then they returned to the Rue des Filles-du-Calvaire, to their home. Marius, side by side with Cosette, triumphant and radiant, climbed that staircase he had been carried up, dying. The poor gathered before the door and shared among themselves the coin bestowed on them, blessed the young couple. There were flowers everywhere. The house was no less perfumed than the church; after incense, roses. They thought they could hear voices singing in the infinite; they had God in their hearts; destiny appeared to them like a ceiling of stars; above their heads they saw a gleam of sunrise. Suddenly the clock struck. Marius looked at Cosette's bewitching bare arm and the rosy flesh he dimly perceived through the lace of her corsage, and Cosette, seeing Marius look, began to blush to the tips of her ears.

A good number of the old friends of the Gillenormand family had been invited; they pressed eagerly around Cosette. They vied with each other in calling her Madame the Baronne.

The officer Théodule Gillenormand, now a captain, had come from Chartres, where he was stationed, to attend the wedding of his cousin Pontmercy. Cosette did not recognize him.

As for him, accustomed to being thought handsome by the women, he remembered Cosette no more than any other.

"How right I was not to believe that story about the lancer!" said Grandfather Gillenormand to himself.

Cosette had never been more tender toward Jean Valjean. She was at one with Grandfather Gillenormand; while he embodied joy in aphorisms and in maxims, she exhaled love and kindness like a perfume. Happiness wishes everybody happy.

She went back, in speaking to Jean Valjean, to the tone of voice of her childhood. She caressed him with smiles.

A banquet had been prepared in the dining room.

Bright illumination is the necessary attendant of great joy. Dusk and obscurity are not accepted by the happy. They do not consent to be dark. Night, yes; darkness, no. If there is no sun, one must be made.

The dining room was a furnace of cheerful things. In the center above the white and glittering table, a Venetian chandelier with flat pendants, with all sorts of colored birds, blue, violet, red, green, perched in the midst of the candles; around the girandoles on the wall, and reflectors with triple and quintuple branches, glasses, crystals, glassware, vessels, porcelains, faïence, pottery, gold and silverware—everything sparkled and rejoiced. The spaces between the candelabra were filled with bouquets, so that wherever there was not a light, there was a flower.

In the anteroom three violins and a flute softly played some Haydn quartets.

Jean Valjean sat in a chair in the drawing room, behind the door, which folded back on him in such a way as almost to hide him. A few moments before they took their seats at the table, Cosette came, as if from a sudden impulse, and made him a low curtsy, spreading out her bridal dress with both hands, and, with a tenderly teasing look, she asked him, "Father, are you pleased?"

"Yes," said Jean Valjean, "I am pleased."

"Well, then, laugh."

Jean Valjean began to laugh.

A few moments later, Basque announced dinner.

The guests, preceded by M. Gillenormand giving his arm to Cosette, entered the dining room, and took their places, according to the appointed order, around the table.

Two large armchairs were placed, to the right and left of the bride, the first for M. Gillenormand, the second for Jean Valjean. M. Gillenormand took his seat. The other armchair remained empty.

All eyes sought "Monsieur Fauchelevent."

He was not there.

M. Gillenormand called Basque.

"Do you know where Monsieur Fauchelevent is?"

"Monsieur," answered Basque. "In fact, Monsieur Fauchelevent told me to say to monsieur that he was suffering a little from his sore hand, and could not dine with Monsieur the Baron and Madame the Baronne. That he begged they would excuse him, that he would come tomorrow morning. He has just gone away."

For a moment this empty armchair chilled the enthusiasm of the nuptial repast. But, if M. Fauchelevent was absent, M. Gillenormand was there, and the grandfather was beaming enough for two. He declared that M. Fauchelevent did well to go to bed early, if he was suffering, but that it was only a "tiny scratch." This declaration was enough. Besides, what is one dark corner in such a deluge of joy? Cosette and Marius were in one of those selfish, blessed moments when we have no faculty except for the perception of happiness. And then, M. Gillenormand had an idea. "By Jove, this armchair is empty. Come here, Marius. Your aunt, although she has a right to you, will allow it. This armchair is for you. It is legal, and it is proper. 'Fortunatus beside Fortunata.' " Applause from the whole table. Marius took Jean Valjean's place at Cosette's side; and things arranged themselves in such a way that Cosette, at first saddened by Jean Valjean's absence, was finally satisfied with it. The moment that Marius was the substitute, Cosette would not have regretted God.

She put her soft little foot encased in white satin on Marius's foot.

The armchair occupied, M. Fauchelevent was effaced; and nothing was missed. And, five minutes later, the whole table was laughing from one end to the other with all the spirit of forgetfulness.

At the dessert, M. Gillenormand standing, a glass of champagne in his hand, filled half full so that the trembling of his ninety-two years should not spill it, toasted the health of the married pair.

"You shall not escape two sermons," he exclaimed. "This morning you had the curé's, tonight you shall have the grandfather's. Listen to me; I am going to give you a piece of advice: Adore one another. I don't make undue flourishes. I go right to the point, be happy. The only sages in creation are the turtledoves. The philosophers say: Moderate your joys. I say: Give them full rein. Be enamored like devils. Be rabid. The philosophers talk nonsense. I would like to cram their philosophy back down their throats. Can there be too many perfumes, too many open rosebuds, too many nightingales singing, too many green leaves, too many dawns in life? Can you love each other too much? Can you please each other too much? Take care, Estelle, you are too pretty! Take care, Némorin, you are too handsome! That's pure absurdity! Can you enchant each other too much, pet each other too much, charm each other too much? Can you be too much alive? Can you be too happy? Moderate your joys. Oh, balderdash! Down with the philosophers! Wisdom is jubilation. Jubilate, jubilate. Are we happy because we are good, or are we good because we are happy? Is the Sancy diamond called that because it belonged to Harlay de Sancy, or because it weighs *cent-six* [a hundred and six] carats? I know nothing about it; life is full of such problems; the important thing is to have the Sancy, and happiness. Be happy without quibbling. Obey the sun blindly. What is the sun? It is love. Who says love says woman. Aha! There is an omnipotence; it is woman. Ask this demagogue of a Marius if he is not the slave of this little tyrant of a Cosette, and with his full consent, the coward. Woman! There is no Robespierre who holds out, woman reigns. I am no longer a royalist except for that royalty. What is Adam? He is the realm of Eve. No 'eighty-nine for Eve. There was the royal scepter surmounted by a fleur-de-lis; there was the imperial scepter surmounted by a globe; there was the scepter of Charlemagne, which was of iron; there was the scepter of Louis XIV, which was of gold, the Revolution twisted them between its thumb and finger like halfpenny wisps of straw; they are finished, they are broken, they are on the ground, there are no more scepters; but get me up some revolutions now against this little embroidered handkerchief smelling of patchouli! I would like to see you at it. Try. Why is it immovable? Because it is a scrap. Ah! You are the nineteenth century! Well, what then? We were the eighteenth! And we were as stupid as you. Don't imagine that you have changed anything much in the universe because your stoop-galant is called the cholera morbus, and because your boree is called the cachucha. At heart you must always love women. I defy you to get away from that. These she-devils are our angels. Yes, love, woman, the kiss, that is a circle I defy you to get out of; and, as for myself, I would like very much to get back into it. Which of you has seen rising into the infinite, calming all beneath her, gazing on the waves like a woman, the star Venus, the great coquette of the abyss, the Célimène of the ocean? The ocean is a rude Alceste. Well, he can scold all he likes, Venus appears, he has to smile. That brutal beast submits. We are all like that. Wrath, tempest, thunderbolts, foam to the sky. A woman enters the scene, a star rises; flat on your face! Marius was fighting six months ago; he is marrying today. Well done. Yes, Marius, yes, Cosette, you are right. Live boldly for one another, my-love one another, make us die with rage that we cannot do as much, idolize each other. Take in your two beaks all the little straws of felicity on earth, and build yourselves a nest for life. By Jove, to love, to be loved, the beautiful miracle when one is young! Don't imagine you have invented it. I too, I have had my dream, my vision, my sighs; I too have had a moonlight soul. Love is a child six thousand years old. Love has a right to a long white beard. Methuselah is a gamin beside Cupid. For sixty centuries, man and woman have gotten out of the scrape by loving. The devil, who is clever, took to hating man; man, who is more clever, took to loving woman. In this way he has done himself more good than the devil has done him harm. This trick was discovered at the time of the earthly paradise. My friends, the invention is old, but it is quite new. Profit by it. Be Daphnis and Chloe, while you are waiting to be Philemon and Baucis. Act in such a way that, when you are with each other, there shall be nothing wanting, and that Cosette may be the sun to Marius, and Marius the universe to Cosette. Cosette, let your fine weather be the smile of your husband; Marius, let your rain be the tears of your wife. And may it never rain in your household. You have filched the good number in the lottery, a love match; you have the big prize, take good care of it, put it under lock and key, don't squander it, worship each other, and snap your fingers at the rest. Believe what I tell you. It is good sense. Good sense cannot lie. Be a religion to each other. Everyone has his own way of worshiping God. The best way to worship God is to love your wife. I love you! That is my catechism. Whoever loves is orthodox. Henry the Fourth's oath puts sanctity between gluttony and drunkenness. *Ventre-saint-gris!* I am not part of the religion of that oath. Woman is forgotten in it. That astonishes me on the part of Henry the Fourth's oath. My friends, long live woman! I am old, they say; it is astonishing how I feel myself growing young again. I would like to go and listen to the bagpipes in the woods. These children who are so fortunate as to be beautiful and happy, that dazzles me. I would get married myself if anybody wished. It is impossible to imagine God has made us for anything but this: To idolize, to coo, to plume, to be pigeons, to be cocks, to bill with our loves from morning to night, to take pride in our little wives, to be vain, to be triumphant, to put on airs—that is the aim of life. That, meaning no offense, is what we thought, we old fellows, in our times when we were the young folks. Oh! What charming women there were in those days, pretty faces, lasses! There's where I made my ravages. So, love each other. If people did not love one another, I really don't see what use there would be in having any spring; and, as for me, I would pray the good Lord to pack up all the pretty things he shows us, and take them away from us, and put the flowers, the birds, and the pretty girls, back into his box. My children, receive the benediction of the old man."

The evening was lively, gay, delightful. The sovereign good humor of the grandfather set the keynote for the whole festival, and everybody adapted to this almost centenarian cordiality. They danced a little, they laughed a great deal; it was a genial wedding. They might have invited the good old man called Formerly. Indeed, he was there in the person of Grandfather Gillenormand.

There was tumult, then silence.

The bride and groom disappeared.

A little after midnight the Gillenormand house became a temple.

Here we stop. On the threshold of wedding nights stands an angel smiling, a finger to his lips.

The soul falls into contemplation before this sanctuary, where the celebration of love is held.

There must be glowing light above such houses. The joy they contain must escape in light through the stones of the walls and shine dimly into the darkness. It is impossible that this sacred festival of destiny should not send a celestial radiation to the infinite. Love is the sublime crucible in which is consummated the fusion of man and woman; the one being, the triple being, the final being—the human trinity springs from it. This birth of two souls into one must be an emotion for space. The lover is priest; the apprehensive maiden submits. Something of this joy goes to God. Where there really is marriage, that is to say where there is love, the ideal is mingled with it. A nuptial bed makes a halo in the darkness. Were it given to the eye of flesh to perceive the fearful and enchanting sights of the superior life, it is likely that we should see the forms of night, the winged stranger, the blue travelers of the invisible, bending, a throng of shadowy heads, over the luminous house, pleased, blessing, showing to one another the sweetly startled maiden bride and wearing the reflection of the human felicity on their divine countenances. If, at that supreme hour, the wedded pair, bewildered with pleasure, and believing themselves alone, were to listen, they would hear in their room a rustling of confused wings. Perfect happiness implies the solidarity of the angels. That obscure little alcove has for its ceiling the whole heavens. When two mouths, made sacred by love, draw near each other to create, it is impossible that above that ineffable kiss there should not be a thrill in the immense mystery of the stars.

These are the true felicities. No joy beyond these joys. Love is the only ecstasy, everything else weeps.

To love or to have loved, that is enough. Ask nothing further. There is no other pearl to be found in the dark folds of life. To love is a consummation.

III

THE INSEPARABLE

What had become of Jean Valjean?

Immediately after having laughed, upon Cosette's playful injunction, with nobody paying any attention to him, Jean Valjean had left his seat and, unperceived, had reached the anteroom. It was that same room that eight months before he had entered, black with mire, blood, and gunsmoke, bringing the grandson home to the grandfather. The old woodwork was garlanded with leaves and flowers; the musicians were seated on the couch on which they had placed Marius. Basque, in a black coat, short breeches, white stockings, and white gloves, was arranging crowns of roses around each of the dishes that was to be served up. Jean Valjean had shown him his arm in a sling, asked him to explain his absence, and gone away.

The windows of the dining room looked out on the street. For some minutes Jean Valjean stood motionless in the darkness under those radiant windows. He listened. The confused sounds of the banquet reached him. He heard the loud and authoritative words of the grandfather, the violins, the clatter of the plates and glasses, the bursts of laughter, and through all that gay uproar he distinguished Cosette's sweet joyful voice.

He left the Rue des Filles-du-Calvaire and returned to the Rue de l'Homme-Armé.

To return, he went by the Rue Saint-Louis, the Rue Culture-Sainte-Catherine, and the Blancs-Manteaux; it was a little longer, but it was the way he used to come every day for three months, from the Rue de l'Homme-Armé to the Rue des Filles-du-Calvaire, with Cosette, to avoid the obstructions and the mud of the Rue Vieille-du-Temple.

This route Cosette had used excluded for him every other road.

Jean Valjean went home. He lit his candle and went upstairs. The apartment was empty. Even Toussaint was no longer there. Jean Valjean's footstep made more noise than usual in the rooms. All the closets were open. He went into Cosette's room. There were no sheets on the bed. The pillow, without a pillowcase and without laces, was laid on the covers folded at the foot of the mattress, whose ticking was visible and on which nobody would sleep from then on. All the little feminine objects Cosette loved had been carried away; there remained only the heavy furniture and the four walls. Toussaint's bed was also stripped. A single bed was made and seemed waiting for somebody; that was Jean Valjean's.

Jean Valjean looked at the walls, shut some closet doors, shuttled back and forth from one room to the other.

Then he found himself in his own room again and he put his candle on the table.

He had released his arm from the sling, and he was using his right hand as though it was not at all painful.

He went over to his bed, and his eye fell—was it by chance, was it intentionally—on the inseparable, of which Cosette had been jealous, on the little case that never left him. On the 4th of June, on arriving in the Rue de l'Homme-Armé, he had placed it on a candle stand at the head of his bed. He went to this stand with a sort of alacrity, took a key from his pocket, and opened the valise.

Slowly he took out the clothes in which, ten years before, Cosette had left Montfermeil; first the little dress, then the black scarf, then the great heavy child's shoes Cosette could still almost have worn, so small was her foot, then the vest of very thick fustian, then the knitted petticoat, then the apron with pockets, then the wool stockings. Those stockings, on which the shape of a little leg was still gracefully marked, were hardly longer than Jean Valjean's hand. They were all black. He had taken these clothes to Montfermeil for her. As he lifted them out of the case, he laid them on the bed. He was thinking. He was remembering. It was in winter, a very cold December, she was shivering half naked in rags, her poor little feet all red in her wooden shoes. He, Jean Valjean, had taken her away from those rags to clothe her in these mourning clothes. The mother must have been pleased in her grave to see her daughter wear mourning for her, and particularly to see that she was dressed, and that she was warm. He thought of that forest of Montfermeil; they had crossed it together, Cosette and he; he thought of the weather, of the trees without leaves, of the forest without birds, of the sky without sun; it didn't matter, it was still charming. He arranged the little things on the bed, the scarf next to the skirt, the stockings beside the shoes, the bodice beside the dress, and he looked at them one after another. She was no taller than that, she had her big doll in her arms, she had put her Louis d'or in the pocket of this apron, she laughed, they walked along holding hands, she had nobody but him in the world.

Then his venerable white head fell on the bed, this old stoical heart broke, his face was swallowed up, so to speak, in Cosette's clothes, and anybody who had passed along the staircase at that moment would have heard irrepressible sobbing.

IV

IMMORTAL JECUR

The formidable old struggle, several phases of which we have already seen, began again.

Jacob wrestled with the angel for one night only. Alas! How many times have we seen Jean Valjean grappling in the darkness with his conscience, desperately wrestling against it.

Unparalleled struggle! At certain moments, the foot slips; at others, the ground gives way. How many times had that conscience furious for the right, grasped and overwhelmed him! How many times had inexorable truth planted her knee on his breast! How many times, thrown to the ground by the light, had he cried to it for mercy! How many times had that implacable light, kindled in him and over him by the bishop, irresistibly dazzled him when he wanted to be blinded! How many times had he risen up in the combat, bound to the rock, supported by sophism, dragged in the dust, sometimes trampling down his conscience, sometimes overwhelmed by it! How many times, after some equivocation, after a treacherous and specious reasoning of selfishness, had he heard his outraged conscience cry in his ear, "Go for a fall! Wretch!" How many times had his refractory thought writhed convulsively under the evidence of duty. Resistance to God. Agonizing sweating. How many secret wounds, whose bleeding he alone could feel! How many chafings of his miserable existence! How many times had he risen bleeding, bruised, lacerated, illuminated, despair in his heart, serenity in his soul, and, conquered, felt himself conqueror. And, having racked, torn, and broken him, his conscience, standing above him, formidable, luminous, tranquil, said to him, "Now, go in peace!"

But, after coming through such a gloomy struggle, what a dreary peace, alas!

That night, however, Jean Valjean felt he was putting up his last struggle.

A poignant question was facing him.

Predestinations are not all straight; they do not develop in a rectilinear avenue in front of the predestined; they're blind alleys, dead ends, obscure windings, disturbing crossroads offering several paths. Just then Jean Valjean had come to a halt at the most dangerous of these crossroads.

He had reached the last intersection of good and evil. He had that dark crossing before his eyes. This time again, as had already happened to him in other painful crises, two roads opened before him; the one tempting, the other terrible. Which should he take?

The one that terrified him was advised by the mysterious indicating finger we all notice whenever we gaze into the shadow.

Once again, Jean Valjean had the choice between the terrible haven and the smiling ambush.

So is it true? The soul may be cured, but not fate. Fearful thing, an incurable destiny!

The question facing him was this:

How should Jean Valjean behave in regard to the happiness of Cosette and Marius? It was he who had willed this happiness, it was he who had made it; he had driven it into his own heart, and at this hour, looking at it, he could have the same satisfaction that an armorer would have recognizing his own mark on a blade, as he withdrew it, bloody, from his own breast.

Cosette had Marius, Marius possessed Cosette. They had everything, even riches. And it was his work.

But now that this happiness existed, now that it was here, what was he to do with it, he, Jean Valjean? Should he impose himself on this happiness? Should he treat it as belonging to him? Unquestionably, Cosette belonged to another; but should he, Jean Valjean, retain all of Cosette that he could? Should he remain the kind of father, scarcely seen, but respected, which he had been hitherto? Should he introduce himself quietly into Cosette's house? Should he, without saying a word, bring his past to this future? Should he present himself there as having a right, and should he come and take his seat, veiled, at that luminous hearth? Smiling at them, should he take the hands of those innocent beings into his two tragic hands? Should he place on the peaceful andirons of the Gillenormand hearth, his feet, which dragged after them the infamous shadow of the law? Should he enter on a sharing of chance with Cosette and Marius? Should he thicken the obscurity on his head and the cloud on theirs? Should he put in his catastrophe as a companion for their two felicities? Should he continue to keep silent? In a word, should he be, by the side of these two happy beings, the ominous mute of destiny?

We have to be accustomed to fatality and its encounter to dare to raise our eyes when certain questions appear to us in their horrible nakedness. Good or evil are behind the stern question. "What are you going to do?" demands the sphinx.

Jean Valjean was accustomed to such trials. He stared intently at the sphinx.

He examined the pitiless problem in all its aspects.

Cosette, that charming existence, was the raft of this shipwreck. What was he to do? Hang on, or let go?

If he clung to it, he escaped disaster, he rose again into the sunshine, he let the bitter water drip from his garments and his hair, he was saved, he lived.

If he let go?

Then, the abyss.

Along these lines he bitterly held counsel with his thoughts, or, to speak more truthfully, he struggled; he thrashed furiously within himself, sometimes against his will, sometimes against his conviction.

It was a good thing for Jean Valjean that he had been able to weep. It gave him light, perhaps. For all that, the beginning was wild. A tempest, more furious than the one that had formerly driven him toward Arras, broke loose within him. The past came back to him face to face with the present; he compared and he sobbed. Once the sluice of tears was opened, the despairing man writhed.

He felt that he was stopped.

Alas! In this unrelenting pugilism between our selfishness and our duty, when we recoil this way step by step before our immutable ideal, bewildered, enraged, exasperated at yielding, disputing the ground, hoping for possible flight, seeking some outlet, how abrupt and ominous is the resistance of the wall behind us!

To feel the sacred shadow that bars the way.

The inexorable invisible, what an obsession!

We are never done with conscience. Choose your course by it, Brutus; choose your course by it, Cato. It is bottomless, being God. We cast into this pit the labor of our whole life, we cast in our fortune, our riches, our success, we cast in our liberty or our country, we cast in our well-being, we cast in our repose, our happiness. More! More! More! Empty the vase! Turn the urn upside down! We must ultimately cast in our heart.

Somewhere in the mist of the old hells there is a vessel like that.

Is it not pardonable to refuse in the end? Can the inexhaustible have a claim? Are endless chains not beyond human strength? Who then would blame Sisyphus and Jean Valjean for saying, "Enough!"

The obedience of matter is limited by friction; is there no limit to the obedience of the soul? If perpetual motion is impossible, can perpetual devotion be demanded?

The first step is nothing; it is the last that is difficult. What was the Champmathieu affair compared to Cosette's marriage and all that it involved? What is this: to return to prison, compared with this: to enter into nothingness?

Oh, first step of descent, how somber! Oh, second step, how black!

How could he not turn his head away this time?

Martyrdom is a sublimation, a corrosive sublimation.

It is a torture of consecration. You consent to it the first hour; you sit on the throne of red-hot iron, you put upon your brow the crown of red-hot iron, you receive the orb of red-hot iron, you take the scepter of red-hot iron, but you have yet to put on the mantle of flame, and is there no moment when miserable flesh revolts, and when you abdicate the torture?

At last Jean Valjean entered the calm of despair.

He weighed, he thought, he considered the alternatives of the mysterious balance of light and shade.

To impose his prison on these two dazzling children, or to consummate by himself his irremediable drowning. On the one side the sacrifice of Cosette, on the other of himself.

What solution did he come to?

What resolution did he make? What, within himself, was his final answer to the incorruptible demand of fate? What door did he decide to open? Which side of his life did he resolve to close and to condemn? Between all these unfathomable precipices that surrounded him, what was his choice? What extremity did he accept? To which of these gulfs did he bow his head?

His whirling reverie lasted all night.

He remained there until dawn, in the same position, doubled over on the bed, prostrated under the enormity of fate, crushed perhaps, alas! His fists clenched, his arms extended at a right angle, like someone taken down from the cross and thrown face to the ground. He stayed there for twelve hours, the twelve hours of a long winter night, chilled, without lifting his head, without uttering a word. He was as motionless as a corpse, while his thought writhed on the ground and flew off, now like the hydra, now like the eagle. To see him motionless like this, one would have thought him dead; suddenly he shuddered convulsively, and his mouth, fixed on Cosette's garments, kissed them; then one saw that he was alive.

What one? Since Jean Valjean was alone, and there was nobody there?

The One who is in the darkness.

Book Seven

THE LAST DROP IN THE CHALICE

I

THE SEVENTH CIRCLE AND THE EIGHTH HEAVEN

The day after a wedding is lonely. The privacy of the happy ones is respected. And therefore their slumber is a little belated. The tumult of visits and felicitations does not begin until later. On the morning of the 17th of February, it was a little after noon when Basque, his cloth and feather duster under his arm, busy "doing his anteroom," heard a light rap at the door. There was no ring, which is considerate on such a day. Basque opened and saw M. Fauchelevent. He led him into the drawing room, still cluttered and topsy-turvy, and looking like the battlefield of the evening's festivities.

"Faith, monsieur," observed Basque, "we are waking up late."

"Is your master up?" inquired Jean Valjean.

"How is monsieur's arm?" answered Basque.

"Better. Is your master up?"

"Which? The old or the new one?"

"Monsieur Pontmercy."

"Monsieur the Baron?" said Basque, drawing himself up.

One is baron to his servants, above all. Something of it reflects onto them; they have what a philosopher would call the spattering of the title, and it flatters them. Marius, to mention it in passing, a militant republican, and so he had proved, was now a baron in spite of himself. A slight revolution had taken place in the family in regard to this title. Now it was M. Gillenormand who clung to it and Marius who made light of it. But Colonel Pontmercy had written, "My son will bear my title." Marius obeyed. And then Cosette, in whom the woman was beginning to dawn, was in raptures at being a baroness.

"Monsieur the Baron?" repeated Basque. "I will go and see. I will tell him that Monsieur Fauchelevent is here."

"No. Do not tell him that it is I. Tell him that somebody would like to speak with him in private, and do not give him any name."

"Ah!" said Basque.

"I want to surprise him."

"Ah!" repeated Basque, giving himself the second "ah!" as an explanation of the first.

And he went off.

Jean Valjean remained alone.

The drawing room, as we have just said, was in total disorder. It seemed that by listening carefully a vague echo of the wedding could still be heard. On the floor, there were all sorts of flowers, which had fallen from garlands and headdresses. The candles, burned to the socket, added stalactites of wax to the pendents of the chandeliers. Not a piece of furniture was in place. In the corners, three or four armchairs drawn up in a circle seemed to be continuing a conversation. Altogether it was joyful. There is still a certain grace in a dead festival. It has been happy. On those chairs in disarray, among those wilting flowers, under those extinguished lights, there have been thoughts of joy. The sun succeeded the chandelier and cheerfully entered the drawing room.

A few minutes elapsed. Jean Valjean was motionless in the spot where Basque had left him. He was very pale. His eyes were hollow, and so sunken in their sockets from lack of sleep that they could hardly be seen. His black coat had the weary folds of a garment that one has spent the night in. The elbows were whitened with that down that is left on cloth by the chafing of linen. Jean Valjean was looking at the window traced by the sun on the floor at his feet.

There was a noise at the door; he looked up.

Marius entered, his head erect, his mouth smiling, an indescribable light upon his face, his forehead radiant, his eye triumphant. He too had not slept.

"It is you, Father!" he exclaimed on seeing Jean Valjean; "that idiot of a Basque with his mysterious air! But you have come too early. It is still only twelve-thirty. Cosette is asleep."

That word "Father" said to M. Fauchelevent by Marius signified supreme felicity. There had always been, as we know, barrier, coldness, and constraint between them; ice to break or to melt. Marius had reached that degree of joy where the barrier was falling, the ice was dissolving, and M. Fauchelevent was to him, as to Cosette, a father.

He continued; words were pouring out of him, which is characteristic of these divine paroxysms of joy, "How glad I am to see you! If you knew how we missed you yesterday! Good morning, Father. How is your hand? Better, I hope?"

And, satisfied with the good reply he made to himself, he went on, "We have both talked a great deal about you. Cosette loves you so much! You will not forget that your room is here. We don't want any more of the Rue de l'Homme-Armé. We don't want any more of it at all. How could you go to live in a street like that, which is sickly, which is scowling, which is ugly, with a barrier at one end, where you are cold, and where no one can drive in? You will come and settle in here. And today. Or you will have to settle with Cosette. She intends to lead us all by the nose, I warn you. You have seen your room, it is close to ours, it looks out on the gardens; the lock has been fixed, the bed is made, everything is ready; you have nothing to do but to come. Cosette has put a great old easy chair of Utrecht velvet beside your bed, and she told it: Stretch out your arms for him. Every spring, a nightingale comes to the clump of acacias in front of your windows, you will have her in two months. You will have her nest at your left and ours at your right. By night she will sing, and by day Cosette will talk. Your room faces full south. Cosette will arrange your books there for you, your voyage of Captain Cook, and the other, Vancouver's, all your things. I believe there is a little valise that you treasure, I have selected a place of honor for it. You have conquered my grandfather, you suit him. We'll live together. Do you play whist? My grandfather will be overjoyed if you know whist. You will take Cosette out for a walk on my court days, you'll give her your arm, you know, the way you used to at the Luxembourg. We have positively decided to be very happy. And you are part of our happiness, do you understand, Father? Come now, will you have breakfast with us today?"

"Monsieur," said Jean Valjean, "I have one thing to tell you. I am a former convict."

The perceptible limit of acute sounds may be crossed just as easily for the mind as for the ear. Those words, "I am a former convict," coming from M. Fauchelevent's mouth and entering Marius's ear, went beyond the possible. Marius did not hear. It seemed to him that something had just been said to him, but he did not know what. He stood aghast.

He then perceived that the man who was talking to him was terrifying. Excited as he was, he had not until this moment noticed that frightful pallor.

Jean Valjean untied the black tie holding up his right arm, took off the cloth wound about his hand, laid his thumb bare, and showed it to Marius.

"There is nothing the matter with my hand," he said.

Marius looked at the thumb.

"There has never been anything the matter with it," continued Jean Valjean.

There was, in fact, no trace of a wound.

Jean Valjean went on, "It was best for me to be absent from your wedding. I kept away as much as I could. I feigned this wound so as not to commit a forgery, so as not to introduce a nullity into the marriage acts, to be excused from signing."

Marius stammered out, "What does this mean?"

"It means," answered Jean Valjean, "that I was in the chain gangs."

"You are driving me mad!" exclaimed Marius in dismay.

"Monsieur Pontmercy," said Jean Valjean, "I spent nineteen years in prison. For robbery. Then I was sentenced for life. For robbery. For a second offense. At this very moment I am illegally at large."

It was useless for Marius to recoil before the reality, to refuse the fact, to resist the evidence; he was compelled to yield. He began to understand, and as always happens in such cases, he understood beyond the truth. He felt the shiver of a horrible interior flash; an idea that made him shudder, crossed his mind. He caught a glimpse in the future of a hideous destiny for himself.

"Tell me everything! Tell me everything!" he cried. "You are Cosette's father!"

And he took two steps backward with an expression of unspeakable horror.

Jean Valjean raised his head with such majestic attitude that he seemed to rise to the ceiling.

"It is necessary for you to believe me in this, monsieur; although the oath of men such as me is not considered valid."

Here he paused, then, with a sort of sovereign, sepulchral authority, he added, articulating slowly and emphasizing his syllables, "—You will believe me. I, the father of Cosette! Before God, no. Monsieur Baron Pontmercy, I am a peasant from Faverolles. I earned my living by pruning trees. My name is not Fauchelevent, my name is Jean Valjean. I am nothing to Cosette. Be reassured."

Marius faltered, "Who proves it to me—"

"I do. Since I say so."

Marius looked at this man. He was mournful, yet self-possessed. No lie could come out of such a calm. What is frozen is sincere. We feel the truth in that sepulchral coldness.

"I believe you," said Marius.

Jean Valjean bowed his head as in acceptance, and continued, "What am I to Cosette? A passerby. Ten years ago, I did not know that she existed. I love her, it is true. A child you have seen when she is little and you are already old, you love. When a man is old, he feels like a grandfather toward all little children. You can, it seems to me, suppose I have something that resembles a heart. She was an orphan. Without father or mother. She needed me. That is why I began to love her. Children are so weak, that anybody, even a man like me, can be their protector. I performed that duty with regard to Cosette. I do not think that one could truly call so little a thing a good deed; but if it is a good deed, well, set it down that I have done it. Make note of that mitigating circumstance. Today Cosette leaves my life; our two roads separate. From now on I can do nothing more for her. She is Madame Pontmercy. Her protector is changed. And Cosette gains by the change. All is well. As for the six hundred thousand francs, you have not spoken of them to me, but I anticipate your thought; that is a trust. How did this trust come into my hands? What does it matter? I have made over the trust. Nothing more can be asked of me. I have completed the restitution by telling you my real name. This concerns me too. I want you to know who I am."

And Jean Valjean looked Marius in the face.

Everything that Marius felt was tumultuous and incoherent. Certain gusts of destiny make such waves in our soul.

We have all had these moments of trouble, in which everything within us is dispersed; we say the first things that come to mind, which are not always precisely those that we should say. There are sudden revelations we cannot bear, that intoxicate like a noxious wine. Marius was so stupefied at the new state of affairs opening before him that he spoke to this man almost as though he were angry with him for his confession.

"But after all," he exclaimed, "why are you telling me all this? What compels you to do so? You could have kept the secret to yourself. You are neither denounced, nor pursued, nor hunted. You have some reason for making, out of mere wantonness, such a revelation. Tell the rest. There is something else. In what connection did you make this admission? From what motive?"

"From what motive?" answered Jean Valjean, in a voice so low and so hollow that one would have said he was speaking to himself rather than to Marius. "From what motive, indeed, did this convict come and say: I am a convict? Well, yes! The motive is strange. It is from honor. Yes, my misfortune is a cord that I have here in my heart, that holds me fast. When one is old these cords are particularly strong. A whole lifetime wastes away around them; they hold fast. If I had been able to rip off that cord, to break it, to untie the knot, or to cut it, to go far away, I would have been saved, I only had to leave; there are coaches in the Rue du Bouloy; you are happy, I could go away. I have tried to break the cord, I have pulled at it, it has held firmly, it did not snap, I was tearing my heart out with it. Then I said I cannot live away from here. I must stay. Well, yes; but you are right, I am a fool, why not just simply stay? You have offered me a room in the house, Madame Pontmercy loves me dearly, she says to that armchair, Stretch out your arms for him; your grandfather asks nothing better than to have me, I suit him, we will all live together, eat in common, I will give my arm to Cosette—to Madame Pontmercy, pardon me, it is out of habit—we will have just one roof, one table, one fire, the same chimney corner in winter, the same stroll in summer, that is joy, that is happiness, that, it is everything. We will live as one family, one family!"

At this word Jean Valjean grew wild. He folded his arms, gazed at the floor at his feet as if he wished to dig an abyss there, and his voice suddenly became piercing.

"One family! No. I belong to no family. I am not part of yours. I am not part of the family of men. In houses where people are at home I am an encumbrance. There are families, but they are not for me. I am the unfortunate; I am outside. Did I have a father and a mother? I almost doubt it. The day I saw the child married, that was all over, I could see she was happy, and that she was with the man she loved, and that there was a good old man here, a household of two angels, every joy in this house, and that it was fine, I said to myself: Don't you enter. I could have lied, it is true, could have deceived you all, have remained Monsieur Fauchelevent. As long as it was for her, I could lie; but now it would be for myself, and I must not do it. It would have been enough to remain silent, it is true, and everything would continue. You ask what forces me to speak? A strange thing: my conscience. Yet to keep silent was very easy. I have spent the night in trying to persuade myself to do so; you are confessing me, and what I have come to tell you is so strange that you have a right to do so; well, yes, I spent the night in giving myself reasons, I have given myself very good reasons, I have done what I could, you know. But there are two things I could not manage; neither to break the cord that holds me by the heart fixed, riveted, and sealed here, nor in silencing someone who speaks softly to me when I am alone. That is why I have come to confess it all to you this morning. All, or almost all. It is useless to you what concerns me alone, I keep that for myself. The essentials you know. So I have taken my mystery, and brought it to you. And I have ripped open my secret under your eyes. It was not an easy decision to make. All night I struggled with myself. Ah! You think I have not said to myself that this is not the Champmathieu affair, that in concealing my name I am not harming anybody, that the name of Fauchelevent was given to me by Fauchelevent himself in gratitude for a service rendered, and I could very well keep it, and that I should be happy in this room that you offer me, that I would interfere with nothing, that I would be in my little corner, and that, while you would have Cosette, I would have the idea of being in the same house with her. Each of us would have had his due share of happiness. To continue being Monsieur Fauchelevent smoothed the way for everything. Yes, except for my soul. There was joy everywhere around me, the depths of my soul were still black. It is not enough to be happy, we must be satisfied with ourselves. That way I would have remained Monsieur Fauchelevent, that way I would have concealed my real face, and, in presence of your cheerfulness, I would have borne an enigma, that way, in the midst of your bright day, I would have been darkness, without openly crying beware, I would have brought the prison to your hearth, I would have sat down at your table with the thought that, if you knew who I was, you would drive me away, I would have let myself be served by servants who, if they had known, would have said: How horrible! I would have touched you with my elbow, which you have a right to shrink from, I would have betrayed your handshake! There would have been in your house a division of respect between venerable white hair and dishonored white hair; at your most intimate hours, when all hearts would have thought themselves open to each other to the core, when we would have all four been together, your grandfather, you two, and myself; there would have been a stranger there! I would have been side by side with you in your existence, having only one care, never to jar the cover of my terrible pit. That way I, a dead man, would have imposed myself on you, who are alive. I would have condemned her to myself forever. You, Cosette, and I, we would have been three heads in the green cap! Aren't you shuddering? I am now only the most depressed of men; I would have been the most monstrous. And I would have committed that crime every day! And I would have acted out that lie every day! And I would have worn this face of night every day! And every day I would have given you your share of my disgrace! Every day! To you, my loved ones, you, my children, you, my innocents! It is nothing to keep my peace? To keep silent is simple? No, it is not simple. There is a silence that lies. And my lie, and my fraud, and my unworthiness, and my cowardice, and my treachery, and my crime, I would have drunk drop by drop, I would have spit it out, then drunk again, I would have finished at midnight and begun again at noon, and my 'good morning' would have lied, and my 'good night,' too, and I would have slept on it, and eaten it with my bread, and I would have looked Cosette in the face, and answered the smile of the angel with the smile of the damned, and I would have been a detestable imposter! What for? To be happy. To be happy, I! Have I any right to be happy? I am outside of life, monsieur."

Jean Valjean stopped. Marius listened. Such a chain of ideas and anguish cannot be interrupted. Jean Valjean lowered his voice again, but it was no longer a hollow voice, it was an ominous voice.

"You ask why I speak? I am neither informed against, nor pursued, nor hunted, you say. Yes! I am informed against! Yes, I am pursued! Yes, I am hunted! By whom? By myself. It is I myself who bar the way before me, and I drag myself, and I urge myself on, and I check myself, and I exert myself, and when a man holds himself in check, he is well held."

And seizing his own coat in his clenched hand and drawing it toward Marius: "Look at this hand, now," he continued. "Don't you think it is holding this collar in such a way as not to let go? Well! Conscience has quite another grasp! If we want to be happy, monsieur, we must never understand duty; for, as soon as we understand it, it is implacable. It is as though it punishes you for understanding it; but no, it rewards you for it; for it puts you in a hell where you feel God at your side. Your heart is not as quickly lacerated when you are at peace with yourself."

And, with bitter emphasis, he added, "Monsieur Pontmercy, this is not common sense, but I am an honest man. It is by degrading myself in your eyes that I raise myself in my own. That has already happened to me once, but it was less painful then; it was nothing. Yes, an honest man. I would not be one if, through my fault, you had continued to think well of me; now that you despise me, I am one. I have this misfortune hanging over me that, never being able to have anything but stolen consideration, that consideration humiliates me and depresses me inwardly, and in order to respect myself, I have to be despised. Then I can hold myself erect. I am a convict who obeys his conscience. I know very well that is improbable. But what would you have me do? That is the way it is. I have assumed commitments toward myself; I keep them. There are accidents that bind us, there are chances that drag us into duties. You see, Monsieur Pontmercy, many things have happened to me in my life!"

Jean Valjean paused again, swallowing his saliva with effort, as if his words had a bitter aftertaste, and went on: "When a person has such a horror hanging over him, he has no right to make others share it without their knowledge, he has no right to communicate his disease to them, he has no right to make them slip down his precipice without warning, he has no right to let his red tunic fall onto them, he has no right to craftily clutter the happiness of others with his own misery. To come close to those who are healthy and touch them in the shadows with his invisible ulcer, that is horrible. Fauchelevent lent me his name, I have no right to use it; he could give it to me, I could not take it. A name is a Me. You see, monsieur, I have thought a little, I have read a little, although I am a peasant; and you see that I express myself tolerably. I form my own idea of things. I have given myself an education of my own. Well, yes, to take a name, and to put yourself under it, is dishonest. The letters of the alphabet can be stolen like a purse or a watch. To be a false signature in flesh and blood, to be a living false key, to enter the houses of honest people by picking their locks, never to look directly out again, but always askance, to be dishonorable within myself, no! No! No! No! It is better to suffer, to bleed, to weep, to scratch the skin off the flesh, to spend the night in writhing, in anguish, to gnaw away body and soul. That is why I come to tell you all this. In mere wantonness, as you say."

He drew a breath with difficulty, and forced out these final words:

"To live, I once stole a loaf of bread; today, to live, I will not steal a name."

"To live!" interrupted Marius. "You don't need that name to live!"

"Ah! I know very well what I mean," answered Jean Valjean, raising and lowering his head several times in succession.

There was a pause. Both were silent, each sunk in thought. Marius had seated himself beside a table, and was resting the corner of his mouth on one of his bent fingers. Jean Valjean was walking back and forth. He stopped before a mirror and stood motionless. Then, as if answering some inward reasoning, he said, looking at that mirror in which he did not see himself, "Whereas at present, I am relieved!"

He began to walk again and went to the other end of the salon. Just as he began to turn, he noticed that Marius was watching him walk. He said to him with an emphasis that went beyond words:

"I drag one leg a little. Now you understand why."

Then he turned the rest of the way around toward Marius:

"And now, monsieur, picture this to yourself: I have said nothing, I have kept on as Monsieur Fauchelevent, I have taken my place in your house, I am one of you, I am in my room, I come to breakfast in the morning in slippers, at night we all three go to the theater, I accompany Madame Pontmercy to the Tuileries and to the Place Royale, we are together, you suppose me your equal; one fine day I am there, you are there, we are chatting, we are laughing, suddenly you hear a voice shout this name: Jean Valjean! And you see that appalling hand, the police, spring out of the shadow and abruptly tear off my mask!"

He stopped again; Marius had risen with a shudder. Jean Valjean went on, "What do you say to that?"

Marius's silence answered.

Jean Valjean continued, "You see very well that I am right in not keeping quiet. Look, be happy, be in heaven, be an angel to an angel, be in the sunshine, and be content with that, and don't trouble yourself about the way a poor condemned man takes to open his heart and do his duty; you have a wretched man before you, monsieur."

Marius crossed the drawing room slowly, and, when he was near Jean Valjean, stretched out his hand to him.

But Marius had to take that hand, which did not respond itself. Jean Valjean was passive, and it seemed to Marius that he was grasping a hand of marble.

"My grandfather has friends," said Marius. "I will procure your pardon."

"That would be useless," answered Jean Valjean. "They think I am dead, that is enough. The dead are not subjected to surveillance. They are supposed to molder tranquilly. Death is the same thing as pardon."

And, disengaging his hand, which Marius was holding, he added with a sort of inexorable dignity, "Besides, to do my duty, that is the friend I have to rely on; and I need the pardon of only one, my conscience."

Just then, at the other end of the salon, the door was softly opened a little way, and Cosette's head appeared. They saw only her sweet face, her hair was in charming disorder, her eyelids still swollen with sleep. She made the movement of a bird poking its head out of the nest, looked first at her husband, then at Jean Valjean, and called out to them with a laugh, you would have thought you saw a smile deep within a rose.

"I'll wager that you're talking politics. How idiotic that is, instead of being with me!"

Jean Valjean gave a start.

"Cosette," faltered Marius—and he stopped. One would have thought they were two culprits.

Cosette, radiant, continued to look at them both. The glint of paradise was in her eyes.

"I'm catching you in the very act," said Cosette. "I just heard my father Fauchelevent say, through the door: 'Conscience—Do his duty.'—It's politics, that is. I won't have it. You shouldn't talk politics the very next day. It's not right."

"You are mistaken, Cosette," answered Marius. "We were talking business. We are talking of the best investment for your six hundred thousand francs—"

"It is not all that important," interrupted Cosette. "I'm coming. Do you want me here?"

And, passing resolutely through the door, she came into the drawing room. She was dressed in a full white dressing gown, with a thousand folds and wide sleeves, which, starting from the neck, fell straight to her feet. In the golden skies of old Gothic pictures are such charming robes fit for angels.

She glanced at herself from head to foot in a large mirror, then exclaimed with a burst of ecstasy, "Once there was a king and a queen. Oh, how happy I am!"

So saying, she curtsied to Marius and to Jean Valjean.

"There," said she, "I am going to settle into an armchair beside you. We will have breakfast in half an hour, you will say all you like; I know very well that men have to talk, I'll be very good."

Marius took her arm, and said to her lovingly, "We are talking business."

"By the way," answered Cosette, "I've opened my window, a whole flock of boisterous sparrows have just come to the garden. It's Ash Wednesday today, but not for the birds."

"I tell you we're talking business. Go, my sweet Cosette, leave us alone for a moment. We are talking figures. It will bore you."

"You have put on a charming tie this morning, Marius. You are very stylish, monseigneur. No, it won't bore me."

"I assure you that it will bore you."

"No. Because it is you. I won't understand you, but I'll listen to you. When we hear voices we love, we don't need to understand the words. To be here together is all I want. I will stay with you; pooh!"

"You are my dearest Cosette! Impossible."

"Impossible!"

"Yes."

"Very well," replied Cosette. "I would have told you the news. I would have told you that grandfather is still asleep, that your aunt is at mass, that the chimney in my father Fauchelevent's room is smoking, that Nicolette has sent for the chimney sweep, that Toussaint and Nicolette have had a quarrel already, that Nicolette makes fun of Toussaint's stuttering. Well, you won't know a thing. Ah, it's impossible? I too, when my turn comes, you'll see, monsieur, I'll say, It's impossible. Then who will be caught? I pray you, my darling Marius, let me stay here with you two."

"I swear to you that we must be alone."

"Well, am I anybody?"

Jean Valjean was not saying a word. Cosette turned to him.

"In the first place, Father, I want you to come and kiss me. What are you doing there, saying nothing, instead of taking my side? Who gave me a father like that? You can plainly see that I am very unfortunate in my domestic affairs. My husband beats me. Come, kiss me this instant."

Jean Valjean came closer.

Cosette turned toward Marius.

"You, sir, I make faces at you."

Then she offered her forehead to Jean Valjean.

Jean Valjean took a step toward her.

Cosette drew back.

"Father, you are so pale. Is your arm hurting?"

"It is healed," said Jean Valjean.

"Did you sleep badly?"

"No."

"Are you sad?"

"No."

"Kiss me. If you're well, if you slept well, if you're happy, I won't scold you."

And again she offered him her forehead.

Jean Valjean kissed that forehead, touched with a celestial reflection.

"Smile."

Jean Valjean obeyed. It was the smile of a specter.

"Now defend me against my husband."

"Cosette!—" said Marius.

"Get angry, Father. Tell him I must stay. Surely you can talk in front of me. So you think me very silly. So it's very astonishing what you are saying! Business, putting money in a bank, that's a great affair. Men play the mysterious for nothing. I want to stay. I am very pretty this morning. Look at me, Marius."

And with an adorable shrug of the shoulders and an inexpressibly exquisite pout, she looked at Marius. It was like a flash between these two beings. That somebody was there mattered little.

"I love you!" said Marius.

"I adore you!" said Cosette.

And they fell irresistibly into each other's arms.

"Now," resumed Cosette, readjusting a fold of her gown with a triumphant little pout, "I'll stay."

"That, no," answered Marius, in a tone of entreaty, "we have something to finish."

"No, still?"

Marius assumed a grave tone of voice, "I assure you, Cosette, it is impossible."

"Ah! You are putting on your man's voice, monsieur.

Very well, I'll go. You, Father, you have not backed me up. Monsieur my husband, Monsieur my papa, you are tyrants. I'm going to tell grandfather about you. If you think that I'll come back and talk nonsense to you, you are mistaken. I am proud. Now I will wait for you, you'll see that it is you who will get bored without me. I'm leaving, very well."

And she went out.

Two seconds later, the door opened again, her fresh rosy face looked once more between the two folds of the door, and she cried out to them, "I'm very angry."

The door closed again and the darkness returned.

It was like a stray sunbeam that, unawares, had suddenly glanced through the night.

Marius made sure that the door was well closed.

"Poor Cosette!" he murmured, "when she knows—"

At these words, Jean Valjean trembled in every limb. He looked at Marius distractedly.

"Cosette! Oh, yes, that's true, you will tell this to Cosette. That is fair. Well, I had not thought of that. People have the strength for some things, but not for others. Monsieur, I beseech you, I entreat you, monsieur, give me your most sacred word, do not tell her. Isn't it enough that you know it yourself? I was able to tell you myself without being forced to, I would have told it to the universe, to all the world, that would be nothing. But she, she doesn't know what it is, it would appal her. A convict, why! You would have to explain it to her, to tell her: It is a man who has been in the prison. She saw the Chain pass by one day. Oh, my God!"

He sank into an armchair and hid his face in his hands. He could not be heard, but by the shaking of his shoulders it was clear that he was weeping. Silent tears, terrible tears.

Sobbing can choke you. A sort of convulsion seized him, he leaned back in the armchair as if to breathe, letting his arms hang down and allowing Marius to see his face bathed in tears, and Marius heard him murmur so low that his voice seemed to come from a bottomless depth: "Oh! I would like to die!"

"Don't worry," said Marius, "I will keep your secret to myself."

And, less softened perhaps than he should have been, but obliged through the past hour to become accustomed to a fearful surprise, bit by bit seeing a convict superimposed before his eyes on M. Fauchelevent, gradually overcome by this dismal reality, and led by the natural tendency of that position to acknowledge the distance that had just been put between this man and himself, Marius added: "It would be impossible for me not to say a word to you about the funds you have so faithfully and so honestly handed over. That is an act of probity. In all fairness you should have a recompense. Set the figure yourself, it will be given to you. Do not be afraid to fix it very high."

"Thank you, monsieur," answered Jean Valjean gently.

He paused thoughtfully for a moment, rubbing the tip of his forefinger against his thumbnail mechanically, then spoke up, "Almost everything is done. There is one thing left—"

"What?"

After what seemed a supreme hesitation, voicelessly, almost breathless, Jean Valjean faltered out rather than said, "Now that you know, do you think, monsieur, you who are the master, that I should not see Cosette again?"

"I think that would be best," answered Marius coldly.

"I will not see her again," murmured Jean Valjean.

And he walked toward the door.

He placed his hand on the knob, the latch yielded, the door began to swing, Jean Valjean opened it wide enough to pass through, stopped for a second motionless, then shut the door, and turned toward Marius.

He was no longer pale, he was livid. There were no longer tears in his eyes, but a sort of tragic flame. His voice had regained its strange calm.

"But, monsieur," he said, "if you are willing, I will come and see her. I assure you that I want that very much. If I had not wanted to see Cosette, I would not have made the admission I made, I would have gone away. But wishing to stay where Cosette is and to continue to see her, I was compelled in all honesty to tell you everything. You follow my reasoning, don't you? That is understandable. You see, for nine years, I have had her near me. First we lived in that wreck on the boulevard, then in the convent, then near the Luxembourg. It was there that you saw her for the first time. You remember her blue plush hat. Then we were near the Invalides where there was an iron gate and a garden. Rue Plumet. I lived in a little back courtyard where I could hear her play the piano. That was my whole life. We never left each other. It lasted nine years and some months. I was like her father, and she was my child. I don't know whether you understand me, Monsieur Pontmercy, but from now on, not to see her again, not to speak to her again, to have nothing left, that would be hard. If you do not think it is wrong, I will come from time to time to see Cosette. I would not come often. I would not stay long. You might say I could be received in the little room downstairs. On the ground floor. I would willingly come in by the back door, the servants' door, but perhaps that would seem strange. It would be better, I suppose, for me to come in the usual door. Monsieur, really, I would truly still like to see Cosette a little. As rarely as you like. Put yourself in my place, it is all that I have. And then, we must be careful. If I were not to come at all, it would not look right, people would think it strange. For instance, what I can do, is to come in the evening, at nightfall."

"You will come every evening," said Marius," and Cosette will expect you."

"You are kind, monsieur," said Jean Valjean.

Marius bowed to Jean Valjean, happiness conducted despair to the door, and the two men separated.

II

THE OBSCURITIES THAT A REVELATION MAY CONTAIN

Marius was completely overwhelmed.

The kind of antipathy he had always felt for the man with whom he saw Cosette was now explained. There was something strangely enigmatic in this person; his instinct had warned him. The enigma was the most hideous disgrace, prison. This M. Fauchelevent was the convict Jean Valjean.

Suddenly finding such a secret in the midst of one's happiness is like the discovery of a scorpion in a nest of turtledoves.

Was the happiness of Marius and Cosette doomed from then on to this contact? Was it a foregone conclusion? Did the acceptance of this man form a part of the marriage that had been consummated? Was there nothing more that could be done?

Was Marius wedded to the convict too?

To be crowned with light and with joy, to be revelling in the royal purple hour of life, happy love, is of no avail; a shock like this would compel even the archangel in his ecstasy, even the demigod in his glory, to shudder.

As always happens in changes of outlook like this, Marius wondered whether he should not partly blame himself. Had he been lacking in perception, in prudence? Had he been involuntarily dazed? A little, perhaps. Had he entered, without enough attention to its surroundings, into this love adventure that had ended in his marriage to Cosette? He recognized—it is this way, in a succession of recognitions by ourselves about ourselves, that life improves us little by little—he recognized the chimeric and visionary side of his nature, a sort of interior cloud peculiar to many organisms, and which, in paroxysms of passion and grief, dilates, changing the temperature of the soul, and pervades the entire man, to the point where he is no more than a consciousness steeped in a fog. More than once we have indicated this characteristic of Marius's personality. He recollected that in the infatuation in the Rue Plumet, during those six or seven ecstatic weeks, he had not even spoken to Cosette of that drama of the Gorbeau lair when the victim had taken the very strange course of silence during the struggle, and of escape after it. How had he managed not to speak of it to Cosette? Yet it was so near and so frightful. How had he managed not even to name the Thénardiers to her, and, particularly, the day that he met Eponine? He had great difficulty now in explaining his earlier silence to himself. He did account for it, however. He recalled his daze, his infatuation with Cosette, love absorbing everything, that transport of one by the other into the ideal, and perhaps too, as the imperceptible quantity of reason mingled with the violent and charming state of the soul, a vague, muffled instinct to hide and erase in his memory that terrible affair whose contact he dreaded, in which he wanted to play no part, which he shunned, and in which he could be neither narrator nor witness without being accuser. Besides, those few weeks had been like a flash; they had had time for nothing except love. Finally, with everything weighed, turned upside down, and examined, if he had told the story of the Gorbeau ambush to Cosette, if he had named the Thénardiers to her, what would have been the consequences? Even if he had discovered Jean Valjean was a convict, would that have changed him, Marius? Would that have changed her, Cosette? Would he have shrunk back? Would he have adored her less? Would he have married her any the less? No. Would it have changed anything in what had taken place? No. So nothing to regret, nothing to reproach himself with. All was well. There is a God for these drunkards who are called lovers. Blind, Marius had followed the route he would have chosen if he had seen clearly. Love had bandaged his eyes, to lead him where? To Paradise.

But this was linked from then on with an infernal complication.

The repulsion Marius had felt toward this man, toward this Fauchelevent become Jean Valjean, was now mingled with horror.

In this horror, we must admit there was some pity, and also a certain surprise.

This robber, this twice-convicted robber, had handed over a trust. And what sort of a trust? Six hundred thousand francs. He alone held the secret. He might have kept everything, he had given it up.

Furthermore, he had revealed his situation of his own accord. Nothing made him do so. If it was known who he was, that was only through him. There was more in that confession than the acceptance of humiliation, there was the acceptance of peril. To a condemned man a mask is not a mask, but a shelter. He had given up that shelter. A false name is security; he had thrown away the false name. He, a convict, could have hidden forever in an honorable family; he had resisted that temptation. And from what motive? For reasons of conscience. He had explained it himself with the irresistible accent of reality. In short, whatever this Jean Valjean might be, he incontestably had an awakened conscience. Some mysterious regeneration had begun in him, and, to all appearances, scruples had long been master of the man. Such paroxysms of justice and goodness do not belong to vulgar natures. An awakening of conscience is greatness of soul.

Jean Valjean was sincere. This sincerity, visible, palpable, unquestionable, evident even in the grief it caused him, made investigation pointless and gave authority to all that the man said. Here, for Marius, a strange inversion of situations. What came from M. Fauchelevent? Distrust. What flowed from Jean Valjean? Confidence.

In the mysterious account that Marius thoughtfully drew up concerning this Jean Valjean, he verified the credit, he verified the debit, he attempted to reach a balance. But it was all as though in a storm. Endeavoring to get a clear idea of the man, and pursuing, so to speak, Jean Valjean in the depths of his thought, Marius lost him and found him again in a fatal haze.

The funds honestly surrendered, the probity of the admission, that was good. It was like a break in the cloud, but the cloud again turned black.

Confused as Marius's recollections were, some trace of them returned to him.

What exactly was that affair in the Jondrette garret? Why, on the arrival of the police, had this man escaped, instead of making his complaint? Here Marius found the answer. Because the man was a fugitive from justice illegally at large.

Another question: Why had this man come into the barricade? For now Marius could see that scene again distinctly, reappearing in these emotions like magic ink in the presence of heat. The man was in the barricade. He did not fight there. What did he come there for? A specter rose with this question and responded. Javert. Now Marius recalled perfectly the grim sight of Jean Valjean dragging Javert outside the barricade, still bound, and again he heard the frightful pistol shot behind the corner of the little Rue Mondétour. There was probably hatred between the sleuth and this convict. The one cramped the other. Jean Valjean had gone to the barricade to avenge himself. He had arrived late. He probably knew that Javert was a prisoner there. The Corsican-style vendetta has penetrated into certain lower depths and is their law; it is so natural that it does not surprise souls half turned back toward the good; and these hearts are so constituted that a repentant criminal may be scrupulous about robbery and not be so about vengeance. Jean Valjean had killed Javert. At least, that seemed evident.

Finally, a last question: But to this one there was no answer. Marius felt this question like a sting. How did it happen that Jean Valjean's existence had been close to Cosette's for so long? What was this gloomy game of providence that had placed the child in contact with this man? Are coupling chains then forged on high too, and does it please God to pair the angel with the demon? So can a crime and an innocence be roommates in the mysterious prisons of misery? In this procession of the condemned, which is called human destiny, can two foreheads pass close to one another, the one childlike, the other terrible, the one all bathed in the divine white of the dawn, the other forever pallid with the glare of an eternal lightning? Who could have decided on this inexplicable fellowship? How, through what prodigy, could community of life have been established between this celestial child and this tormented individual? Who had been able to bind the lamb to the wolf and, still more incomprehensible, attach the wolf to the lamb? For the wolf loved the lamb, the savage being adored the frail being, since during nine years the angel had had the monster for support. Cosette's childhood and adolescence, her coming to the day, her virginal growth toward life and light, had been protected by this monstrous devotion. Here, the questions exfoliated, so to speak, into countless enigmas, abyss opened at the bottom of abysm, and Marius could no longer consider Jean Valjean without vertigo. What then was this man-precipice?

The old symbols from Genesis are eternal; in human society, such as it is and will be, until the day when a greater light changes it, there are always two men, one superior, the other subterranean; the one who follows good is Abel; the one who follows evil is Cain. What was this remorseful Cain? What was this bandit religiously absorbed in the adoration of a virgin, watching over her, bringing her up, guarding her, dignifying her, and enveloping her, himself impure, with purity? What was this cloaca that had venerated this innocence to such an extent as to leave it immaculate? What was this Jean Valjean watching over the education of Cosette? What was this figure of darkness, whose only care was to preserve from all shadow and cloud the rising of a star?

There lay the secret of Jean Valjean; there also lay the secret of God.

Facing this double secret, Marius recoiled. The one in some way reassured him in regard to the other. God was as visible in this as Jean Valjean. God has his instruments. He uses what tool He pleases. He is not responsible to man. Do we know the ways of God? Jean Valjean had labored over Cosette. To some extent, he had formed that soul. That was incontestable. Well, what then? The workman was horrible; but the work admirable. God performs His miracles as He sees fit. He had constructed this enchanting Cosette, and he had employed Jean Valjean for the work. It had pleased Him to choose this strange collaborator. What reckoning have we to ask of Him? Is this the first time the dunghill has helped the spring to make the rose?

Marius gave himself these answers, and declared that they were good. On all the points we have just indicated, he had not dared to press Jean Valjean, without admitting to himself that he did not dare. He adored Cosette, he possessed Cosette. Cosette was resplendently pure. That was enough for him. What explanation did he need? Cosette was a light. Does light need to be explained? He had everything; what more could he desire? Everything, isn't that enough? The personal affairs of Jean Valjean did not concern him. In studying the fatal darkness of this man, he clung to the solemn statement of the miserable being: "I am nothing to Cosette. Ten years ago, I did not know of her existence."

Jean Valjean was a passerby. He had said so, himself. Well, he was passing on. Whatever he might be, his part was finished. From then on Marius was to perform the functions of Providence for Cosette. Cosette had come to find in the azure her mate, her lover, her husband, her celestial male. In taking flight, Cosette, winged and transfigured, left behind her on the ground, empty and hideous, her chrysalis, Jean Valjean.

Whatever the bent of Marius's evolving ideas, he always returned to a certain horror of Jean Valjean. A sacred horror, perhaps, for, as we have just indicated, he felt a *quid divinum* in this man. But, whatever he did, and whatever mitigation he sought, he always had to fall back on this: he was a convict; that is, the creature who has no place on the social ladder, being below the lowest rung. After the lowest of men comes the convict. The convict is no longer, so to speak, the fellow of the living. The law has deprived him of all the humanity it can take from a man. Although a democrat, Marius still adhered upon penal questions to the inexorable system, and in regard to those whom the law smites, he shared all the ideas of the law. He had not yet, let us say, adopted all the ideas of progress. He had not yet come to distinguish between what is written by man and what is written by God, between law and right. He had not examined and weighed the right that man assumes to dispose of the irrevocable and the irreparable. He had not revolted from the word *vengeance*. He thought it natural that certain infractions of the written law should be followed by eternal penalties, and he accepted social damnation as growing out of civilization. He was still at that point, though he was to advance infallibly with time, his nature being good, and basically composed entirely of latent progress.

Through the medium of these ideas, Jean Valjean appeared to him deformed and repulsive. He was the outcast. He was the convict. For him that word was like the sound of the last trumpet; and, after having lengthily considered Jean Valjean, his final action was to turn away his head. *Vade retro.*

We must remember and even emphasize that though he had questioned Jean Valjean to such an extent that Jean Valjean had said to him : "You are confessing me," Marius had not, however, asked him two or three decisive questions. Not that they had not occurred to him, but he was afraid of them. The Jondrette garret? The barricade? Javert? Who knows where the revelations would have stopped? Jean Valjean did not seem the man to shrink, and who knows whether Marius, after having urged him on, would not have desired to restrain him? At certain critical moments, have we not all, after asking a question, stopped our ears so as not to hear the response? We experience this cowardice particularly when we love. It is not wise to question untoward situations to the bitter end, particularly when the indissoluble portion of our own life is fatally interwoven with them. From Jean Valjean's despairing explanations, some appalling light might have sprung, and who knows if that hideous brilliance might have spread as far as Cosette? Who knows whether a sort of infernal glare would have touched the brow of this angel? The spatterings of a flash are still lightning. Fate has such solidarities, whereby innocence itself is impressed with crime by the somber law of tainting reflections. The purest faces may preserve forever the reverberations of a horrible surrounding. Wrongly or rightly Marius had been afraid. He knew too much already. He was trying to blind more than to enlighten himself. In desperation, he carried off Cosette in his arms, closing his eyes on Jean Valjean.

This man belonged to the night, to the living and terrible night. How could he dare to probe it to the bottom? It is appalling to question the shadow. Who knows what answer it will make? The dawn might be blackened by it forever.

In this frame of mind it was bitterly perplexing for Marius to reflect that this man would continue to have any contact whatsoever with Cosette. Now, he almost reproached himself for not having asked these fearful questions, which he had avoided, and from which an implacable and definitive decision might have sprung. He thought he had been too good, too mild, let us say the word, too weak. This weakness had led him to an unwise concession. He had allowed himself to be moved. He had done wrong. He should have simply cast off Jean Valjean. Jean Valjean was the Jonah, he should have done it, and relieved his house of the man. He was vexed with himself; he was vexed with the abruptness of the whirl of emotions that had deafened, blinded, and drawn him on. He was displeased with himself.

Now what should be done? Jean Valjean's visits were deeply repugnant to him. What good did it do to have the man in his house? What should he do? Here he tried to shake off his thoughts; he was unwilling to probe, unwilling to go deeper; he was unwilling to fathom himself. He had promised, he had allowed himself to be led into a promise; Jean Valjean had his promise; even to a convict, particularly to a convict, a man should keep his word. Still, his first duty was toward Cosette. In short, a repulsion that predominated over everything else possessed him.

Marius turned this collection of ideas over in his mind confusedly, passing from one to another, and stirred by all of them. Hence a deep commotion. It was not easy for him to hide this commotion from Cosette, but love is a talent, and Marius succeeded.

Beyond that, with no apparent aim, he put some questions to Cosette who, as candid as a dove is white, suspected nothing; he talked with her of her childhood and her youth, and he convinced himself more and more that every good quality, paternal and venerable, that a man can possess, this convict had shown to Cosette. All that Marius had dimly seen and conjectured was real. The darkly mysterious nettle had loved and protected this lily.

Book Eight

THE TWILIGHT WANE

I

THE BASEMENT ROOM

The next day, at nightfall, Jean Valjean knocked at the Gillenormand carriage gate. Basque let him in. Basque was in the courtyard very conveniently, and as if he had had orders. It sometimes happens that a servant is told: "Watch for Monsieur So-and-so, when he comes."

Without waiting for Jean Valjean to come up to him, Basque addressed him as follows:

"Monsieur the Baron told me to ask monsieur whether he would like to go up or stay downstairs?"

"Stay downstairs," answered Jean Valjean.

Basque, who was in fact absolutely respectful, opened the door of the ground floor room and said, "I will inform madame."

The room Jean Valjean entered was vaulted and damp, used as a storeroom when necessary, looking out on the street, paved with red tiles, and dimly lit by a window with iron bars.

The room was not among those harassed by the brush, the duster, and the broom. The dust in it was undisturbed. There the persecution of the spiders had not been organized. A fine web, broadly spread out, very black, adorned with dead flies, fanned out across one of the windowpanes. The room, small and low, was furnished with a pile of empty bottles heaped up in one corner. The wall had been painted with a wash of yellow ocher, which was scaling off in large flakes. At the end was a wooden mantel, painted black, with a narrow shelf. A fire was kindled, which indicated that somebody had anticipated Jean Valjean's answer: "Stay downstairs."

Two armchairs were placed beside the fireplace. Between the chairs was spread, in guise of a carpet, an old bedside rug, showing more warp than wool.

The room was lit by the fire in the fireplace and the twilight from the window.

Jean Valjean was tired. For some days he had neither eaten nor slept. He let himself fall into one of the armchairs.

Basque came back, set a lighted candle on the mantel, and withdrew. Jean Valjean, his head down and chin on his breast, noticed neither Basque nor the candle.

Suddenly he started up. Cosette was behind him.

He had not seen her come in, but he had felt that she was coming.

He turned. He gazed at her. She was adorably beautiful. But what he looked at with that deep look was not her beauty but her soul.

"Ah, well!" exclaimed Cosette. "Father, I knew you were odd, but I would never have thought of this. What an idea! Marius tells me that you want me to receive you here."

"Yes."

"I expected the answer. Well, I warn you that I'm going to make a scene. Let's begin at the beginning. Father, kiss me."

And she offered her cheek.

Jean Valjean stayed still.

"You are not stirring, so I see. But never mind, I forgive you. Jesus Christ said, 'Offer the other cheek.' Here it is."

And she offered the other cheek.

Jean Valjean did not move. It seemed as though his feet were nailed to the floor.

"This is getting serious," said Cosette. "What have I done to you? I declare I am confused. You owe me amends. You will dine with us."

"I have dined."

"That is not true. I will have Monsieur Gillenormand scold you. Grandfathers are made to scold fathers. Come. Go on up to the drawing room with me. Immediately."

"Impossible."

Here Cosette lost ground a little. She stopped ordering and went on to questions.

"But why not? And you choose the ugliest room in the house to see me in. It is horrible here."

"You know, Cos—" Jean Valjean corrected himself. "Madame, you know I am peculiar, I have my whims."

Cosette clapped her little hands together.

"Madame! There's something new! What does this mean?"

Jean Valjean turned on her that distressing smile to which he sometimes had recourse: "You have wanted to be madame. You are so."

"Not to you, Father."

"Don't call me Father anymore."

"Why not?"

"Call me Monsieur Jean. Jean, if you like."

"You are no longer Father? I am no longer Cosette? Monsieur Jean? What does this mean? But these are revolutions! So, what has happened? Just look me in the eye. And you don't want to live with us! And you don't want my room! What have I done to you? What have I done to you? Is there something the matter?"

"Nothing."

"Well then?"

"Everything is the same as usual."

"Why are you changing your name?"

"You have certainly changed yours."

He smiled again with that same smile and added, "Since you are Madame Pontmercy I can surely be Monsieur Jean."

"I don't understand a thing about it. It's all nonsense; I'll ask my husband's permission for you to be Monsieur Jean. I hope that he won't agree to it. You are hurting me. You may have your whims, but you must not grieve your little Cosette. It's wrong. You have no right to be naughty, you are too good."

He did not answer.

She seized both his hands hastily and, with an irresistible impulse, raising them toward her face, she pressed them against her neck under her chin, which is a deep token of affection.

"Oh!" said she to him, "be good!"

And she went on, "Here is what I call being good: being nice, coming to stay here, going out for our little walks again, there are birds here as well as in the Rue Plumet, living with us, leaving that hole in the Rue de l'Homme-Armé, not giving us riddles to guess, being like other people, dining with us, lunching with us, being my father."

He disengaged his hands.

"You don't need a father anymore, you have a husband."

Cosette could not contain herself.

"I don't need a father anymore! To things like that which don't make common sense, one really doesn't know what to say!"

"If Toussaint were here," replied Jean Valjean, like someone in search of authorities and catching at every straw, "she would be the first to acknowledge that it is true that I always had my peculiar ways. There is nothing new in that. I have always liked my dark corner."

"But it is cold here. We can't see clearly. It is horrid, too, to want to be Monsieur Jean. I don't want you to talk like that to me."

"Just now, on my way here," answered Jean Valjean, "I saw a piece of furniture in the Rue Saint-Louis. At a cabinetmaker's. If I were a pretty woman, I would make myself a present of that piece of furniture. A very fine dressing table, up-to-date, very fashionable. What you call rosewood, I think. It is inlaid. A pretty, large mirror. There are drawers in it. It is handsome."

"Oh! The ugly bear!" replied Cosette.

And with a bewitching sauciness, pressing her teeth together and separating her lips, she blew at Jean Valjean. It was a Grace copying a kitten.

"I am furious," she said. "Since yesterday, you all make me rage. Everybody spites me. I don't understand. You don't defend me against Marius. Marius doesn't uphold me against you, I am all alone. I arrange a room nicely. If I could have put the good Lord into it, I would have done so. You leave me with my room on my hands. My tenant bankrupts me. I order Nicolette to have a nice little dinner. Nobody wants your dinner, madame. And my father Fauchelevent, wants me to called him Monsieur Jean, and to receive him in a hideous, old, ugly, moldy cellar, where the walls have a beard, and where there are empty bottles for vases, and spiders' webs for curtains. You are odd, I admit, that is your way, but a truce is granted to people who get married. You should not have gone back to being odd right away. So you are going to be really satisfied with your awful Rue de l'Homme-Armé. I was very forlorn there, myself! What do you have against me? You give me a great deal of trouble!"

And, growing suddenly serious, she looked fixedly at Jean Valjean, and added, "So you don't like it that I am happy?"

Unconsciously, artlessness sometimes penetrates very deep. This question, simple to Cosette, was profound to Jean Valjean. Cosette wished to scratch; she tore.

Jean Valjean grew pale. For a moment he did not answer, then, with an indescribable accent and talking to himself, he murmured, "Her happiness was the aim of my life. Now, God may beckon me away. Cosette, you are happy; my time is done."

"Ah, you have called me Cosette!" she exclaimed.

And she threw her arms around his neck.

Jean Valjean, in desperation, clasped her to his breast wildly. It seemed to him almost as if he were taking her back.

"Thank you, Father!" said Cosette to him.

The transport was becoming poignant to Jean Valjean. He gently put away Cosette's arms, and took his hat.

"Well?" said Cosette.

Jean Valjean answered, "I will leave you, madame; they are waiting for you."

And, from the door, he added, "I called you Cosette. Tell your husband that it will not happen again. Pardon me."

Jean Valjean went out, leaving Cosette astounded at that enigmatic farewell.

II

OTHER BACKWARD STEPS

The following day, at the same hour, Jean Valjean came.

Cosette did not ask him any questions, was no longer astonished, no longer complained that she was cold, no longer talked of the drawing room, she avoided saying either Father or Monsieur Jean. She let him speak as he liked. She allowed herself to be called madame. Only she showed slightly less joy. She would have been sad, if sadness had been possible for her.

Probably she had had one of those conversations with Marius, in which the beloved man says what he pleases, explains nothing, and satisfies the beloved woman. The curiosity of lovers does not go very far beyond their love.

The ground-floor room had dressed up a little. Basque had eliminated the bottles, and Nicolette the spiders.

Every succeeding evening brought Jean Valjean at the same time. He came every day, not having the strength to take Marius's words otherwise than to the letter. Marius managed to be out when Jean Valjean came. The house became accustomed to M. Fauchelevent's new way of life. Toussaint explained: "Monsieur was always like that," she would repeat. The grandfather decreed: "He is an original!" and everything was said. Besides, past ninety, no further tie is possible; everything is juxtaposition; a newcomer is an annoyance. There is no more room; all the habits are formed. M. Fauchelevent, M. Tranchelevent, Grandfather Gillenormand asked nothing better than to be relieved of "that gentleman." He added, "Nothing is more common than these originals. They do all sorts of odd things. No motive. The Marquis de Canaples was worse. He bought a palace to live in the attic. There are fantastic airs some people put on."

Nobody caught a glimpse of the gloomy underside. Who could have guessed such a thing, actually? There are marshes like that in India; the water seems strange, inexplicable, quivering when there is no wind; agitated where it should be calm. You see on the surface this boiling without cause; you do not notice the Hydra crawling at the bottom.

Many men have a secret monster this way, a disease that they feed, a dragon that gnaws them, a despair that inhabits their night. Such a man seems like others, quite normal. Nobody knows that he has within him a fearful parasitic pain, with a thousand teeth, which lives in the miserable man, who is dying of it. Nobody knows that this man is a gulf. It is stagnant, but deep. From time to time a turmoil, of which we understand nothing, shows up on its surface. A mysterious wrinkle comes along, then vanishes, then reappears; an air bubble rises and bursts. It is a little thing, it is terrible. It is the breathing of the unknown monster.

Certain strange habits—to come at the time when others are gone, shrink away while others make a display, wear on all occasions what might be called the wall-colored mantle, seek the solitary path, prefer the deserted street, not mingle in conversations, avoid gatherings and festivals, seem well provided yet live poorly, have, though rich, one's key in pocket and candle with the doorkeeper, come in by the side door, go up the backstairs—all these insignificant peculiarities, wrinkles, air bubbles, fleeting folds on the surface, often come from an awesome core.

Several weeks went by this way. A new life gradually took possession of Cosette; the relationships marriage creates, the visits, the care of the house, the pleasures, those grand affairs. Cosette's pleasures were not costly; they consisted of a single one: being with Marius. Going out with him, staying at home with him, this was the great occupation of her life. It was a joy still new to them, to go out arm in arm, in full sunlight, in the open street, without hiding, in plain sight, all alone with each other. Cosette had one vexation. Toussaint could not agree with Nicolette, the welding of two old maids being impossible, and went away. The grandfather was in good health; Marius argued a few cases now and then; Aunt Gillenormand calmly led that peripheral life beside the new household, which was enough for her. Jean Valjean came every day.

The disappearance of familiarity, the madame, the Monsieur Jean, all this made him different to Cosette. The care he had taken to detach her from him was working. She became more and more cheerful, and less and less affectionate. Yet she still loved him very much, and he felt it. One day she suddenly said to him, "You were my father, you are no longer my father, you were my uncle, you are no longer my uncle, you were Monsieur Fauchelevent, you are Jean. So who are you? I don't like all that. If I didn't know you were so good, I would be afraid of you."

He still lived in the Rue de l'Homme-Armé, unable to make up his mind to move farther from the quarter where Cosette lived.

At first he would stay with Cosette only a few minutes, then go away.

Little by little he got into the habit of making his visits longer. It was as though he took advantage of the example of the days, which were growing longer: He came earlier and went away later.

One day Cosette inadvertently said to him, "Father." A flash of joy illuminated Jean Valjean's gloomy old face. He corrected her, "Say Jean." "Ah! True," she answered with a burst of laughter, "Monsieur Jean." "That's right," he said, and he turned away so that she would not see him wipe his eyes.

III

THEY REMEMBER THE GARDEN IN THE RUE PLUMET

That was the last time. From that last gleam on, there was complete extinction. No more familiarity, no more good evening with a kiss, never again that word so intensely sweet, "Father!" At his own demand and through his own complicity, he was driven from every happiness in succession; and he endured this misery, that after having wholly lost Cosette in one day, he subsequently had to lose her again little by little.

At last the eye grows accustomed to the light of a cellar. In short, to have a vision of Cosette every day sufficed him. His whole life was concentrated in that hour.

He sat by her side, he looked at her in silence, or rather he talked to her of the years long gone, of her childhood, of the convent, of her friends of those days.

One afternoon—it was one of the early days of April, already warm, still fresh, the season of great cheerfulness in the sunshine, the gardens that lay below Marius's and Cosette's windows were feeling the emotion of awakening, the hawthorn was beginning to peep, a jeweled array of carnations spread out across the old walls, the rosy snapdragons gaped in the cracks between the stones, there was a charming beginning of daisies and buttercups in the grass, the white butterflies of the year made their debut, the wind, that minstrel of the eternal wedding, tried out in the trees the first notes of that grand auroral symphony which the old poets called the renascence—Marius said to Cosette, "We have said that we would go to see our garden in the Rue Plumet again. Let's go. We mustn't be ungrateful." And they flew away like two swallows toward the spring. That garden in the Rue Plumet seemed like the dawn to them. Behind them they already had something like the springtime of their love. The house in the Rue Plumet, held on a lease, still belonged to Cosette. They went to this garden and this house. There they found themselves again; they forgot themselves. That evening, at the usual hour, Jean Valjean came to the Rue-des-Filles-du-Calvaire. "Madame has gone out with monsieur, and has not yet returned," Basque said to him. He sat down in silence, and waited an hour. Cosette did not return. He bowed his head and went away.

Cosette was so intoxicated with her walk to "the garden," and so happy over having "lived a whole day in her past," that she did not speak of anything else the next day. It did not occur to her that she had not seen Jean Valjean.

"How did you get there?" Jean Valjean asked her.

"We walked."

"And how did you return?"

"In a fiacre."

For some time Jean Valjean had noticed the frugal life the young couple led. It annoyed him. Marius's economy was severe, and Jean Valjean took the word in its absolute sense. He ventured a question: "Why don't you have a carriage of your own? A pretty brougham would cost you only five hundred francs a month. You're rich."

"I don't know," answered Cosette.

"It was the same with Toussaint," continued Jean Valjean. "She has gone, and you have not replaced her. Why not?"

"Nicolette is enough."

"But you must have a lady's maid."

"Don't I have Marius?"

"You ought to have a house of your own, servants of your own, a carriage, a box at the theater. There is nothing too good for you. Why not take advantage of being rich? Riches add to happiness."

Cosette did not answer.

Jean Valjean's visits did not grow shorter. Far from it. When the heart is slipping we do not halt on the descent.

When Jean Valjean wanted to prolong his visit, and to make the hours pass unnoticed, he would eulogize Marius; he found him beautiful, noble, courageous, intellectual, eloquent, good. Cosette outdid him. Jean Valjean began again. They were never silent. Marius, this word was inexhaustible; there were volumes in the six letters. In this way Jean Valjean managed to stay a long time. To see Cosette, to forget at her side, was so sweet to him. It was the stanching of his wound. Several times Basque had to come down twice to say, "Monsieur Gillenormand sends me to remind Madame the Baronne that dinner is served."

On those days, Jean Valjean returned home very pensive.

Was there, then, some truth in that comparison of the chrysalis which had occurred to Marius? Was Jean Valjean indeed an obstinate chrysalis, who came to visit his butterfly?

One day he stayed longer than usual. The next day, he noticed that there was no fire in the fireplace. "Well, well," he thought. "No fire." And he explained it to himself: "It is quite simple. Here we are in April. The cold weather is over."

"Goodness! How cold it is here!" exclaimed Cosette as she came in.

"Why, no," said Jean Valjean.

"So it is you who told Basque not to make a fire?"

"Yes. We are almost to May."

"But we have a fire until the month of June. In this cellar, it is needed the year around."

"I thought the fire was unnecessary."

"That is just one of your ideas!" replied Cosette.

The next day there was a fire. But the two armchairs were placed at the other end of the room, near the door. "What does that mean?" thought Jean Valjean.

He went to pick up the armchairs and put them back in their usual place near the fireplace.

The rekindled fire encouraged him, however. He continued the conversation still longer than usual. As he was getting up to go away, Cosette said to him, "My husband said a funny thing yesterday."

"What was it?"

"He said, 'Cosette, we have an income of thirty thousand francs. Twenty-seven that you have, three that my grandfather gives me.' I answered, 'That makes thirty.' 'Would you have the courage to live on three thousand?' I answered, 'Yes, on nothing. Provided it is with you.' And then I asked, 'Why do you say this?' He answered, 'Just to know.' "

Jean Valjean did not say a word. Cosette probably expected some explanation from him; he listened to her in mournful silence. He went back to the Rue de l'Homme-Armé; he was so deeply absorbed that he mistook the door, and instead of his own house, he went into the next one. Not until he had gone up almost two flights did he notice his mistake, and go down again.

His mind was racked with conjectures. It was obvious that Marius had doubts regarding the origin of the six hundred thousand francs, that he feared some impure source, who knows? That he had perhaps discovered that this money came from him, Jean Valjean, that he hesitated in the face of this suspicious fortune, and disliked to take it as his own, preferring to remain poor, he and Cosette, than to be rich with a doubtful wealth.

Beyond that, Jean Valjean was vaguely beginning to feel that he was being shown the door.

The next day, on entering the ground-floor room, he had something of a shock. The armchairs had disappeared. There was not even a chair of any kind.

"Ah now," exclaimed Cosette as she came in, "no chairs! So where are the armchairs?"

"They are gone," answered Jean Valjean.

"That's a pretty business!"

Jean Valjean stammered, "I told Basque to take them away."

"And what for?"

"I'll only stay a few minutes today."

"Staying a little while is no reason for standing up while you do stay."

"I believe that Basque needed some armchairs for the salon."

"What for?"

"You undoubtedly have company this evening."

"Nobody is coming."

Jean Valjean could not say another word.

Cosette shrugged. "To have the chairs taken away! The other day you had the fire put out. How strange you are!"

"Good-bye," murmured Jean Valjean.

He did not say, "Good-bye, Cosette." But he lacked the strength to say, "Good-bye, madame."

He went away overwhelmed.

This time he had understood.

The next day he did not come. Cosette did not notice it until late that night.

"Why," she said, "Monsieur Jean has not come today."

She felt something of a slight pang, but she hardly noticed it, immediately diverted as she was by a kiss from Marius.

The next day he did not come.

Cosette paid no attention to it, spent the evening and slept as usual, and thought of it only on awaking. She was so happy! She sent Nicolette very quickly to Monsieur Jean's to know if he were sick, and why he had not come the day before. Nicolette brought back Monsieur Jean's answer. He was not sick. He was busy. He would come very soon. As soon as he could. However, he was going on a short trip. Madame must remember that he was in the habit of taking trips from time to time. There should be no anxiety. Let them not be troubled about him.

On entering Monsieur Jean's house, Nicolette had repeated to him the very words of her mistress. That madame sent to know "why Monsieur Jean had not come the day before." "It is two days since I have been there," said Jean Valjean mildly.

But the remark escaped the notice of Nicolette, who reported nothing of it to Cosette.

IV

ATTRACTION AND EXTINCTION

During the last months of the spring and the first months of the summer of 1833, the scattered wayfarers in the Marais, the storekeepers, the idlers on the doorsteps, noticed an old man neatly dressed in black, every day, about the same time, at nightfall, come out of the Rue de l'Homme-Armé, in the direction of the Rue Sainte-Croix-de-la-Bretonnerie, pass by the Blancs-Manteaux, to the Rue Culture-Sainte-Catherine, and, reaching the Rue de l'Echarpe, turn to the left, and enter the Rue Saint-Louis.

There he walked slowly, his head bent forward, seeing nothing, hearing nothing, his eye immovably fixed on one point, always the same, which seemed studded with stars to him, and which was nothing more nor less than the corner of the Rue des Filles-du-Calvaire. As he approached the corner of that street, his face lit up; a kind of joy illuminated his eye like an inner aura, he had a fascinated and softened expression, his lips moved vaguely, as if he were speaking to someone whom he did not see, he smiled faintly, and he moved as slowly as he could. You would have said that even while wanting to reach some destination, he dreaded the moment when he would be near it. When there were just a few houses left between him and the street that appeared to attract him, his pace became so slow that at times you might have supposed he had stopped moving. The vacillation of his head and the fixedness of his eye reminded you of the compass needle seeking the pole. However long he managed to defer it, he had to arrive at last; he reached the Rue des Filles-du-Calvaire; then he stopped, he trembled, he poked his head with a kind of gloomy timidity beyond the corner of the last house, and he looked into that street, and in that tragic look there was something like the bewilderment of the impossible, and the reflection of a forbidden paradise. Then a tear, which had gradually gathered in the corner of his eye, grown large enough to fall, slid down his cheek, and sometimes stopped at his mouth. The old man tasted its bitterness. He stayed like that a few minutes, as if he were made of stone; then he returned by the same route and at the same pace; and, with the widening distance, that look gradually faded.

Little by little, the old man stopped going as far as the corner of the Rue des Filles-du-Calvaire; he would stop halfway down the Rue Saint-Louis; sometimes a little farther, sometimes a little nearer. One day, he stopped at the corner of the Rue Culture-Sainte-Catherine, and looked at the Rue des Filles-du-Calvaire from the distance. Then he silently moved his head from right to left as if he were refusing himself something, and retraced his steps.

Very soon he no longer went even as far as the Rue Saint-Louis. He reached the Rue Pavée, shook his head, and went back; then he no longer went beyond the Rue des Trois Pavillons; then he no longer passed the Blancs-Manteaux. It was like a pendulum that has not been wound up, and whose oscillations are growing shorter before they stop.

Every day, he left his house at the same time, began the same walk, did not finish it, and, perhaps unconsciously, he continually shortened it. His whole countenance expressed this single idea: What is the use? His eye was dull; the radiance gone. The tears had also stopped flowing; they no longer gathered at the corner of the lids; that thoughtful eye was dry. The old man's head was still bent forward; his chin quivered at times; the wrinkles of his thin neck were painful to see. Sometimes, when the weather was bad, he carried an umbrella under his arm, which he never opened. The good women of the quarter said, "He is an innocent." The children followed him laughing.

Book Nine

SUPREME SHADOW, SUPREME DAWN

I

PITY FOR THE UNHAPPY, BUT INDULGENCE FOR THE HAPPY

It is a terrible thing to be happy! How pleased we are with it! How all-sufficient we think it! Being in possession of the false aim of life, happiness, how we forget the true aim, duty!

We must say, however, that it would be unjust to blame Marius.

As we have explained, before his marriage, Marius had not asked M. Fauchelevent any questions, and, since then, he had been afraid to put any to Jean Valjean. He had regretted the promise he had reluctantly given. He had reiterated to himself many times that he had done wrong in making that concession to despair. He did nothing more than gradually banishing Jean Valjean from his house, and obliterating him as much as possible from Cosette's mind. He had in a sense constantly placed himself between Cosette and Jean Valjean, sure that in that way she would not notice him, and would never think of him. It was more than obliteration, it was eclipse.

Marius did what he deemed necessary and just. He supposed that, for keeping Jean Valjean away, without harshness, but without weakness, he had serious reasons which we have already seen, and still others, which we shall see further on. Having chanced to meet, in a case he had taken, a former clerk of the house of Laffitte, he had obtained, without seeking it, some mysterious information which he could not, actually, probe to the bottom, out of respect for the secret he had promised to keep, and out of consideration for Jean Valjean's perilous situation. At that very time, he believed that he had a solemn duty to perform, the restitution of the six hundred thousand francs to somebody whom he was seeking as cautiously as possible. In the meantime, he abstained from using that money.

As for Cosette, she was in on none of these secrets; but it would be hard to condemn her, too.

There was an all-powerful magnetism flowing from Marius to her, which made her do, instinctively and almost automatically, whatever Marius wished. In regard to "Monsieur Jean," she felt a strong wish from Marius; she conformed to it. Her husband had had nothing to say to her; she felt the vague but clear pressure of his unspoken wishes, and obeyed blindly. Her obedience in this consisted in not remembering what Marius forgot. That took no effort for her. Without knowing why herself, and without affording any grounds for censure, her soul had so thoroughly become her husband's soul that whatever was covered with shadow in Marius's thoughts was obscured in hers.

We must not go too far, however; in things to do with Jean Valjean, this forgetfulness and obliteration were only superficial. She was thoughtless rather than forgetful. At heart, she really loved the one whom she had so long called father. But she loved her husband still more. It was this that had somewhat swayed the balance of this heart, inclined in a single direction.

It sometimes happened that Cosette spoke of Jean Valjean, and wondered. Then Marius would calm her: "He is away, I think. Didn't he say that he was going off on a trip?" "That is true," thought Cosette. "He was in the habit of disappearing this way. But not for so long." Two or three times she sent Nicolette to ask at the Rue de L'Homme-Armé if Monsieur Jean had returned from his journey. Jean Valjean had the answer sent back that he had not.

Cosette did not inquire further, having but one need on earth, Marius.

We must also say that they, too, Marius and Cosette,

had been away. They had been to Vernon. Marius had taken Cosette to his father's grave.

Marius had little by little drawn Cosette away from Jean Valjean. Cosette was passive.

Moreover, what is called much too harshly, in some cases, the ingratitude of children, is not always as reproachable as is supposed. It is the ingratitude of nature. Nature, as we have said elsewhere, "looks forward." Nature divides living beings into the coming and the going. Those going are turned toward the shadow, those coming toward the light. Hence a separation, which on the side of the old, is a fatality, and, on the side of the young, involuntary. This separation, at first imperceptible, gradually increases, like every separation of branches. The limbs, without parting from the trunk, recede from it. It is not their fault. Youth goes where joy is, to festivals, to brilliant lights, to loves. Old age goes to its end. They do not lose sight of each other, but the ties are loosened. The affection of the young is chilled by life; that of the old by the grave. We must not blame these poor children.

II

THE LAST FLICKERINGS OF THE EXHAUSTED LAMP

One day Jean Valjean went downstairs, took three steps into the street, sat down on a stone block, on that same block where Gavroche, on the night of the 5th of June, had found him musing; he remained there a few minutes, then went upstairs again. This was the last swing of the pendulum. The next day, he did not leave his room. The day after that, he did not leave his bed.

His concierge, who prepared his frugal meal—some cabbage, a few potatoes with a little pork—looked into the brown earthen plate, and exclaimed, "Why, you didn't eat a thing yesterday, poor dear man!"

"Yes, I did," answered Jean Valjean.

"The plate is still full."

"Look at the water pitcher. That is empty."

"That shows that you have drunk; it don't show that you have eaten."

"Well," said Jean Valjean, "suppose I have only been hungry for water?"

"That is called thirst, and, when people don't eat at the same time, it is called fever."

"I will eat tomorrow."

"Or at Christmas. Why not today? Do people say: I'll eat tomorrow! To leave me my whole plateful without touching it! My new potatoes, which were so good!"

Jean Valjean took the old woman's hand, "I promise to eat it," he said to her in his benevolent voice.

"I am not pleased with you," answered the concierge.

Jean Valjean scarcely ever saw any other human being than this good woman. There are streets in Paris in which nobody walks, and houses into which nobody comes. He was in one of those streets, and in one of those houses.

While he still went out, he had bought from a brazier for a few sous a little copper crucifix, which he had hung on a nail opposite his bed. The cross is always good to look at.

A week elapsed, and Jean Valjean had not taken a step in his room. He was still in bed. The concierge said to her husband, "The good man upstairs does not get up anymore, he does not eat anymore, he won't last long. He has trouble, he has. Nobody can get it out of my head that his daughter has made a bad match."

The porter replied, with the accent of the marital sovereignty, "If he is rich, let him have a doctor. If he is not rich, let him not have any. If he doesn't have a doctor, he will die."

"And if he does have one?"

"He will die," said the porter.

With an old knife the concierge began to dig up some grass that was sprouting in what she called her pavement, and, while she was pulling up the grass, she muttered, "It's a pity. An old man who's so nice! He's white as a sheet."

She saw a doctor from the quarter going by at the end of the street; she took it upon herself to beg him to go up.

"It is on the third floor," said she to him. "You can simply walk in. As the good man does not stir from his bed now, the key is in the door all the time."

The physician saw Jean Valjean and spoke with him.

When he came down, the old woman questioned him: "Well, doctor?"

"Your old man is very sick."

"What is the matter with him?"

"Everything and nothing. He is a man who, to all appearances, has lost some dear friend. People die of that."

"What did he tell you?"

"He told me that he was well."

"Will you come again, doctor?"

"Yes," answered the physician. "But another than I should come again."

III

A PEN IS HEAVY TO HIM WHO LIFTED FAUCHELEVENT'S CART

One evening Jean Valjean had difficulty in rising up on his elbow; he felt his wrist and found no pulse; his breathing was shallow and stopped at intervals; he realized that he was weaker than he had been before. Then, undoubtedly under the pressure of some supreme desire, he made an effort, sat up in bed, and got dressed. He put on his old workingman's garb. As he no longer went out, he had returned to it, and he preferred it. He had to stop several times while dressing; the mere effort of putting on his jacket made the sweat roll down his forehead.

Since he had been alone, he had made his bed in the living room, so as to occupy this desolate apartment as little as possible.

He opened the valise and took out Cosette's clothing.

He spread it out on his bed.

The bishop's candlesticks were in their place, on the mantel. He took two wax tapers from a drawer and put them into the candlesticks. Then, although it was still broad daylight, it was in summer, he lit them. You sometimes see candles lit this way in broad daylight, in rooms where the dead are lying.

Each step he took in going from one piece of furniture to another exhausted him, and he had to sit down. It was not ordinary fatigue that spends the strength in order to be renewed; it was the remnant of possible motion; it was exhausted life pressed out drop by drop through overwhelming efforts, never to be repeated.

One of the chairs onto which he sank was standing before that mirror, so fatal for him, so providential for Marius, in which he had read Cosette's note, reversed on the blotter. He saw himself in this mirror, and did not recognize himself. He was eighty years old; before Marius's marriage, one would hardly have thought him fifty; this year had counted for thirty. What now marked his forehead were not the wrinkles of age but the mysterious mark of death. You sensed on it the imprint of the relentless talon. His cheeks were sunken; the skin of his face was of the color that suggests the idea of earth already above it; the corners of his mouth were depressed as in that mask the ancients sculpted on tombs, he was staring into space with a look of reproach; he looked like one of those great tragic beings who rise in judgment.

He was in that state, the last phase of dejection, when sorrow no longer flows; it is as if coagulated, the soul covered with a clot of despair.

Night had fallen. He laboriously drew a table and an old armchair near the fireplace, and put on the table pen, ink, and paper.

Then he fainted. When he regained consciousness he was thirsty. Unable to lift the water pitcher, with great effort he tipped it toward his mouth, and drank a swallow.

Then he turned to the bed, and, still sitting, for he could only stand for a moment, he looked at the little black dress, and all the beloved objects.

Such contemplations last for hours, which seem minutes. Suddenly he shivered, he felt that the chill was coming; he leaned upon the table that was lit by the bishop's candlesticks and picked up the pen.

As neither pen nor ink had been used for a long time, the tip of the pen was bent back, the ink was dried, he was obliged to get up and put a few drops of water into the ink, which he could not do without stopping and sitting down two or three times, and he was compelled to write with the back of the pen. From time to time he wiped his forehead.

His hand trembled. He slowly wrote the few lines, which follow:

"Cosette, I bless you. I am going to explain something to you. Your husband was quite right in giving me to understand that I ought to leave; while there is some mistake in what he believed, he was right. He is very good. Always love him dearly when I am dead. Monsieur Pontmercy, always love my darling child. Cosette, this paper will be found, this is what I want to tell you, you will see the figures, if I have the strength to recall them, listen carefully, the money is really your own. Here is the whole story: White jet comes from Norway, black jet comes from England, the black glass imitation comes from Germany. Jet is lighter, more precious, more costly. We can make imitations in France as well as in Germany. It requires a little anvil two inches square, and a spirit lamp to soften the wax. The wax was formerly made with resin and lamp-black, and cost four francs a pound. I thought of making it with shellac and turpentine. This costs only thirty sous, and it is much better. The buckles are made of violet glass, which is fastened by means of this wax to a light frame of black iron. The glass should be violet for iron trinkets, and black for the gold trinkets. Spain purchases many of them. That is the country for jet—"

Here he stopped, the pen fell from his fingers, he gave way to one of those despairing sobs that rose at times from the depths of his being, the poor man clasped his head with both hands, and reflected.

"Oh!" he cried inwardly (pitiful cries, heard by God alone), "it is all over. I will never see her again. She is a smile that has passed over me. I am going to enter the night without even seeing her again. Oh! A minute, an instant, to hear her voice, to touch her dress, to look at her, the angel! And then to die! It is nothing to die, but it is dreadful to die without seeing her. She would smile at me, she would say a word to me. Would that harm anybody? No, it is over, forever. Here I am, all alone. My God! My God! I shall never see her again."

At that moment there was a knock at his door.

IV

A BOTTLE OF INK THAT SERVES ONLY TO WHITEN

That very day, or rather that very evening, just as Marius had left the table and withdrawn to his office, with a folder of papers to review, Basque had handed him a letter, saying, "The person who wrote the letter is in the anteroom."

Cosette had taken the grandfather's arm and was walking in the garden.

A letter, as well as a man, may have a forbidding appearance. Coarse paper, clumsy fold, the mere sight of certain missives displeases. The letter that Basque brought was of that variety.

Marius took it. It smelled of tobacco. Nothing awakens a reminiscence like an odor. Marius recognized the tobacco. He looked at the address: *To Monsieur, Monsieur the Baron Pommerci. In his hôtel*. The recognition of the tobacco made him recognize the handwriting. One could say that insights come in flashes. Marius was as though illuminated by one of those flashes.

The scent, the mysterious memorandum, revived a whole world within him. Here certainly was the very paper, the way of folding, the paleness of the ink, it was certainly the well-known handwriting; above all, here was the tobacco. The Jondrette garret rose before him.

So, by a strange freak of chance, one of the two trails he had so long sought, the one he had again recently made so many efforts to trace, and believed forever lost, was turning up on its own.

He eagerly broke the seal and read:

"Monsieur Baron,—If the Supreme Being had given me the talents for it, I could have been Baron Thénard, member of the Institute (Academy of Ciences), but I am not so. I merely bear the same name that he does, happy if this remembrance commends me to the excellence of your bounties. The benefit with which you honor me will be reciprocal. I am in possession of a secret conserning an individual. This individual conserns you. I hold the secret at your disposition, desiring to have the honor of being yuseful to you. I will give you the simple means of drivving from your honorable family this individual who has no right in it, Madame the Baronne being of high birth. The sanctuary of virtue could not coabit longer with crime without abdicating.

"I await in the entichamber the orders of Monsieur the Baron.—With respect."

The letter was signed "THÉNARD."

This signature was not false. It was simply a bit abridged.

Besides, the rigmarole and the spelling confirmed it. The certificate of origin was perfect. There was no possible doubt.

Marius felt deeply moved. After the feeling of surprise, he had a feeling of happiness. Let him now find the other man whom he sought, the man who had saved him, and he would have nothing more to wish.

He opened one of his desk drawers, took out some banknotes, put them in his pockets, closed the desk, and rang. Basque appeared.

"Show him in," said Marius.

Basque announced, "Monsieur Thénard."

A man entered.

A new surprise for Marius. The man who came in was completely unknown to him.

This man, old actually, had a large nose, his chin tucked into his tie, green spectacles with a double shade of green silk over his eyes, his hair smooth and slicked down to the eyebrows, like the wigs of English coachmen in high society. His hair was gray. He was dressed in black from head to foot, in a well-worn but tidy black; a bunch of trinkets, hanging from his watch fob, suggested a watch. He held an old hat in his hand. He walked with a stoop, and the crook of his back increased the lowliness of his bow.

What was striking at first was that this person's coat, too full, although carefully buttoned, did not seem to have been made for him. Here a short digression is necessary.

There was in Paris, at that period, in an old hovel, in the Rue Beautreillis, near the Arsenal, an ingenious Jew, whose business it was to change a rascal into an honest man. Not for too long, which could be uncomfortable for the rascal. The change was made instantly, for a day or two, at the rate of thirty sous a day, by means of clothes resembling as closely as possible, that of honest people generally. This costume renter was called "the Changer"; Parisian thieves had given him this name, and knew him by no other. He had a tolerably complete wardrobe. The rags with which he decked his people out were almost respectable. He had specialties and categories; every hook in his shop held a social condition, worn and rumpled, here the magistrate's clothing, there the curé's, there the banker's, in one corner the retired soldier, in another the literary man, farther on the statesman. This man was the costumer of the immense drama skulduggery plays in Paris. His hut was the green room from which robbery issued and swindling returned. A sly customer would come to this wardrobe in rags, lay down thirty sous, and choose, according to the part he wanted to play that day, the clothing that suited him, and when he returned to the streets, the customer was somebody. The next day the clothes were faithfully brought back, and the Changer, who trusted everything to the robbers, was never robbed. These outfits had one inconvenience, they "were not a good fit"; not having been made for those who wore them, they were tight for this man, baggy for that one, and fitted nobody. Every thief beyond the human average at either extreme of size was uncomfortable in the Changer's costumes. He had to be neither too fat nor too lean. The Changer had provided only for the average man. He had taken the measure of the species in the person of the first chance vagabond, who was neither fat nor thin, neither tall nor short, resulting in adaptations, sometimes difficult, whereby the Changer's customers got along as best they could. So much the worse for the exceptions! The stateman's clothing, for instance, black from tip to toe, and consequently suitable, would have been too large for Pitt and too small for Castelcicala. The statesman's suit was described as follows in the Changer's catalogue; we copy: "A black cloth coat, trousers of black double-milled cassimere, a silk waistcoat, boots, and linen." In the margin was written, "Former ambassador," and a note that we also transcribe. "In a separate box, a wig neatly curled, green spectacles, trinkets, and two little quill tubes an inch in length wrapped in cotton." This all went with the statesman, former ambassador. This entire costume was, if we may use the expression, dead tired; the seams were turning white, a vague buttonhole was appearing at one of the elbows; in addition, a button was missing on the breast of the coat; but this was a slight matter; as the stateman's hand should always be inside the coat and over the heart, its function was to conceal the absent button.

If Marius had been familiar with the occult institutions of Paris, he would have recognized immediately, on the back of the visitor whom Basque had just introduced, the statesman's coat borrowed from the Changer's boutique.

Marius's disappointment, on seeing another man enter than the one he was expecting, turned into dislike toward the newcomer. He studied him from head to foot, while the character bowed exaggeratedly, and asked him sharply, "What do you want?"

The man answered with an amiable grin not unlike the smile of a crocodile: "It seems to me impossible that I have not already had the honor of seeing Monsieur the Baron in society. I really think that I met him privately some years ago, at Madame the Princess Bagration's and in the salons of his lordship le Vicomte Dambray, peer of France."

It is always a good tactic in confidence work to pretend to recognize someone you do not know.

Marius listened attentively to the voice of this man. He watched for the tone and gesture eagerly, but his disappointment increased; it was a whining pronunciation, entirely different from the sharp, dry voice he remembered. He was completely bewildered.

"I don't know," he said, "either Madame Bagration or Monsieur Dambray. I have never in my life set foot in the house of either one."

The answer was testy. The person, gracious notwithstanding, persisted, "Then it must be at Chateaubriand's that I have seen monsieur? I know Chateaubriand well. He is very affable. He says to me sometimes: 'Thénard, my friend, won't you have a glass of wine with me?' "

Marius's brow grew more and more severe: "I have never had the honor of being received at Monsieur de Chateaubriand's. Come to the point. What is it you want?"

In view of the harsher voice, the man made a lower bow.

"Monsieur Baron, deign to listen to me. In America, in a region which is near Panama, there is a village called La Joya. This village consists of a single house. A large, square, three-story adobe house, five hundred feet long on each side, each story set back twelve feet from the story below, so as to leave in front a terrace that runs around the building, in the center an interior court in which are provisions and ammunition, no windows, loop-holes, no door, ladders, ladders to climb from the ground to the first terrace, and from the first to the second, and from the second to the third, ladders to go down into the interior court, no doors to the rooms, hatchways, no stairs to the rooms, ladders; at night the hatchways are closed, the ladders drawn up, swivels and carbines are aimed through the portholes; no means of entering; a house by day, a citadel by night, eight hundred inhabitants, such is this village. Why so much precaution? Because the country is dangerous; it is full of cannibals. Then why do people go there? Because it is a wonderful country; gold is found there."

"What are you coming to?" Marius interrupted, who was going from disappointment to impatience.

"To this, Monsieur Baron. I am a weary old diplomat. The old civilization has used me up. I want to try the savages."

"What then?"

"Monsieur Baron, selfishness is the law of the world. The proletarian countrywoman who works by the day turns around when the stagecoach passes, the proprietary countrywoman who works in her own field does not turn around. The poor man's dog barks at the rich man, the rich man's dog barks at the poor man. Every one for himself. Interest is the motive of men. Gold is the lodestone."

"What then? Come to the point."

"I would like to go and establish myself in La Joya. There are three of us. I have my spouse and my daughter, a young lady who is very beautiful. The voyage is long and expensive. I must have a little money."

"How does that concern me?" inquired Marius.

The stranger craned his neck out of his tie, a movement

characteristic of the vulture, and replied, with increased smiles, "Then Monsieur the baron has not read my letter?"

That was not far from true. The fact is, that the contents of the epistle had glanced off Marius. He had seen the handwriting rather than read the letter. He scarcely remembered it. Within a moment a new clue had been given him. He had noticed this remark: My spouse and my young lady. He stared searchingly at the stranger. An examining judge could not have done better. He seemed to be lying in ambush for him. He merely answered, "Explain."

The stranger thrust his hands into his waistcoat pockets, raised his head without straightening his backbone, but scrutinizing Marius in turn with the green gaze of his spectacles.

"Certainly, Monsieur Baron. I will explain. I have a secret to sell you."

"A secret?"

"A secret."

"That concerns me?"

"Somewhat."

"What is the secret?"

Marius examined the man more and more closely, while listening to him.

"I commence gratis," said the stranger. "You will see that I am interesting."

"Go on."

"Monsieur Baron, you have in your house a robber and an assassin."

Marius shuddered.

"In my own house? No," he said.

Imperturbable, the stranger brushed his hat with his sleeve, and continued, "Assassin and robber. Please note, Monsieur Baron, that I do not speak here of acts, old, bygone, and withered, which may be canceled by any statute of limitation in the eyes of the law, and by repentance in the eyes of God. I speak of recent acts, present acts, acts still unknown to justice at this hour. I will proceed. This man has slipped into your confidence, and almost into your family, under a false name. I am going to tell you his true name. And to tell it to you for nothing."

"I am listening."

"His name is Jean Valjean."

"I know that."

"I am going to tell you, also for nothing, who he is."

"Go on."

"He is a former convict."

"I know that."

"You know it since I have had the honor of telling you."

"No. I knew it before."

Marius's cool tone, that double reply, "I know that," his laconic tone, thwarting conversation, excited some suppressed anger in the stranger. He furtively shot at Marius a furious look, immediately extinguished. Quick as it was, this look was one of those that are recognized after they have once been seen; it did not escape Marius. Certain flames can only come from certain souls; the eye, that window of thought, blazes with it; spectacles hide nothing; you might as well put a glass over hell.

The stranger resumed with a smile, "I do not permit myself to contradict Monsieur the Baron. In any event, you must see that I am informed. Now, what I have to tell you is known to myself alone. It concerns the fortune of Madame the Baronne. It is an extraordinary secret. It is for sale. I offer it to you first. Cheap. Twenty thousand francs."

"I know that secret as well as the others," said Marius.

The person felt the necessity of lowering his price a little.

"Monsieur Baron, say ten thousand francs, and I will go on."

"I repeat, that you have nothing to acquaint me with. I know what you want to tell me."

There was a new flash in the man's eye. He exclaimed, "Still I have to eat today. It is an extraordinary secret, I tell you. Monsieur Baron, I am going to speak. I will speak. Give me twenty francs."

Marius looked at him steadily.

"I know your extraordinary secret; just as I knew Jean Valjean's name, just as I know your name."

"My name?"

"Yes."

"That is not difficult, Monsieur Baron. I have had the honor of giving it to you in writing, and telling it to you. Thénard."

"Dier."

"Eh?"

"Thénardier."

"Who is that?"

When in danger the porcupine bristles, the beetle feigns death, the Old Guard forms a square; this man began to laugh.

Then, with a flick, he brushed a speck of dust from his coatsleeve.

Marius went on, "You are also the workingman Jondrette, the comedian Fabantou, the poet Genflot, the Spaniard Don Alvarès, and the woman Balizard."

"The woman what?"

"And you have kept a shabby inn at Montfermeil."

"A shabby inn! Never."

"And I tell you that you are Thénardier."

"I deny it."

"And that you are a scoundrel. Here."

And Marius, taking a banknote from his pocket, threw it in his face.

"Thanks! Pardon! Five hundred francs! Monsieur Baron!"

And the man, bewildered, bowing, catching the note, examined it.

"Five hundred francs!" he repeated in astonishment. And he stammered in an undertone, "A serious *fafiot!*"

Then bluntly, "Well, if that's the way it's going to be," he exclaimed. "Let's be relaxed about this."

And with the agility of a monkey, brushing his hair backward, pulling off his spectacles, removing from his nose and pocketing the two quill tubes we have just mentioned, and which we have already seen elsewhere on another page of this book, he took off his face as one takes off his hat.

His eye kindled; his forehead, uneven, ravined, humped in spots, hideously wrinkled at the top, emerged; his nose became as sharp as a beak; the fierce and cunning profile of the man of prey appeared again.

"Monsieur the Baron is infallible," he said in a clear voice from which all nasality has disappeared. "I am Thénardier."

And he straightened his bent back.

Thénardier, for it was indeed he, was strangely surprised; he would have been disconcerted if he could have been. He had come to bring surprise, and he received it himself. This humiliation had been compensated by five hundred francs, and, all things considered, he accepted it; but he was nonetheless astounded.

He was seeing this Baron Pontmercy for the first time, and, in spite of his disguise, this Baron Pontmercy recognized him, and recognized him thoroughly. And not only was this baron fully informed in regard to Thénardier, but he seemed fully informed in regard to Jean Valjean. Who was this almost beardless young man, so icy and so generous, who knew people's names, who knew all their names, and who opened his purse to them, who abused crooks like a judge and who paid them like a dupe?

Thénardier, it will be remembered, although he had been a neighbor of Marius, had never seen him, which often happens in Paris; he had once heard his daughters talk about a very poor young man named Marius who lived in the house. He had written to him, without knowing him, the letter we have just seen. No connection was possible in his mind between that Marius and M. le Baron Pontmercy.

Through his daughter Azelma, however, whom he had put on the track of the couple married on the 16th of February, and through his own researches, he had succeeded in finding out many things, and, from the depth of his darkness, he had been able to seize more than one mysterious clue. By dint of industry, he had discovered, or at least by dint of induction guessed, who the man was whom he had met on a certain day in the Great Sewer. From the man, he had easily arrived at the name. He knew that Madame the Baronne Pontmercy was Cosette. But, in that respect, he intended to be prudent. Who was Cosette? He did not exactly know himself. He suspected indeed some illegitimacy. Fantine's story had always seemed to him ambiguous; but why speak of it? To get paid for his silence? He had, or thought he had, something better to sell than that. And to all appearances, to come and without any proof make this revelation to Baron Pontmercy: "Your wife is a bastard," would only have attracted the husband's boot toward the revelator's back.

In Thénardier's opinion, the conversation with Marius had not yet begun. He had been obliged to retreat, to modify his strategy, to abandon a position, to change his base; but nothing essential was yet lost, and he had five hundred francs in his pocket. Moreover, he had something decisive to say, and even against this Baron Pontmercy, so well informed and so well armed, he felt strong. To men of Thénardier's nature, every dialogue is a battle. Where did he stand in what was about to begin? He did not know to whom he was speaking, but he knew what he was speaking about. He rapidly made this interior review of his forces, and after saying, "I am Thénardier," he waited.

Marius remained absorbed in thought. At last, then, he had Thénardier; this man, whom he had so much wanted to find again, was facing him. So he would be able to honor Colonel Pontmercy's injunction. He was humiliated that that hero should owe anything to this bandit, and that the bill of exchange drawn by his father from the depth of the grave against him, Marius, should have been outstanding until this day. It also appeared to him, in his complex frame of mind with regard to Thénardier, that here was an opportunity to avenge the colonel for the misfortune of having been saved by such a crook. However that might be, he was pleased. He was about to deliver the colonel's shade at last from his unworthy creditor, and it seemed to him that he was about to release his father's memory from imprisonment for debt.

Besides this duty, he had another to clear up if he could—the source of Cosette's fortune. The opportunity seemed to be there. Perhaps Thénardier knew something. It might be useful to probe this man to the core. He began with that.

Thénardier had slipped the "serious *fafiot*" into his fob, and was looking at Marius with an almost affectionate humility.

Marius broke the silence.

"Thénardier, I have told you your name. Now your secret, what you came to reveal to me, do you want me to tell you that? I too have my sources of information. You will see that I know more about it than you do. Jean Valjean, as you have said, is an assassin and a robber. A robber, because he robbed a rich manufacturer, M. Madeleine, whose ruin he caused. An assassin, because he assassinated the police officer, Javert."

"I don't understand, Monsieur Baron," said Thénardier.

"I will make myself understood. Listen. In some section of the Pas-de-Calais, around 1822, there was a man who had had some old difficulty with justice, and who, under the name of Monsieur Madeleine, had reformed and re-established himself. He had become in the full force of the term an upright man. By means of a factory turning out black glass trinkets, he had made the fortune of an entire city. As for his own personal fortune, he had made that also, but secondarily and, in some sense, incidentally. He was the foster father of the poor. He founded hospitals, opened schools, visited the sick, endowed daughters, supported widows, adopted orphans; he was, as it were, the guardian of the countryside. He had refused the Cross, he had been appointed mayor. A liberated convict knew the secret of a penalty once incurred by this man; he informed against him and had him arrested, and took advantage of the arrest to come to Paris and draw from the banker, Laffitte—I have the fact from the cashier himself—by means of a false signature, a sum of more than half a million, which belonged to Monsieur Madeleine. This convict who robbed Monsieur Madeleine is Jean Valjean. As to the other act, you have just as little to tell me. Jean Valjean killed the officer Javert; he killed him with a pistol. I, who am now speaking to you, I was present."

Thénardier cast at Marius the sovereign glance of a beaten man, catching hold of victory again, who has just recovered in one minute all the ground he had lost. But the smile returned immediately; the inferior before the superior can only have a skulking triumph, and Thénardier merely said to Marius, "Monsieur Baron, we are on the wrong track."

And he emphasized this phrase by giving his bunch of trinkets an expressive twirl.

"What!" replied Marius. "Are you denying this? These are facts."

"They are fantasies. The confidence with which Monsieur the Baron honors me makes it my duty to tell him so. Above all, truth and justice. I do not like to see people accused unjustly. Monsieur Baron, Jean Valjean never robbed Monsieur Madeleine, and Jean Valjean never killed Javert."

"You speak strongly! How can that be?"

"For two reasons."

"What are they? Tell me."

"The first is this: He did not rob Monsieur Madeleine, since it is Jean Valjean himself who was Monsieur Madeleine."

"What are you telling me?"

"And the second is this: He did not assassinate Javert, since Javert himself killed Javert."

"What do you mean?"

"That Javert committed suicide."

"Prove it! Prove it!" cried Marius, beside himself.

Thénardier resumed, scanning his phrase in the fashion of an old Alexandrine:

"The—police—of—ficer—Ja—vert—was—found—drowned—under—a—boat—by—the—Pont—au—Change."

"But prove it!"

Thénardier took from his pocket a large envelope of gray paper, which seemed to contain folded sheets of different sizes.

"I have my documents," he said calmly.

And he added:

"Monsieur Baron, on your behalf, I wanted to learn everything about Jean Valjean. I say that Jean Valjean and Madeleine are the same man; and I say that Javert had no other assassin than Javert; and when I speak I have the proof. Not manuscript proofs—writing is suspicious, writing is complaisant—but proof in print."

While speaking, Thénardier took out of the envelope two newspaper articles, yellow, faded, and strongly saturated with tobacco. One of the two, broken at all the folds, and falling into square pieces, seemed much older than the other.

"Two facts, two proofs," said Thénardier. And unfolding the two papers, he handed them to Marius.

The reader is acquainted with these two newspaper articles. One, the older, from a copy of the *Drapeau Blanc*, of the 25th of July, 1823, whose text can be found on pages 359–360 of this book, established the identity of

M. Madeleine and Jean Valjean. The other, from a *Moniteur* of the 15th of June, 1832, verified the suicide of Javert, adding that it appeared from a verbal report made by Javert to the prefect that, taken prisoner in the barricade of the Rue de la Chanvrerie, he had owed his life to the magnanimity of an insurgent who, though he had him in the sights of his pistol, had instead of blowing out his brains fired into the air.

Marius read. Here was evidence, certain date, unquestionable proof; these two articles had not been printed expressly to support Thénardier's words. The note published in the *Moniteur* was an official communication from the prefecture of police. Marius could not doubt. The information derived from the cashier was false, and he himself was mistaken. Jean Valjean, suddenly elevated, rose above the cloud. Marius could not restrain a cry of joy:

"Well, then, this unhappy person is a wonderful man! That whole fortune was really his own! He is Madeleine, the providence of a whole region! He is Jean Valjean, the savior of Javert! He is a hero! He is a saint!"

"He is not a saint, and he is not a hero," said Thénardier. "He is an assassin and a robber."

And he added with the tone of a man beginning to feel some authority in himself, "Let us be calm."

Robber, assassin; these words, which Marius had supposed gone, but still came back, fell on him like a shower of ice.

"Again!" he said.

"Still," said Thénardier. "Jean Valjean did not rob Madeleine, but he is a robber. He did not kill Javert, but he is a murderer."

"Are you speaking," resumed Marius, "of that petty theft of forty years ago, expiated, as your newspapers themselves show, by a whole life of repentance, abnegation, and virtue?"

"I said assassination and robbery, Monsieur Baron. And I repeat that I am speaking of recent events. What I have to reveal to you is absolutely unknown. It is unpublished. And perhaps you will find in it the source of the fortune adroitly presented by Jean Valjean to Madame the Baronne. I say adroitly, for, by a donation of this kind, to slip into an honorable house, whose comforts he will share and, by the same token, to conceal his crime, enjoy his robbery, bury his name, and to create a family, that would not be unskillful."

"I could interrupt you here," observed Marius, "but continue."

"Monsieur Baron, I will tell you everything, leaving the reward to your generosity. This secret is worth a pile of gold. You will say to me: Why have you not gone to Jean Valjean? For a very simple reason: I know that he has dispossessed himself, and dispossessed in your favor, and I think the contrivance ingenious; but he has not a sou left, he would show me his empty hands, and, since I need some money for my voyage to La Joya, I prefer you, who have everything, to him who has nothing. I am somewhat tired; allow me to take a chair."

Marius sat down, and made sign to him to sit down.

Thénardier settled into a tufted chair, took up the two articles, tucked them back into the envelope, and muttered, striking the *Drapeau Blanc* with his nail: "It cost me some hard work to get this one." This done, he crossed his legs and leaned back in his chair, an attitude characteristic of people who are sure of what they are saying, then broached the subject seriously, emphasizing his words:

"Monsieur Baron, on the sixth of June 1832, about a year ago, the day of the émeute, a man was in the Great Sewer of Paris, near where the sewer empties into the Seine, between the Pont des Invalides and the Pont d'Iéna."

Marius suddenly drew his chair close to Thénardier's. Thénardier noticed this movement, and continued with the deliberation of a speaker holding his listener fast, feeling the palpitation of his adversary beneath his words:

"This man, compelled to conceal himself, for reasons actually foreign to politics, had taken the sewer for his dwelling, and had a key to it. It was, I repeat, the sixth of June; it might have been eight o'clock in the evening. The man heard a noise in the sewer. Very much surprised, he hid and watched. It was a sound of steps, somebody was walking in the darkness; somebody was coming in his direction. Strange to say, there was another man in the sewer besides himself. The grating of the sewer outlet was not far off. A little light coming from there enabled him to recognize the newcomer, and to see that this man was carrying something on his back. He walked bent over. The man who was walking bent over was a former convict, and what he was carrying on his shoulders was a corpse. Assassination in flagrante delicto, if ever there was such a thing. As for the robbery, it hardly needs explaining; nobody kills a man for nothing. This convict was going to throw his corpse into the river. It is a noteworthy fact that before reaching the grating of the outlet, this convict, who had come a great distance in the sewer, had been compelled to pass through a horrible quagmire in which it would seem that he might have left the corpse; but the sewermen working on the quagmire might, the very next day, have found the assassinated man, and that was not the assassin's game. He preferred to go through the quagmire with his load, and his efforts must have been terrible; it is impossible to put one's life in greater peril; I do not understand how he came out of it alive."

Marius's chair drew still nearer. Thénardier took advantage of this to draw a deep breath. He continued, "Monsieur Baron, a sewer is not the Champ-de-Mars. One lacks everything there, even room. When two men are in a sewer, they must meet each other. That is what happened. The resident and the traveler were compelled to greet each other, to their mutual regret. The traveler said to the resident: 'You see what I have on my back, I must get out, you have the key, give it to me.' This convict was a man of terrible strength. There was no refusing him. Still the one who had the key parleyed, merely to gain time. He examined the dead man, but he could see nothing, except that he was young, well dressed, apparently a rich man, and completely disfigured with blood. While he was talking, he found means to cut and tear off from behind, without the assassin perceiving it, a piece of the assassinated man's coat. A piece of evidence, you understand; means of tracing the affair and proving the crime to the criminal. He put this piece of evidence in his pocket. After which he opened the gate, let the man out with his encumbrance on his back, shut the grating again and slipped away, little caring to be mixed up with the remainder of the adventure, and particularly anxious not to be present when the assassin threw the assassinated man into the river. Now you understand. The one who was carrying the corpse was Jean Valjean; the one who had the key is now speaking to you, and the piece of the coat—"

Thénardier finished the phrase by drawing from his pocket and holding up, at eye level, between his thumbs and forefingers, a strip of ragged black cloth, covered with dark stains.

Marius had stood up, pale, hardly breathing, his eye fixed on the scrap of black cloth, and, without uttering a word, without losing sight of this rag, he retreated to the wall and, with his right hand stretched behind him, groped about for a key that was in the lock of a closet near the fireplace. He found the key, opened the closet, and reached into it without looking, and without removing his startled eyes from the fragment that Thénardier held up.

Meanwhile Thénardier continued, "Monsieur Baron, I have the strongest reasons to believe that the assassinated young man was a wealthy stranger drawn into a snare by Jean Valjean, and the bearer of an enormous sum."

"The young man was myself, and there is the coat!" cried Marius, and he threw an old black coat covered with blood onto the carpet.

Then, snatching the fragment from Thénardier's hands, he bent down over the coat, and applied the piece to the cut hem. The edges fitted exactly, and the strip completed the coat.

Thénardier was petrified. He thought, "I am done for."

Marius stood up, quivering, desperate, radiant.

He felt in his pocket, and walked, furious, toward Thénardier, brandishing and almost pushing into his face a fist full of five hundred- and thousand-franc notes.

"You are a wretch! You are a liar, a slanderer, a crook. You came to accuse this man, you have justified him; you wanted to destroy him, you have succeeded only in glorifying him. And it is you who are a robber! And it is you who are an assassin. I saw you, Thénardier, Jondrette, in that den on the Boulevard de l'Hôpital. I know enough about you to send you to prison, and even further, if I wanted to. Here, there are a thousand francs, you braggart!"

And he threw a bill for a thousand francs to Thénardier.

"Ah! Jondrette Thénardier, wretched crook! Let this be a lesson to you, peddler of secrets, trader in mysteries, fumbler in the dark, miserable wretch! Take these five hundred francs, and leave this place! Waterloo protects you."

"Waterloo!" muttered Thénardier, pocketing the five hundred francs with the thousand francs.

"Yes, assassin! You saved the life of a colonel there—"

"Of a general," said Thénardier, raising his head.

"Of a colonel!" replied Marius with a burst of passion. "I would not give a farthing for a general. And you came here to act out your infamy! I tell you that you have committed every crime. Go! Out of my sight! Only be happy, that's all that I desire. Ah! Monster! Here are three thousand francs more. Take them. Tomorrow you will leave for America, with your daughter, for your wife is dead, abominable liar. I will see to your departure, bandit, and then I will count out to you twenty thousand francs. Go and get yourself hung elsewhere!"

"Monsieur Baron," answered Thénardier, bowing to the ground, "eternal gratitude."

And Thénardier went out, understanding nothing, astounded and transported with this sweet burden of sacks of gold and with this thunderbolt bursting over his head in banknotes.

Thunderstruck he was, but happy, too; and he would have been very sorry to have had a lightning rod against that thunderbolt.

Let us be done with this man at once. Two days after the events we are now relating he left, through Marius's care, for America under a false name, with his daughter Azelma, provided with a draft on New York for twenty thousands francs. The abject moral misery of Thénardier, the broken-down bourgeois, was irremediable; in America he was the same thing he had been in Europe. The touch of a wicked man is often enough to corrupt a good deed and to make an evil result spring from it. With Marius's money, Thénardier became a slave trader.

As soon as Thénardier was gone, Marius ran to the garden where Cosette was still walking.

"Cosette! Cosette!" he cried. "Come! Come quickly! We must go. Basque, a fiacre! Cosette, come on. Oh! My

God! It was he who saved my life! Let's not lose a minute! Put on your shawl."

Cosette thought him mad and obeyed.

He did not breathe, he put his hand on his heart to repress its beating. He walked to and fro with rapid strides, he embraced Cosette: "Oh! Cosette! I am an unhappy man!" he said.

Marius was beside himself. He began to see in this Jean Valjean a strangely lofty and saddened form. An unparalleled virtue appeared before him, supreme and mild, humble in its immensity. The convict was transfigured into Christ. Marius was bewildered by this marvel. He did not know exactly what he was seeing, but it was great.

In a moment, a fiacre was at the door.

Marius helped Cosette in and sprang in himself.

"Driver," said he, "Rue de l'Homme-Armé, Number Seven."

The fiacre started.

"Oh! What happiness!" said Cosette. "Rue de l'Homme-Armé! I did not dare speak to you of it again. We are going to see Monsieur Jean."

"Your father! Cosette, your father more than ever. Cosette, I see it. You told me that you never received the letter I sent you by Gavroche. It must have fallen into his hands. Cosette, he went to the barricade to save me. Since he needs to be an angel, he saved others along the way; he saved Javert. He snatched me out of that abyss to give me to you. He carried me on his back through the frightful sewer. Oh! I am an unnatural ingrate. Cosette, after having been your providence, he was mine. Just think, there was a horrible quagmire, enough to drown him a hundred times, to drown him in the mire, Cosette! He carried me through that. I had fainted; I saw nothing, I heard nothing, I couldn't know anything about my own fate. We are going to bring him back, take him with us, whether he wants it or no, he will never leave us again. If only he is at home! If only we find him! I will spend the rest of my life in venerating him. Yes, that must be it, do you see, Cosette? Gavroche must have handed my letter to him. That explains everything. You understand."

Cosette did not understand a word.

"You are right," she said to him.

Meanwhile the fiacre rolled on.

V

NIGHT BEHIND WHICH IS DAWN

At the knock he heard at his door, Jean Valjean turned his head.

"Come in," he said feebly.

The door opened. Cosette and Marius appeared.

Cosette rushed into the room.

Marius remained at the threshold, leaning against the casing of the door.

"Cosette!" said Jean Valjean, and he rose in his chair, his arms stretched out and trembling, haggard, livid, terrible, with immense joy in his eyes.

Cosette, stifled with emotion, fell on Jean Valjean's breast.

"Father!" she said.

Jean Valjean, beside himself, stammered, "Cosette! She? You, madame? Is it you, Cosette? Oh, my God!"

And, clasped in Cosette's arms, he exclaimed, "It is you, Cosette? You are here? You forgive me then!"

Marius, dropping his eyelids so the tears would not fall, stepped forward and murmured between his lips which were contracted convulsively to check the sobs, "Father!"

"And you too, you forgive me!" said Jean Valjean.

Marius could not utter a word, and Jean Valjean added, "Thank you."

Cosette took off her shawl and threw her hat on the bed.

"They are in my way," she said.

And, sitting down on the old man's knees, she stroked his white hair with a tender grace, and kissed his forehead.

Jean Valjean, bewildered, offered no resistance.

Cosette, who had only a very confused understanding of all this, redoubled her caresses, as if she wanted to pay Marius's debt.

Jean Valjean faltered, "How foolish we are! I thought I would never see her again. Only think, Monsieur Pontmercy, that at the moment you came in, I was saying to myself: It is all over. There is her little dress, I am a miserable man, I will never see Cosette again, I was saying that at the very moment you were coming up the stairs. Wasn't I silly? I was as silly as that! But we reckon without God. God said: You think that you are going to be abandoned, idiot? No. No, it shall not come to pass like that. Come, here is a poor man who has need of an angel. And the angel comes; and I see my Cosette again! And I see my darling Cosette again! Oh! I was very miserable!"

For a moment he could not speak, then he continued, "I really needed to see Cosette a little while from time to time. A heart does want a bone to gnaw. Still, I plainly felt I was in the way. I gave myself reasons; they do not need you, stay in your corner, you have no right to go on forever. Oh! Bless God, I am seeing her again! Do you know, Cosette, your husband is very handsome? Ah, you have a pretty embroidered collar, yes, yes. I like that pattern. Your husband chose it, didn't he? And then, Cosette, you must have cashmeres. Monsieur Pontmercy, let me call her Cosette. It will not be very long."

And Cosette interrupted, "How naughty to have left us this way! Where have you been? Why were you away for so long? Your trips did not used to last more than three or four days. I sent Nicolette, the answer always was: He is away. How long have you been back? Why didn't you let us know? Do you know that you are very much changed. Oh! The naughty father! He has been sick, and we did not know it! Here, Marius, feel his hand, how cold it is!"

"So you are here, Monsieur Pontmercy, you forgive me!" repeated Jean Valjean.

At these words, which Jean Valjean was now saying for the second time, all that was welling up in Marius's heart found an outlet, he broke out:

"Cosette, do you hear? That is the way with him! He asks for my pardon, and do you know what he has done for me, Cosette? He saved my life. He has done more. He has given you to me. And, after having saved me, and after having given you to me, Cosette, what did he do with himself? He sacrificed himself. There is the man. And, to me the ungrateful, to me the forgetful, to me the pitiless, to me the guilty, he says: Thank you! Cosette, my whole life spent at the feet of this man would be too little. That barricade, that sewer, that inferno, that cloaca, he went through everything for me, for you, Cosette! He carried me through death in every form, which he kept away from me, and which he accepted for himself. Every courage, every virtue, every heroism, every sanctity, he has it all, Cosette. This man is an angel!"

"Hush! hush!" said Jean Valjean in a whisper. "Why tell all that?"

"But you!" exclaimed Marius, with a passion in which veneration was mingled, "why have not you told it? It is your fault, too. You save people's lives, and you hide it from them! You do more, under pretense of unmasking yourself, you slander yourself. It is frightful."

"I told the truth," answered Jean Valjean.

"No," replied Marius, "the truth is the whole truth; and you did not tell it. You were Monsieur Madeleine, why not have said so? You had saved Javert, why not have said so? I owe my life to you, why not have said so?"

"Because I thought as you did. I felt that you were right. It was necessary for me to go away. If you had known that affair of the sewer, you would have made me stay with you. I would then have had to keep silent. If I had spoken, it would have embarrassed everyone."

"Embarrassed what? Embarrassed whom?" replied Marius. "Do you suppose you are going to stay here? We are going to take you back. Oh! My God! when I think it was by accident that I learned it all! We are going to take you back. You are a part of us. You are her father and mine. You will not spend another day in this awful house. Do not imagine that you will be here tomorrow."

"Tomorrow," said Jean Valjean, "I will not be here, but I will not be at your house."

"What do you mean?" replied Marius. "Ah, now, we won't allow any more trips. You will never leave us again. You belong to us. We will not let you go."

"This time, it is for good," added Cosette. "We have a carriage downstairs. I am going to carry you off. If necessary, I will use force."

And laughing, she made as though to lift the old man in her arms.

"Your room is still in our house," she continued. "If you knew how pretty the garden is now. The azaleas are growing beautifully. The paths are sanded with river sand; there are some little violet shells. You will eat some of my strawberries. I water them myself. And no more madame, and no more Monsieur Jean, we're in a republic, aren't we, Marius? The program is changed. If you only knew, Father, I've had some trouble, there was a robin that had made her nest in a hole in the wall, a horrid cat ate her up for me. My poor pretty little robin who put her head out her window and looked at me! I cried over it. I would have killed the cat! But now, nobody cries anymore. Everybody laughs, everybody is happy. You are coming with us. How glad grandfather will be! You will have your garden bed, you will tend it, and we will see if your strawberries are as fine as mine. And then, I will do whatever you want, and then, you will obey me."

Jean Valjean listened to her without hearing her. He heard the music of her voice rather than the meaning of her words; one of those big tears which are the gloomy pearls of the soul gathered slowly in his eye. He murmured, "The proof that God is good is that she is here."

"Father!" cried Cosette.

Jean Valjean continued, "It is very true that it would be charming to live together. They have their trees full of birds. I could walk with Cosette. To be with people who live, who bid each other good morning, who call each other into the garden, would be sweet. We would see each other as soon as it was morning. We would each cultivate our little corner. She would have me eat her strawberries. I would have her pick my roses. It would be charming. Only—"

He paused and said mildly, "It is a pity."

The tear did not fall, it receded, and Jean Valjean replaced it with a smile.

Cosette took both the old man's hands in her own.

"My God!" she said. "Your hands are still colder. Are you sick? Are you suffering?"

"No," answered Jean Valjean. "I am very well. Only—"

He stopped.

"Only what?"

"I will die in a little while."

Cosette and Marius shuddered.

"Die!" exclaimed Marius.

"Yes, but that is nothing," said Jean Valjean.

He breathed, smiled, and continued.

"Cosette, you are speaking to me, go on, speak again,

so your little robin is dead, speak, let me hear your voice!"

Marius, petrified, gazed at the old man.

Cosette uttered a piercing cry: "Father! My father! You will live. You are going to live. I will have you live, do you hear!"

Jean Valjean raised his head toward her with adoration.

"Oh, yes, forbid me to die. Who knows? Perhaps I will obey. I was just dying when you came. That stopped me, it seemed to me I was born again."

"You are full of strength and life," exclaimed Marius. "Do you think people die just like that? You have had trouble, you shall have no more. I am the one to ask your pardon now, and on my knees! You shall live, and live with us, and live for a long time. We will take you back. Both of us here will have only one thought from now on, your happiness!"

"You see," added Cosette in tears, "Marius says you will not die."

Jean Valjean continued to smile.

"If you were to take me back, Monsieur Pontmercy, would that make me different from what I am? No; God thought as you and I, and he has not changed his mind; it is best that I should go away. Death is a good arrangement. God knows better than we do what we need. That you are happy, that Monsieur Pontmercy has Cosette, that youth espouses morning, that there are about you, my children, lilacs and nightingales, that your life is a beautiful lawn in the sunshine, that all the enchantments of heaven fill your souls, and now, that I who am good for nothing, that I should die; surely all this is good. Look, be reasonable, nothing else is possible now, I am sure it is all over. An hour ago I had a fainting fit. And then, last night, I drank that pitcher full of water. How good your husband is, Cosette! You are much better off than with me."

There was a noise at the door. It was the physician coming in.

"Good day and good-by, doctor," said Jean Valjean. "Here are my poor children."

Marius approached the physician. He addressed this single word to him: "Monsieur?" but in his way of pronouncing it, there was a complete question.

The physician answered the question with an expressive glance.

"Because things are unpleasant," said Jean Valjean, "that is no reason for being unjust toward God."

There was a silence. Every heart was oppressed.

Jean Valjean turned toward Cosette. He began to gaze at her as if he would take a look that should endure through eternity. At the depth of shadow he had already reached, ecstasy was still possible to him while seeing Cosette. The reflection of that sweet countenance illumined his pale face. The sepulcher may have its enchantments.

The physician felt his pulse.

"Ah! It was you he needed!" murmured he, looking at Cosette and Marius.

And, bending toward Marius's ear he added very low, "Too late."

Almost without ceasing to gaze on Cosette, Jean Valjean turned on Marius and the physician a look of serenity. They heard these almost inaudible words come from his lips:

"It is nothing to die; it is horrible not to live."

Suddenly he stood up. These returns of strength are sometimes a sign of approaching death. He walked with a firm step to the wall, brushed aside Marius and the physician, who offered to assist him, took down from the wall the little copper crucifix that hung there, came back, and sat down with all the freedom of motion of perfect health, and said in a loud voice, laying the crucifix on the table, "Behold the great martyr."

Then his chest sank, his head wavered, as if the dizziness of the tomb seized him, and his hands, resting on his knees, began to clutch at his trousers.

Cosette supported his shoulders, and sobbed, and attempted to speak to him but could not. Among the words mingled with the bitter saliva that comes with tears, were phrases repeated over and over: "Father! Do not leave us. Is it possible that we have found you again only to lose you?"

The agony of death may be said to meander. It comes and goes, moves on toward the grave, and turns back toward life. There is a groping in the act of dying.

After this semi-stupor, Jean Valjean gathered strength, shook his head as though to throw off the darkness, and became almost completely lucid once more. He took a fold of Cosette's sleeve, and kissed it.

"He is reviving! Doctor, he is reviving!" cried Marius.

"You are both kind," said Jean Valjean. "I will tell you what has given me pain. What has given me pain, Monsieur Pontmercy, was that you have been unwilling to touch that money. That money really belongs to your wife. I will explain it, my children; that is one reason I am glad to see you. The black jet comes from England, the white jet comes from Norway. All this is in the paper you see there, which you will read. For bracelets, I invented the substitution of clasps made by bending the metal. They are handsomer, better, and cheaper. You understand how much money can be made. So Cosette's fortune is really her own. I am giving you these details so your minds may be at rest."

The concierge had come and was looking through the half-open door. The physician motioned her away, but he could not prevent that good, zealous woman from crying to the dying man before she went, "Do you want a priest?"

"I have one," answered Jean Valjean.

And, with his finger, he seemed to designate a point above his head, where, you would have said, he saw someone.

It is probable that the bishop was indeed a witness of this death.

Cosette slipped a pillow gently under his back.

Jean Valjean resumed: "Monsieur Pontmercy, have no fear, I beg you. The six hundred thousand francs are really Cosette's. I will have wasted my life if you do not enjoy it! We succeeded very well with the glasswork. We rivaled what is called Berlin jewelry. Indeed, the German black glass cannot be compared with it. A gross, which contains twelve hundred grains very well cut, costs only three francs."

When a being who is dear to us is about to die, we look at him with a look that clings to him, and which would like to hold him back. Both of them, dumb with anguish, not knowing what to say to death, despairing and trembling, stood before him, Marius holding Cosette's hand.

From moment to moment, Jean Valjean grew weaker. He was sinking; he was approaching the dark horizon. His breathing had become intermittent, interrupted by slight gasps. He had difficulty moving his arms, his feet had lost all motion, and, at the same time that the distress of the limbs and the failure of the body increased, all the majesty of the soul rose and showed on his forehead. The light of the unknown world was already visible in his eye.

His face grew pale, and at the same time smiled. Life was no longer present, there was something else. His breath died away, his gaze grew wider. It was a corpse on which you could sense the wings.

He motioned to Cosette to approach, then to Marius; it was evidently the last minute of the last hour, and he began to speak to them in a voice so faint it seemed to come from far away, and you would have said that there was already a wall between them and him.

"Come closer, come closer, both of you. I love you dearly. Oh! It is good to die like this! You too, you love me, my Cosette. I knew very well that you still had some affection for your good old father. How kind you are to put this cushion under my back! You will weep for me a little, won't you? Not too much. I do not wish you to have any deep grief. You must live very happily, my children. I forgot to tell you that on buckles without tongues more is earned than on anything else. A gross, twelve dozen, costs ten francs, and sells for sixty. That is really good business. So you should not be surprised at the six hundred thousand francs, Monsieur Pontmercy. It is honest money. You can be rich without concern. You should have a carriage, from time to time a box at the theater, beautiful ball dresses, my Cosette, and then give good dinners to your friends, be very happy. I was writing to Cosette just now. She will find my letter. To her I bequeath the two candlesticks on the mantel. They are silver; but to me they are gold, they are diamonds; they change the candles that are put in them into consecrated tapers. I do not know whether the one who gave them to me is satisfied with me in heaven. I have done what I could. My children, you will not forget that I am a poor man, you will have me buried in the most convenient plot of ground under a stone to mark the spot. That is my wish. No name on the stone. If Cosette will come for a little while sometimes, it will give me pleasure. You too, Monsieur Pontmercy. I must confess to you that I have not always loved you; I ask your pardon. Now, she and you are one to me. I am so grateful to you. I feel that you make Cosette happy. If you knew, Monsieur Pontmercy, how her beautiful rosy cheeks were my joy; when I saw her a little pale, I was sad. There is a five-hundred-franc bill in the bureau. I have not touched it. It is for the poor. Cosette, do you see your little dress, there on the bed? Do you recognize it? Yet it was only ten years ago. How time passes! We have been very happy. It is all over. My children, do not cry, I am not going very far, I will see you from there. You will only have to look at night, you will see me smile. Cosette, do you remember Montfermeil? You were in the woods, you were very frightened; do you remember when I took the handle of the water bucket? That was the first time I touched your poor little hand. It was so cold! Ah! You had red hands in those days, mademoiselle, your hands are very white now. And the big doll! Do you remember? You called her Catherine. You were sorry that you did not carry her to the convent. How you made me laugh sometimes, my sweet angel! When it had rained you launched bits of straw in the gutters, and you would watch them. One day, I gave you a willow racket, and a shuttlecock with yellow, blue, and green feathers. You have forgotten it. You were so sweet when you were little! You played. You hung cherries on your ears. Those are things of the past. The forests through which we have passed with our child, the trees under which we have walked, the convents in which we have hidden, the games, the free laughter of childhood, everything is in shadow. I imagined that all that belonged to me. There was my folly. Those Thénardiers were wicked. We must forgive them. Cosette, the time has come to tell you the name of your mother. Her name was Fantine. Remember that name: Fantine. Fall on your knees whenever you pronounce it. She suffered a great deal. And loved you very much. Her measure of unhappiness was as full as yours of happiness. Such are the distributions of God. He is on high, He sees us all, and He knows what He does in the midst of His great stars. So I am going away, my children. Love each other dearly always. There is scarcely anything else in the world but that: to love one another. Sometimes you will think of the poor old man who died here. O my Cosette! It is not my fault, indeed, if I have not seen you all this time, it broke my heart; I went as far as the corner of the street, I must have seemed strange to the people who saw me go by, I looked like a crazy man, once I went out with no hat. My children, I cannot see very clearly now, I had some more things to say, but it makes no difference. Think of me a little. You are blessed creatures. I do not know what is the matter with me, I see a light. Come nearer. I am dying happy. Let me put my hands on your dear beloved heads."

Cosette and Marius fell on their knees, overwhelmed, choked with tears, each grasping one of Jean Valjean's hands. Those noble hands moved no more.

He had fallen back, the light from the candlesticks fell across him; his white face looked up toward heaven, he let Cosette and Marius cover his hands with kisses; he was dead.

The night was starless and very dark. Without any doubt, in the gloom, some mighty angel was standing, with outstretched wings, waiting for the soul.

VI

GRASS CONCEALS AND RAIN BLOTS OUT

In the Père-Lachaise cemetery, in the neighborhood of the potters' field, far from the elegant quarter of that city of sepulchers, far from all those fantastic tombs that display in presence of eternity the hideous fashions of death, in a deserted corner, beside an old wall, beneath a great yew on which the bindweed climbs, among the dog-grass and the mosses, there is a stone. This stone is exempt no more than the rest from the leprosy of time, from the mold, the lichen, and the birds' droppings. The air turns it black, the water green. It is near no path, and people do not like to go in that direction, because the grass is high, and they would wet their feet. When there is a little sunshine, the lizards come out. All around there is a rustling of wild oats. In spring, the linnets come to sing in the tree.

This stone is entirely blank. The only thought in cutting it was of the essentials of the grave, and there was no other care than to make this stone long enough and narrow enough to cover a man.

No name can be read there.

Only many years ago, a hand wrote on it in pencil these four lines, which have gradually become illegible under the rain and the dust, and are probably gone by now:

> Il dort. Quoique le sort fût pour lui bien étrange,
> Il vivait. Il mourut quand il n'eut plus son ange.
> La chose simplement d'elle-même arriva,
> Comme la nuit se fait lorsque le jour s'en va.[1]

[1] He is asleep. Though his mettle was sorely tried,
He lived, and when he lost his angel, died.
It happened calmly, on its own,
The way night comes when day is done.